ROBIN COOK
THREE COMPLETE NOVELS

ALSO BY ROBIN COOK

ROBIN COOK

THREE COMPLETE NOVELS

CONTAGION

CHROMOSOME 6

INVASION

G. P. PUTNAM'S SONS
NEW YORK

G. P. Putnam's Sons
Publishers Since 1838
a member of
Penguin Putnam Inc.
375 Hudson Street
New York, NY 10014

Library of Congress Cataloging-in-Publication Data

Cook, Robin, date.
[Selections.   1999]
Robin Cook: three complete novels / Robin Cook
p.   cm.
Contents: Contagion—Chromosome 6—Invasion
ISBN 0-399-14538-9
1. Detective and mystery stories, American.   2. Communicable
diseases—Fiction.   3. Forensic pathologists—Fiction.   4. Equatorial
Guinea—Fiction.   5. New York (N.Y.)—Fiction.   I. Title.   II. Title:
Three complete novels.
PS3553.O5545A6   1999
813'.54—dc21   99-24694 CIP

PRINTED IN THE UNITED STATES OF AMERICA

1   3   5   7   9   10   8   6   4   2

This book is printed on acid-free paper. ∞

BOOK DESIGN BY LOVEDOG STUDIO

CONTENTS

CONTAGION

FOR PHYLLIS,
STACY, MARILYN,
DAN, VICKI,
AND BEN

Our leaders should reject market values as a framework for health care and the market-driven mess into which our health system is evolving.

JEROME P. KASSIRER, M.D.
NEW ENGLAND JOURNAL OF MEDICINE
VOL. 333, NO. 1, P. 50, 1995

I would like to thank all my friends and colleagues who are always graciously willing to field questions and offer helpful advice. Those whom I'd particularly like to acknowledge for *Contagion* are:

DR. CHARLES WETLI, Forensic Pathologist and Medical Examiner
DR. JACKI LEE, Forensic Pathologist and Medical Examiner
DR. MARK NEUMAN, Virologist and Virology Laboratory Director
DR. CHUCK KARPAS, Pathologist and Laboratory Supreme Commander
JOE COX, Esquire, Lawyer and Reader
FLASH WILEY, Esquire, Lawyer, Fellow Basketball Player, and Rap Consultant
JEAN REEDS, Social Worker, Critic, and Fabulous Sounding Board

PROLOGUE

June 12, 1991, dawned a near-perfect, late-spring day as the sun's rays touched the eastern shores of the North American continent. Most of the United States, Canada, and Mexico expected clear, sunny skies. The only meteorological blips were a band of potential thunderstorms that was expected to extend from the plains into the Tennessee Valley and some showers that were forecasted to move in from the Bering Strait over the Seward Peninsula in Alaska.

In almost every way this June twelfth was like every other June twelfth, with one curious phenomenon. Three incidents occurred that were totally unrelated, yet were to cause a tragic intersection of the lives of three of the people involved.

11:36 A.M.
DEADHORSE, ALASKA

"Hey! Dick! Over here," shouted Ron Halverton. He waved frantically to get his former roommate's attention. He didn't dare leave his Jeep in the brief chaos at the tiny airport. The morning 737 from Anchorage had just landed and the security people were strict about unattended vehicles in the loading area. Buses and vans were waiting for the tourists and the returning oil company personnel.

Hearing his name and recognizing Ron, Dick waved back and then began threading his way through the milling crowd.

Ron watched Dick as he approached. Ron hadn't seen him since they'd graduated from college the year before, but Dick appeared just as he always did: the picture of normality with his Ralph Lauren shirt and windbreaker jacket, Guess jeans, and a small knapsack slung over his shoulder. Yet Ron knew the real Dick: the ambitious, aspiring microbiologist who would think nothing of flying all the way from Atlanta to Alaska with the hope of finding a new microbe. Here was a guy who loved bacteria and viruses. He collected the stuff the way other people collected baseball cards. Ron smiled and shook his head as he recalled that Dick had even had petri dishes of microbes in their shared refrigerator at the University of Colorado.

When Ron had met Dick during their freshman year, it had taken a bit of time to get used to him. Although he was an indubitably faithful friend, Dick had some peculiar and unpredictable quirks. On the one hand he was a fierce competitor in intramural sports and surely the guy you wanted with you if you mistakenly wandered into the wrong part of town, yet on the other hand he'd been unable to sacrifice a frog in first-year biology lab.

Ron found himself chuckling as he remembered another surprising and embarrassing moment involving Dick. It was during their sophomore year when a whole group had piled into a car for a weekend ski trip. Dick was driving and accidentally ran over a rabbit. His response had been to break down in tears. No one had known what to say. As a result some people began to talk behind Dick's back, especially when it became common knowledge that he would pick up cockroaches at the fraternity house and deposit them outside instead of squishing them and flushing them down the toilet as everybody else did.

As Dick came alongside the Jeep, he tossed his bag into the backseat before grasping Ron's outstretched hand.

They greeted each other enthusiastically.

"I can't believe this," Ron said. "I mean, you're here! In the Arctic."

"Hey, I wouldn't have missed this for the world," Dick said. "I'm really psyched. How far is the Eskimo site from here?"

Ron looked nervously over his shoulder. He recognized several of the security people. Turning back to Dick, he lowered his voice. "Cool it," he murmured. "I told you people are really sensitive about this."

"Oh, come on," Dick scoffed. "You can't be serious."

"I'm dead serious," Ron said. "I could get fired for leaking this to you. No fooling around. I mean, we got to do this hush-hush or we don't do it at all. You're to tell no one, ever! You promised!"

"All right, all right," Dick said with a short, appeasing laugh. "You're right. I promised. I just didn't think it was such a big deal."

"It's a very big deal," Ron said firmly. He was beginning to think he'd made a mistake inviting Dick to visit, despite how much fun it was to see him.

"You're the boss," Dick said. He gave his friend a jab on the shoulder. "My lips are sealed forever. Now chill out and relax." He swung himself into the Jeep. "But let's just buzz out there straightaway and check out this discovery."

"You don't want to see where I live first?" Ron asked.

"I have a feeling I'll be seeing that more than I care to," he said with a laugh.

"I suppose it's not a bad time while everybody is preoccupied with the Anchorage flight and screwing around with the tourists." He reached forward and started the engine.

They drove out of the airport and headed northeast on the only road. It was gravel. To talk they had to shout over the sound of the engine.

"It's about eight miles to Prudhoe Bay," Ron said, "but we'll be turning off to the west in another mile or so. Remember, if anybody stops us, I'm just taking you to the new oilfield."

Dick nodded. He couldn't believe his friend was so uptight about this thing. Looking around at the flat, marshy monotonous tundra and the overcast gunmetal gray sky, he wondered if the place was getting to Ron. He guessed life was not easy on the alluvial plain of Alaska's north slope. To lighten the mood he said: "Weather's not bad. What's the temperature?"

"You're lucky," Ron said. "There was some sun earlier, so it's in the low fifties. This is as warm as it gets up here. Enjoy it while it lasts. It'll probably flurry later today. It usually does. The perpetual joke is whether it's the last snow of last winter or the first snow of next winter."

Dick smiled and nodded but couldn't help but think that if the people up there considered that funny, they were in sad shape.

A few minutes later Ron turned left onto a smaller, newer road, heading northwest.

"How did you happen to find this abandoned igloo?" Dick asked.

"It wasn't an igloo," Ron said. "It was a house made out of peat blocks reinforced with whalebone. Igloos were only made as temporary shelters, like when people went out hunting on the ice. The Inupiat Eskimos lived in peat huts."

"I stand corrected," Dick said. "So how'd you come across it?"

"Totally by accident," Ron said. "We found it when we were bulldozing for this road. We broke through the entrance tunnel."

"Is everything still in it?" Dick asked. "I worried about that flying up here. I mean, I don't want this to be a wasted trip."

"Have no fear," Ron said. "Nothing's been touched. That I can assure you."

"Maybe there are more dwellings in the general area," Dick suggested. "Who knows? It could be a village."

Ron shrugged. "Maybe so. But no one wants to find out. If anybody from the state got wind of this they'd stop construction on our feeder pipeline to the new field. That would be one huge disaster, because we have to have the feeder line functional before winter, and winter starts in August around here."

Ron began to slow down as he scanned the side of the road. Eventually he pulled to a stop abreast of a small cairn. Putting a hand on Dick's arm to keep him in his seat, he turned to look back down the road. When he was convinced that no one was coming, he climbed from the Jeep and motioned for Dick to do the same.

Reaching back into the Jeep, he pulled out two old and soiled anoraks and work gloves. He handed a set to Dick. "You'll need these," he explained. "We'll be down below the permafrost." Then he reached back into the Jeep for a heavy-duty flashlight.

"All right," Ron added nervously. "We can't be here long. I don't want anybody coming along the road and wondering what the hell is going on."

Dick followed Ron as he headed north away from the road. A cloud of mosquitoes mystically materialized and attacked them mercilessly. Looking ahead, Dick could see a fog bank about a half mile away and guessed it marked the coast of the Arctic Ocean. In all other directions there was no relief from the monotony of the flat, windswept, featureless tundra that extended to the horizon. Overhead seabirds circled and cried raucously.

A dozen steps from the road, Ron stopped. After one last glance for approaching vehicles, he bent down and grabbed the edge of a sheet of plywood that had been painted to match the variegated colors of the surrounding tundra. He pulled the wood aside to reveal a hole four feet deep. In the north wall of the hole was the entrance to a small tunnel.

"It looks as if the hut was buried by ice," Dick said.

Ron nodded. "We think that pack ice was blown up from the beach during one of the ferocious winter storms."

"A natural tomb," Dick said.

"Are you sure you want to do this?" Ron asked.

"Don't be silly," Dick said while he donned the parka and pulled on the gloves. "I've come thousands of miles. Let's go."

Ron climbed into the hole and then bent down on all fours. Lowering himself, he entered the tunnel. Dick followed at his heels.

As Dick crawled, he could see very little save for the eerie silhouette of Ron ahead of him. As he moved away from the entrance, the darkness closed in around him like a heavy, frigid blanket. In the failing light he noticed his breath crystalizing. He thanked God that he wasn't claustrophobic.

After about six feet the walls of the tunnel fell away. The floor also slanted downward, giving them an additional foot of headroom. There were about three and a half feet of clearance. Ron moved to the side and Dick crawled up next to him.

"It's colder than a witch's tit down here," Dick said.

Ron's flashlight beam played into the corners to illuminate short vertical struts of beluga rib bones.

"The ice snapped those whalebones like they were toothpicks," Ron said.

"Where are the inhabitants?" Dick asked.

Ron directed his flashlight beam ahead to a large, triangular piece of ice that had punched through the ceiling of the hut. "On the other side of that," he said. He handed the flashlight to Dick.

Dick took the flashlight and started crawling forward. As much as he didn't want to admit it, he was beginning to feel uncomfortable. "You're sure this place is safe?" he questioned.

"I'm not sure of anything," Ron said. "Just that it's been like this for seventy-five years or so."

It was a tight squeeze around the block of dirty ice in the center. When Dick was halfway around he shone the light into the space beyond.

Dick caught his breath while a little gasp issued from his mouth. Although he thought he'd been prepared, the image within the flashlight beam was more ghoulish than he'd expected. Staring back at him was the pale visage of a frozen, bearded Caucasian male dressed in furs. He was sitting upright. His eyes were open and ice blue, and they stared back at Dick defiantly. Around his mouth and nose was frozen pink froth.

"You see all three?" Ron called from the darkness.

Dick allowed the light to play around the room. The second body was supine, with its lower half completely encased in ice. The third body was positioned in a manner similar to the first, propped up against a wall in a half-sitting position. Both were Eskimos with characteristic features, dark hair, and dark eyes. Both also had frozen pink froth around their mouths and noses.

Dick shuddered through a sudden wave of nausea. He hadn't expected such a reaction, but it passed quickly.

"You see the newspaper?" Ron called.

"Not yet," Dick said as he trained his light on the floor. He saw all sorts of debris frozen together, including bird feathers and animal bones.

"It's near the bearded guy," Ron called.

Dick shone the light at the frozen Caucasian's feet. He saw the Anchorage paper immediately. The headlines were about the war in Europe. Even from where he was he could see the date: April 17, 1918.

Dick wriggled back into the antechamber. His initial horror had passed. Now he was excited. "I think you were right," he said. "It looks like all three died of pneumonia, and the date is right on."

"I knew you'd find it interesting," Ron said.

"It's more than interesting," Dick said. "It could be the chance of a lifetime. I'm going to need a saw."

The blood drained from Ron's face. "A saw," he repeated with dismay. "You've got to be joking."

"You think I'd pass up this chance?" Dick questioned. "Not on your life. I need some lung tissue."

"Jesus H. Christ!" Ron murmured. "You'd better promise again not to say anything about this ever!"

"I promised already," Dick said with exasperation. "If I find what I think I'm going to find, it will be for my own collection. Don't worry. Nobody's going to know."

Ron shook his head. "Sometimes I think you're one weird dude."

"Let's get the saw," Dick said. He handed the flashlight to Ron and started for the entrance.

6:40 P.M.
O'HARE AIRPORT, CHICAGO

Marilyn Stapleton looked at her husband of twelve years and felt torn. She knew that the convulsive changes that had racked their family had impacted most on John, yet she still had to think about the children. She glanced at the two girls who were sitting in the departure lounge and nervously looking in her direction, sensing that their life as they knew it was in the balance. John wanted them to move to Chicago where he was starting a new residency in pathology.

Marilyn redirected her gaze to her husband's pleading face. He'd changed over the last several years. The confident, reserved man she had married was now bitter and insecure. He had shed twenty-five pounds, and his once ruddy, full cheeks had hollowed, giving him a lean, haggard look consistent with his new personality.

Marilyn shook her head. It was hard to recall that just two years previously they had been the picture of the successful suburban family with his flourishing ophthalmology practice and her tenured position in English literature at the University of Illinois.

But then the huge health-care conglomerate AmeriCare had appeared on the horizon, sweeping through Champaign, Illinois, as well as numerous other towns, gobbling up practices and hospitals with bewildering speed. John had tried to hold out but ultimately lost his patient base. It was either surrender or flee, and John chose to flee. At first he'd looked for another ophthalmology position, but when it became clear there were too many ophthalmologists and that he'd be forced to work for AmeriCare or a similar organization, he'd made the decision to retrain in another medical specialty.

"I think you would enjoy living in Chicago," John said pleadingly. "And I miss you all terribly."

Marilyn sighed. "We miss you, too," she said. "But that's not the point. If I give up my job the girls would have to go to an inner-city public school. There's no way we could afford private school with your resident's salary."

The public-address system crackled to life and announced that all passengers holding tickets for Champaign had to be on board. It was last call.

"We've got to go," Marilyn said. "We'll miss the flight."

John nodded and brushed away a tear. "I know," he said. "But you will think about it?"

"Of course I'll think about it," Marilyn snapped. Then she caught herself. She sighed again. She didn't mean to sound angry. "It's all I'm thinking about," she added softly.

Marilyn lifted her arms and embraced her husband. He hugged her back with ferocity.

"Careful," she wheezed. "You'll snap one of my ribs."

"I love you," John said in a muffled voice. He'd buried his face in the crook of her neck.

After echoing his sentiments, Marilyn broke away and gathered Lydia and Tamara. She gave the boarding passes to the ticket agent and herded the girls down the ramp. As she walked she glanced at John through the glass partition. As they turned into the jetway she gave a wave. It was to be her last.

"Are we going to have to move?" Lydia whined. She was ten and in the fifth grade.

"I'm not moving," Tamara said. She was eleven and strong-willed. "I'll move in with Connie. She said I could stay with her."

"And I'm sure she discussed that with her mother," Marilyn said sarcastically. She was fighting back tears she didn't want the girls to see.

Marilyn allowed her daughters to precede her onto the small prop plane. She directed the girls to their assigned seats and then had to settle an argument about who was going to sit alone. The seating was two by two.

Marilyn answered her daughters' impassioned entreaties about what the near future would bring with vague generalities. In truth, she didn't know what was best for the family.

The plane's engines started with a roar that made further conversation difficult. As the plane left the terminal and taxied out toward the runway, she put her nose to the window. She wondered how she would have the strength to make a decision.

A bolt of lightning to the southwest jolted Marilyn from her musing. It was an uncomfortable reminder of her disdain for commuter flights. She did not have the same confidence in small planes as she did in regular jets. Unconsciously she cinched her seat belt tighter and again checked her daughters'.

During the takeoff Marilyn gripped the armrests with a force that suggested she thought her effort helped the plane get aloft. It wasn't until the ground had significantly receded that she realized she'd been holding her breath.

"How long is Daddy going to live in Chicago?" Lydia called across the aisle.

"Five years," Marilyn answered. "Until he finishes his training."

"I told you," Lydia yelled to Tamara. "We'll be old by then."

A sudden bump made Marilyn reestablish her death grip on her arm-rests. She glanced around the cabin. The fact that no one was panicking gave her some solace. Looking out the window, she saw that they were entirely enveloped in clouds. A flash of lightning eerily lit up the sky.

As they flew south the turbulence increased, as did the frequency of the lightning. A terse announcement by the pilot that they would try to find smoother air at a different altitude did little to assuage Marilyn's rising fears. She wanted the flight to be over.

The first sign of real disaster was a strange light that filled the plane, followed instantly by a tremendous bump and vibration. Several of the passengers let out half-suppressed screams that made Marilyn's blood run cold. Instinctively she reached over and pulled Tamara closer to her.

The vibration increased in intensity as the plane began an agonizing roll to the right. At the same time the sound of the engines changed from a roar to an earsplitting whine. Sensing that she was being pressed into her seat and feeling disoriented in space, Marilyn looked out the window. At first she didn't see anything but clouds. But then she looked ahead and her heart leaped into her throat. The earth was rushing up at them at breakneck speed! They were flying straight down . . .

10:40 P.M.
MANHATTAN GENERAL HOSPITAL, NEW YORK CITY

Terese Hagen tried to swallow, but it was difficult; her mouth was bone dry. A few minutes later her eyes blinked open, and for a moment she was disoriented. When she realized she was in a surgical recovery room it all came back to her in a flash.

The problem had started without warning that evening just before she and Matthew were about to go out to dinner. There had been no pain. The first thing she was aware of was wetness, particularly on the inside of her thigh. Going into the bathroom, she was dismayed to find that she was bleeding. And it wasn't just spotting. It was active hemorrhaging. Since she was five months pregnant, she was afraid it spelled trouble.

Events had unfolded rapidly from that point. She'd been able to reach her physician, Dr. Carol Glanz, who offered to meet her at the Manhattan General's emergency room. Once there, Terese's suspicions had been confirmed and surgery scheduled. The doctor had said that it appeared as if the embryo had implanted in one of her tubes instead of the uterus—an ectopic pregnancy.

Within minutes of her regaining consciousness, one of the recovery-room nurses was at her side, reassuring her that everything was fine.

"What about my baby?" Terese asked. She could feel a bulky dressing over her disturbingly flat abdomen.

"Your doctor knows more about that than I do," the nurse said. "I'll let her know you are awake. I know she wants to talk with you."

Before the nurse left, Terese complained about her dry throat. The nurse gave her some ice chips, and the cool fluid was a godsend.

Terese closed her eyes. She guessed that she dozed off, because the next thing she knew was that Dr. Carol Glanz was calling her name.

"How do you feel?" Dr. Glanz asked.

Terese assured her she was fine thanks to the ice chips. She then asked about her baby.

Dr. Glanz took a deep breath and reached out and put her hand on Terese's shoulder. "I'm afraid I have double bad news," she said.

Terese could feel herself tense.

"It was ectopic," Dr. Glanz said, falling back on doctor jargon to make a difficult job a bit easier. "We had to terminate the pregnancy and, of course, the child was not viable."

Terese nodded, ostensibly without emotion. She had expected as much and had tried to prepare herself. What she wasn't prepared for was what Dr. Glanz said next.

"Unfortunately the operation wasn't easy. There were some complications, which was why you were bleeding so profusely when you came into the emergency room. We had to sacrifice your uterus. We had to do a hysterectomy."

At first Terese's brain was unable to comprehend what she'd been told. She nodded and looked expectantly at the doctor as if she anticipated more information.

"I'm sure this is very upsetting for you," Dr. Glanz said. "I want you to understand that everything was done that could have been done to avoid this unfortunate outcome."

Sudden comprehension of what she'd been told jolted Terese. Her silent voice broke free from its bounds and she cried: "No!"

Dr. Glanz squeezed her shoulder in sympathy. "Since this was to be your first child, I know what this means to you," she said. "I'm terribly sorry."

Terese groaned. It was such crushing news that for the moment she was beyond tears. She was numb. All her life she had assumed she would have children. It had been part of her identity. The idea that it was impossible was too difficult to grasp.

"What about my husband?" Terese managed. "Has he been told?"

"He has," Dr. Glanz said. "I spoke to him as soon as I'd finished the case. He's downstairs in your room, where I'm sure you'll be going momentarily."

There was more conversation with Dr. Glanz, but Terese remembered little of it. The combined realization that she'd lost her child and would never be able to have another was devastating.

A quarter hour later an orderly arrived to wheel her to her room. The trip went quickly; she was oblivious to her surroundings. Her mind was in turmoil; she needed reassurance and support.

When she reached her room, Matthew was on his cellular phone. As a stockbroker, it was his constant companion.

The floor nurses expertly transferred Terese to her bed and hung her IV on a pole behind her head. After making sure all was in order and encouraging her to call if she needed anything, they left.

Terese looked over at Matthew, who had averted his gaze as he finished his call. She was concerned about his reaction to this catastrophe. They had been married for only three months.

With a definitive click Matthew flipped his phone closed and slipped it into his jacket pocket. He turned to Terese and stared at her for a moment. His tie was loosened and his shirt collar unbuttoned.

She tried to read his expression but couldn't. He was chewing the inside of his cheek.

"How are you?" he asked finally with little emotion.

"As well as can be expected," Terese managed. She desperately wanted him to come to her and hold her, but he kept his distance.

"This is a curious state of affairs," he said.

"I'm not sure I know what you mean," Terese said.

"Simply that the main reason we got married has just evaporated," Matthew said. "I'd say your planning has gone awry."

Terese's mouth slowly dropped open. Stunned, she had to struggle to find her voice. "I don't like your implication," she said. "I didn't get pregnant on purpose."

"Well, you have your reality and I have mine," Matthew said. "The problem is: What are we going to do about it?"

Terese closed her eyes. She couldn't respond. It had been as if Matthew had plunged a knife into her heart. She knew from that moment that she didn't love him. In fact she hated him . . .

CHAPTER 1

"Excuse me," Jack Stapleton said with false civility to the darkly complected Pakistani cabdriver. "Would you care to step out of your car so we can discuss this matter fully?"

Jack was referring to the fact that the cabdriver had cut him off at the intersection of Forty-sixth Street and Second Avenue. In retaliation Jack had kicked the cab's driver-side door when they had both stopped at a red light at Forty-fourth Street. Jack was on his Cannondale mountain bike that he used to commute to work.

This morning's confrontation was not unusual. Jack's daily route included a hair-raising slalom down Second Avenue from Fifty-ninth Street to Thirtieth Street at breakneck speed. There were frequent close calls with trucks and taxicabs and the inevitable arguments. Anyone else would have found the trip nerve-racking. Jack loved it. As he explained to his colleagues, it got his blood circulating.

Choosing to ignore Jack until the light turned green, the Pakistani cab-driver then cursed him soundly before speeding off.

"And to you too!" Jack yelled back. He accelerated standing up until he reached a speed equal to the traffic. Then he settled onto the seat while his legs pumped furiously.

Eventually he caught up with the offending cabdriver, but Jack ignored him. In fact, he whisked past him, squeezing between the taxi and a delivery van.

At Thirtieth Street Jack turned east, crossed First Avenue, and abruptly turned into the loading bay of the Office of the Chief Medical Examiner for the City of New York. Jack had been working there for five months, having been offered a position as an associate medical examiner after finishing his pathology residency and a year's fellowship in forensics.

Jack wheeled his bike past the security office and waved at the uniformed guard. Turning left, he passed the mortuary office and entered the morgue itself. Turning left again, he passed a bank of the refrigerated compartments used to store bodies prior to autopsy. In a corner where simple pine coffins were stored for unclaimed bodies heading for Hart Island, Jack parked his bike and secured it with several Kryptonite locks.

The elevator took Jack up to the first floor. It was well before eight in the morning and few of the daytime employees had arrived. Even Sergeant Murphy wasn't in the office assigned to the police.

Passing through the communications room, Jack entered the ID area. He said hello to Vinnie Amendola, who returned the greeting without looking up from his newspaper. Vinnie was one of the mortuary techs who worked with Jack frequently.

Jack also said hello to Laurie Montgomery, one of the board-certified forensic pathologists. It was her turn in the rotation to be in charge of assigning the cases that had come in during the night. She'd been at the Office of the Chief Medical Examiner for four and a half years. Like Jack, she was usually one of the first to arrive in the morning.

"I see you made it into the office once again without having to come in feet first," Laurie said teasingly. She was referring to Jack's dangerous bike ride. "Coming in feet first" was office vernacular for arriving dead.

"Only one brush with a taxi," Jack said. "I'm accustomed to three or four. It was like a ride in the country this morning."

"I'm sure," Laurie said without belief. "Personally I think you are foolhardy to ride your bike in this city. I've autopsied several of those daredevil bicycle messengers. Every time I see one in traffic I wonder when I'll be seeing him in the pit." The "pit" was office vernacular for the autopsy room.

Jack helped himself to coffee, then wandered over to the desk where Laurie was working.

"Anything particularly interesting?" Jack asked, looking over her shoulder.

"The usual gunshot wounds," Laurie said. "Also a drug overdose."

"Ugh," Jack said.

"You don't like overdoses?"

"Nah," Jack said. "They're all the same. I like surprises and a challenge."

"I had a few overdoses that fit into that category during my first year," Laurie said.

"How so?"

"It's a long story," Laurie said evasively. Then she pointed to one of the names on her list. "Here's a case you might find interesting: Donald Nodelman. The diagnosis is unknown infectious disease."

"That would certainly be better than an overdose," Jack said.

"Not in my book," Laurie said. "But it's yours if you want it. Personally I don't care for infectious disease cases, never have and never will. When I did the external exam earlier, it gave me the creeps. Whatever it was, it was an aggressive bug. He's got extensive subcutaneous bleeding."

"Unknowns can be a challenge," Jack said. He picked up the folder. "I'll be glad to do the case. Did he die at home or in an institution?"

"He was in a hospital," Laurie said. "He was brought in from the Manhattan General. But infectious disease wasn't his admitting diagnosis. He'd been admitted for diabetes."

"It's my recollection that the Manhattan General is an AmeriCare hospital," Jack said. "Is that true?"

"I think so," Laurie said. "Why do you ask?"

"Because it might make this case personally rewarding," Jack said. "Maybe I'll be lucky enough for the diagnosis to be something like Legionnaires' disease. I couldn't think of anything more enjoyable than giving AmeriCare heartburn. I'd love to see that corporation squirm."

"Why's that?" Laurie asked.

"It's a long story," Jack said with an impish smile. "One of these days we should have a drink and you can tell me about your overdoses and I'll tell you about me and AmeriCare."

Laurie didn't know if Jack's invitation was sincere or not. She didn't know much about Jack Stapleton beyond his work at the medical examiner's office; her understanding was that no one else did either. Jack was a superb forensic pathologist, despite the fact that he'd only recently finished his training. But he didn't socialize much, and he was never very personally revealing in his small talk. All Laurie knew was that he was forty-one, unmarried, entertainingly flippant, and came from the Midwest.

"I'll let you know what I find," Jack said as he headed toward the communications room.

"Jack, excuse me," Laurie called out.

Jack stopped and turned around.

"Would you mind if I gave you a bit of advice," she said hesitantly. She was speaking impulsively. It wasn't like her, but she appreciated Jack and hoped that he would be working there for some time.

Jack's impish smile returned. He stepped back to the desk. "By all means," he said.

"I'm probably speaking out of turn," Laurie said.

"Quite the contrary," Jack said. "I honor your opinion. What's on your mind?"

"Just that you and Calvin Washington have been at odds," Laurie said. "I know it's just a clash of personalities, but Calvin has had a long-standing relationship with the Manhattan General, as AmeriCare does with the mayor's office. I think you should be careful."

"Being careful hasn't been one of my strong points for five years," Jack said. "I have utmost respect for the deputy chief. Our only disagreement is that he believes rules to be carved in stone while I see them as guidelines. As for AmeriCare, I don't care for their goals or methods."

"Well, it's not my business," Laurie said. "But Calvin keeps saying he doesn't see you as a team player."

"He's got a point there," Jack said. "The problem is that I've developed an aversion to mediocrity. I'm honored to work with most people around here, especially you. However, there are a few whom I can't deal with, and I don't hide it. It's as simple as that."

"I'll take that as a compliment," Laurie said.

"It was meant as one," Jack said.

"Well, let me know what you find on Nodelman," Laurie said. "Then I'll have at least one more case for you to do."

"My pleasure," Jack said. He turned and headed for the communications room. As he walked past Vinnie, he snatched away his paper.

"Come on, Vinnie," Jack said. "We're going to get a jump on the day."

Vinnie complained but followed. While trying to retrieve his paper he collided with Jack, who had abruptly stopped outside of Janice Jaeger's office. Janice was one of the forensic investigators, frequently referred to as PAs or physician's assistants. Her tour of duty was the graveyard shift, from eleven to seven. Jack was surprised to find her still in her office. A petite woman with dark hair and dark eyes, she was obviously tired.

"What are you still doing here?" Jack asked.

"I've got one more report to finish."

Jack held up the folder in his hand. "Did you or Curt handle Nodelman?"

"I did," Janice said. "Is there a problem?"

"Not that I know about yet," Jack said with a chuckle. He knew Janice to be extremely conscientious, which made her ideal for teasing. "Was it your impression the cause of death was a nosocomial infection?"

"What the hell is a 'nosocomial infection'?" Vinnie asked.

"It's an infection acquired in a hospital," Jack explained.

"It certainly seems so," Janice said. "The man had been in the hospital five days for his diabetes before developing symptoms of an infectious disease. Once he got them, he died within thirty-six hours."

Jack whistled in respect. "Whatever the bug was, it certainly was virulent."

"That's what worried the doctors I spoke with," Janice said.

"Any laboratory results from microbiology?" Jack questioned.

"Nothing has grown out," Janice said. "Blood cultures were negative as of four o'clock this morning. The terminal event was acute respiratory distress syndrome, or ARDS, but sputum cultures have been negative as well. The only positive thing was the gram stain of the sputum. That showed gram-negative bacilli. That made people think of pseudomonas, but it hasn't been confirmed."

"Any question of the patient being immunologically compromised?" Jack asked. "Did he have AIDS or had he been treated with antimetabolites?"

"Not that I could ascertain," Janice said. "The only problem he had listed was diabetes and some of the usual sequelae. Anyway, it's all in the investigative report if you'd care to read it."

"Hey, why read when I can get it from the horse's mouth?" Jack said with a laugh. He thanked Janice and headed for the elevator.

"I hope you are planning to wear your moon suit," Vinnie said. The moon suit, the completely enclosed, impervious outfit complete with a clear plastic face mask, was designed for maximum protection. Air was forced into the suit by a fan worn at the small of the back, pulling air through a filter before circulating it within the headpiece. That provided enough ventilation to breathe but guaranteed sauna-like temperatures inside. Jack detested the setup.

As far as Jack was concerned the moon suit was bulky, restrictive, uncomfortable, hot, and unnecessary. He'd not worn one throughout his training. The problem was that the New York chief, Dr. Harold Bingham, had decreed that the suits be used. Calvin, the deputy chief, was intent on enforcing it. Jack had endured several confrontations as a result.

"This might be the first time the suit is indicated," Jack said, to Vinnie's relief. "Until we know what we are dealing with we have to take all precautions. After all, it could be something like Ebola virus."

Vinnie stopped in his tracks. "You really think it's possible?" he asked, his eyes opened wide.

"Not a chance," Jack said. He slapped him on the back. "Just kidding."

"Thank God," Vinnie said. They started walking again.

"But maybe plague," Jack added.

Vinnie stopped again. "That would be just as bad," he said.

Jack shrugged his shoulders. "All in a day's work," he said. "Come on, let's get it over with."

They changed into scrubs, and then while Vinnie put on his moon suit and went into the autopsy room, Jack went through the contents of Nodelman's folder. It had a case work sheet, a partially completed death certificate, an inventory of medical-legal case records, two sheets for autopsy notes, a telephone notice of death as received that night by communications, a completed identification sheet, Janice's investigative report, a sheet for the autopsy report, and a lab slip for HIV antibody analysis.

Despite having spoken with Janice, Jack read her report carefully as he always did. When he was finished he went into the room next to the pine coffins and put on his moon suit. He took his ventilation unit from where it had been charging and hooked himself up. Then he set out for the autopsy room on the other side of the morgue.

Jack cursed the suit as he walked past most of the 126 refrigerated compartments for bodies. Being encased in the contraption put him in a bad mood, and he eyed his surroundings with a jaundiced eye. The morgue had been state of the art at one time, but it was now in need of repair and upgrading. With its aged, blue tile walls and stained cement floor it looked like a set for an old horror movie.

There was an entrance to the autopsy room directly from the hallway, but that wasn't used any longer except to bring bodies in and out. Instead Jack entered through a small anteroom with a washbasin.

By the time Jack entered the autopsy room Vinnie had Nodelman's body on one of the eight tables and had assembled all the necessary equipment and paraphernalia necessary to do the case. Jack positioned himself on the patient's right, Vinnie on the left.

"He doesn't look so good," Jack said. "I don't think he's going to make it to the prom." It was hard to talk in the moon suit, and he was already perspiring.

Vinnie, who never quite knew how to react to Jack's irreverent comments, didn't respond even though the corpse did look terrible.

"This is gangrene on his fingers," Jack said. He lifted one of the hands and examined the almost-black fingertips closely. Then he pointed to the man's shriveled genitals. "That's gangrene on the end of his penis. Ouch! That must have hurt. Can you imagine?"

Vinnie held his tongue.

Jack carefully examined every inch of the man's exterior. For Vinnie's benefit he pointed out the extensive subcutaneous hemorrhages on the man's abdomen and legs. He told him it was called purpura. Then Jack mentioned there were no obvious insect bites. "That's important," he added. "A lot of serious diseases are transmitted by arthropods."

"Arthropods?" Vinnie questioned. He never knew when Jack was joking.

"Insects," Jack said. "Crustaceans aren't much of a problem as disease vectors."

Vinnie nodded appreciatively, although he didn't know any more than he had when he'd asked his question. He made a mental note to try to remember to look up the meaning of "arthropods" when he had an opportunity.

"What are the chances whatever killed this man is contagious?" Vinnie asked.

"Excellent, I'm afraid," Jack said. "Excellent."

The door to the hallway opened and Sal D'Ambrosio, another mortuary tech, wheeled in another body. Totally absorbed in the external exam of Mr. Nodelman, Jack did not look up. He was already beginning to form a differential diagnosis.

A half hour later six of the eight tables were occupied by corpses awaiting autopsies. One by one the other medical examiners on duty that day began to arrive. Laurie was the first, and she came over to Jack's table.

"Any ideas yet?" she asked.

"Lots of ideas but nothing definitive," Jack said. "But I can assure you this is one virulent organism. I was teasing Vinnie earlier about its being Ebola. There's a lot of disseminated intravascular coagulation."

"My God!" Laurie exclaimed. "Are you serious?"

"No, not really," Jack said. "But from what I've seen so far it's still possible, just not probable. Of course I've never seen a case of Ebola, so that should tell you something."

"Do you think we ought to isolate this case?" Laurie asked nervously.

"I can't see any reason to," Jack said. "Besides, I've already started, and I'll be careful to avoid throwing any of the organs around the room. But I'll tell you what we should do: alert the lab to be mighty careful with the specimens until we have a diagnosis."

"Maybe I'd better ask Bingham's opinion," Laurie said.

"Oh, that would be helpful," Jack said sarcastically. "Then we'll have the blind leading the blind."

"Don't be disrespectful," Laurie said. "He is the chief."

"I don't care if he's the Pope," Jack said. "I think I should just get it done, the sooner the better. If Bingham or even Calvin gets involved it will drag on all morning."

"All right," Laurie said. "Maybe you're right. But let me see any abnormality. I'll be on table three."

Laurie left to do her own case. Jack took a scalpel from Vinnie and was about to make the incision when he noticed that Vinnie had moved away.

"Where are you going to watch this from, Queens?" Jack asked. "You're supposed to be helping."

"I'm a little nervous," Vinnie admitted.

"Oh, come on, man," Jack said. "You've been at more autopsies than I have. Get your Italian ass over here. We've got work to do."

Jack worked quickly but smoothly. He handled the internal organs gently and was meticulously careful about the use of instruments when either his or Vinnie's hands were in the field.

"Whatcha got?" Chet McGovern asked, looking over Jack's shoulder. Chet was also an associate medical examiner, having been hired in the same month as Jack. Of all the colleagues he'd become the closest to Jack, since they shared both a common office and the social circumstance of being single males. But Chet had never been married and at thirty-six, he was five years Jack's junior.

"Something interesting," Jack said. "The mystery disease of the week. And it's a humdinger. This poor bastard didn't have a chance."

"Any ideas?" Chet asked. His trained eye took in the gangrene and the hemorrhages under the skin.

"I got a lot of ideas," Jack said. "But let me show you the internal. I'd appreciate your opinion."

"Is there something I should see?" Laurie called from table three. She'd noticed Jack conversing with Chet.

"Yeah, come on over," Jack said. "No use going through this more than once."

Laurie sent Sal to the sink to wash out the intestines on her case, then stepped over to table one.

"The first thing I want you to look at is the lymphatics I dissected in the throat," Jack said. He had retracted the skin of the neck from the chin to the collarbone.

"No wonder autopsies take so long around here," a voice boomed in the confined space.

All eyes turned toward Dr. Calvin Washington, the deputy chief. He was an intimidating six-foot-seven, two-hundred-and-fifty-pound African-American man who'd passed up a chance to play NFL football to go to medical school.

"What the hell is going on around here?" he demanded half in jest. "What do you people think this is, a holiday?"

"Just pooling resources," Laurie said. "We've got an unknown infectious case that appears to be quite an aggressive microbe."

"So I heard," Calvin said. "I already got a call from the administrator over at the Manhattan General. He's justly concerned. What's the verdict?"

"A bit too soon to tell," Jack said. "But we've got a lot of pathology here."

Jack quickly summarized for Calvin what was known of the history and pointed out the positive findings on the external exam. Then he started back on the internal, indicating the spread of the disease along the lymphatics of the neck.

"Some of these nodes are necrotic," Calvin said.

"Exactly," Jack said. "In fact most of them are necrotic. The disease was spreading rapidly through the lymphatics, presumably from the throat and bronchial tree."

"Airborne, then," Calvin said.

"It would be my first guess," Jack admitted. "Now look at the internal organs."

Jack presented the lungs and opened the areas where he'd made slices.

"As you can see, this is pretty extensive lobar pneumonia," Jack said. "There's a lot of consolidation. But there is also some necrosis, and I believe early cavitation. If the patient had lived longer, I think we would be seeing some abscess formation."

Calvin whistled. "Wow," he said. "All this was happening in the face of massive IV antibiotics."

"It's worrisome," Jack agreed. He carefully slid the lungs back into the pan. He didn't want them sloshing around, potentially throwing infective particles into the air. Next he picked up the liver and gently separated its cut surface.

"Same process," he announced, pointing with his fingers to areas of early abscess formation. "Just not as extensive as with the lungs." Jack put the liver down and picked up the spleen. There were similar lesions throughout the organ. He made sure everyone saw them.

"So much for the gross," Jack said as he carefully replaced the spleen in the pan. "We'll have to see what the microscopic shows, but I actually think we'll be relying on the lab to give us the definitive answer."

"What's your guess at this point?" Calvin asked.

Jack let out a short laugh. "A guess it would have to be," he said. "I haven't seen anything pathognomonic yet. But its fulminant character should tell us something."

"What's your differential diagnosis?" Calvin asked. "Come on, Wonderboy, let's hear it."

"Ummmm," Jack said. "You're kinda putting me on the spot. But okay, I'll tell you what's been going through my head. First, I don't think it could be pseudomonas as suspected at the hospital. It's too aggressive. It could have been something atypical like strep group A or even staph with toxic shock, but I kinda doubt it, especially with the gram stain suggesting it was a bacillus. So I'd have to say it is something like tularemia or plague."

"Whoa!" Calvin exclaimed. "You're coming up with some pretty arcane illnesses for what was apparently a hospital-based infection. Haven't you heard the phrase about when you hear hoofbeats you should think of horses, not zebras?"

"I'm just telling you what's going through my mind. It's just a differential diagnosis. I'm trying to keep an open mind."

"All right," Calvin said soothingly. "Is that it?"

"No, that's not it," Jack said. "I'd also consider that the gram stain could have been wrong and that would let in not only strep and staph but meningococcemia as well. And I might as well throw in Rocky Mountain spotted fever and hantavirus. Hell, I could even throw in the viral hemorrhagic fevers like Ebola."

"Now you're getting out in the stratosphere," Calvin said. "Let's come back to reality. If I made you guess which one it is right now with what you know, what would you say?"

Jack clucked his tongue. He had the irritated feeling he was being put back in medical school, and that Calvin, like many of his medical-school professors, was trying to make him look bad.

"Plague," Jack said to a stunned audience.

"Plague?" Calvin questioned with surprise bordering on disdain. "In March? In New York City? In a hospitalized patient? You got to be out of your mind."

"Hey, you asked me for one diagnosis," Jack said. "So I gave it to you. I wasn't responding by probabilities, just pathology."

"You weren't considering the other epidemiological aspects?" Calvin asked with obvious condescension. He laughed. Then, talking more to the others than Jack, he said: "What the hell did they teach you out there in the Chicago boonies?"

"There are too many unknowns in this case for me to put a lot of weight on unsubstantiated information," Jack said. "I didn't visit the site. I don't know anything about the deceased's pets, travel, or contact with visitors. There are a lot of people coming and going in this city, even in and out of a hospital. And there are certainly more than enough rats around here to support the diagnosis."

For a moment a heavy silence hung over the autopsy room. Neither Laurie nor Chet knew what to say. Jack's tone made them both uncomfortable, especially knowing Calvin's stormy temperament.

"A clever comment," Calvin said finally. "You're quite good at double entendre. I have to give you credit there. Perhaps that's part of pathology training in the Midwest."

Both Laurie and Chet laughed nervously.

"All right, smartass," Calvin continued. "How much are you willing to put on your diagnosis of plague?"

"I didn't know it was customary to gamble around here," Jack said.

"No, it's not common to gamble, but when you come up with a diagnosis of plague, I think it's worthwhile to make a point of it. How about ten dollars?"

"I can afford ten dollars," Jack said.

"Fine," Calvin said. "With that settled, where's Paul Plodgett and that gunshot wound from the World Trade Center?"

"He's down on table six," Laurie said.

Calvin lumbered away and for a moment the others watched him. Laurie broke the silence. "Why do you try to provoke him?" she asked Jack. "I don't understand. You're making it more difficult for yourself."

"I can't help it," Jack said. "He provoked me!"

"Yeah, but he's the deputy chief and it's his prerogative," Chet said. "Besides, you were pushing things with a diagnosis of plague. It certainly wouldn't be on the top of my list."

"Are you sure?" Jack asked. "Look at the black fingers and toes on this patient. Remember, it was called the black death back in the fourteenth century."

"A lot of diseases can cause such thrombotic phenomena," Chet said.

"True," Jack said. "That's why I almost said tularemia."

"And why didn't you?" Laurie asked. In her mind tularemia was equally improbable.

"I thought plague sounded better," Jack said. "It's more dramatic."

"I never know when you are serious," Laurie said.

"Hey, I feel the same way," Jack said.

Laurie shook her head in frustration. At times it was hard to have a serious discussion with Jack. "Anyway," she said, "are you finished with Nodelman? If you are, I've got another case for you."

"I haven't done the brain yet," Jack said.

"Then get to it," Laurie said. She walked back to table three to finish her own case.

CHAPTER 2

**WEDNESDAY, 9:45 A.M., MARCH 20, 1996
NEW YORK CITY**

Terese Hagen stopped abruptly and looked at the closed door to the "cabin," the name given to the main conference room. It was called the cabin because the interior was a reproduction of Taylor Heath's Squam Lake house up in the wilds of New Hampshire. Taylor Heath was the CEO of the hot, up-and-coming advertising firm Willow and Heath, which was threatening to break into the rarefied ranks of the advertising big leagues.

After making sure she was not observed, Terese leaned toward the door and put her ear against it. She heard voices.

With her pulse quickening, Terese hurried down the hall to her own office. It never took long for her anxiety to soar. She'd only been in the office five minutes and already her heart was pounding. She didn't like the idea of a meeting she didn't know about being held in the cabin, the CEO's habitual domain. In her position as the creative director of the firm, she felt she had to know everything that was going on.

The problem was that a lot was going on. Taylor Heath had shocked everybody with his previous month's announcement that he planned to retire as CEO and was designating Brian Wilson, the current president, to succeed him. That left a big question mark about who would succeed Wilson. Terese was in the running. That was for sure. But so was Robert Barker, the firm's executive director of accounts. And on top of that, there was always the worry that Taylor would pick someone from outside.

Terese pulled off her coat and stuffed it into the closet. Her secretary, Marsha Devons, was on the phone, so Terese dashed to her desk and scanned the surface for any telltale message; but there was nothing except a pile of unrelated phone messages.

"There's a meeting in the cabin," Marsha called from the other room after hanging up the phone. She appeared in the doorway. She was a petite woman with raven-black hair. Terese appreciated her because she was intelligent, efficient, and intuitive—all the qualities lacking in the year's previous four secretaries. Terese was tough on her assistants, since she expected commitment and performance equivalent to her own.

"Why didn't you call me at home?" Terese demanded.

"I did, but you'd already left," Marsha said.

"Who's at the meeting?" Terese barked.

"It was Mr. Heath's secretary who called," Marsha said. "She didn't say who would be attending. Just that your presence was requested."

"Was there any indication what the meeting is about?" Terese asked.

"No," Marsha said simply.

"When did it start?"

"The call came through at nine," Marsha said.

Terese snatched up her phone and punched in Colleen Anderson's number. Colleen was Terese's most trusted art director. She was currently heading up a team for the National Health Care account.

"You know anything about this meeting in the cabin?" Terese asked as soon as Colleen was on the line.

Colleen didn't, only that it was going on.

"Damn!" Terese said as she hung up.

"Is there a problem?" Marsha asked solicitously.

"If Robert Barker has been in there all this time with Taylor, there's a problem," Terese said. "That prick never misses a beat to put me down."

Terese snatched the phone again and redialed Colleen. "What's the status on National Health? Do we have any comps or anything I can show right now?"

"I'm afraid not," Colleen said. "We've been brainstorming, but we don't have anything zippy like I know you want. I'm looking for a home run."

"Well, goose your team," Terese said. "I have a sneaking suspicion I'm most vulnerable with National Health."

"No one's been sleeping down here," Colleen said. "I can assure you of that."

Terese hung up without saying good-bye. Snatching up her purse, she ran down the hall to the ladies' room and positioned herself in front of the mirror. She pushed her Medusa's head of highlighted tight curls into a semblance of order, then reapplied some lipstick and a bit of blush.

Stepping back, she surveyed herself. Luckily she'd chosen to wear one of her favorite suits. It was dark blue wool gabardine and seriously severe, hugging her narrow frame like a second skin.

Satisfied with her appearance, Terese hustled to the cabin door. After a deep breath she grasped the knob, turned it, and entered.

"Ah, Miss Hagen," Brian Wilson said, glancing at his watch. He was sitting at the head of a rough-hewn plank table that dominated the room. "I see you're now indulging in banker's hours."

Brian was a short man with thinning hair. He vainly tried to camouflage his bald spot by combing his side hair over it. As per usual he was attired in a white shirt and tie, loosened at the neck, giving him the appearance of a harried newspaper publisher. To complete the journalistic look, his sleeves were rolled up above his elbows and a yellow Dixon pencil was tucked behind his right ear.

Despite the catty comment, Terese liked and respected Brian. He was an able administrator. He had a patented derogatory style, but he was equally demanding of himself.

"I was in the office last night until one A.M.," Terese said. "I certainly would have been here for this meeting if someone had been kind enough to have let me know about it."

"It was an impromptu meeting," Taylor called out. He was standing near the window, in keeping with his laissez-faire management style. He preferred to hover above the group like an Olympian god, watching his demigods and mere mortals hammer out decisions.

Taylor and Brian were opposite in most ways. Where Brian was short, Taylor was tall. Where Brian was balding, Taylor had a dense halo of silver-gray hair. Where Brian appeared as the harried newspaper columnist always with his back against the wall, Taylor was the picture of sophisticated tranquillity and sartorial splendor. Yet no one doubted Taylor's encyclopedic grasp of the business and his uncanny ability to maintain strategic goals in the face of daily tactical disaster and controversy.

Terese took a seat at the table directly across from her nemesis, Robert Barker. He was a tall, thin-faced man with narrow lips who seemed to take a cue from Taylor in regard to his dress. He was always attired nattily in dark silk suits and colorful silk ties. The ties were his trademark. Terese could not remember ever having seen the same tie twice.

Next to Robert was Helen Robinson, whose presence made Terese's racing heart beat even a little faster. Helen worked under Robert as the account executive assigned specifically to National Health. She was a strikingly attractive twenty-five-year-old woman with long, chestnut-colored hair that cascaded to her shoulders, tanned skin even in March, and full, sensuous features. Between her intelligence and looks she was a formidable adversary.

Also sitting at the table was Phil Atkins, the chief financial officer, and Carlene Desalvo, the corporate director of account planning. Phil was an impeccably precise man with his perennial three-piece suit and wire-rimmed glasses. Carlene was a bright, full-figured woman who always dressed in white. Terese was mildly surprised to see both of them at the meeting.

"We've got a big problem with the National Health account," Brian said. "That's why this meeting was called."

Terese's mouth went dry. She glanced at Robert and detected a slight but infuriating smile. Terese wished to God she'd been there since the beginning of the meeting so she could have known everything that had been said.

Terese was aware of trouble with National Health. The company had called for an internal review a month ago, which meant that Willow and Heath had to come up with a new advertising campaign if they expected to keep the account. And everybody knew they had to keep the account. It had mushroomed to somewhere around forty million annually and was still growing. Health-care advertising was in the ascendancy, and would hopefully fill the hole vacated by cigarettes.

Brian turned to Robert. "Perhaps you could fill Terese in on the latest developments," he said.

"I defer to my able assistant, Helen," Robert said, giving Terese one of his condescending smiles.

Helen moved forward in her seat. "As you know, National Health has had misgivings about its advertising campaign. Unfortunately their displeasure has increased. Just yesterday their figures came in for the last open subscriber period. The results weren't good. Their loss of market share to AmeriCare in the New York metropolitan area has increased. After building the new hospital, this is a terrible blow."

"And they blame our ad campaign for that?" Terese blurted out. "That's absurd. They only made a twenty-five-point buy with our sixty-second commercial. That was not adequate. No way."

"That may be your opinion," Helen said evenly. "But I know it is not National Health's."

"I know you are fond of your 'Health care for the modern era' campaign, and it is a good tag line," Robert said, "but the fact of the matter is that National Health has been losing market share from the campaign's inception. These latest figures are just consistent with the previous trend."

"The sixty-second spot has been nominated for a Clio," Terese countered. "It's a damn good commercial. It's wonderfully creative. I'm proud of my team for having put it together."

"And indeed you should be," Brian interjected. "But it is Robert's feeling that the client is not interested in our winning a Clio. And remember, as the Benton and Bowles agency held, 'If it doesn't sell, it isn't creative.' "

"That's equally absurd," Terese snapped. "The campaign is solid. It's just that the account people couldn't get the client to buy adequate exposure. There should have been 'flights' on multiple local stations at a bare minimum."

"With all due respect, they would have bought more time if they'd liked the commercial," Robert said. "I don't think they were ever sold on this idea of 'them versus us,' ancient medicine versus modern medicine. I mean it was humorous, but I don't know if they were convinced the viewer truly associated the ancient methods with National Health Care's competitors, particularly AmeriCare. My personal opinion is that it went over people's heads."

"Your real point is that National Health Care has a very specific type of advertising it wants," Brian said. "Tell Terese what you told me just before she came in here."

"It's simple," Robert said, making an open gesture with his hands. "They want either 'talking heads' discussing actual patient experiences, or a celebrity spokesperson. They couldn't care less whether their ad wins a Clio or any of the other awards. They want results. They want market share, and I want to give it to them."

"Am I hearing that Willow and Heath wants to turn its back on its successes and become a mere vendor shop?" Terese asked. "We're on the edge of becoming one of the big-league firms. And how did we get here? We got here by doing quality advertising. We've carried on in the Doyle-Dane-Bernback tradition. If we start letting clients dictate that we turn out slop, we're doomed."

"What I'm hearing is the usual conflict between the account executive and the creative," Taylor said, interrupting the increasingly heated discussion. "Robert, you think Terese is this self-indulgent child who is bent on alienating the client. Terese, you think Robert is this shortsighted pragmatist who wants to throw out the baby with the bathwater. The trouble is you are both right and both wrong at the same time. You have to use each other as a team. Stop arguing and deal with the problem at hand."

For a moment everyone was quiet. Zeus had spoken and everyone knew he was on target as usual.

"All right," Brian said finally. "Here's our reality. National Health is a vital client to our long-term stability. Thirty-odd days ago it asked for an internal review, which we expected in a couple of months. They now have told us they want it next week."

"Next week!" Terese all but shouted. "My God." It took months to put together a new campaign and pitch it.

"I know that will put the creatives under a lot of pressure," Brian said. "But the reality is National Health is the boss. The problem is that after our pitch, if they are not satisfied, they'll set up an outside review. The account will then be up for grabs, and I don't have to remind you that these health-care giants are going to be the advertising cash cows of the next decade. All the agencies are interested."

"As chief financial officer I think I should make it clear what the loss of the National Health account would do to our bottom line," Phil Atkins said. "We'll have to put off the restructuring because we won't have the funds to buy back our junk bonds."

"Obviously it is in all our best interests that we not lose the account," Brian said.

"I don't know if it is possible to put together a pitch for next week," Terese said.

"You have anything you can show us at the moment?" Brian asked.

Terese shook her head.

"You must have something," Robert said. "I assume you have a team working on it." The smile had returned to the corners of his mouth.

"Of course we have a team on National Health," Terese said. "But we haven't had any 'big ideas' to date. Obviously we thought we had several more months."

"Perhaps you might assign some additional personnel," Brian said. "But I'll leave that up to your judgment." Then to the rest of the group he said: "For now we'll adjourn this meeting until we have something from Creative to look at." He stood up. Everybody else did the same.

Dazed, Terese stumbled out of the cabin and descended to the agency's main studio on the floor below.

Willow and Heath had reversed a trend that began during the seventies and eighties when New York advertising firms had experienced a diaspora to varying chic sections of the city like TriBeCa and Chelsea. The agency returned to the old stamping ground of Madison Avenue, taking over several floors of a modest-sized building.

Terese found Colleen at her drawing board.

"What's the scoop?" Colleen asked. "You look pale."

"Trouble!" Terese exclaimed.

Colleen had been Terese's first hire. She was her most reliable art director. They got along famously both professionally and socially. Colleen was a milky-white-skinned strawberry blonde with a smattering of pale freckles over an upturned nose. Her eyes were a deep blue, a much stronger hue than Terese's. She favored oversized sweatshirts that somehow seemed to accentuate rather than hide her enviable figure.

"Let me guess," Colleen said. "Has National Health pushed up the deadline for the review?"

"How'd you know?"

"Intuition," Colleen said. "When you said 'trouble,' that's the worst thing I could think of."

"The Robert-and-Helen sideshow brought in information that National Health has lost more market share to AmeriCare despite our campaign."

"Damn!" Colleen said. "It's a good campaign and a great sixty-second commercial."

"You know it and I know it," Terese said. "Problem is that it wasn't shown enough. I have an uncomfortable suspicion that Helen undermined us and talked them out of the two-hundred- to three-hundred-point TV commercial buy they had initially intended to make. That would have been saturation. I know it would have worked."

"I thought you told me you had pulled out the stops to guarantee National Health's market share would go up," Colleen said.

"I did," Terese said. "I've done everything I could think of and then some. I mean, it's my best sixty-second spot. You told me yourself."

Terese rubbed her forehead. She was getting a headache. She could still feel her pulse clanging away at her temples.

"You might as well tell me the bad news," Colleen said. She put down her drawing pencil and swung around to face Terese. "What's the new time frame?"

"National Health wants us to pitch a new campaign next week."

"Good Lord!" Colleen said.

"What do we have so far?" Terese asked.

"Not a lot."

"You must have some tissues or some preliminary executions," Terese said. "I know I haven't been giving you any attention lately since we've had deadlines with three other clients. But you have had a team working on this for almost a month."

"We've been having strategy session after strategy session," Colleen said. "A lot of brainstorming, but no big idea. Nothing's jumped out and grabbed us. I mean, I have a sense of what you are looking for."

"Well, I want to see what you have," Terese said. "I don't care how sketchy or preliminary. I want to see what the team has been doing. I want to see it today."

"All right," Colleen said without enthusiasm. "I'll get everybody together."

CHAPTER 3

WEDNESDAY, 11:15 A.M., MARCH 20, 1996

Susanne Hard had never liked hospitals.

A scoliotic back had kept her in and out of them as a child. Hospitals made her nervous. She hated the sense that she was not in control and that she was surrounded by the sick and the dying.

Susanne was a firm believer in the adage If something can go wrong, it will go wrong. She felt this way particularly in relation to hospitals. Indeed, on her last admission, she'd been carted off to urology to face some frightful procedure before she'd finally been able to convince a reluctant technician to read the name on her wristband. They'd had the wrong patient.

On her present admission Susanne wasn't sick. The previous night her labor had started with her second child. In addition to her back problem, her pelvis was distorted, making a normal vaginal delivery impossible. As with her first child, she had to have a cesarean section.

Since she'd just undergone abdominal surgery, her doctor insisted that she stay at least a few days. No amount of cajoling on Susanne's part had been successful in convincing the doctor otherwise.

Susanne tried to relax by wondering what kind of child she'd just birthed. Would he be like his brother, Allen, who had been a wonderful baby? Allen had slept through the night almost from day one. He'd been a delight, and now that he was three and already exerting independence, Susanne was looking forward to a new baby. She thought of herself as a natural mother.

With a start, Susanne awoke. She'd surprised herself by nodding off. What had awakened her was a white-clad figure fiddling with the IV bottles that hung from a pole at the head of her bed.

"What are you doing?" Susanne asked. She felt paranoid about anybody doing anything she didn't know about.

"Sorry to have awakened you, Mrs. Hard," a nurse said. "I was just hanging up a new bottle of fluid. Yours is just about out."

Susanne glanced at the IV snaking into the back of her hand. As an experienced hospital patient, she suggested that it was time for the IV to come out.

"Maybe I should check on that," the nurse said. She then waltzed out of the room.

Tilting her head back, Susanne looked at the IV bottle to see what it was. It was upside down, so she couldn't read the label.

She started to turn over, but a sharp pain reminded her of her recently sutured incision. She decided to stay on her back.

Gingerly she took a deep breath. She didn't feel any discomfort until right at the end of inspiration.

Closing her eyes, Susanne tried again to calm down. She knew that she still had a significant amount of drugs "on board" from the anesthesia, so sleep should be easy. The trouble was, she didn't know if she wanted to be asleep with so many people coming in and out of her room.

A very soft clank of plastic hitting plastic drifted out of the background noise of the hospital and caught Susanne's attention. Her eyes blinked open. She saw an orderly off to the side by the bureau.

"Excuse me," Susanne called.

The man turned around. He was a handsome fellow in a white coat over scrubs. From where he was standing, Susanne could not read his name tag. He appeared surprised to be addressed.

"I hope I didn't disturb you, ma'am," the young man said.

"Everybody is disturbing me," Susanne said without malice. "It's like Grand Central Station in here."

"I'm terribly sorry," the man said. "I can always return later if it would be more convenient."

"What are you doing?" Susanne asked.

"Just filling your humidifier," the man said.

"What do I have a humidifier for?" Susanne said. "I didn't have one after my last cesarean."

"The anesthesiologists frequently order them this time of year," the man said. "Right after surgery, patients' throats are often irritated from the endotracheal tube. It's usually helpful to use a humidifier for the first day or even the first few hours. In what month did you have your last cesarean?"

"May," Susanne said.

"That's probably the reason you didn't have one then," the man said. "Would you like me to return?"

"Do what you have to do," Susanne said.

No sooner had the man left than the original nurse returned. "You were right," she said. "The orders were to pull the IV as soon as the bottle was through."

Susanne merely nodded. She felt like asking the nurse if missing orders was something she did on a regular basis. Susanne sighed. She wanted out of there.

After the nurse had removed the IV, Susanne managed to calm herself enough to fall back asleep. But it didn't last long. Someone was nudging her arm.

Susanne opened her eyes and looked into the face of another smiling nurse. In the foreground and between them was a five-cc syringe.

"I've got something for you," the nurse said as if Susanne were a toddler and the syringe candy.

"What is it?" Susanne demanded. She instinctively pulled away.

"It's the pain shot you requested," the nurse said. "So roll over and I'll give it to you."

"I didn't request a pain shot," Susanne said.

"But of course you did," the nurse said.

"But I didn't," Susanne said.

The nurse's expression changed to exasperation like a cloud passing over the sun. "Well then, it's doctor's orders. You are supposed to have a pain shot every six hours."

"But I don't have much pain," Susanne said. "Only when I move or breathe deeply."

"There you are," the nurse said. "You have to breathe deeply, otherwise you'll get pneumonia. Come on now, be a good girl."

Susanne thought for a moment. On the one hand she felt like being contrary. On the other hand she wanted to be taken care of and there was nothing inherently wrong with a pain shot. It might even make her sleep better.

"Okay," Susanne said.

Gritting her teeth, she managed to roll to the side as the nurse bared her bottom.

CHAPTER 4

WEDNESDAY, 2:05 P.M., MARCH 20, 1996

"You know, Laurie's right," Chet McGovern said.

Chet and Jack were sitting in the narrow office they shared on the fifth floor of the medical examiner's building. They both had their feet up on their respective gray metal desks. They'd finished their autopsies for the day, eaten lunch, and were now supposedly doing their paperwork.

"Of course she's right," Jack agreed.

"But if you know that, why do you provoke Calvin? It's not rational. You're not doing yourself any favors. It's going to affect your promotion up through the system."

"I don't want to rise up in the system," Jack said.

"Come again?" Chet asked. In the grand scheme of medicine, the concept of not wanting to get ahead was heresy.

Jack let his feet fall off the desk and thump onto the floor. He stood up, stretched, and yawned loudly. Jack was a stocky, six-foot man accustomed to serious physical activity. He found that standing at the autopsy table and sitting at a desk tended to cause his muscles to cramp, particularly his quadriceps.

"I'm happy being a low man on the totem pole," Jack said, cracking his knuckles.

"You don't want to become board certified?" Chet asked with surprise.

"Ah, of course I want to be board certified," Jack said. "But that's not the same issue. As far as I'm concerned, becoming board certified is a personal thing. What I don't care about is having supervisory responsibility. I just want to do forensic pathology. To hell with bureaucracy and red tape."

"Jesus," Chet remarked, letting his own feet fall to the floor. "Every time I think I get to know you a little, you throw me a curveball. I mean, we've been sharing this office for almost five months. You're still a mystery. I don't even know where the hell you live."

"I didn't know you cared," Jack teased.

"Come on," Chet said. "You know what I mean."

"I live on the Upper West Side," Jack said. "It's no secret."

"In the seventies?" Chet asked.

"A bit higher," Jack said.

"Eighties?"

"Higher."

"You're not going to tell me higher than the nineties, are you?" Chet asked.

"A tad," Jack said. "I live on a Hundred and Sixth Street."

"Good grief," Chet exclaimed. "You're living in Harlem."

Jack shrugged. He sat down at his desk and pulled out one of his unfinished files. "What's in a name?" he said.

"Why in the world live in Harlem?" Chet asked. "Of all the neat places to live in and around the city, why live there? It can't be a nice neighborhood. Besides, it must be dangerous."

"I don't see it that way," Jack said. "Plus there are a lot of playgrounds in the area and a particularly good one right next door. I'm kind of a pickup basketball nut."

"Now I know you are crazy," Chet said. "Those playgrounds and those pickup games are controlled by neighborhood gangs. That's like having a death wish. I'm afraid we might see you in here on one of the slabs even without the mountain bike heroics."

"I haven't had any trouble," Jack said. "After all, I paid for new backboards and lights and I buy the balls. The neighborhood gang is actually quite appreciative and even solicitous."

Chet eyed his officemate with a touch of awe. He tried to imagine what Jack would look like out running around on a Harlem neighborhood blacktop. He imagined Jack would certainly stand out racially with his light brown hair cut in a peculiar Julius Caesar–like shag. Chet wondered if any of the other players had any idea about Jack, like the fact that he was a doctor. But then Chet acknowledged that he didn't know much more.

"What did you do before you went to medical school?" Chet asked.

"I went to college," Jack said. "Like most people who went to medical school. Don't tell me you didn't go to college."

"Of course I went to college," Chet said. "Calvin is right: you are a smartass. You know what I mean. If you just finished a pathology residency, what did you do in the interim?" Chet had wanted to ask the question for months, but there had never been an opportune moment.

"I became an ophthalmologist," Jack said. "I even had a practice out in Champaign, Illinois. I was a conventional, conservative suburbanite."

"Yeah, sure, just like I was a Buddhist monk." Chet laughed. "I mean I suppose I can see you as an ophthalmologist. After all, I was an emergency-room physician for a few years until I saw the light. But you conservative? No way."

"I was," Jack insisted. "And my name was John, not Jack. Of course, you wouldn't have recognized me. I was heavier. I also had longer hair, and I parted it along the right side of my head the way I did in high school. And as far as dress was concerned, I favored glen-plaid suits."

"What happened?" Chet asked. Chet glanced at Jack's black jeans, blue sports shirt, and dark blue knitted tie.

A knock on the doorjamb caught both Jack's and Chet's attention. They turned to see Agnes Finn, head of the micro lab, standing in the doorway. She was a small, serious woman with thick glasses and stringy hair.

"We just got something a little surprising," she said to Jack. She was clutching a sheet of paper in her hand. She hesitated on the threshold. Her dour expression didn't change.

"Are you going to make us guess or what?" Jack asked. His curiosity had been titillated, since Agnes did not make it a point to deliver lab results.

Agnes pushed her glasses higher onto her nose and handed Jack the paper. "It's the fluorescein antibody screen you requested on Nodelman."

"My word," Jack said after glancing at the page. He handed it to Chet.

Chet looked at the paper and then leaped to his feet. "Holy crap!" he exclaimed. "Nodelman had the goddamn plague!"

"Obviously we were taken aback by the result," Agnes said in her usual monotone. "Is there anything else you want us to do?"

Jack pinched his lower lip while he thought. "Let's try to culture some of the incipient abscesses," he said. "And let's try some of the usual stains. What's recommended for plague?"

"Giemsa's or Wayson's," Agnes said. "They usually make it possible to see the typical bipolar 'safety pin' morphology."

"Okay, let's do that," Jack said. "Of course, the most important thing is to grow the bug. Until we do that, the case is only presumptive plague."

"I understand," Agnes said. She started from the room.

"I guess I don't have to warn you to be careful," Jack said.

"No need," Agnes assured him. "We have a class-three hood, and I intend to use it."

"This is incredible," Chet said when they were alone. "How the hell did you know?"

"I didn't," Jack said. "Calvin forced me to make a diagnosis. To tell the truth, I thought I was being facetious. Of course, the signs were all consistent, but I still didn't imagine I had a snowball's chance in hell of being right. But now that I am, it's no laughing matter. The only positive aspect is that I win that ten dollars from Calvin."

"He's going to hate you for that," Chet said.

"That's the least of my worries," Jack said. "I'm stunned. A case of pneumonic plague in March in New York City, supposedly contracted in a hospital! Of course, that can't be true unless the Manhattan General is supporting a horde of infected rats and their fleas. Nodelman had to have had contact with some sort of infected animal. It's my guess he was traveling recently." Jack snatched up the phone.

"Who are you calling?" Chet asked.

"Bingham, of course," Jack said as he punched the numbers. "There can't be any delay. This is a hot potato I want out of my hands."

Mrs. Sanford picked up the extension but informed Chet that Dr. Bingham was at City Hall and would be all day. He had left specific instructions he was not to be bothered since he'd be closeted with the mayor.

"So much for our chief," Jack said. Without putting down the receiver, he dialed Calvin's number. He didn't have any better luck. Calvin's secretary told him that Calvin had had to leave for the day. There was an illness in the family.

Jack hung up the phone and drummed his fingers on the surface of the desk.

"No luck?" Chet asked.

"The entire general staff is indisposed," Jack said. "We grunts are on our own." Jack suddenly pushed back his chair, got up, and started out of the office.

Chet bounded out of his own chair and followed. "Where are you going?" he asked. He had to run to catch up with Jack.

"Down to talk to Bart Arnold," Jack said. He got to the elevator and hit the Down button. "I need more information. Somebody has to figure out where this plague came from or this city's in for some trouble."

"Hadn't you better wait for Bingham?" Chet asked. "That look in your eye disturbs me."

"I didn't know I was so transparent," Jack said with a laugh. "I guess this incident has caught my interest. It's got me excited."

The elevator door opened and Jack got on. Chet held the door from closing. "Jack, do me a favor and be careful. I like sharing the office with you. Don't ruffle too many feathers."

"Me?" Jack questioned innocently. "I'm Mister Diplomacy."

"And I'm Muammar el Qaddafi," Chet said. He let the elevator door slide closed.

Jack hummed a perky tune while the elevator descended. He was definitely keyed up, and he was enjoying himself. He smiled when he remembered telling Laurie that he'd hoped Nodelman turned out to have something with serious institutional consequences like Legionnaires' disease so he could give AmeriCare some heartburn. Plague was ten times better. And on top of sticking it to AmeriCare, he'd have the pleasure of collecting his ten bucks from Calvin.

Jack exited on the first floor and went directly to Bart Arnold's office. Bart was the chief of the PAs, or physician's assistants. Jack was pleased to catch him at his desk.

"We've got a presumptive diagnosis of plague. I've got to talk with Janice Jaeger right away," Jack said.

"She'll be sleeping," Bart said. "Can't it wait?"

"No," Jack said.

"Bingham or Calvin know about this?" Bart asked.

"Both are out, and I don't know when they'll be back," Jack said.

Bart hesitated a moment, then opened up the side drawer of his desk. After looking up Janice's number, he made the call. When she was on the line, he apologized for having awakened her and explained that Dr. Stapleton needed to speak with her. He handed the phone to Jack.

Jack apologized as well and then told her about the results on Nodelman. Any sign of sleepiness in Janice's voice disappeared instantly.

"What can I do to help?" she asked.

"Did you find any reference to travel in any of the hospital records?" Jack asked.

"Not that I recall," Janice said.

"Any reference to contact with pets or wild animals?" Jack asked.

"Negative," Janice said. "But I can go back there tonight. Those questions were never specifically asked."

Jack thanked her and told her that he'd be looking into it himself. He handed the phone back to Bart and hurried back to his own office.

Chet looked up as Jack dashed in. "Learn anything?" he asked.

"Not a thing," Jack said happily. He pulled out Nodelman's folder and rapidly shuffled through the pages until he found the completed identification sheet. On it were phone numbers for the next of kin. With his index finger marking Nodelman's wife's number, Jack made the call. It was an exchange in the Bronx.

Mrs. Nodelman answered on the second ring.

"I'm Dr. Stapleton," Jack said. "I'm a medical examiner for the City of New York."

At that point Jack had to explain the role of a medical examiner, because even the archaic term "coroner" didn't register with Mrs. Nodelman.

"I'd like to ask you a few questions," Jack said once Mrs. Nodelman understood who he was.

"It was so sudden," Mrs. Nodelman said. She had started to cry. "He had diabetes, that's true. But he wasn't supposed to die."

"I'm very sorry for your loss," Jack said. "But did your late husband do any recent traveling?"

"He went to New Jersey a week or so ago," Mrs. Nodelman said. Jack could hear her blow her nose.

"I was thinking of travel to more distant destinations," Jack said. "Like to the Southwest or maybe India."

"Just to Manhattan every day," Mrs. Nodelman said.

"How about a visitor from some exotic locale?" Jack asked.

"Donald's aunt visited in December," Mrs. Nodelman said.

"And where is she from?"

"Queens," Mrs. Nodelman said.

"Queens," Jack repeated. "That's not quite what I had in mind. How about contact with any wild animals? Like rabbits."

"No," Mrs. Nodelman said. "Donald hated rabbits."

"How about pets?" Jack asked.

"We have a cat," Mrs. Nodelman said.

"Is the cat sick?" Jack asked. "Or has the cat brought home any rodents?"

"The cat is fine," Mrs. Nodelman said. "She's a house cat and never goes outside."

"How about rats?" Jack asked. "Do you see many rats around your house? Have you seen any dead ones lately?"

"We don't have any rats," Mrs. Nodelman said indignantly. "We live in a nice, clean apartment."

Jack tried to think of something else to ask, but for the moment nothing came to mind. "Mrs. Nodelman," he said, "you've been most kind. The reason I'm asking you these questions is because we have reason to believe that your husband died of a serious infectious disease. We think he died of plague."

There was a brief silence.

"You mean bubonic plague like they had in Europe long ago?" Mrs. Nodelman asked.

"Sort of," Jack said. "Plague comes in two clinical forms, bubonic and pneumonic. Your husband seems to have had the pneumonic form, which happens to be the more contagious. I would advise you to go to your doctor and inform him of your potential exposure. I'm sure he'll want you to take some precautionary antibiotics. I would also advise you to take your pet to your vet and tell him the same thing."

"Is this serious?" Mrs. Nodelman asked.

"It's very serious," Jack said. He then gave her his phone number in case she had any questions later. He also asked her to call him if the vet found anything suspicious with the cat.

Jack hung up the phone and turned to Chet. "The mystery is deepening," he said. Then he added cheerfully: "AmeriCare is going to have some severe indigestion over this."

"There's that facial expression again that scares me," Chet said.

Jack laughed, got up, and started out of the room.

"Where are you going now?" Chet asked nervously.

"To tell Laurie Montgomery what's going on," Jack said. "She's supposed to be our supervisor for today. She has to be apprised."

A few minutes later Jack returned.

"What'd she say?" Chet asked.

"She was as stunned as we were," Jack said. He grabbed the phone directory before taking his seat. He flipped open the pages to the city listings.

"Did she want you to do anything in particular?" Chet asked.

"No," Jack said. "She told me to tread water until Bingham is informed. In fact she tried to call our illustrious chief, but he's still incommunicado with the mayor."

Jack picked up the phone and dialed.

"Who are you calling now?" Chet asked.

"The Commissioner of Health, Patricia Markham," Jack said. "I ain't waiting."

"Good grief!" Chet exclaimed, rolling his eyes. "Hadn't you better let Bingham do that? You'll be calling his boss behind his back."

Jack didn't respond. He was busy giving his name to the commissioner's secretary. When she told him to hold on, he covered the mouthpiece with his hand and whispered to Chet: "Surprise, surprise, she's in!"

"I guarantee Bingham is not going to like this," Chet whispered back.

Jack held up his hand to silence Chet. "Hello, Commissioner," Jack said into the phone. "Howya doing. This is Jack Stapleton here, from over at the ME's office."

Chet winced at Jack's breezy informality.

"Sorry to spoil your day," Jack continued, "but I felt I had to call. Dr. Bingham and Dr. Washington are momentarily unavailable and a situation has developed that I believe you should know about. We've just made a presumptive diagnosis of plague in a patient from Manhattan General Hospital."

"Good Lord!" Dr. Markham exclaimed loud enough for Chet to hear. "That's frightening, but only one case, I trust."

"So far," Jack said.

"All right, I'll alert the City Board of Health," Dr. Markham said. "They'll take over and contact the CDC. Thanks for the warning. What was your name again?"

"Stapleton," Jack said. "Jack Stapleton."

Jack hung up with a self-satisfied smile on his lips. "Maybe you should sell short your AmeriCare stock," he told Chet. "The commissioner sounds concerned."

"Maybe you'd better brush off your résumé," Chet said. "Bingham is going to be pissed."

Jack whistled while he leafed through Nodelman's file until he came up with the investigative report. Once he had located the name of the attending physician, Dr. Carl Wainwright, he wrote it down. Then he got up and put on his leather bomber jacket.

"Uh oh," Chet said. "Now what?"

"I'm going over to the Manhattan General," Jack said. "I think I'll make a site visit. This case is too important to leave up to the generals."

Chet swung around in his chair as Jack went through the door.

"Of course, you know that Bingham doesn't encourage us MEs doing site work," Chet said. "You'll be adding insult to injury."

"I'll take my chances," Jack said. "Where I was trained it was considered necessary."

"Bingham thinks it's the job of the PAs," Chet said. "He's told us that time and again."

"This case is too interesting for me to pass up," Jack called from down the hall. "Hold down the fort. I won't be long."

CHAPTER 5

WEDNESDAY, 2:50 P.M., MARCH 20, 1996

It was overcast and threatening rain, but Jack didn't mind. Regardless of the weather, the vigorous bike ride uptown to the Manhattan General was a pleasure after having stood all morning in the autopsy room imprisoned inside his moon suit.

Near the hospital's front entrance Jack located a sturdy street sign to lock his mountain bike to. He even locked up his helmet and bomber jacket with a separate wire lock that also secured the seat.

Standing within the shadow of the hospital, Jack glanced up at its soaring facade. It had been an old, respected, university-affiliated, proprietary hospital in its previous life. AmeriCare had gobbled it up during the fiscally difficult times the government had unwittingly created in health care in the early 1990s. Although Jack knew revenge was far from a noble emotion, he savored the knowledge that he was about to hand AmeriCare a public relations bomb.

Inside Jack went to the information booth and asked about Dr. Carl Wainwright. He learned that the man was an AmeriCare internist whose office was in the attached professional building. The receptionist gave Jack careful directions.

Fifteen minutes later, Jack was in the man's waiting room. After Jack flashed his medical examiner's badge, which looked for all intents and purposes like a police badge, the receptionist wasted no time in letting Dr. Wainwright know he was there. Jack was immediately shown into the doctor's private office, and within minutes the doctor himself appeared.

Dr. Carl Wainwright was prematurely white-haired and slightly stooped over. His face, however, was youthful with bright blue eyes. He shook hands with Jack and motioned for him to sit down.

"It's not every day we're visited by someone from the medical examiner's office," Dr. Wainwright said.

"I'd be concerned if it were," Jack said.

Dr. Wainwright looked confused until he realized Jack was kidding. Dr. Wainwright tittered. "Right you are," he said.

"I've come about your patient Donald Nodelman," Jack said, getting right to the point. "We have a presumptive diagnosis of plague."

Dr. Wainwright's mouth dropped open. "That's impossible," he said when he'd recovered enough to speak.

Jack shrugged. "I guess it's not," he said. "Fluorescein antibody for plague is quite reliable. Of course, we haven't yet grown it out."

"My goodness," Dr. Wainwright managed. He rubbed a nervous palm across his face. "What a shock."

"It is surprising," Jack agreed. "Especially since the patient had been in the hospital for five days before his symptoms started."

"I've never heard of nosocomial plague," Dr. Wainwright said.

"Nor have I," Jack said. "But it was pneumonic plague, not bubonic, and as you know the incubation period is shorter for pneumonic, probably only two to three days."

"I still can't believe it," Dr. Wainwright said. "Plague never entered my thoughts."

"Anybody else sick with similar symptoms?" Jack asked.

"Not that I know of," Dr. Wainwright said, "but you can rest assured that we will find out immediately."

"I'm curious about this man's lifestyle," Jack said. "His wife denied any recent travel or visitors from areas endemic to plague. She also doubted he'd come in contact with wild animals. Is that your understanding as well?"

"The patient worked in the garment district," Dr. Wainwright said. "He did bookkeeping. He never traveled. He wasn't a hunter. I'd been seeing him frequently over the last month, trying to get his diabetes under control."

"Where was he in the hospital?" Jack asked.

"On the medical ward on the seventh floor," Dr. Wainwright said. "Room seven-oh-seven. I remember the number specifically."

"Single room?" Jack asked.

"All our rooms are singles," Dr. Wainwright said.

"That's a help," Jack said. "Can I see the room?"

"Of course," Dr. Wainwright said. "But I think I should call Dr. Mary Zimmerman, who's our infection-control officer. She's got to know about this immediately."

"By all means," Jack said. "Meanwhile, would you mind if I went up to the seventh floor and looked around?"

"Please," Dr. Wainwright said as he gestured toward the door. "I'll call Dr. Zimmerman and we'll meet you up there." He reached for the phone.

Jack retraced his route back to the main hospital building. He took the elevator to the seventh floor, which he found was divided by the elevator lobby into two wings. The north wing housed internal medicine while the south wing was reserved for OB-GYN. Jack pushed through the doors that led into the internal-medicine division.

As soon as the swinging door closed behind Jack, he knew that word of the contagion had arrived. A nervous bustle was apparent, and all the personnel were wearing newly distributed masks. Obviously Wainwright had wasted no time.

No one paid Jack any attention as he wandered down to room 707. Pausing at the door, Jack watched as two masked orderlies wheeled out a masked and confused patient clutching her belongings who was apparently being transferred. As soon as they were gone, Jack walked in.

Seven-oh-seven was a nondescript hospital room of modern design; the interior of the old hospital had been renovated in the not-too-distant past. The metal furniture was typical hospital issue and included a bed, a bureau, a vinyl-covered chair, a night table, and a variable-height bed table. A TV hung from an arm attached to the ceiling.

The air-conditioning apparatus was beneath the window. Jack went over to it, lifted the top, and looked inside. A hot-water and a chill-water pipe poked up through the concrete floor and entered a thermostated fan unit that recirculated room air. Jack detected no holes large enough for any type of rodent much less a rat.

Stepping into the bathroom, Jack glanced around at the sink, toilet, and shower. The room was newly tiled. There was an air return in the ceiling. Bending down, he opened the cabinet below the sink; again there were no holes.

Hearing voices in the other room, Jack stepped back through the door. It was Dr. Wainwright clutching a mask to his face. He was accompanied by two women and a man, all of whom were wearing masks. The women were attired in the long, white professorial coats Jack associated with medical-school professors.

After handing Jack a mask, Dr. Wainwright made the introductions. The taller woman was Dr. Mary Zimmerman, the hospital's infection- control officer and head of the like-named committee. Jack sensed she was a serious woman who felt defensive under the circumstances. As she was introduced, she informed him that she was a board-certified internist with subspecialty training in infectious disease.

Not knowing how to respond to this revelation, Jack complimented her.

"I did not have an opportunity to examine Mr. Nodelman," she added.

"I'm certain you would have made the diagnosis instantly had you done so," Jack said, consciously trying to keep sarcasm out of his voice.

"No doubt," she said.

The second woman was Kathy McBane, and Jack was happy to turn his attention to her, especially since Ms. McBane had a warmer demeanor than her committee chairwoman. He learned she was an RN supervisor and a member of the Infection Control Committee. It was usual for such a committee to have representatives from most if not all the hospital departments.

The man was George Eversharp. He was dressed in a heavy cotton twill blue uniform. As Jack suspected, he was the supervisor of the department of engineering and was also a member of the Infection Control Committee.

"We certainly are indebted to Dr. Stapleton for his rapid diagnosis," Dr. Wainwright said, trying to lighten the atmosphere.

"Just a lucky guess," Jack said.

"We've already begun to react," Dr. Zimmerman said in a deadpan voice. "I've ordered a list to be drawn up of possible contacts to start chemoprophylaxis."

"I think that is wise," Jack said.

"And as we speak, the clinical computer is searching our current patient database for symptom complexes suggestive of plague," she continued.

"Commendable," Jack said.

"Meanwhile we have to discover the origin of the current case," she said.

"You and I are thinking along the same lines," Jack said.

"I'd advise you to wear your mask," she added.

"Okay," Jack said agreeably. He held it up to his face.

Dr. Zimmerman turned to Mr. Eversharp. "Please continue with what you were saying about the air flow."

Jack listened as the engineer explained that the ventilation system in the hospital was designed so that there was a flow from the hall into each room and then its bathroom. The air was then filtered. He also explained that there were a few rooms where the air flow could be reversed for patients with compromised immune systems.

"Is this one of those rooms?" Dr. Zimmerman asked.

"It is not," Mr. Eversharp said.

"So there is no freak way plague bacteria could have gotten into the ventilation system and infected just this room?" Dr. Zimmerman asked.

"No," Mr. Eversharp said. "The air induction in the hall goes into all these rooms equally."

"And the chances of bacteria floating out of this room into the hall would be low," Dr. Zimmerman said.

"Impossible," Mr. Eversharp said. "The only way it could leave would be on some sort of vector."

"Excuse me," a voice called. Everyone turned to see a nurse standing in the doorway. She, too, had a mask pressed against her face. "Mr. Kelley would like you all to come to the nurses' station."

Dutifully everyone started from the room. As Kathy McBane stepped in front of him, Jack got her attention. "Who's Mr. Kelley?" he asked.

"He's the hospital president," Ms. McBane said.

Jack nodded. As he walked he nostalgically reminisced that the head of the hospital used to be called an administrator and was frequently a person who'd had medical training. That was back when patient care was paramount. Now that business was king and the goal was profit, the name had changed to president.

Jack was looking forward to meeting Mr. Kelley. The hospital president was the on-site representative of AmeriCare, and giving him a headache was the equivalent of giving AmeriCare a headache.

The atmosphere at the nurses' station was tense. Word of the plague had spread like wildfire. Everyone who worked on the floor and even some of the ambulatory patients now knew they had been potentially exposed. Charles Kelley was doing his best to reassure them. He told them there was no risk and that everything was under control.

"Yeah, sure!" Jack scoffed under his breath. Jack looked with disgust at this man who had the gall to utter such patently false platitudes. He was intimidatingly tall, a good eight inches taller than Jack's six feet. His handsome face was tanned and his sandy-colored hair was streaked with pure, golden blond as if he'd just returned from a Caribbean vacation. From Jack's perspective, he looked and sounded more like an unctuous car salesman than the business manager that he was.

As soon as Kelley saw Jack and the others approach, he motioned for them to follow him. Breaking off his consoling speech, he made a beeline for the safety of the utility room behind the nurses' station.

As Jack squeezed in behind Kathy McBane, he noticed Kelley wasn't alone. He was being shadowed by a slightly built man with a lantern jaw and thinning hair. In sharp contrast to Kelley's sartorial splendor, this second man was dressed in a threadbare, cheap sports coat over slacks that appeared never to have been pressed.

"God, what a mess!" Kelley said angrily to no one in particular. His demeanor had metamorphosed instantly from slippery salesman to sardonic administrator. He took a paper towel and wiped his perspiring brow. "This is not what this hospital needs!" He crumpled the towel and threw it into the trash. Turning to Dr. Zimmerman and in contrast to what he'd just said out in the nurses' station, he asked her if they were taking a risk just being on the floor.

"I sincerely doubt it," Dr. Zimmerman said. "But we'll have to make certain."

Turning to Dr. Wainwright, Kelley said: "No sooner had I heard about this disaster than I learned you already knew about it. Why didn't you inform me?"

Dr. Wainwright explained that he'd just heard the news from Jack and had not had time to call. He explained he thought it was more important to call Dr. Zimmerman to get corrective measures instituted. He then proceeded to introduce Jack.

Jack stepped forward and gave a little wave. He was unable to suppress a smile. This was the moment he knew he'd savor.

Kelley took in the chambray shirt, the knitted tie, and the black jeans. It was a far cry from his own Valentino silk suit. "Seems to me the Commissioner of Health mentioned your name when she called me," Kelley said. "As I recall, she was impressed you'd made the diagnosis so quickly."

"We city employees are always glad to be of service," Jack said.

Kelley gave a short, derisive laugh.

"Perhaps you'd like to meet one of your dedicated fellow city employees," Kelley said. "This is Dr. Clint Abelard. He's the epidemiologist for the New York City Board of Health."

Jack nodded to his mousy colleague, but the epidemiologist didn't return the greeting. Jack got the sense that Jack's presence was not wholly appreciated. Interdepartmental rivalry was a fact of bureaucratic life he was just beginning to appreciate.

Kelley cleared his throat and then spoke to Wainwright and Zimmerman. "I want this whole episode kept as low-key as possible. The less that's in the media the better. If any reporter tries to talk with either of you, send them to me. I'll be gearing up the PR office to do damage control."

"Excuse me," Jack said, unable to restrain himself from interrupting. "Corporate interests aside, I think you should concentrate on prevention. That means treating contacts and ascertaining where the plague bacteria came from. I think you have a mystery on your hands here, and until that's solved, the media is going to have a field day no matter what damage control you attempt."

"I wasn't aware anyone asked your opinion," Kelley said scornfully.

"I just felt you could use a little direction," Jack said. "You seemed to be wandering a bit far afield."

Kelley's face reddened. He shook his head in disbelief. "All right," he said, struggling to control himself. "With your clairvoyance, I suppose you already have an idea of its origin."

"I'd guess rats," Jack said. "I'm sure there are lots of rats around here." Jack had been waiting to use that comment since it had had such a good effect with Calvin that morning.

"We have no rats here at the Manhattan General," Kelley sputtered. "And if I hear that you've said anything like that to the media, I'll have your head."

"Rats are the classical reservoir for the plague," Jack said. "I'm sure they're around here if you know how to recognize them, I mean find them."

Kelley turned to Clint Abelard. "Do you think rats had anything to do with this case of plague?" he demanded.

"I have yet to begin my investigation," Dr. Abelard said. "I wouldn't want to hazard a guess, but I find it hard to believe that rats could have been involved. We're on the seventh floor."

"I'd suggest you start trapping rats," Jack said. "Start in the immediate neighborhood. The first thing to find out is if plague has infiltrated the local urban rodent population."

"I'd like to switch the conversation away from rats," Kelley said. "I would like to hear about what we should do for people who had direct contact with the deceased."

"That's my department," Dr. Zimmerman said. "Here's what I propose . . ."

While Dr. Zimmerman spoke, Clint Abelard motioned for Jack to accompany him out to the nurses' station.

"I'm the epidemiologist," Clint said in an angry, forced whisper.

"I've never disputed that fact," Jack said. He was surprised and confused by the vehemence of Clint's reaction.

"I'm trained to investigate the origin of diseases in the human community," he said. "It's my job. You, on the other hand, are a coroner . . ."

"Correction," Jack said. "I'm a medical examiner with training in pathology. You, as a physician, should know that."

"Medical examiner or coroner, I couldn't care less what term you guys use for yourselves," Clint said.

"Hey, but I do," Jack said.

"The point is that your training and your responsibility involve the dead, not the origin of disease."

"Wrong again," Jack said. "We deal with the dead so that they speak to the living. Our goal is to prevent death."

"I don't know how to make it much plainer to you," Clint said with exasperation. "You told us a man died of plague. We appreciate that, and we didn't interfere in your work. Now it is for me to figure out how he got it."

"I'm just trying to help," Jack said.

"Thank you, but if I need your help I'll ask for it," Clint said and strode off toward room 707.

Jack watched Clint's figure recede, when a commotion behind him attracted his attention. Kelley had emerged from the utility room and was immediately besieged by the people he'd been speaking with earlier. Jack was impressed by how quickly his plastic smile returned and with what ease he sidestepped all questions. Within seconds, he was on his way down the hall toward the elevators and the safety of the administrative offices.

Dr. Zimmerman and Dr. Wainwright stepped out of the utility room deep in conversation. When Kathy McBane appeared, she was alone. Jack intercepted her.

"Sorry to have been the bearer of bad news," Jack offered.

"Don't be sorry," Kathy said. "From my point of view, we owe you a vote of thanks."

"Well, it's an unfortunate problem," Jack said.

"I'd guess it's the worst since I've been on the Infection Control Committee," she said. "I thought last year's outbreak of hepatitis B was bad. I never dreamed we'd ever see plague."

"What is the Manhattan General's experience in regard to nosocomial infections?" Jack asked.

Kathy shrugged. "Pretty much the equivalent of any large tertiary-care hospital," she said. "We've had our methicillin-resistant staph. Of course, that's an ongoing problem. We even had klebsiella growing in a canister of surgical scrub soap a year ago. That resulted in a whole series of postoperative wound infections until it was discovered."

"How about pneumonias?" Jack asked. "Like this case."

"Oh, yeah, we've had our share of them too," Kathy said with a sigh. "Mostly it's been pseudomonas, but two years ago we had an outbreak of Legionella."

"I hadn't heard about that," Jack said.

"It was kept quiet," Kathy said. "Luckily no one died. Of course, I can't say that about the problem we had just five months ago in the surgical intensive care. We lost three patients to enterobacterial pneumonia. We had to close the unit until it was discovered that some of our nebulizers had become contaminated."

"Kathy!" a voice called out sharply.

Both Jack and Kathy abruptly turned to see that Dr. Zimmerman had come up behind them.

"That is confidential information," Dr. Zimmerman lectured.

Kathy started to say something but then thought better of it.

"We have work to do, Kathy," Dr. Zimmerman said. "Let's go to my office."

Suddenly abandoned, Jack debated what he should do. For a moment he considered going back to room 707, but after Clint's tirade, he thought it best to leave the man alone. After all, Jack had intended to provoke Kelley, not Clint. Then he got an idea: It might be instructive to visit the lab. As defensively as Dr. Zimmerman had responded, Jack thought it was the lab that should have been chagrined. They were the ones who missed the diagnosis.

After inquiring about the location of the lab, Jack took the elevator down to the second floor. Flashing his medical examiner's badge again produced immediate results. Dr. Martin Cheveau, the lab director, materialized and welcomed Jack into his office. He was a short fellow with a full head of dark hair and pencil-line mustache.

"Have you heard about the case of plague?" Jack asked once they were seated.

"No, where?" Martin questioned.

"Here at the Manhattan General," Jack said. "Room seven-oh-seven. I posted the patient this morning."

"Oh, no!" Martin moaned. He sighed loudly. "That doesn't sound good for us. What was the name?"

"Donald Nodelman," Jack said.

Martin swung around in his seat and accessed his computer. The screen flashed all Nodelman's laboratory results for the duration of his admission. Martin scrolled through until he got to the microbiology section.

"I see we had a sputum gram stain showing weakly gram-negative bacilli," Martin said. "There's also a culture pending that was negative for growth at thirty-six hours. I guess that should have told us something, especially where I see pseudomonas was suspected. I mean, pseudomonas would have grown out without any trouble way before thirty-six hours."

"It would have been helpful if Giemsa's or Wayson's stain had been used," Jack said. "The diagnosis could have been made."

"Exactly," Martin said. He turned back to Jack. "This is terrible. I'm embarrassed. Unfortunately, it's an example of the kind of thing that's going to happen more and more often. Administration has been forcing us to cut costs and downsize even though our workload has gone up. It's a deadly combination, as this case of plague proves. And it's happening all over the country."

"You've had to let people go?" Jack asked. He thought that the clinical lab was one place hospitals actually made money.

"About twenty percent," Martin said. "Others we've had to demote. In microbiology we don't have a supervisor any longer; if we had, he probably would have caught this case of plague. With the operating budget we've been allotted we can't afford it. Our old supervisor got demoted to head tech. It's discouraging. It used to be we strove for excellence in the lab. Now we strive for 'adequate,' whatever that means."

"Does your computer say which tech did the gram stain?" Jack asked. "If nothing else, we could turn this episode into a teaching experience."

"Good idea," Martin said. He faced the computer and accessed data. The tech's identity was in code. Suddenly he turned back to Jack.

"I just remembered something," he said. "My head tech thought of plague in relation to a patient just yesterday and asked me what I thought. I'm afraid I discouraged him by telling him the chances were somewhere on the order of a billion to one."

Jack perked up. "I wonder what made him think of plague?"

"I wonder too," Martin said. Reaching over to his intercom system, he paged Richard Overstreet. While they waited for the man to arrive, Martin determined that Nancy Wiggens had signed out on the original gram stain. Martin paged her as well.

Richard Overstreet appeared within minutes. He was a boyish, athletic-looking individual with a shock of auburn hair that fell across his forehead. The hair had a habit of slipping over his eyes. Richard was ever pushing it back with his hand or throwing it back with a snap of his head. He wore a white jacket over surgical scrubs; his jacket pockets were crammed with test tubes, tourniquets, gauze pads, lab chits, and syringes.

Martin introduced Richard to Jack, then asked him about the short discussion they'd had about plague the day before.

Richard seemed embarrassed. "It was just my imagination getting the best of me," he said with a laugh.

"But what made you think of it?" Martin asked.

Richard swept his hair from his face and for a moment left his hand on the top of his head while he thought. "Oh, I remember," he said. "Nancy Wiggens had gone up to get a sputum culture and draw the man's blood. She told me how sick he was and that he appeared to have some gangrene on the tips of his fingers. She said his fingers were black." Richard shrugged. "It made me think of the black death."

Jack was impressed.

"Did you follow up on it at all?" Martin asked.

"No," Richard said. "Not after what you'd said about the probability. As behind as we are in the lab, I couldn't take the time. All of us, including me, have been out drawing blood. Is there some kind of problem?" Richard asked.

"A big problem," Martin said. "The man did have plague. Not only that, but he's already dead."

Richard literally staggered. "My God!" he exclaimed.

"I hope you encourage safety with your techs," Jack said.

"Absolutely," Richard said, regaining his composure. "We have biosafety cabinets, both type two and three. I try to encourage my techs to use one or the other, especially with obviously serious infectious cases. Personally I like the type three, but some people find using the thick rubber gloves too clumsy."

At that moment Nancy Wiggens appeared. She was a shy woman who appeared more like a teenager than a college graduate. She could barely look Jack in the eye as they were introduced. She wore her dark hair parted down the middle of her head, and like that of her immediate boss, Richard, it constantly fell across her eyes.

Martin explained to her what had happened. She was as shocked as Richard had been. Martin assured her she was not being blamed but that they should all try to learn from the experience.

"What should I do about my exposure?" she questioned. "I was the one who got the specimen as well as the one who processed it."

"You'll probably be taking tetracycline by mouth or streptomycin IM," Jack said. "The hospital infection-control officer is working on that at the moment."

"Uh oh!" Martin voiced under his breath but loud enough for the others to hear. "Here comes our fearless leader and the chief of the medical staff, and both look unhappy."

Kelley swept into the room like an irate general after a military defeat. He towered over Martin with his hands on his hips and his reddened face thrust forward. "Dr. Cheveau," he began with a scornful tone. "Dr. Arnold here tells me you should have made this diagnosis before . . ."

Kelley stopped mid-sentence. Although he was content to ignore the two microbiology techs, Jack was a different story.

"What in God's name are you doing down here?" he demanded.

"Just helping out," Jack replied.

"Aren't you overstepping your mandate?" he suggested venomously.

"We like to be thorough in our investigations," Jack said.

"I think you have more than exhausted your official capacity," Kelley snapped. "I want you out of here. After all, this is a private institution."

Jack got to his feet, vainly trying to look the towering Kelley in the eye. "If AmeriCare thinks it can do without me, I think I'll run along."

Kelley's face turned purple. He started to say something else but changed his mind. Instead he merely pointed toward the door.

Jack smiled and waved to the others before taking his leave. He was pleased with his visit. As far as he was concerned, it couldn't have gone better.

CHAPTER 6

WEDNESDAY, 4:05 P.M., MARCH 20, 1996

Susanne Hard was looking through the small, round window of the door to the elevator lobby with rapt attention. The end of the corridor was as far as she was allowed to go on her ambulation. She'd been walking with little steps while supporting her freshly sutured abdomen. As unpleasant as the exercise was, she knew from experience that the sooner she mobilized herself, the sooner she'd be in a position to demand release.

What had caught her attention out in the elevator lobby was the disturbing amount of traffic coming in and out of the medical ward as well as the nervous demeanor of the staff. Susanne's sixth sense told her that something was wrong, especially with most of the people wearing masks.

Before she could put a finger on the cause of the apparent stir, a literal chill passed through her like an icy arctic wind. Turning around, she expected to feel a draft. There wasn't any. Then the chill returned, causing her to tense and shiver until it had passed. Susanne looked down at her hands. They had turned bone white.

Increasingly anxious, Susanne started back to her room. Such a chill could not be a good sign. As an experienced patient she knew there was always the fear of a wound infection.

By the time she entered her room she had a headache behind her eyes. As she climbed back into bed, the headache spread over the top of her head. It wasn't like any headache she'd ever had before. It felt as if someone were pushing an awl into the depths of her brain.

For a few panicky moments Susanne lay perfectly still, hoping that whatever had seemed wrong was now all right. But instead a new symptom developed: the muscles of her legs began to ache. Within minutes she found herself writhing in the bed, vainly trying to find a position that afforded relief.

Close on the heels of the leg pain came an overall malaise that settled over her like a stifling blanket. It was so enervating that she could barely reach across her chest for the nurse's call button. She pressed it and let her arm fall limply back to the bed.

By the time the nurse came into the room, Susanne had developed a cough that chafed her already irritated throat.

"I feel sick," Susanne croaked.

"How so?" the nurse questioned.

Susanne shook her head. It was even hard to talk. She felt so terrible she didn't know where to begin.

"I have a headache," she managed.

"I believe you have a standing order of pain medication," the nurse said. "I'll get it for you."

"I need my doctor," Susanne whispered. Her throat felt as bad as when she'd first awakened from the anesthesia.

"I think we should try the pain medicine before we call your doctor," the nurse said.

"I feel cold," Susanne said. "Terribly cold."

The nurse put a practiced hand on Susanne's forehead, then pulled it back in alarm. Susanne was burning up. The nurse took the thermometer from its container on the bedside table and stuck it into Susanne's mouth. While she waited for the thermometer to equilibrate, she wrapped a blood-pressure cuff around Susanne's arm. The blood pressure was low.

She then took the thermometer out of Susanne's mouth. When she saw what the reading was, she let out a little gasp of surprise. It was 106° Fahrenheit.

"Do I have a fever?" Susanne questioned.

"A little one," the nurse said. "But everything is going to be fine. I'll go and give your doctor a call."

Susanne nodded. A tear came to the corner of her eye. She didn't want this kind of complication. She wanted to go home.

CHAPTER 7

WEDNESDAY, 4:15 P.M., MARCH 20, 1996

"Do you honestly think that Robert Barker deliberately sabotaged our ad campaign?" Colleen asked Terese as they descended the stairs. They were on their way to the studio where Colleen wanted to show Terese what the creative team had put together for a new National Health campaign.

"There's not a doubt in my mind," Terese said. "Of course, he didn't do it himself. He had Helen do it by talking National Health out of buying adequate exposure time."

"But he'd be shooting himself in the foot. If we lose the National Health account and we can't restructure, then his employee participation units are worth the same as ours: zilch."

"Screw his employee participation units," Terese said. "He wants the presidency, and he'll do anything to get it."

"God, bureaucratic infighting disgusts me," Colleen said. "Are you sure you want the presidency?"

Terese stopped dead on the stairs and looked at Colleen as if she'd just blasphemed. "I can't believe you said that."

"But you've complained yourself that the more administrative duties you have, the less time you can spend on creativity."

"If Barker gets the presidency he'll screw up the whole company," Terese said indignantly. "We'll start kowtowing to clients, and there goes creativity and quality in one fell swoop. Besides, I want to be president. It's been my goal for five years. This is my chance, and if I don't get it now, I'll never get it."

"I don't know why you're not happy with what you've already accomplished," Colleen said. "You're only thirty-one and you're already creative director. You should be content and do what you are good at: doing great ads."

"Oh, come on!" Terese said. "You know we advertising people are never satisfied. Even if I make president I'll probably start eyeing CEO."

"I think you should cool it," Colleen said. "You're going to burn out before you're thirty-five."

"I'll cool it when I'm president," Terese said.

"Yeah, sure!" Colleen said.

Once in the studio Colleen directed her friend into the small separate room that was affectionately called the "arena." This was where pitches were rehearsed. The name came from the arenas of ancient Rome where Christians were thrown to the lions. At Willow and Heath the Christians were the low-level creatives.

"You got a film?" Terese questioned. In the front of the room a screen had been pulled down over the chalkboards. At best she thought she'd be looking at sketchy storyboards.

"We threw together a 'ripomatic,' " Colleen explained. A ripomatic was a roughly spliced together amalgam of previously shot video that had been "stolen" from other projects to give a sense of a commercial.

Terese was encouraged. She'd not expected video.

"Now I'm warning you, this is all very preliminary," Colleen added.

"Save the disclaimers," Terese said. "Run what you have."

Colleen waved to one of her underlings. The lights dimmed and the video started. It ran for a hundred seconds. It depicted a darling four-year-old girl with a broken doll. Terese recognized the footage immediately. It was part of a spot they'd done the year before for a national toy chain to promote the company's generous return policy. Colleen had cleverly made it appear as if the child were bringing the doll to the new National Health hospital. The tag line was "We cure anything anytime."

As soon as the video stopped, the lights came on. For a few moments no one spoke. Finally Colleen broke the silence. "You don't like it," she said.

"It's cute," Terese admitted.

"The idea is to make the doll reflect different illnesses and injuries in different commercials," Colleen said. "Of course, we'd have the child speak and extol the virtues of National Health in the video versions. In print we'd make sure the picture told the story."

"The problem is it's too cute," Terese said. "Even if I think it has some merit, I'm sure the client won't like it, since Helen via Robert would certainly trivialize it."

"It's the best that we've come up with so far," Colleen said. "You'll have to give us some direction. We need a creative brief from you; otherwise we'll just keep wandering all over the conceptual landscape. Then there will be no chance to put anything together for next week."

"We have to come up with something that sets National Health apart from AmeriCare even though we know they are equivalent. The challenge is finding that one idea," Terese said.

Colleen motioned for her assistant to leave. Once she had, Colleen took a chair and put it in front of Terese's. "We need more of your direct involvement," she said.

Terese nodded. She knew Colleen was right, but Terese felt mentally paralyzed. "The problem is that it's hard to think with this presidency situation hanging over me like the sword of Damocles."

"I think you've got yourself in overdrive," Colleen said. "You're a ball of nerves."

"So what else is new?" Terese said.

"When was the last time you went out for dinner and a few drinks?" Colleen said.

Terese laughed. "I haven't had time for anything like that for months."

"That's my point," Colleen said. "No wonder your creative juices aren't flowing. You need to relax. Even if it's just for a few hours."

"You really think so?" Terese asked.

"Absolutely," Colleen said. "In fact we're going out tonight. We'll go to dinner and we'll have a few drinks. We'll even try not to talk about advertising for one night."

"I don't know," Terese voiced. "We've got this deadline . . ."

"That's exactly my point," Colleen said. "We need to blow the tubes and clear out the cobwebs. Maybe then we'll come up with that big idea. So don't argue. I'm not taking no for an answer."

CHAPTER 8

Jack navigated his mountain bike between the two Health and Hospital Corporation mortuary vans parked at the receiving bay at the medical examiner's office and rode directly into the morgue. Under normal circumstances he'd have dismounted by then and walked the bike, but he was in too good a mood.

Jack parked his bike by the Hart Island coffins, locked it up, then whistled on his way to the elevators. He waved to Sal D'Ambrosio as he passed the mortuary office.

"Chet, my boy, how are you?" Jack asked as he breezed into their shared fifth-floor office.

Chet laid his pen down on his desk and turned to face his officemate. "The world's been in here looking for you. What have you been doing?"

"Indulging myself," Jack said. He peeled off his leather jacket and draped it over the back of his desk chair before sitting down. He surveyed his row of files, deciding which one to attack first. His in-basket had a newly replenished pile of lab results and PA reports.

"I wouldn't get too comfortable," Chet said. "One of those looking for you was Bingham himself. He told me to tell you to come directly to his office."

"How nice," Jack said. "I was afraid he'd forgotten about me."

"I wouldn't be so flippant about it," Chet said. "Bingham was not happy. And Calvin stopped by as well. He'd like to see you, too, and smoke was coming out of his ears."

"Undoubtedly he's eager to pay me my ten dollars," Jack said. He got up from his desk and patted Chet on the shoulder. "Don't worry about me. I have a strong survival instinct."

"You could have fooled me," Chet said.

As Jack descended in the elevator, he was curious how Bingham would handle the current situation. Since Jack had started working at the ME office, he'd had only sporadic contact with the chief. The day-to-day administrative problems were all handled by Calvin.

"You can go right in," Mrs. Sanford said without even looking up from her typing. Jack wondered how she knew it was he.

"Close the door," Dr. Harold Bingham commanded.

Jack did as he was told. Bingham's office was spacious with a large desk set back under high windows covered with ancient venetian blinds. At the opposite end of the room was a library table with a teaching microscope. A glass-fronted bookcase lined the far wall.

"Sit down," Bingham said.

Dutifully Jack sat.

"I'm not sure I understand you," Bingham said in his deep, husky voice. "You apparently made a rather brilliant diagnosis of plague today and then foolishly took it upon yourself to call my boss, the Commissioner of Health. Either you are a completely apolitical creature or you have a self-destructive streak."

"It's probably a combination of the two," Jack said.

"You're also impertinent," Bingham said.

"That's part of the self-destructive streak," Jack said. "On the positive side, I'm honest." He smiled.

Bingham shook his head. Jack was testing his ability to control himself. "Just so I can try to understand," he said as he entwined the fingers of his shovel-like hands, "did you not think that I would find it inappropriate for you to call the commissioner before talking with me?"

"Chet McGovern suggested as much," Jack said. "But I was more concerned about getting the word out. Ounce of prevention is worth a pound of cure, especially if we're looking at a potential epidemic."

There was a moment of silence while Bingham considered Jack's statement, which he had to admit contained a modicum of validity. "The second thing I wanted to discuss was your visit to the Manhattan General. Frankly, your decision to do this surprises me. During your orientation I know you were told that our policy is to rely on our excellent PAs to do site work. You do remember that, don't you?"

"Certainly I remember," Jack said. "But I felt that the appearance of plague was unique enough to demand a unique response. Besides, I was curious."

"Curious!" Bingham blurted out. He momentarily lost control. "That's the lamest excuse for ignoring established policy I've heard in years."

"Well, there was more," Jack admitted. "Knowing the General was an AmeriCare hospital, I wanted to go over there and rub it in a little. I'm not fond of AmeriCare."

"What in heaven's name do you have against AmeriCare?" Bingham asked.

"It's a personal thing," Jack said.

"Would you care to elaborate?" Bingham asked.

"I'd rather not," Jack said. "It's a long story."

"Suit yourself," Bingham said irritably. "But I'm not going to tolerate your going over there flashing your medical examiner badge for some personal vendetta. That's an egregious misuse of official authority."

"I thought our mandate was to get involved in anything that could affect public health," Jack said. "Certainly a case of plague falls under that rubric."

"Indeed," Bingham pronounced. "But you had already alerted the Commissioner of Health. She in turn alerted the City Board of Health, who immediately dispatched the chief epidemiologist. You had no business being over there, much less causing trouble."

"What kind of trouble did I cause?" Jack asked.

"You managed to irritate hell out of both the administrator and the city epidemiologist," Bingham roared. "Both of them were mad enough to lodge official complaints. The administrator called the mayor's office, and the epidemiologist called the commissioner. Both of these public servants can be considered my boss, and neither one of them was pleased, and both of them let me know about it."

"I was just trying to be helpful," Jack said innocently.

"Well, do me a favor and and don't try to be helpful," Bingham snapped. "Instead I want you to stay around here where you belong and do the work you were hired to do. Calvin informed me that you have a lot of cases pending."

"Is that it?" Jack asked when Bingham paused.

"For now," Bingham said.

Jack got up and headed for the door.

"One last thing," Bingham said. "Remember that you are on probation for the first year."

"I'll keep that in mind," Jack said.

Leaving Bingham's office, Jack passed Mrs. Sanford and went directly across to Calvin Washington's office. The door was ajar. Calvin was busy at his microscope.

"Excuse me," Jack called out. "I understand you were looking for me."

Calvin turned around and eyed Jack. "Have you been in to see the chief yet?" he growled.

"Just came from there," Jack said. "It's reassuring to be in such demand around here."

"Dispense with your smartass talk," Calvin said. "What did Dr. Bingham say?"

Jack told Calvin what had been said and that Bingham had concluded by reminding him that he was on probation.

"Damn straight," Calvin said. "I think you'd better shape up or you'll be out looking for work."

"Meanwhile I have one request," Jack said.

"What is it?" Calvin asked.

"How about that ten dollars you owe me," Jack said.

Calvin stared back at Jack, amazed that under the circumstances Jack had the gall to ask for the money. Finally Calvin rolled to the side in his seat, withdrew his wallet, and pulled out a ten-dollar bill.

"I'll get this back," Calvin vowed.

"Sure you will," Jack said as he took the bill.

With the money comfortably in his pocket, Jack returned upstairs to his office. As he entered he was surprised to find Laurie leaning against Chet's desk. Both she and Chet looked at Jack with expectant concern.

"Well?" Chet questioned.

"Well what?" Jack asked. He squeezed by the others to plop down in his seat.

"Are you still employed?" Chet asked.

"Seems that way," Jack said. He started going through the lab reports in his inbasket.

"You'd better be careful," Laurie advised as she started for the door. "They can fire you at their pleasure during your first year."

"So Bingham reminded me," Jack said.

Pausing at the threshold, Laurie turned back to face Jack. "I almost got fired my first year," she admitted.

Jack looked up at her. "How come?" he asked.

"It had to do with those challenging overdose cases I mentioned this morning," Laurie said. "Unfortunately, while I followed up on them I got on the wrong side of Bingham."

"Is that part of that long story you alluded to?" Jack asked.

"That's the one," Laurie said. "I came this close to being fired." She held up her thumb and index finger about a quarter inch apart. "It was all because I didn't take Bingham's threats seriously. Don't make the same mistake."

As soon as Laurie had gone Chet wanted a verbatim recounting of everything Bingham had said. Jack related what he could remember, including the part about the mayor and the Commissioner of Health calling Bingham to complain about him.

"The complaints were about you specifically?" Chet asked.

"Apparently," Jack said. "And here I was being the Good Samaritan."

"What in God's name did you do?" Chet asked.

"I was just being my usual diplomatic self," Jack said. "Asking questions and offering suggestions."

"You're crazy," Chet said. "You almost got yourself fired for what? I mean, what were you trying to prove?"

"I wasn't trying to prove anything," Jack said.

"I don't understand you," Chet said.

"That seems to be a universal opinion," Jack said.

"All I know about you is that you were an ophthalmologist in a former life and you live in Harlem to play street basketball. What else do you do?"

"That about sums it up," Jack said. "Apart from working here, that is."

"What do you do for fun?" Chet asked. "I mean, what kind of social life do you have? I don't mean to pry, but do you have a girlfriend?"

"No, not really," Jack said.

"Are you gay?"

"Nope. I've just sorta been out of commission for a while."

"Well, no wonder you're acting so weird. I tell you what. We're going out tonight. We'll have some dinner, maybe have a few drinks. There's a comfortable bar in the neighborhood where I live. It will give us time to talk."

"I haven't felt like talking much about myself," Jack said.

"All right, you don't have to talk," Chet said. "But we're going out. I think you need some normal human contact."

"What's normal?" Jack questioned.

CHAPTER 9

Chet turned out to be extraordinarily resolute. No matter what Jack said, he insisted that they have dinner together. Finally Jack relented, and just before eight he'd ridden his bike across Central Park to meet Chet in an Italian restaurant on Second Avenue.

After dinner Chet had been equally insistent about Jack's accompanying him for a few drinks. Feeling beholden to his officemate since Chet had insisted on paying for the dinner, Jack had gone along. Now, as they mounted the steps to the bar, Jack was having second thoughts. For the past several years he'd been in bed by ten and up by five. At ten-fifteen after a half bottle of wine, he was fading fast.

"I'm not sure I'm up for this," Jack said.

"We're already here," Chet complained. "Come on in. We'll just have one beer."

Jack leaned back to look at the facade of the bar. He didn't see a name. "What's this place called?" he asked.

"The Auction House," Chet said. "Get your ass in here." He was holding open the door.

To Jack the interior looked vaguely like his grandmother's living room back in Des Moines, Iowa, except for the mahogany bar itself. The furniture was an odd mishmash of Victorian, and the drapes were long and droopy. The high ceiling was brightly colored embossed tin.

"How about sitting here," Chet suggested. He pointed toward a small table set in the window overlooking Eighty-ninth Street.

Jack complied. From where he was sitting Jack had a good view of the room, which he now noted had a high-gloss hardwood floor, not the usual for a bar. There were about fifty people in the room either standing at the bar or sitting on the couches. They were all well dressed and appeared professional. There was not one backward baseball cap in the group. The mix was about even between male and female.

Jack mused that perhaps Chet had been right to have encouraged him to come out. Jack had not been in such a "normal" social environment in several years. Maybe it was good for him. Having become a loner carried its burdens. He wondered what these attractive people were saying to one another as their easy conversations drifted back to him in a babble of voices. The problem was he had zero confidence he could add to any of the discussions.

Jack's eyes wandered to Chet, who was at the bar, supposedly getting them each a beer. Actually he was in a conversation with a well-endowed, long-haired blonde in a stylish sweatshirt over tight jeans. Accompanying her was a svelte woman in a revealingly simple dark suit. She was not participating in the conversation, preferring to concentrate on her glass of wine.

Jack envied Chet's outgoing personality and the ease with which he indulged in social intercourse. During dinner he'd spoken of himself with utter ease. Among the things Jack learned was that Chet had recently broken off a long-term relationship with a pediatrician and hence was what he called "in between" and available.

While Jack was eyeing his officemate, Chet turned toward him. Almost simultaneously the two women did the same, and then they all laughed. Jack felt his face flush. They were obviously talking about him.

Chet broke away from the bar and headed in Jack's direction. Jack wondered if he should flee or merely dig his fingernails into the tabletop. It was obvious what was coming.

"Hey, sport," Chet whispered. He purposefully positioned himself directly between Jack and the women. "See those two chicks at the bar?" He pointed into his own abdomen to shield the gesture from his new acquaintances. "What do you think? Pretty good, huh? They're both knockouts and guess what? They want to meet you."

"Chet, this has been fun, but . . ." Jack began.

"Don't even think about it," Chet said. "Don't let me down now. I'm after the one in the sweatshirt."

Sensing that resistance would have required considerably more energy than capitulation, Jack allowed himself to be dragged to the bar. Chet made the introductions.

Jack could immediately see what Chet saw in Colleen. She was Chet's equal in terms of blithe repartee. Terese, on the other hand, was a foil for them both. After the introductions, she'd given Jack a once-over with her pale blue eyes before turning back to the bar and her glass of wine.

Chet and Colleen fell into spirited conversation. Jack looked at the back of Terese's head and wondered what the hell he was doing. He wanted to be home in bed, and instead he was being abused by someone as unsociable as himself.

"Chet," Jack called out after a few minutes. "This is a waste of time."

Terese spun around. "Waste of time? For whom?"

"For me," Jack said. He gazed curiously at the rawboned yet sensuously lipped woman standing in front of him. He was taken aback by her vehemence.

"What about for me?" Terese snapped. "Do you think it's a rewarding experience to be pestered by men on the prowl?"

"Wait just one tiny second!" Jack said, with his own ire rising. "Don't flatter yourself. I ain't on the prowl. You can be damn sure about that. And if I were I sure wouldn't . . ."

"Hey, Jack," Chet called out. "Cool it."

"You, too, Terese," Colleen said. "Relax. We're out here to enjoy ourselves."

"I didn't say boo to this lady and she's jumping all over me," Jack explained.

"You didn't have to say anything," Terese said.

"Calm down, you guys." Chet stepped between Jack and Terese, but eyed Jack. "We're out here for some normal contact with fellow human beings."

"Actually, I think I should go home," Terese said.

"You're staying right here," Colleen ordered. She turned to Chet. "She's wound up like a piano wire. That's why I insisted she come out: try to get her to relax. She's consumed by her work."

"Sounds like Jack here," Chet said. "He has some definite antisocial tendencies."

Chet and Colleen were talking as if Jack and Terese couldn't hear, yet they were standing right next to them, staring off in different directions. Both were irritated but both felt foolish at the same time.

Chet and Colleen got a round of drinks and handed them out as they continued to talk about their respective friends.

"Jack's social life revolves around living in a crack neighborhood and playing basketball with killers," Chet said.

"At least he has a social life," Colleen said. "Terese lives in a co-op with a bunch of octogenarians. Going to the garbage chute is the high point of a Sunday afternoon at home."

Chet and Colleen laughed heartily, took long pulls on their respective beers, and then launched into a conversation about a play both of them had seen on Broadway.

Jack and Terese ventured a few fleeting looks at each other as they nursed their own drinks.

"Chet mentioned you were a doctor; are you a specialist?" Terese asked finally. Her tone had mellowed significantly.

Jack explained about forensic pathology. Overhearing this part of the conversation, Chet joined in.

"We're in the presence of one of the future's best and brightest. Jack here made the diagnosis of the day. Against everyone else's impression, he diagnosed a case of plague."

"Here in New York?" Colleen asked with alarm.

"At the Manhattan General," Chet said.

"My God!" Terese exclaimed. "I was a patient there once. Plague is awfully rare, isn't it?"

"Most definitely," Jack said. "A few cases are reported each year in the U.S., but they usually occur in the wilds of the west and during the summer months."

"Is it terribly contagious?" Colleen asked.

"It can be," Jack said. "Especially in the pneumonic form which this patient had."

"Are you worried about having gotten it?" Terese asked. Unconsciously she and Colleen had moved a step backward.

"No," Jack said. "And even if we had, we wouldn't be communicative until after we got pneumonia. So you don't have to stand across the room from us."

Feeling embarrassed, both women stepped closer. "Is there any chance this could turn into an epidemic here in the city?" Terese asked.

"If plague bacteria has infected the urban rodent population, particularly the rats, and if there are adequate rat fleas, it could develop into a problem in the ghetto areas of the city," Jack said. "But chances are it would be self-limited. The last real outbreak of plague in the U.S. occurred in 1919 and there were only twelve cases. And that was before the antibiotic era. I don't anticipate there is going to be a current epidemic, especially since the Manhattan General is taking the episode extremely seriously."

"I trust you contacted the media about this case of plague," Terese said.

"Not me," Jack said. "That's not my job."

"Shouldn't the public be alerted?" Terese asked.

"I don't think so," Jack said. "By sensationalizing it, the media could make things worse. The mere mention of the word 'plague' can evoke panic, and panic would be counterproductive."

"Maybe," Terese said. "But I bet people would feel differently if there was a chance they could avoid coming down with plague if they were forewarned."

"Well, the question is academic," Jack said. "There's no way that the media could avoid hearing about this. It'll be all over the news. Trust me."

"Let's change the subject," Chet said. "What about you guys? What do you do?"

"We're art directors in a relatively large ad agency," Colleen said. "At least I'm an art director. Terese was an art director. Now she's part of the front office. She's creative director."

"Impressive," Chet said.

"And in a strange way we're currently tangentially involved with medicine," she added.

"What do you mean you are involved with medicine?" Jack asked.

"One of our big accounts is National Health," Terese said. "I imagine you've heard of them."

"Unfortunately," Jack said. His tone was flat.

"You have a problem with our working with them?" Terese asked.

"Probably," Jack said.

"Can I ask why?"

"I'm against advertising in medicine," Jack said. "Especially the kind of advertising these new health-care conglomerates are engaged in."

"Why?" Terese asked.

"First of all, the ads have no legitimate function except to increase profits by expanding enrollment. They're nothing but exaggerations, half-truths, or the hyping of superficial amenities. They have nothing to do with the quality of health care. Secondly, the advertising costs a ton of money, and it's being lumped into administrative costs. That's the real crime: It's taking money away from patient care."

"Are you finished?" Terese asked.

"I could probably think up some more reasons if I gave it some thought," Jack said.

"I happen to disagree with you," Terese said with a fervor that matched Jack's. "I think all advertising draws distinctions and fosters a competitive environment which ultimately benefits the consumer."

"That's pure rationalization," Jack said.

"Time out, you guys," Chet said, stepping between Jack and Terese for the second time. "You two are getting out of control again. Let's switch the topic of conversation. Why don't we talk about something neutral, like sex or religion."

Colleen laughed and gave Chet a playful swat on the shoulder.

"I'm serious," Chet said while laughing with Colleen. "Let's discuss religion. It's been getting short shrift lately in bars. Let's have everybody tell what they grew up as. I'll be first . . ."

For the next half hour they indeed did discuss religion, and Jack and Terese forgot their emotional outburst. They even found themselves laughing since Chet was a raconteur of some wit.

At eleven-fifteen Jack happened to glance at his watch and did a double take. He couldn't believe it was so late.

"I'm sorry," he said, interrupting the conversation. "I've got to go. I've got a bicycle ride ahead of me."

"A bike?" Terese questioned. "You ride a bike around this city?"

"He's got a death wish," Chet said.

"Where do you live?" Terese asked.

"Upper West Side," Jack said.

"Ask him how 'upper,' " Chet dared.

"Exactly where?" Terese asked.

"One-oh-six a Hundred and Sixth Street," Jack said. "To be precise."

"But that's in Harlem," Colleen said.

"I told you he has a death wish," Chet said.

"Don't tell me you're going to ride across the park at this hour," Terese said.

"I move pretty quickly," Jack said.

"Well, I think it's asking for trouble," Terese said. She bent down and picked up her briefcase that she'd set on the floor by her feet. "I don't have a bike, but I do have a date with my bed."

"Wait a second, you guys," Chet said. "Colleen and I are in charge. Right, Colleen?" He put his arm loosely around Colleen's shoulder.

"Right!" Colleen said to be agreeable.

"We've decided," Chet said with feigned authority, "that you two can't go home unless you agree to have dinner tomorrow night."

Colleen shook her head as she ducked away from Chet's arm. "I'm afraid we're not available," she said. "We've got an impossible deadline, so we'll be putting in some serious overtime."

"Where were you thinking of having dinner?" Terese asked.

Colleen looked at her friend with surprise.

"How about right around the corner at Elaine's," Chet said. "About eight o'clock. We might even see a couple of celebrities."

"I don't think I can . . ." Jack began.

"I'm not listening to any excuses from you," Chet said, interrupting. "You can bowl with that group of nuns another night. Tomorrow you're having dinner with us."

Jack was too tired to think. He shrugged.

"It's decided, then?" Chet said.

Everyone nodded.

Outside of the bar the women climbed into a cab. They offered Chet a ride home, but he said he lived in the neighborhood.

"Are you sure you don't want to leave that bike here for the night?" Terese asked Jack, who'd finished removing his panoply of locks.

"Not a chance," Jack said. He threw a leg over his bike and powered out across Second Avenue, waving over his head.

Terese gave the cabdriver the address of the first stop, and the taxi made a left onto Second Avenue and accelerated southward. Colleen, who'd kept her eye on Chet out the back window, turned to face her boss.

"What a surprise," she said. "Imagine meeting two decent men at a bar. It always seems to happen when you least expect it."

"They were nice guys," Terese agreed. "I suppose I was wrong about them being out at the meat market, and thank God they didn't spout off about sports or the stock market. Generally that's all men in this city can talk about."

"What tweaks my funny bone is that my mother has forever been encouraging me to meet a doctor," Colleen said with a laugh.

"I don't think either one of them is a typical doctor," Terese said. "Especially Jack. He's got a strange attitude. He's awfully bitter about something, and seems a bit foolhardy. Can you imagine riding a bike around this city?"

"It's easier than thinking about what they do. Can you imagine dealing with dead people all day?"

"I don't know," Terese said. "Mustn't be too different than dealing with account executives."

"I have to say you shocked me when you agreed to have dinner tomorrow night," Colleen said. "Especially with this National Health disaster staring us in the face."

"But that's exactly why I did agree," Terese said. She flashed Colleen a conspiratorial smile. "I want to talk some more with Jack Stapleton. Believe it or not, he actually gave me a great idea for a new ad campaign for National Health! I can't imagine what his reaction would be if he knew. With his philistine attitude about advertising, he'd probably have a stroke."

"What's the idea?" Colleen asked eagerly.

"It involves this plague thing," Terese said. "Since AmeriCare is National Health's only real rival, our ad campaign merely has to take advantage of the fact that AmeriCare got plague in its main hospital. As creepy as the situation is, people should want to flock to National Health."

Colleen's face fell. "We can't use plague," she said.

"Hell, I'm not thinking of using plague specifically," Terese said. "Just emphasizing the idea of National Health's hospital being so new and clean. The contrary will be evoked by inference, and it will be the public who will make the association with this plague episode. I know what the Manhattan General is like. I've been there. It might have been renovated, but it's still an old structure. The National Health hospital is the antithesis. I can see ads where people are eating off the floor at National Health, suggesting it's that clean. I mean, people like the idea that their hospital is new and clean, especially now with all the hullabaloo about bacteria making a comeback and becoming antibiotic-resistant."

"I like it," Colleen said. "If that doesn't increase National Health Care's market share vis-à-vis AmeriCare, nothing will."

"I even have thought up a tag line," Terese said smugly. "Listen: 'We deserve your trust: Health is our middle name.' "

"Excellent! I love it!" Colleen exclaimed. "I'll get the whole team working on it bright and early."

The cab pulled up to Terese's apartment. The women did a high-five before Terese got out.

Leaning back into the cab, Terese said: "Thanks for getting me to go out tonight. It was a good idea for lots of reasons."

"You're welcome," Colleen said, flashing a thumbs-up sign.

CHAPTER 10

THURSDAY, 7:25 A.M., MARCH 21, 1996

As a man of habit, Jack arrived in the vicinity of the medical examiner's office at the same time each day, give or take five minutes. This particular morning he was ten minutes late since he'd awakened with a slight hangover. He'd not had a hangover in so long, he'd completely forgotten how miserable it made him feel. Consequently he'd stayed in the shower a few minutes longer than usual, and on the slalom down Second Avenue, he'd kept his speed to a more reasonable level.

Crossing First Avenue, Jack saw something he'd never seen before at that time of day. There was a TV truck with its main antennae extended sitting in front of the medical examiner's building.

Changing his direction a little, he cruised around the truck. No one was in it. Looking up at the front door to the ME's office, he saw a group of newspeople clustered just over the threshold.

Curious as to what was going on, Jack hustled around to the entrance bay, stashed his bike in the usual place, and went up to the ID room.

As usual Laurie and Vinnie were in their respective seats. Jack said hello but continued through the room to peek out into the lobby area. It was as crowded as he'd ever seen it.

"What the hell's going on?" Jack asked, turning back to Laurie.

"You of all people should know," she said. She was busy making up the day's autopsy schedule. "It's all about the plague epidemic!"

"Epidemic?" Jack questioned. "Have there been more cases?"

"You haven't heard?" Laurie questioned. "Don't you watch morning TV?"

"I don't have a TV," Jack admitted. "In my neighborhood owning one is just inviting trouble."

"Well, two victims came in to us during the night," Laurie said. "One is for sure plague, or at least presumptive since the hospital did its own fluorescein antibody and it was positive. The other is suspected, since clinically it seemed to be plague despite a negative fluorescein antibody. In addition to that, as I understand it, there are several febrile patients who have been quarantined."

"This is all happening at the Manhattan General?" Jack asked.

"Apparently," Laurie said.

"Were these cases direct contacts with Nodelman?" Jack asked.

"I haven't had time to look into that," Laurie said. "Are you interested? If you are, I'll assign them to you."

"Of course," Jack said. "Which one is the presumptive plague?"

"Katherine Mueller," Laurie said. She pushed the patient's folder toward Jack.

Sitting on the edge of the desk where Laurie was working, Jack opened the folder. He leafed through the papers until he found the investigative report. He pulled it out and began reading. He learned the woman had been brought into the Manhattan General emergency room at four o'clock in the afternoon acutely ill with what was diagnosed to be a fulminant case of plague. She'd died nine hours later despite massive antibiotics.

Jack checked on the woman's place of employment and wasn't surprised with what he learned. The woman worked at the Manhattan General. Jack assumed she had to have been a direct contact of Nodelman. Unfortunately the report did not indicate in what department she worked. Jack guessed either nursing or lab.

Reading on in the report, Jack silently complimented Janice Jaeger's work. After the conversation he'd had with her the day before by phone, she added information about travel, pets, and visitors. In the case of Mueller it was all negative.

"Where's the suspected plague?" Jack asked Laurie.

Laurie pushed a second folder toward him.

Jack opened the second file and was immediately surprised. The victim neither worked at the Manhattan General nor had obvious contact with Nodelman. Her name was Susanne Hard. Like Nodelman, she'd been a patient in the General, but not on the same ward as Nodelman. Hard had been on the OB-GYN ward after giving birth! Jack was mystified.

Reading further, Jack learned that Hard had been in the hospital for twenty-four hours when she'd experienced sudden high fever, myalgia, headache, overwhelming malaise, and progressive cough. These symptoms had come on about eighteen hours after undergoing a cesarean section during which she delivered a healthy child. Eight hours after the symptoms appeared, the patient was dead.

Out of curiosity Jack looked up Hard's address, remembering that Nodelman had lived in the Bronx. But Hard had not lived in the Bronx. She had lived in Manhattan on Sutton Place South, hardly a ghetto neighborhood.

Reading on, Jack learned that Hard had not traveled since she'd become pregnant. As far as pets were concerned, she owned an elderly but healthy poodle. Concerning visitors, she had entertained a business associate of her husband's from India three weeks previously who was described as being healthy and well.

"Is Janice Jaeger still here this morning?" Jack asked Laurie.

"She was about fifteen minutes ago when I passed her office," Laurie said.

Jack found Janice where she'd been the previous morning.

"You are a dedicated civil servant," Jack called out from the threshold.

Janice looked up from her work. Her eyes were red from fatigue. "Too many people dying lately. I'm swamped. But tell me: Did I ask the right questions on the infectious cases last night?"

"Absolutely," Jack said. "I was impressed. But I do have a couple more."

"Shoot," Janice said.

"Where's the OB-GYN ward in relation to the medical ward?"

"They're right next to each other," Janice said. "Both are on the seventh floor."

"No kidding," Jack said.

"Is that significant?" Janice asked.

"I haven't the slightest idea," Jack admitted. "Do patients from the OB ward mix with those on the medical ward?"

"You got me there," Janice admitted. "I don't know, but I wouldn't imagine so."

"Nor would I," Jack said. But if they didn't, then how did Susanne Hard manage to get sick? Something seemed screwy about this plague outbreak. Facetiously he wondered if a bunch of infected rats could be living in the ventilation system on the seventh floor.

"Any other questions?" Janice asked. "I want to get out of here, and I have this last report to finish."

"One more," Jack said. "You indicated that Katherine Mueller was employed by the General but you didn't say for what department. Do you know if she worked for nursing or for the lab?"

Janice leafed through her night's notes and came up with the sheet on which she'd recorded Mueller's information. She quickly glanced through it and then looked back up at Jack. "Neither," she said. "She worked in central supply."

"Oh, come on!" Jack said. He sounded disappointed.

"I'm sorry," Janice said. "That's what I was told."

"I'm not blaming you," Jack said with a wave of his hand. "It's just that I'd like there to be some sort of logic to all this. How would a woman in central supply get into contact with a sick patient on the seventh floor? Where's central supply?"

"I believe it's on the same floor with the operating rooms," Janice said. "That would be the third floor."

"Okay, thanks," Jack said. "Now get out of here and get some sleep."

"I intend to," Janice said.

Jack wandered back toward the ID room, thinking that nothing seemed to be making much sense. Usually the course of a contagious illness could be easily plotted sequentially through a family or a community. There was the index case, and the subsequent cases extended from it by contact, either directly or through a vector like an insect. There wasn't a lot of mystery. That wasn't the case so far with this plague outbreak. The only unifying factor was that they all involved the Manhattan General.

Jack absently waved to Sergeant Murphy, who'd apparently just arrived in his cubbyhole office off the communications room. The ebullient Irish policeman waved back with great enthusiasm.

Jack slowed his walk while his mind churned. Susanne Hard had come down with symptoms after only being in the hospital for a day. Since the incubation period for plague was generally thought to be two days at a minimum, she would have been exposed prior to coming into the hospital. Jack went back to Janice's office.

"One more question," Jack called out to her. "Do you happen to know whether the Hard woman visited the hospital in the days prior to her admission?"

"Her husband said no," Janice said. "I asked that question specifically. Apparently she hated the hospital and only came in at the very last minute."

Jack nodded. "Thanks," he said, even more preoccupied. He turned and started back toward the ID room. That information made the situation more baffling, requiring him to postulate that the outbreak had occurred almost simultaneously in two, maybe three locations. That wasn't probable. The other possibility was that the incubation period was extremely short, less than twenty-four hours. That would mean Hard's illness was a nosocomial infection, as he suspected Nodelman's was as well as Mueller's. The problem with that idea was that it would suggest a huge, overwhelming infecting dose, which also seemed unlikely. After all, how many sick rats could be in a ventilation duct all coughing at the same time?

In the ID room Jack wrestled the sports page of the *Daily News* away from a reluctant Vinnie and dragged him down to the pit to begin the day.

"How come you always start so early?" Vinnie complained. "You're the only one. Don't you have a life?"

Jack swatted him in the chest with Katherine Mueller's folder. "Remember the saying 'The early bird gets the worm'?"

"Oh, barf," Vinnie said. He took the folder from Jack and opened it. "Is this the one we're doing first?" he asked.

"Might as well move from the known to the unknown," Jack said. "This one had a positive fluorescein antibody test to plague, so zip up tight in your moon suit."

Fifteen minutes later Jack began the autopsy. He spent a good deal of time on the external exam, looking for any signs of insect bites. It wasn't an easy job, since

Katherine Mueller was an overweight forty-four-year-old with hundreds of moles, freckles, and other minor skin blemishes. Jack found nothing he was sure was a bite, although a few lesions looked mildly suspicious. To be on the safe side he photographed them.

"No gangrene on this body," Vinnie commented.

"Nor purpura," Jack said.

By the time Jack started on the internal exam, a number of the other staff had arrived in the autopsy room and half of the tables were in use. There were a few comments about Jack becoming the local plague expert, but Jack ignored them. He was too engrossed.

Mueller's lungs appeared quite similar to Nodelman's, with extensive lobar pneumonia, consolidation, and early stages of tissue death. The woman's cervical lymphatics were also generally involved, as were the lymph nodes along the bronchial tree.

"This is just as bad or worse than Nodelman," Jack said. "It's frightening."

"You don't have to tell me," Vinnie said. "These infectious cases are the kind that make me wish I'd gone into gardening."

Jack was nearing the end of the internal exam when Calvin came through the door. There was no mistaking his huge silhouette. He was accompanied by another figure who was half his size. Calvin came directly to Jack's table.

"Anything out of the ordinary?" Calvin asked, while peering into the pan of internal organs.

"Internally this case is a repeat of yesterday's," Jack said.

"Good," Calvin said, straightening up. He then introduced Jack to his guest. It was Clint Abelard, the city epidemiologist.

Jack could make out the man's prominent jaw, but because of the reflection off the plastic face mask, he couldn't see the fellow's squirrelly eyes. He wondered if he was still as cantankerous as he'd been the day before.

"According to Dr. Bingham you two have already met," Calvin said.

"Indeed," Jack said. The epidemiologist did not respond.

"Dr. Abelard is trying to discern the origin of this plague outbreak," Calvin explained.

"Commendable," Jack said.

"He's come to us to see if we can add any significant information," Calvin said. "Perhaps you could run through your positive findings."

"My pleasure," Jack said. He started with the external exam, indicating skin abnormalities he thought could have been insect bites. Then he showed all the gross internal pathology, concentrating on the lungs, lymphatics, liver, and spleen. Throughout the entire discourse, Clint Abelard stayed silent.

"There you have it," Jack said as he finished. He put the liver back into the pan. "As you can see it's a severe case, as was Nodelman's, and it's no wonder both patients died so quickly."

"What about Hard?" Clint asked.

"She's next," Jack said.

"Mind if I watch?" Clint asked.

Jack shrugged. "That's up to Dr. Washington," he said.

"No problem," Calvin said.

"If I may ask," Jack said, "have you come up with a theory where this plague came from?"

"Not really," Clint said gruffly. "Not yet."

"Any ideas?" Jack asked, trying to keep sarcasm out of his voice. It seemed Clint was in no better humor than he had been the day before.

"We're looking for plague in the area's rodent population," Clint said condescendingly.

"Splendid idea," Jack said. "And just how are you doing that?"

Clint paused as if he didn't want to divulge any state secrets.

"The CDC is helping," he said finally. "They sent someone up here from their plague division. He's in charge of the trapping and analysis."

"Any luck so far?" Jack asked.

"Some of the rats caught last night were ill," Clint said. "But none with plague."

"What about the hospital?" Jack asked. He persisted despite Clint's apparent reluctance to talk. "This woman we've just autopsied worked in central supply. Seems likely her illness was nosocomial like Nodelman's. Do you think she got it from some primary source in and around the hospital, or do you think she got it from Nodelman?"

"We don't know," Clint admitted.

"If she got it from Nodelman," Jack asked, "any ideas of a possible route of transmission?"

"We've checked the hospital's ventilation and air-conditioning system carefully," Clint said. "All the HEPA filters were in place and had been changed appropriately."

"What about the lab situation?" Jack asked.

"What do you mean?" Clint said.

"Did you know that the chief tech in micro actually suggested plague to the director of the lab purely from his clinical impression, but the director talked him out of following up on it?"

"I didn't know that," Clint mumbled.

"If the chief tech had followed up on it he would have made the diagnosis and appropriate therapy could have been started," Jack said. "Who knows; it could have saved a life. The problem is that the lab has been downsizing because of pressure from AmeriCare to save a few bucks, and they don't have a microbiology supervisor position. It got eliminated."

"I don't know anything about all that," Clint said. "Besides, the case of plague still would have occurred."

"You're right," Jack said. "One way or the other you still have to come up with the origin. Unfortunately, you don't know any more than you did yesterday." Jack smiled inside his mask. He was getting a bit of perverse pleasure out of putting the epidemiologist on the spot.

"I wouldn't go that far," Clint muttered.

"Any sign of illness in the hospital staff?" Jack asked.

"There are several nurses who are febrile and who are quarantined," Clint said. "As of yet there is no confirmation of them having plague, but it is suspected. They were directly exposed to Nodelman."

"When will you be doing Hard?" Calvin asked.

"In about twenty minutes," Jack said. "As soon as Vinnie gets things turned around."

"I'm going around to check on some other cases," Calvin said to Clint. "You want to stay here with Dr. Stapleton or do you want to come with me?"

"I think I'll go with you, if you don't mind," Clint said.

"By the way, Jack," Calvin said before leaving. "There's a bevy of media people upstairs crawling all over the outer office like bloodhounds. I don't want you giving any unauthorized press conferences. Any information coming from the ME's office comes from Mrs. Donnatello and her PR assistant."

"I wouldn't dream of talking to the press," Jack assured him.

Calvin wandered to the next table. Clint stayed at his heels.

"It didn't sound as if that guy wanted to talk with you," Vinnie said to Jack when Calvin and Clint were far enough away. "Not that I can blame him."

"That little mouse has been spleeny since I first met him," Jack said. "I don't know what his problem is. He's kinda a weird duck, if you ask me."

"Now there's the pot calling the kettle black," Vinnie said.

CHAPTER 11

THURSDAY, 9:30 A.M., MARCH 21, 1996
NEW YORK CITY

"Mr. Lagenthorpe, can you hear me?" Dr. Doyle called to his patient. Donald Lagenthorpe was a thirty-eight-year-old African-American oil engineer who had a chronic problem with asthma. That morning, just after three A.M., he'd awakened with progressive difficulty breathing. His prescribed home remedies had not interrupted the attack, and he'd come into the emergency room of the Manhattan General at four. Dr. Doyle had been called at quarter to five after the usual emergency medications had had no effect.

Donald's eyes blinked open. He hadn't been sleeping, just trying to rest. The ordeal had been exhausting and frightening. The feeling of not being able to catch his breath was torture, and this episode had been the worst he'd ever experienced.

"How are you doing?" Dr. Doyle inquired. "I know what you have been through.

You must be very tired." Dr. Doyle was one of those rare physicians who were able to empathize with all his patients with a depth of understanding suggesting he suffered from all the same conditions.

Donald nodded his head, indicating that he was okay. He was breathing through a face mask that made conversation difficult.

"I want you to stay in the hospital for a few days," Dr. Doyle said. "This was a difficult attack to break."

Donald nodded again. No one had to tell him that.

"I want to keep you on the IV steroids for a little while longer," Dr. Doyle explained.

Donald lifted the face mask off his face. "Couldn't I get the steroids at home?" he suggested. As thankful as he was about the hospital's having been there in his hour of need, he much preferred the idea of going home now that his breathing had returned to normal. At home he knew he could at least get some work done. As was always the case, this asthma attack had come at a particularly inconvenient time. He was supposed to go back to Texas the following week for more fieldwork.

"I know you don't want to be in the hospital," Dr. Doyle said. "I'd feel the same way. But I think it is best under the circumstances. We'll get you out just as soon as possible. Not only do I want to continue giving you IV steroids, but I want you breathing humidified, clean, nonirritating air. I also want to follow your peak expiratory flow rate carefully. As I explained to you earlier, it is still not completely back to normal."

"How many days do you estimate I'll have to be in here?" Donald asked.

"I'm sure it will only be a couple," Dr. Doyle said.

"I've got to go back to Texas," Donald explained.

"Oh?" Dr. Doyle said. "When were you there last?"

"Just last week," Donald said.

"Hmm," Dr. Doyle said while he thought. "Were you exposed to anything abnormal while you were there?"

"Just Tex-Mex cuisine," Donald said, managing a smile.

"You haven't gotten any new pets or anything like that, have you?" Dr. Doyle asked. One of the difficulties of managing someone with chronic asthma was determining the factors responsible for triggering attacks. Frequently it was allergenic.

"My girlfriend got a new cat," Donald said. "It has made me itch a bit the last few times I've been over there."

"When was the last time?" Dr. Doyle asked.

"Last night," Donald admitted. "But I was home just a little after eleven, and I felt fine. I didn't have any trouble falling asleep."

"We'll have to look into it," Dr. Doyle said. "Meanwhile I want you in the hospital. What do you say?"

"You're the doctor," Donald said reluctantly.

"Thank you," Dr. Doyle said.

CHAPTER 12

"For chrissake!" Jack murmured under his breath as he was about to start the autopsy on Susanne Hard. Clint Abelard was hovering behind him like a gnat, constantly switching his weight from one leg to the other.

"Clint, why don't you step around the table and stand on the other side," Jack suggested. "You'll be able to see much better."

Clint took the suggestion and stood with his arms behind his back opposite from Jack.

"Now don't move," Jack mumbled to himself. Jack didn't like Clint hanging around, but he had no choice.

"It's sad when you see a young woman like this," Clint said suddenly.

Jack looked up. He hadn't expected such a comment from Clint. It seemed too human. He had struck Jack as an unfeeling, moody bureaucrat.

"How old is she?" Clint asked.

"Twenty-eight," Vinnie said from the head of the table.

"From the looks of her spine she didn't have an easy life," Clint said.

"She had several major back surgeries," Jack said.

"It's a double tragedy since she'd just given birth," Clint said. "Now the child is motherless."

"It was her second child," Vinnie said.

"I suppose I shouldn't forget her husband," Clint said. "It must be upsetting to lose your spouse."

A knifelike stab of emotion went down Jack's spine. He had to fight to keep from reaching across the table and yanking Clint off his feet. Abruptly he left the table and exited to the washroom. He heard Vinnie call after him, but he ignored him. Instead Jack leaned on the edge of the sink and tried to calm himself. He knew that getting angry with Clint was an unreasonable reaction; it was nothing but pure, unadulterated transference. But understanding the origin did not lessen the irritation. It always irked Jack when he heard such clichés from people who truly had no idea.

"Is there a problem?" Vinnie asked. He'd stuck his head through the door.

"I'll be there in a second," Jack said.

Vinnie let the door close.

As long as he was there, Jack washed and regloved his hands. When he was finished he returned to the table.

"Let's get this show on the road," he said.

"I've looked the body over," Clint said. "I don't see anything that looks like an insect bite, do you?"

Jack had to restrain himself from subjecting Clint to a lecture like the one Clint had given to him. Instead, he merely proceeded with his external exam. Only after he'd finished did he speak.

"No gangrene, no purpura, and no insect bites as far as I can see," Jack said. "But by just looking at her I can see some of her cervical lymph nodes are swollen."

Jack pointed out the finding to Clint, who then nodded in agreement.

"That's certainly consistent with plague," Clint said.

Jack didn't answer. Instead he took a scalpel from Vinnie and quickly made the typical Y-shaped autopsy incision. The bold cruelty of the move jolted Clint. He took a step back.

Jack worked quickly but with great care. He knew that the less the internal organs were disturbed, the less chance that any of the infecting microbes would be aerosolized.

When Jack had the organs out, he turned his attention first to the lungs. Calvin had drifted over at this point and towered behind Jack as he made his initial cuts into the obviously diseased organ. Jack spread open the lung like a butterfly.

"Lots of bronchopneumonia and early tissue necrosis," Calvin said. "Looks pretty similar to Nodelman."

"I don't know," Jack said. "Seems to me there is an equal amount of pathology but less consolidation. And look at these nodal areas. They almost look like early granulomas with caseation."

Clint listened to this pathological jargon with little interest or comprehension. He remembered the terms from medical school, but had long since forgotten their meaning. "Does it look like plague?" he asked.

"Consistent," Calvin said. "Let's look at the liver and the spleen."

Jack carefully pulled these organs from the pan and sliced into them. As he'd done with the lung, he spread open their cut surfaces so everyone could see. Even Laurie had stepped over from her table.

"Lots of necrosis," Jack said. "Certainly just as virulent a case as with Nodelman or with the case I did earlier."

"Looks like plague to me," Calvin said.

"But why was the fluorescein antibody negative?" Jack said. "That's telling me something, especially combined with the lung appearance."

"What's with the lungs?" Laurie asked.

Jack moved the liver and the spleen aside and showed Laurie the cut surface of the lung. He explained what he thought of the pathology.

"I see what you mean now that you mention it," Laurie said. "It is different from Nodelman. His lungs definitely had more consolidation. This looks more like some sort of horribly aggressive TB."

"Whoa!" Calvin said. "This isn't TB. No way."

"I don't think Laurie was suggesting it was," Jack said.

"I wasn't," Laurie agreed. "I was just using TB as a way of describing these infected areas."

"I think it is plague," Calvin said. "I mean, I wouldn't if we hadn't just had a case from the same hospital yesterday. Chances are it is plague regardless of what their lab said."

"I don't think it is," Jack said. "But let's see what our lab says."

"How about double or nothing with that ten dollars," Calvin said. "Are you that sure?"

"No, but I'll take you up on it. I know how much the money means to you."

"Are we finished here?" Clint asked. "If so, I think I'll be going."

"I'm essentially finished," Jack said. "I'll do a little more on the lymphatics, and then I'll be obtaining samples for the microscopic. You won't be missing anything if you take off now."

"I'll head out with you," Calvin said.

Calvin and Clint disappeared through the door to the washroom.

"If you don't think this case is plague, what do you think it is?" Laurie asked, looking back at the woman's corpse.

"I'm embarrassed to tell you," Jack said.

"Come on," Laurie urged. "I won't tell anybody."

Jack looked at Vinnie. Vinnie held up his hands. "My lips are sealed."

"Well, I'd have to fall back on my original differential I had for Nodelman," Jack said. "To narrow it down more than that, I have to again go out on thin ice. If it isn't plague, the nearest infectious disease both pathologically and clinically is tularemia."

Laurie laughed. "Tularemia in a twenty-eight-year-old postpartum female in Manhattan?" she questioned. "That would be pretty rare, although not as rare as your diagnosis yesterday of plague. After all, she could have a hobby of rabbit hunting on weekends."

"I know it's not very probable," Jack said. "Once again I'm relying totally on the pathology and the fact that the test for plague was negative."

"I'd be willing to bet a quarter," Laurie said.

"Such a spender!" Jack joked. "Fine! We'll bet a quarter."

Laurie returned to her own case. Jack and Vinnie turned their attention back to Susanne Hard. While Vinnie did his tasks, Jack finished the lymphatic dissection he wanted to do, then took the tissue samples he felt appropriate for microscopic study. When the samples were all in the proper preservatives and appropriately labeled, he helped Vinnie suture the corpse.

Leaving the autopsy room, Jack properly dealt with his isolation equipment. After plugging in his rechargeable ventilator battery, he took the elevator up to the third floor to see Agnes Finn. He found her sitting in front of a stack of petri dishes examining bacterial cultures.

"I've just finished another infectious case that's suspected plague," he told her. "All the samples will be coming up shortly. But there is a problem. The lab over at the Manhattan General claims the patient tested negative. Of course, I want to repeat that, but at the same time I want you to rule out tularemia, and I want it done as quickly as possible."

"That's not easy," she said. "Handling *Francisella tularensis* is hazardous. It's very contagious to laboratory workers if it gets into the air. There is a fluorescein antibody stain for tularemia, but we don't have it."

"How do you make the diagnosis, then?" Jack asked.

"We have to send any samples out," she said. "Because of the risk of handling the bacteria the reagents are generally kept only at reference labs where the personnel are accustomed to dealing with the microbe. There is such a lab here in the city."

"Can you send it right away?" Jack asked.

"We'll messenger it over as soon as it gets here," she said. "If I call and put a rush on it, we'll have a preliminary result in less than twenty-four hours."

"Perfect," Jack said. "I'll be waiting. I've got ten dollars and twenty-five cents riding on the outcome."

Agnes gave Jack a look. He considered explaining, but feared he'd sound even more foolish. Instead he fled upstairs to his office.

CHAPTER 13

THURSDAY, 10:45 A.M., MARCH 21, 1996
NEW YORK CITY

"I'm liking it more and more," Terese said. She straightened up from Colleen's drawing board. Colleen was showing her tissues that her team had comped up just that morning using the theme they'd discussed the night before.

"The best thing is that the concept is consistent with the Hippocratic oath," Colleen said. "Particularly the part about never doing harm to anyone. I love it."

"I don't know why we didn't think about it before," Terese said. "It's such a natural. It's almost embarrassing that it took this damn plague epidemic to make us think of it. Did you catch what's happening on morning TV?"

"Three deaths!" Colleen said. "And several people sick. It's terrible. In fact, it scares me to death."

"I had a headache from the wine last night when I woke up this morning," Terese said. "The first thing that went through my mind was whether I had the plague or not."

"I thought the same thing," Colleen said. "I'm glad you admitted it. I was too embarrassed."

"I hope to hell those guys were right last night," Terese said. "They seemed pretty damn confident it wasn't going to be a big problem."

"Are you worried being around them?" Colleen asked.

"Oh, it's gone through my mind," Terese admitted. "But as I said, they were so confident. I can't imagine their acting that way if there were any risk."

"Are we still on for dinner tonight?" Colleen asked.

"By all means," Terese said. "I have a sneaking suspicion that Jack Stapleton will turn out to be an unknowing fountain of ad ideas. He might be bitter about some-thing, but he's sharp and opinionated, and he certainly knows the business."

"I can't believe how well this is working out," Colleen said. "I was a lot more drawn to Chet; he's fun and open and easy to talk with. I have enough problems of my own, so I'm not attracted to the anguished, brooding type."

"I didn't say anything about being attracted to Jack Stapleton," Terese said. "That's something else entirely."

"What's your gut reaction to this idea of using Hippocrates himself in one of our ads?"

"I think it has fantastic potential," Terese said. "Run with it. Meanwhile I'm going to head upstairs and talk with Helen Robinson."

"Why?" Colleen asked. "I thought she was the enemy."

"I'm taking to heart Taylor's admonition that we creatives and the account people should work together," Terese said breezily.

"Yeah, sure! Likely story!"

"Seriously," Terese said. "There's something I'd like her to do. I need a fifth column. I want Helen to confirm that National Health is clean when it comes to nosocomial or hospital-based infections. If their record is atrocious, the whole cam-paign could backfire. Then, not only would I lose my bid for the presidency, but you and I would probably be out selling pencils."

"Wouldn't we have heard by this time?" Colleen asked. "I mean, they've been clients for a number of years."

"I doubt it," Terese said. "These health-care giants are loath to publicize anything that might adversely affect their stock price. Surely a bad record in regard to noso-comial infections would do that."

Terese gave Colleen a pat on the shoulder and told her to keep cracking the whip, then headed for the stairwell.

Terese emerged breathless onto the administrative floor, having taken the stairs two at a time. From there she marched directly toward the carpeted realm of the account executives. Her mood was soaring; it was the absolute antithesis of the anxiety and dread of the day before. Her intuition told her she was onto something big with National Health and would soon be scoring a deserved triumph. . . .

As soon as the impromptu meeting with Terese had ended and Terese had disap-peared around the corner, Helen returned to her desk and put a call in to her main contact at National Health Care. The woman wasn't immediately available, but Helen didn't expect her to be. Helen merely left her name and number with a request to be called as soon as possible.

With the call accomplished Helen took a brush from her desk and ran it through her hair several times in front of a small mirror on the inside of her closet door. Once she was satisfied with her appearance, she walked out of her office and headed down to Robert Barker's.

"You have a minute?" Helen called to him from his open door.

"For you I have all day," Robert said. He leaned back in his chair.

Helen stepped into the room and turned to close the door. As she did so, Robert surreptitiously turned over the photo of his wife that stood on the corner of the desk. His wife's stern stare made him feel guilty whenever Helen was in his office.

"I just had a visitor," Helen said as she came into the room. As was her custom she sat cross-legged on the arm of one of the two chairs facing Robert's desk.

Robert felt perspiration appear along his hairline in keeping with his quickening pulse. From his vantage point, Helen's short skirt afforded him a view of her thigh that didn't stop.

"It was our creative director," Helen continued. She was very conscious of the effect she was having on her boss, and it pleased her. "She asked me to get some information for her."

"What kind of information?" Robert asked. His eyes didn't move, nor did he blink. It was as if he were hypnotized.

Helen explained what Terese wanted and described the brief conversation about the plague outbreak. When Robert didn't respond immediately, she stood up. That broke the trance. "I tried to tell her not to use it as the basis of an ad campaign," Helen added, "but she thinks it's going to work."

"Maybe you shouldn't have said anything," Robert remarked. He loosened his shirt and took a breath.

"But it's a terrible idea," Helen said. "I couldn't think of anything more tasteless."

"Exactly," Robert said. "I'd like her to propose a tasteless campaign."

"I see your point," Helen said. "I didn't think of that on the spur of the moment."

"Of course not," Robert said. "You're not as devious as I am. But you're a quick study. The problem with the idea about nosocomial infection in general is that it could be a good one. There might possibly be a legitimate difference between National Health and AmeriCare."

"I could always tell her the information wasn't available," Helen said. "After all, it might not be."

"There is always risk in lying," Robert said. "She might already have the information and be testing us to make us look bad. No, go ahead and see what you can find out. But let me know what you learn and what you pass on to Terese Hagen. I want to keep a step ahead of her."

CHAPTER 14

THURSDAY, 12:00 P.M., MARCH 21, 1996

"Hey, sport, how the hell are you?" Chet asked Jack as Jack scooted into their shared office and dumped several folders onto his cluttered desk.

"Couldn't be better," Jack said.

Thursday had been a paper day for Chet, meaning he'd been at his desk and not in the autopsy room. Generally the associate medical examiners only did autopsies three days a week. The other days they spent collating the voluminous paperwork necessary to "sign out" a case. There was always material that needed to be gathered from PA investigators, the lab, the hospital or local doctors, or the police. Plus each doctor had to read the microscopic slides the histology lab processed on every case.

Jack sat down and pushed some of the paper debris away from the center of the desk to give him some room to work.

"You feel all right this morning?" Chet asked.

"A little wobbly," Jack admitted. He rescued his phone from beneath lab reports. Then he opened up one of the folders he'd just brought in with him and began searching through the contents. "And you?"

"Perfect," Chet said. "But I'm accustomed to a little wine and such. Remembering those chicks helped, particularly Colleen. Hey, we still on for tonight?"

"I was going to talk to you about that," Jack said.

"You promised," Chet said.

"I didn't exactly promise," Jack said.

"Come on," Chet pleaded. "Don't let me down. They're expecting both of us. They might not stay if only I show up."

Jack glanced over at his officemate.

"Come on," Chet repeated. "Please!"

"All right, for chrissake," Jack said. "Just this once. But I truly don't understand why you think you need me. You do fine by yourself."

"Thanks, buddy," Chet said. "I owe you one."

Jack found the ID sheet that had the phone numbers for Maurice Hard, Susanne's husband. There was both a home number and an office number. He dialed the home.

"Who you calling?" Chet asked.

"You are a nosy bastard," Jack said jokingly.

"I've got to watch over you so you don't get yourself fired," Chet said.

"I'm calling the spouse of another curious infectious case," Jack said. "I just did the post, and it's got me bewildered. Clinically it looked like plague, but I don't think it was."

A housekeeper picked up the phone. When Jack asked for Mr. Hard, he was told Mr. Hard was at the office. Jack dialed the second number. This time it was answered by a secretary. Jack had to explain who he was and was then put on hold. "I'm amazed," Jack said to Chet, his hand over the receiver. "The man's wife just died and he's at work. Only in America!"

Maurice Hard came on the line. His voice was strained. He was obviously under great stress. Jack was tempted to tell the man he knew something of what he was feeling, but something made him hold back. Instead he explained who he was and why he was calling.

"Do you think I should talk to my lawyer first?" Maurice asked.

"Lawyer? Why your lawyer?"

"My wife's family is making ridiculous accusations," Maurice said. "They're suggesting I had something to do with Susanne's death. They're crazy. Rich, but crazy. I mean, Susanne and I had our ups and downs, but we never would have hurt each other, no way."

"Do they know your wife died of an infectious disease?" Jack questioned.

"I've tried to tell them," Maurice said.

"I don't know what to say," Jack said. "It's really not my position to advise you about your personal legal situation."

"Well, hell, go ahead and ask your questions," Maurice said. "I can't imagine it would make any difference. But let me ask you a question first. Was it plague?"

"That still has not been determined," Jack said. "But I'll call you as soon as we know for sure."

"I'd appreciate that," Maurice said. "Now, what are your questions?"

"I believe you have a dog," Jack said. "Is the dog healthy?"

"For a seventeen-year-old dog he's healthy," Maurice said.

"I'd like to encourage you to take the pet to your vet and explain that your wife died of a serious infectious disease. I want to be sure the dog isn't carrying the illness, whatever it was."

"Is there a chance of that?" Maurice asked with alarm.

"It's small, but there is a chance," Jack said.

"Why didn't the hospital tell me that?" he demanded.

"That I can't answer," Jack said. "I assume they talked to you about taking antibiotics."

"Yeah, I've already started," Maurice said. "But it bums me out about the dog. I should have been informed."

"There's also the issue of travel," Jack said. "I was told your wife didn't do any recent traveling."

"That's right," Maurice said. "She was pretty uncomfortable with her pregnancy, especially with her back problem. We haven't gone anywhere except to our house up in Connecticut."

"When was the last visit to Connecticut?" Jack asked.

"About a week and a half ago," Maurice said. "She liked it up there."

"Is it rural?" Jack asked.

"Seventy acres of fields and forest land," Maurice said proudly. "Beautiful spot. We have our own pond."

"Did your wife ever go out into the woods?" Jack asked.

"All the time," Maurice said. "That was her main enjoyment. She liked to feed the deer and the rabbits."

"Were there many rabbits?" Jack asked.

"You know rabbits," Maurice said. "Every time we went up there there were more of them. I actually thought they were a pain in the neck. In the spring and summer they ate all the goddamn flowers."

"Any problem with rats?"

"Not that I know of," Maurice said. "Are you sure this is all significant?"

"We never know," Jack said. "What about your visitor from India?"

"That was Mr. Svinashan," Maurice said. "He's a business acquaintance from Bombay. He stayed with us for almost a week."

"Hmm," Jack said, remembering the plague outbreak in 1994 in Bombay. "As far as you know, he's healthy and well?"

"As far as I know," Maurice said.

"How about giving him a call," Jack suggested. "If he's been sick, let me know."

"No problem," Maurice said. "You don't think he could have been involved, do you? After all, his visit was three weeks ago."

"This episode has baffled me," Jack admitted. "I'm not ruling anything out. What about Donald Nodelman? Did you or your wife know him?"

"Who's he?" Maurice asked.

"He was the first victim in this plague outbreak," Jack said. "He was a patient in the Manhattan General. I'd be curious if your wife might have visited him. He was on the same floor."

"In OB-GYN?" Maurice questioned with surprise.

"He was on the medical ward on the opposite side of the building. He was in the hospital for diabetes."

"Where did he live?"

"The Bronx," Jack said.

"I doubt it," Maurice said. "We don't know anyone from the Bronx."

"One last question," Jack said. "Did your wife happen to visit the hospital during the week prior to her admission?"

"She hated hospitals," Maurice said. "It was difficult to get her to go even when she was in labor."

Jack thanked Maurice and hung up.

"Now who you calling?" Chet asked as Jack dialed again.

"The husband of my first case this morning," Jack said. "At least we know this case had plague for sure."

"Why don't you let the PAs make these calls?" Chet asked.

"Because I can't tell them what to ask," Jack said. "I don't know what I'm looking for. I just have this suspicion that there is some missing piece of information. Also I'm just plain interested. The more I think about this episode of plague in New York in March, the more unique I think it is."

Mr. Harry Mueller was a far cry from Mr. Maurice Hard. He was devastated by his loss and had trouble speaking despite a professed willingness to be cooperative. Not wishing to add to the man's burden, Jack tried to be quick. After corroborating Janice's report of no pets or travel and no recent visitors, Jack went through the same questions concerning Donald Nodelman as he had with Maurice.

"I'm certain my wife did not know this individual," Harry said, "and she rarely met any patients directly, especially sick patients."

"Did your wife work in central supply for a long time?" Jack asked.

"Twenty-one years," Harry said.

"Did she ever come down with any illness that she thought she'd contracted at the hospital?" Jack asked.

"Maybe if one of her co-workers had a cold," Harry said. "But nothing more than that."

"Thank you, Mr. Mueller," Jack said. "You've been most kind."

"Katherine would have wanted me to help," Harry said. "She was a good person."

Jack hung up the phone but left his hands drumming on the receiver. He was agitated.

"Nobody, including me, has any idea what the hell is going on here," he said.

"True," Chet said. "But it's not your worry. The cavalry has already arrived. I heard that the city epidemiologist was over here observing this morning."

"He was here all right," Jack said. "But it was in desperation. That little twerp hasn't the foggiest notion of what's going on. If it weren't for the CDC's sending someone up here from Atlanta, nothing would be happening. At least someone's out there trapping rats and looking for a reservoir."

Suddenly Jack pushed back from the desk, got up, and pulled on his bomber jacket.

"Uh-oh!" Chet said. "I sense trouble. Where are you going?"

"I'm heading back to the General," Jack said. "My gut sense tells me the missing information is over there at the hospital, and by God I'm going to find it."

"What about Bingham?" Chet said nervously.

"Cover for me," Jack said. "If I'm late for Thursday conference, tell him . . ." Jack paused as he tried to think up some appropriate excuse, but nothing came to mind. "Oh, screw it," he said. "I won't be that long. I'll be back way before conference. If anybody calls, tell them I'm in the john."

Ignoring further pleas to reconsider, Jack left and rode uptown. He arrived in less than fifteen minutes and locked his bike to the same signpost as the day before.

The first thing Jack did was take the hospital elevator up to the seventh floor and reconnoiter. He saw how the OB-GYN and medical wards were completely separate without sharing any common facilities like lounges or lavatories. He also saw that the ventilation system was designed so as to preclude any movement of air from one ward to the other.

Pushing through the swinging doors into the OB-GYN area, Jack walked down to the central desk.

"Excuse me," he said to a ward secretary. "Does this ward share any personnel with the medical ward across the elevator lobby?"

"No, not that I know of," the young man said. He looked about fifteen with a complexion that suggested he had yet to shave. "Except, of course, cleaning people. But they clean all over the hospital."

"Good point," Jack said. He hadn't thought of the housekeeping department. It was something to consider. Jack then asked which room Susanne Hard had occupied.

"Can I ask what this is in reference to?" the ward clerk asked. He had finally noticed that Jack was not wearing a hospital ID. Hospitals all require identification badges of their employees, but then frequently do not have the personnel to enforce compliance.

Jack took out his ME badge and flashed it. It had the desired effect. The ward secretary told Jack that Mrs. Hard had been in room 742.

Jack started out for the room, but the ward clerk called out to him that it was quarantined and temporarily sealed.

Believing that viewing the room would not have been enlightening anyway, Jack left the seventh floor and descended to the third, which housed the surgical suites, the recovery room, the intensive-care units, and central supply. It was a busy area with a lot of patient traffic.

Jack pushed through a pair of swinging doors into central supply and was confronted by an unmanned counter. Beyond the counter was an immense maze of floor-to-ceiling metal shelving laden with all the sundry equipment and supplies needed by a large, busy hospital. In and out of the maze moved a team of people attired in scrubs, white coats, and hats that looked like shower caps. A radio played somewhere in the distance.

After Jack had stood at the counter for a few minutes, a robust and vigorous woman caught sight of him and came over. Her name tag said "Gladys Zarelli, Supervisor." She asked if he needed some help.

"I wanted to inquire about Katherine Mueller," Jack said.

"God rest her soul," Gladys said. She made the sign of the cross. "It was a terrible thing."

Jack introduced himself by displaying his badge, then questioned whether she and her co-workers were concerned that Katherine had died of an infectious disease.

"Of course we're concerned," she said. "Who wouldn't be? We all work closely with one another. But what can you do? At least the hospital is concerned as well. They have us all on antibiotics, and thank God, no one is sick."

"Has anything like this ever happened before?" Jack asked. "What I mean is, a patient died of plague just the day before Katherine. That suggests that Katherine could very well have caught it here at the hospital. I don't mean to scare you, but those are the facts."

"We're all aware of it," Gladys said. "But it's never happened before. I imagine it's happened in nursing, but not here in central supply."

"Do you people have any patient contact?" Jack asked.

"Not really," Gladys said. "Occasionally we might run up to the wards, but it's never to see a patient directly."

"What was Katherine doing the week before she died?" Jack asked.

"I'll have to look that up," Gladys said. She motioned for Jack to follow her. She led Jack into a tiny, windowless office where she cracked open a large, cloth-bound daily ledger.

"Assignments are never too strict," Gladys said. Her finger ran down a row of names. "We all kinda pitch in as needed, but I give some basic responsibility to some of the more senior people." Her finger stopped, then moved across the page. "Okay, Katherine was more or less in charge of supplies to the wards."

"What does that mean?" Jack asked.

"Whatever they needed," Gladys said. "Everything except drugs and that sort of stuff. That comes from pharmacy."

"You mean like things for the patients' rooms?" Jack asked.

"Sure, for the rooms, for the nurses' station, everything," Gladys said. "This is where it all comes from. Without us the hospital would grind to a halt in twenty-four hours."

"Give me an example of the things you deal with for the rooms," Jack said.

"I'm telling you, everything!" Gladys said with a touch of irritation in her voice. "Bedpans, thermometers, humidifiers, pillows, pitchers, soap. Everything."

"You wouldn't have any record of Katherine going up to the seventh floor during the last week or so, would you?"

"No," Gladys said. "We don't keep records like that. I could print out for you everything sent up there, though. That we have a record of."

"Okay," Jack said. "I'll take what I can get."

"It's going to be a lot of stuff," Gladys warned as she made an entry into her computer terminal. "Do you want OB-GYN or medical or both?" she asked.

"Medical," Jack said.

Gladys nodded, pecked at a few more keys on her terminal, and soon her printer was cranking away. In a few minutes she handed Jack a stack of papers. He glanced through them. As Gladys had suggested there were a lot of items. The length of the list gave Jack respect for the logistics of running the institution.

Leaving central supply, Jack descended a floor and wandered into the lab. He did not feel he was making any progress, but he refused to give up. His conviction remained that there was some major missing piece of information. He just didn't know where he would find it.

Jack asked the same receptionist to whom he'd shown his badge the day before for directions to microbiology, which she gave him without question.

Jack walked unchallenged through the extensive lab. It was an odd feeling to see so much impressive equipment running unattended. It reminded Jack of the director's lament the day before that he'd been forced to cut his personnel by twenty percent.

Jack found Nancy Wiggens working at a lab bench plating bacterial cultures.

"Howdy," Jack said. "Remember me?"

Nancy glanced up and then back at her work.

"Of course," she said.

"You guys made the diagnosis on the second plague case just fine," he said.

"It's easy when you suspect it," Nancy said. "But we didn't do so well on the third case."

"I was going to ask you about that," Jack said. "What did the gram stain look like?"

"I didn't do it," Nancy said. "Beth Holderness did. Do you want to talk with her?"

"I would," Jack said.

Nancy slid off her stool and disappeared. Jack took the opportunity to glance around at the microbiology section of the lab. He was impressed. Most labs, particularly microbiology labs, had an invariable clutter. This lab was different. It appeared highly efficient with everything crystal-clean and in its place.

"Hi, I'm Beth!"

Jack turned to find himself before a smiling, outgoing woman in her mid-twenties. She exuded a cheerleader-like zeal that was infectious. Her hair was tightly permed and radiated away from her face as if charged with static electricity.

Jack introduced himself and was immediately charmed by Beth's natural conversation. She was one of the friendliest women he'd ever met.

"Well, I'm sure you didn't come here to gab," Beth said. "I understand you are interested in the gram stain on Susanne Hard. Come on! It's waiting for you."

Beth literally grabbed Jack by the sleeve and pulled him around to her work area. Her microscope was set up with Hard's slide positioned on its platform and the illuminator switched on.

"Sit yourself right here," Beth said as she guided Jack's lower half onto her stool. "How is that? Low enough?"

"It's perfect," Jack said. He leaned forward and peered into the eyepieces. It took a moment for his eyes to adapt. When they did, he could see the field was filled with reddish-stained bacteria.

"Notice how pleomorphic the microbes are," a male voice commented.

Jack looked up. Richard, the head tech, had materialized and was standing to Jack's immediate left, almost touching him.

"I didn't mean to be such a bother," Jack said.

"No bother," Richard said. "In fact, I'm interested in your opinion. We still haven't made a diagnosis on this case. Nothing has grown out, and I presume you know that the test for plague was negative."

"So I heard," Jack said. He put his eyes back to the microscope and peered in again. "I don't think you want my opinion. I'm not so good at this stuff," he admitted.

"But you do see the pleomorphism?" Richard said.

"I suppose," Jack said. "They're pretty small bacilli. Some of them almost look spherical, or am I looking at them on end?"

"I believe you are seeing them as they are," Richard said. "That's more pleomorphism than you see with plague. That's why Beth and I doubted it was plague. Of course, we weren't sure until the fluorescein antibody was negative."

Jack looked up from the scope. "If it's not plague, what do you think it is?"

Richard gave a little embarrassed laugh. "I don't know."

Jack looked at Beth. "What about you? Care to take a chance?"

Beth shook her head. "Not if Richard won't," she said diplomatically.

"Can't someone even hazard a guess?" Jack asked.

Richard shook his head. "Not me. I'm always wrong when I guess."

"You weren't wrong about plague," Jack reminded him.

"That was just lucky," Richard said. He flushed.

"What's going on here," an irritated voice called out.

Jack's head swung around in the opposite direction. Beyond Beth was the director of the lab, Martin Cheveau. He was standing with his legs apart, his hands on his hips, and his mustache quivering. Behind him was Dr. Mary Zimmerman, and behind her was Charles Kelley.

Jack got to his feet. The lab techs slunk back. The atmosphere was suddenly tense. The lab director was clearly irate.

"Are you here in an official capacity?" Martin demanded. "If so, I'd like to know why you didn't have the common courtesy to come to my office instead of sneaking in here? We have a crisis unfolding in this hospital, and this lab is in the middle of it. I am not about to brook interference from anyone."

"Whoa!" Jack said. "Calm down." He hadn't expected this blowup, especially from Martin, who had been so hospitable the day before.

"Don't tell me to calm down," Martin snapped. "What the devil are you doing here, anyway?"

"I'm just doing my job, investigating the deaths of Katherine Mueller and Susanne Hard," Jack said. "I hardly think I'm interfering. In fact I thought I was being rather discreet."

"Is there something in particular you are looking for in my lab?" Martin demanded.

"I was just going over a gram stain with your capable staff," Jack said.

"Your official mandate is to determine the cause and the manner of death," Dr. Zimmerman said, pushing her way in front of Martin. "You've done that."

"Not quite," Jack corrected. "We haven't made a diagnosis on Susanne Hard." He returned the infection-control officer's beady stare. Since she wasn't wearing the mask she'd had on the day before, Jack was able to appreciate how stern her thin-lipped face was.

"You haven't made a specific diagnosis in the Hard case," Dr. Zimmerman corrected, "but you have made a diagnosis of a fatal infectious disease. Under the circumstances I think that is adequate."

"Adequate has never been my goal in medicine," Jack said.

"Nor mine," Dr. Zimmerman shot back. "Nor is it for the Centers for Disease Control or the City Board of Health, who are actively investigating this unfortunate incident. Frankly your presence here is disruptive."

"Are you sure they don't need a little help?" Jack asked. He couldn't hold back the sarcasm.

"I'd say your presence is more than disruptive," Kelley said. "In fact, you've been downright slanderous. You could very well be hearing from our lawyers."

"Whoa!" Jack said again, lifting his hands as if to fend off a bodily attack. "Disruptive I can at least comprehend. Slanderous is ridiculous."

"Not from my point of view," Kelley said. "The supervisor in central supply said you told her Katherine Mueller had contracted her illness on the job."

"And that has not been established," Dr. Zimmerman added.

"Uttering such an unsubstantiated statement is defamatory to this institution and injurious to its reputation," Kelley snapped.

"And could have a negative impact on its stock value," Jack said.

"And that too," Kelley agreed.

"The trouble is I didn't say Mueller had contracted her illness on the job," Jack said. "I said she could have done so. There's a big difference."

"Mrs. Zarelli told us you told her it was a fact," Kelley said.

"I told her 'those were the facts' referring to the possibility," Jack said. "But look, we're quibbling. The real fact is that you people are overly defensive. It makes me wonder about your nosocomial infection history. What's the story there?"

Kelley turned purple. Given the man's intimidating size advantage, Jack took a protective step backward.

"Our nosocomial infection experience is none of your business," Kelley sputtered.

"That's something I'm beginning to question," Jack said. "But I'll save looking into it for another time. It's been nice seeing you all again. Bye."

Jack broke off from the group and strode away. He heard sudden movement behind him and cringed, half expecting a beaker or some other handy piece of laboratory paraphernalia to sail past his ear. But he reached the door to the hallway without incident. Descending a floor, he unlocked his bike and headed south.

Jack weaved in and out of the traffic, marveling at his latest brush with AmeriCare. Most confusing was the sensitivity of the people involved. Even Martin, who'd been friendly the day before, now acted as if Jack were the enemy. What could they all be hiding? And why hide it from Jack?

Jack didn't know who at the hospital had alerted the administration of his presence, but he had a good idea who would be informing Bingham that he'd been there. Jack entertained no illusions about Kelley complaining about him again.

Jack wasn't disappointed. As soon as he came in the receiving bay, the security man stopped him.

"I was told to tell you to go directly to the chief's office," the man said. "Dr. Washington himself gave me the message."

As Jack locked his bike, he tried to think of what he was going to say to Bingham. Nothing came to mind.

While ascending in the elevator, Jack decided he'd switch to offense since he couldn't think of any defense. He was still formulating an idea when he presented himself in front of Mrs. Sanford's desk.

"You're to go right in," Mrs. Sanford said. As usual she didn't look up from her work.

Jack stepped around her desk and entered Bingham's office. Immediately he saw that Bingham wasn't alone. Calvin's huge hulk was hovering near the glass-fronted bookcase.

"Chief, we have a problem," Jack said earnestly. He moved over to Bingham's desk and gave it a tap with his fist for emphasis. "We don't have a diagnosis on the Hard case, and we got to give it to them ASAP. If we don't we're going to look bad, especially the way the press is all stirred up about the plague. I even went all the way over to the General to take a look at the gram stain. Unfortunately, it didn't help."

Bingham regarded Jack curiously with his rheumy eyes. He'd been about to lambaste Jack; now he demurred. Instead of speaking he removed his wire-rimmed spectacles and absently cleaned them while he considered Jack's words. He glanced over at Calvin. Calvin responded by stepping up to the desk. He wasn't fooled by Jack's ruse.

"What the hell are you talking about?" Calvin demanded.

"Susanne Hard," Jack said. "You remember. The case you and I have the ten-dollar double-or-nothing bet on."

"A bet!" Bingham questioned. "Is there gambling going on in this office?"

"Not really, Chief," Calvin said. "It was just a way of making a point. It's not routine."

"I should hope not," Bingham snapped. "I don't want any wagering around here, especially not in regard to diagnoses. That's not the kind of thing I'd like to see in the press. Our critics would have a field day."

"Getting back to Susanne Hard," Jack said. "I'm at a loss as to how to proceed. I'd hoped that by talking directly to the hospital lab people I might have made some headway, but it didn't work. What do you think I should do now?" Jack wanted the conversation to move away from the gambling issue. It might divert Bingham, but Jack knew he'd have hell to pay with Calvin later on.

"I'm a little confused," Bingham said. "Just yesterday I specifically told you to stay around here and get your backload of cases signed out. I especially told you to stay the hell away from the Manhattan General Hospital."

"That was if I were going there for personal reasons," Jack said. "I wasn't. This was all business."

"Then how the hell did you manage to get the administrator all bent out of shape again?" Bingham demanded. "He called the damn mayor's office for the second day in a row. The mayor wants to know if you have some sort of mental problem or whether I have a mental problem for hiring you."

"I hope you reassured him we're both normal," Jack said.

"Don't be impertinent on top of everything else," Bingham said.

"To tell you the honest truth," Jack said, "I haven't the slightest idea why the administrator got upset. Maybe the pressure of this plague episode has gotten to everybody over there, because they're all acting weird."

"So now everyone seems weird to you," Bingham said.

"Well, not everyone," Jack admitted. "But there's something strange going on, I'm sure of it."

Bingham looked up at Calvin, who shrugged and rolled his eyes. He didn't understand what Jack was talking about. Bingham's attention returned to Jack.

"Listen," Bingham said. "I don't want to fire you, so don't make me. You're a smart man. You have a future in this field. But I'm warning you, if you willfully disobey me and continue to embarrass us in the community, I'll have no other recourse. Tell me you understand."

"Perfectly," Jack said.

"Fine," Bingham said. "Then get back to your work, and we'll see you later in conference."

Jack took the cue and instantly disappeared.

For a moment Bingham and Calvin remained silent, each lost in his own thoughts.

"He's an odd duck," Bingham said finally. "I can't read him."

"Nor can I," Calvin said. "His saving grace is that he is smart and truly a hard worker. He's very committed. Whenever he's on autopsy, he's always the first one in the pit."

"I know," Bingham said. "That's why I didn't fire him on the spot. But where does this brashness come from? He has to know it rubs people the wrong way, yet he doesn't seem to care. He's reckless, almost self-destructive, as he admitted himself yesterday. Why?"

"I don't know," Calvin said. "Sometimes I get the feeling it's anger. But directed at what? I haven't the foggiest. I've tried to talk with him a few times on a personal level, but it's like squeezing water out of a rock."

CHAPTER 15

THURSDAY, 8:30 P.M., MARCH 21, 1996

Terese and Colleen climbed out of the cab on Second Avenue between Eighty-ninth and Eighty-eighth Streets a few doors away from Elaine's and walked to the restaurant. They couldn't get out right in front because of several limos inconveniently double-parked.

"How do I look?" Colleen asked as they paused under the canvas awning. She'd pulled off her coat for Terese's inspection.

"Too good," Terese said, and she meant it. Colleen had discarded her signature sweatshirt and jeans for a simple black dress that revealed her ample bust to perfection. Terese felt dowdy by comparison. She still had on her tailored suit that she'd worn to work that day, not having found time to go home to change.

"I don't know why I'm so nervous," Colleen admitted.

"Relax," Terese said. "With that dress Dr. McGovern doesn't stand a chance."

Colleen gave their names to the maître d' who immediately indicated recognition. He motioned for the women to follow him. He started to the rear.

It was an obstacle course of sorts to weave among the densely packed tables and scurrying waiters. Terese had the sensation of being in a fishbowl. Everyone, male and female alike, gave them the once-over as they passed.

The men were at a tiny table squeezed into the far corner. They got to their feet as the women approached. Chet held out Colleen's chair. Jack did the same for Terese. The women draped their coats over the backs of the chairs before sitting down.

"You men must know the owner to have gotten such a great table," Terese said.

Chet, who misinterpreted Terese's remark as a compliment, bragged he'd been introduced to Elaine a year previously. He explained she was the woman seated at the cash register at the end of the bar.

"They tried to seat us up in the front," Jack said. "But we declined. We thought you women wouldn't like the draft from the door."

"How thoughtful," Terese said. "Besides, this is so much more intimate."

"You think so?" Chet questioned. His face visibly brightened. They were, in reality, packed in like proverbial sardines.

"How could you question her?" Jack asked Chet. "She's so sincere."

"All right, enough!" Chet said good-naturedly. "I might be dense, but eventually I catch on."

They ordered wine and appetizers from the waiter who'd immediately appeared after the women had arrived. Colleen and Chet fell into easy conversation. Terese and Jack continued to be teasingly sarcastic with each other, but eventually the wine blunted their witticisms. By the time the main course was served, they were conversing congenially.

"What's the inside scoop on the plague situation?" Terese asked.

"There were two more deaths at the General," Jack said. "Plus a couple of febrile nurses are being treated."

"That was in the morning news," Terese said. "Anything new?"

"Only one of the deaths was actually plague," Jack said. "The other resembled plague clinically, but I personally don't think it was."

Terese stopped a forkful of pasta midway to her mouth. "No?" she questioned. "If it wasn't plague, what was it?"

Jack shrugged. "I wish I knew," he said. "I'm hoping the lab can tell me."

"The Manhattan General must be in an uproar," Terese said. "I'm glad I'm not a patient there now. Being in the hospital is scary enough under the best of circumstances. With the worry of diseases like plague around, it must be terrible."

"The administration is definitely agitated," Jack said. "And for good reason. If it turns out the plague originated there, it will be the first modern episode of nosocomial plague. That's hardly an accolade as far as the hospital is concerned."

"This concept of nosocomial infections is new to me," Terese said. "I'd never thought much about it before you and Chet talked about this current plague problem last night. Do all hospitals have such problems?"

"Absolutely," Jack said. "It's not common knowledge, but usually five to ten percent of hospitalized patients fall victim to infections contracted while they are in the hospital."

"My God!" Terese said. "I had no idea it was such a widespread phenomenon."

"It's all over," Chet agreed. "Every hospital has it, from the academic ivory tower to the smallest community hospital. What makes it so bad is that the hospital is the worst place to get an infection because many of the bugs hanging out there are resistant to antibiotics."

"Oh, great!" Terese said cynically. After she thought for a moment she asked, "Do hospitals differ significantly in their infection rates?"

"For sure," Chet said.

"Are these rates known?" Terese said.

"Yes and no," Chet said. "Hospitals are required by the Joint Commission of Accreditation to keep records of their infection rates, but the rates aren't released to the public."

"That's a travesty!" Terese said with a surreptitious wink at Colleen.

"If the rates go over a certain amount the hospital loses its accreditation," Chet said. "So all is not lost."

"But it's hardly fair to the public," Terese said. "By not having access to those rates people can't make their own decisions about which hospitals to patronize."

Chet opened his hands palms up like a supplicant priest. "That's politics," he said.

"I think it's awful," Terese said.

"Life's not fair," Jack said.

After dessert and coffee Chet and Colleen began campaigning to go someplace where there was dancing, like the China Club. Both Terese and Jack were disinclined. Chet and Colleen tried their best to change their minds, but they soon gave up.

"You guys go," Terese said.

"Are you sure?" Colleen asked.

"We wouldn't want to hold you back," Jack said.

Colleen looked at Chet.

"Let's go for it," Chet said.

Outside the restaurant Chet and Colleen happily piled into a cab. Jack and Terese waved as they drove off.

"I hope they enjoy themselves," Terese said. "I couldn't have thought of anything worse. Sitting in a smoke-filled nightclub assaulted by music loud enough to damage my ears is not my idea of pleasure."

"At least we've finally found something we can agree on," Jack said.

Terese laughed. She was beginning to appreciate Jack's sense of humor. It wasn't too dissimilar from her own.

For a moment of self-conscious indecision they stood at the curbside, each looking in a different direction. Second Avenue was alive with revelers despite a nippy temperature in the high thirties. The air was clear and the sky cloudless.

"I think the weatherman forgot it was the first day of spring," Terese said. She jammed her hands into her coat pockets and hunched up her shoulders.

"We could walk around the corner to that bar where we were last night," Jack suggested.

"We could," Terese said. "But I have a better idea. My agency is over on Madison. It's not too far away. How about a quick visit?"

"You're inviting me to your office despite knowing how I feel about advertising?" Jack asked.

"I thought it was only medical advertising you were against," Terese said.

"The truth is I'm not particularly fond of advertising in general," Jack said. "Last night Chet jumped in before I had a chance to say it."

"But you're not opposed to it per se?" Terese questioned.

"Just the medical kind," Jack said. "For the reasons I gave."

"Then how about a quick visit? We do a lot more than just medical advertising. You might find it enlightening."

Jack tried to read the woman behind the soft, pale blue eyes and sensuous mouth. He was confused because the vulnerability they suggested wasn't in sync with the no-nonsense, goal-oriented, driven woman he suspected she was.

Terese met his stare head-on and smiled back coquettishly. "Be adventuresome!" she challenged.

"Why do I have the feeling you have an ulterior motive?" Jack asked.

"Probably because I do," Terese freely admitted. "I'd like your advice on a new ad campaign. I wasn't going to admit you'd been a stimulus for a new idea, but tonight during dinner I changed my mind about telling you."

"I don't know whether to feel used or complimented," Jack said. "How did I happen to give you an idea for an ad?"

"All this talk about plague at the Manhattan General Hospital," Terese said. "It made me think seriously about the issue of nosocomial infection."

Jack considered this statement for a moment. Then he asked, "And why did you change your mind about telling me and asking my advice?"

"Because it suddenly dawned on me that you might actually approve of the campaign," Terese said. "You told me the reason you were against advertising in medicine was because it didn't address issues of quality. Well, ads concerning nosocomial infections certainly would."

"I suppose," Jack said.

"Oh, come on," Terese said. "Of course it would. If a hospital was proud of its record, why not let the public know?"

"All right," Jack said. "I give up. Let's see this office of yours."

Having made the decision to go, there was the problem of Jack's bike. At that moment it was locked to a nearby No Parking sign. After a short discussion they decided to leave the bike and go together in a cab. Jack would rescue the bike later on his way home.

With little traffic and a wildly fast and reckless Russian-émigré taxi driver, they arrived at Willow and Heath's building in minutes. Jack staggered out of the rear of the taxi.

"God!" he said. "People accuse me of taking a risk riding my bike in this city. It's nothing like riding with that maniac."

As if to underline Jack's statement, the cab shot away from the curb and disappeared up Madison Avenue with its tires screeching.

At ten-thirty the office building was locked up tight. Terese used her night key, and they entered. Their heels echoed noisily in the lonely marble hallway. Even the whine of the elevator seemed loud in the stillness.

"Are you here often after hours?" Jack asked.

Terese laughed cynically. "All the time," she said. "I practically live here."

They rode up in silence. When the doors opened Jack was shocked to find the floor brightly illuminated and bustling with activity as if it were midday. Toiling figures bent over many of the innumerable drawing boards.

"What do you have, two shifts?" Jack asked.

Terese laughed again. "Of course not," she said. "These people have been here since early this morning. Advertising is a competitive world. If you want to make it, you have to put in your time. We have several reviews coming up."

Terese excused herself and walked over to a woman at a nearby drawing table. While they conversed, Jack's eyes roamed the expansive space. He was surprised there were so few partitions. There was only a handful of separate rooms, which shared a common wall with the bank of elevators.

"Alice is going to bring in some material," Terese said when she rejoined Jack. "Why don't we go into Colleen's office."

Terese led him into one of the rooms and turned on the lights. It was tiny, windowless, and claustrophobic when compared to the vast undivided space. It was also cluttered with papers, books, magazines, and videotapes. There were several easels set up with thick pads of drawing paper.

"I'm sure Colleen won't mind if I clear away a little area on her desk," Terese said as she moved aside stacks of orange-colored tracing paper. Gathering up an armload of books, she set them on the floor. No sooner had she finished than Alice Gerber, another of Terese's associates, appeared.

After making introductions, Terese had Alice run through a number of the potential commercial ideas they'd comped up that day.

Jack found himself interested more in the process than the content. He'd never stopped to think about how TV commercials were made, and he came to appreciate the creativity involved and the amount of work.

It took Alice a quarter hour to present what she'd brought in. When she was finished, she gathered up the tissues and looked at Terese for further instructions. Terese thanked her and sent her back to her drawing board.

"So there you have it," Terese said to Jack. "Those're some of the ideas stemming from this nosocomial infection issue. What do you think?"

"I'm impressed with how hard you work on this sort of thing," Jack said.

"I'm more interested in your reaction to the content," Terese said. "What do you think of the idea of Hippocrates coming into the hospital to award it the 'do no harm' medal?"

Jack shrugged. "I don't flatter myself to think I have the ability to intelligently critique a commercial."

"Oh, give me a break," Terese said, rolling her eyes to the ceiling. "I just want your opinion as a human being. This isn't an intellectual quiz. What would you think if you saw this commercial on the TV, say when you were watching the Super Bowl?"

"I'd think it was cute," Jack admitted.

"Would it make you think the National Health hospital might be a good place to go, since its nosocomial infection rates were low?"

"I suppose," Jack said.

"All right," Terese said, trying to keep herself calm. "Maybe you have some other ideas. What else could we do?"

Jack pondered for a few minutes. "You could do something about Oliver Wendell Holmes and Joseph Lister."

"Wasn't Holmes a poet?" Terese asked.

"He was also a doctor," Jack said. "He and Lister probably did more for getting doctors to wash their hands when going from patient to patient than anybody. Well, Semmelweis helped too. Anyway, handwashing was probably the most important lesson that needed to be learned to prevent hospital-based infections."

"Hmm," Terese said. "That sounds interesting. Personally, I love period pieces. Let me tell Alice to get someone to research it."

Jack followed Terese out of Colleen's office and watched her talk with Alice. It only took her a few minutes.

"Okay," Terese said, rejoining Jack. "She'll start the ball rolling. Let's get out of here."

In the elevator Terese had another suggestion. "Why don't we take a run over to your office," she said. "It's only fair now that you have seen mine."

"You don't want to see it," Jack said. "Trust me."

"Try me."

"It's the truth," Jack said. "It's not a pretty place."

"I think it would be interesting," Terese persisted. "I've only seen a morgue in the movies. Who knows, maybe it will give me some ideas. Besides, seeing where you work might help me understand you a little more."

"I'm not sure I want to be understood," Jack said.

The elevator stopped and the doors opened. They walked outside. They paused at the curb.

"What do you say? I can't imagine it would take too long, and it's not terribly late."

"You are a persistent sort," Jack commented. "Tell me: Do you always get your way?"

"Usually," Terese admitted. Then she laughed. "But I prefer to think of myself as tenacious."

"All right," Jack said finally. "But don't say I didn't warn you."

They caught a taxi. After Jack gave the destination the driver looped around and headed south on Park Avenue.

"You give me the impression of being a loner," Terese said.

"You're very perspicacious," Jack said.

"You don't have to be so caustic," Terese said.

"For once I wasn't," Jack said.

The lambent reflections of the streetlights played over their faces as they regarded each other in the half-light of the taxi.

"It's difficult for a woman to know how to feel around you," Terese said.

"I could say the same," Jack said.

"Have you ever been married?" Terese said. "That is, if you don't mind me asking."

"Yes, I was married," Jack said.

"But it didn't work out?" Terese said leadingly.

"There was a problem," Jack admitted. "But I don't really care to talk about it. How about you? Were you ever married?"

"Yes, I was," Terese said. She sighed and looked out her window. "But I don't like talking about it either."

"Now we have two things we agree on," Jack said. "We both feel the same about nightclubs and talking about our former marriages."

Jack had given directions to be dropped off at the Thirtieth Street entrance of the medical examiner's office. He was glad to see that both mortuary vans were gone. He thought their absence was a sign that there wouldn't be any fresh corpses lying around on gurneys. Although Terese had insisted on the visit, he was afraid of offending her sensibilities unnecessarily.

Terese said nothing as Jack led her past the banks of refrigerated compartments. It wasn't until she saw all the simple pine coffins that she spoke. She asked why they were there.

"They're for the unclaimed and unidentified dead," Jack said. "They are buried at city expense."

"Does that happen often?" Terese asked.

"All the time," Jack said.

Jack took her back to the area of the autopsy room. He opened the door to the washroom. Terese leaned in but didn't enter. The autopsy room was visible through a windowed door. The stainless-steel dissecting tables glistened ominously in the half-light.

"I expected this place to be more modern," she said. She was hugging herself to keep from touching anything.

"At one time it was," Jack said. "It was supposed to have been renovated, but it didn't happen. Unfortunately the city is always in some kind of budgetary crisis, and few politicians balk at pulling money away from here. Adequate funding for normal operating expenses is hard to come by, much less money to update the facility. On the other hand we do have a new, state-of-the-art DNA lab."

"Where's your office?" Terese asked.

"Up on the fifth floor," Jack said.

"Can I see it?" she asked.

"Why not?" Jack said. "We've come this far."

They walked back past the mortuary office and waited for the elevator.

"This place is a little hard to take, isn't it?" Jack said.

"It has its gruesome side," Terese admitted.

"We who work here often forget the effect it has on laypeople," Jack said, though he was impressed with the degree of equanimity Terese had demonstrated.

The elevator arrived and they got on. Jack pressed the fifth floor, and they started up.

"How did you ever decide on this kind of career?" Terese asked. "Did you know back in medical school?"

"Heavens, no," Jack said. "I wanted something clean, technically demanding, emotionally fulfilling, and lucrative. I became an ophthalmologist."

"What happened?" Terese asked.

"My practice got taken over by AmeriCare," Jack said. "Since I didn't want to work for them or any similar corporation, I retrained. It's the buzzword these days for superfluous medical specialists."

"Was it difficult?" Terese asked.

Jack didn't answer immediately. The elevator arrived on the fifth floor and the doors opened.

"It was very difficult," Jack said as he started down the hall. "Mostly because it was so lonely."

Terese hazarded a glance in Jack's direction. She'd not expected him to be the type to complain of loneliness. She'd assumed he was a loner by choice. While she was looking, Jack furtively wiped the corner of an eye with his knuckle. Could there have been a tear? Terese was mystified.

"Here we are," Jack announced. He opened his office door with his key and flipped on the light.

The interior was worse than Terese had expected. It was tiny and narrow. The furniture was gray metal and old, and the walls were in need of paint. There was a single, filthy window positioned high on the wall.

"Two desks?" Terese questioned.

"Chet and I share this space," Jack explained.

"Which desk is yours?"

"The messy one," Jack said. "This plague episode has put me farther behind than ususal. I'm generally behind because I'm rather compulsive about my reports."

"Dr. Stapleton!" a voice called out.

It was Janice Jaeger, the PA investigator.

"Security told me you were here when I just came through the receiving bay," she said after being introduced to Terese. "I've been trying to reach you at home."

"What's the problem?" Jack asked.

"The reference lab called this evening," Janice said. "They ran the fluorescein antibody on Susanne Hard's lung tissue as you requested. It was positive for tularemia."

"Are you kidding?" Jack took the paper from Janice and stared at it with disbelief.

"What's tularemia?" Terese asked.

"It's another infectious disease," Jack said. "It's similar in some ways to plague."

"Where was this patient?" Terese asked, although she suspected the answer.

"Also at the General," Jack said. He shook his head. "I truly can't believe it. This is extraordinary!"

"I've got to get back to work," Janice said. "If you need me to do anything just let me know."

"I'm sorry," Jack said. "I didn't mean to have you stand here. Thanks for getting this to me."

"No problem," Janice said. She waved and headed back to the elevators.

"Is tularemia as bad as plague?" Terese asked.

"It's hard to make comparisons," Jack said. "But it's bad, particularly the pneumonic form, which is highly contagious. If Susanne Hard were still here she could tell us exactly how bad it is."

"Why are you so surprised?" Terese asked. "Is it as rare as plague?"

"Probably not," Jack said. "It's seen in a wider area in the U.S. than plague, particularly in southern states like Arkansas. But like plague it's not seen much in the winter, at least not up here in the north. Here it's a late-spring and summer problem, if it exists at all. It needs a vector, just like plague. Instead of the rat flea it's usually spread by ticks and deerflies."

"Any tick or deerfly?" Terese asked. Her parents had a cabin up in the Catskills where she liked to go in the summer. It was isolated and surrounded by forest and fields. There were plenty of ticks and deerflies.

"The reservoir for the bacteria is small mammals like rodents and especially rabbits," Jack said. He started to elaborate but quickly stopped. He'd suddenly recalled that afternoon's conversation with Susanne's husband, Maurice. Jack remembered being told that Susanne liked to go to Connecticut, walk in the woods, and feed wild rabbits!

"Maybe it was the rabbits," Jack mumbled.

"What are you talking about?" Terese asked.

Jack apologized for thinking out loud. Shaking himself out of a momentary daze, he motioned for Terese to follow him into his office and to take Chet's chair. He described his phone conversation with Susanne's husband and explained about the importance of wild rabbits in relation to tularemia.

"Sounds incriminating to me," Terese said.

"The only problem is that her exposure to the Connecticut rabbits was almost two weeks ago," Jack mused. He drummed his fingers on his telephone receiver. "That's a long incubation period, especially for the pneumonic form. Of course, if she didn't catch it in Connecticut, then she had to catch it here in the city, possibly at the General. Of course, nosocomial tularemia doesn't make any more sense than nosocomial plague."

"One way or the other the public has to know about this," Terese said. She nodded toward his hand on the phone. "I hope you are calling the media as well as the hospital."

"Neither," Jack said. He glanced at his watch. It was still before midnight. He picked up the phone and dialed. "I'm calling my immediate boss. The politics of all this are his bailiwick."

Calvin picked up on the first ring but mumbled as if he'd been asleep. Jack cheerfully identified himself.

"This better be important," Calvin growled.

"It is to me," Jack said. "I wanted you to be first to know you owe me another ten dollars."

"Get outta here," Calvin boomed. The grogginess had disappeared from his voice. "I hope to God this isn't some kind of sick joke."

"No joke," Jack assured him. "The lab just reported it in tonight. The Manhattan General had a case of tularemia in addition to its two cases of plague. I'm as surprised as anyone."

"The lab called you directly?" Calvin said.

"Nope," Jack said. "One of the PAs just gave it to me."

"Are you in the office?" Calvin asked.

"Sure am," Jack said. "Working my fingers to the bone."

"Tularemia?" Calvin questioned. "I'd better read up on it. I don't think I've ever seen a case."

"I read up on it just this afternoon," Jack admitted.

"Make sure there are no leaks from our office," Calvin said. "I won't call Bingham tonight, because there's nothing to be done at the moment. I'll let him know first thing in the morning, and he can call the commissioner, and she can call the Board of Health."

"Okay," Jack said.

"So you are going to keep it a secret," Terese said angrily as Jack hung up the receiver.

"It's not my doing," Jack said.

"Yeah, I know," Terese said sarcastically. "It's not your job."

"I already got myself in trouble over the plague episode for calling the commissioner on my own," Jack said. "I don't see any benefit by doing it again. Word will be out in the morning through the proper channels."

"What about people over at the General who are suspected of having plague?" Terese questioned. "They might have this new disease. I think you should let everyone know tonight."

"That's a good point," Jack said. "But it doesn't really matter. The treatment for tularemia is the same as the treatment for plague. We'll wait until morning. Besides, it's only a few hours away."

"What if I alerted the press?" Terese asked.

"I'll have to ask you not to do that," Jack said. "You heard what my boss said. If it were investigated, the source would come back to me."

"You don't like advertising in medicine and I don't like politics in medicine," Terese said.

"Amen," Jack said.

CHAPTER 16

FRIDAY, 6:30 A.M., MARCH 22, 1996

Despite having gone to bed much later than usual for the second night in a row, Jack was wide awake at five-thirty Friday morning. He began mulling over the irony of a case of tularemia appearing in the middle of a plague outbreak. It was a curious coincidence, especially since he'd made the diagnosis. It was a feat certainly worth the ten dollars and twenty-five cents that he stood to win from Calvin and Laurie.

With his mind churning, Jack recognized the futility of trying to go back to sleep. Consequently he got up, ate breakfast, and was on his bike before six. With less traffic than usual, he got to work in record time.

The first thing Jack did was to visit the ID room to look for Laurie and Vinnie. Both had yet to arrive. Passing back through communications, he knocked on Janice's door. She appeared even more beleaguered than usual.

"What a night," she said.

"Busy?" Jack asked.

"That's an understatement," she said. "Especially with these added infectious cases. What's going on over there at the General?"

"How many today?" Jack asked.

"Three," Janice said. "And not one of them tested positive for plague even though that's their presumed diagnosis. Also, all three were fulminant cases. The people all died within twelve or so hours after their first symptoms. It's very scary."

"All of these recent infectious cases have been fulminant," Jack commented.

"Do you think these three new ones are tularemia?" Janice asked.

"There's a good chance," Jack said. "Especially if they tested negative for plague as you say. You didn't mention Susanne's diagnosis to anyone, did you?"

"I had to bite my tongue, but I didn't," Janice said. "I'd learned in the past by sore experience that my role is to gather information, not give it out."

"I had to learn the same lesson," Jack said. "Are you finished with these three folders?"

"They're all yours," Janice said.

Jack carried the folders back to the ID room. Since Vinnie had not arrived Jack made the coffee in the communal pot. Mug in hand, he sat down and began going through the material.

Almost immediately he stumbled onto something curious. The first case was a forty-two-year-old woman by the name of Maria Lopez. What was surprising was that she worked in central supply of the Manhattan General Hospital! Not only that, but she had worked on the same shift as Katherine Mueller!

Jack closed his eyes and tried to think of how two people from central supply could possibly have come down with two different fatal infectious diseases. As far as he was concerned, it could not be a coincidence. He was convinced their illnesses had to be work-related. The question was how?

In his mind's eye, Jack revisited central supply. He could picture the shelving and the aisles, even the outfits the employees wore. But nothing came to mind as a way for the employees to come in contact with contagious bacteria. Central supply had nothing to do with the disposal of hospital waste or even soiled linen, and as the supervisor had mentioned, workers there had little or no contact with patients.

Jack read the rest of Janice's investigative report. As she'd done with the cases since Nodelman, she included information about pets, travel, and visitors. For Maria Lopez, none of the three seemed a factor.

Jack opened the second folder. The patient's name was Joy Hester. In this case Jack felt there was little mystery. She'd been an OB-GYN nurse and had had significant exposure to Susanne Hard just prior to and after the onset of Susanne's symptoms. The only thing that bothered Jack was recalling that he'd read that person-to-person transmission of tularemia rarely occurred.

The third case was Donald Lagenthorpe, a thirty-eight-year-old petroleum engineer who'd been admitted to the hospital the previous morning. He'd come in through the ER with a refractory bout of asthma. He'd been treated with IV steroids and bronchodilators as well as humidified air and bed rest. According to Janice's notes, he'd shown steady improvement and had even been campaigning to be released, when he'd had the sudden onset of a severe frontal headache.

The headache had started in the late afternoon and was followed by shaking chills and fever. There was also an increase in cough and exacerbation of his asthmatic symptoms despite the continued treatment. At that point he was diagnosed to have pneumonia, which was confirmed by X ray. Curiously enough, however, a gram stain of his sputum was negative for bacteria.

Myalgia also had become prominent. Sudden abdominal pain and deep tenderness had suggested a possible appendicitis. At seven-thirty in the evening Lagenthorpe had undergone an appendectomy, but the appendix proved to be normal. After the surgery his situation became progressively grave with apparent multisystem failure. His blood pressure dropped and became unresponsive to treatment. Urine output became negligible.

Reading on in Janice's report, Jack learned that the patient had visited isolated oil rigs in Texas the previous week and had literally been tramping around in desert conditions. Jack also learned that Mr. Lagenthorpe's girlfriend had recently obtained a pet Burmese cat. But he'd not been exposed to any visitors from exotic places.

"Wow! You're here early!" Laurie Montgomery exclaimed.

Jack was shocked out of his concentration in time to see Laurie sweep into the ID room and drape her coat over the desk she used for her early-morning duties. It was the last day of her current rotation as supervisor in charge of determining which of the previous night's cases should be autopsied and who would do them. It was a thankless task that none of the board-certified doctors enjoyed.

"I've got some bad news for you," Jack said.

Laurie paused on her way into communications; a shadow passed over her usually bright, honey-complected face.

Jack laughed. "Hey, relax," he said. "It's not that bad. It's just that you owe me a quarter."

"Are you serious?" she asked. "The Hard case was tularemia?"

"The lab reported a positive fluorescein antibody last night," Jack said. "I think it's a firm diagnosis."

"It's a good thing I didn't bet any more than a quarter," Laurie said. "You are amassing some impressive statistics in the infectious arena. What's your secret?"

"Beginner's luck," Jack said. "By the way, I have three of last night's cases here. They're all infectious and all from the General. I'd like to do at least two of them."

"I can't think of any reason why not," Laurie said. "But let me run over to communications and get the rest."

The moment Laurie left, Vinnie made his appearance. His face was a pasty color and his heavily lidded eyes were red. From Jack's perspective he appeared as if he belonged in one of the coolers downstairs.

"You look like death warmed over," Jack said.

"Hangover," Vinnie remarked. "I went to a buddy's bachelor party. We all got whacked."

Vinnie tossed his newspaper on a desk and went over to the cupboard where the coffee was stored.

"In case you haven't noticed," Jack said, "the coffee is already made."

Vinnie had to stare at the coffee machine with its full pot for several beats until his tired mind comprehended that his current efforts were superfluous.

"How about starting on this instead?" Jack said. He pushed the Maria Lopez folder over to Vinnie. "Might as well get set up. Remember, the early bird . . ."

"Hold the clichés," Vinnie said. He took the folder and let it fall open in his hands. "Frankly, I'm not in the mood for any of your sappy sayings. What bugs me is that you can't come in here when everybody else does."

"Laurie's here," Jack reminded him.

"Yeah, but this is her week for scheduling. You don't have any excuse." He briefly read portions of the folder. "Wonderful! Another infectious case! My favorite! I should have stayed in bed."

"I'll be down in a few minutes," Jack said.

Vinnie irritably snapped up his newspaper and headed downstairs.

Laurie reappeared with an armful of folders and dumped them on her desk. "My, my, but we do have a lot of work to do today," she said.

"I've already sent Vinnie down to get prepared for one of these infectious cases," Jack said. "I hope I'm not overstepping my authority. I know you haven't looked at them yet, but all of them are suspected plague but tested negative. At a minimum I think we have to make a diagnosis."

"No question," Laurie said. "But I should still go downstairs and do my external. Come on, I'll do it right away, and you can get started." She grabbed the master list of all the previous night's deaths.

"What's the story on this first case you want to do?" Laurie asked as they walked.

Jack gave her a quick synopsis of what he knew about Maria Lopez. He emphasized the coincidence of her being employed in central supply at the General. He reminded her that the plague victim from the day before had also worked in that department. They boarded the elevator.

"That's kinda strange, isn't it?" Laurie asked.

"It is to me," Jack agreed.

"Do you think it's significant?" Laurie asked. The elevator bumped to a stop, and they got off.

"My intuition tells me it is," Jack said. "That's why I'm eager to do the post. For the life of me, I can't figure out what the association could be."

As they passed the mortuary office Laurie beckoned to Sal. He caught up to them, and she handed him her master list. "Let's see the Lopez body first," she said.

Sal took the list, referred to his own, then stopped at compartment 67, opened the door, and slid out the tray.

Maria Lopez, like her late co-worker, Katherine Mueller, was an overweight female. Her hair was stringy and dyed a peculiar reddish orange. Several IVs were still in place. One was taped to the right side of her neck, the other to her left arm.

"A fairly young woman," Laurie commented.

Jack nodded. "She was only forty-two."

Laurie held Maria Lopez's full-body X ray up to the ceiling light. Its only abnormality was patchy infiltration in her lungs.

"Go to it," Laurie said.

Jack turned on his heels and headed toward the room where his moon-suit ventilator was charging.

"Of the other two cases you had upstairs, which one would you want to do if you only do one?" Laurie called after him.

"Lagenthorpe," Jack said.

Laurie gave him a thumbs-up.

Despite his hangover, Vinnie had been his usual efficient self in setting up the autopsy on Maria Lopez. By the time Jack read over the material in Maria's folder for the second time and had climbed into his moon suit, all was ready.

With no distractions from anyone in the pit besides himself and Vinnie, Jack was able to concentrate. He spent an inordinate amount of time on the external exam. He was determined to find an insect bite if there had been one. He was not successful. As with Mueller, there were a few questionable blemishes, which he photographed, but none he felt were bites.

Jack's concentration was inadvertently aided by Vinnie's hangover. Preferring to nurse his headache, Vinnie remained silent, sparing Jack his usual quips and running commentary on sports trivia. Jack reveled in the thought-provoking silence.

Jack handled the internal exam the same way he'd handled those of the previous infectious cases. He was extraordinarily careful to avoid unnecessary movement of the organs to keep bacterial aerosolization to a minimum.

As the autopsy progressed, Jack's overall impression was that Lopez's case mirrored that of Susanne Hard, not Katherine Mueller. Hence, his preliminary diagnosis remained tularemia, not plague. This only highlighted his confusion of how two women from central supply had managed to catch these illnesses while other, more exposed hospital workers had avoided them.

When he finished with the internal exam and had taken the samples he wanted, he put aside a special sample of lung to take up to Agnes Finn. Once he had similar samples from Joy Hester and Donald Lagenthorpe, he planned to have them all sent immediately to the reference lab to be tested for tularemia.

By the time Jack and Vinnie had commenced stitching up Maria Lopez, they began to hear voices in the washroom and out in the hall.

"Here come the normal, civilized people," Vinnie commented.

Jack didn't respond.

Presently the door to the washroom opened. Two figures entered in their moon suits and ambled over to Jack's table. It was Laurie and Chet.

"Are you guys finished already?" Chet said.

"It's not my doing," Vinnie said. "The mad biker has to start before the sun is up."

"What do you think?" Laurie asked. "Plague or tularemia?"

"My guess is tularemia," Jack said.

"That will be four cases if these other two are tularemia as well," Laurie said.

"I know," Jack said. "It's weird. Person-to-person spread is supposed to be rare. It doesn't make a lot of sense, but that seems par for the course with these recent cases."

"How is tularemia spread?" Chet asked. "I've never seen a case."

"It's spread by ticks or direct contact with an infected animal, like a rabbit," Jack said.

"I've got you scheduled for Lagenthorpe next," Laurie told Jack. "I'm going to do Hester myself."

"I'm happy to do Hester as well," Jack said.

"No need," Laurie said. "There aren't that many autopsies today. A lot of last night's deaths didn't need to be posted. I can't let you have all the fun."

Bodies began arriving. They were being pushed into the autopsy room by other mortuary techs and lifted onto their designated tables. Laurie and Chet moved off to do their own cases.

Jack and Vinnie returned to their suturing. When they were finished, Jack helped Vinnie move the body onto a gurney. Then Jack asked how quickly Vinnie could have Lagenthorpe ready to go.

"What a slave driver," Vinnie complained. "Aren't we going to have coffee like everybody else?"

"I'd rather get it over with," Jack said. "Then you can have coffee for the rest of the day."

"Bull," Vinnie said. "I'll be reassigned back in here helping someone else."

Still complaining, Vinnie pushed Maria Lopez out of the autopsy room. Jack wandered over to Laurie's table. Laurie was engrossed in the external exam but straightened up when she caught sight of Jack.

"This poor woman was thirty-six," Laurie said wistfully. "What a waste."

"What have you found? Any insect bites or cat scratches?"

"Nothing except a shaving nick on her lower leg," Laurie said. "But it's not inflamed, so I'm convinced it's incidental. There is something interesting. She has definite eye infections."

Laurie carefully lifted the woman's eyelids. Both eyes were deeply inflamed, although the corneas were clear.

"I can also feel enlarged preauricular lymph nodes," Laurie said. She pointed to visible lumps in front of the patient's ears.

"Interesting," Jack commented. "That's consistent with tularemia, but I didn't see it on the other cases. Give a yell if you come across anything else unusual."

Jack stepped over to Chet's table. He was happily engrossed in a multiple gunshot wound case. At the moment he was busy photographing the entrance and exit wounds. When he saw Jack he handed the camera to Sal, who was helping him, and pulled Jack aside.

"How was your time last night?" Chet asked.

"This is hardly the best time to discuss it," Jack said. Conversation in the moon suits was difficult at best.

"Oh, come on," Chet said. "I had a blast with Colleen. After the China Club we went back to her pad on East Sixty-sixth."

"I'm happy for you," Jack said.

"What did you guys end up doing?" Chet asked.

"You wouldn't believe me if I told you," Jack said.

"Try me," Chet challenged. He leaned closer to Jack.

"We went over to her office, and then we came over here to ours," Jack said.

"You're right," Chet said. "I don't believe you."

"The truth is often difficult to accept," Jack said.

Jack used Vinnie's arrival with Lagenthorpe's corpse as an excuse to return to his table. Jack pitched in to help set up the case because it was preferable to further grilling by Chet. Besides, it made it possible to start the case that much sooner.

On the external exam the most obvious abnormality was the freshly sutured, two-inch-long appendectomy incision. But Jack quickly discovered more pathology. When he examined the corpse's hands he found subtle evidence of early gangrene on the tips of the fingers. He found some even fainter evidence of the same process on the man's earlobes.

"Reminds me of Nodelman," Vinnie said. "It's just less, and he doesn't have any on his pecker. Do you think it's plague again?"

"I don't know," Jack said. "Nodelman didn't have an appendectomy."

Jack spent twenty minutes diligently searching the rest of the body for any signs of insect or animal bites. Since Lagenthorpe was a moderately dark-skinned African-American, this was more difficult than it had been with the considerably lighter-skinned Lopez.

Although Jack's diligence didn't reward him with any bite marks, it did make it possible for him to appreciate another subtle abnormality. On Lagenthorpe's palms and soles there was a faint rash. Jack pointed it out to Vinnie, but Vinnie said he couldn't see it.

"Tell me what I'm looking for," Vinnie said.

"Flat, pinkish blotches," Jack said. "Here's more on the underside of the wrist." Jack held up Lagenthorpe's right arm.

"I'm sorry," Vinnie said. "I don't see it."

"No matter," Jack said. He took several photographs even though he doubted the rash would show up. The flash often washed out such subtle findings.

As Jack continued the external exam he found himself progressively mystified. The patient had come in with a presumed diagnosis of pneumonic plague, and externally he resembled a plague victim, as Vinnie had pointed out. Yet there were discrepancies. The record indicated he'd had a negative test for plague, which made Jack suspect tularemia.

But tularemia seemed implausible because the patient's sputum test had shown no free bacteria. To complicate things further, the patient had had severe enough abdominal symptoms to suggest appendicitis, which he proved not to have. And on top of that he had a rash on his palms and soles.

At that point Jack had no idea what he was dealing with. As far as he was concerned, he doubted the case was either plague or tularemia!

Starting the internal exam, he immediately came across strong presumptive evidence that substantiated his belief. The lymphatics were minimally involved.

Slicing open the lung, Jack also detected a difference even on gross from what he'd expect to see in either plague or tularemia. To Jack's eye Lagenthorpe's lung resembled heart failure more than it did infection. There was plenty of fluid but little consolidation.

Turning to the other internal organs, Jack found almost all of them involved in the pathological process. The heart seemed acutely enlarged, as were the liver, the spleen, and the kidneys. Even the intestines were engorged, as if they had stopped functioning.

"Got something interesting?" a husky voice demanded.

Jack had been so absorbed, he hadn't noticed that Calvin had nudged Vinnie aside.

"I believe I do," Jack managed.

"Another infectious case?" another gruff voice asked.

Jack's head swung around to his left. He'd recognized the voice immediately, but he had to confirm his suspicion. He was right. It was the chief!

"It came in as a presumed plague," Jack said. He was surprised to see Bingham; the chief rarely came into the pit unless it was a highly unusual case or one that had immediate political ramifications.

"Your tone suggests you don't think it is," Bingham said. He leaned over the open body and glanced in at the swollen, glistening organs.

"You are very perceptive, sir," Jack said. He made a specific effort to keep his patented sarcasm from his voice. This was one time he meant the compliment.

"What do you think you have?" Bingham asked. He poked the swollen spleen gingerly with his gloved hand. "This spleen looks huge."

"I haven't the faintest idea," Jack said.

"Dr. Washington informed me this morning that you'd made an impressive diagnosis on a case of tularemia yesterday," Bingham said.

"A lucky guess," Jack said.

"Not according to Dr. Washington," Bingham said. "I'd like to compliment you. Following on the heels of your astute and rapid diagnosis of the case of plague, I'm impressed. I'm also impressed you left it up to me to inform the proper authorities. Keep up the good work. You make me happy I didn't fire you yesterday."

"Now that's a backhanded compliment," Jack said. He chuckled, and so did Bingham.

"Where's the Martin case?" Bingham asked Calvin.

Calvin pointed. "Table three, sir," he said. "Dr. McGovern's doing it. I'll be over in a second."

Jack watched Bingham long enough to see Chet's double take when he recognized the chief. Jack turned back to Calvin. "My feelings are hurt," he said jokingly. "For a moment I thought the chief came all the way down here and suited up just to pay me a compliment."

"Dream on," Calvin said. "You were an afterthought. He really came down about that gunshot wound Dr. McGovern is doing."

"Is it a problem case?" Jack asked.

"Potentially," Calvin said. "The police claim the victim was resisting arrest."

"That's not so uncommon," Jack said.

"The problem is whether the bullets went in the front or the back," Calvin said. "Also there were five of them. That's a bit heavy-handed."

Jack nodded. He understood all too well and was glad he wasn't doing the case.

"The chief didn't come down here to compliment you, but he did it just the same," Calvin said. "He was impressed about the tularemia, and I have to admit I was too. That was a rapid and clever diagnosis. It's worth ten bucks. But I'll tell you something: I didn't appreciate that little ruse you pulled in the chief's office yesterday about our bet. You might have confused the chief for a moment, but you didn't fool me."

"I assumed as much," Jack said. "That's why I changed the subject so quickly."

"I just wanted you to know," Calvin said. Leaning over Lagenthorpe's open corpse, he pushed on the spleen just as Bingham had done. "The chief was right," he said. "This thing is swollen."

"So's the heart and just about everything else," Jack said.

"What's your guess?" Calvin asked.

"This time I don't even have a guess," Jack admitted. "It's another infectious disease, but I'm only willing to bet it's not plague or tularemia. I'm really starting to question what they are doing over there at the General."

"Don't get carried away," Calvin said. "New York is a big city and the General is a big hospital. The way people move around today and with all the flights coming into Kennedy day in and day out, we can see any disease here, any time of the year."

"You've got a point," Jack conceded.

"Well, when you have an idea what it is, let me know," Calvin said. "I want to win that twenty dollars back."

After Calvin left, Vinnie moved back into place. Jack took samples from all the organs and Vinnie saw to it that they were placed in preservative and properly labeled. After all the samples had been taken, they both sutured Lagenthorpe's incision.

Leaving Vinnie to take care of the body, Jack wandered over to Laurie's table. He had her show him the cut surfaces of the lungs, liver, and spleen. The pathology mirrored that of Lopez and Hard. There were hundreds of incipient abscesses with granuloma formation.

"Looks like another case of tularemia," Laurie said.

"I can't argue with you," Jack said. "But this issue of person-to-person spread being so rare bugs me. I don't know how to explain it."

"Unless they all were exposed to the same source," Laurie said.

"Oh sure!" Jack exclaimed scornfully. "They all happened to go to the same spot in Connecticut and feed the same sick rabbit."

"I'm just suggesting the possibility," Laurie complained.

"I'm sorry," Jack said. "You're right. I shouldn't jump on you. It's just that these infectious disease cases are driving me bananas. I feel like I'm missing something important, and yet I have no idea what it could be."

"What about Lagenthorpe?" Laurie asked. "Do you think he had tularemia as well?"

"No," Jack said. He seems to have had something completely different, and I have no idea what."

"Maybe you are getting too emotionally involved," Laurie suggested.

"Could be," Jack said. He was feeling a bit guilty about wishing the worst for AmeriCare regarding the first case. "I'll try to calm down. Maybe I should go do more reading on infectious diseases."

"That's the spirit," Laurie said. "Instead of stressing yourself out, you should treat these cases as an opportunity to learn. After all, that's part of the fun of this job."

Jack tried vainly to peer through Laurie's plastic face mask to get an idea of whether she was being serious or just mocking him. Unfortunately with all the reflections from the overhead lights, he couldn't tell.

Leaving Laurie, Jack stopped briefly at Chet's table. Chet was not in a good mood.

"Hell," he said. "It's going to take me all day to trace these bullet paths the way Bingham suggested. If he wants to be this particular, I wonder why he doesn't do the case himself."

"Yell if you need any help," Jack said. "I'll be happy to come down and lend a hand."

"I might do that," Chet said.

Jack disposed of his protective gear, changed into his street clothes, and made sure his ventilation charger was plugged in. Then he got the autopsy folders for Lopez and Lagenthorpe. From Hester's folder he looked up her next of kin. A sister was listed whose address was the same as the deceased. Jack surmised they were roommates. He copied down the phone number.

Next Jack sought out Vinnie, whom he found coming out of the walk-in cooler where he'd just deposited Lagenthorpe's corpse.

"Where are all the samples from our two cases?" Jack asked.

"I got 'em all under control," Vinnie said.

"I want to take them upstairs myself," Jack said.

"Are you sure?" Vinnie asked. Running up the samples to the various labs was always an excuse for a coffee break.

"I'm positive," Jack said.

Once he was armed with all the samples plus the autopsy folders Jack set out for his office. But he made two detours. The first was to the microbiology lab, where he sought out Agnes Finn.

"I was impressed with your diagnosis of tularemia," Agnes said.

"I'm getting a lot of compliments out of that one," Jack said.

"Got something for me today?" Agnes asked, eyeing Jack's armful of samples.

"I do, indeed," Jack said. He found the appropriate sample from Lopez and put it on the corner of Agnes's desk. "This is another probable tularemia. Another sample will come up from a case Laurie Montgomery is doing as we speak. I want them both tested for tularemia."

"The reference lab is very eager to follow up on the Hard case, so that won't be difficult. I should have results back today. What else?"

"Well, this one is a mystery," Jack said. He put several samples from Lagenthorpe on Agnes's desk. "I don't have any idea what this patient had. All I know is that it's not plague, and it's not tularemia."

Jack went on to describe the Lagenthorpe case, giving Agnes all the positive findings. She was especially interested that no bacteria had been reported on the gram stain of the sputum.

"Have you thought of virus?" Agnes asked.

"As much as my limited infectious disease knowledge would allow," Jack admitted. "Hantavirus crossed my mind, but there was not a lot of hemorrhage."

"I'll start some viral screening with tissue cultures," Agnes said.

"I plan to do some reading and maybe I'll have another idea," Jack said.

"I'll be here," Agnes assured him.

Leaving microbiology, Jack went up to the fifth-floor histology lab.

"Wake up, girls, we have a visitor," one of the histology techs shouted. Laughter echoed around the room.

Jack smiled. He always enjoyed visiting histology. The entire group of women who worked there always seemed to be in the best of moods. Jack was particularly fond of Maureen O'Conner, a busty redhead with a devilish twinkle in her eye. He was pleased when he saw her round the corner of the lab bench, wiping her hands on a towel. The front of her lab coat was stained a rainbow of colors.

"Well now, Dr. Stapleton," she said in her pleasant brogue. "What can we do for the likes of you?"

"I need a favor," Jack said.

"A favor, he says," Maureen repeated. "You hear that, girls? What should we ask in return?"

More laughter erupted. It was common knowledge that Jack and Chet were the only two unmarried male doctors, and the histology women liked to tease them.

Jack unloaded his armful of sample bottles, separating Lagenthorpe's from Lopez's.

"I'd like to do frozen sections on Lagenthorpe," he said. "Just a few slides from each organ. Of course, I want a set of the regular slides as well."

"What about stains?" Maureen asked.

"Just the usual," Jack said.

"Are you looking for anything in particular?" Maureen inquired.

"Some sort of microbe," Jack said. "But that's all I can tell you."

"We'll give you a call," Maureen said. "I'll get right on it."

Back in his office, Jack went through his messages. There was nothing of interest. Clearing a space in front of himself, he set down Lopez's and Lagenthorpe's folders intending to dictate the autopsy findings and then call the next of kin. He even intended to call the next of kin of the case Laurie was doing. But instead his eye caught sight of his copy of Harrison's textbook of medicine.

Pulling out the book, Jack cracked it open to the section on infectious disease and began reading. There was a lot of material: almost five hundred pages. But he was able to scan quickly since much of it was information he'd committed to memory at some point in his professional career.

Jack had gotten to the chapters on specific bacterial infections when Maureen called. She said that the frozen section slides were ready. Jack immediately walked down to the lab to retrieve them. He carried them back to his office and moved his microscope to the center of the desk.

The slides were organized by organ. Jack looked at the sections of the lung first. What impressed him most was the amount of swelling of the lung tissue and the fact that he saw no bacteria.

Looking at the heart sections, he could immediately see why the heart had appeared swollen. There was a massive amount of inflammation, and the spaces between the heart muscle cells were filled with fluid.

Switching to a higher power of magnification, Jack immediately appreciated the primary pathology. The cells lining the blood vessels that coursed through the heart were severely damaged. As a result, many of these blood vessels had become occluded with blood clots, causing multiple tiny heart attacks!

With a shot of adrenaline coursing through his own circulation from the excitement of discovery, Jack quickly switched back to the section of lung. Using the same high power he saw identical pathology in the walls of the tiny blood vessels, a finding he hadn't noticed on his first examination.

Jack exchanged the lung section with one from the spleen. Adjusting the focus, he saw the same pathology. Obviously it was a significant finding, one that immediately suggested a possible diagnosis.

Jack pushed back from his desk and made a quick trip back to the micro lab and sought out Agnes. He found her at one of the lab's many incubators.

"Hold up on the tissue cultures on Lagenthorpe," he said breathlessly. "I got some new information you're going to love."

Agnes regarded him curiously through her thick glasses.

"It's an endothelial disease," Jack said excitedly. "The patient had an acute infectious disease without bacteria seen or cultured. That should have given it away. He also had the faintest beginnings of a rash that included his palms and soles. Plus he'd been suspected of having appendicitis. Guess why?"

"Muscle tenderness," Agnes said.

"Exactly," Jack said. "So what does that make you think of?"

"Rickettsia," Agnes said.

"Bingo," Jack said, and he punched the air for emphasis. "Good old Rocky Mountain spotted fever. Now, can you confirm it?"

"It's as difficult as tularemia," Agnes said. "We'll have to send it out again. There is a direct immunofluorescent technique, but we don't have the reagent. But I know the city reference lab has it, because there'd been an outbreak of Rocky Mountain spotted fever in the Bronx in eighty-seven."

"Get it over there right away," Jack said. "Tell them we want a reading as soon as they can get it to us."

"Will do," Agnes said.

"You're a doll," Jack said.

He started for the door. Before he got there Agnes called out to him: "I appreciate you letting me know about this as soon as you did," she said. "Rickettsias are extremely dangerous for us lab workers. In an aerosol form it is highly contagious. It's as bad or worse than tularemia."

"Needless to say, be careful," Jack told her.

CHAPTER 17

FRIDAY, 12:15 P.M., MARCH 22, 1996

Helen Robinson brushed her hair with quick strokes. She was excited. Having just hung up the phone with her main contact at National Health's home office, she wanted to get in to see Robert Barker as soon as possible. She knew he was going to love what she had to tell him.

Stepping back from the mirror, Helen surveyed herself from both the right and the left. Satisfied, she closed the closet door and headed out of her office.

Her usual method of contacting Robert was merely to drop in on him. But she thought the information she now had justified a more formal approach; she'd asked one of the secretaries to call ahead. The secretary had reported back that Robert was available at that very moment, not that Helen was surprised.

Helen had been cultivating Robert for the last year. She started when it became apparent to her that Robert could ascend to the presidency. Sensing the man had a salacious streak, she'd deliberately fanned the fires of his imagination. It was easy, although she knew she treaded a fine line. She wanted to encourage him, but not to the point where she would have to openly deny him. In reality, she found him physically unpleasant at best.

Helen's goal was Robert's position. She wanted to be executive director of accounts and could see no reason why she shouldn't be. Her only problem was that she was younger than the others in the department. She felt that was the handicap that her "cultivation" of Robert could overcome.

"Ah, Helen, my dear," Robert said as Helen demurely stepped into his office. He leaped to his feet and closed the door behind her.

Helen perched on the arm of the chair as was her custom. She crossed her legs and her skirt hiked up well above her knee. She noticed the photo of Robert's wife was lying facedown as usual.

"How about some coffee?" Robert offered, taking his seat and assuming his customary hypnotic stare.

"I've just spoken with Gertrude Wilson over at National Health," Helen began. "I'm sure you know her."

"Of course," Robert said. "She's one of the more senior vice presidents."

"She's also one of my most trusted contacts," Helen said. "And she is a fan of Willow and Heath."

"Uh-huh," Robert said.

"She told me two very interesting things," Helen said. "First of all, National Health's main hospital here in the city compares very favorably with other similar hospitals when it comes to hospital-based infections, or what they like to call nosocomial infections."

"Uh-huh," Robert repeated.

"National Health has followed all the recommendations of the CDC and the Joint Commission on Accreditation," Helen said.

Robert shook his head slightly, as if waking up. It had taken a moment for Helen's comments to penetrate his preoccupied brain. "Wait a second," he said. He looked away to organize his thoughts. "This doesn't sound like good news to me. I thought my secretary told me you had good news."

"Hear me out," Helen said. "Although they have an overall good nosocomial record, they've had some recent troubles in their New York facility that they're very sensitive about and would hate to be made public. There were three episodes in particular. One involved an extended outbreak of staph in the intensive-care units. That gave them a real problem until it was discovered a number of the nursing staff were carriers and had to be given courses of antibiotics. I tell you, this stuff is frightening when you hear about it."

"What were the other problems?" Robert asked. For the moment he tried to avoid looking at Helen.

"They had another kind of bacterial problem originate in their kitchen," Helen said. "A lot of patients got serious diarrhea. A few even died. And the last problem was an outbreak of hospital-based hepatitis. That killed several as well."

"That doesn't sound like such a good record to me," Robert said.

"It is when you compare it with some of the other hospitals," Helen said. "I tell you, it's scary. But the point is that National Health is sensitive about this nosocomial infection issue. Gertrude specifically told me that National Health would never in a million years consider running an ad campaign based on it."

"Perfect!" Robert exclaimed. "That is good news. What have you told Terese Hagen?"

"Nothing, of course," Helen said. "You told me to brief you first."

"Excellent job!" Robert said. He pushed himself up onto his long, thin legs and paced. "This couldn't be better. I've got Terese just where I want her."

"What do you want me to tell her?" Helen asked.

"Just tell her that you have confirmed National Health has an excellent record vis-à-vis nosocomial infection," Robert said. "I want to encourage her to go ahead with her campaign, because it will surely bomb."

"But we'll lose the account," Helen said.

"Not necessarily," Robert said. "You've found out in the past that they are interested in 'talking heads' spots with celebrities. We've communicated that to Terese time and time again and she has ignored it. I'm going to go behind her back and line up a few of the stars from some of the current hospital-based TV dramas. They'd be perfect for testimonials. Terese Hagen will bomb and we'll be able to step in with our own campaign."

"Ingenious," Helen said. She slid off the arm of her chair. "I'll start the ball rolling by calling Terese Hagen immediately."

Helen scooted back to her own office and had a secretary put in a call to Terese. As she waited, she complimented herself on the conversation she'd just had with Robert. It couldn't have gone any better had she scripted it. Her position in the firm was looking better and better.

"Miss Hagen is downstairs in the arena," the secretary reported. "Do you want me to call down there?"

"No," Helen said. "I'll head down there in person."

Leaving the carpeted tranquillity of the account executive area, Helen descended the stairs to the studio floor. Her pumps echoed loudly on the metal steps. She liked the idea of talking with Terese in person, although she'd not wanted to go to Terese's office, where she'd feel intimidated.

Helen rapped loudly on the doorjamb before entering. Terese was sitting at a large table covered with storyboards and tissues. Also present were Colleen Anderson, Alice Gerber, and a man Helen did not know. He was introduced as Nelson Friedman.

"I've got the information you requested," Helen said to Terese. She forced her face into a broad smile.

"Good news or bad?" Terese asked.

"I'd say very good," Helen said.

"Let's have it," Terese said. She leaned back in her chair.

Helen described National Health's positive nosocomial record. She even told Terese something she hadn't told Robert: National Health's hospital infection rates were better than AmeriCare's at the General.

"Fabulous," Terese said. "That's just what I wanted to know. You've been a big help. Thank you."

"Glad to be of service," Helen said. "How are you coming with the campaign?"

"I feel good about it," Terese said. "By Monday we'll have something for Taylor and Brian to see."

"Excellent," Helen said. "Well, if I can do anything else, just let me know."

"Certainly," Terese said. She walked Helen to the door, then waved as Helen disappeared into the stairwell.

Terese returned to the table and sat back down.

"Do you believe her?" Colleen asked.

"I do," Terese said. "Accounts wouldn't risk lying about stats that we could presumably get elsewhere."

"I don't see how you can trust her," Colleen said. "I hate that plastic smile. It's unnatural."

"Hey, I said I believed her," Terese said. "I didn't say I trusted her. That's why I didn't share with her what we are doing here."

"Speaking of what we are doing here," Colleen said, "you haven't exactly said you like it."

Terese sighed as her eyes ranged around at the scattered storyboards. "I like the Hippocrates sequence," she said. "But I don't know about this Oliver Wendell Holmes and this Joseph Lister material. I understand how important washing hands is even in a modern hospital, but it's not zippy."

"What about that doctor who was up here with you last night?" Alice asked. "Since he suggested this handwashing stuff, maybe he'll have more of an idea now that we've sketched it out."

Colleen glanced up at Terese. She was dumbfounded. "You and Jack came here last night?" she asked.

"Yeah, we stopped by," Terese said casually. She reached out and adjusted one of the storyboards so she could see it better.

"You didn't tell me that," Colleen said.

"You didn't ask," Terese said. "But it's no secret, if that's what you are implying. My relationship with Jack is not romantic."

"And you guys talked about this ad campaign?" Colleen asked. "I didn't think you wanted him to know about it, especially since he'd been kinda responsible for the idea."

"I changed my mind," Terese said. "I thought he might like it since it deals with the quality of medical care."

"You're full of surprises," Colleen commented.

"Having Jack and Chet take a look at this is not a bad idea," Terese said. "A professional response might be helpful."

"I'd be happy to make the call," Colleen offered.

CHAPTER 18

Jack had been on the phone for over an hour, calling the next of kin of that day's three infectious disease cases. He'd talked with Laurie before calling Joy Hester's sister and roommate. Jack didn't want Laurie to think he was trying to take over her case, but she assured him she didn't mind.

Unfortunately Jack did not learn anything positive. All he was able to do was to confirm a series of negatives, such as that none of the patients had had contact with wild animals in general or wild rabbits in particular. Only Donald Lagenthorpe had had contact with a pet, and that was his girlfriend's newly acquired cat, which was alive and well.

Hanging up at the end of the final call, Jack slouched down in his chair and stared moodily at the blank wall. The adrenaline rush he'd felt earlier with the tentative diagnosis of Rocky Mountain spotted fever had given way to frustration. He seemed to be making no headway.

The phone startled Jack and pulled him out of his gloom. The caller identified himself as Dr. Gary Eckhart, a microbiologist at the city reference lab.

"Are you Dr. Stapleton?"

"Yes, I am," Jack said.

"I'm reporting a positive reaction for *Rickettsia rickettsii*," Dr. Eckhart said. "Your patient had Rocky Mountain spotted fever. Will you be reporting this to the Board of Health or do you want me to do it?"

"You do it," Jack said. "I'm not even sure I'd know whom to call."

"Consider it done," Dr. Eckhart said. He hung up.

Jack slowly replaced the receiver. That his diagnosis had been confirmed was as much of a shock as it had been when his diagnoses of the plague and tularemia had been confirmed. These developments were incredible. Within three days he'd seen three relatively rare infectious diseases.

Only in New York, he thought. In his mind's eye he saw all those planes Calvin had made reference to arriving at Kennedy Airport from all over the world.

But Jack's shock began to metamorphose to disbelief. Even with all the planes and all the people arriving from exotic locales carrying all manner of vermin, bugs, and microbes, it seemed too much of a coincidence to see back-to-back cases of plague, tularemia, and now Rocky Mountain spotted fever. Jack's analytical mind tried to imagine what the probability of such an occurrence would be.

"I'd say about zero," he said out loud.

Suddenly Jack pushed back from his desk and stormed out of his office. His disbelief was now changing to something akin to anger. Jack was sure something weird was going on, and for the moment he was taking it personally. Believing that something had to be done, he headed downstairs and presented himself to Mrs. Sanford. He demanded to talk with the chief.

"I'm afraid Dr. Bingham is over at City Hall meeting with the mayor and the chief of police," Mrs. Sanford said.

"Oh, hell!" Jack exclaimed. "Is he moving in over there or what?"

"There's a lot of controversy surrounding that gunshot case this morning," Mrs. Sanford said warily.

"When will he be back?" Jack demanded. Bingham's being unavailable was adding to his frustration.

"I just don't know," Mrs. Sanford said. "But I'll be sure to tell him you want to speak with him."

"What about Dr. Washington?"

"He's at the same meeting," Mrs. Sanford said.

"Oh, great!"

"Is there something I can help you with?" Mrs. Sanford asked.

Jack thought for a moment. "How about a piece of paper," he said. "I think I'll leave a note."

Mrs. Sanford handed him a sheet of typing paper. In block letters Jack wrote: *LAGENTHORPE HAD ROCKY MOUNTAIN SPOTTED FEVER.* Then he drew a half dozen large question marks and exclamation points. Beneath that he wrote: *THE CITY BOARD OF HEALTH HAS BEEN NOTIFIED BY THE CITY MICROBIO-LOGICAL REFERENCE LAB.*

Jack handed the sheet to Mrs. Sanford, who promised that she'd personally see to it that Dr. Bingham got it as soon as he came in. Then she asked Jack where he'd be if the chief wanted to speak with him.

"Depends on when he gets back," Jack said. "I plan to be out of the office for a while. Of course, he might hear about me before he hears from me."

Mrs. Sanford regarded him quizzically, but Jack didn't elaborate.

Jack returned to his office and grabbed his jacket. Then he descended to the morgue and unlocked his bike. Bingham's exhortations notwithstanding, Jack was on his way to the Manhattan General Hospital. For two days he'd had the suspicion that something unusual was going on over there; now he was sure of it.

After a quick ride, Jack locked his bike to the same sign he'd used on his previous visits and entered the hospital. With visiting hours just beginning, the lobby was jammed with people, particularly around the information booth.

Jack wormed his way through the crowd and climbed the stairs to the second floor. He went directly to the lab and waited in line to speak with the receptionist. This time he asked to see the director, even though his impulse was to march right in.

Martin Cheveau made Jack wait for a half hour before seeing him. Jack tried to use the time to calm himself. He recognized that over the last four or five years he'd become less than tactful in the best of circumstances; when he was upset, as he was now, he could be abrasive.

A laboratory tech eventually came out and informed Jack that Dr. Martin Cheveau would see him now.

"Thanks for seeing me so promptly," Jack said as he entered the office. Despite his best intentions he couldn't avoid a touch of sarcasm.

"I'm a busy man," Martin said, not bothering to stand up.

"I can well imagine," Jack said. "With the string of rare infectious diseases emanating from this hospital on a daily basis, I'd think you'd be putting in overtime."

"Dr. Stapleton," Martin said in a controlled voice. "I have to tell you that I find your attitude distinctly disagreeable."

"I find yours confusing," Jack said. "On my first visit you were the picture of hospitality. On my second visit, you were just the opposite."

"Unfortunately I don't have time for this conversation," Martin said. "Is there something in particular you wanted to say to me?"

"Obviously," Jack said. "I didn't come over here just for abuse. I wanted to ask your professional opinion about how you think three rare, arthropod-borne diseases have mysteriously occurred in this hospital. I've been cultivating my own opinion, but as the director of the lab I'm curious about yours."

"What do you mean three diseases?" Martin asked.

"I just got confirmation that a patient named Lagenthorpe who expired here in the General last night had Rocky Mountain spotted fever."

"I don't believe you," Martin said.

Jack eyed the man and tried to decide if he was a good actor or truly surprised.

"Well then, let me ask you a question," Jack said. "What would I accomplish by coming over here and telling you something that wasn't true? Do you think of me as some sort of health-care provocateur?"

Martin didn't answer. Instead he picked up the phone and paged Dr. Mary Zimmerman.

"Calling in reinforcements?" Jack asked. "Why can't you and I have a talk?"

"I'm not sure you are capable of normal conversation," Martin said.

"Good technique," Jack commented. "When defense doesn't work, switch to offense. The problem is, strategies won't change the facts. Rickettsias are extremely dangerous in the laboratory. Maybe we should make sure whoever handled Lagenthorpe's specimens did so with proper precautions."

Martin pressed his intercom button and paged his chief microbiology tech, Richard Overstreet.

"Another thing I'd like to discuss," Jack said. "On my first visit here you told me how discouraging it was to run your lab with the budgets foisted on you by AmeriCare. On a scale of one to ten, how disgruntled are you?"

"What are you implying?" Martin demanded ominously.

"At the moment I'm not implying anything," Jack said. "I'm just asking."

The phone rang and Martin picked it up. It was Dr. Mary Zimmerman. Martin asked her if she could come down to the lab since something important had just come up.

"The problem as I see it is that the probability of these three illnesses popping up as they have is close to zero," Jack said. "How would you explain it?"

"I don't have to listen to this," Martin snarled.

"But I think you have to consider it," Jack said.

Richard Overstreet appeared in the doorway dressed as he'd been before, in a white lab coat over surgical scrubs. He appeared harried.

"What is it, Chief?" he asked. He nodded a greeting to Jack, who returned the gesture.

"I've just learned a patient by the name of Lagenthorpe expired from Rocky Mountain spotted fever," Martin said gruffly. "Find out who got the samples and who processed them."

Richard stood for a moment, obviously shocked by the news. "That means we had rickettsia in the lab," he said.

"I'm afraid so," Martin said. "Get right back to me." Richard vanished and Martin turned back to Jack. "Now that you have brought us this happy news, perhaps you could do us the favor and leave."

"I'd prefer to hear your opinion as to the origin of these diseases," Jack said.

Martin's face flushed, but before he could respond Dr. Mary Zimmerman appeared at his door.

"What can I do for you, Martin?" she asked. She started to tell him that she'd just been paged to the ER when she caught sight of Jack. Her eyes narrowed. She was obviously no happier than Martin to see Jack.

"Howdy, Doctor," Jack said cheerfully.

"I was assured we would not see you again," Dr. Zimmerman said.

"You can never believe everything you hear," Jack said.

Just then Richard returned, clearly distraught. "It was Nancy Wiggens," he blurted out. "She's the one who got the sample and processed it herself. She called in sick this morning."

Dr. Zimmerman consulted a note she held in her hand. "Wiggens is one of the patients I've just been called to see in the ER," she said. "Apparently she's suffering from some sort of fulminant infection."

"Oh, no!" Richard said.

"What's going on here?" Dr. Zimmerman demanded.

"Dr. Stapleton just brought news that a patient of ours died from Rocky Mountain spotted fever," Martin said. "Nancy was exposed."

"Not here in the lab," Richard said. "I've been a bear about safety. Ever since the plague case I have insisted all infectious material be handled in the biosafety III cabinet. If she were exposed it had to be from the patient."

"That's not likely," Jack said. "The only other possibility is that the hospital is lousy with ticks."

"Dr. Stapleton, your comments are tasteless and inappropriate," Dr. Zimmerman said.

"They are a lot worse than that," Martin said. "Just before you got here, Dr.

Zimmerman, he slanderously suggested that I had something to do with the spread of these latest illnesses."

"That's not true," Jack corrected. "I was merely implying that the idea of deliberate spread has to be considered when the probability of them occurring by chance is so negligible. It only makes sense. What's wrong with you people?"

"I think such thoughts are the product of a paranoid mind," Dr. Zimmerman said. "And frankly I don't have time for this nonsense. I've got to get to the ER. In addition to Miss Wiggens, there are two other employees with the same severe symptoms. Good-bye, Dr. Stapleton!"

"Just a minute," Jack said. "Let me guess what areas these two other stricken employees work in. Could they be from nursing and central supply?"

Dr. Zimmerman, who was already several steps away from Martin's door, paused and looked back at Jack. "How did you know that?" she asked.

"I'm beginning to see a pattern," Jack said. "I can't explain it, but it's there. I mean, the nurse is regrettable but understandable. But someone from central supply?"

"Listen, Dr. Stapleton," Dr. Zimmerman said. "Perhaps we're in your debt for once again having alerted us to a dangerous disease. But we will take over from here, and we certainly don't need any of your paranoid delusions. Good day, Dr. Stapleton."

"Hold on a minute," Martin called out to Dr. Zimmerman. "I'll come with you to the ER. If this is rickettsial disease I want to be sure all samples are handled safely."

Martin grabbed his long white lab coat from a hook behind the door and ran after Dr. Zimmerman.

Jack shook his head in disbelief. Every visit he'd made to the General had been strange, and this one was no exception. On previous occasions he'd been chased out. This time he'd been all but deserted.

"Do you really think these illnesses could have been spread deliberately?" Richard asked.

Jack shrugged. "To tell you the truth, I don't know what to think. But there certainly has been some defensive behavior, particularly on the part of those two who just left. Tell me, is Dr. Cheveau generally mercurial? He seemed to turn on me rather suddenly."

"He's always been a gentleman with me," Richard said.

Jack got to his feet. "It must be me, then," he said. "And I suppose our relations won't improve after today. Such is life. Anyway, I'd better be going. I sure hope Nancy is okay."

"You and me both," Richard said.

Jack wandered out of the lab debating what to do next. He thought about either going to the emergency room to see about the three sick patients or heading up to central supply for another visit. He decided on the emergency room. Even though Dr. Zimmerman and Dr. Cheveau had headed down there, Jack thought the chance of another run-in was remote, given the size of the ER and the constant activity there.

As soon as he arrived he detected a general panic. Charles Kelley was anxiously conferring with several other administrators. Then Clint Abelard came dashing through the main ambulance entry only to disappear down the central corridor.

Jack went over to one of the nurses who was busy behind the main counter. He introduced himself and asked if the hubbub was about the three sick hospital staff.

"It most certainly is," she said. "They're trying to decide how best to isolate them."

"Any diagnosis?" Jack asked.

"I just heard they suspect Rocky Mountain spotted fever," the nurse said.

"Pretty scary," Jack said.

"Very," the nurse said. "One of the patients is a nurse."

Out of the corner of his eye Jack saw Kelley approaching. Jack quickly faced away. Kelley came to the desk and asked the nurse for the phone.

Jack left the bustling ER. He thought about going up to central supply, but decided against it. Having come close to another confrontation with Charles Kelley, he thought it best to head back to the office. Although he hadn't accomplished anything, at least he was leaving on his own volition.

"Uh-oh! Where have you been?" Chet asked as Jack came into their office.

"Over at the General," Jack admitted. He started organizing the clutter on his desk.

"At least you must have behaved yourself; there haven't been any frantic calls from the front office."

"I was a good boy," Jack said. "Well, reasonably good. The place is in an uproar. They have another outbreak. This one is Rocky Mountain spotted fever. Can you believe it?"

"That's incredible," Chet said.

"That's my feeling exactly," Jack said. He went on to tell Chet how he'd implied to the head of the lab that outbreaks of three rare, infectious, arthropod-borne diseases in as many days couldn't occur naturally.

"I bet that went over well," Chet said.

"Oh, he was indignant," Jack said. "But then he got preoccupied with some fresh cases and forgot about me."

"I'm surprised you weren't thrown out again," Chet said. "Why do you do this to yourself?"

"Because I'm convinced that there's 'something rotten in the state of Denmark,' " Jack said. "But enough about me. How did your case go?"

Chet gave a short, scornful laugh. "And to think I used to like gunshot cases," he said. "This one is kicking up a storm. Three of the five bullets entered through the back."

"That's going to give the police department a headache," Jack said.

"And me too," Jack said. "Oh, by the way, I got a call from Colleen. She wants you and me to come by their studio when we leave work tonight. Listen to this: They want our opinion about some ads. What do you say?"

"You go," Jack said. "I've got to get some of these cases of mine signed out. I'm so far behind it's scaring me."

"But they want both of us," Chet said. "Colleen specifically said that. In fact, she said they particularly wanted you there because you had helped already. Come on, it will be fun. They are going to show us a bunch of sketches outlining some potential TV commercials."

"Is that really your idea of fun?" Jack asked.

"Okay," Chet admitted. "I've an ulterior motive. I'm enjoying spending time with Colleen. But they want both of us. Help me out."

"All right," Jack said. "But for the life of me I don't understand why you think you need me."

CHAPTER 19

FRIDAY, 9:00 P.M., MARCH 22, 1996

Jack had insisted on working late. Chet had obliged by fetching Chinese takeout so Jack could continue. Once Jack got started, he hated to stop. By eight-thirty Colleen had called, wondering where they were. Chet had to nag Jack to get him to turn off his microscope and lay down his pen.

The next problem was Jack's bike. After much discussion it was decided that Chet would take a taxi and Jack would ride as he normally did. They then met in front of Willow and Heath after having arrived almost simultaneously.

A night watchman opened the door for them and made them sign in. They boarded the only functioning elevator, and Jack promptly pressed the eleventh floor.

"You really were here," Chet said.

"I told you I was," Jack said.

"I thought you were pulling my leg," Chet remarked.

When the doors opened Chet was as surprised as Jack had been the night before. The studio was in full swing, as if it were still sometime between nine and five, instead of almost nine in the evening.

The two men stood for a few minutes watching the bustle. They were totally ignored.

"Some welcoming party," Jack commented.

"Maybe someone should tell them it's after quitting time," Chet said.

Jack peered into Colleen's office. The lights were on but no one was there. Turning around, he recognized Alice toiling at her drawing board. He walked over to her, but she didn't look up.

"Excuse me?" Jack said. She was working with such concentration he hated to bother her. "Hello, hello."

Finally Alice's head bobbed up, and when she caught sight of him, her face reflected instant recognition.

"Oh, gosh, sorry," she said, wiping her hands on a towel. "Welcome!" She acted self-conscious; she'd not seen them arrive as she stood and motioned for them to follow her. "Come on! I'm supposed to take you down to the arena."

"Uh-oh," Chet said. "That doesn't sound good. They must think we're Christians."

Alice laughed. "Creatives are sacrificed in the arena, not Christians," she explained.

Terese and Colleen greeted them with air kisses: the mere touching of cheeks accompanied by a smacking sound. It was the kind of ritual that made Jack feel distinctly uncomfortable.

Terese got right to business. She had the men sit at the table while she and Colleen began putting storyboards in front of them, maintaining a running commentary on what the storyboards represented.

Both Jack and Chet were entertained from the start. They were particularly taken by the humorous sketches involving Oliver Wendell Holmes and Joseph Lister visiting the National Health hospital and inspecting the hospital's hand-washing protocols. At the conclusion of each commercial these famous characters in the history of medicine commented on how much more scrupulously the National Health hospital followed their teachings than that "other" hospital.

"Well, there you have it," Terese said after the last storyboard was explained and withdrawn. "What do you men think?"

"They're cute," Jack admitted. "And probably effective. But they are hardly worth the money that's going to be spent on them."

"But they deal with something associated with the quality of care," Terese said defensively.

"Barely," Jack said. "The National Health subscribers would be better off if the millions spent on this were put into actual health care."

"Well, I love them," Chet said. "They're so fresh and delightfully humorous. I think they're great."

"I assume the 'other' hospital refers to the competition," Jack said.

"Most assuredly," Terese said. "We feel it would be in bad taste to mention the General by name, especially in light of the problems it's been having."

"Their problems are getting worse," Jack said. "They've had an outbreak of another serious disease. This makes three in three days."

"Good God!" Terese exclaimed. "That's awful. I certainly hope this gets to the media, or is this one going to be a secret?"

"I don't know why you keep making this an issue," Jack snapped. "There's no way it can be kept a secret."

"It would be if AmeriCare had its way," Terese said heatedly.

"Hey, are you guys at it again?" Chet said.

"It's an ongoing argument," Terese said. "I just can't get over the fact that Jack does not feel it is his job as a public servant to let the media and hence the public know about these awful diseases."

"I told you I've been specifically informed it is not my job," Jack shot back.

"Wait! Time out," Chet called out. "Listen, Terese, Jack is right. We can't go to the media ourselves. That's the chief's domain via the PR office. But Jack is no slouch in all this. Today he went flying over to the General and implied right to their faces that these recent outbreaks aren't natural."

"What do you mean, not 'natural'?" Terese asked.

"Exactly that," Chet said. "If they are not natural, then they are deliberate. Somebody is causing them."

"Is that true?" Terese asked Jack. She was shocked.

"It's gone through my mind," Jack admitted. "I'm having trouble explaining scientifically everything that has been going on over there."

"Why would someone do that?" Terese wondered. "It's absurd."

"Is it?" Jack asked.

"Could it be the work of some crazy person?" Colleen offered.

"That I'd doubt," Jack said. "There is too much expertise involved. And these bugs are dangerous to handle. One of the current victims is a lab technician."

"What about a disgruntled employee?" Chet suggested. "Someone with the knowledge and a grudge who's snapped."

"That I think is more likely than some madman," Jack said. "In fact, the director of the hospital lab is unhappy with the management of the hospital. He told me so himself. He's had to lay off twenty percent of his workforce."

"Oh my God," Colleen exclaimed. "Do you think it could be him?"

"Actually I don't," Jack said. "Frankly, too many arrows would point to the director of the lab. He'd be the first suspect. He's been acting defensive, but he's not stupid. I think that if this series of diseases has been spread deliberately it has to be for a more venal reason."

"Like what?" Terese said. "I think we're all jumping off the deep end here."

"Maybe so," Jack said. "But we have to remember that AmeriCare is first and foremost a business. I even know something about their philosophy. Believe me, it is bottom-line oriented all the way."

"You're suggesting that AmeriCare might be spreading disease in its own facility?" Terese asked incredulously. "That doesn't make any sense."

"I'm just thinking out loud," Jack explained. "For the sake of argument let's assume these illnesses have been deliberately spread. Now, let's look at the index case in each incidence. First, there was Nodelman, who had diabetes. Second, there was Hard, who had a chronic orthopedic problem, and lastly there was Lagenthorpe, who suffered from chronic asthma."

"I see what you're suggesting," Chet said. "All of the index cases were the type of patient prepaid plans hate because they lose money on them. They simply use too much medical care."

"Oh, come on!" Terese complained. "This is ridiculous. No wonder you doctors make such horrid businessmen. AmeriCare would never risk this kind of public relations disaster to rid itself of three problem patients. It would make no sense. Give me a break!"

"Terese is probably right," Jack admitted. "If AmeriCare was behind all this, they certainly could have done it more expeditiously. What truly worries me is that infectious agents are involved. If these outbreaks have been deliberate, the individual behind them wants to start epidemics, not just eliminate specific patients."

"That's even more diabolical," Terese said.

"I agree," Jack said. "It kind of forces us back to considering the improbable idea of a crazy person."

"But if someone is trying to start epidemics, why hasn't there been one?" Colleen asked.

"For several reasons," Jack said. "First of all, the diagnosis has been made relatively rapidly in all three cases. Second, the General has taken these outbreaks seriously and has taken appropriate steps to control them. And third, the agents involved are poor choices for creating an epidemic here in New York in March."

"You'll have to explain," Colleen said.

"Plague, tularemia, and Rocky Mountain spotted fever can be transmitted by airborne spread, but it is not their usual route. The usual route is through an arthropod vector, and those specific bugs are not available this time of year, especially not in a hospital."

"What do you think of all this?" Terese asked Chet.

"Me?" Chet asked with a self-conscious laugh. "I don't know what to think."

"Come on," Terese prodded. "Don't try to protect your friend here. What's your gut reaction?"

"Well, it is New York," Chet said. "We see a lot of infectious diseases, so I suppose I'm dubious about this notion of a deliberate spread. I guess I'd have to say it sounds a little paranoid to me. I do know that Jack dislikes AmeriCare."

"Is that true?" Terese asked Jack.

"I hate them," Jack admitted.

"Why?"

"I'd rather not talk about it," Jack said. "It's personal."

"Well," Terese said. She put her hand on top of the stack of storyboards. "Dr. Stapleton's disdain for medical advertising aside, you men think these sketches are okay?"

"I told you, I think they're great," Chet said.

"I imagine they will be effective," Jack grudgingly agreed.

"Do either of you have any other suggestions we could use regarding preventing hospital infections?" Terese asked.

"Maybe you could do something concerning steam sterilization for instruments and devices," Jack said. "Hospitals differ in their protocols. Robert Koch was involved with that advance, and he was a colorful character."

Terese wrote down the suggestion. "Anything else?" she asked.

"I'm afraid I'm not very good at this," Chet admitted. "But why don't we all head over to the Auction House for a couple of drinks. With the proper lubricant, who knows what I might come up with?"

The women declined. Terese explained that they had to continue working on the sketches. She said that by Monday they had to have something significant to show to the president and the CEO.

"How about tomorrow night?" Chet suggested.

"We'll see," Terese said.

Five minutes later Jack and Chet were heading down in the elevator.

"That was the bum's rush," Chet complained.

"They are driven women," Jack said.

"How about you?" Chet asked. "Want to stop for a beer?"

"I think I'll head home and see if the guys are playing basketball," Jack said. "I could use some exercise. I feel wired."

"Basketball at this hour?" Chet questioned.

"Friday night is a big night in the neighborhood," Jack said.

The two men parted company in front of the Willow and Heath building. Chet jumped into a cab, and Jack undid his medley of locks. Climbing on his bike, Jack pedaled north on Madison, then crossed over to Fifth Avenue at Fifty-ninth Street. From there he entered Central Park.

Although his usual style was to ride fast, Jack kept his pace slow. He was mulling over the conversation he'd just had. It had been the first time that he'd put his suspicions into words; he felt anxious as a result.

Chet had suggested he was paranoid, and Jack had to admit there had to be some truth in it. Ever since AmeriCare had effectively gobbled up his practice, Jack felt that death had been stalking him. First it had robbed him of his family, then it had threatened his own life with depression. It had even filled his daily routine with the second specialty he'd chosen. And now death seemed to be teasing him with these outbreaks, even mocking him with inexplicable details.

As Jack rode deeper into the dark, deserted park, its gloomy and somber views added to his disquietude. In areas where he'd seen beauty that morning on his way to work, now he saw ghastly skeletons of leafless trees silhouetted against an eerily bleached sky. Even the distant sawtooth skyline of the city seemed ominous.

Jack put muscle into his pedaling, and his bike gained speed. For an irrational moment he was afraid to look back over his shoulder. He had the creepy feeling that something was bearing down on him.

Jack streaked into a puddle of light beneath a lonely streetlight, braked, and skidded to a stop. He forced himself to turn around and face his pursuer. But there was nothing there. Jack strained to see into the distant shadows, and as he did, he understood that what was threatening him was coming from inside his own head. It was the depression that had paralyzed him after his family's tragedy.

Angry with himself, Jack began pedaling again. He was embarrassed by his child-like fear. He thought he had more control. Obviously he was letting this episode with the outbreaks affect him far too much. Laurie had been right: he was too emotionally involved.

Having faced his fears, Jack felt better, but he noticed that the park still looked sinister. People had warned him about riding in the park at night, but Jack had always ignored their admonitions. Now, for the first time, he wondered if he was being foolish.

Emerging from the park onto Central Park West was like escaping from a night-mare. From the dark, scary loneliness of the park's interior he was instantly thrust into a rallylike bustle of yellow cabs racing northward. The city had come alive. There were even people calmly walking on the sidewalks.

The farther north Jack rode the more the environment deteriorated. Beyond 100th Street the buildings became noticeably shabbier. Some were even boarded up and appeared abandoned. There was more litter in the street. Stray dogs plundered overturned trash cans.

Jack turned left onto 106th Street. As he rode along his street the neighborhood seemed more depressed than usual to him. The minor epiphany in the park had opened Jack's eyes to just how dilapidated the area was.

Jack stopped at the playground where he played basketball by grabbing onto the chain-link fence that separated it from the street. His feet remained snug in his toe clips.

As Jack had expected, the court was in full use. The mercury vapor lights that he'd paid to be installed were ablaze. Jack recognized many of the players as they surged up and down the court. Warren, by far the best player, was there, and Jack could hear him urging his teammates to greater effort. The team that lost would have to sit out, since a bevy of other players waited impatiently on the sidelines. The competition was always fierce.

While Jack was watching, Warren sank the final basket of the game and the losing team slunk off the court, momentarily disgraced. As the new game was being organized Warren caught sight of Jack. He waved and strutted over. It was the winning team walk.

"Hey, Doc, whatcha know?" Warren asked. "You coming out to run or what?"

Warren was a handsome African-American with a shaved head, a groomed mustache, and a body like one of the Greek statues in the Metropolitan Museum. It had taken Jack several months to cultivate Warren's acquaintance. They had developed a friendship of sorts, but it was based more on a shared love of street basketball than anything else. Jack didn't know much about Warren except that he was the best basketball player and also the de facto leader of the local gang. Jack suspected that the two positions went hand in hand.

"I was thinking about coming out for a run," Jack said. "Who's got winners?"

Getting into the game could be a tricky business. When Jack had first moved to the neighborhood, it had taken him a month of coming to the court and patiently waiting until he'd been invited to play. Then he'd had to prove himself. Once he'd demonstrated he was capable of putting the ball in the basket on a consistent basis, he'd been tolerated.

Things got a bit better when Jack had paid to have the lights installed and the backboards refurbished, but not a lot. There were only two other honkies besides Jack who were allowed to play. Being Caucasian was a definite disadvantage on the neighborhood playground: you had to know the rules.

"Ron's got winners and then Jake," Warren said. "But I can get you on my team. Flash's old lady wants him home."

"I'll be out," Jack said. He pushed off from the fence and rode the rest of the way to his building.

Jack got off his bike and hefted it up onto his shoulder. Before he entered his building he looked up at its facade. In his current critical state of mind he had to admit it wasn't pretty. In fact, it was a downright sorry structure, although at one time it must have been rather fancy, because a small segment of highly decorative cornice still clung precariously to the roofline. Two of the windows on the third floor were boarded up.

The building was six stories, constructed of brick, and had two apartments per floor. Jack shared the fourth floor with Denise, a husbandless teenager with two children.

Jack pushed the front door open with his foot. It had no lock. He started up the stairs, careful to avoid any debris. As Jack passed the second floor he heard the sorry sounds of a vehement argument, followed by the noise of breaking glass. Unfortunately, this was a nightly occurrence.

With the bike balanced on his shoulder, it took Jack some maneuvering to get himself situated in front of his apartment door. He was fumbling in his pocket for his key when he noticed he didn't need it. The doorjamb opposite his lock was splintered.

Jack pushed his door open. It was dark inside. He listened but only heard renewed yelling from 2A and the traffic out in the street. His apartment was eerily quiet. He put his bike down and reached in and turned on the overhead light.

The living room was in shambles. Jack didn't have much furniture, but what he had was either tipped over, emptied, or broken. He noticed that a small radio that usually stood on the desk was gone.

Jack wheeled the bike into the room and leaned it against the wall. He took off his jacket and draped it over the bike. Then he walked over to the desk. The drawers had been pulled out and dumped. Amid the rubble on the floor was a photo album. Jack bent down and picked it up. He opened the cover and breathed a sigh of relief. It was unscathed. It was the only possession he cared about.

Jack placed the photo album on the windowsill and walked into the bedroom.

He switched on the light and saw a similar scene. Most of his clothes had been pulled from his closet and from his bureau and tossed onto the floor.

The condition of the bathroom mirrored that of the living room and the bedroom. The contents of the medicine cabinet had been dumped into the bathtub.

Jack walked from the bedroom to the kitchen. Expecting more of the same, he flipped on the light. A slight gasp escaped from his lips.

"We were beginning to wonder about you," a large African-American male said. He was sitting at Jack's table, dressed totally in black leather, including gloves and a visorless hat. "We'd run out of your beer and we were getting antsy."

There were three other men dressed in identical fashion to the first. One was half sitting on the windowsill. The two others were to Jack's immediate right, leaning against the kitchen cabinet. On the table was an impressive array of weaponry, including machine pistols.

Jack didn't recognize any of these men. He was shocked that they were still there. He'd been robbed before but nobody had stayed to drink his beer.

"How about coming over and sitting yourself down?" the large black man said.

Jack hesitated. He knew the door to the hall was open. Could he make it before they picked up their guns? Jack doubted it, and he wasn't about to try.

"Come on, man," the black man said. "Get your white ass over here!"

Reluctantly Jack did as he was told. Warily he sat down and faced his uninvited visitor.

"We might as well be civilized about this," the black man said. "My name is Twin. This here's Reginald." Twin pointed to the man at the window.

Jack glanced in Reginald's direction. He was toying with a toothpick and sucking his teeth. He regarded Jack with obvious disdain. Although he wasn't quite as muscular as Warren, he was in the same category. Jack could see he had the words "Black Kings" tattooed on the volar surface of his right forearm.

"Now Reginald is pissed," Twin continued, "because you ain't got shit here in this apartment. I mean, there isn't even a TV. You see, part of the deal was that we'd have pickings over your stuff."

"What kind of deal are you talking about?" Jack asked.

"Let's put it this way," Twin said. "Me and my brothers are being paid some small change to come way the hell over here to rough you up a bit. Nothing major, despite the artillery you see on the table. It's supposed to be some kind of warning. Now, I don't know the details, but apparently you've been making a pain of yourself at some hospital and got a bunch of people all riled up. I'm supposed to remind you to do your job and let them do theirs. Does that make any more sense to you than it does to me? I mean, I've never done anything like this before."

"I think I catch your drift," Jack said.

"I'm glad," Twin said. "Otherwise we'd have to break a few fingers or something. We weren't supposed to hurt you bad, but when Reginald starts, it's hard to stop him, especially when he's pissed. He needs something. Are you sure you don't have a TV or something hidden around here?"

"He just came in with a bike," one of the other men said.

"What about that, Reginald?" Twin asked. "You want a new bike?"

Reginald leaned forward so he could see into the living room. He shrugged his shoulders.

"I think you got yourself a deal," Twin said. He stood up.

"Who's paying you to do this?" Jack asked.

Twin raised his eyebrows and laughed. "Now, it wouldn't be kosher of me to tell you that, now would it? But at least you've got the balls to ask."

Jack was about to ask another question when he was viciously cold-cocked by Twin. The force of the sucker punch knocked Jack over backward, and he sprawled limply on the floor. The room swam before his eyes. Hovering close to unconsciousness, he felt his wallet being pulled from his trousers. There was muffled laughter followed by a final agonizing kick in the stomach. Then there was absolute blackness.

CHAPTER 20

FRIDAY, 11:45 P.M., MARCH 22, 1996

The first thing Jack was aware of was a ringing in his head. Slowly he opened his eyes and found himself staring directly up at the ceiling fixture in the kitchen. Wondering what he was doing on the kitchen floor, he tried to get up. When he moved he felt a sharp pain in his jaw that made him lie back down. That was when he realized the ringing was intermittent and it wasn't in his head: it was the wall phone directly above him.

Jack rolled over onto his stomach. From that position he pushed himself up onto his knees. He'd never been knocked out before, and he couldn't believe how weak he felt. Gingerly he felt along his jawline. Thankfully he didn't feel any jagged edges of broken bones. Equally carefully he palpated his tender abdomen. That was less painful than the jaw, so he assumed there'd been no internal damage.

The phone continued to ring insistently. Finally Jack reached up and took it off the hook. As he said hello he eased himself into a sitting position on the floor with his back against the kitchen cabinets. His voice sounded strange even to himself.

"Oh, no! I'm sorry," Terese said when she heard his voice. "You've been asleep. I shouldn't have called so late."

"What time is it?" Jack asked.

"It's almost twelve," Terese said. "We're still here in the studio, and sometimes we forget that the rest of the world sleeps normal hours. I wanted to ask a question about sterilization, but I'll call you tomorrow. I'm sorry to have awakened you."

"Actually I've been unconscious on my kitchen floor," Jack said.

"Is that some kind of joke?" Terese asked.

"I wish," Jack said. "I came home to a ransacked apartment, and unfortunately the ransackers were still here. To add insult to injury they also kind of beat me up."

"Are you all right?" Terese asked urgently.

"I think so," Jack said. "But I think I chipped a tooth."

"Were you really unconscious?" Terese asked.

"I'm afraid so," Jack said. "I still feel weak."

"Listen," Terese said decisively. "I want you to call the police immediately, and I'm coming over."

"Wait a sec," Jack said. "First of all, the police won't do anything. I mean, what can they do? It was four gang members, and there's a million of them in the city."

"I don't care, I want you to call the police," Terese said. "I'll be over there in fifteen minutes."

"Terese, this isn't the best neighborhood," Jack said. He could tell she'd made up her mind, but he persisted. "You don't have to come. I'm okay. Honest!"

"I don't want to hear any excuses about not calling the police," Terese said. "I should be there in fifteen minutes."

Jack found himself holding a dead telephone. Terese had hung up.

Dutifully Jack dialed 911 and gave the information. When he was asked if he was in any current danger, he said no. The operator said the officers would be there as soon as possible.

Jack pushed himself up onto wobbly legs and walked out into his living room. Briefly he looked for his bike, but then vaguely remembered something about his attackers wanting it. In the bathroom he bared his teeth and examined them. As he'd suspected from touching it with his tongue, his left front tooth had a small chip. Twin must have had something like brass knuckles under his gloves.

To Jack's surprise the police arrived within ten minutes. There were two officers, an African-American by the name of David Jefferson and a Latino, Juan Sanchez. They listened politely to Jack's tale of woe, wrote down the particulars, including the make of the missing bike, and asked Jack if he'd care to come to the precinct to look at mug shots of various local gang members.

Jack declined. Through Warren he understood that the gangs did not fear the police. Consequently, Jack knew the police could not protect him from the gangs, so he decided not to tell the police everything. But at least he'd satisfied Terese's demand and would be able to collect insurance on his bike.

"Excuse me, Doc," David Jefferson said as the police were leaving. Jack had informed them he was a medical examiner. "How come you live in this neighborhood? Aren't you asking for trouble?"

"I ask myself the same question," Jack said.

After the police had left, Jack closed his splintered door and leaned against it while surveying his apartment. Somehow he would have to find the energy to clean it up. At the moment it seemed like an overwhelming task.

A knock that he could feel more than hear made him reopen the door. It was Terese.

"Ah, thank God it's you," Terese said. She came into the apartment. "You weren't kidding when you said this wasn't the best neighborhood. Just climbing these stairs was a trauma. If it hadn't been you opening the door I might have screamed."

"I tried to warn you," Jack said.

"Let me look at you," Terese said. "Where's the best light?"

Jack shrugged. "You choose," he said. "Maybe the bathroom."

Terese dragged Jack into the bathroom and examined his face. "You have a tiny cut over your jawbone," she said.

"I'm not surprised," Jack said. He then showed her the chipped tooth.

"Why did they beat you up?" Terese said. "I hope you weren't playing hero."

"Quite the contrary," Jack said. "I was terrified into total immobility. I was sucker-punched. This was evidently some kind of warning for me to stay out of the Manhattan General."

"What on earth are you talking about?" Terese demanded.

Jack told her all the things he hadn't told the police. He even told her why he hadn't told the police.

"This is getting more and more unbelievable," Terese said. "What are you going to do?"

"To tell the truth, I haven't had a lot of time to think about it," Jack said.

"Well, I know one thing you are going to do," Terese said. "You are going to the emergency room."

"Come on!" Jack complained. "I'm fine. My jaw is sore, but big deal."

"You were knocked out," Terese reminded him. "You should be seen. I'm not even a doctor and I know that much."

Jack opened his mouth to protest further, but he didn't; he knew she was right. He should be seen. After a head injury serious enough to render him unconscious, there was the worry of intracranial hemorrhage. He should have a basic neurological exam.

Jack rescued his jacket from the floor. Then he followed Terese down the stairs to the street. To catch a cab they walked to Columbus Avenue.

"Where do you want to go?" Terese asked once they were in the taxi.

"I think I'll stay away from the General for the time being," Jack said with a smile. "Let's go uptown to Columbia-Presbyterian."

"Fine," Terese said. She gave directions to the cabdriver and settled back in her seat.

"Terese, I really appreciate your coming over," Jack said. "You didn't have to, and I certainly didn't expect it. I'm touched."

"You would have done it for me," Terese said.

Would he have? Jack wondered. He didn't know. The whole day had been confusing.

The visit to the emergency room went smoothly. They had to wait as auto accidents, knife wounds, and heart attacks were given priority. But eventually Jack was seen. Terese insisted on staying the whole time and even accompanied him into the examining room.

When the ER resident learned Jack was a medical examiner, he insisted Jack be seen by the neurology consult. The neurology resident went over Jack with utmost care. He declared him fit and said he didn't even think an X ray was indicated unless Jack felt strongly otherwise. Jack didn't.

"The one thing I do recommend is that you be observed overnight," the neurology resident said. He then turned to Terese and said: "Mrs. Stapleton, just wake him up occasionally and make sure he behaves normally. Also check that his pupils remain the same size. Okay?"

"Okay," Terese said.

Later as they were walking out of the hospital Jack commented that he was impressed with her equanimity when she'd been addressed as Mrs. Stapleton.

"I thought it would have embarrassed the man to have corrected him," Terese said. "But I'm going to take his recommendations quite seriously. You are coming home with me."

"Terese . . ." Jack complained.

"No arguments!" Terese commanded. "You heard the doctor. There's no way I'd allow you to go back to that hellhole of yours tonight."

With his head mildly throbbing and his jaw aching and his stomach sore, Jack surrendered. "Okay," he said. "But this is all far beyond the call of duty."

Jack felt truly grateful as they rode up in the elevator in Terese's posh high-rise. No one had been as gracious to him as Terese in years. Between her concern and generosity he felt that he'd misjudged her.

"I've a guest room that I'm confident you'll find comfortable," she said as they walked down a carpeted hallway. "Whenever my folks come to town it is hard to get them to leave."

Terese's apartment was picture perfect. Jack was amazed how neat it was. Even the magazines were arranged carefully on the coffee table, as if she expected *Architectural Digest* to do a photo shoot.

The guest room was quaint with flower-print drapes, carpet, and bedspread that all matched. Jack joked that he hoped he didn't get disoriented since he might have trouble finding the bed.

After providing Jack with a bottle of aspirin, Terese left him to shower. After he'd finished, he donned a terry-cloth bathrobe, which she'd laid out. Thus attired, he poked his head out into the living room and saw her sitting on the couch reading. He walked out and sat across from her.

"Aren't you going to bed?" he asked.

"I wanted to be sure you were okay," she said. She leaned forward to stare directly into his face. "Your pupils look equal to me."

"To me too," Jack said. He laughed. "You are taking those doctor's orders seriously."

"You'd better believe it," she said. "I'll be coming in to wake you up, so be prepared."

"I know better than to argue," Jack said.

"How do you feel in general?" Terese asked.

"Physically or mentally?"

"Mentally," Terese said. "Physically I have a pretty good idea."

"To be truthful, the experience has scared me," Jack admitted. "I know enough about these gangs to be afraid of them."

"That's why I wanted you to call the police," Terese said.

"You don't understand," Jack said. "The police can't really help me. I mean, I didn't even bother to tell them the possible name of the gang or the first names of the intruders. Even if the police picked them up, all they'd do is slap their wrists. Then they'll be back on the street."

"So what are you going to do?" Terese asked.

"I suppose I'm going to stay the hell away from the General," Jack said. "Seems like that's going to make everybody happy. Even my own boss told me not to go. I suppose I can do my job without going over there."

"I'm relieved," Terese said. "I was worried you'd try to be a hero and take the warning as a challenge."

"You said that before," Jack said. "But don't worry. I'm no hero."

"What about this bike-riding around this city?" Terese asked. "And riding through the park at night? And what about living where you do? The fact is, I do worry. I worry that you're either oblivious to danger or courting it. Which is it?"

Jack looked into Terese's pale blue eyes. She was asking questions that he strictly avoided. The answers were too personal. But after the concern that she'd demonstrated that evening and the effort she'd expended on his behalf, he felt she deserved some explanation. "I suppose I have been courting danger," he said.

"Can I ask why?"

"I guess I haven't been worried about dying," Jack said. "In fact, there was a time when I felt dying would be a relief. A few years back I had trouble with depression, and I suppose it's always going to be there in the background."

"I can relate to that," Terese said. "I had a bout with depression as well. Was yours associated with a particular event, if I may ask?"

Jack bit the inside of his lip. He felt uncomfortable talking about such issues, but now that he'd started it was hard to turn back.

"My wife died," Jack managed. He couldn't get himself to mention the children.

"I'm sorry," Terese said empathetically. She paused a moment and then said: "Mine was due to the death of my only child."

Jack turned his head away. Terese's admission brought instant tears to his eyes. He took a deep breath and then looked back at this complicated woman. She was a hard-driving executive; of that he was sure from the moment he'd met her. But now he knew there was more.

"I guess we have more in common than just disliking discos," he said in an attempt to lighten the atmosphere.

"I think we've both been emotionally scarred," Terese said. "And we've both overly invested ourselves in our careers."

"I'm not so sure we share that," Jack said. "I'm not as committed to my career as I once was, nor as I think you are. The changes that have come to medicine have robbed me of some of that."

Terese stood up. Jack did the same. They were standing close enough to appreciate each other physically.

"I guess I meant more that we both are afraid of emotional commitment," Terese said. "We've both been wounded."

"That I can agree to," Jack said.

Terese kissed the tips of her fingers and then touched them gently to Jack's lips. "I'll be in to wake you in a few hours," she said. "So be prepared."

"I hate to be putting you through all this," Jack said.

"I'm enjoying this little bit of mothering," Terese said. "Sleep well."

They parted. Jack walked back toward the guest room, but before he got to the door, Terese called out: "One more question: Why do you live in that awful slum?"

"I guess I don't feel as if I deserve to be all that happy," Jack said.

Terese thought about that for a moment, then smiled. "Well, I shouldn't imagine I'd understand everything," she said. "Good night."

"Good night," Jack echoed.

CHAPTER 21

SATURDAY, 8:30 A.M., MARCH 23, 1996

True to her word, Terese had come into Jack's room and awakened him several times during the night. Each time they'd talked for a few minutes. By the time Jack awakened in the morning he felt conflicted. He was still thankful for Terese's ministrations, but he felt embarrassed by how much of himself he'd revealed.

As Terese made him breakfast, it became apparent that she felt as awkward as he. At eight-thirty, with mutual relief, they parted company in front of Terese's building. She was off to the studio for what she thought would be a marathon session. He headed for his apartment.

Jack spent a few hours cleaning up the debris left by the Black Kings. With some rudimentary tools he even repaired his door as best he could.

With his apartment taken care of, Jack headed to the morgue. He wasn't scheduled to work that weekend, but he wanted to spend more time on his backlog of autopsies that had yet to be signed out. He also wanted to check on any infectious cases that might have come in during the night from the General. Knowing that there had been three reportedly fulminant cases of Rocky Mountain spotted fever in the emergency room the day before, he was afraid of what he might find.

Jack missed his bike and thought about getting another one. To get to work he took the subway, but it wasn't convenient. He had to change trains twice. The New York subway system was fine for getting from north to south, but west to east was another story entirely.

Even with the multiple train changing Jack still had to walk six blocks. With a light rain falling and no umbrella, he was wet by the time he got to the medical examiner's office at noon.

Weekends were far different than weekdays at the morgue. There was much less commotion. Jack used the front entrance and had the receptionist buzz him into the ID area. A distraught family was in one of the identification rooms. Jack could hear sobbing as he passed by.

Jack found the schedule that listed the doctors on call for the weekend and was pleased to see that Laurie was among them. He also found the master list of cases that had come in the previous night. Scanning it, he was sickened to see a familiar name. Nancy Wiggens had been brought in at four A.M.! The provisional diagnosis was Rocky Mountain spotted fever.

Jack found two more cases with the same diagnosis: Valerie Schafer, aged thirty-three, and Carmen Chavez, aged forty-seven. Jack assumed they were the other two cases in the General's emergency room the day before.

Jack went downstairs and peeked into the autopsy room. Two tables were in use. Jack couldn't tell who the doctors were, but judging by height he guessed one of them was Laurie.

After changing into scrubs and donning protective gear, Jack entered through the washroom.

"What are you doing here?" Laurie asked when she caught sight of Jack. "You're supposed to be off enjoying yourself."

"Just can't keep away," Jack quipped. He leaned over to see the face of the patient Laurie was working on and his heart sank. Staring up at him with lifeless eyes was Nancy Wiggens. In death she appeared even younger than she had in life.

Jack quickly looked away.

"Did you know this individual?" Laurie asked. Her own emotional antennae had instantly picked up Jack's reaction.

"Vaguely," Jack admitted.

"It's a terrible thing when health-care workers succumb to their patients' illnesses," Laurie remarked. "The patient I did before this one was a nurse who'd ministered to the patient you did yesterday."

"I'd assumed as much," Jack said. "What about the third case?"

"I did her first," Laurie said. "She was from central supply. I couldn't quite figure how she contracted it."

"Tell me about it," Jack said. "I've done two other people from central supply. One with plague and one with tularemia. I can't understand it either."

"Somebody better figure it out," Laurie said.

"I couldn't agree more," Jack said. Then he pointed to Nancy's organs. "What'd you find?"

"It's all been consistent with Rocky Mountain spotted fever," Laurie said. "Are you interested to see?"

"I sure am," Jack said.

Laurie took time out to show all the relevant pathology to Jack. Jack told her the findings were the mirror image of those he'd seen with Lagenthorpe.

"It makes you wonder why just three got sick, since they were so sick," Laurie said. "The interval from the onset of symptoms to the time of death was a lot shorter than usual. It suggests that the microbes were particularly pathogenic, yet if they were, where are the other patients? Janice told me that as far as the hospital knows there are no more cases."

"There was a similar pattern with the other diseases," Jack said. "I can't explain it, just like I can't explain so many other aspects of these outbreaks. That's why they've been driving me crazy."

Laurie glanced up at the clock and was surprised by the time. "I've got to get a move on here," she said. "Sal has to leave early."

"Why don't I help?" Jack offered. "Tell Sal he can go now."

"Are you serious?" Laurie asked.

"Absolutely," Jack said. "Let's get it done."

Sal was happy to leave a little early. Laurie and Jack worked well together and finished up the case in good time. They walked out of the autopsy room together.

"How about a bite up in the lunchroom?" Laurie asked. "My treat."

"You're on," Jack said.

They disposed of their isolation gear and disappeared into their respective locker rooms. When Jack was dressed, he went out into the hall and waited for Laurie to appear.

"You didn't have to wait for . . ." Laurie began to say, but stopped. "Your jaw is swollen," she said.

"That's not all," Jack said. He bared his teeth and pointed to his left incisor. "See the chip?" he asked.

"Of course I do," Laurie said. Her hands went onto her hips and her eyes narrowed. She looked like an irate mother confronting a naughty child. "Did you fall off of that bike?" she asked.

"I wish," Jack said with a mirthless laugh. He then told her the whole story minus the part about Terese. Laurie's expression changed from mock anger to disbelief.

"That's extortion," she said indignantly.

"I suppose it is in a way," Jack said. "But come on, let's not let it upset our gourmet lunch."

They did the best they could with the vending machines on the second floor. Laurie got a soup while Jack settled on a tuna-fish salad sandwich. They took their food to a table and sat down.

"The more I think about what you've told me, the crazier I think it sounds," Laurie said. "How's your apartment?"

"A bit dilapidated," Jack said. "But it wasn't so great before this happened, so it doesn't much matter. The worst thing is that they took my bike."

"I think you should move," Laurie said. "You shouldn't be living there anyway."

"It's only the second break-in," Jack said.

"I hope you're not planning on staying in tonight," Laurie said. "How depressing."

"No, I'm busy tonight," Jack said. "I've got a group of nuns coming into town who I'm supposed to show around."

Laurie laughed. "Hey, my folks are having a little dinner party tonight. Would you care to come along? It would be a lot more cheerful than sitting in your plundered apartment."

"That's very thoughtful of you," Jack said. As with Terese's actions the night before, this invitation was totally unexpected. Jack was moved.

"I would enjoy your company," Laurie said. "What do you say?"

"You do realize that I'm not particularly social," Jack said.

"I'm aware of that," Laurie said. "I don't mean to put you on the spot. You don't even have to tell me now. The dinner is at eight and you can call me a half hour before if you decide to come. Here's my number." She wrote it on a napkin and handed it to him.

"I'm afraid I'm not such good company at dinner parties," Jack said.

"Well, it's up to you," Laurie said. "The invitation stands. Now, if you'll excuse me, I've got two more cases to do."

Jack watched Laurie leave. He'd been impressed with her from the first day, but he'd always thought of her as one of his more talented colleagues, nothing more. But now suddenly he saw how strikingly attractive she was with her sculptured features, soft skin, and beautiful auburn hair.

Laurie waved before slipping out the door, and Jack waved back. Disconcertedly he stood up, discarded his trash, and headed up to his office. In the elevator he wondered what was happening to him. It had taken him years to stabilize his life, and now his well-constructed cocoon seemed to be unraveling.

Once inside his office Jack sat down at his desk. He rubbed his temples to try to calm himself. He was becoming agitated again, and he knew that when he became agitated he could be impulsive.

As soon as he felt capable of concentrating he pulled the closest folder toward him and flipped it open. Then he went to work.

By four o'clock Jack had accomplished as much paperwork as he could handle. Leaving the medical examiner's office, he took the subway. As he sat in the bouncing rail cars with the other silent, zombielike people, he told himself he had to get another bike. Commuting underground like a mole was not going to work for him.

Arriving home, Jack lost no time. He took his stairs two at a time. Finding a drunk, homeless person asleep on the first landing didn't faze him. He just stepped over the man and continued. With his anxiety Jack needed exercise, and the sooner he got out on the basketball court the happier he'd be.

Jack hesitated briefly at his door. It seemed to be in the same shape as he'd left it. He unlocked it and peered into the apartment. It, too, seemed undisturbed. Somewhat superstitiously Jack walked over to the kitchen and looked in. He was relieved to see that no one was there.

In the bedroom Jack pulled out his basketball gear: oversized sweatpants, a turtleneck, and a sweater. He quickly changed. After lacing up his hightops, he grabbed a headband, a basketball, and was back out the door.

Saturday afternoon was always a big day at the playground, provided the weather cooperated. Usually twenty to thirty people showed up ready to run, and this particular Saturday was no exception. The morning rain had long since stopped. As Jack approached the court he counted fourteen people waiting to play. That meant he'd probably have to wait through two more games beyond the present match before he could hope to join.

Jack nodded subdued greetings to some of the people he recognized. The etiquette required that no emotion be shown. After he'd stood on the sidelines for the appropriate amount of time he asked who had winners. He was told that David had winners. Jack was acquainted with David.

Careful to suppress the eagerness he felt, Jack sidled up to David.

"You got winners?" Jack asked, pretending to be uninterested.

"Yeah, I got winners," David said. He went through some minor ducking and weaving that Jack had learned to recognize as posturing. Jack had also learned by sore experience not to imitate it.

"You got five?" Jack asked.

David already had his team lined up so Jack had to go through the same process with the next fellow who had winners. That was Spit, whose nickname was based on one of his less endearing mannerisms. Luckily for Jack, Spit only had four players and since he knew Jack's outside shooting ability, he agreed to add Jack to his roster.

With his entrance into the game now assured, Jack took his ball to one of the unused side baskets and began warming up. He had a mild headache and his jaw ached, but otherwise he felt better than he'd expected. He'd been more concerned about his stomach once he started running around, but that didn't bother him in the slightest.

While Jack was busy shooting foul shots Warren showed up. After he'd gone through the same process that Jack had done in order to get into the game, he wandered over to where Jack was practicing.

"Hey, Doc, what's happening?" Warren asked. He snatched the ball from Jack's hands and quickly tossed in a shot that hit nothing but net. Warren's movements were uncannily fast.

"Not much," Jack said, which was the correct reply. Warren's question was really a greeting in disguise.

136 / ROBIN COOK

They shot for a while in a ritual fashion. First Warren would shoot until he missed, which wasn't often. Then Jack would do the same. While one was shooting the other rebounded.

"Warren, let me ask you a question," Jack said during one of his turns shooting. "You ever hear of a gang by the name of the Black Kings?"

"Yeah, I think so," Warren said. He fed Jack the ball after Jack had put in one of his patented long-distance jump shots. "I think they're a bunch of losers from down near the Bowery. How come you're asking?"

"Just curious," Jack said. He sank another long jump shot. He was feeling good.

Warren snatched the ball out of the air as it came through the basket. But he didn't pass it back to Jack. Instead he walked it to Jack.

"What do you mean, 'curious'?" Warren asked. He drilled Jack with his gun-barrel eyes. "You ain't been curious about any gangs before."

One of the other things that Jack knew about Warren was that he was keenly intelligent. Had he had the opportunity, Jack was sure he'd be a doctor or a lawyer or some other professional.

"I happened to see it tattooed on a guy's forearm," Jack said.

"The guy dead?" Warren asked. He was aware of what Jack did for a living.

"Not yet," Jack said. He rarely risked sarcasm with his playground acquaintances, but on this occasion it had just slipped out.

Warren regarded him warily and continued to hold the ball. "You pulling my chain, or what?"

"Hell no," Jack said. "I might be white, but I ain't stupid."

Warren smiled. "How come you got banged up on your jaw?"

Warren didn't miss a trick. "Just caught an elbow," Jack said. "I was in the wrong place at the wrong time."

Warren handed over the ball. "Let's warm up with a little one-on-one," he said. "Hit-or-miss for the ball."

Warren got in the game before Jack, but Jack eventually played, and played well. Spit's players seemed unbeatable, to the chagrin of Warren, who had to play against them on several occasions. By six o'clock Jack was exhausted and soaked to the skin.

Jack was perfectly happy to leave when everyone else departed en masse for dinner and their usual Saturday-night revelry. The basketball court would be empty until the following afternoon.

A long, hot postgame shower was a distinct pleasure for Jack. When he was finished he dressed in clean clothes and looked into his refrigerator. It was a sad scene. All his beer had been drunk by the Black Kings. As far as food was concerned he was limited to an old wedge of cheddar cheese and two eggs of dubious age. Jack closed the refrigerator. He wasn't all that hungry anyway.

In the living room Jack sat on his threadbare couch and picked up one of his medical journals. His usual evening routine was to read until nine-thirty or ten and then fall asleep. But tonight he was still restless despite the exercise, and he found he couldn't concentrate.

Jack tossed the journal aside and stared at the wall. He was lonely, and although he was lonely almost every night, he felt it more keenly at that moment. He kept thinking about Terese and how compassionate she'd been the night before.

Jack impulsively went to the desk, got out the phone book, and called Willow and Heath. He wasn't sure if the phones would be manned after hours, but eventually someone answered. After several wrong extensions he finally got Terese on the phone.

With his heart inexplicably pounding in his chest, Jack casually told her he was thinking of getting something to eat.

"Is this an invitation?" Terese questioned.

"Well," Jack said hesitantly. "Maybe you'd like to come along, provided you haven't eaten yet."

"This is the most roundabout invitation I've gotten since Marty Berman asked me to the junior prom," Terese said with a laugh. "You know what he did? He used the conditional. He said: 'What would you say if I asked you?' "

"I guess Marty and I have some things in common," Jack said.

"Hardly," Terese said. "Marty was a skinny runt. But as for dinner, I'll have to take a rain check. I'd love to see you, but you know about this deadline we have. We're hoping that we can get it under control tonight. I hope you understand."

"Absolutely," Jack said. "No problem."

"Call me tomorrow," Terese said. "Maybe in the afternoon we can get together for coffee or something."

Jack promised he'd call and wished her good luck. Then he hung up the phone, feeling even lonelier for having made an effort to be sociable after so many years and having been turned down.

Surprising himself anew, Jack found Laurie's number and called her. Trying to cover his nervousness with humor, he told her that the group of nuns he was expecting had to cancel.

"Does that mean you'd like to come to dinner?" Laurie asked.

"If you'll have me," Jack said.

"I'd be delighted," Laurie said.

CHAPTER 22

SUNDAY, 9:00 A.M., MARCH 24, 1996

Jack was poring over one of his forensic science journals when his phone rang. Since he had yet to speak that morning his voice was gravelly when he answered.

"I didn't wake you, did I?" Laurie asked.

"I've been up for hours," Jack assured her.

"I'm calling because you asked me to," Laurie said. "Otherwise I wouldn't call this early on a Sunday morning."

"It's not early for me," Jack said.

"But it was late when you went home," Laurie said.

"It wasn't that late," Jack said. "Besides, no matter what time I go to bed I always wake up early."

"Anyway, you wanted me to let you know if there were any infectious deaths from the General last night," Laurie said. "There weren't. Janice even told me before she left that there wasn't even anyone ill with Rocky Mountain spotted fever in the hospital. That's good news, isn't it?"

"Very good news," Jack agreed.

"My parents were quite impressed with you last night," Laurie added. "I hope you enjoyed yourself."

"It was a delightful evening," Jack said. "Frankly I'm embarrassed I stayed so long. Thank you for inviting me and thank your parents. They couldn't have been more hospitable."

"We'll have to do it again sometime," Laurie said.

"Absolutely," Jack said.

After they had said good-byes, Jack hung up the phone and tried to go back to reading. But he was momentarily distracted by thoughts of the previous evening. He had enjoyed himself. In fact he'd enjoyed himself much more than he could have imagined, and that confused him. He'd purposefully kept to himself for five years, and now without warning he found himself enjoying the company of two very different women.

What he liked about Laurie was how easy she was to be with. Terese, on the other hand, could be overbearing even while she was being warmly caring. Terese was more intimidating than Laurie, but she was also challenging in a way that was more consistent with Jack's reckless lifestyle. But now that he'd had the opportunity to see Laurie interact with her parents, he appreciated her open, warm personality all the more. He imagined having a pompous cardiovascular surgeon for a father couldn't have been easy.

Laurie had tried to engage Jack in personal conversation after the older generation had retired, but Jack had resisted, as was his habit. Yet he'd been tempted. Having opened up a little with Terese the night before, it had surprised him how good it felt to talk with someone caring. But Jack had fallen back on his usual stratagem of turning the conversation back to Laurie, and he'd learned some unexpected things.

Most surprising was that she was unattached. Jack had just assumed someone as desirable and sensitive as Laurie would have been involved with someone, but Laurie insisted she didn't even date much. She'd explained that she'd had a relationship with a police detective for a time, but it hadn't worked out.

Eventually Jack got back to his journal. He read until hunger drove him to a neighborhood deli. On his way home from lunch he saw that a group of guys was already beginning to appear on the basketball court. Eager for more physical activity, Jack dashed home, changed, and joined them.

Jack played for several hours. Unfortunately his shot wasn't as smooth or accurate as on the previous day. Warren teased him unmercifully, especially when he guarded Jack during several of the games. Warren was making up for the ignominy of the previous day's defeats.

At three o'clock after another loss, which meant Jack would be sitting out for at least three games, maybe more, he gave up and returned to his apartment. After a shower he sat down to try to read again, but found himself thinking about Terese.

Concerned about being rejected a second time, Jack had not planned on calling her. But by four he relented; after all, she had asked him to call. More important, he truly wanted to talk with her. Having partially opened up to her, he felt curiously disturbed not to have told her the whole story. He felt he owed her more.

Even more anxious than he had been the evening before, Jack dialed the number. This time Terese was much more receptive. In fact, she was ebullient.

"We made great progress last night," she announced proudly. "Tomorrow we're going to knock the socks off the president and the CEO. Thanks to you this idea of hospital cleanliness and low infection rate is a great hook. We're even having some fun with your sterilization idea."

Finally Jack got around to asking her if she'd like to get together for some coffee. He reminded her it had been her suggestion.

"I'd love it," Terese said without hesitation. "When?"

"How about right now?" Jack said.

"Fine by me," Terese said.

They met at a small French-style café on Madison Avenue between Sixty-first and Sixty-second conveniently close to the Willow and Heath building. Jack got there ahead of Terese and took a table in the window and ordered an espresso.

Terese arrived soon after. She waved through the window, and after entering, she forced Jack into a repeat of the cheek-pressing routine. She was vibrant. She ordered a decaf cappuccino from the attentive waiter.

As soon as they were alone, she leaned across the table and grasped Jack's hand. "How are you?" she asked. She looked directly into his eyes and then at his jawline. "Your pupils are equal, and you look okay. I thought you'd be black and blue."

"I'm better than I would have expected," Jack admitted.

Terese then launched into an excited monologue about her upcoming review and how wonderfully everything was falling into place. She explained what a "ripomatic" was and how they had managed to put one together with tape sequences from their previous National Health campaign. She said it was terrific and gave a good impression of the Do-No-Harm Hippocrates idea.

Jack let her carry on until she'd exhausted the subject. After taking a few gulps of her cappuccino, she asked him what he'd been doing.

"I've been thinking a lot about the conversation we had Friday night," he said. "It's been bothering me."

"How so?" Terese asked.

"We were being open with each other, but I wasn't completely forthright," Jack said. "I'm not accustomed to talking about my problems. The truth is: I didn't tell you the whole story."

Terese put her coffee cup down and studied Jack's face. His dark blue eyes were intense. His face was stubbled; he'd obviously not shaved that day. She thought that under different circumstances Jack could appear intimidating, maybe even scary.

"My wife wasn't the only person who died," Jack said haltingly. "I lost my two daughters as well. It was a commuter plane crash."

Terese swallowed with difficulty. She'd felt a welling of emotion clog her throat. Jack's story was hardly what she'd expected.

"The problem is, I've always felt so damn responsible," he continued. "If it hadn't been for me they wouldn't have been on that plane."

Terese felt an intense stab of empathy. After a few moments she said: "I wasn't entirely forthright either. I told you I'd lost my child. What I didn't say is that it was an unborn child, and at the same time I lost the child, I lost my ability to have any more. To add insult to injury, the man I'd married deserted me."

For a few emotionally choked minutes neither Jack nor Terese spoke. Finally, Jack broke the silence: "It sounds like we're trying to outdo each other with our personal tragedies," he said, managing a smile.

"Just like a couple of depressives," Terese agreed. "My therapist would love this."

"Of course, what I've told you is for your ears only," Jack said.

"Don't be silly," Terese assured him. "Same goes for you. I haven't told my story to anyone but my therapist."

"I haven't told anybody," Jack said. "Not even a therapist."

Feeling a sense of relief from having both bared their innermost secrets, Jack and Terese went on to talk about happier things. Terese, who'd grown up in the city, was shocked to hear how little of the area Jack had visited since he'd been there. She talked about taking him to the Cloisters when spring had truly arrived.

"You'll love it," she promised.

"I'll look forward to it," Jack said.

CHAPTER 23

MONDAY, 7:30 A.M., MARCH 25, 1996

Jack was irritated at himself. He'd had time to buy a new bike on Saturday, but he'd failed to do so. Consequently, he had to use the subway again to commute to work, although he'd considered jogging. The problem with jogging was that he'd have to have a change of clothes in his office. To give him the option in the future he brought some to work in a small shoulder bag.

Coming in from First Avenue, Jack again entered the medical examiner's facility through the front entrance. As he passed through the glass door, he was impressed with the number of families waiting in the outer reception area. It was highly unusual for so many people to be there that early. Something must be up, he surmised.

Jack had himself buzzed in. He walked into the scheduling room and saw George Fontworth sitting at the desk Laurie had occupied each morning the previous week.

Jack was sorry Laurie's week as supervisor was over. George had rotated to the position. He was a short, moderately overweight doctor of whom Jack had a low opinion. He was perfunctory and often missed important findings.

Ignoring George, Jack headed over to Vinnie and pushed down the edge of his newspaper.

"Why are there so many people out in the ID area?" Jack asked.

"Because there's a minor disaster over at the General," George said, answering for Vinnie. Vinnie treated Jack to a jaunty but disdainful expression and went back to his paper.

"What kind of disaster?" Jack asked.

George patted the top of a stack of folders. "A whole bunch of meningococcal deaths," he said. "Could be an epidemic in the making. We've got eight so far."

Jack rushed over to George's desk and snapped up a folder at random. He opened it and shuffled through its contents until he came to the investigative report. Scanning it quickly, he learned that the patient's name was Robert Caruso, and that he had been a nurse on the orthopedic floor at the General.

Jack tossed the folder back onto the desk and literally ran through communications to the offices of the PAs. He was relieved to see Janice was still there, putting in overtime as usual.

She looked terrible. The dark circles under her eyes were so distinct, she resembled a battered woman. She put her pen down and leaned back. She shook her head. "I might have to get another job," she said. "I can't keep this up. Thank God I have tomorrow and the next day off."

"What happened?" Jack asked.

"It started on the shift before mine," Janice said. "The first case was called in around six-thirty. Apparently the patient had died about six P.M."

"An orthopedic patient?" Jack asked.

"How'd you know?"

"I just saw a folder from an orthopedic nurse," Jack said.

"Oh, yeah, that was Mr. Caruso," Janice said with a yawn. She excused herself before continuing. "Anyway, I started getting called shortly after I arrived at eleven. Since then it's been nonstop. I've been back and forth all night. In fact, I just got back here twenty minutes ago. I tell you, this is worse than the the other outbreaks. One of the patients is a nine-year-old girl. What a tragedy."

"Was she related to the first case?" Jack asked.

"She was a niece," Janice said.

"Had she been in to visit her uncle?" Jack asked.

"Around noon yesterday," Janice said. "You don't think that could have contributed to her death, do you? I mean, that was only about twelve hours before her death."

"Under certain circumstances meningococcus has a frightful capacity to kill, and kill incredibly swiftly," Jack said. "In fact, it can kill in just a few hours."

"Well, the hospital is in a panic."

"I can imagine," Jack said. "What was the name of the first case?"

"Carlo Pacini," Janice said. "But that's about all I know. He came in on the shift before mine. Steve Mariott handled it."

"Could I ask a favor?" Jack asked.

"That depends," Janice said. "I'm awfully tired."

"Just leave word for Bart that I want you PAs to get all the charts of the index case in each of these outbreaks. Let's see, that's Nodelman with the plague, Hard with tularemia, Lagenthorpe with Rocky Mountain spotted fever, and Pacini with meningococcus. Do you think that will be a problem?"

"Not at all," Janice said. "They are all active ME cases."

Jack stood up and gave Janice a pat on the back. "Maybe you should go over to the clinic on your way home," he said. "Some chemoprophylaxis might not be a bad idea."

Janice's eyes widened. "You think that is necessary?"

"Better safe than sorry," Jack said. "Anyway, discuss it with one of the infectious disease gurus. They know better than I. There's even a tetravalent vaccine, but that takes a few days to kick in."

Jack dashed back to the ID room and asked George for Carlo Pacini's folder.

"It's not here," George said. "Laurie came in early, and when she heard about what was going on, she requested the case. She's got the folder."

"Where is she?" Jack asked.

"Up in her office," Vinnie responded from behind his paper.

Jack hustled up to Laurie's office. Contrary to the way Jack worked, she liked to go over each folder in her office before doing the autopsy.

"Pretty frightening, I'd say," Laurie said as soon as she saw Jack.

"It's terrifying," Jack said. He grabbed Laurie's officemate's chair, pulled it over to Laurie's desk, and sat down. "This is just what I've been worrying about. This could be a real epidemic. What have you learned about this index case?"

"Not much," Laurie admitted. "He'd been admitted Saturday evening with a fractured hip. Apparently he'd had a brittle bone problem; he'd had a whole string of fractures over the last few years."

"Fits the pattern," Jack said.

"What pattern?" Laurie asked.

"All the index cases from these recent outbreaks have had some sort of chronic illness," Jack said.

"A lot of people who are hospitalized have chronic illnesses," Laurie said. "In fact, most of them. What does that have to do with anything?"

"I'll tell you what's on his paranoid, sick mind," Chet said. Chet had appeared at Laurie's door. He stepped into the room and leaned against the second desk. "He's got this thing about AmeriCare and wants to see conspiracy behind all this trouble."

"Is that true?" Laurie asked.

"I think it's less that I want to see conspiracy than it's staring me in the face," Jack said.

"What do you mean by 'conspiracy'?" Laurie asked.

"He has this notion that these unusual illnesses are being spread deliberately," Chet said. Chet summarized Jack's theory that the culprit was either someone at AmeriCare trying to protect its bottom line or some crazy person with terrorist inclinations.

Laurie looked questioningly at Jack. Jack shrugged.

"There are a lot of unanswered questions," Jack offered.

"As there are in just about any outbreak," Laurie said. "But really! This is all a bit far-fetched. I hope you didn't mention this theory to the powers that be over at the General."

"Yeah, I did," Jack said. "In fact I sort of asked the director of the lab if he was involved. He's rather disgruntled with his budget. He immediately informed the infection-control officer. I imagine they've let the administration know."

Laurie let out a short, cynical laugh. "Oh, brother," she said. "No wonder you've become persona non grata around there."

"You have to admit there's been an awful lot of questionable nosocomial infection at the General," Jack said.

"I'm not even so sure about that," Laurie said. "Both the tularemic patient and the patient with Rocky Mountain spotted fever developed their illnesses within forty-eight hours of admission. By definition, they are not nosocomial infections."

"Technically that's true," Jack admitted. "But . . ."

"Besides, all these illnesses have been seen in New York," Laurie said. "I've done some recent reading myself. There was a serious outbreak of Rocky Mountain spotted fever in eighty-seven."

"Thank you, Laurie," Chet said. "I tried to tell Jack the same thing. Even Calvin has told him."

"What about the series of cases coming from central supply?" Jack asked Laurie. "And what about the rapidity with which the patients with Rocky Mountain spotted fever developed their illnesses? You were questioning that just this Saturday."

"Of course I'd question those things," Laurie said. "They're the type of questions that have to be asked in any epidemiological situation."

Jack sighed. "I'm sorry," he said. "But I'm convinced something highly unusual is going on. All along I've been worried that we might see a real epidemic crop up. This outbreak of meningococcus may be it. If it peters out like the other outbreaks, I'll be relieved, of course, in human terms. But it will only add to my suspicions. This pattern of multiple fulminant cases, then nothing, is highly unusual in itself."

"But this is the season for meningococcus," Laurie said. "It's not so unusual."

"Laurie's right," Chet said. "But regardless, my concern is that you're going to get yourself into real trouble. You're like a dog with a bone. Calm down! I don't want to see you fired. At least reassure me you're not going back to the General."

"I can't say that," Jack said. "Not with this new outbreak. This one doesn't depend on some arthropods that aren't around. This is an airborne problem, and as far as I'm concerned, it changes the rules."

"Just a moment," Laurie said. "What about that warning you got from those thugs?"

"Now what?" Chet questioned. "What thugs?"

"Jack had a cozy visit from some charming members of a gang," Laurie said. "It seems that at least one of the New York gangs is going into the extortion business."

"Somebody has to explain," Chet said.

Laurie told Chet what she knew of Jack's beating.

"And you're still thinking of going over there?" Chet asked when she was through.

"I'll be careful," Jack said. "Besides, I haven't exactly decided to go yet."

Chet rolled his eyes to the ceiling. "I think I would have preferred you as a suburbanite ophthalmologist."

"What do you mean, ophthalmologist?" Laurie questioned.

"Come on, you guys," Jack said. He stood up. "Enough is enough. We've got work to do."

Jack, Laurie, and Chet did not emerge from the autopsy room until after one in the afternoon. Although George had questioned the need to post all the meningococcal cases, the triumvirate had insisted; George relented in the end. Doing some on their own and some together, they autopsied the initial patient, one orthopedic resident, two nurses, one orderly, two people who'd visited the patient, including the nine-year-old girl, and particularly important as far as Jack was concerned, one woman from central supply.

After the marathon they all changed back to their street clothes and met up in the lunchroom. Relieved to be away from the mayhem and a bit overwhelmed by the findings, they didn't talk at first. They merely got their selections from the vending machines and sat down at one of the free tables.

"I haven't done many meningococcal cases in the past," Laurie said finally. "But these today were a lot more impressive than the ones I did do."

"You won't see a more dramatic case of the Waterhouse-Friderichsen syndrome," Chet said. "None of these people had a chance. The bacteria marched through them like a Mongol horde. The amount of internal hemorrhage was extraordinary. I tell you, it scares the pants off me."

"It was one time that I actually didn't mind being in the moon suit," Jack agreed. "I couldn't get over the amount of gangrene on the extremities. It was even more than on the recent plague cases."

"What surprised me was how little meningitis was involved," Laurie said. "Even the child had very little, and I would have thought at least she would have had extensive involvement."

"What puzzles me," Jack said, "is the amount of pneumonitis. Obviously it is an airborne infection, but it usually invades the upper part of the respiratory tree, not the lungs."

"It can get there easily enough once it gets into the blood," Chet said. "Obviously all these people had high levels coursing through their vascular systems."

"Have either of you heard if any more cases have come in today?" Jack asked.

Chet and Laurie exchanged glances. Both shook their heads.

Jack scraped back his chair and went to a wall phone. He called down to communications and posed the same question to one of the operators. The answer was no. Jack walked back to the table and reclaimed his seat.

"Well, well," he said. "Isn't this curious. No new cases."

"I'd say it was good news," Laurie said.

"I'd second that," Chet said.

"Does either of you know any of the internists over at the General?" Jack asked.

"I do," Laurie said. "One of my classmates from medical school is over there."

"How about giving her a call and seeing if they have many meningococcal cases under treatment?" Jack asked.

Laurie shrugged and went to use the same phone Jack had just used.

"I don't like that look in your eye," Chet said.

"I can't help it," Jack said. "Just like with the other outbreaks, little disturbing facts are beginning to appear. We've just autopsied some of the sickest meningococcal patients any of us has ever seen and then, boom! No more cases, as if a faucet had been turned off. It's just what I was talking about earlier."

"Isn't that characteristic of the disease?" Chet asked. "Peaks and valleys."

"Not this fast," Jack said. Then he paused. "Wait a second," he added. "I just thought of something else. We know who the first person was to die in this outbreak, but who was the last?"

"I don't know, but we've got all the folders," Chet said.

Laurie returned. "No meningococcal cases presently," she said. "But the hospital doesn't consider itself out of the woods. They've instituted a massive campaign of vaccination and chemoprophylaxis. Apparently the place is in an uproar."

Both Jack and Chet merely grunted at this news. They were preoccupied with going through the eight folders and jotting down notations on their napkins.

"What on earth are you guys doing?" Laurie asked.

"We're trying to figure out who was the last to die," Jack said.

"What on earth for?" Laurie asked.

"I'm not sure," Jack said.

"This is it," Chet said. "It was Imogene Philbertson."

"Honest?" Jack questioned. "Let me see."

Chet turned around the partially filled-out death certificate that listed the time of death.

"I'll be damned," Jack said.

"Now what?" Laurie asked.

"She was the one who worked in central supply," Jack said.

"Is that significant?" Laurie asked.

Jack pondered for a few minutes, then shook his head. "I don't know," he said. "I'll have to look back at the other outbreaks. As you know, each outbreak has included someone from central supply. I'll see if it is a pattern I'd missed."

"You guys weren't particularly impressed with my news that there are currently no more cases of meningococcal disease over at the General."

"I am," Chet said. "Jack sees it as confirmation of his theories."

"I'm worried it is going to frustrate our hypothetical terrorist," Jack said. "It's also going to teach him an unfortunate lesson."

Both Laurie and Chet rolled their eyes to the ceiling and let out audible groans.

"Come on, you guys," Jack said. "Hear me out. Let's just say for the sake of argument that I'm right about some weirdo spreading these microbes in hopes of starting an epidemic. At first he picks the scariest, most exotic diseases he can think of, but he doesn't know that they won't really spread patient to patient. They are spread by arthropods having access to an infected reservoir. But after a few flops he figures this out and turns to a disease that is spread airborne. But he picks meningococcus. The problem with meningococcus is that it really isn't a patient-to-patient disease either: it's a carrier disease that's mainly spread by an immune individual walking around and giving it to others. So now our weirdo is really frustrated, but he truly knows what he needs. He needs a disease that is spread mainly patient-to-patient by aerosol."

"And what would you choose in this hypothetical scenario?" Chet asked superciliously.

"Let's see," Jack said. He pondered for a moment. "I'd use drug-resistant diphtheria, or maybe even drug-resistant pertussis. Those old standbys are making some devastating comebacks. Or you know what else would be perfect? Influenza! A pathological strain of influenza."

"What an imagination!" Chet commented.

Laurie stood up. "I've got to get back to work," she said. "This conversation is too hypothetical for me."

Chet did the same.

"Hey, isn't anybody going to comment?" Jack said.

"You know how we feel," Chet said. "This is just mental masturbation. It seems like the more you think and talk about this stuff the more you believe it. I mean, really, if it were one disease, okay, but now we're up to four. Where would someone get these microbes? They are not the kind of thing you can go into your neighborhood deli and order. I'll see you upstairs."

Jack watched Laurie and Chet dispose of their trash and leave the lunchroom. He sat for a few moments and considered what Chet had said. Chet had a good point, one that Jack had not even considered. Where would someone get pathological bacteria? He really had no idea.

Jack got up and stretched his legs. After discarding his tray and sandwich wrappings, he followed the others up to the fifth floor. By the time he got to the office, Chet was already engrossed and didn't look up.

Sitting down at his desk, Jack got all the folders together plus his notes and looked up the time of death of each of the women victims from central supply. To date, central supply had lost four people. Jack imagined that the department head would have to be actively recruiting to keep up with that type of attrition.

Next Jack looked up the time of death of each of the other infectious cases. For the times of death of the few he'd not autopsied, he called down to Bart Arnold, the chief PA.

When Jack had all the information it became immediately apparent that with each outbreak, it had been the woman from central supply to be the last to succumb. That suggested, but certainly didn't prove, that in each instance those from central supply were the last to become infected. Jack asked himself what that meant, but couldn't come up with an answer. Still, it was an extremely curious detail.

"I have to go back to the General," Jack said suddenly. He stood up.

Chet didn't even bother to look up. "Do what you have to do," he said with resignation. "Not that my opinion counts."

Jack pulled on his bomber jacket. "Don't take it personally," he said. "I appreciate your concern, but I've got to go. I've got to look into this strange central supply connection. It could just be a coincidence, I agree, but it seems unlikely."

"What about Bingham and what about those gang members Laurie mentioned?" Chet asked. "You're taking a lot of risk."

"Such is life," Jack said. He gave Chet a tap on the shoulder on his way to the hallway. Jack had just reached the threshold when his phone rang. He debated whether to take the time to answer it. It was usually someone from one of the labs.

"Want me to get it?" Chet offered when he saw Jack hesitate.

"No, I'm here, and I might as well," Jack said. He returned to his desk and picked up the receiver.

"Thank God you are there!" Terese said with obvious relief. "I was terrified I wouldn't get you, at least not in time."

"What on earth is the matter?" Jack asked. His pulse quickened. He could tell by the sound of her voice that she was acutely upset.

"There's been a catastrophe," she said. "I have to see you immediately. Can I come over to your office?"

"What happened?" Jack asked.

"I can't talk now," Terese said. "I can't risk it with everything that has happened. I've just got to see you."

"We're sort of in the middle of an emergency ourselves," Jack said. "And I'm just on my way out."

"It's very important," Terese said. "Please!"

Jack immediately relented, especially with Terese's selfless response to his emergency Friday night.

"All right," Jack said. "Since I was just leaving, I'll come to you. Where would you like to meet?"

"Were you going uptown or downtown?" Terese asked.

"Uptown," Jack said.

"Then let's meet at the café where we had coffee on Sunday," Terese said.

"I'll be right there," Jack said.

"Wonderful!" Terese asserted. "I'll be waiting." Then she hung up.

Jack replaced the receiver and self-consciously looked over at Chet. "Did you hear any of that?" Jack asked.

"It was hard not to," Chet said. "What do you think happened?"

"I haven't the faintest idea," Jack said.

True to his word, Jack left immediately. Exiting from the front of the medical examiner facility, he caught a cab on First Avenue. Despite the normal afternoon traffic, he made it uptown in reasonable time.

The café was crowded. He found Terese sitting toward the rear at a small banquette. He took the seat opposite her. She didn't make any motion to get up. She was dressed as usual in a smart suit. Her jaw was clenched. She looked angry.

She leaned forward. "You are not going to believe this," she said in a forced whisper.

"Did the president and the CEO not like your presentation?" Jack asked. It was the only thing he could think of.

Terese made a motion of dismissal with her hand. "I canceled the presentation," she said.

"Why?" Jack asked.

"Because I'd had the sense to schedule an early breakfast with a woman acquaintance at National Health," Terese said. "She's a vice president in marketing who I happened to have gone to Smith College with. I'd had a brainstorm about leaking the campaign to some higher-ups through her. I was so confident. But she shocked me by telling me that under no circumstances would the campaign fly."

"But why?" Jack asked. As much as he disliked medical advertising, he'd considered the ads Terese had come up with the best he'd seen.

"Because National Health is deathly afraid of any reference to nosocomial infections," Terese said angrily. Then she leaned forward again and whispered. "Apparently they have had some of their own trouble lately."

"What kind of trouble?" Jack asked.

"Nothing like the Manhattan General," Terese said. "But serious nonetheless, even with a few deaths. But the real point is that our own account executive people, specifically Helen Robinson and her boss, Robert Barker, knew all this and didn't tell me."

"That's counterproductive," Jack said. "I thought you corporate types were all working toward the same end."

"Counterproductive!" Terese practically shouted, causing the nearby diners to turn their heads. Terese closed her eyes for a moment to collect herself.

" 'Counterproductive' is not the term I'd use," Terese said, keeping her voice down. "The way I'd describe it would make a sailor blush. You see, this was not an oversight. It was done deliberately to make me look bad."

"I'm sorry to hear this," Jack said. "I can see it's upsetting for you."

"That's an understatement," Terese said. "It's the death of my presidential aspirations if I don't come up with an alternative campaign in the next couple of days."

"A couple of days?" Jack questioned. "From what you've shown me about how this process works, that's a mighty tall order."

"Exactly," Terese said. "That's why I had to see you. I need another hook. You came up with this infection idea, or at least you were the source of it. Can you come up with another concept? Something that I can construct an ad campaign around. I'm desperate!"

Jack looked off and tried to think. The irony of the situation didn't escape him; as much as he despised medical advertising, here he was racking his brains for some sort of an idea. He wanted to help; after all, Terese had been so willing to help him.

"The reason I think medical advertising is such a waste of money is that it ultimately has to rely on superficial amenities," he said. "The problem is that without quality being an issue there just isn't enough difference between AmeriCare and National Health or any of the other big conglomerates."

"I don't care," Terese said. "Just give me something I can use."

"Well, the only thing that comes to my mind at the moment is the issue about waiting," Jack said.

"What do you mean, 'waiting'?" Terese asked.

"You know," Jack said. "Nobody likes waiting for the doctor, but everybody does. It's one of those irritating universal annoyances."

"You're right!" Terese said excitedly. "I love it. I can already see a tag line like: No waiting with National Health! Or even better: We wait for you, you don't wait for us! God, that's great! You're a genius at this. How about a job?"

Jack chuckled. "Wouldn't that be a trip," he said. "But I'm having enough trouble with the one I have."

"Is there something wrong?" Terese asked. "What did you mean when you said you were in the middle of an emergency?"

"There's more trouble at the Manhattan General," Jack said. "This time it's an illness caused by meningococcus bacteria. It can be extremely deadly, as it has been in this instance."

"How many cases?"

"Eight," Jack said. "Including a child."

"How awful," Terese said. She was appalled. "Do you think it will spread?"

"I was worried at first," Jack said. "I thought we were going to have a bona fide epidemic on our hands. But the cases just stopped. So far it hasn't spread beyond the initial cohort."

"I hope this isn't going to be kept a secret like whatever killed the people at National Health," Terese said.

"No worry on that account," Jack said. "This episode is no secret. I've heard the hospital is in an uproar. But I'll find out firsthand. I'm on my way over there."

"Oh, no you're not!" Terese commanded. "Is your memory so short that Friday night is already a blur?"

"You sound like several of my colleagues," Jack said. "I appreciate your concern, but I can't stay away. I have a sense that these outbreaks are deliberate, and my conscience won't let me ignore them."

"What about those people who beat you up?" she demanded.

"I'll have to be careful," Jack said.

Terese made a disparaging sound. "Being careful hardly sounds adequate," she said. "It's certainly not consistent with how you described those hoodlums Friday night."

"I'll just have to take my chances and improvise," Jack said. "I'm going over to the General no matter what anybody says."

"What I can't understand is why you are so agitated about these infections. I've read that infectious diseases are generally on the rise."

"That's true," Jack said. "But that's not due to deliberate spread. That's from the injudicious use of antibiotics, urbanization, and the invasion of primeval habitats."

"Give me a break," Terese commented. "I'm concerned about you getting yourself hurt or worse, and you're giving me a lecture."

Jack shrugged. "I'm going to the General," he said.

"Fine, go!" Terese said. She stood up. "You're being that ridiculous hero I was afraid you'd be." Then she softened. "Do what you must, but if you need me, call me."

"I will," Jack said. He watched her hurry out of the restaurant, thinking that she was a bewildering blend of ambition and solicitude. It was no wonder he was confused by her: one minute attracted, the next minute mildly put off.

Jack tossed down the remains of his coffee and stood up. After leaving an appropriate tip, he, too, hurried out of the café.

CHAPTER 24

Jack walked rapidly toward the General. After the conversation with Terese he needed some fresh air. She had a way of agitating him. Not only was she emotionally confusing, but she was also right about the Black Kings. As much as Jack didn't want to think about it, he was taking a chance defying their threat. The questions were: Whom had he irritated enough to send a gang to threaten him, and did the threat confirm his suspicions? Unfortunately there was no way to know. As he'd told Terese, he would have to be careful. The problem with that flippant answer, of course, was that he had no idea with whom he had to be careful. He assumed it would have to be Kelley, Zimmerman, Cheveau, or Abelard because those were the people he'd irritated. The trick was to avoid them all.

As Jack rounded the final corner, it was immediately apparent that things were abnormal at the hospital. Several wooden police sawhorses stood on the sidewalk, and two New York City uniformed policemen lounged on either side of the main door. Jack stopped to watch them for a moment, since they seemed to be spending more time talking with each other than anything else.

Feeling confused about their role, Jack went up to them and asked.

"We were supposed to discourage people from going into the hospital," one officer said. "There was some kind of epidemic in there, but they think it's under control."

"We're really here more for crowd control," the other officer admitted. "They were expecting trouble earlier when they were toying with the idea of quarantining the facility, but things have settled down."

"For that we can all be thankful," Jack said. He started forward, but one of the officers restrained him.

"You sure you want to go in?" he asked.

"Afraid so," Jack said.

The officer shrugged and let Jack pass.

The minute Jack entered through the door he was confronted by a uniformed hospital security officer wearing a surgical mask.

"I'm sorry," the officer said. "No visitors today."

Jack pulled out his medical examiner's badge.

"Sorry, Doctor," the officer said. He stepped aside.

Although calm outside, the inside of the hospital was still in a minor furor. The lobby was filled with people. What gave the scene a surrealistic aura was that everyone was wearing a mask.

With the sudden cessation of new meningococcal cases some twelve hours earlier, Jack was reasonably confident that a mask was superfluous. Yet he wanted one, not so much for protection as for disguise. He asked the security officer if they were available. He was directed to the unmanned information desk, where he found several boxes. Jack took one out and put it on.

Next he located the doctors' coatroom. He entered when one of the staff doctors was exiting. Inside he took off his bomber jacket and searched for an appropriately sized long white coat. When he found one, he put it on, then returned to the lobby.

Jack's destination was central supply. He felt that if he was to learn anything on this visit, it would be there. He got off the elevator on the third floor and was impressed with how much less patient traffic there was than there had been on his visit the previous Thursday. A glance through the glass portal on the OR suite doors told him why. Apparently the OR's had been temporarily shut down. With some knowledge of hospital cash flow, Jack surmised that AmeriCare must be having a financial stroke.

Jack pushed through the swinging doors into central supply. Even there the level of activity was a quarter of what it had been on his first visit. He only saw two women near the end of one of the long aisles between the floor-to-ceiling shelving. Like everyone else he'd seen so far, they were wearing masks. Obviously the hospital was taking this last outbreak particularly seriously.

Avoiding the aisle with the women, Jack set off for Gladys Zarelli's office. She'd been receptive on his first visit, and she was the supervisor. Jack couldn't think of a better person with whom to talk.

As he walked through the department, Jack eyed the myriad hospital supplies and equipment stacked on the shelves. Seeing such a profusion of items made him wonder if there had been anything unique sent from central supply to the index cases. It was an interesting thought, he reasoned, but he couldn't imagine how it would matter. There was still the question of how the women in central supply could have come in contact with the patient and the infecting bacteria. As he'd been told, the employees rarely, if ever, even saw a patient.

Jack found Gladys in her office. She was on the phone, but when she saw him standing at her door, she motioned exuberantly for him to come in. Jack sat down on a straight-back chair opposite her narrow desk. With the size of the office, he could not help overhearing both sides of Gladys's conversation. As he might have imagined, she was busy recruiting.

"Sorry to keep you waiting," she said when she finished her call. Despite her problems she was as affable as the last time Jack had talked with her. "But I'm in desperate need of more help."

Jack reintroduced himself, but Gladys said she'd recognized him despite the mask. So much for the disguise, Jack thought glumly.

"I'm sorry about what's happened," Jack said. "It must be difficult for you for all sorts of reasons."

"It's been terrible," she admitted. "Just terrible. Who would have guessed? Four wonderful people!"

"It's shocking," Jack said. "Especially since it's so unusual. As you said last time I was here, no one in this department had ever caught anything serious before."

Gladys raised her uplifted hands. "What can you do?" she said. "It's in God's hands."

"It might be in God's hands," Jack said. "But usually there is some way to explain this kind of contagion. Have you given it any thought at all?"

Gladys nodded vigorously. "I've thought about it until I was blue in the face," she said. "I don't have a clue. Even if I didn't want to think about it, I've had to because everybody has been asking me the same question."

"Really," Jack said with a twinge of disappointment. He'd had the idea he was exploring virginal territory.

"Dr. Zimmerman was in here right after you on Thursday," Gladys said. "She came with this cute little man who kept sticking his chin out as if his collar button were too tight."

"That sounds like Dr. Clint Abelard," Jack said, realizing he truly was strolling a beaten path.

"That was his name," Gladys said. "He sure could ask a lot of questions. And they've been back each time someone else has gotten sick. That's why we're all wearing our masks. They even had Mr. Eversharp down here from engineering, thinking there might have been something messed up with our air-conditioning system, but apparently that's fine."

"So they haven't come up with any explanation?" Jack said.

"Nope," Gladys said. "Unless they haven't told me. But I doubt that. It's been like Grand Central in here. Used to be no one came. Some of these doctors, though, they're a little strange."

"How so?" Jack asked.

"Just weird," Gladys said. "Like the doctor from the lab. He's come down here plenty of times lately."

"Is that Dr. Cheveau?" Jack asked.

"I think so," Gladys said.

"In what way was he strange?" Jack asked.

"Just unfriendly," Gladys said. She lowered her voice as if telling a secret. "I asked him if I could help him a couple of times, and he bites my head off. He says he just wants to be left alone. But, you know, this is my department. I'm responsible for all this inventory. I don't like people wandering around, even doctors. I had to tell him."

"Who else has been around?" Jack asked.

"A bunch of the bigwigs," Gladys said. "Even Mr. Kelley. Usually I'd only see him at the Christmas party. Last couple of days he's been down here three or four times, always with a bunch of people. Once with that little doctor."

"Dr. Abelard?" Jack asked.

"That's the one," Gladys said. "I can never remember his name."

"I hate to ask you the same questions as the others," Jack said. "But did the women who died perform similar tasks? I mean, did they share some specific job?"

"Like I told you last time," Gladys said, "we all pitch in."

"None of them went up to the patients' rooms who died of the same illnesses?" Jack asked.

"No, nothing like that," Gladys said. "That was the first thing that Dr. Zimmerman checked."

"Last time I was here you printed out a big list of all the stuff that you'd sent up to the seventh floor," Jack said. "Could you make the same list for an individual patient?"

"That would be more difficult," Gladys said. "The order usually comes from the floor, and then it is the floor that enters it into the patient's data."

"Is there any way you could come up with such a list?" Jack asked.

"I suppose," Gladys said. "When we do inventory there is a way of double-checking through billing. I could tell billing I'm doing that kind of check even though we're not officially doing inventory."

"I'd appreciate it," Jack said. He took out one of his cards. "You could either call me or just send it over."

Gladys took the card and examined it. "I'll do anything that might help," she said.

"One other thing," Jack said. "I've had my own run-in with Mr. Cheveau and even a few of the other people around here. I'd appreciate it if this was just between you and me."

"Isn't he weird!" Gladys said. "Sure, I won't tell anybody."

Easing out from in front of Gladys's desk, Jack bid good-bye to the robust woman and exited central supply. He wasn't in the best of moods. After beginning with high expectations, the only thing of note he'd been told was something he already knew: Martin Cheveau was irascible.

Jack pushed the down button at the bank of elevators while he pondered his next move. He had two choices: either he could just leave and minimize his risk, or he could make a careful visit to the lab. Ultimately, he decided in favor of the lab. Chet's comment about the lack of availability of pathological bacteria carried the day, since it had raised a question Jack needed to answer.

When the elevator doors opened, Jack started to board, but then he hesitated. Standing directly in front of the crowded car was Charles Kelley. Jack recognized him instantly despite his mask.

Jack's first impulse was to back away and let the elevator go. But such a move would have only drawn attention. Instead he put his head down, proceeded onto the elevator, and immediately turned to face the closing door. The administrator was standing right behind him. Jack half expected a tap on the shoulder.

Luckily, Kelley had not recognized him. The administrator was deep in conversation with a colleague about how much it was costing the hospital to transport the ER patients by ambulance and the clinic patients by bus to their nearest facility.

Kelley's agitation was palpable. He said their self-imposed semi-quarantine would have to end.

Kelley's companion assured him that everything was being done that could be done, since the city and state regulatory people were all there making an evaluation.

When the doors opened on the second floor, Jack exited with great relief, especially when Kelley didn't get off as well. With such a close call, Jack wondered if he was doing the right thing, but after a moment of indecision he elected to continue with a quick visit to the lab. After all, he was right there.

In contrast to the rest of the hospital, the lab was in full swing. The outer lobby area was thronged with hospital personnel, all of whom were masked.

Jack was confused as to why so many hospital employees were there but thankful because it was easy to blend in with the crowd. With his mask and white lab coat he fit in perfectly. Since Martin's office was just off this main reception, Jack had worried that he'd be apt to run into him. Now he felt the chances were next to nil.

At the far end of the room was a series of cubicles used by the technicians to draw blood or obtain other samples from clinic patients. Near them the crowd concentrated. As Jack wormed his way past this area it dawned on him what was going on. The entire hospital staff was having throat cultures taken.

Jack was impressed. It was an appropriate response to the current outbreak. Since most meningococcal epidemics resulted from a carrier state, there was always a chance the carrier was a hospital employee. It had happened in the past.

A glance into the last cubicle made Jack do a double take. Despite a mask and even a surgical cap, Jack recognized Martin. He literally had his sleeves rolled up as he worked as a technician, swabbing throat after throat. Next to him on a tray the used swabs were piling up in an impressive pyramid. Obviously, everyone in the lab was pitching in.

Feeling even more confident, Jack slipped through the doors into the lab itself. No one paid him any attention. In sharp contrast to the comparative pandemonium in reception, the lab's interior was a study in automated solitude. The only sounds were a muted chorus of mechanical clicks and low-pitched beeps. There were no technicians in sight.

Jack made a beeline for the microbiology section. His hope was to run across either the head tech, Richard, or the vivacious Beth Holderness. But when he arrived he found no one. The micro area appeared as deserted as the rest of the lab.

Jack approached the spot where Beth had been working on his last visit. There he found something encouraging. A Bunsen burner was aflame. Next to it was a tray of throat culture swabs and a large stack of fresh agar plates. On the floor stood a plastic trash barrel brimming with discarded culture tubes.

Sensing that Beth must be in the immediate area, Jack began to explore. The microbiology section was a room about thirty feet square divided by two rows of countertop. Jack walked down the center aisle. Along the back wall were several biosafety cabinets. Jack rounded the lab bench to his right and glanced into a small office. It had a desk and a file cabinet. On a bulletin board he could see some photos. Without going into the room, Jack recognized Richard, the head tech, in several of them.

Moving on, Jack came abreast of several polished aluminum insulated doors that looked like walk-in refrigerators. Glancing over to the opposite side of the room, he saw a regular door that he thought could lead into a storeroom. As he was about to head in that direction one of the insulated doors opened with a loud click that made him jump.

Beth Holderness emerged along with a waft of warm, moist air and nearly collided with Jack. "You scared me to death," she said, pressing a hand to her chest.

"I'm not sure who scared whom more," Jack said. He then reintroduced himself.

"Don't worry, I remember you," Beth said. "You caused quite a stir, and I don't think you should be here."

"Oh?" Jack questioned innocently.

"Dr. Cheveau is really mad at you," Beth said.

"Is he now?" Jack said. "I've noticed he's been rather grumpy."

"He can be cranky," Beth admitted. "But Richard said something about your accusing him of spreading the bacteria that we've been experiencing here at the General."

"Actually, I didn't accuse your boss of anything," Jack said. "It was only an implication I made after he irritated me. I'd come over here just to have a conversation with him. I really wanted his opinion about the plausibility of all these relatively rare illnesses having appeared so close together and at this time of year. But for reasons unknown to me, he was in as inhospitable a mood as he'd been on my previous visit."

"Well, I must admit I was surprised how he treated you the day we met," Beth said. "Same with Mr. Kelley and Dr. Zimmerman. I just thought you were trying to help."

Jack had to restrain himself from giving this lively young woman a hug. It seemed as if she were the only person on the planet who appreciated what he was doing.

"I was so sorry about your co-worker, Nancy Wiggens," Jack said. "I imagine it's been difficult for you all."

Beth's cheerful face clouded over to the point just shy of tears.

"Maybe I shouldn't have said anything," Jack said when he noticed her reaction.

"It's all right," Beth managed. "But it was a terrible shock. We all worry about such a thing, but hope it will never happen. She was such a warm person, although she could be a bit reckless."

"How so?" Jack asked.

"She just wasn't as careful as she should have been," Beth said. "She took chances, like not using one of the hoods when it was indicated or not wearing her goggles when she was supposed to."

Jack could understand that attitude.

"She didn't even take the antibiotic Dr. Zimmerman prescribed for her after the plague case," Beth said.

"How unfortunate," Jack said. "That might have protected her against the Rocky Mountain spotted fever."

"I know," Beth said. "I wish that I had tried harder to convince her. I mean, I took it, and I don't think I was exposed."

"Did she happen to say she did anything different when she got samples from Lagenthorpe?" Jack asked.

"No, she didn't," Beth said. "That's why we feel she was exposed down here in the lab when she processed the samples. Rickettsia are notoriously dangerous in the lab."

Jack was about to respond when he noticed that Beth had begun to fidget and look over his shoulder. Jack glanced in the direction she was looking, but there was no one there.

"I really should be getting back to work," Beth said. "And I shouldn't be talking with you. Dr. Cheveau told us specifically."

"Don't you find that strange?" Jack said. "After all, I am a medical examiner in this city. Legally I have a right to investigate the deaths of the patients assigned to us."

"I guess I do," Beth admitted. "But what can I say? I just work here." She stepped around Jack and went back to her workstation.

Jack followed her. "I don't mean to be a pest," he said. "But my intuition tells me something weird is going on here; that's why I keep coming back. A number of people have been acting defensive, including your boss. Now there could be an explanation. AmeriCare and this hospital are a business, and these outbreaks have been tremendously disruptive economically. That's reason enough for people to be acting strangely. But from my point of view it's more than that."

"So what do you want from me?" Beth asked. She'd taken her seat and gone back to transferring the throat cultures to the agar plates.

"I'd like to ask you to look around," Jack said. "If pathological bacteria are being deliberately spread they have to come from somewhere, and the microbiology lab would be a good place to start looking. I mean, the equipment is here to store and handle the stuff. It's not as if plague bacteria is something you'd find anywhere."

"It wouldn't be so strange to find it on occasion in any standard lab," Beth said.

"Really?" Jack questioned. He'd assumed that outside of the CDC and maybe a few academic centers, plague bacteria would be a rarity.

"Intermittently labs have to get cultures of all different bacteria to test the efficacy of their reagents," Beth said as she continued to work. "Antibodies, which are often the main ingredient in many modern reagents, can deteriorate, and if they do the tests would give false negatives."

"Oh, of course," Jack said. He felt stupid. He should have remembered all this. All laboratory tests had to be constantly checked.

"Where do you get something like plague bacteria?"

"From National Biologicals in Virginia," Beth said.

"What's the process for getting it?" Jack asked.

"Just call up and order it," Beth said.

"Who can do that?" Jack asked.

"Anybody," Beth said.

"You're joking," Jack said. Somehow he'd thought the security at a minimum would be comparable to that involved in getting a controlled drug like morphine.

"I'm not joking," Beth said. "I've done it many times."

"You don't need some special permit?" Jack asked.

"I have to get the signature of the director of the lab on the purchase order," Beth said. "But that's just to guarantee that the hospital will pay for it."

"So let me get this straight," Jack said. "Anyone can call these people up and have plague sent to them?"

"As long as their credit is okay," Beth said.

"How do the cultures come?" Jack said.

"Usually by mail," Beth said. "But if you pay extra and need it faster you can get overnight service."

Jack was appalled, but he tried to hide his reaction. He was embarrassed at his own naveté. "Do you have this organization's phone number?" he asked.

Beth pulled open a file drawer to her immediate right, leafed through some files, and pulled out a folder. Opening it up, she took out a sheet and indicated the letterhead.

Jack wrote the number down. Then he pointed to the phone. "Do you mind?" he asked.

Beth pushed the phone in his direction but glanced up at the clock as she did so.

"I'll just be a second," Jack said. He still couldn't believe what he'd just been told.

Jack dialed the number. The phone was answered and a recording gave him the name of the company and asked him to make a selection. Jack pressed two for sales. Presently a charmingly friendly voice came on the line and asked if she could be of assistance.

"Yes," Jack said. "This is Dr. Billy Rubin and I'd like to place an order."

"Do you have an account with National Biologicals?" the woman asked.

"Not yet," Jack said. "In fact, for this order I'd just like to use my American Express card."

"I'm sorry, but we only accept Visa or MasterCard," the woman said.

"No problem," Jack said. "Visa will be fine."

"Okay," the woman said cheerfully. "Could I have your first order?"

"How about some meningococcus," Jack said.

The woman laughed. "You'll have to be more specific," she said. "I need the serologic group, the serotype, and the subtype. We have hundreds of meningococcus subspecies."

"Uh-oh!" Jack said, pretending to have been suddenly paged. "An emergency has just come up! I'm afraid I'll have to call back."

"No problem," the woman said. "Call anytime. As you know, we're here twenty-four hours a day to serve your culture needs."

Jack hung up the phone. He was stunned.

"I have the feeling you didn't believe me," Beth said.

"I didn't," Jack admitted. "I didn't realize the availability of these pathogens. But I'd still like you to look around here and see if these offending bugs might somehow be stashed here now. Could you do that?"

"I suppose," Beth said without her usual enthusiasm.

"But I want you to be discreet," Jack said. "And careful. I want this just between you and me."

Jack took out one of his cards and wrote his home number on the back. He handed it to her. "You can call me anytime, day or night, if you find anything or if you get into any trouble because of me. Okay?"

Beth took the card, examined it briefly, and then stuck it into her lab coat pocket. "Okay," she said.

"Would you mind if I asked for your number?" Jack said. "I might have some more questions myself. Obviously microbiology isn't my forte."

Beth thought for a moment, then relented. She got out a piece of paper and wrote her phone number down. She handed it to Jack, who put it into his wallet.

"I think you'd better go now," she said.

"I'm on my way," Jack said. "Thanks for your help."

"You're welcome," Beth said. She was her old self again.

Preoccupied, Jack walked out of the microbiology section and headed across the main portion of the lab. He still couldn't believe how easy it was to order pathological cultures.

About twenty feet from the double swinging doors that connected the lab to the reception area, Jack stopped dead in his tracks. Backing through the doors was a figure that looked alarmingly like Martin. The individual was carrying a tray loaded with prepared throat swabs ready for plating.

Jack felt like a criminal caught in the act. For a fraction of a second he contemplated fleeing or trying to hide. But there was no time. Besides, irritation at the absurdity of his fear of being recognized inspired him to stand his ground.

Martin held the door open for a second figure Jack recognized as Richard. He, too, was carrying a tray of throat swabs. It was Richard who saw Jack first.

Martin was a quick second. He recognized Jack immediately, despite the mask.

"Hi, folks," Jack said.

"You . . . !" Martin cried.

"It is I," Jack said cheerfully. He grabbed the end of his face mask with his thumb and forefinger and pulled it away from his face to give Martin an unobstructed look.

"You've been warned about sneaking around in here," Martin snapped. "You're trespassing."

"Not so," Jack said. He produced his medical examiner badge and pointed it toward Martin's face. "Just making an official site visit. There've been a few more regrettable infectious deaths over here at the General. At least this time you were able to make the diagnosis on your own."

"We'll see whether this is a legitimate site visit," Martin said. He heaved the tray of throat swabs onto the countertop and snatched up the nearest phone. He told the operator to put him through to Charles Kelley.

"Couldn't we just discuss this like grown-ups?" Jack asked.

Martin ignored the question as he waited for Kelley.

"Out of curiosity, maybe you could just tell me why you were so accommodating on my first visit and so nasty on my next," Jack said.

"In the interim Mr. Kelley informed me what your attitude had been on that first day," Martin said. "And he told me he had learned that you were here without authorization."

Jack was about to respond when it became clear that Kelley had come on the line. Martin informed the administrator that he'd again found Dr. Stapleton lurking in the lab.

While Martin listened to an apparent monologue from Kelley, Jack moved over and leaned casually against the nearest countertop. Richard, on the other hand, stood rooted in place, still supporting his tray of throat swabs.

Martin punctuated Kelley's apparent tirade with a few strategically placed yeses and a final "Yes sir!" at the end of the conversation. As he hung up the phone he treated Jack to a supercilious smile.

"Mr. Kelley told me to inform you," Martin said haughtily, "that he will be personally calling the mayor's office, the Commissioner of Health, and your chief. He'll be lodging a formal complaint concerning your harassment of this hospital while we've been making every effort to deal with a state of emergency. He also told me to inform you that our security will be up here in a few moments to escort you off the premises."

"That's terribly considerate of him," Jack said. "But I really don't need to be shown the way out. In fact, I was on my way when we happened to bump into each other. Good day, gentlemen."

CHAPTER 25

MONDAY, 3:15 P.M., MARCH 25, 1996

"So there you have it," Terese said as she looked out on the expanded team of creatives for the National Health account. In the present emergency she and Colleen had pulled key people away from other projects. Right now they needed all the man- and womanpower they could muster to concentrate on the new campaign.

"Any questions?" Terese asked. The entire group was squeezed into Colleen's office. With no room to sit they were wedged in like sardines, cheek by jowl. Terese had outlined the "no wait" idea in an expanded form that she and Colleen had devised based on Jack's initial suggestion.

"We only have two days for this?" Alice questioned.

"I'm afraid so," Terese said. "I might be able to squeeze out another day, but we can't count on it. We've got to go for broke."

There was a murmur of incredulity.

"I know I'm asking a lot," Terese said. "But the fact of the matter is, as I've told you, we were sabotaged by the accounts department. We've even got confirmation that they are expecting to present a 'talking heads' spot with one of the *ER* stars. They are counting on us to self-destruct with the old idea."

"Actually I think the 'no wait' concept is better than the 'cleanliness' concept," Alice said. "The 'cleanliness' idea was getting too technical with that asepsis malarkey. People are going to understand 'no waiting' much better."

"There's also a lot more opportunity for humor," another voice commented.

"I like it too," someone else said. "I hate waiting for the gynecologist. By the time I get in there I'm as tense as a banjo wire."

A wave of tension-relieving laughter rippled through the group.

"That's the spirit," Terese said. "Let's get to work. Let's show them what we can do when our backs are against the wall."

People started to leave, eager to get to their drawing boards.

"Hold up!" Terese shouted over the buzz of voices that had erupted. "One other thing. This has to stay quiet. Don't even tell other creatives unless absolutely necessary. I don't want accounts to have any inkling of what's going on. Okay?"

A murmur of agreement arose.

"All right!" Terese yelled. "Get to it!"

The room emptied as if there had been a fire. Terese flopped back into Colleen's chair, exhausted from the emotional effort of the day. Typical of her life in advertising, she'd started out that morning on a high, then sank to a new low, and was now somewhere in between.

"They're enthusiastic," Colleen said. "You made a great presentation. I kind of wish someone from National Health were here."

"At least it's a good idea for a campaign," Terese said. "The question is whether they can put it together enough for a real presentation."

"They'll certainly give it their best shot," Colleen said. "You really motivated them."

"God, I hope so," Terese said. "I can't let Barker have a free field with his stupid 'talking heads' junk. That's like taking advertising back to pre-Bernbach days. It would be an embarrassment for the agency if the client liked it, and we had to actually do it."

"God forbid," Colleen said.

"We'll be out of a job if that happens," Terese said.

"Let's not get too pessimistic," Colleen warned.

"Ah, what a day," Terese complained. "On top of everything else I've got to worry about Jack."

"How so?" Colleen asked.

"When I met with him and he gave me the 'no wait' idea he told me he was going back to the General."

"Uh-oh," Colleen said. "Isn't that where those gang members warned him against going?"

"Exactly," Terese said. "Talk about a Taurus, he's the epitome. He's so damn bullheaded and reckless. He doesn't have to go over there. They have people at the medical examiner's office whose job it is to go out to hospitals. It must be some male thing, like he has to be a hero. I don't understand it."

"Are you starting to get attached to him?" Colleen asked gingerly, aware it was a touchy subject with Terese. Colleen knew enough about her boss to know that she eschewed romantic entanglements, though she had no idea why.

Terese only sighed. "I'm attracted to him and put off by him at the same time," she said. "He got me to open up a little, and apparently I coaxed him out a little too. I think both of us felt good talking to someone who seemed to care."

"That sounds encouraging," Colleen said.

Terese shrugged, then smiled. "We're both carrying around a lot of emotional baggage," she said. "But enough about me. How about you and Chet?"

"It's going great," Colleen said. "I could really fall for that guy."

Jack felt as if he were sitting through the same movie for the third time. Once again he was literally on Bingham's carpet enduring a protracted tirade about how his chief had been called by every major civil servant in the city to complain bitterly about Jack Stapleton.

"So what do you have to say for yourself?" Bingham demanded, finally running out of steam with his ranting. He was literally out of breath.

"I don't know what to say," Jack admitted. "But in my defense, I haven't gone over there with the intention of irritating people. I was just looking for information. There's a lot about this series of outbreaks that I don't understand."

"You're a goddamn paradox," Bingham remarked as he visibly calmed down. "At the same time you've been such a pain in the butt you've made some commendable diagnoses. I was impressed when Calvin told me about the tularemia and the Rocky Mountain spotted fever. It's like you're two different people. What am I to do?"

"Fire the irritating one and keep the other?" Jack suggested.

Bingham grunted a reluctant chuckle, but any sign of amusement quickly faded. "The main problem from my perspective," he grumbled, "is that you are so god-damned contumacious. You've specifically disobeyed my orders to stay away from the General, not once but twice."

"I'm guilty," Jack said, raising his hands as if to surrender.

"Is all this motivated by that personal vendetta you have against AmeriCare?" Bingham demanded.

"No," Jack said. "That was a minor factor to begin with, but my interest in the matter has gone way beyond that. I told you last time that I thought something strange was going on. I feel even more strongly now, and the people over there are continuing to act defensive."

"Defensive?" Bingham questioned querulously. "I was told that you accused the General's lab director of spreading these illnesses."

"That story has been blown way out of proportion," Jack said. He then explained to Bingham that he'd merely implied as much by reminding the lab director that he, the director, was disgruntled about the budget AmeriCare was giving him.

"The man was acting like an ass," Jack added. "I was trying to ask his opinion about the possible intentional spread of these illnesses, but he never gave me a chance, and I got mad at him. I suppose I shouldn't have said what I did, but sometimes I can't help myself."

"So you're convinced about this idea yourself?" Bingham asked.

"I don't know if I'm convinced," Jack admitted. "But it is hard to ascribe them all to coincidence. On top of that is the way people at the General have been acting, from the administrator on down." Jack thought about telling Bingham about his being beaten up and threatened, but he decided against it. He feared it might get him grounded altogether.

"After Commissioner Markham called me," Bingham said, "I asked her to have the chief epidemiologist, Dr. Abelard, get in touch with me." When he did, I asked him what he thought of this intentional spread idea. You want to know what he said?"

"I can't wait," Jack said.

"He said except for the plague case, which he still cannot explain but is working on with the CDC, he feels the others all have very reasonable explanations. The Hard woman had been in contact with wild rabbits, and Mr. Lagenthorpe had been out in the desert in Texas. And as far as meningococcus is concerned, it's the season for that."

"I don't think the time sequences are correct," Jack said. "Nor are the clinical courses consistent with—"

"Hold on," Bingham interrupted. "Let me remind you that Dr. Abelard is an epidemiologist. He's got a Ph.D. as well as an M.D. His whole job is to figure out the where and the why of disease."

"I don't doubt his credentials," Jack said. "Just his conclusions. He didn't impress me from the start."

"You certainly are opinionated," Bingham said.

"I might have ruffled feathers on past visits to the General," Jack admitted, "but this time all I did was talk to the supervisor of central supply and one of the microbiology techs."

"From the calls I got you were deliberately hampering their efforts to deal with the meningococcal outbreak," Bingham said.

"God is my witness," Jack said, holding up his hand. "All I did was talk to

Ms. Zarelli and Ms. Holderness, who happen to be two pleasant, cooperative people."

"You do have a way of rubbing people the wrong way," Bingham said. "I suppose you know that."

"Usually, I only have that effect on those I intend to provoke," Jack said.

"I get the feeling I'm one of those people," Bingham snapped.

"Quite the contrary," Jack said. "Irritating you is entirely unintentional."

"I wouldn't have known," Bingham said.

"In speaking with Ms. Holderness, the lab tech, I did uncover an interesting fact," Jack said. "I learned that just about anyone with reasonable credit can call up and order pathological bacteria. The company doesn't do any background check."

"You don't need a license or a permit?" Bingham asked.

"Apparently not," Jack said.

"I suppose I'd never thought about it," Bingham said.

"Nor had I," Jack said. "Needless to say, thought-provoking."

"Indeed," Bingham said. He appeared to ponder this for a moment as his rheumy eyes glazed over. But then they quickly cleared.

"Seems to me you've managed to get this conversation off track," he said, regaining his gruff posture. "The issue here is what to do with you."

"You could always send me on vacation to the Caribbean," Jack suggested. "It's nice down there this time of year."

"Enough of your impertinent humor," Bingham snapped. "I'm trying to be serious with you."

"I'll try to control myself," Jack said. "My problem is that during the last five years of my life cynicism has led to reflex sarcasm."

"I'm not going to fire you," Bingham announced. "But I've got to warn you again, you've come very close. In fact when I hung up the phone from the mayor's office, I was going to let you go. I've changed my mind for now. But there is one thing that we have to be clear on: You are to stay away from the General. Do we have an understanding?"

"I think it's finally getting through," Jack said.

"If you need more information, send the PAs," Bingham said. "For chrissake that's what they're here for."

"I'll try to remember that," Jack said.

"All right, get out of here," Bingham said with a sweep of his hand.

With relief Jack stood up and left Bingham's office. He went straight up to his own. When he arrived he found Chet talking with George Fontworth. Jack squeezed by the two of them and draped his coat over the back of his chair.

"Well?" Chet asked.

"Well what?" Jack asked back.

"The daily question," Chet said. "Are you still employed here?"

"Very funny," Jack said. He was perplexed by the stack of four large manila envelopes at the center of his desk. He picked one up. It was about two inches thick. There were no markings on the exterior. Opening the latch, he slid out the contents. It was a copy of Susanne Hard's hospital chart.

"You've seen Bingham?" Chet asked.

"I just came from there," Jack said. "He was sweet. He wanted to commend me on my diagnoses of tularemia and Rocky Mountain spotted fever."

"Bull!" Chet exclaimed.

"Honest," Jack said with a chuckle. "Of course, he also bawled me out for going over to the General." While Jack was talking, he took the contents out of all the manila envelopes. He now had copies of the hospital charts of the index cases of each outbreak.

"Was your visit worth it?" Chet asked.

"What do you mean, 'worth it'?" Jack asked.

"Did you learn enough to justify stirring up the pot once more?" Chet said. "We heard you got everyone over there angry again."

"Not a lot of secrets around here," Jack commented. "But I did learn something that I didn't know." Jack explained to Chet and George about the ease of ordering pathological bacteria.

"I knew that," George said. "I worked in a micro lab during summers while I was in college. I remember the supervisor ordering a cholera culture. When it came in I picked it up and held it. It gave me a thrill."

Jack glanced at George. "A thrill?" he questioned. "You're weirder than I thought."

"Seriously," George said. "I know other people who had the same reaction. Comprehending how much pain, suffering, and death the little buggers had caused and could cause was both scary and stimulating at the same time, and holding it in my hand just blew me away."

"I guess my idea of a thrill and yours are a bit different," Jack said. He went back to the charts and organized them chronologically so that Nodelman was on top.

"I hope the mere availability of pathological bacteria doesn't encourage your paranoid thinking," Chet said. "I mean, that's hardly proof of your theory."

"Umm hmm," Jack murmured. He was already beginning to go over the charts. He planned to read through them rapidly to see if anything jumped out at him. Then he would go back over them in detail. What he was looking for was any way the cases could have been related that would suggest they were not random occurrences.

Chet and George went back to their conversation when it was apparent Jack was preoccupied. Fifteen minutes later George got up and left. As soon as he did Chet went to the door and closed it.

"Colleen called me a little while ago," he said.

"I'm happy for you," Jack said, still trying to concentrate on the charts.

"She told me what had happened over there at the agency," Chet said. "I think it stinks. I can't imagine one part of the same company undermining another. It doesn't make sense."

Jack looked up from his reading. "It's the business mentality," he said. "Lust for power is the major motivator."

Chet sat down. "Colleen also told me that you gave Terese a terrific idea for a new campaign."

"Don't remind me," Jack said. He redirected his attention to the charts. "I really don't want to be a part of it. I don't know why she asked me. She knows how I feel about medical advertising."

"Colleen also said that you and Terese are hitting it off," Chet said.

"Really now?" Jack said.

"She said that you two had gotten each other to open up. I think that is terrific for both of you."

"Did she give any specifics?" Jack asked.

"I didn't get the sense she had any specifics," Chet said.

"Thank God," Jack said without looking up.

When Jack answered Chet's next few questions with mere grunts, it dawned on Chet that Jack was again engrossed in his reading. Chet gave up trying to have a conversation and turned his attention to his own work.

By five-thirty Chet was ready to call it a day. He got up and stretched noisily, hoping that Jack would respond. Jack didn't. In fact, Jack had not moved for the last hour or so except to turn pages and jot down more notes.

Chet got his coat from the top drawer of his file cabinet and cleared his throat several times. Still Jack did not respond. Finally Chet resorted to speech.

"Hey, old sport," Chet called out. "How long are you going to work on that stuff?"

"Until I'm done," Jack said without looking up.

"I'm meeting Colleen for a quick bite," Chet said "We're meeting at six. Are you interested? Maybe Terese could join us. Apparently they are planning to work most of the night."

"I'm sticking here," Jack said. "Enjoy yourselves. Say hello for me."

Chet shrugged, pulled on his coat, and left.

Jack had been through the charts twice. So far the only genuine similarity among the four cases was the fact that their infectious disease symptoms had started after they had been admitted for other complaints. But as Laurie had pointed out, by definition, only Nodelman was a nosocomial case. In the other three situations the symptoms had come on within forty-eight hours of admission.

The only other possible similarity was the one that Jack had already considered: namely that all four patients were people who'd been hospitalized frequently and hence were economically undesirable in a capitated system. But other than that, Jack found nothing.

The ages ranged from twenty-eight to sixty-three. Two had been on the medical ward, one in OB-GYN, and one in orthopedics. There were no medications common to them all. Two were on "keep open" IVs. Socially they ranged from lower- to upper-middle class, and there was no indication that any of the four knew any of the others. There was one female and three males. Even their blood types differed.

Jack tossed his pen onto his desk and leaned back in his chair to stare at the ceiling. He didn't know what he expected from the charts, but so far he hadn't learned anything.

"Knock, knock," a voice called.

Jack turned to see Laurie standing in the doorway.

"I see you made it back from your foray to the General," she said.

"I don't think I was in any danger until I got back here," Jack said.

"I know what you mean," Laurie said. "Rumor had it that Bingham was fit to be tied."

"He wasn't happy, but we managed to work it out," Jack said.

"Are you worried about the threat from the people who beat you up?" Laurie asked.

"I suppose," Jack said. "I haven't thought too much about it. I'm sure I'll feel differently when I get to my apartment."

"You're welcome to come over to mine," Laurie said. "I have a sad couch in my living room that pulls out into a decent bed."

"You're kind to offer," Jack said. "But I have to go home sometime. I'll be careful."

"Did you learn anything to explain the central supply connection?" Laurie asked.

"I wish," Jack said. "Not only didn't I learn anything, but I found out that a number of people, including the city epidemiologist and the hospital infection control officer, have been in there beating the bushes for clues. I had the mistaken notion it was a novel idea."

"Are you still thinking of the conspiracy slant?" Laurie asked.

"In some form or fashion," Jack admitted. "Unfortunately, it seems to be a lonely stance."

Laurie wished him good luck. He thanked her, and she left. A minute later she was back.

"I'm planning on getting a bite on the way home," Laurie said. "Are you interested?"

"Thanks, but I've started on these charts, and I want to keep at it while the material is fresh in my mind."

"I understand. Good night."

"Good night, Laurie," Jack said.

No sooner had Jack opened Nodelman's chart for the third time than the phone rang. It was Terese.

"Colleen is about to leave to meet up with Chet," Terese said. "Can I talk you into coming out for a quick dinner? We could all eat together."

Jack was amazed. For five years he'd been avoiding social attachments of any kind. Now suddenly two intelligent, attractive women were both asking him to dine with them on the same night.

"I appreciate the offer," Jack said. He then told Terese the same thing he'd told Laurie about the charts he was working on.

"I keep hoping you'll give up on that crusade," Terese said. "It hardly seems worth the risks, since you've already been beaten up and threatened with the loss of your job."

"If I can prove someone is behind this affair it will certainly be worth the risks," Jack said. "My fear is that there might be a real epidemic."

"Chet seems to think you're acting foolishly," Terese persisted.

"He's entitled to his opinion," Jack said.

"Please be careful when you go home," Terese intoned.

"I will," Jack said. He was getting weary of everyone's solicitude. The danger of going home that evening was something he'd considered as early as that morning.

"We'll be working most of the night," she added. "If you need to call, call me at work."

"Okay," Jack said. "Good luck."

"Good luck to you," Terese said. "And thanks for this 'no waiting' idea. Everyone loves it so far. I'm very grateful. 'Bye!"

Jack went back to Nodelman's chart as soon as he put the phone down. He was attempting to get through the reams of nurses' notes. But after five minutes of reading the same paragraph over and over, he acknowledged he wasn't concentrating. His mind kept mulling over the irony of both Laurie and Terese asking him to dine with them. Thinking about the two women led to pondering again the similarities and differences in their personalities, and once he started thinking about personality, Beth Holderness popped into his mind. As soon as he thought about Beth, he began musing about the ease of ordering bacteria.

Jack closed Nodelman's chart and drummed his fingers on his desk. He began to wonder. If someone had obtained a culture of a pathological bacteria from National Biologicals and then intentionally spread it to people, could National Biologicals tell it had been their bacteria?

The idea intrigued him. With the advances in DNA technology he thought it was scientifically possible for National Biologicals to tag their cultures, and for reasons of both liability and economic protection, he thought it was a reasonable thing to do. The question then became whether they did it or not.

Jack searched for the phone number. Once he found it, he put through a second call to the organization.

Early that afternoon on Jack's first call he'd pressed "two" for sales. This time he pressed "three" for "support." After being forced to listen to a rock music station for a few minutes, Jack heard a youthful-sounding male voice give his name, Igor Krasnyansky, and ask how he could be of assistance.

Jack introduced himself properly on this occasion and inquired if he could pose a theoretical question.

"Of course," Igor said with a slight Slavic accent. "I will try to answer."

"If I had a culture of bacteria," Jack began, "is there any way that I could determine that it had originally come from your company even if it had gone through several passages in vivo?"

"That's an easy one," Igor said. "We phage-type all our cultures. So, sure, you could tell it came from National Biologicals."

"What's the identification process?" Jack asked.

"We have a fluorescein-labeled DNA probe," Igor said. "It's very simple."

"If I wanted to make such an identification, would I have to send the sample to you?" Jack asked.

"Either that or I could send you some of the probe," Igor said.

Jack was pleased. He gave his address and asked for the probe to be shipped via overnight express. He said he wanted it as soon as possible.

Hanging up the phone, Jack felt pleased with himself. He thought he'd come up with something that might lend considerable weight to his theory of intentional spread if any of the patients' bacteria tested positive.

Jack looked down at the charts and considered giving up on them for the time being. After all, if the opposite turned out to be the case, and none of the bacteria was from National Biologicals, perhaps he would have to rethink the whole affair.

Jack scraped back his chair and stood up. He'd had enough for one day. Pulling on his jacket, he prepared to head home. Suddenly the idea of some vigorous exercise had a strong appeal.

CHAPTER 26

MONDAY, 6:00 P.M., MARCH 25, 1996

Beth Holderness had stayed late to get all the throat cultures of the hospital employees planted. The evening crew had come in at the usual time, but at that moment they were down in the cafeteria having their dinner. Even Richard had disappeared, although Beth wasn't sure if he'd left for the day or not.

Since the micro section of the lab was deserted except for her, Beth thought that if she were to do any clandestine searching, this was as good a time as any. Sliding off her stool, she walked over to the door to the main part of the lab. She didn't see a soul, which encouraged her further.

Turning back to microbiology, Beth headed over to the insulated doors. She wasn't sure she should be doing what she was doing, but having said she would, she felt some obligation. She was confused about Dr. Jack Stapleton, but she was even more confused about her own boss, Dr. Martin Cheveau. He'd always been temperamental, but lately that moodiness had reached ridiculous proportions.

That afternoon he'd stormed in after Dr. Stapleton had left, demanding to know what she had told the medical examiner. Beth had tried to say that she'd told him nothing of consequence and had tried to get him to leave, but Dr. Cheveau wouldn't listen. He even threatened to fire Beth for willfully disobeying him. His ranting had brought her close to tears.

After he'd left Beth had thought about Dr. Stapleton's comment that people at the hospital, including her boss, had been acting defensively. Considering Dr. Cheveau's behavior, she'd thought Dr. Stapleton might be right. It made her even more willing to follow up on Dr. Stapleton's request.

Beth stood in front of the two insulated doors. The one on the left was the walk-in freezer, the other the walk-in incubator. She debated which one to search first. Since she'd been in and out of the incubator all day with the throat cultures, she decided to tackle that first. After all, there was only a small area in the incubator where the contents were unfamiliar to her.

Beth pulled open the door and entered. Immediately she was enveloped by the moist, warm air. The temperature was kept close to body temperature, at 98.6° Fahrenheit. Many bacteria and viruses, especially those that affected humans, had understandably evolved to grow best at human body temperature.

The door behind Beth closed automatically to seal in the heat. The compartment was about eight by ten. The lighting came from two bulbs covered with wire mesh mounted on the ceiling. The shelving was perforated stainless steel. It extended floor to ceiling on both walls, along the back, and down the center, creating two narrow aisles.

Beth made her way to the rear of the compartment. There were stainless-steel boxes back there that she'd seen on numerous occasions but had never examined.

Grasping one of the boxes with both hands, Beth slid it out from its shelf and put it on the floor. It was about the size of a shoe box. When she tried to open it, she realized it had a latch that was secured with a miniature padlock!

Beth was amazed and instantly suspicious. Few things in the lab were kept under lock and key. Picking the box up, Beth slid it back into place. Moving along the shelf, she reached around each box in turn. Every one of them had the same type of lock.

Bending down, Beth did the same on the lower shelf. The condition of the fifth box was different. As Beth stuck her hand around its back, she could feel that the padlock's clasp had not been closed.

Insinuating her fingers between the unlocked box and its neighbors, Beth was able to slide it out. As she lifted it, she could tell it wasn't quite as heavy as the first locked box; she feared it would be empty. But it wasn't. As she lifted its cover, she saw that it contained a few petri dishes. She also noted that the petri dishes did not bear the customary label that was used in the lab. Instead they only had grease-pencil alphanumeric designators.

Beth gingerly reached into the box and lifted out a petri dish labeled A-81. She lifted the top and looked in at expanding bacterial colonies. They were transparent and mucoid and they were growing on a medium she recognized as chocolate agar.

A sharp mechanical click of the insulated door opening startled Beth. Her pulse raced. Like a child caught in a forbidden act, she frantically tried to get the petri dish back in the box and the box back on the shelf before whoever was entering saw what she was doing.

Unfortunately, there wasn't enough time. She'd only had a chance to close the box and pick it up before she found herself face-to-face with Dr. Martin Cheveau. Ironically, he was at that moment carrying a box identical to the one she was holding.

"What are you doing?" he snarled.

"I'm . . ." Beth voiced, but that was all she could say. Under the pressure of the circumstance, no potential explanation came to mind.

Dr. Cheveau noisily stashed his box on one of the shelves, then grabbed Beth's away from her. He looked at the open latch.

"Where's the lock?" he growled.

Beth extended her hand and then opened it. In her palm was the open padlock. Martin snatched it and examined it.

"How did you get it open?" he demanded.

"It was open," Beth asserted.

"You're lying," Martin snapped.

"I'm not," Beth said. "Honest. It was open and it made me curious."

"Likely story," Martin yelled. His voice reverberated around the confined space.

"I didn't disturb anything," Beth said.

"How do you know you didn't disturb anything?" Martin said. He opened the box and glanced inside. Seemingly satisfied, he closed it and locked it. He tested the lock. It held.

"I only lifted the cover and looked at one culture dish," Beth said. She was beginning to regain some composure, although her pulse was still racing.

Martin slipped the box into its position. Then he counted them all. When he was finished, he ordered her out of the incubator.

"I'm sorry," Beth said after Martin had closed the insulated door behind them. "I didn't know that I wasn't supposed to touch those boxes."

At that moment Richard appeared in the doorway. Martin ordered him over, then angrily related how he'd caught Beth handling his research cultures.

Richard acted as upset as Martin when he heard. Turning to Beth, he demanded to know why she would do such a thing. He wondered whether they weren't giving her enough work to do.

"No one told me not to touch them," Beth protested. She was again close to tears. She hated confrontations and had already weathered a previous one only hours earlier.

"No one told you to handle them either," Richard snapped.

"Did that Dr. Stapleton put you up to this?" Martin demanded.

Beth hesitated, not knowing how to respond. As far as Martin was concerned her hesitation was incriminating. "I thought as much," he snapped. "He probably even told you about his preposterous idea that the plague cases and the others were started on purpose."

"I told him I wasn't supposed to talk with him," Beth cried.

"But talk he did," Martin said. "And obviously you listened. Well, I'm not going to stand for it. You are fired, Miss Holderness. Take your things and get out. I don't want to see your face again."

Beth sputtered a protest and with it came tears.

"Crying is not going to get you anywhere," Martin spat out. "Nor are excuses. You made your choice, now live with the consequences. Get out."

Twin reached across the scarred desk and hung up the phone. His real name was Marvin Thomas. He'd gotten the nickname "Twin" because he'd had an identical twin. No one had been able to tell the two of them apart until one of them got killed in a protracted disagreement between the Black Kings and a gang from the East Village over crack territories.

Twin looked across the desk at Phil. Phil was tall and skinny and hardly imposing, but he had brains. It had been his brains, not his bravado or muscles, that had caused Twin to elevate him to number-two man in the gang. He had been the only person to know what to do with all the drug money they'd been raking in. Up until Phil took over, they'd been burying the greenbacks in PVC pipe in the basement of Twin's tenement.

"I don't understand these people," Twin said. "Apparently that honky doctor didn't get our message, and he's been out doing just what he damned well pleases. Can you believe it? I hit that sucker with just about everything I got, and three days later he's giving us the finger. I don't call that respect, no way."

"The people want us to talk to him again?" Phil asked. He'd been on the visit to Jack's apartment and witnessed how hard Twin had hit the man.

"Better than that," Twin said. "They want us to ice the bastard. Why they didn't have us do it the first time is anybody's guess. They're offering us five big ones." Twin laughed. "Funny thing is, I would have done it for nothing. We can't have people ignoring us. We'd be out of business."

"Should we send Reginald?" Phil asked.

"Who else?" Twin questioned. "This is the kind of activity he loves."

Phil got to his feet and ground out his cigarette. He left the office and walked down the litter-strewn hallway to the front room, where a half dozen members were playing cards. Cigarette smoke hung heavily in the air.

"Hey, Reginald," Phil called out. "You up for some action?"

Reginald glanced up from his cards. He adjusted the toothpick protruding from his mouth. "It depends," he said.

"I think you'd like this one," Phil said. "Five big ones to do away with the doctor whose bike you got."

"Hey, man, I'll do it," BJ said. BJ was the nickname for Bruce Jefferson. He was a stocky fellow with thighs as thick as Phil's waist. He'd also been on the visit to Jack's.

"Twin wants Reginald," Phil said.

Reginald stood up and tossed his cards on the table. "I had a crap hand anyway," he said. He followed Phil back to the office.

"Did Phil tell you the story?" Twin asked when they entered.

"Just that the doctor goes," Phil said. "And five big ones for us. Anything else?"

"Yeah," Twin said. "You gotta do a white chick too. Might as well do her first. Here's the address."

Twin handed over a scrap of paper with Beth Holderness's name and address written on it.

"You care how I do these honkies?" Reginald asked.

"I couldn't care less," Twin said. "Just be sure you get rid of them."

"I'd like to use the new machine pistol," Reginald said. He smiled with the toothpick still stuck in the corner of his mouth.

"It'll be good to see if it's worth the money we paid for it," Twin said. Twin opened up one of the desk drawers and withdrew a new Tec pistol. It still had some packing grease on the handle. He gave the gun a shove across the desk. Reginald snapped it up before it got to the edge. "Enjoy yourself," Twin added.

"I intend to," Reginald said.

Reginald made it a point never to show any emotion, but that didn't mean he didn't feel it. As he walked out of the building, his mood was soaring. He loved this kind of work.

He unlocked the driver's-side door of his jet-black Camaro and slipped in behind the wheel. He put the Tec pistol on the passenger seat and covered it with a newspaper. As soon as the motor was humming, he turned on his tape deck and pushed in his current favorite rap cassette. The car had a sound system that was the envy of the gang. It had enough subwoofer power to loosen ceramic tile in whatever neighborhood Reginald cruised.

With one last glance at Beth Holderness's address and with his head bobbing with the music, Reginald pulled away from the curb and headed uptown.

Beth hadn't gone directly home. In her distressed state, she needed to talk with someone. She'd stopped at a friend's house and even had had a glass of wine. After talking the situation over, she felt somewhat better, but was still depressed. She couldn't believe she'd been fired. There was also the gnawing possibility that she'd stumbled onto something significant in the incubator.

Beth lived in a five-story tenement on East Eighty-third Street between First and Second Avenues. It wasn't the greatest neighborhood, but it wasn't bad either. The only problem was that her building was not one of the best. The landlord did the least possible in terms of repair, and there was always trouble with something. As Beth arrived, she saw there was a new problem. The outer front door had been sprung open with a crowbar. Beth sighed. It had happened before and it had taken three months for the landlord to fix it.

For several months Beth had been intending to move out of the building, and had been saving her money for a deposit on a new apartment. Now that she was out of work, she'd have to dip into her savings. She probably couldn't move, at least not for the foreseeable future.

As she climbed the last flight of stairs she told herself that as bad as things seemed, they could be worse. She reminded herself that at least she was healthy.

Outside of her door, Beth fumbled with the clutter in the depths of her purse to find her apartment key, which she kept separate from the building key. Her idea was that if she lost one, she wouldn't necessarily lose the other.

Finally coming up with the key, she let herself into her apartment. She closed and locked the door, as was her habit. After taking off her coat and hanging it up, Beth again searched through her purse for Jack Stapleton's card. When she found it, she sat on the couch and gave him a call.

Although it was after seven, Beth called the medical examiner's office. An operator told her that Dr. Stapleton had left for the day. Turning the card over, she tried Jack's home number. She got his answering machine.

"Dr. Stapleton," Beth said after Jack's beep sounded. "This is Beth Holderness. I have something to tell you." Beth choked back tears from a sudden surge of emotion. She considered hanging up to collect herself, but instead she cleared her throat and continued haltingly: "I have to talk with you. I did find something. Unfortunately I was also fired. So please call."

Beth depressed the disconnect and then hung up the phone. For a second she debated calling back to describe what she found, but she decided against it. She'd wait for Jack to call her.

Beth was about to stand up when a tremendous crash shocked her into complete immobility. The door to her apartment had burst open, and it slammed back against the wall hard enough to drive the doorknob into the plaster. The deadbolt that she'd felt so secure about had splintered the doorjamb as if the jamb had been made of balsa wood.

A figure stood on the threshold like a magician appearing out of a cloud of smoke. He was dressed from head to foot in black leather. He glanced at Beth, then turned and yanked the door closed. Quiet returned to the apartment with the same suddenness as the explosive crash. At the moment only the muffled sound of a TV in a neighboring apartment could be heard.

If Beth could have envisioned this situation she would have thought she'd scream or flee or both, but she didn't do either. She'd been paralyzed. She'd even been holding her breath, which she now let out with an audible sigh.

The man advanced toward her. His face was expressionless. A toothpick jauntily stuck out of his mouth. In his left hand he brandished the largest pistol Beth had ever seen. Its ammunition clip protruded down almost a foot.

The man stopped directly in front of Beth. He didn't say a word. Instead he slowly raised the pistol and pointed it at her forehead. Beth closed her eyes . . .

Jack exited the subway at 103rd Street and jogged north. The weather was fine and the temperature reasonable. He expected a big turnout at the playground, and he wasn't disappointed. Warren saw him through the chain-link fence and told him to get his ass in gear and get over there.

Jack jogged the rest of the way home. As he approached his building, thoughts of Friday night and his uninvited visitors unwelcomely entered his mind. Having been at the General that day and having been discovered, Jack thought it was very possible that the Black Kings would be back. If they were, Jack wanted to know about it.

Instead of going in the front door, Jack descended a few steps and walked down a dank tunnel that connected the front and the back of his building. It reeked of urine. He emerged in the backyard, which looked like a junkyard. In the half-light he could make out the twisted remains of discarded bedsprings, broken baby carriages, bald car tires, and other unwanted trash.

Against the back of the building was a fire escape. It didn't descend all the way to the ground. The last segment was a metal ladder with a cement counterweight. By turning over a garbage can and standing on its base, Jack was able to reach up and grab the lowest rung. As soon as he put his weight on it, it came down with a clatter.

Jack climbed up the ladder. When he stepped off onto the grate of the first landing, the ladder retracted to its original position with equal clamor. Jack stood still for a few minutes to be sure that the din didn't disturb anyone. When no one stuck their head out of a window to complain, Jack continued climbing.

On each floor Jack had ample opportunity to glance in at the various domestic scenes, but he assiduously avoided doing so. It wasn't pretty. When he saw it close-up, Jack found true poverty enervating. Jack also kept his eyes elevated to avoid looking down. He'd always been afraid of heights, and climbing the fire escape was a test of his fortitude.

As Jack approached his own floor he slowed down. The fire escape serviced both his kitchen window and his bedroom window, both of which were ablaze with light. When he'd left that morning, he'd left all the lights on.

Jack sidled up to the kitchen window first and peered in. The room was empty. A grouping of fruit he'd left on the table was undisturbed. From where he was standing he could also see through to his door to the common hall. His repair was still in place. The door had not been forced open.

Moving to the second window, Jack made sure that the bedroom was as he'd left it. Satisfied, he opened the window and climbed in. He knew he'd been taking a chance leaving the bedroom window unlocked, but he thought it worth the risk. Once inside his apartment, he made a rapid final check. It was empty with no sign of any unexpected visitors having been there.

Jack quickly changed into his basketball gear and exited the same way he'd entered. Given his acrophobia, descent was more difficult than ascent, but Jack forced himself to do it. Under the circumstances, he wasn't wild about stepping out of his front door unprotected.

When Jack got to the street end of the tunnel, he paused in the shadows to view the area immediately in front of his building. He was particularly concerned about seeing any groups of men sitting in cars. When he was reasonably confident there were no hostile gang members waiting for him, he jogged down to the playground.

Unfortunately, during the time he'd taken to climb up and down the fire escape and change clothes the crowd at the playground had swelled. It took Jack even longer than usual to get into the game, and when he did, he ended up on a comparatively poor team.

Although Jack's shot was on, particularly his long jumper, his teammates' weren't. The game was a rout, to Warren's delight; his team had been winning all night.

Disgusted with his luck, Jack went to the sidelines and picked up his sweatshirt. Pulling it over his head, he started for the gate.

"Hey, man, you leaving already?" Warren called out. "Come on, stick around. We'll let you win one of these days." Warren guffawed. He wasn't being a bad sport; ridiculing the defeated was part of the accepted playground behavior. Everybody did it and everybody expected it.

"I don't mind getting whipped if it's by a decent team," Jack shot back. "But losing to a bunch of pansies is embarrassing."

"Ohhhh," Warren's teammates crooned. Jack's retort had been a good one.

Warren strutted over to Jack and stuck his index finger into Jack's chest. "Pansies, huh?" he said. "I tell you what. My five would devastate any five you could put together right now! You pick, we play."

Jack's eyes swept around the court. Everybody was looking in their direction. Jack considered the challenge and weighed the pluses and the minuses. First of all, he wanted more exercise so he did want to play, and he knew that Warren could make it happen.

At the same time, Jack understood that picking four people out of the crowd would irritate the ones he didn't pick. These were people Jack had been painstakingly cultivating over the past months to accept him. Beyond that, the people who were supposed to have winners would be especially vexed, not at Warren, who was insulated from such emotion, but at Jack. Considering all the angles, Jack decided it wasn't worth it.

"I'm going running in the park," Jack said.

Having bested Jack's retort and willing to accept Jack's refusal to meet his challenge as another victory, Warren bowed in recognition of his team's cheering. He high-fived with one of them and then swaggered back onto the court. "Let's run!" he yelled.

Jack smiled to himself, thinking how much the dynamics of the playground basketball court revealed about current intra-city society. Vaguely he wondered if any psychologist had ever thought about studying it from an academic point of view. He thought it would be fruitful indeed.

Jack stepped through the chain-link gate onto the sidewalk and started jogging. He ran due east. Ahead, at the end of the block he could see the dark silhouettes of jagged rocks and leafless trees. He knew that in a few minutes he'd leave behind the bustle of the city and enter the placid interior of Central Park. It was his favorite place to run.

Reginald had been stymied. There was no way he could have walked out into a playground in a hostile neighborhood. Having found the doc playing b-ball, he'd resigned himself to waiting in his Camaro. His hope was that Jack would separate himself from the crowd, perhaps by heading for one of the nearby delis for a drink.

When he'd seen Jack quit the game and pull on his sweater, he'd been encouraged enough to reach under the newspaper and snap the safety off the Tec. But then he heard Warren's challenge and was sure he'd be sitting through at least another game.

He was wrong. To his delight, a few minutes later Jack came out of the playground. But he didn't head west in the direction of the shops as Reginald had anticipated. Instead he headed east!

Cursing under his breath, Reginald had to make a U-turn right in the middle of all the traffic. A cabdriver complained bitterly by leaning on his horn. It was all Reginald could do to keep from reaching for the Tec. The cabdriver was one of those guys from the Far East whom Reginald would have loved to surprise with a couple of bursts.

Reginald's disappointment turned back to delight when he became aware of Jack's destination. As Jack sprinted across Central Park West, Reginald quickly parked. Leaping from the car, he grabbed the Tec along with the newspaper. Cradling the package in his hands, he, too, dashed across Central Park West, dodging the traffic.

At that point an entrance to the park's West Drive continued eastward into the park. Nearby was a sweeping stone stairway that rose up around a rocky outcropping. Lampposts partially lit the walkway before it disappeared into the blackness.

Reginald started up the stairs where he'd seen Jack go seconds earlier. Reginald was pleased. He couldn't believe his luck. In fact, chasing his prey into the dark, deserted park was making the job almost too easy.

From Jack's point of view at that moment the park's desolate darkness was more a source of comfort than uneasiness, unlike when he'd crossed the park on his bike Friday night. He felt consolation in the fact that although his vision was hampered, so was everyone else's. He firmly believed if the Black Kings were to harass him it would be in and around his apartment.

The terrain where Jack's run began was surprisingly hilly and rocky. The area was called the Great Hill for good reason. He was following an asphalt walkway that twisted, turned, and tunneled beneath the leafless branches of the surrounding trees. The lights from the lampposts illuminated the branches in an eerie fashion, giving the impression the park was covered by a giant spider's web.

Although he felt winded at first, Jack settled into a comfortable pace and began to relax. With the city out of view, he had a chance to think more clearly. He began to wonder if his crusade was based on his hatred for AmeriCare, as Chet and Bingham had implied. From his present perspective Jack had to agree it was possible.

After all, the idea of the intentional spread of the four diseases was implausible if not preposterous. And if he found the people at the General defensive, maybe he'd made them respond that way. As Bingham had reminded him: Jack could be abrasive.

In the middle of his musings Jack became aware of a new sound that coincided with his own footfalls. It was a metallic click, as if his basketball shoes had heel-savers. Perplexed, Jack altered his pace. The sound went out of sync for a moment but then gradually merged back.

Jack hazarded a glance behind him. When he did, he saw a figure running in his direction and closing. At the moment Jack spotted the figure, the man was passing under a lamppost. Jack could see he was not dressed as a jogger. In fact, he was wearing black leather, and in his hand he brandished a gun!

Jack's heart leaped in his chest. Aided by an adrenaline rush, he put on a burst of speed. Behind him he could hear his pursuer do likewise.

Jack frantically tried to figure the fastest way out of the park. If he was able to get among traffic and other people he might have a chance. All he knew for sure was that the closest way to the city was through the foliage to his right. He had no idea how far. It could have been a hundred feet or a hundred yards.

Sensing his pursuer was staying with him and perhaps even gaining, Jack veered right and plunged into the forest. Within the woods it was considerably darker than on the walkway. Jack could barely see where he was going as he stumbled up a steep grade. He was in a full panic, crashing over underbrush and scrambling through dense evergreens.

The hill leveled off at the summit and Jack burst through to an area with considerably less undergrowth. It was just as dark, but there were only dead leaves to contend with as he ran between the closely spaced tree trunks.

Happening upon a massive oak tree, Jack slipped behind and leaned against its rough surface. He was breathing hard. He tried to control his panting to listen. All he could hear was the sound of distant traffic that reverberated like the muffled roar of a waterfall. Only occasional car horns and undulating sirens punctuated the night.

Jack stayed behind the broad trunk of the oak for several minutes. Hearing no more footfalls, he pushed off the tree and continued heading west. Now he moved slowly and as silently as possible, nudging his feet forward in the leaves to keep the noise down. His heart was racing.

Jack's foot hit up against something soft, and to his horror it seemed to explode in front of him. For a second Jack had no idea what was happening. With great commotion a phantom figure swathed in rags lurched out of the ground as if resurrecting itself from the dead. The creature whirled about like a dervish, flailing at the air and shouting "Bastards" over and over again.

Instantly another figure loomed up as well, equally frantic. "You're not gonna get our shopping cart," the second man yelled. "We'll kill you first."

Jack had only managed to take a single step backward when the first figure threw himself at him, smothering him with a wretched stench and ineffectual blows. Jack tried to push him away, but the man reached up and drew his fingernails down Jack's face.

Jack marshaled his strength to rid himself of this fetid vagrant who clung to his chest. Before Jack could shake him loose, a burst of gunfire shattered the night. Jack felt himself sprayed with fluid as the tramp stiffened, then collapsed forward. Jack had to push him aside to keep from being knocked over backward.

The other vagrant's keening brought forth a second burst of gunfire. His wails of grief were cut off suddenly with a gurgle.

Having seen the direction from which the second burst of gunfire had come, Jack turned and fled in the opposite direction. Once again he was in headlong flight despite the darkness and the obstacles. Suddenly the ground dropped off, and Jack stumbled down a steep hillside, barely keeping his feet under him until he plunged into a dense undergrowth of vines and thornbushes.

Jack clawed his way through the thick bushes until he burst out onto a walkway with such suddenness, he fell to his hands and knees. Ahead he could see a flight of dimly lit, granite stairs. Scrambling to his feet, he dashed toward the stairs and took them two at a time. As he neared the top a single shot rang out. A bullet ricocheted off the stone to Jack's right and whined off into the night.

Trying to duck and weave, Jack reached the top of the stairs and emerged onto a terrace. A fountain that had been turned off for the winter stood empty in its center. Three sides of the terrace were enclosed by an arcade. In the center of the rear arcade was another stone stairway leading to another level.

Jack heard the rapid metallic clicks of his pursuer's shoes start up the stone stairway behind him. He would be there in an instant. Jack knew he had no time to make it to the second stairway, so he ran into the interior of the arcade. Within the arched space the darkness was complete. Jack advanced blindly by holding his hands out in front of him.

The pounding footfalls on the first stairway abruptly stopped. Jack knew his pursuer had reached the terrace. Jack continued forward, moving faster, heading for the second run of stairs. To his horror he collided in the blackness with a metal trash can. The noise was loud and unmistakable as the can tipped over and rolled to a stop. Almost immediately a burst of gunfire sounded. The bullets entered the arcade and ricocheted wildly off the granite walls. Jack lay flat, clasping his arms over his head until the final shell whined off into the night.

Standing up again, Jack continued forward, more slowly this time. When he reached the corner he encountered more obstacles: bottles and beer cans were strewn on the floor with no way for Jack to avoid them.

Jack winced every time one of his feet struck an object and the resulting noise echoed in the arcade. But there was no stopping. Ahead a faint glow indicated where the second stairway rose up to the next level. As soon as Jack reached it, he started climbing, moving more quickly now that there was light enough to see where to put his feet.

Jack was almost to the top when a sharp, authoritative command rang out in the stillness.

"Hey, man, hold up or you're gone!"

Jack could tell from the sound of the man's voice that he was at the foot of the stairs. At that range Jack had no choice. He stopped.

"Turn around!"

Jack did as he was told. He could see that his pursuer had a huge pistol leveled at him.

"Remember me? I'm Reginald."

"I remember you," Jack said.

"Come down here!" Reginald ordered in between breaths. "I'm not climbing another stair for you. No way."

Jack descended slowly. When he got to the third stair he stopped. The only light was a suffused glow from the surrounding city reflected off the cloud cover. Jack could barely make out the man's features. His eyes appeared to be bottomless holes.

"Man, you got balls," Reginald said. Slowly he let his hand holding the Tec pistol fall until it was dangling at his side. "And you're in shape. I gotta hand you that."

"What do you want from me?" Jack asked. "Whatever it is you can have it."

"Hey, I'm not expecting anything," Reginald said. " 'Cause I can tell you ain't got much. Certainly not in those threads, and I've already been to that shithole apartment of yours. To be honest, I'm just supposed to ice you. Word has it you didn't take Twin's recommendation."

"I'll pay you," Jack said. "Whatever you're being paid to do this, I'll pay you more."

"Sounds interesting," Reginald said. "But I can't deal. Otherwise I'd have to answer to Twin, and you couldn't pay me enough to take on that kind of shit. No way."

"Then tell me who's paying you," Jack said. "Just so I know."

"Hey, to tell you the truth, I don't even know," Reginald said. "All I know is that the money's good. We're getting five big ones just for me to chase you around the park for fifteen minutes. I'd say that's not bad."

"I'll pay a thousand," Jack said. He was desperate to keep Reginald talking.

"Sorry," Reginald said. "Our little rap is over and your number's up." As slowly as Reginald had lowered the gun, now he raised it.

Jack couldn't believe he was going to be shot at point-blank range by someone he didn't know and who didn't know him. It was preposterous. Jack knew he had to get Reginald talking, but as glib as Jack was, he couldn't think of anything more to say. His gift for repartee had deserted him as he watched the gun rise up to the point where he was staring directly down the barrel.

"My bad," Reginald said. It was a comment that Jack understood from his street basketball. It meant that Reginald was taking responsibility for what he was about to do.

The gun fired, and Jack winced reflexively. Even his eyes closed. But he didn't feel anything. Then he realized that Reginald was toying with him like a cat with a captured mouse. Jack opened his eyes. As terrorized as he felt, he was determined not to give Reginald any satisfaction. But what he saw shocked him. Reginald had disappeared.

Jack blinked several times, as if he thought his eyes were playing tricks on him. When he looked more closely he could just make out Reginald's body sprawled on the paving stones. A dark stain like an octopus's ink was spreading out from his head.

Jack swallowed but didn't move. He was transfixed. Out of the shadows of the arcade stepped a man. He was wearing a baseball hat backward. In his hand he held a pistol similar to the one Reginald had been carrying. He went first to Reginald's gun, which had skidded ten feet away, and picked it up. He examined it briefly, then thrust it into the top of his trousers. He stepped over to the dead man and with the tip of his foot turned Reginald's head over to look at the wound. Satisfied, he bent down and frisked the body until he found a wallet. He pulled it out, pocketed it, then stood up.

"Let's go, Doc," the man said.

Jack descended the last three steps. When he got to the bottom he recognized his rescuer. It was Spit!

"What are you doing here?" Jack asked in a forced whisper. His throat had gone bone dry.

"This ain't no time for rapping, man," Spit said. He then indulged in the act that had been the source of his sobriquet. "We gotta get the hell out of here. One of those bums back on the hill was only winged, and he's going to have this place crawling with cops."

From the moment Spit's gun had gone off in the arcade, Jack's mind had been spinning. Jack had no idea how Spit happened to be there at such a crucial time, or why he was now hustling him out of the park.

Jack tried to protest. He knew leaving a murder scene was a felony, and there had been two murders, not one. But Spit was not to be dissuaded. In fact, when Jack finally stopped running and started to explain why they shouldn't flee, Spit slapped him. It wasn't a gentle slap; it was a blow with vengeance.

Jack put his hand to his face. His skin was hot where he'd been struck.

"What the hell are you doing?" Jack asked.

"Trying to knock some sense into you, man," Spit said. "We got to get our asses over to Amsterdam. Here, you carry this mother." Spit thrust Reginald's machine pistol into Jack's hands.

"What am I supposed to do with it?" Jack asked. As far as he was concerned it was a murder weapon that should be handled with latex gloves and treated as evidence.

"Stick it under your sweater," Spit said. "Let's get."

"Spit, I don't think I can run away like this," Jack said. "You go if you must, and take this thing." Jack extended the gun toward Spit.

Spit exploded. He grabbed Reginald's gun out of Jack's hand and immediately pressed the barrel against Jack's forehead. "You're pissing me off, man," he said. "What's the matter with you? There still could be some of these Black King assholes hanging around here. I tell you what: If you don't get your ass in gear I'm going to waste you. You understand? I mean I wouldn't be out here risking my black ass if it hadn't been for Warren telling me to do it."

"Warren?" Jack questioned. Everything was getting too complicated. But he believed Spit's threat, so he didn't try to question him further. Jack knew Spit to be an impulsive man on the basketball court with a quick temper. Jack had never been willing to argue with him.

"Are you coming or what?" Spit demanded.

"I'm coming," Jack said. "I'm bowing to your better judgment."

"Damn straight," Spit said. He handed the machine pistol back to Jack and gave Jack a shove to move out.

On Amsterdam Spit used a pay phone while Jack waited nervously. All at once the ubiquitous sirens heard in the distance in New York City had a new meaning for Jack. So did the concept of being a felon. For years Jack had been thinking of himself as a victim. Now he was the criminal.

Spit hung up the phone and gave Jack a thumbs-up sign. Jack had no idea what the gesture meant, but he smiled anyway since Spit seemed to be content.

Less than fifteen minutes later a lowered maroon Buick pulled to the curb. The intermittent thud of rap music could be heard through the tinted windows. Spit opened the back door and motioned for Jack to slide in. Jack complied. Events were clearly not in his control.

Spit gave a final look around before climbing into the front seat. The car shot away from the curb.

"What's happening?" the driver asked. His name was David. He was also a regular on the b-ball court.

"A lot of shit," Spit said. He rolled his window down and noisily expectorated.

Jack winced each time the bass sounded in one of the many stereo speakers. He slipped the machine pistol out from under his sweater. Having the thing close to his body gave him a distinctly unpleasant feeling. "What do you want me to do with this?" Jack asked Spit. He had to talk loudly to be heard over the sound of the music.

Spit swung around and took the gun. He showed it to David, who whistled in admiration. "That's the new model," he commented.

With little talk the threesome drove north to 106th Street and turned right. David braked across from the playground. The basketball game was still in progress.

"Wait here," Spit said. He got out of the car and headed into the playground.

Jack watched Spit as he walked to the basketball court and stood on the sidelines as the game swept back and forth in front of him. Jack was tempted to ask David what was happening, but his intuition told him to keep still. Eventually Spit got Warren's attention and Warren stopped the game.

After a brief conversation during which Spit passed Reginald's wallet to Warren, the two men came back to David's car. David lowered the window. Warren stuck his head in and looked at Jack. "What the hell have you been doing?" he demanded angrily.

"Nothing," Jack said. "I'm the victim here. Why be angry with me?"

Warren didn't answer. Instead, he ran his tongue around the inside of his dry mouth while he thought. Perspiration lined his forehead. All at once he stood up and opened the door for Jack. "Get out," he said. "We have to talk. Let's go up to your place."

Jack slid out of the car. He tried to look Warren in the eye, but Warren avoided his stare. Warren started out across the street, and Jack followed. Spit came behind Jack.

They climbed Jack's stairs in silence.

"You got anything to drink?" Warren asked once they were inside.

"Gatorade or beer," Jack said. He had restocked his refrigerator.

"Gatorade," Warren said. He walked over to Jack's couch and sat heavily.

Jack offered Spit the same choices. He took beer.

After Jack had provided the drinks he sat in the chair opposite the couch. Spit preferred to lean against the desk.

"I want to know what's going on," Warren said.

"You and I both," Jack said.

"I don't want to hear any shit," Warren said. " 'Cause you haven't been straight with me."

"What do you mean?" Jack asked.

"Saturday you asked me about the Black Kings," Warren reminded him. "You said you were just curious. Now tonight one of those mothers tries to knock you off. Now I know something about those losers. They're into drugs big time. You catch my drift? What I want you to know is if you're mixed up with dealing, I don't want you in this neighborhood. It's as simple as that."

Jack let out a short laugh of incredulity. "Is that what this is about?" he asked. "You think I'm dealing drugs?"

"Doc, listen to me," Warren said. "You're a strange dude. I never understood why you're living here. But it's okay as long as you don't screw up the neighborhood. But if you're here because of drugs, you gotta rethink your situation."

Jack cleared his throat. He then admitted to Warren that he'd not been truthful with him when he'd asked about the Black Kings. He told him that the Black Kings had beaten him up, but that it involved something concerning his work that even he didn't totally understand.

"You sure you're not dealing?" Warren asked again. He looked at Jack out of the corner of his eye. " 'Cause if you're not straight with me now you're going to be one sorry shit."

"I'm being entirely truthful," Jack assured him.

"Well, then you're a lucky man," Warren said. "Had David and Spit not recognized that dude who came cruising around the neighborhood in his Camaro, you'd be history right now. Spit says he was fixing to blow you away."

Jack looked up at Spit. "I'm very grateful," he said.

"It was nothing, man," Spit said. "That mother was so fixed on getting you that he never once looked behind him. We'd been on his tail almost the moment he turned on a Hundred and Sixth."

Jack rubbed his head and sighed. Only now was he truly beginning to calm down. "What a night," he said. "But it's not over. We've got to go to the police."

"Hell we do," Warren said, his anger returning. "Nobody's going to the police."

"But there's someone dead," Jack said. "Maybe two or three, counting those homeless guys."

"There'll be four if you go," Warren warned. "Listen, Doc, don't get yourself involved in gang business, and this has become gang business. This Reginald dude knew he wasn't supposed to be up here. No way. I mean, we can't have them thinking they can just breeze into our neighborhood and knock somebody off, even if it is only you. Next they'd be icing one of the brothers. Leave it be, Doc. The police don't give a shit anyway. They're happy when us brothers are knocking each other off. All you can do is cause you and us trouble, and if you go to the police, you're no friend of ours, no way."

"But leaving the scene of a crime is a—" Jack began.

"Yeah, I know," Warren interrupted. "It's a felony. Big deal. Who the hell cares? And let me tell you something else. You still got a problem. If the Black Kings want you dead, you'd better be our friend, because we're the only ones who can keep you alive. The cops can't, believe me."

Jack started to say something, but he changed his mind. With his knowledge of gang life in New York City, he knew that Warren was right. If the Kings wanted him dead, which they apparently did—and would all the more now with Reginald's death—there was no way for the police to prevent it short of secret-service–type twenty-four-hour guard.

Warren looked up at Spit. "Somebody's going to have to stick tight to Doc for the next few days," he said.

Spit nodded. "No problem," he said.

Warren stood up and stretched. "What pisses me off is that I had the best team I've had in weeks tonight, and this shit has cut it short."

"I'm sorry," Jack said. "I'll let you win next time I play against you."

Warren laughed. "One thing I can say about you, Doc," he said. "You can sure rap with the best of them."

Warren motioned to Spit to leave. "We'll be seeing you, Doc," Warren said at the door. "Now don't do anything foolish. You going to run tomorrow night?"

"Maybe," Jack said. He didn't know what he was going to do in the next five minutes, much less the following night.

With a final wave Warren and Spit departed. The door closed behind them.

Jack sat for a few minutes. He felt shell-shocked. Then he got up, went into the bathroom. When he looked into the mirror he cringed. At the time he and Spit had been waiting for David to arrive with the car, a few people had glanced at Jack, but no one had stared. Now Jack wondered why they hadn't. Jack's face and sweater were spattered with blood, presumably from the vagrant. There was also a nasty series of parallel scratches from the vagrant's fingernails down his forehead and over his nose. A cross-hatching of scratches marred his cheeks, from the underbrush, no doubt. He looked like he'd been in a war.

Jack climbed into his tub and took a shower. By then his mind was going a mile a minute. He couldn't remember ever being in such a state of confusion, except after his family had perished. But that was different. He'd been depressed then. Now he was just confused.

Jack got out of the shower and dried himself off. He was still half debating whether or not to contact the police. In a state of indecision, he went to the phone. That's when he noticed that his answering machine was blinking. He pushed the play button and listened to Beth Holderness's disturbing message. Instantly he called her back. He let her phone ring ten times before giving up. What could she have found? he wondered. He also felt responsible for her having been fired. Somehow he was sure he was to blame.

Jack got a beer and took it into the living room. Sitting on the windowsill, he could see a sliver of 106th Street. There was the usual traffic and parade of people. He watched with unseeing eyes as he wrestled with his dilemma regarding calling the police.

Hours passed. Jack realized that by not making a decision he was in essence making one. By not calling the police he was agreeing with Warren. He'd become a felon.

Jack went back to the phone and tried Beth for the tenth time. It was now after midnight. The phone rang interminably. Jack started to worry. He hoped she'd simply fled to a friend's house for solace after losing her job. Yet not being able to get in touch with her nagged at him along with everything else.

CHAPTER 27

The first thing Jack did when he woke up was to try calling Beth Holderness. When she'd still not answered he'd tried to be optimistic about her visiting a friend, but in the face of everything that had happened, the inability to get ahold of her was progressively more distressing.

Still without a bike, Jack was forced back into the subway for his commute. But he wasn't alone. From the moment Jack had emerged from his tenement he'd been trailed by one of the younger members of the local gang. His name was Slam, in deference to his dunking ability with the basketball. Even though he was Jack's height, he could outjump Jack by at least twelve inches.

Jack and Slam did not talk during the train ride. They sat opposite each other, and although Slam didn't try to avoid eye contact, his expression never changed from one of total indifference. He was dressed like most of the younger African-Americans in the city, with oversized clothes. His sweatshirt was tentlike, and Jack preferred not to imagine what it concealed. Jack didn't believe that Warren would have sent the young man out to protect Jack without some significant weaponry.

As Jack crossed First Avenue and mounted the steps in front of the medical examiner's office, he glanced behind him. Slam had paused on the sidewalk, obviously confused as to what he should do. Jack hesitated as well. The unreasonable thought went through Jack's mind of inviting the man in so that he could pass the time in the second-floor canteen, but that was clearly out of the question.

Jack shrugged. Although he appreciated Slam's efforts on his behalf, it was Slam's problem what he was going to do for the day.

Jack turned back to the building, steeling himself for the possibility of having to face one or more bodies in whose death he somehow felt complicit.

Gathering his courage, Jack pulled open the door and entered.

Even though he was scheduled for a "paper day" and no autopsies, Jack wanted to see what had come in during the night. Not only was he concerned about Reginald and the vagrants, he was also concerned about the possibility of more meningococcus cases.

Jack had the receptionist buzz him into the ID area. Walking into the scheduling room, Jack knew instantly that it was not going to be a normal day. Vinnie was not sitting in his usual location with his morning newspaper.

"Where's Vinnie?" Jack asked George.

Without looking up, George told Jack that Vinnie was already in the pit with Bingham.

Jack's pulse quickened. Given his guilt about the previous evening's events, he had the irrational thought that Bingham could have been called in to do Reginald. At this stage of his career Bingham rarely did autopsies unless they were of particular interest or importance.

"What's Bingham doing in this early?" Jack asked, trying to sound disinterested.

"It's been a busy night," George said. "There was another infectious death over at the General. Apparently it's got the city all worked up. During the night the city epidemiologist called the Commissioner of Health, who called Bingham."

"Another meningococcus?" Jack asked.

"Nope," George said. "They think this one is a viral pneumonia."

Jack nodded and felt a chill descend his spine. His immediate concern was hantavirus. He knew there had been a case on Long Island the previous year in the early spring. Hantavirus was a scary proposition, although it was still not an illness with much patient-to-patient spread.

Jack could see there were more than the usual number of folders on the desk in front of George. "Anything else interesting last night?" Jack asked. He shuffled through the folders looking for Reginald's name.

"Hey," George complained. "I got these things in order." He looked up, then did a double take. "What the hell happened to you?"

Jack had forgotten how bad his face looked.

"I tripped when I was out jogging last night," Jack said. Jack didn't like to lie. What he said was true, but hardly the whole story.

"What did you fall into?" George asked. "A roll of barbed wire?"

"Any gunshot wounds last night?" Jack asked, to change the subject.

"You'd better believe it," George said. "We got four. Too bad it's a paper day for you. I'd give you one."

"Which ones are they?" Jack asked. He glanced around the desk.

George tapped the top of one of his stacks of folders.

Jack reached over and picked up the first one. When he opened the cover, his heart sank. He had to reach out and steady himself against the desk. The name was Beth Holderness.

"Oh, God, no," Jack murmured.

George's head shot up again. "What's the matter?" he asked. "Hey, you're as white as a sheet. You okay?"

Jack sat in a nearby chair and put his head down between his legs. He'd felt dizzy.

"Is it someone you know?" George asked with concern.

Jack straightened up. The dizziness had passed. He took a deep breath and nodded. "She was an acquaintance," he said. "But I'd spoken with her just yesterday." Jack shook his head. "I can't believe it."

George reached over and took the folder from Jack's hands. He opened it up. "Oh, yeah," he said. "This is the lab tech from over at the General. Sad! She was only twenty-eight. Supposed to be shot through the forehead for a TV and some cheap jewelry. What a waste."

"What are the other gunshot wounds?" Jack asked. For the moment he remained seated.

George consulted his master sheet. "I've got a Hector Lopez, West Hundred and Sixtieth Street, a Mustafa Aboud, East Nineteenth Street, and Reginald Winthrope, Central Park."

"Let me see Winthrope," Jack said.

George handed Jack the folder.

Jack opened it up. He wasn't looking for anything in particular, but his sense of involvement made him want to check the case. The strangest thing was that had it not been for Spit, Jack himself would have been represented there on George's desk with his own folder. Jack shuddered. He handed Reginald's folder back to George.

"Is Laurie here yet?" Jack asked.

"She came in just before you did," George said. "She wanted some folders, but I told her that I'd not made out the schedule yet."

"Where is she?" Jack asked.

"Up in her office, I guess," George said. "I really don't know."

"Assign her the Holderness and the Winthrope cases," Jack said. Jack stood up. He anticipated feeling dizzy again, but he didn't.

"How come?" George asked.

"George, just do it," Jack said.

"All right, don't get mad," George said.

"I'm sorry," Jack said. "I'm not mad. Just preoccupied."

Jack walked back through communications. He passed Janice's office, where she was putting in her usual overtime. Jack didn't bother her. He was too absorbed by his own thoughts. Beth Holderness's death made him feel unhinged. Feeling guilty about his complicity in her losing her job was bad enough; the idea that she might have lost her life because of his actions was unthinkable.

Jack pressed the button for the elevator and waited. The attempt on his own life the night before had given more weight to his suspicions. Someone had tried to kill him after he refused to heed the warning. The very same night Beth Holderness had been murdered. Could it have been in the course of an unrelated robbery or could it have been because of Jack, and, if so, what did that mean about Martin Cheveau? Jack didn't know. But what he did know was that he could not involve anyone else in this affair for fear of putting them in jeopardy. From that moment on, Jack knew he had to keep everything to himself.

As George had surmised, Laurie was in her office. While waiting for George to assign the day's cases, she was using the time profitably, working on some of her uncompleted cases. She took one look at Jack and recoiled. Jack offered the same explanation he'd given George, but he could tell that Laurie wasn't quite convinced.

"Did you hear that Bingham is down in the pit?" Jack asked, to move the conversation away from his previous night's experiences.

"I did," Laurie said. "I was shocked. I didn't think there was anything that could get him here before eight, much less in the autopsy room."

"Do you know anything about the case?" Jack asked.

"Just that it was atypical pneumonia," Laurie said. "I spoke with Janice for a moment. She said they'd had preliminary confirmation it was influenza."

"Uh-oh!" Jack said.

"I know what you're thinking," Laurie said, wagging her finger. "Influenza was one of the diseases you said you'd use if you were a terrorist type trying to start an epidemic. But before you go jumping off using this as confirmation of your theory, just remember that it is still influenza season."

"Primary influenza pneumonia is not very common," Jack said, trying to stay calm. The mention of the word "influenza" had his pulse racing again.

"We see it every year," Laurie said.

"Maybe so," Jack said. "But I tell you what. How about calling that internist friend of yours and asking if there are any more cases?"

"Right now?" Laurie asked. She glanced at her watch.

"It's as good a time as any," Jack said. "She'll probably be making her rounds. She can use the computer terminal at one of the nurses' stations."

Laurie shrugged and picked up her phone. A few minutes later she had her friend on the line. She asked the question, then waited. While she waited she looked up at Jack. She was worried about him. His face was not only scratched up, it was now flushed.

"No cases," Laurie repeated into the phone when her friend came back on the line. "Thanks, Sue. I appreciate it. Talk to you soon. Bye."

Laurie hung up the phone. "Satisfied?" she said.

"For the moment," Jack said. "Listen: I asked George to assign you two particular cases this morning. The names are Holderness and Winthrope."

"Is there some specific reason?" Laurie asked. She could see that Jack was trembling.

"Do it as a favor," Jack said.

"Of course," Laurie said.

"One thing I'd like you to do is look for any hairs or fibers on the Holderness woman's body," Jack said. "And find out if homicide had a criminologist at the scene to do the same. If there are any hairs, see if there is a DNA match with Winthrope."

Laurie didn't say anything. When she found her voice, she asked: "You think that Winthrope killed Holderness?" Her voice reflected her disbelief.

Jack looked off and sighed. "There's a chance," he said.

"How would you know?" Laurie asked.

"Let's call it a disturbing hunch," Jack said. He would have liked to tell Laurie more, but with the new pact he had with himself, he didn't. He wasn't about to put anyone else at risk in any form or fashion.

"Now you really have my curiosity going," Laurie said.

"I'd like to ask one more favor," Jack said. "You told me that you had a relationship with a police detective who's now a friend."

"That's true," Laurie said.

"Do you think you could give him a call?" Jack said. "I'd like to talk with him sorta off the record."

"You are scaring me," Laurie said. "Are you in some kind of trouble?"

"Laurie," Jack said. "Please don't ask any questions. The less you know right now the better off you are. But I think I should talk to someone high up in law enforcement."

"You want me to call him now?"

"Whenever is convenient," Jack said.

Laurie blew out through pursed lips as she dialed Lou Soldano's number. She'd not talked to him in a few weeks, and she felt it was a little awkward calling about a situation she knew so little about. But she was definitely worried about Jack and wanted to help.

When police headquarters answered and Laurie asked for Lou, she was told the detective wasn't available. She left a message on his voice mail for him to call her.

"That's the best I could do," Laurie said as she hung up. "Knowing Lou, he'll be back to me as soon as he can."

"I appreciate it," Jack said. He gave her shoulder a squeeze. He had the comforting sense she was a true friend.

Jack went back to his own office just in time to run into Chet. Chet took one look at Jack's face and whistled.

"And what did the other guy look like?" Chet asked jokingly.

"I'm not in the mood," Jack said. He took off his jacket and hung it over his chair.

"I hope this doesn't have anything to do with those gang members who visited you Friday," Chet said.

Jack gave the same explanation he'd given to the others.

Chet flashed a wry smile as he stowed his coat in his file cabinet. "Sure, you fell while jogging," he said. "And I'm dating Julia Roberts. But, hey, you don't have to tell me what happened; I'm just your friend."

That was exactly the point, Jack mused. After checking to see if he had any phone messages, he started back out of the office.

"You missed a nice little dinner last night," Chet said. "Terese came along. We talked about you. She's a fan of yours, but she's as concerned as I am about your monomania concerning these infectious cases."

Jack didn't even bother to answer. If Chet or Terese knew what had really happened last night, they'd be more than concerned.

Returning to the first floor, Jack looked into Janice's office. Now he wanted to ask her about the influenza case that was being posted by Bingham, but she'd left. Jack descended to the morgue level and changed into his isolation gear.

He went into the autopsy room and walked up to the only table in operation. Bingham was on the patient's right, Calvin on the left, and Vinnie at the head. They were almost done.

"Well, well," Bingham said when Jack joined them. "Isn't this convenient? Here's our in-house infectious expert."

"Perhaps the expert would like to tell us what this case is," Calvin challenged.

"I've already heard," Jack said. "Influenza."

"Too bad," Bingham said. "It would have been fun to see if you truly have the nose for this stuff. When it came in early this morning there was no diagnosis yet. The suspicion was some sort of viral hemorrhagic fever. It had everybody up in arms."

"When did you learn it was influenza?" Jack asked.

"A couple of hours ago," Bingham answered. "Just before we started. It's a good case, though. You want to see the lungs?"

"I would," Jack said.

Bingham reached into the pan and lifted out the lungs. He showed the cut surface to Jack.

"My God, the whole lung is involved!" Jack commented. He was impressed. In some areas there was frank hemorrhage.

"Even some myocarditis," Bingham said. He put the lung back and lifted up the heart and displayed it for Jack. "When you can see the inflammation grossly like this, you know it's extensive."

"Looks like a virulent strain," Jack said.

"You'd better believe it," Bingham said. "This patient's only twenty-nine years old, and his first symptoms occurred around six last night. He was dead at four A.M. It reminds me of a case I did back in my residency during the pandemic of fifty-seven and fifty-eight."

Vinnie rolled his eyes. Bingham had a mind-numbing habit of comparing every case to one that he'd had in his long career.

"That case was also a primary influenza pneumonia," Bingham continued. "Same appearance of the lung. When we looked at it histologically we were amazed at the degree of damage. It gave us a lot of respect for certain strains of influenza."

"Seeing this case concerns me," Jack said. "Especially in light of the other diseases that have been popping up."

"Now, don't head off into left field!" Bingham warned, remembering some of Jack's comments the day before. "This isn't out of the ordinary, like the plague case or even the tularemia. It's flu season. Primary influenza pneumonia is a rare complication, but we see it. In fact we had a case just last month."

Jack listened, but Bingham wasn't making him feel any more comfortable. The patient in front of them had had a lethal infection with an agent that had the capability of spreading from patient to patient like wildfire. Jack's only consolation was the call Laurie had made to her internist friend who'd said there were no other cases in the hospital.

"Mind if I take some washings?" Jack asked.

"Hell no!" Bingham said. "Be my guest. But be careful what you do with them."

"Obviously," Jack said.

Jack took the lungs over to one of the sinks, and with Vinnie's help prepared some samples by washing out some of the small bronchioles with sterile saline. He then sterilized the outside of the containers with ether.

Jack was on his way out when Bingham asked him what he was going to do with the samples.

"Take them up to Agnes," Jack said. "I'd like to know the subtype."

Bingham shrugged and looked across at Calvin.

"Not a bad idea," Calvin said.

Jack did exactly what he said he would. But he was disappointed when he presented the bottles to Agnes up on the third floor.

"We don't have the capability of subtyping it," she said.

"Who does?" Jack asked.

"The city or state reference lab," Agnes said. "Or even over at the university lab. But the best place would be the CDC. They have a whole section devoted to influenza. If it were up to me, I'd send it there."

Jack got some viral transport medium from Agnes and transferred the washings into it. Then he went up to his office. Sitting down, he placed a call to the CDC and was put through to the influenza unit. A pleasant-sounding woman answered, introducing herself as Nicole Marquette.

Jack explained what he wanted, and Nicole was accommodating. She said she'd be happy to see that the influenza was typed and subtyped.

"If I manage to get the sample to you today," Jack said, "how long would it take for you to do the typing?"

"We can't do this overnight," Nicole said, "if that's what you have in mind."

"Why not?" Jack asked impatiently.

"Well, maybe we could," Nicole corrected herself. "If there is a sufficient viral titer in your sample, meaning enough viral particles, I suppose it is possible. Do you know what the titer is?"

"I haven't the faintest idea," Jack said. "But the sample was taken directly from the lung of a patient who passed away from primary influenza pneumonia. The strain is obviously virulent, and I'm worried about a possible epidemic."

"If it is a virulent strain, then the titer might be high," Nicole said.

"I'll find a way to get it to you today," Jack promised. He then gave Nicole his telephone number both at the office and at home. He told her to call anytime she had any information.

"We'll do the best we can," Nicole said. "But I have to warn you, if the titer is too low it might be several weeks before I get back to you."

"Weeks!" Jack complained. "Why?"

"Because we'll have to grow the virus out," Nicole explained. "We usually use ferrets, and it takes a good two weeks for an adequate antibody response which guarantees we'll have a good harvest of virus. But once we have the virus in quantity, we can tell you a lot more than just its subtype. In fact, we can sequence its genome."

"I'll keep my fingers crossed that my samples have a high titer," Jack said. "And one other question. What subtype would you think was the most virulent?"

"Whoa!" Nicole said. "That's a hard question. There are a lot of factors involved, particularly host immunity. I'd have to say the most virulent would be an entirely new pathological strain, or one that hasn't been around for a long time. I suppose the subtype that caused the pandemic of 1918 to 1919 that killed twenty-five million people worldwide might get the dubious honor of having been the most virulent."

"What subtype was that?" Jack asked.

"No one knows for sure," Nicole said. "The subtype doesn't exist. It disappeared years ago, maybe right after the epidemic wore itself out. Some people think it was similar to the subtype that caused that swine-flu scare back in seventy-six."

Jack thanked Nicole and again assured her he'd get the samples to her that day. After he hung up, he called Agnes back and asked her opinion on shipping. She told him the name of the courier service they used, but she said she didn't know if they shipped interstate.

"Besides," Agnes added, "it will cost a small fortune. I mean overnight is one thing, but you're talking about the same day. Bingham will never authorize it."

"I don't care," Jack said. "I'll pay for it myself."

Jack called the courier company. They were delighted with the request and put Jack through to one of the supervisors, Tony Liggio. When Jack explained what he wanted, Tony said no problem.

"Can you come to pick it up now?" Jack asked. He was encouraged.

"I'll send someone right away," Tony said.

"It will be ready," Jack said.

Jack was about to hang up when he heard Tony add: "Aren't you interested in the cost? I mean, this is not like taking something over to Queens. Also, there's the question of how you plan to pay."

"Credit card," Jack said. "If that's okay."

"Sure, no problem, Doc," Tony said. "It's going to take me a little while to figure out the exact charge."

"Just give me a ballpark figure," Jack said.

"Somewhere between one and two thousand dollars," Tony said.

Jack winced but didn't complain. Instead, he merely gave Tony his credit card number. He'd envisioned the cost would be two or three hundred dollars, but then he hadn't thought about the fact that someone might have to fly round-trip to Atlanta.

While Jack had been engaged in giving his credit card information, one of the secretaries from the front office had appeared at his door. She'd handed him an overnight Federal Express package and departed without saying a word. As Jack hung up from the courier service he saw that the parcel was from National Biologicals. It was the DNA probes he'd requested the day before.

Taking the probes and his viral samples, Jack went back down to Agnes. He told her about the arrangements he'd made with the courier service.

"I'm impressed," Agnes said. "But I'm not going to ask how much it's costing."

"Don't," Jack advised. "How should I package the samples?"

"We'll take over," she said. She called in the department secretary and commissioned her to do it with appropriate biohazard containers and labels.

"Looks like you have something else for me," she said, eyeing the vials containing the probes.

Jack explained what they were and what he wanted, namely to have the DNA lab use the probes to see if they reacted with the nucleoproteins of the cultures taken from any of the four recent infectious disease cases he'd been working on. What he didn't tell her was why he wanted it done.

"All I need to know is whether it is positive or not," Jack said. "It doesn't have to be quantitative."

"I'll have to handle the rickettsia and the tularemia agent myself," Agnes said. "I'm afraid to have any of the techs working with them."

"I really appreciate all this," Jack said.

"Well, it's what we're here for," Agnes said agreeably.

After leaving the lab Jack went downstairs to the scheduling room and helped himself to some coffee. He'd been so frantic since he'd arrived that he'd not had much time to think. Now, as he stirred his coffee, he realized that neither of the homeless men that he'd inadvertently run into in his flight from Reginald had been brought in. That meant that they were either in some hospital, or they were still out there in the park.

Carrying his coffee back upstairs, Jack sat down at his desk. With both Laurie and Chet in the autopsy room, he knew he could count on some peace and quiet.

Before he could enjoy his solitude, the phone interrupted. It was Terese.

"I'm mad at you," she said without preamble.

"That's wonderful," Jack said with his usual sarcasm. "Now my day is complete."

"I am angry," Terese maintained, but her voice had softened considerably. "Colleen just hung up from talking with Chet. He told her you were beaten up again."

"That was Chet's personal interpretation," Jack said. "The fact is, I wasn't beaten up again."

"You weren't?"

"I explained to Chet that I'd fallen while jogging," Jack said.

"But he told Colleen . . ."

"Terese," Jack said sharply. "I wasn't beaten up. Can we talk about something else?"

"Well, if you weren't assaulted, why are you sounding so irritable?"

"It's been a stressful morning," Jack admitted.

"Care to talk about it?" she asked. "That's what friends are for. I've certainly bent your ear about my problems."

"There's been another infectious death at the General," Jack said. He would have liked to tell her what was really on his mind—his sense of guilt about Beth Holderness—but he dared not.

"That's terrible!" Terese said. "What is wrong with that place? What is it this time?"

"Influenza," Jack said. "A very virulent case. It's the kind of illness I've been truly worried we'd see."

"But the flu is around," Terese said. "It's flu season."

"That's what everybody says," Jack admitted.

"But not you?"

"Put it this way," Jack said. "I'm worried, especially if it is a unique strain. The deceased was a young patient, only twenty-nine. In the face of what else has been popping up over there at the General, I'm worried."

"Are some of your colleagues worried as well?" Terese asked.

"At the moment, I'm on my own," Jack admitted.

"I guess we're lucky to have you," Terese said. "I have to admire your dedication."

"That's kind of you to say," Jack said. "Actually, I hope I'm wrong."

"But you're not going to give up, are you?"

"Not until I have some proof one way or the other," Jack said. "But let's talk about you. I hope you are doing better than I."

"I appreciate your asking," Terese said. "Thanks in no small part to you, I think we have the makings of a good ad campaign. Plus, I've managed to have the in-house presentation put off until Thursday, so we have another whole day of breathing room. At the moment things are looking reasonable, but in the advertising world that could change at any moment."

"Well, good luck," Jack said. He wanted to get off the phone.

"Maybe we could have a quick dinner tonight," Terese suggested. "I'd really enjoy it. There's a great little Italian restaurant just up the street on Madison."

"It's possible," Jack said. "I'll just have to see how the day progresses."

"Come on, Jack," Terese complained. "You have to eat. We both could use the relaxation, not to mention the companionship. I can hear the tension in your voice. I'm afraid I'm going to have to insist."

"All right," Jack said, relenting. "But it might have to be a short dinner." He realized there was some truth to what Terese was saying, although at the moment it was hard for him to think as far ahead as dinnertime.

"Fantastic," Terese said happily. "Call me later and we'll decide on the time. If I'm not here, I'll be home. Okay?"

"I'll call you," Jack promised.

After they exchanged good-byes, Jack hung up the phone. For a few minutes he stared at it. He knew that conventional wisdom held that talking about a problem was supposed to relieve anxiety. But at the moment, having talked about the case of influenza with Terese, he only felt more anxious. At least the viral sample was on its way to the CDC and the DNA lab was working with the probe from National Biologicals. Maybe soon he'd start to get some answers.

CHAPTER 28

Phil came through the outer door of the abandoned building the Black Kings had taken over. The door was a piece of three-quarter-inch plywood bolted to an aluminum frame.

Phil passed the front room with the invariable pall of cigarette smoke and interminable card game and rushed directly back to the office. He was relieved to see Twin at the desk.

Phil waited impatiently for Twin to wrap up a payoff from one of their eleven-year-old pushers and send the kid away.

"There's a problem," Phil said.

"There's always a problem," Twin said philosophically. He was re-counting the ragged stack of greenbacks the kid had brought in.

"Not like this one," Phil said. "Reginald's been tagged."

Twin looked up from the money with an expression as if he'd just been slapped. "Get out!" he said. "Where'd you hear that shit?"

"It's true," Phil insisted. He took one of the several beat-up straight-backed chairs standing against the wall and turned it around so he could sit on it backward. The pose provided visual harmony with the backward baseball cap he always wore.

"Who says?" Twin asked.

"It's all over the street," Phil said. "Emmett heard it from a pusher up in Times Square. Seems that the doc is being protected by the Gangsta Hoods from Manhattan Valley on the Upper West Side."

"You mean one of the Hoods iced Reginald?" Twin asked in total disbelief.

"That's the story," Phil said. "Shot him through the head."

Twin slammed his open palm on the desk hard enough to send the tattered stack of greenbacks wafting off into the air. He leaped to his feet and paced. He gave the metal wastebasket a hard kick.

"I can't believe this," he said. "What the hell is this world coming to? I don't understand it. They'd do a brother for some white honky doctor. It doesn't make sense, no way."

"Maybe the doc is doing something for them," Phil suggested.

"I don't care what the hell he's doing," Twin raged. He towered over Phil, and Phil cringed. Phil was well aware that Twin could be ruthless and unpredictable when he was pissed, and he was royally pissed at the moment.

Returning to the desk, Twin pounded it again. "I don't understand this, but there is one thing that I do know. It can't stand. No way! The Hoods can't go around knocking off a Black King without a response. I mean, at a minimum we gotta do the doc like we agreed."

"Word is that the Hoods have a tail on the doc," Phil said. "They are still protecting him."

"It's unbelievable," Twin said as he retook his seat at the desk. "But it makes things easier. We do the doc and the tail at the same time. But we don't do it in the Hoods' neighborhood. We do it where the doc works."

Twin pulled open the center drawer of his desk and rummaged around. "Where the hell is that sheet about the doc," he said.

"Side drawer," Phil said.

Twin glared at Phil. Phil shrugged. He didn't want to aggravate Twin, but he remembered Twin putting the sheet in the side drawer.

Twin got the sheet out and read it over quickly. "All right," he said. "Go get BJ. He's been itching for action."

Phil disappeared for two minutes. When he reappeared he had BJ with him. BJ lumbered into the office, his pace belying his notorious quickness.

Twin explained the circumstances.

"Think you can handle this?" Twin asked.

"Hey, no problem," BJ said.

"You want a backup?" Twin asked.

"Hell, no," BJ said. "I'll just wait until the two mothers are together, then nail them both."

"You'll have to pick the doc up where he works," Twin said. "We can't risk going up into the Hoods' neighborhood unless we go in force. You understand?"

"No problem," BJ said.

"You got a machine pistol?" Twin asked.

"No," BJ said.

Twin opened the lower drawer of the desk and took out a Tec like the one he'd given to Reginald. "Don't lose this," he said. "We only have so many."

"No problem," BJ said. He took the gun and handled it with reverence, turning it over slowly in his hands.

"Well, what are you waiting for?" Twin asked.

"You finished?" BJ asked.

"Of course I'm finished," Twin said. "What do you want, me to come along and hold your hand? Get out of here so you can come back and tell me it's done."

Jack could not concentrate on his other cases no matter how hard he tried. It was almost noon, and he'd accomplished a pitifully small amount of paperwork. He couldn't stop worrying about the influenza case and wondering what had happened to Beth Holderness. What could she have found?

Jack threw down his pen in disgust. He wanted desperately to go to the General and visit Cheveau and his lab, but he knew he couldn't. Cheveau would undoubtedly call in the marines at a minimum, and Jack would get himself fired. Jack knew he had to wait for the results with the probe from National Biologicals to give him some ammunition before he approached anyone in authority.

Giving up on his paperwork, Jack impulsively went up to the DNA lab on the sixth floor. In contrast to most of the rest of the building, this lab was a state-of-the-art facility. It had been renovated recently and outfitted with the latest equipment. Even the white lab coats worn by the personnel seemed crisper and whiter than in any of the other labs.

Jack sought out the director, Ted Lynch, who was on his way to lunch.

"Did you get those probes from Agnes?" Jack asked.

"Yup," Ted said. "They're in my office."

"I guess that means there're no results yet," Jack said.

Ted laughed. "What are you talking about?" he questioned. "We haven't even gotten the cultures yet. Besides, I think you might be underestimating what the process is going to be. We don't just throw the probes into a soup of bacteria. We have to isolate the nuclear protein, then run it through the PCR in order to have enough substrate. Otherwise we wouldn't see the fluorescence even if the probe reacted. It's going to take some time."

Sufficiently chastised, Jack returned to his office to stare at the wall behind his desk. Although it was lunchtime, he wasn't hungry in the slightest.

Jack decided to call the city epidemiologist. Jack was interested in the man's reaction to this case of influenza; he thought he could give the epidemiologist a chance to redeem himself.

Jack got the number from the city directory and placed the call. A secretary answered. Jack asked to speak with Dr. Abelard.

"Who should I say is calling?" the secretary asked.

"Dr. Stapleton," Jack said, resisting the temptation to be humorously sarcastic. Knowing Abelard's sensitive ego, Jack would have liked to have said he was the mayor or the Secretary of Health.

Jack twisted a paper clip mindlessly as he waited. When the phone was picked up again, he was surprised it was again the secretary.

"Excuse me," she said. "But Dr. Abelard told me to tell you that he does not wish to speak with you."

"Tell the good doctor that I am in awe of his maturity," Jack said.

Jack slammed the phone down. His first impression had been correct: the man was an ass. Anger now mixed with his anxiety, which made his current inaction that much more difficult to bear. He was like a caged lion. He had to do something. What he wanted to do was go to the General despite Bingham's admonitions. Yet if he went over there whom could he talk with? Jack made a mental checklist of the people he knew at the hospital. Suddenly he thought of Kathy McBane. She'd been both friendly and open, and she was on the Infection Control Committee.

Jack snatched up the phone again and called the Manhattan General. Kathy was not in her office, so he had her paged. She picked up the page from the cafeteria. Jack could hear the usual babble of voices and clink of tableware in the background. He introduced himself and apologized for interrupting her lunch.

"It doesn't matter," Kathy said agreeably. "What can I do for you?"

"Do you remember me?" Jack asked.

"Absolutely," Kathy said. "How could I forget after the reaction you got out of Mr. Kelley and Dr. Zimmerman?"

"They are not the only people I seem to have offended in your hospital," Jack admitted.

"Everybody has been on edge since these infectious cases," Kathy said. "I wouldn't take it personally."

"Listen," Jack said. "I'm concerned about the same cases, and I'd love to come over and talk to you directly. Would you mind? But it will have to be just between the two of us. Is that too much to ask?"

"No, not at all," Kathy said. "When did you have in mind? I'm afraid I have meetings scheduled for most of the afternoon."

"How about right now?" Jack said. "I'll pass up lunch."

"Now that's dedication," Kathy said. "How can I refuse? My office is in administration on the first floor."

"Uh-oh," Jack voiced. "Is there a chance I'd run into Mr. Kelley?"

"The chances are slim," Kathy said. "There's a group of bigwigs in from AmeriCare, and Mr. Kelley is scheduled to be locked up with them all day."

"I'm on my way," Jack said.

Jack exited from the front entrance on First Avenue. He was vaguely aware of Slam straightening up from where he was leaning against a neighboring building, but Jack was too preoccupied to take much notice. He flagged a cab and climbed in. Behind him he saw Slam following suit.

BJ had not been entirely confident he'd recognize Jack from the visit to the doc's apartment, but the moment Jack appeared at the door of the medical examiner's office, BJ knew it was him.

While he'd been waiting BJ had tried to figure out who was supposedly protecting Jack. For a while a tall muscular dude had loitered on the corner of First Avenue and Thirtieth Street, smoking, and intermittently looking up at the medical examiner building's door. BJ had thought he was the one, but eventually he'd left. So BJ had been surprised when he'd seen Slam stiffen in response to Jack's appearance.

"He's no more than a goddamn kid," BJ had whispered to himself. He was disgusted. He expected a more formidable opponent.

No sooner had BJ gotten his hand around the butt of his machine pistol, which he had in a shoulder holster under his hooded sweatshirt, than he saw first Jack and then Slam jump into separate cabs. Letting go of his gun, BJ stepped out into the street and flagged his own taxi.

"Just head north," BJ told the cabdriver. "But push it, man."

The Pakistani cabdriver gave BJ a questioning look, but then did as he was told. BJ kept Slam's cab in sight, aided by the fact that it had a broken taillight.

Jack jumped out of the cab and dashed into the General and across the lobby. The masks had been dispensed with now that the meningococcal scare had passed, so Jack couldn't use one to hide behind. Concerned about being recognized, he wanted to spend the least time possible in the hospital's public places.

He pushed through the doors into the administrative area, hoping that Kathy had been right about Kelley's being occupied. The sounds of the hospital died away as the doors closed behind him. He was in a carpeted hall. Happily, he saw no one he recognized.

Jack approached the first secretary he came upon and asked for Kathy McBane's office. He was directed to the third door on the right. Losing no time, Jack hustled down there and stepped in.

"Hello," Jack called out as he closed the door behind him. "I hope you don't mind my shutting us in like this. I know it's presumptuous, but as I explained there are a few people I don't want to see."

"If it makes you feel better, by all means," Kathy said. "Come and sit down."

Jack took one of the seats facing the desk. It was a small office with barely enough room for a desk, two facing chairs, and a file cabinet. The walls had a series of diplomas and licenses attesting to Kathy's impressive credentials. The decoration was spartan but comfortable. There were family photos on the desk.

Kathy herself appeared as Jack remembered her: friendly and open. She had a round face with small, delicate features. Her smile came easily.

"I'm very concerned about this recent case of primary influenza pneumonia," Jack said, losing no time. "What's been the reaction of the Infection Control Committee?"

"We've not met yet," Kathy said. "After all, the patient just passed away last night."

"Have you spoken about it with any of the other members?" Jack asked.

"No," Kathy admitted. "Why are you so concerned? We've seen a lot of influenza this season. Frankly, this case hasn't bothered me anywhere near the way the others did, particularly the meningococcus."

"It bothers me because of a pattern," Jack said. "It presented as a fulminant form of a pneumonia just like the other, rarer diseases. The difference is that with influenza the infectivity is higher. It doesn't need a vector. It spreads person to person."

"I understand that," Kathy said. "But as I've pointed out we've been seeing influenza all winter long."

"Primary influenza pneumonia?" Jack questioned.

"Well, no," Kathy admitted.

"This morning I had someone check to see if there were any other similar cases currently in the hospital," Jack said. "There weren't. Do you know if there are now?"

"Not that I am aware of," Kathy said.

"Could you check?" Jack asked.

Kathy turned to her terminal and punched in a query. The answer flashed back in an instant. There were no cases of influenza pneumonia.

"All right," Jack said. "Let's try something else. The patient's name was Kevin Carpenter. Where was his room in the hospital?"

"He was on the orthopedic floor," Kathy said.

"His symptoms started at six P.M.," Jack said. "Let's see if any of the orthopedic nurses on the evening shift are sick."

Kathy hesitated for a moment, then turned back to her computer terminal. It took her several minutes to get the list and the phone numbers.

"You want me to call them now?" Kathy asked. "They're due in for their shift in just a couple of hours."

"If you don't mind," Jack said.

Kathy started making the calls. On her second call, to a Ms. Kim Spensor, she discovered that the woman was ill. In fact, she'd just been preparing to call in sick. She admitted to severe flu symptoms with a temperature of almost 104°.

"Would you mind if I talked with her?" Jack asked.

Kathy asked Kim if she'd be willing to speak to a doctor who was in her office. Kim apparently agreed, because Kathy handed the phone to Jack.

Jack introduced himself, but not as a medical examiner. He commiserated with her about her illness, and then inquired about her symptoms.

"It started abruptly," Kim said. "One minute I was fine; the next minute I had a terrible headache and a shaking chill. Also, my muscles are aching, particularly my lower back. I've had the flu before, but this is the worst I've ever felt."

"Any cough?" Jack asked.

"A little," Kim said. "And it's been getting worse."

"How about substernal pain?" Jack asked. "Behind your breastbone when you breathe in?"

"Yes," Kim said. "Does that mean anything in particular?"

"Did you have much contact with a patient by the name of Carpenter?" Jack asked.

"I did," Kim said. "And so did the LPN, George Haselton. Mr. Carpenter was a demanding patient once he started complaining of headache and chills. You don't think my contact with him could be the cause of my symptoms, do you? I mean, the incubation period for the flu is more than twenty-four hours."

"I'm not an infectious disease specialist," Jack said. "I truly don't know. But I'd recommend you take some rimantadine."

"How is Mr. Carpenter?" Kim asked.

"If you give me the name of your local pharmacy I'll call you in a prescription," Jack said, purposefully ignoring Kim's question. Obviously his fulminant course started after Kim's shift had departed.

As soon as he could, Jack terminated the conversation. He handed the phone back to Kathy. "I don't like this," Jack said. "It's just what I was afraid of."

"Aren't you being an alarmist?" Kathy questioned. "I'd guess two to three percent of the hospital personnel are out with the flu currently."

"Let's call George Haselton," Jack said.

George Haselton turned out to be even sicker than Kim; he'd already called in sick to the floor supervisor. Jack didn't talk to him. He simply listened to Kathy's side of the conversation.

Kathy hung up slowly. "Now you're starting to get me worried," she admitted.

They called the rest of the evening shift for the orthopedic floor, including the ward secretary. No one else was ill.

"Let's try another department," Jack said. "Someone from the lab must have been in to see Carpenter. How can we check?"

"I'll call Ginny Whalen in personnel," Kathy said, picking up the phone again.

A half hour later they had the full picture. Four people had symptoms of a bad case of the flu. Besides the two nurses, one of the evening microbiology techs had abruptly experienced sore throat, headache, shaking chill, muscle pain, cough, and substernal discomfort. His contact with Kevin Carpenter had occurred about ten o'clock in the evening, when he'd visited the patient to obtain a sputum culture.

The final person from the evening shift who was similarly ill was Gloria Hernandez. To Kathy's surprise but not Jack's, she worked in central supply and had had no contact with Kevin Carpenter.

"She can't be related to the others," Kathy said.

"I wouldn't be too sure," Jack said. He then reminded her that someone from central supply had perished with each of the other recent infectious cases. "I'm surprised this hasn't been a topic of debate with the Infection Control Committee. I know for a fact that both Dr. Zimmerman and Dr. Abelard are aware of the connection, because they have been to central supply to talk to the supervisor, Mrs. Zarelli."

"We haven't had a formal committee meeting since all this started," Kathy said. "We meet on the first Monday of each month."

"Then Dr. Zimmerman is not keeping you informed," Jack said.

"It wouldn't be the first time," Kathy said. "We've never been on the best of terms."

"Speaking of Mrs. Zarelli," Jack said. "She'd promised me printouts of everything central supply had sent to each of the index cases. Could we see if she has them and, if so, have her bring them down?"

Having absorbed some of Jack's anxiety about the influenza, Kathy was eager to help. After talking briefly to Mrs. Zarelli and ascertaining that the printouts were available, Kathy had one of the administrative secretaries run up to get them.

"Let me have Gloria Hernandez's phone number," Jack said. "In fact, give me her address as well. This central supply connection is a mystery that for the life of me, I can't understand. It can't be coincidence and could be key to understanding what is going on."

Kathy got the information from the computer, wrote it down, and handed it to Jack.

"What do you think we should do here at the hospital?" she asked.

Jack sighed. "I don't know," he admitted. "I guess you'll have to discuss that with friendly Dr. Zimmerman. She's the local expert. In general, quarantine is not very effective for influenza since it spreads so quickly. But if this is some special strain, perhaps it would be worth a try. I think I'd get those hospital personnel who are sick in here and isolate them: worst case, it's an inconvenience; best case, it could help avert a disaster."

"What about rimantadine?" Kathy asked.

"I'm all for it," Jack said. "I'll probably get some myself. It has been used to control some nosocomial influenza in the past. But again that should be up to Dr. Zimmerman."

"I think I'll give her a call," Kathy said.

Jack waited while Kathy spoke to Dr. Zimmerman. Kathy was deferential but firm in explaining the apparent connection between the sick personnel and the deceased, Kevin Carpenter. Once she had spoken, she was reduced to silence punctuated only by repetitions of "yes" at certain intervals.

Eventually, Kathy hung up. She rolled her eyes. "That woman is impossible," she said. "At any rate, she's reluctant to do anything extraordinary, as she puts it, with just one confirmed case. She's afraid Mr. Kelley and the AmeriCare executives would be against it for PR reasons until it was undeniably indicated."

"What about the rimantadine?" Jack asked.

"On that she was a little more receptive," Kathy said. "She said she'd authorize the pharmacy to order in enough for the staff, but she wasn't going to prescribe it just yet. At any rate, I got her attention."

"At least that's something," Jack agreed.

The secretary knocked and came in with the printouts Jack had wanted from central supply. He thanked the woman, and immediately began scanning them. He was impressed; it was rather extraordinary what each patient utilized. The lists were long and included everything short of medications, food, and linen.

"Anything interesting?" Kathy asked.

"Nothing that jumps out at me," Jack admitted. "Except how similar they are. But I realize I should have asked for a control. I should have asked for a similar list from a random patient."

"That shouldn't be hard to get," Kathy said. She called Mrs. Zarelli back and asked her to print one out.

"Want to wait?" Kathy said.

Jack got to his feet. "I think I've overstretched my luck as it is," he said. "If you could get it and have it sent over to the medical examiner's office, I'd be appreciative. As I mentioned, this central supply connection could be important."

"I'd be happy to do it," Kathy said.

Jack went to the door and furtively glanced out into the hall. Turning back to Kathy, he said, "It's hard to get used to acting like a criminal."

"I think we're in your debt for your perseverance," Kathy said. "I apologize for those who have misinterpreted your intentions."

"Thank you," Jack said sincerely.

"Can I ask you a personal question?" Kathy asked.

"How personal?" Jack asked.

"Just about your face," Kathy asked. "What happened? Whatever it was, it looks like it must have been painful."

"It looks worse than it is," Jack said. "It's merely a reflection of the rigors of jogging in the park at night."

Jack walked quickly through administration and across the lobby. As he stepped out into the early-spring sunshine, he felt relief. It had been the first time he'd been able to visit the General without stirring up a hornet's nest of protest.

Jack turned right and headed east. On one of his prior visits he'd noticed a chain drugstore two blocks from the hospital. He went directly there. Kathy's suggestion of rimantadine was a good one, and he wanted to get some for himself, especially given his intention of visiting Gloria Hernandez.

Thinking of the Hernandez woman made Jack reach into his pocket to be sure he'd not misplaced her address. He hadn't. Unfolding the paper, he looked at it. She lived on West 144th Street, some forty blocks north of Jack.

Arriving at the drugstore, Jack pulled open the door and entered. It was a large store with a bewildering display of merchandise. Everything, including cosmetics, school supplies, cleaning agents, stationery, greeting cards, and even automotive products, was crammed onto metal shelving. The store had as many aisles as a supermarket.

It took Jack a few minutes to find the pharmacy section, which occupied a few square feet in the back corner of the store. With as little respect as pharmacy was given, Jack felt there was a certain irony they even called the establishment a drugstore.

Jack waited in line to speak to the pharmacist. When he finally did he asked for a prescription blank, which he quickly filled out for rimantadine.

The pharmacist was dressed in an old-fashioned white, collarless pharmacist jacket with the top button undone. He squinted at the prescription and then told Jack it would take about twenty minutes.

"Twenty minutes!" Jack questioned. "Why so long? I mean, all you have to do is count out the tablets."

"Do you want this or don't you?" the pharmacist asked acidly.

"I want it," Jack muttered. The medical establishment had a way of bullying people; doctors were no longer immune.

Jack turned back to the main part of the store. He had to entertain himself for twenty minutes. With no goal in mind, he wandered down aisle seven and found himself before a staggering variety of condoms.

BJ liked the idea of the drugstore from the moment he saw Jack enter. He knew it would be close quarters, and as an added attraction, there was a subway entrance right out the door. The subway was a great place to disappear.

After a quick glance up and down the street, BJ pulled open the door and stepped inside. He eyed the glass-enclosed manager's office near the entrance, but experience told him it wouldn't be a problem. It might take a short burst from his machine pistol just to keep everybody's head down when he was on his way out, but that would be about it.

BJ advanced beyond the checkout registers and started glancing down the aisles, looking for either Jack or Slam. He knew if he found one, he'd quickly find the other. He hit pay dirt in aisle seven. Jack was at the very end, with Slam loitering less than ten feet away.

As BJ moved quickly down aisle six, he reached under his sweatshirt and let his hand wrap around the butt of his Tec pistol. He snapped off the safety with his thumb. When he arrived at the cross-aisle in the middle of the store, he slowed, stepped laterally, and stopped. Carefully he leaned around a display of Bounty paper towels and glanced down the remainder of aisle seven.

BJ felt his pulse quicken in anticipation. Jack was standing in the same spot, and Slam had moved over next to him. It was perfect.

BJ's heart skipped a beat when he felt a finger tap his shoulder. He swung around. His hand was still under his sweatshirt, holding on to the holstered Tec.

"May I help you?" a bald-headed man asked.

Anger seared through BJ at having been interrupted at precisely the wrong moment. He glared at the jowled clerk and felt like busting him in the chops, but instead he decided to ignore him for the moment. He couldn't pass up the opportunity with Jack and Slam standing nose to nose.

BJ spun back around, and as he did so he drew out the machine pistol. He started forward. He knew a single step would bring the aisle into full view.

The clerk was shocked by BJ's sudden movement, and he didn't see the gun. If he had, he never would have shouted "Hey" the way he did.

Jack felt on edge and jittery. He disliked the store, especially after his run-in with the pharmacist. The background elevator music and the smell of cheap cosmetics added to his discomfort. He didn't want to be there.

As wired as he was, when he heard the clerk yell, his head shot up, and he looked in the direction of the commotion. He was just in time to see a stocky African-American leaping into the center of the aisle brandishing a machine pistol.

Jack's reaction was pure reflex. He threw himself into the condom display. As his body made contact with the shelving an entire unit tipped over with a clatter. Jack found himself in the center of aisle eight on top of a mountain of disarranged merchandise and collapsed shelves.

While Jack leaped forward, Slam hit the floor, extracting his own machine pistol in the process. It was a skillful maneuver, suggesting the poise and expertise of a Green Beret.

BJ was the first to fire. Since he held his pistol in only one hand, the burst of shots went all over the store, ripping divots in the vinyl flooring and poking holes in the tin ceiling. But most of the shots screamed past the area where Jack and Slam had been standing seconds before, and pounded into the vitamin section below the pharmacy counter.

Slam let out a burst as well. Most of his bullets traveled the length of aisle seven, shattering one of the huge plate-glass windows facing the street.

BJ had pulled himself back the moment he'd seen the element of surprise had been lost. Now he stood, crouched over behind the Bounty paper towels, trying to decide what to do next.

Everyone else in the store was screaming, including the clerk who'd tapped BJ on the shoulder. They began rushing to the exits, fleeing for their lives.

Jack scrambled to his feet. He'd heard Slam's burst of gunfire, and now he was hearing another burst from BJ. Jack wanted out of the store.

Keeping his head down, he dashed back into the pharmacy area. There was a door that said "Employees Only," and Jack rushed through. He found himself in a lunchroom. A handful of open soft drinks and half-eaten packaged pastries on the table told him that people had just been there.

Convinced that there was a way out through the back, Jack began opening doors. The first was a bathroom, the second a storeroom.

He heard more sustained gunfire and more screams out in the main part of the store.

Panicked, Jack tried a third door. To his relief it led out into an alley lined with trash cans. In the distance he could see people running. Among those fleeing, he recognized the pharmacist's white coat. Jack took off after them.

CHAPTER 29

TUESDAY, 1:30 P.M., MARCH 26, 1996

Detective Lieutenant Lou Soldano pulled his unmarked Chevy Caprice into the parking area at the loading bay of the medical examiner's office. He parked behind Dr. Harold Bingham's official car and took the keys out of the ignition. He gave them to the security man in case the car had to be moved. Lou was a frequent visitor to the morgue, although he hadn't been there for over a month.

He got on the elevator and pushed five. He was on his way to Laurie's office. He'd gotten her message earlier but hadn't been able to call until a few minutes ago as he was on his way across the Queensboro Bridge. He'd been over in Queens supervising the investigation on a homicide of a prominent banker.

Laurie had been telling him about one of the medical examiners when Lou had interrupted to tell her he was in the neighborhood and could stop by. She'd immediately agreed, telling him she'd be waiting in her office.

Lou got off the elevator and walked down the hall. It brought back memories. There had been a time when he'd thought that he and Laurie could have had a future together. But it hadn't worked out. Too many differences in their backgrounds, Lou thought.

"Hey, Laur," Lou called out when he caught sight of her working at her desk. Every time he saw her she looked better to him. Her auburn hair fell over her shoulders in a way that reminded him of shampoo commercials. "Laur" was the nickname his son had given her the first time he'd met her. The name had stuck.

Laurie got up and gave Lou a big hug.

"You're looking great," she said.

Lou shrugged self-consciously. "I'm feeling okay," he said.

"And the children?" Laurie asked.

"Children?" Lou commented. "My daughter is sixteen now going on thirty. She's boy crazy, and it's driving me crazy."

Laurie lifted some journals off the spare chair she and her officemate shared. She gestured for Lou to sit down.

"It's good to see you, Laurie," Lou said.

"It's good to see you too," she agreed. "We shouldn't let so much time go by without getting together."

"So what's this big problem you wanted to talk to me about?" Lou asked. He wanted to steer the conversation away from potentially painful arenas.

"I don't know how big it is," Laurie said. She got up and closed her office door. "One of the new doctors on staff would like to talk to you off the record. I'd mentioned that you and I were friends. Unfortunately, he's not around at the moment. I checked when you said you were coming over. In fact, no one knows where he is."

"Any idea what it's about?" Lou asked.

"Not specifically," Laurie said. "But I'm worried about him."

"Oh?" Lou settled back.

"He asked me to do two autopsies this morning. One on a twenty-nine-year-old Caucasian woman who'd been a microbiology tech over at the General. She'd been shot in her apartment last night. The second was on a twenty-five-year-old African-American who'd been shot in Central Park. Before I did the cases he suggested that I try to see if the two were in any way related: through hair, fiber, blood . . ."

"And?" Lou asked.

"I found some blood on his jacket which preliminarily matches the woman's," Laurie said. "Now that's just by serology. The DNA is pending. But it's not a common type: B negative."

Lou raised his eyebrows. "Did this medical examiner give any explanation for his suspicion?" he asked.

"He said it was a hunch," Laurie said. "But there's more. I know for a fact that he'd been beaten up recently by some New York gang members—at least once, maybe twice. When he showed up this morning he looked to me like it might have happened again, although he denied it."

"Why was he beaten up?" Lou asked.

"Supposedly as a warning for him not to go to the Manhattan General Hospital," Laurie said.

"Whoa!" Lou said. "What are you talking about?"

"I don't know the details," Laurie said. "But I do know he's been irritating a lot of people over there, and for that matter, over here as well. Dr. Bingham has been ready to fire him on several occasions."

"How's he been irritating everyone?" Lou asked.

"He has it in his mind that a series of infectious diseases that have appeared over at the General have been spread intentionally."

"You mean like by a terrorist or something?" Lou asked.

"I suppose," Laurie said.

"You know this is sounding familiar," Lou said.

Laurie nodded. "I remember how I felt about that series of overdoses five years ago and the fact that no one believed me."

"What do you think of your friend's theory?" Lou said. "By the way, what's his name?"

"Jack Stapleton," Laurie said. "As to his theory, I don't really have all the facts."

"Come on, Laurie," Lou said. "I know you better than that. Tell me your opinion."

"I think he's seeing conspiracy because he wants to see conspiracy," Laurie said. "His officemate told me he has a long-standing grudge against the health-care giant AmeriCare, which owns the General."

"But even so, that doesn't explain the gang connection or the fact that he might have knowledge of the woman's murder. What're the names of the homicide victims?"

"Elizabeth Holderness and Reginald Winthrope," Laurie said.

Lou wrote down the names in the small black notebook he carried.

"There wasn't much criminologist work done on either case," Laurie said.

"You of all people know how limited our personnel is," Lou said. "Did they have a preliminary motive for the woman?"

"Robbery," Laurie said.

"Rape?"

"No."

"How about the man?" Lou asked.

"He was a member of a gang," Laurie said. "He was shot in the head at relatively close range."

"Unfortunately, that's all too common," Lou said. "We don't spend a lot of time investigating those. Did the autopsies show anything?"

"Nothing unusual," Laurie said.

"Do you think your friend Dr. Stapleton comprehends how dangerous these gangs can be?" Lou asked. "I have a feeling that he's walking on the edge."

"I don't know much about him," Laurie said. "But he's not a New Yorker. He's from the Midwest."

"Uh-oh," Lou said. "I think I'd better have a talk with him about the realities of city life, and I'd better do it sooner rather than later. He might not be around long."

"Don't say that," Laurie said.

"Is your interest in him more than professional?" Lou asked.

"Now let's not get into that kind of discussion," Laurie said. "But the answer is no."

"Don't get steamed up," Lou said. "I just like to know the lay of the land." He stood up. "Anyway, I'll help the guy, and it sounds like he needs help."

"Thank you, Lou," Laurie said. She got up herself and gave the detective another hug. "I'll have him call you."

"Do that," Lou said.

Leaving Laurie's office, Lou took the elevator down to the first floor. Walking through the communications area, he stopped in to see Sergeant Murphy, who was permanently assigned to the medical examiner's office. After they talked for a while about the prospects of the Yankees and the Mets in the upcoming baseball season, Lou sat down and put his feet up on the corner of the sergeant's desk.

"Tell me something, Murph," Lou said. "What's your honest take on this new doctor by the name of Jack Stapleton?"

After having fled from the drugstore, Jack had run the length of the alley and then another four blocks before stopping. When he had, he was winded from the exertion. In between breaths he heard the undulating wails of converging police sirens. He assumed the police were on their way to the store. He hoped that Slam had fared as well as he.

Jack walked until both his breathing and his pulse were back to a semblance of normal. He was still shaking. The experience in the store had unnerved him as much as the ordeal in the park, even though the store episode had taken only seconds. The knowledge that once again he'd been stalked in an attempt to kill him was mind numbing.

Additional sirens now competed with the normal clatter of the city, and Jack wondered if he should go back to the scene to talk to the police and perhaps help if anyone had been struck with a bullet. But Warren's admonitions about talking to the police about gang affairs came to mind. After all, Warren had been right about Jack needing his protection. If it had not been for Slam, Jack sensed he would have been killed.

Jack shuddered. There had been a time in the not-too-distant past when he'd not cared particularly if he lived or died. But now, having come close to death twice, he felt differently. He wanted to live, and that desire made him question why the Black Kings wanted him dead. Who was paying them? Did they think Jack knew something that he didn't, or was it just because of his suspicions concerning the outbreaks at the Manhattan General?

Jack had no answer to these questions, but this second attempt on his life made him more confident that his suspicions were correct. Now he had only to prove them.

In the middle of these musings Jack found himself in front of a second drugstore. But in contrast to the first, it was a small, neighborhood concern. Entering, Jack approached the pharmacist who was manning the store by himself. His name tag said simply "Herman."

"Do you carry rimantadine?" Jack asked.

"We did last time I looked," Herman said with a smile. "But it's a prescription item."

"I'm a doctor," Jack said. "I'll need a script."

"Can I see some identification?" Herman asked.

Jack showed him his New York State medical license.

"How much do you want?"

"Enough for at least a couple of weeks," Jack said. "Why don't you give me fifty tablets. I might as well err on the plus side."

"You got it," Herman said. He started working behind a counter.

"How long will it take?" Jack asked.

"How long does it take to count to fifty?" Herman replied.

"The last store I was in told me it would take twenty minutes," Jack said.

"It was a chain store, right?" Herman said.

Jack nodded.

"Those chain stores don't care a whit about service," Herman said. "It's a crime. And for all their poor service, they're still forcing us independents out of business. It's got me angrier than hell."

Jack nodded. He knew the feeling well. These days no part of the medical landscape was sacrosanct.

Herman came out from behind his counter carrying a small plastic vial of orange tablets. He plunked it next to the cash register. "Is this for you?" he asked.

Jack nodded again.

Herman rattled off a list of possible side effects as well as contraindications. Jack was impressed. After Jack paid for the drug, he asked Herman for a glass of water. Herman gave him some in a small paper cup. Jack took one of the tablets.

"Come again," Herman said as Jack left the store.

With the rimantadine coursing through his system, Jack decided it was time to visit Gloria Hernandez from central supply.

Stepping out into the street, Jack caught a cab. At first the driver demurred about going up into Harlem, but he agreed after Jack reminded him of the rules posted on the back of the front seat.

Jack sat back as the taxi first headed north and then across town on St. Nicholas Avenue after passing Central Park. He looked out the window as Harlem changed from predominantly African-American neighborhoods to Hispanic ones. Eventually all the signs were in Spanish.

When the cab pulled up to his destination, Jack paid the fare and stepped out into a street alive with people. He looked up at the building he was about to enter. At one time it had been a fine, proud single-family home in the middle of an upscale neighborhood. Now it had seen better days, much like Jack's own tenement.

A few people eyed Jack curiously as he mounted the brownstone steps and entered the foyer. The black-and-white mosaic on the floor was missing tiles.

The names on a broken line of mailboxes indicated that the Hernandez family lived on the third floor. Jack pushed the doorbell for that apartment even though his sense was that it didn't work. Next he tried the inner door. Just as in his own building, the lock on the door had been broken long ago and never repaired.

Having climbed the stairs to the third floor, Jack knocked on the Hernandezes' door. When no one answered he knocked again, only louder. Finally he heard a child's voice ask who was there. Jack called out he was a doctor and wanted to speak with Gloria Hernandez.

After a short, muffled discussion that Jack could hear through the door, the door was pulled open to the limit of a chain lock. Jack saw two faces. Above was a middle-aged woman with disheveled, bleached-blond hair. Her eyes were red and sunken with dark shadows. She was wearing a quilted bathrobe and was coughing intermittently. Her lips had a slight purplish cast.

Below was a cherubic child of nine or ten. Jack wasn't sure if it was a boy or a girl. The child's hair was shoulder length, coal black, and combed straight back from the forehead.

"Mrs. Hernandez?" Jack questioned the blond-haired woman.

After Jack showed his medical examiner's badge and explained he'd just come from Kathy McBane's office at the Manhattan General, Mrs. Hernandez opened the door and invited him inside.

The apartment was stuffy and small, although an attempt had been made to decorate it with bright colors and movie posters in Spanish. Gloria immediately retreated to the couch where she'd apparently been resting when Jack knocked. She drew a blanket up around her neck and shivered.

"I'm sorry you are so sick," Jack said.

"It's terrible," Gloria said. Jack was relieved that she spoke English. His Spanish was rusty at best.

"I don't mean to disturb you," Jack said. "But as you know, lately people from your department have become ill with serious diseases."

Gloria's eyes opened wide. "I just have the flu, don't I?" she asked with alarm.

"I'm sure that's correct," Jack said. "Katherine Mueller, Maria Lopez, Carmen Chavez, and Imogene Philbertson had completely different illnesses than you have, that is certain."

"Thank the Lord," Gloria said. She made the sign of the cross with the index finger of her right hand. "May their souls rest in peace."

"What concerns me," Jack continued, "is that there was a patient by the name of Kevin Carpenter on the orthopedic floor last night who possibly had an illness

212 / ROBIN COOK

similar to your own. Does that name mean anything to you? Did you have any contact with him?"

"No," Gloria said. "I work in central supply."

"I'm aware of that," Jack said. "And so did those other unfortunate women I just mentioned. But in each case there had been a patient with the same illness the women caught. There has to be a connection, and I'm hoping you can help me figure out what it is."

Gloria looked confused. She turned to her child, whom she addressed as "Juan." Juan began speaking in rapid Spanish. Jack gathered he was translating for him; Gloria had not quite understood what he'd said.

Gloria nodded and said "si" many times while Juan spoke. But as soon as Juan finished, Gloria looked up at Jack, shook her head, and said: "No!"

"No?" Jack asked. After so many yeses he didn't expect such a definitive no.

"No connection," Gloria said. "We don't see patients."

"You never go to patient floors?" Jack asked.

"No," Gloria said.

Jack's mind raced. He tried to think what else to ask. Finally he said: "Did you do anything out of the ordinary last night?"

Gloria shrugged and again said no.

"Can you remember what you did do?" Jack asked. "Try to give me an idea of your shift."

Gloria started to speak, but the effort brought on a serious bout of coughing. At one point Jack was about to pound her on her back, but she raised her hand to indicate she was all right. Juan got her a glass of water, which she drank thirstily.

Once she could speak, she tried to recall everything she'd done the evening before. As she described her duties, Jack struggled to think if any of her activities put her in contact with Carpenter's virus. But he couldn't. Gloria insisted she had not left central supply for the entire shift.

When Jack could not think of any more questions, he asked if he could call if something else came to mind. She agreed. Jack then insisted she call Dr. Zimmerman at the General to let her know how sick she was.

"What could she do?" Gloria asked.

"She might want to put you on a particular medication," Jack said. "As well as the rest of your family." He knew that rimantadine not only could prevent flu, but if it was started early enough in an established case, it might reduce the duration and possibly the severity of symptoms by as much as fifty percent. The problem was, it wasn't cheap, and Jack knew that AmeriCare was loath to spend money on patient care it didn't feel it had to.

Jack left the Hernandez apartment and headed toward Broadway where he thought he could catch a cab. Now, on top of being agitated from the attempt on his life, he was also discouraged. The visit to Gloria had accomplished nothing other than to expose him to Gloria's influenza, which he feared might be the strain that so readily killed Kevin Carpenter.

Jack's only consolation was that he'd started his own course of rimantadine. The problem was, he knew rimantadine wasn't one hundred percent effective in preventing infection, particularly with a virulent strain.

It was late afternoon by the time Jack was dropped off at the medical examiner's office. Feeling stressed and despondent, he entered and allowed himself to be buzzed in. As he passed the ID area, he did a double take. In one of the small rooms set aside for families identifying their dead, Jack saw David. He didn't know David's last name, but it was the same David who had driven Jack and Spit back to the neighborhood after the episode in the park.

David also caught sight of Jack, and for the second their eyes made contact, Jack sensed anger and contempt.

Resisting the impulse to approach, Jack immediately descended to the morgue level. With his heels echoing loudly on the cement floor he walked around the refrigerated compartments, fearful of what he was going to find. There in the hall was a single gurney bearing a newly dead body. It was directly beneath the harsh glare of a hooded overhead light.

The sheets had been arranged so that only the face could be seen. It had been so posed for a Polaroid picture to be taken. Such a picture was the current method for families to identify their dead. Photographs were considered more humane than having the bereaved families view the often mutilated remains.

A lump formed in Jack's throat as he looked down on Slam's placid face. His eyes were closed; he truly appeared to be asleep. In death he looked even younger than he had in life. Jack would have guessed around fourteen.

Depressed beyond words, Jack took the elevator up to his office. He was thankful that Chet was not in. He slammed his door, sat down at his desk, and held his head in his hands. He felt like crying, but no tears came. He knew indirectly he was responsible for yet another individual's death.

Before he'd had a chance to wallow in guilt, there was a knock on his door. At first Jack ignored it, hoping whoever it was would go away. But then the would-be visitor knocked again. Finally he called out irritably for whoever it was to come in.

Laurie opened the door hesitantly. "I don't mean to be a bother," she said. She could sense Jack's agitation immediately. His eyes were fierce, like the needle ends of darts.

"What do you want?" Jack asked.

"Just to let you know that I spoke with Detective Lou Soldano," Laurie said. "As you asked me to do." She took several steps into the room and placed Lou's phone number on the edge of Jack's desk. "He's expecting your call."

"Thanks, Laurie," Jack said. "But I don't think at the moment I am in the mood to talk to anyone."

"I think he could help," Laurie said. "In fact—"

"Laurie!" Jack called out sharply to interrupt her. Then, in a softer tone, he said: "Please, just leave me alone."

"Sure," Laurie said soothingly. She backed out and closed the door behind her.

For a second she stared at the door. Her concerns skyrocketed. She'd never seen Jack this way. It was a far cry from his normally flippant demeanor and reckless, seemingly carefree ways.

Hurrying back to her own office, Laurie closed her door and called Lou immediately.

"Dr. Stapleton just came in a few minutes ago," she said.

"Fine," Lou said. "Have him give me a call. I'll be here for at least another hour."

"I'm afraid he's not going to call," Laurie said. "He's acting worse now than he was this morning. Something has happened. I'm sure of it."

"Why won't he call?" Lou said.

"I don't know," Laurie said. "He won't even talk to me. And as we speak there is another apparent gang murder down in the morgue. The shooting took place in the vicinity of the Manhattan General."

"You think it involved him in some way?" Lou asked.

"I don't know what to think," Laurie admitted. "I'm just worried. I'm afraid something terrible is about to happen."

"All right, calm down," Lou advised. "Leave it up to me. I'll think of something."

"Promise?" Laurie asked.

"Have I ever let you down?" Lou questioned.

Jack rubbed his eyes forcibly, then blinked them open. He glanced around at the profusion of unfinished autopsy cases that littered his desk. He knew there was no chance he'd be able to concentrate enough to work on them.

Then his eyes focused on two unfamiliar envelopes. One was a large manila envelope, the other was business size. Jack opened the manila one first. It contained the copy of a hospital chart. There was also a note from Bart Arnold saying that he'd taken it upon himself to get a copy of Kevin Carpenter's chart to add to the others Jack had requested.

Jack was pleased and impressed. Such initiative was commendable and spoke well for the entire PA investigative team. Jack opened the chart and glanced through it. Kevin had been admitted for an ACL repair of the right knee, which had gone smoothly Monday morning.

Jack stopped reading and thought about the fact that Kevin had been immediately postoperative when he'd come down with his symptoms. Putting Kevin's chart aside, he picked up Susanne Hard's and confirmed that she, too, had been immediately post-op, having had a cesarean section. Looking at Pacini's, he confirmed the same.

Jack wondered if having had surgery had anything to do with their having contracted their respective illnesses. It didn't seem probable, since neither Nodelman nor Lagenthorpe had undergone surgery. Even so, Jack thought he'd keep the operative connection in mind.

Going back to Kevin's chart, Jack learned that the flu symptoms started abruptly at six P.M. and progressed steadily and relentlessly until a little after nine. At that time they were considered worrisome enough to warrant transferring the patient to the intensive-care unit. In the unit he developed the respiratory distress syndrome that ultimately led to his death.

Jack closed the chart and put it on the stack with the others. Opening the smaller envelope—addressed simply to "Dr. Stapleton"—Jack found a computer printout and a Post-it note from Kathy McBane. The note simply thanked him again for his attention to the affairs of the General. In a short postscript Kathy added that she hoped the enclosed printout would help him.

Jack opened the printout. It was a copy of everything that had been sent from central supply to a patient by the name of Broderick Humphrey. The man's diagnosis wasn't mentioned, but his age was: forty-eight.

The list was just as long as the lists he had for the infectious disease index cases. Like the other lists, it appeared to be random. It was not in alphabetical order, nor were similar products or equipment lumped together. Jack guessed the list was generated in the sequence the items were ordered. That idea was bolstered by the fact that all five lists started out identically, presumably because as each patient was admitted, he required standard, routine equipment.

The random nature of the lists made them hard to compare. Jack's interest was finding any ways that the control list differed from the others. After spending fifteen wasted minutes going back and forth among the lists, Jack decided to use the computer.

The first thing he did was create separate files for each patient. Into each file he copied each list. Since he was hardly the world's best typist, this activity took him a considerable amount of time.

Several hours drifted by. In the middle of the transcription process Laurie again knocked on his door to say good night and to see if she could do anything for him. Jack was preoccupied, but he assured her that he was fine.

When all the data were entered, Jack asked the computer to list the ways the infectious cases differed from the control case. What he got was disheartening: another long list! Looking at it, he realized the problem. In contrast to the control case, all five infectious cases had had sojourns in the intensive-care unit. In addition, all five infectious cases had died and the control hadn't.

For a few minutes Jack thought that his painstaking efforts had been for naught, but then he got another idea. Since he'd typed the lists into the computer in the same order they'd been originally, he asked the computer to make the comparison prior to the first product used in the ICU.

As soon as Jack pushed his execute button the computer flashed its answer. The word "humidifier" appeared on the screen. Jack stared. Apparently the infectious cases had all used humidifiers from central supply; the control hadn't. But was it a significant difference? From Jack's childhood, he remembered his mother had put a humidifier in his room when he'd had the croup. He remembered the device as a small, boiling cauldron that sputtered and steamed at his bedside. So Jack could not imagine a humidifier having anything to do with spreading bacteria. At 212° Fahrenheit, it would boil bacteria.

But then Jack remembered the newer type of humidifier: the ultrasonic, cold humidifier. That, he realized, could be a totally different story.

Jack snatched up his phone and called the General. He asked to be put through to central supply. Mrs. Zarelli was off, so he asked to speak to the evening supervisor. Her name was Darlene Springborn. Jack explained who he was and then asked if central supply at the General handled the humidifiers.

"Certainly do," Darlene said. "Especially during the winter months."

"What kind does the hospital use?" Jack asked. "The steam type or the cold type?"

"The cold type almost exclusively," Darlene said.

"When a humidifier comes back from a patient room what happens to it?" Jack asked.

"We take care of it," Darlene said.

"Do you clean it?" Jack asked.

"Certainly," Darlene said. "Plus we run them for a while to be sure they still function normally. Then we empty them and scrub them out. Why?"

"Are they always cleaned in the same location?" Jack asked.

"They are," Darlene said. "We keep them in a small storeroom that has its own sink. Has there been a problem with the humidifiers?"

"I'm not sure," Jack said. "But if so, I'll let you or Mrs. Zarelli know."

"I'd appreciate it," Darlene said.

Jack disconnected but kept the phone in the crook of his shoulder while he got out Gloria Hernandez's phone number. He punched in the digits and waited. A man answered who could speak only Spanish. After Jack struggled with a few broken phrases, the man told Jack to wait.

A younger voice came on the line. Jack assumed it was Juan. He asked the boy if he could speak to his mother.

"She's very sick," Juan said. "She's coughing a lot and having trouble breathing."

"Did she call the hospital like I urged?" Jack asked.

"No, she didn't," Juan said. "She said she didn't want to bother anybody."

"I'm going to call an ambulance to come and get her," Jack said without hesitation. "You tell her to hold on, okay?"

"Okay," Juan said.

"Meanwhile, could you ask her one question," Jack said. "Could you ask her if she cleaned any humidifiers last night? You know what humidifiers are, don't you?"

"Yeah, I know," Juan said. "Just a minute."

Jack waited nervously, tapping his fingers on top of Kevin Carpenter's chart. To add to his guilt, he thought he should have followed up on his suggestion for Gloria to call Zimmerman. Juan came back on the line.

"She says thank you about the ambulance," Juan said. "She was afraid to call herself because AmeriCare doesn't pay unless a doctor says okay."

"What about the humidifiers?" Jack asked.

"Yeah, she said she cleaned two or three. She couldn't remember exactly."

After Jack hung up from talking to the Hernandez boy he called 911 and dispatched an ambulance to the Hernandez residence. He told the dispatcher to inform the EMTs that it was an infectious case and that they should at least wear masks. He also told her that the patient should go to the Manhattan General and no place else.

With growing excitement, Jack placed a call to Kathy McBane. As late as it was, he didn't expect to get her, but he was pleasantly surprised. She was still in her office. When Jack commented on the fact that she was still there after six, she said she'd probably be there for some time.

"What's going on?" Jack asked.

"Plenty," Kathy said. "Kim Spensor has been admitted into the intensive care unit with respiratory distress syndrome. George Haselton is also in the hospital and is worsening. I'm afraid your fears were well grounded."

Jack quickly added that Gloria Hernandez would be coming to the emergency room soon. He also recommended that the contacts of all these patients be immediately started on rimantadine.

"I don't know if Dr. Zimmerman will go for the rimantadine for contacts," Kathy said. "But at least I've talked her into isolating these patients. We've set up a special ward."

"That might help," Jack said. "It's certainly worth a try. What about the microbiology tech?"

"He's on his way in at the moment," Kathy said.

"I hope by ambulance rather than public transportation," Jack said.

"That was my recommendation," Kathy said. "But Dr. Zimmerman followed up on it. I honestly don't know what the final decision was."

"That printout you sent over was helpful," Jack said, finally getting around to why he'd called. "Remember when you told me about the General's nebulizers getting contaminated in the intensive-care unit three months ago? I think there might have been a similar problem with the hospital's humidifiers."

Jack told Kathy how he'd come to this conclusion, particularly about Gloria Hernandez having admitted to handling humidifiers the previous evening.

"What should I do?" Kathy said with alarm.

"At the moment I don't want you to do anything," Jack said.

"But I should at least take the humidifiers out of service until their safety is assured," Kathy said.

"The problem is I don't want you to become involved," Jack said. "I'm afraid doing something like that might be dangerous."

"What are you talking about?" Kathy demanded angrily. "I am already involved."

"Don't get upset," Jack said soothingly. "I apologize. I'm afraid I'm handling this badly." Jack had not wanted to draw anyone else into the web of his suspicions for fear of their safety, yet at the moment he didn't seem to have any choice. Kathy was right: the humidifiers had to be taken out of service.

"Listen, Kathy," Jack said. Then, as succinctly as possible, he explained his theory about the recent illnesses being intentionally spread. He also told her there was a possibility Beth Holderness had been killed because he'd asked her to search the microbiology lab for the offending agents.

"That's a rather extraordinary story," Kathy said haltingly. Then she added: "It's a little hard to swallow all at once."

"I'm not asking you necessarily to subscribe to it," Jack said. "My only interest in telling you now is for your safety. Whatever you do or say to anyone, please keep what I have told you in mind. And for God's sake, don't mention my theory to anyone. Even if I'm right, I have no idea who's behind it."

"Well," Kathy said with a sigh. "I don't know what to say."

"You don't have to say anything," Jack said. "But if you want to help, there is something you could do."

"Like what?" Kathy asked warily.

"Get some bacterial culture medium and viral transport medium from the micro-biology lab," Jack said. "But don't tell anyone why you want them. Then get some-one from engineering to open the elbow drain below the sink in the storeroom where the humidifiers are kept. Put aliquots from the trap into the two mediums and take them to the city reference lab. Ask them to see if they can isolate any one of the five agents."

"You think some of the microorganisms would still be there?" Kathy asked.

"It's a possibility," Jack said. "It's a long shot, but I'm trying to find proof whatever way I can. At any rate, what I'm suggesting you do is not going to hurt anyone except possibly yourself if you are not careful."

"I'll think about it," Kathy said.

"I'd do it myself except for the reception I invariably get over there," Jack said. "I was able to get away with visiting your office, but trying to get bacterial samples out of a trap in central supply is another thing entirely."

"I'd have to agree with you there," Kathy said.

After he hung up, Jack wondered about Kathy's reaction to his revelations. From the moment he'd voiced his suspicions she'd sounded subdued, almost wary. Jack shrugged. At the moment there wasn't anything else he could say to convince her. All he could do was hope she'd heed his warnings.

Jack had one more call to make, and as he dialed the long-distance number he superstitiously crossed the middle and index fingers of his left hand. He was calling Nicole Marquette at the CDC, and Jack was hoping for two things. First, he wanted to hear that the sample had arrived. Second, he wanted Nicole to say that the titer was high, meaning there were enough viral particles to test without having to wait to grow it out.

As the call went through Jack glanced at his watch. It was nearing seven P.M. He scolded himself for not having called earlier, thinking he'd have to wait until morning to reach Nicole. But after dialing the extension for the influenza unit, he got Nicole immediately.

"It arrived here fine," Nicole said in response to his query. "And I have to give you credit for packing it so well. The refrigerant pack and the Styrofoam kept the sample well preserved."

"What about the titer?" Jack asked.

"I was impressed with that too," Nicole said. "Where was this sample from?"

"Bronchiole washings," Jack said.

Nicole gave a short whistle. "With this concentration of virus it's got to be one hell of a virulent strain. Either that, or a compromised host."

"It's a virulent strain all right," Jack said. "The victim was a young healthy male. Besides that, one of the nurses taking care of him is already in the ICU herself in acute respiratory distress. That's in less than twenty-four hours after exposure."

"Wow! I'd better do this typing immediately. In fact, I'll stay here tonight. Are there any more cases besides the nurse?"

"Three others that I know about," Jack said.

"I'll call in the morning," Nicole said. Then she hung up.

Jack was mildly taken aback by the precipitous end to the conversation, but he was pleased that Nicole was as motivated as she'd apparently become.

Jack replaced the phone receiver, and as he did so, he noticed the tremble of his hand. He took a few deep breaths and tried to decide what to do. He was concerned about going home. He had no way of gauging Warren's reaction to Slam's death. He also wondered if yet another assassin would be sent after him.

The unexpected ring of the telephone interrupted his thoughts. He reached for the phone but didn't pick it up while he tried to think who it could be. As late as it was, he had to shake off some irrational thoughts, like the worry it might be the man who'd tried to kill him that afternoon.

Finally, Jack picked up the phone. To his relief, it was Terese.

"You promised you would call," she said accusingly. "I hope you're not going to tell me you forgot."

"I've been on the phone," Jack said. "In fact, I just this second got off."

"Well, all right," Terese said. "But I've been ready to eat for an hour. Why don't you come to the restaurant directly from work?"

"Oh, jeez, Terese," Jack voiced. With everything that had happened he'd totally forgotten about their dinner plans.

"Don't tell me you are going to try to cop out," Terese said.

"I've had a wicked day," Jack said.

"So have I," Terese countered. "You promised, and as I said this morning, you have to eat. Tell me, did you have lunch?"

"No," Jack said.

"Well, there you go," Terese said. "You can't skip dinner as well as lunch. Come on! I'll understand if you have to go back to work. I might myself."

Terese was making a lot of sense. He needed to eat something even if he wasn't hungry, and he needed to relax. Besides, knowing Terese's persistence he didn't expect she'd take no for an answer, and Jack did not have the energy for an argument.

"Are you thinking or what?" Terese asked impatiently. "Jack, please! I've been looking forward to seeing you all day. We can compare war stories and have a vote whose day was the worst."

Jack was weakening. Suddenly having dinner with Terese sounded wonderfully appealing. He was concerned about putting her at risk simply through proximity, but he doubted anyone was trailing him now. If they were, he could certainly shake them on the way to the restaurant.

"What's the name of the restaurant?" Jack asked finally.

"Thank you," Terese said. "I knew you'd come through. It's called Positano. It's just up the street from me on Madison. You'll love it. It's small and very relaxing. Very un-New-Yorkish."

"I'll meet you there in a half hour," Jack said.

"Perfect," Terese said. "I'm really looking forward to this. It's been a stressful few days."

"I can attest to that," Jack said.

Jack locked up his office and went down to the first floor. He did not know how to ensure that no one followed him, but he thought that he should at least glance out the front to see if anyone suspicious was lurking there. As he passed through communications he noticed that Sergeant Murphy was still in his cubbyhole talking with someone Jack didn't recognize.

Jack and the sergeant exchanged waves. Jack wondered if there had been an unusual number of unidentified dead over the last several days. Murphy usually left at five like clockwork.

Reaching the front door, Jack scanned the area outside. He immediately recognized the futility of what he was doing. Particularly with the homeless facility next door in the old Bellevue Hospital building, there were any number of people loitering who could have qualified as suspicious.

For a few moments Jack watched the activity on First Avenue. Rush hour was still in full swing with bumper-to-bumper traffic heading north. The buses were all filled to overflowing. All the cabs were occupied.

Jack debated what to do. The idea of standing in the street, trying to catch a taxi, had no appeal whatsoever. He'd be too exposed. Someone might even attack him right there, especially if they had been willing to try to shoot him in a drugstore.

A passing delivery van gave Jack an idea. Turning back into the building, he descended to the morgue floor and walked into the mortuary office. Marvin Fletcher, one of the evening mortuary techs, was having coffee and doughnuts.

"Marvin, I have a favor to ask," Jack said.

"What's that?" Marvin asked, washing down a mouthful with a gulp of his coffee.

"I don't want you to tell anyone about this," Jack said. "It's personal."

"Yeah?" Marvin questioned. His eyes opened wider than usual. He was interested.

"I need a ride up to New York Hospital," Jack said. "Could you take me in one of the mortuary vans?"

"I'm not supposed to drive—" Marvin began.

"There's a good reason," Jack said, interrupting Marvin. "I'm trying to duck a girlfriend, and I'm afraid she's outside. I'm sure a good-looking guy like you has had similar problems."

Marvin laughed. "I suppose," he said.

"It will only take a second," Jack said. "We shoot up First and cut over to York. You'll be back here in a flash, and here's a ten-spot for your trouble." Jack laid a ten-dollar bill on the desk.

Marvin eyed the bill and looked up at Jack. "When do you want to go?"

"Right now," Jack said.

Jack climbed into the passenger-side door of the van and then stepped back into the van's cargo area. He held on to whatever handhold he could find while Marvin backed out onto Thirtieth Street. As they waited for the light at the corner of First Avenue, Jack made sure he stayed well out of sight.

Despite the traffic they made good time to New York Hospital. Marvin dropped Jack off at the busy front entrance, and Jack immediately went inside. Within the lobby he stood off to the side for five minutes. When no one even vaguely suspicious entered, Jack headed for the emergency room.

Having been in the hospital on multiple occasions, Jack had no trouble finding his way. Once in the emergency room he stepped out on the receiving dock and waited for a cab to bring in a patient. He didn't have to wait long.

As soon as the patient got out of the cab, Jack got in. He told the cab-driver to take him to the Third Avenue entrance of Bloomingdale's.

Bloomingdale's was as crowded as Jack assumed it would be. Jack rapidly traversed the store's main floor, emerging on Lexington where he caught a second cab. He had this taxi drop him off a block away from Positano.

To be a hundred percent certain he was safe, Jack stood within the entrance of a shoe store for another five minutes. The vehicular traffic on Madison Avenue was moderate, as was the number of pedestrians. In contrast to the area around the morgue, everyone was dressed nattily. Jack saw no one he would have thought was a gang member.

Feeling confident and patting himself on the back for his ingenuity, Jack set out for the restaurant. What he didn't know was that two men sat waiting inside a shiny black Cadillac that had recently parked between the shoe store and Positano. As Jack walked past he couldn't see inside because the windows were tinted dark enough to make them appear like mirrors.

Jack opened the door to the restaurant and entered a canvas tent of sorts designed to keep the winter chill away from the people seated near the entrance.

Pulling a canvas flap aside, Jack found himself in a warm, comfortable environment. To his left was a small mahogany bar. The dining tables were grouped to the right and they extended back into the depths of the restaurant. The walls and ceiling were covered with white lattice into which was woven silk ivy that looked astonishingly real. It was as if Jack had suddenly walked into a garden restaurant in Italy.

From the savory aroma that informed the place, Jack could tell that the chef had the same respect for garlic that he had. Earlier Jack had felt he wasn't hungry. Now he was famished.

The restaurant was crowded but without the frenzied atmosphere of many New York restaurants. With the lattice on the ceiling the sounds of the patrons' conversations and the clink of the china were muted. Jack assumed that the peacefulness of the place was what Terese had meant when she said it was un-New-Yorkish.

The maître d' greeted Jack and asked if he could be of assistance. Jack said he was to meet a Ms. Hagen. The waiter bowed and gestured for Jack to follow him. He showed Jack to a table against the wall just beyond the bar.

Terese rose to give Jack a hug. When she saw his face, she paused.

"Oh, my!" she said. "Your face looks painful."

"People have been saying that my whole life," Jack quipped.

"Jack, please," Terese said. "Don't joke. I'm being serious. Are you really okay?"

"To tell you the honest truth," Jack said, "I'd totally forgotten about my face."

"It looks like it would be so tender," Terese said. "I'd like to give you a kiss, but I'm afraid."

"Nothing wrong with my lips," Jack said.

Terese shook her head, smiled, and waved her hand at him. "You are too much," she said. "I considered myself adept at repartee until I met you."

They sat down.

"What do you think of the restaurant?" Terese asked as she repositioned her napkin and moved her work aside.

"I liked it immediately," Jack said. "It's cozy, and you can't say that about too many restaurants in this city. I never would have known it was here. The sign outside is so subtle."

"It's one of my favorite places," Terese said.

"Thanks for insisting I come out," Jack said. "I hate to admit you were right, but you were. I'm starved."

Over the next fifteen minutes they studied their respective menus, listened to a remarkably long list of special entrées from their waiter, and placed their orders.

"How about some wine?" Terese asked.

"Why not," Jack said.

"Do you want to pick?" Terese asked, extending the wine list in his direction.

"I have a suspicion that you'll know better than I what to order," Jack said.

"Red or white?" Terese asked.

"I can go either way," Jack said.

With the wine opened and two glasses poured, both Terese and Jack leaned back and tried to relax. Both were tense. In fact, Jack wondered if Terese wasn't more tense than he. He caught her furtively glancing at her watch.

"I saw that," Jack said.

"Saw what?" Terese asked innocently.

"I saw you looking at your watch," Jack said. "I thought we were supposed to be relaxing. That's why I've been purposefully avoiding asking about your day or telling you about mine."

"I'm sorry," Terese said. "You're right. I shouldn't be doing it. It's just reflex. I know Colleen and the crew are still in the studio working, and I suppose I feel guilty being out here enjoying myself."

"Should I ask how the campaign is going?" Jack asked.

"It's going fine," Terese said. "In fact, I got nervous today and called my contact over at National Health and had lunch with her. When I told her about the new campaign she was so excited she begged me to allow her to leak it to her CEO. She called back this afternoon to say that he liked it so much that he's thinking of upping the advertising budget by another twenty percent."

Jack made a mental calculation of what a twenty percent increase meant. It was millions, and it made him ill since he knew the money would essentially be coming from patient-care funds. But not wishing to spoil their evening, he did not let Terese know his thoughts. Instead, he congratulated her.

"Thank you," she said.

"It hardly sounds like you had a bad day," Jack commented.

"Well, hearing that the client likes the concept is just the beginning," Terese said. "Now there is the reality of actually putting the presentation together and then actually doing the campaign itself. You have no idea of the problems that arise making a thirty-second TV spot."

Terese took a sip of her wine. As she set her glass back on the table she again glanced at her watch.

"Terese!" Jack said with mock anger. "You did it again!"

"You're right!" Terese said, slapping a hand to her forehead. "What am I going to do with myself. I'm an impossible workaholic. I admit it. But wait! I do know what I can do. I can take the damn thing off!" She unbuckled her wristwatch and slipped it into her purse. "How's that?" she asked.

"Much better," Jack said.

"The trouble is this dude is probably thinking he's some kind of superman or something," Twin said. "He's probably saying those brothers don't know what the hell they are doing. I mean, it's all pissing me off. You know what I'm saying?"

"So why don't you do this yourself?" Phil asked. "Why me?" Dots of perspiration stood out like cabochon diamonds along his hairline.

Twin was draped over the steering wheel of his Cadillac. Slowly he turned his head to regard his heir apparent in the half-light of the car's interior. Headlights of the passing vehicles alternately illuminated Phil's face.

"Be cool," Twin warned. "You know I can't walk in there. The doc would recognize me right off and the game would be over. The element of surprise is important."

"But I was there in the doc's apartment too," Phil complained.

"But the mother wasn't looking you in the eye," Twin said. "Nor did you tag him with a sucker punch. He won't remember you. Trust me."

"But why me," Phil whined. "BJ wanted to do it, especially after things got screwed up in the drugstore. He wants another chance."

"After the drugstore the doc might recognize BJ," Twin said. "Besides, it's an opportunity for you. Some of the brothers have been complaining that you've never done anything like this and that you shouldn't be next in line in the gang. Trust me, I know what I'm doing."

"But I'm not good at this stuff," Phil complained. "I've never shot anyone."

"Hey, it's easy," Twin said. "First time maybe you wonder, but it's easy. Pop! It's over. In a way it's kinda a letdown, because you get yourself all keyed up."

"I'm keyed up, all right," Phil admitted.

"Relax, kid," Twin said. "All you have to do is walk in there and not say a word to anyone. Keep the gun in your pocket and don't take it out until you are standing right in front of the doc. Then draw it out and pop! Then get your black ass outta there and away we go. It's that easy."

"What if the doc runs?" Phil asked.

"He won't run," Twin said. "He'll be so surprised he won't lift a finger. If a dude thinks he might be knocked off he has a chance, but if it comes out of the blue like a sucker punch, there's no way. Nobody moves. I've seen it done ten times."

"I'm nervous, though," Phil admitted.

"Okay, so you're a little nervous," Twin said. "Let me look at you." Twin reached over and pushed Phil's shoulder back. "How's your tie?"

Phil reached up and felt the knot in his tie. "I think it's okay," he said.

"You look great," Twin said. "Looks like you're on your way to church, man. You look like a damn banker or lawyer." Twin laughed and slapped Phil repeatedly on the back.

Phil winced as he absorbed the blows. He hated this. It was the worst thing he'd ever done, and he wondered if it was worth it. Yet at this point he knew he didn't have much choice. It was like going on the roller coaster and clanking up that first hill.

"Okay, man, it's time to blow the mother away," Twin said. He gave Phil a final pat, then reached in front of him to open the passenger-side door.

Phil got out onto rubbery legs.

"Phil," Twin called.

Phil bent down and looked into the car.

"Remember," Twin said. "Thirty seconds from the time you go in the door, I'll be pulling up to the restaurant. You get out of there fast and into the car. Got it?"

"I guess so," Phil said.

Phil straightened up and began walking toward the restaurant. He could feel the pistol bumping up against his thigh. He had it in his right hip pocket.

———

When Jack had first met Terese he'd had the impression that she was so goal oriented, she'd be incapable of small talk. But he had to admit he'd been wrong. When he'd started to tease her unmercifully about her inability to leave her work behind, she'd not only borne the brunt of the gibes with equanimity but had been able to dish out as good as he gave. By their second glasses of wine they had each other laughing heartily.

"I certainly didn't think I'd be laughing like this earlier today," Jack said.

"I'll take that as a compliment," Terese said.

"And indeed you should," Jack said.

"Excuse me," Terese said as she folded her napkin. "I imagine our entrées will be out momentarily. If you don't mind, I'd like to use the ladies' room before they get here."

"By all means," Jack said. He grasped the edge of the table and pulled it toward him to give Terese more room to get out. There was not much space between tables.

"I'll be right back," Terese said. She gave Jack's shoulder a squeeze. "Don't go away," she teased.

Jack watched her approach the maître d', who listened to her and then pointed toward the rear of the restaurant. Jack continued to watch her as she gracefully weaved her way down the length of the room. As usual, she was wearing a simple, tailored suit that limned her slim, athletic body. It wasn't hard for Jack to imagine that she approached physical exercise with the same dogged determination she devoted to her career.

When Terese disappeared from view Jack turned his attention back to the table. He picked up his wine and took a sip. Someplace he'd read that red wine was capable of killing viruses. That thought made him think of something he hadn't considered but perhaps should have. He'd been exposed to influenza, and while he felt confident given the measures he was taking regarding his health, he certainly didn't want to expose anyone else to it, particularly not Terese.

Thinking about the possibility, Jack reasoned that since he didn't have any symptoms, he could not be manufacturing virus. Therefore, he could not be infective. At least he hoped that to be the case. Thinking of influenza reminded him of his rimantadine. Reaching into his pocket, he took out the plastic vial, extracted one of the orange tablets, and took it with a swallow of water.

After putting the drug away, Jack let his eyes roam around the restaurant. He was impressed that every table was occupied, yet the waiters seemed to maintain a leisurely pace. Jack attributed it to good planning and training.

Looking to the right, Jack saw that there were a few couples and single men having drinks at the bar, possibly waiting for tables. Just then, he noticed that the canvas curtain at the entrance was thrown aside as a smartly dressed, young, African-American man stepped into the restaurant.

Jack wasn't sure why the individual caught his attention. At first he thought it might have been because the man was tall and thin; he reminded Jack of several of the men he played ball with. But whatever the reason was, Jack continued to watch the man as he hesitated at the door, then began to walk down the central aisle, apparently searching for friends.

The gait wasn't the high-stepping, springy, jaunty playground walk. It was more of a shuffle, as if the man were carrying a load on his back. His right hand was thrust into his trouser pocket while his left hung down stiffly at his side. Jack couldn't help but notice the left arm didn't swing. It was as if it were a prosthesis instead of a real arm.

Captivated by the individual, Jack watched as the man's head swung from side to side. The man had advanced twenty feet when the maître d' intercepted him, and they had a conversation.

The conversation was short. The maître d' bowed and gestured into the restaurant. The man started forward once again, continuing his search.

Jack lifted his wineglass to his lips and took a sip. As he did so the man's eyes locked onto his. To Jack's surprise the man headed directly for him. Jack slowly put his wineglass down. The man came up to the table.

As if in a dream Jack saw the man start to raise his right hand. In it was a gun. Before Jack could even take a breath the barrel was aimed straight at him.

Within the confines of the narrow restaurant the sound of a pistol seemed deafening. By reflex Jack's hands had grasped the tablecloth and pulled it toward him as if he could hide behind it. In the process he knocked the wineglasses and the wine bottle to the floor, where they shattered.

The concussion of the gunshot and the shattering of glass was followed by stunned silence. A moment later, the body fell forward onto the table. The gun clattered to the floor.

"Police," a voice called out. A man rushed to the center of the room, holding a police badge aloft. In his other hand he held a .38 detective special. "No one move. Do not panic!"

With a sense of disgust Jack pushed the table away. It was pinning him against the wall. When he did so the man rolled off the side and fell heavily to the floor.

The policeman holstered his gun and pocketed his badge before quickly kneeling at the side of the body. He felt for a pulse, then barked an order for someone to call 911 for an ambulance.

Only then did the restaurant erupt with screams and sobs. Terrified diners began to stand up. A few in the front of the restaurant fled out the door.

"Stay in your seats," the policeman commanded to those remaining. "Everything is under control."

Some people followed his orders and sat. Others stood immobilized, their eyes wide.

Having regained a semblance of composure, Jack squatted beside the policeman.

"I'm a doctor," Jack said.

"Yeah, I know," the policeman said. "Give a check. I'm afraid he's a goner."

Jack felt for a pulse while wondering how the policeman knew he was a doctor. There was no pulse.

"I didn't have a lot of choice," the policeman said defensively. "It happened so fast and with so many people around, I shot him in the left side of his chest. I must have hit the heart."

Jack and the policeman stood up.

The policeman looked Jack up and down. "Are you all right?" he asked.

In shocked disbelief, Jack examined himself. He could have been shot without having felt it. "I guess so," he said.

The policeman shook his head. "That was a close one," he said. "I never expected anything to happen to you in here."

"What do you mean?" Jack asked.

"If there was to be trouble, I expected it to be after you left the restaurant," the policeman said.

"I don't know what you are talking about," Jack said. "But I'm awfully glad you happened to be here."

"Don't thank me," the policeman said. "Thank Lou Soldano."

Terese came out of the rest room, confused as to what was going on. She hurried back to the table. When she saw the body her hands flew to her face to cover her mouth. Aghast, she looked at Jack.

"What happened?" she asked. "You're as white as a ghost."

"At least I'm alive," Jack said. "Thanks to this policeman."

In confusion Terese turned to the policeman for an explanation, but the sound of multiple sirens could be heard converging on the restaurant, and the policeman began moving people out of the way and urging them to sit down.

CHAPTER 30

TUESDAY, 8:45 P.M., MARCH 26, 1996

Jack looked out the window of the speeding car and watched the night-time scenery flash by with unseeing eyes. Jack was in the front passenger seat of Shawn Magoginal's unmarked car as it cruised south on the FDR Drive. Shawn was the plainclothes policeman who had mysteriously materialized at the crucial moment to save Jack from sure death.

Over an hour had passed since the event, but Jack was no more relaxed. In fact, now that he'd had time to think about this third attempt on his life he was more agitated than right after the event. He was literally shaking. In an attempt to hide this belated reaction from Shawn he clutched both hands to his knees.

Earlier, when the police cars and the ambulance had arrived at the restaurant, chaos had reigned. The police wanted everyone's names and addresses. Some people balked, others complied willingly. At first Jack had assumed he'd be treated similarly, but then Shawn had informed him that Detective Lieutenant Lou Soldano wanted to talk with him at police headquarters.

Jack had not wanted to go, but he'd been given no choice. Terese had insisted on coming along, but Jack had talked her out of it. She'd only relented once he'd promised to call her later. She'd told him that she'd be at the agency. After such an experience she didn't want to be alone.

Jack ran his tongue around the inside of his mouth. A combination of the wine and tension had made it as dry as the inside of a sock. He didn't want to go to police headquarters for fear they might detain him. He'd failed to report Reginald's murder and he'd been at the scene of the drugstore homicide. To top it off, he'd said enough to Laurie to indicate a potential link between Reginald and Beth's murder.

Jack sighed and ran a worried hand through his hair. He wondered how he'd respond to the inevitable questions he'd be asked.

"You okay?" Shawn questioned. He glanced at Jack, sensing his anxiety.

"Yeah, fine," Jack said. "It's been a wonderful evening in New York. It's a city where you can never get bored."

"That's a positive way to look at it," Shawn agreed.

Jack shot a look at the policeman, who seemed to have taken his comment literally.

"I have a couple of questions," Jack said. "How the hell did you happen to be there at the restaurant? And how did you know I was a doctor? And how is it that I have Lou Soldano to thank?"

"Lieutenant Soldano got a tip you might be in danger," Shawn said.

"How'd you know I was at the restaurant?" Jack asked.

"Simple," Shawn said. "Sergeant Murphy and I tailed you from the morgue."

Jack again looked out at the dark city as it sped by and shook his head imperceptibly. He was embarrassed for having thought he'd been so clever to ensure he'd not been followed. It was painfully obvious that he was out of his league.

"You almost gave us the slip at Bloomies," Shawn said. "But I guessed what you were up to by then."

Jack turned back to the detective. "Who gave Lieutenant Soldano the tip?" he asked. He assumed it had to have been Laurie.

"That I don't know," Shawn said. "But you'll soon be able to ask him yourself."

The FDR Drive imperceptibly became the South Street Viaduct. Ahead Jack could see the familiar silhouette of the Brooklyn Bridge come into view. Against the pale night sky it looked like a gigantic lyre.

They turned off the freeway just north of the bridge and were soon pulling into police headquarters.

Jack had never seen the building and was surprised by its modernity. Inside he had to pass through a metal detector. Shawn accompanied him to Lou Soldano's office, then took his leave.

Lou stood up and offered his hand, then pulled over a straight-backed chair. "Sit down, Doc," Lou said. "This is Sergeant Wilson." Lou gestured toward a uniformed African-American police officer who got to his feet as he was introduced. He was a striking man, and his uniform was impeccably pressed. His well-groomed appearance stood in sharp contrast to Lou's rumpled attire.

Jack shook hands with the sergeant and was impressed with the man's grip. In contrast Jack was ashamed of his own trembling, damp palm.

"I asked Sergeant Wilson down because he's heading up our Anti-Gang Violence Unit in Special Ops," Lou said as he returned to his desk and sat down.

Oh, wonderful, Jack thought, concerned that this meeting might get back to Warren. Jack tried to smile, but it was hesitant and fake; he was afraid his nervousness was all too transparent. Jack worried that both these experienced law-enforcement people could tell he was a felon the moment he walked through the door.

"I understand you had a bad experience tonight," Lou said.

"That's an understatement," Jack said. He regarded Lou. The man was not what he'd expected. After Laurie had implied that she'd been involved with him, Jack had assumed he'd be more physically imposing: taller and more stylish. Instead, Jack thought he was a shorter version of himself considering his stocky, muscular frame and close-cropped hair.

"Can I ask you a question?" Jack asked.

"By all means," Lou said, spreading his hands. "This isn't an inquisition. It's a discussion."

"What made you have Officer Magoginal follow me?" Jack asked. "Mind you, I'm not complaining. He saved my life."

"You have Dr. Laurie Montgomery to thank for that," Lou said. "She was worried about you and made me promise that I would do something. Putting a tail on you was the only thing I could think of."

"I'm certainly appreciative," Jack said. He wondered what he could say to Laurie to thank her.

"Now, Doc, there's a lot going on here that we'd like to know about," Lou said. He steepled his hands with his elbows on his desk. "Maybe you should just tell us what's happening."

"I truly don't know yet," Jack said.

"Okay, fair enough," Lou said. "But, Doc, remember! You can relax! Again, this is a discussion."

"As shaken up as I am, I'm not sure I'm capable of much of a conversation."

"Maybe I should let you know what I know already," Lou said. Lou quickly outlined what Laurie had told him. He emphasized that he knew that Jack had been beaten up at least once and now had had an attempt on his life made by a member of a Lower East Side gang. Lou mentioned Jack's dislike of AmeriCare and his tendency to see conspiracy in the recent series of outbreaks of infectious disease at the Manhattan General. He also mentioned that Jack had apparently irritated a number of people at that hospital. He concluded with Jack's suggestion to Laurie that two apparently unrelated homicides might be linked and that preliminary tests had substantiated this surprising theory.

Jack visibly swallowed. "Wow," he said. "I'm beginning to think you know more than I do."

"I'm sure that's not the case," Lou said with a wry smile. "But maybe all this information gives you a sense of what else we need to know to prevent any more violence to you and others. There was another gang-related killing in the vicinity of the General this afternoon. Is that anything you know about?"

Jack swallowed again. He didn't know what to say. Warren's admonition reverberated in his mind, as did his fleeing from two crime scenes and abetting a murderer. He was, after all, a felon.

"I'd rather not talk about this right now," Jack said.

"Oh?" Lou questioned. "And why is that, Doc?"

Jack's mind raced for answers, and he was loath to lie. "I guess because I'm concerned about certain people's safety," he said.

"That's what we are here for," Lou said. "People's safety."

"I understand that," Jack said. "But this is a rather unique situation. There are a lot of things going on. I'm worried we might be on the brink of a real epidemic."

"Of what?" Lou asked.

"Influenza," Jack said. "A type of influenza with a high morbidity."

"Have there been a lot of cases?" Lou asked.

"Not a lot so far," Jack said. "But I'm worried nonetheless."

"Epidemics scare me, but they are out of my area of expertise," Lou said. "But homicide isn't. When do you think you might be willing to talk about these murders we've been discussing if you're not inclined at the moment?"

"Give me a day," Jack said. "This epidemic scare is real. Trust me."

"Hmmmm . . ." Lou voiced. He looked at Sergeant Wilson.

"A lot can happen in a day," the sergeant said.

"That's my concern too," Lou said. He redirected his attention to Jack. "What worries us is that the two gang members who've been killed were from different gangs. We don't want to see a gang war erupt around here. Whenever they do, a lot of innocent people get killed."

"I need twenty-four hours," Jack repeated. "By then I hope to be able to prove what I'm trying to prove. If I can't, I'll admit I was wrong, and I'll tell you everything I know, which, by the way, is not much."

"Listen, Doc," Lou said. "I could arrest you right now and charge you with accessory after the fact. You are willfully obstructing the investigation of several homicides. I mean, you do understand the reality of what you are doing, don't you?"

"I think I do," Jack said.

"I could charge you, but I'm not going to do that," Lou said. He sat back in his chair. "Instead I'm going to bow to your judgment concerning this epidemic stuff. In deference to Dr. Montgomery, who seems to think you are a good guy, I'll be patient about my area of expertise. But I want to hear from you tomorrow night. Understand?"

"I understand," Jack said. Jack looked from the lieutenant to the sergeant and then back. "Is that it?"

"For now," Lou said.

Jack got up and headed for the door. Before he reached it, Sergeant Wilson spoke up: "I hope you understand how dangerous dealing with these gangs is. They feel they have little to lose and consequently have little respect for life, either their own or others'."

"I'll keep that in mind," Jack said.

Jack hurried from the building. As he emerged into the night he felt enormous relief, as if he'd been granted a reprieve.

While he waited for a taxi to appear in Park Row in front of the police head-quarters, he thought about what he should do. He was afraid to go home. At the moment he didn't want to see the Black Kings or Warren. He thought about going back to see Terese, but he feared endangering her more than he already had.

With few alternatives Jack decided to find a cheap hotel. At least he'd be safe and so would his friends.

CHAPTER 31

WEDNESDAY, 6:15 A.M., MARCH 27, 1996

The first symptom Jack noticed was a sudden rash that appeared on his forearms. As he was examining it, the rash spread quickly to his chest and abdomen. With his index fingers he spread the skin at the site of one of the blotches to see if it would blanch with pressure. Not only did it not blanch, the pressure deepened the color.

Then, as quickly as the skin eruption appeared, it began to itch. At first Jack tried to ignore the sensation, but it increased in intensity to the point where he had to scratch. When he did, the rash began to bleed. Each blotch was transformed into an open sore.

With the bleeding and the sores came a fever. It started to rise slowly, but once it got past a hundred degrees, it shot up. Soon Jack's forehead was awash with perspiration.

When he looked at himself in the mirror and saw his face flushed and spotted with open sores, he was horrified. A few minutes later he began to experience difficulty breathing. Even with deep breaths he was gasping for air.

Then Jack's head began to pound like a drum with each beat of his heart. He had no idea what he'd contracted, but its seriousness was all too obvious. Intuitively Jack knew he had only moments to make the diagnosis and determine treatment.

But there was a problem. To make the diagnosis he needed a blood sample, but he had no needle. Perhaps he could get a sample with a knife. It would be messy, but it might work. Where could he find a knife?

Jack's eyes blinked open. For a second he frantically searched the nightstand for a knife, but then he stopped. He was disoriented. A deep clang sounded again and again. Jack could not place it. He lifted his arm to look at his rash, but it had disappeared. Only then did Jack realize where he was and that he'd been dreaming.

Jack estimated the temperature in the hotel room to be ninety degrees. With disgust he kicked off the blankets. He was drenched in sweat. Sitting up, he put his legs over the side of the bed. The clanging noise was coming from the radiator, which was also steaming and sputtering. It sounded like someone was striking the riser with a sledgehammer.

Jack went to the window and tried to open it. It wouldn't budge. It was as if it had been nailed shut. Giving up, he went to the radiator. It was so hot he couldn't touch the valve. He got a towel from the bathroom, but then found the valve was stuck in the open position.

In the bathroom Jack was able to open a frosted window. A refreshing breeze blew in. For a few minutes he didn't move. The cool tiles felt good on his feet. He leaned on the sink and recoiled at the remembrance of his nightmare. It had been so frighteningly real. He even looked at his arms and abdomen again to make sure he didn't have a rash. Thankfully, he didn't. But he still had a headache, which he assumed was from being overheated. He wondered why he hadn't awakened sooner.

Looking into the mirror, he noticed that his eyes were red. He was also in dire need of a shave. He hoped that there was a sundry shop in the lobby, because he had no toilet articles with him.

Jack returned to the bedroom. The radiator was now silent and the room temperature had dropped to a tolerable level, with cool air flowing in from the bathroom.

Jack began to dress so he could go downstairs. As he did so he recalled the events of the previous evening. The image of the gun barrel came back to his mind's eye with terrifying clarity. He shuddered. Another fraction of a second and he would have been gone.

Three times in twenty-four hours Jack had come close to death. Each episode made him realize how much he wanted to live. For the first time he began to wonder if his response to his grief for his wife and daughters—his reckless behavior—might be a disservice to their memory.

Down in the seedy lobby Jack was able to purchase a disposable razor and a miniature tube of toothpaste with a toothbrush attached. As he waited for the elevator to return to his room he caught sight of a bound stack of the *Daily News* outside of an unopened newsstand. Above the lurid headlines was: "Morgue Doc Nearly Winds Up on the Slab in Trendy Restaurant Shoot-out! See page three."

Jack set down his purchases and tried to tease out a copy of the paper, but he couldn't. The securing band was too tough to snap.

Returning to the front desk, he managed to convince the morose night receptionist to come out from behind his desk and cut the band with a razor blade. Jack paid for the paper and saw the receptionist pocket the money.

On the way up in the elevator Jack was shocked to see a picture of himself on page three coming out of the Positano restaurant with Shawn Magoginal holding his upper arm. Jack couldn't remember a picture being taken. The caption read: "Dr. Jack Stapleton, a NYC medical examiner, being led by plainclothes detective Shawn Magoginal from the scene of the doctor's attempted assassination. A NYC gang member was killed in the incident."

Jack read the article. It wasn't long; he was finished before he got back to his room. Somehow the writer had learned that Jack had had run-ins with the same gang in the past. There was an unmistakably scandalous implication. He tossed the paper aside. He was disgusted at the unexpected exposure and was concerned it could hinder his cause. He expected to have a busy day, and he didn't want interference resulting from this unwanted notoriety.

Jack showered, shaved, and brushed his teeth. He felt a world of difference from when he'd awakened, but he did not feel up to par. He still had a headache and the muscles of his legs were sore. So was his lower back. He couldn't help but worry that he was having early symptoms of the flu. He didn't have to remind himself to take his rimantadine.

When Jack arrived at the medical examiner's office, he had the taxi drop him off at the morgue receiving bay to avoid any members of the press who might be lying in wait.

Jack headed directly upstairs to scheduling. He was worried about what had come in during the night. As he stepped into the room, Vinnie lowered his newspaper.

"Hey, Doc," Vinnie said. "Guess what? You're in the morning paper."

Jack ignored him and went over to where George was working.

"Aren't you interested?" Vinnie called out. "There's even a picture!"

"I've seen it," Jack said. "It's not my best side."

"Tell me what happened," Vinnie demanded. "Heck, this is like a movie or something. Why'd this guy want to shoot you?"

"It was a case of mistaken identity," Jack said.

"Aw, no!" Vinnie said. He was disappointed. "You mean he thought you were someone else?"

"Something like that," Jack said. Then, addressing George, he asked if there had been any more influenza deaths.

"Did someone actually fire a gun at you?" George asked, ignoring Jack's question. He was as interested as Vinnie. Other people's disasters hold universal appeal.

"Forty or fifty times," Jack said. "But luckily it was one of those guns that shoots Ping-Pong balls. Those I wasn't able to duck bounced off harmlessly."

"I guess you don't want to talk about it," George said.

"That's perceptive of you, George," Jack said. "Now, have any influenza deaths come in?"

"Four," George said.

Jack's pulse quickened.

"Where are they?" Jack asked.

George tapped one of his stacks. "I'd assign a couple of them to you, but Calvin already called to tell me he wants you to have another paper day. I think he saw the newspaper too. In fact, he didn't even know if you'd be coming in to work today."

Jack didn't respond. With as much as he had to do that day, having another paper day was probably a godsend. Jack opened the charts quickly to read the names. Although he could have guessed their identities, it was still a shock. Kim Spensor, George Haselton, Gloria Hernandez, and a William Pearson, the evening lab tech, had all passed away during the night with acute respiratory distress syndrome. The worry that the influenza strain was virulent was no longer a question; it was now a fact. These victims had all been healthy, young adults who'd died within twenty-four-plus hours of exposure.

All of Jack's anxiety came back in a rush. His fear of a major epidemic soared. His only hope was that if he was right about the humidifier being the source, all of these cases represented index cases in that all had been exposed to the infected humidifier. Hence, none of these deaths represented person-to-person transfer, the key element for the kind of epidemic he feared.

Jack rushed from the room, ignoring more questions from Vinnie. Jack didn't know what he should do first. From what had happened with the plague episode, he thought he should wait to talk to Bingham and have Bingham call the city and state authorities. Yet now that Jack's worry about a potential epidemic had increased, he hated to let any time pass.

"Dr. Stapleton, you've had a lot of calls," Marjorie Zankowski said. Marjorie was the night communications operator. "Some left messages on your voice mail, but here's a list. I was going to take them up to your office, but since you are here. . ." She pushed a stack of pink phone messages toward Jack. Jack snatched them up and continued on.

He scanned the list as he went up in the elevator. Terese had called several times, the last time being four o'clock in the morning. The fact that she'd called so many times gave Jack a stab of guilt. He should have called her from the hotel, but in truth he hadn't felt like talking with anyone.

To his surprise there were also messages from Clint Abelard and Mary Zimmerman. His first thought was that Kathy McBane might have told them everything he'd said. If she had, then Clint's and Mary's messages might be of the unpleasant sort. They had called one after the other just after six A.M.

Most intriguing and worrisome of all the calls were two from Nicole Marquette from the CDC. One was around midnight, the other at five forty-five.

Rushing into his office, Jack stripped off his coat, plopped himself at his desk, and returned Nicole's call. When he got her on the line, she sounded exhausted.

"It's been a long night," she admitted. "I tried to call you many times both at work and at home."

"I apologize," Jack said. "I should have called to give you an alternate number."

"One of the times I called your apartment the phone was answered by an individual called Warren," Nicole said. "I hope he's an acquaintance. He didn't sound all that friendly."

"He's a friend," Jack said, but the news disturbed him. Facing Warren was not going to be easy.

"Well, I don't know quite where to begin," Nicole said. "One thing I can assure you is that you've caused a lot of people to lose a night's sleep. The sample of influenza you sent has ignited a fire down here. We ran it against our battery of antisera to all known reference strains. It didn't react with any one of them to any significant degree. In other words, it had to be a strain that was either entirely new or had not been seen for as many years as we've been keeping antisera."

"That's not good news, is it?" Jack said.

"Hardly," Nicole said. "It was very scary news, particularly in light of the strain's pathogenicity. We understand there now have been five deaths."

"How did you know?" Jack asked. "I just found out myself there'd been four more victims last night."

"We've already been in contact with the state and local authorities during the night," Nicole said. "That was one of the reasons I tried so hard to get ahold of you. We consider this to be an epidemiological emergency; I didn't want you to feel you were out of the loop. You see, we did finally find something that reacted with the virus. It was a sample of frozen sera we have that we suspect contains antisera to the influenza strain that caused the great epidemic in 1918 and 1919!"

"Good God!" Jack exclaimed.

"As soon as I discovered this, I called my immediate boss, Dr. Hirose Nakano," Nicole said. "He, in turn, called the director of the CDC. He's been on the phone with everyone from the Surgeon General on down. We're mobilizing to fight a war here. We need a vaccine, and we need it fast. This is the swine-flu scare of seventy-six all over again."

"Is there anything I can do?" Jack asked even though he already knew the answer.

"Not at this time," Nicole said. "We owe you a debt of gratitude for alerting us to the problem as soon as you did. I told as much to the director. I wouldn't be surprised if he gave you a call himself."

"So the hospital has been notified?" Jack asked.

"Most definitely," Nicole said. "A CDC team will be coming up there today to assist in any way it can, including helping the local epidemiologist. Needless to say, we'd love to find out where this virus came from. One of the mysteries of influenza is where the dormant reservoirs are. Birds, particularly ducks, and pigs are suspected, but no one knows for sure. It's astonishing, to say the least, that a strain that hasn't been seen for some seventy-five years comes back to haunt us."

A few minutes later, Jack hung up the phone. He was stunned, yet also relieved to a degree. At least his warnings of a possible epidemic had been heeded, and the proper authorities mobilized. If an epidemic was to be averted, the only people who could make that happen were now involved.

But there was still the question of where these infectious agents had come from. Jack certainly did not think it was a natural source like another animal or a bird for the influenza. He thought it was either a person or an organization, and now he could concentrate on that issue.

Before Jack did anything else, he called Terese. He found her at home. She was extremely relieved to hear his voice.

"What happened to you?" she asked. "I've been worried sick."

"I stayed the night in a hotel," Jack said.

"Why didn't you call like you said you would?" Terese asked. "I've called your apartment a dozen times."

"I'm sorry," Jack said. "I should have called. But by the time I left the police headquarters and found a hotel, I wasn't feeling much like talking to anyone. I can't tell you how stressful the last twenty-four hours has been. I'm afraid I'm not myself."

"I suppose I understand," Terese said. "After that horrid incident last night I'm amazed you are functioning at all today. Didn't you consider just staying home? I think that's what I would have done."

"I'm too caught up in everything that is happening," Jack said.

"That's just what I was afraid of," Terese said. "Jack, listen to me. You've been beat up and now almost killed. Isn't it time to let other people take over, and you get back to your normal job?"

"It's already happening to an extent," Jack said. "Officials from the Centers for Disease Control are on their way up here in force to contain this influenza outbreak. All I have to do is make it through today."

"What is that supposed to mean?" Terese asked.

"If I don't solve this mystery of mine by tonight I'm giving up on it," Jack said. "I had to promise as much to the police."

"That's music to my ears," Terese said. "When can I see you? I have some exciting news to tell."

"After last night I would have thought you'd consider me dangerous to be around," Jack said.

"I'm assuming that once you stop this crusade of yours people will leave you alone."

"I'll have to call you," Jack said. "I'm not sure how the day is going to play out."

"You'd promised to call last night and didn't," Terese said. "How can I trust you?"

"You'll just have to give me another chance," Jack said. "And now I have to get to work."

"Aren't you going to ask me about my exciting news?" Terese asked.

"I thought you'd tell me if you wanted to," Jack said.

"National Health canceled the internal review," Terese said.

"Is that good?" Jack asked.

"Absolutely," Terese said. "The reason they canceled it is because they are so sure they'll like our 'no waiting' campaign that I leaked yesterday. So instead of having to throw the presentation together haphazardly we have a month to do it properly."

"That's wonderful," Jack said. "I'm pleased for you."

"And that's not all," Terese said. "Taylor Heath called me in to congratulate me. He also told me he'd learned what Robert Barker had tried to do, so Barker is out and I'm in. Taylor all but assured me I'll be the next president of Willow and Heath."

"That calls for a celebration," Jack said.

"Exactly," Terese said. "A good way to do it would be to have lunch today at the Four Seasons."

"You certainly are persistent," Jack said.

"As a career woman I have to be," Terese said.

"I can't have lunch, but maybe dinner," Jack said. "That is, unless I'm in jail."

"Now what does that mean?" Terese asked.

"It would take too long to explain," Jack said. "I'll call you later. Bye, Terese." Jack hung up before Terese could get in another word. As tenacious as she was, Jack had the feeling she'd keep him on the phone until she got her way.

Jack was about to head up to the DNA lab when Laurie appeared in his doorway.

"I can't tell you how glad I am to see you," Laurie said.

"And I have you to thank for my being here," Jack said. "A few days ago I might have thought of you as having interfered. But not now. I appreciate whatever you said to Lieutenant Soldano, because it saved my life."

"He called me last night and told me what happened," Laurie said. "I tried to call you at your apartment a number of times."

"You and everyone else," Jack said. "To tell you the truth, I was scared to go home."

"Lou also told me he thought you were taking a lot of risks with these gangs involved," Laurie said. "Personally, I think you should call off whatever you are doing."

"Well, you are siding with the majority if it is any consolation," Jack said. "And I'm sure my mother would agree if you were to call her in South Bend, Indiana, and ask her opinion."

"I don't understand how you can be flippant in light of everything that has happened," Laurie said. "Besides, Lou wanted me to make sure you understand that he can't protect you with twenty-four-hour security. He doesn't have the manpower. You're on your own."

"At least I'll be working with someone I've spent a lot of time with," Jack said.

"You are impossible!" Laurie said. "When you don't want to talk about something you hide behind your clever repartee. I think you should tell everything to Lou. Tell him about your terrorist idea and turn it over to him. Let him investigate it. He's good at it. It's his job."

"That might be," Jack said. "But this is a unique circumstance in a lot of ways. I think it requires knowledge that Lou doesn't have. Besides, I sense it might do a world of good for my self-confidence to follow this thing through. Whether it's obvious or not, my ego has taken a beating over the last five years."

"You are a mystery man," Laurie said. "Also stubborn, and I don't know enough about you to know when you are joking and when you are serious. Just promise to be more careful than you've been the last few days."

"I'll make you a deal," Jack said. "I'll promise if you agree to take rimantadine."

"I did notice there were more influenza deaths downstairs," Laurie said. "You think it warrants rimantadine?"

"Absolutely," Jack said. "The CDC is taking this outbreak very seriously, and you should as well. In fact, they think it might be the same strain that caused the disastrous influenza outbreak in 1918. I've started rimantadine myself."

"How could it be the same strain?" Laurie asked. "That strain doesn't exist."

"Influenza has a way of hiding out," Jack said. "It's one of the things that has the CDC so interested."

"Well, if that were the case, it sure shoots holes in your terrorist theory," Laurie said. "There's no way for someone to deliberately spread something that doesn't exist outside of some unknown natural reservoir."

Jack stared at Laurie for a minute. She was right, and he wondered why he hadn't thought of it.

"I don't mean to rain on your parade," Laurie said.

"That's okay," Jack said, preoccupied. He was busy wondering if the influenza episode could be a natural phenomenon, while the other outbreaks were intentional. The problem with that line of thinking was that it violated a cardinal rule in medical diagnostics: single explanations are sought even for seemingly disparate events.

"Nevertheless, the influenza threat is obviously real," Laurie said. "So I'll take the drug, but to make sure you hold up your side of the bargain, I want you to keep in touch with me. I noticed that Calvin took you off autopsy, so if you leave the office you have to call me at regular intervals."

"Maybe you've been talking to my mother after all," Jack said. "Sounds remarkably like the orders she gave me during my first week at college."

"Take it or leave it," Laurie said.

"I'll take it," Jack said.

After Laurie left, Jack headed to the DNA lab to seek out Ted Lynch. Jack was glad to get out of his office. Despite the good intentions involved he was tiring of people giving him advice and he was afraid Chet would soon be arriving. Undoubtedly he'd voice the same concerns just expressed by Laurie.

As Jack mounted the stairs he thought more about Laurie's point concerning the influenza's source. He couldn't believe he'd not thought of it himself, and it undermined his confidence. It also underlined how much he was depending on a positive result with the probe National Biologicals had sent. If they were all negative he'd have scant hope of proving his theory. All he'd have left would be the improbable cultures he'd hoped Kathy McBane had obtained from the sink trap in central supply.

The moment Ted Lynch caught sight of Jack approaching, he pretended to hide behind his lab bench.

"Shucks, you found me," Ted joked when Jack came around the end of the counter. "I was hoping not to see you until the afternoon."

"It's your unlucky day," Jack said. "I'm not even on autopsy, so I've decided to camp out here in your lab. I don't suppose you've had a chance to run my probes . . ."

"Actually, I stayed late last night and even came in early to prepare the nucleoproteins. I'm ready to run the probes now. If you give me an hour or so, I should have some results."

"Did you get all four cultures?" Jack asked.

"Sure did," Ted said. "Agnes was on the ball as usual."

"I'll be back," Jack said.

With some time to kill, Jack went down to the morgue and changed into his moon suit before entering the autopsy room.

The morning routine was well under way. Six of the eight tables were in various stages of the autopsy procedure. Jack walked down the row until he recognized one of the cases. It was Gloria Hernandez. For a moment he looked at her pale face and tried to comprehend the reality of death. Having just spoken with her in her apartment the day before, it seemed an inconceivable transition.

The autopsy was being done by Riva Mehta, Laurie's officemate. She was a petite woman of Indian extraction who had to stand on a stool to do the procedure. At that moment she was just entering the chest.

Jack stayed and watched. When the lungs were removed he asked to see the cut surface. It was identical to Kevin Carpenter's from the day before, complete with pinpoint hemorrhages. There was no doubt it was a primary influenza pneumonia.

Moving on, Jack found Chet, who was busy with the nurse, George Haselton. Jack was surprised; it was Chet's usual modus operandi to stop into the office before doing his day's autopsies. When Chet saw it was Jack, he seemed annoyed.

"How come you didn't answer your phone last night?" Chet demanded.

"It was too long a reach," Jack said. "I wasn't there."

"Colleen called to tell me what happened," Chet said. "I think this whole thing has gone far enough."

"Chet, instead of talking, how about showing me the lung," Jack said.

Chet showed Jack the lung. It was identical to Gloria Hernandez's and Kevin Carpenter's. When Chet started to talk again, Jack merely moved on.

Jack stayed in the autopsy room until he'd seen the gross on all the influenza cases. There were no surprises. Everyone was impressed by the pathogenicity of the virus.

Changing back into his street clothes, Jack went directly up to the DNA lab. This time Ted acted glad to see him.

"I'm not sure what you wanted me to find," Ted said. "But you are batting five hundred. Two of the four were positive."

"Just two?" Jack asked. He'd prepared himself for either all positive or all negative. Like everything else associated with these outbreaks, he was surprised.

"If you want I can go back and fudge the results," Ted joked. "How many do you want to be positive?"

"I thought I was the jokester around here," Jack said.

"Do these results screw up some theory of yours?" Ted asked.

"I'm not sure yet," Jack said. "Which two were positive?"

"The plague and the tularemia," Ted said.

Jack walked back to his office while he pondered this new information. By the time he was sitting down he'd decided that it didn't make any difference how many of the cultures were positive. That fact that any of them were positive supported his theory. Unless an individual was a laboratory worker it would be hard to come in contact with an artificially propagated culture of a bacteria.

Pulling his phone over closer to himself, Jack put in a call to National Biologicals. He asked to speak with Igor Krasnyansky, since the man had already been accommodating enough to send the probes.

Jack reintroduced himself.

"I remember you," Igor said. "Did you have any luck with the probes?"

"I did," Jack said. "Thank you again for sending them. But now I have a few more questions."

"I'll try to answer them," Igor said.

"Does National Biologicals also sell influenza cultures?" Jack asked.

"Indeed," Igor said. "Viruses are a big part of our business, including influenza. We have many strains, particularly type A."

"Do you have the strain that caused the epidemic in 1918?" Jack asked. He just wanted to be one hundred percent certain.

"We wish!" Igor said with a laugh. "I'm sure that strain would be popular with researchers. No, we don't have it, but we have some that are probably similar, like the strain of the '76 swine-flu scare. It's generally believed that the 1918 strain was a permutation of H1N1, but exactly what, no one knows."

"My next question concerns plague and tularemia," Jack said.

"We carry both," Igor said.

"I'm aware of that," Jack said. "What I would like to know is who has ordered either of those two cultures in the last few months."

"I'm afraid we don't usually give that information out," Igor said.

"I can understand that," Jack said. For a moment Jack feared he would have to get Lou Soldano involved just to get the information he wanted. But then he thought he could possibly talk Igor into giving it to him. After all, Igor had been careful to say that such information wasn't "usually" given out.

"Perhaps you'd like to talk to our president," Igor suggested.

"Let me tell you why I want to know," Jack said. "As a medical examiner I've seen a couple of deaths recently with these pathogens. We'd just like to know which labs we should warn. Our interest is preventing any more accidents."

"And the deaths were due to our cultures?" Igor asked.

"That was why I wanted the probes," Jack said. "We suspected as much but needed proof."

"Hmm," Igor said. "I don't know if that should make me feel more or less inclined to give out information."

"It's just an issue of safety," Jack said.

"Well, that sounds reasonable," Igor said. "It's not as if it's a secret. We share our customer lists with several equipment manufacturers. Let me see what I can find here at my workstation."

"To make it easier for you, narrow the field to labs in the New York metropolitan area," Jack said.

"Fair enough," Igor said. Jack could hear the man typing on his keyboard. "We'll try tularemia first. Here we go."

There was a pause.

"Okay," Igor said. "We have sent tularemia to the National Health hospital and to the Manhattan General Hospital. That's it; at least for the last couple of months."

Jack sat more upright, especially knowing that National Health was the major competitor of AmeriCare. "Can you tell me when these cultures went out?"

"I think so," Igor said. Jack could hear more typing. "Okay, here we are. The National Health shipment went out on the twenty-second of this month, and the Manhattan General shipment went out on the fifteenth."

Jack's enthusiasm waned slightly. By the twenty-second he'd already made the diagnosis of tularemia in Susanne Hard. That eliminated National Health for the time being. "Does it show who the receiver was on the Manhattan General shipment?" Jack asked. "Or was it just the lab itself?"

"Hold on," Igor said as he switched screens again. "It says that the consignee was a Dr. Martin Cheveau."

Jack's pulse quickened. He was uncovering information that very few people would know could be discoverable. He doubted that even Martin Cheveau was aware that National Biologicals phage-typed their cultures.

"What about plague?" Jack asked.

"Just a moment," Igor said while he made the proper entries.

There was another pause. Jack could hear Igor's breathing.

"Okay, here it is," Igor said. "Plague's not a common item ordered on the East Coast outside of academic or reference labs. But there was one shipment that went out on the eighth. It went to Frazer Labs."

"I've never heard of them," Jack said. "Do you have an address?"

"Five-fifty Broome Street," Igor said.

"How about a consignee?" Jack asked as he wrote down the address.

"Just the lab itself," Igor said.

"Do you do much business with them?" Jack asked.

"I don't know," Igor said. He made another entry. "They send us orders now and then. It must be a small diagnostic lab. But there's one thing strange."

242 / ROBIN COOK

"What's that?" Jack asked.

"They always pay with a cashier's check," Igor said. "I've never seen that before. It's okay, of course, but customers usually have established credit."

"Is there a telephone number?" Jack asked.

"Just the address," Igor said, which he repeated.

Jack thanked Igor for his help and hung up the phone. Taking out the phone directory, he looked up Frazer Labs. There was no listing. He tried information but had the same luck.

Jack sat back. Once again he'd gotten information he didn't expect. He now had two sources of the offending bacteria. Since he already knew something about the lab at the Manhattan General, he thought he'd better visit Frazer Labs. If there was some way he could establish an association with the two labs or with Martin Cheveau personally, he'd turn everything over to Lou Soldano.

The first problem was the concern about being followed. The previous evening he'd thought he'd been so clever but had been humbled by Shawn Magoginal. Yet to give himself credit, he had to remember that Shawn was an expert. The Black Kings certainly weren't. But to make up for their lack of expertise, the Black Kings were ruthless. Jack knew he'd have to lose a potential tail rapidly since they had clearly demonstrated a total lack of compunction about attacking him in public.

There was also the collateral worry about Warren and his gang. Jack didn't know what to think about them. He had no idea of Warren's state of mind. It was something Jack would have to face in the near future.

To lose any tail Jack wanted a crowded location with multiple entrances and exits. Immediately Grand Central Terminal and the Port Authority Bus Terminal came to mind. He decided on the former since it was closer.

Jack wished there were some underground way of getting over to the NYU Medical Center to help him get away from the office, but there wasn't. Instead he settled on a radio-dispatched taxi service. He directed the dispatcher to have the car pick him up at the receiving bay of the morgue.

Everything seemed to work perfectly. The car came quickly. Jack slipped in from the bay. They managed to hit the light at First Avenue; at no time was Jack a sitting duck in a motionless car. Still, he hunched low in his seat, out of view, sparking the driver's curiosity. The cabbie kept stealing looks at Jack in his rearview mirror.

As they drove up First Avenue, Jack raised himself up and watched out the back. He saw nothing suspicious. No cars suddenly pulled into the traffic. No one ran out to flag a cab.

They turned left on Forty-second Street. Jack had the driver pull up directly in front of Grand Central. The moment the car came to a stop, Jack was out and running. He dashed through the entrance and merged quickly with the crowd. To be absolutely sure he was not being followed, he descended into the subway and boarded the Forty-second Street shuttle.

When the train was about to leave and the doors had started to close, Jack impeded their closing and jumped off the train. He ran up into the station proper and exited back onto Forty-second Street through a different entrance than he used when he arrived.

Feeling confident, Jack hailed a taxi. At first he told the driver to take him to the World Trade Center. During the trip down Fifth Avenue he watched to see if any cars, taxis, or trucks could have been following. When none seemed to be doing so, Jack told the driver to take him to 550 Broome Street.

Jack finally began to relax. He sat back in the seat and put his hands to his temples. The headache he'd awakened with in the overheated hotel room had never completely gone away. He'd been ascribing the lingering throb to anxiety, but now there were new symptoms. He had a vague sore throat accompanied by mild coryza. There was still a chance it was all psychosomatic, but he was still worried.

After rounding Washington Square, the taxi driver went south on Broadway before turning east on Houston Street. At Eldridge he made a right.

Jack looked out at the scenery. He'd not had any idea where Broome Street was, although he'd assumed it was someplace downtown, south of Houston. That entire section of the city was one of the many parts of New York he had yet to explore, and there were many street names with which he was unfamiliar.

The cab made a left-hand turn off Eldridge, and Jack caught a glimpse of the street sign. It was Broome Street. Jack looked out at the buildings. They were five and six stories tall. Many were abandoned and boarded up. It seemed an improbable place to have a medical lab.

At the next corner the neighborhood improved slightly. There was a plumbing-supply store with thick metal grates covering its windows. Sprinkled down the rest of the block were other building-supply concerns. On the floors above the street-level stores were a few loft apartments. Otherwise, it seemed to be vacant commercial space.

In the middle of the following block, the cabdriver pulled to the side of the street. Five-fifty Broome Street was not Frazer Labs. It was a combination check-cashing place, mailbox rental, and pawnshop stuck between a package store and a shoe repair shop.

Jack hesitated. At first he thought he'd gotten the wrong address. But that seemed unlikely. Not only had he written it down, but Igor had mentioned it twice. Jack paid his fare and climbed from the cab.

Like all the other stores in the area, this one had an iron grille that could be pulled across its front at night and locked. In the window was a miscellaneous mixture of objects that included an electric guitar, a handful of cameras, and a display of cheap jewelry. A large sign over the door said: "Personal Mailboxes." Painted on the door glass were the words "Checks Cashed."

Jack stepped up to the window. By standing directly in front of the electric guitar, he could see beyond the display into the store itself. There was a glass-topped counter that ran down the right side. Behind the counter was a mustached man with a punk-rock hairstyle. He was dressed in military camouflage fatigues. In the rear of the shop was a Plexiglas-enclosed cubicle that looked like a bank teller's window. On the left side of the store was a bank of mailboxes.

Jack was intrigued. The fact that Frazer Labs might be using this tacky shop as a mail drop was certainly suspicious if it was true. At first he was tempted to walk in and ask. But he didn't. He was afraid by doing so he might hinder other methods of finding out. He knew that such personal mailbox establishments were loath to give out any information. Privacy was the main reason people rented the boxes in the first place.

What Jack truly wanted was not only to find out if Frazer Labs had a box there, but to entice a Frazer Labs representative to come to the shop. Slowly an elaborate plan began to form in Jack's mind.

Being careful not to be seen by the clerk within the store, Jack quickly walked away. The first thing he needed was a telephone directory. Since the area around the pawnshop was comparatively deserted, Jack walked south to Canal Street. There he found a drugstore.

From the phone directory Jack copied down four addresses: a nearby uniform shop, a van rental agency, an office supply store, and a Federal Express office. Since the clothing shop was the closest, Jack went there first.

Once in the store Jack realized that he couldn't remember what Federal Express courier uniforms looked like. But he wasn't terribly concerned. If he couldn't remember, he didn't think the clerk in the pawnshop would know either. Jack bought a pair of blue cotton twill pants and a white shirt with flap pockets and epaulets. He also bought a plain black belt and blue tie.

"Would you mind if I put these on?" Jack asked the clerk.

"Of course not," the clerk said. He showed Jack to a makeshift dressing room.

The pants were slightly too long, but Jack was satisfied. When he looked at himself in the mirror he thought he needed something else. He ended up adding a blue peaked cap to his outfit. After Jack paid for his purchases, the clerk was happy to wrap up Jack's street clothes. Just before the package was sealed, Jack thought to rescue his rimantadine. With the symptoms he was feeling he didn't want to miss a dose.

The next stop was the office-supply store, where Jack selected wrapping paper, tape, a medium-sized box, string, and a packet of "rush" labels. To Jack's surprise he even found "biohazard" labels, so he tossed a box of them into his shopping cart. In another part of the store he found a clipboard and a pad of printed receipt forms. Once he had everything he wanted he took them to the checkout register and paid.

The next stop was the Federal Express office. From their supply stand Jack took several address labels with the clear plastic envelopes used to attach them to a parcel.

The final destination was a car rental agency, where Jack rented a cargo van. That took the most time, since Jack had to wait while someone went to another location to bring the van to the agency. Jack used the opportunity to prepare the parcel. First he put together the box. Wanting to give it the feeling of having contents, Jack eyed a triangular piece of wood on the floor near the entrance. He assumed it was a doorstop.

When no one at the rental counter was looking Jack picked up the object and slipped it into the box. He then crumpled up multiple sheets of a *New York Post* that he found in the waiting area. He hefted the box and gave it a shake. Satisfied, he taped it shut.

After the wrapping paper and the string were applied, Jack plastered the outside with "rush" and "biohazard" labels.

The final touch was the Federal Express label, which Jack carefully filled out, addressing it to Frazer Labs. For the return address Jack used National Biologicals's. After throwing away the top copy, Jack inserted one of the carbons into the plastic envelope and secured it to the front of the box. He was pleased. The package appeared official indeed, and with all the "rush" labels, he hoped it would have the desired effect.

When the van arrived, Jack went out and put the package, the remains of the wrapping material, and the parcel containing his clothes in the back. Climbing behind the wheel, he drove off.

Before going back to the pawnshop Jack made two stops. He returned to the drugstore where he'd used the phone book and bought some throat lozenges for his irritated throat, which seemed to be getting worse. He also stopped at a deli for some takeout. He wasn't hungry, but it was already afternoon, and he'd eaten nothing that day. Besides, after he delivered the package he had no idea how long he'd have to wait.

While driving back to Broome Street Jack opened one of the orange-juice containers he'd bought and used the juice to take a second dose of rimantadine. In view of his progressive symptoms he wanted to keep the drug's concentration high in his blood.

Jack pulled up directly in front of the pawnshop, leaving the engine running and the emergency blinkers blinking. Clutching his clipboard, he got out and went around to the rear to get the package. Then he entered the store.

The door had bells secured to the top edge, and Jack's entrance was heralded by a raucous ringing. As had been the case earlier, there were no customers in the shop. The mustached man in the camouflage fatigues looked up from a magazine. With his hair standing on end he had the look of perpetual surprise.

"I've got a rush delivery for Frazer Labs," Jack said. He plopped the parcel down on the glass counter and shoved the clipboard under the man's nose. "Sign there at the bottom," he added while proffering his pen to the man.

The man took the pen but hesitated and eyed the box.

"This is the right address, isn't it?" Jack asked.

"I reckon," the man said. He stroked his mustache and looked up at Jack. "What's the rush?"

"I was told there was dry ice in there," Jack said. Then he leaned forward as if to tell a secret. "My supervisor thinks it's a shipment of live bacteria. You know, for research and all."

The man nodded.

"I was surprised I wasn't delivering this directly to the lab," Jack said. "It can't sit around. I mean, I don't think it will leak out or anything; at least I don't think so. But it might die and then it will be useless. I assume you have a way of getting in touch with your customers?"

"I reckon," the man repeated.

"I'd advise you to do that," Jack said. "Now sign and I'll be on my way."

The man signed his name. Reading upside down, Jack made out "Tex Hartmann." Tex pushed the clipboard back toward Jack, and Jack slipped it under his arm. "I'm sure glad to get that thing off my truck," Jack said. "I've never been much of a fan of bacteria and viruses. Did you hear about those cases of plague that were here in New York last week? They scared me to death."

The man nodded again.

"Take care," Jack said with a wave. He walked out of the store and climbed into his truck. He wished that Tex had been a bit more talkative. Jack wasn't sure if he would be calling Frazer Labs or not. But just as Jack was releasing the emergency brake he could see Tex through the window dialing his phone.

Pleased with himself, Jack drove several blocks down Broome Street, then circled the block. He parked about a half block from the pawn shop and turned off the motor. After locking the doors, he broke out the deli food. Whether he was hungry or not, he was going to make himself eat something.

"Are you sure we should be doing this?" BJ questioned.

"Yeah, man, I'm sure," Twin said. He was maneuvering his Cadillac around Washington Square Park looking for someplace to park. It wasn't looking good. The park was crammed full of people entertaining themselves in a bewildering variety of ways. There was skateboarding, in-line skating, Frisbee throwing, break dancing, chess playing, and drug dealing. Baby carriages dotted the park. It was a carnival-like atmosphere, which was exactly why Twin had suggested the park for the upcoming meeting.

"Shit, man, I feel naked without some kind of ordnance. It's not right."

"Shut your mouth, BJ, and look for a spot for this ride of mine," Twin said. "This is going to be a meeting of the brothers. There's no need for any firepower."

"What if they bring some?" BJ asked.

"Hey, man, don't you trust nobody?" Twin asked. At that moment he saw a delivery van pulling away from the curb. "What do you know, we're in luck."

Twin expertly guided his car into the spot and pushed on the emergency brake.

"It says for commercial vehicles only," BJ said. He had his face pressed up against the window to see the parking sign.

"With all the crack we've moved this year I think we qualify," Twin said with a laugh. "Come on, get your black ass in gear."

They got out of the car and crossed the street to enter the park. Twin checked his watch. They were a little early despite the trouble parking. That was how Twin liked it for this kind of meeting. He wanted a chance to scope the place out. It wasn't that he didn't trust the other brothers, it was just that he liked to be careful.

But Twin was in for a surprise. When his eyes swept the area for the agreed-upon meeting he found himself transfixed by the stare of one of the more physically imposing men he'd seen in some time.

"Uh-oh," Twin said under his breath.

"What's the matter?" BJ demanded, instantly alert.

"The brothers have gotten here before us," Twin said.

"What do you want me to do?" BJ asked. His own eyes raced around the park until they, too, settled on the same man Twin had spotted.

"Nothing," Twin said. "Just keep walking."

"He looks so goddamn relaxed," BJ said. "It makes me worried."

"Shut up!" Twin commanded.

Twin walked right up to the man whose piercing eyes had never left his. Twin formed his right hand into the form of a gun, pointed at the man, and said: "Warren!"

"You got it," Warren said. "How's it going?"

"Not bad," Twin said. He then ritualistically raised his right hand to head height. Warren did the same and they high-fived. It was a perfunctory gesture, akin to a couple of rival investment bankers shaking hands.

"This here's David," Warren said, motioning toward his companion.

"And this here's BJ," Twin said, mimicking Warren.

David and BJ eyed each other but didn't move or speak.

"Listen, man," Twin said. "Let me say one thing right off. We didn't know the doc was living in your hood. I mean, maybe we should have known, but we didn't think about it with him being white."

"What kind of a relationship did you have with the doc?" Warren asked.

"Relationship?" Twin questioned. "We didn't have no relationship."

"How come you've been trying to ice him?" Warren asked.

"Just for some small change," Twin said. "A white dude who lives down our way came to us and offered us some cash to warn the doc about something he was doing. Then, when the doc didn't take our advice, the dude offered us more to take him out."

"So you're telling me the doc hasn't been dealing with you people?" Warren asked.

"Shit no," Twin said with a derisive laugh. "We don't need no honky doctor for our operation, no way."

"You should have come to us first," Warren said. "We would have set you right about the doc. He's been running with us on the b-ball court for four or five months. He's not half bad neither. So I'm sorry about Reginald. I mean, it wouldn't have happened if we'd talked."

"I'm sorry about the kid," Twin said. "That shouldn't have happened neither.

Trouble was, we were so pissed about Reginald. We couldn't believe a brother would get shot over a honky doctor."

"That makes us even," Warren said. "That's not counting what happened last night, but that didn't involve us."

"I know," Twin said. "Can you imagine that doc? He's like a cat with nine lives. How the hell did that cop react so fast? And why was he in there? He must think he's Wyatt Earp or something."

"The point is that we have a truce," Warren said.

"Damn straight," Twin said. "No more brother shooting brother. We've got enough trouble without that."

"But a truce means you lay off the doc too," Warren said.

"You care what happens to that dude?" Twin asked.

"Yeah, I do," Warren said.

"Hey, then it's your call, man," Twin said. "It wasn't like the money was that good anyway."

Warren stuck out his hand palm up. Twin slapped it. Then Warren slapped Twin's.

"Be good," Warren said.

"You too, man," Twin said.

Warren motioned to David that they were leaving. They walked back toward the Washington Arch at the base of Fifth Avenue.

"That wasn't half bad," David said.

Warren shrugged.

"You believe him?" David asked.

"Yeah, I do," Warren said. "He might deal in drugs, but he's not stupid. If this thing goes on, we all lose."

CHAPTER 32

WEDNESDAY, 5:45 P.M., MARCH 27, 1996

Jack felt uncomfortable. Among other problems he was stiff and now all his muscles ached. He'd been sitting in the van for more hours than he cared to count, watching customers going in and out of the pawnshop. There'd never been a crowd, but it was steady. Most of the people looked seedy. It occurred to Jack that the shop was trafficking in illicit activities like gambling or drugs.

It was not a good neighborhood. Jack had sensed that the moment he'd arrived that morning. The point had been driven home as darkness fell and someone tried to break into the van with Jack sitting there. The man had approached the passenger-side door with a flat bar, which he proceeded to insert between the glass and the door frame. Jack had to knock on the glass and wave to get the man's attention. The moment he saw Jack he ran off.

Jack was now popping throat lozenges at a regular rate with little relief. His throat was worse, and to add to his increasing misery he'd developed a cough. It wasn't a bad cough, merely a dry hack. But it further irritated his throat and increased his anxiety that he had indeed caught the flu from Gloria Hernandez. Although two rimantadine tablets were recommended as the daily dose, Jack took a third when the coughing started.

Just about the time Jack was contemplating admitting to himself that his clever ploy with the package had been a failure, his patience paid off. The man involved did not attract Jack's attention initially. He'd arrived on foot, which was not what Jack expected. He was dressed in an old nylon ski parka with a hood just like a few of the individuals who'd preceded him. But when he came out he was carrying the parcel. Despite the failing light and the distance, Jack could see the "rush" and "biohazard" labels plastered haphazardly over the exterior.

Jack had to make a rapid decision as the man walked briskly toward the Bowery. He hadn't expected to be following a pedestrian, and he debated if he should get out of the van and follow on foot or stay in the van, circle around, and try to follow the man while driving.

Thinking that a slowly moving van would attract more attention than a pedestrian, Jack got out of the truck. He followed at a distance until the man turned right on Eldridge Street. Jack then ran until he reached the corner.

He peeked around just in time to see the man entering a building across the street, midway down the block.

Jack quickly walked to the building. It was five stories, like its immediate neighbors. Each floor had two large, storefront-sized windows with smaller, sashed windows on either side. A fire escape zigzagged down the left side of the facade to end in a counterweighted ladder pivoted some twelve feet from the sidewalk. The ground-floor commercial space was vacant with a For Rent sign stuck to the inside of the glass.

The only lights were in the second-floor windows. From where Jack was standing it appeared to be a loft apartment, but he couldn't be certain. There were no drapes or other obvious signs of domesticity.

While Jack was eyeing the building, vaguely wondering what to do next, the lights went on up on the fifth floor. While he watched he saw someone raise the sash of the smaller window to the left. Jack was unable to see if it had been the man he followed, but he suspected it was.

After making certain he wasn't being observed, Jack quickly moved over to the door where the man had entered. He tried it, and it opened. Stepping over the threshold, he found himself in a small foyer. A group of four mailboxes was set into the wall to the left. Only two had names. The second floor was occupied by G. Heilbrunn. The fifth-floor tenant was R. Overstreet. There was no Frazer Labs.

Four buzzers bordered a small grille which Jack assumed covered a speaker. He vaguely contemplated ringing the fifth floor but had trouble imagining what he could say. He stood there for a few minutes thinking, but nothing came to mind. Then he noticed that the mailbox for the fifth floor appeared to be unlocked.

Jack was about to reach up to the mailbox when the inner door to the building proper abruptly opened. It startled Jack and he jumped, but he had the presence of mind to keep himself turned away from whoever was exiting the building. The person hastily brushed by Jack with obvious distress. Jack caught a fleeting glimpse of the same nylon ski parka. A second later the man was gone.

Jack reacted quickly, getting his foot into the inner door before it closed. As soon as he was certain the man was not immediately returning, Jack entered the building. He let the door close behind him. A stairway wound up surrounding a wide elevator built of a steel frame covered by heavy wire mesh. Jack assumed the elevator had been for freight, not only because of its size but also because its doors closed horizontally instead of vertically, and its floor was rough-hewn planks.

Jack got into the elevator and pushed five.

The elevator was noisy, bumpy, and slow, but it got Jack to the fifth floor. Getting off, he faced a plain, heavy door. There was no name and no bell. Hoping the apartment was empty, Jack knocked. When there was no answer even after a second, louder rapping, Jack tried the door. It was locked.

Since the stairway rose up another floor, Jack climbed to see if he could get to the roof. The door opened but would lock behind him once he was outside. Before he ventured onto the roof he had to find something to wedge between the door and doorjamb so he could return to the stairwell. Just over the threshold he found a short length of two-by-four, which he guessed was there for that very purpose.

With the door propped open Jack stepped out onto the dark roof and gingerly walked toward the front of the building. Ahead of him he could see the arched handrails of the fire-escape ladder silhouetted against the night sky.

Arriving at the front parapet, Jack grasped the handrails and looked down. The view down to the street awakened his fear of heights, and the idea of lowering himself over the edge made him feel momentarily weak. Yet just twelve feet down was the fire-escape landing for the fifth floor. It was generously illuminated by the light coming from within the apartment.

Despite his phobia, Jack knew this was a chance he couldn't pass up. He had to at least take a look into the window.

First he sat on the parapet facing the rear of the building. Then, holding on to the handrail, he stood up. Keeping his eyes fixed on each rung, Jack lowered himself down the short run of ladder. He moved slowly and deliberately until his foot hit up against the grate of the landing. Never once did he look down.

Maintaining one hand on the ladder, he leaned over and peered through the window. The space was indeed a loft as Jack had surmised, but he could see it was partially divided with six-foot-high partitions. Immediately in front of him was a living area with a bed to the right and a small kitchen built against the left wall. On a round table was the opened remains of Jack's parcel. The doorstop and the crumpled newspaper were strewn about the floor.

What interested Jack more was what he could just see over the partition: It was the top of a stainless-steel appliance that did not look as if it belonged in an apartment.

With the window in front of him invitingly open, Jack could not control his urge to climb into the apartment for a better look. Besides, he rationalized, he could exit into the stairwell rather than subject himself to climbing the fire-escape ladder again.

Although he continued to avoid looking down, it took Jack a moment to convince himself to let go of the ladder. By the time he had slithered into the apartment headfirst, he was perspiring heavily.

Jack quickly collected himself. Once inside with his feet planted on the floor, he had no compunction about peering back out the window and down at the street. He wanted to make sure the man in the ski parka wasn't coming back, at least not for the moment.

Satisfied, Jack turned back to the apartment. He went from the combination kitchen-bedroom into a living room dominated by a storefront-sized window. There were two couches facing each other and a coffee table on a small hooked rug. The walls of the partitions were decorated with posters announcing international microbiological symposia. The magazines on the coffee table were all microbiological journals.

Jack was encouraged. Perhaps he had found Frazer Labs after all. But there was also something that disturbed him. A large, glass-fronted gun cabinet stood against the far partition. The man in the ski parka was not only interested in bacteria; he was also a gun enthusiast.

Moving quickly, Jack passed through the living room intent on locating the door to the stairwell. But as soon as he passed beyond the living room's partition, he came to a stop. The entire rest of the large, multicolumned loft was occupied by a lab. The stainless-steel appliance he'd seen from the fire escape was similar to the walk-in incubator he'd seen in the General's lab. In the far right-hand corner was a type III biosafety hood whose exhaust vented out the top of the sashed window.

Although Jack had suspected he'd find a private lab when he climbed through the window, the comprehensiveness of the one he'd discovered stunned him. He knew that such equipment was not cheap, and the combination living quarters/lab was unusual to say the least.

A generous commercial freezer caught Jack's attention. Standing to the side were several large cylinders of compressed nitrogen. The freezer had been converted to using liquid nitrogen as its coolant, making it possible to take the interior temperature down into the minus-fifty-degree range.

Jack tried to open the freezer, but it was locked.

A muffled noise that resembled a bark caught Jack's attention, and he looked up from the freezer. He heard it again. It came from the very back of the lab where there was a shed about twenty feet square. Jack walked closer to examine the odd structure. A vent duct exited from its rear and exhausted through the top of one of the rear windows.

Jack cracked the door. A feral odor drifted out as well as a few sharp barks. Opening the door farther, Jack saw the edges of metal cages. He flipped on a light. He saw a few dogs and cats, but for the most part the room was filled with rats and mice. The animals stared back at him blankly. A few dogs wagged their tails in hopeful anticipation.

Jack shut the door. In Jack's mind the man in the parka was becoming some kind of fiendish microbiological devotee. Jack didn't even want to think about what kind of experiments were in progress with the animals he'd discovered.

A sudden, distant high-pitched whine of electrical machinery made Jack's heart skip a beat. He knew instantly what it was: the elevator!

With rapidly mounting panic, Jack frantically searched for the door to the hall. The spectacle of the lab had diverted his attention from locating it. It didn't take long to find, but by the time Jack reached it, he feared the elevator would be nearing the fifth floor.

Jack's initial thought had been to dash up the stairs to the roof and then exit the building after the man in the parka had entered his apartment. But now with the elevator fast approaching, Jack thought he'd be seen. That left exiting the apartment the way he'd entered. But when the elevator motor stopped and the metal doors clanged open, he knew there wasn't time.

Jack had to hide quickly, preferably close to the door to the hall. About ten feet away was a blank door. Jack rushed to it and opened it. It was a bathroom. Jack jumped in and pulled the door closed behind him. He had to hope the man in the parka had other things on his mind than using the toilet or washing his hands.

Hardly had Jack shut the bathroom door than he heard keys turning the locks of the outer door. The man came in, locked the door after him, then walked briskly away. The sound of his footsteps receded, then disappeared.

For a second Jack hesitated. He gauged how much time he needed to get to the door to the hall and unlock it. Once he got to the stairs he felt confident he could outrun the man in the parka. With all his basketball playing, Jack was in better shape than most.

As quietly as possible, Jack opened the door. At first he only cracked it to be able to listen. Jack heard nothing. Slowly he opened the door further so that he could peer out.

From Jack's vantage point he could see a large part of the lab. The man was not to be seen. Jack pushed the door open just enough to squeeze through. He eyed the door to the hall. There was a deadbolt a few inches above the knob.

Glancing around the lab once more, Jack slipped out of the bathroom and rushed silently over to the outer door. He grasped the knob with his left hand while his right hand went to the deadbolt. But there was an agonizing problem. The deadbolt had no knob. A key was required from both inside and out. Jack was locked in!

Panicked, Jack retreated to the bathroom. He felt desperate, like one of the poor animals penned in the makeshift shelter. His only hope was that the man in the parka would leave before using the bathroom. But it was not to be. After only a few agonizing minutes, the bathroom door was suddenly whisked open. The man, sans parka, started in but collided with Jack. Both men gasped.

Jack was about to say something clever when the man stepped back and slammed the door hard enough to bring down the shower curtain and rod.

Jack immediately went for the door handle for fear of being locked in. Putting his shoulder into it, Jack rammed the door. Unexpectedly the door opened without hindrance. Jack stumbled out of the bathroom, struggling to stay on his feet. Once he had his balance, his eyes darted around the loft. The man had disappeared.

Jack headed for the kitchen and the open window. He had no other choice. But he only made it as far as the living room. The man had also run there to snatch a large revolver out of a drawer in the coffee table. As Jack appeared, the man leveled the gun at him and told him to freeze.

Jack immediately complied. He even raised his hands. With such a large gun pointing at him, Jack wanted to be as cooperative as possible.

"What the hell are you doing here?" the man snarled. His hair fell across his forehead, making him snap his head back to keep it out of his eyes.

It was that gesture more than anything else that made Jack recognize the man. It was Richard, the head tech from the Manhattan General's lab.

"Answer me!" Richard demanded.

Jack raised his hands higher, hoping the gesture might satisfy Richard, while his mind desperately sought some reasonable explanation of why he was there. But none came to mind. Under the circumstances Jack couldn't even think of anything clever to say.

Jack kept his eyes riveted to the gun barrel, which had moved to within three feet of his nose. He noticed the tip trembled, suggesting that Richard was not only angry but also acutely agitated. In Jack's mind such a combination was particularly dangerous.

"If you don't answer me I'm going to shoot you right now," Richard hissed.

"I'm a medical examiner," Jack blurted out. "I'm investigating."

"Bull!" Richard snapped. "Medical examiners don't go busting into people's apartments."

"I didn't break in," Jack explained. "The window was open."

"Shut up," Richard said. "It's all the same. You're trespassing and meddling."

"I'm sorry," Jack said. "Couldn't we just talk about this?"

"Were you the one who sent me that fake package?" Richard demanded.

"What package?" Jack asked innocently.

Richard's eyes left Jack's, and they swept down to Jack's feet and then back up to his face. "You've even got on a fake deliveryman outfit. That took thought and effort."

"What are you talking about?" Jack asked. "I dress like this all the time when I'm not at the morgue."

"Bull!" Richard repeated. He pointed toward one of the couches with the gun. "Sit down!" he yelled.

"All right already," Jack said. "You only have to ask nicely." The initial shock was passing and his wits were returning. He sat where Richard indicated.

Richard backed up to the gun cabinet without taking his eyes off Jack. He groped for keys in his pocket and then tried to get the gun cabinet open without looking at what he was doing.

"Can I give you a hand?" Jack asked.

"Shut up!" Richard yelled. Even his hand with the key was shaking. When he got the glazed door open, he reached in and pulled out a pair of handcuffs.

"Now, that's a handy item to have around," Jack said.

Handcuffs in hand, Richard started back toward Jack, keeping the gun pointed at his face.

"I tell you what," Jack said. "Why don't we call the police. I'll confess, and they can take me away. Then I'll be out of your hair."

"Shut up," Richard ordered. He then motioned for Jack to get to his feet.

Jack complied and lifted his hands again.

"Move!" Richard said, motioning toward the main part of the lab.

Jack backed up. He was afraid to take his eyes off the gun. Richard kept coming toward him, the handcuffs dangling from his left hand.

"Over by the column," Richard snapped.

Jack did as he was instructed. He stood against the column. It was about fifteen inches in diameter.

"Face it," Richard commanded.

Jack turned around.

"Reach around it with your hands and grasp them together," Richard said.

When he did what Richard had insisted, Jack felt the handcuffs snap over each wrist. He was now locked to the column.

"Mind if I sit down?" Jack asked.

Richard didn't bother to answer. He hurried back into the living area. Jack lowered himself to the floor. The most comfortable position was embracing the column with his legs wrapped around it as well as his arms.

Jack could hear Richard dialing a telephone. Jack considered yelling for help when Richard started his conversation, but quickly scrapped the idea as suicidal, considering how nervous Richard was acting. Besides, whomever Richard was calling probably wouldn't care about Jack's plight.

"Jack Stapleton is here!" Richard blurted without preamble. "I caught him in my goddamn bathroom. He knows about Frazer Labs and he's been snooping around in here. I'm sure of it. Just like Beth Holderness at the lab."

The hairs on the back of Jack's neck rose up when he heard Richard mention Beth's name.

"Don't tell me to calm down!" Richard shouted. "This is an emergency. I shouldn't have gotten myself involved in this. You'd better get over here fast. This is your problem as well as it is mine."

Jack heard Richard slam down the telephone. The man sounded even more agitated. A few minutes later Richard reappeared without his gun.

He came over to Jack and looked down at him. Richard's lips were quivering. "How did you find out about Frazer Labs?" he demanded. "I know you sent the phony package, so there's no use lying."

Jack looked up into the man's face. Richard's pupils were widely dilated. He looked half crazy.

Without warning, Richard slapped Jack with an open palm. The blow split Jack's lower lip. A trickle of blood appeared at the corner of his mouth.

"You'd better start talking," Richard snarled.

Jack gingerly felt the damaged part of his lip with his tongue. It was numb. He tasted the saltiness of his blood.

"Maybe we should wait for your colleague," Jack said, to say something. His intuition told him he soon would be seeing Martin Cheveau or Kelley or possibly even Zimmerman.

The slap must have hurt Richard as well as Jack because he opened and closed his hand a few times and then disappeared back into the living area. Jack heard what he thought was the refrigerator being opened, then an ice tray being dumped.

A few minutes later Richard reappeared to glare at Jack. He had a dish towel wrapped around his hand. He commenced pacing, pausing every now and again to glance at his watch.

Time dragged by. Jack would have liked to have been able to take one of his throat lozenges, but it was impossible. He also noticed that his cough was increasing and that he now felt just plain sick. He guessed he had a fever.

The distant, high-pitched sound of the elevator brought Jack's head up from where it had slumped against the column. Jack considered the fact that the buzzer hadn't sounded. That meant that whoever was on their way up had a key.

Richard heard the elevator motor as well. He went to the door and opened it to wait in the hall.

Jack heard the elevator arrive with a thump. The motor switched off and the elevator door clanged open.

"Where is he?" an angry voice demanded.

Jack was facing away from the door when he heard Richard and his visitor come into the loft. He heard the door close and be locked.

"He's over there," Richard said with equal venom. "Handcuffed to the column."

Jack took a breath and turned his head as he heard footsteps close in on him. When he caught sight of who it was, he gasped.

CHAPTER 33

"You bastard!" Terese snapped. "Why couldn't you let sleeping dogs lie. You and your stubbornness! You're screwing everything up, just when things are finally starting to go right."

Jack was dumbstruck. He looked up into her blue eyes, which he had only recently seen as soft. Now they looked as hard as pale sapphires. Her mouth was no longer sensuous. Her bloodless lips formed a grim line.

"Terese!" Richard yelled. "Don't waste time trying to talk with him. We got to figure out what we're going to do. What if someone knows he is here?"

Terese broke off from glaring at Jack to look at Richard. "Are those stupid cultures of yours in this lab?" she demanded.

"Of course they're here," Richard said.

"Then get rid of them," Terese said. "Flush them down the toilet."

"But, Terese!" Richard cried.

"Don't 'but, Terese' me. Get rid of them. Now!"

"Even the influenza?" Richard questioned.

"Especially the influenza!" Terese snapped.

Morosely Richard went over to the freezer, unlocked it, and began rummaging through its contents.

"What am I going to do with you?" Terese asked, redirecting her attention to Jack. She was thinking out loud.

"For starters you could take off these handcuffs," Jack said. "Then we could all go for a quiet dinner at Positano, and you can let your friends know we are there."

"Shut up!" Terese exclaimed. "I've had it with your repartee."

Abruptly Terese left Jack and moved over next to Richard. She watched him gathering a handful of frozen vials. "All of it, now!" she warned. "There cannot be any evidence here, you understand?"

"It was the worst decision of my life to help you," Richard complained. When he had all the vials he disappeared into the bathroom.

"How are you involved in all this?" Jack asked Terese.

Terese didn't answer. Instead she walked around the partition into the living room. Behind him Jack heard the toilet flush, and he hated to think what had just been sent into the city's sewers to infect the sewer rats.

Richard reappeared and followed Terese into the living area. Jack couldn't see them, but given the high, unadorned ceiling he could hear them as if they were right next to him.

"We've got to get him out of here immediately," Terese said.

"And do what?" Richard asked moodily. "Dump him in the East River?"

"No, I think he should just disappear," Terese said. "What about Mom and Dad's farmhouse up in the Catskills?"

"I never thought of that," Richard said. His voice brightened. "But, yeah, that's a good idea."

"How will we get him up there?" Terese asked.

"I'll bring around my Explorer," Richard said.

"The problem is getting him into it and then keeping him quiet," Terese said.

"I've got ketamine," Richard said.

"What's that?" Terese asked.

"It's an anesthetic agent," Richard said. "It's used a lot in veterinary medicine. There are some uses for humans, but it can cause hallucinations."

"I don't care if it causes hallucinations," Terese said. "All I care about is whether it will knock him out or not. Actually, it would be best just to have him tranquilized."

"Ketamine is all I've got," Richard said. "I can get it because it's not a scheduled drug. I use it with the animals."

"I don't want to hear about any of that," Terese said. "Is it possible just to give him enough to make him dopey?"

"I don't know for sure," Richard said. "But I'll try."

"How do you give it?" Terese asked.

"Injection," Richard said. "But it's short-acting, so we might have to do it several times."

"Let's give it a try," Terese said.

Jack found himself perspiring heavily when Terese and Richard reappeared from the living room. Jack didn't know if it was from a fever or from the worry engendered by the conversation he'd just overheard. He did not like the idea of being an unwilling experimental subject with a potent anesthetic agent.

Richard went to a cabinet and got out a handful of syringes. From another cabinet he got the drug, which came in a glass vial with a rubber top. He then stopped to figure out a dose.

"What do you think he weighs?" Richard asked Terese as if Jack were an uncomprehending animal.

"I'd guess about one-eighty, give or take five pounds," Terese said.

Richard did some simple calculations, then filled one of the syringes. As he came at Jack, Jack had to fight off a panic attack. He wanted to scream, but he didn't. Richard injected the ketamine into his right upper arm. Jack winced. It burned like crazy.

"Let's see what that does," Richard said, stepping away. He discarded the used syringe. "While we wait I'll go get my car."

Terese nodded. Richard got his ski parka and pulled it on. At the door he told Terese he'd be back in ten minutes.

"So, this is a sibling operation," Jack commented when he and Terese were alone.

"Don't remind me," Terese said, shaking her head. She began to pace as Richard had earlier.

The first effect Jack experienced from the ketamine was a ringing in his ears. Then his image of Terese began to do strange things. Jack blinked and shook his head. It was as if a cloud of heavy air were settling over him, and he was outside of himself watching it happen. Then he saw Terese at the end of a long tunnel. Suddenly her face expanded to an enormous size. She was speaking but the sound echoed interminably. Her words were incomprehensible.

The next thing Jack was aware of was that he was walking. But it was a strange, uncoordinated walk, since he had no idea where the various parts of his body were. He had to look down to see his feet sweep out of the periphery of his vision and then plant themselves. When he tried to look where he was going he saw a fragmented image of brightly colored shapes and straight lines that were constantly moving.

He felt mild nausea, but when he shook himself it passed. He blinked and the colored shapes came together and merged into a large shiny object. A hand came into his field of vision and it touched the object. That was when Jack realized it was his hand and the object was a car.

Other elements of his immediate environment became recognizable. There were lights and a building. Then he realized that there were people on either side of him holding him up. They were speaking but their voices had a deep, mechanical sound as if they were synthesized.

Jack felt himself falling, but he couldn't stop himself. It seemed as if he fell for several minutes before landing on a hard surface. Then he could only see dark shapes. He was lying on a carpeted surface with something firm jutting into his stomach. When he tried to move he found that his wrists were restrained.

Time passed. Jack had no idea how long. It could have been minutes or it could have been hours. But at last he'd regained orientation, and he was no longer hallucinating. He realized that he was on the floor of the backseat of a moving car, and his hands were handcuffed to the undercarriage of the front passenger seat. Presumably they were on their way to the Catskills.

To relieve the discomfort of the driveshaft pressing against his stomach, Jack drew his knees underneath him to assume a crouched-over position. It was far from ideal but better than it had been. But his discomfort was from more than his cramped posture. The flu symptoms were much worse, and combined with a hangover from the ketamine, he felt about as bad as he'd ever felt.

Several violent sneezes caused Terese to look over the back of the seat.

"Good God!" she exclaimed.

"Where are we?" Jack asked. His voice was hoarse, and the effort of speaking caused him to cough repeatedly. He was having a problem with his nose running, but with his hands secured he couldn't do anything about it.

"I think you better just shut up or you'll choke to death," Richard said.

Terese turned to Richard: "Is this coughing and sneezing from the shot you gave him?"

"How the hell do I know? It's not as if I've ever given ketamine to a person before."

"Well, it's not so far-fetched to imagine you might have an idea," Terese snapped. "You use it on those poor animals."

"I resent that," Richard said indignantly. "You know I treat those animals like my pets. That's why I have the ketamine in the first place."

Jack sensed that the anxiety that Terese and Richard had evidenced earlier about his presence had metamorphosed into irritation. From the way they were speaking it seemed to be mostly directed at each other.

After a brief silence, Richard spoke up. "You know, this whole thing was your idea, not mine," he said.

"Oh no!" Terese voiced. "I'm not about to let you get away with that misconception. You were the one who suggested causing AmeriCare trouble with nosocomial infection. It never would have even crossed my mind."

"I only suggested it after you complained so bitterly about AmeriCare gobbling up National Health's market share despite your stupid ad campaign," Richard said. "You begged me to help."

"I wanted some ideas," Terese said. "Something to use with the ads."

"Hell you did!" Richard said. "You don't go to a grocery store and ask for hardware. I don't know squat about advertising. You knew my field was microbiology. You knew what I'd suggest. It was what you were hoping."

"I never thought about it until you mentioned it," Terese countered. "Besides, all you suggested was that you could arrange some bad press by nuisance infections. I thought you meant colds, or diarrhea, or the flu."

"I did use the flu," Richard said.

"Yes, you used the flu," Terese said. "But was it regular flu? No, it was some weird stuff that has everybody all up in arms, including Doctor Detective in the backseat. I thought you were going to use common illnesses, not the plague, for chrissake. Or those other ones. I can't even remember their names."

"You didn't complain when the press jumped all over the outbreaks and the market share trend rapidly reversed," Richard said. "You were happy."

"I was appalled," Terese said. "And scared. I just didn't say it."

"You're full of crap!" Richard said heatedly. "I talked with you the day after the plague broke out. You didn't mention it once. It even hurt my feelings since it took some effort on my part."

"I was afraid to say anything about it," Terese said. "I didn't want to associate myself with it in any way. But as bad as it was, I thought that was it. I didn't know you were planning on more."

"I can't believe I'm hearing this," Richard said.

Jack became aware they were slowing down. He lifted his head as high as his handcuffed hands would allow. The glare of artificial light penetrated the car. They'd been driving in darkness for some time.

Suddenly there were bright lights, and they'd come to a complete stop under an overhang. When Jack heard the driver's-side window going down, he realized they were at a tollbooth. He started to yell for help, but his voice was weak and raspy.

Richard reacted swiftly by reaching around and smacking Jack with a hard object. The blow impacted on Jack's head. He collapsed onto the floor.

"Don't hit him so hard," Terese said. "You don't want blood on the inside of the car."

"I thought shutting him up was more important," Richard said. He threw a handful of coins into the bin of the automatic gate.

Jack's headache was now worse from the blow. He closed his eyes. He tried to find the most comfortable position, but there weren't many choices. Mercifully, he finally fell into a troubled sleep despite being thrown from side to side. After the toll they were driving on a winding and twisting road.

The next thing Jack knew, they were stopped again. Carefully he raised his head. Again there were lights outside of the car.

"Don't even think about it," Richard said. He had the revolver in his hand.

"Where are we?" Jack asked groggily.

"At an all-night convenience store," Richard said. "Terese wanted to get some basics."

Terese came back to the car with a bag of groceries.

"Did he stir?" she asked, as she climbed in.

"Yeah, he's awake," Richard said.

"Did he try to yell again?"

"Nope," Richard said. "He didn't dare."

They drove for another hour. Terese and Richard intermittently continued to bicker about whose fault the whole mess was. Neither was willing to give in.

Finally they turned off the paved road and bounced along a rutted gravel drive. Jack winced as his tender body thumped against the floor and the driveshaft hump.

Eventually they made a sharp turn to the left and came to a stop. Richard switched off the motor. Both he and Terese then got out.

Jack was left in the car by himself. Lifting his head as high as he could, he was only able to see a swatch of night sky. It was very dark.

Getting his legs under him, Jack tried to see if he could possibly rip the handcuffs from beneath the seat. But it wasn't possible. The handcuffs had been looped around a stout piece of steel.

Collapsing back down, he resigned himself to waiting. It was half an hour before they came back for him. When they did they opened both doors on the passenger side.

Terese unlocked one side of the handcuffs.

"Out of the car!" Richard commanded. He held his gun aimed at Jack's head.

Jack did as he was told. Terese then quickly stepped forward and recuffed Jack's free hand.

"In the house!" Richard said.

Jack started walking on wobbly legs through the wet grass. It was much colder than in the city, and he could see his breath. Ahead a white farmhouse loomed in the darkness. There were lights in the windows facing a balustraded porch. Jack could make out smoke and a few sparks issuing from the chimney.

As they reached the porch, Jack glanced around. To the left he could see the dark outline of a barn. Beyond that was a field. Then there were mountains. There were no distant lights; it was an isolated, private hideaway.

"Come on!" Richard said, poking Jack in the ribs with the barrel of the gun. "Inside."

The interior was decorated as a comfortable weekend/summer house with an English country flair. There were matching calico couches facing each other in front of a massive fieldstone chimney. In the fireplace was a roaring, freshly kindled fire. An oriental rug covered most of the wide-board floor.

Through a large arch was a country kitchen with a center table and ladder-back chairs. Beyond the table was a Franklin stove. Against the far wall was a large 1920s-style porcelain kitchen sink.

Richard marched Jack into the kitchen and motioned for him to get down on the rag rug in front of the sink. Sensing he was about to be shackled to the plumbing, Jack asked to use the rest room.

The request brought on a new argument between brother and sister. Terese wanted Richard to go into the bathroom with Jack, but Richard flatly refused. He told Terese she could do it, but she thought it was Richard's role. Finally they agreed to let Jack go in by himself, since the guest bathroom had only one tiny window, one that was too small for Jack to climb through.

Left to himself, Jack got out the rimantadine and took one of the tablets. He'd been discouraged that the drug had not prevented his infection, but he did think it was slowing the flu's course. No doubt his symptoms would be far worse if he weren't taking it.

When Jack came out of the bathroom, Richard took him back to the kitchen, and as Jack had anticipated, locked the handcuffs around the kitchen drainpipe. While Terese and Richard retired to the couches in front of the fire, Jack eyed the plumbing with the intent of escaping. The problem was that the pipes were old-fashioned. They weren't PVC or even copper. They were brass and cast iron. Jack tried putting pressure on them, but they didn't budge.

Resigned for the moment, Jack assumed the most comfortable position. It was lying on his back on the rag rug. He listened to Terese and Richard, who for the moment had gotten past their attempts to blame each other for the present catastrophe. They were now being more rational. They knew they had to make some decisions.

Jack's position on his back made his nasal discharge run down the back of his throat. His coughing jags returned, as did a round of violent sneezes. When he finally got himself under control he found himself looking up into Terese's and Richard's faces.

"We have to know how you found out about Frazer Labs," Richard said, gun once again in hand.

Jack feared that if they found out he was the only person who knew about Frazer Labs, they'd probably kill him then and there.

"It was easy," Jack said.

"Give us an idea how easy," Terese said.

"I just called up National Biologicals and asked if anyone had recently ordered plague bacteria. They told me Frazer Labs had."

Terese reacted as if she'd been slapped. Angrily she turned to Richard. "Don't tell me you ordered the stuff," she said with disbelief. "I thought you had all these bugs in your so-called collection."

"I didn't have plague," Richard said. "And I thought plague would make the biggest media impact. But what difference does it make? They can't trace where the bacteria came from."

"That's where you are wrong," Jack said. "National Biologicals tags their cultures. We all found out about it at the medical examiner's office when we did the autopsy."

"You idiot!" Terese shouted. "You've left a goddamn trail right to your door."

"I didn't know they tagged their cultures," Richard said meekly.

"Oh, God!" Terese said, rolling her eyes to the ceiling. "That means everybody at the ME's office knows the plague episode was artificial."

"What should we do?" Richard asked nervously.

"Wait a second," Terese said. She looked down at Jack. "I'm not sure he's telling the truth. I don't think that fits with what Colleen said. Hang on. Let me call her."

Terese's conversation with Colleen was short. Terese told her underling that she was worried about Jack and asked if Colleen could call Chet to inquire about Jack's conspiracy theory. Terese wanted to know if anyone else at the medical examiner's office subscribed to it. Terese concluded by telling Colleen that she was unreachable but would call back in fifteen minutes.

During the interim, there was little conversation except for Terese asking Richard if he was sure he'd disposed of all the cultures. Richard assured her that he'd flushed everything down the toilet.

When the fifteen minutes was up, Terese redialed Colleen as promised. At the end of their brief conversation Terese thanked Colleen and hung up.

"That's the first good news tonight," Terese said to Richard. "No one else at the ME's office gives any credence to Jack's theory. Chet told Colleen that everyone chalks it up to Jack's grudge against AmeriCare."

"So no one else must know about Frazer Labs and the tagged bacteria," Richard said.

"Exactly," Terese said. "And that simplifies things dramatically. Now all we have to do is get rid of Jack."

"And how are we going to do that?" Richard asked.

"First you are going to go out and dig a hole," Terese said. "I think the best spot would be on the other side of the barn by the blueberry patch."

"Now?" Richard questioned.

"This isn't something we can blithely put off, you idiot," Terese said.

"The ground's probably frozen," Richard complained. "It will be like digging in granite."

"You should have thought of that when you dreamed up this catastrophe," Terese said. "Get out there and get it done. There should be a shovel and a pick in the barn."

Richard grumbled as he pulled on his parka. He took the flashlight and went out the front door.

"Terese," Jack called out. "Don't you think you've taken this a bit too far?"

Terese got off the couch and came into the kitchen. She leaned against the cabinet and eyed Jack.

"Don't try to make me feel sorry for you," she said. "If I warned you once, I warned you a dozen times to leave well enough alone. You've only yourself to blame."

"I can't believe your career can be this important to you," Jack said. "People have died, and more people can die still. Not just me."

"I never intended that anybody die," Terese said. "That only happened thanks to my harebrained brother, who's had this love affair with microbes ever since he was in high school. He's collected bacteria the way a survivalist collects guns. Just having them around was a weird turn-on for him. Maybe I should have known he'd do something crazy sometime; I don't know. Right now I'm just trying to get us out of this mess."

"You're rationalizing," Jack said. "You're an accomplice, just as guilty as he is."

"You know something, Jack?" Terese said. "At this moment I couldn't care less what you think."

Terese walked back to the fire. Jack could hear more logs being added. He rested his head on his forearm and closed his eyes. He was miserable, both sick and frightened. He felt like a condemned man vainly waiting for a reprieve.

When the door burst open an hour later Jack jumped. He'd fallen asleep again. He also noticed a new symptom: now his eyes hurt when he looked from side to side.

"Digging the hole was easier than I thought," Richard reported. He peeled off his coat. "Wasn't any frost at all. It must have been a bog in that area at one time, because there weren't even any rocks."

"I hope you made it deep enough," Terese said, tossing aside a book. "I don't want any more screwups, like having him wash up in the spring rain."

"It's plenty deep enough," Richard said. He disappeared into the bathroom to wash his hands. When he came out Terese was putting on her coat. "Where are you going?"

"Out," Terese said. She headed for the door. "I'll go for a walk while you kill Jack."

"Wait a second," Richard said. "Why me?"

"You're the man," Terese said with a scornful smile. "That's a man's work."

"The hell it is," Richard said. "I'm not going to kill him. I couldn't. I couldn't shoot someone while he's handcuffed."

"I don't believe you," Terese yelled. "You're not making sense. You had no compunction about putting lethal bacteria into defenseless people's humidifiers, which sure as hell killed them."

"It was the bacteria that killed them," Richard said. "It was a fight between the bacteria and the person's immune system. I didn't do the killing directly. They had a chance."

"Give me patience!" Terese cried, rolling her eyes heavenward. She collected herself and took a breath. "Okay, fine. With the patients it wasn't you, it was the bacteria. In this case it will be the bullet, not you. How's that? Does that satisfy this weird sense of responsibility of yours?"

"This is different," Richard said. "It's not the same at all."

"Richard, we don't have any choice. Otherwise you'll go to jail for the rest of your life."

Richard hesitantly looked over at the gun on the coffee table.

"Get it!" Terese commanded when she saw him eyeing the pistol.

Richard wavered.

"Come on, Richard," Terese urged.

Richard went over and irresolutely picked up the gun. Holding it by the barrel as well as the handle, he cocked it.

"Good!" Terese said encouragingly. "Now go over there and do it."

"Maybe if we take off the handcuffs, and he tries to run, I can . . ." Richard began. But he stopped in midsentence when Terese strode over to him with her eyes blazing. Without warning she slapped him. Richard recoiled from the blow, and his own anger flared.

"Don't even talk like that, you fool," Terese spat. "We are not taking any more chances. Understand?"

Richard put a hand to his face and then looked at it as if he expected to see blood. His initial fury quickly abated. He realized that Terese was right. Slowly he nodded.

"Okay, now get to it," Terese said. "I'll be outside."

Terese strode to the door. "Do it quickly, but don't make a mess," she said. Then she was gone.

Silence settled over the room. Richard didn't move. He only turned the gun over slowly in his hands, as if he were inspecting it. Finally, Jack spoke up: "I don't know whether I'd listen to her. You might face prison for the outbreaks if they can prove it was you behind them, but killing me like this in cold blood means the death penalty here in New York."

"Shut up," Richard screamed. He rushed into the kitchen and assumed a shooting stance directly behind Jack.

A full minute went by which seemed like an hour to Jack. He'd been holding his breath. Unable to hold it any longer, he exhaled—and immediately began coughing uncontrollably.

The next thing he knew, Richard tossed the gun onto the kitchen table. Then he ran to the door. He opened it and shouted out into the night: "I can't do it!"

Almost immediately Terese reappeared. "You goddamned coward!" she told him.

"Why don't you do it yourself?" Richard spat back.

Terese started to respond, but instead she strode to the kitchen table, snapped up the gun, and walked around to face Jack. Holding the pistol in both hands, she pointed it at his face. Jack stared back at her, directly into her eyes.

The tip of the gun barrel began to waver. All at once Terese let out a barrage of profanity and threw the gun back onto the table.

"Ah, iron woman isn't as hard as she thought," Richard taunted.

"Shut up," Terese said. She stalked back to the couch and sat down. Richard sat across from her. They eyed each other irritably.

"This is becoming a bad joke," she said.

"I think we are all strung out," Richard said.

"That's probably the first thing you've said that's true," Terese said. "I'm exhausted. What time is it?"

"It's after midnight," Richard said.

"No wonder," Terese said. "I've got a headache."

"I'm not feeling so great myself," Richard admitted.

"Let's sleep," Terese said. "We'll deal with this problem in the morning. Right now I can't even see straight."

Jack woke up at four-thirty in the morning, shivering. The fire had gone out and the temperature in the room had fallen. The rag rug had provided some warmth. Jack had managed to pull it over him.

The room was almost completely dark. Terese and Richard had not left on any lights when they'd retired to separate bedrooms. What little light there was drifted in from outside through the window over the sink. It was just enough for Jack to discern the vague shapes of the furniture.

Jack didn't know what made him feel worse: fear or the flu. At least his cough had not worsened. The rimantadine had seemingly protected him from developing primary influenza pneumonia.

For a few minutes Jack allowed himself the luxury of contemplating being rescued. The problem was that the chances were minuscule. The only person who knew that the National Biologicals probe test was positive with the plague culture was Ted Lynch, not that he could know what it meant. Agnes might, but there was no reason for Ted to tell Agnes what he'd found.

If rescue was not a viable possibility, then he'd have to rely on escape. With numb fingers Jack felt up and down the length of drainpipe to which he was shackled.

He tried to feel for any imperfections, but there were none. He positioned the handcuffs at various heights and, with his feet against the pipes, pushed until the handcuffs cut into his skin. The pipes were there to stay.

If he were to escape it would have to occur when he was allowed to go to the bathroom. How he would actually do it, he had no idea. All he could hope was that they'd become careless.

Jack shuddered when he thought of what morning might bring. A good night's sleep would only toughen Terese's resolve. The fact that neither Terese nor Richard could shoot him in cold blood the night before was scant reassurance. As self-centered as they both were, he couldn't bank on that continuing indefinitely.

Using his legs, Jack succeeded in getting the rag rug to fold over him again. Settling down as best he could, he tried to rest. If an opportunity of escape presented itself, he hoped he'd be physically able to take full advantage of it.

CHAPTER 34

THURSDAY, 8:15 A.M., MARCH 28, 1996
CATSKILL MOUNTAINS, NEW YORK

The hours had passed slowly and miserably for Jack. He'd not been able to fall back asleep. Nor could he even find a comfortable position with his shivering. When Richard finally staggered into the room with his hair standing on end, Jack was almost glad to see him.

"I've got to use the bathroom," Jack called out.

"You'll have to wait for Terese to get up," Richard said. He was busy rebuilding the fire.

The door to Terese's room opened a few minutes later. Terese was dressed in an old bathrobe; she didn't look any better than Richard. Her normal helmet of highlighted curls looked more like a mop. She was without makeup, and the contrast with her normal appearance made her seem exceptionally pale.

"I've still got my headache," Terese complained. "And I slept lousy."

"Me too," Richard said. "It's the stress, and we never really had any dinner."

"But I'm not hungry," Terese said. "I can't understand it."

"I've got to go to the bathroom," Jack repeated. "I've been waiting for hours."

"Get the gun," Terese said to Richard. "I'll unlock the handcuffs."

Terese came into the kitchen and bent down to reach under the sink with the handcuff key.

"Sorry you didn't sleep well," Jack said. "You should have joined me out here in the kitchen. It's been delightful."

"I don't want to hear any mouth from you," Terese warned. "I'm not in the mood."

The handcuff snapped open. Jack rubbed his chafed wrist as he stiffly got to his feet. A wave of dizziness spread over him, forcing him to lean against the kitchen table. Terese quickly relocked the handcuff around Jack's free wrist. Jack wouldn't have been able to resist even if he'd had the intention.

"Okay, march!" Richard said. He was training the gun on Jack.

"In a second," Jack said. The room was still spinning.

"No tricks!" Terese said. She stepped away from him.

As soon as he could, Jack walked to the bathroom on rubbery legs. The first order of business was to relieve himself. The second was to take a dose of the rimantadine with a long drink of water. Only then did he hazard a look in the mirror. What he saw surprised him. He wasn't sure he would have recognized himself. He looked like a vagrant. His eyes were bright red and slightly swollen. Dried blood was on the left side of his face and spattered on the shoulder of his uniform shirt, apparently from the blow he'd received in the car at the tollbooth. His lip was swollen where Richard had split it. Dried mucus stuck to his formidable stubble.

"Hurry up in there," Terese commanded through the door.

Jack ran water in the sink and washed his face. Using his index finger, he brushed his teeth. Then with a little water he smoothed his hair.

"It's about time," Terese said when Jack emerged.

Jack suppressed the urge to give a clever retort. He felt he was walking a tightrope with these people, and he didn't want to push his luck. He hoped they wouldn't lock him back to the kitchen drain, but the wish was in vain. He was marched right back to the sink and secured.

"We should eat something," Richard said.

"I got cold cereal last night," Terese said.

"Fine," Richard said.

They sat at the table a mere four feet away from Jack. Terese ate very little. She again mentioned that she just wasn't hungry. They didn't offer any cereal to Jack.

"Have you thought about what we're going to do?" Richard asked.

"What about those people who were supposed to kill Jack in the city? Who were they?"

"It's a gang from down where I live," Richard said.

"How do you contact them?" Terese asked.

"I usually call them up or just go over to the building they occupy," Richard said. "I've been dealing with a man called Twin."

"Well, let's get him the hell up here," Terese said.

"He might come," Richard said. "If the money is right."

"Call him," Terese said. "How much were you going to pay them?"

"Five hundred," Richard said.

"Offer him a thousand if you have to," Terese said. "But say it's a rush job and that he's got to come today."

Richard scraped back his chair and went into the living room to get the phone.

268 / ROBIN COOK

He brought it back to the kitchen table. He wanted her to listen in case they had to up the ante; he didn't know how Twin would respond to the idea of coming all the way to the Catskills.

Richard dialed and Twin answered. Richard told him he wanted to talk once again about knocking off the doctor.

"Hey, man, we're not interested," Twin said.

"I know there was trouble in the past," Richard said. "But this time it will be a snap. We have him handcuffed and hidden away outside the city."

"If that's the case, you don't need us," Twin said.

"Wait!" Richard said hastily. He'd sensed Twin was about to hang up. "We still need you. In fact, to make it worth your while driving out here, we'll pay double."

"A thousand bucks?" Twin asked.

"You got it," Richard said.

"Don't come, Twin," Jack shouted. "It's a setup!"

"Shit!" Richard barked. He told Twin to hold the line for a second. In a fit of fury, Richard cracked Jack over the head with the butt of his gun.

Jack closed his eyes hard enough to bring tears. The pain in his head was intense. Again he felt blood drip down the side of his scalp.

"Was that the doc?" Twin asked.

"Yeah, that was the doc," Richard said angrily.

"What did he mean, 'setup'?" Twin asked.

"Nothing," Richard said. "He's just running off at the mouth. We've got him handcuffed to the kitchen drainpipe."

"Let me get this straight," Twin said. "You're paying a thousand bucks for us to come out and ice the doc while he's chained to a pipe."

"It'll be a like a turkey shoot," Richard assured him.

"Where are you?" Twin asked.

"About a hundred miles north of the city," Richard said. "In the Catskills."

There was a pause.

"What do you say?" Richard asked. "It's easy money."

"Why don't you do it yourself?" Twin asked.

"That's my business," Richard said.

"All right," Twin said. "Give me directions. But if there is any funny stuff, you'll be one unhappy dude."

Richard gave directions to get to the farmhouse and told Twin they'd be waiting for him.

Richard slowly replaced the receiver while he looked triumphantly at Terese.

"Well, thank God!" Terese said.

"I'd better call in sick," Richard said, picking up the phone again. "I should have been at work already."

After he finished his call Terese made a similar one to Colleen. Then she went to take a shower. Richard went to fill the wood box.

Wincing against the pain, Jack pushed himself back to a sitting position. At least the bleeding had stopped. The prospect of the Black Kings' arrival spelled doom. From bitter experience, Jack knew these gang members would have no qualms about shooting him no matter what state he was in.

For a few seconds Jack lost total control of himself. Like a child in a temper tantrum he yanked inconsequentially at his shackles. All he managed to do was cut into his wrists and knock over some detergent containers. There was no way he was about to break either the drainpipe or the handcuffs.

After the fit had passed, Jack slumped over and cried. But even that didn't last long. Wiping his face on his left sleeve, he sighed and sat up. He knew he had to escape. On his next trip to the bathroom he'd have to try something. It was his only chance, and he didn't have much time.

Three-quarters of an hour later Terese reappeared in her clothes. She dragged herself to the couch and plopped down. Richard was on the other couch flipping through an old 1950s *Life* magazine.

"I really don't feel too good," Terese admitted. "My headache is still killing me. I feel like I'm coming down with a cold."

"Me too," Richard said without looking up.

"I have to use the bathroom again," Jack called out.

Terese rolled her eyes. "Give me a break!" she said.

No one moved or spoke for five minutes.

"I suppose I can just let loose right here," Jack said, breaking the silence.

Terese sighed and threw her legs over the side of the couch. "Come on, stalwart warrior," she said disparagingly to Richard.

They used the same method as before. Terese unlocked the handcuffs while Richard stood poised with the gun.

"Do I really need these handcuffs while I'm in the bathroom?" Jack asked when Terese started to relock them.

"Absolutely," Terese said.

Once inside the bathroom Jack took another rimantadine and a long drink of water. Then, leaving the water running, he stepped on the closed toilet seat, grasped the window trim with both hands, and began to pull. He increased the pressure to see if the window casing would come loose.

Just then the door opened.

"Get down from there!" Terese snarled.

Jack stepped down from the toilet and cringed. He was afraid that Richard was about to hit him on the head again. Instead Richard just crowded into the bathroom, holding the gun out in front of him trained on Jack's face. The gun was cocked.

"Just give me a reason to shoot," he hissed.

For a second no one moved. Then Terese ordered Jack back to the kitchen sink.

"Can't you think of another place?" Jack said. "I'm getting tired of the view."

"Don't push me," Terese warned.

With the cocked gun just a few feet away, there was nothing Jack could do. In a matter of seconds he was handcuffed to the drainpipe yet again.

A half hour later Terese decided to go out to the store to get some aspirin and some soup. She asked Richard if he wanted anything. He told her to get some ice cream; he thought it might feel good on his sore throat.

After Terese had left, Jack told Richard that he had to go to the bathroom again.

"Yeah, sure," Richard said without budging from the couch.

"I do," Jack averred. "I didn't get to go last time."

Richard gave a short laugh. "Tough shit," he said. "It was your own fault."

"Come on," Jack said. "It will only take a minute."

"Listen!" Richard yelled. "If I come in there it will be to crack you over the head again. Understand?"

Jack understood all too well.

Twenty minutes later Jack heard the unmistakable sound of a car approaching along the gravel drive. He felt a rush of adrenaline in his system. Was it the Black Kings? His panic returned, and he stared forlornly at the unbudgable drainpipe.

The door opened. To Jack's relief it was Terese. She dropped a bag of groceries on the kitchen table, then retreated to the couch and lay down and closed her eyes. She told Richard to put the groceries away.

Richard got up without enthusiasm. He put what had to be kept cold in the refrigerator and the ice cream in the freezer. Then he placed the cans of soup in the cupboard. In the bottom of the bag he found aspirin and a bunch of small cellophane-wrapped packages of peanut-butter crackers.

"You might give some of the crackers to Jack," Terese said.

Richard looked down at Jack. "You want some?" he asked.

Jack nodded. Although he still felt ill, his appetite had returned. He'd not eaten anything since the deli food in the van.

Richard fed Jack peanut butter crackers whole, like a mother bird dropping food into a waiting chick's gaping mouth. Jack hungrily devoured five of them and then asked for water.

"For chrissake!" Richard voiced. He was annoyed this job had fallen to him.

"Give it to him," Terese said.

Reluctantly Richard did as he was told. After a long drink Jack thanked him. Richard told Jack to thank Terese, not him.

"Bring me a couple of aspirin and some water," Terese said.

Richard rolled his eyes. "What am I, the servant?"

"Just do it," Terese said petulantly.

Three-quarters of an hour later another car could be heard coming up the driveway.

"Finally," Richard said as he tossed a magazine aside and heaved himself off the couch. "They must have driven by way of Philadelphia, for chrissake." He headed for the door while Terese pushed herself up to a sitting position.

Jack swallowed nervously. He could feel his pulse pounding in his temples. He realized he didn't have long to live.

Richard pulled open the door. "Shit!" he voiced.

Terese sat bolt upright. "What's the matter?"

"It's Henry, the goddamn caretaker!" Richard croaked. "What are we going to do?"

"You cover Jack!" Terese barked in panic. "I'll talk to Henry." She stood up and swayed for a moment as a wave of dizziness overcame her. Then she went out the door.

Richard dashed over to Jack. En route he'd picked up the gun, which he now held by the barrel as if it were a hatchet. "One word and so help me I'll bash your head in," he growled.

Jack looked up at Richard. He could see the man's determination. Outside he could hear a car come to a stop followed by the muffled sound of Terese's voice.

Jack was faced with an unreasonable quandary. He could yell, but how much sound he could make before being incapacitated by Richard was questionable. Yet if he didn't try, he'd soon be facing the Black Kings and certain death. He decided to go for it.

Jack put his head back and started to scream for help. As expected, Richard brought the handle of his gun crashing down on Jack's forehead. Jack's scream was cut off before he could form any words. A merciful darkness intervened with the suddenness of a light being switched off.

Jack regained consciousness in stages. The first thing he was aware of was that his eyes wouldn't open. But after a struggle the right one did, and a minute later so did the left. When he wiped his face on his sleeve he realized that his lids had been sealed together with coagulated blood.

With his forearm, Jack could feel that he had a sizable lump centered at his hairline. He knew it was a good place to be hit if you had to take a wallop. That part of the skull was by far the thickest.

He blinked to clear his vision and looked at his watch. It was just after four, a fact confirmed by the anemic quality of the late-afternoon sunlight coming through the window over the sink.

Jack glanced around the living room, which he could see from under the kitchen table. The fire had burned down significantly. Terese and Richard were sprawled on their respective couches.

Jack changed his position and in the process tipped over a container of window cleaner.

"What's he doing now?" Richard asked.

"Who the hell cares," Terese said. "What time is it?"

"It's after four," Richard said.

"Where are these gang friends of yours?" Terese demanded. "Are they coming by bicycle?"

"Should I call and check?" Richard asked.

272 / ROBIN COOK

"No, let's just wait here for a week," Terese said irritably.

Richard put the phone on his chest and dialed. When the phone was answered he had to ask for Twin. After a long wait Twin came on the line.

"Why the hell aren't you here?" Richard complained. "We've been waiting all day."

"I'm not coming, man," Twin said.

"But you said you were," Richard rejoined.

"I can't do it, man," Twin said. "I can't come."

"Not even for a thousand dollars?"

"Nope," Twin said.

"But why?" Richard demanded.

" 'Cause I gave my word," Twin said.

"You gave your word? What does that mean?" Richard asked.

"Just what I said," Twin said. "Don't you understand English?"

"But this is ridiculous," Richard said.

"Hey, it's your party," Twin said. "You have to do your own shit."

Richard found himself holding a dead telephone. He slammed the receiver down. "That worthless bum," he spat. "He won't do it. I can't believe it."

Terese pushed herself up into a sitting position. "So much for that idea. That puts us back to square one."

"Don't look at me. I'm not doing it," Richard snapped. "I've made that crystal clear. It's up to you, sister. Hell, all this was for your benefit, not mine."

"Supposedly," Terese retorted. "But you got some perverted enjoyment out of it. You finally got to use those bugs you've been playing with all your life. Yet now you can't do this simple thing. You're some sort of . . ." She struggled for the word: "Degenerate!" she said finally.

"Well, you're no Snow White yourself," Richard yelled. "No wonder that husband of yours left you."

Terese's face flushed. She opened her mouth but no words came out. Suddenly she lunged for the gun.

Richard took a step backward. He feared he'd overdone it by mentioning the unmentionable. For a second he thought Terese was about to use the gun on him. But instead she flew into the kitchen, cocking the gun as she went. She stepped up to Jack and pointed the gun at his bloodied face.

"Turn away!" she commanded.

Jack felt as if his heart had stopped. He looked up the quivering barrel and into Terese's arctic blue eyes. He was paralyzed, incapable of following her command.

"Damn you!" Terese said through a sudden flood of tears.

Uncocking the gun, she tossed it aside, then rushed back to the couch to bury her head in her hands. She was sobbing.

Richard felt guilty. He knew he shouldn't have said what he had. Losing her baby and then her husband was his sister's Achilles' heel. Meekly he went over to her and sat on the edge of the couch.

"I didn't mean it," Richard said, stroking her back gently. "It slipped out. I'm not myself."

Terese sat up and wiped her eyes. "I'm not myself either," she admitted. "I can't believe these tears. I'm a wreck. I feel awful too. Now my throat's sore."

"You want another aspirin?" Richard asked.

Terese shook her head. "What do you think Twin meant about giving his word?" she asked.

"I don't know," Richard said. "That's why I asked him."

"Why didn't you offer him more money?" Terese said.

"He didn't give me a chance," Richard said. "He hung up."

"Well, call him back," Terese said. "We have to get out of here."

"How much should I offer?" Richard said. "I don't have the kind of money you have."

"Whatever it takes," Terese said. "At this point money shouldn't be a limiting factor."

Richard picked up the phone and dialed. This time when he asked for Twin he was told Twin was out. He wouldn't be back for an hour. Richard hung up.

"We have to wait," he said.

"What else is new?" Terese commented.

Terese lay back on the couch and pulled a crocheted afghan over her. She shivered. "Is it getting cold in here or is it just me?" she asked.

"I had a couple of chills myself," Richard said. He went to the fire and piled on more logs. Then he got a blanket from his bedroom before reclining on his couch. He tried to read, but he couldn't concentrate. He was intermittently shivering despite the blanket. "I just thought of a new worry," he said.

"What now?" Terese asked. Her eyes were closed.

"Jack's been sneezing and coughing. You don't think he was exposed to my flu strain, the one I put in the humidifier?"

With the blanket wrapped around him, Richard got up and went into the kitchen and asked Jack about it. Jack didn't answer.

"Come on, Doc," Richard urged. "Don't make me have to hit you again."

"What difference does it make?" Terese called from the couch.

"It makes a lot of difference," Richard said. "There's a good chance my strain was the strain that caused the great flu epidemic of 1918. I got it in Alaska from a couple of frozen Eskimos who died of pneumonia. The time frame was right."

Terese joined him in the kitchen. "Now you're getting me worried," she said. "Do you think he has it and has exposed us?"

"It's possible," Richard said.

"That's terrifying!" She looked down at Jack. "Well?" she demanded. "Were you exposed?"

Jack wasn't sure if he should admit to his exposure or not. He didn't know which would anger them more. The truth or his silence.

"I don't like it that he's not answering," Richard said.

"He's a medical examiner," Terese said. "He had to have been exposed. They brought the dead people to him. He told me on the phone."

"I'm not afraid of that," Richard said. "The exposure to worry about is to a living, breathing, sneezing, coughing person, not a dead body."

"Medical examiners don't take care of live people," Terese said. "All their patients are dead."

"That's true," Richard admitted.

"Besides," Terese said, "Jack is hardly sick. He's got a cold. Big deal. Wouldn't he be really ill by now if he'd contracted your flu bug?"

"You're right," Richard said. "I'm not thinking straight; if he had the 1918 flu bug he'd be flat out by now."

Brother and sister returned to their couches and collapsed.

"I can't take much more of this," Terese said. "Especially the way I feel."

At five-fifteen, exactly one hour after the previous call, Richard phoned Twin. This time Twin himself picked up.

"What the hell are you pestering me for?" Twin asked.

"I want to offer more money," Richard said. "Obviously a thousand wasn't enough. I understand. It's a long drive up here. How much are you looking for?"

"You didn't understand me, did you?" Twin said irritably. "I told you I couldn't do it. That's it. Game's over."

"Two thousand," Richard said. He looked over at Terese. She nodded.

"Hey, man, are you deaf or what?" Twin said. "How many times . . ."

"Three thousand," Richard said, and Terese again nodded.

"Three thousand bucks?" Twin repeated.

"That's correct," Richard said.

"You are sounding desperate," Twin said.

"We're willing to pay three thousand dollars," Richard said. "That should speak for itself."

"Hmmm," Twin said. "And you say you have the doc handcuffed."

"Exactly," Richard said. "It will be a piece of cake."

"I tell you what," Twin said. "I'll send someone up there tomorrow morning."

"You're not going to do what you did this morning, are you?" Richard asked.

"No," Twin said. "I guarantee I'll have someone up there to take care of things."

"For three thousand," Richard said. He wanted to be sure they understood each other.

"Three thousand will be just fine," Twin said.

Richard replaced the receiver and looked over at Terese.

"Do you believe him?" she asked.

"This time he guaranteed it," Richard said. "And when Twin guarantees something, it happens. He'll be here in the morning. I'm confident."

Terese sighed. "Thank God for small favors," she said.

Jack wasn't so relieved. His panic rekindled, he determined he had to find a way to escape that night. Morning would bring the apocalypse.

Afternoon dragged into evening. Terese and Richard fell asleep. Unattended, the fire died down. A chill came with the darkness. Jack wracked his brains for ideas of escape, but unless he was freed from the drainpipe, he didn't see how he could get away.

Around seven both Richard and Terese began to cough in their sleep. At first they seemed more to be clearing their throats than coughing, but soon the hacking became more forceful and productive. Jack considered the development significant. It gave support to a concern he'd been harboring since they both began complaining of chills: namely, that they had caught the dreaded flu from him just as Richard suspected.

Thinking back to the long car ride from the city, Jack realized it would have been hard for them not to have contracted his illness. During the ride Jack's symptoms were peaking, and symptoms of the flu often peaked with maximum viral production. Each of Jack's sneezes and coughs had undoubtedly sent millions of the infective virions into the car's confined space.

Still, Jack couldn't be sure. Besides, his real worry was facing the Black Kings in the morning. He had more pressing concerns than the health of his captors.

Jack yanked futilely at the drain with the short chain between the handcuffs. All he succeeded in doing was to make a racket and abrade his wrists more than they already were.

"Shut up!" Richard yelled after having been awakened by the clamor. He switched on a table lamp, then was immediately overwhelmed by a fit of coughing.

"What's happening?" Terese asked groggily.

"The animal is restless," Richard rasped. "God, I need some water." He sat up, waited for a moment, then got to his feet. "I'm dizzy," he said. "I might even have a fever."

He walked hesitantly into the kitchen and got a glass. As he was filling it, Jack thought about knocking his legs out from under him. But he decided that would only win him another blow to the head.

"I have to go to the bathroom," Jack said.

"Shut up," Richard said.

"It's been a long time," Jack said. "It's not as if I'm asking to go for a run in the yard. And if I don't go, it's going to be unpleasant around here."

Richard shook his head in resignation. After he took a drink of water, he called out to Terese that her services were needed. Then he got the gun from the kitchen table.

Jack heard Richard cock the gun. The move narrowed Jack's options.

Terese appeared with the key. Jack noticed her eyes had a glazed, feverish look. She bent down under the sink and unlocked one side of the handcuffs without a word. She backed away as Jack got to his feet. As before, the room swam before his eyes. Some escape artist, he thought cynically. He was weak from lack of food, sleep, and liquids. Terese relocked the handcuffs.

Richard marched directly behind Jack with the gun at the ready. There was nothing that Jack could do. When he got to the bathroom he tried to close the door.

"Sorry," Terese said, using her foot to block it. "You lost that privilege."

Jack looked from one to the other. He could tell there was no use arguing. He shrugged and turned around to relieve himself. When he was finished he motioned toward the sink. "How about my washing my face," he asked.

"If you must," Terese said. She coughed but then held herself in check. It was obvious her throat was sore.

Jack stepped to the sink, which was out of the line of Terese's sight. After turning on the water, Jack surreptitiously got out his rimantadine and took one of the tablets. In his haste he almost dropped the vial before getting it back into his pocket.

He glanced at himself in the mirror and recoiled. He looked significantly worse than he had that morning, thanks to the new laceration high on his forehead. It was gaping and needed stitches if it was to heal without a scar. Jack laughed at himself. What a time to worry about cosmetics!

The trip back to the spot of Jack's internment was without incident. There were a few moments when Jack was tempted to try something, but each time his courage failed him. By the time Jack was again locked up under the sink he felt disappointed in himself and correspondingly despondent. He had the disheartening sense that he'd just let his last chance of escape slip by.

"Do you want any soup?" Terese asked Richard.

"I'm really not hungry," Richard admitted. "All I want is a couple of aspirin. I feel like I've been run over by a truck."

"I'm not hungry either," Terese said. "This is more than a cold. I'm sure I have a fever too. Do you think we should be worried?"

"Obviously we've got what Jack has," Richard said. "I guess he's just more stoic. Anyway, we'll see a doctor tomorrow after Twin's visit if we think we should. Who knows, maybe a night's sleep is all we need."

"Let me have a couple of those aspirins," Terese said.

After taking their analgesic Terese and Richard returned to the living room. Richard spent a few moments building up the dying fire. Terese made herself as comfortable as possible on her couch. Soon Richard went back to his. They both seemed exhausted.

Jack was surer than ever that both his captors had the deadly strain of the flu. He didn't know what his ethics dictated he do. The problem was his rimantadine, and the fact that it possibly could thwart the flu's progress. Jack agonized silently over whether he should tell them of his exposure and talk them into taking the drug to potentially save their lives even though they were totally committed to ending his and were responsible for the deaths of other innocent victims. With that in mind, did he owe Terese and Richard compassion in the face of their callous indifference? Should his oath as a physician prevail?

Jack took no comfort at the notion of poetic justice being done. Yet if he shared the rimantadine with them, they might deny it to him. After all, they weren't choosy about the way he died as long as it wasn't directly by their hand.

Jack sighed. It was an impossible decision. He couldn't choose. But not making a decision was, in effect, a decision. Jack understood its ramifications.

By nine o'clock Terese's and Richard's breathing had become stertorous, punctuated by frequent coughing episodes. Terese's condition seemed worse than Richard's. Around ten a markedly violent fit of coughing woke Terese up, and she moaned for Richard.

"What's the matter?" Richard questioned lethargically.

"I'm feeling worse," Terese said. "I need some water and another aspirin."

Richard got up and woozily made his way into the kitchen. He gave Jack a halfhearted kick to move him out of the way. Needing little encouragement, Jack scrambled to the side as much as his shackled hands would allow. Richard filled a glass with water and stumbled back to Terese.

Terese sat up to take the aspirin and the water, while Richard helped support the glass. When she was finished with the water, she pushed the glass away and wiped her mouth with her hand. Her movements were jerky. "With the way I'm feeling, do you think we should head back to the city tonight?" she questioned.

"We have to wait for morning," Richard said. "As soon as Twin comes we'll be off. Besides, I'm too sleepy to drive now anyway."

"You're right," Terese said as she flopped back. "At the moment I don't think I could stand the drive either. Not with this cough. It's hard to catch my breath."

"Sleep it off," Richard said. "I'll leave the rest of the water right here next to you." He put the glass on the coffee table.

"Thanks," Terese murmured.

Richard made his way back to his couch and collapsed. He drew the blanket up around his neck and sighed loudly.

Time dragged, and with it Terese and Richard's congested breathing slowly got worse. By ten-thirty Jack noticed that Terese's respiration was labored. Even from as far away as the kitchen he could see that her lips had become dusky. He was amazed she'd not awakened. He guessed the aspirin had brought her fever down.

In spite of his ambivalence, Jack was finally moved to say something. He called out to Richard and told him Terese didn't sound or look good.

"Shut up!" Richard yelled back between coughs.

Jack stayed silent for another half hour. By then he was convinced he could hear faint popping noises at the end of each of Terese's inspirations that sounded like moist rales. If they were, it was an ominous sign, suggesting to Jack that Terese was slipping into acute respiratory distress.

"Richard!" Jack called out, despite Richard's warning to stay quiet. "Terese is getting worse."

There was no response.

"Richard!" Jack called louder.

"What?" Richard answered sluggishly.

"I think your sister needs to be in an intensive care unit," Jack said.

Richard didn't respond.

"I'm warning you," Jack called. "I'm a doctor, after all, and I should know. If you don't do something it's going to be your fault."

Jack had hit a nerve, and to his surprise Richard leaped off the couch in a fit of rage. "My fault?" he snarled. "It's your fault for giving us whatever we have!" Frantically he looked for the gun, but he couldn't remember what he'd done with it after Jack's last visit to the bathroom.

The search for the pistol only lasted for a few seconds. Richard suddenly grabbed his head with both hands and moaned about his headache. Then he swayed before collapsing back onto the couch.

Jack sighed with relief. Touching off a fit of rage in Richard had not been expected. He tried not to imagine what might have happened had the gun been handy.

Jack resigned himself to the horror of witnessing the spectacle of a virulently pathogenic influenza wreaking its havoc. With Terese's and Richard's rapidly worsening clinical state, he recalled stories that had been told about the terrible influenza pandemic of 1918–19. People were said to have boarded a subway in Brooklyn with mild symptoms, only to be dead by the time they'd reached their destination in Manhattan. When Jack had heard such stories he'd assumed they had been exaggerations. But now that he was being forced to observe Terese and Richard, he no longer thought so. Their swift deterioration was a frightening display of the power of contagion.

By one A.M. Richard's breathing was as labored as Terese's had been. Terese was now frankly cyanotic and barely breathing. By four Richard was cyanotic, and Terese was dead. At six A.M. Richard made a few feeble gurgling sounds and then stopped breathing.

CHAPTER 35

FRIDAY, 8:00 A.M., MARCH 29, 1996

Morning came slowly. At first pale fingers of sunlight tentatively limned the edge of the porcelain sink. From where Jack was sitting he could see a spiderweb of leafless tree branches against the gradually brightening sky. He hadn't slept a wink.

When the room was completely filled with morning light, Jack hazarded a look over his shoulder. It was not a pretty scene. Terese and Richard were both dead, with bloody froth exuding from their dusky blue lips. Both had started to bloat slightly, particularly Terese. Jack assumed it was from the heat of the fire, which was now reduced to mere embers.

Jack looked back despairingly at the drainpipe that so effectively nailed him to his spot. It was an inconceivable predicament. Twin and his Black Kings were probably now on their way. Even without the three thousand dollars, the gang had ample reason to kill him given his role in two of their members' deaths.

Throwing back his head, Jack screamed at the top of his voice for help. He knew it was futile and soon stopped when he was out of breath. He rattled the handcuffs against the brass pipe, and even put his head in under the sink to examine the lead seal where the brass pipe joined the cast-iron pipe below the trap. With a fingernail he tried to dig into the lead, but without result.

Eventually Jack sat back. His anxiety was enervating, coupled with his lack of sleep, food, and water. It was hard to think clearly, but he had to try; he didn't have much time.

Jack considered the faint possibility that the Black Kings wouldn't show up as they'd failed to show the day before, yet that prospect wasn't any rosier. Jack would be sentenced to an agonizing death from exposure and lack of water. Of course, if he couldn't take his rimantadine, the flu might get him first.

Jack fought back tears. How could he have been so stupid to have allowed himself to get caught in such an impossible situation? He chided himself for his inane heroic crusade idea, and the juvenile thought of wanting to prove something to himself. He'd been as reckless in this episode as he'd been each day he'd ridden his bike down Second Avenue thumbing his nose at death.

Two hours passed before Jack heard the faint beginnings of the dread sound: the crackling of car tires on gravel. The Black Kings had arrived.

In a fit of panic, Jack repeatedly kicked the drainpipe as he'd done numerous times over the previous day and a half with the same result.

He stopped and listened again. The car was closer. Jack looked at the sink. Suddenly an idea occurred to him. The sink was a huge, old cast-iron monstrosity with a large bowl and expansive drainage area for dishes. Jack imagined it weighed several hundred pounds. It was hung on the wall in addition to being supported by the heavy drain.

Getting his feet under him, Jack rested the underlip of the sink on his biceps and tried to pry the sink upward. It moved slightly and bits of mortar at the sink's junction with the wall fell into the bowl.

Jack twisted like a contortionist to put his right foot against the sink's lip. He could hear the car come to a halt the moment he pushed with his leg. There was a cracking sound. Jack positioned himself so that both his feet were under the edge of the sink. Straining with all his might, he exerted the maximum force he could muster.

With a snap and a grinding sound the sink detached from the wall. A bit of plaster rained down on Jack's face. Unattached, the sink teetered on the drain.

With another thrust of his legs, Jack got the sink to fall forward. The copper water-supply pipes snapped off at their soldered ends and water began spraying. The drain remained intact until the lead seal gave way. At that moment the brass pipe slipped out of the cast iron. The sink made an enormous crashing noise as it crushed a ladder-back chair before thumping heavily on the wooden floor.

Jack was soaked from the spraying water, but he was free! He scrambled to his feet as heavy footfalls sounded on the front porch. He knew the door was unlocked and that the Black Kings would be inside in a moment. They'd undoubtedly heard the crash of the sink.

With no time to look for the pistol Jack lunged for the back door. Frantically he fumbled with the deadbolt and threw the door open. In an instant he was outside, hurling himself down the few steps to the dew-covered grass.

Hunching down to stay out of view, Jack ran from the house as fast as he could manage with his hands still handcuffed. Ahead was a pond. It occupied the area he'd imagined was a field on his arrival the previous night. To the left of the pond and about a hundred feet from the house stood the barn. Jack ran to it. It was his only hope of a hiding place. The surrounding forest was barren and leafless.

With heart pounding, Jack reached the barn door. To his relief it was unlocked. He yanked it open, dashed inside, and pulled it closed behind him.

The interior of the barn was dark, dank, and uninviting. The only light came through a single, west-facing window. The rusted remains of an old tractor loomed in the half-light.

With utter panic Jack stumbled around in the darkness searching for a hiding place. His eyes began to adjust. He looked into several deserted animal stalls, but there was no way to conceal himself. There was a loft above, but it was devoid of hay.

Looking down at the plank flooring, Jack vainly looked for a trapdoor, but there wasn't any. In the very back of the barn there was a small room filled with garden tools but still no place to hide. Jack was about to give up when he spotted a low wooden chest the size of a coffin. He ran to it and raised its hinged lid. Inside were malodorous bags of fertilizer.

Jack's blood ran cold. Outside he heard a male voice yell: "Hey, man, around here! There's tracks in the grass!"

With little other choice Jack emptied the chest of the bags of fertilizer. Then he climbed in and lowered the lid.

Shivering from fear and the damp cold, Jack was still perspiring. His breaths were coming in short gasps. He tried to calm down. If the hiding place was to work, he'd have to be silent.

It wasn't long before he heard the door to the barn creak open followed by the sound of muffled voices. Footsteps sounded on the plank flooring. Then there was a crash as something was overturned. Jack heard curses. Then another crash.

"You got your machine pistol cocked?" one husky voice said.

"What'd you think I am, stupid?" another replied.

Jack heard footsteps approach. He held his breath, tried to contain his shivering, and fought the urge to cough. There was a pause, then the footsteps receded. Jack allowed himself to breathe out.

"Somebody's in here, I'm sure of it," a voice said.

"Shut up and keep looking," the other answered.

Without warning the cover to Jack's hiding place was whisked open. It happened with such unexpected suddenness, Jack was totally unprepared. He let out a muffled screech. The black man looking down at him did the same, letting the lid slam back into place.

The lid was quickly yanked open again. Jack could see that the man was holding a machine pistol in his free hand. On his head was a black knit cap.

Jack and the black man locked eyes for a moment, then the man looked toward his partner.

"It's the doc all right," he called out. "He's here in a box."

Jack was afraid to move. He heard footsteps approaching. He tried to prepare himself for Twin's mocking smile. But Jack's expectations weren't met. When he looked up, it wasn't Twin's face he saw; it was Warren's!

"Shit, Doc," Warren said. "You look like you fought the Vietnam War all by yourself."

Jack swallowed. He looked at the other man and now recognized him as one of the basketball regulars. Jack's eyes darted back to Warren. Jack was confused, afraid this was all a hallucination.

"Come on, Doc," Warren said, reaching a hand toward Jack. "Get the hell out of the box so we can see if the rest of you looks as bad as your face."

Jack allowed himself to be helped to stand up. He stepped out onto the floor. He was soaking wet from the broken water pipes.

"Well, everything else looks like it's in working order," Warren said. "But you don't smell great. And we've got to get these cuffs off."

"How did you get here?" Jack asked, finally finding his voice.

"We drove," Warren said. "How'd you think we got here? The subway?"

"But I expected the Black Kings," Jack said. "A guy by the name of Twin."

"Sorry to disappoint you, man," Warren said. "You've got to settle for me."

"I don't understand," Jack said.

"Twin and I made a deal," Warren said. "We called a truce so there'd be no more brothers shooting brothers. Part of the terms were that they wouldn't ice you. Then Twin called me and told me you were being held up here and that if I wanted to save your ass, I'd better get mine up to the mountains. So here we are: the cavalry."

"Good Lord!" Jack said, shaking his head. It was unsettling to learn how much one's fate was in the hands of others.

"Hey, those people back in the house don't look so good," Warren said. "And they smell worse than you. How'd they happen to die?"

"Influenza," Jack said.

"No shit!" Warren said. "So it's up here too. I heard about it on the news last night. There's a lot of people down in the city all revved up about it."

"And for good reason," Jack said. "I think you'd better tell me what you've heard."

EPILOGUE

The game to eleven was tied at ten apiece. The rules dictated a win by two, so a one-point layup wouldn't clinch it but a long two-pointer would. This was in the back of Jack's mind as he dribbled upcourt. He was being mercilessly hounded by an aggressive player by the name of Flash whom Jack knew was faster than he.

The competition was fierce. Players on the sidelines waiting to play were loudly supporting the other team, a sharp contrast to their typical studied indifference. The reason for the change was the fact that Jack's team had been winning all night, mainly because Jack was teamed up with a particularly good mix of players that included Warren and Spit.

Jack normally didn't bring the ball downcourt. That was Warren's job. But on the previous play, to Jack's chagrin, Flash had made a driving layup to tie the game, and after the ball had passed through the basket it had ended up in Jack's hands. In order to get the ball downcourt as fast as possible, Spit had stepped out. When Jack gave him the ball, Spit gave it right back.

As Jack pulled up at the top of the key, Warren faked one direction and then made a rush for the basket. Jack saw this maneuver out of the corner of his eye and cocked his arm with the intent of passing the ball to Warren.

Flash anticipated the pass and dropped back in hopes of intercepting it. All at once Jack was in the clear, and he changed his mind about passing. Instead he let fly one of his normally reliable jumpers. Unfortunately the ball hit the back of the rim and bounced directly into Flash's waiting hands.

The tide then swept back in the other direction, to the glee of the onlookers.

Flash brought the ball rapidly downcourt. Jack was intent on denying him the opportunity of repeating his driving layup, but inadvertently gave him too much room. To Jack's surprise, since Flash was not an outside shooter, Flash pulled up and from "downtown" let fly his own jumper.

To Jack's horror it was "nothing-but-net" as the shot passed through the basket. A cheer rose up from the sidelines. The game had been won by the underdogs.

Flash high-stepped around the court holding his arms straight and stiffly to his sides with his palms out. All his teammates slapped his palms in a congratulatory ritual, as did some of the onlookers.

Warren drifted over to Jack with a disgusted look on his face.

"You should have passed the friggin' ball," Warren said.

"My bad," Jack said. He was embarrassed. He'd made three mistakes in a row.

"Shit," Warren said. "With these new kicks of mine I didn't think I could lose."

Jack looked down at the spanking-new pair of Nikes Warren was referring to and then at his own scuffed and scarred Filas. "Maybe I need some new kicks myself."

"Jack! Hey, Jack!" a female voice called out. "Hello!"

Jack looked through the chain-link fence separating the playground from the sidewalk. It was Laurie.

"Hey, kid!" Warren said to Jack. "Looks like your shortie has decided to pay the courts a visit."

The game-winning celebration stopped. All eyes turned to Laurie. Girlfriends and wives didn't come to the courts. Whether they weren't inclined or whether they were actively excluded, Jack didn't know. But the infraction of Laurie's unexpected arrival made him feel uncomfortable. He'd always tried to play by the playground's mostly unspoken rules.

"I think she wants to rap," Warren said. Laurie was waving Jack over.

"I didn't invite her," Jack said. "We were supposed to meet later."

"No problem," Warren said. "She's a looker. You must be a better lover than you are a b-ball player."

Jack laughed in spite of himself, then walked over to Laurie. Behind him he heard the celebration recommence, and he relaxed a degree.

"Now I know the stories are all true," Laurie said. "You really do play basketball."

"I hope you didn't see the last three plays," Jack said. "You wouldn't have guessed I played much if you had."

"I know we weren't supposed to meet until nine, but I couldn't wait to talk to you," Laurie said.

"What's happened?" Jack asked.

"You got a call from a Nicole Marquette from the CDC," Laurie said. "Apparently she was so disappointed not to get you that Marjorie, the operator, put her through to me. Nicole asked me to relay a message to you."

"Well?" Jack questioned.

"The CDC is officially putting the crash vaccine program on hold," Laurie said. "There hasn't been a new case of the Alaska-strain influenza for two weeks. The quarantine efforts have worked. Apparently the outbreak has been contained just the way the seventy-six swine flu was."

"That's great news!" Jack said. Over the past week he'd been praying that this would happen, and Laurie knew it. After fifty-two cases with thirty-four deaths there had been a lull. Everyone involved was holding his breath.

"Did she offer any explanations as to why they think this has occurred?" Jack asked.

"She did," Laurie said. "Their studies have shown that the virus is unusually unstable outside of a host. They believe that the temperature must have varied in the buried Eskimo hut and might have even approached thawing on occasion. That's a far cry from the usual minus fifty degrees at which viruses are typically stored."

"Too bad it didn't affect its pathogenicity as well," Jack said.

"But at least it made the CDC-engineered quarantine effective," Laurie said, "which everyone knows isn't the usual case with influenza. Apparently with the Alaska strain, contacts had to have relatively sustained close contact with an infected individual for transmission to occur."

"I think we were all very lucky," Jack said. "The pharmaceutical industry deserves a lot of credit too. They came through with all the rimantadine needed in record time."

"Are you finished playing basketball?" Laurie asked. She looked over Jack's shoulder and could see that another game had commenced.

"I'm afraid so," Jack said. "My team lost, thanks to me."

"Is that man you were talking with when I arrived Warren?" Laurie asked.

"That's right," Jack said.

"He's just as you described," Laurie said. "He looks impressive. But there's one thing I don't understand. How do those shorts of his stay on? They are so oversized and he has such narrow hips."

Jack let out a laugh. He looked back at Warren casually shooting foul shots like a machine. The funny thing was that Laurie was right: Warren's shorts defied Newton's law of gravity. Jack was just so accustomed to the hip-hop gear, he'd never questioned it.

"I guess it's a mystery to me too," Jack said. "You'll have to ask him yourself."

"Okay," Laurie said agreeably. "I'd like to meet him anyway."

Jack turned back to her with a quizzical look.

"I'm serious," she said. "I'd like to meet this man you are in awe of and who saved your life."

"Don't ask him about his drawers," Jack cautioned. He had no idea how that would go over.

"Please!" Laurie said. "I do have some social sense."

Jack called out to Warren and waved him over. Warren sauntered to the fence, dribbling his basketball. Jack was unsure of the situation and didn't know what to expect. He introduced the two people, and to his surprise they got along well.

"It's probably not my place to say this . . ." Laurie began after they had spoken for a while. "And Jack might wish I didn't, but . . ."

Jack cringed. He had no idea what Laurie was about to say.

". . . I'd like to thank you personally for what you did for Jack."

Warren shrugged. "I might not have taken my ride all the way up there if I knew he wasn't going to pass me the ball tonight."

Jack formed his hand into a semi-fist and cuffed the top of Warren's head.

Warren flinched and ducked out of the way. "Nice meeting you, Laurie," he said. "I'm glad you stopped by. Me and some of the other brothers have been a bit worried about the old man here. We're glad to see that he has a shortie after all."

"What's a shortie?" Laurie asked.

"Girlfriend," Jack translated.

"Come anytime, Laurie," Warren said. "You sure are better-looking than this kid." He took a swipe at Jack and then dribbled back to where he'd been shooting foul shots.

" 'Shortie' for girlfriend?" Laurie questioned.

"It's just rap-talk," Jack said. "Shortie is a lot more flattering than some of the terms. But you're not supposed to take any of it literally."

"Don't get me wrong! I wasn't offended," Laurie said. "In fact, why don't you ask him and his 'shortie' to come to dinner with us. I'd like to get to know him better."

Jack shrugged and looked back at Warren. "That's an idea," he said. "I wonder if he'd come."

"You'll never know unless you ask," Laurie said.

"I can't argue with you there," Jack said.

"I assume he has a girlfriend," Laurie said.

"To tell you the truth, I don't know," Jack said.

"You mean to tell me you were quarantined with the man for a week and you don't even know if he has a girlfriend?" Laurie said. "What did you men talk about all that time?"

"I can't remember," Jack said. "Hold on. I'll be right back."

Jack walked over to Warren and asked him if he'd come to dinner with them and bring his "shortie."

"That is, if you have one," Jack added.

"Of course I have one," Warren said. He stared at Jack for a beat, then looked over at Laurie. "Was it her idea?"

"Yeah," Jack admitted. "But I think it's a good one. The reason I never asked in the past is because I never thought you'd come."

"Where?"

"A restaurant called Elios on the East Side," Jack said. "At nine. It's my treat."

"Cool," Warren said. "How you getting over there?"

"I suppose we'll take a taxi from my place," Jack said.

"No need," Warren said. "My ride's handy. I'll pick you up at quarter of nine."

"See you then," Jack said. He turned and started back toward Laurie.

"This doesn't mean I'm not still pissed that you didn't pass me the ball on that last run," Warren called out.

Jack smiled and waved over his shoulder. When he got back to Laurie he told her that Warren was coming.

"Wonderful," Laurie said.

"I agree," Jack said. "I'll be dining with two of the four people who saved my life."

"Where are the other two?" Laurie asked.

"Unfortunately, Slam is no longer with us," Jack said regretfully. "That's a story I have yet to tell you. Spit is the fellow over on the sidelines in the bright red sweatshirt."

"Why not ask him to dinner too," Laurie suggested.

"Another night," Jack said. "I'd rather this not be a party. I'm looking forward to the conversation. You learned more about Warren in two minutes than I've learned in months."

"I'll never understand what you men talk about," Laurie said.

"Listen, I've got to shower and dress," Jack said. "Do you mind coming up to my place?"

"Not at all," Laurie said. "I'm kind of curious, the way you've described it."

"It's not pretty," Jack warned.

"Lead on!" Laurie commanded.

Jack was pleased there were no homeless people asleep in the hall of his tenement, but to make up for that blessing the endless argument on the second floor was as loud as ever. Nevertheless, Laurie didn't seem to mind and had no comment until they were safely inside Jack's apartment. There she glanced around and said it looked warm and comfortable, like an oasis.

"It'll only take me a few minutes to get ready," Jack said. "Can I offer you something? Actually I don't have much. How about a beer?"

Laurie declined and told Jack to go ahead and shower. He tried to give her something to read, but she declined that as well.

"I don't have a TV," Jack said apologetically.

"I noticed," Laurie said.

"In this building a TV is too much of a temptation," Jack said. "It would walk out of here too fast."

"Talking about TV," Laurie said, "have you seen those National Health commercials everyone is talking about, the 'no wait' ones?"

"No, I haven't," Jack said.

"You should," Laurie said. "They're amazingly effective. One of them has become an overnight classic. It's the one with the tag line 'We wait for you, you don't wait for us.' It's very clever. If you can believe it, it's even caused National Health's stock to go up."

"Could we talk about something else?" Jack said.

"Of course," Laurie said. She cocked her head to the side. "What's the matter? Did I say something wrong?"

"No, it's not you, it's me," Jack said. "Sometimes I'm overly sensitive. Medical advertising has always been a pet peeve of mine, and lately I feel even more strongly about it. But don't worry; I'll explain it later."

CHROMOSOME 6

FOR AUDREY AND BARBARA

Thanks for being wonderful mothers.

ACKNOWLEDGMENTS

MATTHEW J. BANKOWSKI, PH.D.,
*Director of Clinical Virology, Molecular Medicine,
and Research-Development, DSI Laboratories*

JOE COX, J.D., L.L.M., *tax and corporate law*

JOHN GILATTO, V.M.D., PH.D., *Associate Professor
of Veterinary Pathology, Tufts University
School of Veterinary Medicine*

JACKI LEE, M.D., *Chief Medical Examiner,
Queens, New York*

MATTS LINDEN, *Captain Pilot, American Airlines*

MARTINE PIGNEDE, *Director of NIWA
Private Game Reserve, Cameroon*

JEAN REEDS, *School Psychologist, reader, and critic*

CHARLES WETLI, M.D., *Chief Medical Examiner,
Suffolk County, New York*

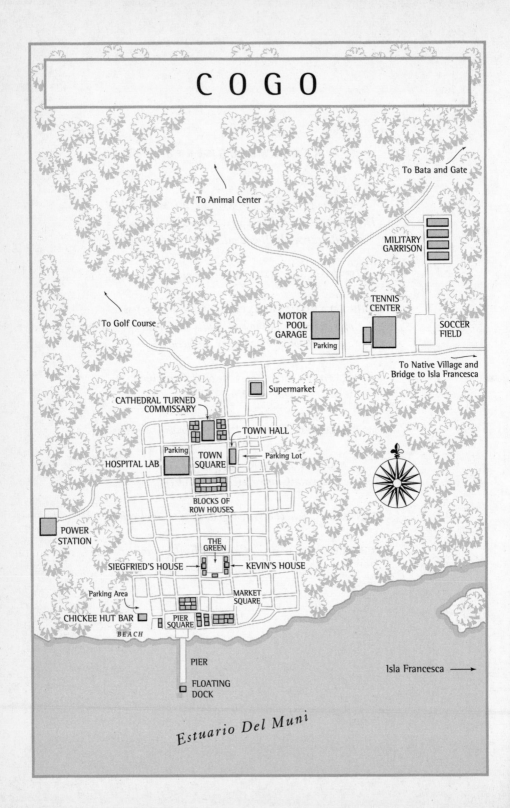

COGO

To Bata and Gate

To Animal Center

MILITARY
GARRISON

To Golf Course

TENNIS
CENTER

MOTOR
POOL
GARAGE

Parking

SOCCER
FIELD

To Native Village and
Bridge to Isla Francesca

Supermarket

CATHEDRAL TURNED
COMMISSARY

TOWN HALL

Parking

HOSPITAL LAB

TOWN
SQUARE

Parking Lot

BLOCKS OF
ROW HOUSES

POWER
STATION

THE
GREEN

SIEGFRIED'S HOUSE

KEVIN'S HOUSE

Parking Area

MARKET
SQUARE

CHICKEE HUT BAR

PIER
SQUARE

BEACH

Isla Francesca

PIER

FLOATING
DOCK

Estuario Del Muni

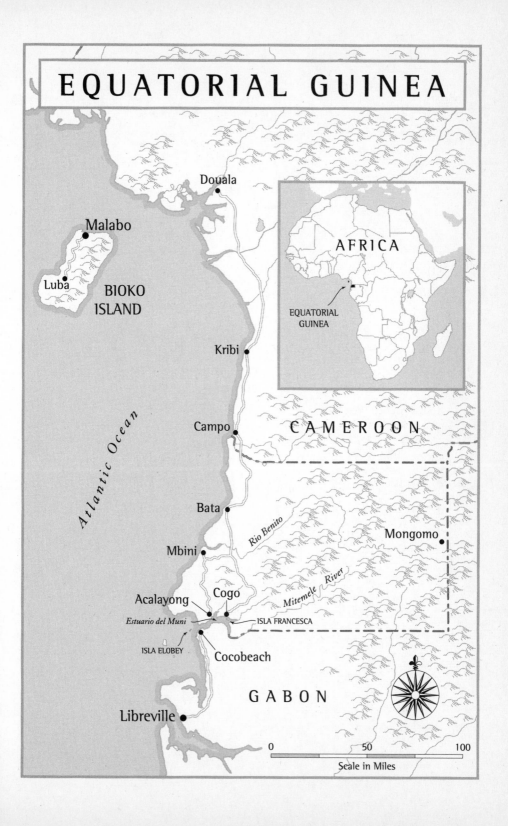

EQUATORIAL GUINEA

Douala

Malabo

Luba   BIOKO
        ISLAND

AFRICA

EQUATORIAL
GUINEA

Kribi

Atlantic Ocean

Campo   C A M E R O O N

Bata

Rio Benito

Mbini   Mongomo

Cogo   *Mitemele River*

Acalayong

Estuario del Muni   ISLA FRANCESCA

ISLA ELOBEY   Cocobeach

G A B O N

Libreville

0   50   100

Scale in Miles

PROLOGUE

Given a Ph.D. in molecular biology from MIT that had been earned in close co-operation with the Massachusetts General Hospital, Kevin Marshall found his squeamishness regarding medical procedures a distinct embarrassment. Although he'd never admitted it to anyone, just having a blood test or a vaccination was an ordeal for him. Needles were his specific bête noire. The sight of them caused his legs to go rubbery and a cold sweat to break out on his broad forehead. Once he'd even fainted in college after getting a measles shot.

At age thirty-four, after many years of postgraduate biomedical research, some of it involving live animals, he'd expected to outgrow his phobia, but it hadn't happened. And it was for that reason he was not in operating room 1A or 1B at the moment. Instead he'd chosen to remain in the intervening scrub room, where he was leaning against the scrub sink, a vantage that allowed him to look through angled windows into both ORs—until he felt the need to avert his eyes.

The two patients had been in their respective rooms for about a quarter hour in preparation for their respective procedures. The two surgical teams were quietly conversing while standing off to the side. They were gowned and gloved and ready to commence.

There'd been little technical conversation in the ORs except between the anesthesiologist and the two anesthetists as the patients were inducted under general anesthesia. The lone anesthesiologist had slipped back and forth between the two rooms to supervise and to be available at any sign of trouble.

But there was no trouble. At least not yet. Nonetheless, Kevin felt anxious. To his surprise he did not experience the same sense of triumph he had enjoyed during three previous comparable procedures when he'd exalted in the power of science and his own creativity.

Instead of jubilation Kevin felt a mushrooming unease. His discomfort had started almost a week previously, but it was now, watching these patients and contemplating their different prognoses, that Kevin felt the disquietude with disturbing poignancy. The effect was similar to his thinking about needles: perspiration appeared on his forehead and his legs trembled. He had to grasp the edge of the scrub sink to steady himself.

The door to operating room 1A opened suddenly, startling Kevin. He was confronted by a figure whose pale blue eyes were framed by a hood and a face mask. Recognition was rapid: It was Candace Brickmann, one of the surgical nurses.

"The IVs are all started, and the patients are asleep," Candace said. "Are you sure you don't want to come in? You'll be able to see much better."

"Thank you, but I'm fine right here," Kevin said.

"Suit yourself," Candace said.

The door swung shut behind Candace as she returned to one of the surgeries. Kevin watched her scurry across the room and say something to the surgeons. Their response was to turn in Kevin's direction and give him a thumbs-up sign. Kevin self-consciously returned the gesture.

The surgeons went back to their conversation, but the effect of the wordless communication with Kevin magnified his sense of complicity. He let go of the scrub sink and took a step backward. His unease was now tinged with fear. What had he done?

Spinning on his heels, Kevin fled from the scrub room and then from the operating suite. A puff of air followed him as he left the mildly positive pressure aseptic OR area and entered his gleaming, futuristic laboratory. He was breathing heavily as if out of breath from exertion.

On any other day, merely walking into his domain would have filled him with anticipation just at the thought of the discoveries awaiting his magic hand. The series of rooms literally bristled with hi-tech equipment the likes of which used to be the focus of his fantasies. Now these sophisticated machines were at his beck and call, day and night. Absently he ran his fingers lightly along the stainless-steel cowlings, casually brushing the analogue dials and digital displays as he headed for his office. He touched the hundred-and-fifty-thousand-dollar DNA sequencer and the five-hundred-thousand-dollar globular NMR machine that sprouted a tangle of wires like a giant sea anemone. He glanced at the PCRs, whose red lights blinked like distant quasars announcing successive DNA-strand doublings. It was an environment that had previously filled Kevin with hope and promise. But now each Eppendorf microcentrifuge tube and each tissue-culture flask stood as mute reminders of the building foreboding he was experiencing.

Advancing to his desk, Kevin looked down at his gene map of the short arm of chromosome 6. His area of principal interest was outlined in red. It was the major histocompatibility complex. The problem was that the MHC was only a small portion of the short arm of chromosome 6. There were large blank areas that represented millions and millions of base pairs, and hence hundreds of other genes. Kevin did not know what they did.

A recent request for information concerning these genes that he'd put out over the Internet had resulted in some vague replies. Several researchers had responded that the short arm of chromosome 6 contained genes that were involved with muscular-skeletal development. But that was it. There were no details.

Kevin shuddered involuntarily. He raised his eyes to the large picture window above his desk. As usual it was streaked with moisture from the tropical rain that swept across the view in undulating sheets. The droplets slowly descended until enough had fused to reach a critical mass. Then they raced off the surface like sparks from a grinding wheel.

Kevin's eyes focused into the distance. The contrast between the gleaming, air-conditioned interior with the outside world was always a shock. Roiling, gun-metal gray clouds filled the sky despite the fact that the dry season was supposed to have begun three weeks previously. The land was dominated by riotous vegetation that was so dark green as to almost appear black. Along the edge of the town it rose up like a gigantic, threatening tidal wave.

Kevin's office was in the hospital-laboratory complex that was one of the few new structures in the previously decaying and deserted Spanish colonial town of Cogo in the little-known African country of Equatorial Guinea. The building was three stories tall. Kevin's office was on the top floor, facing southeast. From his window he could see a good portion of the town as it sprawled haphazardly toward the Estuario del Muni and its contributory rivers.

Some of the neighboring buildings had been renovated, some were in the process, but most had not been touched. A half dozen previously handsome haciendas were enveloped by vines and roots of vegetation that had gone wild. Over the whole scene hung the perennial mist of super-saturated warm air.

In the immediate foreground Kevin could see beneath the arched arcade of the old town hall. In the shadows were the inevitable handful of Equatoguinean soldiers in combat fatigues with AK-47's haphazardly slung over their shoulders. As usual they were smoking, arguing, and consuming Cameroonean beer.

Finally Kevin let his eyes wander beyond the town. He'd been unconsciously avoiding doing so, but now he focused on the estuary whose rain-lashed surface looked like beaten tin. Directly south he could just make out the forested shoreline of Gabon. Looking to the east he followed the trail of islands that stretched toward the interior of the continent. On the horizon he could see the largest of the islands, Isla Francesca, named by the Portuguese in the fifteenth century. In contrast to the other islands, Isla Francesca had a jungle-covered limestone escarpment that ran down its center like the backbone of a dinosaur.

Kevin's heart skipped a beat. Despite the rain and the mist, he could see what he'd feared he'd see. Just like a week ago there was the unmistakable wisp of smoke lazily undulating toward the leaden sky.

Kevin slumped into his desk chair and cradled his head in his hands. He asked himself what he'd done. Having minored in the Classics as an undergraduate, he knew about Greek myths. Now he questioned if he'd made a Promethean mistake. Smoke meant fire, and he had to wonder if it was the proverbial fire inadvertently stolen from the gods.

6:45 P.M.
BOSTON, MASSACHUSETTS

While a cold March wind rattled the storm windows, Taylor Devonshire Cabot reveled in the security and warmth of his walnut-paneled study in his sprawling Manchester-by-the-Sea home north of Boston, Massachusetts. Harriette Livingston Cabot, Taylor's wife, was in the kitchen supervising the final stages of dinner scheduled to be served at seven-thirty sharp.

On the arm of Taylor's chair balanced a cut-crystal glass of neat, single-malt whiskey. A fire crackled in the fireplace as Wagner played on the stereo, the volume turned low. In addition there were three built-in televisions tuned respectively to a local news station, CNN, and ESPN.

Taylor was the picture of contentment. He'd spent a busy but productive day at the world headquarters of GenSys, a relatively new biotechnology firm he'd started eight years previously. The company had constructed a new building along the Charles River in Boston to take advantage of the proximity of both Harvard and MIT for recruitment purposes.

The evening commute had been easier than usual, and Taylor hadn't had time to finish his scheduled reading. Knowing his employer's habits, Rodney, his driver, had apologized for getting Taylor home so quickly.

"I'm sure you'll be able to come up with a significant delay tomorrow night to make up," Taylor had quipped.

"I'll do my best," Rodney had responded.

So Taylor wasn't listening to the stereo or watching the TVs. Instead he was carefully reading the financial report scheduled to be released at the GenSys stockholders' meeting scheduled the following week. But that didn't mean he was unaware of what was going on around him. He was very much aware of the sound of the wind, the sputtering of the fire, the music, and alert to the various reporters' banters on the TVs. So when the name Carlo Franconi was mentioned, Taylor's head snapped up.

The first thing Taylor did was lift the remote and turn up the sound of the central television. It was the local news on the CBS affiliate. The anchors were Jack Williams and Liz Walker. Jack Williams had mentioned the name Carlo Franconi, and was going on to say that the station had obtained a videotape of the killing of this known Mafia figure who had some association with Boston crime families.

"This tape is quite graphic," Jack warned. "Parental discretion is recommended. You might remember that a few days ago we reported that the ailing Franconi had disappeared after his indictment, and many had feared he'd jumped bail. But then he'd just reappeared yesterday with the news that he'd struck a deal with the New York City DA's office to plea-bargain and enter the witness-protection program. However, this evening while emerging from a favorite restaurant, the indicted racketeer was fatally shot."

Taylor was transfixed as he watched an amateur video of an overweight man emerge from a restaurant accompanied by several people who looked like policemen. With a casual wave, the man acknowledged the crowd who'd assembled and then headed to an awaiting limousine. He assiduously ignored questions from any journalists angling to get close to him. Just as he was bending to enter the car, Franconi's body jerked, and he staggered backward with his hand clasping the base of his neck. As he fell to his right, his body jerked again before hitting the ground. The men who'd accompanied him had drawn their guns and were frantically turning in all directions. The pursuing journalists had all hit the deck.

"Whoa!" Jack commented. "What a scene! Sort'a reminds me of the killing of Lee Harvey Oswald. So much for police protection."

"I wonder what effect this will have on future similar witnesses?" Liz asked.

"Not good, I'm sure," Jack said.

Taylor's eyes immediately switched to CNN, which was at that moment about to show the same video. He watched the sequence again. It made him wince. At the end of the tape, CNN went live to a reporter outside the Office of the Chief Medical Examiner for the City of New York.

"The question now is whether there were one or two assailants," the reporter said over the sound of the traffic on First Avenue. "It's our impression that Franconi was shot twice. The police are understandably chagrined over this episode and have refused to speculate or offer any information whatsoever. We do know that an autopsy is scheduled for tomorrow morning, and we assume that ballistics will answer the question."

Taylor turned down the sound on the television, then picked up his drink. Walking to the window, he gazed out at the angry, dark sea. Franconi's death could mean trouble. He looked at his watch. It was almost midnight in West Africa.

Snatching up the phone, Taylor called the operator at GenSys and told him he wanted to speak with Kevin Marshall immediately.

Replacing the receiver, Taylor returned his gaze out the window. He'd never felt completely comfortable about this project although financially it was looking very profitable. He wondered if he should stop it. The phone interrupted his thoughts.

Picking the receiver back up, Taylor was told that Mr. Marshall was available. After some static Kevin's sleepy voice crackled over the line.

"Is this really Taylor Cabot?" Kevin asked.

"Do you remember a Carlo Franconi?" Taylor demanded, ignoring Kevin's question.

"Of course," Kevin said.

"He's been murdered this afternoon," Taylor said. "There's an autopsy scheduled for the morning in New York City. What I want to know is, could that be a problem?"

There was a moment of silence. Taylor was about to question whether the connection had been broken when Kevin spoke up.

"Yes, it could be a problem," Kevin said.

"Someone could figure out everything from an autopsy?"

"It's possible," Kevin said. "I wouldn't say probable, but it is possible."

"I don't like possible," Taylor said. He disconnected from Kevin and called the operator back at GenSys. Taylor said he wanted to speak immediately to Dr. Raymond Lyons. He emphasized that it was an emergency.

NEW YORK CITY

Excuse me," the waiter whispered. He'd approached Dr. Lyons from the left side, having waited for a break in the conversation the doctor was engaged in with his young, blond assistant and current lover, Darlene Polson. Between his gracefully graying hair and conservative apparel, the good doctor looked like the quintessential, soap-opera physician. He was in his early fifties, tall, tanned, and enviably slender with refined, patrician good looks.

"I'm sorry to intrude," the waiter continued. "But there is an emergency call for you. Can I offer you our cordless phone or would you prefer to use the phone in the hall?"

Raymond's blue eyes darted back and forth between Darlene's affable but bland face and the considerate waiter whose impeccable demeanor reflected Aureole's 26 service rating in Zagat's restaurant guide. Raymond did not look happy.

"Perhaps I should tell them you are not available," the waiter suggested.

"No, I'll take the cordless," Raymond said. He couldn't imagine who could be calling him on an emergency basis. Raymond had not been practicing medicine since he'd lost his medical license after having been convicted of a major Medicare scam he'd been carrying on for a dozen years.

"Hello?" Raymond said with a degree of trepidation.

"This is Taylor Cabot. There's a problem."

Raymond visibly stiffened and his brow furrowed.

Taylor quickly summarized the Carlo Franconi situation and his call to Kevin Marshall.

"This operation is your baby," Taylor concluded irritably. "And let me warn you: it is small potatoes in the grand scheme of things. If there is trouble, I'll scrap the entire enterprise. I don't want bad publicity, so handle it."

"But what can I do?" Raymond blurted out.

"Frankly, I don't know," Taylor said. "But you'd better think of something, and you'd better do it fast."

"Things couldn't be going any better from my end," Raymond interjected. "Just today I made positive contact with a physician in L.A. who treats a lot of movie stars and wealthy West Coast businessmen. She's interested in setting up a branch in California."

"Maybe you didn't hear me," Taylor said. "There isn't going to be a branch anyplace if this Franconi problem isn't resolved. So you'd better get busy. I'd say you have about twelve hours."

The resounding click of the disconnection made Raymond's head jerk. He looked at the phone as if it had been responsible for the precipitate termination of the conversation. The waiter, who'd retreated to an appropriate distance, stepped forward to retrieve the phone before disappearing.

"Trouble?" Darlene questioned.

"Oh, God!" Raymond voiced. Nervously he chewed the quick of his thumb. It was more than trouble. It was potential disaster. With his attempts at retrieving his medical license tied up in the quagmire of the judicial system, his current work situation was all he had, and things had only recently been clicking. It had taken him five years to get where he was. He couldn't let it all go down the drain.

"What is it?" Darlene asked. She reached out and pulled Raymond's hand away from his mouth.

Raymond quickly explained about the upcoming autopsy on Carlo Franconi and repeated Taylor Cabot's threat to scrap the entire enterprise.

"But it's finally making big money," Darlene said. "He won't scrap it."

Raymond gave a short, mirthless laugh. "It isn't big money to someone like Taylor Cabot and GenSys," he said. "He'd scrap it for certain. Hell, it was difficult to talk him into it in the first place."

"Then you have to tell them not to do the autopsy," Darlene said.

Raymond stared at his companion. He knew she meant well, and he'd never been attracted to her for her brain power. So he resisted lashing out. But his reply was sarcastic: "You think I can just call up the medical examiner's office and tell them not to do an autopsy on such a case? Give me a break!"

"But you know a lot of important people," Darlene persisted. "Ask them to call."

"Please, dear . . ." Raymond said condescendingly, but then he paused. He began to think that unwittingly Darlene had a point. An idea began to germinate.

"What about Dr. Levitz?" Darlene said. "He was Mr. Franconi's doctor. Maybe he could help."

"I was just thinking the same thing," Raymond said. Dr. Daniel Levitz was a Park Avenue physician with a big office, high overhead, and a dwindling patient base, thanks to managed care. He'd been easy to recruit and had been one of the first doctors to join the venture. On top of that, he'd brought in many clients, some of them in the same business as Carlo Franconi.

Raymond stood up, extracted his wallet, and plopped three crisp one-hundred-dollar bills on the table. He knew that was more than enough for the tab and a generous tip. "Come on," he said. "We've got to make a house call."

"But I haven't finished my entrée," Darlene complained.

Raymond didn't respond. Instead he whisked Darlene's chair out from the table, forcing her to her feet. The more he thought about Dr. Levitz, the more he thought the man could be the savior. As the personal physician of a number of competing New York crime families, Levitz knew people who could do the impossible.

CHAPTER 1

Jack Stapleton bent over and put more muscle into his pedaling as he sprinted the last block heading east along Thirtieth Street. About fifty yards from First Avenue he sat up and coasted no-hands before beginning to brake. The upcoming traffic light was not in his favor, and even Jack wasn't crazy enough to sail out into the mix of cars, buses, and trucks racing uptown.

The weather had warmed considerably and the five inches of slush that had fallen two days previously was gone save for a few dirty piles between parked cars. Jack was pleased the roads were clear since he'd not been able to commute on his bike for several days. The bike was only three weeks old. It was a replacement for one that had been stolen a year previously.

Originally, Jack had planned on replacing the bike immediately. But he'd changed his mind after a terrifyingly close encounter with death made him temporarily conservative about risk. The episode had nothing to do with bike riding in the city, but nonetheless it scared him enough to acknowledge that his riding style had been deliberately reckless.

But time dimmed Jack's fears. The final prod came when he lost his watch and wallet in a subway mugging. A day later, Jack bought himself a new Cannondale mountain bike, and as far as his friends were concerned, he was up to his old tricks. In reality, he was no longer tempting fate by squeezing between speeding delivery vans and parked cars; he no longer slalomed down Second Avenue; and for the most part he stayed out of Central Park after dark.

Jack came to a stop at the corner to wait for the light, and as his foot touched down on the pavement he surveyed the scene. Almost at once he became aware of a bevy of TV vans with extended antennae parked on the east side of First Avenue in front of his destination: the Office of the Chief Medical Examiner for the City of New York, or what some people called simply, the morgue.

Jack was an associate medical examiner, and he'd been in that position for almost a year and a half so he'd seen such journalistic congestion on numerous occasions. Generally it meant that there had been a death of a celebrity, or at least someone made momentarily famous by the media. If it wasn't a single death, then it was a mass disaster like an airplane crash or a train wreck. For reasons both personal and public Jack hoped it was the former.

With a green light, Jack pedaled across First Avenue and entered the morgue through the receiving dock on Thirtieth Street. He parked his bike in his usual location near the Hart Island coffins used for the unclaimed dead and took the elevator up to the first floor.

It was immediately apparent to Jack that the place was in a minor uproar. Several of the day secretaries were busily manning the phones in the communications room: they normally didn't arrive until eight. Their consoles were awash with blinking red lights. Even Sergeant Murphy's cubicle was open and the overhead light was on, and his usual modus operandi was to arrive sometime after nine.

With curiosity mounting, Jack entered the ID room and headed directly for the coffeepot. Vinnie Amendola, one of the mortuary techs, was hiding behind his newspaper as per usual. But that was the only normal circumstance for that time of the morning. Generally Jack was the first pathologist to arrive, but on this particular day the deputy chief, Dr. Calvin Washington, Dr. Laurie Montgomery, and Dr. Chet McGovern were already there. The three were involved in a deep discussion along with Sergeant Murphy and, to Jack's surprise, Detective Lieutenant Lou Soldano from homicide. Lou was a frequent visitor to the morgue, but certainly not at seven-thirty in the morning. On top of that, he looked like he'd never been to bed, or if he had, he'd slept in his clothes.

Jack helped himself to coffee. No one acknowledged his arrival. After adding a dollop of half-and-half as well as a cube of sugar to his cup, Jack wandered to the door to the lobby. He glanced out, and as he'd expected the area was filled to overflowing with media people talking among themselves and drinking take-out coffee. What he didn't expect was that many were also smoking cigarettes. Since smoking was strictly taboo, Jack told Vinnie to go out there and inform them.

"You're closer," Vinnie said, without looking up from his newspaper.

Jack rolled his eyes at Vinnie's lack of respect but had to admit Vinnie was right. So Jack walked over to the locked glass door and opened it. Before he could call out his no smoking pronouncement, he was literally mobbed.

Jack had to push the microphones away that were thrust into his face. The simultaneous questions precluded any real comprehension of what the questions were other than about an anticipated autopsy.

Jack shouted at the top of his lungs that there was no smoking, then had to literally peel hands off his arm before he was able to get the door closed. On the other side the reporters surged forward, pressing colleagues roughly against the glass like tomatoes in a jar of preserves.

Disgusted, Jack returned to the ID room.

"Will someone clue me in to what's going on?" he called out.

Everyone turned in Jack's direction, but Laurie was the first to respond. "You haven't heard?"

"Now, would I be asking if I'd heard?" Jack said.

"It's been all over the TV for crissake," Calvin snapped.

"Jack doesn't own a TV," Laurie said. "His neighborhood won't allow it."

"Where do you live, son?" Sergeant Murphy asked. "I've never heard of neighbors not allowing each other to have a television." The aging, red-faced, Irish policeman had a pronounced paternal streak. He'd been assigned to the medical examiner's office for more years than he was willing to admit and thought of all the employees as family.

"He lives in Harlem," Chet said. "Actually his neighbors would love him to get a set so they could permanently borrow it."

"Enough, you guys," Jack said. "Fill me in on the excitement."

"A Mafia don was gunned down yesterday late afternoon," Calvin's booming voice announced. "It's stirred up a hornet's nest of trouble since he'd agreed to cooperate with the DA's office and was under police protection."

"He was no Mafia don," Lou Soldano said. "He was nothing but a midlevel functionary of the Vaccarro crime family."

"Whatever," Calvin said with a wave of his hand. "The key point is that he was whacked while literally boxed in by a number of New York's finest, which doesn't say much about their ability to protect someone in their charge."

"He was warned not to go to that restaurant," Lou protested. "I know that for a fact. And it's almost impossible to protect someone if the individual refuses to follow suggestions."

"Any chance he could have been killed by the police?" Jack asked. One of the roles of a medical examiner was to think of all angles, especially when situations of custody were concerned.

"He wasn't under arrest," Lou said, guessing what was going through Jack's mind. "He'd been arrested and indicted, but he was out on bail."

"So what's the big deal?" Jack asked.

"The big deal is that the mayor, the district attorney, and the police commissioner are all under a lot of heat," Calvin said.

"Amen," Lou said. "Particularly the police commissioner. That's why I'm here. It's turning into one of those public-relations nightmares that the media loves to blow way out of proportion. We've got to apprehend the perpetrator or perpetrators ASAP, otherwise heads are going to roll."

"And not to discourage future potential witnesses," Jack said.

"Yeah, that too," Lou said.

"I don't know, Laurie," Calvin said, getting back to the discussion they'd been having before Jack's interruption. "I appreciate you coming in early and offering to do this autopsy, but maybe Bingham might want to do it himself."

"But why?" Laurie complained. "Look, it's a straightforward case, and I've recently done a lot of gunshot wounds. Besides, with Dr. Bingham's budget meeting this morning at City Hall, he can't be here until almost noon. By then I can have the autopsy done and whatever information I come up with will be in the hands of the police. With their time constraint, it makes the most sense."

Calvin looked at Lou. "Do you think five or six hours will make a difference with the investigation?"

"It could," Lou admitted. "Hell, the sooner the autopsy is done the better. I mean, just knowing if we're looking for one or two people will be a big help."

Calvin sighed. "I hate this kind of decision." He shifted his massive two-hundred-and-fifty-pound muscular bulk from one foot to the other. "Trouble is, half the time I can't anticipate Bingham's reaction. But what the hell! Go for it, Laurie. The case is yours."

"Thanks, Calvin," Laurie said gleefully. She snatched up the folder from the table. "Is it okay if Lou observes?"

"By all means," Calvin said.

"Come on, Lou!" Laurie said. She rescued her coat from a chair and started for the door. "Let's head downstairs, do a quick external exam, and have the body X-rayed. In the confusion last night it apparently wasn't done."

"I'm right behind you," Lou said.

Jack hesitated for a moment then hurried after them. He was mystified why Laurie was so interested in doing the autopsy. From his perspective she would have done better to stay clear. Such politically charged cases were always hot potatoes. You couldn't win.

Laurie was moving quickly, and Jack didn't catch up to her and Lou until they were beyond communications. Laurie stopped abruptly to lean into Janice Jaeger's office. Janice was one of the forensic investigators, also called physicians' assistants or PAs. Janice ran the graveyard shift and took her job very seriously. She always stayed late.

"Will you be seeing Bart Arnold before you leave?" Laurie asked Janice. Bart Arnold was the chief of the PAs.

"I usually do," Janice said. She was a tiny, dark-haired woman with prominent circles under her eyes.

"Do me a favor," Laurie said. "Ask him to call CNN and get a copy of the video of Carlo Franconi's assassination. I'd like to have it as soon as possible."

"Will do," Janice said cheerfully.

Laurie and Lou continued on their way.

"Hey, slow down, you two," Jack said. He had to run a couple of steps to catch up to them.

"We've got work to do," Laurie said without breaking stride.

"I've never seen you so eager to do an autopsy," Jack said. He and Lou flanked her as she hurried to the autopsy room. "What's the attraction?"

"A lot of things," Laurie said. She reached the elevator and pressed the button.

"Give me an example," Jack said. "I don't mean to rain on your parade, but this is a politically sensitive case. No matter what you do or say, you'll be irritating someone. I think Calvin was right. This one ought to be done by the chief."

"You're entitled to your opinion," Laurie said. She hit the button again. The back elevator was inordinately slow. "But I feel differently. With the work I've been doing on the forensics of gunshot wounds, I'm fascinated to have a case where there is a video of the event to corroborate my reconstruction of what happened. I was planning on writing a paper on gunshot wounds, and this could be the crowning case."

"Oh, dear," Jack moaned, raising his eyes heavenward. "And her motivations were so noble." Then looking back at Laurie he said: "I think you should reconsider! My intuition tells me you're only going to get yourself into a bureaucratic headache. And there's still time to avoid it. All you have to do is turn around and go back and tell Calvin you've changed your mind. I'm warning you, you're taking a risk."

Laurie laughed. "You are the last person to advise me about risk." She reached out and touched Jack on the end of his nose with her index finger. "Everyone who knows you, me included, pleaded with you not to get that new bike. You're risking your life, not a headache."

The elevator arrived, and Laurie and Lou boarded. Jack hesitated but then squeezed through the doors just before they closed.

"You are not going to talk me out of this," Laurie said. "So save your breath."

"Okay," Jack said, raising his hands in mock surrender. "I promise: no more advice. Now, I'm just interested in watching this story unfold. It's a paper day for me today, so if you don't mind, I'll watch."

"You can do more than that if you want," Laurie said. "You can help."

"I'm sensitive about horning in on Lou." His double entendre was intended.

Lou laughed, Laurie blushed, but the comment went unacknowledged.

"You implied there were other reasons for your interest in this case," Jack said. "If you don't mind my asking, what are they?"

Laurie cast a quick glance at Lou that Jack saw but couldn't interpret.

"Hmmm," Jack said. "I'm getting the feeling there's something going on here that isn't any of my business."

"Nothing like that," Lou volunteered. "It's just an unusual connection. The victim, Carlo Franconi, had taken the place of a midlevel crime hoodlum named Pauli Cerino. Cerino's position had become vacant after Cerino was thrown in the slammer, mostly due to Laurie's persistence and hard work."

"And yours, too," Laurie added as the elevator jerked to a stop and the doors opened.

"Yeah, but mostly yours," Lou said.

The three got off on the basement level and headed in the direction of the mortuary office.

"Did the Cerino case involve that series of overdoses you've made reference to?" Jack asked Laurie.

"I'm afraid so," Laurie said. "It was awful. The experience terrified me, and the problem is some of the characters are still around, including Cerino, although he's in jail."

"And not likely to be released for a long time," Lou added.

"Or so I'd like to believe," Laurie said. "Anyway, I'm hoping that doing the post on Franconi might provide me with some closure. I still have nightmares occasionally."

"They sealed her in a pine coffin to abduct her from here," Lou said. "She was taken away in one of the mortuary vans."

"My God!" Jack said to Laurie. "You never told me about that."

"I try not to think about it," Laurie said. Then without missing a beat she added: "You guys wait out here."

Laurie ducked into the mortuary office to get a copy of the list of refrigerator compartments assigned to the cases that had come in the previous night.

"I can't imagine getting closed in a coffin," Jack said. He shuddered. Heights were his main phobia but tight, confining spaces came a close second.

"Nor can I," Lou agreed. "But she was able to recover remarkably. An hour or so after being released she had the presence of mind to figure out how to save us both. That was particularly humbling since I'd gone there to save her."

"Jeez!" Jack said with a shake of his head. "Up until this minute I thought my getting handcuffed to a sink by a couple of killers who were arguing over who was going to do me in was the worst-case scenario."

Laurie came out of the office waving a sheet of paper. "Compartment one eleven," she said. "And I was right. The body wasn't X-rayed."

Laurie took off like a power walker. Jack and Lou had to hustle to catch up with her. She made a beeline for the proper compartment. Once there she slipped the autopsy folder under her left arm and used her right hand to release the latch. In one, smooth, practiced motion, she swung open the door and slid out the tray on its ball bearings.

Laurie's brow furrowed.

"That's odd!" she remarked. The tray was empty save for a few bloodstains and hardened secretions.

Laurie slid the tray back in and closed the door. She rechecked the number. There'd been no mistake. It was compartment one eleven.

After looking at the list once again to make certain she'd not misread the number, she reopened the compartment door, shielded her eyes from the glare of the overhead lights, and peered into the depths of the dark interior. There was no doubt: the compartment did not contain Carlo Franconi's remains.

"What the hell!" Laurie complained. She slammed the insulated door. And just to be sure there wasn't some stupid logistic error, she opened up all the neighboring compartments one after the other. In those which contained bodies, she checked the names and accession numbers. But it soon became obvious: Carlo Franconi was not among them.

"I don't believe this," Laurie said with angry frustration. "The damn body is gone!"

A smile had appeared on Jack's face from the moment compartment one eleven had proved to be empty. Now, facing Laurie's exasperated frown, he couldn't help himself. He laughed heartily. Unfortunately his laughter further piqued Laurie.

"I'm sorry," Jack managed. "My intuition told me this case was going to give you a bureaucratic headache. I was wrong. It's going to give the bureaucracy a headache."

CHAPTER 2

MARCH 4, 1997
1:30 P.M.
COGO, EQUATORIAL GUINEA

Kevin Marshall put down his pencil and looked out the window above his desk. In contrast to his inner turmoil, the weather outside was rather pleasant with the first patches of blue sky that Kevin had seen for months. The dry season had finally begun. Of course it wasn't dry; it just didn't rain nearly as much as during the wet season. The downside was that the more consistent sun made the temperature soar to ovenlike levels. At the moment it hovered at one hundred and fifteen degrees in the shade.

Kevin had not worked well that morning nor had he slept during the night. The anxiety he'd felt the previous day at the commencement of the surgery had not abated. In fact, it had gotten worse, especially after the unexpected call from the GenSys CEO, Taylor Cabot. Kevin had only spoken with the man on one previous occasion. Most people in the company equated the experience with talking with God.

Adding to Kevin's unease was seeing another wisp of smoke snaking its way up into the sky from Isla Francesca. He'd noticed it when he'd first arrived at the lab that morning. As near as he could tell it was coming from the same location as the day before: the sheer side of the limestone escarpment. The fact that the smoke was no longer apparent failed to comfort him.

Giving up on any attempt at further work, Kevin peeled off his white lab coat and draped it over his chair. He wasn't particularly hungry, but he knew his house-keeper, Esmeralda, would have made lunch, so he felt obliged to make an appearance.

Kevin descended the three flights of stairs in a preoccupied daze. Several co-workers passed him and said hello, but it was as if Kevin did not see them. He was too preoccupied. In the last twenty-four hours he'd come to realize that he would have to take action. The problem wasn't going to pass as he'd hoped it would a week previously when he'd first glimpsed the smoke.

Unfortunately, he had no idea what to do. He knew he was no hero; in fact, over the years he'd come to think of himself as a coward of sorts. He hated confrontation and avoided it. As a boy, he had even shunned competition except for chess. He'd grown up pretty much a loner.

Kevin paused at the glass door to the exterior. Across the square he could see the usual coterie of Equatoguinean soldiers beneath the arches of the old town hall. They were up to their usual sedentary pursuits, aimlessly passing the time of the day. Some were sitting in old rattan furniture playing cards, others were leaning up against the building arguing with each other in strident voices. Almost all of them were smoking. Cigarettes were part of their wages. They were dressed in soiled, jungle-camouflage fatigues with scuffed combat boots and red berets. All of them had automatic assault rifles either slung over their shoulders or within arm's reach.

From the moment of Kevin's arrival at Cogo five years previously, the soldiers had scared him. Cameron McIvers, head of security, who had initially shown Kevin around, told him that GenSys had hired a good portion of the Equatoguinean army for protection. Later Cameron had admitted that the army's so-called employment was in reality an additional payoff to the government as well as to the Minister of Defense and the Minister of Territorial Administration.

From Kevin's perspective the soldiers looked more like a bunch of aimless teen-agers than protectors. Their complexions were like burnished ebony. Their blank expressions and arched eyebrows gave them a look of superciliousness that reflected their boredom. Kevin always had the uncomfortable sense they were itching to have an excuse to use their weapons.

Kevin pushed through the door and walked across the square. He didn't look in the direction of the soldiers, but from past experience he knew at least some of them were watching him, and it made his skin crawl. Kevin didn't know a word of Fang, the major local dialect, so he had no idea what they were saying.

Once out of sight of the central square Kevin relaxed a degree and slowed his pace. The combination of heat and hundred-percent humidity was like a perpetual steam bath. Any activity caused a sweat. After only a few minutes, Kevin could feel his shirt beginning to adhere to his back.

Kevin's house was situated a little more than halfway between the hospital-lab complex and the waterfront, a distance of only three blocks. The town was small but had obviously been charming in its day. The buildings had been constructed primarily of brightly colored stucco with red tile roofs. Now the colors had faded to pale pastels. The shutters were the type that hinged at the top. Most were in a terrible state of disrepair except for the ones on the renovated buildings. The streets had been laid out in an unimaginative grid but had been paved over the years with imported granite that had served as sailing ships' ballast. In Spanish colonial times the town's wealth had come from agriculture, particularly cocoa and coffee production, and it had graciously supported a population of several thousand people.

But the town's history changed dramatically after 1959, the year of Equatorial Guinea's independence. The new president, Macias Nguema, quickly meta-morphosed from a popularly elected official to the continent's worst, sadistic dictator whose atrocities managed to outclass even those of Idi Amin of Uganda and Jean-Bedel Bokassa of the Central African Republic. The effect on the country was apocalyptic. After fifty thousand people were murdered, a third of the population of the entire country fled, including all the Spanish settlers. Most of the country's towns were decimated, particularly Cogo, which had been completely abandoned. The road connecting Cogo to the rest of the country fell into ruin and quickly became impassable.

For a number of years, the town was fated to be a mere curiosity for the occasional visitor arriving by small motorboat from the coastal town of Acalayong. The jungle had begun to reclaim the land by the time a representative of GenSys had happened upon it seven years previously. This individual recognized Cogo's isolation and its limitless surrounding rain forest as the perfect spot for GenSys's intended primate facility. Returning to Malabo, the capital of Equatorial Guinea, the GenSys official immediately commenced negotiations with the current Equatoguinean government. Since the country was one of the poorest of Africa and consequently desperate for foreign exchange, the new president was eager and negotiations proceeded apace.

Kevin rounded the last corner and approached his house. It was three stories like most of the other buildings in the town. It had been tastefully renovated by GenSys to give it storybook appeal. In fact it was one of the more desirable houses in the whole town and a source of envy of a number of the other GenSys employees, particularly head of security, Cameron McIvers. Only Siegfried Spallek, manager of the Zone, and Bertram Edwards, chief veterinarian, had accommodations that were equivalent. Kevin had attributed his good luck to intercession on his behalf by Dr. Raymond Lyons, but he didn't know for certain.

The house had been built in the mid-nineteenth century by a successful import/ exporter in traditional Spanish style. The first floor was arched and arcaded like the town hall and had originally housed shops and storage facilities. The second floor was the main living floor with three bedrooms, three baths, a large through-and-through living room, a dining room, a kitchen, and a tiny maid's apartment. It was surrounded by a veranda on all four sides. The third floor was an enormous open room with wide-plank flooring illuminated with two huge, cast-iron chandeliers. It was capable of holding a hundred people with ease and had apparently been used for mass meetings.

Kevin entered and climbed a central stairway that led up to a narrow hall. From there he went into the dining room. As he expected, the table had been laid for lunch.

The house was too big for Kevin, especially since he didn't have a family. He'd said as much when he'd first been shown the property, but Siegfried Spallek had told him the decision had been made in Boston and warned Kevin not to complain. So Kevin accepted the assignment, but his co-workers' envy often made him feel uncomfortable.

As if by magic Esmeralda appeared. Kevin wondered how she did it so consistently. It was as if she were always on the lookout for his approaching the house. She was a pleasant woman of indeterminate age with rounded features and sad eyes. She dressed in a shift of brightly colored print fabric with a matching scarf wrapped tightly around her head. Besides her native tongue, she spoke fluent Spanish and passable English that improved on a daily basis.

Esmeralda lived in the maid's quarters Monday through Friday. Over the weekend she stayed with her family in a village that GenSys had constructed to the east along the banks of the estuary to house the many local workers employed in the Zone, as the area occupied by GenSys's Equatoguinean operation was called. She and her family had been moved there from Bata, the main city on the Equatoguinean mainland. The capital of the country, Malabo, was on an island called Bioko.

Kevin had encouraged Esmeralda to go home in the evenings during the week if she so desired, but she declined. When Kevin persisted, she told him she'd been ordered to remain in Cogo.

"There is a phone message for you," Esmeralda said.

"Oh," Kevin said nervously. His pulse quickened. Phone messages were rare, and in his current state he did not need any more unexpected events. The call in the middle of the night from Taylor Cabot had been disturbing enough.

"It was from Dr. Raymond Lyons in New York," Esmeralda said. "He wants you to call him back."

The fact that the call was from overseas did not surprise Kevin. With the satellite communications GenSys had installed in the Zone, it was far easier to call Europe or the U.S. than Bata, a mere sixty miles to the north. Calls to Malabo were almost impossible.

Kevin started for the living room. The phone was on a desk in the corner.

"Will you be eating lunch?" Esmeralda asked.

"Yes," Kevin said. He still wasn't hungry but he didn't want to hurt Esmeralda's feelings.

Kevin sat down at his desk. With his hand on the phone he quickly calculated it was about eight o'clock in the morning in New York. He pondered what Dr. Lyons had called about but guessed it had something to do with his brief conversation with Taylor Cabot. Kevin did not like the idea of an autopsy on Carlo Franconi, and he didn't imagine that Raymond Lyons would either.

Kevin had first met Raymond six years previously. It was during a meeting in New York of the American Association for the Advancement of Science where Kevin presented a paper. Kevin hated giving papers and rarely did, but on this occasion he'd been forced to do so by the chief of his department at Harvard. Dating back to his Ph.D. thesis his interest was the transposition of chromosomes: a process by which chromosomes exchanged bits and pieces to enhance species adaption and hence evolution. This phenomenon happened particularly frequently during the generation of sex cells: a process known as meiosis.

By coincidence, during the same meeting and at the same time Kevin was scheduled to present, James Watson and Francis Crick gave an immensely popular talk on the anniversary of their discovery of the structure of DNA. Consequently, very few people came to hear Kevin. One of the attendees had been Raymond. It was after this talk that Raymond first approached Kevin. The conversation resulted in Kevin's leaving Harvard and coming to work for GenSys.

With a slightly shaky hand Kevin picked up the receiver and dialed. Raymond answered on the first ring, suggesting he'd been hovering over the phone. The connection was crystal clear as if he were in the next room.

"I've got good news," Raymond said as soon as he knew it was Kevin. "There's to be no autopsy."

Kevin didn't respond. His mind was a jumble.

"Aren't you relieved?" Raymond asked. "I know Cabot called you last night."

"I'm relieved to an extent," Kevin said. "But autopsy or no autopsy, I'm having second thoughts about this whole operation."

Now it was Raymond's turn to be silent. No sooner had he solved one potential problem than another was rearing its unwelcome head.

"Maybe we've made a mistake," Kevin said. "What I mean is, maybe I've made a mistake. My conscience is starting to bother me, and I'm getting a little scared. I'm really a basic science person. This applied science is not my thing."

"Oh, please!" Raymond said irritably. "Don't complicate things! Not now. I mean, you've got that lab you've always wanted. I've beat my brains out getting you every damn piece of equipment that you've asked for. And on top of that, things are going so well, especially with my recruiting. Hell, with all the stock options you're amassing, you'll be a rich man."

"I've never intended on being rich," Kevin said.

"Worse things could happen," Raymond said. "Come on, Kevin! Don't do this to me."

"And what good is being rich when I have to be out here in the heart of darkness?" Kevin said. Unwittingly his mind conjured up the image of the manager, Siegfried Spallek. Kevin shuddered. He was terrified of the man.

"It's not forever," Raymond said. "You told me yourself, you're almost there, that the system is nearly perfect. When it is and you've trained someone to take your place, you can come back here. With your money you'll be able to build the lab of your dreams."

"I've seen more smoke coming from the island," Kevin said. "Just like last week."

"Forget the smoke!" Raymond said. "You're letting your imagination run wild. Instead of working yourself up into a frenzy over nothing, concentrate on your work so you can finish. If you've got some free time, start fantasizing about the lab you'll be building back here state-side."

Kevin nodded. Raymond had a point. Part of Kevin's concern was that if what he'd been involved with in Africa became common knowledge, he might never be able to go back to academia. No one would hire him much less give him tenure. But if he had his own lab and an independent income, he wouldn't have to worry.

"Listen," Raymond said. "I'll be coming to pick up the last patient when he's ready, which should be soon. We'll talk again then. Meanwhile just remember that we're almost there and money is pouring into our offshore coffers."

"All right," Kevin said reluctantly.

"Just don't do anything rash," Raymond said. "Promise me!"

"All right," Kevin repeated with slightly more enthusiasm.

Kevin hung up the phone. Raymond was a persuasive person, and whenever Kevin spoke to him, Kevin inevitably felt better.

Kevin pushed back from the desk and walked back to the dining room. Following Raymond's advice he tried to think of where he'd build his lab. There were some strong arguments for Cambridge, Massachusetts, because of the associations Kevin had with both Harvard and MIT. But then again maybe it would be better to be out in the countryside like up in New Hampshire.

Lunch was a white fish that Kevin didn't recognize. When he inquired about it, Esmeralda gave him only the name in Fang, which meant nothing to Kevin. He surprised himself by eating more than he'd expected. The conversation with Raymond had had a positive effect on his appetite. The idea of having his own lab still held inordinate appeal.

After eating, Kevin changed his damp shirt for a clean, freshly ironed one. He was eager to get back to work. As he was about to descend the stairs, Esmeralda inquired when he wanted dinner. He told her seven, the usual time.

While Kevin had been lunching a leaden group of gray lavender clouds had rolled in from the ocean. By the time he emerged from his front door, it was pouring, and the street in front of his house was a cascade as the runoff raced down to the waterfront. Looking south over the Estuario del Muni, Kevin could see a line of bright sunshine as well as the arch of a complete rainbow. The weather in Gabon was still clear. Kevin was not surprised. There had been times when it had rained on one side of the street and not the other.

Guessing the rain would continue for at least the next hour, Kevin skirted his house beneath the protection of the arcade and climbed into his black Toyota utility vehicle. Although it was a ridiculously short drive back to the hospital, Kevin felt it was better to ride than be wet for the rest of the afternoon.

CHAPTER 3

MARCH 4, 1997
8:45 A.M.
NEW YORK CITY

"Well, what do you want to do?" Franco Ponti asked while looking at his boss, Vinnie Dominick, in the rearview mirror. They were in Vinnie's Lincoln Towncar. Vinnie was in the backseat, leaning forward with his right hand holding onto the overhead strap. He was looking out at 126 East Sixty-fourth Street. It was a brownstone built in a French rococo style with high-arched, multipaned windows. The first-floor windows were heavily barred for protection.

"Looks like pretty posh digs," Vinnie said. "The good doctor is doing okay for himself."

"Should I park?" Franco asked. The car was in the middle of the street, and the taxi behind them was honking insistently.

"Park!" Vinnie said.

Franco drove ahead until he came to a fire hydrant. He pulled to the curb. The taxi went past, the driver frantically giving them the finger. Angelo Facciolo shook his head and made a disparaging comment about expatriate Russian taxi drivers. Angelo was sitting in the front passenger seat.

Vinnie climbed out of the car. Franco and Angelo quickly followed suit. All three men were impeccably dressed in long, Salvatore Ferragamo overcoats in varying shades of gray.

"You think the car will be okay?" Franco asked.

"I anticipate this will be a short meeting," Vinnie said. "But put the Police Benevolent Association Commendation on the dash. Might as well save fifty bucks."

Vinnie walked back to number 126. Franco and Angelo trailed in their perpetually vigilant style. Vinnie looked at the door intercom. "It's a duplex," Vinnie said. "I guess the doctor isn't doing quite as well as I thought." Vinnie pressed the button for Dr. Raymond Lyons and waited.

"Hello?" a feminine voice inquired.

"I'm here to see the doctor," Vinnie said. "My name is Vinnie Dominick."

There was a pause. Vinnie played with a bottle cap with the tip of his Gucci loafer. Franco and Angelo looked up and down the street.

The intercom crackled back to life. "Hello, this is Dr. Lyons. Can I help you?"

"I believe so," Vinnie said. "I need about fifteen minutes of your time."

"I'm not sure I know you, Mr. Dominick," Raymond said. "Could you tell me what this is in reference to?"

"It's in reference to a favor I did for you last night," Vinnie said. "The request had come through a mutual acquaintance, Dr. Daniel Levitz."

There was a pause.

"I trust you are still there, Doctor," Vinnie said.

"Yes, of course," Raymond said. A raucous buzzing sounded. Vinnie pushed open the heavy door and entered. His minions followed.

"I don't think the good doctor is terribly excited to see us," Vinnie quipped as they rode up in the small elevator. The three men were pressed together like cigars in a triple pack.

Raymond met his visitors as they exited the lift. He was obviously nervous as he shook hands with all three after the introductions. He gestured for them to enter his apartment and then showed them into a small, mahogany-paneled study.

"Coffee anyone?" Raymond asked.

Franco and Angelo looked at Vinnie.

"I wouldn't turn down an espresso if it's not too much trouble," Vinnie said. Franco and Angelo said they'd have the same.

Raymond used his desk phone to place the order.

Raymond's worst fears had materialized the moment he'd caught sight of his uninvited guests. From his perspective they appeared like stereotypes from a grade-B movie. Vinnie was about five-ten, darkly complected and handsome, with full features and slicked-back hair. He was obviously the boss. The other two men were both over six feet and gaunt. Their noses and lips were thin and their eyes were beady and deeply set. They could have been brothers. The main difference in their appearance was the condition of Angelo's skin. Raymond thought it looked like the far side of the moon.

"Can I take your coats?" Raymond asked.

"We don't intend on staying too long," Vinnie said.

"At least sit down," Raymond said.

Vinnie relaxed into a leather armchair. Franco and Angelo sat stiffly on a velvet-covered settee. Raymond sat behind his desk.

"What can I do for you gentlemen?" Raymond said, trying to assume a confident air.

"The favor we did for you last night was not easy to pull off," Vinnie said. "We thought you'd like to know how it was arranged."

Raymond let out a little, mirthless laugh through a weak smile. He held up his hands as if to ward off something coming his way. "That's not necessary. I'm certain you . . ."

"We insist," Vinnie interrupted. "It makes good business sense. You see, we wouldn't like you to think that we didn't make a significant effort on your behalf."

"I wouldn't think that for a moment," Raymond said.

"Well, just to be sure," Vinnie said. "You see, getting a body out of the morgue is no easy task, since they are open for business twenty-four hours a day, and they have a uniformed security man on duty at all times."

"This isn't necessary," Raymond said. "I'd rather not be privy to the details, but I'm very appreciative of your efforts."

"Be quiet, Dr. Lyons, and listen!" Vinnie said. He paused for a moment to organize his thoughts. "We were lucky because Angelo here knows a kid named Vinnie Amendola, who works in the morgue. This kid was beholden to Pauli Cerino, a guy Angelo used to work for but who is currently in jail. Angelo now works for me, and knowing what he knows, he was able to convince the kid to tell us exactly where Mr. Franconi's remains were stored. The kid was also able to tell us some other information so we'd have some reason to be there in the middle of the night."

At that moment the espressos arrived. They were brought in by Darlene Polson, whom Raymond introduced as his assistant. As soon as the coffees were distributed, Darlene left.

"Good-looking assistant," Vinnie said.

"She's very efficient," Raymond commented. Unconsciously, he wiped his brow.

"I hope we're not making you feel uncomfortable," Vinnie said.

"No, not at all," Raymond said a bit too quickly.

"So we got the body out okay," Vinnie said. "And we disposed of it so it is gone. But as you can understand, it was not a walk in the park. In fact it was one big pain in the ass since we had so little time to plan it."

"Well, if there is ever some favor I can do for you," Raymond commented after an uncomfortable pause in the conversation.

"Thank you, Doctor," Vinnie said. He polished off his espresso like he was drinking a shot. He put the cup and saucer on the corner of the desk. "You've said exactly what I was hoping you'd say, which brings me to why I'm here. Now, you probably know I'm a client just like Franconi was. More important, my eleven-year-old son, Vinnie Junior, is also a client. In fact, he's more apt to need your services than I am. So we're facing two tuitions, as you people call it. What I'd like to propose is that I don't pay anything this year. What do you say?"

Raymond's eyes dropped to his desk surface.

"What we're talking about is a favor for a favor," Vinnie said. "It's only fair."

Raymond cleared his throat. "I'll have to talk to the powers that be," he said.

"Now, that's the first unfriendly thing you've said," Vinnie added. "My information is that *you* are the so-called 'powers that be.' So I find this foot-dragging insulting. I'll change my offer. I won't pay any tuition this year or next year. I hope you comprehend the direction this conversation is taking."

"I understand," Raymond said. He swallowed with obvious effort. "I'll take care of it."

Vinnie stood up. Franco and Angelo did likewise. "That's the spirit," Vinnie said. "So I'll count on your talking with Dr. Daniel Levitz and let him know about our understanding."

"Of course," Raymond said. He got to his feet.

"Thank you for the coffee," Vinnie said. "It hit the spot. My compliments to your assistant."

Raymond closed the apartment door after the hoodlums had left and leaned against it. His pulse was racing. Darlene appeared in the doorway leading to the kitchen.

"Was it as bad as you feared?" she asked.

"Worse!" Raymond said. "They behaved perfectly in character. Now I've got to deal with petty mobsters demanding a free ride. I tell you, what else can go wrong?"

Raymond pushed off the door and started toward his study. After only two steps he wobbled. Darlene reached out and supported his arm.

"Are you okay?" she demanded.

Raymond waited for a moment before nodding. "Yeah, I'm all right," he said. "Just a bit dizzy. Thanks to this Franconi flap, I didn't sleep a wink last night."

"Maybe you should put off the meeting you've planned with the new prospective doctor," Darlene suggested.

"I think you're right," Raymond said. "In this state, I probably couldn't convince anyone to join our group even if they were on their way to bankruptcy court."

CHAPTER 4

Laurie finished preparing the salad greens, put a paper towel over the bowl, and slipped it into the refrigerator. Then she mixed the dressing, a simple combination of olive oil, fresh garlic, and white vinegar, with just a touch of balsamic. She put that in the refrigerator as well. Turning her attention to the lamb loin, she trimmed off the small amount of fat the butcher had left, put the meat into a marinade she'd made earlier, and then stuck it into the refrigerator with the other makings. The last chore was preparing the artichokes. It took only a moment to cut off the excess base and a few of the large, stringy leaves.

Wiping her hands on the dish towel, Laurie glanced up at the wall clock. Familiar with Jack's schedule, she thought it was exactly the time to call. She used the wall phone next to the sink.

As the connection went through, she could imagine Jack coming up the cluttered stairwell in his dilapidated building. Although she thought she understood why he'd originally rented his apartment, she had trouble comprehending why he stayed. The building was so depressing. On the other hand, as she glanced around at her own flat, she had to admit, there wasn't a lot of difference once Jack got inside his unit except he had almost double the space.

The phone rang at the other end. Laurie counted the rings. When she got to ten she began to doubt her familiarity with his schedule. She was about to hang up when Jack answered.

"Yeah?" he said unceremoniously. He was out of breath.

"Tonight's your lucky night," Laurie said.

"Who is this?" Jack asked. "Is that you, Laurie?"

"You sound out of breath," Laurie said. "Does that mean you lost at basketball?"

"No, it means I ran up four flights of stairs to get the phone," Jack said. "What's happening? Don't tell me you're still at work?"

"Heavens, no," Laurie said. "I've been home for an hour."

"So why is this my lucky night?" Jack asked.

"I stopped by Gristede's on the way home and picked up the makings of your favorite dinner," Laurie said. "It's all ready to go into the broiler. All you have to do is shower and get yourself down here."

"And I thought I owed you an apology for laughing at the vanishing mafioso," Jack said. "If amends are needed it's surely from my side."

"There's no atonement involved," Laurie said. "I would just enjoy your company. But there's one condition."

"Uh-oh," Jack said. "What?"

"No bike tonight," Laurie said. "You have to come by cab or the deal's off."

"Taxis are more dangerous than my bike," Jack complained.

"No argument," Laurie said. "Take it or leave it. If and when you slide under a bus and end up on a slab in the pit, I don't want to feel responsible." Laurie felt her face flush. It was an issue she didn't even like to joke about.

"Okay," Jack said agreeably. "I should be there in thirty-five to forty minutes. Shall I bring some wine?"

"That would be great," Laurie said.

Laurie was pleased. She'd been unsure if Jack would accept the invitation. Over the previous year they had been seeing each other socially, and several months ago, Laurie had admitted to herself that she'd fallen in love with him. But Jack seemed reluctant to allow the relationship to progress to the next level of commitment. When Laurie tried to force the issue, Jack had responded by distancing himself. Feeling rejected, Laurie had responded with anger. For weeks, they only spoke on a professional basis.

Over the last month their relationship had slowly improved. They were seeing each other again casually. This time Laurie realized that she had to bide her time. The problem was that at age thirty-seven it was not easy. Laurie had always wanted to become a mother someday. With forty fast approaching, she felt she was running out of time.

With the dinner essentially prepared, Laurie went around her small one-bedroom apartment straightening up. That meant putting odd books back into their spots on the shelves, stacking medical journals neatly, and emptying Tom's litter box. Tom was her six-and-a-half-year-old tawny tabby who was still as wild as he'd been as a kitten. Laurie straightened the Klimt print that the cat always knocked askew on his daily route from the bookcase to the top of the valance over the window.

Next Laurie took a quick shower, changed into a turtleneck and jeans, and put on a touch of makeup. As she did so she glared at the crow's feet that had been developing at the corners of her eyes. She didn't feel any older than when she'd gotten out of medical school, yet there was no denying the advance of years.

Jack arrived on schedule. When Laurie looked through the peephole, all she could see was a bloated image of his broadly grinning face, which he had positioned a mere inch from the lens. She smiled at his antics as she undid the host of locks that secured her door.

"Get in here, you clown!" Laurie said.

"I wanted to be sure you recognized me," Jack said as he stepped past her. "My chipped, upper-left incisor has become my trademark."

Just as Laurie was closing her door she caught a glimpse of her neighbor, Mrs. Engler, who'd cracked her door to see who was visiting Laurie. Laurie glared at her. She was such a busybody.

The dinner was a success. The food was perfect and the wine was okay. Jack's excuse was that the liquor store closest to his apartment specialized in jug wine, not the better stuff.

During the course of the evening, Laurie had to continually bite her tongue to keep the conversation away from sensitive areas. She would have loved to talk about their relationship, but she didn't dare. She sensed that some of Jack's hesitance stemmed from his extraordinary personal tragedy. Six years previously, his wife and two daughters had been tragically killed in a commuter-plane crash. Jack had told Laurie about it after they had been dating for several months, but then refused to talk about it again. Laurie sensed that this loss was the biggest stumbling block to their relationship. In a way, this belief helped her to take Jack's reluctance to commit himself less personally.

Jack had no trouble keeping the conversation light. He'd had a good evening playing pickup basketball at his neighborhood playground and was happy to talk about it. By chance he'd been teamed up with Warren, an all-around impressive African-American, who was the leader of the local gang and by far the best player. Jack and Warren's team didn't lose all evening.

"How is Warren?" Laurie asked. Jack and Laurie had frequently double-dated with Warren and his girlfriend, Natalie Adams. Laurie hadn't seen either of them since before she and Jack had their falling-out.

"Warren's Warren," Jack said. He shrugged. "He's got so much potential. I've tried my best to get him to take some college courses, but he resists. He says my value system isn't his, so I've given up."

"And Natalie?"

"Fine, I guess," Jack said. "I haven't seen her since we all went out."

"We should do it again," Laurie said. "I miss seeing them."

"That's an idea," Jack said evasively.

There was a pause. Laurie could hear Tom's purring. After eating and cleaning up, Jack moved to the couch. Laurie sat across from him in her art-deco club chair she'd purchased in the Village.

Laurie sighed. She felt frustrated. It seemed juvenile that they couldn't talk about emotionally important issues.

Jack checked his watch. "Uh-oh!" he said. He moved himself forward so that he was sitting on the very edge of the couch. "It's quarter to eleven," Jack added. "I've got to be going. It's a school night and bed is beckoning."

"More wine?" Laurie asked. She held up the jug. They'd only drunk a quarter of it.

"I can't," Jack said. "I've got to keep my reflexes sharp for the cab ride home." He stood up and thanked Laurie for the meal.

Laurie put down the wine and got to her feet. "If you don't mind, I'd like to ride with you as far as the morgue."

"What?" Jack questioned. He scrunched up his face in disbelief. "You're not going to work at this hour? I mean, you're not even on call."

"I just want to question the night mortuary tech and security," Laurie said, as she went to the hall closet for their coats.

"What on earth for?" Jack asked.

"I want to figure out how Franconi's body disappeared," Laurie said. She handed Jack his bomber jacket. "I talked to the evening crew when they came on this afternoon."

"And what did they tell you?"

"Not a whole bunch," Laurie said. "The body came in around eight forty-five with an entourage of police and media. Apparently it was a circus. I guess that's why the X ray was overlooked. Identification was made by the mother—a very emotional scene by all reports. By ten forty-five the body was placed in the fridge in compartment one eleven. So I think it's pretty clear the abduction occurred during the night shift from eleven to seven."

"Why are you worrying yourself about this?" Jack said. "This is the front office's problem."

Laurie pulled on her coat and got her keys. "Let's just say that I've taken a personal interest in the case."

Jack rolled his eyes as they exited into the hall. "Laurie!" he intoned. "You're going to get yourself in trouble over this. Mark my word."

Laurie pushed the elevator button then glared at Mrs. Engler, who'd cracked her door as usual.

"That woman drives me crazy," Laurie said as they boarded the elevator.

"You're not listening to me," Jack said.

"I'm listening," Laurie said. "But I'm still going to look into this. Between this stunt and my run-in with Franconi's predecessor, it irks me that these two-bit mobsters think they can do whatever they please. They think laws are for other people. Pauli Cerino, the man Lou mentioned this morning, had people killed so that he didn't have to wait too long to have corneal transplants. That gives you an idea of their ethics. I don't like the idea that they think they can just come into our morgue and walk off with the body of a man they just killed."

They emerged onto Nineteenth Street and walked toward First Avenue. Laurie put up her collar. There was a breeze off the East River, and it was only in the twenties.

"What makes you think the mobsters are behind this?" Jack asked.

"You don't have to be a rocket scientist to assume as much," Laurie said. She put up her hand as a cab approached, but it zoomed past without slowing. "Franconi was going to testify as part of a plea bargain. The higher-ups of the Vaccarro organization got angry or scared or both. It's an old story."

"So they killed him," Jack said. "Why take the body?"

Laurie shrugged. "I'm not going to pretend I can put my mind into a mobster's," she said. "I don't know why they wanted the body. Maybe to deny him a proper burial. Maybe they're afraid an autopsy would provide a clue to the killer's identity. Hell, I don't know. But ultimately it doesn't matter why."

"I have a sense the 'why' might be important," Jack said. "I think by getting involved you'll be skating on thin ice."

"Maybe so," Laurie said. She shrugged again. "I get caught up in things like this. I suppose part of the problem is that at the moment my main focus in life is my job."

"Here comes a free cab," Jack said, deliberately avoiding having to respond to Laurie's last comment. He sensed the implications and was reluctant to get drawn into a more personal discussion.

It was a short cab ride down to the corner of First Avenue and Thirtieth Street. Laurie climbed out and was surprised when Jack did the same.

"You don't have to come," Laurie said.

"I know," Jack said. "But I'm coming anyway. In case you haven't guessed, you have me concerned."

Jack leaned back inside the cab and paid the driver.

Laurie was still insisting that Jack's presence was not needed as they walked between the Health and Hospital's mortuary vans. They entered the morgue through the Thirtieth Street entrance. "I thought you told me your bed was beckoning?"

"It can wait," Jack said. "After Lou's story about your getting carted out of here nailed in a coffin, I think I should tag along."

"That was a totally different situation," Laurie said.

"Oh, yeah?" Jack questioned. "It involved mobsters just like now."

Laurie was about to protest further when Jack's comment struck a chord. She had to admit there were parallels.

The first person they came to was the night security man sitting in his cubbyhole office. Carl Novak was an elderly, affable, gray-haired man who appeared to have shrunk inside his uniform that was at least two sizes too big. He was playing solitaire but looked up when Laurie and Jack passed by his window and stopped in his open doorway.

"Can I help you?" Carl asked. Then he recognized Laurie and apologized for not having done so sooner.

Laurie asked him if he'd been informed of Franconi's body's disappearance.

"By all means," Carl said. "I got called at home by Robert Harper, head of security. He was up in arms about it and asked me all sorts of questions."

It didn't take Laurie long to learn that Carl had little light to shed on the mystery. He insisted that nothing out of the ordinary happened. Bodies had come in and bodies had gone out, just the way they did every night of the year. He admitted having left his post twice during his shift to visit the men's room. He emphasized that on both occasions, he'd only been gone for a few minutes and that each time he'd informed the night mortuary tech, Mike Passano.

"What about meals?" Laurie asked.

Carl pulled open a file drawer of his metal desk and lifted out an insulated lunch box. "I eat right here."

Laurie thanked him and moved on. Jack followed.

"The place certainly looks different at night," Jack commented as they passed the wide hall that led down to the refrigerators and the autopsy room.

"It's a bit sinister without the usual daytime hubbub," Laurie admitted.

They looked into the mortuary office and found Mike Passano busy with some receiving forms. A body had recently been brought in that had been fished out of the ocean by the Coast Guard. He looked up when he sensed company.

Mike was in his early thirties, spoke with a strong Long Island accent, and looked decidedly Southern Italian. He was slight of build with sharply defined facial features. He had dark hair, dark skin, and dark eyes. Neither Laurie nor Jack had worked with him although they had met him on multiple occasions.

"Did you docs come in to see the floater?" Mike asked.

"No," Jack said. "Is there a problem?"

"No problem," Mike said. "It's just in bad shape."

"We've come to talk about last night," Laurie said.

"What about it?" Mike asked.

Laurie posed the same questions she'd put to Carl. To her surprise, Mike quickly became irritated. She was about to say as much when Jack tugged on her arm and motioned for her to retreat to the hall.

"Ease off," Jack recommended when they were beyond earshot.

"Ease off from what?" Laurie asked. "I'm not being confrontational."

"I agree," Jack said. "I know I'm the last person to be an expert in office politics or interpersonal relations, but Mike sounds defensive to me. If you want to get any information out of him, I think you have to take that into consideration and tread lightly."

Laurie thought for a minute then nodded. "Maybe you're right."

They returned to the mortuary office, but before Laurie could say anything, Mike said: "In case you didn't know, Dr. Washington telephoned this morning and woke me up about all this. He read me the riot act. But I did my normal job last night, and I certainly didn't have anything to do with that body disappearing."

"I'm sorry if I implied that you did," Laurie said. "All I'm saying is that I believe the body disappeared during your shift. That's not saying you are responsible in any way."

"It sort'a sounds that way," Mike said. "I mean, I'm the only one here besides security and the janitors."

"Did anything happen out of the ordinary?" Laurie asked.

Mike shook his head. "It was a quiet night. We had two bodies come in and two go out."

"What about the bodies that arrived?" Laurie asked. "Did they come in with our people?"

"Yup, with our vans," Mike said. "Jeff Cooper and Peter Molina. Both bodies were from local hospitals."

"What about the two bodies that went out?" Laurie asked.

"What about them?"

"Well, who was it that came to pick them up?"

Mike grabbed the mortuary logbook from the corner of his desk and cracked it open. His index finger traced down the column then stopped. "Spoletto Funeral Home in Ozone Park and Dickson Funeral Home in Summit, New Jersey."

"What were the names of the deceased?" Laurie asked.

Mike consulted the book. "Frank Gleason and Dorothy Kline. Their accession numbers are 100385 and 101455. Anything else?"

"Were you expecting these particular funeral homes to come?" Laurie asked.

"Yeah, of course," Mike said. "They'd called beforehand just like always."

"So you had everything ready for them?"

"Sure," Mike said. "I had the paperwork all done. They just had to sign off."

"And the bodies?" Laurie asked.

"They were in the walk-in cooler as usual," Mike said. "Right in the front on gurneys."

Laurie looked at Jack. "Can you think of anything else to ask?"

Jack shrugged. "I think you've pretty well covered the bases except when Mike was off the floor."

"Good point!" Laurie said. Turning back to Mike she said: "Carl told us that when he left for the men's room twice last night, he contacted you. Do you contact Carl whenever you need to leave your post?"

"Always," Mike said. "We're often the only ones down here. We have to have someone guarding the door."

"Were you away from the office very long last night?" Laurie asked.

"Nope," Mike said. "No more than usual. Couple of times to the head and a half hour for lunch up on the second floor. I'm telling you, it was a normal night."

"What about the janitors?" Laurie asked. "Were they around?"

"Not during my shift," Mike said. "Generally they clean down here evenings. The night shift is upstairs unless there is something out of the ordinary going on."

Laurie tried to think of additional questions but couldn't. "Thanks, Mike," she said.

"No problem," Mike said.

Laurie started for the door but stopped. Turning around she asked: "By any chance did you happen to see Franconi's body?"

Mike hesitated a second before admitting that he had.

"What was the circumstance?" Laurie asked.

"When I get to work Marvin, the evening tech, usually briefs me about what's going on. He was kind of psyched about the Franconi situation because of all the police and the way the family carried on. Anyway, he showed me the body."

"When you saw it, was it in compartment one eleven?"

"Yup."

"Tell me, Mike," Laurie said. "If you had to guess, how do you think the body disappeared?"

"I don't have the foggiest idea," Mike said. "Unless he walked out of here." He laughed, then seemed embarrassed. "I don't mean to joke around. I'm as confused as everybody else. All I know is only two bodies went out of here last night, and they were the two I checked out."

"And you never looked at Franconi again after Marvin showed him to you?"

"Of course not," Mike said. "Why would I?"

"No reason," Laurie said. "Do you happen to know where the van drivers are?"

"Upstairs in the lunchroom," Mike said. "That's where they always are."

Laurie and Jack took the elevator. As they were riding up, Laurie noticed Jack's eyelids were drooping.

"You look tired," Laurie commented.

"No surprise. I am," Jack said.

"Why don't you go home?" Laurie said.

"I've stuck it out this far," Jack said. "I think I'll see it to the bitter end."

The bright fluorescent lighting of the lunchroom made both Laurie and Jack squint. They found Jeff and Pete at a table next to the vending machines, poring over newspapers while snacking on potato chips. They were dressed in rumpled blue coveralls with Health and Hospital Corporation patches on their upper arms. Both had ponytails.

Laurie introduced herself, explained about her interest in the missing body, and asked if there was anything unique about the previous night, particularly about the two bodies they'd brought in.

Jeff and Pete exchanged a look, then Pete responded.

"Mine was a mess," Pete said.

"I don't mean the bodies themselves," Laurie said. "I'm wondering if there was anything unusual about the process. Did you see anyone in the morgue you didn't recognize? Did anything out of the ordinary happen?"

Pete glanced again at Jeff then shook his head. "Nope. It was just like usual."

"Do you remember what compartment you put your body into?" Laurie asked.

Pete scratched the top of his head. "Not really," he said.

"Was it near to one eleven?" Laurie asked.

Pete shook his head. "No, it was around the other side. Something like fifty-five. I don't remember exactly. But it's written downstairs."

Laurie turned to Jeff.

"My body went into twenty-eight," Jeff said. "I remembered because that's how old I am."

"Did either of you see Franconi's body?" Laurie asked.

The two drivers again exchanged glances. Jeff spoke: "Yeah, we did."

"What time?"

"Around now," Jeff said.

"What was the circumstance?" Laurie said. "You guys don't normally see bodies that you don't transport."

"After Mike told us about it, we wanted to look because of all the excitement. But we didn't touch anything."

"It was only for a second," Pete added. "We just opened the door and looked in."

"Were you with Mike?" Laurie asked.

"No," Pete said. "He just told us which compartment."

"Has Dr. Washington talked to you about last night?" Laurie asked.

"Yeah, and Mr. Harper, too," Jeff said.

"Did you tell Dr. Washington about looking at the body?" Laurie asked.

"No," Jeff said.

"Why not?" Laurie asked.

"He didn't ask," Jeff said. "I guess we know we're really not supposed to do it. I mean we don't usually. But, as I said, with all the commotion, we were curious."

"Maybe you should tell Dr. Washington," Laurie suggested. "Just so he has all the facts."

Laurie turned around and headed back to the elevator. Jack dutifully followed.

"What do you think?" Laurie asked.

"It's getting harder and harder for me to think the closer it gets to midnight," Jack said. "But I wouldn't make anything of those two peeking at the body."

"But Mike didn't mention it," Laurie said.

"True," Jack said. "But they all know they were bending the rules. It's human nature in such a situation not to be completely forthcoming."

"Maybe so," Laurie said with a sigh.

"Where to now?" Jack asked as they boarded the elevator.

"I'm running out of ideas," Laurie said.

"Thank God," Jack said.

"Don't you think I should ask Mike why he didn't tell us about the van drivers looking at Franconi?" Laurie asked.

"You could, but I think you're just spinning your wheels," Jack said. "Truly, I can't imagine it was anything but harmless curiosity."

"Then let's call it a night," Laurie said. "Bed is sounding good to me, too."

CHAPTER 5

MARCH 5, 1997
10:15 A.M.
COGO, EQUATORIAL GUINEA

Kevin replaced the tissue culture flasks in the incubator and closed the door. He'd been working since before dawn. His current quest was to find a transponase to handle a minor histocompatibility gene on the Y chromosome. It had been eluding him for over a month despite his use of the technique that had resulted in his finding and isolating the transponases associated with the short arm of chromosome 6.

Kevin's usual schedule was to arrive at the lab around eight-thirty, but that morning he'd awakened at four A.M. and had not been able to fall back to sleep. After tossing and turning for three-quarters of an hour, he'd decided he might as well use the time for good purpose. He'd arrived at his lab at five A.M. while it was still pitch-dark.

What was troubling Kevin's sleep was his conscience. The nagging notion that he'd made a Promethean mistake resurfaced with a vengeance. Although Dr. Lyons's mention of building his own lab had assuaged him at the time, it didn't last. Lab of his dreams or no, he couldn't deny the horror he feared was evolving on Isla Francesca.

Kevin's feelings had nothing to do with seeing more smoke. He hadn't, but as dawn broke, he'd also consciously avoided looking out the window, much less in the direction of the island.

Kevin realized he couldn't go on like this. He decided that the most rational course of action would be to find out if his fears were justified. The best way to do it, he surmised, was to approach someone close to the situation who might be able to shed some light on Kevin's area of concern. But Kevin didn't feel comfortable talking with many people in the Zone. He'd never been very social, especially in Cogo, where he was the sole academician. But there was one person working in the Zone with whom he felt slightly more comfortable, mainly because he admired his work: Bertram Edwards, the chief veterinarian.

Impulsively Kevin removed his lab coat, draped it over his chair, and headed out of his office. Descending to the first floor, he exited into the steamy heat of the parking area north of the hospital. The morning weather was clear, with white, puffy cumuli clouds overhead. There were some dark rain clouds looming, but they were out over the ocean in a clump along the western horizon; if they brought rain, it wouldn't be before the afternoon.

Kevin climbed into his Toyota four-wheel drive and turned right out of the hospital parking lot. Traversing the north side of the town square, he passed the old Catholic church. GenSys had renovated the building to function as the recreational center. On Friday and Saturday nights they showed movies. Monday nights they had bingo. In the basement was a commissary serving American hamburgers.

Bertram Edwards's office was at the veterinary center that was part of the far larger animal unit. The entire complex was bigger than Cogo itself. It was situated north of the town in a dense equatorial rain forest and separated from the town by a stretch of virgin jungle.

Kevin's route took him east as far as the motor-pool facility, where he turned north. The traffic, which was considerable for such a remote spot, reflected the difficult logistics of running an operation the size of the Zone. Everything from toilet paper to centrifuge tubes had to be imported, which necessitated moving a lot of goods. Most supplies came by truck from Bata, where there was a crude deep-water port and an airport capable of handling large jet aircraft. The Estuario del Muni with access to Libreville, Gabon, was only served by motorized canoes.

At the edge of town the granite cobblestone street gave way to newly laid asphalt. Kevin let out a sigh of relief. The sound and the vibration that came up the steering column from the cobblestones was intense.

After fifteen minutes of driving through a canyon of dark green vegetation, Kevin could see the first buildings of the state-of-the-art animal complex. They were constructed of prestressed concrete and cinder block that was stuccoed and painted white. The design had a Spanish flare to complement the Colonial architecture of the town.

The enormous main building looked more like an airport terminal than a primate housing facility. Its front facade was three stories tall and perhaps five hundred feet long. From the back of the structure projected multiple wings that literally disappeared into the canopy of vegetation. Several smaller buildings faced the main one. Kevin wasn't sure of their purpose except for two buildings in the center. One housed the complex's contingent of Equatoguinean soldiers. Just like their comrades in the town square, these soldiers were aimlessly sprawled about with their rifles, cigarettes, and Cameroonean beer. The other building was the headquarters of a group that Kevin found even more disturbing than the teenage soldiers. These were Moroccan mercenaries who were part of the Equatoguinean presidential guard. The local president didn't trust his own army.

These foreign special-forces commandos dressed in inappropriate and ill-fitting dark suits and ties, with obvious bulges from their shoulder holsters. Every one of them had dark skin, piercing eyes, and a heavy mustache. Unlike the soldiers they were rarely seen, but their presence was felt like a sinister evil force.

The sheer size of the GenSys animal center was a tribute to its success. Recognizing the difficulties attached to primate biomedical research, GenSys had sited their facility in Equatorial Africa where the animals were indigenous. This move cleverly sidestepped the industrialized West's inconvenient web of import/export restrictions associated with primates, as well as the disruptive influence of animal-rights zealots. As an added incentive, the foreign exchange–starved local government and its venal leaders were inordinately receptive to all a company like GenSys had to offer. Obstructive laws were conveniently overlooked or abolished. The legislature was so accommodating that it even passed a law making interference with GenSys a capital offense.

The operation proved to be extraordinarily successful so quickly that GenSys expanded it to serve as a convenient spot for other biotechnology companies, especially pharmaceutical giants, to out-source their primate testing. The growth shocked the GenSys economic forecasters. From every point of view, the Zone was an impressive financial success.

Kevin parked next to another four-wheel-drive vehicle. He knew it was Dr. Edwards's from the bumper sticker that said: Man is an Ape. He pushed through the double doors with "Veterinary Center" stenciled on the glass. Dr. Edwards's office and examining rooms were just inside the door.

Martha Blummer greeted him. "Dr. Edwards is in the chimpanzee wing," she said. Martha was the veterinary secretary. Her husband was one of the supervisors at the motor pool.

Kevin set off for the chimpanzee wing. It was one of the few areas in the building he was at all acquainted with. He went through a second pair of double doors and walked the length of the central corridor of the veterinary hospital. The facility looked like a regular hospital, down to its employees who were all dressed in surgical scrubs, many with stethoscopes draped over their necks.

A few people nodded, others smiled, and some said hello to Kevin. He returned the greetings self-consciously. He didn't know any of these people by name.

Another pair of double doors brought him into the main part of the building that housed the primates. The air had a slightly feral odor. Intermittent shrieks and howls reverberated in the corridor. Through doors with windows of wire-embedded glass, Kevin caught glimpses of large cages where monkeys were incarcerated. Outside the cages were men in coveralls and rubber boots, pulling hoses.

The chimpanzee wing was one of the ells that extended from the back of the building into the forest. It, too, was three stories tall. Kevin entered on the first floor. Immediately the sounds changed. Now there was as much hooting as shrieking.

Cracking a door off the central corridor, Kevin got the attention of one of the workers in the coveralls. He asked about Dr. Edwards and was told the vet was in the bonobo unit.

Kevin found a stairwell and climbed to the second floor. He thought it was a coincidence that Dr. Edwards happened to be in the bonobo unit just when Kevin was looking for him. It was through bonobos that Kevin and Dr. Edwards had met.

Six years ago Kevin had never heard of a bonobo. But that changed rapidly when bonobos were selected as the subjects for his GenSys project. He now knew they were exceptional creatures. They were cousins of chimpanzees but had lived in isolation in a twenty-five-thousand-square-mile patch of virginal jungle in central Zaire for one and a half million years. In contrast to chimps, bonobo society was matriarchal with less male aggression. Hence, the bonobos were able to live in larger groups. Some people called them pygmy chimpanzees but the name was a misnomer because some bonobos were actually larger than some chimpanzees, and they were a distinct species.

Kevin found Dr. Edwards in front of a relatively small acclimatization cage. He was reaching through the bars making tentative contact with an adult female bonobo.

Another female bonobo was sitting against the back wall of the cage. Her eyes were nervously darting around her new accommodations. Kevin could sense her terror.

Dr. Edwards was hooting softly in imitation of one of the many bonobo and chimpanzee sounds of communication. He was a relatively tall man, a good three or four inches over Kevin's five foot ten. His hair was a shocking white which contrasted dramatically with his almost black eyebrows and eyelashes. The sharply demarcated eyebrows combined with a habit of wrinkling his forehead gave him a perpetually surprised look.

Kevin watched for a moment. Dr. Edwards's obvious rapport with the animals had been something Kevin had appreciated from their first meeting. Kevin sensed it was an intuitive talent and not something learned, and it always impressed him.

"Excuse me," Kevin said finally.

Dr. Edwards jumped as if he'd been frightened. Even the bonobo shrieked and fled to the back of the cage.

"I'm terribly sorry," Kevin said.

Dr. Edwards smiled and put a hand to his chest. "No need to be sorry. I was just so intent I didn't hear you approach."

"I certainly didn't mean to frighten you, Dr. Edwards," Kevin began, "but I . . ."

"Kevin, please! If I've told you once, I've told you a dozen times: my name is Bertram. I mean, we've known each other for five years. Don't you think first names are more appropriate?"

"Of course," Kevin said.

"It's serendipitous you should come," Bertram said. "Meet our two newest breeding females." Bertram gestured toward the two apes who'd inched away from the back wall. Kevin's arrival had frightened them, but they were now curious.

Kevin gazed in at the dramatically anthropomorphic faces of the two primates. Bonobo's faces were less prognathous than their cousins, the chimpanzees, and hence considerably more human. Kevin always found looking into bonobos' eyes disconcerting.

"Healthy-appearing animals," Kevin commented, not knowing how else to respond.

"They were just trucked in from Zaire this morning," Bertram said. "It's about a thousand miles as the crow flies. But by the circuitous route they had to take to get across the borders of the Congo and Gabon, they probably traveled three times that."

"That's the equivalent of driving across the U.S.," Kevin said.

"In terms of distance," Bertram agreed. "But here they probably didn't see more than short stretches of pavement. It's an arduous trip no matter how you look at it."

"They look like they are in good shape," Kevin said. He wondered how he'd appear if he'd made the journey jammed into wooden boxes and hidden in the back of a truck.

"By this time I've got the drivers pretty well trained," Bertram said. "They treat 'em better than they treat their own wives. They know if the apes die, they don't get paid. It's a pretty good incentive."

"With our demand going up they'll be put to good use," Kevin said.

"You'd better believe it," Bertram said. "These two are already spoken for, as you know. If they pass all the tests, which I'm certain they will, we'll be over to your lab in the next couple of days. I want to watch again. I think you are a genius.

And Melanie . . . Well, I've never seen such hand-eye coordination, even if you include an eye surgeon I used to know back in the States."

Kevin blushed at the reference to himself. "Melanie is quite talented," he said to deflect the conversation. Melanie Becket was a reproductive technologist. GenSys had recruited her mainly for Kevin's project.

"She's good," Bertram said. "But the few of us lucky enough to be associated with your project know that you are the hero."

Bertram looked up and down the space between the wall of the corridor and the cages to make sure that none of the coverall-clad workers were in earshot.

"You know, when I signed on to come over here I thought my wife and I would do well," Bertram said. "Moneywise I thought it would be as lucrative as going to Saudi Arabia. But we're doing better than I'd ever dreamed. Through your project and the stock options that come along with it, we're going to get rich. Just yesterday I heard from Melanie that we have two more clients from New York City. That will put us over one hundred."

"I hadn't heard about the two additional clients," Kevin said.

"No? Well it's true," Bertram said. "Melanie told me last night when I bumped into her at the rec center. She said she spoke with Raymond Lyons. I'm glad she informed me so I could send the drivers back to Zaire for another shipment. All I can say is that I hope our pygmy colleagues in Lomako can keep up their end of the bargain."

Kevin looked back into the cage at the two females. They returned his stare with pleading expressions that melted Kevin's heart. He wished he could tell them that they had nothing to fear. All that would happen to them was that they would become pregnant within the month. During their pregnancies they'd be kept indoors and would be treated to special, nutritious diets. After their babies were born, they'd be put in the enormous bonobo outdoor enclosure to rear the infants. When the youngsters reached age three the cycle would be repeated.

"They sure are human-looking," Bertram said, interrupting Kevin's musing. "Sometimes you can't help but wonder what they are thinking."

"Or worry what their offspring are capable of thinking," Kevin said.

Bertram glanced at Kevin. His black eyebrows arched more than usual. "I don't follow," he said.

"Listen, Bertram," Kevin said. "I came over here specifically to talk to you about the project."

"How marvelously convenient," Bertram said. "I was going to call you today and have you come over to see the progress we've made. And here you are. Come on!"

Bertram pulled open the nearest door to the corridor, motioned for Kevin to follow, and set out with long strides. Kevin had to hurry to catch up.

"Progress?" Kevin questioned. Although he admired Bertram, the man's tendency toward manic behavior was disconcerting. Under the best of circumstances Kevin would have had trouble discussing what was on his mind. Just broaching the issue was difficult, and Bertram was not helping. In fact, he was making it impossible.

"You bet'cha progress!" Bertram said enthusiastically. "We solved the technical problems with the grid on the island. It's on line now as you'll see. We can locate any individual animal with the push of a button. It's just in time, I might add. With twelve square miles and almost a hundred individuals, it was fast becoming impossible with the handheld trackers. Part of the problem is that we didn't anticipate the creatures would split into two separate sociological groups. We were counting on their being one big happy family."

"Bertram," Kevin said between breaths, marshaling his courage. "I wanted to talk to you because I've been anxious . . ."

"It's no wonder," Bertram said as Kevin paused. "I'd be anxious, too, if I put in the hours that you put in without any form of relaxation or release. Hell, sometimes I see the light in your lab as late as midnight when the wife and I come out of the rec center after a movie. We've even commented on it. We've invited you to dinner at our house on several occasions to draw you out a little. How come you never come?"

Kevin groaned inwardly. This was not the conversation he wanted to get into.

"All right, you don't have to answer," Bertram said. "I don't want to add to your anxiety. We'd enjoy having you over, so if you change your mind, give us a call. But what about the gym or the rec center or even the pool? I've never seen you in any of those places. Being stuck here in this hothouse part of Africa is bad enough, but making yourself a prisoner of your lab or house just makes it worse."

"I'm sure you are right," Kevin said. "But . . ."

"Of course I'm right," Bertram said. "But there is another side to this that I should warn you about. People are talking."

"What do you mean?" Kevin asked. "Talking about what?"

"People are saying that you're aloof because you think you are superior," Bertram said. "You know, the academician with all his fancy degrees from Harvard and MIT. It's easy for people to misinterpret your behavior, especially if they are envious."

"Why would anybody be envious of me?" Kevin asked. He was shocked.

"Very easy," Bertram said. "You obviously get special treatment from the home office. You get a new car every two years, and your quarters are as good as Siegfried Spallek's, the manager for the entire operation. That's bound to raise some eyebrows, particularly from people like Cameron McIvers who was stupid enough to bring his whole damn family out here. Plus you got that NMR machine. The hospital administrator and I have been lobbying for an MRI since day one."

"I tried to talk them out of giving me the house," Kevin said. "I said it was too big."

"Hey, you don't have to defend your perks to me," Bertram said. "I understand because I'm privy to your project. But very few other people are, and some of them aren't happy. Even Spallek doesn't quite understand although he definitely likes participating in the bonus your project has brought those of us who are lucky enough to be associated."

Before Kevin could respond, Bertram was stopped for a series of corridor consultations. He and Bertram had been traversing the veterinary hospital. Kevin used the interruption to ponder Bertram's comments. Kevin had always thought of himself as being rather invisible. The idea that he'd engendered animosities was hard to comprehend.

"Sorry," Bertram offered after the final consult. He pushed through the last of the double doors. Kevin followed.

Passing his secretary, Martha, he picked up a small stack of phone messages. He leafed through them as he waved Kevin into his inner office. He closed his door.

"You're going to love this," Bertram said, tossing the messages aside. He sat down in front of his computer and showed Kevin how to bring up a graphic of Isla Francesca. It was divided into a grid. "Now give me the number of whatever creature you want to locate."

"Mine," Kevin said. "Number one."

"Coming up," Bertram said. He entered the information and clicked. Suddenly a red blinking light appeared on the map of the island. It was north of the limestone escarpment but south of the stream that had been humorously dubbed Rio Diviso. The stream bisected the six-by-two-mile island lengthwise, flowing east to west. In the center of the island was a pond they'd called Lago Hippo for obvious reasons.

"Pretty slick, huh?" Bertram said proudly.

Kevin was captivated. It wasn't so much by the technology, although that interested him. It was more because the red light was blinking exactly where he would have imagined the smoke to have been coming from.

Bertram got up and pulled open a file drawer. It was filled with small handheld electronic devices that looked like miniature notepads with small LCD screens. An extendable antenna protruded from each.

"These work in a similar fashion," Bertram said. He handed one to Kevin. "We call them locators. Of course, they are portable and can be taken into the field. It makes retrieval a snap compared to the struggles we had initially."

Kevin played with the keyboard. With Bertram's help, he soon had the island graphic with the red blinking light displayed. Bertram showed how to go from successive maps with smaller and smaller scales until the entire screen represented a square fifty feet by fifty feet.

"Once you are that close, you use this," Bertram said. He handed Kevin an instrument that looked like a flashlight with a keypad. "On this you type in the same information. What it does is function as a directional beacon. It pings louder the closer it comes to pointing at the animal you're looking for. When there is a clear visual sighting, it emits a continuous sound. Then all you have to do is use the dart gun."

"How does this tracking system operate?" Kevin asked. Having been immersed in the biomolecular aspects of the project, he'd not paid any attention to the logistics. He'd toured the island five years previously at the commencement of the venture, but that had been it. He'd never inquired about the nuts and bolts of everyday operation.

"It's a satellite system," Bertram said. "I don't pretend to know the details. Of course each animal has a small microchip with a long-lasting nickel cadmium battery embedded just under the derma. The afferent signal from the microchip is minuscule, but it's picked up by the grid, magnified, and transmitted by microwave."

Kevin started to give the devices back to Bertram, but Bertram waved them away. "Keep them," he said. "We've got plenty of others."

"But I don't need them," Kevin protested.

"Come on, Kevin," Bertram chided playfully while thumping Kevin on the back. The blow was hard enough to knock Kevin forward. "Loosen up! You're much too serious." Bertram sat at his desk, picked up his phone messages, and absently began to arrange them in order of importance.

Kevin glanced at the electronic devices in his hands and wondered what he'd do with them. They were obviously costly instruments.

"What was it about your project that you wanted to discuss with me?" Bertram asked. He looked up from his phone messages. "People are always complaining I don't allow them to get a word in edgewise. What's on your mind?"

"I'm concerned," Kevin stammered.

"About what?" Bertram asked. "Things couldn't be going any better."

"I've seen the smoke again," Kevin managed.

"What? You mean like that wisp of smoke you mentioned to me last week?" Bertram asked.

"Exactly," Kevin said. "And from the same spot on the island."

"Ah, it's nothing," Bertram declared, with a wave of his hand. "We've been having electrical storms just about every other night. Lightning starts fires; everybody knows that."

"As wet as everything is?" Kevin said. "I thought lightning starts fires in savannas during the dry season, not in dank, equatorial rain forests."

"Lightning can start a fire anyplace," Bertram said. "Think of the heat it generates. Remember, thunder is nothing but expansion of air from the heat. It's unbelievable."

"Well, maybe," Kevin said. He was unconvinced. "But even if it were to start a fire, would it last?"

"You're like a dog with a bone," Bertram commented. "Have you mentioned this crazy idea to anybody else?"

"Only to Raymond Lyons," Kevin said. "He called me yesterday about another problem."

"And what was his response?" Bertram asked.

"He told me not to let my imagination run wild," Kevin said.

"I'd say that was good advice," Bertram said. "I second the motion."

"I don't know," Kevin said. "Maybe we should go out there and check."

"No!" Bertram snapped. For a fleeting moment his mouth formed a hard line and his blue eyes blazed. Then his face relaxed. "I don't want to go to the island except for a retrieval. That was the original plan and by golly we're sticking with it. As well as everything is going, I don't want to take any chances. The animals are to remain isolated and undisturbed. The only person who goes there is the pygmy, Alphonse Kimba, and he goes only to pull supplementary food across to the island."

"Maybe I could go by myself," Kevin suggested. "It wouldn't take me long, and then I can stop worrying."

"Absolutely not!" Bertram said emphatically. "I'm in charge of this part of the project, and I forbid you or anyone else to go on the island."

"I don't see that it would make that much difference," Kevin said. "I wouldn't bother the animals."

"No!" Bertram said. "There are to be no exceptions. We want these to be wild animals. That means minimal contact. Besides, with as small as this enclave is, visits will provoke talk, and we don't want that. And on top of that it could be dangerous."

"Dangerous?" Kevin questioned. "I'd stay away from the hippos and the crocs. The bonobos certainly aren't dangerous."

"One of the pygmy bearers was killed on the last retrieval," Bertram said. "We've kept that very quiet for obvious reasons."

"How was he killed?" Kevin asked.

"By a rock," Bertram said. "One of the bonobos threw a rock."

"Isn't that unusual?" Kevin asked.

Bertram shrugged. "Chimps are known to throw sticks on occasion when they are stressed or scared. No, I don't think it's unusual. It was probably just a reflex gesture. The rock was there so he threw it."

"But it's also aggressive," Kevin said. "That's unusual for a bonobo, especially one of ours."

"All apes will defend their group when attacked," Bertram said.

"But why should they have felt they were being attacked?" Kevin asked.

"That was the fourth retrieval," Bertram said. He shrugged again. "Maybe they're learning what to expect. But whatever the reason, we don't want anyone going to the island. Spallek and I have discussed this, and he's in full agreement."

Bertram got up from the desk and draped an arm over Kevin's shoulders. Kevin tried to ease himself away, but Bertram held on. "Come on, Kevin! Relax! This kind of wild flight of imagination of yours is exactly what I was talking about earlier. You've got to get out of your lab and do something to divert that overactive mind of yours. You're going stir-crazy and you're obsessing. I mean, this fire crap is ridiculous. The irony is that the project is going splendidly. How about reconsidering that offer for coming over for dinner? Trish and I would be delighted."

"I'll give it serious thought," Kevin said. He felt distinctly uncomfortable with Bertram's arm around his neck.

"Good," Bertram said. He gave Kevin a final pat on his back. "Maybe the three of us could take in a movie as well. There's a terrific double-feature scheduled for this week. I mean, you ought to take advantage of the fact that we get the latest movies. It's a big effort on GenSys's part to fly them in here on a weekly basis. What do you say?"

"I guess," Kevin said evasively.

"Good," Bertram said. "I'll mention it to Trish, she'll give you a call. Okay?"

"Okay," Kevin said. He smiled weakly.

Five minutes later, Kevin climbed back into his vehicle more confused than before he'd come to see Bertram Edwards. He didn't know what to think. Maybe his imagination was working overtime. It was possible, but short of visiting Isla Francesca there was no way of knowing for sure. And on top of that was this new worry that people were feeling resentful toward him.

Braking at the exit of the parking area, Kevin glanced up and down the road in front of the animal complex. He waited for a large truck to rumble by. As he was about to pull out, his eye caught the sight of a man standing motionlessly in the window of the Moroccan headquarters. Kevin couldn't see him well because of the sunlight reflecting off the glass, but he could tell it was one of the mustached guards. He could also tell the man was watching him intently.

Kevin shivered without exactly knowing why.

The ride back to the hospital was uneventful and quick, but the seemingly impenetrable walls of dark green vegetation gave Kevin an uncomfortable claustrophobic feeling. Kevin's response was to press down on the accelerator. He was relieved to reach the edge of town.

Kevin parked in his spot. He opened his door, but hesitated. It was close to noon, and he debated heading home for lunch or going up to his lab for an hour or so. The lab won out. Esmeralda never expected him before one.

Just with the short walk from the car to the hospital, Kevin could appreciate the intensity of the noontime sun. It was like an oppressive blanket that made all movement more difficult, even breathing. Until he'd come to Africa, he'd never experienced true tropical heat. Once inside, enveloped with cool, air-conditioned air, Kevin grasped the edge of his collar and pulled his shirt away from his back.

He started up the stairs, but he didn't get far.

"Dr. Marshall!" a voice called.

Kevin looked behind him. He wasn't accustomed to being accosted in the stairwell.

"Shame on you, Dr. Marshall," a woman said, standing at the base of the stairs. Her voice had a lilting quality that suggested she was being less than serious. She was clad in surgical scrubs and a white coat. The sleeves of the coat were rolled up to her mid-forearms.

"Excuse me?" Kevin said. The woman looked familiar, but he couldn't place her.

"You haven't been to see the patient," the woman said. "With other cases you came each day."

"Well, that's true," Kevin said self-consciously. He'd finally recognized the woman. It was the nurse, Candace Brickmann. She was part of the surgical team that flew in with the patient. This was her fourth trip to Cogo. Kevin had met her briefly on all three previous visits.

"You've hurt Mr. Winchester's feelings," Candace said, wagging her finger at

Kevin. She was a vivacious gamine in her late twenties. With fine, light-blond hair done up in a French twist. Kevin couldn't remember a time he'd seen her that she wasn't smiling.

"I didn't think he'd notice," Kevin stammered.

Candace threw back her head and laughed. Then she covered her mouth with her hand to suppress further giggles when she saw Kevin's confused expression.

"I'm only teasing," she said. "I'm not even sure Mr. Winchester remembers meeting you on that hectic day of arrival."

"Well, I meant to come and see how he was doing," Kevin said. "I've just been too busy."

"Too busy in this place in the middle of nowhere?" Candace asked.

"Well, I guess it's more that I've been preoccupied," Kevin admitted. "A lot has been happening."

"Like what?" Candace asked, suppressing a smile. She liked this shy, unassuming researcher.

Kevin made some fumbling gestures with his hands while his face flushed. "All sorts of things," he said finally.

"You academic types crack me up," Candace said. "But, teasing aside, I'm happy to report that Mr. Winchester is doing just fine, and I understand from the surgeon that's largely thanks to you."

"I wouldn't go that far," Kevin said.

"Oh, modest, too!" Candace commented. "Smart, cute, and humble. That's a killing combination."

Kevin stuttered but no words came out.

"Would it be out of bounds for me to invite you to join me for lunch?" Candace said. "I thought I'd walk over and get a hamburger. I'm a little tired of the hospital cafeteria food, and it would be nice to get a little air now that the sun is out. What do you say?"

Kevin's mind whirled. The invitation was unexpected, and under normal circumstances he would have found reason to decline for that reason alone. But with Bertram's comments fresh in his mind, he wavered.

"Cat got your tongue?" Candace asked. She lowered her head and flirtatiously peered at him beneath arched eyebrows.

Kevin gestured up toward his lab, then mumbled words to the effect that Esmeralda was expecting him.

"Can't you give her a call?" Candace asked. She had the intuitive feeling Kevin wanted to join her, so she persisted.

"I guess," Kevin said. "I suppose I could call from my lab."

"Fine," Candace said. "Do you want me to wait here or come with you?"

Kevin had never met such a forward female, not that he had a lot of opportunity or experience. His last and only love other than a couple of high school crushes had been a fellow doctorate candidate, Jacqueline Morton. That relationship had taken months to develop out of long hours working together; she'd been as shy as Kevin.

Candace came up the five stairs to stand next to Kevin. She was about five-three in her Nikes. "If you can't decide, and it's all the same to you, why don't I come up."

"Okay," Kevin said.

Kevin's nervousness quickly abated. Usually what bothered him in social circumstances with females was the stress of trying to think of things to talk about. With Candace, he didn't have time to think. She maintained a running conversation. During the ascent of the two flights of stairs she managed to bring up the weather, the town, the hospital, and how the surgery had gone.

"This is my lab," Kevin said, after opening the door.

"Fantastic!" Candace said with sincerity.

Kevin smiled. He could tell she was truly impressed.

"You go ahead and make your call," Candace said. "I'll just look around if it's okay."

"If you'd like," Kevin said.

Although Kevin was concerned about giving Esmeralda so little warning he'd not be there for lunch, she surprised him with her equanimity. Her only response was to ask when Kevin wanted dinner.

"At the usual time," Kevin said. Then after a brief hesitation, he surprised himself by adding: "I might have company. Would that be a problem?"

"Not at all," Esmeralda said. "How many persons?"

"Just one," Kevin said. He hung up the phone and wiped his palms together. They were a little damp.

"Are we on for lunch?" Candace called from across the room.

"Let's go!" Kevin said.

"This is some lab!" she commented. "I never would have expected to find it here in the heart of tropical Africa. Tell me, what is it that you're doing with all this fantastic equipment?"

"I'm trying to perfect the protocol," Kevin said.

"Can't you be more specific?" Candace asked.

"You really want to know?" Kevin asked.

"Yes," Candace said. "I'm interested."

"At this stage I'm dealing with minor histocompatibility antigens. You know, proteins that define you as a unique, separate individual."

"And what do you do with them?"

"Well, I locate their genes on the proper chromosome," Kevin said. "Then I search for the transponase that's associated with the genes, if there's any, so I can move the genes."

Candace let out a little laugh. "You've lost me already," she admitted. "I haven't the foggiest notion what a transponase is. In fact, I'm afraid a lot of this molecular biology is over my head."

"It really isn't," Kevin said. "The principles aren't that complicated. The critical fact few people realize is that some genes can move around on their chromosome.

This happens particularly in B lymphocytes to increase the diversity of antibodies. Other genes are even more mobile and can change places with their twins. You do remember that there are two copies of every gene."

"Yup," Candace said. "Just like there are two copies of each chromosome. Our cells have twenty-three chromosome pairs."

"Exactly," Kevin said. "When genes exchange places on their chromosome pairs it's called homologous transposition. It's a particularly important process in the generation of sex cells, both eggs and sperms. What it does is help increase genetic shuffling, and hence the ability of species to evolve."

"So this homologous transposition plays a role in evolution," Candace said.

"Absolutely," Kevin agreed. "Anyway, the gene segments that move are called transposons, and the enzymes that catalyze their movement are called transposases."

"Okay," Candace said. "I follow you so far."

"Well, right now I'm interested in transposons that contain the genes for minor histocompatibility antigens," Kevin said.

"I see," Candace said, nodding her head. "I'm getting the picture. You're goal is to move the gene for a minor histocompatibility antigen from one chromosome to another."

"Exactly!" Kevin said. "The trick, of course, is finding and isolating the transposase. That's the difficult step. But once I've found the transposase, it's relatively easy to locate its gene. And once I've located and isolated the gene, I can use standard recombinant DNA technology to produce it."

"Meaning getting bacteria to make it for you," Candace said.

"Bacteria or mammalian tissue culture," Kevin said. "Whatever works best."

"Phew!" Candace commented. "This brain game is reminding me how hungry I am. Let's get some hamburgers before my blood sugar bottoms out."

Kevin smiled. He liked this woman. He was even starting to relax.

Descending the hospital stairs, Kevin felt a little giddy while listening and responding to Candace's entertaining, nonstop questions and chatter. He couldn't believe he was going to lunch with such an attractive, engaging female. It seemed to him that more things had happened in the last couple of days than during the previous five years he'd been in Cogo. He was so preoccupied, he didn't give a thought to the Equatoguinean soldiers as he and Candace crossed the square.

Kevin had not been in the rec center since his initial orientation tour. He'd forgotten its quaintness. He'd also forgotten how blasphemous it was that the church had been recycled to provide worldly diversion. The altar was gone, but the pulpit was still in place off to the left. It was used for lectures and for calling out the numbers on bingo night. In place of the altar was the movie screen: an unintended sign of the times.

The commissary was in the basement and was reached by a stairway in the narthex. Kevin was surprised at how busy it was. A babble of voices echoed off the harsh, concrete ceiling. He and Candace had to stand in a long line before ordering. Then after they'd gotten their food, they had to search in the confusion for a place to sit. The tables were all long and had to be shared. The seats were benches attached like picnic tables.

"There are some seats," Candace called out over the chatter. She pointed toward the rear of the room with her tray. Kevin nodded.

Kevin glanced furtively at the faces in the crowd as he weaved his way after Candace. He felt self-conscious, given Bertram's insight into popular opinion, yet no one paid him the slightest attention.

Kevin followed Candace as she squeezed between two tables. He held his tray high to avoid hitting anyone, then put it down at an empty spot. He had to struggle to get his legs over the seat and under the table. By the time he was situated, Candace had already introduced herself to the two people sitting on the aisle. Kevin nodded to them. He didn't recognize either one.

"Lively place," Candace said. She reached for catsup. "Do you come here often?"

Before Kevin could respond, someone called out his name. He turned and recognized the lone familiar face. It was Melanie Becket, the reproductive technologist.

"Kevin Marshall!" Melanie exclaimed again. "I'm shocked. What are you doing here?"

Melanie was about the same age as Candace; she'd celebrated her thirtieth birthday the previous month. Where Candace was light, she was dark, with medium-brown hair and coloration that seemed Mediterranean. Her dark brown eyes were nearly black.

Kevin struggled to introduce his lunchmate, and was horrified to realize that for the moment he couldn't remember her name.

"I'm Candace Brickmann," Candace said without missing a beat. She reached out a hand. Melanie introduced herself and asked if she could join them.

"By all means," Candace said.

Candace and Kevin were sitting side by side. Melanie sat opposite.

"Are you responsible for our local genius's presence at the ptomaine palace?" Melanie asked Candace. Melanie was a sharp-witted, playfully irreverent woman who'd grown up in Manhattan.

"I guess," Candace said. "Is this unusual for him?"

"That's the understatement of the year," Melanie said. "What's your secret? I've asked him to come over here so many times to no avail that I finally gave up, and that was several years ago."

"You never asked me specifically," Kevin said in his own defense.

"Oh, really?" Melanie questioned. "What did I have to do—draw you a map? I used to ask if you wanted to grab a burger. Wasn't that specific enough?"

"Well," Candace said, straightening up in her seat. "This must be my lucky day."

Melanie and Candace fell into easy conversation, exchanging job descriptions. Kevin listened but concentrated on his hamburger.

"So we're all three part of the same project," Melanie commented when she heard that Candace was the intensive-care nurse of the surgical team from Pittsburgh. "Three peas in a pod."

"You're being generous," Candace said. "I'm just one of the low men on the therapeutic totem pole. I wouldn't put myself on the same level with you guys. You're the ones that make it all possible. If you don't mind my asking, how on earth do you do it?"

"She's the hero," Kevin said, speaking up for the first time and nodding toward Melanie.

"Come on, Kevin!" Melanie complained. "I didn't develop the techniques I use the way you did. There are lots of people who could have done my job, but only you could have done yours. It was your breakthrough that was key."

"No arguing, you two," Candace said. "Just tell me how it's done. I've been curious from day one, but everything has been so hush-hush. Kevin's explained the science to me, but I still don't understand the logistics."

"Kevin gets a bone-marrow sample from a client," Melanie said. "From that, he isolates a cell preparing to divide so that the chromosomes are condensed, preferably a stem cell if I'm correct."

"It's pretty rare to find a stem cell," Kevin said.

"Well, then you tell her what you do," Melanie said to Kevin, with a dismissive wave of her hand. "I'll get it all balled up."

"I work with a transposase that I discovered almost seven years ago," Kevin said. "It catalyzes the homolygous transposition or crossing over of the short arms of chromosome six."

"What's the short arm of chromosome six?" Candace asked.

"Chromosomes have what's called a centromere that divides them into two segments," Melanie explained. "Chromosome six has particularly unequal segments. The little ones are called the short arms."

"Thank you," Candace said.

"So . . ." Kevin said, trying to organize his thoughts. "What I do is add my secret transposase to a client's cell that is preparing to divide. But I don't let the crossing-over go to completion. I halt it with the two short arms detached from their respective chromosomes. Then I extract them."

"Wow!" Candace remarked. "You actually take these tiny, tiny strands out of the nucleus. How on earth can you do that!"

"That's another story," Kevin said. "Actually I use a monoclonal antibody system that recognizes the backside of the transposase."

"This is getting over my head," Candace said.

"Well, forget how he gets the short arms out," Melanie said. "Just accept it."

"Okay," Candace said. "What do you do with these detached short arms?"

Kevin pointed toward Melanie. "I wait for her to work her magic."

"It's not magic," Melanie said. "I'm just a technician. I apply in vitro fertilization techniques to the bonobos, the same techniques that were developed to increase the fertility of captive mountain gorillas. Actually, Kevin and I have to coordinate our efforts because what he wants is a fertilized egg that has yet to divide. Timing is important."

"I want it just ready to divide," Kevin said. "So it's Melanie's schedule that determines mine. I don't start my part until she gives me the green light. When she delivers the zygote, I repeat exactly the same procedure that I'd just done with the client's cell. After removing the bonobo short arms, I inject the client's short arms into the zygote. Thanks to the transponase they hook right up exactly where they are supposed to be."

"And that's it?" Candace said.

"Well, no," Kevin admitted. "Actually I introduce four transponases, not one. The short arm of chromosome six is the major segment that we're transferring, but we also transfer a relatively small part of chromosomes nine, twelve, and fourteen. These carry the genes for the ABO blood groups and a few other minor histocompatibility antigens like CD-31 adhesion molecules. But that gets too complicated. Just think about chromosome six. It's the most important part."

"That's because chromosome six contains the genes that make up the major histocompatibility complex," Candace said knowledgeably.

"Exactly," Kevin said. He was impressed and smitten. Not only was Candace socially adept, she was also smart and informed.

"Would this protocol work with other animals?" Candace asked.

"What kind would you have in mind?" Kevin asked.

"Pigs," Candace said. "I know other centers in the U.S. and England have been trying to reduce the destructive effect of complement in transplantation with pig organs by inserting a human gene."

"Compared with what we are doing that's like using leaches," Melanie said. "It's so old-fashioned because it is treating the symptom, not eliminating its cause."

"It's true," Kevin said. "In our protocol there is no immunological reaction to worry about. Histocompatibility-wise we're offering an immunological double, especially if I can incorporate a few more of the minor antigens."

"I don't know why you are agonizing over them," Melanie said. "In our first three transplants the clients haven't had any rejection reaction at all. Zilch!"

"I want it perfect," Kevin said.

"I'm asking about pigs for several reasons," Candace said. "First, I think using bonobos may offend some people. Second, I understand there aren't very many of them."

"That's true," Kevin said. "The total world population of bonobos is only about twenty thousand."

"That's my point," Candace said. "Whereas pigs are slaughtered for bacon by the hundred of thousands."

"I don't think my system would work with pigs," Kevin said. "I don't know for sure, but I doubt it. The reason it works so well in bonobos, or chimps for that matter, is that their genomes and ours are so similar. In fact, they differ by only one and a half percent."

"That's all?" Candace questioned. She was amazed.

"It's kind of humbling, isn't it," Kevin said.

"It's more than humbling," Candace said.

"It's indicative of how close bonobos, chimps, and humans are evolutionarily," Melanie said. "It's thought we and our primate cousins have descended from a common ancestor who lived around seven million years ago."

"That underscores the ethical question about using them," Candace said, "and why some people might be offended by their use. They look so human. I mean, doesn't it bother you guys when one of them has to be sacrificed?"

"This liver transplant with Mr. Winchester is only the second that required a sacrifice," Melanie said. "The other two were kidneys, and the animals are fine."

"Well, how did this case make you feel?" Candace asked. "Most of us on the surgical team were more upset this time even though we thought we were prepared, especially since it was the second sacrifice."

Kevin looked at Melanie. His mouth had gone dry. Candace was forcing him to face an issue he'd struggled to avoid. It was part of the reason the smoke coming from Isla Francesca upset him so much.

"Yeah, it bothers me," Melanie said. "But I guess I'm so thrilled with the involved science and what it can do for a patient, that I try not to think about it. Besides, we never expect to have to use many of them. They are more like insurance in case the clients might need them. We don't accept people who already need transplant organs unless they can wait the three plus years it takes for their double to come of age. And we don't have to interact with these creatures. They live off on an island by themselves. That's by design so that no one here has the chance to form emotional bonds of any sort."

Kevin swallowed with difficulty. In his mind's eye he could see the smoke lazily snaking its way into the dull, leaden sky. He could also imagine the stressed bonobo picking up a rock and throwing it with deadly accuracy at the pygmy during the retrieval process.

"What's the term when animals have human genes incorporated into them?" Candace asked.

"Transgenic," Melanie said.

"Right," Candace said. "I just wish we could be using transgenic pigs instead of bonobos. This procedure bothers me. As much as I like the money and the GenSys stock, I'm not so sure I'm going to stick with the program."

"They're not going to like that," Melanie said. "Remember, you signed a contract. I understand they are sticklers about holding people to their original agreements."

Candace shrugged. "I'll give them back all the stock, options included. I can live without it. I'll just have to see how I feel. I'd be much happier if we were using pigs. When we put that last bonobo under anesthesia, I could have sworn he was trying to communicate with us. We had to use a ton of sedative."

"Oh, come on!" Kevin snapped, suddenly furious. His face was flushed.

Melanie's eyes opened wide. "What in heaven's name has gotten into you?"

Kevin instantly regretted his outburst. "Sorry," he said. His heart was still pounding. He hated the fact that he was always so transparent, or felt he was.

Melanie rolled her eyes for Candace's benefit, but Candace didn't catch it. She was watching Kevin.

"I have a feeling you were as bummed out as I was," she said to him.

Kevin breathed out noisily then took a bite of hamburger to avoid saying anything he'd later regret.

"Why don't you want to talk about it?" Candace asked.

Kevin shook his head while he chewed. He guessed his face was still beet-red.

"Don't worry about him," Melanie said. "He'll recover."

Candace faced Melanie. "The bonobos are just so human," she commented, going back to one of her original points, "so I guess we shouldn't be shocked that their genomes differ by only one and a half percent. But something just occurred to me. If you guys are replacing the short arms of chromosome six as well as some other smaller segments of the bonobo genome with human DNA, what percentage do you think you're dealing with?"

Melanie looked at Kevin while she made a mental calculation. She arched her eyebrows. "Hmmm," she said. "That's a curious point. That would be over two percent."

"Yeah, but the one and a half percent is not all on the short arm of chromosome six," Kevin snapped again.

"Hey, calm down, bucko," Melanie said. She put down her soft drink, reached across the table and put her hand on Kevin's shoulder. "You're out of control. All we're doing is having a conversation. You know, it's sort of normal for people to sit and talk. I know you find that weird since you'd rather interact with your centrifuge tubes, but what's wrong?"

Kevin sighed. It went against his nature, but he decided to confide in these two bright, confident women. He admitted he was upset.

"As if we didn't know!" Melanie said with another roll of her eyes. "Can't you be more specific? What's bugging you?"

"Just what Candace is talking about," Kevin said.

"She's said a lot of things," Melanie said.

"Yeah, and they're all making me feel like I've made a monumental mistake."

Melanie took her hand away and stared into the depths of Kevin's topaz-colored eyes. "In what regard?" she questioned.

"By adding so much human DNA," Kevin said. "The short arm of chromosome six has millions of base pairs and hundreds of genes that have nothing to do with the major histocompatibility complex. I should have isolated the complex instead of taking the easy route."

"So the creatures have a few more human proteins," Melanie said. "Big deal!"

"That's exactly how I felt at first," Kevin said. "At least until I put an inquiry out over the Internet, asking if anyone knew what other kinds of genes were on the short arm of chromosome six. Unfortunately, one of the responders informed me there was a large segment of developmental genes. Now I have no idea what I've created."

"Of course you do," Candace said. "You've created a transgenic bonobo."

"I know," Kevin said with his eyes blazing. He was breathing rapidly and perspiration had appeared on his forehead. "And by doing so I'm terrified I've overstepped the bounds."

CHAPTER 6

MARCH 5, 1997
1:00 P.M.
COGO, EQUATORIAL GUINEA

Bertram pulled his three-year-old Jeep Cherokee into the parking area behind the town hall and yanked on the brake. The car had been giving him trouble and had spent innumerable days being repaired in the motor pool. But the problem had persisted, and that fact made him particularly irritated when Kevin Marshall pretended not to know how lucky he was to get a new Toyota every two years. Bertram wasn't scheduled for a new car for another year.

Bertram took the stairs that rose up behind the first-floor arcade to reach the veranda that ringed the building. From there he walked into the central office. By Siegfried Spallek's choice, it had not been air-conditioned. A large ceiling fan lazily rotated with a particular wavering hum. The long, flat blades kept the sizable room's warm, moist air on the move.

Bertram had called ahead, so Siegfried's secretary, a broad-faced black man named Aurielo from the island of Bioko, was expecting him and waved him into the inner office. Aurielo had been trained in France as a schoolteacher, but had been unemployed until GenSys founded the Zone.

The inner office was larger than the outer and extended the entire width of the building. It had shuttered windows overlooking the parking lot in the back and the town square in the front. The front windows yielded the impressive view of the new hospital/laboratory complex. From where Bertram was standing, he could even see Kevin's laboratory windows.

"Sit down," Siegfried said, without looking up. His voice had a harsh, guttural quality, with a slight Germanic accent. It was commandingly authoritarian. He was signing a stack of correspondence. "I'll be finished in a moment."

Bertram's eyes wandered around the cluttered office. It was a place that never made him feel comfortable. As a veterinarian and moderate environmentalist, he did not appreciate the decor. Covering the walls and every available horizontal surface were glassy-eyed, stuffed heads of animals, many of which were endangered species. There were cats such as lions, leopards, and cheetahs. There was a bewildering variety of antelope, more than Bertram knew existed. Several enormous rhino heads peered blankly down from positions of prominence on the wall behind Spallek. On top of the bookcase were snakes, including a rearing cobra. On the floor was an enormous crocodile with its mouth partially ajar to reveal its fearsome teeth. The table next to Bertram's chair was an elephant's foot topped with a slab of mahogany. In the corners stood crossed elephant tusks.

Even more bothersome to Bertram than the stuffed animals were the skulls. There were three of them on Siegfried's desk. All three had their tops sawn off. One had an apparent bullet hole through the temple. They were used respectively for paper clips, ashtray, and to hold a large candle. Although the Zone's electric power was the most reliable in the entire country, it did go off on rare occasions because of lightning strikes.

Most people, especially visitors from GenSys, assumed the skulls were from apes. Bertram knew differently. They were human skulls of people executed by the Equatoguinean soldiers. All three of the victims had been convicted of the capital offense of interfering with GenSys operations. In actuality, they had been caught poaching wild chimps on the Zone's designated hundred-square-mile land. Siegfried considered the area his own private hunting reserve.

Years previously, when Bertram had gently questioned the wisdom of displaying the skulls, Siegfried had responded by saying that they kept the native workers on their toes. "It's the kind of communication they comprehend," Siegfried had explained. "They understand such symbols."

Bertram didn't wonder that they got the message. Especially in a country which had suffered the atrocities of a diabolically cruel dictator. Bertram always remembered Kevin's response to the skulls. Kevin had said that they reminded him of the deranged character Kurtz in Joseph Conrad's *Heart of Darkness*.

"There," Siegfried said, pushing the signed papers aside. With his accent it sounded more like "zair." "What's on your mind, Bertram? I hope you don't have a problem with the new bonobos."

"Not at all. The two breeding females are perfect," Bertram said. He eyed the Zone's site boss. His most obvious physical trait was a grotesque scar that ran from beneath his left ear, down across his cheek, and under his nose. Over the years its gradual contraction had pulled up the corner of Siegfried's mouth in a perpetual sneer.

Bertram did not technically report to Siegfried. As the chief vet of the world's largest primate research and breeding facility, Bertram dealt directly with a GenSys senior vice president of operations back in Cambridge, Massachusetts, who had direct access to Taylor Cabot. But on a day-to-day basis, particularly in relation to the bonobo project, it was in Bertram's best interest to maintain a cordial working relationship with the site boss. The problem was, Siegfried was short-tempered and difficult to deal with.

He'd started his African career as a white hunter, who, for a price, could get a client anything he wanted. Such a reputation required a move from East Africa to West Africa, where game laws were less rigidly enforced. Siegfried had built up a large organization, and things went well until some trackers failed him in a crucial situation, resulting in his being mauled by an enormous bull elephant and the client couple being killed.

The episode ended Siegfried's career as a white hunter. It also left him with his facial scar and a paralyzed right arm. The extremity hung limp and useless from its shoulder connection.

Rage over the incident had made him a bitter and vindictive man. Still, GenSys had recognized his bush-based organizational skills, his knowledge of animal behavior, and his heavy-handed but effectual way of dealing with the indigenous African personality. They thought he was the perfect individual to run their multimillion-dollar African operation.

"There's another wrinkle with the bonobo operation," Bertram said.

"Is this new concern in addition to the weird worry of yours that the apes have divided into two groups?" Siegfried asked superciliously.

"Recognizing a change in social organization is a damn legitimate concern!" Bertram said, his color rising.

"So you said," Siegfried remarked. "But I've been thinking about it, and I can't imagine it matters. What do we care if they hang out in one group or ten? All we want them to do is stay put and stay healthy."

"I disagree," Bertram said. "Splitting up suggests they are not getting along. That would not be typical bonobo behavior, and it could spell trouble down the road."

"I'll let you, the professional, worry about it," Siegfried said. He leaned back in his chair, and it squeaked. "I personally don't care what those apes do as long as nothing threatens this windfall money and stock options. The project is turning into a gold mine."

"The new problem has to do with Kevin Marshall," Bertram said.

"Now what in God's name could that skinny simpleton do to get you to worry?" Siegfried asked. "With your paranoia, it's a good thing you don't have to do my job."

"The nerd has worked himself up because he's seen smoke coming from the island," Bertram said. "He's come to me twice. Once last week and then again this morning."

"What's the big deal about smoke?" Siegfried asked. "Why does he care? He sounds worse than you."

"He thinks the bonobos might be using fire," Bertram said. "He hasn't said so explicitly, but I'm sure that's what is on his mind."

"What do you mean 'using fire'?" Siegfried asked. He leaned forward. "You mean like making a campfire for warmth or cooking?" Siegfried laughed without disturbing his omnipresent sneer. "I don't know about you urban Americans. Out here in the bush you're scared of your own shadow."

"I know it's preposterous," Bertram said. "Of course no one else has seen it, or if they have, it's probably from a lightning storm. The problem is, he wants to go out there."

"No one goes near the island!" Siegfried growled. "Only during a harvest, and it's only the harvest team! That's a directive from the home office. There are no exceptions save for Kimba, the pygmy, delivering the supplementary food."

"I told him the same thing," Bertram said. "And I don't think he'll do anything on his own. Still, I thought I should tell you about it just the same."

"It's good that you did," Siegfried said irritably. "The little prick. He's a god-damned thorn in my side."

"There is one other thing," Bertram said. "He told Raymond Lyons about the smoke."

Siegfried slapped the surface of his desk with his good hand loud enough to cause Bertram to jump. He stood up and stepped to the shuttered window overlooking the town square. He glared over at the hospital. He'd never liked the epicene bookish researcher from their first meeting. When he'd learned Kevin was to be coddled and accommodated in the second best house in the town, Siegfried had boiled over. He'd wanted to assign the house as a perk to one of his loyal underlings.

Siegfried balled his good hand into a fist and gritted his teeth. "What a meddling pain in the ass," he said.

"His research is almost done," Bertram said. "It would be a shame if he was to muck things up just when everything is going so well."

"What did Lyons say?" Siegfried asked.

"Nothing," Bertram said. "He accused Kevin of letting his imagination run wild."

"I might have to have someone watch Kevin," Siegfried said. "I will not have anyone destroy this program. That's all there is to it. It's too lucrative."

Bertram stood up. "That's your department," he said. He started for the door, confident he'd planted the appropriate seed.

CHAPTER 7

MARCH 5, 1997
7:25 A.M.
NEW YORK CITY

The combination of cheap red wine and little sleep slowed Jack's pace on his morning bicycle commute. His customary time of arrival in the ID room of the medical examiner's office was seven-fifteen. But as he got off the elevator on the first floor of the morgue en route to the ID room, he noticed it was already seven twenty-five, and it bothered him. It wasn't as if he were late, it was just that Jack liked to keep to a schedule. Discipline in relation to his work was one of the ways he'd learned to avoid depression.

His first order of business was to pour himself a cup of coffee from the communal pot. Even the aroma seemed to have a beneficial effect, which Jack attributed to Pavlovian conditioning. He took his first sip. It was a heavenly experience. Though he doubted the caffeine could work quite so quickly, he felt like his mild hangover headache was already on the mend.

He stepped over to Vinnie Amendola, the mortuary tech whose day shift overlapped the night shift. He was ensconced as usual at one of the office's government-issued metal desks. His feet were parked on the corner, and his face hidden behind his morning newspaper.

Jack pulled the edge of the paper down to expose Vinnie's Italianate features to the world. He was in his late twenties, in sorry physical shape, but handsome. His dark, thick hair was something Jack envied. Jack had been noticing over the previous year a decided thinning of his gray-streaked brown hair on the crown of his head.

"Hey, Einstein, what's the paper say about the Franconi body incident?" Jack asked. Jack and Vinnie worked together on a frequent basis, both appreciating the other's flippancy, quick wit, and black humor.

"I don't know," Vinnie said. He tried to pull his beloved paper from Jack's grasp. He was embroiled in the Knicks stats from the previous night's basketball game.

Jack's forehead furrowed. Vinnie might not have been an academic genius, but about current news items, he was something of a resident authority. He read the newspapers cover to cover every day and had impressive recall.

"There's nothing about it in the paper?" Jack questioned. He was shocked. He'd imagined the media would have had a field day with the embarrassment of the body disappearing from the morgue. Bureaucratic mismanagement was a favorite journalistic theme.

"I didn't notice it," Vinnie said. He yanked harder, freed the paper, and reburied his face.

Jack shook his head. He was truly surprised and wondered how Harold Bingham, the chief medical examiner, had managed such a media coverup. Just as Jack was about to turn away, he caught the headlines. It said: MOB THUMBS NOSE AT AUTHORITY. The subhead read: "Vaccarro crime family kills one of its own then steals the body out from under the noses of city officials."

Jack snatched the entire paper from the surprised Vinnie's grasp. Vinnie's legs fell to the floor with a thump. "Hey, come on!" he complained.

Jack folded the paper then held it so that Vinnie was forced to stare at the front page.

"I thought you said the story wasn't in the paper," Jack said.

"I didn't say it wasn't in there," Vinnie said. "I said I didn't see it."

"It's the headlines, for crissake!" Jack said. He pointed at them with his coffee cup for emphasis.

Vinnie lunged out to grab his paper. Jack pulled it away from his grasp.

"Come on!" Vinnie whined. "Get your own freakin' paper."

"You've got me curious," Jack said. "As methodical as you are, you'd have read this front-page story on your subway ride into town. What's up, Vinnie?"

"Nothing!" Vinnie said. "I just went directly to the sports page."

Jack studied Vinnie's face for a moment. Vinnie looked away to avoid eye contact.

"Are you sick?" Jack asked facetiously.

"No!" Vinnie snapped. "Just give me the paper."

Jack slipped out the sports pages and handed them over. Then he went over to the scheduling desk and started the article. It began on the front page and concluded on the third. As Jack anticipated, it was written from a sarcastic, mocking point of view. It cast equal aspersion on the police department and the medical examiner's office. It said the whole sordid affair was just another glowing example of the gross incompetence of both organizations.

Laurie breezed into the room and interrupted Jack. As she removed her coat, she told him that she hoped he felt better than she.

"Probably not," Jack admitted. "It was that cheap wine I brought over. I'm sorry."

"It was also the five hours of sleep," Laurie said. "I had a terrible time hauling myself out of bed." She put her coat down on a chair. "Good morning, Vinnie," she called out.

Vinnie stayed silent behind his sports page.

"He's pouting because I violated his paper," Jack said. Jack got up so Laurie could sit down at the scheduling desk. It was Laurie's week to divvy up the cases for autopsy among the staff. "The headlines and cover story are about the Franconi incident."

"I wouldn't wonder," Laurie said. "It was all over the local news, and I heard it announced that Bingham will be on *Good Morning America* to attempt damage control."

"He's got his hands full," Jack said.

"Have you looked at today's cases?" Laurie asked, as she started glancing through the twenty or so folders.

"I just got here myself," Jack admitted. He continued reading the article.

"Oh, this is good!" Jack commented after a moment's silence. "They're alleging that there is some kind of conspiracy between us and the police department. They suggest we might have deliberately disposed of the body for their benefit. Can you imagine! These media people are so paranoid that they see conspiracy in everything!"

"It's the public who is paranoid," Laurie said. "The media likes to give them what they want. But that kind of wild theory is exactly why I'm going to find out how that body disappeared. The public has to know we are impartial."

"I was hoping you'd have a change of heart and given up on that quest after a night's sleep," Jack mumbled while continuing to read.

"Not a chance," Laurie said.

"This is crazy!" Jack said, slapping the page of newsprint. "First they suggest we here at the ME office were responsible for the body disappearing, and now they say the mob undoubtedly buried the remains in the wilds of Westchester so they will never be found."

"The last part is probably correct," Laurie said. "Unless the body turns up in the spring thaw. With the frost it's hard to dig more than a foot below the surface."

"Gads, what trash!" Jack commented as he finished the article. "Here, you want to read it?" He offered the front pages of the paper to Laurie.

Laurie waved them off. "Thanks, but I already read the version in the *Times*," she said. "It was caustic enough. I don't need the *New York Post*'s point of view."

Jack went back over to Vinnie and quipped that he was willing to return his paper to its virginal state. Vinnie took the pages without comment.

"You are awfully sensitive today," Jack said to the tech.

"Just leave me alone," Vinnie snapped.

"Whoa, watch out, Laurie!" Jack said. "I think Vinnie has pre-mental tension. He's probably planning on doing some thinking and it's got his hormones all out of whack."

"Uh-oh!" Laurie called out. "Here's that floater that Mike Passano mentioned last night. Who should I assign it to? Trouble is I don't think I'm mad at anyone and to forestall guilt I'll probably end up doing it myself."

"Give it to me," Jack said.

"You don't care?" Laurie asked. She hated floaters, especially those which had been in the water for a long time. Such autopsies were unpleasant and often difficult jobs.

"Nah," Jack said. "Once you get past the smell, you got it licked."

"Please!" Laurie murmured. "That's disgusting."

"Seriously," Jack said. "They can be a challenge. I like them better than gunshot wounds."

"This one is both," Laurie commented, as she put Jack down for the floater.

"How delightful!" Jack commented. He walked back to the scheduling desk and looked over Laurie's shoulder.

"There's a presumptive, close range shotgun blast to the upper-right quadrant," Laurie said.

"It's sounding better and better," Jack said. "What's the victim's name?"

"No name," Laurie said. "In fact, that will be part of your challenge. The head and the hands are missing."

Laurie handed Jack the folder. He leaned on the edge of the desk and slid out the contents. There wasn't much information. What there was came from the forensic investigator, Janice Jaeger.

Janice wrote that the body had been discovered in the Atlantic Ocean way out off Coney Island. It had been inadvertently found by a Coast Guard cutter which had been lying in wait under the cover of night for some suspected drug runners. The Coast Guard had acted on an anonymous tip, and, at the time of the discovery, had been essentially dead in the water with their lights out and radar on. The cutter had literally bumped up against the body. The presumption was that it was the remains of the drug runner/informer.

"Not a lot to go on," Jack said.

"All the more challenge," Laurie teased.

Jack slipped off the desk and headed for the communications room en route to the elevator. "Come on, grouchy!" he called to Vinnie. He gave Vinnie's paper a slap and his arm a tug as he passed. "Time's a wasting." But at the door he literally bumped into Lou Soldano. The detective lieutenant had his mind on his goal: the coffee machine.

"Jeez," Jack commented. "You should try out for the New York Giants." Some of his coffee had sloshed out onto the floor.

"Sorry," Lou said. "I'm in sorry need of some java."

Both men went to the coffeepot. Jack used some paper towels to dab at the spill down the front of his corduroy jacket. Lou filled a cup to the brim with a shaky hand, then sipped enough to allow for plenty of cream and sugar.

Lou sighed. "It's been a grueling couple of days."

"Have you been partying all night again?" Jack said.

Lou's face was stubbled with a heavy growth of whiskers. He had on a wrinkled blue shirt with the top button undone and his tie loosened and askew. His Colombo-style trench coat looked like something a homeless person would wear.

"I wish," Lou grunted. "I've seen about three hours of sleep in the last two nights." He walked over, said hello to Laurie, and sat down heavily in a chair next to the scheduling desk.

"Any progress on the Franconi case?" Laurie asked.

"Nothing that pleases the captain, the area commander, or the police commissioner," Lou said dejectedly. "What a mess. The worry is, some heads are going to roll. We in Homicide are starting to worry we might be set up as scapegoats unless we can come up with a break in the case."

"It wasn't your fault Franconi was murdered," Laurie said indignantly.

"Tell that to the commissioner," Lou commented. He took a loud sip from his coffee. "Mind if I smoke?" He looked at Laurie and Jack. "Forget it," he said the moment he saw their expressions. "I don't know why I asked. Must have been a moment of temporary insanity."

"What have you learned?" Laurie asked. Laurie knew that prior to being assigned to Homicide, Lou had been with the Organized Crime unit. With his experience, there was no one more qualified to investigate the case.

"It was definitely a Vaccarro hit," Lou said. "We learned that from our informers. But since Franconi was about to testify, we'd already assumed as much. The only real lead is that we have the murder weapon."

"That should help," Laurie said.

"Not as much as you'd think," Lou said. "It's not so unusual during a mob hit that the weapon is left behind. We found it on a rooftop across from the Positano Restaurant. It was a scoped 30-30 Remington with two rounds missing from its magazine. The two casings were on the roof."

"Fingerprints?" Laurie asked.

"Wiped clean," Lou said, "but the crime boys are still going over it."

"Traceable?" Jack asked.

"Yeah," Lou said with a sigh. "We did that. The rifle belonged to a hunting freak out in Menlo Park. But it was the expected dead end. The guy's place had been robbed the day before. The only thing missing was the rifle."

"So what's next?" Laurie asked.

"We're still following up leads," Lou said. "Plus there are more informers that we've not been able to contact. But mostly we're just keeping our fingers crossed for some sort of break. What about you guys? Any idea how the body walked out of here?"

"Not yet, but I'm looking into it personally," Laurie said.

"Hey, don't encourage her," Jack said. "That's for Bingham and Washington to do."

"He's got a point, Laurie," Lou said.

"Damn straight I got a point," Jack said. "Last time Laurie got involved with the mob she got carried out of here nailed in a coffin. At least that's what you told me."

"That was then and this is now," Laurie said. "I'm not involved in this case the way I was in that one. I think it is important to find out how the body disappeared for the sake of this office, and frankly I'm not convinced either Bingham or Washington will make the effort. From their point of view, it is better to let the episode just fade."

"I can understand that," Lou said. "In fact, if the goddamned media would only let up, the commissioner might even want us to ease up. Who knows?"

"I'm going to find out how it happened," Laurie repeated with conviction.

"Well, knowing the who and the how could help my investigation," Lou said. "It was most likely the same people from the Vaccarro organization. It just stands to reason."

Jack threw up his hands. "I'm getting out of here," he said. "I can tell neither of you will listen to reason." He again tugged on Vinnie's shirt on the way out the door.

Jack poked his head into Janice's office. "Anything I should know about this floater that's not in the folder?" he asked the investigator.

"The little there is, is all there," Janice said. "Except for the coordinates where the Coast Guard picked up the body. They told me that someone would have to call today to make sure it wasn't classified or something. But I can't imagine that information will matter. It's not like anyone could go out there and find the head and the hands."

"I agree," Jack said. "But have someone call anyway. Just for the record."

"I'll leave a note for Bart," Janice said. Bart Arnold was the chief forensic investigator.

"Thanks, Janice," Jack said. "Now get out of here and get some sleep." Janice was so committed to her job that she always worked overtime.

"Wait a second," Janice called out. "There was one other thing that I forgot to note in my report. When the body was picked up, it was naked. Not a stitch of clothing."

Jack nodded. That was a curious piece of information. Undressing a corpse was added effort on the part of the murderer. Jack pondered for a moment, and when he did, he decided it was consistent with the murderer's wish to hide the victim's identity, a fact made obvious by the missing head and hands. Jack waved goodbye to Janice.

"Don't tell me we're doing a floater," Vinnie whined as he and Jack headed for the elevator.

"You sure do tune out when you read the sports page," Jack said. "Laurie and I discussed it for ten minutes."

They boarded the elevator and started down to the autopsy room floor. Vinnie refused to make eye contact with Jack.

"You are in a weird mood," Jack said. "Don't tell me you're taking this Franconi disappearance personally."

"Lay off," Vinnie said.

While Vinnie went off to don his moon suit, lay out all the paraphernalia necessary to do the autopsy, and then get the body into the morgue and onto the table, Jack went through the rest of the folder to make absolutely certain he'd not missed anything. Then he went and found the X rays that had been taken when the body had arrived.

Jack put on his own moon suit, unplugged the power source that had been charging over night, and hooked himself up. He hated the suit in general, but to work on a decomposing floater he hated it less. As he'd teased with Laurie earlier, the smell was the worst part.

At that time in the morning, Jack and Vinnie were the only ones in the autopsy room. To Vinnie's chagrin, Jack invariably insisted on getting a jump on the day. Frequently, Jack was finishing his first case when his colleagues were just starting theirs.

The first order of business was to look at the X rays, and Jack snapped them up on the viewer. With his hands on his hips, Jack took a step back and gazed at the anterioposterior full-body shot. With no head and no hands, the image was decidedly abnormal, like the X ray of some primitive, nonhuman creature. The other abnormality was a bright, dense blob of shotgun pellets in the area of the right upper quadrant. Jack's immediate impression was that there had been multiple shotgun blasts, not just one. There were too many beebee-like pellets.

The pellets were opaque to the X rays and obscured any detail they covered. On the light box they appeared white.

Jack was about to switch his attention to the lateral X ray when something about the opacity caught his attention. At two locations the periphery appeared strange, more lumpy than the usual beebee contour.

Jack looked at the lateral film and saw the same phenomena. His first impression was that the shotgun blasts might have carried some radio-opaque material into the wound. Perhaps it had been some part of the victim's clothing.

"Whenever you're ready, Maestro," Vinnie called out. He had everything prepared.

Jack turned from the X-ray view box and approached the autopsy table. The floater was ghastly pale in the raw fluorescent light. Whoever the victim had been, he'd been relatively obese and had not made any recent trips to the Caribbean.

"To use one of your favorite quotes," Vinnie said. "It doesn't look like he's going to make it to the prom."

Jack smiled at Vinnie's black humor. It was much more in keeping with his personality, suggesting that he had recovered from his early-morning pique.

The body was in sad shape although bobbing around in the water had washed it clean. The good news was that it had obviously been in the water for only a short time. The trauma went far beyond the multiple shotgun blasts to the upper abdomen. Not only were the head and the hands hacked off, but there was a series of wide, deep gashes in the torso and thighs that exposed swaths of greasy adipose tissue. The edges of all the wounds were ragged.

"Looks like the fish have been having a banquet," Jack said.

"Oh, gross!" Vinnie commented.

The shotgun blasts had bared and damaged many of the internal abdominal organs. Some strands of intestines were visible as was one dangling kidney.

Jack picked up one of the arms and looked at the exposed bones. "A hacksaw would be my guess," he said.

"What are all these huge cuts?" Vinnie asked. "Somebody try to slice him up like a holiday turkey?"

"Nah, I'd guess he'd been run over with a boat," Jack said. "They look like propeller injuries."

Jack then began a careful examination of the exterior of the corpse. With so much obvious trauma, he knew it was easy to miss more subtle findings. He worked slowly, frequently stopping to photograph lesions. His meticulousness paid off. At the ragged base of the neck just anterior to the collarbone he found a small circular lesion. He found another similar one on the left side below the rib cage.

"What are they?" Vinnie asked.

"I don't know," Jack said. "Puncture wounds of some sort."

"How many times do you suppose they shot him in the abdomen?" Vinnie asked.

"Hard to say," Jack said.

"Boy, they weren't taking any chances," Vinnie said. "They sure as hell wanted him dead."

A half hour later, when Jack was about to commence the internal part of the autopsy, the door opened and Laurie walked in. She was gowned and held a mask to her face, but she didn't have on her moon suit. Since she was a stickler for rules and since moon suits were now required in the "pit," Jack was immediately suspicious.

"At least your case wasn't in the water for long," Laurie said, looking down at the corpse. "It's not decomposed at all."

"Just a refreshing dip," Jack quipped.

"What a shotgun wound!" Laurie marveled, gazing at the fearsome wound. Then looking at the multiple gashes, she added, "These look like they were done by a propeller."

Jack straightened up. "Laurie, what's on your mind? You didn't come down here just to help us, did you?"

"No," Laurie admitted. Her voice wavered behind her mask. "I guess I wanted a little moral support."

"About what?" Jack questioned.

"Calvin just reamed me out," Laurie said. "Apparently the night tech, Mike Passano, complained that I had been in last night accusing him of being involved in the theft of Franconi's body. Can you imagine? Anyway, Calvin was really angry, and you know how I hate confrontation. I ended up crying, which made me furious at myself."

Jack blew out through pursed lips. He tried to think of something to say other than "I told you so," but nothing came to mind.

"I'm sorry," Jack said limply.

"Thanks," Laurie said.

"So you shed a few tears," Jack said. "Don't be so hard on yourself."

"But I hate it," Laurie complained. "It's so unprofessional."

"Ah, I wouldn't worry about it," Jack said. "Sometimes I wish I could shed tears. Maybe if we could do some kind of partial trade, we'd both be better off."

"Anytime!" Laurie said with conviction. This was the closest Jack had come to an admission of what Laurie had long suspected: his bottled-up grief was the major stumbling block for his own happiness.

"So, at least now you'll drop your minicrusade," Jack said.

"Heavens, no!" Laurie said. "If anything, it makes me more committed because it suggests just what I feared. Calvin and Bingham are going to try to sweep the episode under the carpet. It's not right."

"Oh, Laurie!" Jack moaned. "Please! This little run-in with Calvin will only be the beginning. You're going to bring yourself nothing but grief."

"It's the principle," Laurie said. "So don't lecture me. I came to you for support."

Jack sighed, fogging up his plastic face mask for a moment. "Okay," he said. "What do you want me to do?"

"Nothing in particular," Laurie said. "Just be there for me."

Fifteen minutes later, Laurie left the autopsy room. Jack had showed her all the external findings on his case, including the two puncture wounds. She'd listened with half an ear, obviously preoccupied with the Franconi business. Jack had had to restrain himself to keep from telling her again how he felt.

"Enough of this external stuff," Jack said to Vinnie. "Let's move on to the internal part of the autopsy."

"It's about time," Vinnie complained. It was now after eight and bodies were coming in along with their assigned techs and medical examiners. Despite the early start, he and Jack were not significantly ahead of the others.

Jack ignored the friendly banter evoked by his hapless corpse. With all the obvious trauma, Jack had to vary the traditional autopsy technique and that took concentration. In contrast to Vinnie, Jack was oblivious to the passage of time. But again his meticulousness paid off. Although the liver had essentially been obliterated by the shotgun blasts, Jack discovered something extraordinary that might have been missed by someone doing a more haphazard, cursory job. He found the tiny remains of surgical sutures in the vena cava and in the ragged end of the hepatic artery. Sutures in such an area were uncommon. The hepatic artery brought blood to the liver, whereas the vena cava was the largest vein in the abdomen. Jack didn't find any sutures in the portal vein, because that vessel was almost entirely obliterated.

"Chet, get over here," Jack called. Chet McGovern was Jack's office mate. He was busy at a neighboring table.

Chet put down his scalpel and stepped over to Jack's table. Vinnie moved to the head to give him space.

"What'cha got?" Chet asked. "Something interesting?" He peered into the hole where Jack was working.

"I sure do," Jack said. "I got a bunch of shotgun pellets, but I also have some vascular sutures."

"Where?" Chet asked. He couldn't make out any anatomical landmarks.

"Here," Jack said. He pointed with the handle of a scalpel.

"Okay, I see them," Chet said with admiration. "Nice pickup. There's not a lot of endothelialization. I'd say they weren't that old."

"That's my thought," Jack said. "Probably within a month or two. Six months at the extreme."

"What do you think it means?"

"I think the chances of me making an identification just went up a thousand percent," Jack said. He straightened up and stretched.

"So the victim had abdominal surgery," Chet said. "Lots of people have had abdominal surgery."

"Not the kind of surgery this guy apparently had," Jack said. "With sutures in the vena cava and the hepatic artery, I'm betting he's in a pretty distinguished group. My guess is that he'd had a liver transplant not too long ago."

CHAPTER 8

Raymond Lyons pulled up his cuff-linked sleeve and glanced at his wafer-thin Piaget watch. It was exactly ten o'clock. He was content. He liked to be punctual especially for business meetings, but he did not like to be early. As far as he was concerned being early reeked of desperation, and Raymond had a penchant for bargaining from a position of strength.

For the previous few minutes he'd been standing on the corner of Park Avenue and Seventy-eighth Street, waiting for the hour to arrive. Now that it had, he straightened his tie, adjusted his fedora, and started walking toward the entrance of 972 Park Avenue.

"I'm looking for Dr. Anderson's office," Raymond announced to the liveried doorman who'd opened the heavy wrought-iron and glass door.

"The doctor's office has its own entrance," the doorman replied. He reopened the door behind Raymond, stepped out onto the sidewalk and pointed south.

Raymond touched the tip of his hat in appreciation before moving down to this private entrance. A sign of engraved brass read: PLEASE RING AND THEN ENTER. Raymond did as he was told.

As the door closed behind him, Raymond was immediately pleased. The office looked and even smelled like money. It was sumptuously appointed with antiques and thick oriental carpets. The walls were covered with nineteenth-century art.

Raymond advanced to an elegant, boulle-work French desk. A well-dressed, matronly receptionist glanced up at him over her reading glasses. A nameplate sat on the desk facing Raymond. It said: MRS. ARTHUR P. AUCHINCLOSS.

Raymond gave his name, being sure to emphasize the fact that he was a physician. He was well aware that some doctors' receptionists could be uncomfortably imperious if they didn't know a visitor was a member of the trade.

"The doctor is expecting you," Mrs. Auchincloss said. Then she politely asked Raymond to wait in the waiting room.

"It's a beautiful office," Raymond said to make conversation.

"Indeed," Mrs. Auchincloss said.

"Is it a large office?" Raymond asked.

"Yes, of course," Mrs. Auchincloss said. "Dr. Anderson is a very busy man. We have four full examining rooms and an X-ray room."

Raymond smiled. It wasn't difficult for him to guess the astronomical overhead that Dr. Anderson had been duped into assuming by so-called productivity experts during the heyday of "fee-for-service" medicine. From Raymond's point of view, Dr.

Anderson was the perfect quarry as a potential partner. Although the doctor undoubtedly still had a small backlog of wealthy patients willing to pay cash to retain their old, comfortable relationship, Dr. Anderson had to have been being squeezed by managed care.

"I suppose that means a large staff," Raymond said.

"We're down to one nurse," Mrs. Auchincloss said. "It's hard to find appropriate help these days."

Yeah, sure, Raymond mused. One nurse for four examining rooms unquestionably meant the doctor was struggling. But Raymond didn't vocalize his thoughts. Instead he let his eyes roam around the carefully wallpapered walls and said: "I've always admired these old-school, Park Avenue offices. They are so civilized and serene. They can't help but impart a feeling of trust."

"I'm sure our patients feel the same way," Mrs. Auchincloss said.

An interior door opened and a bejeweled, Gucci-draped, elderly woman stepped into the reception area. She was painfully thin and had suffered so many face-lifts that her mouth was drawn into a taut, unremitting smirk. Behind her was Dr. Waller Anderson.

Raymond's and Waller's eyes crossed for a fleeting moment as the doctor guided his patient to the receptionist and gave instructions of when he should see her next.

Raymond assessed the doctor. He was tall and had a refined look that Raymond sensed he possessed as well. But Waller wasn't tanned. In fact, his complexion had a grayish cast, and he looked strained with sad eyes and hollow cheeks. As far as Raymond was concerned, hard times were written all over his face.

After warm goodbyes to his patient, Waller motioned Raymond to follow him. He led down a long corridor that gave access to the examining rooms. At the end he preceded Raymond into his private office, then closed the door after them.

Waller introduced himself cordially but with obvious reserve. He took Raymond's hat and coat, which he carefully hung in a small closet.

"Coffee?" Waller asked.

"By all means," Raymond said.

A few minutes later, both with coffee, and with Waller behind his desk and Raymond sitting in a chair in front, Raymond began his pitch.

"These are tough times to be practicing medicine," Raymond said.

Waller made a sound that was akin to a laugh, but it was bereft of humor. Obviously he wasn't amused.

"We can offer you an opportunity to significantly augment your income as well as provide a state-of-the-art service to select patients," Raymond said. For the most part Raymond's presentation was a practiced speech that he'd perfected over the years.

"Is there anything illegal about this?" Waller interjected. His tone was serious, almost irritable. "If there is, I'm not interested."

"Nothing illegal," Raymond assured him. "Just extremely confidential. From our phone call, you said you would be willing to keep this conversation just among you, me, and Dr. Daniel Levitz."

"As long as my silence is not felonious in and of itself," Waller said. "I will not be duped into being an accessory."

"No need to worry," Raymond said. He smiled. "But if you do decide to join our group, you will be asked to sign an affidavit concerning confidentiality. Only then will you be told the specific details."

"I don't have any trouble with signing an affidavit," Waller said. "As long as I'm not breaking any law."

"Well, then," Raymond said. He put his coffee cup on the edge of Waller's desk to free up his hands. He fervently believed that hand gestures were important for impact. He started by telling about his chance meeting seven years previously with Kevin Marshall who'd given a poorly attended presentation at a national meeting that dealt with homologous transposition of chromosome parts between cells.

"Homologous transposition?" Waller questioned. "What the devil is that?" Having been through medical school prior to the revolution in molecular biology, he was unfamiliar with the terms.

Raymond patiently explained and used for his example the short arms of chromosome 6.

"So this Kevin Marshall developed a way to take a piece of chromosome from one cell and exchange it for the same piece in the same location of another cell," Waller said.

"Exactly," Raymond said. "And for me it was like an epiphany. I immediately saw the clinical application. Suddenly it was potentially possible to create an immunological double of an individual. As I'm sure you are aware, the short arm of chromosome six contains the major histocompatibility complex."

"Like an identical twin," Waller said with growing interest.

"Even better than an identical twin," Raymond said. "The immunological double is created in an appropriately sized animal species that can be sacrificed on demand. Few people would be able to have an identical twin sacrificed."

"Why wasn't this published?" Waller asked.

"Dr. Marshall fully intended to publish," Raymond said. "But there were some minor details he wanted to work out before he did so. It was his department head that forced him to present at the meeting. Lucky for us!

"After hearing the talk, I approached him and convinced him to go private. It wasn't easy, but what tipped the scales in our favor was that I promised him the lab of his dreams with no interference from academia. I assured him that he would be given any and every piece of equipment he wanted."

"You had such a lab?" Waller asked.

"Not at the time," Raymond admitted. "Once I had agreement from him, I approached an international biotechnology giant, which will go nameless until you agree to join our group. With some difficulty I sold them on the idea of creatively marketing this phenomenon."

"And how is that done?" Waller asked.

Raymond moved forward in his chair and locked eyes with Waller. "For a price we create an immunological double for a client," he said. "As you can well imagine, it is a significant price but not unreasonable for the peace of mind it affords. But how we really make money is that the client must pay a yearly tuition to maintain his double."

"Sort of like an initiation fee and then dues," Waller said.

"That's another way to look at it," Raymond agreed.

"How do I benefit?" Waller asked.

"Myriad ways," Raymond said. "I've constructed the business like a merchandising pyramid. For every client you recruit, you get a percentage, not only of the initial price but each year from the tuition. On top of that, we will encourage you to recruit other physicians like yourself with collapsing patient bases but who still have a number of wealthy, health-conscious, cash-paying patients. With every successful physician recruitment, you get percentages from each of his recruitment efforts. For instance, if you choose to join, Dr. Levitz, who recommended you, will receive percentages from all your successes. You don't have to be an accountant to understand that with a little effort you could be earning a substantial income. And as an added incentive, we can offer the payments offshore so they will accrue tax-free."

"Why all the secrecy?" Waller asked.

"For obvious reasons as far as the offshore accounts are concerned," Raymond said. "As for the whole program, there have been ethical issues that have been overlooked. Consequently, the biotechnology company that is making this all possible is paranoid about bad publicity. Frankly, the use of animals for transplantation offends some people, and we certainly do not want to be forced to deal with animal-rights zealots. Besides, this is an expensive operation and can be made available to only a few highly select people. That violates the concept of equality."

"May I ask how many clients have taken advantage of this plan?"

"Laymen or physicians?" Raymond asked.

"Laymen," Waller said.

"Around one hundred," Raymond said.

"Has anybody had to utilize the resource?"

"As a matter of fact, four have," Raymond said. "Two kidneys and two livers have been transplanted. All are doing superbly without medication and without any signs of rejection. And, I might add, there is a substantial additional charge for the harvest and transplantation, and the involved physicians get the same percentages of these fees."

"How many physicians are involved?" Waller asked.

"Fewer than fifty," Raymond said. "We started slowly on recruitment, but it is now speeding up."

"How long has this program been going on?" Waller asked.

"About six years," Raymond said. "It's been a significant outlay of capital and a lot of effort, but it is now beginning to pay off handsomely. I should remind you that you will be getting in at a relatively early date, so the pyramid structure will benefit you greatly."

"It sounds interesting," Waller said. "God knows I could use some additional income with my falling patient base. I've got to do something before I lose this office."

"It would be a pity," Raymond agreed.

"Can I think about it for a day or so?" Waller asked.

Raymond stood up. Experience told him he'd made another score. "By all means," he said graciously. "I'd also invite you to call Dr. Levitz. He'd recommended you highly, and he's extraordinarily satisfied with the arrangements."

Five minutes later Raymond exited onto the sidewalk and turned south down Park Avenue. His walk had an extra bounce to it. With the blue sky, the clear air, and the hint of spring, he felt on top of the world, especially with the pleasurable rush of adrenaline that a successful recruitment always gave him. Even the unpleasantness of the previous couple of days seemed insignificant. The future was bright and full of promise.

But then near disaster came out of nowhere. Distracted by his victory, Raymond almost stepped from the curb into the path of a speeding city bus. Wind from the hurling vehicle blew off his hat while filthy gutter water sprayed the front of his cashmere coat.

Raymond staggered back, dazed from his narrow escape from what might have been a horrible death. New York was a city of sudden extremes.

"You okay, buddy?" a passerby asked. He handed Raymond his dented fedora.

"I'm fine, thank you," Raymond said. He looked down at the front of his coat and felt ill. The episode seemed metaphorical and brought back the anxiety he'd experienced over the unfortunate Franconi business. The muck reminded him of having to deal with Vinnie Dominick.

Feeling chastened, Raymond crossed the street with much more care. Life was full of dangers. As he walked toward Sixty-fourth Street, he began to worry about the other two transplant cases. He'd never considered the problem an autopsy posed to his program until the Franconi dilemma.

All at once, Raymond decided he'd better check the status of the other patients. There was no doubt in his mind that Taylor Cabot's threat had been real. If one of the patients happened to be autopsied sometime in the future for whatever reason, and the media got hold of the results, it could spell disaster. GenSys would probably drop the whole operation.

Raymond quickened his pace. One patient lived in New Jersey, the other in Dallas. He thought he'd better get on the phone and talk with the recruiting doctors.

CHAPTER 9

"Hello!" Candace's voice called out. "Anybody home?"

Kevin's hand flinched at the unexpected noise. The lab techs had long since left for the day, and the laboratory had been silent save for the low hum of the refrigeration units. Kevin had stayed to run another southern blot analysis to separate DNA fragments, but at the sound of Candace's voice, he'd missed one of the wells with the micropipette. The fluid had run out over the surface of the gel. The test was ruined; he'd have to start again.

"Over here!" Kevin yelled. He put down the pipette and stood up. Through the reagent bottles atop the lab bench, he could see Candace across the room, standing in the doorway.

"Am I coming at a bad time?" Candace asked as she approached.

"No, I was just finishing up," Kevin said. He hoped he wasn't being too transparent.

Although he was frustrated about the wasted time he'd spent on the procedure, Kevin was pleased to see Candace. During lunch that day, he'd worked up the courage to invite Candace and Melanie to his house for tea. Both had accepted with alacrity. Melanie had admitted that she'd always been curious to see what the house looked like on the inside.

The afternoon had been a big success. Undoubtedly, the key ingredient for the afternoon's success was the personalities of the two ladies. There was never a pause in the conversation. Another contributing factor had been the wine that they'd all decided upon instead of tea. As a member of the Zone's elite, Kevin was given a regular allotment of French wine which he rarely drank. Consequently, he had an impressive cellar.

The major topic of conversation had been the U.S., a favorite pastime for temporary American expatriates. Each of the three had extolled and argued the virtues of their hometown. Melanie loved New York and contended it was in a class all its own; Candace said that Pittsburgh's quality of life was rated one of the highest; and Kevin praised the intellectual stimulation of Boston. What they had purposefully avoided discussing was Kevin's emotional outburst at the commissary during lunch.

At the time, both Candace and Melanie questioned what he'd meant by being terrified of overstepping the bounds. But they didn't persist when it became clear that Kevin was overly upset and reluctant to explain. Intuitively, the women had decided it best to change the subject, at least for the time.

"I've come to see if I can drag you over to meet Mr. Horace Winchester," Candace said. "I told him about you, and he'd like to thank you in person."

"I don't know if that is a good idea," Kevin said. He could feel himself tense.

"On the contrary," Candace said. "After what you said at lunch, I think you should see the good side of what you have been able to accomplish. I'm sorry that what I said made you feel so terrible."

Candace's remark was the first reference to Kevin's lunch outburst since its occurrence. Kevin's pulse quickened.

"It wasn't your fault," he said. "I'd been upset before your comments."

"Then come meet Horace," Candace said. "His recovery is fantastic. He's doing so well, in fact, that an intensive-care nurse like me is just about unnecessary."

"I wouldn't know what to say," Kevin mumbled.

"Oh, it doesn't matter what you say," Candace said. "The man is so thankful. Just a few days ago, he was so sick he thought he was going to die. Now he feels like he's been given a new lease on life. Come on! It can't help but make you feel good."

Kevin struggled to think up a reason not to go and then was saved by another voice. It was Melanie.

"Ah, my two favorite drinking buddies," Melanie said, coming into the room. She'd caught sight of Candace and Kevin through the open door. She'd been on her way to her own lab down the hall. She was dressed in blue coveralls which had ANIMAL CENTER embroidered on the breast pocket.

"Are either of you guys hungover?" Melanie asked. "I've still got a little buzz. God, we went through two bottles of wine. Can you believe it?"

Neither Candace or Kevin responded.

Melanie looked back and forth between their faces. She sensed something was wrong.

"What is this—a wake?" she asked.

Candace smiled. She loved Melanie's outspoken irreverence. "Hardly," Candace said. "Kevin and I are at a standoff. I was just trying to talk him into going over to the hospital to meet Mr. Winchester. He's already out of bed and feeling chipper. I told him about you guys, and he'd like to meet both of you."

"I hear he owns a string of resort hotels," Melanie said with a wink. "Hey, maybe we can finagle some vouchers for complimentary drinks."

"As appreciative and as wealthy as he is, you could very well do better than that," Candace said. "The problem is that Kevin doesn't want to go."

"How come, sport?" Melanie asked.

"I thought it would be a good idea for him to see the good side of what he's been able to accomplish," Candace added.

Candace caught Melanie's eye. Melanie understood Candace's motivations immediately.

"Yeah," Melanie said. "Let's get some positive feedback from a real, live patient. That should justify all this hard work and give us a boost."

"I think it will make me feel worse," Kevin said. Ever since getting back to the lab, he'd been trying to concentrate on basic research to avoid facing his fears. The ploy had worked to an extent until his curiosity made him call up the Isla Francesca graphic on his computer terminal. Playing with the data had had an effect as bad as the smoke.

Melanie put her hands on her hips. "Why?" she asked. "I don't understand."

"It's hard to explain," Kevin said evasively.

"Try me," Melanie challenged.

"Because seeing him will remind me of things I'm trying not to think about," Kevin said. "Like what happened to the other patient."

"You mean his double, the bonobo?" Melanie asked.

Kevin nodded. His face was now flushed, almost as bad as it had been at the commissary.

"You're taking this animal-rights issue even more seriously than I am," Candace remarked.

"I'm afraid it goes beyond animal rights," Kevin said.

A tense silence intervened. Melanie glanced at Candace. Candace shrugged, suggesting she was at a loss.

"Okay, enough is enough!" Melanie said with sudden resolve. She reached up, placed both hands on Kevin's shoulders, and pushed him down onto his laboratory stool.

"Up until this afternoon I thought we were just colleagues," she said. She leaned over and put her sharp-featured face close to Kevin's. "But now I feel differently. I got to know you a little bit, which I must say I appreciated, and I no longer think of you as an icy, aloof, intellectual snob. In fact I think we are friends. Am I right?"

Kevin nodded. He was forced to look up into Melanie's black, marblelike eyes.

"Friends talk to each other," Melanie said. "They communicate. They don't hide their feelings and make others feel uncomfortable. Do you know what I'm saying?"

"I think so," Kevin said. He'd never considered the idea his behavior was capable of making others uncomfortable.

"Think so?" Melanie chided. "How can I explain it so that you know so!"

Kevin swallowed. "I guess I know so."

Melanie rolled her eyes in frustration. "You are so evasive, it drives me bananas. But that's okay; I can deal with it. What I can't deal with is your outburst at lunch. And when I tried to ask you what's wrong, you gave some vague comment about 'overstepping the bounds' and then clammed up, unable to talk about it. You can't let this fester, whatever it is that's bothering you. It will only hurt you and impede your friendships."

Candace nodded agreement with all that Melanie had expressed.

Kevin looked back and forth between the two outspoken and tenacious women. As much as he resisted expressing his fears, at the moment he didn't think he had much choice, especially with Melanie's face inches away from his own. Not knowing how to begin he said: "I've seen smoke coming from Isla Francesca."

"What's Isla Francesca?" Candace asked.

"It's the island where the transgenic bonobos go once they reach age three," Melanie said. "So what's with smoke?"

Kevin stood and motioned for the women to follow him. He walked over to his desk. With his index finger he pointed out the window toward Isla Francesca. "I've seen the smoke three times," he said. "It's always from the same place just to the left of the limestone ridge. It's only a little curl snaking up into the sky, but it persists."

Candace squinted. She was mildly nearsighted, but for vanity reasons didn't wear glasses. "Is it the farthest island?" she asked. She thought she could just make out some brownish smudges on its spine that could have been rock. In the late-afternoon sunlight, the other islands in the chain appeared like homogeneous mounds of dark green moss.

"That's the one," Kevin said.

"So, big deal!" Melanie commented. "A couple of little fires. With all the lightning around here it's no wonder."

"That's what Bertram Edwards suggested," Kevin said. "But it can't be lightning."

"Who's Bertram Edwards?" Candace asked.

"Why can't it be lightning?" Melanie asked, ignoring Candace. "Maybe there's some metal ore in that rocky ridge."

"Ever hear the expression lightning never strikes the same place twice?" Kevin questioned. "The fire is not from lightning. Besides, the smoke persisted and has never moved."

"Maybe some native people live out there," Candace said.

"GenSys was very sure that was not the case before choosing the island," Kevin said.

"Maybe some local fishermen visit," Candace suggested.

"All the locals know it is forbidden," Kevin said. "Because of the new Equatoguinean law it would be a capital offense. There's nothing out there that would be worth dying for."

"Then who started the fires?" Candace asked.

"Good God, Kevin!" Melanie exclaimed suddenly. "I'm beginning to get an idea what you're thinking. But let me tell you, it's preposterous."

"What's preposterous?" Candace asked. "Will someone clue me in?"

"Let me show you something else," Kevin said. He turned to his computer terminal and with a few keystrokes called up the graphic of the island. He explained the system to the women, and as a demonstration, brought up the location of Melanie's double. The little red light blinked just north of the escarpment very close to where his own had the day before.

"You have a double?" Candace asked. She was dumbfounded.

"Kevin and I were the guinea pigs," Melanie said. "Our doubles were the first. We had to prove that the technology really works."

"Okay, now that you women know how the locator system operates," Kevin said, "let me show you what I did an hour ago, and we'll see if we get the same disturbing result." Kevin's fingers played over the keyboard. "What I'm doing is instructing the computer to automatically locate all seventy-three of the doubles sequentially. The creatures' numbers will occur in the corner followed by the blinking light on the graphic. Now watch." Kevin clicked to start.

The system worked smoothly with only a short delay between the number appearing and then the red blinking light.

"I thought there were closer to a hundred animals," Candace said.

"There are," Kevin said. "But twenty-two of them are less than three years old. They are in the bonobo enclosure at the animal center."

"Okay," Melanie said after a few minutes of watching the computer function. "It's working just as you said. What's so disturbing?"

"Just hold on," Kevin said.

All at once the number 37 appeared but no blinking red light. After a few moments, a prompt flashed onto the screen. It said: ANIMAL NOT LOCATED: CLICK TO RECOMMENCE.

Melanie looked at Kevin. "Where's number thirty-seven?"

Kevin sighed. "What's left is in the incinerator," he said. "Number thirty-seven was Mr. Winchester's double. But that's not what I wanted to show you." Kevin clicked and the program restarted. Then it stopped again at forty-two.

"Was that Mr. Franconi's double?" Candace asked. "The other liver transplant?"

Kevin shook his head. He pressed several keys, asking the computer the identity of forty-two. The name Warren Prescott appeared.

"So where's forty-two?" Melanie asked.

"I don't know for sure, but I know what I fear," Kevin said. Kevin clicked and again the numbers and red lights alternately flashed on the screen.

When the entire program had run its course, it had indicated that seven of the bonobo doubles were unaccounted for, not including Franconi's, which had been sacrificed.

"Is this what you found earlier?" Melanie asked.

Kevin nodded. "But it wasn't seven, it was twelve. And although some of the ones that were missing this morning are still missing, most of them have reappeared."

"I don't understand," Melanie said. "How can that be?"

"When I toured that island way back before all this started," Kevin said, "I remember seeing some caves in that limestone cliff. What I'm thinking is that our creations are going into the caves, maybe even living in them. It's the only way I can think of to explain why the grid would fail to pick them up."

Melanie brought up a hand to cover her mouth. Her eyes reflected a flicker of horror and dismay.

Candace saw Melanie's reaction. "Hey, come on, guys," she pleaded. "What's wrong? What are you thinking?"

Melanie lowered her hand. Her eyes were locked on Kevin's. "What Kevin was referring to when he said he was terrified he'd overstepped the bounds," she explained in a slow, deliberate voice, "was the fear that he'd created a human."

"You're not serious!" Candace exclaimed, but a glance at Kevin and then at Melanie indicated that she was.

For a full minute no one spoke.

Finally Kevin broke the silence. "I'm not suggesting a real human being in the guise of an ape," Kevin said finally. "I'm suggesting that I've inadvertently created a kind of protohuman. Maybe something akin to our distant ancestral forebears who spontaneously appeared in nature from apelike animals four or five million years ago. Maybe back then the critical mutations responsible for the change occurred in the developmental genes I've subsequently learned are on the short arm of chromosome six."

Candace found herself blankly gazing out the window, while her mind replayed the scene two days previous in the OR when the bonobo was about to be inducted under anesthesia. He'd made curious humanlike sounds and tried desperately to keep his hands free so that he could continue to make the same wild gesture. He'd been constantly opening and closing his fingers and then sweeping his hands away from his body.

"You're talking about some early hominidlike creature, something on the order of Homo erectus," Melanie said. "It's true we noticed the infant transgenic bonobos tended to walk upright more than their mothers. At the time we just thought it was cute."

"Not so early a hominid as not to have used fire," Kevin said. "Only true early man has used fire. And that's what I'm worried I've been seeing on the island: campfires."

"So, to put it bluntly," Candace said, turning away from the window. "We've got a bunch of cavemen out there like back in prehistoric time."

"Something like that," Kevin said. As he'd expected the women were aghast. Strangely, he actually felt a little better now that he'd voiced his anxieties.

"What are we going to do?" Candace demanded. "I'm certainly not going to be involved with sacrificing any more until this is resolved one way or the other. I was having a hard enough time dealing with the situation when I thought the victim was an ape."

"Wait a sec," Melanie said. She spread her hands with fingers apart. Her eyes were blazing anew. "Maybe we're jumping to conclusions here. There's no proof of all this. Everything we've been talking about is circumstantial at best."

"True, but there's more," Kevin said. He turned back to the computer and instructed it to display the locations of all the bonobos on the island simultaneously. Within seconds, two red splotches began pulsating. One was in the location where Melanie's double had been. The other was north of the lake. Kevin looked up at Melanie. "What does this data suggest to you?"

"It suggests there are two groups," she said. "Do you think it is permanent?"

"It was the same earlier," Kevin said. "I think it is a real phenomenon. Even Bertram mentioned it. That's not typical of bonobos. They get along in larger social groups than chimps, plus these are all relatively young animals. They should all be in one group."

Melanie nodded. Over the previous five years she'd learned a lot about bonobo behavior.

"And there is something else more upsetting," Kevin said. "Bertram told me one of the bonobos killed one of the pygmies on the retrieval of Winchester's double. It wasn't an accident. The bonobo aggressively threw a rock. That kind of aggression is more associated with human behavior than with bonobos."

"I'd have to agree," Melanie said. "But it's still circumstantial. All of it."

"Circumstantial or not," Candace said, "I'm not going to have it on my conscience."

"I feel the same way," Melanie said. "I've spent today getting two new female bonobos started on the egg-collection protocol. I'm not going to proceed until we find out if this wild idea about these possible protohumans is valid or not."

"That's not going to be easy," Kevin said. "To prove it, somebody has to go to the island. The trouble is there are only two people who can authorize a visit: Bertram Edwards or Siegfried Spallek. I already tried to talk with Bertram, and even though I brought up the issue about the smoke, he made it very clear that no one was allowed near the island except for a pygmy who brings supplementary food."

"Did you tell him what you are worried about?" Melanie asked.

"Not in so many words," Kevin said. "But he knew. I'm sure of it. He wasn't interested. The problem is that he and Siegfried have been included in the project bonuses. Consequently, they are going to make damn sure nothing threatens it. I'm afraid they're venal enough not to care what's on the island. And on top of their venality we have to weigh in Siegfried's sociopathy."

"Is he that bad?" Candace asked. "I'd heard rumors."

"Whatever you heard, it's ten times worse," Melanie said. "He's a major sleazeball. To give you an example, he executed some impoverished Equatoguinean men because they'd been caught poaching in the Zone, where he likes to hunt."

"He killed them himself?" Candace questioned with shock and revulsion.

"Not by himself," Melanie said. "He had the men tried in a kangaroo court here in Cogo. Then they were executed by a handful of Equatoguinean soldiers at the soccer field."

"And to add insult to injury," Kevin said, "he uses the skulls as bowls for odds and ends on his desk."

"Sorry I asked," Candace said with a shiver.

"What about Dr. Lyons?" Melanie asked.

Kevin laughed. "Forget it. He's more venal than Bertram. This whole operation is his baby. I tried to talk to him about the smoke, too. He was even less receptive. Claimed it was my imagination. Frankly I don't trust him, although I have to give him credit for being generous with bonuses and stocks. He's cleverly given everyone connected with the project a real stake in the venture, particularly Bertram and Siegfried."

"So, that leaves it all up to us," Melanie said. "Let's find out if it's your imagination or not. What do you say the three of us take a quick trip to Isla Francesca?"

"You're joking," Kevin said. "It's a capital offense without authorization."

"It's a capital offense for locals," Melanie said. "That can't apply to us. In our case, Siegfried has to answer to GenSys."

"Bertram specifically forbade visits," Kevin said. "I offered to go by myself, and he said no."

"Well, big deal," Melanie said. "So he gets mad. What is he going to do, fire us? I've been here long enough so that I don't think that would be half bad. Besides, they can't do without you. That's the reality."

"Do you think it might be dangerous?" Candace asked.

"Bonobos are peaceful creatures," Melanie said. "Much more so than chimps, and chimps aren't dangerous unless you corner them."

"What about the man who was killed?" Candace said.

"That was during a retrieval," Kevin said. "They had to get close enough to shoot a dart gun. Also, it was the fourth retrieval."

"All we want to do is observe," Melanie said.

"Okay, how do we get there?" Candace asked.

"Drive, I guess," Melanie said. "That's how they go when they do a release or a retrieval. There must be some kind of bridge."

"There's a road that goes east along the coast," Kevin said. "It's paved to the native village then it becomes a track. That's how I went on the visit to the island before we started the program. For a hundred feet or so the island and the mainland are only separated by a channel thirty feet wide. Back then there was a wire suspension bridge stretched between two mahogany trees."

"Maybe we can view the animals without even going across," Candace said. "Let's do it."

"You ladies are fearless," Kevin remarked.

"Hardly," Melanie said. "But I don't see any problem with driving up there and checking the situation out. Once we know what we're dealing with, we can make a better decision about what we want to do."

"When do you want to do this?" Kevin questioned.

"I'd say now," Melanie replied. She glanced at her watch. "There's no better time. Ninety percent of the population of the town is either at the waterfront chickee bar, splashing around in the pool, or sweating buckets at the athletic center."

Kevin sighed, let his arms fall limply to his sides, and capitulated. "Whose car should we take?" he asked.

"Yours," Melanie said without hesitation. "Mine doesn't even have four-wheel drive."

As the trio descended the stairs and made their way across the sweltering blacktop of the parking area, Kevin had the gnawing sense they were making a mistake. But in the face of the women's resolve, he felt reluctant to voice his reservations.

On the east exit of the town, they passed the athletic center's tennis courts, which were chockful of players. Between the humidity and heat, the players looked as drenched as if they'd jumped into a swimming pool with their tennis outfits on.

Kevin drove. Melanie sat in the front passenger seat, while Candace sat in the back. The windows were all open, since the temperature had fallen into the high eighties. The sun was low in the west, directly behind them and peeking in and out of clouds along the horizon.

Just beyond the soccer field the vegetation closed in around the road. Brightly colored birds flitted in and out of the deepening shadows. Large insects annihilated themselves against the windshield like miniature kamikaze pilots.

"The jungle looks dense," Candace said. She'd never traveled east from the town.

"You have no idea," Kevin said. When he'd first arrived he'd tried to take some hikes in the area, but with the profusion of vines and creepers, it was all but impossible without a machete.

"I just had a thought about the aggression issue," Melanie said. "The passivity of bonobo society is generally attributed to its matriarchal character. Because of the skewed demand for male doubles, our program has a population that's mostly male. There has to be a lot of competition for the few females."

"That's a good point," Kevin agreed. He wondered why Bertram hadn't thought of it.

"Sounds like my type of place," Candace joked. "Maybe I should book Isla Francesca instead of Club Med on my next vacation."

Melanie laughed. "Let's go together," she said.

They passed a number of Equatoguineans on their way home from work in Cogo. Most of the women carried jugs and parcels on top of their heads. The men were generally empty-handed.

"It's a strange culture," Melanie commented. "The women do the lion's share of the work: growing the food, carrying the water, raising the kids, cooking the meals, taking care of the house."

"What do the men do?" Candace asked.

"Sit around and discuss metaphysics," Melanie said.

"I just had an idea," Kevin said. "I don't know why I didn't think of it before. Maybe we should talk to the pygmy who takes out the food to the island first and hear what he has to say."

"Sounds like a good idea to me," Melanie said. "Do you know his name?"

"Alphonse Kimba," Kevin said.

When they reached the native village, they pulled to a stop in front of the busy general store and got out. Kevin went inside to inquire after the pygmy.

"This place is almost too charming," Candace said as she looked around the neighborhood. "It looks African but like something you'd see in Disneyland."

GenSys had built the village with the cooperation of the Equatoguinean Minister of the Interior. The homes were circular, whitewashed mud brick with thatched roofs. Corrals for domestic animals were made of reed mats lashed to wooden stakes. The structures appeared traditional, but every one of them was new and spotless. They also had electricity and running water. Buried underground were powerlines and modern sewers.

Kevin returned quickly. "No problem," he said. "He lives close by. Come on, we'll walk."

The village was alive with men, women, and children. Traditional cooking fires were in the process of being lit. Everyone acted happy and friendly from having been recently freed from the captivity of the interminable rainy season.

Alphonse Kimba was less than five feet tall with skin as black as onyx. A constant smile dominated his wide, flat face as he welcomed his unexpected visitors. He tried to introduce his wife and child, but they were shy and shrunk back into the shadows.

Alphonse invited his guests to sit on a reed mat. He then got four glasses and poured a dollop of clear fluid into each from an old green bottle that had at one time contained motor oil.

His visitors warily swirled the fluid. They didn't want to seem ungrateful, but they were reluctant to drink.

"Alcohol?" Kevin asked.

"Oh, yes!" Alphonse said. His smile broadened. "It is lotoko from corn. Very good! I bring it from my home in Lomako." He sipped with intense enjoyment. In contrast to the Equatoguineans, Alphonse's English was accented with French, not Spanish. He was a member of the Mongandu people from Zaire. He'd been brought to the Zone with the first shipment of bonobos.

Since the drink contained alcohol, which would presumably kill potential micro-organisms, the guests cautiously tasted the brew. All of them made faces in spite of good intentions not to do so. The drink was powerfully pungent.

Kevin explained that they had come to ask about the bonobos on the island. He didn't mention his concern that their number included a strain of protohumans. He asked only if Alphonse thought they were acting like bonobos back in his home province in Zaire.

"They are all very young," Alphonse said. "So they are very unruly and wild."

"Do you go on the island often?" Kevin asked.

"No, I am forbidden," Alphonse said. "Only when we retrieve or release, and only then with Dr. Edwards."

"How do you get the extra food to the island?" Melanie asked.

"There is a small float," Alphonse said. "I pull it across the water with a rope, then pull it back."

"Are the bonobos aggressive with the food or do they share?" Melanie asked.

"Very aggressive," Alphonse said. "They fight like crazy, especially for the fruit. I also saw one kill a monkey."

"Why?" Kevin asked.

"I think to eat," Alphonse said. "He carried it away after the food I brought was all gone."

"That sounds more like a chimp," Melanie said to Kevin.

Kevin nodded. "Where on the island have the retrievals taken place?" he asked.

"All have been on this side of the lake and stream," Alphonse said.

"None have been over by the cliff?" Kevin asked.

"No, never," Alphonse said.

"How do you get to the island for the retrieval?" Kevin asked. "Does everybody use the float?"

Alphonse laughed heartily. He had to dry his eyes with his knuckle. "The float is too small. We'd all be supper for the crocs. We use the bridge."

"Why don't you use the bridge for the food?" Melanie asked.

"Because Dr. Edwards has to make the bridge grow," Alphonse said.

"Grow?" Melanie questioned.

"Yes," Alphonse said.

The three guests exchanged glances. They were confused.

"Have you seen any fire on the island?" Kevin asked, changing the subject.

"No fire," Alphonse said. "But I've seen smoke."

"And what did you think?" Kevin asked.

"Me?" Alphonse questioned. "I didn't think anything."

"Have you ever seen one of the bonobos do this?" Candace asked. She opened and closed her fingers then swept her hand away from her body in imitation of the bonobo in the operating room.

"Yes," Alphonse said. "Many do that when they finish dividing up the food."

"How about noise?" Melanie asked. "Do they make a lot of sounds?"

"A lot," Alphonse said.

"Like the bonobos back in Zaire?" Kevin asked.

"More," Alphonse said. "But back in Zaire I don't see the same bonobos so often as I do here, and I don't feed them. Back home they get their own food in the jungle."

"What kind of noise do they make?" Candace asked. "Can you give us an example."

Alphonse laughed self-consciously. He glanced around at his wife to make sure she wasn't listening. Then he softly vocalized: "Eeee, ba da, loo loo, tad tat." He laughed again. He was embarrassed.

"Do they hoot like chimps?" Melanie asked.

"Some," Alphonse said.

The guests looked at each other. They'd run out of questions for the moment. Kevin got up. The women did the same. They thanked Alphonse for his hospitality and handed back their unfinished drinks. If Alphonse was offended, he didn't show it. His smile didn't falter.

"There's one other thing," Alphonse said just before his guests departed. "The bonobos on the island like to show off. Whenever they come for the food, they make themselves stand up."

"All the time?" Kevin asked.

"Mostly," Alphonse said.

The group walked back through the village to the car. They didn't talk until Kevin had started the motor.

"Well, what do you guys think?" Kevin asked. "Should we continue? The sun's already set."

"I vote yes," Melanie said. "We've come this far."

"I agree," Candace said. "I'm curious to see this bridge that grows."

Melanie laughed. "Me, too. What a charming fellow."

Kevin drove away from the store, which was now busier than earlier. But he wasn't sure of his direction. The road into the village had simply expanded into the parking area for the store, and there was no indication of the track leading further east. To find it, he had to cruise the parking lot's perimeter.

Once on the track, they were impressed with how much easier it had been to travel on the improved road. The track was narrow, bumpy, and muddy. Grass about three feet tall grew down the median strip. Frequently branches stretched from one side to the other, slapping against the windshield and poking through the open windows. To avoid being hit by the snapping branches, they had to raise the windows. Kevin clicked on the air conditioner and the lights. The beams reflected off the surrounding vegetation and gave the impression of driving through a tunnel.

"How far do we have to go on this cow path?" Melanie asked.

"Only three or four miles," Kevin said.

"It's a good thing we have four-wheel drive," Candace remarked. She was holding on tightly to the overhead strap and still bouncing around. The seat belt wasn't helping. "The last thing I'd want to do is get stuck out here." She glanced out the side window at the inky black jungle and shivered. It was eerie. She couldn't see a thing despite patches of luminous sky above. And then there was the noise. Just during their short visit with Alphonse, the night creatures of the jungle had commenced their loud and monotonous chorus.

"What did you make of the things Alphonse said?" Kevin asked finally.

"I'd say the jury is still out," Melanie said. "But they're certainly deliberating."

"I think his comment about the bonobos being bipedal when they come to get the food is very disturbing," Kevin said. "The circumstantial evidence is adding up."

"The suggestion that they are communicating impressed me," Candace said.

"Yeah, but chimps and gorillas have been taught sign language," Melanie said. "And we know bonobos are more bipedal than any other apes. What impressed me was the aggressive behavior, although I stand by my idea that it might be from our mistake not to have produced more females to maintain the balance."

"Can chimps make those sounds that Alphonse imitated?" Candace asked.

"I don't think so," Kevin said. "And that's an important point. It suggests maybe their larynges are different."

"Do chimps really kill monkeys?" Candace asked.

"They do occasionally," Melanie said. "But I've never heard of a bonobo doing so."

"Hang on!" Kevin shouted as he braked.

The car lurched over a log strewn across the track.

"Are you okay?" he asked Candace, while glancing up into the rearview mirror.

"No problem," Candace said, although she'd been severely jolted. Luckily the seat belt had worked, and it had kept her head from hitting the roof.

Kevin slowed considerably for fear of encountering another log. Fifteen minutes later, they entered a clearing which marked the termination of the track. Kevin came to a halt. Directly ahead the headlight beams washed the front of a single-story cinder-block building with an overhead garage door.

"Is this it?" Melanie questioned.

"I guess," Kevin said. "The building is new to me."

Kevin switched off the lights and the engine. With the clearing open to the sky the level of illumination was adequate. For a moment no one moved.

"What's the story?" Kevin asked. "Are we going to check it out or what?"

"Might as well," Melanie said. "We've come this far." She opened her door and got out. Kevin did the same.

"I think I'll stay in the car," Candace said.

Kevin went to the building and tried the door. It was locked. He shrugged. "I can't imagine what's in there." Kevin slapped a mosquito on his forehead.

"How do we get to the island?" Melanie asked.

Kevin pointed to the right. "There's a track over there. It's only about fifty yards to the water's edge."

Melanie glanced up at the sky. It was a pale lavender. "It's going to be dark pretty soon. Do you have a flashlight in the car?"

"I think so," Kevin said. "More important, I have some mosquito spray. We're going to get eaten alive out here unless we use it."

They went back to the car. Just as they arrived, Candace climbed out.

"I can't stay in here by myself," she said. "It's too spooky."

Kevin got the mosquito spray. While the women doused themselves, he searched for the flashlight. He found it in the glove compartment.

After spraying himself, Kevin motioned for the women to follow him. "Stay close," he said. "The crocodiles and the hippos come out of the water at night."

"Is he joking?" Candace asked Melanie.

"I don't think so," Melanie said.

As soon as they entered the path, the illumination fell considerably although it was still light enough to walk without the flashlight. Kevin led while the two women crowded behind. The closer they got to the water the louder the chorus of insects and frogs became.

"How did I get myself into this?" Candace questioned. "I'm no outdoors person."

I can't even conceive of a crocodile or a hippo outside of a zoo. Hell, any bug bigger than my thumbnail terrifies me, and spiders, forget it."

All of the sudden, there was a crashing noise off to the left. Candace let out a muffled scream, as she grabbed Melanie who then did likewise. Kevin whimpered and switched on the light. He pointed the beam in the direction of the noise, but it only penetrated a few feet.

"What was that?" Candace demanded when she could find her voice.

"Probably a duiker," Kevin said. "They're a small breed of antelope."

"Antelope or elephant," Candace said. "It scared me."

"It scared me, too," Kevin said. "Maybe we should go back and return in the daytime."

"We've come all this way, for crissake," Melanie said. "We're there. I can hear the water."

For a moment no one moved. Sure enough, they could hear water lapping against the shore.

"What happened to all the night creatures?" Candace asked.

"Good question," Kevin said. "The antelope must have scared them as well."

"Turn the light off," Melanie said.

As soon as Kevin did, they all could see the shimmering surface of the water through the vegetation. It looked like liquid silver.

Melanie led the way as the chorus of night creatures recommenced. The path opened up into another clearing at the edge of the river. In the middle of the clearing was a dark object almost the size of the garage back where they'd left the car. Kevin walked up to it. It wasn't hard to figure out what it was: it was the bridge.

"It's a telescoping mechanism," Kevin said. "That's why Alphonse said that it could grow."

About thirty feet across the water was Isla Francesca. In the fading light, its dense vegetation appeared midnight-blue. Directly across from the telescoping bridge was a concrete structure that served as the support for the bridge when it was extended. Beyond that was an expansive clearing that extended to the east.

"Try extending the bridge," Melanie suggested.

Kevin switched on the flashlight. He found the control panel. There were two buttons: one red, the other green. He pushed the red one. When nothing happened, he pushed the green. When there still wasn't a reaction, he noticed a keyhole with the slot aligned with OFF.

"You need a key," he called.

Melanie and Candace had walked over to the water's edge.

"There's a bit of current," Melanie said. Leaves and other debris floated by slowly.

Candace looked up. The top branches of some of the trees that lined either bank almost touched. "Why do the creatures stay on the island?" she asked.

"Apes and monkeys don't go in the water, particularly deep water," Melanie explained. "That's why zoos only need a moat for their primate exhibits."

"What about crossing in the trees?" Candace asked.

Kevin joined the women at the riverbank. "The bonobos are relatively heavy fellows," he explained, "particularly ours. Most of them are already over a hundred pounds, and the branches up there aren't nearly strong enough to support their weight. Back before we put the first animals on the island, there were a couple of questionable places so those trees were cut down. But colobus monkeys still go back and forth."

"What are all those square objects in the field?" Melanie asked.

Kevin shined the flashlight. Its beam wasn't strong enough to make much difference at that distance. He turned it off and squinted in the half light. "They look like transport cages from the animal center," he said.

"I wonder what they are doing out there?" Melanie asked. "There're so many of them."

"No idea," Kevin said.

"How can we get some of the bonobos to appear?" Candace asked.

"By this time they're probably settling down for the night," Kevin said. "I doubt if we can."

"What about the float?" Melanie asked. "The mechanism that pulls it across must be like a clothesline. If it makes noise, they might hear it. It would be like a dinner bell and might bring them around."

"Guess it's worth a try," Kevin said. He glanced up and down the water's edge. "Trouble is, we don't have any idea where the float may be."

"I can't imagine it would be far," Melanie said. "You go east, I'll go west."

Kevin and Melanie walked in opposite directions. Candace stayed were she was, wishing she were back in her room in the hospital quarters.

"Here it is!" Melanie called out. She'd followed a path in the dense foliage for a short distance before coming to a pulley attached to a thick tree. A heavy rope hung around the pulley. One end disappeared into the water. The other end was tied to a four-foot square float nestled against the shore.

Kevin and Candace joined her. Kevin shined the flashlight across to the island. On the other side a similar pulley was attached to a similar tree.

Kevin handed the flashlight to Melanie and grasped the rope that drooped into the water. When he pulled, he could see the pulley on the other side swing out from the trunk of the tree.

Kevin pulled on the rope hand over hand. The pulleys complained bitterly with high-pitched squeaking noises. The float immediately moved away from the shore on its way to the other side.

"This might work," Kevin said. While he pulled, Melanie swept the other shore with the flashlight beam. When the float was halfway across, there was a loud splash to their right as a large object dropped into the water from the island.

Melanie shined the light in the direction of the splash. Two glowing slits of light reflected back from the surface of the water. Peering at them was a large crocodile.

"Good lord!" Candace said as she stepped back from the water.

"It's okay," Kevin said. He let go of the rope, reached down and picked up a stout stick. He threw the stick at the croc. With another loud splash the crocodile disappeared beneath the water.

"Oh, great!" Candace said. "Now we have no idea where he is."

"He's gone," Kevin said. "They're not dangerous unless you're in the water or they're very hungry."

"Who's to say he's not hungry?" Candace commented.

"There's plenty for them to eat out here," Kevin said as he picked up the rope and recommenced pulling. When the float reached the other side, he switched ropes and started pulling it back.

"Ah, it's too late," he said. "This isn't going to work. The closest nesting area we saw on the computer graphic is over a mile away. We'll have to try this in the daytime."

No sooner had these words escaped from his mouth when the night was shattered by a number of fearsome screams. At the same time, there was wild commotion in the bushes on the island as if a stampeding elephant was about to appear.

Kevin dropped the rope. Both Candace and Melanie fled back along the path a few steps before stopping. With pulses pounding they froze, waiting for another scream. With a shaking hand, Melanie shined the flashlight at the area where the commotion had occurred. Everything was still. Not a leaf moved.

Ten tense seconds passed that seemed more like ten minutes. The group strained their ears to pick up the slightest sound. There was nothing but utter silence. All the night creatures had fallen silent. It was as if the entire jungle was waiting for a catastrophe.

"What in heaven's name was that?" Melanie asked finally.

"I'm not sure I want to find out," Candace said. "Let's get out of here."

"It must have been a couple of the bonobos," Kevin said. He reached out and grabbed the rope. The float was being buffeted in midstream. He quickly hauled it in.

"I think Candace is right," Melanie said. "It's gotten too dark to see much even if they did appear. I'm spooked. Let's go!"

"You'll not get an argument from me," Kevin said as he made his way over to the women. "I don't know what we're doing here at this hour. We'll come back in the daylight."

They hurried along the path to the clearing as best they could. Melanie led with the flashlight. Candace was behind her, holding on to her blouse. Kevin brought up the rear.

"It would be great to get a key for this bridge," Kevin said as they passed the structure.

"And how do you propose to do that?" Melanie asked.

"Borrow Bertram's," Kevin said.

"But you told us he forbid anyone to go to the island," Melanie said. "He's certainly not going to lend the key."

"We'll have to borrow it without his knowledge," Kevin said.

"Oh, yeah, sure," Melanie said sarcastically.

They entered the tunnel-like path leading up to the car. Halfway to the parking area Melanie said: "God, it's dark. Am I holding the light okay for you guys?"

"It's fine," Candace said.

Melanie slowed then stopped.

"What's the matter?" Kevin asked.

"There's something strange," she said. She cocked her head to the side, listening.

"Now don't get me scared," Candace warned.

"The frogs and crickets haven't restarted their racket," Melanie said.

In the next instant all hell broke loose. A loud, repetitive stuttering noise splintered the jungle stillness. Branches, twigs, and leaves rained down on the group. Kevin recognized the noise and reacted by reflex. Extending his arms, he literally tackled the women so that all three fell to the moist insect-infested earth.

The reason Kevin recognized the sound was because he once had inadvertently witnessed the Equatoguinean soldiers practicing. The noise was the sound of a machine gun.

CHAPTER 10

MARCH 5, 1997
2:15 P.M.
NEW YORK CITY

"Excuse me, Laurie," Cheryl Myers said, standing in the doorway to Laurie's office. Cheryl was one of the forensic investigators. "We just received this overnight package, and I thought you might want it right away."

Laurie stood up and took the parcel. She was curious about what it could be. She looked at the label to find out the sender. It was CNN.

"Thanks, Cheryl," Laurie said. She was perplexed. She had no idea for the moment what CNN could have sent her.

"I see Dr. Mehta is not in," Cheryl said. "I brought up a chart for her that came in from University Hospital. Should I put it on her desk?" Dr. Riva Mehta was Laurie's office mate. They'd shared the space since both had started at the medical examiner's office six and a half years previously.

"Sure," Laurie said, preoccupied with her parcel. She got her finger under the flap and pulled it open. Inside was a videotape. Laurie looked at the label. It said: CARLO FRANCONI SHOOTING, MARCH 3, 1997.

After having finished her final autopsy that morning, Laurie had been ensconced in her office, trying to complete some of the twenty-odd cases that she had pending. She'd been busy reviewing microscopic slides, laboratory results, hospital records, and police reports, and for several hours had not thought of the Franconi business.

The arrival of the tape brought it all back. Unfortunately the video was meaningless without the body.

Laurie tossed the tape into her briefcase and tried to get back to work. But after fifteen minutes of wasted effort, she turned the light off under her microscope. She couldn't concentrate. Her mind kept toying with the baffling question of how the body had disappeared. It was as if it had been an amazing magic trick. One minute the body was safely stored in compartment one eleven and viewed by three employees, then poof, it was gone. There had to be an explanation, but try as she might, Laurie could not fathom it.

Laurie decided to head down to the basement to visit the mortuary office. She'd expected at least one tech to be available, but when she arrived the room was unoccupied. Undaunted, Laurie went over to the large, leather-bound log. Flipping the page, she looked for the entries that Mike Passano had shown her the previous night. She found them without difficulty. Taking a pencil from a collection in a coffee mug and a sheet of scratch paper, Laurie wrote down the names and accession numbers of the two bodies that had come in during the night shift: Dorothy Kline #101455 and Frank Gleason #100385. She also wrote down the names of the two funeral homes: Spoletto in Ozone Park, New York, and the Dickson in Summit, New Jersey.

Laurie was about to leave when her eye caught the large Rolodex on the corner of the desk. She decided to call each home. After identifying herself, she asked to speak to the managers.

What had sparked her interest in telephoning was the outside chance that either one of the pickups could have been bogus. She thought the chances were slim, since the night tech, Mike Passano, had said the homes had called before coming and presumably he was familiar with the people.

As Laurie expected, the pickups indeed were legitimate, both managers attesting to the fact that the bodies had come in to their respective homes and were at that time on view.

Laurie went back to the logbook and looked again at the names of the two arrivals. To be complete, she copied them down along with their accession numbers. The names were familiar to her, since she'd assigned them as autopsies the following morning to Paul Plodgett. But she wasn't as interested in the arrivals as the departures. The arrivals had come in with longtime ME employees, whereas the bodies that had gone out had done so with strangers.

Feeling frustrated, Laurie drummed her pencil on the desk surface. She was sure she had to be missing something. Once again, her eye caught the Rolodex which was open to the Spoletto Funeral Home. In the very back of Laurie's mind, the name made a hazy association. For a moment, she struggled with her memory. Why was that name familiar? Then she remembered. It had been during the Cerino affair. A man had been murdered in the Spoletto Funeral Home on orders from Paul Cerino, Franconi's predecessor.

Laurie pocketed her memo, pushed away from the desk and returned to the fifth floor. She walked directly to Jack's office. The door was ajar. She knocked on the jamb. Both Jack and Chet looked up from their respective labors.

"I had a thought," Laurie said to Jack.

"Just one?" Jack quipped.

Laurie threw her pencil at him, which he easily evaded. She plopped down in the chair to his right and told him about the mob connection with the Spoletto Funeral Home.

"Good grief, Laurie," Jack complained. "Just because there is a mob hit in a funeral home, doesn't mean that it is mob-connected."

"You don't think so?" Laurie asked. Jack didn't have to answer. She could see by his expression. And, now that she thought about her idea, she understood it was a ridiculous notion. She'd been grabbing for straws.

"Besides," Jack said. "Why won't you just leave this alone?"

"I told you," Laurie said. "It's a personal thing."

"Maybe I can channel your efforts into a more positive direction," Jack said. He motioned toward his microscope. "Take a look at a frozen section. Tell me what you think."

Laurie got up from the chair and leaned over the microscope. "What is this, the shotgun entrance wound?" she asked.

"Just as sharp as usual," Jack commented. "You're right on the money."

"Well, it's not a hard call," Laurie said. "I'd say the muzzle was within inches of the skin."

"My opinion exactly," Jack said. "Anything else?"

"My gosh, there's absolutely no extravasation of blood!" Laurie said. "None at all, so this had to have been a postmortem wound." She raised her head and looked at Jack. She was amazed. She'd assumed it had been the mortal wound.

"Ah, the power of modern science," Jack commented. "This floater you foisted on me is turning into a bastard of a case."

"Hey, you volunteered," Laurie said.

"I'm teasing," Jack said. "I'm glad I got the case. The shotgun wounds were definitely postmortem, so was the decapitation and removal of the hands. Of course the propeller injuries were, too."

"What was the cause of death?" Laurie asked.

"Two other gunshot wounds," Jack said. "One through the base of the neck." He pointed to an area just above his right collarbone. "And another in the left side that shattered the tenth rib. The irony was that both slugs ended up in the mass of shotgun pellets in the right upper abdominal area and were difficult to be seen on the X ray."

"Now that's a first," Laurie said. "Bullets hidden by shotgun pellets. Amazing! The beauty of this job is that you see new things every day."

"The best is yet to come," Jack said.

"This is a 'beaut,' " Chet said. He'd been listening to the conversation. "It'll be perfect for one of the forensic pathology dinner seminars."

"I think the shotgun blasts were an attempt to shield the victim's identity as much as the decapitation and removal of the hands," Jack said.

"In what way?" Laurie asked.

"I believe this patient had had a liver transplant," Jack said. "And not that long ago. The killer must have understood that such a procedure put the patient in a relatively small group, and hence jeopardized the chances of hiding the victim's identity."

"Was there much liver left?" Laurie asked.

"Very little," Jack said. "Most of it was destroyed by the shotgun injury."

"And the fish helped," Chet said.

Laurie winced.

"But I was able to find some liver tissue," Jack said. "We'll use that to corroborate the transplant. As we speak, Ted Lynch up in DNA is running a DQ alpha. We'll have the results in an hour or so. But for me the clincher was the sutures in the vena cava and the hepatic artery."

"What's a DQ alpha?" Laurie asked.

Jack laughed. "Makes me feel better that you don't know," he said, "because I had to ask Ted the same question. He told me it is a convenient and rapid DNA marker for differentiating two individuals. It compares the DQ region of the histocompatibility complex on chromosome six."

"What about the portal vein?" Laurie asked. "Were there sutures in it as well?"

"Unfortunately, the portal vein was pretty much gone," Jack said. "Along with a lot of the intestines."

"Well," Laurie said. "This should all make identification rather easy."

"My thought exactly," Jack said. "I've already got Bart Arnold hot on the trail. He's been in contact with the national organ procurement organization UNOS. He's also in the process of calling all the centers actively doing liver transplants, especially here in the city."

"That's a small list," Laurie said. "Good job, Jack."

Jack's face reddened slightly, and Laurie was touched. She thought he was immune to such compliments.

"What about the bullets?" Laurie asked. "Same gun?"

"We've packed them off to the police lab for ballistics," Jack said. "It was hard to say if they came from the same gun or not because of their distortion. One of them made direct contact with the tenth rib and was flattened. Even the second one wasn't in good shape. I think it grazed the vertebral column."

"What caliber?" Laurie asked.

"Couldn't tell from mere observation," Jack said.

"What did Vinnie say?" Laurie asked. "He's become pretty good at guessing."

"Vinnie's worthless today," Jack said. "He's been in the worst mood I've ever seen him in. I asked him what he thought, but he wouldn't say. He told me it was my job, and that he wasn't paid enough to be giving his opinions all the time."

"You know, I had a case similar to this back during that awful Cerino affair,"

Laurie said. She stared off and for a moment, her eyes glazed over. "The victim was a secretary of the doctor who was involved with the conspiracy. Of course, she'd not had a liver transplant, but the head and the hands were gone, and I did make the identification because of her surgical history."

"Someday you'll have to tell me that whole grisly story," Jack said. "You keep dropping tantalizing bits and pieces."

Laurie sighed. "I wish I could just forget the whole thing. It still gives me nightmares."

Raymond glanced at his watch as he opened the Fifth Avenue door to Dr. Daniel Levitz's office. It was two forty-five. Raymond had called the doctor three times starting just after eleven A.M., without success. On each occasion, the receptionist had promised Dr. Levitz would phone back, but he hadn't. In his agitated state, Raymond found the discourtesy aggravating. Since Dr. Levitz's office was just around the corner from Raymond's apartment, Raymond thought it was better to walk over than sit by the phone.

"Dr. Raymond Lyons," Raymond said with authority to the receptionist. "I'm here to see Dr. Levitz."

"Yes, Dr. Lyons," the receptionist said. She had the same cultivated, matronly look as Dr. Anderson's receptionist. "I don't have you down on my appointment sheet. Is the doctor expecting you?"

"Not exactly," Raymond said.

"Well, I'll let the doctor know you are here," the receptionist said noncommittally.

Raymond took a seat in the crowded waiting room. He picked up one of the usual doctor waiting-room magazines and flipped the pages without focusing on the images. His agitation was becoming tinged with irritation, and he began to wonder if it had been a bad decision to come to Dr. Levitz's office.

The job of checking on the first of the other two transplant patients had been easy. With one phone call Raymond had spoken with the recruiting doctor in Dallas, Texas. The doctor had assured Raymond that his kidney-transplant patient, a prominent local businessman, was doing superbly and was in no way a possible candidate for an autopsy. Before hanging up the doctor had promised Raymond to inform him if the situation were ever to change.

But with Dr. Levitz's failure to return Raymond's phone call, Raymond had not been able to check on the last case. It was frustrating and anxiety-producing.

Raymond's eyes roamed the room. It was as sumptuously appointed as Dr. Anderson's, with original oils, deep burgundy-colored walls, and oriental carpets. The patients patiently waiting were all obviously well-to-do as evidenced by their clothes, bearing, and jewels.

As the minutes ticked by, Raymond found his irritation mounting. What was adding insult to injury at the moment was Dr. Levitz's obvious success. It reminded Raymond of the absurdity of his own medical license being in legal limbo just because he'd gotten caught padding his Medicare claims. But here was Dr. Levitz working away in all this splendor with at least part of his receipts coming from taking care of a number of crime families. Obviously, it all represented dirty money. And on top of that Raymond was sure Levitz padded his Medicare claims. Hell, everybody did.

A nurse appeared and cleared her throat. Expectantly, Raymond moved to the edge of his seat. But the nurse called out another name. While the summoned patient got up, replaced his magazine, and disappeared into the bowels of the office, Raymond slouched back against the sofa and fumed. Being at the mercy of such people made Raymond long for financial security all the more. With this current "doubles" program he was so close. He couldn't let the whole enterprise crumble for some stupid, unexpected, easily remedied reason.

It was three-fifteen when finally Raymond was ushered into Daniel Levitz's inner sanctum. Levitz was a small, balding man with multiple nervous tics. He had a mustache but it was sparse and decidedly unmanly. Raymond had always wondered what it was about the man that apparently inspired confidence in so many patients.

"It's been one of those days," Daniel said by way of explanation. "I didn't expect you to drop by."

"I hadn't planned on it myself," Raymond said. "But when you didn't return my calls, I didn't think I had a choice."

"Calls?" Daniel questioned. "I didn't get any calls from you. I'll have to have another talk with that receptionist of mine. Good help is so difficult to come by these days."

Raymond was tempted to tell Daniel to cut the bull, but he resisted. After all, he was finally talking to the man, and turning the meeting into a confrontation wouldn't solve anything. Besides, as irritating as Daniel Levitz could be, he was also Raymond's most successful recruit. He had signed up twelve clients for the program as well as four doctors.

"What can I do for you?" Daniel asked. His head twitched several times in its usual and disconcerting way.

"First I want to thank you for helping out the other night," Raymond said. "From the absolute pinnacles of power it was thought to be an emergency. Publicity at this point would have meant an end to the whole enterprise."

"I was glad to be of service," Daniel said. "And pleased that Mr. Vincent Dominick was willing to help out to preserve his investment."

"Speaking of Mr. Dominick," Raymond said. "He paid me an unexpected visit yesterday morning."

"I hope on a cordial note," Daniel said. He was quite familiar with Dominick's career as well as his personality, and surmised that extortion would not be out of the question.

"Yes and no," Raymond admitted. "He insisted on telling me details I didn't want to know. Then he insisted on paying no tuition for two years."

"It could have been worse," Daniel said. "What does that mean to my percentage?"

"The percentage stays the same," Raymond said. "It's just that it becomes a percentage of nothing."

"So, I help and then get penalized!" Daniel complained. "That's hardly fair."

Raymond paused. He'd not thought about Daniel's loss of his cut of Dominick's tuition, yet it was something that had to be faced. At present, Raymond was reluctant to upset the man.

"You have a valid point," Raymond conceded. "Let's say we'll discuss it in the near future. At the moment, I have another concern. What's the status of Cindy Carlson?"

Cindy Carlson was the sixteen-year-old daughter of Albright Carlson, the Wall Street junk-bond mogul. Daniel had recruited Albright and his daughter as clients. As a youngster the daughter had suffered from glomerulonephritis. The malady had worsened during the girl's early teens to the point of kidney failure. Consequently, Daniel not only had the record number of clients, he also had the record number of harvests, two: Carlo Franconi and Cindy Carlson.

"She's been doing fine," Daniel said. "At least healthwise. Why do you ask?"

"This Franconi business has made me realize how vulnerable the enterprise is," Raymond admitted. "I want to be sure there are no other possible loose ends."

"Don't worry about the Carlsons," Daniel said. "They certainly aren't going to cause us any trouble. They couldn't be any more grateful. In fact, just last week Albright was talking about getting his wife out to the Bahamas to give a bone-marrow sample so she can become a client as well."

"That's encouraging," Raymond said. "We can always use more clients. But it's not the demand side of the enterprise that has me worried. Financially we couldn't be doing any better. We're ahead of all projections. It's the unexpected that has me worried, like Franconi."

Daniel nodded and then twitched. "There's always uncertainty," he said philosophically. "That's life!"

"The lower the level of uncertainty, the better I'll feel," Raymond said. "When I asked you about Cindy Carlson's status, you qualified your positive response as healthwise. Why?"

"Because she's a basket case mentally," Daniel said.

"How do you mean?" Raymond asked. Once again his pulse quickened.

"It's hard to imagine a kid not being a bit crazy growing up with a father like Albright Carlson," Daniel said. "Think about it. And then add the burden of a chronic illness. Whether that contributed to her obesity, I don't know. The girl is quite overweight. That's tough enough for anybody but especially so for a teen. The poor kid is understandably depressed."

"How depressed?" Raymond asked.

"Depressed enough to attempt suicide on two occasions," Daniel said. "And they weren't just childish bids for attention. They were bona fide attempts, and the only reason she's still with us is because she was discovered almost immediately and because she'd tried drugs the first time and hanging herself the second. If she'd had a gun she surely would have succeeded."

Raymond groaned out loud.

"What's the matter?" Daniel asked.

"All suicides are medical examiner cases," Raymond said.

"I hadn't thought of that," Daniel said.

"This is the kind of loose end I was referring to," Raymond said. "Damn! Just our luck!"

"Sorry to be the bearer of bad tidings," Daniel said.

"It's not your fault," Raymond said. "The important thing is that we recognize it for what it is, and that we understand we can't sit idly by and wait for catastrophe."

"I don't think we have much choice," Daniel said.

"What about Vincent Dominick?" Raymond said. "He's helped us once and with his own child ill, he has a vested interest in our program's future."

Dr. Daniel Levitz stared at Raymond. "Are you suggesting . . . ?"

Raymond didn't reply.

"This is where I draw the line," Daniel said. He stood up. "I'm sorry, but I have a waiting-room full of patients."

"Couldn't you call Mr. Dominick and just ask?" Raymond said. He felt a wave of desperation wash over him.

"Absolutely not," Daniel said. "I might take care of a number of criminally connected individuals, but I certainly don't get involved with their business."

"But you helped with Franconi," Raymond complained.

"Franconi was a corpse on ice at the medical examiner's office," Daniel said.

"Then give me Mr. Dominick's phone number," Raymond said. "I'll call him myself. And I'll need the Carlsons' address."

"Ask my receptionist," Daniel said. "Just tell her you're a personal friend."

"Thank you," Raymond said.

"But just remember," Daniel said. "I deserve and want the percentages that are due to me regardless of what happens between you and Vinnie Dominick."

At first the receptionist was reluctant to give Raymond the phone number and the addresses, but after a quick call to her boss, she relented. Wordlessly, she copied the information onto the back of one of Dr. Daniel Levitz's business cards and handed it to Raymond.

Raymond wasted no time getting back to his apartment on Sixty-fourth Street. As he came through the door, Darlene asked how the meeting with the doctor had gone.

"Don't ask," Raymond said curtly. He went into his paneled study, closed the door, and sat down at his desk. Nervously, he dialed the phone. In his mind's eye, he could see Cindy Carlson either scrounging around in the medicine cabinet for her mother's sleeping pills or hanging out in the local hardware store buying a length of rope.

"Yeah, what is it?" a voice said on the other end of the line.

"I'd like to speak to Mr. Vincent Dominick," Raymond said with as much authority as he could muster. He detested the necessity to deal with the likes of these people, but he had little choice. Seven years of intense labor and commitment were on the line, not to mention his entire future.

"Who's calling?"

"Dr. Raymond Lyons."

There was a pause before the man said: "Hang on!"

To Raymond's surprise he was put on hold with one of Beethoven's sonatas playing in the background. To Raymond it seemed like some sort of oxymoron.

A few minutes later Vinnie Dominick's dulcet voice came over the line. Raymond could picture the man's practiced and deceptive banality as if Vinnie were a well-dressed character actor playing himself.

"How did you get this number, Doctor?" Vinnie asked. His tone was nonchalant, yet somehow more threatening because of it. Raymond's mouth went bone-dry. He had to cough.

"Dr. Levitz gave it to me," Raymond managed.

"What can I do for you, Doctor?" Vinnie asked.

"Another problem has come up," Raymond croaked. He cleared his throat again. "I'd like to see you to discuss it."

There was a pause that went on for longer than Raymond could tolerate. Just when he was about to ask if Vinnie was still there, the mobster responded: "When I got involved with you people I thought it was supposed to give me peace of mind. I didn't think it was supposed to make my life more complicated."

"These are just minor growing pains," Raymond said. "In actuality, the project is going extremely well."

"I'll meet you in the Neopolitan Restaurant on Corona Avenue in Elmhurst in a half hour," Vinnie said. "Think you can find it?"

"I'm certain I can," Raymond said. "I'll take a cab, and I'll leave immediately."

"See you there," Vinnie said before hanging up.

Raymond rummaged hastily through the top drawer of his desk for his New York City map that included all five boroughs. He spread the map out on his desk, and using the index, located Corona Avenue in Elmhurst. He estimated that he could make it easily in half an hour provided the traffic wasn't bad on the Queensboro Bridge. That was a concern because it was almost four o'clock: the beginning of rush hour.

As Raymond came flying out of his study, pulling his coat back on, Darlene asked him where he was going. He told her he didn't have time to explain. He said he'd be back in an hour or so.

Raymond ran to Park Avenue, where he caught a cab. It was a good thing he'd brought his map along because the Afghan taxi driver had no idea even where Elmhurst was, much less Corona Avenue.

The trip was not easy. Just getting across the East Side of Manhattan took almost a quarter of an hour. And then the bridge was stop-and-go. By the time Raymond was supposed to be at the restaurant, his cab had just reached Queens. But from there it was easy going, and Raymond was only fifteen minutes late when he walked into the restaurant and pushed aside a heavy, velvet curtain.

It was immediately apparent the restaurant was not open for business. Most of the chairs were upside down on top of the tables. Vinnie Dominick was sitting by himself in one of the curved, red velvet–upholstered booths that lined the walls. In front of him were a newspaper and a small cup of espresso. A lighted cigarette lay in a glass ashtray.

Four other men were smoking at the bar, sprawled on bar stools. Two of them Raymond recognized from their visit to his apartment. Behind the bar was an over-weight bearded man washing glassware. The rest of the restaurant was empty.

Vinnie waved Raymond to his booth.

"Sit down, Doc," Vinnie said. "A coffee?"

Raymond nodded as he slid into the banquette. It took some effort because of the nap of the velvet. The room was chilly, damp, and smelled of the previous night's garlic and the accumulated smoke of five-years' worth of cigarettes. Raymond was happy to keep on his hat and coat.

"Two coffees," Vinnie called out to the man behind the bar. Wordlessly, the man turned to an elaborate Italian espresso machine and began manipulating the controls.

"You surprised me, Doc," Vinnie said. "I truly never expected to hear from you again."

"As I mentioned on the phone there's another problem," Raymond said. He leaned forward and spoke in a low voice just above a whisper.

Vinnie spread his hands. "I'm all ears."

As succinctly as he could, Raymond outlined the situation with Cindy Carlson. He emphasized the fact that all suicides were medical examiner cases and had to be autopsied. There were no exceptions.

The overweight man from behind the bar brought out the coffees. Vinnie didn't respond to Raymond's monologue until the bartender had gone back to his glassware.

"Is this Cindy Carlson the daughter of Albright Carlson?" Vinnie asked. "The Wall Street legend?"

Raymond nodded. "That's partly why this situation is so important," he said. "If she commits suicide it will undoubtedly garner considerable media attention. The medical examiners will be particularly vigilant."

"I get the picture," Vinnie said as he took a sip of his coffee. "What is it exactly that you would want us to do?"

"I wouldn't presume to offer any suggestions," Raymond said nervously. "But you can appreciate that this problem is on a par with the Franconi situation."

"So you want this sixteen-year-old girl to just conveniently disappear," Vinnie said.

"Well, she has tried to kill herself twice," Raymond said limply. "In a way, we'd just be doing her a favor."

Vinnie laughed. He picked up his cigarette, took a drag, and then ran his hand over the top of his head. His hair was slicked back smoothly from his forehead. He regarded Raymond with his dark eyes.

"You're a piece of work, Doc," Vinnie said. "I gotta give you credit for that."

"Perhaps I can offer another year of free tuition," Raymond said.

"That's very generous of you," Vinnie said. "But you know something, Doc, it's not enough. In fact, I'm getting a little fed up with this whole operation. And I'll tell you straight: if it weren't for Vinnie Junior's kidney problems, I'd probably just ask for my money back, and we'd go our separate ways. You see, I'm already looking at potential problems from the first favor I did for you. I got a call from my wife's brother who runs the Spoletto Funeral Home. He's all upset because a Dr. Laurie Montgomery called asking embarrassing questions. Tell me, Doc. Do you know this Dr. Laurie Montgomery?"

"No, I don't," Raymond said. He swallowed loudly.

"Hey, Angelo, come over here!" Vinnie called out.

Angelo slid off his bar stool and came to the table.

"Sit down, Angelo," Vinnie said. "I want you to tell the good doctor here about Laurie Montgomery."

Raymond had to move farther into the booth to give room for Angelo. He felt distinctly uncomfortable being sandwiched between the two men.

"Laurie Montgomery is a smart, persistent individual," Angelo said with his husky voice. "To put it bluntly, she's a pain in the ass."

Raymond avoided looking at Angelo. His face was mostly scar tissue. Since his eyes didn't close properly, they were red and rheumy.

"Angelo had an unfortunate run-in with Laurie Montgomery a few years back," Vinnie explained. "Angelo, tell Raymond what you learned today after we heard from the funeral home."

"I called Vinnie Amendola, our contact in the morgue," Angelo said. "He told me that Laurie Montgomery specifically said that she was going to make it her personal business to find out how Franconi's body disappeared. Needless to say he's very concerned."

"See what I mean," Vinnie said. "We got a potential problem here just because we did you a favor."

"I'm very sorry," Raymond said lamely. He couldn't think of any other response.

"It brings us back to this tuition issue," Vinnie said. "Under the circumstances I think the tuition should just be waived. In other words, no tuition for me or Vinnie Junior forever."

"I do have to answer to the parent corporation," Raymond squeaked. He cleared his throat.

"Fine," Vinnie said. "Doesn't bother me in the slightest. Explain to them it's a valid business expense. Hey, maybe you could even use it as a deduction on your taxes." Vinnie laughed heartily.

Raymond shuddered imperceptibly. He knew he was being unfairly muscled, yet he had little choice. "Okay," he managed.

"Thank you," Vinnie said. "Gosh, I guess this is going to work out after all. We've become sort'a business partners. Now I trust you have Cindy Carlson's address?"

Raymond fumbled in his pocket and produced Dr. Levitz's business card. Vinnie took it, copied down the address from the back, and handed it back. Vinnie gave the address to Angelo.

"Englewood, New Jersey," Angelo said, reading aloud.

"Is that a problem?" Vinnie asked.

Angelo shook his head.

"Then, it's arranged," Vinnie said, looking back at Raymond. "So much for your latest problem. But I advise you not to come up with any more. With our current tuition understanding it seems to me you're out of bargaining chips."

A few minutes later, Raymond was out on the street. He realized he was shaking as he looked at his watch. It was close to five and getting dark. Stepping off the curb, he raised his hand to flag a cab. *What a disaster!* he thought. Somehow he would have to absorb the cost of maintaining Vinnie Dominick's and his son's doubles for the rest of their lives.

A cab pulled over. Raymond climbed in and gave his home address. As he sped away from the Neopolitan Restaurant, he began to feel better. The actual cost of maintaining the two doubles was minuscule, since the animals lived in isolation on a deserted island. So the situation wasn't that bad, especially since the potential problem with Cindy Carlson was now solved.

By the time Raymond entered his apartment his mood had improved significantly, at least until he got in the door.

"You've had two calls from Africa," Darlene reported.

"Problems?" Raymond asked. There was something about Darlene's voice that set off alarm bells.

"There was good news and bad news," Darlene said. "The good news was from the surgeon. He said that Horace Winchester is doing miraculously and that you should start planning on coming to pick him and the surgical team up."

"What's the bad news?" Raymond asked.

"The other call was from Siegfried Spallek," Darlene said. "He was a little vague. He said there was some trouble with Kevin Marshall."

"What kind of trouble?" Raymond asked.

"He didn't elaborate," Darlene said.

Raymond remembered specifically asking Kevin not to do anything rash. He wondered if the researcher had not heeded his warning. It must have had something to do with that stupid smoke Kevin had seen.

"Did Spallek want me to call back tonight?" Raymond asked.

"It was eleven o'clock his time when he called," Darlene said. "He said he could talk to you tomorrow."

Raymond groaned inwardly. Now he'd have to spend the entire night worrying. He wondered when it was all going to end.

CHAPTER 11

MARCH 5, 1997
11:30 P.M.
COGO, EQUATORIAL GUINEA

Kevin heard the heavy metal door open at the top of the stone stairs and a crack of light cascaded in. Two seconds later, the string of bare lightbulbs in the ceiling of the corridor went on. Through the bars of his cell, he could see Melanie and Candace in their respective cells. They were squinting as he was in the sudden glare.

Heavy footfalls on the granite stairs preceded Siegfried Spallek's appearance. He was accompanied by Cameron McIvers and Mustapha Aboud, chief of the Moroccan guards.

"It's about time, Mr. Spallek!" Melanie snapped. "I demand to be let out of here this instant, or you'll be in serious trouble."

Kevin winced. It was not the way to talk with Siegfried Spallek on any occasion, much less in their current circumstance.

Kevin, Melanie, and Candace had been huddling in utter blackness in separate cells in the oppressively hot, dank jail in the basement of the town hall. Each cell had a small, arched window that opened into a window well in the rear arcade of the building. The openings were barred but without glass, so vermin could pass through unimpeded. All three prisoners had been terrified by the sounds of scampering creatures, especially since they'd seen several tarantulas before the lights had been turned out. The only source of comfort had been that they could easily talk to each other.

The first five minutes of the evening's ordeal had been the worst. As soon as the sound of the burst of machine-gun fire died out, Kevin and the women were blinded by large hand-held lights. When their eyes had finally adjusted, they saw that they'd walked into an ambush of sorts. They were surrounded by a jeering group of youthful Equatoguinean soldiers who'd delighted in casually aiming their AK-47's at them. Several had been brazen enough to poke the women with the muzzles of their weapons.

Fearing the worst, Kevin and the others hadn't moved a muscle. They'd been scared witless by the indiscriminate gunfire and terrified it might begin again at the slightest provocation.

Only at the appearance of several of the Moroccan guards did the unruly soldiers back off. Kevin had never imagined the intimidating Arabs as potential saviors, but that's how it had turned out. The guards had assumed custody of Kevin and the women. Then the guards drove them in Kevin's car, first to the Moroccan guard building across from the animal center, where they'd been placed in a windowless room for several hours, and then finally into town, where they'd been incarcerated in the old jail.

"This is outrageous treatment," Melanie persisted.

"On the contrary," Siegfried said. "I have been assured by Mustapha that you have been treated with all due respect."

"Respect!" Melanie sputtered. "To be shot at with machine guns! And kept in this shithole in the dark! That's respect?"

"You were not shot at," Siegfried corrected. "Those were merely a few warning shots directed over your heads. You had, after all, violated an important rule here in the Zone. Isla Francesca is off-limits. Everyone knows that."

Siegfried motioned to Cameron toward Candace. Cameron opened her cell with a large, antique key. Candace wasted no time getting out of the cell. She hastily dusted off her clothes to make sure there were no bugs. She was still dressed in her surgical scrubs from the hospital.

"My apologies to you," Siegfried said to Candace. "I imagine you were led astray by our resident researchers. Perhaps you were not even aware of the rule against visiting the island area."

Cameron opened Melanie's cell and then Kevin's.

"As soon as I heard about your detention, I tried to call Dr. Raymond Lyons," Siegfried said. "I wanted to ask his opinion as to the best way to handle this situation. Since he was unavailable, I have to take responsibility myself. I am releasing you all on your own recognizance. I trust that you now know the seriousness of your actions. Under Equatoguinean law it could be considered a capital offense."

"Oh, bull!" Melanie spat.

Kevin cringed. He was afraid Melanie would anger Siegfried enough to order them back into the cells. Benevolence was not a part of Siegfried's character.

Mustapha extended Kevin's car keys to him. "Your vehicle is out back," he said with a heavy French accent.

Kevin took the keys. His hand shook enough to cause them to jingle until he got his hand and the keys into his pocket.

"I'm sure I will be speaking to Dr. Lyons sometime tomorrow," Siegfried said. "I will contact you individually. You may go."

Melanie started to speak again, but Kevin surprised himself by grabbing her arm and propelling her toward the stairs.

"I've had enough manhandling," Melanie sputtered. She tried to pull her arm from Kevin's grasp.

"Let's just get into the car," Kevin whispered harshly through clenched teeth. He forced her to keep moving.

"What a night!" Melanie complained. At the base of the stairs, she managed to yank her arm free. Irritably, she started up.

Kevin waited for Candace to precede him, then followed the women up to the ground floor. They emerged into an office used by the Equatoguinean soldiers that were constantly seen lounging in front of the town hall. There were four of them present.

With the base manager, the head of security, and the chief of the Moroccan guards in the building, the soldiers were a good deal more attentive than usual. All four were standing in their interpretation of attention, with their assault rifles over their shoulders. When Kevin and the women appeared, their expressions suggested they were confused.

Melanie gave them the finger as Kevin herded her and Candace out the door into the parking lot.

"Please, Melanie," Kevin begged. "Don't provoke them!"

Whether the soldiers did not understand the meaning of Melanie's gesture or were bewildered by the anomalous circumstances, Kevin didn't know. One way or the other, they didn't come flying out after them as Kevin feared they might.

They got to the car. Kevin opened the passenger-side door. Candace climbed in eagerly. But not Melanie. She turned to Kevin with her eyes blazing in the dim light.

"Give me the keys," she demanded.

"What?" Kevin asked, even though he'd heard her.

"I said give me the keys," Melanie repeated.

Confused by this unexpected request but not wishing to incite her more than she already was, Kevin handed her the car keys. Melanie immediately went around to the other side of the car and got in behind the wheel. Kevin climbed into the passenger seat. He didn't care who drove as long as they got themselves out of there.

Melanie started the car, spun the tires, and drove out of the parking lot.

"Jeez, Melanie," Kevin said. "Slow down!"

"I'm pissed," Melanie said.

"As if I couldn't tell," Kevin said.

"I'm not going home just yet," Melanie said. "But I'd be happy to take you guys home if you want."

"Where do you want to go?" Kevin asked. "It's almost midnight."

"I'm going out to the animal center," Melanie said. "I'm not going to tolerate being treated like this without finding out what the hell is going on."

"What's at the animal center?" Kevin asked.

"The keys to that goddamned bridge," Melanie said. "I want one, because for me this affair has gone beyond curiosity."

"Maybe we should stop and talk about this," Kevin suggested.

Melanie jammed on the brakes, bringing them to a lurching stop. Both Kevin and Candace had to push themselves back into their respective seats.

"I'm going to the animal center," Melanie repeated. "You guys can either come along or I'll drop you off. It's your call."

"Why tonight?" Kevin asked.

"One, because I'm really ticked off right now," Melanie said. "And two, because they wouldn't suspect it. Obviously, they intend for us to go home and quake in our beds. That's why we were so mistreated. But you know something, that's not my style."

"That's my style," Kevin said.

"I think Melanie is right," Candace said from the backseat. "They were deliberately trying to scare us."

"And I think they did a damn good job," Kevin said. "Or am I the only sane one in the group?"

"Let's do it," Candace said.

"Oh, no!" Kevin groaned. "I'm outnumbered."

"We'll take you home," Melanie said. "No problem." She started to put the car in reverse.

Kevin reached out and stayed her hand. "How do you propose to get the keys? You don't even know where they'd be."

"I think it's pretty clear they'd be in Bertram's office," Melanie said. "He's the one in charge of logistics for the bonobo program. Hell, you're the one who suggested he had them."

"Okay, they're in Bertram's office," Kevin said. "But what about security? Offices are locked."

Melanie reached into the breast pocket of her animal-center coveralls and pulled out a magnetic card. "You're forgetting that I'm part of the animal-center hierarchy. This is a master card, and not the kind that competes with Visa. This thing gets me in every door of the animal center twenty-four hours a day. Remember, my work with the bonobo project is only a part of the fertility work I do."

Kevin looked over the back of his seat at Candace. Her blond hair was luminous in the half light of the car interior. "If you're game, Candace, I guess I'm game," he said.

"Let's go!" Candace said.

Melanie accelerated and turned north beyond the motor pool. The motor pool was in full operation, with huge mercury-vapor lamps illuminating the entire staging area. The motor pool's night shift was larger than either the day or evening shifts since that's when truck traffic between the Zone and Bata was at its peak.

Melanie zipped past a number of tractor trailers until the turnoff to Bata fell behind. From that point, all the way to the animal center, they didn't see another vehicle.

The animal center worked three shifts just like the motor pool did, although in the animal center the night shift was the smallest. The majority of the night staff worked in the veterinary hospital. Melanie took advantage of this fact by pulling Kevin's Toyota up to one of the animal-hospital doors. There the car had lots of company.

Melanie turned off the ignition and gazed at the animal-center entrance that led directly into the veterinary hospital. She drummed her fingers on the steering wheel.

"Well?" Kevin said. "We're here, what's the plan?"

"I'm thinking," Melanie said. "I can't decide what's best: whether you guys wait here or come with me."

"This place is huge," Candace said. She'd leaned forward and was gazing at the building in front of them. It ran from the street all the way back to where it disappeared into the jungle foliage. "For as many times as I've been to Cogo, I've never been out here at the animal center. I didn't have any idea it was so large. Is this part we're facing the hospital?"

"Yup," Melanie said. "This whole wing."

"I'd be interested to see it," Candace said. "I've never been in a veterinary hospital let alone one that's so palatial."

"It's state-of-the-art," Melanie said. "You should see the ORs."

"Oh my God," Kevin sighed. He rolled his eyes. "I've been ensnared by the insane. We've just had the most harrowing experience in our lives, and you're talking about taking a tour."

"It's not going to be a tour," Melanie said as she alighted from the car. "Come on, Candace. I'm sure I can use your help. Kevin, you can wait here if you'd like."

"Fine by me," Kevin said. But it only took him a few moments of watching the women trudge toward the entrance before he, too, climbed out of the car. He decided that the anxiety of waiting would be worse than the stress of going.

"Wait up," Kevin called out. He had to run a few steps until he'd caught up with the others.

"I don't want to hear any complaining," Melanie told Kevin.

"Don't worry," Kevin said. He felt like a teenager being chastised by his mother.

"I don't anticipate any problems," Melanie said. "Bertram Edwards's office is in the administration part of the building, which at this time will be deserted. But just to be sure we don't arouse any suspicion, once we're inside, we'll head down to the locker room. I want you guys in animal center coveralls. Okay? I mean it's not really the time anyone would expect to encounter visitors."

"Sounds like a good idea to me," Candace said.

"All right," Bertram said into the phone. His eye caught the luminous dial of his bedside clock. It was quarter past midnight. "I'll meet you at your office in five minutes."

Bertram swung his legs over the edge of the bed and parted the mosquito netting.

"Trouble?" Trish, his wife, asked. She'd pushed herself up on one elbow.

"Just a nuisance," Bertram said. "Go back to sleep! I'll be back in a half hour or so."

Bertram closed the door to the bedroom before turning on the dressing-room light. He dressed quickly. Although he'd downplayed the situation to Trish, Bertram was anxious. He had no idea what was going on, but it had to be trouble. Siegfried had never called him in the middle of the night with a request to come to his office.

Outside, it was as bright as daytime with a nearly full moon having risen in the east. The sky was filled with silvery-purple cumulus clouds. The night air was heavy and humid and perfectly still. The sounds of the jungle were an almost constant cacophony of buzzes, chirps, and squawks interrupted with occasional short screams. It was a noise Bertram had grown accustomed to over the years, and it didn't even register in his mind.

Despite the distance to the town hall being only a few hundred yards, Bertram drove. He knew it would be faster, and every minute that passed raised his curiosity. As he pulled into the parking lot, he could see that the usually lethargic soldiers were strangely agitated, moving around the army post, clutching their rifles. They eyed him nervously as he turned off his headlights and alighted from the car.

Approaching the building on foot, Bertram could see meager light flickering through the slats of the shutters covering Siegfried's second-floor office windows. He went up the stairs, passed through the dark reception area normally occupied by Aurielo, and entered Siegfried's office.

Siegfried was sitting at his desk with his feet propped up on the corner. In the hand of his good arm he held and was gently swirling a brandy snifter. Cameron McIvers, head of security, was sitting in a rattan chair with a similar glass. The only illumination in the room was coming from the candle in the skull. The low level of shimmering light cast dark shadows and gave a lifelike quality to the menagerie of stuffed animals.

"Thanks for coming out at such an ungodly hour," Siegfried said with his usual German accent. "How about a splash of brandy?"

"Do I need it?" Bertram asked, as he pulled a rattan chair over to the desk.

Siegfried laughed. "It can never hurt."

Cameron got the drink from a sideboard. He was a hefty, full-bearded Scotsman with a bulbous, red nose and a strong bias toward alcohol of any sort, although scotch was understandably his favorite. He handed the snifter to Bertram and re-claimed his seat and his own drink.

"Usually when I'm called out in the middle of the night it is a medical emergency with an animal," Bertram said. He took a sip of the brandy and breathed in deeply. "Tonight I have the sense it is something else entirely."

"Indeed," Siegfried said. "First I have to commend you. Your warning this af-ternoon about Kevin Marshall was well-founded and timely. I asked Cameron to have him watched by the Moroccans, and sure enough this evening he, Melanie Becket, and one of the surgical nurses drove all the way out to the landing area for Isla Francesca."

"Damnation!" Bertram exclaimed. "Did they go on the island?"

"No," Siegfried said. "They merely played with the food float. They'd also stopped to talk with Alphonse Kimba."

"This irritates me to death!" Bertram exclaimed. "I don't like anyone going near that island, and I don't like anyone talking to that pygmy."

"Nor do I," Siegfried agreed.

"Where are they now?" Bertram questioned.

"We let them go home," Siegfried said. "But not before putting the fear of God into them. I don't think they will be doing it again, at least not for a while."

"This is not what I need!" Bertram complained. "I hate to have to worry about this on top of the bonobos splitting into two groups."

"This is worse than the animals living in two groups," Siegfried said.

"They're both bad," Bertram said. "Both have the potential of interrupting the smooth operation of the program and possibly putting an end to it. I think my idea of caging them all and bringing them into the animal center should be reconsidered. I've got the cages out there. It wouldn't be difficult, and it will make retrievals a hell of a lot easier."

From the moment Bertram had determined the bonobos were living in two social groups, he'd thought it best to round up the animals and keep them in separate cages where they could be watched. But he'd been thwarted by Siegfried. Bertram had considered going over Siegfried's head by appealing to his boss in Cambridge, Massachusetts, but had decided against it. Doing so would have alerted the GenSys hierarchy that there was potential trouble with the bonobo program.

"We're not opening that discussion!" Siegfried said emphatically. "We're not giving up on the idea of keeping them isolated on the island. We all decided back when this started that was the best idea. I still think it is. But with this episode with Kevin Marshall, the bridge has me worried."

"Why?" Bertram asked. "It's locked."

"Where are the keys?" Siegfried asked.

"In my office," Bertram said.

"I think they should be here in the main safe," Siegfried said. "Most of your staff has access to your office, including Melanie Becket."

"Perhaps you have a point," Bertram said.

"I'm glad you agree," Siegfried said. "So I'd like you to get them. How many are there?"

"I don't recall exactly," Bertram said. "Four or five. Something like that."

"I want them here," Siegfried said.

"Fine," Bertram said agreeably. "I don't have a problem with that."

"Good," Siegfried said. He let his legs drop from the desk and stood up. "Let's go. I'll come with you."

"You want to go now?" Bertram asked with disbelief.

"Why put off until tomorrow what you can do today?" Siegfried said. "Isn't that an expression you Americans espouse? With the keys in the safe, I know I'll sleep a lot better tonight."

"Would you want me to come along as well?" Cameron asked.

"It's not necessary," Siegfried said. "I'm sure Bertram and I can handle it."

———

Kevin looked at himself in the full-length mirror at the end of the banks of lockers in the men's room. The trouble with the coveralls was that the small was too small and the medium was a little too big. He had to roll up the sleeves and the pant legs.

"What the hell are you doing in there?" Melanie's voice called out. She'd pushed open the door from the hall.

"I'm coming," Kevin said. He closed the locker where he'd stored his own clothes and hurried out into the hall.

"I thought women were supposed to take a long time dressing," Melanie complained.

"I couldn't decide which size was best," Kevin said.

"Did anybody come in while you were in there?" Melanie asked.

"Not a soul," Kevin said.

"Good," Melanie said. "Same for us in the ladies' room. Let's go!"

Melanie motioned for the others to follow her as she started up the stairs. "To get to the administration area from here, we have to pass through part of the veterinary hospital. I think it's best to avoid the main floor, which has the emergency room and the acute-care unit. There's always a lot of activity there. So let's go up to the second floor and go through the fertility unit. I can even say I'm checking on patients if someone asks."

"Cool," Candace said.

They passed the first floor and climbed to the second. Entering the main corridor, they encountered their first animal-center employee. If the man thought that there was anything abnormal about Kevin and Candace's presence in the middle of the night, he didn't give any evidence. He passed by with merely a nod.

"That was easy," Candace whispered.

"It's the coveralls," Melanie said.

They turned left through a set of double doors and entered a brightly lit, narrow hallway lined with a number of blank doors. Melanie cracked one of them and stuck her head inside. Quietly, she closed the door. "It's one of my patients. She's a lowland gorilla who's almost ready for egg retrieval. They can get a little rambunctious with the hormone level we have to achieve, but she's sleeping soundly."

"Can I see?" Candace asked.

"I suppose," Melanie said. "But be quiet and don't make any sudden movements."

Candace nodded. Melanie opened the door and slipped inside. Candace followed. Kevin stayed by the door, holding it open.

"Shouldn't we be doing what we came here for?" Kevin whispered.

Melanie put her finger to her lips.

There were four large cages in the room, only one of which was occupied. A large gorilla was sleeping on a bed of straw. The illumination came from overhead recessed lighting that was dimmed down to a point of being almost off.

Gently touching the bars of the cage, Candace leaned forward to get a better look. She'd never been so close to a gorilla. If she'd been inclined, she could have touched the huge animal.

With speed that defied belief, the female gorilla awoke and then bounced off the front of the cage. In the next instant, she was pounding the floor with her fists like kettle drums and shrieking.

Candace let out a scream of her own as she leapt back out of harm's way. Melanie grabbed her.

"It's okay," Melanie said.

The gorilla then made another lunge for the front of the cage. She also hurled a handful of fresh feces in the process, which splattered against the far wall.

Melanie directed Candace out the door and Kevin let it shut.

"I'm terribly sorry," Melanie said to Candace. Candace's Nordic complexion was even paler than usual. "Are you all right?"

"I guess," Candace said. She checked the front of her coveralls.

"A little PMS, I'm afraid," Melanie said. "She didn't hit you with any of her poop, did she?"

"I don't think so," Candace said. She ran a hand through her hair and then examined it.

"Let's get the keys," Kevin said. "We're pushing our luck."

They walked the length of the fertility unit and pushed through a second pair of swinging doors to enter a large room divided into bays. Each bay had several cages, and most of the cages were occupied by youthful primates of different species.

"This is the pediatric unit," Melanie whispered. "Just act natural."

There were four people working in the unit. They were all dressed in surgical scrubs with stethoscopes draped around their necks. Everyone was friendly but busy and preoccupied, and the trio passed through, garnering nothing more than a couple of smiles and nods.

After another set of double doors and a short corridor, they came to a heavy, locked fire door. Melanie had to use her card to open it.

"Here we are!" Melanie whispered, as she let the fire door close quietly behind them. After the bustle they'd just witnessed, the silence and darkness seemed absolute. "This is the administration area. The stairwell is down the hall to the left. So hold on."

There was groping in the dark until Candace got her hand on Melanie's shoulder and Kevin got his on Candace's.

"Come on!" Melanie encouraged. She began to inch her way along the corridor, while running her hand against the wall. The others allowed themselves to be pulled along. Gradually, their eyes adjusted and by the time the group neared the door to the stairwell, they could appreciate the small amount of moonlight that seeped through the cracks.

Inside the stairwell, it was comparatively bright. Large windows on each landing flooded the stairs with moonlight.

The first-floor hall was much easier to walk in than the second-floor hall because of the windows in the main-entrance doors.

Melanie led them to a position just outside Bertram's office.

"Now comes the acid test," Kevin said, as Melanie tried her card in the lock.

There was an immediate, reassuring click. The door opened.

"No problem," Melanie said buoyantly.

The three stepped inside the room and were again thrust into almost complete darkness. The only light was a meager glow that filtered through the open door into the inner office.

"What now?" Kevin questioned. "We're not going to find anything in the dark."

"I agree," Melanie said. She felt along the wall for the switch. As soon as her finger touched it, she switched it on.

For a moment, they blinked at each other. "Whoa, seems awfully bright," Melanie said.

"I hope it doesn't wake up those Moroccan guards across the street," Kevin said.

"Don't even joke about it," Melanie said. She walked into the inner office and turned on the light. Kevin and Candace joined her.

"I think we should be methodical about this," Melanie said. "I'll take the desk. Candace, you take the file cabinet, and, Kevin, why don't you take the outer office and, while you're at it, keep an eye on the hall. Give a yell if anybody appears."

"Now that's a happy thought," Kevin said.

Siegfreid turned left at the motor pool and accelerated his new Toyota LandCruiser toward the animal center. The vehicle had been modified for his disability so that he could shift with his left hand.

"Does Cameron have any idea why we are so concerned about the security of Isla Francesca?" Bertram asked.

"No, not at all," Siegfried said.

"Has he asked?"

"No, he's not that kind of person. He takes orders. He doesn't question them."

"What about telling him and cutting him in on a small percentage?" Bertram suggested. "He could be very helpful."

"I'm not diluting our percentages!" Siegfried said. "Don't even suggest it. Besides, Cameron is already helpful. He does whatever I tell him to do."

"What worries me the most about this episode with Kevin Marshall is that he must have said something to those women," Bertram said. "The last thing I want is for them to start thinking the bonobos on the island are using fire. If that gets out, it's just a matter of time before we have animal-rights zealots coming out of the woodwork. GenSys will shut the program down faster than you can blink your eye."

"What do you think we should do?" Siegfried asked. "I could arrange to have the three of them just disappear."

Bertram glanced at Siegfried and shivered. He knew the man was not joking.

"No, that could be worse," Bertram said. He looked back out through the windshield. "That might stimulate a major State-side investigation. I'm telling you, I think we should dart the bonobos, put them in the cages I brought out there, and bring them in. Sure as hell, they won't be using fire in the animal center."

"No, goddamn it!" Siegfried snapped. "The animals stay on the island. If they're brought in, you won't be able to keep it a secret. Even if they don't use fire, we know they're cunning little bastards from the problems we've had during retrievals, and maybe they'll start doing something else equally as weird. If they do, handlers will start talking. We'll be in worse shape."

Bertram sighed and ran a nervous hand through his white hair. Reluctantly, he admitted to himself that Siegfried had a point. Still, he thought it best to bring the animals in, mainly to keep them isolated from each other.

"I'll be talking to Raymond Lyons tomorrow," Siegfried said. "I tried to call him earlier. I figured that since Kevin Marshall had already talked to him, we might as well get his opinion about what to do. After all, this whole operation is his creation. He doesn't want trouble any more than we do."

"True," Bertram said.

"Tell me something," Siegfried said. "If the animals are using fire, how do you think they got it? You still think it was lightning?"

"I'm not sure," Bertram said. "It could have been lightning. But, then again, they managed to steal a bunch of tools, rope, and other stuff when we had the crew out there constructing the island side of the bridge mechanism. No one even thought about the possibility of theft. I mean, everything was secured in toolboxes. Anyway, they might have gotten matches. Of course, I have no idea how they could have figured out how to use them."

"You just gave me an idea," Siegfried said. "Why don't we tell Kevin and the women there's been a crew going out to the island over the past week to do some kind of work like cutting trails. We can say that we've just found out that they have been starting the fires."

"Now that's a damn good idea!" Bertram said. "It makes perfect sense. We've even considered putting a bridge over the Rio Diviso."

"Why the hell didn't we think of it earlier?" Siegfried questioned. "It's so obvious."

Ahead the LandCruiser's headlights illuminated the first of the animal-center's buildings.

"Where do you want me to park?" Siegfried asked.

"Pull right up to the front," Bertram said. "You can wait in the car. It will only take me a second."

Siegfried took his foot off the accelerator and began to brake.

"What the hell!" Bertram said.

"What's the matter?"

"There's a light on in my office," Bertram answered.

"This looks promising," Candace called out as she pulled a large folder from the top drawer of the file cabinet. The folder was dark blue and closed with an attached elastic. In the upper right-hand corner it said: ISLA FRANCESCA.

Melanie pushed in the drawer of the desk she'd been searching and walked over to Candace. Kevin appeared from the outer office and joined them.

Candace snapped off the elastic and opened the folder. She slid the contents out onto a library table. There were wiring diagrams of electronic equipment, computer printouts, and numerous maps. There was also a large and lumpy manila envelope that had the words STEVENSON BRIDGE written across its top.

"Now we're cooking," Candace said. She opened the envelope, reached in, and pulled out a ring with five identical keys.

"Voilà," Melanie said. She took the ring and began to remove one of the keys.

Kevin peeked at the maps and picked up a detailed contour map. He had it partially unfolded when he became aware of a flickering light out of the corner of his eye. Glancing at the window, he saw the reflections of headlight beams dancing along the slats of the half open blinds. Stepping over to the window, he peeked out.

"Uh-oh!" Kevin croaked. "It's Siegfried's car."

"Quick!" Melanie said. "Get this all back into the file cabinet."

Melanie and Candace hastily crammed everything back into the folder, got the folder into the file cabinet, and closed the drawer. No sooner was it closed than they heard the rattle of the front door of the building as it was opened.

"This way!" Melanie whispered frantically. She motioned toward a door behind Bertram's desk. Quickly, the three went through the door. As Kevin closed it, he could hear the door to the outer office being pulled open.

They had entered one of Bertram's examining rooms. It was constructed of white tile and had a central stainless-steel examining table. Like Bertram's inner office it had windows covered with blinds. Enough light filtered in to allow them to rush over to the door to the hall. Unfortunately, en route Kevin kicked a stainless-steel pail standing on the floor next to the examining table.

The pail clanged up against the table leg. In the stillness, it sounded like a gong at an amusement park. Melanie reacted by throwing open the door to the hall and racing toward the stairwell. Candace followed. As Kevin dashed into the hall, he heard the door to Bertram's office slam open. He had no idea if he'd been seen or not.

In the stairwell, Melanie descended as fast as the moonlight would allow. She could hear Candace and Kevin behind her. She slowed at the foot of the stairs to grope for the door to the basement level. She got it open none too soon. Above they heard the first-floor stairwell door open, followed by heavy footfalls on the metal stairs.

The basement was utterly black save for a dim rectangular outline of light in the distance. Holding on to each other, they made their way toward the light. It wasn't until they had reached it that Kevin and Candace realized it was a fire door with light seeping around its periphery. Melanie had it open with her magnetic card once she'd located the slot.

Beyond the fire door was a brightly lit hallway which allowed them to run full tilt. Melanie pulled them to an abrupt halt halfway down the narrow passageway. There she opened a door marked PATHOLOGY.

"Inside," Melanie barked. Wordlessly, everyone complied.

Closing the door, Melanie locked it with a throw bolt.

They were standing in an anteroom for two autopsy theaters. There were scrub sinks, several desks, and a large insulated door leading to a refrigerated room.

"Why did we come in here?" Kevin said with panic in his voice. "We're trapped."

"Not quite," Melanie said breathlessly. "This way." She motioned for them to follow her around the corner. To Kevin's surprise there was an elevator. Melanie pounded the call-button, which brought forth an immediate whine of its machinery. At the same time, the floor indicator illuminated to show the elevator cab was on the third floor.

"Come on!" Melanie pleaded as if her urging could speed up the apparatus. Since it was a freight elevator, it was agonizingly slow. It was just passing the second floor when the door to the hallway rattled on its hinges followed by a muffled expletive.

The three exchanged panicky glances. "They'll be in here in the next few seconds," Kevin said. "Is there another way out?"

Melanie shook her head. "Only the elevator."

"We have to hide," Kevin said.

"What about the refrigerator?" Candace offered.

With no time to argue, the three darted to the refrigerator. Kevin got the door open. A cool mist flowed out to layer itself along the floor. Candace went in first, followed by Melanie and then Kevin. Kevin pulled the door shut. Its hardware clicked soundly.

The room was twenty feet square, with stainless-steel shelving from floor to ceiling that lined the periphery as well as forming a central island. The hulks of a number of dead primates lay on the shelves. The most impressive was the body of a huge silver-back male gorilla on the middle shelf of the central island. The illumination in the room came from bare light bulbs within wire cages attached to the ceiling at intervals along the walkways.

Instinctively, the three rushed around to the back of the central island and squatted down. Their heavy breathing formed fleeting spheres of mist in the frigid temperature. The smell was not pleasant with a hint of ammonia, but it was tolerable.

Surrounded by heavy insulation, Kevin and the others could not hear a sound inside the refrigerator, not even the whine of the elevator. At least not until they heard the unmistakable click of the refrigerator door's latch.

Kevin felt his heart skip a beat as the door was pulled open. Preparing himself to see the sneering face of Siegfried, Kevin slowly raised his head to look over the bulk of the dead gorilla. To his surprise it wasn't Siegfried. It was two men in scrub suits carrying in the body of a chimpanzee.

Wordlessly, the men placed the remains of the dead ape on a shelf to the right just inside the door and then left. Once the door was closed, Kevin looked down at Melanie and sighed. "This has to have been the worst day of my life."

"It's not over yet," Melanie said. "We still have to get out of here. But at least we got what we came for." She opened her fist and held up the key. Light glinted off its chrome-colored surface.

Kevin looked at his own hand. Without realizing it, he was still clutching the detailed contour map of Isla Francesca.

Bertram turned on the light in the hallway as he exited the stairwell. He'd gone up to the second floor and had entered the pediatric unit. He'd asked the crew if anybody had just run through. The answer was no.

Entering his examination room, he switched on the light in there as well. Siegfried appeared at the door to Bertram's office.

"Well?" Siegfried questioned.

"I don't know if someone was in here or not," Bertram said. He looked down at the stainless-steel pail that had moved from its normal position under the edge of the examining table.

"Did you see anyone?" Siegfried asked.

"Not really," Bertram said. He shook his head. "Maybe the janitorial crew left the lights on."

"Well, it underlines my concerns about the keys," Siegfried said.

Bertram nodded. He reached out with his foot and pushed the stainless-steel bucket back to its normal position. He turned out the light in the examining room before following Siegfried back into his office.

Bertram opened the top drawer of the file cabinet and pulled out the Isla Francesca folder. He unsnapped the securing elastic and pulled out the contents.

"What's the matter?" Siegfried asked.

Bertram had hesitated. As a compulsively neat individual he could not imagine having crammed everything into the folder so haphazardly. Fearing the worst, it was with some relief that he lifted the Stevenson Bridge envelope and felt the lump made by the ring of keys.

CHAPTER 12

MARCH 5, 1997
6:45 P.M.
NEW YORK CITY

"This is the damndest thing," Jack said. He was peering into his microscope at one particular slide and had been doing so intently for the previous half hour. Chet had tried to talk with him but had given up. When Jack was concentrating, it was impossible to get his attention.

"I'm glad you are enjoying yourself," Chet said. He'd just stood up in preparation to leave and was about to heft his briefcase.

Jack leaned back and shook his head. "Everything about this case is screwy." He looked up at Chet and was surprised to see he had his coat on. "Oh, are you leaving?"

"Yeah, and I've been trying to say goodbye for the last fifteen minutes."

"Take a look at this before you go," Jack said. He motioned toward his microscope as he pushed away from the desk to give Chet room.

Chet debated. He checked his watch. He was due at his gym for a seven o'clock aerobics class. He'd had his eye on one of the girls who was a regular. In an effort to build up the courage to approach her, he'd been taking the class himself. The problem was that she was in far better shape than he, so that at the end of the class he was always too winded to talk.

"Come on, sport," Jack said. "Give me your golden opinion."

Chet let go of his briefcase, leaned over, and peered into the eyepieces of Jack's microscope. With no explanation from Jack, he first had to figure out what the tissue was. "So, you're still looking at this frozen section of liver," he said.

"It's been entertaining me all afternoon," Jack said.

"Why not wait for the regular fixed sections?" Chet said. "These frozen sections are so limiting."

"I've asked Maureen to get them out as soon as she can," Jack said. "But meanwhile this is all I have. What do you think of the area under the pointer?"

Chet played with the focus. One of the many problems with frozen sections was they were often thick and the cellular architecture appeared fuzzy.

"I'd say it looks like a granuloma," Chet said. A granuloma was the cellular sign of chronic, cell-mediated inflammation.

"That was my thought as well," Jack said. "Now move the field over to the right. It will show a part of the liver surface. What do you see there?"

Chet did as he was told, while worrying that if he was late to the gym, there wouldn't be a spot in the aerobics class. The instructor was one of the most popular.

"I see what looks like a large, scarred cyst," Chet said.

"Does it look at all familiar?" Jack asked.

"Can't say it does," Chet said. "In fact, I'd have to say it looks a little weird."

"Well said," Jack remarked. "Now, let me ask you a question."

Chet raised his head and looked at his office mate. Jack's domed forehead was wrinkled with confusion.

"Does this look like a liver that you'd expect to see in a relatively recent transplant?"

"Hell, no!" Chet said. "I'd expect some acute inflammation but certainly not a granuloma. Especially if the process could be seen grossly as suggested by the collapsed surface cyst."

Jack sighed. "Thank you! I was beginning to question my judgment. It's reassuring to hear you've come to the same conclusion."

"Knock, knock!" a voice called out.

Jack and Chet looked up to see Ted Lynch, the director of the DNA lab, standing in the doorway. He was a big man, almost in Calvin Washington's league. He'd been an all-American tackle for Princeton before going on to graduate school.

"I got some results for you, Jack," Ted said. "But I'm afraid it's not what you want to hear, so I thought I'd come down and tell you in person. I know you've been thinking you've got a liver transplant here, but the DQ alpha was a perfect match, suggesting it was the patient's own liver."

Jack threw up his hands. "I give up," he said.

"Now there was still a chance it was a transplant," Ted said. "There are twenty-one possible genotypes of the DQ alpha sequence, and the test fails to discriminate about seven percent of the time. But I went ahead and ran the ABO blood groups on chromosome nine, and it was a perfect match as well. Combining the two results, the chances are mighty slim it's not the patient's own liver."

"I'm crushed," Jack said. With his fingers intertwined, he let his hands fall onto the top of his head. "I even called a surgeon friend of mine and asked if there would be any other reason to find sutures in the vena cava, the hepatic artery, and the biliary system. He said no: that it had to be a transplant."

"What can I say?" Ted commented. "Of course, for you I'd be happy to fudge the results." He laughed, and Jack pretended to take a swipe at him with his hand.

Jack's phone jangled insistently. Jack motioned for Ted to stay, while he picked up the receiver. "What?" he said rudely.

"I'm out of here," Chet said. He waved to Jack and pushed past Ted.

Jack listened intently. Slowly, his expression changed from exasperation to interest. He nodded a few times as he glanced up at Ted. For Ted's benefit he held up a finger and mouthed, "One minute."

"Yeah, sure," Jack said into the phone. "If UNOS suggests we try Europe, give it a try." He glanced at his watch. "Of course it's the middle of the night over there, but do what you can!"

Jack hung up the phone. "That was Bart Arnold," he said. "I've had the entire forensics department searching for a missing recent liver transplant."

"What's UNOS?" Ted asked.

"United National Organ Sharing," Jack said.

"Any luck?" Ted asked.

"Nope," Jack said. "It's baffling. Bart's even checked with all the major centers doing liver transplants."

"Maybe it wasn't a transplant," Ted said. "I'm telling you, the probability of my two tests matching by chance is very small indeed."

"I'm convinced it was a transplant," Jack said. "There's no rhyme or reason to take out a person's liver and then put it back."

"You're sure?"

"Of course I'm sure," Jack said.

"You seem committed to this case," Ted commented.

Jack gave a short derisive laugh. "I've decided that I'm going to unravel this mystery come hell or high water," he said. "If I can't, I'll lose respect for myself.

There just aren't that many liver transplants. I mean, if I can't solve this one, I might as well hang it up."

"All right," Ted said. "I'll tell you what I can do. I can run a polymarker which compares areas on chromosomes four, six, seven, nine, eleven, and nineteen. A chance match will be in the billions to one. And for my own peace of mind, I'll even sequence the DQ alpha on both the liver sample and the patient to try to figure out how they could have matched."

"I'll be appreciative whatever you can do," Jack said.

"I'll even go up and start tonight," Ted said. "That way I can have the results tomorrow."

"What a sport!" Jack said. He put out his hand and Ted slapped it.

After Ted left, Jack switched off the light under his microscope. He felt as if the slide had been mocking him with its puzzling details. He'd been looking at it for so long his eyes hurt.

For a few minutes, Jack sat at his desk and gazed at the clutter of unfinished cases. Folders were stacked in uneven piles. Even his own conservative estimate had the figure somewhere between twenty-five and thirty. That was more than usual. Paperwork had never been Jack's forte, and it got worse when he became enmeshed in a particular case.

Cursing under his breath from frustration at his own ineptitude, Jack pushed back from his desk and grabbed his bomber jacket from the hook on the back of his office door. He'd had as much sitting and thinking as he was capable of. He needed some mindless, hard exercise, and his neighborhood basketball court was beckoning.

The view of the New York City skyline from the George Washington Bridge was breathtaking. Franco Ponti tried to turn his head to appreciate it, but it was difficult because of the rush-hour traffic. Franco was behind the wheel of a stolen Ford sedan on the way to Englewood, New Jersey. Angelo Facciolo was sitting in the front passenger seat, staring out the windshield. Both men were wearing gloves.

"Get a load of the view to the left," Franco said. "Look at all those lights. You can see the whole freakin' island, even the Statue of Liberty."

"Yeah, I've seen it already," Angelo said moodily.

"What's the matter with you?" Franco asked. "You're acting like you're on the rag."

"I don't like this kind of job," Angelo said. "It reminds me of when Cerino went berserk and sent me and Tony Ruggerio all over the goddamn city doing the same kind of shit. We should stick to our usual work, dealing with the usual people."

"Vinnie Dominick is not Pauli Cerino," Franco said. "And what's so bad about picking up some easy extra cash?"

"The cash is fine," Angelo agreed. "It's the risk I don't like."

"What do you mean?" Franco questioned. "There's no risk. We're professionals. We don't take risks."

"There's always the unexpected," Angelo said. "And as far as I'm concerned, the unexpected has already occurred."

Franco glanced over at Angelo's scarred face silhouetted in the half light of the car's interior. He could tell that Angelo was dead serious. "What are you talking about?" he questioned.

"The fact that this Laurie Montgomery is involved," Angelo said. "She gives me nightmares. Tony and I tried to whack her, but we couldn't. It was like God was protecting her."

Franco laughed in spite of Angelo's seriousness. "This Laurie Montgomery would be flattered that someone with your reputation has nightmares about her. That's hilarious."

"I don't find it funny at all," Angelo said.

"Don't get sore at me," Franco said. "Besides, she's hardly involved in what we're doing here."

"It's related," Angelo said. "And she told Vinnie Amendola that she's going to make it her personal business to find out how we managed to get Franconi's body out of the morgue."

"But how is she going to do that?" Franco said. "And worse comes to worse we send Freddie Capuso and Richie Herns to do the actual dirty work. I think you're jumping to conclusions here."

"Oh yeah?" Angelo questioned. "You don't know this woman. She's one persistent bitch."

"All right!" Franco said with resignation. "You want to be bummed out, fine by me."

As they reached the New Jersey side of the bridge, Franco bore right onto the Palisades Interstate Parkway. With Angelo insisting on sulking, he reached over and turned on the radio. After pushing a few buttons he found a station that played "oldies but goodies." Turning up the volume he sang "Sweet Caroline" along with Neil Diamond.

By the second refrain, Angelo leaned forward and turned off the radio. "You win," he said. "I'll cheer up if you promise not to sing."

"You don't like that song?" Franco questioned as if he were hurt. "It's got such sweet memories for me." He smacked his lips as if he were tasting. "It reminds me of making out with Maria Provolone."

"I'm not going to touch that one," Angelo said, laughing despite himself. He appreciated working with Franco Ponti. Franco was a professional. He also had a sense of humor, which Angelo knew he himself lacked.

Franco exited the parkway onto Palisades Avenue, passed Route 9W, and headed west down a long hill into Englewood, New Jersey. The environment quickly changed from franchise fast-food restaurants and service stations to upper-class suburban.

"You got the map and the address handy?" Franco asked.

"I got it right here," Angelo said. He reached up and turned on the map light. "We're looking for Overlook Place," he said. "It will be on the left."

Overlook Place was easy to find, and five minutes later, they were cruising along a winding, tree-lined street. The lawns that stretched up to the widely spaced houses were so expansive they looked like fairways on a golf course.

"Can you imagine living in a place like this?" Franco commented, his head swinging from side to side. "Hell, I'd get lost trying to find the street from my front door."

"I don't like this," Angelo said. "It's too peaceful. We're going to stick out like a sore thumb."

"Now don't get yourself all bent out of shape," Franco said. "At this point, all we're doing is reconnoitering. What number are we looking for?"

Angelo consulted the piece of paper in his hand. "Number Eight Overlook Place."

"That means it's going to be on our left," Franco said. They were just passing number twelve.

A few moments later Franco slowed and pulled over to the right side of the road. He and Angelo stared up a serpentine driveway lined with carriage lamps to a massive Tudor-style house set against a backdrop of soaring pine trees. Most of the multipaned windows were aglow with light. The property was the size of a football field.

"Looks like a goddamn castle," Angelo complained.

"I must say, it's not what I was hoping for," Franco said.

"Well, what are we going to do?" Angelo asked. "We can't just sit here. We haven't seen a car since we pulled off the main drag back there."

Franco put the car in gear. He knew Angelo was right. They couldn't wait there. Someone would undoubtedly spot them, become suspicious, and call the police. They'd already passed one of those stupid NEIGHBORHOOD WATCH signs with the silhouette of a guy wearing a bandana.

"Let's find out more about this sixteen-year-old chick," Angelo said. "Like, where she goes to school, what she likes to do, and who are her friends. We can't risk going up to the house. No way."

Franco grunted in agreement. Just as he was about to press on the accelerator, he saw a tiny figure come out the front of the house. From such a distance he couldn't tell if it was male or female. "Somebody just came out," he said.

"I noticed," Angelo said.

The two men watched in silence as the figure descended a few stone stairs and then started down the driveway.

"Whoever it is, is kind of fat," Franco said.

"And they got a dog," Angelo said.

"Holy Madonna," Franco said after a few moments. "It's the girl."

"I don't believe this," Angelo said. "Do you think it really is Cindy Carlson? I'm not used to things happening this easy."

Astounded, the two men watched as the girl continued down the driveway as if she were coming directly to greet them. Ahead of her walked a tiny, caramel-colored toy poodle with its little pompom tail sticking straight up.

"What should we do?" Franco questioned. He didn't expect an answer; he was thinking out loud.

"How about the police act?" Angelo suggested. "It always worked for Tony and me."

"Sounds good," Franco said. He turned to Angelo and stuck out his hand. "Let me use your Ozone Park police badge."

Angelo reached into the vest pocket of his Brioni suit and handed over the wal- letlike badge cover.

"You stay put for the moment," Franco said. "No reason to scare her right off the bat with that face of yours."

"Thanks for the compliment," Angelo said sourly. Angelo cared about his ap- pearance and dressed to the nines in a vain attempt to compensate for his face, which was severely scarred from a combination of chicken pox as a child, severe acne as a teenager, and third-degree burns from an explosion five years previously. Ironically, the explosion had been ignited thanks to Laurie Montgomery.

"Ah, don't be so touchy," Franco teased. He cuffed Angelo on the back of the head. "You know we love you, even though you look like you should be in a horror movie."

Angelo fended off Franco's hand. There were only two people he allowed even to make reference to his facial problem: Franco and his boss, Vinnie Dominick. Still, he didn't appreciate it.

The girl was now nearing the street. She was dressed in a pink down-filled ski parka, which only made her look heavier. Her facial features indented a puffy face with mild acne. Her hair was straight and parted down the middle.

"She look anything like Maria Provolone?" Angelo questioned, to get in a dig at Franco.

"Very funny," Franco said. He reached for the door handle and got out of the car.

"Excuse me!" Franco called out as sweetly as possible. Having smoked heavily from age eight, he had a voice that normally had a harsh, raspy quality. "Could you, by any chance, be the popular Cindy Carlson?"

"Maybe," the teenager said. "Who wants to know?" She'd stopped at the foot of the driveway. The dog lifted his leg against the gate post.

"We're police officers," Franco said. He held up the badge so that the light from the streetlamp glinted off its polished surface. "We're investigating several of the boys in town and we were told you might be able to help us."

"Really?" Cindy questioned.

"Absolutely," Franco said. "Please come over here so my colleague can talk to you."

Cindy glanced up and down the street, even though not a car had passed in the last five minutes. She crossed the street, pulling her dog who'd been intently sniffing the base of an elm tree.

Franco moved out of the way so that Cindy Carlson could bend over to look into the front seat of the car at Angelo. Before a word was spoken, Franco pushed her into the car headfirst.

Cindy let out a squeal but it was quickly smothered by Angelo who wrestled her into the car.

Franco swiftly yanked the leash out of Cindy's hand and shooed the dog away. Then he squeezed into the front seat, crushing Cindy against Angelo. He put the car in gear and drove away.

Laurie had surprised herself. After the delivery of the Franconi videotape, she'd been able to redirect her attention to her paperwork. She'd worked efficiently and made significant progress. There was now a gratifying stack of completed folders on the corner of her desk.

Taking the remaining tray of histology slides, she started on the final case, which could be completed with the material and reports she had. As she peered into her microscope to examine the first slide, she heard a knock on her open door. It was Lou Soldano.

"What are you doing here so late?" Lou asked. He sat down heavily in the chair next to Laurie's desk. He made no effort to take off his coat or hat, which was tipped way back on his head.

Laurie glanced at her watch. "My gosh!" she remarked. "I had no idea of the time."

"I tried to call you at home as I was coming across the Queensboro Bridge," Lou said. "When I didn't get you, I decided to stop here. I had a sneaking suspicion you'd still be at it. You know, you work too hard!"

"You should talk!" Laurie said with playful sarcasm. "Look at you! When was the last time you got any sleep? And I'm not talking about a catnap at your desk."

"Let's talk about more pleasant things," Lou suggested. "How about grabbing a bite to eat? I've got to run down to headquarters to do about an hour's worth of dictating, then I'd love to go out someplace. The kids are with their aunt, God love her. What do you say to some pasta?"

"Are you sure you're up for going out?" Laurie questioned. The circles under Lou's dark eyes were touching his smile creases. His stubble was more than a five o'clock shadow. Laurie guessed it was at least two days' worth.

"I gotta eat," Lou said. "Are you planning on working much longer?"

"I'm on my last case," Laurie said. "Maybe another half hour."

"You gotta eat, too," Lou said.

"Have you made any progress in the Franconi case?" Laurie asked.

Lou let out an exasperated puff of air. "I wish," he said. "And the trouble is with these mob hits, if you don't score quickly, the trail cools mighty fast. We haven't gotten the break I've been hoping for."

"I'm sorry," Laurie said.

"Thanks," Lou said. "How about you? Any more of an idea how Franconi's body got out of here?"

"That trail is about equally as cool," Laurie said. "Calvin even gave me a reaming out for interrogating the night mortuary tech. All I did was talk to the man. I'm afraid administration just wants the episode to fade."

"So Jack was right about telling you to lay off," Lou said.

"I suppose," Laurie reluctantly agreed. "But don't tell him that."

"I wish the commissioner would let it fade," Lou said. "Hell, I might get demoted over this thing."

"I did have one thought," Laurie said. "One of the funeral homes that picked up a body the night Franconi disappeared is called Spoletto. It's in Ozone Park. Somehow the name was familiar to me. Then I remembered that one of the more grisly murders of a young mobster took place there back during the Cerino case. Do you think that it's just a coincidence they happened to be making a pickup here the night Franconi disappeared?"

"Yeah," Lou said. "And I'll tell you why. I'm familiar with that funeral home from my years in Queens fighting organized crime. There is a loose and innocent connection by marriage with the Spoletto Funeral Home and the New York crime establishment. But it's with the wrong family. It's with the Lucia people, not with the Vaccarros, who killed Franconi."

"Oh, well," Laurie said. "It was just a thought."

"Hey, I'm not knocking your questioning it," Lou said. "Your recall always impresses me. I'm not sure I would have made the association. Anyway, what about some dinner?"

"As tired as you look, how about just coming over to my apartment for some spaghetti?" Laurie suggested. Lou and Laurie had become best of friends over the years. After being thrust together on the Cerino case five years previously, they'd flirted with a romantic relationship. But it hadn't worked out. Becoming friends had been a mutual decision. In the years since, they made it a point to have dinner together every couple of weeks.

"You wouldn't mind?" Lou asked. The idea of kicking back on Laurie's couch sounded like heaven.

"Not at all," Laurie said. "In fact, I'd prefer it. I've got some sauce in the freezer and plenty of salad makings."

"Great!" Lou said. "I'll grab some Chianti on my way downtown. I'll give you a call when I'm leaving headquarters."

"Perfect," Laurie said.

After Lou had left, Laurie went back to her slide. But Lou's visit had broken her concentration by reawakening the Franconi business. Besides, she was tired of looking through the microscope. Leaning back, she rubbed her eyes.

"Damn it all!" she murmured. She sighed and gazed up at the cobwebbed ceiling. Every time she questioned how Franconi's body could have gotten out of the morgue, she agonized anew. She also felt guilty that she couldn't provide even a modicum of help to Lou.

Laurie got up and got her coat, snapped shut her briefcase, and walked out of her office. But she didn't leave the morgue. Instead, she went down for another visit to the mortuary office. There was a question that was nagging her and which she'd forgotten to ask Marvin Fletcher, the evening mortuary tech, the previous late afternoon.

She found Marvin at his desk busily filling out the required forms for the scheduled pickups for that evening. Marvin was one of Laurie's favorite coworkers. He'd been on the day shift before Bruce Pomowski's tragic murder during the Cerino affair. After that event, Marvin had been switched to evenings. It had been a promotion because the evening mortuary tech had a lot of responsibility.

"Hey, Laurie! What's happening?" Marvin said the moment he caught sight of her. Marvin was a handsome African-American, with the most flawless skin Laurie had ever seen. It seemed to glow as if lit internally.

Laurie chatted with Marvin for a few minutes, catching him up on the intraoffice gossip of the day before getting down to business. "Marvin, I've got to ask you something, but I don't want you to feel defensive." Laurie couldn't help remembering Mike Passano's reaction to her questioning, and she certainly didn't want Marvin complaining to Calvin.

"About what?" Marvin asked.

"Franconi," Laurie said. "I wanted to ask why you didn't X-ray the body."

"What are you talking about?" Marvin questioned.

"Just what I said," Laurie remarked. "There was no X-ray slip in the autopsy folder and there were no films down here with others when I looked prior to finding out that the body had disappeared."

"I took X rays," Marvin said. He acted hurt that Laurie would suggest that he hadn't. "I always take X rays when a body comes in unless one of the doctors tells me otherwise."

"Then where's the slip and where are the films?" Laurie asked.

"Hey, I don't know what happened to the slip," Marvin said. "But the films: They went with Doctor Bingham."

"Bingham took them?" Laurie questioned. Even that was odd, yet she recognized that Bingham probably was planning on doing the post the following morning.

"He told me he was taking them up to his office," Marvin said. "What am I supposed to do, tell the boss he can't take the X rays. No way! Not this dude."

"Right, of course," Laurie said vaguely. She was preoccupied. Here was a new surprise. X rays existed of Franconi's body! Of course, it didn't matter much without the body itself, but she wondered why she'd not been told. Then again she'd not seen Bingham until after it was known that Franconi's body had been stolen.

"Well, I'm glad I spoke to you," Laurie said, coming out of her musing. "And I apologize for suggesting that you'd forgotten to take the films."

"Hey, it's cool," Marvin said.

Laurie was about to leave when she thought about the Spoletto Funeral Home. On a whim, she asked Marvin about it.

Marvin shrugged. "What do you want to know?" he asked. "I don't know much. I've never been there, you know what I'm saying."

"What are the people like who come here from the home?" Laurie asked.

"Normal," Marvin said with another shrug. "I've probably only seen them a couple of times. I mean, I don't know what you want me to say."

Laurie nodded. "It was a silly question. I don't know why I asked."

Laurie left the mortuary office and exited the morgue through the loading area onto Thirtieth Street. It seemed to her that nothing about the Franconi case was routine.

As Laurie commenced walking south along First Avenue another whim hit her. Suddenly, the idea of visiting the Spoletto Funeral Home seemed very appealing. She hesitated for a second while considering the idea and then stepped out into the street to hail a cab.

"Where to, lady?" the driver asked. Laurie could see from his hackney license that his name was Michael Neuman.

"Do you know where Ozone Park is?" Laurie asked.

"Sure, it's over in Queens," Michael said. He was an older man who, Laurie guessed, was in his late sixties. He was sitting on a foam rubber–stuffed pillow with a lot of foam rubber visible. His backrest was constructed of wooden beads.

"How long would it take to get there?" Laurie asked. If it was going to take hours, she wouldn't do it.

Michael made a questioning expression by compressing his lips while thinking. "Not long," he said vaguely. "Traffic's light. In fact, I was just out at Kennedy Airport, and it was a breeze."

"Let's go," Laurie said.

As Michael promised, the trip took only a short time, especially once they got on the Van Wyck Expressway. While they were traveling, Laurie found out that Michael had been driving a cab for over thirty years. He was a loquacious and opinionated man who also exuded a paternal charm.

"Would you know where Gold Road is in Ozone Park?" Laurie asked. She felt privileged to have found an experienced taxi driver. She'd remembered the address of the Spoletto Funeral Home from the Rolodex in the mortuary office. The street name had stuck in her mind as making a metaphorical statement about the undertaking business.

"Gold Road," Michael said. "No problem. It's a continuation of Eighty-ninth Street. You looking for a house or what?"

"I'm looking for the Spoletto Funeral Home," Laurie said.

"I'll have you there in no time," Michael said.

Laurie sat back with a contented feeling, only half listening to Michael's nonstop chatter. For the moment luck seemed to be on her side. The reason she'd decided to visit the Spoletto Funeral Home was because Jack had been wrong about it. The home did have a mob connection, and even though it was with the wrong family according to Lou, the fact that it was associated at all was suspicious to Laurie.

True to his promise, within a surprisingly short time Michael pulled up to a three-storied white clapboard house wedged between several brick tenements. It had Greek-style columns holding up the roof of a wide front porch. A glazed, internally lit sign in the middle of a postage stamp–sized lawn read: "Spoletto Funeral Home, a family business, two generations of caring."

The establishment was in full operation. Lights were on in all the windows. A few cigarette smokers were on the porch. Other people were visible through the ground-floor windows.

Michael was about to terminate the meter when Laurie spoke up: "Would you mind waiting for me?" she asked. "I'm certain I'll only be a few minutes, and I imagine it would be hard catching a cab from here."

"Sure, lady," Michael said. "No problem."

"Would you mind if I left my briefcase?" Laurie asked. "There's absolutely nothing of value in it."

"It will be safe just the same," Michael said.

Laurie got out and started up the front walk, feeling unnerved. She could remember as if it were yesterday the case Dr. Dick Katzenburg had presented at the Thursday afternoon conference five years earlier. A man in his twenties had been essentially embalmed alive in the Spoletto Funeral Home after having been involved in throwing battery acid in Pauli Cerino's face.

Laurie shuddered but forced herself up the front steps. She was never going to be completely free from the Cerino affair.

The people smoking cigarettes ignored her. Soft organ music could be heard through the closed front door. Laurie tried the door. It was unlocked, and she walked in.

Save for the music there was little sound. The floors were heavily carpeted. Small groups of people were standing around the entrance hall but they conversed in hushed whispers.

To Laurie's left was a room full of elaborate coffins and urns on display. To the right was a viewing room with people seated in folding chairs. At the far end of the room was a coffin resting on a bed of flowers.

"May I help you?" a soft voice enquired.

A thin man about Laurie's age with an ascetic face and sad features had come up to her. He was dressed in black except for his white shirt. He was obviously part of the staff. To Laurie, he looked like her image of a puritan preacher.

"Are you here to pay respects to Jonathan Dibartolo?" the man asked.

"No," Laurie said. "Frank Gleason."

"Excuse me?" the man enquired.

Laurie repeated the name. There was a pause.

"And your name is?" the man asked.

"Dr. Laurie Montgomery."

"Just one moment if you will," the man said as he literally ducked away.

Laurie looked around at the mourners. This was a side of death that she'd experienced only once. It was when her brother had died from an overdose when he was nineteen and Laurie was fifteen. It had been a traumatic experience for her in all regards, but especially since she'd been the one who had found him.

"Dr. Montgomery," a soft, unctuous voice intoned. "I'm Anthony Spoletto. I understand you are here to pay respects to Mr. Frank Gleason."

"That's correct," Laurie said. She turned to face a man also dressed in a black suit. He was obese and as oily as his voice. His forehead glistened in the soft incandescent light.

"I'm afraid that will be impossible," Mr. Spoletto said.

"I called this afternoon and was told he was on view," Laurie said.

"Yes, of course," Mr. Spoletto said. "But that was this afternoon. At the family's request this afternoon's four P.M. to six P.M. viewing was to be the last."

"I see," Laurie said, nonplussed. She'd not had any particular plan in mind concerning her visit and had intended on viewing the body as a kind of jumping-off place. Now that the body was not available, she didn't know what to do.

"Perhaps I could just sign the register book anyway," Laurie said.

"I'm afraid that, too, is impossible," Mr. Spoletto said. "The family has already taken it."

"Well, I guess that's it," Laurie said with a limp gesture of her arms.

"Unfortunately," returned Mr. Spoletto.

"Would you know when the burial is planned?" Laurie asked.

"Not at the moment," Mr. Spoletto said.

"Thank you," Laurie said.

"Not at all," Mr. Spoletto said. He opened the door for Laurie.

Laurie walked out and got into the cab.

"Now where?" Michael asked.

Laurie gave her address on Nineteenth Street and leaned forward to look out at the Spoletto Funeral Home as the taxi pulled away. It had been a wasted trip. Or had it? After she'd been talking with Mr. Spoletto for a moment, she'd realized that his forehead wasn't oily. The man had been perspiring despite the temperature inside the funeral parlor being decidedly on the cool side. Laurie scratched her head, wondering if that meant anything or if it were just another example of her grabbing at straws.

"Was it a friend?" Michael asked.

"Was who a friend?"

"The deceased," Michael said.

Laurie let out a little mirthless laugh. "Hardly," she said.

"I know what you mean," Michael said, looking at Laurie in the rearview mirror. "Relationships today are very complicated. And I'll tell you why it is . . ."

Laurie smiled as she settled back to listen. She loved philosophical taxi drivers, and Michael was a regular Plato of his profession.

When the cab pulled up outside Laurie's building, Laurie saw a familiar figure in the foyer. It was Lou Soldano slouched over against the mailboxes, clutching a bottle of wine in a straw basket. Laurie paid Michael the fare along with a generous tip, then hurried inside.

"I'm sorry," Laurie offered. "I thought you were going to call before you came over."

Lou blinked as if he'd been asleep. "I did," he said, after a brief coughing spree. "I got your answering machine. So I left the message that I was on my way."

Laurie glanced at her watch as she unlocked the inner door. She'd only been gone for a little over an hour, which was what she'd expected.

"I thought you were only going to work for another half hour," Lou said.

"I wasn't working," Laurie said, as she called for the elevator. "I took a trip out to the Spoletto Funeral Home."

Lou frowned.

"Now don't give me extra grief," Laurie said as they boarded the elevator.

"So what did you find? Franconi lying in state?" Lou asked sarcastically.

"I'm not going to tell you a thing if you're going to act that way," Laurie complained.

"Okay, I'm sorry," Lou said.

"I didn't find anything," Laurie admitted. "The body I went to see was no longer on view. The family had cut it off at six P.M."

The elevator opened. While Laurie struggled with her locks, Lou curtsied for Debra Engler, whose door opened against its chain as usual.

"But the director acted a little suspicious," Laurie said. "At least I think he did."

"How so?" Lou asked as they entered Laurie's apartment. Tom came running out of the bedroom to purr and rub against Laurie's leg.

Laurie put her briefcase on the small half moon–shaped hall console table in order to bend down to scratch Tom vigorously behind his ear.

"He was perspiring while I was talking with him," Laurie said.

Lou paused with his coat half off. "Is that all?" he asked. "The man was perspiring?"

"Yes, that's it," Laurie said. She knew what Lou was thinking; it was written all over his face.

"Did he start perspiring after you asked him difficult and incriminating questions about Franconi's body?" Lou asked. "Or was he perspiring before you began talking with him?"

"Before," Laurie admitted.

Lou rolled his eyes. "Whoa! Another Sherlock Holmes incarnate," he said. "Maybe you should take over my job. I don't have your powers of intuition and inductive reasoning!"

"You promised not to give me grief," Laurie said.

"I never promised," Lou said.

"All right, it was a wasted trip," Laurie said. "Let's get some food. I'm starved."

Lou switched the bottle of wine from one hand to the other, allowing him to swing his arm out of his trench coat. When he did, he clumsily knocked Laurie's briefcase to the floor. The impact caused it to spring open and scatter the contents. The crash terrified the cat, who disappeared back into the bedroom after a desperate struggle to gain traction on the highly polished wood floor.

"What a klutz," Lou said. "I'm sorry!" He bent down to retrieve the papers, pens, microscope slides, and other paraphernalia and bumped into Laurie in the process.

"Maybe it's best you just sit down," Laurie suggested with a laugh.

"No, I insist," Lou said.

After they'd gotten most of the contents back into the briefcase, Lou picked up the videotape. "What's this, your favorite X-rated feature?"

"Hardly," Laurie commented.

Lou turned it over to read the label. "The Franconi shooting?" he questioned. "CNN sent you this out-of-the-blue?"

Laurie straightened up. "No, I requested it. I was going to use the tape to corroborate the findings when I did the autopsy. I thought it could make an interesting paper to show how reliable forensics can be."

"Mind if I look at it?" Lou asked.

"Of course not," Laurie said. "Didn't you see it on TV?"

"Along with everyone else," Lou said. "But it would still be interesting to see the tape."

"I'm surprised you don't have a copy at police headquarters," Laurie said.

"Hey, maybe we do," Lou said. "I just haven't seen it."

"Man, this ain't your night," Warren teased Jack. "You must be getting too old."

Jack had decided when he'd gotten to the playground late and had had to wait to get into the game, that he was going to win no matter whom he was teamed up with. But it didn't happen. In fact, Jack lost every game he played in because Warren and Spit had gotten on the same team and neither could miss. Their team had won every game including the last, which had just been capped off with a sweet "give and go" that gave Spit an easy final lay-up.

Jack walked over to the sidelines on rubbery legs. He'd played his heart out and was perspiring profusely. He pulled a towel from where he'd jammed it into the chain-link fence and wiped his face. He could feel his heart pounding in his chest.

"Come on, man!" Warren teased from the edge of the court, where he was dribbling a basketball back and forth between his legs. "One more run. We'll let you win this time."

"Yeah, sure!" Jack called back. "You never let nobody win nothing." Jack made it a point to adapt his syntax for the environment. "I'm out'a here."

Warren sauntered over and hooked one of his fingers through the fence and leaned against it. "What's up with your shortie?" he asked. "Natalie's been driving me up the wall asking questions about her since we haven't seen nothing of you guys, you know what I'm saying?"

Jack looked at Warren's sculpted face. To add insult to injury, as far as Jack was concerned, Warren wasn't even perspiring, nor was he breathing particularly heavily. And to make matters worse, he'd been playing before Jack had arrived. The only evidence of exertion was a tiny triangle of sweat down the front of his cut-off sweatshirt.

"Reassure Natalie that Laurie's fine," Jack said. "She and I were just taking a little vacation from each other. It was mostly my fault. I just wanted to cool things down a bit."

"I hear you," Warren said.

"I was with her last night," Jack added. "And things are looking up. She was asking me about you and Natalie, so you weren't alone."

Warren nodded. "You sure you're finished or do you want to run one more?"

"I'm finished," Jack said.

"Take care, man," Warren said as he pushed off the fence. Then he yelled out to the others: "Let's run, you bad asses."

Jack shook his head in dismay as he watched Warren amble away. He was envious of the man's stamina. Warren truly wasn't tired.

Jack pulled on his sweatshirt and started for home. He'd not won a single game, and although during the play the inability to win had seemed overwhelmingly frustrating, now it didn't matter. The exercise had cleared his mind, and for the hour and a half he'd played, he hadn't thought about work.

But Jack wasn't even all the way across 106th Street when the tantalizing mystery of his floater began troubling him again. As he climbed his refuse-strewn stairs, he wondered if there was a chance that Ted had made a mistake with the DNA analysis. As far as Jack was concerned the victim had had a transplant.

Jack was rounding the third-floor landing when he heard the telltale sound of his phone. He knew it was his because Denise, the single mother of two who lived on his floor, didn't have a phone.

With some effort, Jack encouraged his tired quadriceps to propel him up the final flight. Clumsily, he fumbled with his keys at his door. The moment he got it open, he heard his answering machine pick up with a voice that Jack refused to believe was his own.

He got to the phone and snatched it up, cutting himself off in mid-sentence.

"Hello," he gasped. After an hour and a half of full-court, all-out basketball, the dash up the final flight of stairs had put him close to collapse.

"Don't tell me you're just coming in from your basketball," Laurie said. "It's going on nine o'clock. That's way off your schedule."

"I didn't get home until after seven-thirty," Jack explained between breaths. He wiped his face to keep his perspiration from dripping on the floor.

"That means you haven't eaten yet," Laurie said.

"You got that right," Jack said.

"Lou is over here, and we were going to have salad and spaghetti," Laurie said. "Why don't you join us?"

"I wouldn't want to break up the party," Jack said jokingly. At the same time he felt a mild stab of jealousy. He knew about Laurie's and Lou's brief romantic involvement and half wondered if the two friends were starting something up.

Jack knew he had no right to such feelings, considering the ambivalence he had about becoming involved with any woman. After the loss of his family, he'd been unsure if he ever wanted to make himself vulnerable to such pain again. At the same time, he'd come to admit both his loneliness and how much he enjoyed Laurie's company.

"You won't be breaking up any party," Laurie assured him. "It's going to be a very, very casual dinner. But we have something we want to show you. Something that is going to surprise you and maybe even make you want to give yourself a boot in the rear end. As you can probably tell, we're pretty excited."

"Oh?" Jack questioned. His mouth had gone dry. Hearing Lou laughing in the background, and putting two and two together, Jack knew what they wanted to show him; it had to be a ring! Lou must have proposed!

"Are you coming?" Laurie asked.

"It's kind of late," Jack said. "I've got to shower."

"Hey, you old sawbones," Lou said. He'd snatched the phone from Laurie. "Get your ass over here. Laurie and I are dying to share this with you."

"Okay," Jack said with resignation. "I'll jump in the shower and be there in forty minutes."

"See ya, dude," Lou said.

Jack hung up the phone. "Dude?" he mumbled. That didn't sound like Lou. Jack mused that the detective must be on cloud nine.

"I wish I knew what I could do to cheer you up," Darlene said. She'd made the effort to put on a slinky silk teddy from Victoria's Secret, but Raymond hadn't even noticed.

Raymond was stretched out on the sofa with an ice pack on his head and his eyes closed.

"Are you sure you don't want anything to eat?" Darlene asked. She was a tall woman over five feet ten, with bleached blond hair and a curvaceous body. She was twenty-six years old, and as she and Raymond joked, halfway to his fifty-two. She'd been a fashion model before Raymond had met her in a cozy East Side bar called the Auction House.

Raymond slowly took his ice pack off and glared at Darlene. Her bubbly vivaciousness was only an irritation.

"My stomach is in a knot," he said deliberately. "I'm not hungry. Is that so difficult to understand?"

"Well, I don't know why you are so upset," Darlene persisted. "You just got a call from the doctor in Los Angeles, and she's decided to come on board. That means we'll soon have some movie stars as clients. I think we should celebrate."

Raymond replaced the ice pack and closed his eyes. "The problems haven't been about the business side. That's all been going like clockwork. It's these unexpected snafus, like Franconi and now Kevin Marshall." Raymond was loath to explain about Cindy Carlson. In fact, he'd been trying to avoid even thinking about the girl himself.

"Why are you still worried about Franconi?" Darlene asked. "That problem has been taken care of."

"Listen," Raymond said, trying to be patient, "maybe it would be best if you go watch some TV and let me suffer in peace."

"How about some toast or a little cereal?" Darlene asked.

"Leave me alone!" Raymond shouted. He'd sat up suddenly and was clutching his ice pack in his hand. His eyes were bulging and his face was flushed.

"Okay, I can tell when I'm not wanted," Darlene pouted. As she was leaving the room, the phone rang. She looked back at Raymond. "Want me to get it?" she asked.

Raymond nodded and told her to take the call in the study. He also said that if the call was for him, she should be vague about where he was, since he wasn't up to talking with anyone.

Darlene reversed her direction and disappeared into the study. Raymond breathed a sigh of relief and put the ice pack back on his head. Lying back, he tried to relax. He was just getting comfortable when Darlene returned.

"It's the intercom, not the phone," she said. "There's a man downstairs who wants to see you. His name is Franco Ponti, and he said it was important. I told him that I'd see if you were here. What do you want me to say?"

Raymond sat back up with a new jolt of anxiety. For a moment, he couldn't place the name, but he didn't like the sound of it. Then it hit him. It was one of Vinnie Dominick's men who'd accompanied the mobster to the apartment the previous morning.

"Well?" Darlene questioned.

Raymond swallowed loudly. "I'll talk to him." Raymond reached behind the couch and picked up the telephone extension. He tried to sound authoritative when he said hello.

"Howdy, Doc," Franco said. "I was going to be disappointed if you hadn't been at home."

"I'm about to go to bed," Raymond said. "It's rather late for you to be calling."

"My apologies for the hour," Franco said. "But Angelo Facciolo and I have something we'd like to show you."

"Why don't we do this tomorrow?" Raymond said. "Say between nine and ten."

"It can't wait," Franco said. "Come on, Doc! Don't give us a hard time. It's Vinnie Dominick's express wish that you become intimately acquainted with our services."

Raymond struggled to come up with an excuse to avoid going downstairs. But given his headache, nothing came to mind.

"Two minutes," Franco said. "That's all I'm asking."

"I'm awfully tired," Raymond said. "I'm afraid . . ."

"Hold on, Doc," Franco said. "Listen, I have to insist you come down here or you're going to be very sorry. I hope I'm making myself clear."

"All right," Raymond said, recognizing the inevitable. He was not naive enough to believe that Vinnie Dominick and his people made idle threats. "I'll be right down."

Raymond went to the hall closet and got his coat.

Darlene was amazed. "You're going out?"

"It appears that I don't have a lot of choice," Raymond said. "I suppose I should be happy they're not demanding to come inside."

As Raymond descended in the elevator, he tried to calm himself, but it was difficult since his headache had only gotten worse. This unexpected, unwanted visit was just the kind of turn that was making his life miserable. He had no idea what these people wanted to show him, although he guessed it had something to do with how they were going to deal with Cindy Carlson.

"Good evening, Doc," Franco said as Raymond appeared. "Sorry to trouble you."

"Let's just make this short," Raymond said, sounding more confident than he felt.

"It will be short and sweet, trust me," Franco said. "If you don't mind." He pointed up the street where the Ford sedan had been pulled to the curb next to a fire hydrant. Angelo was half-sitting, half-leaning against the trunk, smoking a cigarette.

Raymond followed Franco to the car. Angelo responded by straightening up and stepping to the side.

"We just want you to take a quick look in the trunk," Franco said. He reached the car and keyed the luggage compartment. "Come right over here so you can see. The light's not so good."

Raymond stepped between the Ford and the car behind it, literally inches away from the trunk's lid as Franco raised it.

In the next second, Raymond thought his heart had stopped. The instant he glimpsed the ghoulish sight of Cindy Carlson's dead body crammed into the trunk, there was a flash of light.

Raymond staggered back. He felt sick with the image of the obese girl's porcelain face imprinted in his brain and dizzy from the flash of light which he quickly realized was from a Polaroid camera.

Franco closed the trunk and wiped his hands. "How'd the picture come out?" he asked Angelo.

"Gotta wait a minute," Angelo said. He was holding the edges of the photo as it was developing.

"Just a second longer," Franco said to Raymond.

Raymond involuntarily moaned under his breath, while his eyes scanned the immediate area. He was terrified anybody else had seen the corpse.

"Looks good," Angelo said. He handed the picture to Franco who agreed.

Franco reached out with the photo so Raymond could see it.

"I'd say that's your best side," Franco said.

Raymond swallowed. The picture accurately depicted his shocked terror as well as the awful image of the dead girl.

Franco pocketed the picture. "There, that's it, Doc," he said. "I told you we wouldn't need a lot of your time."

"Why did you do this?" Raymond croaked.

"It was Vinnie's idea," Franco said. "He thought it best to have a record of the favor he'd done for you just in case."

"In case of what?" Raymond asked.

Franco spread his hands. "In case of whatever."

Franco and Angelo got into the car. Raymond stepped up onto the sidewalk. He watched until the Ford had gone to the corner and disappeared.

"Good Lord!" Raymond murmured. He turned and headed back to his door on unsteady legs. Every time he solved one problem another emerged.

The shower had revived Jack. Since Laurie had not included any injunction about riding his bike this time, Jack decided to ride. He cruised south at a good clip. Given the bad experiences he'd had in the park the previous year, he stayed on Central Park West all the way to Columbus Circle.

From Columbus Circle, Jack shot across Fifty-ninth Street to Park Avenue. At that time of the evening, Park Avenue was a dream, and he took it all the way to Laurie's street. He secured his bike with his collection of locks and went to Laurie's door. Before ringing her bell, he took a moment to compose himself, determining how best to act and what to say.

Laurie met him at the door, with a wide grin on her face. Before he could even say a word, she threw her free arm around his neck to give him a hug. In her other hand, she was balancing a glass of wine.

"Uh-oh," she said, stepping back. She eyed the wild state of his close-cropped hair. "I forgot about the bike issue. Don't tell me you rode down here."

Jack shrugged guiltily.

"Well, at least you made it," Laurie said. She unzipped his leather jacket and peeled it off his back.

Jack could see Lou sitting on the sofa, with a grin that rivaled the Cheshire cat's.

Laurie took Jack's arm and pulled him into the living room. "Do you want the surprise first or do you want to eat first?" she asked.

"Let's have the surprise," Jack said.

"Good," Lou said. He bounded off the couch and went to the TV.

Laurie guided Jack to the spot Lou had just vacated. "Do you want a glass of wine?"

Jack nodded. He was confused. He hadn't seen any ring, and Lou was intently studying the VCR remote. Laurie disappeared into the kitchen but was soon back with Jack's wine.

"I don't know how to do this," Lou complained. "At home, my daughter runs the VCR."

Laurie took the remote, then told Lou that he had to turn on the TV first.

Jack took a sip of the wine. It wasn't much better than what he'd brought the previous night.

Laurie and Lou joined Jack on the couch. Jack looked from one to the other, but they were ignoring him. They were intently watching the TV screen.

"What's this surprise?" Jack asked.

"Just watch," Laurie said, pointing toward the electronic snow on the TV.

More confused than ever, Jack looked at the screen. All of a sudden, there was music and the CNN logo followed by the image of a moderately obese man coming out of a Manhattan restaurant Jack recognized as Positano. The man was surrounded by a group of people.

"Should I put on the sound?" Laurie asked.

"Nah, it's not necessary," Lou said.

Jack watched the sequence. When it was over he looked at Laurie and Lou. Both had huge smiles.

"What is going on here?" Jack questioned. "How much wine have you two been drinking?"

"Do you recognize what you've just seen?" Laurie asked.

"I'd say it was somebody getting shot," Jack said.

"It's Carlo Franconi," Laurie said. "After watching it, does it remind you of anything?"

"Sort of reminds me of those old tapes of Lee Harvey Oswald getting shot," Jack said.

"Show it to him again," Lou suggested.

Jack watched the sequence for the second time. He divided his attention between the screen and watching Laurie and Lou. They were captivated.

After the second run-through, Laurie again turned to Jack and said: "Well?"

Jack shrugged. "I don't know what you want me to say."

"Let me run certain sections in slow motion," Laurie said. She used the remote to isolate the sequence to where Franconi was about to climb into the limo. She ran it in slow motion, and then stopped it exactly at the moment he was shot. She walked up to the screen and pointed at the base of the man's neck. "There's the entry point," she said.

Using the remote again, she advanced to the moment of the next impact when the victim was falling to his right.

"Well, I'll be damned!" Jack remarked with astonishment. "My floater might be Carlo Franconi!"

Laurie spun around from facing the TV. Her eyes were blazing. "Exactly!" she said triumphantly. "Obviously, we haven't proved it yet but with the entrance wounds and the paths of the bullets in the floater, I'd be willing to bet five dollars."

"Whoa!" Jack commented. "I'll take you up on a five-dollar wager, but I want to remind you that's a hundred percent higher than any bet you've ever made in my presence."

"I'm that sure," Laurie said.

"Laurie is so fast at making associations," said Lou. "She picked up on the similarities right away. She always makes me feel stupid."

"Get out of here!" Laurie said, giving Lou a friendly shove.

"Is this the surprise you guys wanted to tell me about?" Jack asked cautiously. He didn't want to get his hopes up.

"Yes," Laurie said. "What's the matter? Aren't you as excited as we are?"

Jack laughed with relief. "Oh, I'm just tickled pink!"

"I can never tell when you are serious," Laurie said. She detected a certain amount of Jack's typical sarcasm in his reply.

"It's the best news I've heard in days," Jack added. "Maybe weeks."

"All right, let's not overdo it," Laurie said. She turned off the TV and the VCR. "Enough of the surprise, let's eat."

Over dinner the conversation turned to why no one even considered that the floater might be Franconi.

"For me it was the shotgun wound," Laurie said. "Which I knew Franconi didn't have. Also I was thrown off by the body's being found way out off Coney Island. Now, if it had been fished out of the East River, it might have been a different story."

"I suppose I was thrown off for the same reasons," Jack said. "And then, when I realized the shotgun wound was postmortem, I was already engrossed in the issue about the liver. By the way, Lou, did Franconi have a liver transplant?"

"Not that I know of," Lou said. "He'd been sick for a number of years, but I never knew the diagnosis. I hadn't heard anything about a liver transplant."

"If he didn't have a liver transplant, then the floater isn't Franconi," Jack said. "Even though the DNA lab is having a hard time confirming it, I'm personally convinced the floater has a donated liver."

"What else can you people do to confirm that the floater and Franconi are the same person?" Lou asked.

"We can request a blood sample from the mother," Laurie said. "Comparing the mitochondrial DNA which all of us inherit only from our mothers, we could tell right away if the floater is Franconi. I'm sure the mother will be agreeable, since she'd been the one to come to identify the body initially."

"Too bad an X ray wasn't taken when Franconi came in," Jack said. "That would have done it."

"But there was an X ray!" Laurie said with excitement. "I just found out this evening. Marvin had taken one."

"Where the hell did it go?" Jack asked.

"Marvin said that Bingham took it," Laurie said. "It must be in his office."

"Then I suggest we make a little foray to the morgue," Jack said. "I'd like to settle this issue."

"Bingham's office will be locked," Laurie said.

"I think this situation calls for some creative action," Jack said.

"Amen," Lou said. "This might be that break I've been hoping for."

As soon as they had finished eating and cleaning up the kitchen, which Jack and Lou had insisted on doing, the three took a cab down to the morgue. They entered through the receiving dock and went directly into the mortuary office.

"My God!" Marvin commented when he saw both Jack and Laurie. It was rare for two medical examiners to show up at the same time during the evening. "Has there been a natural disaster?"

"Where are the janitors?" Jack asked.

"In the pit last time I looked," Marvin said. "Seriously, what's up?"

"An identity crisis," Jack quipped.

Jack led the others to the autopsy room and cracked the door. Marvin had been right. Both janitors were busy mopping the expansive terrazzo floor.

"I assume you guys have keys to the chief's office," Jack said.

"Yeah, sure," Daryl Foster said. Daryl had been working for the medical examiner's office for almost thirty years. His partner, Jim O'Donnel, was a relatively new employee.

"We've got to get in there," Jack said. "Would you mind opening it?"

Daryl hesitated. "The chief's kind'a sensitive about people being in his office," he said.

"I'll take responsibility," Jack said. "This is an emergency. Besides we have Lieutenant Detective Soldano with us from the police department, who will keep our thievery to a minimum."

"I don't know," Daryl said. He was obviously uncomfortable, as well as unimpressed, with Jack's humor.

"Then give me the key," Jack said. He stuck out his hand. "That way you won't be involved."

With obvious reluctance, Daryl removed two keys from his key chain and handed them to Jack. "One's for the outer office, and one is for Dr. Bingham's inner office."

"I'll have them back for you in five minutes," Jack said.

Daryl didn't respond.

"I think the poor guy was intimidated," Lou commented as the three rose up to the first floor in the elevator.

"Once Jack is on a mission, look out!" Laurie said.

"Bureaucracy irks me," Jack said. "There's no excuse for the X ray to be squirreled away in the chief's office in the first place."

Jack opened the front office's outer door and then Dr. Bingham's inner door. He turned on the lights.

The office was large, with a big desk beneath high windows to the left and a large library table to the right. Teaching paraphernalia, including a blackboard and an X-ray view box, were at the head of the table.

"Where should we look?" Laurie asked.

"I was hoping they'd just be on that view box," Jack said. "But I don't see them. I tell you what, I'll take the desk and the file cabinet, you look around the view box."

"Fine," Laurie said.

"What do you want me to do?" Lou asked.

"You just stand there and make sure we don't steal anything," Jack scoffed.

Jack pulled out several of the file drawers, but closed them quickly. The full-body X rays that were taken by the morgue came in large folders. It wasn't something easily hidden.

"This looks promising," Laurie called out. She'd found a stash of X rays in the cabinet directly under the view box. Lifting the folders out onto the library table, she scanned the names. She found Franconi's and pulled them free of the others.

Returning to the basement level, Jack got the X rays of the floater and took both folders back to the autopsy room. He gave Bingham's office keys to Daryl and thanked him. Daryl merely nodded.

"Okay, everybody!" Jack said, walking over to the view box. "The critical moment has arrived." First he slipped up Franconi's X rays and then the headless floater's.

"What do you know," Jack said after only a second's inspection. "I owe Laurie five dollars!"

Laurie gave a cry of triumph, as Jack gave her the money. Lou scratched his head and leaned closer to the light box to stare at the films. "How can you guys tell so quickly?" he asked.

Jack pointed out the lumpy shadows of the bullets almost obscured by the mass of shotgun pellets in the floater's X rays and showed how they corresponded to the bullets on the Franconi films. Then he pointed to identical healed clavicular fractures that appeared on the X rays of the two bodies.

"This is great," Lou said, rubbing his hands together with enthusiasm that almost matched Laurie's. "Now that we have a corpus delicti, we might be able to make some headway in this case."

"And I'll be able to figure out what the hell's going on concerning this guy's liver," Jack said.

"And maybe I'll go on a shopping spree with my money," Laurie said, giving the five-dollar bill a kiss. "But not until I figure out the how and the why this body left here in the first place."

Unable to sleep despite having taken two sleeping pills, Raymond slipped out of bed so as not to disturb Darlene. Not that he was terribly worried. Darlene was such a sound sleeper that the ceiling could fall in without her so much as moving.

Raymond padded into the kitchen and turned on the light. He wasn't hungry but he thought that perhaps a little warm milk might help to settle his roiling stomach. Ever since the shock of having been forced to view the terrible sight in the trunk of the Ford, he'd been suffering with heartburn. He'd tried Maalox, Pepcid AC, and finally Pepto-Bismol. Nothing had helped.

Raymond was not handy in the kitchen, mainly because he didn't know where anything was located. Consequently, it took him some time to heat the milk and find an appropriate glass. When it was ready, he carried it into his study and sat at his desk.

After taking a few sips, he noticed that it was three-fifteen in the morning. Despite the fuzziness in his brain from the sleeping pills, he was able to figure out that at the Zone it was after nine, a good time to call Siegfried Spallek.

The connection was almost instantaneous. At that hour, phone traffic with North America was at a minimum. Aurielo answered promptly and put Raymond through to the director.

"You are up early," Siegfried commented. "I was going to call you in four or five hours."

"I couldn't sleep," Raymond said. "What's going on over there? What's the problem with Kevin Marshall?"

"I believe the problem is over," Siegfried said. Siegfried summarized what had happened and gave credit to Bertram Edwards for alerting him about Kevin so that he could be followed. He said that Kevin and his friends had been given such a scare that they wouldn't dare go near the island again.

"What do you mean 'friends'?" Raymond asked. "Kevin has always been such a loner."

"He was with the reproductive technologist and one of the surgical nurses," Siegfried said. "Frankly, even that surprised us since he's always been such a schlemiel, or what do you Americans call such a socially inept person?"

"A nerd," Raymond said.

"That's it," Siegfried said.

"And presumably the stimulus for this attempted visit to the island was the smoke that's been bothering him?"

"That's what Bertram Edwards says," Siegfried said. "And Bertram had a good idea. We're going to tell Kevin that we've had a work crew out there building a bridge over the stream that divides the island in two."

"But you haven't," Raymond said.

"Of course not," Siegfried said. "The last work crew we had out there was when we built the landing for the extension bridge to the mainland. Of course, Bertram had some people there when he moved those hundred cages out there."

"I don't know anything about cages on the island," Raymond said. "What are you talking about?"

"Bertram has been lobbying lately to give up on the island isolation idea," Siegfried said. "He thinks that the bonobos should be brought to the animal center and somehow hidden."

"I want them to stay on the island," Raymond said emphatically. "That was the agreement I worked out with GenSys. They could shut the program down if we bring the animals in. They're paranoid about publicity."

"I know," Siegfried said. "That's exactly what I told Bertram. He understands but wants to leave the cages there just in case. I don't see any harm in that. In fact, it is good to be prepared for unexpected contingencies."

Raymond ran a nervous hand through his hair. He didn't want to hear about any "unexpected contingencies."

"I was going to ask you how you wanted us to handle Kevin and the women," Siegfried said. "But with this explanation about the smoke and having given them a good scare, I think the situation is under control."

"They didn't get onto the island, did they?" Raymond asked.

"No, they were only at the staging area," Siegfried said.

"I don't even like people nosing around there," Raymond said.

"I understand," Siegfried said. "I don't think Kevin will go back for the reasons I've given. But just to be on the safe side, I'm leaving a Moroccan guard and a contingent of the Equatoguinean soldiers out there for a few days, provided you think it's a good idea."

"That's fine," Raymond said. "But tell me, what's your feeling about smoke coming out of the island, assuming that Kevin is right about it?"

"Me?" Siegfried questioned. "I couldn't care less what those animals do out there. As long as they stay there and stay healthy. Does it bother you?"

"Not in the slightest," Raymond said.

"Maybe we should send over a bunch of soccer balls," Siegfried said. "That might keep them entertained." He laughed heartily.

"I hardly think this is a laughing matter," Raymond said irritably. Raymond was not fond of Siegfried, although he appreciated his disciplined managerial style. Raymond could picture the director at his desk, surrounded by his stuffed menagerie and those skulls dotting his desk.

"When are you coming for the patient?" Siegfried asked. "I've been told he's doing fantastically well and ready to go."

"So I've heard," Raymond said. "I put in a call to Cambridge, and as soon as the GenSys plane is available, I'll be over. It should be in a day or so."

"Let me know," Siegfried said. "I'll have a car waiting for you in Bata."

Raymond replaced the receiver and breathed a small sigh of relief. He was glad he'd called Africa, since part of his current anxiety had stemmed from Siegfried's disturbing message about there being a problem with Kevin. It was good to know the crisis had been taken care of. In fact, Raymond thought that if he could just get the image of that snapshot of him hovering over Cindy Carlson's body out of his mind, he'd feel almost like himself again.

CHAPTER 13

Kevin was totally unaware of the time when a knock interrupted the intense concentration he'd been directing toward his computer screen for several hours. He opened his laboratory door and was promptly greeted by Melanie as she swooped into the room. She was carrying a large paper bag.

"Where are your techs?" she asked.

"I gave them the day off," Kevin said. "There was no way I was going to get any work done today so I told them to enjoy the sun. It's been a long rainy season, and it will be back before we know it."

"Where's Candace?" Melanie asked. She put down her parcel on the lab bench.

"I don't know," Kevin said. "I haven't seen or talked with her since we dropped her off at the hospital this morning."

It had been a long night. After having hid in the pathology cooler for over an hour, Melanie had talked both Kevin and Candace into sneaking up to the on-call room Melanie had at the animal center. The three had stayed there getting very little sleep, until the early-morning shift change. Blending in with all the employees coming and going, the group had made it back to Cogo without incident.

"Do you know how to get in touch with her?" Melanie asked.

"I guess just call the hospital and have her paged," Kevin suggested. "Unless she's in her room in the Inn, which is what I'd guess since Horace Winchester is doing so well." The Inn was the name given to the temporary quarters for transient hospital personnel. It was physically part of the hospital/laboratory complex.

"Good point!" Melanie said. She picked up the phone and had the operator put her through to Candace's room. Candace answered on the third ring. It was apparent she'd been asleep.

"Kevin and I are going to the island," Melanie said without preamble. "You want to come or hang in here?"

"What are you talking about?" Kevin asked nervously.

Melanie motioned for him to be quiet.

"When?" Candace asked.

"As soon as you get over here," Melanie said. "We're in Kevin's lab."

"It will take me a good half hour," Candace said. "I've got to shower."

"We'll be waiting," Melanie said. She hung up the phone.

"Melanie, are you crazy?" Kevin said. "We've got to let some time go by before we hazard another try at the island."

"This girl doesn't think so," Melanie said, giving herself a poke in the chest.

"The sooner we go, the better. If Bertram finds out a key is missing, he could change the lock, and we'll be back to square one. Besides, like I said last night, they expect us to be terrified. Going out there right away will catch them off-guard."

"I don't think I'm up for this," Kevin said.

"Oh really?" Melanie questioned superciliously. "Hey, you're the one who's brought up this worry about what we've created. And now I'm really worried. I saw some more circumstantial evidence this morning."

"Like what?" Kevin asked.

"I went into the bonobo enclosure out at the animal center," Melanie said. "I made sure no one saw me go in, so don't get yourself all worked up. It took me over an hour, but I managed to find a mother with one of our infants."

"And?" Kevin questioned. He wasn't sure he wanted to hear the rest.

"The infant walked around on its hindlegs—just like you and I—the whole time I was able to observe," Melanie said. Her dark eyes flashed with emotion akin to anger. "Behavior we used to call cute is definitely bipedal."

Kevin nodded and looked away. He found Melanie's intensity unnerving, and her conversation was underlining all his own fears.

"We have to find out for sure what the status is of these creatures," Melanie said. "And we can do that only by going out there."

Kevin nodded.

"So, I made some sandwiches," Melanie said, pointing toward the paper bag she'd brought in with her. "We'll call it a picnic."

"I came across something disturbing this morning as well," Kevin said. "Let me show you." He grabbed a stool and pushed it over to his computer terminal. He motioned for Melanie to sit down, while he took his own chair. His fingers played over the keyboard. Soon the screen displayed the computer graphic of Isla Francesca.

"I programmed the computer to follow all seventy-three bonobos on the island for several hours of real-time activity," Kevin explained. "Then I had the data condensed so I could watch it in fast-forward. Look what resulted."

Kevin clicked his mouse to start the sequence. The multitude of little red dots rapidly traced out weird geometric designs. It only took a few seconds.

"Looks like a bunch of chicken scratches," Melanie said.

"Except for these two dots," Kevin said. He pointed to two pinpoints.

"They apparently didn't move much," Melanie said.

"Exactly," Kevin said. "Creature number sixty and creature number sixty-seven." Kevin reached over and picked up the detailed contour map he'd inadvertently taken from Bertram's office. "I located creature number sixty to a marshy clearing just south of Lago Hippo. According to the map, there are no trees there."

"What's your explanation?" Melanie asked.

"Hang on," Kevin said. "What I did next was reduce the scale of the grid so that it represented a fifty-by-fifty-foot portion of the island right where creature number sixty was located. Let me show you what happened."

Kevin keyed in the information and then clicked to start the sequence again. Once again the red light for creature number sixty was a pinpoint.

"He didn't move at all," Melanie said.

"I'm afraid not," Kevin said.

"You think he's sleeping?"

"In the middle of the morning?" Kevin asked. "And with such a scale, even turning over in his sleep should result in some movement. The system is that sensitive."

"If he's not sleeping, what is he doing?" Melanie asked.

Kevin shrugged. "I don't know. Maybe he found a way to remove his computer chip."

"I never thought of that," Melanie said. "That's a scary idea."

"The only other thing I could think of is the bonobo died," Kevin said.

"I suppose that's a possibility," Melanie said. "But I don't think it is very probable. Those are young, extraordinarily healthy animals. We've made sure of that. And they are in an environment without natural enemies and have more than enough food."

Kevin sighed. "Whatever it is, it is disturbing, and when we go out there, I think we should check it out."

"I wonder if Bertram knows about this?" Melanie asked. "It doesn't bode well for the program in general."

"I suppose I should tell him," Kevin said.

"Let's wait until we make our visit," Melanie said.

"Obviously," Kevin said.

"Did you come across anything else with this real-time program?"

"Yup," Kevin said. "I pretty much confirmed my earlier suspicion they are using the caves. Watch!"

Kevin changed the coordinates of the displayed grid on the computer screen to correspond to a specific portion of the limestone escarpment. He then asked the computer to trace the activity of his own double, creature number one.

Melanie watched as the red dot traced a geometric shape then disappeared. It then reappeared at the identical spot and traced a second shape. Then a similar sequence repeated itself for a third time.

"I guess I'd have to agree," Melanie said. "It sure looks like your double is going in and out of the rock face."

"When we go out there, I think we should make it a point to see our doubles," Kevin said. "They are the oldest of the creatures, and if any of the transgenic bonobos are acting like protohumans, it should be them."

Melanie nodded. "The idea of facing my double gives me the creeps. But we're not going to have a lot of time out there. And given the twelve-square-mile island it will be extraordinarily difficult for us to find a specific creature."

"You're wrong," Kevin said. "I've got the instruments they use for retrievals."

He got up from the computer and went to his desk. When he returned, he was carrying the locator and the directional beacon that Bertram had given to him. He showed the apparatuses to Melanie and explained their use. Melanie was impressed.

"Where is that girl?" Melanie asked as she checked her watch. "I wanted to get this island visit over during lunch hour."

"Did Siegfried talk to you this morning?" Kevin asked.

"No, Bertram did," Melanie said. "He acted really mad and said he was disappointed in me. Can you imagine? I mean, is that supposed to break me up or what?"

"Did he give you any explanation about the smoke I've seen?" Kevin asked.

"Oh, yeah," Melanie said. "He went on at length how he'd just been told that Siegfried had a work crew out there building a bridge and burning trash. He said it was being done without his knowledge."

"I thought so," Kevin said. "Siegfried called me over just after nine. He gave me the same story. He even told me he'd just talked with Dr. Lyons and that Dr. Lyons was disappointed in us as well."

"It's enough to make you cry," Melanie said.

"I don't think he was telling the truth about the work crew," Kevin said.

"Of course he wasn't," Melanie said. "I mean, Bertram makes it a point to know everything that's going on about Isla Francesca. It makes you wonder if they think we were born yesterday."

Kevin stood up, fidgeted, and stared out his window at the distant island.

"What's wrong now?" Melanie questioned.

"Siegfried," Kevin said. He looked back at Melanie. "About his warning to apply Equatoguinean law to us. He reminded us that going to the island could be considered a capital offense. Don't you think we should take that threat seriously?"

"Hell, no!" Melanie said.

"How can you be so sure," Kevin said. "Siegfried scares me."

"He'd scare me, too, if I was an Equatoguinean," Melanie said. "But we're not. We're Americans. While we're here in the Zone, good old American law applies to us. The worst thing that can happen is we get fired. And as I said last night, I'm not sure I wouldn't welcome it. Manhattan is sounding awfully good to me these days."

"I wish I felt as confident as you," Kevin said.

"Has your playing around with the computer this morning confirmed that the bonobos are remaining in two groups?"

Kevin nodded. "The first group is the largest and stays around the caves. It includes most of the older bonobos, including your double and mine. The other group is in a forest area on the north side of the Rio Diviso. It's composed mostly of younger animals, although the third oldest is with them. That's Raymond Lyons's double."

"Very curious," Melanie said.

"Hi, everybody," Candace called out while coming through the door, without knocking. "How'd I do timewise? I didn't even blow-dry my hair." Instead of her normal French twist, her damp hair was combed back straight off her forehead.

"You did great," Melanie assured her. "And you were the only smart one to get some sleep. I have to admit, I'm exhausted."

"Did Siegfried Spallek get in touch with you?" Kevin asked.

"At about nine-thirty," Candace said. "He woke me up out of a sound sleep. I hope I made sense."

"What did he say?" Kevin asked.

"He was very nice, actually," Candace said. "He even apologized for what happened last night. He also had an explanation about the smoke coming from the island. He said it was from a work crew burning brush."

"We got the same message," Kevin said.

"What's your take on it?" Candace asked.

"We don't buy it," Melanie said. "It's too convenient."

"I sort of assumed as much," Candace said.

Melanie grabbed her paper bag. "Let's get this show on the road."

"Do you have the key?" Kevin questioned. He picked up the locator and the directional beacon.

"Of course I have the key," Melanie said.

As they went out the door Melanie told Candace she'd brought some lunch for them.

"Great!" Candace said. "I'm famished."

"Hold on a second," Kevin said when they reached the stairs. "Something just dawned on me. We must have been followed yesterday. That's the only way I can explain the way they surprised us. Of course, that really means I must have been followed, since I was the one who talked about the smoke situation with Bertram Edwards."

"That's a good point," Melanie said.

The three people stared at each other for a moment.

"What should we do?" Candace asked. "We don't want to be followed."

"The first thing is that we shouldn't use my car," Kevin said. "Where's yours, Melanie? With this dry weather we can manage without four-wheel drive."

"Downstairs in the parking lot," Melanie said. "I just drove in from the animal center."

"Was anybody following you?"

"Who knows?" Melanie said. "I wasn't watching."

"Hmmm," Kevin pondered. "I still think they'll be following me if they follow anybody. So, Melanie, go down and get in your car and head home."

"What will you guys do?"

"There's a tunnel in the basement that goes all the way out to the power station. Wait about five minutes at your house and pick us up at the power station. There's a side door that opens directly onto the parking lot. You know where I mean?"

"I think so," Melanie said.

"All right," Kevin said. "See you there."

They split up at the first floor, with Melanie going out into the noonday heat while Candace and Kevin descended to the basement level.

After walking for fifteen minutes, Candace commented on what a maze the hallways were.

"All the power comes from the same source," Kevin explained. "The tunnels connect all the main buildings except for the animal center, which has its own power station."

"One could get lost down here," Candace said.

"I did," Kevin admitted. "A number of times. But during the middle of the rainy season, I find these tunnels handy. They're both dry and cool."

As they neared the power station they could hear and feel the vibration of the turbines. A flight of metal steps took them up to the side door. As soon as they appeared, Melanie, who'd been parked under a malapa tree, cruised over and picked them up.

Kevin got in the back so Candace could climb into the front. Melanie pulled away immediately. The car's air-conditioning felt good given the heat and hundred-percent humidity.

"See anything suspicious?" Kevin asked.

"Not a thing," Melanie said. "And I drove around for a while pretending I was on errands. There wasn't anyone following me. I'm ninety-nine percent sure."

Kevin looked out the back window of Melanie's Honda and watched the area around the power station as it fell behind, then disappeared as they rounded a corner. No people had appeared, and there were no cars in pursuit.

"I'd say it looks good," Kevin said. He scrunched down on the backseat to be out of sight.

Melanie drove around the north rim of the town. While she did so, Candace broke out the sandwiches.

"Not bad," Candace said, taking a bite of a tuna fish on whole wheat.

"I had them made up at the animal-center commissary," Melanie explained. "There are drinks in the bottom of the bag."

"You want some, Kevin?" Candace called.

"I suppose," Kevin said. He stayed on his side. Candace passed him a sandwich and a soft drink between the front bucket seats.

They were soon on the road that led east out of town toward the native village. From Kevin's perspective, all he could see was the tops of the liana-covered trees that lined the road, plus a strip of hazy blue sky. After so many months of cloud cover and rain, it was good to see the sun.

"Anybody following us?" Kevin asked, after they'd driven for some time.

Melanie glanced in the rearview mirror. "I haven't seen a car," she said. There'd been no vehicular traffic in either direction, although there were plenty of native women carrying various burdens on their heads.

After they passed the parking lot in front of the general store at the native village and entered the track that led to the island staging area, Kevin sat up. He was no longer worried about being seen. Every few minutes, he looked behind to make sure they weren't being followed. Although he didn't admit it to the women, he was a nervous wreck.

"That log we hit last night should be coming up soon," Kevin warned.

"But we didn't go over it when they brought us out," Melanie said. "They must have moved it."

"You're right," Kevin said. He was impressed that Melanie remembered. After the machine-gun fire, the details of the previous night were murky in Kevin's mind.

Guessing they were getting close, Kevin moved forward so he could see out the front windshield between the two front seats. Despite the noontime sun the ability to see into the dense jungle lining the road was hardly any better than it had been the evening before. Little light penetrated the vegetation; it was like moving between two walls.

They drove into the clearing and stopped. The garage stood to their left while to the right they could see the mouth of the track that led down to the water's edge and the bridge.

"Should I drive down to the bridge?" Melanie asked.

Kevin's nervousness increased. Coming into a dead end bothered him. He debated driving down to the water's edge but guessed there wouldn't be enough room to turn around. That would mean they'd have to back out.

"My suggestion would be to park here," Kevin said. "But let's turn the car around first."

Kevin expected an argument, but Melanie put the car in gear without so much as a whimper. They left unspoken the fact that they would now have to walk past the spot where they'd been fired upon.

Melanie completed her three-point turn. "Okay, everybody, here we are," she said airily, as she pulled on the emergency brake. She was trying to buoy everyone's spirits. They were all tense.

"I just had an idea which I don't like," Kevin said.

"Now what?" Melanie asked, looking at him in the rearview mirror.

"Maybe I should quietly walk down to the bridge and make sure no one is around," Kevin said.

"Like who?" Melanie asked, but the thought of unwanted company had occurred to her as well.

Kevin took a deep breath to bolster his sagging courage and climbed out. "Anybody," he said. "Even Alphonse Kimba." He hiked up his pants and started off.

The track down toward the water was so thickly shrouded with vegetation, it was even more like a tunnel than the track in from the road. As soon as Kevin entered it, it twisted to the right. The canopy of trees and vines blocked out much of the light. The center strip of vegetation was so tall that the track was more like two parallel trails.

Kevin rounded the first bend, then stopped. The unmistakable sound of boots running on the damp ground combined with the jingling of metal against metal made his stomach turn. Ahead, the track turned to the left. Kevin held his breath. In the next instant, he saw a group of Equatoguinean soldiers in their camouflage fatigues, rounding the bend and coming in his direction. All were carrying Chinese assault rifles.

Kevin spun on his heels and sprinted back up the trail like he'd never sprinted before. As he reached the clearing, he yelled to Melanie to get the hell out of there. Reaching the car he threw open the rear door and dived in.

Melanie was trying to start the car. "What happened?" she screamed.

"Soldiers!" Kevin croaked. "A bunch of them!"

The car engine caught and roared to life. At the same time, the soldiers spilled into the clearing. One of them yelled as Melanie stomped on the accelerator.

The little car leaped forward, and Melanie fought the wheel. There was a burst of gunfire and the rear window of the Honda shattered into a million cubic shards. Kevin flattened himself against the backseat. Candace screamed as her window was blown out as well.

The track turned left just beyond the clearing. Melanie managed to keep the car in the tracks and then pushed the car to its limit. After they'd gone seventy yards, there was another distant burst of gunfire. A few stray bullets whined over the car as Melanie navigated another slight turn.

"Good God!" Kevin said, as he sat up and brushed the glass from the rear window off his torso.

"Now I'm really mad," Melanie said. "That was hardly a burst over our heads. Look at that rear window!"

"I think I want to retire," Kevin said. "I've always been afraid of those soldiers and now I know why."

"I guess the key to the bridge is not going to do us much good," Candace said. "What a waste after all the effort we went through to get it."

"It's damn irritating," Melanie agreed. "We're just going to have to come up with an alternate plan."

"I'm going to bed," Kevin said. He couldn't believe these women; they seemed fearless. He put a hand over his heart; it was beating more rapidly than it ever had before.

CHAPTER 14

With a burst of speed, Jack made the green light at the intersection of First Avenue and Thirtieth Street and sailed across without slowing down. Angling the bike up the morgue's driveway, he didn't brake until the last minute. Moments later, he had the bike locked and was on his way to the office of Janice Jaeger, the night forensic investigator.

Jack was keyed up. After near conclusive identification of his floater as Carlo Franconi, Jack had gotten little sleep. He'd been on and off the phone with Janice, finally imploring her to get copies of all of Franconi's records from the Manhattan General Hospital. Her preliminary investigation had determined that Franconi had been hospitalized there.

Jack had also had Janice get the phone numbers of the European human organ distribution organizations from Bart Arnold's desk. Because of the six-hour-time difference, Jack had started calling after three A.M. He was most interested in the organization called Euro Transplant Foundation in the Netherlands. When they had no record of a Carlo Franconi as a recent liver recipient, Jack called all the national organizations whose numbers he had. They included organizations in France, England, Italy, Sweden, Hungary, and Spain. No one had heard of Carlo Franconi. On top of that, most of the people he had spoken with said that it would be rare for a foreign national to get such a transplant because most of the countries had waiting lists comprised of their own citizens.

After only a few hours of sleep, Jack's curiosity had awakened him. Unable to get back to sleep, he'd decided to get into the morgue early to go over the material that Janice had collected.

"My word, you are eager," Janice commented as Jack came into her office.

"This is the kind of case that makes forensics fun," Jack said. "How'd you do at the MGH?"

"I got a lot of material," Janice said. "Mr. Franconi had multiple admissions over the years, mostly for hepatitis and cirrhosis."

"Ah, the plot thickens," Jack said. "When was the last admission?"

"About two months ago," Janice said. "But no transplant. There is mention of it, but if he had one, he didn't have it at the MGH." She handed Jack a large folder.

Jack hefted the package and smiled. "Guess I got a lot of reading to do."

"It looked pretty repetitive to me," Janice said.

"What about his doctor?" Jack asked. "Has he had one in particular or has he been playing the field?"

"One for the most part," Janice said. "Dr. Daniel Levitz on Fifth Avenue between Sixty-fourth and Sixty-fifth Street. His office number is written on the outside of your parcel."

"You are efficient," Jack said.

"I try to do my best," Janice said. "Have any luck with those European organ distribution organizations?"

"A complete strikeout," Jack said. "Have Bart give me a call as soon as he comes in. We have to go back and retry all the transplant centers in this country now that we have a name."

"If Bart's not in by the time I leave, I'll put a note on his desk," Janice said.

Jack whistled as he walked through communications on his way to the ID room. He could taste the coffee already while dreaming of the euphoria that the first cup of the day always gave him. But when he arrived he could see he was too early. Vinnie Amendola was just in the process of making it.

"Hurry up with that coffee," Jack said, as he dropped his heavy package onto the metal desk Vinnie used to read his newspaper. "It's an emergency this morning."

Vinnie didn't answer, which was out of character, and Jack noticed. "Are you still in a bad mood?" he asked.

Vinnie still didn't answer, but Jack's mind was already elsewhere. He'd seen the headlines on Vinnie's paper: FRANCONI'S BODY FOUND. Beneath the headline in slightly smaller print was: "Franconi's corpse languishing in the Medical Examiner's Office for twenty-four hours before identity established."

Jack sat down to read the article. As usual, it was written in a sarcastic bent with the implication that the city's medical examiners were bunglers. Jack thought it was interesting that while the journalist had had enough information to write the article, he didn't appear to know that the body had been headless and handless in a deliberate attempt to conceal its identity. Nor did it mention anything about the shotgun wound to its right upper quadrant.

After finishing with the coffee preparation, Vinnie came over to stand next to the desk while Jack read. Impatiently, he shifted his weight from one foot to the other. When Jack finally looked up Vinnie said irritably: "Do you mind! I'd like to have my paper."

"You see this article?" Jack asked, slapping the front page.

"Yeah, I seen it," Vinnie said.

Jack resisted the temptation to correct his English. Instead he said: "Did it surprise you? I mean, when we did the autopsy yesterday, did it ever cross your mind it might have been the missing Franconi?"

"No, why should it?" Vinnie said.

"I'm not saying it should," Jack said. "I'm just asking if it did."

"No," Vinnie said. "Let me have my paper! Why don't you buy your own? You're always reading mine."

Jack stood up, pushed Vinnie's paper toward him, and lifted the bundle from

Janice. "You really are out of sorts lately. Maybe you need a vacation. You're fast becoming a grumpy old man."

"At least I'm not a cheapskate," Vinnie said. He picked up his paper and read-justed the pages that Jack had gotten out of alignment.

Jack went to the coffeemaker and poured himself a brimming cup. He took it over to the scheduling desk. While sipping contentedly, he went through the mul-titude of Franconi's hospital admissions. On his first perusal of the material, he just wanted the basics, so he read each discharge summary page. As Janice had already told him, the admissions were mostly due to liver problems starting from a bout of hepatitis he contracted in Naples, Italy.

Laurie arrived next. Before she even had her coat off, she asked Jack if he'd seen the paper or heard the morning news. Jack told her he'd seen the *Post*.

"Was it your doing?" Laurie asked, as she folded her coat and put it on a chair.

"What are you talking about?"

"The leak that we tentatively identified Franconi as your floater," Laurie said.

Jack gave a little laugh of disbelief. "I'm surprised you'd even ask. Why would I do such a thing?"

"I don't know, except you were so excited about it last night," Laurie said. "But I didn't mean any offense. I was just surprised to see it in the news so quickly."

"You and me both," Jack said. "Maybe it was Lou."

"I think that would surprise me even more than you," Laurie said.

"Why me?" Jack said. He sounded hurt.

"Last year you leaked the plague story," Laurie said.

"That was a completely different situation," Jack said defensively. "That was to save people."

"Well, don't get mad," Laurie said. To change the subject she asked: "What kind of cases do we have for today?"

"I didn't look," Jack admitted. "But the pile is small and I have a request. If possible, I'd like to have a paper day or really a research day."

Laurie bent over and counted the autopsy folders. "Only ten cases; no problem," she said. "I think I'll only do one myself. Now that Franconi's body is back, I'm even more interested to find out how it left here in the first place. The more I've thought about it, the more I believe it had to have been an inside job in some form or fashion."

There was a splashing sound followed by loud cursing. Both Laurie and Jack looked over at Vinnie, who'd jumped up to a standing position. He'd spilled his coffee all over his desk and even onto his lap.

"Watch out for Vinnie," Jack warned Laurie. "He's again in a foul mood."

"Are you all right, Vinnie?" Laurie called out.

"I'm okay," Vinnie said. He walked stiff-legged over to the coffeepot to get some paper towels.

"I'm a little confused," Jack said to Laurie. "Why does Franconi's return make you more interested in his disappearance?"

"Mainly because of what you found during the autopsy," Laurie said. "At first I thought that whoever stole the body had done it out of pure spite, like the killer wanted to deny the man a proper funeral, something like that. But now it seems that the body was taken to destroy the liver. That's weird. Initially I thought that solving the riddle of how the body disappeared was simply a challenge. Now I think if I can figure out how the body disappeared, we might be able to find out who did it."

"I'm beginning to understand what Lou said about feeling stupid about your ability to make associations," Jack said. "With Franconi's disappearance I always thought the 'why' was more important than the 'how.' You're suggesting they are related."

"Exactly," Laurie said. "The 'how' will lead to the 'who,' and the 'who' will explain the 'why.' "

"And you think someone who works here is involved," Jack said.

"I'm afraid I do," Laurie said. "I don't see how they could have pulled it off without someone on the inside. But I still have no clue how it happened."

After his call to Siegfried, Raymond's brain had finally succumbed to the high levels of hypnotic medication circulating in his bloodstream from the two sleeping pills. He slept soundly through the remaining early hours. The next thing he was aware of was Darlene opening the curtains to let in the daylight. It was almost eight o'clock, the time he'd asked to be awakened.

"Feel better, dear?" Darlene asked. She made Raymond sit forward so she could fluff up his pillow.

"I do," Raymond admitted, although his mind was fuzzy from the sleeping pills.

"I even made you your favorite breakfast," Darlene said. She went over to the bureau and lifted a wicker tray. She carried it over to the bed and placed it across Raymond's lap.

Raymond's eyes traveled around the tray. There was fresh-squeezed orange juice, two strips of bacon, a single-egg omelette, toast, and fresh coffee. In a side pocket was the morning paper.

"How's that?" Darlene asked proudly.

"Perfect," Raymond said. He reached up and gave her a kiss.

"Let me know when you want more coffee," Darlene said. Then she left the room.

With childlike pleasure Raymond buttered his toast and sipped his orange juice. As far as he was concerned, there was nothing quite so wonderful as the smell of coffee and bacon in the morning.

Taking a bite of both bacon and omelette at the same time to savor the combined tastes, Raymond lifted the paper, opened it, and glanced at the headlines.

He gasped, inadvertently inhaling some of his food. He coughed so hard, he bucked the wicker tray off the bed. It crashed upside down on the carpet.

Darlene came running into the room and stood wringing her hands, while Raymond went through a series of coughing jags that turned him tomato red.

"Water!" he squeaked between fits.

Darlene dashed into the bathroom and returned with a glass. Raymond clutched it and managed to drink a small amount. The bacon and egg that he'd had in his mouth was now distributed in an arc around the bed.

"Are you all right?" Darlene asked. "Should I call 911?"

"The wrong way down," Raymond croaked. He pointed to his Adam's apple.

It took Raymond five minutes to recover. By that time, his throat was sore and his voice hoarse. Darlene had cleaned up most of the mess he'd caused except for the coffee stain on the white carpet.

"Did you see the paper?" Raymond asked Darlene.

She shook her head, so Raymond spread it out for her.

"Oh, my," she said.

"Oh, my!" Raymond repeated sarcastically. "And you were wondering why I was still worried about Franconi!" Raymond forcibly crumpled the paper.

"What are you going to do?" Darlene asked.

"I suppose I have to go back and see Vinnie Dominick," Raymond said. "He promised me the body was gone. Some job he did!"

The phone rang and Raymond jumped.

"Do you want me to answer it?" Darlene asked.

Raymond nodded. He wondered who could be calling so early.

Darlene picked up the phone and said hello followed by several yeses. Then she put the phone on hold.

"It's Dr. Waller Anderson," Darlene said with a smile. "He wants to come on board."

Raymond exhaled. Until then he'd not been aware he'd been holding his breath. "Tell him we're pleased, but that I'll have to call him later."

Darlene did as she was told and then hung up the phone. "At least that was good news," she said.

Raymond rubbed his forehead and audibly groaned. "I just wish everything would go as well as the business side."

The phone rang again. Raymond motioned for Darlene to answer it. After saying hello and listening for a moment, her smile quickly faded. She put the phone on hold and told Raymond it was Taylor Cabot.

Raymond swallowed hard. His already irritated throat had gone dry. He took a quick swig of water and took the receiver.

"Hello, sir!" Raymond managed. His voice was still hoarse.

"I'm calling from my car phone," Taylor said. "So I won't be too specific. But I have just been informed of the reemergence of a problem I thought had been taken care of. What I said earlier about this issue still stands. I hope you understand."

"Of course, sir," Raymond squeaked. "I will . . ."

Raymond stopped speaking. He took the phone away from his ear and looked at it. Taylor had cut him off.

"Just what I need," Raymond said, as he handed the phone back to Darlene. "Another threat from Cabot to close down the program."

Raymond put his feet over the side of the bed. As he stood up and slipped on his robe, he could still feel the remnants of yesterday's headache. "I have to go find Vinnie Dominick's number. I need another miracle."

By eight o'clock Laurie and the others were down in the "pit" starting their autopsies. Jack had stayed in the ID room to read through the records of Carlo Franconi's hospital admissions. When he noticed the time, he went back to the forensics area to find out why the chief investigator, Bart Arnold, had not come in that day. Jack was surprised when he found the man in his office.

"Didn't Janice talk to you this morning?" Jack asked. He and Bart were good enough friends so that Jack thought nothing of marching right into Bart's office and plopping himself down.

"I just came in fifteen minutes ago," Bart said. "Janice was already gone."

"Wasn't there a message on your desk?" Jack asked.

Bart started to peek around under the clutter. Bart's desk looked strikingly similar to Jack's. Bart pulled out a note which he read aloud: "Important! Call Jack Stapleton immediately." It was signed "Janice."

"Sorry," Bart said. "I'd have seen it eventually." He smiled weakly, knowing there was no excuse.

"I suppose you've heard that my floater has been just about conclusively identified as Carlo Franconi," Jack said.

"So I've heard," Bart said.

"That means I want you to go back to UNOS and all the centers that do liver transplantation with the name."

"That's a lot easier than asking them to check if any of their recent transplants is missing," Bart said. "With all the phone numbers handy I can do that in a flash."

"I spent most of the night on the phone with the organizations in Europe responsible for organ allocation," Jack said. "I came up with zilch."

"Did you talk to Euro Transplant in the Netherlands?" Bart asked.

"I called them first," Jack said. "They had no record of a Franconi."

"Then it's pretty safe to say that Franconi didn't have his transplant in Europe," Bart said. "Euro Transplant keeps tabs on the whole continent."

"The next thing I want is for someone to go visit Franconi's mother and talk her into giving a blood sample. I want Ted Lynch to run a mitochondrial DNA match with the floater. That will clinch the identity, so it will no longer be presumptive. Also have the investigator ask the woman if her son had a liver transplant. It will be interesting to hear what she has to say."

Bart wrote Jack's requests down. "What else?" Bart asked.

"I think that's it for now," Jack said. "Janice told me Franconi's doctor's name is Daniel Levitz. Is that anyone you have come in contact with?"

"If it's the Levitz on Fifth, then I've come in contact with him."

"What was your take?" Jack asked.

"High-profile practice with wealthy clientele. He's a good internist as far as I could tell. The curious thing is that he takes care of a lot of the crime families, so it's not surprising he was taking care of Carlo Franconi."

"Different families?" Jack questioned. "Even families in competition with each other?"

"Strange, isn't it?" Bart said. "It must be one big headache for the poor receptionist who does the scheduling. Can you imagine having two rival crime figures with their bodyguards in the waiting room at the same time?"

"Life's stranger than fiction," Jack said.

"Do you want me to go to Dr. Levitz and get what I can on Franconi?" Bart asked.

"I think I'll do that myself," Jack said. "I have a sneaking suspicion that when talking with Franconi's doctor what's unsaid is going to be more important than what is said. You concentrate on finding out where Franconi got his transplant. I think that's going to be the key piece of information in this case. Who knows, it might just explain everything."

"There you are!" a robust voice boomed. Both Jack and Bart looked up to see the doorway literally filled with the imposing figure of Dr. Calvin Washington, the deputy chief.

"I've been looking all over for you, Stapleton," Calvin growled. "Come on! The chief wants to see you."

Jack gave Bart a wink before getting to his feet. "Probably just another of the many awards he's given me."

"I wouldn't be so glib if I were you," Calvin snapped, as he made room for Jack to pass. "Once again, you got the old man all riled up."

Jack followed Calvin to the administration area. Just before going into the front office, Jack caught a glimpse of the waiting room. There were more than the usual number of journalists.

"Something going on?" Jack asked.

"As if I have to tell you," Calvin grunted.

Jack didn't understand, but he didn't have a chance to ask more. Calvin was already asking Mrs. Sanford, Bingham's secretary, if they could go into the chief's office.

As it turned out, the timing wasn't good, and Jack was relegated to sitting on the bench that faced Mrs. Sanford's desk. Obviously, she was as upset as her boss and treated Jack to several disapproving looks. Jack felt like a naughty schoolboy waiting to see the principal. Calvin used the time by disappearing into his own office to make a few phone calls.

Having a reasonable idea of what the chief was upset about, Jack tried to come up with an explanation. Unfortunately, none came to mind. After all, he could have waited to get Franconi's X rays until Bingham's arrival that morning.

"You can go in now," Mrs. Sanford said, without looking up from her typing.

She'd noticed the light on her extension phone had gone out, meaning the chief was off the phone.

Jack entered the chief's office with a sense of déjà vu. A year ago, during a series of infectious disease cases, Jack had managed to drive the chief to distraction, and there had been several such confrontations.

"Get in here and sit down," Bingham said roughly.

Jack took the seat in front of the man's desk. Bingham had aged in the last few years. He looked considerably older than sixty-three. He glared at Jack through his wire-rimmed glasses. Despite his jowls and sagging flesh, Jack saw that his eyes were as intense and intelligent as ever.

"I was just beginning to think you were really fitting in around here, and now this," Bingham said.

Jack didn't respond. He felt it best not to say anything until he was asked a question.

"Can I at least ask why?" Bingham said obligingly in his deep, husky voice.

Jack shrugged. "Curiosity," Jack said. "I was excited and I couldn't wait."

"Curiosity!" Bingham roared. "That was the same lame excuse you used last year when you disregarded my orders and went over to the MGH."

"At least I'm consistent," Jack said.

Bingham moaned. "And now here comes the impertinence. You really haven't changed much, have you?"

"My basketball has improved," Jack said.

Jack heard the door open. He turned to see Calvin slip into the room. Calvin folded his massive arms across his chest and stood to the side like an elite harem guard.

"I'm not getting anywhere with him," Bingham complained to Calvin, as if Jack were no longer in the room. "I thought you said his behavior had improved."

"It had, until this episode," Calvin said. He then glared down at Jack. "What irks me," Calvin said, finally addressing Jack, "is that you know damn well that releases from the medical examiner's office are to come from Dr. Bingham or through public relations, period! You examiner grunts are not to take it upon yourselves to divulge information. The reality is that this job is highly politicized, and in the face of our current problems we certainly don't need more bad press."

"Time out," Jack said. "Something's not right here. I'm not sure we're talking the same language."

"You can say that again," Bingham asserted.

"What I mean is," Jack said, "I don't think we are talking about the same issue. When I came in here, I thought I was being called onto the carpet because I bullied the janitor into giving me keys for this office so I could find Franconi's films."

"Hell, no!" Bingham yelled. He pointed his finger at Jack's nose. "It's because you leaked the story about Franconi's body being discovered here at the morgue after it had been stolen. What did you think? This would somehow advance your career?"

"Hold up," Jack said. "First, I'm not all that excited about advancing my career. Second, I was not responsible for this story getting to the media."

"You're not?" Bingham asked.

"Certainly, you're not suggesting that Laurie Montgomery was responsible?" Calvin asked.

"Not at all," Jack said. "But it wasn't me. Look, to tell you the truth, I don't even think it's a story."

"That's not how the media feels," Bingham said. "Nor the mayor for that matter. He's already called me twice this morning, asking what kind of circus we're running around here. This Franconi business continues to make us look bad in the eyes of the entire city—particularly when news about our own office takes us by surprise."

"The real story about Franconi isn't about his body going on an overnight out of the morgue," Jack said. "It's about the fact that the man seemingly had a liver transplant that no one knows about, that's hard to detect by DNA analysis, and that somebody wanted to hide it."

Bingham looked up at Calvin, who raised his hands defensively. "This is the first I've heard about this," he said.

Jack gave a rapid summary of his autopsy findings and then told about Ted Lynch's confusing DNA analysis results.

"This sounds weird," Bingham said. He took off his glasses and wiped his rheumy eyes. "It also sounds bad, considering that I want this whole Franconi business to fade away. If there is something truly screwy going on like Franconi getting an unauthorized liver, then that's not going to happen."

"I'll know more today," Jack said. "I've got Bart Arnold contacting all the transplant centers around the country, John DeVries up in the lab running assays for immuno suppressants, Maureen O'Conner in histology pushing through the slides, and Ted doing a six polymarker DNA test, which he contends is foolproof. By this afternoon, we'll know for sure whether there'd been a transplant, and, if we're lucky, where it had taken place."

Bingham squinted across his desk at Jack. "And you're sure you didn't leak today's newspaper story to the media?"

"Scout's honor," Jack said, holding up two fingers to form a V.

"All right, I apologize," Bingham said. "But listen, Stapleton, keep this all under your hat. And don't go irritating everyone under the sun, so that I start getting calls complaining about your behavior. You have a knack for getting under people's skin. And finally, promise me that nothing goes to the media unless it goes through me. Understand?"

"As clear as a crystal," Jack said.

Jack could rarely find an excuse to get out on his mountain bike during the day, so that it was with a good deal of pleasure that he pedaled with the traffic up First Avenue on his way to visit Dr. Daniel Levitz. There was no sun, but the temperature was pleasantly in the fifties, heralding the coming spring. For Jack, spring was the best season in New York City.

With his bike safely secured to a NO PARKING sign, Jack walked up to the sidewalk entrance of Dr. Daniel Levitz's office. Jack had called ahead to make sure the doctor was in, but he'd specifically avoided making an appointment. It was Jack's feeling that a surprise visit might be more fruitful. If Franconi had had a transplant, there was definitely something surreptitious about it.

"Your name please?" the silver-haired matronly receptionist asked.

Jack flashed open his medical examiner badge. Its shiny surface and official appearance confused most people into thinking it was a police badge. In situations like this, Jack didn't explain the difference. The badge never failed to cause a reaction.

"I must see the doctor," Jack said, slipping his badge back inside his pocket. "The sooner the better."

When the receptionist regained her voice, she asked for Jack's name. When he gave it, he left off the title of doctor so as not to clarify the nature of his employ.

The receptionist immediately scraped back her chair and disappeared into the depths of the office.

Jack's eyes roamed the waiting room. It was generous in size and lavishly decorated. It was a far cry from the utilitarian waiting room he'd had when he'd been a practicing ophthalmologist. That had been before the retraining necessitated by the managed-care invasion. To Jack, it seemed like a previous life, and in many ways it was.

There were five well-dressed people in the waiting room. All eyed Jack clandestinely as they continued to peruse their respective magazines. As they noisily flipped the pages, Jack sensed an aura of irritation, as if they knew he was about to upset the schedule and relegate them to additional waiting. Jack hoped none of them were notorious crime figures who might consider such an inconvenience a reason for revenge.

The receptionist reappeared, and with embarrassing subservience, she guided Jack back to the doctor's private study. Once Jack was inside, she closed the door.

Dr. Levitz was not in the room. Jack sat in one of the two chairs facing the desk and surveyed the surroundings. There were the usual framed diplomas and licenses, the family pictures, and even the stacks of unread medical journals. It was all familiar to Jack and gave him a shudder. From his current vantage point, he wondered how he'd lasted as long as he had in a similar, confining environment.

Dr. Daniel Levitz came through a second door. He was dressed in his white coat complete with a pocket full of tongue depressors and assorted pens. A stethoscope hung from his neck. Compared with Jack's muscular, thick-shouldered, six-foot frame, Dr. Levitz was rather short and almost fragile in appearance.

Jack immediately noticed the man's nervous tics, which involved slight twists and nods of his head. Dr. Levitz gave no indication he was aware of these movements. He shook hands stiffly with Jack and then retreated behind the vast expanse of his desk.

"I'm very busy," Dr. Levitz said. "But, of course, I always have time for the police."

"I'm not the police," Jack said. "I'm Dr. Jack Stapleton from the Office of the Chief Medical Examiner of New York."

Dr. Levitz's head twitched as did his sparse mustache. He appeared to swallow. "Oh," he commented.

"I wanted to talk to you briefly about one of your patients," Jack said.

"My patients' conditions are confidential," Dr. Levitz said, as if by rote.

"Of course," Jack said. He smiled. "That is, of course, until they have died and become a medical examiner's case. You see, I want to ask you about Mr. Carlo Franconi."

Jack watched as Dr. Levitz went through a number of bizarre motions, making Jack glad the man had not gone into brain surgery.

"I still respect my patients' confidentiality," he said.

"I can understand your position from an ethical point of view," Jack said. "But I should remind you that we medical examiners in the State of New York have subpoena power in such a circumstance. So, why don't we just have a conversation? Who knows, we might be able to clear things up."

"What do you want to know?" Dr. Levitz asked.

"I learned from reading Mr. Franconi's extensive hospital history that he'd had a long bout with liver problems leading to liver failure," Jack said.

Dr. Levitz nodded, which caused his right shoulder to jerk several times. Jack waited until these involuntary movements subsided.

"To come right to the point," Jack said, "the big question is whether or not Mr. Franconi had a liver transplant."

At first Levitz did not speak. He merely twitched. Jack was determined to wait the man out.

"I don't know anything about a liver transplant," Dr. Levitz said finally.

"When did you see him last?" Jack asked.

Dr. Levitz picked up his phone and asked one of his assistants to bring in Mr. Carlo Franconi's record.

"It will just be a moment," Dr. Levitz said.

"In one of Mr. Franconi's hospital admissions about three years ago, you specifically wrote that it was your opinion that a transplant would be necessary. Do you remember writing that?"

"Not specifically," Dr. Levitz said. "But I was aware of a deteriorating condition, as well as Mr. Franconi's failure to stop drinking."

"But you never mentioned it again," Jack said. "I found that surprising when it was easy to see a gradual but relentless deterioration in his liver function tests over the next couple of years."

"A doctor can only do so much to influence his patient's behavior," Dr. Levitz said.

The door opened and the deferential receptionist brought in a fat folder. Wordlessly she placed it on Dr. Levitz's desk and withdrew.

Dr. Levitz picked it up and, after a quick glance, said that he'd seen Carlo Franconi a month previously.

"What did you see him for?"

"An upper respiratory infection," Dr. Levitz said. "I prescribed some antibiotic. Apparently, it worked."

"Did you examine him?"

"Of course!" Dr. Levitz said with indignation. "I always examine my patients."

"Had he had a liver transplant?"

"Well, I didn't do a complete physical," Dr. Levitz explained. "I examined him appropriately in reference to his complaint and his symptoms."

"You didn't even feel his liver, knowing his history?" Jack asked.

"I didn't write it down if I did," Dr. Levitz said.

"Did you do any blood work that would reflect liver function?" Jack asked.

"Only a bilirubin," Dr. Levitz said.

"Why only a bilirubin?"

"He'd been jaundiced in the past," Dr. Levitz said. "He looked better, but I wanted to document it."

"What was the result?" Jack asked.

"It was within normal limits," Dr. Levitz said.

"So, except for his upper respiratory infection, he was doing quite well," Jack said.

"Yes, I suppose you could say that," Dr. Levitz said.

"Almost like a miracle," Jack said. "Especially as you've already mentioned the man was unwilling to curb his alcohol intake."

"Perhaps he finally had stopped," Dr. Levitz said. "After all, people can change."

"Would you mind if I looked at his record?" Jack asked.

"Yes, I would mind," Dr. Levitz said. "I've already stated my ethical position about confidentiality. If you want these records, you will have to subpoena them. I'm sorry. I don't mean to be obstructive."

"That's quite all right," Jack said agreeably. He stood up. "I'll let the state's attorney's office know how you feel. Meanwhile, thanks for your time, and if you don't mind, I'll probably be talking with you in the near future. There's something very strange about this case, and I intend to get to the bottom of it."

Jack smiled to himself, as he undid the locks on his bike. It was so obvious that Dr. Levitz knew more than he was willing to say. How much more, Jack didn't know, but certainly it added to the intrigue. Jack had an intuitive sense that not only was this the most interesting case he'd had so far in his forensics career, it might be the most interesting case he'd ever have.

Returning to the morgue, he stashed his bike in the usual location, went up to his office to drop off his coat, then went directly to the DNA lab. But Ted wasn't ready for him.

"I need a couple more hours," Ted said. "And I'll call you! You don't have to come up here."

Disappointed but undeterred, Jack descended a floor to histology and checked on the progress of his permanent microscopic sections on what was now labeled the Franconi case.

"My god!" Maureen complained. "What do you expect, miracles? I'm rushing your slides through ahead of everybody else, but still you'll be lucky to get them today."

Still trying to keep his spirits up and his curiosity at bay, Jack rode the elevator down to the second floor and sought out John DeVries in the lab.

"The assays for cyclosporin A and FK506 are not easy," John snapped. "Besides, we're backed up as it is. You can't expect instant service with the budget I have to work with."

"Okay!" Jack said agreeably, as he backed out of the lab. He knew that John was an irascible individual, and if aroused, he could be passive aggressive. If that happened, it might be weeks before Jack got the test results.

Descending yet another floor, Jack went into Bart Arnold's office and implored the man to give him something since he'd struck out every place else.

"I've made a lot of calls," Bart said. "But you know the situation with voice mail. You almost never get anyone on the phone anymore. So, I got a lot of messages out there, waiting for callbacks."

"Jeez," Jack complained. "I feel like a teenage girl with a new dress, waiting to get asked to the prom."

"Sorry," Bart said. "If it's any consolation, we did manage to get a blood sample from Franconi's mother. It's already up in the DNA lab."

"Was the mother asked whether her son had a liver transplant?"

"Absolutely," Bart said. "Mrs. Franconi assured the investigator that she didn't know anything about a transplant. But she did admit that her son had been much healthier lately."

"To what did she attribute his sudden health?" Jack asked.

"She says he went away to a spa someplace and came back a new man."

"Did she happen to say where?" Jack questioned.

"She didn't know," Bart said. "At least that's what she told the investigator, and the investigator told me that she thought she was telling the truth."

Jack nodded as he got to his feet. "Figures," he said. "Getting a bona fide tip from the mother would have been much too easy."

"I'll keep you informed as soon as I start getting callbacks," Bart said.

"Thanks," Jack said.

Feeling frustrated, Jack walked through communications to the ID room. He thought maybe some coffee would cheer him up. He was surprised to find Lieutenant Detective Lou Soldano busily helping himself to a cup.

"Uh-oh," Lou said. "Caught red-handed."

Jack eyed the homicide detective. He looked better than he had in days. Not only was the top button of his shirt buttoned, but his tie was cinched up in place. On top of that, he was close shaven and his hair was combed.

"You look almost human today," Jack said.

"I feel that way," Lou said. "I got my first decent night's sleep in days. Where's Laurie?"

"In the pit, I presume," Jack said.

"I gotta pat her on the back again for making that association with your floater after watching the video," Lou said. "All of us down at headquarters think it might lead to a break in this case. Already we've gotten a couple of good tips from our informers because it's stimulated a lot of talk in the streets, especially over in Queens."

"Laurie and I were surprised to see it in the papers this morning," Jack commented. "That was a lot faster than we expected. Do you have any idea who was the source?"

"I was," Lou said innocently. "But I was careful not to give any details other than the fact that the body had been identified. Why, is there a problem?"

"Only that Bingham went mildly ballistic," Jack said. "And I was hauled in as the culprit."

"Gosh, I'm sorry," Lou said. "It didn't dawn on me it could cause a problem here. I guess I should have run it by you. Well, I owe you."

"Forget it," Jack said. "It's already patched up." He poured himself some coffee, shoveled in some sugar, and added a dollop of cream.

"At least it had the desired effect on the street," Lou said. "And we learned something important already. The people who killed him were definitely not the same people who took his body and mauled it."

"Doesn't surprise me," Jack said.

"No?" Lou questioned. "I thought that was the general consensus around here. At least that's what Laurie said."

"She now thinks the people that took the body did it because they didn't want anyone to know he'd had a liver transplant," Jack said. "I still favor the idea it was done to conceal the individual's identity."

"Really," Lou said pensively, sipping his coffee. "That doesn't make any sense to me. You see we're reasonably sure the body was taken on orders from the Lucia crime family, the direct competitors of the Vaccarros, who we understand had Franconi killed."

"Good grief!" Jack exclaimed. "Are you sure about that?"

"Reasonably," Lou said. "The informer who divulged it is usually reliable. Of course, we don't have any names. That's the frustrating part."

"Just the idea that organized crime is involved is appalling," Jack said. "It means that the Lucia people are somehow involved in organ transplants. If that doesn't make you lose sleep, nothing will."

"Calm down!" Raymond yelled into the phone. The moment he'd been about to leave the apartment, the phone had rung. When he heard it was Dr. Daniel Levitz on the line, he'd taken the call.

"Don't tell me to calm down!" Daniel shouted back. "You've seen the papers. They have Franconi's body! And already a medical examiner by the name of Dr. Jack Stapleton has been in my office asking for Franconi's records."

"You didn't give them, did you?" Raymond asked.

"Of course not!" Daniel snapped. "But he condescendingly reminded me that he could subpoena them. I'm telling you, this guy was very direct and very aggressive, and he vowed to get to the bottom of the case. He suspects Franconi had a transplant. He asked me directly."

"Do your records have any information at all about his transplant or our program?" Raymond asked.

"No, I followed your suggestions in that regard to the letter," Daniel said. "But it's going to look very strange if anybody looks at my records. After all, I'd been documenting Franconi's deteriorating status for years. Then all of a sudden, his liver function studies are normal without any explanation, nothing! Not even a comment. I'm telling you there'll be questions, and I don't know whether I can handle them. I'm very upset. I wish I'd never gotten involved in all this."

"Now let's not get carried away," Raymond said with a calmness that he himself did not feel. "There's no way Stapleton could get to the bottom of the case. Our concern about an autopsy was purely hypothetical and based on an infinitesimally small chance someone with the IQ of Einstein could figure out the source of the transplant. It's not going to happen. But I appreciate your calling me about Dr. Stapleton's visit. As it turns out, I'm on my way this very minute to have a meeting with Vinnie Dominick. With his resources, I'm sure he'll be able to take care of everything. After all, to a large measure, he's responsible for the present situation."

As soon as he could, Raymond got off the phone. Appeasing Dr. Daniel Levitz wasn't doing anything for his own anxiety. After advising Darlene what to say in the unlikely chance Taylor Cabot called back, he left the apartment. Catching a taxi at the corner of Madison and Sixty-fourth, he instructed the cabbie how to get to Corona Avenue in Elmhurst.

The scene at the Neopolitan Restaurant was exactly the same as it had been the day before, with the addition of the stale smell of a couple of hundred more cigarettes. Vinnie Dominick was sitting in the same booth and his minions were lounging on the same bar stools. The obese bearded man was again busily washing glassware.

Raymond lost no time. After coming through the heavy red velvet drape at the door, he made a beeline for Vinnie's booth and slid in without invitation. He pushed forward the crumpled newspaper, which he'd painstakingly smoothed out, across the table.

Vinnie gazed down at the headlines nonchalantly.

"As you can see, there's a problem," Raymond said. "You promised me the body was gone. Obviously, you screwed up."

Vinnie picked up his cigarette, took a long drag, then blew the smoke at the ceiling.

"Doc," Vinnie said. "You never fail but to amaze me. You either have a lot of nerve or you're crazy. I don't tolerate this kind of disrespect even from my trusted lieutenants. Either you reword what you just said to me or get up and get yourself lost before I get really pissed."

Raymond swallowed hard while he got a finger between his neck and his shirt and adjusted his collar. Remembering to whom he was speaking gave him a chill. A mere nod from Vinnie Dominick could find him bobbing around in the East River.

"I'm sorry," Raymond said meekly. "I'm not myself. I'm very upset. After I saw the headlines, I got a call from the CEO of GenSys, threatening the whole program. I also got a call from Franconi's doctor, who told me he'd been approached by one of the medical examiners. An ME named Jack Stapleton dropped by his office wanting to see Franconi's records."

"Angelo!" Vinnie called out. "Come over here!"

Angelo ambled over to the booth. Vinnie asked him if he knew a Dr. Jack Stapleton at the morgue. Angelo shook his head.

"I've never seen him," Angelo said. "But Vinnie Amendola mentioned him when he called this morning. He said Stapleton was all fired up about Franconi because Franconi is his case."

"You see, I've gotten a few calls myself," Vinnie said. "Not only did I get a call from Vinnie Amendola who's still sweating it because we leaned on him to help us get Franconi out of the morgue. I also got another call from my wife's brother who runs the funeral home that took the body out. Seems that Dr. Laurie Montgomery paid a visit and was asking about a body that doesn't exist."

"I'm sorry that this has all gone so badly," Raymond said.

"You and me both," Vinnie said. "To tell you the truth, I can't understand how they got the body back. We went to some effort knowing the ground was too hard to bury it out in Westchester. So we took it way the hell out off Coney Island and dumped it into the ocean."

"Obviously, something went wrong," Raymond said. "With all due respect, what can be done at this point?"

"As far as the body is concerned, we can't do anything. Vinnie Amendola told Angelo that the autopsy was already done. So that's that."

Raymond moaned and cradled his head. His headache had intensified.

"Just a second, Doc," Vinnie said. "I want to reassure you about something. Since I knew the reason why an autopsy might cause problems for your program, I had Angelo and Carlo destroy Franconi's liver."

Raymond raised his head. A ray of hope had appeared on the horizon. "How did you do that?" he asked.

"With a shotgun," Vinnie said. "They blasted the hell out of the liver. They totally destroyed this whole portion of the abdomen." Vinnie made a circling motion with his hand over his right upper quadrant. "Right, Angelo?"

Angelo nodded. "The entire magazine of a pump action Remington. The guy's gut looked like hamburger."

"So I don't think you have as much to worry about as you think," Vinnie said to Raymond.

"If Franconi's liver was totally destroyed, why is Jack Stapleton asking whether Franconi had a transplant?" Raymond asked.

"Is he?" Vinnie asked.

"He asked Dr. Levitz directly," Raymond said.

Vinnie shrugged. "He must have gotten a clue some other way. At any rate, the problem now seems to be focused on these two characters: Dr. Jack Stapleton and Dr. Laurie Montgomery."

Raymond raised his eyebrows expectantly.

"As I already told you, Doc," Vinnie continued. "If it weren't for Vinnie Junior and his bum kidneys, I wouldn't have gotten involved in all this. The fact that I've since gotten my wife's brother into this situation compounds my problem. Now that I got him involved I can't leave him dangling, you see what I'm saying? So, here's what I'm thinking. I'll have Angelo and Franco pay a visit to these two doctors and take care of things. Would you mind that, Angelo?"

Raymond looked hopefully at Angelo, and for the first time since Raymond had seen Angelo, Angelo smiled. It wasn't much of a smile because all the scar tissue precluded most facial movement, but it was a smile nonetheless.

"I've been looking forward to meeting Laurie Montgomery for five years," Angelo said.

"I suspected as much," Vinnie said. "Can you get their addresses from Vinnie Amendola?"

"I'm sure he'll be happy to give us Dr. Stapleton's," Angelo said. "He wants this messy situation cleared up as much as anybody. As far as Laurie Montgomery is concerned, I already know her address."

Vinnie stubbed out his cigarette and raised his own eyebrows. "So, Doc, what do you think of the idea of Angelo and Franco visiting the two pesky medical examiners and convincing them to see things our way? They have to be convinced that they are causing us considerable inconvenience, if you know what I mean." A wry smile appeared on his face, and he winked.

Raymond let out a little laugh of relief. "I can't think of a better solution." He worked his way along the curved, velvet banquette seat and stood up. "Thank you, Mr. Dominick. I'm much obliged, and apologize again for my thoughtless outburst when I first arrived."

"Hold on, Doc," Vinnie said. "We haven't discussed compensation yet."

"I thought this would be covered under the rubric of our prior agreement," Raymond said, trying to sound businesslike without offending Vinnie. "After all, Franconi's body was not supposed to reappear."

"That's not the way I see it," Vinnie said. "This is an extra. Since you've already bargained away the tuition issue, I'm afraid we're now talking about recouping some of my initiation fee. What about twenty thousand? That sounds like a nice round figure."

Raymond was outraged, but he managed to stifle a response. He also remembered what happened the last time he tried to bargain with Vinnie Dominick: the cost doubled.

"It might take me a little time to get that kind of money together," Raymond said.

"That's fine, Doc," Vinnie said. "Just as long as we have an agreement. From my end, I'll get Angelo and Franco right on it."

"Wonderful," Raymond managed to say before leaving.

"Are you serious about this?" Angelo asked Vinnie.

"I'm afraid so," Vinnie said. "I guess it wasn't such a smart idea to get my brother-in-law involved in all this, although at the time we didn't have much choice. One way or the other, I got to clean it up, otherwise my wife will have my balls. The only good part is that I was able to get the good doc to pay for what I'd have to do anyway."

"When do you want us to take care of those two?" Angelo asked.

"The sooner the better," Vinnie said. "In fact, you'd better do it tonight!"

CHAPTER 15

MARCH 6, 1997
7:30 P.M.
COGO, EQUATORIAL GUINEA

"At what time did you expect your guests?" Esmeralda asked Kevin. Her body and head were wrapped in a handsome bright orange-and-green fabric.

"Seven o'clock," Kevin said, happy for the distraction. He'd been sitting at his desk, trying to fool himself into believing he was reading one of his molecular biology journals. In reality, he was tortured by repeatedly running through the harrowing events of that afternoon.

He could still see the soldiers in their red berets and jungle camouflage fatigues seemingly coming out of nowhere. He could hear their boots pounding against the moist earth and the jangle of their equipment as they ran. Worse yet, he could feel the same sickening terror that he'd felt when he'd turned to flee, expecting at any instant to hear the sound of machine-gun fire.

The dash across the clearing to the car and the wild ride had been somehow anticlimactic to that initial fright. The windows being shot out had an almost surreal quality that somehow couldn't compare to his first glimpse of those soldiers.

Melanie had once again responded to the event completely differently than Kevin. It made Kevin wonder if growing up in Manhattan had somehow toughened her for such experiences. Rather than expressing fear, Melanie was more angry than afraid. She was furious at the soldiers' wanton destruction of what she considered her property, even though the car technically belonged to GenSys.

"The dinner is prepared," Esmeralda said. "I shall keep it warm."

Kevin thanked his attentive housekeeper, and she disappeared back into the kitchen. Tossing aside his journal, Kevin got up from his desk and walked out onto the veranda. Night had fallen, and he was beginning to worry about where Melanie and Candace could be.

Kevin's house fronted a small grassy square illuminated by old-fashioned street lamps. Directly across the square was Siegfried Spallek's house. It was similar to Kevin's with an arcaded first floor, a veranda around the second, and dormers in its steeply pitched roof. At present, there were lights only in the kitchen end of the house. Apparently, the manager had not yet come home.

Hearing laughter to his left, Kevin turned in the direction of the waterfront. There had been a tropical downpour for an hour that had just ended fifteen minutes previously. The cobblestones were steaming since they'd still been hot from the sun. Into this lighted mist walked the two women, arm in arm, laughing merrily.

"Hey, Kevin!" Melanie shouted, spying Kevin on his balcony. "How come you didn't send a carriage?"

The women walked to a point directly beneath Kevin who was embarrassed by their revelry.

"What are you talking about?" Kevin asked.

"Well, you didn't expect us to get soaked, did you?" Melanie joked. Candace giggled.

"Come on up," Kevin encouraged. His eyes roamed around the small square, hoping that his neighbors weren't being disturbed.

The women came up the stairs with great commotion. Kevin met them in the hall. Melanie insisted on giving Kevin a kiss on both cheeks. Candace did likewise.

"Sorry we're late," Melanie said. "But the rain forced us to take shelter at the Chickee Bar."

"And a friendly group of men from the motor pool insisted on buying us piña coladas," Candace said gaily.

"It's okay," Kevin said. "But dinner is ready."

"Fantastic," Candace said. "I'm famished."

"Me too," Melanie said. She reached down and slipped off her shoes. "I hope you don't mind my going barefoot. My shoes got a little wet on the way up here."

"Me too," Candace said as she followed suit.

Kevin motioned toward the dining room and trailed the women in. Esmeralda had laid the table at one end since it was large enough for twelve. There was a small tablecloth just covering the area under the dishes. There were also candles burning in glass holders.

"How romantic," Candace commented.

"I hope we're having wine," Melanie said as she took the seat closest to her.

Candace went around and sat opposite Melanie, leaving the head of the table for Kevin.

"White or red?" Kevin asked.

"Any color," Melanie said. Then she laughed.

"What are we eating?" Candace asked.

"It's a local fish," Kevin said.

"A fish! How appropriate," Melanie said, which caused both women to laugh to the point of tears.

"I don't get it," Kevin said. He had the distinct feeling that when he was around these two women, he wasn't in control of anything and understood less than half the conversation.

"We'll explain later," Melanie managed. "Get the wine. That's more important."

"Let's have white," Candace said.

Kevin went into the kitchen and got the wine that he had earlier put into the refrigerator. He avoided looking at Esmeralda, worried what she must be thinking with these tipsy women as guests. Kevin didn't know what to think himself.

As he opened the wine, he could hear them carrying on with lively conversation and laughter. The good side, he reminded himself, was that with Melanie and Candace there were never any uncomfortable silences.

"What kind of wine are we having?" Melanie asked when Kevin reappeared. Kevin showed her the bottle. "Oh, my," she said with feigned condescension. "Montrachet! Aren't we lucky tonight."

Kevin had had no idea what he'd picked from his collection of wine bottles, but he was pleased Melanie was impressed. He poured the wine as Esmeralda appeared with the first course.

The dinner was an unqualified success. Even Kevin began to relax after attempting to keep up with the women as far as the wine was concerned. About halfway through the meal he was forced to return to the kitchen for another bottle.

"You can't guess who else was at the Chickee Bar," Melanie said as the entrée dishes were being cleared. "Our fearless leader Siegfried."

Kevin choked on his wine. He wiped his face with his napkin. "You didn't talk to him, did you?"

"It would have been hard not to," Melanie said. "He graciously asked if he could join us and even bought a round, not only for us but also for the guys from the motor pool."

"He was actually quite charming," Candace said.

Kevin felt a chill descend down his spine. The second ordeal of the afternoon which scared him almost as much as the first was a visit to Siegfried's office. No sooner had they evaded the Equatoguinean soldiers then Melanie had insisted on driving there. It made no difference what Kevin said in an attempt to talk her out of it.

"I'm not going to stand for this kind of treatment," Melanie had said as they mounted the stairs. She didn't even bother to speak with Aurielo. She just sailed into Siegfried's office and demanded that he personally see to it that her car was repaired.

Candace had gone in with Melanie, but Kevin had held back, watching from just beyond Aurielo's desk.

"Last night I lost my sunglasses," Melanie had said. "So we go out there just to see if we can find them, and we get shot at again!"

Kevin had expected Siegfried to explode. But he didn't. Instead, he was immediately apologetic, said that the soldiers were only out there to keep people away from the island, and that they shouldn't have fired their guns. He agreed not only to fix Melanie's car but to make sure she got a loaner in the interim. He also offered to have the soldiers scour the area for the lost sunglasses.

Esmeralda appeared with the dessert. The women were pleased. It was made with locally grown cocoa.

"Did Siegfried mention anything about what happened today?" Kevin asked.

"He apologized again," Candace said. "He said he spoke with the Moroccan guard and assured us that there won't be any more shooting. He said that if anybody wanders out there by the bridge, they will just be spoken to and told that the area is off-limits."

"Likely story," Kevin said. "As trigger-happy as those kids they call soldiers are, it's not going to happen."

Melanie laughed. "Talk about the soldiers, Siegfried said that they spent hours searching for the nonexistent sunglasses. Serves them right!"

"He did ask us if we wanted to talk with some of the workers who'd been on the island and who'd been burning underbrush," Candace said. "Can you believe it?"

"And how did you respond?" Kevin asked.

"We told him it wasn't necessary," Candace said. "I mean, we don't want him to think we're still concerned about the smoke, and we definitely don't want him to think we're planning on visiting the island."

"But we're not," Kevin said. He eyed the women while they smiled at each other conspiratorially. "Are we?" As far as Kevin was concerned, getting shot at twice had been more than enough to convince him that visiting the island was out of the question.

"You wondered why we laughed when you told us we were having fish for dinner," Melanie said. "Remember?"

"Yeah," Kevin said with concern. He had the distinct feeling he wasn't going to like what Melanie was about to say.

"We laughed because we spent a good deal of the late afternoon talking to fishermen who come to Cogo a couple of times a week," Melanie said. "Probably the ones who caught the fish we just ate. They come from a town called Acalayong about ten to twelve miles east of here."

"I know the town," Kevin said. It was the jumping-off place for people going from Equatorial Guinea to Cocobeach, Gabon. The route was served by motorized canoes called pirogues.

"We rented one of their boats for two or three days," Melanie said proudly. "So we don't have to even go near the bridge. We can visit Isla Francesca by water."

"Not me," Kevin said emphatically. "I've had it. Frankly, I think we're lucky to be alive. If you guys want to go, go! I know that nothing I could ever say would influence what you do."

"Oh, that's great!" Melanie said derisively. "You're giving up already! If that's the case, how do you intend to find out whether you and I have created a race of protohumans? I mean, you're the one who's raised this issue and got us all upset."

Melanie and Candace stared at Kevin across the table. For a few minutes, no one said a word. The night sounds of the jungle drifted in, which until then no one had heard.

After feeling progressively uncomfortable, Kevin finally broke the silence. "I don't know what I'm going to do yet," he said. "I'll think of something."

"Like hell you will," Melanie said. "You already said the only way to find out what those animals are doing is to visit the island. Those were your words. Have you forgotten?"

"No, I haven't forgotten," Kevin said. "It's just that . . . well . . ."

"That's okay," Melanie said condescendingly. "If you're too chicken to go and find out what you might have done with your genetic tinkering, fine. We were counting on you coming to help run the motor in the pirogue, but that's okay. Candace and I can manage. Right, Candace?"

"Right," Candace said.

"You see we've planned this out pretty carefully," Melanie said. "Not only did we rent the large, motorized canoe, but we had them bring back a smaller, paddle version as well. We plan to tow the paddle boat. Once we get to the island, we'll paddle up the Rio Diviso. Maybe we won't even have to go on land at all. All we want to do is observe the animals for a while."

Kevin nodded. He looked back and forth between the two women who were relentlessly staring at him. Acutely uncomfortable, he scraped back his chair and started from the room.

"Where are you going?" Melanie asked.

"To get more wine," Kevin said.

With strange emotion akin to anger, Kevin got a third bottle of white Burgundy, opened it, and brought it back into the dining room. He gestured with it toward Melanie and she nodded. Kevin filled her glass. He did the same to Candace. Then he filled his own.

After taking his seat, Kevin took a healthy swig of wine. He coughed a little after swallowing, and then asked when they planned on going on their great expedition.

"Tomorrow, bright and early," Melanie said. "We figure it will take a little over an hour to get to the island, and we'd like to be back before the sun gets really strong."

"We already got food and drink from the commissary," Candace said. "And I got a portable cooler from the hospital to pack it in."

"We'll stay far away from the bridge and the staging area," Melanie said. "So that won't be a problem."

"I think it's going to be kind of fun," Candace said. "I'd love to see a hippopotamus."

Kevin took another gulp of wine.

"I suppose you don't mind if we take those electronic gizmos to locate the animals," Melanie said. "And we could use the contour map. Of course, we'll be careful with them."

Kevin sighed and sagged in his chair. "All right, I give up. What time is this mission scheduled?"

"Oh goody," Candace said, clapping her hands together. "I knew you'd come."

"The sun comes up after six," Melanie said. "I'd like to be in the boat and on our way by then. My plan is to head west, then swing way out into the estuary before going east. That way we won't evoke any suspicions here in town if anyone sees us getting into the boat. I'd like them to think we were going off to Acalayong."

"What about work?" Kevin asked. "Won't you be missed?"

"Nope," Melanie said. "I told the people in the lab I'd be unreachable at the animal center. Whereas the people in the animal center I told . . ."

"I get the picture," Kevin interjected. "What about you, Candace?"

"No problem," Candace said. "As long as Mr. Winchester keeps doing as well as he's doing, I'm essentially unemployed. The surgeons are golfing and playing tennis all day. I can do what I like."

"I'll call my head tech," Kevin said. "I'll tell him I'm under the weather with an acute attack of insanity."

"Wait a second," Candace said suddenly. "I just thought of a problem."

Kevin sat bolt upright. "What?" he asked.

"I don't have any sunblock," Candace said. "I didn't bring any because on my three previous visits I never saw the sun."

CHAPTER 16

MARCH 6, 1997
2:30 P.M.
NEW YORK CITY

With all the tests on Franconi pending, Jack had forced himself to go to his office and try to concentrate on some of his other outstanding cases. To his surprise, he'd made reasonable headway until the phone rang at two-thirty.

"Is this Dr. Stapleton?" a female voice with an Italian accent asked.

"It is indeed," Jack said. "Is this Mrs. Franconi?"

"Imogene Franconi. I got a message to call you."

"I appreciate it, Mrs. Franconi," Jack said. "First let me extend my sympathies to you in regards to your son."

"Thank you," Imogene said. "Carlo was a good boy. He didn't do any of those things they said in the newspapers. He worked for the American Fresh Fruit Company here in Queens. I don't know where all that talk about organized crime came from. The newspapers just make stuff up."

"It's terrible what they'll do to sell papers," Jack said.

"The man that came this morning said that you got his body back," Imogene said.

"We believe so," Jack said. "That's why we needed some blood from you to confirm it. Thank you for being cooperative."

"I asked him why he didn't want me to come down there and identify it like I did last time," Imogene said. "But he told me he didn't know."

Jack tried to think of a graceful way of explaining the identity problem, but he couldn't think of any. "Some parts of the body are still missing," he said vaguely, hoping that Mrs. Franconi would be satisfied.

"Oh?" Imogene commented.

"Let me tell you why I called," Jack said quickly. He was afraid that if Mrs. Franconi became offended, she might not be receptive to his question. "You told the investigator that your son's health had improved after a trip. Do you remember saying that?"

"Of course," Imogene said.

"I was told you don't know where he went," Jack said. "Is there any way you could find out?"

"I don't think so," Imogene said. "He told me it had nothing to do with his work and that it was very private."

"Do you remember when it was?" Jack asked.

"Not exactly," Imogene said. "Maybe five or six weeks ago."

"Was it in this country?" Jack asked.

"I don't know," Imogene said. "All he said was that it was very private."

"If you find out where it was, would you give me a call back?" Jack asked.

"I suppose," Imogene said.

"Thank you," Jack said.

"Wait," Imogene said. "I just remembered he did say something strange just before he left. He said that if he didn't come back that he loved me very much."

"Did that surprise you?" Jack asked.

"Well, yes," Imogene said. "I thought that was a fine thing to say to your mother."

Jack thanked Mrs. Franconi again and hung up the phone. Hardly had he had his hand off the receiver when it rang again. It was Ted Lynch.

"I think you'd better come up here," Ted said.

"I'm on my way," Jack said.

Jack found Ted sitting at his desk, literally scratching his head.

"If I didn't know better I'd think you were trying to put one over on me," Ted spat. "Sit down!"

Jack sat. Ted was holding a ream of computer-generated paper plus a number of sheets of developed film with hundreds of small dark bands. Ted reached over and dropped the mass into Jack's lap.

"What the hell's this?" Jack questioned. He picked up several of the celluloid sheets and held them up to the light.

Ted leaned over and with the eraser end of an old-fashioned wooden pencil pointed to the films. "These are the results of the DNA polymarker test." He fingered the computer printout. "And this mass of data compares the nucleotide sequences of the DQ alpha regions of the MHC."

"Come on, Ted!" Jack urged. "Talk English to me, would you please? You know I'm a babe in the woods when it comes to this stuff."

"Fine," Ted exclaimed as if vexed. "The polymarker test shows that Franconi's DNA and the DNA of the liver tissue you found inside him could not be any more different."

"Hey, that's good news," Jack said. "Then, it was a transplant."

"I guess," Ted said without conviction. "But the sequence with the DQ alpha is identical, right down to the last nucleotide."

"What does that mean?" Jack asked.

Ted spread his hands like a supplicant and wrinkled his forehead. "I don't know. I can't explain it. Mathematically, it couldn't happen. I mean the chances are so infinitesimally small, it's beyond belief. We're talking about an identical match of thousands upon thousands of base pairs even in areas of long repeats. Absolutely identical. That's why we got the results that we did with the DQ alpha screen."

"Well, the bottom line is that it was a transplant," Jack said. "That's the issue here."

"If pressed, I'd have to agree it was a transplant," Ted said. "But how they found a donor with the identical DQ alpha is beyond me. It's the kind of coincidence that smacks of the supernatural."

"What about the test with the mitochondrial DNA to confirm the floater is Franconi?" Jack asked.

"Jeez, you give a guy an inch and he wants a mile," Ted complained. "We just got the blood, for chrissake. You'll have to wait on the results. After all, we turned the lab upside down to get what you got so quickly. Besides I'm more interested in this DQ alpha situation compared to the polymarker results. Something doesn't jibe."

"Well, don't lose any sleep over it," Jack said. He stood up and gave Ted back all the material Ted had dumped in his lap. "I appreciate what you've done. Thanks! It's the information I needed. And when the mitochondrial results are back, give me a call."

Jack was elated by Ted's results, and he wasn't worried about the mitochondrial study. With the correlation of the X rays, he was already confident the floater and Franconi were one and the same.

Jack got on the elevator. Now that he'd documented that it had been a transplant, he was counting on Bart Arnold to come up with the answers to solve the rest of the mystery. As he descended, Jack found himself wondering about Ted's emotional reaction to the DQ alpha results. Jack was aware that Ted didn't get excited about too many things. Consequently, it had to be significant. Unfortunately, Jack didn't know enough about the test to have much of an opinion. He vowed that when he had the chance he'd read up on it.

Jack's elation was short-lived; it faded the moment he walked into Bart's office. The forensic investigator was on the phone, but he shook his head the moment he caught sight of Jack. Jack interpreted the gesture as bad news. He sat down to wait.

"No luck?" Jack asked as soon as Bart disconnected.

"I'm afraid not," Bart said. "I really expected UNOS to come through, and when they said that they had not provided a liver for Carlo Franconi and that he'd not even been on their waiting list, I knew the chances of tracing where he'd gotten the liver fell precipitously. Just now I was on the phone with Columbia-Presbyterian, and it wasn't done there. So I've heard from just about every center doing liver transplants, and no one takes credit for Carlo Franconi."

"This is crazy," Jack said. He told Bart that Ted's findings confirmed that Franconi had had a transplant.

"I don't know what to say," Bart commented.

"If someone didn't get their transplant in North America or Europe, where could it have taken place?" Jack asked.

Bart shrugged. "There are a few other possibilities. Australia, South Africa, even a couple of places in South America, but having talked to my contact at UNOS, I don't think any of them are likely."

"No kidding?" Jack said. He was not hearing what he wanted to hear.

"It's a mystery," Bart commented.

"Nothing about this case is easy," Jack complained as he got to his feet.

"I'll keep at it," Bart offered.

"I'd appreciate it," Jack said.

Jack wandered out of the forensic area, feeling mildly depressed. He had the uncomfortable sensation that he was missing some major fact, but he had no idea what it could be or how to go about finding out what it was.

In the ID room he got himself another cup of coffee, which was more like sludge than a beverage by that time of the day. With cup in hand, he climbed the stairs to the lab.

"I ran your samples," John DeVries said. "They were negative for both cyclosporin A and FK506."

Jack was astounded. All he could do was stare at the pale, gaunt face of the laboratory director. Jack didn't know what was more surprising: the fact that John had already run the samples or that the results were negative.

"You must be joking," Jack managed to say.

"Hardly," John said. "It's not my style."

"But the patient had to be on immunosuppressants," Jack said. "He'd had a recent liver transplant. Is it possible you got a false negative?"

"We run controls as standard procedure," John said.

"I expected one or the other drug to be present," Jack said.

"I'm sorry that we don't gear our results to your expectations," John said sourly. "If you'll excuse me, I have work to do."

Jack watched the laboratory director walk over to an instrument and make some adjustments. Then Jack turned and made his way out of the lab. Now he was more depressed. Ted Lynch's DNA results and John DeVries's drug assays were contradictory. If there'd been a transplant, Franconi had to be on either cyclosporin A or FK506. That was standard medical procedure.

Getting off the elevator on the fifth floor, he walked down to histology while trying to come up with some rational explanation for the facts he'd been given. Nothing came to mind.

"Well, if it isn't the good doctor yet again," Maureen O'Conner said in her Irish brogue. "What is it? You only have one case? Is that why you are dogging us so?"

"I only have one that is driving me bananas," Jack said. "What's the story with the slides?"

"There's a few that are ready," Maureen said. "Do you want to take them or wait for the whole batch?"

"I'll take what I can get," Jack said.

Maureen's nimble fingers picked out a sampling of the sections that were dry and placed them in a microscopic slide holder. She handed the tray to Jack.

"Are there liver sections among these?" Jack asked hopefully.

"I believe so," Maureen said. "One or two. The rest you'll have later."

Jack nodded and walked out. A few doors down the hall, he entered his office. Chet looked up from his work and smiled.

"Hey, sport, how's it going?" Chet said.

"Not so good," Jack said. He sat down and turned on his microscope light.

"Problems with the Franconi case?" Chet asked.

Jack nodded. He began to hunt through the slides for liver sections. He only found one. "Everything about it is like squeezing water from a rock."

"Listen, I'm glad you came back," Chet said. "I'm expecting a call from a doctor in North Carolina. I just want to find out if a patient had heart trouble. I have to duck out to get passport photos taken for my upcoming trip to India. Would you take the call for me?"

"Sure," Jack said. "What's the patient's name?"

"Clarence Potemkin," Chet said. "The folder is right here on my desk."

"Fine," Jack said, while slipping the sole liver section onto his microscope's stage. He ignored Chet as Chet got his coat from behind the door and left. Jack ran the microscopic objective down to the slide and was about to peer into the eyepieces, when he paused. Chet's errand had started him thinking about international travel. If Franconi had gotten his transplant out of the country, which seemed increasingly probable, there might be a way to find out where he'd been.

Jack picked up his phone and called police headquarters. He asked for Lieutenant Detective Lou Soldano. He expected to have to leave a message and was pleasantly surprised to get the man himself.

"Hey, I'm glad you called," Lou said. "Remember what I told you this morning about the tip it was the Lucia people who stole Franconi's remains from the morgue? We just got confirmation from another source. I thought you might like to know."

"Interesting," Jack said. "Now I have a question for you."

"Shoot," Lou said.

Jack outlined the reasons for his belief that Carlo Franconi might have traveled abroad for his liver transplant. He added that according to the man's mother, he'd taken a trip to a supposed spa four to six weeks previously.

"What I want to know is, is there a way to find out by talking to Customs if Franconi left the country recently, and if so, where did he go?"

"Either Customs or the Immigration and Naturalization," Lou said. "Your best bet would be Immigration unless, of course, he brought back so much stuff he had to pay duty. Besides, I have a friend in Immigration. That way I can get the information much faster than going through the usual bureaucratic channels. Want me to check?"

"I'd love it," Jack said. "This case is bugging the hell out of me."

"My pleasure," Lou said. "As I said this morning, I owe you."

Jack hung up the phone with a tiny glimmer of hope that he'd thought of a new angle. Feeling a bit more optimistic, he leaned forward, looked into his microscope, and began to focus.

Laurie's day had not gone anything like she'd anticipated. She'd planned on doing only one autopsy but ended up doing two. And then George Fontworth ran into trouble with his multiple gunshot wound case, and Laurie volunteered to help him. Even with no lunch, Laurie didn't get out of the pit until three.

After changing into her street clothes, Laurie was on her way up to her office when she caught sight of Marvin in the mortuary office. He'd just come on duty and was busy putting the office in order after the tumult of a normal day. Laurie made a detour and stuck her head in the door.

"We found Franconi's X rays," she said. "And it turned out that floater that came in the other night was our missing man."

"I saw it in the paper," Marvin said. "Far out."

"The X rays made the identification," Laurie said. "So I'm extra glad you took them."

"It's my job," Marvin said.

"I wanted to apologize again for suggesting you didn't take them," Laurie said.

"No problem," Marvin said.

Laurie got about four steps away, when she turned around and returned to the mortuary office. This time she entered and closed the door behind her.

Marvin looked at her questioningly.

"Would you mind if I asked you a question just between you and me?" Laurie asked.

"I guess not," Marvin said warily.

"Obviously, I've been interested in how Franconi's body was stolen from here," Laurie said. "That's why I talked to you the afternoon before last. Remember?"

"Of course," Marvin said.

"I also came in that night and talked with Mike Passano," Laurie said.

"So I heard," Marvin said.

"I bet you did," Laurie said. "But believe me I wasn't accusing Mike of anything."

"I hear you," Marvin said. "He can be sensitive now and then."

"I can't figure out how the body was stolen," Laurie said. "Between Mike and security, there was always someone here."

Marvin shrugged. "I don't know, either," he said. "Believe me."

"I understand," Laurie said. "I'm sure you would have said something to me if you had any suspicions. But that's not what I wanted to ask. My feeling at this point is that there had to be some help from inside. Is there any employee here at the morgue that you think might have been involved in this somehow? That's my question."

Marvin thought for a minute and then shook his head. "I don't think so."

"It had to have happened on Mike's shift," Laurie said. "The two drivers, Pete and Jeff, do you know them very well?"

"Nope," Marvin said. "I mean, I've seen them around and even talked with them a few times, but since we're on different shifts, we don't have a lot of contact."

"But you don't have any reason to suspect them?"

"Nope, no more than anybody else," Marvin said.

"Thanks," Laurie said. "I hope my question didn't make you feel uncomfortable."

"No problem," Marvin said.

Laurie thought for a minute, while she absently chewed on her lower lip. She knew she was missing something. "I have an idea," she said suddenly. "Maybe you should describe to me the exact sequence you go through when a body leaves here."

"You mean everything that happens?" Marvin said.

"Please," Laurie said. "I mean, I have a general idea, but I don't know the specifics."

"Where do you want me to start?" Marvin asked.

"Right from the beginning," Laurie said. "Right from the moment you get the call from the funeral home."

"Okay," Marvin said. "The call comes in, and they say they're from so-and-so funeral home and they want to do a pickup. So they give me the name and the accession number."

"That's it?" Laurie asked. "Then you hang up."

"No," Marvin said. "I put them on hold while I enter the accession number into the computer. I gotta make sure the body has been released by you guys and also find out where it is."

"So then you go back to the phone and say what?"

"I say it's okay," Marvin said. "I tell them I'll have the body ready. I guess I usually ask when they think they'll be here. I mean, no sense rushing around if they're not going to be here for two hours or something."

"Then what?" Laurie said.

"I get the body and check the accession number," Marvin said. "Then I put it in the front of the walk-in cooler. We always put them in the same place. In fact, we line them up in the order we expect them to go out. It makes it easier for the drivers."

"And then what happens?" Laurie asked.

"Then they come," Marvin said with another shrug.

"And what happens when they arrive?" Laurie asked.

"They come in here and we fill out a receipt," Marvin said. "It's all got to be documented. I mean they have to sign to indicate they have accepted custody."

"Okay," Laurie said. "And then you go back and get the body?"

"Yeah, or one of them gets it," Marvin said. "All of them have been in and out of here a million times."

"Is there any final check?" Laurie asked.

"You bet," Marvin said. "We always check the accession number one more time before they wheel the body out of here. We have to indicate that being done on the documents. It would be embarrassing if the drivers got back to the home and realized they had the wrong corpse."

"Sounds like a good system," Laurie said, and she meant it. With so many checks it would be hard to subvert such a procedure.

"It's been working for decades without a screwup," Marvin said. "Of course, the computer helps. Before that, all they had was the logbook."

"Thanks, Marvin," Laurie said.

"Hey, no problem, Doc," Marvin said.

Laurie left the mortuary office. Before going up to her own she stopped off on the second floor to get a snack out of the vending machines in the lunch room. Reasonably fortified, she went up to the fifth floor. Seeing Jack's office door ajar, she walked over and peeked in. Jack was at his microscope.

"Something interesting?" she asked.

Jack looked up and smiled. "Very," he said. "Want to take a look?"

Laurie glanced into the eyepieces as Jack leaned to the side. "It looks like a tiny granuloma in a liver," she said.

"That's right," Jack said. "It's from one of those tiny pieces I was able to find of Franconi's liver."

"Hmmm," Laurie commented, continuing to look into the microscope. "That's weird they would have used an infected liver for a transplant. You'd think they would have screened the donor better. Are there a lot of these tiny granulomas?"

"Maureen has only given me one slide of the liver so far," Jack said. "And that's the only granuloma I found, so my guess would be that there aren't a lot. But I did see one on the frozen section. Also on the frozen section were tiny collapsed cysts on the surface of the liver which would have been visible to the naked eye. The transplant team must have known and didn't care."

"At least there's no general inflammation," Laurie said. "So the transplant was being tolerated pretty well."

"Extremely well," Jack said. "Too well, but that's another issue. What do you think that is under the pointer?"

Laurie played with the focus so that she could visually move up and down in the section. There were a few curious flecks of basophilic material. "I don't know. I can't even be sure it's not artifact."

"Don't know, either," Jack said. "Unless it's what stimulated the granuloma."

"That's a thought," Laurie said. She straightened up. "What did you mean by the liver being tolerated too well?"

"The lab reported that Franconi had not been taking any immunosuppressant drugs," Jack said. "That seems highly improbable since there is no general inflammation."

"Are we sure it was a transplant?" Laurie asked.

"Absolutely," Jack said. He summarized what Ted Lynch had reported to him.

Laurie was as puzzled as Jack. "Except for identical twins I can't imagine two people's DQ alpha sequences being exactly the same," she said.

"It sounds like you know more about it than I do," Jack said. "Until a couple of days ago, I'd never even heard of DQ alpha."

"Have you made any headway as to where Franconi could have had this transplant?" Laurie asked.

"I wish," Jack said. He then told Laurie about Bart's vain efforts. Jack explained that he himself had spent a good portion of the previous night calling centers all over Europe.

"Good Lord!" Laurie remarked.

"I've even enlisted Lou's help," Jack said. "I found out from Franconi's mother that he'd gone off to what she thought was a spa and came home a new man. I'm thinking that's when he might have gotten the transplant. Unfortunately, she has no idea where he went. Lou's checking Immigration to see if he'd gone out of the country."

"If anyone can find out, Lou can," Laurie said.

"By the way," Jack said, assuming a teasingly superior air, "Lou 'fessed up that he was the source of the leak about Franconi to the newspapers."

"I don't believe it," Laurie said.

"I got it from the horse's mouth," Jack said. "So I expect an abject apology."

"You've got it," Laurie said. "I'm amazed. Did he give any reason?"

"He said they wanted to release the information right away to see if it would smoke out any more tips from informers. He said it worked to an extent. They got a tip which was later confirmed that Franconi's body had been taken under orders from the Lucia crime family."

"Good grief!" Laurie said and shuddered. "This case is starting to remind me too much of the Cerino affair."

"I know what you mean," Jack said. "Instead of eyes, it's livers."

"You don't suppose there's a private hospital here in the United States that's doing undercover liver transplants, do you?" Laurie asked.

"I can't imagine," Jack said. "No doubt there could be big money involved, but there is the issue of supply. I mean, there's seven thousand plus people in this country waiting for livers as it is. Few of these people have the money to make it worthwhile."

"I wish I were as confident as you," Laurie said. "The profit motive has taken over American medicine by storm."

"But the big money in medicine is in volume," Jack said. "There are too few wealthy people who need livers. The investment in the physical plant and the requisite secrecy wouldn't pay off, especially without a supply of organs. You'd have to postulate some modern version of Burk and Hare, and although such a scenario might work in a B movie, in reality it would be too risky and uncertain. No businessman in his right mind would go for it, no matter how venal."

"Maybe you have a point," Laurie said.

"I'm convinced there's something else involved here," Jack said. "There are just too many unexplained facts from the DQ alpha nonsense to the fact that Franconi wasn't taking any immunosuppressant drugs. We're missing something: something key, something unexpected."

"What an effort!" Laurie exclaimed. "One thing is for sure, I'm glad I foisted this case onto you."

"Thanks for nothing," Jack quipped. "It's certainly a frustrating case. On a happier note, last night at basketball, Warren told me that Natalie has been asking about you. What do you say that we all get together this weekend for dinner and maybe a movie, provided they don't have any plans?"

"I'd enjoy that very much," Laurie said. "I hope you told Warren that I was asking about them as well."

"I did," Jack admitted. "Not to change the subject, but how was your day? Did you make any headway in figuring out how Franconi managed to go on his overnight? I mean, Lou telling us that a crime family was responsible isn't telling us a whole bunch. We need specifics."

"Unfortunately, no," Laurie admitted. "I was caught in the pit until just a little while ago. I've gotten nothing done that I'd planned."

"Too bad," Jack said with a smile. "With my lack of progress, I might have to rely on you providing the breakthrough."

After promises to talk with each other by phone that evening, specifically about the weekend plans, Laurie headed to her own office. With good intentions she sat down at her desk and started to go through the lab reports and other correspondence that had come in that day involving her uncompleted cases. But she found it difficult to concentrate.

Jack's generosity in crediting her with providing the breakthrough in the Franconi case only made her feel guilty for not coming up with a working hypothesis about how Franconi's body was taken. Seeing the effort Jack was expending on the case made her want to redouble her efforts.

Pulling out a fresh sheet of paper, Laurie began to write down everything Marvin had related. Her intuition told her that Franconi's mysterious abduction had to involve the two bodies that went out the same night. And now that Lou had said the Lucia crime family was implicated, she was more convinced than ever that the Spoletto Funeral Home was somehow involved.

Raymond replaced the phone and raised his eyes to Darlene, who'd come into his study.

"Well?" Darlene asked. She had her blond hair pulled back into a ponytail. She'd been working out on an exercise bike in the other room and was clothed in sexy workout gear.

Raymond leaned back in his desk chair and sighed. He even smiled. "Things seem to be working out," he said. "That was the GenSys operational officer up in Cambridge, Mass. The plane will be available tomorrow evening so I'll be on my way to Africa. Of course, we'll stop to refuel, but I don't know where yet."

"Can I come?" Darlene asked hopefully.

"I'm afraid not, dear," Raymond said. He reached out and took her by the hand. He knew he'd been difficult over the previous couple of days and felt badly. He guided her around the desk and urged her to sit on his lap. As soon as she did, he was sorry. She was, after all, a big woman.

"With the patient and the surgical team, there'll be too many people on the plane on the return trip," he managed, even though his face was becoming red.

Darlene sighed and pouted. "I never get to go anywhere."

"Next time," Raymond croaked. He patted her on her back and eased her up into a standing position. "It's just a short trip. There and back. It's not going to be fun."

With a sudden burst of tears Darlene fled from the room. Raymond considered following her to console her, but a glance at his desk clock changed his mind. It was after three and therefore after nine in Cogo. If he wanted to talk to Siegfried, he felt he'd better try now.

Raymond called the manager's home. The housekeeper put Siegfried on the line.

"Things still going okay?" Raymond asked expectantly.

"Perfectly," Siegfried said. "My last update on the patient's condition was fine. He couldn't be doing any better."

"That's reassuring," Raymond said.

"I suppose that means our harvest bonuses will be forthcoming," Siegfried said.

"Of course," Raymond said, although he knew there would be a delay. With the necessity of raising twenty thousand cash for Vinnie Dominick, bonuses would have to wait until the next initiation fee came in.

"What about the situation with Kevin Marshall?" Raymond asked.

"Everything is back to normal," Siegfried said. "Except for one incident when they went back to the staging area around lunch time."

"That hardly sounds normal," Raymond complained.

"Calm down," Siegfried said. "They only went back to look for Melanie Becket's sunglasses. Nevertheless, they ended up getting fired at again by the soldiers I'd posted out there." Siegfried laughed heartily.

Raymond waited until Siegfried had calmed down.

"What's so funny?" Raymond asked.

"Those numbskull soldiers shot out Melanie's rear window," Siegfried said. "It made her very angry, but it had the desired effect. Now I'm really sure they won't be going out there again."

"I should hope not," Raymond said.

"Besides, I had an opportunity to have a drink with the two women this afternoon," Siegfried said. "I have a feeling our nerdy researcher has something risqué going on."

"What are you talking about?" Raymond asked.

"I don't believe he'll be having the time or the energy to worry about smoke from Isla Francesca," Siegfried said. "I think he's got himself involved in a ménage à trois."

"Seriously?" Raymond asked. Such an idea seemed preposterous for the Kevin Marshall Raymond knew. In all of Raymond's dealing with Kevin Marshall he'd never expressed the slightest interest in the opposite sex. The idea he'd have the inclination and stamina for one woman let alone two seemed ludicrous.

"That was the implication I got," Siegfried said. "You should have heard the two women carrying on about their cute researcher. That's what they called him. And they were on their way to Kevin's for a dinner party. That's the first dinner party he's ever had as far as I know, and I live right across from him."

"I suppose we should be thankful," Raymond said.

"Envious is a better word," Siegfried said, with another burst of laughter that grated on Raymond's nerves.

"I've called to say that I'll be leaving here tomorrow evening," Raymond said. "I can't say when I'll arrive in Bata because I don't know where we'll refuel. I'll have to call from the refueling stop or have the pilots radio ahead."

"Anyone else coming with you?" Siegfried asked.

"Not that I know of," Raymond said. "I doubt it because we'll be almost full on the way back."

"We'll be waiting for you," Siegfried said.

"See you soon," Raymond said.

"Maybe you could bring our bonuses with you," Siegfried suggested.

"I'll see if it can be arranged," Raymond said.

He hung up the phone and smiled. He shook his head in amazement concerning Kevin Marshall's behavior. "You never know!" Raymond commented out loud as he got up and started from the room. He wanted to find Darlene and cheer her up. He thought that maybe as a consolation they should go out to dinner at her favorite restaurant.

Jack had scoured the single liver section Maureen had given him from one end to the other. He'd even used his oil-immersion lens to stare vainly at the basophilic specks in the heart of the tiny granuloma. He still had no idea whether they were a true finding, and if they were, what they were.

Having exhausted his histological and pathological knowledge with respect to the slide, he was about to take it over to the pathology department at New York University Hospital when his phone rang. It was Chet's call from North Carolina, so Jack asked the appropriate question and wrote down the response. Hanging up the phone, Jack got his jacket from the file cabinet. With the jacket on, he picked up the microscopic slide only to have the phone ring again. This time it was Lou Soldano.

"Bingo!" Lou said cheerfully. "I got some good news for you."

"I'm all ears," Jack said. He slipped out of his bomber jacket and sat down.

"I put in a call to my friend in Immigration, and he just phoned me back," Lou said. "When I asked him your question, he told me to hang on the line. I could even hear him entering the name into the computer. Two seconds later, he had the info. Carlo Franconi entered the country exactly thirty-seven days ago on January twenty-ninth at Teterboro in New Jersey."

"I've never heard of Teterboro," Jack said.

"It's a private airport," Lou said. "It's for general aviation, but there's lots of fancy corporate jets out there because of the field's proximity to the city."

"Was Carlo Franconi on a corporate jet?" Jack asked.

"I don't know," Lou said. "All I got is the plane's call letters or numbers or whatever they call it. You know, the numbers and letters on the airplane's tail. Let's see, I got it right here. It was N69SU."

"Was there any indication where the plane had come from?" Jack asked as he wrote down the alphanumeric characters and the date.

"Oh yeah," Lou said. "That's gotta be filed. The plane came from Lyon, France."

"Nah, it couldn't have," Jack said.

"That's what's in the computer," Lou said. "Why don't you think it's correct?"

"Because I talked with the French organ allocation organization early this morning," Jack said. "They had no record of an American with the name of Franconi, and they categorically denied they'd be transplanting an American since they have a long waiting list for French citizens."

"The information that Immigration has must correlate with the flight plan filed with both the FAA and the European equivalent," Lou said. "At least that's how I understand it."

"Do you think your friend in Immigration has a contact in France?" Jack asked.

"It wouldn't surprise me," Lou said. "Those upper-echelon guys have to cooperate with each other. I can ask him. Why would you like to know?"

"If Franconi was in France I'd like to find out the day he arrived," Jack said. "And I'd like to know any other information the French might have on where he went in the country. They keep close tabs on most non-European foreigners through their hotels."

"Okay, let me see what I can do," Lou said. "Let me call him, and I'll call you back."

"One other thing," Jack said. "How can we find out who owns N69SU?"

"That's easy," Lou said. "All you have to do is call the FAA Control Aviation Center in Oklahoma City. Anybody can do it, but I've got a friend there, too."

"Jeez, you have friends in all the convenient places," Jack remarked.

"It comes with the territory," Lou said. "We do favors for each other all the time. If you have to wait for everything to go through channels, nothing gets done."

"It's certainly convenient for me to take advantage of your web of contacts," Jack said.

"So you want me to call my friend at the FAA?" Lou asked.

"I'll be much obliged," Jack said.

"Hey, it's my pleasure," Lou said. "I have a feeling that the more I help you the more I'm helping myself. I'd like nothing better than to have this case solved. It might save my job."

"I'm leaving my office to run over to the University Hospital," Jack said. "What if I call you back in a half hour or so?"

"Perfect," Lou said before disconnecting.

Jack shook his head. Like everything else with this case, the information he'd gotten from Lou was both surprising and confusing. France probably was the last country Jack suspected Franconi to have visited.

After donning his coat for the second time, Jack left his office. Given the proximity of the University Hospital, he didn't bother with his bike. It only took ten minutes by foot.

Inside the busy medical center, Jack took the elevator up to the pathology department. He was hoping that Dr. Malovar would be available. Peter Malovar was a giant in the field, and even at the age of eighty-two he was one of the sharpest pathologists Jack had ever met. Jack made it a point to go to seminars Dr. Malovar offered once a month. So when Jack had a question about pathology, he didn't go to Bingham because Bingham's strong point was forensics, not general pathology. Instead, Jack went to Dr. Malovar.

"The professor's in his lab as usual," the harried pathology department secretary said. "You know where it is?"

Jack nodded and walked down to the aged, frosted-glass door which led to what was known as "Malovar's lair." Jack knocked. When there was no response, he tried the door. It was unlocked. Inside, he found Dr. Malovar bent over his beloved microscope. The elderly man looked a little like Einstein with wild gray hair and a full mustache. He also had kyphotic posture as if his body had been specifically designed to bend over and peer into a microscope. Of his five senses only his hearing had deteriorated over the years.

The professor greeted Jack cursorily while hungrily eyeing the slide in his hand. He loved people to bring him problematic cases, a fact that Jack had taken advantage of on many occasions.

Jack tried to give a little history of the case as he passed the slide to the professor, but Dr. Malovar lifted his hand to quiet him. Dr. Malovar was a true detective who didn't want anyone else's impressions to influence his own. The aged professor replaced the slide he'd been studying with Jack's. Without a word, he scanned it for all of one minute.

Raising his head, Dr. Malovar put a drop of oil on the slide and switched to his oil-immersion lens for higher magnification. Once again, he examined the slide for only a matter of seconds.

Dr. Malovar looked up at Jack. "Interesting!" he said, which was a high compliment coming from him. Because of his hearing problem, he spoke loudly. "There's a small granuloma of the liver as well as the cicatrix of another. Looking at the granuloma, I think I might be seeing some merozoites, but I can't be sure."

Jack nodded. He assumed that Dr. Malovar was referring to the tiny basophilic flecks Jack had seen in the core of the granuloma.

Dr. Malovar reached for his phone. He called a colleague and asked him to come over for a moment. Within minutes, a tall, thin, overly serious, African-American man in a long white coat appeared. Dr. Malovar introduced him as Dr. Colin Osgood, chief of parasitology.

"What's your opinion, Colin?" Dr. Malovar asked as he gestured toward his microscope.

Dr. Osgood looked at the slide for a few seconds longer than Dr. Malovar had before responding. "Definitely parasitic," he intoned with his eyes still glued to the eye pieces. "Those are merozoites, but I don't recognize them. It's either a new species or a parasite not seen in humans. I recommend that Dr. Lander Hammersmith view it and render his opinion."

"Good idea," Dr. Malovar said. He looked at Jack. "Would you mind leaving this overnight? I'll have Dr. Hammersmith view it in the morning."

"Who is Dr. Hammersmith?" Jack asked.

"He's a veterinary pathologist," Dr. Osgood said.

"Fine by me," Jack said agreeably. Having the slide reviewed by a veterinary pathologist was something he'd not thought of.

After thanking both men, Jack went back out to the secretary and asked if he could use a phone. The secretary directed him to an empty desk and told him to push nine for an outside line. Jack called Lou at police headquarters.

"Hey, glad you called," Lou said. "I think I'm getting some interesting stuff here. First of all, the plane is quite a plane. It's a G4. Does that mean anything to you?"

"I don't think so," Jack said. From Lou's tone it sounded as if it should have.

"It stands for Gulfstream 4," Lou explained. "It's what you would call the Rolls Royce of the corporate jet. It's like twenty million bucks."

"I'm impressed," Jack said.

"You should be," Lou said. "Okay, let's see what else I learned. Ah, here it is: The plane is owned by Alpha Aviation out of Reno, Nevada. Ever hear of them?"

"Nope," Jack said. "Have you?"

"Not me," Lou said. "Must be a leasing organization. Let's see, what else? Oh, yeah! This might be the most interesting. My friend from Immigration called his counterpart in France at his home, if you can believe it, and asked about Carlo Franconi's recent French holiday. Apparently, this French bureaucrat can access the Immigration mainframe from his own PC, because guess what?"

"I'm on pins and needles," Jack said.

"Franconi never visited France!" Lou said. "Not unless he had a fake passport and fake name. There's no record of his entering or departing."

"So what's this about the plane incontrovertibly coming from Lyon, France?" Jack demanded.

"Hey, don't get testy," Lou said.

"I'm not," Jack said. "I was only responding to your point that the flight plan and the Immigration information had to correlate."

"They do!" Lou said. "Saying the plane came from Lyon, France, doesn't mean anybody or everybody got out. It could have refueled for all I know."

"Good point," Jack said. "I didn't think of that. How can we find out?"

"I suppose I can call my friend back at the FAA," Lou said.

"Great," Jack said. "I'm heading back to my office at the morgue. You want me to call you or you call me?"

"I'll call you," Lou said.

After Laurie had written down all that she could remember from her conversation with Marvin concerning how bodies were picked up by funeral homes, she'd put the paper aside and ignored it while she did some other busywork. A half hour later, she picked it back up.

With her mind clear, she tried to read it with fresh eyes. On the second read-through, something jumped out at her: namely, how many times the term "accession number" appeared. Of course, she wasn't surprised. After all, the accession number was to a body what a Social Security number was to a living individual. It was a form of identification that allowed the morgue to keep track of the thousands of bodies and consequent paperwork that passed through its portals. Whenever a body arrived at the medical examiner's office, the first thing that happened was that it was given an accession number. The second thing that happened was that a tag with the number was tied around the big toe.

Looking at the word "accession," Laurie realized to her surprise that if asked she wouldn't have been able to define it. It was a word she'd just accepted and used on a daily basis. Every laboratory slip and report, every X-ray film, every investigator's report, every document intramurally had the accession number. In many ways, it was more important than the victim's name.

Taking her American Heritage dictionary from its shelf, Laurie looked up the word "accession." As she began reading the definitions, none of them made any sense in the context of the word's use at the morgue, until the next to last entry. There it was defined as "admittance." In other words, the accession number was just another way of saying admittance number.

Laurie searched for the accession numbers and names of the bodies that had been picked up during the night shift of March fourth when Franconi's body disappeared. She found the piece of scratch paper beneath a slide tray. On it was written: Dorothy Kline #101455 and Frank Gleason #100385.

Thanks to her musing about accession numbers, Laurie noticed something she'd not paid any attention to before. The fact that the accession numbers differed by over a thousand! That was strange because the numbers were given out sequentially. Knowing the approximate volume of bodies processed through the morgue, Laurie estimated that there must have been several weeks separation between the arrivals of these two individuals.

The time differential was strange since bodies rarely stayed at the morgue more than a couple of days, so Laurie keyed Frank Gleason's accession number into her computer terminal. His was the body picked up by the Spoletto Funeral Home.

What popped up on the screen surprised her.

"Good grief!" Laurie exclaimed.

Lou was having a great time. Contrary to the general public's romantic image of detective work, actual gumshoeing was an exhausting, thankless task. What Lou was doing now, namely sitting in the comfort of his office and making productive telephone calls, was both entertaining and fulfilling. It was also nice to say hello to old acquaintances.

"My word, Soldano!" Mark Servert commented. Mark was Lou's contact at the FAA in Oklahoma City. "I don't hear from you for a year and then twice in the same day. This must be some case."

"It's a corker," Lou said. "And I have a follow-up question. We found out that the G4 plane I called you about earlier had flown from Lyon, France, to Teterboro, New Jersey, on January twenty-ninth. However, the guy we're interested in didn't pass through French Immigration. So, we're wondering if it's possible to find out where N69SU came from before it landed in Lyon."

"Now that's a tricky question," Mark said. "I know the ICAO . . ."

"Wait a second," Lou interrupted. "Keep the acronyms to a minimum. What's the ICAO?"

"International Civil Aviation Organization," Mark said. "I know they file all flight plans in and out of Europe."

"Perfect," Lou said. "Anybody there you can call?"

"There's someone I can call," Mark said. "But it wouldn't do you much good. The ICAO shreds all their files after fifteen days. It's not stored."

"Wonderful," Lou commented sarcastically.

"The same goes for the European Air Traffic Control Center in Brussels," Mark said. "There's just too much material, considering all the commercial flights."

"So, there's no way," Lou remarked.

"I'm thinking," Mark said.

"You want to call me back?" Lou said. "I'll be here for another hour or so."

"Yeah, let me do that," Mark said.

Lou was about to hang up when he heard Mark yell his name.

"I just thought of something else," Mark said. "There's an organization called Central Flow Management with offices in both Paris and Brussels. They're the ones who provide the slot times for takeoffs and landings. They handle all of Europe except for Austria and Slovenia. Who knows why those countries aren't involved? So, if N69SU came from anyplace other than Austria or Slovenia, their flight plan should be on file."

"Do you know anybody in that organization?" Lou asked.

"No, but I know somebody who does," Mark said. "Let me see if I can find out for you."

"Hey, I appreciate it," Lou said.

"No problem," Mark said.

Lou hung up the phone and then drummed his pencil on the surface of his scarred and battle-worn gray-metal desk. There were innumerable burn marks where he'd left smoldering cigarette butts. He was thinking about Alpha Aviation and wondering how to run down the organization.

First, he tried telephone information in Reno. There was no listing for Alpha Aviation. Lou wasn't surprised. Next, he called the Reno police department. He explained who he was and asked to be connected to his equivalent, the head of Homicide. His name was Paul Hersey.

After a few minutes of friendly banter, Lou gave Paul a thumbnail sketch of the Franconi case. Then he asked about Alpha Aviation.

"Never heard of them," Paul said.

"The FAA said it was out of Reno, Nevada," Lou said.

"That's because Nevada's an easy state to incorporate in," Paul explained. "And here in Reno we've got a slew of high-priced law firms who spend their time doing nothing else."

"What's your suggestion about getting the lowdown on the organization?" Lou asked.

"Call the Office of the Nevada Secretary of State in Carson City," Paul said. "If Alpha Aviation is incorporated in Nevada, it will be on public record. Want us to call for you?"

"I'll call," Lou said. "At this point, I'm not even sure what I want to know."

"We can at least give you the number," Paul said. He went off the line for a moment, and Lou could hear him bark an order to an underling. A moment later, he was back and gave Lou the telephone number. Then he added: "They should be helpful, but if you have any trouble, call me back. And if you need any assistance in Carson City for whatever reason call Todd Arronson. He's head of Homicide down there, and he's a good guy."

A few minutes later Lou was on the line with the Office of the Nevada Secretary of State. An operator connected him to a clerk, who couldn't have been nicer or more cooperative. Her name was Brenda Whitehall.

Lou explained that he was interested to find out all he could about Alpha Aviation out of Reno, Nevada.

"Just a moment, please," Brenda said. Lou could hear the woman typing the name onto a keyboard. "Okay, here it is," she added. "Hang on and let me pull the folder."

Lou lifted his feet up onto his desk and leaned back in his chair. He felt an almost irresistible urge to light up, but he fought it.

"I'm back," Brenda said. Lou could hear the rustle of papers. "Now what is it that you want to know?"

"What do you have?" Lou asked.

"I have the Articles of Incorporation," Brenda said. There was a short period of silence while she read, then she added: "It's a limited partnership and the general partner is Alpha Management."

"What does that mean in plain English?" Lou asked. "I'm not a lawyer or a businessman."

"It simply means that Alpha Management is the corporation that runs the limited partnership," Brenda said patiently.

"Does it have any people's names?" Lou asked.

"Of course," Brenda said. "The Articles of Incorporation have to have the names and addresses of the directors, the registered agent for service of process, and the officers of the corporation."

"That sounds encouraging," Lou said. "Could you give them to me?"

Lou could hear the sound of rustling papers.

"Hmmmm," Brenda commented. "Actually, in this instance there's only one name and address."

"One person is wearing all those hats?"

"According to this document," Brenda said.

"What's the name and address?" Lou asked. He reached for a piece of paper.

"It's Samuel Hartman of the firm, Wheeler, Hartman, Gottlieb, and Sawyer. Their address is Eight Rodeo Drive, Reno."

"That sounds like a law firm," Lou said.

"It is," Brenda said. "I recognize the name."

"That's no help!" Lou said. He knew that the chances of getting any information out of a law firm were unlikely.

"A lot of Nevada corporations are set up like this," Brenda explained. "But let's see if there are any amendments."

Lou was already thinking of calling Paul back to get the rundown on Samuel Hartman, when Brenda made a murmur of discovery.

"There are amendments," she said. "At the first board meeting of Alpha Management, Mr. Hartman resigned as president and secretary. In his place Frederick Rouse was appointed."

"Is there an address for Mr. Rouse?" Lou asked.

"There is," Brenda said. "His title is Chief Financial Officer of the GenSys Corporation. The address is 150 Kendall Square, Cambridge, Massachusetts."

Lou got all the information written down and thanked Brenda. He was particularly appreciative because he couldn't imagine getting the same service from his own Secretary of State's Office in Albany.

Lou was about to call Jack to give him the information about the ownership of the plane, when the phone literally rang under his hand. It was Mark Servert calling back already.

"You are in luck," Mark said. "The fellow I'm acquainted with who knows people in the Central Flow Management organization in Europe happened to be on the job when I called him. In fact, he's in your neck of the woods. He's out at Kennedy Airport, helping direct air traffic across the north Atlantic. He talks to these Central Flow Management people all the time, so he slipped in a query about N69SU on January twenty-ninth. Apparently, it popped right up on the screen. N69SU flew into Lyon from Bata, Equatorial Guinea."

"Whoa!" Lou said. "Where's that?"

"Beats me," Mark said. "Without looking at a map, I'd guess West Africa."

"Curious," Lou said.

"It's also curious that as soon as the plane touched down in Lyon, France, it radioed to obtain a slot time to depart for Teterboro, New Jersey," Mark said. "Near as I can figure, it just sat on the runway until it got clearance."

"Maybe it refueled," Lou offered.

"Could be," Mark said. "Even so, I would have expected them to have filed a through-flight plan with a stop in Lyon, rather than two separate flight plans. I mean, they could have gotten hung up in Lyon for hours. It was taking a chance."

"Maybe they just changed their minds," Lou said.

"It's possible," Mark agreed.

"Or maybe they didn't want anyone knowing they were coming from Equatorial Guinea," Lou suggested.

"Now, that's an idea that wouldn't have crossed my mind," Mark admitted. "I suppose that's why you're an engaging detective, and I'm a boring FAA bureaucrat."

Lou laughed. "Engaging I'm not. On the contrary, I'm afraid this job has made me cynical and suspicious."

"It's better than being boring," Mark said.

Lou thanked his friend for his help, and after they exchanged the usual well-meaning promises to get together, they hung up.

For a few minutes, Lou sat and marveled at why a twenty-million-dollar airplane was carrying a midlevel crime boss from Queens, New York, from some African country Lou had never heard of. Such a third-world backwater certainly wasn't a medical mecca where a person would go to have sophisticated surgery like a liver transplant.

After entering Frank Gleason's accession number into the computer, Laurie sat pondering the apparent discrepancy for some time. She'd tried to imagine what the information meant in terms of the Franconi body disappearance. Slowly, an idea took root.

Suddenly pushing back from her desk, Laurie headed to the morgue level to look for Marvin. He wasn't in the mortuary office. She found him by stepping into the walk-in cooler. He was busy moving the gurneys around to prepare for body pickups.

The moment Laurie entered the cooler, she flashed on the horrid experience she'd had during the Cerino affair inside the walk-in unit. The memory made her distinctly uncomfortable, and she decided against attempting to have a conversation with Marvin while inside. Instead, she asked him to meet her back in the mortuary office when he was finished.

Five minutes later, Marvin appeared. He plopped a sheaf of papers on the desk and then went to a sink in the corner to wash his hands.

"Everything in order?" Laurie asked, just to make conversation.

"I think so," Marvin said. He came to the desk and sat down. He began arranging the documents in the order that the bodies were to be picked up.

"After talking with you earlier, I learned something quite surprising," Laurie said, getting to the point of her visit.

"Like what?" Marvin said. He finished arranging the papers and sat back.

"I entered Frank Gleason's accession number into the computer," Laurie said. "And I found out that his body had come into the morgue over two weeks ago. There was no name associated with it. It was an unidentified corpse!"

"No shit!" Marvin exclaimed. Then realizing what he'd said, he added: "I mean, I'm surprised."

"So was I," Laurie said. "I tried to call Dr. Besserman, who'd done the original autopsy. I wanted to ask if the body had been recently identified as Frank Gleason, but he's out of the office. Do you think it was surprising that Mike Passano didn't know the body was still labeled in the computer as an unidentified corpse?"

"Not really," Marvin said. "I'm not sure I would have, either. I mean, you enter the accession number just to find out if the body is released. You don't really worry too much about the name."

"That was the impression you gave me earlier," Laurie said. "There was also something else you said that I've been mulling over. You said that sometimes you don't get the body yourself but rather one of the funeral home people does."

"Sometimes," Marvin said. "But it only happens if two people come and if they've been here lots of times so they know the process. It's just a way of speeding things up. One of them goes to the cooler to get the body while me and the other guy finish the documents."

"How well do you know Mike Passano?" Laurie asked.

"As well as I know most of the other techs," Marvin said.

"You and I have known each other for six years," Laurie said. "I think of us as friends."

"Yeah, I suppose," Marvin said warily.

"I'd like you to do something for me as a friend," Laurie said. "But only if it doesn't make you feel uncomfortable."

"Like what?" Marvin said.

"I'd like you to call Mike Passano and tell him that I found out that one of the bodies that he sent out the night Franconi disappeared was an unidentified corpse."

"That's strange, man!" Marvin said. "Why would I be calling him rather than just waiting for him to come on duty?"

"You can act like you just heard it, which is the case," Laurie said. "And you can say that you thought he should know right away since he was on duty that night."

"I don't know, man," Marvin said, unconvinced.

"The key thing is that coming from you, it won't be confrontational," Laurie said. "If I call, he'll think I'm accusing him, and I'm interested to hear his reaction without his feeling defensive. But more important, I'd like you to ask him if there were two people from Spoletto Funeral Home that night, and if there were two, whether he can remember who actually went to get the body."

"That's like setting him up, man," Marvin complained.

"I don't see it that way," Laurie said. "If anything, it gives him a chance to clear himself. You see, I think the Spoletto people took Franconi."

"I don't feel comfortable calling him," Marvin said. "He's going to know something is up. Why don't you call him yourself, you know what I'm saying?"

"I already told you, I think he'll be too defensive," Laurie said. "Last time he was defensive when I asked him purely vague questions. But okay, if you feel uncomfortable, I don't want you to do it. Instead, I want you to go on a little hunt with me."

"Now what?" Marvin asked. His patience was wearing thin.

"Can you produce a list of all the refrigerator compartments that are occupied at the moment?" Laurie asked.

"Sure, that's easy," Marvin said.

"Please," Laurie said, while gesturing toward Marvin's computer terminal. "While you're at it, make two copies."

Marvin shrugged and sat down. Using a relatively rapid hunt-and-peck style, he directed the computer to produce the list Laurie wanted. He handed the two sheets to her the moment they came out of the printer.

"Excellent," Laurie said, glancing at the sheets. "Come on!" As she left the mortuary office, she waved over her shoulder. Marvin followed at her heels.

They walked down the stained cement corridor to the giant island that dominated the morgue. On opposite sides were the banks of refrigerated compartments used to store the bodies before autopsy.

Laurie handed one of the lists to Marvin.

"I want to search every compartment that is not occupied," Laurie said. "You take this side and I'll take the other."

Marvin rolled his eyes but took the list. He started opening the compartments, peering inside, then slamming the doors. Laurie went around to the other side of the island and did the same.

"Uh-oh!" Marvin intoned after five minutes.

Laurie paused. "What is it?"

"You'd better come over here," Marvin said.

Laurie walked around the island. Marvin was standing at the far end of the island, scratching his head while staring at his list. In front of him was an open refrigerated compartment.

"This one is supposed to be empty," Marvin said.

Laurie glanced within and felt her pulse race. Inside, was a naked male corpse with no tag on its big toe. The number of the compartment was ninety-four. It wasn't too far away from number one eleven, where Franconi was supposed to have been.

Marvin slid out the tray. It rattled on its ball bearings in the stillness of the deserted morgue. The body was a middle-aged male with signs of extensive trauma to the legs and torso.

"Well, this explains it," Laurie said. Her voice reflected an improbable mixture of triumph, anger, and fear. "It's the unidentified corpse. He'd been a hit-and-run accident on the FDR Drive."

Jack stepped off the elevator and could hear a phone ringing insistently. As he proceeded down the hall he became progressively aware it had to be his phone, especially since his office was the only one with an open door.

Jack picked up speed and then almost missed his door as he slid on the vinyl flooring. He snapped the phone off the hook just in time. It was Lou.

"Where the hell have you been?" Lou complained.

"I got stuck over at the University Hospital," Jack said. After Jack had last talked with Lou, Dr. Malovar had appeared and had him look at some forensic slides for him. So soon on the heels of his consulting Malovar, Jack didn't feel he could refuse.

"I've been calling every fifteen minutes," Lou remarked.

"Sorry," Jack said.

"I've got some surprising information that I've been dying to give you," Lou said. "This is one weird case."

"That's not telling me anything I didn't already know," Jack said. "What did you learn?"

Movement out of the corner of Jack's eye attracted his attention. Turning his head, he saw Laurie standing in the doorway. She did not look normal. Her eyes were blazing, her mouth was set in an angry grimace, and her skin was the color of ivory.

"Wait a sec!" Jack said, interrupting Lou. "Laurie, what the hell is the matter?"

"I have to talk with you," Laurie sputtered.

"Sure," Jack said. "But could it wait for two minutes?" He pointed at the phone to indicate that he was talking with someone.

"Now!" Laurie barked.

"Okay, okay," Jack repeated. It was clear to him she was as tense as a piano wire about to snap.

"Listen, Lou," Jack said into the phone. "Laurie just came in, and she's upset. Let me call you right back."

"Hold on!" Laurie snapped. "Is that Lou Soldano you're talking with?"

"Yeah," Jack said hesitantly. For an irrational instant, he thought that Laurie was overwrought because he was talking with Lou.

"Where is he?" Laurie demanded.

Jack shrugged. "I guess he's in his office."

"Ask him," Laurie snapped.

Jack posed the question, and Lou answered in the affirmative. Jack nodded to Laurie. "He's there," he said.

"Tell him we're coming down to see him," Laurie said.

Jack hesitated. He was confused.

"Tell him!" Laurie repeated. "Tell him we're leaving right away."

"Did you hear that?" Jack asked Lou. Laurie then disappeared down the corridor toward her office.

"I did," Lou said. "What's going on?"

"Damned if I know," Jack said. "She just barreled in. Unless I call you right back, we'll be there."

"Fine," Lou said. "I'll wait."

Jack hung up the phone and rushed out into the hall. Laurie was already on her way back and was struggling into her coat. She eyed him as she brushed past on her way to the elevators. Jack hustled to catch up with her.

"What's happened?" Jack asked hesitantly. He was afraid to upset her any more than she already was.

"I'm about ninety-nine percent sure how Franconi's body was taken from here," Laurie said angrily. "And two things are becoming clear. First, the Spoletto Funeral Home was involved and second, the abduction was surely abetted by someone who works here. And to tell you the truth, I'm not sure which of these two things bothers me more."

"Jeez, look at that traffic," Franco Ponti said to Angelo Facciolo. "I'm sure as hell glad we're going into Manhattan instead of going out."

Franco and Angelo were in Franco's black Cadillac, heading west on the Queensboro Bridge. It was five-thirty, the height of rush hour. Both men were dressed as if they were going to a ritzy dinner.

"What order do you want to do this in?" Franco asked.

Angelo shrugged. "Maybe the girl first," he said. His face twisted into a slight smile.

"You're looking forward to this, aren't you?" Franco commented.

Angelo raised his eyebrows as much as his facial scar tissue would allow. "Five years I've been dreaming about seeing this broad professionally," he said. "I guess I never thought I would get my chance."

"I know I don't have to remind you that we follow orders," Franco said. "To the letter."

"Cerino was never so specific," Angelo said. "He'd just tell us to do a job. He didn't tell us how to do it."

"That's why Cerino is in jail and Vinnie is running the show," Franco said.

"I'll tell you what," Angelo said. "Why don't we do a drive by Jack Stapleton's place. I've already been inside Laurie Montgomery's apartment, so I know what we're getting ourselves into. But I'm a little surprised by this other address. West One Hundred-sixth Street isn't where I'd expect a doctor to be living."

"I think a drive-by sounds smart," Franco said.

When they reached Manhattan, Franco continued west on Fifty-ninth Street. He rounded the southern end of Central Park and headed north on Central Park West.

Angelo thought back to the fateful day on the pier of the American Fresh Fruit Company when Laurie caused the explosion. Angelo had had skin problems from chicken pox and acne, but it had been the burns he suffered because of Laurie Montgomery that had turned him into what he called a "freak."

Franco posed a question, but Angelo hadn't heard him because of his angry musings. He had to ask him to repeat it.

"I bet you'd like to stick it to that Laurie Montgomery," Franco said. "If it had been me, I sure would."

Angelo let out a sarcastic laugh. Unconsciously, he moved his left arm so that he could feel the reassuring mass of his Walther TPH auto pistol snuggled into its shoulder holster.

Franco turned left onto One Hundred-sixth Street. They passed a playground on the right that was in full use, particularly the basketball court. There were lots of people standing on the sidelines.

"It must be on the left," Franco said.

Angelo consulted the piece of paper he was holding with Jack's address. "It's coming up," he said. "It's the building with the fancy top."

Franco slowed and then stopped to double-park a few buildings short of Jack's on the opposite side of the street. A car behind beeped. Franco lowered his window and motioned for the car to pass. There was cursing as the car did so. Franco shook his head. "You hear that guy? Nobody in this city has any manners."

"Why would a doctor live there?" Angelo said. He was eyeing Jack's building through the front windshield.

Franco shook his head. "Doesn't make any sense to me. The building looks like a dump."

"Amendola said he was a little strange," Angelo said. "Apparently, he rides a bike from here all the way down to the morgue at First Avenue and Thirtieth Street every day."

"No way!" Franco commented.

"That's what Amendola said," Angelo said.

Franco's eyes scanned the area. "The whole neighborhood is a dump. Maybe he's into drugs."

Angelo opened the car door and got out.

"Where are you going?" Franco asked.

"I want to check to make sure he lives here," Angelo said. "Amendola said his apartment is the fourth floor rear. I'll be right back."

Angelo rounded the car and waited for a break in the traffic. He crossed the street and climbed to the stoop in front of Jack's building. Calmly, he pushed open the outer door and glanced at the mailboxes. Many were broken. None had locks that worked.

Quickly, Angelo sorted through the mail. As soon as he came across a catalogue addressed to Jack Stapleton, he put it all back. Next, he tried the inner door. It opened with ease.

Stepping into the front hall, Angelo took a breath. There was an unpleasant musty odor. He eyed the trash on the stairs, the peeling paint, and the broken light bulbs in the once-elegant chandelier. Up on the second floor, he could hear the sounds of a domestic fight with muffled screaming. Angelo smiled. Dealing with Jack Stapleton was going to be easy. The tenement looked like a crack house.

Returning to the front of the house, Angelo took a step away to determine which underground passageway belonged to Jack's building. Each house had a sunken corridor reached by a half dozen steps. These corridors led to the backyards.

After deciding which was the appropriate one, Angelo gingerly walked its length. There were puddles and refuse which threatened his Bruno Magli shoes.

The backyard was a tumult of decaying and collapsed fencing, rotting mattresses, abandoned tires, and other trash. After carefully picking his way a few feet from the building, Angelo turned to look at the fire escape. On the fourth floor two windows had access. The windows were dark. The doctor wasn't at home.

Angelo returned and climbed back into the car.

"Well?" Franco asked.

"He lives there all right," Angelo said. "The building is worse on the inside if you can believe it. It's not locked. I could hear a couple fighting on the second floor and someone else's TV on full blast. The place is not pretty but for our purposes it's perfect. It'll be easy."

"That's what I like to hear," Franco said. "Should we still do the woman first?"

Angelo smiled as best he could. "Why deny myself?"

Franco put the car in gear. They headed south on Columbus Avenue to Broadway then cut across town to Second Avenue. Soon they were on Nineteenth Street. Angelo didn't need the address. He pointed out Laurie's building without difficulty. Franco found a convenient no-parking zone and parked.

"So, you think we should go up the back way?" Franco said, while eyeing the building.

"For several reasons," Angelo said. "She's on the fifth floor, but her windows face the back. To tell if she's there, we have to go back there anyway. Also she's got a nosy neighbor who lives in the front, and you can see her lights are on. This woman opened her door to gawk at me the two times I was up at Montgomery's front door. Besides, Montgomery's apartment has access to the back stairs, and the back stairs dump directly into the backyard. I know because we chased her out that way."

"I'm convinced," Franco said. "Let's do it."

Franco and Angelo got out of the car. Angelo opened up the backseat and lifted out his bag of lock-picking tools along with a Halligan bar, a tool firefighters use to get through doors in cases of emergency.

The two men headed for the passageway to the backyard.

"I heard she got away from you and Tony Ruggerio," Franco said. "At least for a while. She must be quite a number."

"Don't remind me," Angelo said. "Of course, working with Tony was like carrying around a bucket of sand."

Emerging into the backyard, which was a dark warren of neglected gardens, Franco and Angelo carefully moved away from the building far enough to see up to the fifth floor. The windows were all dark.

"Looks like we have time to prepare a nice homecoming," Franco said.

Angelo didn't answer. Instead, he took his lock-picking tools over to the metal fire door that led to the back stairs. He slipped on a tight-fitting pair of leather gloves, while Franco readied the flashlight.

At first Angelo's hands shook from sheer anticipatory excitement of coming face-to-face with Laurie Montgomery after five years of smoldering resentment. When the lock resisted Angelo's efforts, he made a point to control himself and concentrate. The lock responded, and the door opened.

Five floors up, Angelo didn't bother with the lock-picking tools. He knew that Laurie had several dead bolts. He used the Halligan bar. With a quiet splintering sound, it made short work of the door. Within twenty seconds, they were inside.

For a few minutes, the two men stood motionless in the darkness of Laurie's pantry so that they could listen. They wanted to be certain there were no sounds suggestive that their forced entry had been noticed by any of the other tenants.

"Jesus Christ!" Franco forcibly whispered. "Something just touched my leg!"

"What is it?" Angelo demanded. He'd not expected such an outburst, and it caused his heart to flutter.

"Oh, it's only a goddamn cat!" Franco said with relief. All at once, both men could hear the animal purring in the darkness.

"Aren't we lucky," Angelo said. "That will be a nice touch. Bring it along."

Slowly, the men made their way from the pantry through the dark kitchen and into the living room. There they could see significantly better with the city night light coming through the windows.

"So far so good," Angelo said.

"Now we just have to wait," Franco said. "Maybe I'll see if there's any beer or wine in the refrigerator. Are you interested?"

"A beer would be nice," Angelo said.

At police headquarters, Laurie and Jack had to get ID badges and go through a metal detector before they were allowed to go up to Lou's floor. Lou was at the elevator to welcome them.

The first thing he did was take Laurie by the shoulders, look her in the eye, and ask what had happened.

"She's okay," Jack said, patting Lou reassuringly on the back. "She's back to her old, rational, calm self."

"Really?" Lou questioned, still giving Laurie a close inspection.

Laurie couldn't help but smile under Lou's intense scrutiny. "Jack's right," she said. "I'm fine. In fact, I'm embarrassed I made us rush down here."

Lou breathed a sigh of relief. "Well, I'm happy to see both of you. Come on back to my palace." He led the way to his office.

"I can offer you coffee, but I strongly advise against it," Lou said. "At this time of day the janitorial staff considers it strong enough to clean out sink drains."

"We're fine," Laurie said. She took a chair.

Jack did likewise. He glanced around the spartan quarters with an unpleasant shiver. The last time he'd been there about a year ago, it had been after he'd narrowly escaped an attempt on his life.

"I think I figured out how Franconi's body was taken from the morgue," Laurie began. "You teased me about suspecting the Spoletto Funeral Home, but now I think you're going to have to take that back. In fact, I think it's time that you took over."

Laurie then outlined what she thought had happened. She told Lou that she suspected that someone from the medical examiner's office had given the Spoletto people the accession number of a relatively recent, unidentified body as well as the location of Franconi's remains.

"Often when two drivers come to pick up a body for a funeral home, one of them goes in the walk-in cooler while the other handles the paperwork with the mortuary tech," Laurie explained. "In these instances, the mortuary tech prepares the body for pickup by covering it with a sheet and positioning its gurney in a convenient location just inside the cooler door. In the Franconi situation, I believe the driver took the body whose accession number he had, removed its tag, stashed the body in one of the many unoccupied refrigerator compartments, replaced Franconi's tag with that one, and then calmly appeared outside the mortuary office with Franconi's remains. All the tech did at that point was check the accession number."

"That's quite a scenario," Lou said. "Can I ask if you have any proof of this or is it all conjecture?"

"I found the body whose accession number Spoletto called in," Laurie said. "It was in a compartment which was supposed to be vacant. The name Frank Gleason was bogus."

"Ahhhh!" Lou said, becoming much more interested. He leaned forward on his desk. "I'm beginning to like this very much, especially considering the matrimonial association between the Spoletto and the Lucia people. This could be something important. It kind'a reminds me of getting Al Capone on tax evasion. I mean, it would be fantastic if we could get some of the Lucia people on body theft!"

"Of course, it also raises the specter of an organized crime connection to illicit liver transplantation," Jack said. "This could be a frightening association."

"Dangerous as well," Lou said. "So I must insist on no more amateur sleuthing on your part. We take over from here. Do I have your word on that?"

"I'm happy to let you take over," Laurie said. "But there is also the issue of a mole in the medical examiner's office."

"I think it's best I deal with that, too," Lou said. "With the involvement of organized crime, I'd expect some element of extortion or criminal coercion. But I'll deal directly with Bingham. I shouldn't have to warn you that these people are dangerous."

"I learned that lesson all too well," Laurie said.

"I'm too preoccupied with my end of the mystery to interfere," Jack said. "What did you learn for me?"

"Plenty," Lou said. He reached over to the corner of his desk and hefted a large book the size of a coffee-table art book. With a grunt, he handed it to Jack.

With a look of confusion, Jack cracked the book. "What the hell!" he commented. "What's an atlas for?"

"Because you're going to need it," Lou said. "I can't tell you how long it took me to scrounge one up here at police headquarters."

"I don't get it," Jack said.

"My contact at the FAA was able to call someone who knew someone who works in a European organization that doles out landing and takeoff times all over Europe," Lou explained. "They also get the flight plans and store them for over sixty days. Franconi's G4 came to France from Equatorial Guinea."

"Where?" Jack questioned as his eyebrows collided in an expression of total confusion. "I never even heard of Equatorial Guinea. Is it a country?"

"Check out page one hundred fifty-two!" Lou said.

"What's this about a Franconi and a G4?" Laurie asked.

"A G4 is a private jet," Lou explained. "I was able to find out for Jack that Franconi had been out of the country. We thought he'd been in France until I got this new information."

Jack got to page 152 in the atlas. It was a map labeled "the Western Congo Basin," covering a huge portion of western Africa.

"All right, give me a hint," Jack said.

Lou pointed over Jack's shoulder. "It's this little tiny country between Cameroon and Gabon. The city that the plane flew out of is Bata, on the coast." He pointed to the appropriate dot. The atlas depicted the country as mostly uninterrupted green.

Laurie got up from her chair and looked over Jack's other shoulder. "I think I remember hearing about that country one time. I think that's where the writer Frederick Forsyth went to write *Dogs of War.*"

Lou slapped the top of his head in utter amazement. "How do you remember stuff like that? I can't remember where I had lunch last Tuesday."

Laurie shrugged. "I read a lot of novels," she said. "Writers interest me."

"This doesn't make any sense whatsoever," Jack complained. "This is an undeveloped part of Africa. This country must be covered with nothing but jungle. In fact, this whole part of Africa is nothing but jungle. Franconi couldn't have gotten a liver transplant there."

"That was my reaction, too," Lou said. "But the other information makes a little more sense. I tracked Alpha Aviation through its Nevada management corporation to its real owner. It's GenSys Corp in Cambridge, Massachusetts."

"I've heard of GenSys," Laurie said. "It's a biotech firm that's big in vaccines and lymphokines. I remember because a girlfriend of mine who's a broker in Chicago recommended the stock. She's forever giving me tips, thinking I've got tons of money to invest."

"A biotech company!" Jack mused. "Hmmm. That's a new twist. It must be significant, although I don't quite know how. Nor do I know what a biotech firm would be doing in Equatorial Guinea."

"What's the meaning of this indirect corporate trail in Nevada?" Laurie asked. "Is GenSys trying to hide the fact that they own an aircraft?"

"I doubt it," Lou said. "I was able to learn the connection too easily. If GenSys was trying to conceal ownership, the lawyers in Nevada would have continued to be the directors and officers of record for Alpha Aviation. Instead, at the first board meeting the chief financial officer of GenSys assumed the duties of president and secretary."

"Then why Nevada for an airplane owned by a Massachusetts-based company?" Laurie asked.

"I'm no lawyer," Lou admitted. "But I'm sure it has something to do with taxes and limitation of liability. Massachusetts is a terrible state to get sued in. I imagine GenSys leases its plane out for the percentage of the time it doesn't use it, and insurance for a Nevada-based company would be a lot less."

"How well do you know this broker friend of yours?" Jack asked Laurie.

"Really well," Laurie said. "We went to Wesleyan University together."

"How about giving her a call and asking her if she knows of any connection between GenSys and Equatorial Guinea," Jack said. "If she recommended the stock, she'd probably thoroughly researched the company."

"Without a doubt," Laurie said. "Jean Corwin was one of the most compulsive students I knew. She made us premeds seem casual by comparison."

"Is it all right if Laurie uses your phone?" Jack asked Lou.

"No problem," Lou said.

"You want me to call this minute?" Laurie asked with surprise.

"Catch her while she's still at work," Jack said. "Chances are if she has any file, it would be there."

"You're probably right," Laurie admitted. She sat down at Lou's desk and called Chicago information.

While Laurie was on the phone, Jack quizzed Lou in detail about how he was able to find out what he had. He was particularly interested and impressed with the way Lou had come up with Equatorial Guinea. Together, they looked more closely at the map, noticing the country's proximity to the equator. They even noticed that its major city, presumably its capital, wasn't on the mainland but rather on an island called Bioko.

"I just can't imagine what it's like in a place like that," Lou said.

"I can," Jack said. "It's hot, buggy, rainy, and wet."

"Sounds delightful," Lou quipped.

"Not the place someone would choose to vacation," Jack said. "On the other hand, it's off the beaten track."

Laurie hung up the phone and twisted around in Lou's desk chair to face the others. "Jean was as organized as I expected," she said. "She was able to put her finger on her GenSys material in a flash. Of course, she had to ask me how much of the stock I'd bought and was crushed when I admitted I hadn't bought any. Apparently, the stock tripled and then split."

"Is that good?" Lou asked facetiously.

"So good I might have missed my opportunity to retire," Laurie said. "She said this is the second successful biotech company started by its CEO, Taylor Cabot."

"Did she have anything to say about Equatorial Guinea?" Jack asked.

"For sure," Laurie said. "She said that one of the main reasons the company has been doing so well is that it established a huge primate farm. Initially, the farm was to do in-house research for GenSys. Then someone hit on the idea of creating an opportunity for other biotech companies and pharmaceutical firms to out-source their primate research to GenSys. Apparently, the demand for this service has trampled even the most optimistic forecasts."

"And this primate farm is in Equatorial Guinea?" Jack asked.

"That's right," Laurie said.

"Did she suggest any reason why?" Jack asked.

"A memorandum she had from an analyst said that GenSys chose Equatorial Guinea because of the favorable reception they received from the government, which even passed laws to aid their operation. Apparently, GenSys has become the government's major source of much-needed foreign currency."

"Can you imagine the amount of graft that must be involved in that kind of scenario?" Jack asked Lou.

Lou merely whistled.

"The memorandum also pointed out that most of the primates they use are indigenous to Equatorial Guinea," Laurie added. "It allows them to circumvent all the international restrictions in exportation and importation of endangered species like chimpanzees."

"A primate farm," Jack repeated while shaking his head. "This is raising even more bizarre possibilities. Could we be dealing with a xenograft?"

"Don't start that doctor jargon on me," Lou complained. "What in God's name is a xenograft?"

"Impossible," Laurie said. "Xenografts cause hyper-acute rejections. There was no evidence of inflammation in the liver section you showed me, neither humoral nor cell-mediated."

"True," Jack said. "And he wasn't even on any immunosuppressant drugs."

"Come on, you guys," Lou pleaded. "Don't make me beg. What the hell is a xenograft?"

"It's when a transplant organ is taken from an animal of a different species," Laurie said.

"You mean like that Baby Fae baboon heart fiasco ten or twelve years ago?" Lou asked.

"Exactly," Laurie said.

"The new immunosuppressant drugs have brought xenografts back into the picture," Jack explained. "And with considerable more success than with Baby Fae."

"Especially with pig heart valves," Laurie said.

"Of course, it poses a lot of ethical questions," Jack said. "And it drives animal-rights people berserk."

"Especially now that they are experimenting with inserting human genes into the pigs to ameliorate some of the rejection reaction," Laurie added.

"Could Franconi have gotten a primate liver while he was in Africa?" Lou asked.

"I can't imagine," Jack said. "Laurie's point is well taken. There was no evidence of any rejection. That's unheard of even with a good human match short of identical twins."

"But Franconi was apparently in Africa," Lou said.

"True, and his mother said he came home a new man," Jack said. He threw up his hands and stood up. "I don't know what to make of it. It's the damndest mystery. Especially with this organized crime aspect thrown in."

Laurie stood up as well.

"Are you guys leaving?" Lou asked.

Jack nodded. "I'm confused and exhausted," he said. "I didn't sleep much last night. After we made the identification of Franconi's remains, I was on the phone for hours. I called every European organ allocation organization whose phone number I could get."

"How about we all head over to Little Italy for a quick dinner?" Lou suggested. "It's right around the corner."

"Not me," Jack said. "I've got a bike ride ahead of me. At this point, a meal would do me in."

"Nor I," Laurie said. "I'm looking forward to getting home and taking a shower. It's been two late nights for me in a row, and I'm frazzled."

Lou admitted to having another half hour of work to do, so Laurie and Jack said goodbye and descended to the first floor. They returned their temporary-visitor badges and left police headquarters. In the shadow of City Hall, they caught a cab.

"Feel better?" Jack asked Laurie, as they headed north up the Bowery. A kaleidoscope of light played across their faces.

"Much," Laurie admitted. "I can't tell you how relieved I am to dump it all in Lou's capable lap. I'm sorry I got myself so worked up."

"No need to apologize," Jack said. "It's unsettling, to say the least, there's a potential spy in our midst and that organized crime has an interest in liver transplants."

"And how are you bearing up?" Laurie asked. "You're getting a lot of bizarre input on the Franconi case."

"It's bizarre, but it's also intriguing," Jack said. "Especially this association with a biotech giant like GenSys. The scary part about these corporations is that their research is all behind closed doors. Cold-war style secrecy is their modus operandi. No one knows what they are doing in their quest for return on investment. It's a big difference from ten or twenty years ago when the NIH funded most biomedical research in a kind of open forum. In those days, there was oversight in the form of peer review, but not today."

"Too bad there's no one like Lou that you can turn the case over to," Laurie said with a chuckle.

"Wouldn't that be nice," Jack said.

"What's your next step?" Laurie asked.

Jack sighed. "I'm running out of options. The only thing that's scheduled is for a veterinary pathologist to review the liver section."

"So, you already thought about a xenograft?" Laurie asked with surprise.

"No, I didn't," Jack admitted. "The suggestion to have a veterinary pathologist look at the slide wasn't my idea. It came from a parasitologist over at the hospital who thought the granuloma was due to a parasite, but one he didn't recognize."

"Maybe you should mention the possibility of a xenograft to Ted Lynch," Laurie suggested. "As a DNA expert he might have something in his bag of tricks that could say yes or no definitively."

"Excellent idea!" Jack said with admiration. "How can you come up with such a great suggestion when you're so beat? You amaze me! My mind has already shut down for the night."

"Compliments are always welcome," Laurie teased. "Especially in the dark, so you can't see me blush."

"I'm starting to think that the only option that might be open to me if I really want to solve this case is a quick trip to Equatorial Guinea."

Laurie twisted around in the seat so she could look directly into Jack's broad face. In the half light, it was impossible to see his eyes. "You're not serious. I mean you're joking, right?"

"Well, there's no way I could phone GenSys or even go up to Cambridge and walk into their home office and say: 'Hi folks, what's going on in Equatorial Guinea?'"

"But we're talking about Africa," Laurie said. "That's crazy. It's halfway around the world. Besides, if you don't think you'd learn anything going up to Cambridge, what makes you think you'd learn anything going to Africa?"

"Maybe because they wouldn't expect it," Jack said. "I don't suppose they get many visitors."

"Oh, this is insane," Laurie said, flapping her hands into the air and rolling her eyes.

"Hey, calm down," Jack said. "I didn't say I was going. I just said it was something I was beginning to think about."

"Well, stop thinking about it," Laurie said. "I've got enough to worry about."

Jack smiled at her. "You really are concerned. I'm touched."

"Oh, sure!" Laurie remarked cynically. "You're never touched by my pleas not to ride your mountain bike around the city."

The taxi pulled up in front of Laurie's apartment building and came to a halt. Laurie started to get some money out. Jack put a hand on her arm. "My treat."

"All right, I'll get it next time," Laurie said. She started to climb out of the cab, then stopped. "If you were to promise to take a cab home, I think we could rustle up something to eat in my apartment."

"Thanks, but not tonight," Jack said. "I've got to get the bike home. I'd probably fall asleep on a full stomach."

"Worse things could happen," Laurie said.

"Let me take a rain check," Jack said.

Laurie climbed out of the cab and then leaned back in. "Just promise me one thing: you won't leave for Africa tonight."

Jack took a playful swipe at her, but she easily evaded his hand.

"Good night, Jack," Laurie said with a warm smile.

"Good night, Laurie," Jack said. "I'll call you later after I talk with Warren."

"Oh, that's right," Laurie said. "With everything that's happened, I'd forgotten. I'll be waiting for your call."

Laurie closed the taxi door and watched the cab until it disappeared around the corner on First Avenue. She turned toward her door, musing that Jack was a charming but complicated man.

As she rode up in her elevator, Laurie began to anticipate her shower and the warmth of her terry-cloth robe. She vowed she'd turn in early.

Laurie treated Debra Engler to an acid smile before keying her multiple locks. She slammed her door behind her to give Mrs. Engler an extra message. Moving her mail from one hand to the other, she removed her coat. In the darkness of the closet, she groped for a hanger.

It wasn't until Laurie entered the living room that she flipped the wall switch that turned on a floor lamp. She got two steps toward the kitchen when she let out a muffled scream and dropped her mail on the floor. There were two men in the living room. One was in her art-deco chair, the other sitting on the couch. The one on the couch was petting Tom, who was asleep on his lap.

The other thing Laurie noticed was a large handgun with an attached silencer on the arm of the art-deco chair.

"Welcome home, Dr. Montgomery," Franco said. "Thank you for the wine and beer."

Laurie's eyes went to the coffee table. There was an empty beer bottle and wineglass.

"Please come over and sit down," Franco said. He pointed to a side chair they'd put in the middle of the room.

Laurie didn't move. She was incapable of it. She thought vaguely about running into the kitchen for the phone but immediately dismissed the idea as ridiculous. She even thought about fleeing back to her front door, but with all the locks, she knew it would be a futile gesture.

"Please!" Franco repeated with a false politeness that only augmented Laurie's terror.

Angelo moved the cat to the side and stood up. He took a step toward Laurie and, without warning, backhanded her viciously across the face. The blow propelled Laurie back against the wall, where her legs gave way. She slumped to her hands and knees. A few drops of bright red blood dropped from her split upper lip, splattering on the hardwood floor.

Angelo grabbed her by the upper arm and roughly hoisted her to her feet. Then he powered her over to the chair and pushed her into a sitting position. Laurie's terror made her incapable of resisting.

"That's better," Franco said.

Angelo leaned over and stuck his face in Laurie's. "Recognize me?"

Laurie forced herself to look up into the man's horribly scarred face. He looked like a character in a horror movie. She swallowed; her throat had gone dry. Incapable of speech, all she could do was shake her head.

"No?" Franco questioned. "Doctor, I'm afraid you are going to hurt Angelo's feelings and, under the circumstances, that's a dangerous thing to do."

"I'm sorry," Laurie squeaked. But no sooner had the words come out, then Laurie associated the name with the fact that the man standing in front of her had been burned. It was Angelo Facciolo, Cerino's main hit man, now obviously out of jail.

"I've been waiting five years," Angelo snarled. Then he struck Laurie again, half knocking her off the chair. She ended up with her head down. There was more blood. This time it came from her nose and soaked into the carpet.

"Okay, Angelo!" Franco said. "Remember! We've got to talk with her."

Angelo trembled for a moment over Laurie, as if struggling to restrain himself. Abruptly, he went back to the couch and sat down. He picked the cat back up and began roughly petting it. Tom didn't mind and began to purr.

Laurie managed to right herself. With her hand, she felt both her lip and her nose. Her lip was already beginning to swell. She pinched her nose to halt the bleeding.

"Listen, Doctor Montgomery," Franco said. "As you might imagine, it was very easy for us to come in here. I say this so you will comprehend how vulnerable you are. You see, we have a problem that you can help us with. We're here to ask you nicely to leave the Franconi thing alone. Am I making myself clear?"

Laurie nodded. She was afraid not to.

"Good," Franco said. "Now, we are very reasonable people. We'll consider this a favor on your part, and we're willing to do a favor in return. We happen to know who killed Mr. Franconi, and we're willing to pass that information on to you. You see, Mr. Franconi wasn't a nice man, so he was killed. End of story. Are you still with me?"

Laurie nodded again. She glanced at Angelo but quickly averted her eyes.

"The killer's name is Vido Delbario," Franco continued. "He's not a nice person, either, although he did do the world a favor in getting rid of Franconi. I've even taken the trouble to write the name down." Franco leaned forward and put a piece of paper on the coffee table. "So, a favor for a favor."

Franco paused and looked expectantly at Laurie.

"You do understand what I'm saying, don't you?" Franco asked after a moment of silence.

Laurie nodded for the third time.

"I mean, we're not asking much," Franco said. "To be blunt, Franconi was a bad guy. He killed a bunch of people and deserved to die himself. Now, as far as you are concerned, I hope you will be sensible because in a city this size there's no way to protect yourself, and Angelo here would like no better than have his way with you. Lucky for you, our boss is not heavy-handed. He's a negotiator. Do you understand?"

Franco paused again. Laurie felt compelled to respond. With difficulty, she managed to say she understood.

"Wonderful!" Franco said. He slapped his knees and stood up. "When I heard how intelligent and resourceful you are, Doc, I was confident we could see eye to eye."

Franco slipped his handgun into his shoulder holster and put on his Ferragamo coat. "Come on, Angelo," he said. "I'm sure the doctor wants to shower and have her dinner. She looks kind'a tired to me."

Angelo got up, took a step in Laurie's direction, and then viciously wrenched the cat's neck. There was a sickening snap, and Tom went limp without a sound. Angelo dumped the dead cat in Laurie's lap, and followed Franco out the front door.

"Oh, no!" Laurie whimpered as she cradled her pet of six years. She knew its neck had been cruelly broken. She stood up on rubbery legs. Out in the hall, she heard the elevator arrive and then descend.

With sudden panic she rushed to the front door and relocked all the locks while still clutching Tom's body. Then, realizing the intruders had to have come in the back door, she raced there only to find it wide open and splintered. She forced it closed as best she could.

Back in the kitchen she took the phone off the hook with trembling hands. Her first response was to call the police, but then she hesitated, hearing Franco's voice in the back of her mind warning her how vulnerable she was. She also could see Angelo's horrid face and the intensity of his eyes.

Recognizing she was in shock and fighting tears, Laurie replaced the receiver. She thought she'd call Jack, but she knew he wouldn't be home yet. So, instead of calling anyone for the moment, she tenderly packed her pet in a Styrofoam box with several trays of ice cubes. Then she went into the bathroom to check out her own wounds.

Jack's bike ride from the morgue home was not the ordeal he expected. In fact, once he got under way, he felt better than he had for most of the day. He even allowed himself to cut through Central Park. It had been the first time he'd been in the park after dark for a year. Although he was uneasy, it was also exhilarating to sprint along the dark, winding paths.

For most of the trip, he'd pondered about GenSys and Equatorial Guinea. He wondered what it was really like in that part of Africa. He'd joked earlier with Lou that it was buggy, hot, and wet, but he didn't know for sure.

He also thought about Ted Lynch and wondered what Ted would be able to do the following day. Before Jack had left the morgue, he'd called him at home to outline the unlikely possibility of a xenograft. Ted said that he thought he'd be able to tell by checking an area on the DNA that specified ribosomal proteins. He'd explained that the area differed considerably from species to species and that the information to make a species identification was available on a CD-ROM.

Jack turned onto his street with the idea of going to the local bookstore to see if there was any material on Equatorial Guinea. But as he approached the playground with its daily late afternoon and evening game of basketball under way, he had another idea. It occurred to him that there might be expatriate Equatoguineans in New York. After all, the city harbored people from every country in the world.

Turning his bike into the playground, Jack dismounted and leaned it up against the chain-link fence. He didn't bother to lock it, though most people would have thought the neighborhood a risky place to leave a thousand-dollar bike. In reality, the playground was the only place in New York Jack felt he didn't have to lock up.

Jack walked over to the sidelines and nodded to Spit and Flash, who were part of the crowd waiting to play. The game in progress swept up and down the court as the ball changed hands or baskets were made. As usual, Warren was dominating the play. Before each of his shots he'd say "money," which was aggravating to the opponents because ninety percent of the time, the ball would sail through the basket.

A quarter hour later the game was decided by one of Warren's "money" shots, and the losers slunk off the court. Warren caught sight of Jack and strutted over.

"Hey, man, you going to run or what?" Warren asked.

"I'm thinking about it," Jack said. "But I've got a couple of questions. First of all, how about you and Natalie getting together with Laurie and me this weekend?"

"Hell, yes," Warren said. "Anything to shut my shortie up. She's been ragging on me fierce about you and Laurie."

"Secondly, do you know any brothers from a tiny African country called Equatorial Guinea?"

"Man, I never know what's going to come out of your mouth," Warren complained. "Let me think."

"It's on the west coast of Africa," Jack said. "Between Cameroon and Gabon."

"I know where it is," Warren said indignantly. "It was supposedly discovered by the Portuguese and colonized by the Spanish. Actually, it was discovered a long time earlier by black people."

"I'm impressed you know of it," Jack said. "I'd never heard of the country."

"I'm not surprised," Warren said. "I'm sure you didn't take any black history courses. But to answer your question, yes, I do know a couple of people from there, and one family in particular. Their name is Ndeme. They live two doors down from you, toward the park."

Jack looked over at the building, then back at Warren. "Do you know them well enough to introduce me?" Jack asked. "I've developed a sudden interest in Equatorial Guinea."

"Yeah, sure," Warren said. "The father's name is Esteban. He owns the Mercado Market over on Columbus. That's his son over there with the orange kicks."

Jack followed Warren's pointing finger until he spotted the orange sneakers. He recognized the boy as one of the basketball regulars. He was a quiet kid and an intense player.

"Why don't you come down and run a few games?" Warren suggested. "Then I'll take you over and introduce you to Esteban. He's a friendly dude."

"Fair enough," Jack said. After being revived by the bicycle ride, he was looking for an excuse to play basketball. The events of the day had him in knots.

Jack went back and got his bike. Hurrying over to his building, he carried the bicycle up the stairs. He unlocked his door without even taking it off his shoulder. Once inside, he made a beeline for his bedroom and his basketball gear.

Within five minutes, Jack was already on his way out when his phone rang. For a moment, he debated answering it, but thinking it might be Ted calling back with a bit of arcane DNA trivia, Jack picked it up. It was Laurie, and she was beside herself.

Jack crammed enough bills through the Plexiglas partition in the taxi to more than cover the fare and jumped out. He was in front of Laurie's apartment building, where he'd been less than an hour earlier. Dressed in his basketball gear he raced to the front door and was buzzed in. Laurie met him in the elevator foyer on her floor.

"My god!" Jack wailed. "Look at your lip."

"That will heal," Laurie said stoically. Then she caught Debra Engler's eye peering through the crack in her door. Laurie lunged at the woman and shouted for her to mind her own business. The door snapped shut.

Jack put his arm around Laurie to calm her and led her into her apartment.

"All right," Jack said, after getting Laurie seated on the couch. "Tell me what happened."

"They killed Tom," Laurie whimpered. After the initial shock, Laurie had cried for her pet, but her tears had dried until Jack's question.

"Who?" Jack demanded.

Laurie waited until she had her emotions under control. "There were two of them, but I only knew one," she said. "And he's the one who struck me and killed Tom. His name is Angelo. He's the person I've had nightmares about. I had a terrible run-in with him during the Cerino affair. I thought he was still in prison. I can't imagine how or why he is out. He's horrid to look at. His face is terribly scarred from burns, and I'm sure he blames me."

"So this visit was for revenge?" Jack asked.

"No," Laurie said. "This was a warning for me. In their words I'm to 'leave the Franconi thing alone.' "

"I don't believe this," Jack said. "I'm the one investigating the case, not you."

"You warned me. I've obviously irritated the wrong people by trying to find out how Franconi's body was lifted from the morgue," Laurie said. "For all I know it was my visit to the Spoletto Funeral Home that set them off."

"I'm not going to take any credit for foreseeing this," Jack said. "I thought you would get in trouble with Bingham, not mobsters."

"Angelo's warning was presented in the guise of a favor for a favor," Laurie said. "His favor was to tell me who killed Franconi. In fact, he wrote the name down." Laurie lifted the piece of paper from the coffee table and handed it to Jack.

"Vido Delbario," Jack read. He looked back at Laurie's battered face. Both her nose and lip were swollen, and she was developing a black eye. "This case has been bizarre from the start, now it's getting out of hand. I think you'd better tell me everything that happened."

Laurie related to Jack the details from the moment she'd walked in the door until she'd called him on the phone. She even told him why she'd hesitated calling 911.

Jack nodded. "I understand," he said. "There's little the local precinct could do at this point."

"What am I going to do?" Laurie asked rhetorically. She didn't expect an answer.

"Let me look at the back door," Jack said.

Laurie led him through the kitchen and into the pantry.

"Whoa!" Jack said. Because of the multiple dead bolts the entire edge split when the door had been forced. "I'll tell you one thing, you're not staying here tonight."

"I suppose I could go home to my parents," Laurie said.

"You're coming home with me," Jack said. "I'll sleep on the couch."

Laurie looked into the depths of Jack's eyes. She couldn't help but wonder if there were more to this sudden invitation than the issue of her safety.

"Get your things," Jack said. "And pack for a few days. It will take that long to replace this door."

"I hate to bring this up," Laurie said. "But I have to do something with poor Tom."

Jack scratched the back of his head. "Do you have access to a shovel?"

"I have a gardening trowel," Laurie said. "What are you thinking?"

"We could bury him in the backyard," Jack said.

Laurie smiled. "You are a softie, aren't you?"

"I just know what it's like to lose things you love," Jack said. His voice caught. For a painful moment he recalled the phone call that had informed him of his wife and daughters' deaths in a commuter plane crash.

While Laurie packed her things, Jack paced her bedroom. He forced his mind to concentrate on current concerns. "We're going to have to tell Lou about this," Jack said, "and give him Vido Delbario's name."

"I was thinking the same thing," Laurie said from the depths of her walk-in closet. "Do you think we should do it tonight?"

"I think we should," Jack said. "Then he can decide when he wants to act on it. We'll call from my house. Do you have his home number?"

"I do," Laurie said.

"You know, this episode is disturbing for more reasons than just your safety," Jack said. "It adds to my worry that organized crime is somehow involved in liver transplantation. Maybe there is some kind of black-market operation going on."

Laurie came out of her closet with a hangup bag. "But how can it be transplantation when Franconi wasn't on immunosuppressant drugs? And don't forget the strange results Ted got with his DNA testing."

Jack sighed. "You're right," he admitted. "It doesn't fit together."

"Maybe Lou can make sense of it all," Laurie said.

"Wouldn't that be nice," Jack said. "Meanwhile, this episode makes the idea of going to Africa a lot more appealing."

Laurie stopped short on her way into the bathroom. "What on earth are you talking about?" she demanded.

"I haven't had any personal experience with organized crime," Jack said. "But I have with street gangs, and I believe there's a similarity that I learned the hard way. If either of these groups gets it in their mind to get rid of you, the police can't protect you unless they are committed to guarding you twenty-four hours a day. The problem is, they don't have the manpower. Maybe it would be good for both of us to get out of town for a while. It could give Lou a chance to sort this out."

"I'd go, too?" Laurie asked. Suddenly the idea of going to Africa had a very different connotation. She'd never been to Africa, and it could be interesting. In fact, it might even be fun.

"We'd consider it a forced vacation," Jack said. "Of course, Equatorial Guinea might not be a prime destination, but it would be . . . different. And perhaps, in the process, we'll be able to figure out exactly what GenSys is doing there and why Franconi made the trip."

"Hmmm," Laurie said. "I'm starting to warm to the idea."

After Laurie had her things ready, she and Jack took Tom's Styrofoam casket into the backyard. In the far corner of the garden where there was loose loam, they dug a deep hole. The chance discovery of a rusted spade made the job easy, and Tom was put to rest.

"My word!" Jack complained as he hauled Laurie's suitcase out the front door. "What did you put in here?"

"You told me to pack for several days," Laurie said defensively.

"But you didn't have to bring your bowling ball," Jack quipped.

"It's the cosmetics," Laurie said. "They are not travel size."

They caught a cab on First Avenue. En route to Jack's they stopped at a bookstore on Fifth Avenue. While Jack waited in the taxi, Laurie dashed inside to get a book on Equatorial Guinea. Unfortunately, there weren't any, and she had to settle for a guidebook for all of Central Africa.

"The clerk laughed at me when I asked for a book on Equatorial Guinea," Laurie said, when she got back in the cab.

"That's one more hint it's not a top vacation destination," Jack said.

Laurie laughed. She reached over and gave Jack's arm a squeeze. "I haven't thanked you yet for coming over," she said. "I really appreciated it, and I'm feeling much better."

"I'm glad," Jack said.

Once in Jack's building, Jack had to struggle with Laurie's suitcase up the cluttered stairs. After a series of exaggerated grunts and groans, Laurie asked him if he wanted her to carry it. Jack told her that her punishment for packing such a heavy bag was to listen to him complain.

Eventually, he got it outside his door. He fumbled for his key, got it into the cylinder and turned. He heard the dead bolt snap back.

"Hmmm," he commented. "I don't remember double-locking the door." He turned the key again to release the latch bolt and pushed open the door. Because of the darkness, he preceded Laurie into the apartment to flip on the light. Laurie followed and collided with him because he'd stopped suddenly.

"Go ahead, turn it on," a voice said.

Jack complied. The silhouettes he'd glimpsed a moment before were now men dressed in long, dark coats. They were seated on Jack's sofa, facing into the room.

"Oh my God!" Laurie said. "It's them!"

Franco and Angelo had made themselves at home, just as they had at Laurie's. They'd even helped themselves to beers. The half-empty bottles were on the coffee table, along with a handgun and its attached silencer. A straight-backed chair had been brought into the center of the room to face the couch.

"I assume you are Dr. Jack Stapleton," Franco said.

Jack nodded, as his mind began to go over ways of handling the situation. He knew the front door behind him was still ajar. He berated himself for not being more suspicious to have found it double-locked. The problem was he'd gone out so quickly, he couldn't remember which locks he'd secured.

"Don't do anything foolish," Franco admonished as if reading Jack's mind. "We won't be staying long. And if we'd known that Dr. Montgomery was going to be here, we could have saved ourselves a trip to her place, not to mention the effort of going over the same message twice."

"What is it you people are afraid we might learn that makes you want to come and threaten us?" Jack asked.

Franco smiled and looked at Angelo. "Can you believe this guy? He thinks we made all this effort to get in here to answer questions."

"No respect," Angelo said.

"Doc, how about getting another chair for the lady," Franco said to Jack. "Then we can have our little talk, and we'll be on our way."

Jack didn't move. He was thinking about the gun on the coffee table and wondering which of the men was still armed. As he tried to gauge their strength, he noticed that both were on the thin side. He figured they were most likely out of shape.

"Excuse me, Doc," Franco said. "Are you with us or what?"

Before Jack could answer, there was a commotion behind him and someone roughly bumped him to the side. Another person shouted: "Nobody move!"

Jack recovered from his momentary confusion to comprehend that three African-Americans had leaped into the room, each armed with machine pistols. The guns were trained unwaveringly on Franco and Angelo. These newcomers were all dressed in basketball gear, and Jack quickly recognized them. It was Flash, David, and Spit, all of whom were still sweating from activity on the playground.

Franco and Angelo were taken completely unawares. They simply sat there, eyes wide. Since they were accustomed to being on the other side of lethal weapons, they knew enough not to move.

For a moment there was frozen silence. Then Warren strutted in. "Man, Doc, keeping you alive has become a full-time job, you know what I'm saying? And I'm going to have to tell you, you're dragging down the neighborhood, bringing in this kind of white trash."

Warren took the machine pistol away from Spit and told Spit to frisk the visitors. Wordlessly, Spit relieved Angelo of his Walther auto pistol. After frisking Franco, he collected the gun from the coffee table.

Jack noisily let out a breath of air. "Warren, old sport, I don't know how you manage to drop in on such a timely basis in my life, but it's appreciated."

"These scumbags were seen casing this place earlier tonight," Warren explained. "It's as if they think they're invisible, despite their expensive threads and that big, black, shiny Cadillac. It's kind of a joke."

Jack rubbed his hands together in appreciation of the sudden change of power. He asked Angelo and Franco their names but got cold stares in return.

"That one is Angelo Facciolo," Laurie said, while pointing toward her nemesis.

"Spit, get their wallets," Warren ordered.

Spit complied and read out their names and addresses. "Uh-oh, what's this?" he questioned when he opened the wallet containing the Ozone Park police badge. He held it up for Warren to see.

"They're not police officers," Warren said with a wave of dismissal. "Don't worry."

"Laurie," Jack said. "I think it's time to give Lou a call. I'm sure he'd like nothing better than to talk with these gentlemen. And tell him to bring the paddy wagon in case he'd like to invite them to stay the night at the city's expense."

Laurie disappeared into the kitchen.

Jack walked over to Angelo and towered above him.

"Stand up," Jack said.

Angelo got to his feet and glowered insolently at Jack. To everyone's surprise, especially Angelo, Jack sucker punched him as hard as he could in the face. There was a crunching sound as Angelo was knocked backward over the sofa to land in a heap on the floor.

Jack winced, cursed, and grabbed his hand. Then he shook it up and down. "Jeez," he complained. "I've never hit anybody like that. It hurts!"

"Hold up," Warren warned Jack. "I don't like beatin' on these dog turds. It's not my style."

"I'm all done," Jack said, still shaking his injured hand. "You see, that dog turd on the other side of the couch beat up on Laurie earlier this evening after they broke into her apartment. I'm sure you noticed her face."

Angelo pushed himself up to a sitting position. His nose angled to the right. Jack invited him to come back around the couch and sit down. Angelo moved slowly, while cupping his hand beneath his nose to catch the dripping blood.

"Now, before the police get here," Jack said to the two men, "I'd like to ask you guys again about what you're afraid Laurie and I might learn. What is going on with this Franconi nonsense?"

Angelo and Franco stared at Jack as if he weren't there. Jack persisted and asked what they knew about Franconi's liver, but the men remained stone silent.

Laurie returned from the kitchen. "I got Lou," she reported. "He's on his way, and I have to say he's excited, especially about the Vido Delbario tip."

An hour later, Jack found himself comfortably ensconced in Esteban Ndeme's apartment along with Laurie and Warren.

"Sure, I'll have another beer," Jack said in response to Esteban's offer. Jack was feeling a pleasant buzz from his first beer and progressively euphoric that the evening had worked out so auspiciously after such a bad start.

Lou had arrived at Jack's with several patrolmen less than twenty minutes after Laurie's call. He'd been ecstatic to take Angelo and Franco downtown to book them on breaking and entering, possession of unauthorized firearms, assault and battery, extortion, and impersonation of a police officer. His hope was to hold them long enough to get some real information out of them about New York City organized crime, particularly the Lucia organization.

Lou had been disturbed by the threats Laurie and Jack had received, so when Jack mentioned that he and Laurie were thinking of going out of town for a week or so, Lou was all for it. Lou was concerned enough that in the interim, he'd assigned a guard for Laurie and Jack. To make the job easier, Jack and Laurie agreed to stay together.

At Jack's urging, Warren had taken him and Laurie to the Mercado Market and to meet Esteban Ndeme. As Warren had intimated, Esteban was an amiable and gracious man. He was close to Jack's age of forty-two, but his body type was the opposite of Jack's. Where Jack was stocky, Esteban was slender. Even his facial features seemed delicate. His skin was a deep, rich brown, many shades darker than Warren's. But his most noticeable physical trait was his high-domed forehead. He'd lost his hair in the front so that his hairline ran from ear to ear over the top of his head.

As soon as he'd learned Jack was considering a trip to Equatorial Guinea, he'd invited Jack, Laurie, and Warren back to his apartment.

Teodora Ndeme had turned out to be as congenial as her husband. After the group had been in the apartment for only a short time, she'd insisted everyone stay for dinner.

With savory aromas drifting from the kitchen, Jack sat back contentedly with a second beer. "What brought you and Teodora to New York City?" he asked Esteban.

"We had to flee our country," Esteban said. He went on to describe the the reign of terror of the ruthless dictator Nguema that forced a third of the population, including all of Spanish descent, to leave. "Fifty thousand people were murdered,"

Esteban said. "It was terrible. We were lucky to get out. I was a schoolteacher trained in Spain and therefore suspect."

"Things have changed, I hope," Jack said.

"Oh, yes," Esteban said. "A coup in 1979 has changed a lot. But it is a poor country, although there is some talk of offshore oil, as was discovered off Gabon. Gabon is now the wealthiest country in the region."

"Have you been back?" Jack asked.

"Several times," Esteban said. "The last time, a few years ago," Esteban said. "Teodora and I still have family there. Teodora's brother even has a small hotel on the mainland in a town called Bata."

"I've heard of Bata," Jack said. "I understand it has an airport."

"The only one on the mainland," Esteban said. "It was built in the eighties for a Central African Congress. Of course, the country couldn't afford it, but that is another story."

"Have you heard of a company called GenSys?" Jack asked.

"Most definitely," Esteban said. "It is the major source of foreign currency for the government, especially since cocoa and coffee prices have fallen."

"So I've heard," Jack said. "I've also heard GenSys has a primate farm. Do you know if that is in Bata?"

"No, it is in the south," Esteban said. "They built it in the jungle near an old deserted Spanish town called Cogo. They have rebuilt much of the town for their people from America and Europe, and they have built a new town for local people who work for them. They employ many Equatoguinean people."

"Do you know if GenSys built a hospital?" Jack asked.

"Yes, they did," Esteban said. "They built a hospital and laboratory on the old town square facing the town hall."

"How do you know so much about it?" Jack asked.

"Because my cousin used to work there," Esteban said. "But he quit when the soldiers executed one of his friends for hunting. A lot of people like GenSys because they pay well, but others don't like GenSys because they have too much power with the government."

"Because of money," Jack said.

"Yes, of course," Esteban said. "They pay a lot of money to the ministers. They even pay part of the army."

"That's cozy," Laurie commented.

"If we were to go to Bata, would we be able to visit Cogo?" Jack asked.

"I suppose," Esteban said. "After the Spanish left twenty-five years ago, the road to Cogo was abandoned and became impassable, but GenSys has rebuilt it so the trucks can go back and forth. But you'd have to hire a car."

"Is that possible?" Jack asked.

"If you have money, anything is possible in Equatorial Guinea," Esteban said. "When are you planning to go? Because it's best to go in the dry season."

"When's that?" Jack asked.

"February and March," Esteban said.

"That's convenient," Jack said. "Because Laurie and I are thinking of going tomorrow night."

"What?" Warren spoke for the first time since they'd arrived at Esteban's apartment. He'd not been privy to Jack and Lou's conversation. "I thought me and Natalie were going out on the town with you guys this weekend. I've already told Natalie."

"Ohhhh!" Jack commented. "I forgot about that."

"Hey, man, you gotta wait 'til after Saturday night, otherwise I'm in deep shit, you know what I'm saying. I told you how much she's been ragging on me to see you guys."

In his euphoric mood Jack had another suggestion. "I have a better idea. Why don't you and Natalie come along with Laurie and me to Equatorial Guinea? It will be our treat."

Laurie blinked. She wasn't sure she'd heard correctly.

"Man, what are you talking about?" Warren said. "You're out'a your friggin' mind. You're talking about Africa."

"Yeah, Africa," Jack said. "If Laurie and I have to go, we might as well make it as fun as possible. In fact, Esteban, why don't you and your wife come, too? We'll make it a party."

"Are you serious?" Esteban asked.

Laurie's expression was equally as incredulous.

"Sure, I'm serious," Jack said. "The best way to visit a country is to go with someone who used to live there. That's no secret. But tell me, do we all need visas?"

"Yes, but the Equatorial Guinean Embassy is here in New York," Esteban said. "Two pictures, twenty-five dollars, and a letter from a bank saying you're not poor gets you a visa."

"How do you get to Equatorial Guinea?" Jack asked.

"For Bata the easiest is through Paris," Esteban said. "From Paris there is daily service to Douala, Cameroon. From Douala there's daily service to Bata. You can go through Madrid, too, but that's only twice a week to Malabo on Bioko."

"Sounds like Paris wins out," Jack said gaily.

"Teodora!" Esteban called out to his wife in the kitchen. "You'd better come in here."

"You're crazy, man," Warren said to Jack. "I knew it the first day you walked out on that basketball court. But, you know something, I'm beginning to like it."

CHAPTER 17

Kevin's alarm went off at six-fifteen. It was still completely dark outside. Emerging from his mosquito net, he turned on the light to find his robe and slippers. A cottony feeling in his mouth and a mild bitemporal headache reminded him of the wine he'd drunk the night before. With a shaky hand he took a long drink of the water he had at his bedside. Thus fortified, he set out on shaky legs to knock on his guest rooms' doors.

The previous night, he and the women had decided that it made sense for Melanie and Candace to spend the night. Kevin had plenty of room, and they all agreed being together would make the departure in the morning far easier and probably elicit less attention. Consequently, at about eleven P.M., amid lots of laughter and gaiety, Kevin had driven the women to their respective quarters to collect their overnight necessities, a change of clothes, and the food they'd gotten from the commissary.

While the women had been packing, Kevin had made a quick detour to his lab to get the locator, the directional beacon, a flashlight, and the contour map.

On each guest room door, Kevin had to knock twice. Once quite softly, and when there was no response, he rapped more vigorously until he heard a response. He sensed the women were hungover, especially after it took them significantly longer than they planned to show up in the kitchen. Both of them poured themselves a mug of coffee and drank the first cup without conversation.

After breakfast they all revived significantly. In fact, as they emerged from Kevin's house they felt exhilarated, as if they were setting off on a holiday. The weather was as good as could be expected in that part of the world. Dawn was breaking and the pink and silver sky was generally clear overhead. To the south, there was a line of small puffy clouds. On the horizon to the west, there were ominous purple storm clouds, but they were way out over the ocean and would most likely stay there for the day.

As they walked toward the waterfront, they were enthralled by the profusion of bird life. There were blue turacos, parrots, weaverbirds, African fish eagles, and a kind of African blackbird. The air was filled with their color and shrieks.

The town seemed deserted. There were no pedestrians or vehicles, and the homes were still shuttered against the night. The only person they saw was a local mopping the floor in the Chickee Hut Bar.

They walked out on the impressive pier GenSys had built. It was twenty feet wide and six feet high. The rough-hewn planks were wet from the humid night air.

At the end of the pier, there was a wooden ramp that led down to a floating dock. The dock seemed to be mysteriously suspended; the surface of the perfectly calm water was hidden by a layer of mist that extended as far as the eye could see.

As the women had promised, there was a motorized thirty-foot-long pirogue languidly moored to the end of the dock. Long ago, it had been painted red with a white interior, but the paint had faded or had been scraped off in large areas. A thatched roof supported by wooden poles extended over three-quarters of the boat's length. Under the shelter were benches. The motor was an antique Evinrude outboard. Tethered to the stern was a small canoe with four narrow benches extending from gunwale to gunwale.

"Not bad, eh?" Melanie said, as she grabbed the mooring line and pulled the boat to the dock.

"It's bigger than I expected," Kevin said. "As long as the motor keeps going, we should be fine. I wouldn't want to paddle it very far."

"Worst-case scenario we float back," Melanie said undaunted. "After all, we are going upriver."

They got the gear and food aboard. While Melanie continued to stand on the pier, Kevin made his way to the stern to examine the motor. It was self-explanatory with instructions written in English. He put the throttle on start and pulled the cord. To his utter surprise, the engine started. He motioned for Melanie to hop in, shifted the motor into forward, and they were off.

As they pulled away from the pier, they all looked back at Cogo to see if anyone took note of their departure. The only person they saw was the lone man cleaning the Chickee Hut, and he didn't bother to look in their direction.

As they had planned, they motored west as if they were going to Acalayong. Kevin advanced the throttle to half-open and was pleased at the speed. The pirogue was large and heavy but it had very little draw. He checked the canoe they had in tow; it was riding easily in the water.

The sound of the motor made conversation difficult so they were content to enjoy the scenery. The sun had yet to come up, but the sky was brighter and the eastern ends of the cumulus clouds over Gabon were edged in gold. To their right, the shoreline of Equatorial Guinea appeared as a solid mass of vegetation that abruptly dumped into the water. Dotted about the wide estuary were other pirogues moving ghostlike through the mist that still layered the surface of the water.

When Cogo had fallen significantly astern, Melanie tapped Kevin on the shoulder. Once she had his attention, she made a wide sweeping motion with her hand. Kevin nodded and began to steer the boat to the south.

After traveling south for ten minutes, Kevin began a slow turn to the west. They were now at least a mile offshore, and when they passed Cogo, it was difficult to make out specific buildings.

When the sun did finally make its appearance, it was a huge ball of reddish gold. At first, the equatorial mists were so dense that the sun could be examined directly without the need to shield one's eyes. But the heat of the sun began to evaporate the mist which, in turn, rapidly made the sun's rays stronger. Melanie was the first to slip on her sunglasses, but Candace and Kevin quickly did the same. A few minutes later, everyone began to peel off layers of clothing they'd donned against the comparative morning chill.

To their left was the string of islands that hugged the Equatoguinean coast. Kevin had been steering north to complete the wide circle around Cogo. Now he pushed over the helm to point the bow directly toward Isla Francesca, which loomed in the distance.

Once the mists had dissipated from the sun's glare, a welcome breeze stirred the water, and waves began to mar the hitherto glassy surface. Pushing into a mounting headwind the pirogue began to slap against the crests, occasionally sprinkling its passengers with spray.

Isla Francesca looked different than her sister islands, and the closer they got, the more apparent it became. Besides being considerably larger, Isla Francesca's limestone escarpment gave it a much more substantial appearance. There were even bits of cloudlike mist that clung to its summits.

An hour and fifteen minutes after they had left the pier in Cogo, Kevin cut back on the throttle and the pirogue slowed. A hundred feet ahead was the dense shoreline of the southwestern tip of Isla Francesca.

"From this vantage point it looks sort of forbidding," Melanie yelled over the sound of the engine.

Kevin nodded. There was nothing about the island that was inviting. There was no beach. The entire shoreline appeared to be covered with dense mangroves.

"We've got to find Rio Diviso's outlet," Kevin yelled back. After approaching the mangroves as close as he thought prudent, he pushed the helm to starboard and headed along the western shore. In the lee of the island, the waves disappeared. Kevin stood up in hopes of seeing possible underwater obstructions. But he couldn't. The water was an impenetrable muddy color.

"What about where all those bulrushes are?" Candace called out from the bow. She pointed ahead to an expansive marsh that had appeared.

Kevin nodded and cut back on the throttle even farther. He nosed the boat toward the six-foot reeds.

"Can you see any obstructions underwater?" he called out to Candace.

Candace shook her head. "It's too murky," she said.

Kevin turned the boat so that they were again moving parallel with the island shoreline. The reeds were dense, and the marsh now extended inland for a hundred yards.

"This must be the river outlet," Kevin said. "I hope there is a channel or we're out of luck. There's no way we could get the canoe through those reeds."

Ten minutes later, without having found a break in the reeds, Kevin turned the boat around. He was careful not to foul the towline for the small canoe.

"I don't want to go any further in this direction," Kevin said. "The width of the marsh is decreasing. I don't think we're going to find a channel. Besides, I'm afraid of getting too close to the staging area where the bridge is."

"I agree," Melanie said. "What about going to the other end of the island where Rio Diviso has its inlet?"

"That was exactly my thought," Kevin said.

Melanie raised her hand.

"What are you doing?" Kevin asked.

"It's called a high five, you jerk," Melanie teased.

Kevin slapped her hand with his and laughed.

They motored back the way they'd come and rounded the island to head east along its length. Kevin opened up the throttle to about half speed. The route gave them a good view of the southern aspect of the island's mountainous backbone. From that angle, no limestone was visible. The island appeared to be an uninterrupted mountain of virgin jungle.

"All I see are birds," Melanie yelled over the sound of the engine.

Kevin nodded. He'd seen lots of ibises and shrikes.

The sun had now risen enough so that the thatched shelter was useful. They all crowded into the stern to take advantage of the shade. Candace put on some sunblock that Kevin had found in his medicine cabinet.

"Do you think the bonobos on the island are going to be as skittish as bonobos normally are?" Melanie yelled.

Kevin shrugged. "I wish I knew," he yelled back. "If they are, it might be difficult for us to see any of them, and all this effort will have been in vain."

"They did have diminishing contact with humans until they were there in the bonobo enclosure at the animal center," Melanie yelled. "I think we have a good chance as long as we don't try to get too close."

"Are bonobos timid in the wild?" Candace asked Melanie.

"Very much so," Melanie said. "As much or more than chimpanzees. Chimps unexposed to humans are almost impossible to see in the wild. They're inordinately timid, and their sense of hearing and smell is so much more acute than ours that people cannot get near them."

"Are there still truly wild areas left in Africa?" Candace asked.

"Oh, my Lord, yes!" Melanie said. "Essentially, from this coastal part of Equatorial Guinea and extending west northwest there are huge tracts that are still essentially unexplored virginal rain forest. We're talking about as much as a million square miles."

"How long is that going to last?" Candace questioned.

"That's another story," Melanie said.

"How about handing me a cold drink," Kevin yelled.

"Coming up," Candace said. She moved over to the Styrofoam chest and lifted the lid.

Twenty minutes later, Kevin again throttled back on the motor and turned north around the eastern end of Isla Francesca. The sun was higher in the sky and it was significantly hotter. Candace pushed the Styrofoam chest over to the port side of the pirogue to keep it in the shade.

"There's another marsh coming up," Candace said.

"I see it," Kevin said.

Kevin again guided the boat in close to the shore. In terms of size, the marsh appeared to be similar to the one on the western end of the island. Once again, the jungle dropped back to approximately a hundred yards from the edge of the water.

Just when Kevin was about to announce that they had again been foiled, an opening appeared in the otherwise unremitting wall of reeds.

Kevin turned the canoe toward the opening and throttled back even more. The boat slowed. About thirty feet away, Kevin put the motor into neutral and then turned it off.

As the sound of the engine died off, they were thrust into a heavy stillness.

"God, my ears are ringing," Melanie complained.

"Does it look like a channel?" Kevin asked Candace, who'd again gone up to the bow.

"It's hard to tell," Candace said.

Kevin grabbed the back of the motor and tilted it up out of the water. He didn't want to foul the propeller in underwater vegetation.

The pirogue entered among the reeds. It scraped against the stems, then glided to a halt. Kevin reached behind the boat to keep the towed canoe from banging into the pirogue's stern.

"It looks like it goes forward in a meandering fashion," Candace said. She was standing on the gunwale and holding onto the thatched roof of the shelter so she could see over the top of the reeds.

Kevin snapped off a stem and broke it into small pieces. He tossed them into the water next to the boat and watched them. They drifted slowly but inexorably in the direction they were pointing.

"There seems to be some current," Kevin said. "I think that's a good sign. Let's give it a try with the canoe." Kevin moved the smaller boat alongside the larger.

With difficulty because of the canoe's unsteadiness, they managed to get themselves into the smaller boat along with their gear and the food chest. Kevin sat in the stern while Candace took the bow. Melanie sat in the middle but not on one of the seats. Canoes made her nervous; she preferred to sit on the bottom.

By a combination of paddling, pulling on reeds, and pulling on the pirogue, they managed to get ahead of the larger boat. Once in what they hoped was the channel, the going was considerably easier.

With Kevin paddling in the rear and Candace in the front they were able to move at the pace of a slow walk. The narrow six-foot-wide passage twisted and turned as it worked its way across the marsh. The sun was now evidencing its equatorial power even though it was only eight o'clock in the morning. The reeds blocked the breeze, effectively raising the temperature even higher.

"There're not many trails on this island," Melanie commented. She'd unfolded the contour map and was studying it.

"The main one is from the staging area to Lago Hippo," Kevin said.

"There are a few more," Melanie said. "All leading away from Lago Hippo. I suppose they'd been made to facilitate retrievals."

"That would be my guess," Kevin said.

Kevin looked into the dark water. He could see strands of plant life trailing in the direction they were paddling, suggesting there was current. He was encouraged.

"Why don't you try the locator?" Kevin said. "See if bonobo number sixty has moved since we last checked."

Melanie entered the information and clicked.

"He doesn't appear to have moved," she said. She reduced the scale until it was equivalent to the scale on the contour map, then located the red dot. "He's still in the same spot in the marshy clearing."

"At least we can solve that mystery, even if we don't see any of the others," Kevin said.

Ahead, they approached the hundred-foot-high wall of jungle. As they rounded the final bend in the marsh, they could see the channel disappear into the riot of vegetation.

"We'll be in shade in a moment," Candace said. "That should make it a lot cooler."

"Don't count on it," Kevin said.

Pushing branches to the side, they silently slid into the perpetual darkness of the forest. Contrary to Candace's hopes it was like a muggy, claustrophobic hot house. There was not a breath of air, and everything dripped moisture. Although the thick canopy of tree limbs, twisted vines, and hanging mosses completely blocked the sunlight, it also held in the heat like a heavy woolen blanket. Some of the leaves were up to a foot in diameter. Everyone was shocked by how dark it was in the tunnel of vegetation until their eyes began to adjust. Slowly details appeared out of the dank gloom until the scene resembled late twilight just before nightfall.

Almost from the moment the first branches snapped in place behind them, they were assaulted by swarms of insects: mosquitoes, deer flies, and trigona bees. Melanie frantically located the insect repellant. After dousing herself, she passed it to the others.

"It smells like a damn swamp," Melanie complained.

"This is scary," Candace commented from her position in the bow. "I just saw a snake, and I hate snakes."

"As long as we stay in the boat, we'll be fine," Kevin said.

"So, let's not tip over," Melanie said.

"Don't even suggest it!" Candace moaned. "You guys have to remember I'm a newcomer. You've been in this part of the world for years."

"All we have to worry about are the crocs and hippos," Kevin said. "When you see one, let me know."

"Oh, great!" Candace complained nervously. "And just what do we do when we see one?"

"I didn't mean to worry you," Kevin said. "I don't think we'll see any until we come to the lake."

"And what then?" Candace questioned. "Maybe I should have asked about the dangers of this trip before I signed on."

"They won't bother us," Kevin said. "At least that's what I've been told. As long as they are in the water, all we have to do is stay a reasonable distance away. It's when they're caught on land that they can be unpredictably aggressive, and both crocs and hippos can run faster than you'd think."

"All of a sudden, I'm not enjoying this at all," Candace admitted. "I thought it was going to be fun."

"It wasn't supposed to be a picnic," Melanie said. "We're not sightseeing. We're here for a reason."

"Let's just hope we're successful," Kevin said. He could appreciate Candace's state of mind. Kevin marveled that he'd been talked into coming himself.

Besides the insects, the dominant wildlife were the birds. They ceaselessly flitted among the branches, filling the air with melodies.

On either side of the channel the forest was impenetrably dense. Only occasionally could Kevin or the others see for more than twenty feet in any direction. Even the shoreline was invisible, hidden behind a tangle of water plants and roots.

As he paddled Kevin looked down into the inky water that was covered with a plethora of darting water spiders. The disturbance he caused with each stroke made fetid bubbles rise to the surface.

The channel soon became straighter than it had been in the marsh, making the paddling considerably easier. By observing the rate at which they floated by the passing tree trunks, Kevin estimated that they were moving at about the speed of a fast walk. At this rate, he figured they'd arrive at the Lago Hippo in ten to fifteen minutes.

"How about putting the locator on scan?" Kevin suggested to Melanie. "If you narrow the graphic to this area, we'll know if there are any bonobos in the neighborhood."

Melanie was huddled over the compact computer, when there was a sudden commotion in the branches to their left. A moment later, deeper into the forest, they heard twigs snapping.

Candace had a hand clasped to her chest. "Oh my," she said. "What the hell was that?"

"I'd guess another one of those duikers," Kevin said. "Those little antelopes are common even on these islands."

Melanie redirected her attention to the locator. Soon she was able to report that there were no bonobos in the area.

"Of course not," Kevin said. "That would have been too easy."

Twenty minutes later, Candace reported that she could see a lattice of sunlight coming through the branches directly ahead.

"That must be the lake," Kevin said.

After a few more paddle strokes, the canoe glided out into the open water of Lago Hippo. The trio blinked in the bright sunlight, then scrambled for their sunglasses.

The lake was not large. In fact, it was more like an elongated pond dotted with several lushly thicketed islands chock-a-block with white ibises. The shore was lined with dense reeds. Here and there on the surface of the lake were pure white water lilies. Patches of free-floating vegetation thick enough to allow small birds to walk across them turned lazily in slow circles, pushed by the gentle breezes.

The wall of surrounding forest dropped away on both sides to form grassy fields, some as big as an acre. A few of these fields were peppered with pockets of palm trees. To the left, above the line of the forest rim, the very top of the limestone escarpment was clearly discernible against the hazy morning sky.

"It's actually quite beautiful," Melanie said.

"It reminds me of paintings of prehistoric times," Kevin said. "I could almost imagine a couple of brontosauruses in the foreground."

"Oh my God, I see hippos over to the left!" Candace called out with alarm. She pointed with her paddle.

Kevin looked in the direction she was indicating. Sure enough, the heads and small ears of a dozen of these huge mammals were just visible in the water. Standing on their crowns were a number of white birds preening.

"They're okay," Kevin assured Candace. "See how they are slowly moving away from us. They won't be any trouble."

"I've never been much of a nature lover," Candace admitted.

"You don't have to explain," Kevin said. He could remember clearly his unease about wildlife during his first year in Cogo.

"According to the map, there should be a trail not too far away from the left bank," Melanie said, while studying the contour map.

"If I remember correctly, there's a trail that goes around the whole eastern end of the lake," Kevin said. "It originates at the bridge."

"That's true, but it comes closest to our left," Melanie said.

Kevin angled the canoe toward the left shore and began looking for an opening in the reeds. Unfortunately, there wasn't one.

"I think we'll just have to try to paddle right through the vegetation," Kevin said.

"I'm certainly not getting out of this boat until there's dry land," Melanie announced.

Kevin told Candace not to paddle as he aimed the canoe at the six-foot-high wall of reeds and took a number of forceful strokes. To everyone's surprise, the boat skimmed through the vegetation with no trouble at all, despite the scraping noise of the reeds on the hull. Sooner than they expected, they bumped against dry land.

"That was easy," Kevin said. He looked behind at the path they'd created to the lake, but already the reeds were springing back to their original position.

"Am I supposed to get out?" Candace said. "I can't see the ground. What if there are bugs and snakes?"

"Make yourself a clearing with your paddle," Kevin suggested.

As soon as Candace climbed out of the bow, Kevin paddled against the vegetation and succeeded to force the canoe still further onto the shore. Melanie got out easily.

"What about the food?" Kevin asked as he moved forward.

"Let's leave it here," Melanie said. "Just bring the bag with the directional beacon and flashlight. I've got the locator and the contour map."

The women waited for Kevin to get out of the boat, then motioned for him to go ahead of them. With the gear bag over his shoulder, he pushed aside the reeds and began moving inland. The ground was marshy and the muck sucked at his shoes. But within ten feet, he emerged onto the grassy field.

"This looks like a field, but it's actually a swamp," Melanie complained as she looked down at her tennis shoes. They were already black with mud and completely soaked.

Kevin struggled with the contour map to get his bearings, then pointed off to the right. "The transmitting chip from bonobo number sixty should be no more than a hundred feet from here in the direction of that cul de sac of trees," he said.

"Let's get this over with," Melanie said. With her new tennis shoes ruined, even she was beginning to question if they should have come. In Africa, nothing was easy.

Kevin struck off with the women following. At first, walking was difficult because of the unstable footing. Although the grass appeared generally uniform, it grew in small, lumpy hummocks surrounded by muddy water. But the going became easier about fifty feet from the pond, where the ground rose and became comparatively drier. A moment later, they came across a trail.

They were surprised to discover that the trail looked well-used. It ran parallel with the shoreline of the lake.

"Siegfried must send work crews out here more than we thought," Melanie said. "This trail has been maintained."

"I'd have to agree," Kevin said. "I suppose they'd need to keep them up for retrievals. The jungle is so thick and grows so fast out here. Lucky for us, they'll certainly help us get around as well. As I recall, this one heads up to the limestone cliff."

"If they come out here to maintain trails, maybe there is something to Siegfried's story about workmen making the fires," Melanie said.

"Wouldn't that be nice," Kevin said.

"I smell something bad," Candace said, while sniffing the air. "In fact, it smells putrid."

Hesitantly, the others sniffed and agreed.

"That's not a good sign," Melanie said.

Kevin nodded and moved off in the direction of the cul de sac. A few minutes later, with their fingers pinching their nostrils shut, the three stared down at a disgusting sight: It was the remains of bonobo number sixty. The carcass was in the process of being devoured by insects. Larger scavengers had also taken a toll.

Far more gruesome than the state of the corpse was the evidence of how the animal had died. A wedge-shaped piece of limestone had struck the poor creature between the eyes, effectively splitting his head in two. The rock was still in place. Exposed soft eyeballs stared off in opposite directions.

"Ugh!" Melanie said. "It's what we didn't want to see. This suggests that not only the bonobos have split into two groups, but they're killing each other. I wonder if number sixty-seven is dead, too."

Kevin kicked the rock out of the decomposing head. All three stared at it.

"That's also what we didn't want to see," Kevin said.

"What are you talking about?" Candace asked.

"That rock was shaped artificially," Kevin said. With the toe of his shoe, he pointed to an area along the side of the rock where there appeared to be freshly made gouges. "That suggests tool-making."

"More circumstantial evidence, I'm afraid," Melanie said.

"Let's move upwind," Kevin managed. "Before I get sick. I can't stand this smell."

Kevin got three steps away in an easterly direction when someone grabbed his arm and yanked him to a stop. He turned to see Melanie with her index finger pressed against her lips. Then she pointed to the south.

Kevin turned his gaze in that direction, then caught his breath. About fifty yards away in the shadows of the very back of the cul de sac was one of the bonobos! The animal was standing ramrod straight and absolutely motionless, as if he were a military honor guard. He appeared to be staring back at Kevin and the others just as they were staring at him.

Kevin was surprised at the creature's size. The animal was well over five feet tall. It also seemed oversized in terms of weight. Given its enormously muscular torso, Kevin guessed the bonobo weighed between one hundred twenty-five and one hundred fifty pounds.

"He's taller than the bonobos that have been brought in for transplant surgery," Candace said. "At least I think he is. Of course, the bonobos for the transplants were already sedated and strapped to a gurney by the time they got to me."

"Shhhhhh," Melanie admonished. "Let's not scare him. This might be our only chance to see one."

Being careful not to move too quickly, Kevin pulled the gear bag off his shoulder and got out the directional beacon. He turned it on to scan. It began to quietly beep until he pointed it toward the bonobo; then it let out a continuous note. Kevin looked at the LCD screen and gasped.

"What's the matter?" Melanie whispered. She had seen Kevin's expression change.

"It's number one!" Kevin whispered back. "It's my double."

"Oh my God!" Melanie whispered. "I'm jealous. I'd like to see mine, too."

"I wish we could see better," Candace said. "Do we dare try to get closer?"

Kevin was struck by two things. First was the coincidence that the first live bonobo they'd come across would happen to be his double. Secondly, if he had inadvertently created a race of protohumans, then he was in some metamorphic way meeting himself six million years earlier. "This is too much," Kevin couldn't help but whisper aloud.

"What are you talking about?" Melanie asked.

"In some ways that's me standing over there," Kevin answered.

"Now let's not jump the gun," Melanie said.

"He's certainly standing like a human," Candace remarked. "But he's hairier than any human I've ever been out with."

"Very funny," Melanie said without laughing.

"Melanie, use the locator to scan the area," Kevin said. "Bonobos usually travel together. Maybe there are more around that we can't see. They could be hiding in the bushes."

Melanie played with the instrument.

"I can't believe how still he is," Candace said.

"He's probably scared stiff," Kevin said. "I'm sure he doesn't know what to make of us. Or if Melanie is right about there not being enough females out here, maybe he's smitten with you two."

"That I don't find funny at all," Melanie said, without looking up from the keyboard of the locator.

"Sorry," Kevin said.

"What's he got around his waist?" Candace asked.

"I was wondering that, too," Kevin said. "I can't make it out, unless it's just a vine that got caught on him when he came through the bushes."

"Look at this," Melanie said with excitement. She held up the instrument so the others could see. "Kevin, you were right. There's a whole group of bonobos in the trees behind your double."

"Why would he venture out on his own?" Candace asked.

"Maybe he's like an alpha male in chimp society," Melanie said. "Since there are so few females, it stands to reason these bonobos might act more like chimps. If that's the case, he might be proving himself to be courageous."

Several minutes passed. The bonobo did not move.

"This is like a Mexican standoff," Candace complained. "Come on! Let's see how close we can get. What do we have to lose? Even if he runs off, I'd say this little episode is encouraging that we'll see more."

"All right," Kevin said. "But no sudden movement. I don't want to scare him. That would only ruin our chances for seeing the others."

"You guys first," Candace said.

The three advanced carefully, moving forward step by step. Kevin was in the lead followed immediately by Melanie. Candace brought up the rear. When they reached the midway mark, between them and the bonobo, they stopped. Now they could see the bonobo much better. He had prominent eyebrows and a sloped forehead like a chimp, but the lower half of his face was significantly less prognathous than even a normal bonobo. His nose was flat, his nostrils flared. His ears were smaller than those of either chimps or bonobos and flush against the side of his head.

"Are you guys thinking what I'm thinking?" Melanie whispered.

Candace nodded. "He reminds me of the pictures I saw in the third grade. Of very early cavemen."

"Uh, oh, can you guys see his hands?" Kevin whispered.

"I think so," Candace said softly. "What's wrong with them?"

"It's the thumb," Kevin whispered. "It's not like a chimp's. His thumb juts out from the palm."

"You're right," Melanie whispered. "And that means he might be able to oppose his thumb with his fingers."

"Good God! The circumstantial evidence keeps mounting," Kevin whispered. "I suppose if the developmental genes responsible for the anatomical changes necessary for bipedalism are on the short arm of chromosome six, then it's entirely possible that the ones for the opposable thumb are, too."

"It is a vine around his waist," Candace commented. "Now I can see it clearly."

"Let's try moving closer," Melanie suggested.

"I don't know," Kevin said. "I think we're pushing our luck. Frankly, I'm surprised he hasn't bolted already. Maybe we should just sit down right here."

"It's hotter than blazes here in the sun," Melanie said. "And it's not even nine o'clock, so it'll only get worse. When we decide to sit and observe, I vote we do it in the shade. I'd also like to have the food chest."

"I agree," Candace said.

"Of course, you agree," Kevin said mockingly. "I'd be surprised if you didn't." Kevin was becoming tired of Melanie making a suggestion only to have Candace eagerly support it. It had already gotten him into trouble.

"That's not very nice," Candace said indignantly.

"I'm sorry," Kevin said. He'd not meant to hurt her feelings.

"Well, I'm going closer," Melanie announced. "Jane Goodall was able to get right up next to her chimps."

"True," Kevin said. "But that was after months of acclimatization."

"I'm still going to try," Melanie said.

Kevin and Candace let Melanie get ten feet in front of them before they looked at each other, shrugged, and joined her.

"You don't have to do this for me," Melanie whispered.

"Actually, I want to get close enough to see if my double has any facial expression," Kevin whispered. "And I want to look into his eyes."

With no more talk and by moving slowly and deliberately, the three were able to come within twenty feet of the bonobo. Then they stopped again.

"This is incredible," Melanie whispered without taking her eyes from the animal's face. The only way it was apparent the bonobo was alive was an occasional blink, movements of his eyes, and a flaring of his nostrils with each respiration.

"Look at those pectorals," Candace said. "It looks like he's spent most of his life in a gym."

"How do you think he got that scar?" Melanie asked.

The bonobo had a thick scar that ran down the left side of his face almost to his mouth.

Kevin leaned forward and stared into the animal's eyes. They were brown just like his own. Since the sun was in the bonobo's face, his pupils were pinpoint. Kevin strained to detect intelligence, but it was difficult to tell.

Without the slightest warning the bonobo suddenly clapped his hands with such force that an echo reverberated between the leafy walls of the cul de sac. At the same time he yelled: "Atah!"

Kevin, Melanie, and Candace leaped from fright. Having worried from the start that the bonobo was about to flee at any moment, they'd not considered the possibility of him acting aggressively. The violent clap and yell panicked them, and made them fear the animal was about to attack. But he didn't. He reverted back to his stonelike state.

After a moment's confusion they recovered a semblance of their previous poise. They eyed the bonobo nervously.

"What was that all about?" Melanie asked.

"I don't think he's as scared of us as we'd thought," Candace said. "Maybe we should just back away."

"I agree," Kevin said uneasily. "But let's go slowly. Don't panic." Following his own advice, he took a few careful steps backward and motioned for the women to do likewise.

The bonobo responded by reaching around behind his back and grabbing a tool he had suspended by the vine around his waist. He held the tool aloft over his head and cried "Atah" again.

The three froze, wide-eyed with terror.

"What can 'Atah' mean?" Melanie whined after a few moments when nothing happened. "Can it be a word? Could he be talking?"

"I don't have any idea," Kevin sputtered. "But at least he hasn't come toward us."

"What is he holding?" Candace asked apprehensively. "It looks like a hammer."

"It is," Kevin managed. "It's a regular carpenter's clawhammer. It must be one of the tools the bonobos stole when the bridge was being built."

"Look at the way he is grasping it. Just the way you or I would," Melanie said. "There's no question he has an opposable thumb."

"We got to get away from here!" Candace half cried. "You two promised me these creatures were timid. This guy is anything but!"

"Don't run!" Kevin said, keeping his eyes glued to the bonobo's.

"You can stay if you want, but I'm going back to the boat," Candace said desperately.

"We'll all go, but slowly," Kevin said.

Despite warnings not to do so, Candace turned on her heels and started to run. But she only went a few steps before she froze and let out a scream.

Kevin and Melanie turned in her direction. Both of them caught their breaths when they saw what had shocked her: Twenty more bonobos had silently emerged from the surrounding forest and had arrayed themselves in an arc, effectively blocking the exit from the cul de sac.

Candace slowly backed up until she bumped against Melanie.

For a full minute no one spoke or moved, not even any of the bonobos. Then bonobo number one repeated his cry: "Atah!" Instantly, the animals began to circle around the humans.

Candace moaned as she, Kevin, and Melanie backed into each other, forming a tight triangle. The ring the animals formed around them began to close like a noose. The bonobos came closer a step at a time. The humans could now distinctly smell them. Their odor was strong and feral. The animals' faces were expressionless but intent. Their eyes flashed.

The animals stopped advancing when they were an arm's length from the three friends. Their eyes ran up and down the humans' bodies. Some of them were holding stone wedges similar to the one that had killed bonobo number sixty.

Kevin, Melanie, and Candace did not move. They were paralyzed with fear. All the animals looked as powerful as bonobo number one.

Bonobo number one remained outside the tight ring. He was still clutching the clawhammer but no longer had it raised over his head. He advanced and made a full circuit of the group, staring at the humans between the heads of his compatriots. Then he let out a string of sounds accompanied by hand gestures.

Several of the other animals answered him. Then one of them reached out his hand toward Candace. Candace moaned.

"Don't move," Kevin managed to say. "I think the fact that they haven't harmed us is a good sign."

Candace swallowed with difficulty as the bonobo's hand caressed her hair. He seemed enthralled by its blond color. It took all the resolve she could muster not to scream or duck away.

Another animal began to speak and gesture. He then pointed to his side. Kevin saw a long healing surgical scar. "It's the animal whose kidney went to the Dallas businessman," Kevin said fearfully. "See how he's pointing at us. I think he's connecting us to the retrieval process."

"That can't be good," Melanie whispered.

Another animal reached out tentatively and touched Kevin's comparatively hairless forearm. Then he touched the directional beacon Kevin was holding in his hand. Kevin was surprised when he didn't try to take it away from him.

The bonobo standing directly in front of Melanie reached out and pinched the fabric of her blouse between his thumb and forefinger as if feeling its texture. Then he gently touched the locator she was holding with just the tip of his index finger.

"They seem mystified by us," Kevin said hesitantly. "And strangely respectful. I don't think they are going to hurt us. Maybe they think we are gods."

"How can we encourage that belief?" Melanie asked.

"I'll try to give them something," Kevin said. Kevin considered the objects he had on his person and immediately settled on his wristwatch. Moving slowly, he put the directional beacon under his arm and slipped the watch from his wrist. Holding it by its bracelet, he extended it toward the animal in front of him.

The animal tilted his head, eyeing the watch, then reached for it. No sooner had he had it in his hand than bonobo number one vocalized the sound: "Ot." The animal with the watch responded by quickly giving it up. Bonobo number one examined the watch, then slipped it onto his forearm.

"My God!" Kevin voiced. "My double is wearing my watch. This is a nightmare."

Bonobo number one appeared to admire the watch for a moment. Then he brought his thumbs and forefinger together to form a circle while saying: "Randa."

One of the bonobos immediately ran off and disappeared for a moment into the forest. When he reappeared, he was carrying a length of rope.

"Rope?" Kevin said with trepidation. "Now what?"

"Where did they get rope?" Melanie asked.

"They probably stole it with the tools," Kevin said.

"What are they going to do?" Candace asked nervously.

The bonobo went directly to Kevin and looped the rope around his waist. Kevin watched with a mixture of fear and admiration as the animal tied a crude knot and then cinched it tight against Kevin's abdomen.

Kevin looked up at the women. "Don't struggle," he said. "I think everything is going to be okay as long as we don't anger them or scare them."

"But I don't want to be tied up," Candace cried.

"As long as we're not hurt it's okay," Melanie said, hoping to calm Candace.

The bonobo roped Melanie and then Candace in a similar fashion. When he was finished, he stepped back, still holding the long end of the rope.

"Obviously, they want us to stay for a while," Kevin said, trying to make light of the situation.

"Don't be mad if I don't laugh," Melanie said.

"At least they don't mind our talking," Kevin said.

"Strangely enough, they seem to find it interesting," Melanie said. Each time one of them spoke the nearest bonobo would cock its head as if listening.

Bonobo number one suddenly opened and closed his fingers while sweeping his hands away from his chest. At the same time he said: "Arak."

Immediately, the group started moving, including the animal holding the rope. Kevin, Melanie, and Candace were forced forward.

"That gesture was the same as the bonobo did in the operating room," Candace said.

"Then it must mean 'go' or 'move' or 'away,' " Kevin said. "It's incredible. They're speaking!"

They left the cul de sac and moved across the field until they came to the trail. At that point they were led right. While they walked, the bonobos remained silent but vigilant.

"I suspect that it isn't Siegfried who maintains these trails," Melanie said. "I think it's the bonobos."

The trail curved to the south and soon entered the jungle. Even in the forest it was well cleared and the ground underfoot was packed smooth.

"Where are they taking us?" Candace asked nervously.

"I guess toward the caves," Kevin said.

"This is ridiculous," Melanie said. "We're being taken for a walk like dogs on a leash. If they're so impressed with us, maybe we should resist."

"I don't think so," Kevin said. "I think we should make every effort not to get them riled up."

"Candace?" Melanie asked. "What are you thinking?"

"I'm too scared to think," Candace said. "I just want to get back to the canoe."

The bonobo leading with the rope turned and gave the rope a yank. The tug almost knocked all three people down. The bonobo repeatedly waved his hand palm down while whispering: "Hana."

"My God, is he strong or what?" Melanie commented as she regained her footing.

"What do you think he means?" Candace asked.

"If I had to guess, I'd say he's telling us to be quiet," Kevin said.

All at once, the entire group stopped. There were some hand signals among the bonobos. Several pointed up toward the trees to the right. A small group of bonobos slipped silently into the vegetation. Those remaining formed a wide circle, except for three who climbed directly up into the canopy of the forest with an ease that defied gravity.

"What's happening?" Candace whispered.

"Something important," Kevin said. "They all seem to be tense."

Several minutes went by. None of the bonobos on the ground moved or made the slightest noise. Then suddenly, there was a tremendous commotion to the right, accompanied by high-pitched shrieks. At once, the trees were alive with desperately fleeing colobus monkeys on a course bringing them directly toward the bonobos who'd climbed up into the trees.

The terrified monkeys tried to change direction, but in their haste several of them lost their hold on the branches and fell to the ground. Before they could recover they were set upon by waiting bonobos on the ground who killed them instantly with stone wedges.

Candace winced in horror, then turned away.

"I'd say that was a good example of coordinated hunting," Melanie whispered. "That requires a high level of cooperation." Despite the circumstances, she couldn't help but be impressed.

"Don't rub it in," Kevin whispered. "I'm afraid the jury is in, and the verdict is bad. We've only been on the island for an hour, but the question that brought us here has already been answered. Besides collective hunting, we've seen totally upright posture, opposable thumbs, toolmaking, and even rudimentary speech. I sense they can vocalize just like you and I."

"It's extraordinary," Melanie whispered. "These animals have gone through four or five million years of human evolution in the few years they've been out here."

"Oh, shut up!" Candace cried. "We're prisoners of these beasts and you two are having a scientific discussion."

"It's more than a scientific discussion," Kevin said. "We're acknowledging a terrible mistake, and I'm responsible. The reality is worse than I feared when I saw the smoke coming from this island. These animals are protohumans."

"I have to share some of the blame," Melanie said.

"I disagree," Kevin said. "I'm the one who created the chimeras by adding the human chromosome segments. That wasn't your doing."

"What are they doing now?" Candace asked.

Kevin and Melanie turned to see bonobo number one coming toward them, carrying the bloodied corpse of one of the colobus monkeys. He was still wearing the wristwatch, which only underlined the beast's odd position between man and ape.

Bonobo number one brought the dead monkey directly to Candace and held it out toward her in both his hands and said: "Sta."

Candace moaned and turned her head. She looked like she was about to get sick.

"He's offering it to you," Melanie told Candace. "Try to respond."

"I can't look at it," Candace said.

"Try!" Melanie pleaded.

Candace slowly turned. Her face reflected her disgust. The monkey's head had been crushed.

"Just bow or do something," Melanie encouraged.

Candace smiled weakly and bowed her head.

Bonobo number one bowed and then withdrew.

"Incredible," Melanie said, watching the animal leave. "Although he's obviously the alpha male, there must still be remnants of the typical matriarchal bonobo society."

"Candace, you did great," Kevin said.

"I'm a wreck," Candace said.

"I knew I should have been a blond," Melanie said with her own attempt at humor.

The bonobo holding the rope gave a tug significantly less forceful than the previous one. The group was on the move again and Kevin, Melanie, and Candace were forced to follow.

"I don't want to go any farther," Candace said tearfully.

"Pull yourself together," Melanie said. "Everything is going to be okay. I'm starting to think Kevin's suggestion was right. They think of us like gods, especially you with that blond hair. They could have killed us instantly if they'd been inclined, just like they killed the monkeys."

"Why did they kill the monkeys?" Candace asked.

"I assume for food," Melanie said. "It is a little surprising since bonobos are not carnivorous, but chimps can be."

"I was afraid they were human enough for the killing to be for sport," Candace said.

The group passed through a marshy area, then began a climb. Fifteen minutes later, they emerged from the forest twilight onto a rocky but grassy area at the foot of the limestone escarpment.

Halfway up the rock face was the opening of a cave that appeared to be accessible only by a series of extremely steeply tiered ledges. At the lip of the cave were a dozen more bonobos. Most were female. They were striking their chests with the flat of their hands and yelling "bada" over and over again.

The bonobos with Kevin, Melanie, and Candace did the same and then held up the dead colobus monkeys. That resulted in hooting from the females that Melanie said reminded her of chimps.

Then the group of bonobos at the base of the cliff parted. Kevin, Melanie, and Candace were pulled forward. At the sight of them, the females above fell silent.

"Why do I have the feeling the females aren't so happy to see us?" Melanie whispered.

"I'd rather think they were just confused," Kevin whispered back. "They hadn't expected company."

Finally bonobo number one said "zit" and pointed up with his thumb. The group surged forward pulling Kevin, Melanie, and Candace along.

CHAPTER 18

MARCH 7, 1997
6:15 A.M.
NEW YORK CITY

Jack's lids blinked open, and he was instantly awake. He sat up and rubbed his gritty eyes. He was still tired from the poor night's sleep the night before last and from having stayed up later than he planned the previous evening, but he was too keyed up to fall back asleep.

Getting up off the couch, Jack wrapped himself in his blanket against the morning chill and went to the bedroom door. He listened for a moment. Convinced that Laurie was still sound asleep, he cracked the door. As he'd expected, Laurie was on her side under a mound of covers, breathing deeply.

As quietly as possible, Jack tiptoed across the bedroom and entered the bathroom. Once the door was closed, he quickly shaved and showered. When he reappeared, he was pleased to see that Laurie had not budged.

Getting fresh clothes from his closet and bureau, Jack carried them out into the living room and got dressed. A few minutes later, he emerged from his building into the predawn light. It was raw and cold with a few snowflakes dancing in the gusts of wind.

Across the street was a squad car with two uniformed policemen drinking coffee and reading the morning papers with the help of the interior light. They recognized Jack and waved. Jack waved back. Lou had kept his word.

Jack jogged down the street to the local deli on Columbus Avenue. One of the policemen dutifully followed. Jack thought about buying him a donut but decided against it; he didn't want the cop to take it the wrong way.

With an armload of juice, coffee, fruit, and fresh bagels, he returned to the apartment. Laurie was up and was in the shower. Jack knocked on the door to announce that breakfast was served whenever she was ready.

Laurie appeared a few minutes later clad in Jack's robe. Her hair was still wet. The sequelae from the previous night's run-in with Angelo did not look bad. All that was apparent was a mild black eye.

"Now that you've had a night's sleep to think about this trip, do you still feel the same?" Laurie asked.

"Absolutely," Jack said. "I'm psyched."

"Are you really going to pay for everyone's ticket?" she asked. "This could get expensive."

"What else do I have to spend my money on?" Jack said. He glanced around his apartment. "Certainly not my lifestyle, and the bike is all paid for."

"Seriously," Laurie said. "I can understand Esteban to some extent, but Warren and Natalie?"

The previous night when the proposal had been presented to Teodora, she had reminded her husband that one of them had to stay in the city to mind the market and be there for their teenage son. The decision that Esteban would go instead of Teodora had been decided by the flip of a coin.

"I was serious about making it fun," Jack said. "Even if we don't learn anything, which is a possibility, it will at least be a great trip. I could see in Warren's eyes his interest to visit that part of Africa. And on the way back, we'll spend a night or two in Paris."

"You don't have to convince me," Laurie said. "I was against your going at first, but now I'm excited myself."

"Now all we have to do is convince Bingham," Jack said.

"I don't think that will be a problem," Laurie said. "Neither of us has taken the vacation time they've wanted us to. And Lou said he'd put in his two cents about the threats. He'd like to get us out of town."

"I never trust bureaucracy," Jack said. "But I'll be optimistic. And assuming we're going, let's divvy up the errands. I'll go ahead and get the tickets while you, Warren, and Natalie take care of the visa situation. Also, we've got to arrange for some shots and start malaria prophylaxis. We really should have more time for immunizations, but we'll do the best we can, and we'll take a lot of insect repellant."

"Sounds good," Laurie said.

Because of Laurie, Jack left his beloved mountain bike in his apartment. Together, they cabbed down to the medical examiner's office. When they walked into the ID room Vinnie lowered his newspaper and looked at them as if they were ghosts.

"What are you guys doing here?" he asked with a voice that broke. He cleared his throat.

"What kind of question is that?" Jack asked. "We work here, Vinnie. Have you forgotten?"

"I just didn't think you two were on call," Vinnie said. He hastily took a drink from his coffee cup before coughing again.

Jack and Laurie went to the coffee urn. "He's been in a weird mood for the last couple of days," Jack whispered.

Laurie glanced back at Vinnie over her shoulder. Vinnie had gone back behind his newspaper.

"That was a strange reaction," she agreed. "I noticed he was nervous around me yesterday."

Jack and Laurie's eyes met. They regarded each other for a moment.

"Are you thinking what I'm thinking?" Laurie asked.

"Maybe," Jack said. "It kind of fits. He certainly has access."

"I think we should say something to Lou," Laurie said. "I'd hate it to be Vinnie, but we have to find out who's been giving out confidential information around here."

Conveniently for Laurie, her week-long rotation as the day chief was over, and Paul Plodgett's was starting. Paul was already at the desk, going over the cases that had come in the previous night. Laurie and Jack told him they were planning on taking vacation time and wanted to skip doing any autopsies that day unless there was a glut. Paul assured them that the case load was light.

Laurie was more politically minded than Jack, and it was her opinion that they should approach Calvin about their vacation plans before they talked with Bingham. Jack bowed to her better judgment. Calvin's response was to merely grunt that they could have given more notice.

As soon as Bingham arrived, Laurie and Jack went to his office. He regarded them curiously over the tops of his wire-rimmed glasses. He was clutching the morning mail, which he was in the process of going through.

"You want two weeks starting today?" he questioned with disbelief. "What's the rush? Is this some sort of an emergency?"

"We're planning on an adventure-type trip," Jack said. "We'd like to leave this evening."

Bingham's watery eyes went back and forth between Laurie and Jack. "You two aren't planning on getting married, are you?"

"Not that adventuresome," Jack said.

Laurie sputtered with laughter. "We're sorry not to have given more notice," she said. "The reason for the haste is because last night both of us were threatened over the Franconi case."

"Threatened?" Bingham questioned. "Does it have anything to do with that shiner you've got?"

"I'm afraid so," Laurie said. She'd tried to cover the bruise with makeup but had only been partially successful.

"Who was behind these threats?" Bingham asked.

"One of the New York crime families," Laurie said. "Lieutenant Louis Soldano offered to fill you in on it as well as talk to you about a possible mole for the crime family here in the medical examiner's office. We think we have figured out how Franconi's body was taken from here."

"I'm listening," Bingham said. He put the mail down and leaned back in his chair.

Laurie explained the story, emphasizing that the Spoletto Funeral Home had to have been given the accession number of the unidentified case.

"Did Detective Soldano think it wise for you two to leave town?" Bingham asked.

"Yes, he did," Laurie said.

"Fine," Bingham said. "Then you're out of here. Am I supposed to call Soldano or is he calling me?"

"It was our understanding that he was going to call you," Laurie said.

"Good," Bingham said. Then he looked directly at Jack. "What about the liver issue?"

"That's up in the air," Jack said. "I'm still waiting on some more tests."

Bingham nodded and commented: "This case is a goddamned pain in the ass. Just make sure I'm informed of any breaking news while you're away. I don't want any surprises." He looked down at his desk and picked up the mail. "You people have a good trip and send me a postcard."

Laurie and Jack went out into the hall and smiled at each other.

"Well, it looks good," Jack said. "Bingham was the major potential stumbling block."

"I wonder if we should have told him we're going to Africa because of the liver issue?" Laurie asked.

"I don't think so," Jack said. "He might have changed his mind about letting us go. As far as he's concerned, he wishes this case would just disappear."

Retiring to their separate offices, Laurie phoned the Equatoguinean Embassy about the visas, while Jack called the airlines. She quickly learned that Esteban had been right about the ease of getting a visa and that it could be done that morning. Jack found Air France happy to make all the arrangements, and he agreed to stop by their office that afternoon to pick up the tickets.

Laurie appeared in Jack's office. She was beaming. "I'm beginning to think this is really going to happen," she said excitedly. "How'd you do?"

"Fine," Jack said. "We leave tonight at seven-fifty."

"I can't believe this," Laurie said. "I feel like a teenager going on my first trip."

After making arrangements with the travel and immunization office at the Manhattan General Hospital, they called Warren. He agreed to get in touch with Natalie and meet them at the hospital.

The nurse practitioner gave each of them a battery of shots as well as prescriptions for antimalarial drugs. She also urged them to wait a full week before exposure. Jack explained that was impossible. The nurse's response was to say that she was glad they were going and not she.

In the hall outside the travel office, Warren asked Jack what the woman meant.

"It takes up to a week for these shots to take effect," Jack explained. "That is, except for the gamma globulin."

"Are we taking a risk, then?" Warren asked.

"Life's a risk," Jack quipped. "Seriously, there's some risk, but each day our immune systems will be better prepared. The main problem is the malaria, but I intend to take a hell of a lot of insect repellant."

"So you're not concerned?" Warren asked.

"Not enough to keep me home," Jack said.

After leaving the hospital, they all went to a passport photo place and had snapshots taken. With those in hand, Laurie, Warren, and Natalie left to visit the Equatoguinean Embassy.

Jack caught a taxi and directed it to the University Hospital. Once there, he went directly up to Dr. Peter Malovar's lab. As usual he found the aged pathologist bent over his microscope. Jack waited respectfully until the professor had finished studying his current slide.

"Ahhh, Dr. Stapleton," Dr. Malovar said, catching sight of Jack. "I'm glad you came. Now, where is that slide of yours?"

Dr. Malovar's lab was a dusty clutter of books, journals, and hundreds of slide trays. The wastebaskets were perennially overflowing. The professor steadfastly refused to allow anybody into his work space to clean lest they disturb his structured disorder.

With surprising speed, the professor located Jack's slide on top of a veterinary pathology book. His nimble fingers picked it up and slipped it under the microscope's objective.

"Dr. Osgood's suggestion to have this reviewed by Dr. Hammersmith was crackerjack," Dr. Malovar said as he focused. When he was satisfied, he sat back, picked up the book, and opened it to the page indicated by a clean microscope slide. He handed the book to Jack.

Jack looked at the page Dr. Malovar indicated. It was a photomicrograph of a section of liver. There was a granuloma similar to the one on Jack's slide.

"It's the same," Dr. Malovar said. He motioned for Jack to compare by looking into the microscope.

Jack leaned forward and studied the slide. The images did seem identical.

"This is certainly one of the more interesting slides you have brought to me," Dr. Malovar said. He pushed a lock of his wild, gray hair out of his eyes. "As you can read from the book, the offending organism is called hepatocystis."

Jack straightened up from looking at his slide to glance back at the book. He'd never heard of hepatocystis.

"Is it rare?" Jack asked.

"In the New York City morgue I'd have to say yes," Dr. Malovar said. "Extremely rare! You see, it is only found in primates. And not only that, but it is only found in Old World primates, meaning primates found in Africa and Southeast Asia. It's never been seen in the New World and never in humans."

"Never?" Jack questioned.

"Put it this way," Dr. Malovar said. "I've never seen it, and I've seen a lot of liver parasites. More important, Dr. Osgood has never seen it, and he has seen more liver parasites than I. With that kind of combined experience, I'd have to say it does not exist in humans. Of course, in the endemic areas, it might be a different story, but even there it would have to be rare. Otherwise we'd have seen a case or two."

"I appreciate your help," Jack said distractedly. He was already wrestling with the implications of this surprising bit of information. It was a much stronger suggestion that Franconi had had a xenotransplant than the mere fact that he'd gone to Africa.

"This would be an interesting case to present at our grand rounds," Dr. Malovar said. "If you are interested, let me know."

"Of course," Jack said noncommittally. His mind was in a whirl.

Jack left the professor, took the hospital elevator down to the ground floor, and started toward the medical examiner's office. Finding an Old World primate parasite in a liver sample was very telling evidence. But then there were the confusing results that Ted Lynch had gotten on the DNA analysis to contend with. And on top of that was the fact there was no inflammation in the liver with no immunosuppressant drugs. The only thing that was certain was that it all didn't make sense.

Arriving back at the morgue, Jack went directly up to the DNA lab with the intention of grilling Ted in the hope that he could come up with some hypothesis to explain what was going on. The problem as Jack saw it was that Jack didn't know enough about current DNA science to come up with an idea on his own. The field was changing too rapidly.

"Jesus, Stapleton, where the hell have you been!" Ted snapped the moment he saw Jack. "I've been calling all over creation and nobody's seen you."

"I've been out," Jack said defensively. He thought for a second about explaining what was going on then changed his mind. Too much had happened in the previous twelve hours.

"Sit down!" Ted commanded.

Jack sat.

Ted searched around on his desktop until he located a particular sheet of developed film covered with hundreds of minute dark bands. He handed it to Jack.

"Ted, why do you do this to me?" Jack complained. "You know perfectly well I have no idea what I'm looking at with these things."

Ted ignored Jack, while he searched for another similar piece of celluloid. He found it under a laboratory budget he was working on. He handed the second one to Jack.

"Hold them up to the light," Ted said.

Jack did as he was told. He looked at the two sheets. Even he could tell they were different.

Ted pointed to the first sheet of celluloid. "This is a study of the region of the DNA that codes for ribosomal protein of a human being. I just picked a case at random to show you what it looks like."

"It's gorgeous," Jack said.

"Let's not be sarcastic," Ted said.

"I'll try," Jack said.

"Now, this other one is a study of Franconi's liver sample," Ted said. "It's the same region using the same enzymes as the first study. Can you see how different it is?"

"That's the only thing I can see," Jack said.

Ted snatched away the human study and tossed it aside. Then he pointed at the film Jack was still holding. "As I told you yesterday this information is on CD-ROM so I was able to let the computer make a match of the pattern. It came back that it was most consistent with a chimpanzee."

"Not definitely a chimpanzee?" Jack asked. Nothing seemed to be definite about this case.

"No, but close," Ted said. "Kind of like a cousin of a chimpanzee. Something like that."

"Do chimps have cousins?" Jack asked.

"You got me," Ted said with a shrug. "But I've been dying to give you this information. You have to admit it's rather impressive."

"So from your perspective it was a xenograft," Jack said.

Ted shrugged again. "If you made me guess, I'd have to say yes. But taking the DQ alpha results into consideration, I don't know what to say. Also I've taken it upon myself to run the DNA for the ABO blood groups. So far that's coming up just like the DQ alpha. I think it's going to be a perfect match for Franconi, which only confuses things further. It's a weird case."

"Tell me about it!" Jack said. He then related to Ted the discovery of an Old World primate parasite.

Ted made an expression of confusion. "I'm glad this is your case and not mine," he said.

Jack placed the sheet of celluloid on Ted's desk. "If I'm lucky, I might have some answers in the next few days," he said. "Tonight I'm off to Africa to visit the same country Franconi did."

"Is the office sending you?" Ted asked with surprise.

"Nope," Jack said. "I'm going on my own. Well, that's not quite true. I mean, I'm paying for it, but Laurie is going, too."

"My God, you are thorough," Ted said.

"Dogged is probably a better word," Jack said.

Jack got up to go. When he reached the door, Ted called out to him: "I did get the results of the mitochondrial DNA back. There was a match with Mrs. Franconi, so at least your identification was right."

"Finally something definitive," Jack said.

Jack was again about to leave when Ted called out again.

"I just had a crazy idea," Ted said. "The only way I could explain the results I've been getting is if the liver was transgenic."

"What the hell does that mean?" Jack asked.

"It means the liver contains DNA from two separate organisms," Ted said.

"Hmmmm," Jack said. "I'll have to think about that one."

COGO, EQUATORIAL GUINEA

Bertram looked at his watch. It was four o'clock in the afternoon. Raising his eyes to look out the window, he noticed that the sudden, violent tropical rainstorm which had totally darkened the sky only fifteen minutes earlier had already vanished. In its place was a steamy sunny African afternoon.

With sudden resolve Bertram reached for his phone and called up to the fertility center. The evening tech by the name of Shirley Cartwright answered.

"Have the two new breeding bonobo females got their hormone shots today?" Bertram asked.

"Not yet," Shirley said.

"I thought the protocol called for them to get the shots at two P.M.," Bertram said.

"That's the usual schedule," Shirley said hesitantly.

"Why the delay?" Bertram asked.

"Miss Becket hasn't arrived yet," Shirley explained reluctantly. The last thing she wanted to do was get her immediate boss in trouble, but she knew she couldn't lie.

"When was she due?" Bertram asked.

"No particular time," Shirley said. "She'd told the day staff she'd be busy all morning in her lab over at the hospital. I imagine she got tied up."

"She didn't leave instructions for the hormones to be given by someone else if she didn't arrive by two?" Bertram asked.

"Apparently not," Shirley said. "So I expect her at any minute."

"If she doesn't come in the next half hour, go ahead and give the scheduled doses," Bertram said. "Will that be a problem?"

"No problem whatsoever, Doctor," Shirley said.

Bertram disconnected and then dialed Melanie's lab in the hospital complex. He was less familiar with the staff and didn't know the person who answered. But the person knew Bertram and told him a disturbing story. Melanie hadn't been in that day because she'd been tied up at the animal center.

Bertram hung up and nervously tapped the top of the phone with the nail of his index finger. Despite Siegfried's assertions that he'd taken care of the potential problem with Kevin and his reputed girlfriends, Bertram was skeptical. Melanie was a conscientious worker. It certainly wasn't like her to miss a scheduled injection.

Snapping up the phone again, Bertram tried calling Kevin, but there was no answer.

With his suspicions rising, Bertram got up from his desk and informed Martha, his secretary, that he'd be back in an hour. Outside, he climbed into his Cherokee and headed for town.

As he drove Bertram became increasingly certain that Kevin and the women had managed to go to the island, and it angered him. He berated himself for allowing Siegfried to lull him into a false sense of security. Bertram had a growing premonition that Kevin's curiosity was going to cause major trouble.

At the point of transition from asphalt to cobblestones at the edge of town, Bertram had to brake abruptly. In his mounting vexation, he'd been unaware of his speed. The wet cobblestones from the recent downpour were as slick as ice, so Bertram's car skidded several yards before coming to a complete stop.

Bertram parked in the hospital parking lot. He climbed to the third floor of the lab and pounded on Kevin's door. There was no response. Bertram tried the door. It was locked.

Returning to his car, Bertram drove around the town square and parked behind the town hall. He nodded to the lazy group of soldiers lounging in broken rattan chairs in the shade of the arcade.

Taking the stairs by twos, Bertram presented himself to Aurielo and said he had to speak to Siegfried.

"He's with the chief of security at the moment," Aurielo said.

"Let him know I'm here," Bertram said, as he began to pace the outer office. His irritation was mounting.

Five minutes later, Cameron McIvers emerged from the inner office. He said hello to Bertram, but Bertram ignored him in his haste to get in to see Siegfried.

"We've got a problem," Bertram said. "Melanie Becket didn't show up for a scheduled injection this afternoon, and Kevin Marshall is not in his lab."

"I'm not surprised," Siegfried said calmly. He sat back and stretched with his good arm. "They were both seen leaving early this morning with the nurse. The ménage-à-trois seems to be blossoming. They even had a dinner party late into the night at Kevin's house, and then the women stayed over."

"Truly?" Bertram questioned. That the nerdy researcher could be involved in such a liaison seemed impossible.

"I should know," Siegfried said. "I live across the green from Kevin. Besides, I met the women earlier at the Chickee Bar. They were already tipsy and told me they were on their way to Kevin's."

"Where did they go this morning?" Bertram asked.

"I assume to Acalayong," Siegfried said. "They were seen leaving in a pirogue before dawn by a member of the janitorial staff."

"Then they have gone to the island by water," Bertram snapped.

"They were seen going west, not east," Siegfried said.

"It could have been a ruse," Bertram said.

"It could have," Siegfried agreed. "And I thought of the possibility. I even discussed it with Cameron. But both of us are of the opinion that the only way to visit the island by water is to land at the staging area. The rest of the island is surrounded by a virtual wall of mangroves and marsh."

Bertram's eyes rose up to stare at the huge rhino heads on the wall behind Siegfried. Their brainless carcasses reminded him of the site manager, yet Bertram had to admit in this instance he had a point. In fact, when the island was initially considered for the bonobo project its inaccessibility by water had been one of its attractions.

"And they couldn't have landed at the staging area," Siegfried continued, "because the soldiers are still out there itching to have an excuse to use their AK-47's." Siegfried laughed. "It tickles me every time I think of their shooting out Melanie's car windows."

"Maybe you're right," Bertram said grudgingly.

"Of course I'm right," Siegfried said.

"But I'm still concerned," Bertram said. "And suspicious. I want to get into Kevin's office."

"For what reason?" Siegfried asked.

"I was stupid enough to show him how to tap into the software we'd developed for locating the bonobos," Bertram said. "Unfortunately, he's been taking advantage of it. I know because he's accessed it on several occasions for long periods of time. I'd like to see if I can find out what he'd been up to."

"I'd say that sounds quite reasonable," Siegfried said. He called out to Aurielo to see to it that Bertram had an entrance card for the lab. Then he said to Bertram: "Let me know if you find anything interesting."

"Don't worry," Bertram said.

Armed with the magnetic pass card, Bertram returned to the lab and entered Kevin's space. Locking the door behind him, he first went through Kevin's desk. Finding nothing, he made a quick tour of the room. The first sign of trouble was a stack of computer paper next to the printer that Bertram recognized as printouts of the island graphic.

Bertram examined each page. He could tell that they represented varying scales. What he couldn't figure out was the meaning of all the surcharged geometric shapes.

Putting the pages aside, Bertram went to Kevin's computer and began to search through his directories. It wasn't long before he found what he was looking for: the source of the information on the printouts.

For the next half hour, Bertram was transfixed by what he found: Kevin had devised a way to follow individual animals in real time. After Bertram played with this capability for a while, he came across Kevin's stored information documenting the animals' movement over a period of several hours. From this information, Bertram was able to reproduce the geometric shapes.

"You are too clever for your own good," Bertram said out loud as he allowed the computer to run sequentially through the movements of each animal. By the time the program had run its course, Bertram had seen the problem with bonobo numbers sixty and sixty-seven.

With mounting anxiety, Bertram tried to get the indicators for the two animals to move. When he couldn't, he went back to real time and displayed the two animals' current position. They'd not changed one iota.

"Good lord!" Bertram moaned. All at once, the worry about Kevin vanished and was replaced with a more pressing problem. Turning off the computer, Bertram snapped up the printed island graphics, and ran out of the lab. Outside, he passed up his car to run directly across the square to the town hall. He knew it would take less time on foot.

He raced up the stairs. As he entered the outer office, Aurielo looked up. Bertram ignored him. He burst into Siegfried's office unannounced.

"I've got to talk with you immediately," Bertram sputtered to Siegfried. He was out of breath.

Siegfried was meeting with his food-service supervisor. Both appeared stunned by Bertram's arrival.

"It's an emergency," Bertram added.

The food-service supervisor stood up. "I can return later," he said and left.

"This better be important," Siegfried warned.

Bertram waved the computer printouts. "It's very bad news," he said. He took the chair vacated by the supervisor. "Kevin Marshall figured out a way to follow the bonobos over time."

"So what?" Siegfried said.

"At least two of the bonobos don't move," Bertram said. "Number sixty and number sixty-seven. And they haven't moved for more than twenty-four hours. There's only one explanation. They're dead!"

Siegfried raised his eyebrows. "Well, they're animals," he said. "Animals die. We have to expect some attrition."

"You don't understand," Bertram said with a tinge of disdain. "You made light of my concern that the animals had split into two groups. I told you that it was significant. This, unfortunately, is proof. As sure as I'm standing here, those animals are killing each other!"

"You think so?" Siegfried asked with alarm.

"There's no doubt in my mind," Bertram said. "I've been agonizing over why they split up into two groups. I decided it had to have been because we forgot to maintain the balance between males and females. There's no other explanation, and it means the males are fighting over the females. I'm sure of it."

"Oh my God!" Siegfried exclaimed, with a shake of his head. "That's terrible news."

"It's more than terrible," Bertram said. "It's intolerable. It will be the ruin of the whole program provided we don't act."

"What can we do?" Siegfried asked.

"First, we tell no one!" Bertram said. "If there is ever an order to harvest either sixty or sixty-seven, we'll deal with that particular problem then. Second, and more important, we must bring the animals in like I've been advocating. The bonobos won't be killing each other if they're in separate cages."

Siegfried had to accept the white-haired veterinarian's advice. Although he'd always favored the animals being off by themselves for logistical and security reasons, its time was past. The animals could not be allowed to kill each other. In a very real way, there was no choice.

"When should we retrieve them?" Siegfried asked.

"As soon as possible," Bertram said. "I can have a team of security-cleared animal handlers ready by dawn tomorrow. We'll begin by darting the splinter group. Once we have all the animals caged, which should take no more than two or three days, we'll move them at night to a section of the animal center that I will prepare."

"I suppose I'd better recall that contingent of soldiers out by the bridge," Siegfried said. "The last thing we need is for them to shoot the animal handlers."

"I didn't like having them out there in the first place," Bertram said. "I was afraid they might have shot one of the animals for sport or soup."

"When should we inform our respective bosses at GenSys?" Siegfried asked.

"Not until it is done," Bertram said. "Only then will we know how many animals have been killed. Maybe we'll also have a better idea of the best ultimate disposition. My guess is we'll have to build a separate, new facility."

"For that, we'd need authorization," Siegfried said.

"Obviously," Bertram said. He stood up. "All I can say is that it is a damn good thing I had the foresight to move all those cages out there."

NEW YORK CITY

Raymond felt better than he had in days. Things seemed to have gone well from the moment he'd gotten up. Just after nine he'd called Dr. Waller Anderson, and not only was the doctor going to join, he already had two clients ready to plunk down their deposits and head out to the Bahamas for the bone marrow aspirations.

Then around noon Raymond had gotten a call from Dr. Alice Norwood, whose office was on Rodeo Drive in Beverly Hills. She'd called to say that she'd recruited three physicians with large private practices who were eager to come on board. One was in Century City, another in Brentwood, and the last was in Bel-Air. She was convinced that these doctors would soon provide a flood of clients because the market on the West Coast for the service Raymond was offering was nothing short of phenomenal.

But what had pleased Raymond the most during the day was whom he didn't hear from. There were no calls from either Vinnie Dominick or Dr. Daniel Levitz.

Raymond took this silence to mean that the Franconi business had finally been put to bed.

At three-thirty, the door buzzer went off. Darlene answered it and with a tearful voice told Raymond that his car was waiting.

Raymond took his girlfriend in his arms and patted her on the back. "Next time maybe you can go," Raymond said consolingly.

"Really?" she asked.

"I can't guarantee it," Raymond said. "But we'll try." Raymond had no control over the GenSys flights. Darlene had been able to go on only one of the trips to Cogo. On all the other occasions, the plane had been full on one of the segments. As standard procedure, the plane flew from the States to Europe and then on to Bata. On the return trip the same general itinerary was followed, although it was always a different European city.

After promising to call as soon as he arrived in Cogo, Raymond carried his bag downstairs. He climbed into the waiting sedan and luxuriously leaned back.

"Would you like the radio on, sir?" the driver asked.

"Sure, why not," Raymond said. He was already beginning to enjoy himself.

The drive across town was the most difficult part of the trip. Once they were on the West Side Highway, they were able to make good time. There was a lot of traffic, but since rush hour had not begun, the traffic moved fluidly. It was the same situation on the George Washington Bridge. In less than an hour Raymond was dropped off at Teterboro Airport.

The GenSys plane had not yet arrived, but Raymond was not concerned. He positioned himself in the lounge, where he had a view of the runway and ordered himself a scotch. Just as he was being served, the sleek GenSys jet swooped in low out of the clouds and touched down. It taxied over to a position directly in front of Raymond.

It was a beautiful aircraft painted white with a red stripe along its side. Its only markings were its call sign, N69SU, and a tiny American flag. Both were on the fin of the tail assembly.

As if in slow motion, a forward door opened and self-contained steps extended down toward the tarmac. An impeccably dressed steward in dark-blue livery appeared in the doorway, descended the stairs and entered the general aviation building. His name was Roger Perry. Raymond remembered him well. Along with another steward named Jasper Devereau, he'd been on the plane every trip Raymond had made.

Once inside the building, Roger scanned the lounge. The moment he spotted Raymond, he walked over and greeted him with a salute.

"Is this the extent of your luggage, sir?" Roger asked as he picked up Raymond's bag.

"That's it," Raymond said. "Are we leaving already? Isn't the plane going to refuel?" That had been the procedure on previous flights.

"We're all set," Roger said.

Raymond got to his feet and followed the steward out into the gray, raw March afternoon. As he approached the luxurious private jet, Raymond hoped there were people watching him. At times like this, he felt as if he were living the life that was meant for him. He even told himself that he was lucky he'd lost his medical license.

"Tell me, Roger," Raymond called out just before they reached the stairs. "Are we full on the flight to Europe?" On every flight Raymond had been on, there'd been other GenSys executives.

"Only one other passenger," Roger said. He stepped to the side at the base of the stairs and gestured for Raymond to precede him.

Raymond smiled as he climbed. With only one other passenger and two stewards, the flight was going to be even more enjoyable than he'd anticipated. The troubles that he'd had over the previous few days seemed a small price to pay for such luxury.

Just inside the plane, he was met by Jasper. Jasper took his overcoat and jacket and asked if Raymond wanted a drink before takeoff.

"I'll wait," Raymond said gallantly.

Jasper pulled aside the drape that separated the galley from the cabin. Swelling with pride, Raymond passed into the main part of the plane. He was debating which of the deeply cushioned leather chairs to take when his eyes passed over the face of the other passenger. Raymond froze. At the same time, he felt a sinking feeling in his gut.

"Hello, Dr. Lyons. Welcome aboard."

"Taylor Cabot!" Raymond croaked. "I didn't expect to see you."

"I suppose not," Taylor said. "I'm surprised to see myself." He smiled and gestured toward the seat next to him.

Raymond quickly sat down. He berated himself for not taking the drink Jasper had offered. His throat had gone bone-dry.

"I'd been informed of the plane's flight plan," Taylor explained, "and since there was a window of opportunity in my schedule, I thought it wise for me to personally check on our Cogo operation. It was a last-minute decision. Of course, we'll be making a stop in Zurich for me to have a short meeting with some bankers. I hope you won't find that inconvenient."

Raymond shook his head. "No, not at all," he stammered.

"And how are things going with the bonobo project?" Taylor asked.

"Very well," Raymond managed. "We're expecting a number of new clients. In fact, we're having trouble keeping up with demand."

"And what about that regrettable episode with Carlo Franconi?" Taylor enquired. "I trust that has been successfully dealt with."

"Yes, of course," Raymond sputtered. He tried to smile.

"Part of the reason I'm making this trip is to be reassured that project is worth supporting," Taylor said. "My chief financial officer assures me that it is now turning a small profit. But my operations officer has reservations about jeopardizing our primate research business. So, I have to make a decision. I hope you will be willing to help me."

"Certainly," Raymond squeaked, as he heard the characteristic whine of the jet engines starting.

It was like a party at the bar in the international departure lounge at JFK airport. Even Lou was there having a beer and popping peanuts into his mouth. He was in a great mood and acted as if he were going on the trip.

Jack, Laurie, Warren, Natalie, and Esteban were sitting with Lou at a round table in the corner of the bar. Over their heads was a television tuned to a hockey game. The frantic voice of the announcer and the roar of the fans added to the general din.

"It's been a great day," Lou yelled to Jack and Laurie. "We picked up Vido Delbario, and he's singing to save his ass. I think we'll be making a major dent in the Vaccarro organization."

"What about Angelo Facciolo and Franco Ponti?" Laurie asked.

"That's another story," Lou said with a laugh. "For once the judge sided with us and set bail at two million each. What did the trick was the police impersonation charge."

"How about Spoletto Funeral Home?" Laurie asked.

"That's going to be a gold mine," Lou said. "The owner is the brother of the wife of Vinnie Dominick. You remember him, don't you, Laurie?"

Laurie nodded. "How can I forget?"

"Who's Vinnie Dominick?" Jack asked.

"He played a surprising role in the Cerino affair," Laurie explained.

"He's with the competing Lucia organization," Lou said. "They've been having a field day after Cerino's fall. But my gut feeling tells me we're going to puncture their balloon."

"What about the mole in the medical examiner's office?" Laurie asked.

"Hey, first things first," Lou said. "We'll get to that. Don't worry."

"When you do, check out one of the techs by the name of Vinnie Amendola," Laurie said.

"Any particular reason?" Lou asked, as he wrote down the name in the small notebook he carried in the side pocket of his jacket.

"Just a suspicion," Laurie said.

"Consider it done," Lou said. "You know, this episode shows how fast things can change. Yesterday I was in the dog house, whereas today I'm the golden boy. I even got a call from the captain about a possible commendation. Can you believe it?"

"You deserve it," Laurie said.

"Hey, if I get one, you guys should get one, too," Lou said.

Jack felt someone tap on his arm. It was the waitress. She asked if they wanted another round.

"Hey, everybody?" Jack called out above the babble of voices. "More beer?"

Jack looked first at Natalie who put her hand over her glass to indicate she was fine. She looked radiant in a dark purple jumpsuit. She was a third-grade teacher at a public school in Harlem, but didn't look like any teacher Jack could remember. From Jack's perspective her features were reminiscent of the Egyptian sculptures in the Metropolitan Museum that Laurie had dragged him in to see. Her eyes were almond-shaped and her lips were full and generous. Her hair was done up in the most elaborate corn-row style that Jack had ever seen. Natalie had said that it was her sister's forte.

When Jack looked at Warren to see whether he wanted more beer, he shook his head. Warren was sitting next to Natalie. He was wearing a sport jacket over a black T-shirt that somehow managed to hide his powerful physique. He looked happier than Jack had ever seen him. His mouth harbored a half smile instead of his normal expression of hard-lipped determination.

"I'm fine," Esteban called out. He, too, was smiling, even more broadly than Warren.

Jack looked at Laurie. "No more for me. I want to save some room for wine with dinner on the plane." Laurie had her auburn hair braided and was wearing a loose-fitting velour top with leggings. With her relaxed, ebullient demeanor and casual clothes Jack thought she looked like she was in college.

"Yeah, sure, I'll have another beer," Lou said.

"One beer," Jack told the waitress. "Then the check."

"How'd you guys make out today?" Lou asked Jack and Laurie.

"We're here," Jack said. "That was the goal. Laurie and the others got the visas, and I got the tickets." He patted his stomach. "I also got a bunch of French francs and a money belt. I was told that the French franc was the hard currency of choice for that part of Africa."

"What's going to happen when you arrive?" Lou asked.

Jack pointed over to Esteban. "Our expatriate traveling companion has taken care of the arrangements. His cousin's meeting us at the airport, and his wife's brother has a hotel."

"You should be fine," Lou said. "What's your plan?"

"Esteban's cousin has arranged for us to rent a van," Jack said. "So we'll drive to Cogo."

"And just drop in?" Lou asked.

"That's the idea," Jack said.

"Good luck," Lou said.

"Thanks," Jack said. "We'll probably need it."

A half hour later the group—minus Lou—merrily boarded the 747. They found their seats and stowed their carry-on baggage. No sooner had they gotten themselves situated than the huge plane lurched and was pulled from the gate.

Later when the engines began to scream and the plane began its dash down the runway to takeoff, Laurie felt Jack take her hand. He gripped it fiercely.

"Are you okay?" she asked.

Jack nodded. "I've just learned not to like air travel," he said.

Laurie understood.

"We're on our way," Warren exclaimed gleefully. "Africa, here we come!"

CHAPTER 19

MARCH 8, 1997
2:00 A.M.
COGO, EQUATORIAL GUINEA

"Are you asleep?" Candace whispered.

"Are you kidding?" Melanie whispered back. "How am I supposed to sleep on rock with just a few branches strewn over it?"

"I can't sleep either," Candace admitted. "Especially with all this snoring going on. What about Kevin?"

"I'm awake," Kevin said.

They were in a small side cave jutting off the main chamber just behind the main entrance. The darkness was almost absolute. The only light came from meager moonlight reflected from outside.

Kevin, Melanie, and Candace had been shuttled into this small cave immediately on their arrival. It measured about ten feet wide with a downward sloping ceiling that started at a maximum height roughly equivalent to Kevin's five feet ten inches. There was no back wall to this cave; the chamber simply narrowed to a tunnel. Earlier in the evening, Kevin had explored the tunnel with the help of the flashlight in hopes of finding another way out, but the tunnel abruptly ended after about thirty feet.

The bonobos had treated them well, even after the initially cold reception by the females. Apparently, the animals were mystified by the humans and intended to keep them alive and well. They'd provided them with muddy water in gourds and a variety of food. Unfortunately, the food was in the form of grubs, maggots, and other insects along with some kind of sedge from Lago Hippo.

Later in the afternoon, the animals had started a fire at the cave's entrance. Kevin was particularly interested in how they started it, but he'd been too far back to observe their method. A group of the bonobos had formed a tight circle, and then a half an hour later a fire was going.

"Well, that answers the question about the smoke," Kevin had said.

The animals had skewered the colobus monkeys and roasted them over the fire. The monkeys were then torn apart and distributed with great fanfare. Given all the hooting and vocalizations it had been obvious to the humans that this monkey meat was considered a great treat.

Bonobo number one had placed a few morsels of the feast on a large leaf and brought them back to the humans. Only Kevin had been willing to try it. He'd said it was the toughest thing he'd ever chewed. As far as taste was concerned, he'd told the women that it was strangely similar to the elephant he'd once sampled. The previous year, Siegfried had bagged a forest elephant on one of his hunting forays and after taking the tusks, he'd had some of the meat cooked up by the central kitchen.

The bonobos had not tried to imprison the humans and had not tried to inhibit Kevin and the women from untying the rope that bound them together. At the same time, the bonobos had made it clear that they were to stay in the small cave. At all times, at least two of the larger male bonobos remained in the immediate vicinity. Each time Kevin or one of the women tried to venture forth, these guards would screech and howl at the top of their lungs. Even more threatening, they would ferociously charge with bared teeth only to pull up short at the last minute. Thus they effectively kept the humans in their place.

"We're going to have to do something," Melanie said. "We can't stay here forever. And it's pretty apparent we'll have to do it while they are all sleeping, like now."

Every bonobo in the cave, including the supposed guards, were fast asleep on primitive pallets constructed of branches and leaves. Most were snoring.

"I don't think we should take the chance of angering them," Kevin said. "We're lucky they've treated us as well as they have."

"Being offered maggots to eat is not what I'd call being well treated," Melanie said. "Seriously, we have to do something. Besides, they might turn on us. There's no way to anticipate what they'll do."

"I prefer to wait," Kevin said. "We're a novelty now, but they'll lose interest in us. Besides, we're undoubtedly missed back in town. It won't take Siegfried or Bertram that long to figure out what we've done. Then they'll come for us."

"I'm not convinced," Melanie said. "Siegfried might take our disappearance as a godsend."

"Siegfried might, but Bertram won't," Kevin said. "He's basically a nice person."

"What do you think, Candace?" Melanie asked.

"I don't know what to think," Candace said. "This situation is so far beyond anything I'd ever thought I'd be involved in, that I don't know how to react. I'm numb."

"What are we going to do when we do get back?" Kevin said. "We haven't talked about that."

"*If* we get back," Melanie said.

"Don't talk that way," Candace said.

"We have to face facts," Melanie said. "That's why I think we should do something now while they're all asleep."

"We have no idea how soundly they sleep," Kevin said. "Trying to walk out of here will be like walking through a mine field."

"One thing is for sure," Candace said. "I'm not going to be involved in any more harvests. I began to feel uncomfortable when I thought they were apes. Now that we know they're protohumans, I can't do it. I know that much about myself."

"That's a foregone conclusion," Kevin said. "I can't imagine any sensitive human being would feel differently. But that's not the issue. The issue is that this new race exists, and if they're not to be used for transplants, what's to be done with them?"

"Will they be able to reproduce?" Candace asked.

"Most assuredly," Melanie said. "Nothing was done to them to affect their fertility."

"Oh, my," Candace said. "This is a horror."

"Maybe they should be rendered infertile," Melanie said. "Then there'd only be a single generation to consider."

"I wish I'd thought of all this before I started this project," Kevin said. "The problem was that once I stumbled onto the ability to interchange chromosomal parts, the intellectual stimulation was so strong I never considered other consequences."

There was a sudden, bright flash of lightning momentarily illuminating the interior of the cave, followed by a loud clap of thunder. The concussion seemed to shake the entire mountain. The violent display was nature's way of announcing that one of the almost daily thunderstorms was about to inundate the island.

"Now, that's an argument in favor of my position," Melanie said, after the sound of the thunder died away.

"What are you talking about?" Kevin asked.

"That thunder was loud enough to wake the dead," Melanie explained. "And not one of the bonobos so much as blinked."

"It's true," Candace said.

"I think at least one of us should try to get out of here," Melanie said. "That way we could be sure that Bertram will be alerted as to what is happening out here. Bertram can also make arrangements for someone to come here and rescue the others."

"I guess I agree," Candace said.

"Of course you do," Melanie said.

There were a few moments of silence. Finally, Kevin broke it: "Wait a second. You guys are not suggesting that I go?"

"I couldn't get in the canoe much less paddle it," Melanie said.

"I could get in it, but I doubt I could paddle it in the dark," Candace said.

"And you two think I could?" Kevin asked.

"Certainly better than we could," Melanie said.

Kevin shivered. The idea of trying to get to the canoe in the dark knowing the hippos were out grazing was a scary thought. Even more scary was trying to paddle across the pond, knowing it was filled with crocodiles.

"Maybe you could hide in the canoe until it gets light," Melanie suggested. "The important thing is to get out of this cave and away from these creatures while they are sleeping."

The idea of waiting in the canoe was better than trying to cross the lake in the darkness, but it did not address the potential problem of running into the hippos in the marshy field.

"Remember it was your suggestion to come out here," Melanie reminded him.

Kevin started to strongly protest, but he stopped. In a way, it was true. He'd said that the only way to learn whether the bonobos were protohumans was to come to the island. But from then on, Melanie had been the one to call the shots.

"It was your suggestion," Candace said. "I remember it well. We were in your office. It was when you first raised the question about the smoke."

"But I only said . . ." Kevin began, but he stopped. From past experience, he knew he was ill-equipped to argue with Melanie, and especially when Candace supported her as she was now doing. Besides, from where Kevin was sitting, he could see a clear path of moonlight along the cave floor all the way to the entrance. Except for a few rocks and branches, there were no obstructions.

Kevin began to think maybe he could do it. Maybe it was best not to think of the hippos. Maybe it was true that the creatures' hospitality could not be counted upon, not because of the bonobo part of their heritage but because of the human part.

"All right," Kevin said with sudden resolve. "I'll try."

"Hooray," Melanie said.

Kevin pushed himself up onto his hands and knees. He was already trembling with the knowledge that there were fifty powerful and wild animals in the immediate environment that wanted him to stay where he was.

"If something goes wrong," Melanie said, "just get yourself back here in a hurry."

"You make it sound so easy," Kevin said.

"It will be," Melanie said. "Bonobos and chimps fall asleep as soon as it gets dark and sleep until dawn. You're not going to have any trouble."

"But what about the hippos?" Kevin said.

"What about them?" Melanie asked.

"Never mind," Kevin said. "I've got enough to worry about."

"Okay, good luck," Melanie whispered.

"Yeah, good luck," Candace echoed.

Kevin tried to stand up and start out, but he couldn't. He kept telling himself that he'd never been a hero, and this was no time to start.

"What's the matter?" Melanie asked.

"Nothing," Kevin said. Then suddenly from some place deep within himself, Kevin found the courage. He rose to a hunched-over position and began to pick his way along the path of moonlight toward the mouth of the cave.

As Kevin moved, he debated whether he would do better to move at a snail's pace or make an out-and-out dash for the canoe. It was an argument between caution and getting the ordeal over with. Caution won out. He moved with painstaking baby steps. Every time his foot made the slightest noise, he winced and froze in the darkness. All around him, he could hear the stertorous breathing of the sleeping creatures.

Twenty feet from the cave's entrance one of the bonobos moved so suddenly, the branches in his bed snapped. Again Kevin stopped in mid-stride, his heart pounding. But the bonobo had only stirred and was still breathing heavily, a sign of sleep. With additional light from the proximity of the cave entrance, Kevin could clearly see the bonobos sprawled about him. The sight of so many sleeping beasts was enough to stop him dead in his tracks. After a full minute of paralysis Kevin recommenced his progress toward freedom. He even began to feel the first wave of relief as the smell of the damp jungle replaced the feral scent of the bonobos. But that relief was short-lived.

Another clap of thunder followed by a sudden tropical downpour scared Kevin to the point that he almost lost his balance. It was only after frantic arm swinging that he managed to stay upright and in his planned path. He shuddered to think how close he'd come to stepping on one of the sleeping bonobos.

With another ten feet to go, Kevin could now see the black silhouette of the jungle below. The nocturnal sounds of the jungle were now audible over the bonobos' snores.

Kevin was close enough to begin worrying about how to make the steep descent to the ground when calamity struck. His heart leaped into his throat as he felt a hand on his leg! Something had grabbed him around the ankle with such force that instant tears formed in his eyes. Looking down in the half light, the first thing he saw was his watch. It was on the hairy wrist of the powerful bonobo number one.

"Tada," shouted the bonobo as he leaped to his feet, upending Kevin in the process. Luckily, the floor of that part of the cave was covered with refuse which broke Kevin's fall. Nevertheless, he landed on his left hip in a jarring fashion.

Bonobo number one's yell brought the other bonobos to their feet. For a moment, there was utter chaos until they all understood that there was no danger.

Bonobo number one let go of Kevin's ankle only to reach down and grasp him by his upper arms. In an amazing demonstration of strength, he picked Kevin up and held him off the ground at arm's length.

The bonobo gave a loud, long, angry vocalization. All Kevin could do was wince in pain at the animal's tight grip.

At the end of his tirade, bonobo number one marched into the depths of the cave and literally tossed Kevin into the smaller chamber. After a final angry word, he went back to his pallet.

Kevin managed to push himself up to a sitting position. He'd again landed on his hip, and it felt numb. He'd also sprained a wrist and scraped an elbow. But considering the fact that he'd been literally thrown through the air, he was better off than he'd anticipated.

More cries echoed inside of the cave, presumably from bonobo number one, but Kevin couldn't tell for certain in the darkness. He felt his right elbow. He knew that the sticky warmth had to be blood.

"Kevin?" Melanie whispered. "Are you okay?"

"As good as can be expected," Kevin said.

"Thank God," Melanie said. "What happened?"

"I don't know," Kevin said. "I'd thought I'd made it. I was right at the cave's entrance."

"Are you hurt?" Candace asked.

"A little," Kevin admitted. "But no broken bones. At least, I don't think so."

"We couldn't see what happened," Melanie said.

"My double scolded me," Kevin said. "At least that's what I think he was doing. Then he threw me back in here. I'm glad I didn't land on either of you."

"I'm so sorry I encouraged you to go," Melanie said. "I guess you were right."

"It's good of you to say," Kevin said. "Well, it almost worked. I was so close."

Candace switched on the flashlight with her hand shielding the front lens. She held it near Kevin's arm to check his elbow.

"I guess we're going to have to count on Bertram Edwards," Melanie said. She shuddered and then sighed. "It's hard to believe: we're prisoners of our own creations."

CHAPTER 20

MARCH 8, 1997
4:40 P.M.
BATA, EQUATORIAL GUINEA

Jack realized he'd been clenching his teeth. He was also holding Laurie's hand much harder than was reasonable. Consciously, he tried to relax. The problem had been the flight from Douala, Cameroon, to Bata. The airline was a fly-by-night outfit that used small, old commuter planes, just the kind of aircraft that plagued Jack's nightmares about his late family.

The flight had not been easy. The plane constantly dodged thunderstorms whose towering clouds varied in color from whipped-cream white to deep purple. Lightning had flashed constantly, and the turbulence was fierce.

The previous part of the trip had been a dream. The flight from New York to Paris had been smooth and blissfully uneventful. Everyone had slept at least a few hours.

Arrival in Paris had been ten minutes early, so they'd had ample time to make their connection with Cameroon Airlines. Everyone slept even more on the flight south to Douala. But that final leg to Bata was a hair-raiser.

"We're landing," Laurie said to Jack.

"I hope it is a controlled landing," Jack quipped.

He looked out the dirty window. As he'd expected, the landscape was a carpet of uninterrupted green. As the tops of the trees came closer and closer, he hoped there was a runway ahead.

Eventually, they touched down onto tarmac, and Jack and Warren breathed simultaneous sighs of relief.

As the weary travelers climbed out of the small, aged plane, Jack looked across the ill-maintained runway and saw a strange sight. It was a resplendent white jet sitting all by itself against the dark green of the jungle. At four points surrounding the plane were soldiers in camouflage fatigues and red berets. Although ostensibly standing upright, they'd all assumed varying postures of repose. Automatic rifles were casually slung over their shoulders.

"Whose plane?" Jack asked Esteban. With no markings it was apparent it was a private jet.

"I can't imagine," Esteban said.

Everyone except Esteban was unprepared for the chaos in the airport arrival area. All foreign arrivals had to go through Customs. The group was taken along with their luggage to a side room. They were led to this unlikely spot by two men in dirty uniforms with automatic pistols holstered in their belts.

At first Esteban had been excluded from the room, but after a loud argument on his part in a local dialect, he was allowed in. The men opened all the bags and spread the contents onto a picnic-sized table.

Esteban told Jack the men expected bribes. At first Jack refused on principle. When it became apparent that the standoff was going to last for hours, Jack relented. Ten French francs solved the problem.

As they exited into the main part of the airport, Esteban apologized. "It's a problem here," he said. "All government people take bribes."

They were met by Esteban's cousin whose name was Arturo. He was a heavyset, enormously friendly individual with bright eyes and flashing teeth who shook hands enthusiastically with everyone. He was attired in native African costume: flowing robes in a colorful print and a pillbox hat.

They stepped out of the airport into the hot, humid air of equatorial Africa. The vistas in all directions seemed immense since the land was relatively flat. The late-afternoon sky was a faraway blue directly overhead, but enormous thunderheads were nestled all along the horizon.

"Man, I can't believe this," Warren said. He was gazing around like a kid in a toy store. "I've been thinking about coming here for years, but I never thought I'd make it." He looked at Jack. "Thanks, man. Give it here!" Warren stuck out his hand. He and Jack exchanged palm slaps as if they were back on the neighborhood basketball court.

Arturo had the rented van parked at curbside. He slipped a couple of bills into the palm of a policeman and gestured for everyone to climb in.

Esteban insisted that Jack ride in the front passenger seat. Too tired to argue, Jack climbed in. The vehicle was an old Toyota with two rows of benches behind the front bucket seats. Laurie and Natalie squeezed into the very back while Warren and Esteban took the middle.

As they exited the airport they had a view out over the ocean. The beach was broad and sandy. Gentle waves lapped the shore.

After a short distance, they passed a large unfinished concrete structure that was weathered and crumbling. Rusted rebars stuck out of the top like the spines of sea urchins. Jack asked what it was.

"It was supposed to be a tourist hotel," Arturo said. "But there was no money and no tourists."

"That's a bad combination for business," Jack said.

While Esteban played tour guide and pointed out various sights, Jack asked Arturo if they had far to go.

"No, ten minutes," Arturo said.

"I understand you worked for GenSys," Jack said.

"For three years," Arturo said. "But no more. The manager is a bad person. I prefer to stay in Bata. I'm lucky to have work."

"We want to tour the GenSys facility," Jack said. "Do you think we'll have any trouble?"

"They don't expect you?" Arturo asked with bewilderment.

"Nope," Jack said. "It's a surprise visit."

"Then you may have trouble," Arturo said. "I don't think they like visitors. When they repaired the only road to Cogo, they built a gate. It's manned twenty-four hours a day by soldiers."

"Uh-oh!" Jack said. "That doesn't sound good." He'd not expected restricted access to the town and had counted on being able to drive in directly. Where he expected to have trouble was getting into the hospital or the labs.

"When Esteban called to say you were going to Cogo, I thought you'd been invited," Arturo said. "I didn't think to mention the gate."

"I understand," Jack said. "It's not your fault. Tell me, do you think the soldiers would take money to let us in?"

Arturo flashed a glance in Jack's direction. He shrugged. "I don't know. They're better paid than regular soldiers."

"How far is the gate from the town?" Jack asked. "Could someone walk through the forest and just pass the gate?"

Arturo glanced at Jack again. The conversation had taken a turn in a direction he'd not expected.

"It is quite far," Arturo said, evincing some unease. "Maybe five kilometers. And it is not easy to walk in the jungle. It can be dangerous."

"And there is only one road?" Jack asked.

"Only one road," Arturo agreed.

"I saw on a map that Cogo is on the water," Jack said. "What about arriving by boat?"

"I suppose," Arturo said.

"Where could someone find a boat?" Jack asked.

"In Acalayong," Arturo said. "There are many boats there. That's how to go to Gabon."

"And there would be boats to rent?" Jack asked.

"With enough money," Arturo said.

They were now passing through the center of Bata. It was composed of surprisingly broad tree-lined, litter-strewn streets. There were lots of people out and about but relatively few vehicles. The buildings were all low concrete structures.

On the south side of town, they turned off the main street and made their way along a rutted unpaved road. There were large puddles from a recent rain.

The hotel was an unimposing two-story concrete building with rusted rebars sticking out the top for potential future upward expansion. The façade had been painted blue but the color had faded to an indistinct pastel.

The moment they stopped, an army of congenial children and adults emerged from the front door. Everyone was introduced down to the youngest, shy child. It turned out that several multigenerational families lived on the first floor. The second floor was the hotel.

The rooms turned out to be tiny but clean. They were all situated on the outside of the U-shaped building. Access was by way of a veranda open to the courtyard. There was a toilet and a shower on each end of the "U."

After putting his bag in his room and appreciating the mosquito netting around the inordinately narrow bed, Jack went out onto the veranda. Laurie came out of her room. Together, they leaned on the balustrade and peered down into the courtyard. It was an interesting combination of banana trees, discarded tires, naked infants, and chickens.

"Not quite the Four Seasons," Jack said.

Laurie smiled. "It's charming. I'm happy. There's not a bug in my room. That had been my main worry."

The proprietors, Esteban's brother-in-law, Florenico, and his wife, Celestina, had prepared a huge feast. The main course was a local fish served with a turniplike plant called "malanga." For dessert there was a type of pudding along with exotic fruit. An ample supply of ice-cold Cameroonean beer helped wash it all down.

The combination of plentiful food and beer took a toll on the exhausted travelers. It wasn't long before all of them were fighting drooping eyelids. With some effort, they dragged themselves upstairs to their separate rooms, full of plans to rise early and head south in the morning.

Bertram climbed the stairs to Siegfried's office. He was exhausted. It was almost eight-thirty at night, and he'd been up since five-thirty that morning to accompany the animal handlers out to Isla Francesca to help get the mass retrieval under way. They'd worked all day and only returned to the animal center an hour earlier.

Aurielo had long since gone home, so Bertram walked directly into the manager's office. Siegfried was by the window facing the square with a glass in his hand. He was staring over at the hospital. The only light in the room was from the candle in the skull, just as it had been three nights before. Its flame flickered from the action of the overhead fan, sending shadows dancing across the stuffed animal trophies.

"Make yourself a drink," Siegfried said, without turning around. He knew it was Bertram, since they'd talked on the phone a half an hour earlier and made plans to meet.

Bertram was more of a wine drinker than an imbiber of hard alcohol, but under the circumstances he poured himself a double scotch. He sipped the fiery fluid as he joined Siegfried at the window. The lights of the hospital lab complex glowed warmly in the moist tropical night.

"Did you know Taylor Cabot was coming?" Bertram asked.

"I hadn't the faintest idea," Siegfried said.

"What did you do with him?" Bertram asked.

Siegfried gestured toward the hospital. "He's at the Inn. I had the chief surgeon move out of what we call the presidential suite. Of course, he was none too happy. You know how these egotistical doctors are. But what was I supposed to do? It's not like I'm running a hotel here."

"Do you know why Cabot came?" Bertram asked.

"Raymond said that he came specifically to evaluate the bonobo program," Siegfried said.

"I was afraid of that," Bertram said.

"It's just our luck," Siegfried complained. "The program has been running like a Swiss clock for years on end, and just when we have a problem, he shows up."

"What did you do with Raymond?" Bertram asked.

"He's over there, too," Siegfried said. "He's a pain in the ass. He wanted to be away from Cabot, but where was I supposed to put him: in my house? No thank you!"

"Has he asked about Kevin Marshall?" Bertram asked.

"Of course," Siegfried said. "As soon as he got me aside, it was his first question."

"What did you say?"

"I told the truth," Siegfried said. "I told him Kevin had gone off with the reproductive technologist and the intensive care nurse and that I had no idea where he was."

"What was his reaction?"

"He got red in the face," Siegfried said. "He wanted to know if Kevin had gone to the island. I told him that we didn't think so. Then he ordered me to find him. Can you imagine? I don't take orders from Raymond Lyons."

"So Kevin and the women have not reappeared?" Bertram asked.

"No, and not a word," Siegfried said.

"Have you made any effort to find them?" Bertram asked.

"I sent Cameron over to Acalayong to check out those cheap hotels along the waterfront, but he didn't have any luck. I'm thinking they might have gone over to Cocobeach in Gabon. That's what makes the most sense, but why they didn't tell anyone is beyond me."

"What a God-awful mess," Bertram commented.

"How did you do on the island?" Siegfried asked.

"We did well, considering how fast we had to put the operation together," Bertram said. "We got an all-terrain vehicle over there with a wagon. It was all we could think of to get that many animals back to the staging area."

"How many animals did you get?"

"Twenty-one," Bertram said. "Which is a tribute to my crew. It suggests we'll be able to finish up by tomorrow."

"So soon," Siegfried commented. "That's the first encouraging news all day."

"It's easier than we anticipated," Bertram said. "The animals seem enthralled by us. They are trusting enough to let us get close with the dart gun. It's like a turkey shoot."

"I'm glad something is going right," Siegfried said.

"The twenty-one animals we got today were all part of the splinter group living north of the Rio Diviso. It was interesting how they were living. They'd made crude huts on stilts with roofs of layered lobelia leaves."

"I don't give a damn how those animals were living," Siegfried snapped. "Don't tell me you're going soft, too."

"No, I'm not going soft," Bertram said. "But I still find it interesting. There was also evidence of campfires."

"So, it's good we're putting them in the cages," Siegfried said. "They won't be killing each other, and they won't be playing around with fire."

"That's one way to look at it," Bertram agreed.

"Any sign of Kevin and the women on the island?" Siegfried asked.

"Not in the slightest," Bertram said. "And I made it a point to look. But even in areas they would have left footprints, there was nothing. We spent part of today building a log bridge over the Rio Diviso, so tomorrow we'll start retrievals near the limestone cliffs. I'll keep my eyes open for signs they'd been there."

"I doubt you'll find anything, but until they are located we shouldn't rule out the possibility they went to the island. But I'll tell you, if they did go, and they come back here, I'll turn them over to the Equatoguinean minister of justice with the charge that they have severely compromised the GenSys operation. Of course, that means they'll be lined up out in the soccer field in front of a firing squad before they knew what hit them."

"Nothing like that could happen until Cabot and the others leave," Bertram said with alarm.

"Obviously," Siegfried said. "Besides, I mentioned the soccer field only figuratively. I'd tell the minister they'd have to be taken out of the Zone to be shot."

"Any idea when Cabot and the others will be taking the patient back to the States?"

"No one has said anything," Siegfried said. "I guess it's up to Cabot. I hope it will be tomorrow, or at the very latest, the following day."

CHAPTER 21

MARCH 9, 1997
4:30 A.M.
BATA, EQUATORIAL GUINEA

Jack awakened at four-thirty and was unable to get back to sleep. Ironically, the racket made by tree frogs and crickets in the courtyard banana trees was too much even for someone fully adjusted to the noisy sirens and general din of New York City.

Taking his towel and his soap, Jack stepped out on the veranda and started for the shower. Midway, he bumped into Laurie on her way back.

"What are you doing up?" Jack asked. It was still pitch dark outside.

"We went to bed around eight," Laurie said. "Eight hours: that's a reasonable night's sleep for me."

"You're right," Jack said. He'd forgotten how early it was when they'd all collapsed.

"I'll go down into the kitchen area and see if I can find any coffee," Laurie said.

"I'll be right down," Jack said.

By the time Jack got downstairs to the dining room, he was surprised to find the rest of his group already having breakfast. Jack got a cup of coffee and some bread and sat down between Warren and Esteban.

"Arturo mentioned to me that he thought you were crazy to go to Cogo without an invitation," Esteban said.

With his mouth full, all Jack could do was nod.

"He told me you won't get in," Esteban said.

"We'll see," Jack said after swallowing. "I've come this far, so I'm not going to turn back without making an effort."

"At least the road is good, thanks to GenSys," Esteban said.

"Worst case, we've had an interesting drive," Jack said.

An hour later, everyone met again in the dining room. Jack reminded the others that going to Cogo wasn't a command performance, and that those people who preferred to stay in Bata should do so. He said that he'd been told it might take four hours each way.

"You think you can make out on your own?" Esteban asked.

"Absolutely," Jack said. "It's not as if we'll be getting lost. The map indicates only one main road heading south. Even I can handle that."

"Then I think I'll stay," Esteban said. "I have more family I'd like to see."

By the time they were on the road with Warren in the front passenger seat and the two women in the middle seat, the eastern sky was just beginning to show a faint glow of dawn. As they drove south they were shocked at how many people were walking along the road on their way into the city. There were mostly women and children and most of the women were carrying large bundles on their heads.

"They don't seem to have much, but they appear happy," Warren commented. Many of the children stopped to wave at the passing van. Warren waved back.

The outskirts of Bata dragged by. The concrete buildings eventually changed to simple whitewashed mud brick structures with thatched roofs. Reed mats formed corrals for goats.

Once completely out of Bata, they began to see stretches of incredibly lush jungle.

Traffic was almost nonexistent save for occasional large trucks going in the opposite direction. As the trucks went by, the wind jostled the van.

"Man, those truckers move," Warren commented.

Fifteen miles south of Bata, Warren got out the map. There was one fork and one turn in the road that they had to navigate appropriately or lose considerable time. Signs were almost nonexistent.

When the sun came up, they all donned their sunglasses. The scenery became monotonous, uninterrupted jungle except for occasional tiny clusters of thatched huts. Almost two hours after they'd left Bata, they turned onto the road that led to Cogo.

"This is a much better road," Warren commented as Jack accelerated up to cruising speed.

"It looks new," Jack said. The previous road had been reasonably smooth, although its surface appeared like a patchwork quilt from all the separate repairs.

They were now heading southeast away from the coast and into considerably denser jungle. They also began to climb. In the distance they could see low, jungle-covered mountains.

Seemingly out of nowhere came a violent thunderstorm. Just prior to its arrival the sky became a swirling mass of dark clouds. Day turned to night in the space of several minutes. Once the rain started, it came down in sheets, and the van's old, ragged windshield wipers could not keep up with the downpour. Jack had to slow to less than twenty miles an hour.

Fifteen minutes later, the sun poked out between massive clouds, turning the road into a ribbon of rising steam. On a straight stretch, a group of baboons crossing the road looked as if they were walking on a cloud.

After passing through the mountains, the road turned back to the southeast. Warren consulted the map and told everyone they were within twenty miles of their destination.

Rounding another turn, they all saw what looked like a white building in the middle of the road.

"What the hell's this?" Warren said. "We're not there yet, no way."

"I think it's a gate," Jack said. "I was told about this only last night. Keep your fingers crossed. We might have to switch to plan B."

As they got closer, they could see that on either side of the central structure were enormous white, latticework fences. They were on a roller mechanism so they could be drawn out of the way to permit vehicles to pass.

Jack braked and brought the van to a stop about twenty feet from the fence. Out of the two-story gate house stepped three soldiers dressed similarly to those who'd been guarding the private jet at the airport. Like the soldiers at the airport, these men were carrying assault rifles, only these men were holding their guns waist high, aimed at the van.

"I don't like this," Warren said. "These guys look like kids."

"Stay cool," Jack said. He rolled his window down. "Hi, guys. Nice day, huh?"

The soldiers didn't move. Their blank expressions didn't change.

Jack was about to ask them kindly to open the gate, when a fourth man stepped out into the sunlight. To Jack's surprise, this man was pulling on a black suit jacket over a white shirt and tie. In the middle of the steaming jungle it was absurd. The other surprising thing was that the man wasn't black. He was Arab.

"Can I help you?" the Arab asked. His tone was not friendly.

"I hope so," Jack said. "We're here to visit Cogo."

The Arab glanced at the windshield of the vehicle, presumably looking for some identification. Not seeing it, he asked Jack if he had a pass.

"No pass," Jack admitted. "We're just a couple of doctors interested in the work that's going on here."

"What is your name?" the Arab asked.

"Dr. Jack Stapleton. I've come all the way from New York City."

"Just a minute," the Arab said before disappearing back into the gate house.

"This doesn't look good," Jack said to Warren out of the corner of his mouth. He smiled at the soldiers. "How much should I offer him? I'm not good at this bribing stuff."

"Money must mean a lot more here than it does in New York," Warren said. "Why don't you overwhelm him with a hundred dollars. I mean, if it's worth it to you."

Jack mentally converted a hundred dollars into French francs, then extracted the bills from his money belt. A few minutes later, the Arab returned.

"The manager says that he does not know you and that you are not welcome," the Arab said.

"Shucks," Jack said. Then he extended his left hand with the French francs casually stuck between his index finger and his ring finger. "We sure do appreciate your help."

The Arab eyed the money for a moment before reaching out and taking it. It disappeared into his pocket in the blink of an eye.

Jack stared at him for a moment, but the man didn't move. Jack found it difficult to read his expression because the man's mustache obscured his mouth.

Jack turned to Warren. "Didn't I give him enough?"

Warren shook his head. "I don't think it's going to happen."

"You mean he just took my money and that's that?" Jack asked.

"Be my guess," Warren said.

Jack turned his attention back to the man in the black suit. Jack estimated he was about a hundred and fifty pounds, definitely on the thin side. For a moment Jack entertained the idea of getting out of the car and asking for his money back, but a glance at the soldiers made him think otherwise.

With a sigh of resignation Jack did a three-point turn and headed back the way they'd come.

"Phew!" Laurie said from the backseat. "I did not like that one bit."

"You didn't like it?" Jack questioned. "Now I'm pissed."

"What's plan B?" Warren asked.

Jack explained about his idea of approaching Cogo by boat from Acalayong. He had Warren look at the map. Given how long it had taken them to get where they were, he asked Warren to estimate how long it would take to get to Acalayong.

"I'd say three hours," Warren said. "As long as the road stays good. The problem is we have to backtrack quite a way before heading south."

Jack glanced at his watch. It was almost nine A.M. "That means we'd get there about noon. I'd judged we could get from Acalayong to Cogo in an hour, even in the world's slowest boat. Say we stay in Cogo for a couple hours. I think we'd still get back at a reasonable hour. What do you guys say?"

"I'm cool," Warren said.

Jack looked in the rearview mirror. "I could take you ladies back to Bata and come back tomorrow."

"My only reservation about any of us going is those soldiers with the assault rifles," Laurie said.

"I don't think that's a problem," Jack said. "If they have soldiers at the gate then they don't need them in the town. Of course there's always the chance they patrol the waterfront, which would mean I'd be forced to use plan C."

"What's plan C?" Warren asked.

"I don't know," Jack said. "I haven't come up with it yet."

"What about you, Natalie?" Jack asked.

"I'm finding it all interesting," Natalie said. "I'll go along with the crowd."

It took almost an hour to get to the point where a decision had to be made. Jack pulled to the side of the road.

"What's it going to be, gang?" he asked. He wanted to be absolutely sure. "Back to Bata or on to Acalayong?"

"I think I'll be more worried if you go by yourself," Laurie said. "Count me in."

"Natalie?" Jack said. "Don't be influenced by these other crazies. What do you want to do?"

"I'll go," Natalie said.

"Okay," Jack said. He put the car in gear and turned left toward Acalayong.

Siegfried got up from his desk with his coffee mug in hand and walked to the window overlooking the square. He was mystified. The Cogo operation had been up and running for six years and never had they had someone come to the gate house and request entrance. Equatorial Guinea was not a place people visited casually.

Siegfried took a swig of his coffee and wondered if there could be any connection between this abnormal event and the arrival of Taylor Cabot, the CEO of GenSys. Both were unanticipated, and both were particularly unwelcome since they came just when there was a major problem with the bonobo project. Until that unfortunate situation was taken care of, Siegfried didn't want any stray people around, and he put the CEO in that category.

Aurielo poked his head in the door and said that Dr. Raymond Lyons was there and wished to see him.

Siegfried rolled his eyes. He didn't want Raymond around, either. "Send him in," Siegfried said reluctantly.

Raymond came into the room, looking as tanned and healthy as ever. Siegfried envied the man's aristocratic appearance, and the fact that he had two good arms.

"Have you located Kevin Marshall yet?" Raymond demanded.

"No, we haven't," Siegfried said. He took immediate offense at Raymond's tone.

"I understand it's been forty-eight hours since he's been seen," Raymond said. "I want him found!"

"Sit down, Doctor!" Siegfried said sharply.

Raymond hesitated. He didn't know whether to get angry or be intimidated by the manager's sudden aggressiveness.

"I said sit!" Siegfried said.

Raymond sat. The white hunter with his horrid scar and limp arm could be imposing, particularly surrounded by evidence of his extensive kills.

"Let us clear up a point involving the chain of command," Siegfried said. "I do not take orders from you. In fact, when you are here as a guest, you take orders from me. Is that understood?"

Raymond opened his mouth to protest but thought better of it. He knew Siegfried was technically correct.

"And while we are talking so directly," Siegfried added, "where is my retrieval bonus? In the past, I've always gotten it when the patient left the Zone on his way back to the States."

"That's true," Raymond said tautly. "But there have been major expenses. Money is coming in shortly from new clients. You'll be paid as soon as it comes in."

"I don't want you to think you can give me the runaround," Siegfried warned.

"Of course not," Raymond blurted out.

"And one other thing," Siegfried said. "Isn't there some way you can hasten the CEO's departure? His presence here in Cogo is disrupting. Can't you use the patient's needs in some way?"

"I don't see how," Raymond said. "He's been informed the patient is capable of traveling. What more can I say?"

"Think of something," Siegfried said.

"I'll try," Raymond said. "Meanwhile, please locate Kevin Marshall. His disappearance concerns me. I'm afraid he might do something rash."

"We believe he went to Cocobeach in Gabon," Siegfried said. He was gratified with the appropriate subservience in Raymond's voice.

"You're sure he didn't go to the island?" Raymond asked.

"We can't be totally sure," Siegfried admitted. "But we don't think so. Even if he did, he wouldn't be apt to stay there. He would have been back by now. It's been forty-eight hours."

Raymond stood up and sighed. "I wish he would turn up. Worrying about him is driving me up the wall, especially with Taylor Cabot here. It's just something else in a long string of problems going on in New York that have threatened the program and made my life miserable."

"We'll continue to search," Siegfried assured him. He tried to sound sympathetic, but in actuality, he was wondering how Raymond was going to respond when he heard the bonobos were being rounded up to be brought into the animal center. All other problems paled in the face of the animals killing each other.

"I'll try to think of something to say to Taylor Cabot," Raymond said as he started for the door. "If you could, I'd appreciate being informed the moment you hear about Kevin Marshall."

"Certainly," Siegfried said obligingly. He watched with satisfaction as the previously proud doctor beat a meek retreat. Just as Raymond disappeared from view, Siegfried remembered that Raymond was from New York.

Siegfried dashed to his door, catching Raymond on his way down the stairs.

"Doctor," Siegfried called out with false deference.

Raymond paused and looked back.

"Do you happen to know a doctor by the name of Jack Stapleton?"

The blood drained from Raymond's face.

This reaction was not lost on Siegfried. "I think you'd better come back into my office," the manager said.

Siegfried closed the door behind Raymond, who immediately wanted to know how in the world the name "Jack Stapleton" had come up.

Siegfried walked around his desk and sat down. He gestured toward a chair for Raymond. Siegfried was not happy. He'd briefly thought of relating the unexpected request for a site visit by strange doctors to Taylor Cabot. He'd not thought of relating it to Raymond.

"Just before you arrived I got an unusual call from our gate house," Siegfried said. "The Moroccan guard told me that there was a van full of people who wanted to tour the facility. We've never had uninvited visitors before. The van was driven by Dr. Jack Stapleton of New York City."

Raymond wiped the perspiration that had appeared on his forehead. Then he ran both hands simultaneously through his hair. He kept telling himself that this couldn't be happening since Vinnie Dominick was supposed to have taken care of Jack Stapleton and Laurie Montgomery. Raymond hadn't called to find out what had happened to the two; he didn't really want to know the details. For twenty thousand dollars, details weren't something he should have to worry about—or so he thought. If pressed, he would have guessed that Stapleton and Montgomery were somewhere floating in the Atlantic Ocean about now.

"Your reaction to this is starting to concern me," Siegfried said.

"You didn't let Stapleton and his friends in?" Raymond asked.

"No, of course not," Siegfried said.

"Maybe you should have," Raymond said. "Then we could have dealt with them. Jack Stapleton is a very big danger to the program. I mean, is there a way here in the Zone to take care of such people?"

"There is," Siegfried said. "We just turn them over to the Equatoguinean minister of justice or the minister of defense along with a sizable bonus. Punishment is both discreet and very rapid. The government is eager to ensure that nothing threatens the goose that lays the golden egg. All we need to say is that they are seriously interfering with GenSys operations."

"Then if they come back, I think you should let them in," Raymond said.

"Perhaps you should tell me why," Siegfried said.

"Do you remember Carlo Franconi?" Raymond asked.

"Carlo Franconi the patient?" Siegfried asked.

Raymond nodded.

"Of course," Siegfried said.

"Well, it started with him," Raymond said as he began the complicated story.

"You think it is safe?" Laurie asked. She was looking at a huge hollowed-out log canoe with a thatched canopy that was pulled halfway up the beach. On the back was a sizable, beat-up outboard motor. It was leaking fuel as evidenced by an opalescent scum that ringed the stern.

"Reportedly it goes all the way to Gabon twice a day," Jack said. "That's farther than Cogo."

"How much rent did you have to pay?" Natalie asked. It had taken Jack a half hour of negotiations to get it.

"A bit more than I expected," Jack said. "Apparently, some people rented one a couple of days ago, and it hasn't been seen since. That episode has driven the rental price up, I'm afraid."

"More than a hundred or less?" Warren asked. He, too, wasn't impressed with the craft's apparent seaworthiness. "Because if it was more than a C note you got took."

"Well, let's not quibble," Jack said. "In fact, let's get the show on the road unless you guys want to back out."

There was a moment of silence while the group eyed each other.

"I'm not a great swimmer," Warren admitted.

"I can assure you that we are not planning on going into the water," Jack said.

"All right," Warren said. "Let's go."

"You ladies concur?" Jack asked.

Both Laurie and Natalie nodded without a lot of enthusiasm. At the moment, the noonday sun was enervating. Despite being on the shore of the estuary, there was not a breath of air.

With the women positioned in the stern to help lift the bow, Jack and Warren pushed the heavy pirogue off the shore and jumped in one after the other. Everyone helped paddle out about fifty feet. Jack attended to the motor, compressing the small hand pump on top of the red fuel tank. He'd had a boat as a child on a lake in the Midwest and had a lot of experience fussing with an outboard.

"This canoe is a lot more stable than it looks," Laurie said. Even with Jack moving around in the stern it was barely rocking.

"And no leaks," Natalie said. "That was my concern."

Warren stayed silent. He had a white-knuckle grip on the gunwale.

To Jack's surprise, the engine started after only two pulls. A moment later, they were off, motoring almost due east. After the oppressive heat the breeze felt good.

The drive to Acalayong had been accomplished quicker than they'd anticipated, even though the road deteriorated in comparison to the road north of the Cogo turnoff. There was no traffic save for an occasional northward-bound van inconceivably packed with passengers. Even the luggage racks on the tops had two or three people holding on for dear life.

Acalayong had brought smiles to everyone's face. It was indicated as a city on the map but turned out to consist of no more than a handful of tawdry concrete shops, bars, and a few hotels. There was a cinder-block police post with several men in dirty uniforms sprawled in rattan chairs in the shade of the porch. They'd eyed Jack and the others with soporific disdain as the van had passed by.

Although they had found the town comically honky-tonk and litter strewn, they'd been able to get something to eat and drink as well as procure the boat. With some unease, they'd parked the van in sight of the police station, hoping it would be there on their return.

"How long did you estimate it would take us?" Laurie shouted over the noise of the outboard. It was particularly loud because a portion of its cowling was missing.

"An hour," Jack yelled back. "But the boat owner told me it would be more like twenty minutes. It's apparently just around the headland directly ahead."

At that moment, they were crossing the two-mile-wide mouth of Rio Congue. The jungle-covered shorelines were hazy with mist. Thunderheads loomed above; two thunderstorms had hit while they'd been in the van.

"I hope we don't get caught out here in the rain," Natalie said. But Mother Nature ignored her wish. Less than five minutes later, it was pouring so hard that some of the huge drops splashed river water into the boat. Jack slowed the engine and allowed the boat to guide itself, while he joined the others under the thatched canopy. To everyone's pleasant surprise, they stayed completely dry.

As soon as they rounded the headland, they saw Cogo's pier. Constructed of heavy pressure-treated timber, it was a far cry from the rickety docks at Acalayong. As they got closer, they could see there was a floating portion off the tip.

The first view of Cogo impressed everyone. In contrast with the dilapidated and haphazardly constructed buildings with flat, corrugated metal roofs endemic to Bata and all of Acalayong, Cogo was comprised of attractive, tiled, whitewashed structures reflecting a rich colonial ambiance. To the left and almost hidden by the jungle was a modern power station. Its presence was obvious only because of its improbably tall smokestack.

Jack cut the engine way back as the town approached so they could hear each other speak. Tied along the dock were several pirogues similar to the one they were in, though these others were piled high with fish netting.

"I'm glad to see other boats," Jack said. "I was afraid our canoe would stand out like a sore thumb."

"Do you think that large, modern building is the hospital?" Laurie said while pointing.

Jack followed her line of sight. "Yup, at least according to Arturo, and he should know. He was part of the initial building crew out here."

"I suppose that's our destination," Laurie said.

"I'd guess," Jack said. "At least initially. Arturo said the animal complex is a few miles away in the jungle. We might try to figure out a way to get out there."

"The town is bigger than I expected," Warren said.

"I was told it was an abandoned Spanish colonial town," Jack explained. "Not all of it has been renovated, but from here it sure looks like it has."

"What did the Spanish do here?" Natalie asked. "It's nothing but jungle."

"They grew coffee and cocoa," Jack said. "At least that's my understanding. Of course, I don't have any idea where they grew it."

"Uh-oh, I see a soldier," Laurie said.

"I see him, too," Jack said. His eyes had been searching along the waterfront as they came closer.

The soldier was dressed in the same jungle camouflage fatigues and red beret as the ones at the gate. He was aimlessly pacing a cobblestone square immediately at the base of the pier with an assault rifle slung over his shoulder.

"Does that mean we switch to plan C?" Warren questioned teasingly.

"Not yet," Jack said. "Obviously, he's where he is to interdict people coming off the pier. But look at that Chickee Hut built on the beach. If we got in there, we'd be home free."

"We can't just run the canoe up onto the beach," Laurie said. "He'll see that as well."

"Look how high that pier is," Jack said. "What if we were to slip underneath, beach the canoe there and then walk to the Chickee Hut? What do you think?"

"Sounds cool," Warren said. "But this boat is not going to fit under that pier, no way."

Jack stood up and made his way over to one of the poles that supported the thatched roof. It disappeared into a hole in the gunwale. Grasping it with both hands, he pulled it up. "How convenient!" he said. "This canoe is a convertible."

A few minutes later, they had all the poles out, and the thatched roof had been converted to a pile of sticks and dried leaves. They distributed it along both sides under the benches.

"The owner's not going to be happy about this," Natalie commented.

Jack angled the boat so that the pier shielded them as much as possible from the line of sight from the square. Jack cut the engine just at the moment they glided into the shade under the pier. Grasping the timbers they guided the boat toward shore, being careful to duck under crossbeams.

The boat scraped up the shady patch of shore and came to a stop.

"So far so good," Jack said. He encouraged the women and Warren to get out. Then, with Warren pulling and Jack paddling, they got the boat high on the beach.

Jack got out and pointed to a stone wall that ran perpendicular to the base of the pier before disappearing into the gently rising sand of the beach. "Let's hug the wall. When we clear it, head for the Chickee Bar."

A few minutes later, they were in the bar. The soldier had not paid them any heed. Either he didn't see them or he didn't care.

The bar was deserted except for a black man carefully cutting up lemons and limes. Jack motioned toward the stools and suggested a celebratory drink. Everyone was happy to comply. It had been hot in the canoe after the sun came out and especially after the canopy had come down.

The bartender came over immediately. His name tag identified him as Saturnino. In contradiction to his name, he was a jovial fellow. He was wearing a wild print shirt and a pillbox hat similar to the one Arturo had on when he picked them up at the airport the previous afternoon.

Following Natalie's lead, everyone had Coke with a slice of lemon.

"Not much business today," Jack commented to Saturnino.

"Not until after five," the bartender said. "Then we are very busy."

"We're new here," Jack said. "What money do we use?"

"You can sign," Saturnino said.

Jack looked at Laurie for permission. Laurie shook her head. "We'd rather pay," he said. "Are dollars okay?"

"What you like," Saturnino said. "Dollars or CFA. It makes no difference."

"Where is the hospital?" Jack asked.

Saturnino pointed over his shoulder. "Up the street until you get to the main square. It is the big building on the left."

"What do they do there?" Jack asked.

Saturnino looked at Jack as if he were crazy. "They take care of people."

"Do people come from America just to go to the hospital?" Jack asked.

Saturnino shrugged. "I don't know about that," he said. He took the bills Jack had put on the bar and turned to the cash register.

"Nice try," Laurie whispered.

"It would have been too easy," Jack agreed.

Refreshed after their cold drinks, the group headed out into the sunlight. They passed within fifty feet of the soldier who continued to ignore them. After a short walk up a hot cobblestone street, they came to a small green surrounded by plantation-style homes.

"It reminds me of some of the Caribbean Islands," Laurie said.

Five minutes later, they entered the tree-lined town square. The group of soldiers lolling in front of the town hall diagonally across from where they were standing spoiled the otherwise idyllic tableau.

"Whoa," Jack said. "There's a whole battalion."

"I thought you said that if there were soldiers at the gate they wouldn't have to have any in the town," Laurie said.

"I've been proved wrong," Jack acknowledged. "But there's no need to go over and announce ourselves. This is the hospital lab complex in front of us."

From the corner of the square, the building appeared to take up most of a Cogo city block. There was an entrance facing the square, but there was also one down the side street to their left. To avoid remaining in view of the lounging soldiers, they went to the side entrance.

"What are you going to say if we're questioned?" Laurie asked with some concern. "And walking into a hospital, you know it's bound to happen."

"I'm going to improvise," Jack said. He yanked the door open and ushered his friends in with an exaggerated bow.

Laurie glanced at Natalie and Warren and rolled her eyes. At least Jack could still be charming even when he was most exasperating.

After entering the building, everyone shivered with delight. Never had air conditioning felt quite so good. The room they found themselves in appeared to be a lounge, complete with wall-to-wall carpeting, club chairs, and couches. A large bookcase lined one wall. Some of the shelving was on an angle to display an impressive collection of periodicals from *Time* to *National Geographic*. There were about a half dozen people sitting in the room, all of them reading.

In the back wall at desk height was an opening fronted with sliding glass panels. Behind the glass a black woman in a blue uniform dress was sitting at a desk. To the right of the opening was a hall with several elevators.

"Could all these people be patients?" Laurie asked.

"Good question," Jack said. "Somehow, I don't think so. They all look too healthy and too comfortable. Let's talk to the secretary or whoever she is."

Warren and Natalie were intimidated by the hospital environment. They silently followed after Jack and Laurie.

Jack rapped softly on the glass. The woman looked up from her work and slid the glass open.

"Sorry," she said. "I didn't see you arrive. Are you checking in?"

"No," Jack said. "All my bodily functions are working fine at the moment."

"Excuse me?" the woman questioned.

"We're here to see the hospital, not use its services," Jack said. "We're doctors."

"This isn't the hospital," the woman said. "This is the Inn. You can either go out and come in the front of the building or follow the hall to your right. The hospital is beyond the double doors."

"Thank you," Jack said.

"My pleasure," the woman said. She leaned forward and watched as Jack and the others disappeared around the corner. Perplexed, the woman sat back and picked up her phone.

Jack led the others through the double doors. Immediately, the surroundings looked more familiar. The floors were vinyl and the walls were painted a soothing hospital green. A faint antiseptic smell was detectable.

"This is more like it," Jack said.

They entered a room whose windows fronted on the square. Between the windows were a large pair of doors leading to the outside. There were a few couches and chairs on area rugs forming distinct conversational groupings, but it was nothing like the lounge they'd initially entered. But like the lounge, this space had a glass-fronted information cubbyhole.

Jack again knocked on the glass. Another woman slid open the glass partition. She was equally as cordial.

"We have a question," Jack said. "We're doctors, and we'd like to know if there are currently any transplant patients in the hospital?"

"Yes, of course, there's one," the woman said with a confused look on her face. "Horace Winchester. He's in 302 and ready to be discharged."

"How convenient," Jack said. "What organ was transplanted?"

"His liver," the woman said. "Are you all from the Pittsburgh group?"

"No, we're part of the New York group," Jack said.

"I see," the woman said, although her expression suggested she didn't see at all.

"Thank you," Jack said to the woman as he herded the group toward the elevators that could be seen to the right.

"Luck is finally going our way," Jack said excitedly. "This is going to make it easy. Maybe all we have to do is get a look at the chart."

"As if that's going to be easy," Laurie commented.

"True," Jack said after a moment's thought. "So maybe we should just drop in on Horace and get the lowdown from the horse's mouth."

"Hey, man," Warren said, pulling Jack to a stop. "Maybe Natalie and I should wait down here. We're not used to being in a hospital, you know what I'm saying?"

"I suppose," Jack said reluctantly. "But I kind of think it's important for us to stick together in case we have to mosey down to the canoe sooner than we'd like. You know what I'm saying?"

Warren nodded and Jack pressed the elevator call button.

Cameron McIvers was accustomed to false alarms. After all, most of the time he or the Office of Security was called, it was a false alarm. Accordingly, as he entered the front door of the Inn, he was not concerned. But it was his job or one of his deputies' to check out all potential problems.

As he crossed to the information desk, Cameron noted that the lounge was as subdued as usual. The calm scene bolstered his suspicions that this call would be like all the others.

Cameron tapped on the glass, and it was slid open.

"Miss Williams," Cameron said, while touching the brim of his hat in a form of salute. Cameron and the rest of the security force wore khaki uniforms with an Aussi hat when on duty. There was also a leather belt with shoulder strap. A holstered Beretta was attached to the belt on the right side and a hand-held two-way radio on the left side.

"They went that way," Corrina Williams said excitedly. She lifted herself out of her chair to point around the corner.

"Calm down," Cameron said gently. "Who exactly are you talking about?"

"They didn't give any names," Corrina said. "There were four of them. Only one spoke. He said he was a doctor."

"Hmmm," Cameron voiced. "And you've never seen them before?"

"Never," Corrina said anxiously. "They took me by surprise. I thought maybe they were to stay at the Inn since we had new arrivals yesterday. But they said they had come to see the hospital. When I told them how to get there, they left straight-away."

"Were they black or white?" Cameron asked. Maybe this wouldn't be a typical false alarm after all.

"Half and half," Corrina said. "Two blacks, two whites. But I could tell from the way they were dressed they were all American."

"I see," Cameron said, while he stroked his beard and pondered the unlikely possibility of any of the Zone's American workers coming into the Inn to say they wanted to see the hospital.

"The one who was talking also said something strange about his bodily functions working fine," Corrina said. "I didn't know how to respond."

"Hmmm," Cameron repeated. "Could I use your phone?"

"Of course," Corrina said. She pulled the phone over from the side of her desk and faced it out toward Cameron.

Cameron punched the manager's direct line. Siegfried answered immediately.

"I'm here at the Inn," Cameron explained. "I thought you should be apprised of a curious story. Four strange doctors presented themselves here to Miss Williams with the wish to see the hospital."

Siegfried's response was an angry tirade that forced Cameron to hold the receiver away from his ear. Even Corrina cringed.

Cameron handed the phone back to the receptionist. He'd not heard every word of Siegfried's invective but the meaning was clear. Cameron was to get reinforcements over there immediately and detain the alien doctors.

Cameron unsnapped the straps over both his Beretta and the radio simultaneously. He pulled the radio free and made an emergency call to base while he started for the hospital.

Room 302 turned out to be in the front of the building with a fine view out over the square looking east. Jack and the others had found the room without difficulty. No one had challenged them. In fact, they hadn't seen a person as they'd made their way from the elevator to the room's open door.

Jack had knocked but it was obvious the room was momentarily empty although there'd been plenty of evidence the room was occupied. A television with a built-in VCR was on, and it was showing an old Paul Newman movie. The hospital bed was moderately disheveled. An open, half-packed suitcase was poised on a luggage stand.

The mystery was solved when Laurie noticed the sounds of a shower behind the closed bathroom door.

When the water stopped running, Jack had knocked, but it wasn't until almost ten minutes later that Horace Winchester appeared.

The patient was in his mid-fifties and corpulent. But he looked happy and healthy. He cinched up the tie on his bathrobe and padded over to the club chair by the bed. He sat down with a satisfied sigh.

"What's the occasion?" he asked, smiling at his guests. "This is more company than I've had the whole time I've been here."

"How are you feeling?" Jack asked. He grabbed a straight-back chair and sat down directly in front of Horace. Warren and Natalie lurked just outside the door. They felt reluctant to enter the room. Laurie went to the window. After seeing the group of soldiers, she'd become progressively anxious. She was eager to make the visit short and get back to the boat.

"I'm feeling just great," Horace said. "It's a miracle. I came here at death's door and as yellow as a canary. Look at me now! I'm ready for thirty-six holes of golf at one of my resorts. Hey, any of you people are invited to any of my places for as long as you want to stay, and it will all be on the house. Do you like to ski?"

"I do," Jack said. "But I'd rather talk about your case. I understand you had a liver transplant here. I'd like to ask where the liver came from?"

A half smile puckered Horace's face as he regarded Jack out of the corner of his eye. "Is this some kind of test?" he asked. "Because if it is, it's not necessary. I'm not going to be telling anyone. I couldn't be more grateful. In fact, as soon as I can, I'm going to have another double made."

"Exactly what do you mean by a 'double'?" Jack asked.

"Are you people part of the Pittsburgh team?" Horace asked. He looked over at Laurie.

"No, we're part of the New York team," Jack said. "And we're fascinated by your case. We're glad you are doing so well, and we're here to learn." Jack smiled and spread his hands palms up. "We're all ears. Why don't you start from the beginning?"

"You mean how I got sick?" Horace asked. He was plainly confused.

"No, how you arranged to have your transplant here in Africa," Jack said. "And I'd like to know what you mean by a double. Did you by any chance get a liver taken from some kind of ape?"

Horace gave a little nervous laugh and shook his head. "What's going on here?" he questioned. He glanced again at Laurie and then at Natalie and Warren, who were still standing in the doorway.

"Uh-oh!" Laurie suddenly voiced. She was staring out the window. "There's a bunch of soldiers running this way across the square."

Warren quickly crossed the room and looked out. "Shit, man. They mean business!"

Jack stood up, reached out, and grasped Horace by the shoulders. He leaned his face close to the patient's. "You are really going to disappoint me if you don't answer my questions, and I do the strangest things when I'm disappointed. What kind of animal was it, a chimpanzee?"

"They're coming to the hospital," Warren yelled. "And they all have AK-47's."

"Come on!" Jack urged Horace while giving the man a little shake. "Talk to me. Was it a chimpanzee?" Jack tightened his hold on the man.

"It was a bonobo," Horace squeaked. He was terrified.

"Is that a type of ape?" Jack demanded.

"Yes," Horace managed.

"Come on, man!" Warren encouraged. He was back at the door. "We got to get our asses out of here."

"And what did you mean by a double?" Jack asked.

Laurie grabbed Jack's arm. "There's no time. Those soldiers will be up here in a minute."

Reluctantly, Jack let go of Horace and allowed himself to be dragged to the door. "Damn, I was so close," he complained.

Warren was waving frantically for them to follow him and Natalie down the central corridor toward the back of the building, when the elevator door opened. Out stepped Cameron with his Beretta clutched in his hand.

"Everyone halt!" Cameron shouted the moment he saw the strangers. He grabbed his gun in both hands and trained it on Warren and Natalie. Then he swept it around to aim at Jack and Laurie. For Cameron, the problem was that his adversaries were on either side of him. When he was looking at one group, he couldn't see the other.

"Hands on top of your heads," Cameron commanded. He motioned with the barrel of his gun.

Everyone complied, although every time Cameron swung the gun toward Jack and Laurie, Warren approached another step toward him.

"No one is going to get hurt," Cameron said as he brought the gun back toward Warren.

Warren had gotten within range of a kick, and with lightning speed his foot lashed out and connected with Cameron's hands. The gun bounced off the ceiling.

Before Cameron could react to his gun's sudden disappearance, Warren closed in on him and hit him twice, once in the lower abdomen and then on the tip of the nose. Cameron collapsed backwards in a heap on the floor.

"I'm glad you're on my team for this run," Jack said.

"We got to get ourselves back to that boat!" Warren blurted without humor.

"I'm open to suggestions," Jack said.

Cameron moaned and pushed himself over onto his stomach.

Warren looked both ways down the hall. A few minutes earlier, he'd thought of running down the main corridor toward the rear, but that was no longer a reasonable alternative. Halfway down the corridor he could see some nurses gathering and pointing in his direction.

Across from the elevators at eye-level was a sign in the form of an arrow that pointed down the hall beyond Horace's room. It said: OR.

Knowing they had little time to debate, Warren motioned in the direction of the arrow. "That way!" he barked.

"The operating room?" Jack questioned. "Why?"

"Because they won't expect it," Warren said. He grabbed a stunned Natalie by the hand and propelled her into a jog.

Jack and Laurie followed. They passed Horace's room but the chubby man had locked himself in his bathroom.

The operating suite was set off from the rest of the hospital by the usual swinging doors. Warren hit them and went through with a straight arm like a football running back. Jack and Laurie were right behind.

There were no cases under way nor were there any patients in the recovery room. There weren't even any lights on except for those in a supply room halfway down the hall. The supply room's door was ajar, emitting a faint glow.

Hearing the repetitive thumps on the operating room doors, a woman appeared from the supply room. She was dressed in a scrub suit with a disposable cap. She caught her breath as she saw the four figures hurtling in her direction.

"Hey, you can't come in here in street clothes," she yelled as soon as she'd recovered from her initial shock. But Warren and the others had already passed. Perplexed, she watched the intruders run all the way down the rest of the corridor to disappear through the doors leading to the lab.

Turning back into the supply room, she went for the wall phone.

Warren skidded to a stop where the corridor formed a "T." He looked in either direction. To the left at the far end was a red wall light indicating a fire alarm. Above it was an exit sign.

"Hold up!" Jack said, as Warren was preparing to dash down to what he imagined would be a stairwell.

"What's the matter, man?" Warren questioned anxiously.

"This looks like a laboratory," Jack said. He stepped over to a glazed door and looked inside. He was immediately impressed. Although they were in the middle of Africa, it was the most modern lab he'd ever seen. Every piece of equipment looked brand new.

"Come on!" Laurie snapped. "There's no time for curiosity. We've got to get out of here."

"It's true, man," Warren said. "Especially after hitting that security type back there, we've got to make tracks."

"You guys go," Jack said distractedly. "I'll meet you at the boat."

Warren, Laurie, and Natalie exchanged anxious glances.

Jack tried the door. It was unlocked. He opened it and walked inside.

"Oh, for crissake," Laurie complained. Jack could be so frustrating. It was one thing for him to have little concern for his own safety, but it was quite another thing for him to compromise others.

"This place is going to be crawling with security dudes and soldiers in nothing flat," Warren said.

"I know," Laurie said. "You guys go. I'll get him to come as soon as I can."

"I can't leave you," Warren said.

"Think of Natalie," Laurie said.

"Nonsense," Natalie said. "I'm no frail female. We're in this together."

"You ladies go in there and talk some sense into that man," Warren said. "I'm going to run down the hall and pull the fire alarm."

"What on earth for?" Laurie asked.

"It's an old trick I learned as a teenager," Warren said. "Whenever there's trouble cause as much chaos as you can. It gives you a chance to slip away."

"I'll take your word for it," Laurie said. She motioned for Natalie to follow and entered the lab.

They found Jack already engaged in pleasant conversation with a laboratory technician wearing a long white coat. She was a freckle-faced redhead with an amiable smile. Jack already had her laughing.

"Excuse me!" Laurie said, struggling to keep her voice down. "Jack, we have to go."

"Laurie, meet Rolanda Phieffer," Jack said. "She's originally from Heidelberg, Germany."

"Jack!" Laurie intoned through clenched teeth.

"Rolanda's been telling me something very interesting," Jack said. "She and her colleagues here are working on the genes for minor histocompatibility antigens. They're moving them from a specific chromosome in one cell and sticking them into the same location on the same chromosome in another cell."

Natalie, who'd walked over to a large picture window overlooking the square, hastily turned back into the room. "It's getting worse. An entire car load of those Arabs in black suits are arriving."

At that moment, the fire alarm in the building went off. It featured alternating sequences of three ear-splitting shrieks of a horn followed by a disembodied voice: "Fire in the laboratory! Please proceed immediately to stairwells for evacuation! Do not use the elevators!"

"Oh, my word!" Rolanda said. She looked around quickly to see what she should take with her.

Laurie grabbed Jack by both arms and shook him. "Jack, be reasonable! We have to get out of here."

"I've figured it out," Jack said with a wry smile.

"I don't give a good goddamn," Laurie spat. "Come on!"

They rushed out into the hall. Other people were appearing as well. Everyone seemed confused as they looked up and down the hall. Some were sniffing. There was animated conversation. Many people were carrying their lap-top computers.

Without rushing they moved en masse to the stairwell. Jack, Laurie, and Natalie met up with Warren who was holding the door. He'd also managed to find white coats which he distributed to the others. They all pulled them on over their clothes. Unfortunately, they were the only ones wearing shorts.

"They have created some kind of chimera with these apes called bonobos," Jack said excitedly. "That's the explanation. No wonder the DNA tests were so screwy."

"What's he carrying on about now?" Warren asked with irritation.

"Don't ask," Laurie said. "It will only encourage him."

"Whose idea was it to pull the fire alarm?" Jack asked. "It was brilliant."

"Warren's," Laurie said. "At least one of us is thinking."

The stairwell opened up into a parking lot on the north side. People were milling about, looking back at the building, and talking in small groups. It was deathly hot since the sun was out and the parking lot was blacktop. A wailing fire siren could be heard coming from the northeast.

"What should we do?" Laurie asked. "I'm relieved we've gotten as far as we have. I didn't think it was going to be so easy to get out of the building."

"Let's walk over to the street and turn left," Jack said while pointing. "We can circle around the area to the west and get back to the waterfront."

"Where are all those soldiers?" Laurie asked.

"And the Arabs?" Natalie added.

"I'd guess they're looking for us in the hospital," Jack said.

"Let's go before all these lab people start going back into the building," Warren said.

They tried not to rush to avoid attracting any attention. As they neared the street they all glanced behind them for fear they were being watched, but no one was even looking in their direction. Everybody was captivated by the fire crew who'd arrived.

"So far so good," Jack said.

Warren was the first to reach the street. As he got a look to the west around the corner, he stopped abruptly and put his arms out to block the others. He backed up a step.

"We're not going that way," he said. "They've got a roadblock at the end of the street."

"Uh-oh," Laurie said. "Maybe they've sealed off the area."

"You remember that power station we saw?" Jack said.

Everyone nodded.

"That power has to get over here to the hospital," Jack said. "I'd bet there's a tunnel."

"Maybe," Warren said. "But the trouble is we don't know how to find it. Besides, I'm not thrilled about going back inside. Not with all those kids with AK-47's."

"Then let's try walking across the square," Jack said.

"Toward where we saw the soldiers?" Laurie questioned with dismay.

"Hey, if they're over here at the hospital, there should be no problem," Jack said.

"That's a point," Natalie agreed.

"Of course, we could always give ourselves up and say we're sorry," Jack said. "I mean, what can they do to us besides kick us the hell out. I think I've gotten what I came for, so it wouldn't bother me in the slightest."

"You're joking," Laurie said. "They're not going to accept a mere apology. Warren struck that man; we've done more than trespass."

"I'm joking to an extent," Jack agreed. "But the man was sticking a gun in our face. That's at least an explanation. Besides, we can leave a bunch of our French francs behind. Supposedly, that solves everything in this country."

"It didn't get us past the gate," Laurie reminded him.

"All right, everything but get us in here," Jack said. "But I'll be very surprised if it doesn't get us out."

"We've got to do something," Warren said. "The fire crew are already waving for the people to come back in the building. We're going to be standing out here in this god-awful heat by ourselves."

"So they are," Jack said, squinting against the sunlight. He found his sunglasses and put them on. "Let's try crossing the square before the soldiers return."

Once again, they tried to walk calmly as if they were strolling. They got almost to the grass, when they became aware of a commotion at the door into the building. They all turned to see a number of the black-suited Arabs push their way past the lab techs who were entering.

The Arabs rushed out into the sundrenched parking lot with their neckties flapping and their eyes squinting. Each brandished an automatic pistol in his hand. Behind the Arabs came several soldiers. Out of breath, they stood in the hot sun, panting while scanning the neighborhood.

Warren froze, and the rest of the group did the same.

"I don't like this," Warren said. "The six of them have enough fire power to rob the Chase Manhattan Bank."

"They kind of remind me of the Keystone Kops," Jack said.

"I don't find anything about this comical at all," Laurie said.

"Strangely enough, I think we're going to have to walk back inside," Warren said. "With these lab coats on they're going to wonder why we're standing out here."

Before anyone could respond to Warren's suggestion Cameron came out the door accompanied by two other men. One was dressed like Cameron: clearly a member of the security force. The other was shorter with a limp right arm. He, too, was dressed in khaki but without any of the martial embellishments the other two sported.

"Uh-oh," Jack said. "I have a feeling we'll be forced to use the apology approach after all."

Cameron was holding a blood-spotted handkerchief to his nose, but it didn't obstruct his vision. He spotted the group immediately and pointed. "That's them!" he yelled.

The Moroccans and the soldiers responded immediately by surrounding the trespassers. Every gun was pointed at the group, who raised their hands without being told.

"I wonder if they'll be impressed with my medical examiner badge?" Jack quipped.

"Don't do anything foolish!" Laurie warned.

Cameron and his companions walked over immediately. Silently, the ring around the Americans opened to allow them through. Siegfried stepped to the forefront.

"We'd like to apologize for any inconvenience," Jack began.

"Shut up!" Siegfried snapped. He walked around the group to eye them from all directions. When he got back to where he started, he asked Cameron if these were the people he'd encountered in the hospital.

"No doubt in my mind," Cameron said while glaring directly into Warren's face. "I hope you will indulge me, sir."

"Of course," Siegfried said with a slight wave of dismissal.

Without warning, Cameron punched Warren in the side of the face with a roundhouse blow. The sound was like a telephone directory falling to the floor. A plaintive whine escaped from Cameron's lips as he grabbed his hand and gritted his teeth. Warren did not move a muscle. He may not have blinked.

Cameron swore under his breath and stepped away.

"Search them," Siegfried commanded.

"We are sorry if we—" Jack began but Siegfried didn't let him finish. He slapped him with an open fist hard enough to turn Jack's head in the direction of the blow and raise a red welt on his cheek.

Cameron's deputy quickly relieved Jack and the others of their passports, wallets, money, and car keys. He gave them to Siegfried, who slowly went through them. After he looked at Jack's passport, he raised his eyes and glowered at him.

"I've been told you are a troublemaker," Siegfried said with disdain.

"I'd rather think of myself as a tenacious competitor," Jack said.

"Ah, arrogant as well," Siegfried snarled. "I hope your tenacity comes in handy once you are turned over to the Equatoguinean military."

"Perhaps we can call the American Embassy and resolve this," Jack said. "We are, after all, government employees."

Siegfried smiled, which actually only increased his scar-induced sneer. "American Embassy?" he questioned with uncamouflaged scorn. "In Equatorial Guinea! What a joke! Unfortunately for you, it's out on the island of Bioko." He turned to Cameron. "Put them in the jail but separate the men and the women!"

Cameron snapped his fingers for his deputy. He wanted the four handcuffed first. While this was in progress he and Siegfried drew off to the side.

"Are you really going to hand them over to the Equatoguineans?" Cameron asked.

"Absolutely," Siegfried said. "Raymond told me all about Stapleton. They have to disappear."

"When?" Cameron asked.

"As soon as Taylor Cabot leaves," Siegfried said. "I want this whole episode kept quiet."

"I understand," Cameron said. He touched the brim of his hat and then went back to supervise the transfer of the prisoners to the jail in the basement of the town hall.

CHAPTER 22

MARCH 9, 1997
4:15 P.M.
ISLA FRANCESCA

"Something very strange is going on," Kevin said.

"But what?" Melanie said. "Should we get our hopes up?"

"Where could all the other animals be?" Candace questioned.

"I don't know whether to be encouraged or concerned," Kevin said. "What if they're having Armageddon with the other group, and the fighting spreads to here?"

"God almighty," Melanie commented. "I never thought of that."

Kevin and the women had been virtual prisoners for over two days. They had not been allowed to leave the small cave the entire time of their confinement, and it now smelled as bad or worse than the outer cave. To relieve themselves, they'd been forced to go back into the tunnel which reeked like a mini-cesspool.

They themselves didn't smell much better. They were filthy from wearing the same clothes and sleeping on the rock and dirt floor. Their hair was hopelessly matted. Kevin's face was covered with a two-day stubble. They were all weak from lack of exercise and food although each had eaten some of what was brought to them.

Around ten o'clock that morning, there'd been a sense that something abnormal was happening. The animals had become agitated. Some had rushed out only to return moments later, making loud cries. Early on, bonobo number one had gone out but had yet to return. That in itself was abnormal.

"Wait a second," Kevin said suddenly. He put up his hands to keep the women from making any noise. He strained to hear by turning his head slowly from side to side.

"What is it?" Melanie asked urgently.

"I thought I heard a voice," Kevin said.

"A human voice?" Candace questioned.

Kevin nodded.

"Wait, I just heard it!" Melanie said with excitement.

"I did, too," Candace said. "I'm sure it was a human voice. It sounded like someone yelling 'okay.' "

"Arthur heard it, too," Kevin said. They'd named the bonobo who most often stood guard at the lip of the small cave Arthur for no particular reason other than to have a way to refer to him. Over the long hours, they'd had what could have been called a dialogue. They'd even been able to guess at some of the meanings of the bonobo words and gestures.

The ones they were the most sure of included "arak," which meant "away" especially when accompanied by the spreading of fingers and a sweeping arm motion, the same gesture Candace had seen in the operating room. There was also "hana" for "quiet" and "zit" for "go." They were very sure of "food" and "water," which were "bumi" and "carak" respectively. A word they weren't too sure of was "sta" accompanied by holding up one's hands with palms out. They thought it might be the pronoun "you."

Arthur stood up and loudly vocalized to the few bonobos remaining in the cave. They listened and then immediately disappeared out the front.

The next thing Kevin and the others heard were several reports from a rifle: not an ordinary gun but rather an air gun. A few minutes later, two figures in animal-center coveralls appeared silhouetted against the hazy, late-afternoon sky at the cave's entrance. One was carrying a gun, the other a strong, battery-powered lamp.

"Help!" Melanie shouted. She averted her eyes from the strong beam of light but waved her hands frantically lest the men not see her.

There was a loud thump that echoed around the inside of the cave. Simultaneously, Arthur let out a whimper. With a confused expression on his flat face he looked down at a red-tailed dart that protruded from his chest. His hand came up to grasp it, but before he could, he began to wobble. As if in slow motion, he sagged to the floor and rolled over onto his side.

Kevin, Melanie, and Candace emerged from their doorless cell and tried to stand upright. It took a moment for them to stretch. By the time they did the men were kneeling at the side of the bonobo to give the animal an additional dose of tranquilizer.

"My God, are we glad to see you," Melanie said. She had to steady herself with a hand against the rock. For a moment, the cave had begun to spin.

The men stood up and shined the bright light on the women and then on Kevin. The former captives all had to shield their eyes.

"You people are a mess," the man with the light said.

"I'm Kevin Marshall and this is Melanie Becket and Candace Brickmann."

"I know who you are," the man said flatly. "Let's get out of this shithole."

Kevin and the women were happy to comply on rubbery legs. The two men followed. Once out of the cave, the three friends had to squint in the bright, hazy sunlight. Below the face of the cliff were a half dozen more animal handlers. They were busy rolling up tranquilized bonobos in reed mats and lifting them onto a trailer where they were carefully positioned side by side.

"There's one more up here in this cave," the man with the flashlight yelled down to the others.

"I know you two," Melanie said once she got a good view of the men who'd come into the cave. "You're Dave Turner and Daryl Christian."

The men ignored Melanie. Dave, the taller of the two, pulled a two-way radio out of a holder at his waist. Daryl started climbing down the giant steps.

"Turner to base," Dave said into the instrument.

"I hear you loud and clear," Bertram said on the other end.

"We got the last of the bonobos and we're loading up," Dave said.

"Excellent work," Bertram said.

"We found Kevin Marshall and the two women in a cave," Dave said.

"In what state?" Bertram asked.

"Filthy but otherwise apparently healthy," Dave said.

"Give me that thing!" Melanie said, reaching for Dave's radio. Suddenly, she didn't like being talked about disparagingly by an underling.

Dave fended her off. "What do you want me to do with them?"

Melanie put her hands on her hips. She was incensed. "What do you mean 'what to do with them'?"

"Bring them to the animal center," Bertram said. "I'll inform Siegfried Spallek. I'm sure he'll want to talk with them."

"Ten-four," Dave said. He snapped off the radio.

"What's the meaning of this kind of treatment?" Melanie demanded. "We've been prisoners out here for more than two days."

Dave shrugged. "We just follow orders, ma'am. It seems as if you two have riled up the front office big time."

"What on earth is happening to the bonobos?" Kevin asked. When he'd first seen what the men were doing, he'd assumed it had all been for the purpose of their rescue. But the more he thought about it he couldn't understand why the animals were being loaded onto a trailer.

"The bonobos' good life on the island is a thing of the past," Dave said. "They've been warring out here and killing each other. We've found four corpses as evidence, all bashed with stone wedges. So we're caging them at the staging area in preparation for taking them all to the animal center. It'll be six-foot concrete cells from now on as far as I know."

Kevin's mouth slowly fell open. In spite of his hunger, exhaustion, and aches and pains, he felt a profound sadness for these unfortunate creatures who'd not asked to be created or born. Their lives had suddenly and arbitrarily been doomed to monotonous incarceration. Their human potential was not to be realized, and their striking accomplishments thus far would be lost.

Daryl and three other men were now on their way up with a litter.

Kevin turned to look back inside the cave. In the far shadows, he could see Arthur's profile near the lip of the chamber where Kevin and the women had been kept. A tear formed in the corner of Kevin's eye as he imagined how Arthur was going to feel when he awoke to find himself encased in steel.

"All right, you three," Dave said. "Let's start back. Are you strong enough to walk or you want to ride on the trailer?"

"How do you move the trailer?" Kevin asked.

"We've got an all-terrain vehicle on the island," Dave said.

"I'll walk, thank you," Melanie said icily.

Kevin and Candace nodded in agreement.

"We're awfully hungry, though," Kevin said. "The animals have only been offering us insects, worms, and marsh grass."

"We've got some candy bars and soft drinks in a locker on the front of the trailer," Dave said.

"That should be just fine," Kevin said.

The climb down the rock face was the hardest part of the trip. Once on the flat, the walking was easy, especially since the animal handlers had cleared the trail for the all-terrain vehicle.

Kevin was impressed with how much the workers had accomplished in so short a time. As he emerged into the marshy field south of Lago Hippo, he wondered if the canoe was still hidden in the reeds. He guessed it probably was. There was no reason it would have been found.

Candace was elated when she saw the earth-covered timber bridge and said as much. She'd been worrying how they were going to get across the Rio Diviso.

"You people have been busy," Kevin commented.

"We had no choice," Dave said. "We had to round up these animals in the quickest time possible."

Kevin, Melanie, and Candace began to get seriously fatigued on the last mile segment from the Rio Diviso bridge to the staging area. It was especially apparent when they had to step off the trail for the all-terrain vehicle to pass on its way back for the last trailer-load of bonobos. Stopping and standing just for a moment made their legs feel like lead.

Everybody breathed a sigh of relief when they emerged from the twilight of the jungle into the bustling staging area in the clearing. Another half dozen bluecoveralled workers were toiling under the hot sun. They were quickly unloading the bonobos from a second trailer and getting them into individual steel cages before the animals revived.

The cages were four-foot square steel boxes, making it impossible for all but the youngest animals to stand up. The only source of ventilation was through the bars in the doors. The doors were secured by an angled hasp that latched around the side beyond the animal's reach. Kevin was able to catch glimpses of terrified bonobos cowering within the cages' shadows.

Such small cages were supposed to be used only for transport, but a forklift was laboriously moving them into the shade of the north-facing wall of the jungle, suggesting they were staying on the island. One of the workers was manning a hose from a gasoline-powered pump and spraying the cages and the animals with river water.

"I thought you said the bonobos were going to the animal center?" Kevin asked.

"Not today," Dave said. "For the moment, there is no place to put them. It'll be tomorrow or the next day at the very latest."

There was no trouble getting over to the mainland because the telescoping bridge had been deployed. It was constructed of steel and had a hollow, drumlike sound as they trodded across. Parked alongside the bridge mechanism was Dave's pickup truck.

"Hop in," Dave said, while pointing into the truck's bed.

"Just one minute!" Melanie snapped. They were her first words since leaving the cave. "We're not riding in the back of a truck."

"Then you'll walk," Dave said. "You're not riding in my cab."

"Come on, Melanie," Kevin urged. "It will be more pleasant back here in the open air." Kevin gave Candace a hand.

Dave went around and got in behind the wheel.

Melanie resisted for another minute. With her hands on her hips, her legs spread apart, and her lips pressed together, she looked like a young girl on the verge of a temper tantrum.

"Melanie, it's not that far," Candace said. She reached out her hand. Reluctantly, Melanie took it.

"I didn't expect a hero's welcome," Melanie complained. "But I didn't expect this kind of treatment."

After the damp oppressiveness of the cave and the moist hothouse of the jungle, the breezy ride in the back of the truck was unexpectedly pleasant. The bed was filled with reed mats that had been used to transport the animals, and they provided adequate cushion. The mats had a rather rank smell, but the group guessed they did, too.

They lay on their backs and watched patches of the late-afternoon sky appear between the branches of the overhead canopy of trees.

"What do you think they are going to do to us?" Candace said. "I don't want to go back in that jail."

"Let's hope they just fire us on the spot," Melanie said. "I'm ready to pack my bag and say goodbye to the Zone, the project, and Equatorial Guinea. I've had it."

"I can only hope it will be that easy," Kevin said. "I'm also worried about the animals. They've been given life sentences."

"There's not much we can do," Candace said.

"I wonder," Kevin said. "I wonder what animal-rights groups would say about this situation."

"Now, don't say anything like that until we get the hell out of here," Melanie said. "That would drive everybody bananas."

They entered the eastern end of town, passing the soccer field and tennis center on their right. Both were in use, particularly the tennis center. Every court was taken.

"An experience like this makes you feel less important than you thought you were," Melanie commented while glancing at the players. "You're hidden away for two agonizing days and everything goes on just as it did before."

They all pondered Melanie's comment as they unconsciously braced for the sharp right-hand turn they knew was coming up to take them to the animal center. But instead, after the truck slowed, it stopped. Kevin sat up and looked ahead. He saw Bertram's Jeep Cherokee.

"Siegfried wants you to drive directly to Kevin's house," Bertram called to Dave.

"Okay!" Dave called back.

The truck lurched forward as Dave pulled out behind Bertram.

Kevin lay back down. "Well, that's a surprise. Maybe we're not going to be treated that badly after all."

"Maybe we can get them to drop Candace and me at our places," Melanie said. "They're more or less on the way." She looked down at herself. "The first thing I'm going to do is take a shower and change clothes. Only then am I going to eat."

Kevin got his legs under him and kneeled behind the truck's cab. He rapped on the rear window until he got Dave's attention. He then relayed Melanie's request. The response from Dave was a wave of dismissal.

Kevin repositioned himself on his back. "I guess you have to go to my house first," he said.

As soon as they hit the cobblestones, the ride was so jarring that they all sat up. Rounding the last turn, Kevin looked ahead expectantly. He was as eager to take a shower as Melanie. Unfortunately what he saw was not encouraging. Siegfried and Cameron were standing out in front of his house along with four heavily armed Equatoguinean soldiers. One of the soldiers was an officer.

"Uh-oh," Kevin said. "This doesn't look promising after all."

The truck came to a halt. Dave hopped out and came around to put down the tailgate. Kevin was the first to climb out on stiff legs. Melanie and Candace followed.

Preparing himself for the inevitable, Kevin walked over to where Siegfried and Cameron were standing. He knew Melanie and Candace were right behind. Bertram, who'd parked in front of the pickup truck, joined them. No one looked particularly happy.

"We had hoped you'd taken an unannounced holiday," Siegfried said scornfully. "Instead, we find you have willfully disobeyed standing orders not to trespass on Isla Francesca. You're all to be confined to quarters here, in this house." He pointed over his shoulder at Kevin's.

Kevin was about to explain why they'd done what they had when Melanie pushed past him. She was exhausted and irate.

"I'm not staying here and that's final," she spat. "In fact, I quit. I'll be leaving the Zone just as soon as I can make arrangements."

Siegfried's upper lip hiked itself up to exaggerate his sneer. After a quick step forward, he backhanded Melanie viciously, knocking her down. Reflexively Candace dropped to one knee to aid her friend.

"Don't touch her," Siegfried shouted, as he drew his hand back as if to strike Candace.

Candace ignored him and helped Melanie up into a sitting position. Melanie's left eye was beginning to swell, and a trickle of blood slowly ran down her cheek.

Kevin winced and looked away, expecting to hear another blow. He admired Candace's courage and wished that he shared some. But he was terrified of Siegfried and afraid to move.

When another blow did not materialize, Kevin looked back. Candace had Melanie standing shakily on her feet.

"You'll be leaving the Zone soon enough," Siegfried snarled at Melanie. "But it will be in the company of the Equatoguinean authorities. You can try your insolence on them."

Kevin swallowed with difficulty. Being given to the Equatoguineans was what he'd feared most.

"I'm an American," Melanie sobbed.

"But you are in Equatorial Guinea," Siegfried snapped. "And you've violated Equatoguinean law."

Siegfried stepped back. "I've confiscated all of your passports. Just so you know, they will be given to the local authorities along with your persons. In the meantime, you are to stay here in this house. And I warn you that these soldiers and this officer have been ordered to shoot if you so much as take one step outside. Have I made myself clear?"

"I need some clothes," Melanie cried.

"I've had clothes for both of you women brought from your quarters and thrown into upstairs guest rooms," Siegfried said. "Believe me, we have thought of every-thing."

Siegfried turned to Cameron. "See that these people are taken care of."

"Of course, sir," Cameron said. He touched the tip of his hat before turning to Kevin and the women.

"Okay, you've heard the manager," he barked. "Upstairs you go and no trouble, please."

Kevin started forward but he detoured enough to go by Bertram. "They were using more than fire. They were making tools and even talking with each other."

Kevin walked on. He'd not seen any reaction in Bertram's face other than a slight movement of his perpetually elevated eyebrows. But Kevin was certain Bertram had heard him.

As Kevin wearily climbed to the second floor, he saw Cameron already organizing an area for the soldiers and the officer to occupy at the base of the stairs.

Up in the front hall Kevin, Melanie, and Candace eyed each other. Melanie was still sobbing intermittently.

Kevin breathed out. "This is not good news," he said.

"They can't do this to us," Melanie whimpered.

"The point is they are going to try," Kevin said. "And without our passports we'd have trouble leaving the country even if we were to walk out of here."

Melanie put her hands on either side of her face and squeezed. "I've got to get ahold of myself," she said.

"I feel numb again," Candace admitted. "We've gone from one form of captivity to another."

Kevin sighed. "At least they didn't put us in the jail."

Outside they heard multiple car engines start and vehicles pull away. Kevin went out onto the veranda and saw all the cars leaving except for Cameron's. Glancing up into the sky, he noted that twilight was deepening into night. A few stars were visible.

Turning back into the house, Kevin went directly to the phone. Picking it up, he heard what he'd expected to hear: nothing.

"Is there a dial tone?" Melanie asked from behind him.

Kevin replaced the receiver. He shook his head. "I'm afraid not."

"I didn't expect so," Melanie said.

"Let's take showers," Candace suggested.

"Good idea," Melanie said, making an effort to sound positive.

After agreeing to meet in a half hour, Kevin walked back through the dining room and pushed open the kitchen door. As dirty as he was, he didn't want to enter. The smell of roast chicken teased his nose.

Esmeralda had leaped to her feet the moment the door opened.

"Hello, Esmeralda," Kevin said.

"Welcome, Mr. Marshall," Esmeralda said.

"You didn't come out to greet us like you always do," Kevin said.

"I was afraid the manager was still here," Esmeralda said. "He and the security man had come up earlier to say you were coming home and that you would not be able to leave the house."

"That's what they told me, too," Kevin said.

"I've made food for you," Esmeralda said. "Are you hungry?"

"Very much," Kevin said. "But there are two guests."

"I know," Esmeralda said. "The manager told me that as well."

"Can we eat in a half hour?" Kevin asked.

"Certainly."

Kevin nodded. He was lucky to have Esmeralda. He turned to leave, but Esmeralda called out to him. He hesitated, holding the door ajar.

"There are many bad things happening in the town," she said. "Not only for you and your friends, but also for strangers. I have a cousin who works at the hospital. She told me that four Americans came from New York and went into the hospital. They talked with the patient who got the liver from the bonobo."

"Oh?" Kevin questioned. Strangers coming from New York to talk to one of the transplant patients was a thoroughly unanticipated development.

"They just walked in," Esmeralda continued. "They were not supposed to be there. They said they were doctors. Security was called, and the army and the guards came to take them away. They are in the jail."

"My word," Kevin commented, while his mind veered off on a tangent. New York reminded him of the surprising call he'd gotten a week previously in the middle of the night from the GenSys CEO, Taylor Cabot. It had been about the patient Carlo Franconi, who'd been killed in New York. Taylor Cabot had asked if someone could figure out what had happened to Carlo from an autopsy.

"My cousin knows some of the soldiers who were there," Esmeralda continued. "They said that the Americans will be given to the Ministers. If they are, they will be killed. I thought you should know."

Kevin felt a chill descend his spine. He knew such a fate was what Siegfried had in mind for him, Melanie, and Candace. But who were these Americans? Had they been involved with the autopsy on Carlo Franconi?

"It is all very serious," Esmeralda said. "And I am afraid for you. I know you went to the forbidden island."

"How do you know that?" Kevin questioned with amazement.

"In our town people talk," Esmeralda said. "When I said you were gone unexpectedly and that the manager was looking for you, Alphonse Kimba told my husband that you had gone to the island. He was sure."

"I appreciate your concern," Kevin said evasively and preoccupied with his thoughts. "Thank you for what you have told me."

Kevin went back to his own room. When he looked at himself in the mirror, he was surprised how exhausted and filthy he appeared. Running a hand over his beginning beard, he noticed something more disturbing. He was beginning to look a lot like his double!

After a shave, shower, and clean clothes, Kevin felt revived. The entire time, he mused about the Americans in the jail under the town hall. He was very curious and would have liked nothing better than to go and talk with them.

Kevin found the two women were equally refreshed. The shower had transformed Melanie into her irrepressible self, and she complained bitterly about the selection of clothes she'd been offered. "Nothing goes with anything," she complained.

They settled in the dining room, and Esmeralda began serving the meal. Melanie laughed, after looking around at the surroundings. "You know, I find it almost funny that a few hours ago we were living like Neanderthals. Then, presto, we're in the lap of luxury. It's like a time machine."

"If only we didn't have to worry about what tomorrow will bring," Candace said.

"Let's at least enjoy our last supper," Melanie said with her typical wry humor. "Besides, the more I think about it, the less likely I think it is that they can just foist us off on the Equatoguineans. I mean, they wouldn't be able to get away with it. This is almost the beginning of the third millennium. The world is too small."

"But I'm worried . . ." Candace began.

"Excuse me," Kevin interrupted. "Esmeralda told me something curious that I'd like to share with you." Kevin started by mentioning the phone call he got in the middle of the night from Taylor Cabot. Then he told the story about the arrival and subsequent incarceration of the New Yorkers in the town's jail.

"Well, this's just what I'm talking about," Melanie said. "A couple of smart people do an autopsy in New York, and they end up here in Cogo. And we thought we were so isolated. I tell you the world's getting smaller every day."

"So you think these Americans came here following a trail that started with Franconi?" Kevin asked. His intuition was telling him the same thing, but he wanted reinforcement.

"What else could it be?" Melanie questioned. "There's no question in my mind."

"Candace, what do you think?" Kevin asked.

"I agree with Melanie," Candace said. "Otherwise, it's too much of a coincidence."

"Thank you, Candace!" Melanie said. While twirling her empty wineglass, she looked menacingly at Kevin. "I hate to interrupt this fascinating conversation, but where's some of that great wine of yours, bucko?"

"Gosh, I totally forgot," Kevin said. "Sorry!" He pushed back from the table and went into the butler's pantry that he'd filled with his mostly untouched wine allocation. As he was looking through the labels, which held little meaning for him, he was suddenly struck by how much wine he had. Counting the bottles in a small area and extrapolating it to allow for the entire room, he realized he had more than three hundred bottles.

"My word," Kevin said as a plan began to form in his head. He grabbed an armload of bottles and pushed through the swinging door into the kitchen.

Esmeralda got up from where she was sitting having her own dinner.

"I have a favor to ask," Kevin said. "Would you take these bottles of wine and a corkscrew down to the soldiers at the foot of the stairs?"

"So many?" she questioned.

"Yes, and I'd like you to take even more to the soldiers in the town hall. If they ask what the occasion is, tell them that I'm going away, and I wanted them to enjoy the wine, not the manager."

A smile spread across Esmeralda's face. She looked at Kevin. "I think I understand." From a cupboard she got the canvas bag that she used for shopping and loaded it with wine bottles. A moment later, she disappeared through the butler's pantry, heading for the front hall.

Kevin made several trips back and forth from his wine collection to the kitchen table. Soon he had several dozen bottles lined up, including a couple bottles of port.

"What's going on?" Melanie enquired after sticking her head into the kitchen. "We're waiting and where's the wine?"

Kevin handed her one of the bottles. He said he'd be a few minutes more and they should start eating without him. Melanie rolled the bottle over to look at the label.

"Oh, my, Château Latour!" she said. She flashed Kevin an appreciative grin, before ducking back into the dining room.

Esmeralda returned to say that the soldiers were very pleased. "But I thought I'd take them some bread," she added. "It will stimulate their thirst."

"Marvelous idea," Kevin said. He filled the canvas bag with wine and tested its weight. It was heavy, but he thought Esmeralda could handle it.

"Let me know how many soldiers are at the town hall," Kevin said as he handed her the bag. "We want to make sure there is plenty for everyone."

"There are usually four at night," Esmeralda said.

"Then ten bottles should be fine," Kevin said. "At least for starters." He smiled, and Esmeralda smiled back.

Taking a deep breath, Kevin pushed through the door into the dining room. He wanted to see what the women thought of his idea.

Kevin rolled over and looked at the clock. It was just before midnight, so he sat up and put his feet over the side of the bed. He turned off the alarm clock that had been set to go off at twelve P.M. sharp. Then he stretched.

During dinner, Kevin's proposed plan had sparked a lively discussion. In a co-operative effort, the idea had been refined and expanded. Ultimately, all three thought it was worth attempting.

After making what preparations they could, they all decided to try to get a little rest. But Kevin had been unable to sleep despite his exhaustion. He was too keyed up. There was also the problem of the gradually increasing noise from the soldiers. At first, it had just been animated chatter, but during the last half hour, loud, drunken singing had reverberated from below.

Esmeralda had visited both groups of soldiers twice during the evening. When she returned, she reported that the expensive French wine was a big hit. After her second visit, she told Kevin that the initial deliveries of bottles had been almost drained.

Kevin dressed quickly in the dark, then ventured out into the hall. He did not want to turn on any lights. Luckily, the moon was bright enough for him to see his way to the guest rooms. He knocked first on Melanie's door. He was startled when it was opened instantly.

"I've been waiting," Melanie whispered. "I couldn't sleep."

Together, they went to Candace's room. She, too, was ready.

In the living room they picked up the small canvas bags each had prepared and walked out onto the veranda. The vista was enticingly exotic. It had rained several hours earlier, but now the sky was filled with puffy, silver-blue clouds. A gibbous moon was high in the sky, and its light made the mist-filled town glow eerily. The jungle sounds were shockingly loud in the hot, moist air.

They had discussed this first stage in detail so there was no need for talk now. At the far end of the veranda in the rear corner they secured the end of three sheets that had been tied together. The other end was dropped over the side to the ground.

Melanie had insisted on going first. She climbed nimbly over the balustrade, and lowered herself to the ground with inspiring ease. Candace was next, and her cheer-leading experience stood her in good stead. She had no trouble making it down.

Kevin was the one who had difficulty. Trying to imitate Melanie, he pushed off with his feet. But then as he swung back toward the building he got twisted in the sheets so that he collided with the stucco, scraping his knuckles.

"Damn," he whispered, when he finally was standing on the cobblestones. He shook his hand and squeezed his fingers.

"Are you okay?" Melanie whispered.

"I think so," Kevin said.

The next stage of their escape was more worrisome. In single file, they inched along the back of the building within the shadow of the arcade. Each step took them closer to the central stairwell, where they could hear the soldiers. A cassette recorder playing African music at low volume had been added to the festivities.

They reached the stall where Kevin kept his Toyota LandCruiser and slipped in along the passenger side until they reached the front. According to previously made plans, Kevin eased around the car to the driver's-side door and quietly opened it. At that point, he was within fifteen to twenty feet from the inebriated soldiers who were on the opposite side of a reed mat suspended from the ceiling.

Kevin released the emergency brake and put the car in neutral. Returning to the women, he motioned to start pushing.

At first, the heavy vehicle resisted their efforts. Kevin lifted his foot to push against the house's foundation. That added amount of leverage made the difference; the car eased out of its parking slot.

At the lip of the arcade, the cobblestones of the street slanted downward in a gentle slope so rainwater would run away from the house. As soon as the rear wheels of the vehicle passed this point, the car gained momentum. All at once, Kevin realized that no additional force was needed.

"Uh-oh!" Kevin cried, as the car began to gain speed.

Kevin ran around the side of the car and tried to get the driver's-side door open. Given the car's increasing momentum, this wasn't easy. The car was now halfway across the alley and beginning to curve to the right down the hill toward the water-front.

Finally Kevin succeeded in opening the door. In one swift move, he dove in behind the wheel. He got in position as quickly as possible, then jammed on the brakes. At the same time, he turned the steering wheel hard to the left so as to better align the vehicle with the street.

Fearful their efforts might have attracted the soldiers' attention, Kevin looked their way to check. The men were gathered around a small table supporting the cassette player and a half dozen empty wine bottles. The soldiers were happily clapping and stomping their feet, oblivious to Kevin's maneuverings with the car.

Kevin breathed a sigh of relief. The passenger-side door opened and Melanie climbed in. Candace got in the back.

"Don't close the door," Kevin whispered. He was still holding his ajar.

Kevin eased up on the brake. The car did not move at first, so he shifted his weight back and forth until he got the car rolling down the incline toward the waterfront. Kevin looked out the rear window, steering the vehicle as it began gathering speed.

They rolled for two blocks. At that point, the hill began to flatten out, and the car eventually came to a stop. Only then did Kevin slip the key into the ignition and start the engine. They all closed their doors.

They looked at each other in the half light of the car's interior. They were all keyed up and their pulses were racing. Everyone smiled.

"We did it!" Melanie asserted.

"So far so good," Kevin agreed.

Kevin put the car in gear. He turned right for several blocks to give his house a wide berth and headed for the motor pool.

"You're pretty sure no one will give us trouble at the garage," Melanie said.

"Well, there's no way to know for sure," Kevin said. "But I don't think so. The motor-pool people live a life of their own. Besides, Siegfried has probably kept the story of our disappearance and reappearance a secret. He'd have to if he were truly planning on handing us over to the Equatoguinean authorities."

"I hope you are right," Melanie said. She sighed. "I'm half wondering if we shouldn't just try to drive out of the Zone behind one of the trucks instead of bothering with four Americans we've never met."

"Those people got in here somehow," Kevin said. "I'm counting on their having had a plan to get out. Running the main gate should be considered our last-ditch option."

They pulled into the busy motor-pool facility. They had to squint under the glare of the mercury-vapor lights. They continued until they came to the repair section. Kevin parked behind a bay with the cab of a semi up on the hydraulic lift. Several greasy mechanics were standing under it, scratching their heads.

"Wait here," Kevin said, as he alighted from the Toyota.

He walked inside and greeted the men.

Melanie and Candace watched. Candace literally had her fingers crossed.

"Well, at least they didn't bolt for the telephone the moment they saw him," Melanie said.

The women watched as one of the mechanics sauntered off and disappeared through a door in the rear of the facility. He reappeared a moment later, carrying a lengthy hunk of heavy chain. He gave it to Kevin who staggered under its weight.

As his face turned a progressively brighter shade of red, Kevin stumbled back toward the LandCruiser. Sensing he was about to drop the chain, Melanie hopped out of the car to open the luggage area.

The vehicle lurched as Kevin dropped the chain onto the tailgate.

"I told them I wanted heavy chain," Kevin managed. "It didn't have to be this heavy."

"What did you say to those men?" Melanie asked.

"I said that your car got stuck in some mud," Kevin said. "They didn't bat an eyelash. Of course, they didn't offer to come and help, either."

Kevin and Melanie returned inside the Toyota, and they started back toward town.

"You're sure this is going to work?" Candace asked from the rear seat.

"No, but I can't think of anything else," Kevin said.

For the rest of the trip, no one spoke. They all knew this was the most difficult part of the whole plan. The tension mounted as they turned into the parking lot for the town hall and doused the headlights.

The room occupied by the army post was ablaze with light. As they got closer Kevin, Melanie, and Candace could hear the music. This group of soldiers also had a cassette player, only theirs was cranking out African music at full volume.

"That's the kind of party I was counting on," Kevin said. He made a wide turn and then backed toward the building. He could just make out the window wells for the subterranean jail within the shadows of the ground-floor arcade.

He stopped the car within five feet of the building and put on the emergency brake. All three gazed into the room occupied by the soldiers. They couldn't see much of the room and none of the soldiers because the line of sight was on an angle through an unglazed window. The window's shutter had been raised and hooked to the ceiling of the arcade. A number of empty wine bottles were on the sill.

"Well, it's now or never," Kevin said.

"Can we help?" Melanie asked.

"No, stay put," Kevin said.

Kevin climbed from the car and walked in under the nearest arch to stand within the shelter of the arcade. The sound of the music was deafening. Kevin's major concern was that if someone looked out the window, Kevin would be seen immediately. There was nothing to hide behind.

Looking down at the window well, Kevin could see the barred opening. Beyond the bars was utter darkness. There was not the faintest light within the cell.

Getting down on his hands and knees first, Kevin lay on the stone floor with his head over the lip of the window well. With his face close to the bars, he called out over the noise of the music: "Hello! Anybody in there?"

"Just us tourists," Jack said. "Are we invited to the party?"

"I understand you are Americans," Kevin said.

"Like apple pie and baseball," Jack said.

Kevin could suddenly hear other voices in the dark, but they were unintelligible.

"You people have to realize what a dangerous situation you've gotten yourselves into," Kevin said.

"Really," Jack said. "We thought this was how all visitors to Cogo were treated."

Kevin thought that whomever he was speaking with would certainly get along well with Melanie.

"I'm going to try to pull these bars out," Kevin said. "Are you all in the same cell?"

"No, we have two beautiful ladies in the cell to my left."

"Okay," Kevin said. "Let's see what I can do with these bars first."

Kevin got up and went back for the chain. Returning to the window well, he threaded one end through the bars into the abyss.

"Hook this around one of the bars a number of times," Kevin said.

"I like this," Jack said. "It reminds me of an old Western movie."

Back at the Toyota, Kevin secured the chain to the trailer hitch. When he got back to the window well he gently pulled on the chain. He could see it was tied securely around the central bar.

"Looks good," Kevin said. "Let's see what happens."

He climbed back into the vehicle and made sure it was in its lowest four-wheel drive gear. Looking out the back window, Kevin cautiously eased the car forward to take the slack out of the chain.

"All right, here we go," Kevin said to Melanie and Candace. He began to press on the accelerator. The heavy-duty Toyota engine strained, but Kevin couldn't hear it. The hum of the motor was drowned out by the frenzied beat of a popular Zairean rock group.

Suddenly, the vehicle lurched forward. Hastily, Kevin braked. Behind them they heard a terrible clanging over the sound of the music like someone hitting a fire escape with a curbstone.

Kevin and the women winced. They looked back at the opening into the army post. To their relief, no one appeared to check out the awful sound.

Kevin jumped out of the Toyota with the intention of going back to see what had happened when he almost ran into an impressively muscled black man heading right for him.

"Good job, man! My name's Warren and this is Jack." Jack had come up alongside Warren.

"I'm Kevin."

"Cool," Warren said. "You back these wheels up, and we'll see what we can do with the other opening."

"How did you get out so quickly?" Kevin asked.

"Man, you pulled out the whole friggin' frame," Warren said.

Kevin climbed into the car and slowly backed up. He could see the two men had already detached the chain.

"It worked!" Melanie said. "Congratulations."

"I must admit it was better than I thought," Kevin said.

A moment later, someone thumped on the back of the Toyota. When Kevin looked, he could see one of the men wave for him to go forward.

Kevin used the same driving technique he'd used the first episode. With approximately the same amount of power there was the same sudden release and unfortunately the same clanging noise. This time a soldier had appeared at the window.

Kevin didn't move, and he prayed the two men he'd just met did the same. The soldier proceeded to bring a wine bottle to his lips and in the process knocked several of the empties off the sill. They shattered on the stone pavement. Then he turned and disappeared back into the room.

Kevin got out of the vehicle in time to see two women being extracted from the second window well. As soon as they were free, all four rushed for the car. Kevin went around to detach the chain but found that Warren was already in the process of doing so.

They all climbed into the Toyota without discussion. Jack and Warren squeezed into the jump seats in the back while Laurie and Natalie joined Candace on the middle bench.

Kevin put the car in gear. After a final glance at the army post, he drove from the parking lot. He didn't switch on the lights until they were away from town hall.

The escape had been a heady experience for everyone: triumph for Kevin, Melanie, and Candace; surprise and utter relief for the crew from New York. The seven exchanged terse introductions; then the questions started. At first, everyone spoke at the same time.

"Wait a second, everybody!" Jack shouted over the babble. "We need some order in this chaos. Only one person at a time."

"Well, damn!" Warren said. "I'm going first! I just want to thank you guys for coming when you did."

"I'll second that," Laurie said.

Having cleared the central part of town, Kevin pulled into the parking lot for the main supermarket. There were several other cars. He stopped and turned off the lights and the engine.

"Before we talk about anything else," Kevin said. "We've got to talk about getting out of this town. We don't have a lot of time. How did you people originally plan on leaving?"

"By the same boat we came in on," Jack said.

"Where's the boat?" Kevin asked.

"We assume it's where we left it," Jack said. "Pulled up on the beach under the pier."

"Is it big enough for all of us?" Kevin asked.

"With room to spare," Jack said.

"Perfect!" Kevin said with excitement. "I was hoping you'd come by boat. That way we can go directly to Gabon." He faced around quickly and restarted the engine. "Let's just pray it's not been found."

He drove out of the parking lot and began a circuitous route to the waterfront. He wanted to stay as far from the town hall and his own house as possible.

"We have a problem," Jack said. "We have no identification or money. Everything was taken from us."

"We're not much better off," Kevin said. "But we do have some money, both cash and travelers checks. Our passports were confiscated when we were put under house arrest this afternoon. We were destined for the same fate as you: to be turned over to the Equatoguinean authorities."

"Would that have been a problem?" Jack asked.

Kevin let out a little derisive laugh. In the back of his mind, he could see the skulls on Siegfried's desk. "It would have been more than a problem. It would have meant a hush-hush mock trial followed by a firing squad."

"No shit!" Warren said.

"In this country, it is a capital offense to interfere with GenSys operations," Kevin said. "And the manager is the one who decides whether someone is interfering or not."

"A firing squad?" Jack repeated with horror.

"I'm afraid so," Kevin said. "The army here is good at it. They've had a lot of practice over the years."

"Then we're even more in debt to you people than we thought," Jack said. "I'd no idea."

Laurie looked out the side window of the car and shuddered. It was just sinking in how seriously her life was on the line and that the threat was not yet over.

"How come you guys were in the soup?" Warren asked.

"It's a long story," Melanie said.

"So is ours," Laurie said.

"I have a question," Kevin said. "Did you people come here because of Carlo Franconi?"

"Whoa!" Jack said. "Such clairvoyance! I'm impressed, and intrigued. How did you guess? What exactly is your role here in Cogo?"

"Me, in particular?" Kevin asked.

"Well, all of you," Jack said.

Kevin, Melanie, and Candace looked at each other to see who wanted to speak first.

"We were all part of the same program," Candace said. "But I was just a minor player. I'm an intensive-care nurse for a surgical transplant team."

"I'm a reproductive technologist," Melanie said. "I provide the raw materials for Kevin to work his magic, and once he has, I see to it that his creations are brought to fruition."

"I'm a molecular biologist," Kevin explained with a sigh of regret. "Someone who overstepped his bounds and committed a Promethean blunder."

"Hold up," Jack said. "Don't go too literary on me. I know I've heard of Prometheus, but I can't remember who he was."

"Prometheus was a Titan in Greek mythology," Laurie said. "He stole fire from Olympus and gave it to man."

"I inadvertently gave fire to some animals," Kevin said. "I stumbled on the way to move chromosome parts, particularly the short arm of chromosome six from one cell to another, from one species to another."

"So you took chromosome parts from humans and put them into an ape," Jack said.

"Into the fertilized egg of an ape," Kevin said. "A bonobo to be exact."

"And what you were really doing," Jack continued, "was custom-designing the perfect organ transplant source for a specific individual."

"Exactly," Kevin said. "It wasn't what I had in mind in the beginning. I was just a pure researcher. What I ended up doing was something I was lured into because of its economic potential."

"Wow!" Jack commented. "Ingenious and impressive, but also a little scary."

"It's more than scary," Kevin said. "It's a tragedy of sorts. The problem is I transferred too many human genes. I've accidently created a race of protohumans."

"You mean like Neanderthals?" Laurie asked.

"More primitive by millions of years," Kevin said. "More like Lucy. But they're intelligent enough to use fire, make tools, and even converse. I think they are the way we were four or five million years ago."

"Where are these creatures?" Laurie asked with alarm.

"They're on a nearby island," Kevin said, "where they have been living in comparative freedom. Unfortunately, that's all about to change."

"Why is that?" Laurie asked. In her mind's eye, she could see these protohumans. As a child she'd been fascinated by cavemen.

Kevin quickly told the story of the smoke eventually bringing him, Melanie, and Candace to the island. He related how they'd been captured and then rescued. He also told them about the creatures' fate of facing lifelong internment in tiny concrete cells purely because they were too human.

"That's awful," Laurie commented.

"It's a disaster!" Jack said with a shake of his head. "What a story!"

"This world isn't ready for a new race," Warren said. "We've got enough trouble with what we have already."

"We're coming up on the waterfront," Kevin announced. "The square at the base of the pier is around the next bend."

"Then stop here," Jack said. "There was a soldier there when we arrived."

Kevin pulled over to the side of the road and turned off the headlights. He kept the engine running for the air-conditioning. Jack and Warren got out the back and ran down to the corner. Carefully, they peeked around the bend.

"If our boat is not there, are there other boats around here?" Laurie asked.

"I'm afraid not," Kevin said.

"Is there another way out of town besides the main gate?" Laurie asked.

"That's it," Kevin said.

"Heaven help us," Laurie commented.

Jack and Warren came back quickly. Kevin lowered his window.

"There's a soldier," Jack said. "He's none too attentive. In fact, he might even be asleep. But we'll still have to deal with him. I think it best you all stay here."

"Fine by me," Kevin said. He was more than happy to leave such business up to others. If left to him, he wouldn't have had any idea what to do.

Jack and Warren returned to the corner and disappeared.

Kevin raised his window.

Laurie looked at Natalie and shook her head. "I'm sorry about all this. I suppose I should have known. Jack seems to have a penchant for finding trouble."

"No need to apologize," Natalie said. "It's certainly not your fault. Besides, things are looking a lot better than they did only fifteen or twenty minutes ago."

Jack and Warren reappeared in a surprisingly short time. Jack was holding a handgun, while Warren was carrying an assault rifle. They got into the back of the Toyota.

"Any problem?" Kevin asked.

"Nope," Jack said. "He was very accommodating. Of course, Warren can be very persuasive when he wants to be."

"Does the Chickee Hut Bar have a parking area?" Warren asked.

"It does," Kevin said.

"Drive there!" Warren said.

Kevin backed up, took a right and then the first left. At the end of the block he pulled into an expansive asphalt parking lot. The darkened Chickee Hut Bar was silhouetted ahead. Beyond the bar was the sparkling expanse of the broad estuary. Its surface shimmered in the moonlight.

Kevin drove directly up to the bar and stopped.

"You all wait here," Warren said. "I'll check on the boat." He climbed out with the assault rifle and quickly disappeared around the bar.

"He moves quickly," Melanie commented.

"You have no idea," Jack said.

"Is that Gabon on the other side of the water?" Laurie asked.

"It sure is," Melanie said.

"How far is it?" Jack asked.

"About four miles straight across," Kevin said. "But we should try to get to Cocobeach. That's about ten miles away. From there we can contact the American Embassy in Libreville who will certainly be able to help us."

"How long will it take to get to Cocobeach?" Laurie asked.

"I'd estimate a little more than an hour," Kevin said. "Of course, it depends on the speed of the boat."

Warren reappeared and came to the car. Kevin lowered his window again.

"We're cool," Warren said. "The boat's there. No problem."

"Hooray," everybody replied in unison. They piled out of the car. Kevin, Melanie, and Candace brought their canvas bags.

"Is that your luggage?" Laurie teased.

"This is it," Candace said.

Warren led the group into the darkened bar and around to where there were steps to the beach.

"Let's move quickly until we get behind the retaining wall," Warren said. He motioned for the others to precede him.

It was dark beneath the pier, and everyone had to move slowly. Along with the sound of the small waves lapping against the shore was the noise of large crabs scampering into their sand burrows.

"We've got a couple of flashlights," Kevin said. "Should we use them?"

"Let's not take the chance," Jack said as he literally bumped into the boat. He made sure it was reasonably stable before telling everyone to climb in and move to the stern. As soon as everyone had done so, Jack could feel the bow become lighter. Leaning against the boat, he began to push it out.

"Watch out for the crossbeams," Jack said as he jumped aboard.

Everyone helped by reaching for the wood piles and pulling the boat silently along. It took them only a few minutes to travel to the end of the pier which was blocked by the floating dock. At that point they angled the boat out into moonlit open water.

There were only four paddles. Besides the men, Melanie insisted on paddling.

"I want to get about a hundred yards away from the shore before I start the motor," Jack explained. "There's no sense taking any chances."

Everyone looked back at peaceful-appearing Cogo whose whitewashed buildings shrouded in mist glimmered in the silver moonlight. The surrounding jungle limned the town with midnight blue. The walls of vegetation were like tidal waves about to break.

The night sounds of the jungle fell astern. The only noise became the gurgle of the paddles passing through the water or their scraping along the side of the boat. For a time, no one spoke. Racing hearts slowed, and breathing tended toward normal. There was time to think and even look around. The newcomers in particular were captivated by the arresting beauty of the nocturnal African landscape. Its sheer size was overwhelming. Everything seemed bigger in Africa, even the night sky.

For Kevin it was different. His relief of having escaped Cogo and having helped others to do so as well only made his anguish about the fate of his chimeric bonobos that much more poignant. It had been a mistake to have created them, but abandoning them to a lifetime of captivity in a tiny cage compounded his guilt.

After a time, Jack picked up his oar and dropped it into the bottom of the boat. "Time to start the engine," he announced. He grasped the outboard and tilted it down into the water.

"Wait a second," Kevin said suddenly. "I have a request. Something I have no right to ask of you people, but it is important."

Jack straightened up from bending over the gas tank. "What's on your mind, sport?" he asked.

"See that island, the last one in the chain?" Kevin said while pointing toward Isla Francesca. "That's where all the bonobos are. They're in cages at the foot of a bridge to the mainland. I'd like nothing better than to go over there and release them."

"What would that accomplish?" Laurie asked.

"A lot if I could get them to cross the bridge," Kevin said.

"Wouldn't your Cogo friends just round them up again?" Jack asked.

"They'd never find them," Kevin said, warming to his idea. "They'd vanish. From this part of Equatorial Guinea and stretching for a thousand miles inland is mostly virginal rain forest. It encompasses not only this country but vast regions of Gabon, Cameroon, Congo, and Central African Republic. It's got to be a million square miles, parts of which are still literally unexplored."

"Just let them go by themselves?" Candace asked.

"That's exactly the point," Kevin said. "They'd have a chance, and I think they'd make it! They're resourceful. Look at our ancestors. They had to live through the Pleistocene ice age. That was more of a challenge than living in a rain forest."

Laurie looked at Jack. "I like the idea."

Jack glanced at the island, then asked which direction was Cocobeach.

"We'd be going out of our way," Kevin admitted, "but it's not far. Twenty minutes tops."

"What if you let them out and they stay on the island?" Warren said.

"At least I could tell myself I tried," Kevin said. "I feel that I have to do something."

"Hey, why not?" Jack said. "I think I like the idea too. What does everybody else say?"

"To tell you the truth, I'd like to see one of these animals," Warren said.

"Let's go," Candace said enthusiastically.

"Okay by me," Natalie said.

"I couldn't think of a better idea," Melanie said. "Let's do it!"

Jack gave the engine cord a few pulls. The outboard roared to life. Pushing over the helm, Jack steered toward Isla Francesca.

CHAPTER 23

MARCH 10, 1997
1:45 A.M.
COGO, EQUATORIAL GUINEA

Siegfried had dreamed the dream a hundred times, and each time it had gotten a little worse. In it, he was approaching a female elephant with a young calf. He didn't like doing it, but a client couple demanded it. It was the wife who wanted to see the baby up close.

Siegfried had sent trackers out laterally to protect the flank while he and the couple neared the mother. But the trackers to the north became terrified when a huge bull elephant appeared. They ran, and to compound their cowardice, they failed to warn Siegfried of the danger.

The sound of the enormous elephant charging through the underbrush was like the thunder of an oncoming train. Its shrieks built to a crescendo, and just before impact Siegfried woke up bathed in sweat.

Panting, Siegfried rolled over and sat up. Reaching through the mosquito netting, he found a glass of water and took a drink. The problem with his dream was that it was too real. This was the incident through which he'd lost the use of his right arm and had the skin of his face flayed open.

Siegfried sat on the edge of his bed for a few moments before he realized the shrieking he'd thought was from his dream was coming from outside his window. A moment later, he realized the source: loud West African rock music emanating from a cheap cassette player.

Siegfried looked at the clock. Seeing that it was close to two A.M., he became instantly incensed. Who could be so insolent to make such noise at that time in the morning?

Sensing the noise was coming across the green in front of his house, he got out of bed and stepped onto the veranda. To his surprise and dismay the music was coming from Kevin Marshall's. In fact, Siegfried could see who was responsible: It was the soldiers guarding the house.

Anger coursed through Siegfried's body like a bolt of electricity. Ducking back inside his bedroom, he called Cameron and ordered the security director to meet him over at Kevin's. Siegfried slammed the phone down. He pulled on his clothes. As he left the house he grabbed one of his old hunting carbines.

Siegfried walked directly across the green. The closer he got to Kevin's, the louder the music became. The soldiers were in a puddle of light beneath a bare light bulb. Sprinkled across the ground at their feet were numerous empty bottles of wine. Two of the soldiers were singing along with the music while playing imaginary instruments. The other two appeared to have passed out.

By the time Siegfried got to the scene, Cameron's car had careened down the cobblestone street and screeched to a halt. Cameron jumped out. He was still buttoning his shirt as he approached Siegfried. He glanced at the inebriated soldiers and was clearly appalled.

Cameron started to apologize when Siegfried cut him off. "Forget about explanations and excuses," he said. "Get upstairs and make sure Mr. Marshall and his two friends are tucked in for the night."

Cameron touched the tip of hat in faint salute. He disappeared up the stairs. Siegfried could hear him pounding on the door. A moment later, several lights went on in the living quarters.

Siegfried fumed as he watched the soldiers. They hadn't even noticed his presence or Cameron's.

Cameron came back looking pale and shaking his head. "They're not there."

Siegfried tried to control his anger enough to think. The level of incompetence with which he had to work was astounding.

"What about his LandCruiser?" Siegfried snapped.

"I'll check," Cameron said. He ran back, literally pushing his way through the singing soldiers. He returned almost instantly. "It's gone."

"What a surprise!" Siegfried said sarcastically. Then he snapped his fingers and motioned toward Cameron's car.

Siegfried got in the front seat while Cameron climbed in behind the wheel.

"Call and alert your security force," Siegfried ordered. "I want Kevin's car found immediately. And call the gate. Make sure it hasn't left the Zone. Meanwhile, take me to town hall."

Cameron used his car phone as he maneuvered his vehicle around the block. Both numbers were stored in his phone's autodialer so it was a hands-free operation. Stomping on the accelerator, he headed north.

By the time they neared the town hall, the official search for Kevin's car had been initiated. It was readily determined that the vehicle had not tried to go through the gate. As they turned into the parking lot both heard the music.

"Uh-oh!" Cameron said.

Siegfried stayed silent. He was trying to prepare himself for what he now suspected.

Cameron pulled to a halt at the building. His headlights picked up the debris that had resulted when the bar frames had been yanked out of the wall. The pile of chain was visible.

"This is a disaster," Siegfried said with a tremulous voice. He stepped out of the car with the carbine. Although he had to hold the gun with one hand, he was an accomplished marksman. In quick succession he pulled off three rounds and three of the empty wine bottles on the windowsill of the army post burst into shards of glass. But the music did not falter.

Gripping the gun tightly in his good hand, Siegfried went over to the army-post window and looked in. The cassette player was on the desk with its volume pegged at max. The four soldiers were passed out either on the floor or slouched in the rickety furniture.

Siegfried raised the gun. He pulled the trigger and the cassette player flew off the desk. In an instant, the scene was thrust into a painful silence.

Siegfried went back to Cameron. "Call the colonel of the garrison. Tell him what has happened. Tell him I want these men court-martialed. Tell him to get a contingent of soldiers here immediately with a vehicle."

"Yes, sir!" Cameron intoned.

Siegfried stepped beneath the arcade and looked at the bars that had been pulled from the jail-cell windows. They were hand forged. Looking at the openings, he could tell why they'd come out so easily. The mortar between the bricks under the stucco had turned to sand.

To get himself under control, Siegfried walked all the way around the town hall.

By the time he rounded the final corner, headlights were coming along the road. They turned into the parking lot. With screeching tires the security patrol car came to a halt next to Cameron's car, and the duty officer jumped out.

Siegfried cursed under his breath as he approached. With Kevin and the women plus the Americans missing, the bonobo project was in serious jeopardy. They had to be found.

"Mr. Spallek," Cameron said. "I have some information. Officer O'Leary thinks he saw Kevin Marshall's car ten minutes ago. Of course, we can quickly confirm it if it is still there."

"Where?" Siegfried asked.

"In the lot by the Chickee Hut Bar," O'Leary said. "I noticed it on my last tour."

"Did you see any people?"

"No, sir! Not a soul."

"There's supposed to be a guard down there," Siegfried said. "Did you see him?"

"Not really, sir," O'Leary said.

"What do you mean 'not really'?" Siegfried growled. He was fed up with incompetence.

"We don't make it a point to pay much attention to the soldiers," O'Leary said.

Siegfried looked off in the distance. In a further attempt to control his anger, he forced himself to notice how the moonlight reflected off the vegetation. The beauty calmed him to a degree, and he reluctantly admitted that he didn't pay much attention to the soldiers, either. Rather than serving any truly utilitarian purpose, they were just there; one of the costs of doing business with the Equatoguinean government. But why would Kevin's car be at the Chickee Hut Bar? Then it dawned on him.

"Cameron, was it determined how the Americans got into town?" Siegfried asked.

"I'm afraid not," Cameron said.

"Was a boat searched for?" Siegfried asked.

Cameron looked at O'Leary, who reluctantly replied. "I didn't know anything about looking for a boat."

"What about when you relieved Hansen at eleven?" Cameron asked. "When he briefed you, did he mention he'd looked for a boat?"

"Not a word, sir," O'Leary said.

Cameron swallowed. He turned to Siegfried. "I'll just have to follow up on this and get back to you later."

"In other words, no one looked for a goddamn boat!" Siegfried snapped. "This is a comedy around here, but I'm not laughing."

"I gave specific orders for a search for a boat," Cameron said.

"Obviously, orders are not enough, you lunkhead," Siegfried spat. "You are supposed to be in charge. You are responsible."

Siegfried closed his eyes and gritted his teeth. He'd lost both groups. All he could do at this point was have the colonel call the army post in Acalayong in the unlikely event the escapees might land there. But Siegfried was far from optimistic. He knew that if the tables were turned and he'd been the one fleeing, he'd go to Gabon.

All of a sudden, Siegfried's eyes popped open. Another thought occurred to him: a more worrisome thought.

"Is there a guard out at Isla Francesca?" he asked.

"No, sir. None was requested."

"What about at the bridge on the mainland?" Siegfried persisted.

"There was until you ordered it removed," Cameron said.

"Then, we're going right now," Siegfried said. He started for Cameron's car. As he did so, three vehicles sped down the street and turned into the parking lot. They were army jeeps. They swooped over to the two parked vehicles and stopped. All of them were filled with soldiers bristling with guns.

From the front jeep stepped Colonel Mongomo. In contrast to the slovenly soldiers, he was impeccably attired in his martial finery complete with medals. Despite the fact that it was night, he wore aviator sunglasses. He saluted Siegfried stiffly and said he was at his service.

"I'd be very appreciative if you took care of those drunk soldiers," Siegfried said in a controlled fashion, while pointing toward the post. "There's another group where Officer O'Leary can take you. And tell one of these jeeps full of soldiers to follow us. We may need their firepower."

Kevin motioned for Jack to slow down. Jack cut back on the throttle and the heavy pirogue quickly lost momentum. They had entered the narrow channel between Isla Francesca and the mainland. It was significantly darker than out in the open water because the trees on either side formed a canopy.

Kevin was worried about the rope for the feeding float and he'd positioned himself in the bow. He'd explained it to Jack so Jack was prepared.

"It's eerie in here," Laurie said.

"Listen to how loud the animals are," Natalie said.

"What you are hearing are mostly frogs," Melanie said. "Romantically inclined frogs."

"It's coming up just ahead," Kevin said.

Jack cut the engine then stood in order to tip the outboard out of the water.

There was a soft thud and a scraping noise as the boat passed over the rope.

"Let's paddle," Kevin said. "It's only a little way farther, and I wouldn't want to hit a log in the dark."

The dense jungle on the right fell away as they reached the staging area clearing. Once again they were in moonlight.

"Oh, no!" Kevin cried from the bow. "The bridge is not deployed. Damn!"

"That shouldn't be a problem," Melanie said. "I still have the key." She held it up, and it glinted in the low light. "I had a feeling it would come in handy someday."

"Oh, Melanie!" Kevin gushed. "You're wonderful. For a moment there, I thought all was lost."

"A deployable bridge that needs a key?" Jack questioned. "That's mighty sophisticated for out here in the jungle."

"There's a dock coming up on our right," Kevin said. "That's where we'll tie the boat up."

Jack was in the stern. He used his oar to back paddle so the bow turned toward the island. A few minutes later, they quietly bumped against wood planking.

"Okay, everybody," Kevin said. He took a breath. He was nervous. He knew he was out of character since he was about to to do something he'd never done before: be a hero of sorts. "Here's what I suggest. You all stay in the boat. At least for now. I really don't know how these animals are going to react to me. They're unbelievably strong, so there is a risk. I'm willing to take it for the reasons I've already talked about, but I don't want to put any of you in jeopardy. Is that reasonable?"

"It's reasonable, but I don't know if I agree," Jack said. "Seems to me you are going to need some help."

"Besides, with this AK-47 it's not as if we can't defend ourselves," Warren said.

"No shooting!" Kevin said. "Please. Particularly not for my benefit. That's why I want you all to stay here. If things go badly, just leave."

Melanie stood up. "I'm almost as responsible as you for these creatures' existence. I'm helping whether you like it or not, bucko."

Kevin made an expression of exasperation.

"No pouting," Melanie said. She climbed out of the boat onto the dock.

"Sounds like a party," Jack said. He stood up to follow Melanie's lead.

"You sit down!" Melanie said sternly. "At the moment, it's a private party."

Jack sat.

Kevin got out his flashlight and joined Melanie on the dock. "We'll work very quickly," he promised.

The first line of business was the bridge. Without it, the plan would fail no matter what the response was from the animals. Kevin put in the key. As he turned it on and pressed the green button, he held his breath. Almost immediately he heard the whine of a battery-driven electric motor from the mainland side. Then in slow motion the telescoping bridge extended across the dark river to make contact with the concrete stanchion on the island.

Kevin climbed up on it to make sure it was solidly seated. He tried to shake it but it was rigidly in place. Satisfied, he got down, and he and Melanie hiked in the direction of the forest. They couldn't see the cages because of the darkness of the shadows, but they knew where they were.

"Do you have any plan or are we just going to let them all out en masse?" Melanie asked as they walked across the field. Kevin had the flashlight on so they could see where they were stepping.

"The only idea that came to my mind was to find my double, bonobo number one," Kevin said. "Unlike me, he's a leader. If I can make him understand, maybe he'll take the others." Kevin shrugged. "Can you think of a better idea?"

"Not at the moment," Melanie said.

The cages were all lined up in a long row. The smell was rank since some of the animals had been in their tiny prisons for more than twenty-four hours. As Kevin and Melanie walked along, Kevin shined the light in each enclosure. The animals awoke immediately. Some backed against the rear wall, trying to shield themselves from the glare. Others stood their ground obstinately, their eyes flashing red.

"How are you going to recognize him?" Melanie asked.

"I wish I could count on seeing my watch," Kevin said. "But the chances of that are slim. I suppose it's up to recognizing that awful scar he has."

"It's rather ironic that he and Siegfried have almost the same scar," Melanie said.

"Don't even mention that man's name," Kevin said. "My gosh, look!" The light illuminated bonobo number one's frightfully scarred face. He stared back defiantly.

"It's him," Melanie cried.

"Bada," Kevin said. He patted his chest as the bonobo females had done when he, Melanie, and Candace had first been brought to the cave.

Bonobo number one tilted his head and the skin between his eye furrowed.

"Bada," Kevin repeated.

Slowly, the bonobo raised his hand and patted his chest. Then he said "bada" as clearly as Kevin had.

Kevin looked at Melanie. They were both shocked. Although they had tentatively conversed with Arthur, it had been in such a different context, they'd never been entirely sure they were actually communicating. This was different.

"Atah," Kevin said. It was a word they'd heard frequently starting from the moment bonobo number one had yelled it when they'd first encountered him. They thought it meant "come."

Bonobo number one didn't respond.

Kevin repeated the word then looked at Melanie. "I don't know what else to say."

"Neither do I," Melanie said. "Let's go for it and open the door. Maybe he'll respond then. I mean it is hard for him to 'come' when he's locked up."

"Good point," Jack said. He stepped around Melanie to reach back along the right side of the cage. With trepidation, Kevin released the latch and opened the door.

Kevin and Melanie stepped back. Kevin directed the flashlight toward the ground rather than shine it in the animal's face. Bonobo number one emerged slowly and stood up to his full height. He looked to his left and then to his right before redirecting his attention at the two humans.

"Atah," Kevin said again while backing up. Melanie stayed in step.

Bonobo number one started forward, stretching as he walked like an athlete warming up.

Kevin turned his body around so he could walk easier. He repeated "atah" several more times. The animal's facial expression didn't change as he followed.

Kevin led to the bridge and climbed up on it. He again repeated "atah."

Bonobo number one hesitantly climbed onto the concrete stanchion. Kevin backed up until he was standing in the middle of the span. The bonobo came out onto the bridge warily. He glanced frequently from side to side.

Kevin then tried something they'd not tested on Arthur. Kevin strung bonobo words together. He used "sta," from the episode when bonobo number one tried to give the dead monkey to Candace. He used "zit," which bonobo number one had used to get them to go to the cave. And finally he used "arak," which they were quite sure meant "away."

"Sta zit arak," Kevin said. He opened his fingers and swept his hand away from his chest, the gesture that Candace had described in the operating room. Kevin hoped his amalgamated sentence said: "You go away."

After repeating the phrase once again, Kevin pointed to the northeast in the direction of the limitless rain forest.

Bonobo number one rose up on the balls of his feet and looked over Kevin's shoulder at the dark wall of mainland jungle. He then looked back in the direction of the cages. Spreading his arms he vocalized a series of sounds Kevin and Melanie had not heard, or at least not associated with any specific activity.

"What's he doing?" Kevin asked. At that point the animal was facing away from him.

"I could be wrong," Melanie said, "but I think he's making reference to his people."

"My God!" Kevin said. "I think he might have understood my meaning. Let's let more of the animals out."

Kevin walked forward. The bonobo sensed his movement and turned to face him. Kevin hesitated. The bridge was about ten feet wide, and Kevin was concerned about coming too close. He remembered all too well how easy it had been for the bonobo to pick him up and throw him like a rag doll.

Kevin stared into the animal's face to try to see any emotion, but he couldn't. All he got was a repeat of the uncanny sensation that he was looking into an evolutionary mirror.

"What's the matter?" Melanie asked.

"He's scary," Kevin admitted. "I don't know whether to pass him or not."

"Please, not another Mexican standoff," Melanie said. "We don't have much time."

"Okay," Kevin said. He took a breath and inched around the animal while teetering on the edge. The bonobo watched him but didn't move.

"This is so nerve wracking!" Kevin complained when he climbed down from the bridge.

"Do we want him to stay here?" Melanie asked.

Kevin scratched his head. "I don't know. He might be a lure to get the others over here, but then again, maybe he should come back with us."

"Why don't we just start walking?" Melanie said. "We'll let him decide."

Melanie and Kevin set out for the animal cages. They were pleased when bonobo number one immediately climbed from the bridge and followed.

They walked quickly, conscious that Candace and the other people were waiting. When they got to the cages they didn't hesitate. Kevin opened the door on the first cage while Melanie did the second.

The animals emerged quickly and immediately exchanged words with bonobo number one. Kevin and Melanie went to the next two cages.

Within only a few minutes, there were a dozen animals milling about, vocalizing and stretching.

"It's working," Kevin said. "I'm sure of it. If they were just going to run off in the forest here on the island, they would have already done so. I think they all know they have to leave."

"Maybe I should get Candace and our new friends," Melanie said. "They should witness this, and they can help speed things up."

"Good idea," Kevin said. He looked at the long row of cages. He knew there were over seventy.

Melanie ran off into the night while Kevin went to the next cage. He noticed that bonobo number one stayed nearby to greet each newly freed animal.

By the time Kevin had released a half dozen more animals, the humans arrived. At first, they were intimidated by the creatures and didn't know how to act. The animals ignored them except for Warren whom they gave a wide berth. Warren had brought the assault rifle, which Kevin guessed reminded the animals of the dart gun.

"They are so quiet," Laurie said. "It's spooky."

"They're depressed," Kevin said. "It could be from the tranquilizer or from having been imprisoned. But don't go too close. They might be quiet, but they are very strong."

"What can we do to help?" Candace asked.

"Just open the cage doors," Kevin said.

With seven people working, it took only a few minutes to get all the cages open. As soon as the last animal had emerged into the night, Kevin motioned for everyone to start toward the bridge.

Bonobo number one, who'd been shadowing Kevin, clapped his hands loudly just as he'd done when Kevin and the women had first come upon him in the cul-de-sac of the marshy field. Then he vocalized raucously before starting after the humans. Immediately the rest of the bonobos quietly followed.

The seven humans led the seventy-one transgenic bonobos in a procession across the clearing to the bridge of their freedom. Arriving at the span, the humans stepped aside. Bonobo number one stopped at the concrete stanchion.

"Sta zit arak," Kevin repeated as he spread his fingers and swept his hand away from his chest for the final time. Then he pointed toward the unexplored African interior.

Bonobo number one bowed his head momentarily before leaping up on top of the stanchion. Looking out over his people, he vocalized for a final time before turning his back on Isla Francesca and crossing the bridge to the mainland. The mass of the bonobos silently followed.

"It's like watching the Exodus," Jack quipped.

"Don't be blasphemous," Laurie teased. But, as with all teasing, there was an element of truth. She was truly awed by the spectacle.

As if by magic the animals melted into the dark jungle without a sound. One minute they were a restive crowd milling about the base of the bridge; the next minute they were gone like water soaking into a sponge.

The humans didn't move or talk for a moment. Finally, Kevin broke the silence. "They did it, and I'm pleased," he said. "Thank you all for helping. Maybe now I can come to terms with what I did in creating them." He stepped up to the bridge and pressed the red button. With a whine, the bridge retracted.

The group turned away from the stanchion and began to trudge back to the pirogue.

"That was one of the strangest pageants I've ever seen," Jack said.

Halfway to the canoe, Melanie suddenly stopped and cried: "Oh, no! Look!"

Everyone's eyes darted across the river in the direction she was pointing. Headlight beams from several vehicles could be intermittently seen through the foliage. The vehicles were descending the track leading to the bridge mechanism.

"We can't get to the boat!" Warren blurted. "They'll see us."

"We can't stay here, either," Jack said.

"Back to the cages!" Kevin cried.

They all turned and ran toward the bulwark of the jungle. The moment they ducked behind the cages, the headlight beams swept across the clearing as the vehicles turned to the west. The vehicles stopped, but the headlights stayed on and the engines kept running.

"It's a group of Equatoguinean soldiers," Kevin said.

"And Siegfried," Melanie said. "I can recognize him anywhere. And that's Cameron McIvers's patrol car."

A searchlight snapped on. Its high-intensity light played along the row of cages then swept the bank of the river. It quickly found the canoe.

Even fifty yards away, they could hear excited voices responding to the discovery of the boat.

"This is not good," Jack said. "They know we're here."

A sudden and sustained burst of heavy gunfire shattered the tranquillity of the night.

"What on earth are they shooting at?" Laurie asked.

"I'm afraid they're destroying our boat," Jack said. "I suppose that's bad news for my deposit."

"This is no time for humor," Laurie complained.

An explosion rocked the night air, and a fireball briefly illuminated the soldiers. "That must have been the gas tank," Kevin said. "So much for our transportation."

A few minutes later, the searchlight went out. Then the first vehicle made a U-turn and disappeared back up the track leading to Cogo.

"Does anybody have an idea what's happening?" Jack asked.

"My guess is Siegfried and Cameron are going back to town," Melanie said. "Knowing we're on the island, they probably feel pretty confident."

The headlights on the second vehicle suddenly went out, thrusting the entire area into darkness. Even the moonlight was meager since the moon had sunk low in the western sky.

"I preferred it when we had some idea where they were and what they were doing," Warren said.

"How big is this island?" Jack asked.

"About six miles long and two wide," Kevin said. "But . . ."

"They're making a fire," Warren said, interrupting Kevin.

A dot of golden light illuminated part of the bridge mechanism, then flared up into a campfire. The ghostly figures of the soldiers could be seen moving in the periphery of the light.

"Isn't that nice," Jack said. "Looks like they're making themselves at home."

"What are we going to do?" Laurie questioned despairingly.

"We don't have a lot of choice with them sitting at the base of the bridge," Warren said. "I count six of them."

"Let's hope they're not planning on coming over here," Jack said.

"They won't come until dawn," Kevin said. "There's no way they'd come over here in the dark. Besides, there's no need. They don't expect us to be going anywhere."

"What about swimming across that channel?" Jack said. "It's only about thirty or forty feet wide and there's no current to speak of."

"I'm not a good swimmer," Warren said nervously. "I told you that."

"This whole area is also infested with crocodiles," Kevin said.

"Oh, God!" Laurie said. "Now he tells us."

"But, listen! We don't have to swim," Kevin said. "At least, I don't think so. The boat that Melanie, Candace, and I used to get here is most likely where we left it, and it's big enough for all of us."

"Fantastic!" Jack said. "Where is it?"

"I'm afraid it's going to require a little hike," Kevin said. "It's a little more than a mile, but at least there's a freshly cleared trail."

"Sounds like a walk in the park," Jack said.

"What time is it?" Kevin asked.

"Three-twenty," Warren said.

"Then we only have approximately an hour and a half before daylight," Kevin said. "We'd better start now."

What Jack had facetiously labeled a walk in the park turned out to be one of the most harrowing experiences that any of them had ever had. Unwilling to use the flashlights for the first two to three hundred yards, they had proceeded by a process that could only be termed the blind leading the blind. The interior of the jungle had been entirely devoid of light. It was so utterly dark it had been difficult for anyone to even know whether their eyes were open or not.

Kevin had gone first to feel his way along the ground, making frequent wrong choices that required backtracking to find the trail. Knowing what kind of creatures inhabited the forest, Kevin held his breath each time he extended his hand or his foot into the blackness.

Behind Kevin, the others had aligned themselves in snakelike single file, each holding on to the unseen figure ahead. Jack had tried to make light of the situation, but after a time even his usually resourceful flippancy failed him. From then on, they were all victims of their own fears as the noctural creatures chattered, chirped, bellowed, twittered, and occasionally screamed around them.

When they finally deemed it safe to use the flashlights, they made better progress. At the same time, they shuddered when they saw the number of snakes and insects that they encountered, knowing that prior to the use of the flashlights they had been passing these same creatures unawares.

By the time they reached the marshy fields around Lago Hippo, the eastern horizon was faintly beginning to lighten. Leaving the darkness of the forest, they mistakenly believed the worst was behind them. But it wasn't the case. The hippo-potami were all out of the water grazing. The animals looked enormous in the predawn twilight.

"They may not look it but they are very dangerous," Kevin warned. "More humans are killed by them than you'd think."

The group took a circuitous route to give the hippopotami wide berth. But as they neared the reeds where they hoped the small canoe was still hidden, they had to pass close by two particularly large hippos. The animals seemed to regard them sleepily until without warning they charged.

Luckily, they charged for the lake with a huge amount of commotion and crashing noise. Each multi-ton animal created a new wide trail through the reeds to the water. For a moment, everyone's heart fluttered in his chest.

It took a few minutes for everyone to recover before pushing on. The sky was now progressively brightening, and they knew they had no time to lose. The short hike had taken much more time than they had anticipated.

"Thank God it's still here," Kevin said when he separated the reeds and found the small canoe. Even the Styrofoam food chest was still in place.

But reaching the canoe posed another problem. It was quickly decided the boat was too small and too dangerous to carry seven people. After a difficult discussion, it was decided that Jack and Warren would stay in the reeds to wait for Kevin to bring the small canoe back.

Waiting was hell. Not only did the sky continue to get lighter and lighter, pre-saging imminent dawn and the possible appearance of the soldiers, but there was always the worry that the motorized canoe had disappeared. Jack and Warren ner-vously alternated between looking at each other and their watches, while fighting off clouds of insatiable insects. And on top of everything else, their exhaustion was total.

Just when they were thinking that something terrible had happened to the others, Kevin appeared at the edge of the reeds like a mirage and silently paddled in.

Warren scrambled into the canoe followed by Jack.

"The power boat's okay?" Jack asked anxiously.

"At least it was there," Kevin said. "I didn't try to start the engine."

They backed out of the reeds and started for the Rio Diviso. Unfortunately, there were lots of hippos and even a few crocodiles forcing them to paddle twice the usual distance just to keep clear.

Before they slipped into the foliage hiding the mouth of the jungle-lined river they caught a glimpse of some soldiers entering the clearing in the distance.

"Do you think they saw us?" Jack asked from his position in the bow.

"There's no way to know," Kevin said.

"We're getting out of here by the skin of our teeth," Jack said.

The waiting was as hard on the women as it had been on Jack and Warren. When the small canoe pulled alongside, there were literal tears of relief.

The final worry was the outboard motor. Jack agreed to attend to it because of his experience with similar engines as a teenager. While he checked it over, the others paddled the heavy canoe out of the reeds into the open water.

Jack pumped the gas, then with a little prayer, pulled the cord.

The engine sputtered and caught. It was loud in the morning stillness. Jack looked at Laurie. She smiled and gave him the thumbs-up sign.

Jack put the motor in gear, gave it a full throttle, and steered directly south, where they could see Gabon as a line of green along the horizon.

EPILOGUE

MARCH 18, 1997
3:45 P.M.
NEW YORK CITY

Lou Soldano glanced at his watch as he flashed his police badge to get him into the Customs area of the international arrivals building at Kennedy Airport. He'd hit more traffic than he'd expected in the midtown tunnel, and hoped he was not too late to greet the returning world travelers.

Going up to one of the skycaps, he asked which carousel was Air France.

"Way down the end, brother," the skycap said with a wave of his hand.

Just my luck, thought Lou as he broke into a slow jog. After a short distance he slowed, and for the one millionth time vowed to stop smoking.

As he got closer, it was easy to see which carousel he was looking for. Air France in block letters showed on a monitor. Around it, the people were four deep.

Lou made a half circuit before seeing the group. Even though they were facing away, he could recognize Laurie's hair.

He insinuated himself between other passengers and gave Laurie's arm a squeeze. She turned around indignantly but quickly recognized him. Then she gave him a hug so fierce, his face turned red.

"Okay, okay, I give up," Lou managed. He laughed.

Laurie let him go so that he could give Jack and Warren a handshake. Lou gave Natalie a peck on the cheek.

"So, you guys have a good trip, or what?" Lou questioned. It was apparent he was all keyed up.

Jack shrugged and looked at Laurie. "It was okay," he said noncommittally.

"Yeah, it was okay," Laurie agreed. "The trouble was nothing happened."

"Really?" Lou said. "I'm surprised. You know, being Africa and all. I haven't been there, but I've heard."

"What have you heard, man?" Warren asked.

"Well, there's lots of animals," Lou said.

"Is that it?" Natalie asked.

Lou shrugged embarrassingly. "I guess. Animals and the Ebola virus. But like I said, I've never been there."

Jack laughed, and when he did, so did all the others.

"What's going on here?" Lou said. "Are you guys pulling my leg?"

"I'm afraid so," Laurie said. "We had a fabulous trip! The first part was a little harrowing, but we managed to survive that, and once we got to Gabon, we had a ball."

"Did you see any animals?" Lou asked.

"More than you could imagine," Laurie said.

"There, see, that's what everybody says," Lou remarked. "Maybe someday I'll go over there myself."

The luggage came, and they hoisted it onto their shoulders. They breezed through Customs and passed through the terminal. Lou's unmarked car was at the curb.

"One of the few perks," he explained.

They put the luggage in the trunk, and climbed in. Laurie sat next to Lou. Lou drove out of the airport, and they were immediately bogged down in traffic.

"How about you?" Laurie asked. "Have you been making any headway back here?"

"I was afraid you weren't going to ask," Lou said. "Things have been going down like you wouldn't believe. It was that Spoletto Funeral Home that was the gold mine. Right now, everybody is lining up to plea-bargain. I even got an indictment on Vinnie Dominick."

"That's fantastic," Laurie said. "What about that awful pig, Angelo Facciolo?"

"He's still in the slammer," Lou said. "We have him nailed on stealing Franconi's body. I know it's not much, but remember Al Capone was reeled in on tax evasion."

"What about the mole in the medical examiner's office?" Laurie said.

"Solved," Lou said. "In fact, that's how we have Angelo nailed. Vinnie Amendola has agreed to testify."

"So, it was Vinnie!" Laurie said with a mixture of vindication and regret.

"No wonder he's been acting so weird," Jack said from the backseat.

"There was one unexpected twist," Lou said. "There was someone else mixed up in all this who has taken us by surprise. He's apparently out of the country at the moment. When he comes back into the country, he's going to be arrested for murder of a teenager by the name of Cindy Carlson over in Jersey. We believe Franco Ponti and Angelo Facciolo did the actual killing, but it was at this guy's behest. His name is Dr. Raymond Lyons. Do either of you guys know him?"

"Never heard of him," Jack said.

"Nor I," Laurie said.

"Well, he had something to do with that organ transplant stuff you people were so interested in," Lou said. "But later for that. Right now I'd like to hear about the first part of your trip: the harrowing part."

"For that you'll have to buy us dinner," Laurie said. "It's kind of a long story."

GLOSSARY

BONOBO: An anthropoid ape classified as a species in 1933. Related to chimpanzees, they occasionally walk upright and are found only in a localized area of Zaire. The estimated population is less than twenty thousand.

CENTROMERE: A specialized portion of a chromosome that plays an important role in the reduplication of the chromosome during cellular division.

CHIMERA: A combination of a lion, a goat, and a serpent in Greek mythology. In literature, a chimera is a creation of the imagination: an impossible mixture. In biology, a chimera is an organism that contains genetically distinct cell types. In genetics, a chimera is an entity containing a mixture of DNA from different sources.

CHROMOSOME: An elongated structure in the nucleus of a cell that contains DNA. In humans and anthropoid apes, there are twenty-three pairs of chromosomes for a total of forty-six.

CICATRIX: A scar.

CROSSING OVER: The exchange of parts of chromosomes between chromosome pairs during meiosis.

DNA: The acronym for deoxyribonucleic acid, which encodes genetic information.

ENDOTHELIALIZATION: The healing of the inner surface of blood vessels by the cells that cover such surfaces.

FORENSIC PATHOLOGY: A branch of pathology that relates pathological science with civil and criminal law.

GENE: A functional unit of heredity that is composed of a sequence of DNA located at a specific locus or place on the chromosome.

GENOME: The complete complement of genes of an organism. In humans, the genome contains approximately one hundred thousand genes.

GRANULOMA: A growth of a mixture of specialized cells as a result of chronic inflammation.

HISTOCOMPATIBILITY: A state when two or more organisms can share organs or tissue (e.g., identical twins).

HOMOLOGOUS CHROMOSOME: Chromosomes that are similar with respect to their genes and visible structure: e.g., each chromosome of a chromosome pair.

HOMOLOGOUS TRANSPOSITION: The exchange of corresponding portions of DNA between homologous chromosomes.

LYMPHOKINE: An immunologically active hormone produced by certain immune cells called lymphocytes.

MEIOSIS: A special type of cellular division that occurs during the creation of sex cells (eggs and sperm), resulting in each sex cell having half the usual number of chromosomes. In humans, each sex cell has twenty-three chromosomes.

MEROZOITE: A stage in the life cycle of some parasites that enables the organism to disperse and infect additional cells within the host.

MITOCHONDRIA: Self-replicating entities in cells that produce energy.

MITOCHONDRIAL DNA: DNA necessary for mitochondrial replication. It is inherited only through the maternal line.

PARASITE: An organism that lives on or in another organism (or host). A parasite does not help the host; in fact, it typically harms the host.

PARASITOLOGY: A branch of biology dealing with parasites.

PATHOLOGY: A branch of medical science involving the cause, the process, the anatomic effects, and the consequence of disease.

RECOMBINANT DNA: A composite molecule of DNA that has been formed in the laboratory with DNA from separate sources.

RECOMBINANT DNA TECHNOLOGY: The applied science of separating, producing, and recombining segments of DNA or genes.

RIBOSOMAL PROTEINS: The proteins that form a ribosome. The DNA that codes for these proteins is species specific and is used to identify the species of tissue (e.g., to determine if blood is human blood or blood of a particular species of animal).

RIBOSOME: A cellular entity responsible for manufacturing all cellular protein.

TRANSGENIC: An organism whose genome contains one or more genes from another species (e.g., pigs containing human genes to facilitate human reception of pig heart valves).

VACCINE: A substance given to an individual to produce resistance to disease or infection.

XENOGRAFT: An organ or tissue taken from one species and transplanted into another species. Generally, a xenograft refers to an animal organ or tissue that is transplanted into a human (e.g., a pig heart valve).

INVASION

PROLOGUE

In the frigid vastness of interstellar space a pinpoint of matter–antimatter fluctuated from the void, creating an intense flash of electromagnetic radiation. To the human retina, the phenomena would have appeared as the sudden emergence and expansion of a blip of colors representing the full spectrum of visual light. Of course, the gamma rays, the X rays, and even the infrared and radio waves would not have been visible to a human's limited vision.

Simultaneous with the burst of colors, the human witness would have seen the emergence of an astronomical number of atoms in the form of a rotating, black disciform concretion. The phenomenon would have appeared like a video run in reverse of the object falling into a crystalline pool of fluid whose ripples were the warping of space and time.

Still traveling at nearly the speed of light, the huge number of coalesced atoms rocketed into the distant reaches of the solar system, streaking past the orbits of the bloated outer gaseous planets of Neptune, Uranus, Saturn, and Jupiter. By the time the concretion reached the orbit of Mars its rotation and velocity had slowed significantly.

The object could now be seen for what it was: an intergalactic spaceship whose gleaming outer surface looked like highly polished onyx. The only deformity of its disciform shape was a series of bulges along the top surface of its outer edge. The contours of each of these bulges mirrored the silhouette of the massive mother ship. There were no other distortions of the outer skin: no portholes or exhaust vents or antennae. There weren't even any structural seams.

Streaking into the outer fringes of the earth's atmosphere, the outside temperature of the space ship soared. A burning tail appeared to light up the night sky behind the ship as the heat-excited atmospheric atoms gave off photons in protest.

The ship continued to slow both in terms of rotation and velocity. Far below, the twinkling lights of an unsuspecting city appeared. The preprogrammed ship ignored the lights; it was by luck that the impact occurred in a rocky, boulder-strewn, arid landscape. Despite the relatively slow speed it was more of a controlled crash than a landing, sending rock, sand, and dust billowing into the air. When the craft finally came to a stop, it was half buried in earth. Debris sent skyward in the impact rained down on its polished topside.

After the surface temperature had fallen below two hundred degrees centigrade, a vertical slitlike opening appeared along the ship's outer edge. It was not like a mechanical door. It was as if the molecules themselves worked in concert to create the penetration of the ship's seamless exterior.

Vapor escaped through the slit, evidence that the interior of the craft was deep-space frigid. Inside, banks of computers busily ran automatic sequences. Samples of the earth's atmosphere and soil were hauled inside to be analyzed. These automated procedures functioned as planned, including the isolation of prokaryotic life forms (bacteria) from the dirt. Analysis of all the samples, including the DNA contained therein, confirmed that the proper destination had been reached. The arming sequence was then initiated. Meanwhile, an antenna was extended up into the night sky to prepare for quasar frequency transmission to announce that Magnum had arrived.

CHAPTER 1

10:15 P.M.

"Hey, hello!" Candee Taylor said as she tapped Jonathan Sellers on the shoulder. At the moment Jonathan was busily kissing her neck. "Earth to Jonathan, come in please!" Candee added while she began rapping on Jonathan's head with her knuckles.

Both Candee and Jonathan were seventeen and juniors at Anna C. Scott High School. Jonathan had recently gotten his driver's license, and although he was not yet permitted to use the family car, he'd been able to borrow Tim Appleton's VW. Despite it being a school night, Candee and Jonathan had managed to sneak out and drive up to the bluff overlooking the city. Each had eagerly anticipated this first visit to the school's favorite "lover's lane." To help set the mood, as if they'd needed any help, the radio was tuned to KNGA, home of nonstop top forty hits.

"What's the matter?" Jonathan questioned while probing the tender spot on the top of his head. Candee had had to hit him pretty hard to divert his attention. Jonathan was tall for his age and thin. His adolescent growth spurt had been all vertical, much to his basketball coach's delight.

"I wanted you to see the shooting star." As a gymnast, Candee was significantly more physically developed than Jonathan. Her body was the source of the admiration of the boys and the envy of the girls. She could have dated almost anyone, but she chose Jonathan because of a combination of his cuddly good looks and his interest in and abilities with computers. Computers happened to be one of her interests as well.

"So what's the big deal about a shooting star?" Jonathan whined. He glanced up at the stars but quickly returned his gaze to Candee. He couldn't be sure of it, but he thought that one of the buttons of her blouse that had been buttoned when they'd arrived was now mysteriously unbuttoned.

"It went all the way across the sky," Candee said. She traced her index finger across the windshield for emphasis. "It was awesome!"

In the half-light of the car's interior, Jonathan could just make out the imperceptible rise and fall of Candee's breasts with her breathing. He found that more awesome than any stars. He was about to lean over and try to kiss her when the radio seemingly self-destructed.

First the volume jumped to an ear-splitting level, followed instantly by a loud popping and hissing noise. Sparks leaped out of the dashboard and smoke billowed up.

"Shit!" Jonathan and Candee screeched in unison as they reflexively tried to push themselves away from the sparking receiver. Both leaped from the car. From the safety of the exterior they peered back inside, half expecting to see flames. Instead the sparking stopped as abruptly as it had started. Straightening up, they eyed each other across the top of the car.

"What the hell am I going to tell Tim?" Jonathan moaned.

"Look at the antenna!" Candee said.

Even in the darkness Jonathan could see that its tip was blackened.

Candee reached out and touched it. "Ouch!" she exclaimed. "It's hot."

Hearing a babble of voices, Jonathan and Candee looked around them. Other kids had gotten out of their cars as well. A pall of acrid smoke hung over the scene. Every radio that had been on, whether playing rap music, rock, or classical, had blown its fuse. At least that's what everybody was saying.

10:15 P.M.

Dr. Sheila Miller lived in one of the city's few residential high-rises. She liked the view, the breezes from the desert, and the proximity to the University Medical Center. Of the three, the last was the most important.

At age thirty-five, she felt as if she'd been through two lives. She married early in college to a fellow premed student. They'd had so much in common. Both thought that medicine was to be their consuming interest and that they should share the dream. Unfortunately, reality had been brutally unromantic because of their arduous schedules. Still, their relationship might have survived if George hadn't had the irritating idea that his career as a surgeon was more valuable than Sheila's path, first in internal medicine and then in emergency medicine. As far as domestic responsibility was concerned, it had all fallen on her shoulders.

George's undiscussed decision to accept a two-year fellowship in New York had been the straw that broke the camel's back. The idea that George expected her to follow him to New York when she'd recently accepted the position of head of the University Medical Center emergency department showed Sheila how mismatched they were. What romance had once been between them had long since evaporated, so with little argument and no passion they divided up their collection of CDs and back issues of medical journals and went their separate ways. As far as Sheila was concerned, the only legacy was a mild bitterness about assumed male prerogatives.

On that particular night like most nights Sheila was busy reading her unending pile of medical journals. At the same time she was taping a TV presentation of an old movie classic with the idea of watching it over the weekend. Consequently her apartment was quiet save for the occasional tinkle of her wind chimes on her patio.

Sheila did not see the shooting star that Candee saw, but at the same moment

Candee and Jonathan were startled by the destruction of Tim's car radio, Sheila was equally shocked by a somewhat similar catastrophe with her VCR. Suddenly it began to spark and whir as if it were about to launch into orbit.

Startled from the depths of concentration, Sheila still had the presence of mind to yank out the power cord. Unfortunately that maneuver had little effect. It wasn't until she disengaged the cable line that the machine fell silent although it continued to smoke. Gingerly Sheila felt the top of the console. It was warm to the touch but certainly not about to catch fire.

Silently cursing, Sheila went back to her reading. She vaguely toyed with the idea of bringing the VCR to the hospital the following day to see if one of the electronic technicians could fix it. She justified the idea with her busy schedule. There was no way she could take the time to schlep the thing to the appliance store where she'd bought it.

10:15 P.M.

Pitt Henderson had been slowly easing himself down so that he was now practically horizontal. He was sprawled on the threadbare couch squeezed into his third-floor dorm room on campus in front of his black-and-white thirteen-inch TV. His parents had given him the set on his previous birthday. The screen might have been tiny, but the reception was good, and the image was clear as a bell.

Pitt was a senior at the university and scheduled to graduate that year. He was premed and had majored in chemistry. Although he'd been only a slightly above average student, he'd been able to snare a position in the medical school by evidencing hard work and commitment. He was the only chemistry major who had opted for the work-study program and had been working in the University Medical Center since his freshman year, mostly in the labs. Currently he was on a work rotation and clerking in the emergency department. Over the years Pitt had developed a habit of making himself useful wherever in the hospital he was assigned.

A huge yawn brought tears to his eyes and the NBA game he was watching began to fade as his mind began to drift toward sleep. Pitt was a stocky, muscular twenty-one-year-old who'd been a star football player in high school but had failed to make the team in college. He'd weathered the disappointment and turned it into a positive experience by concentrating that much more on his goal of becoming a doctor.

Just when Pitt's eyelids touched, the picture tube of his beloved TV blew up, scattering shards of glass over his abdomen and chest. It had been at the same instant that Candee and Jonathan's radio as well as Sheila's VCR had gone crazy.

For a second Pitt didn't move. He was stunned and confused, unsure if the disturbance that had shocked him awake had been external or internal, like one of the jerks he'd get on occasion just before falling asleep. After pushing his glasses up on the bridge of his nose and finding himself staring into the depths of a burned-out cathode ray tube, he knew that he'd not been dreaming.

"Holy crap!" he remarked as he heaved himself to his feet and gingerly brushed the thin shards of glass from his lap. Out in the hall he heard multiple doors creaking against their hinges.

Stepping out into the hall, Pitt glanced up and down the corridor. A number of students in all manner of dress, male and female, were looking at each other with dazed expressions.

"My computer just blew a fuse," John Barkly said. "I was on the Internet." John lived in the room right next to Pitt's.

"My freakin' TV exploded," announced another student.

"My Bose clock-radio practically caught fire," said another student. "What the hell's going on? Is this some sort of prank?"

Pitt closed his door and eyed the sad remains of his beloved TV. Some prank, he mused. If he caught the guy responsible, he'd beat the crap out of him . . .

CHAPTER 2

7:30 A.M.

Pulling off Main Street into Costa's 24-hour Diner, the right rear tire of Beau Stark's black Toyota 4Runner hit the curb and the vehicle bounced. Sitting in the front passenger seat, Cassy Winthrope's head bumped against the passenger-side window. She wasn't hurt, but the jolt had been unexpected. Luckily she had her seat belt on.

"My God!" Cassy exclaimed. "Where'd you learn to drive, Kmart?"

"Very funny," Beau said sheepishly. "I turned a little too soon, okay?"

"You should let me drive if you're preoccupied," Cassy said.

Beau drove across the crowded gravel parking lot and pulled to a stop in a slot in front of the diner. "How do you know I'm preoccupied?" he asked. He pulled on the brake and killed the engine.

"When you live with someone you begin to read all sorts of little clues," Cassy said as she undid her seat belt and alighted from the car. "Especially someone you're engaged to."

Beau did the same, but as his foot made contact with the ground, it slipped on a rock. He grabbed onto the open door to keep from falling.

"That settles it," Cassy said, having caught Beau's latest sign of inattentiveness and temporary lack of coordination. "After breakfast, I'm driving."

"I can drive fine," Beau said irritably as he slammed the car door and locked the car with his remote. He met up with Cassy at the rear of the car and they trudged toward the diner's entrance.

"Sure, just like you can shave fine," Cassy said.

Beau had a small forest of tissue paper plastered to the various nicks and cuts he'd inflicted on himself that morning.

"And pour coffee," Cassy added. Earlier Beau had dropped the pot of coffee and broken one of their mugs in the process.

"Well, maybe I am a little preoccupied," Beau reluctantly admitted.

Beau and Cassy had been living together for the last eight months. They were both twenty-one and seniors, like Pitt. They'd known of each other from their freshman year, but had never dated, each certain that the other was always involved with someone else. When they'd finally been brought together inadvertently by their mutual friend, Pitt, who'd been casually dating Cassy at the time, they'd clicked as if their relationship were meant to be.

Most people thought they resembled each other and could almost be brother and sister. Both had thick, dark brown hair, flawless olive-complected skin, and shockingly crystalline blue eyes. Both were also athletically inclined and frequently worked out together. Some people had joked that they were a brunette version of Ken and Barbie.

"Do you really think that you are going to hear from the Nite people?" Cassy asked as Beau held the door open for her. "I mean, Cipher is only the largest software company in the world. I think you are just setting yourself up for big-time rejection."

"No question that they'll call," Beau said confidently, entering the restaurant behind Cassy. "After the resume I sent, they'll be calling any minute." He pulled aside his Cerruti jacket to flash the tip of his cellular phone stuck in his inner pocket.

Beau's snappy attire that morning was no accident. He made it a point to dress nattily every day. It was his feeling that looking successful bred success. Luckily, his professional parents were able and willing to indulge his inclinations. To his credit he was a hard worker, studied diligently, and got outstanding grades. Confidence was not something he lacked.

"Hey, guys!" Pitt called from a booth beneath the front windows. "Over here!"

Cassy waved and wormed her way through the crowd. Costa's Diner, affectionately labeled the "greasy spoon," was a popular university hangout, especially for breakfast. Cassy slid into the seat across from Pitt. Beau did likewise.

"Did you have any trouble with your TV or radio last night?" Pitt asked excitedly before any hellos were exchanged. "Did you have anything turned on around ten-fifteen?"

Cassy made an expression of exaggerated disdain.

"Unlike other people," Beau said with feigned haughtiness, "we study on school nights."

Pitt unceremoniously bounced a piece of wadded-up napkin off Beau's forehead. He'd been nervously toying with the paper while waiting for Beau and Cassy to arrive.

"For those of you nerds who have no idea of what's going on in the real world, last night at quarter past ten a whole shitload of radios and TVs were knocked out all over the city," Pitt said. "Mine included. Some people think it was a prank by some guys in the physics department, and I'll tell you, I'm steamed."

"It would be nice if it happened over the entire country," Beau said. "Within a week of no TV the national average IQ would probably go up."

"Orange juice for everyone?" Marjorie the waitress asked. She'd appeared at the tableside. Before anyone could answer she began pouring. It was all part of the normal morning ritual. Then Marjorie took their orders and barked them in Greek over the counter to the two short-order cooks.

While everyone was enjoying their juice, Beau's cellular phone's muted ring could be heard under the fabric of his jacket. In his haste to get to it, he knocked over his juice glass. Pitt had to react instinctively to avoid a lap full of OJ.

Cassy shook her head captiously as she pulled out a half-dozen napkins from the holder and blotted up the spilled juice. She rolled her eyes for Pitt's benefit and mentioned that Beau had been pulling off equivalent stunts all morning.

Beau's expression brightened when he realized his hopes had been answered: the call was coming from Randy Nite's organization. He even made certain to pronounce the name, Cipher, very clearly for Cassy's benefit.

Cassy explained to Pitt that Beau was looking for employment with the Pope.

"I'd be happy to come for an interview," Beau was saying with studied calmness. "It would be my pleasure indeed. Whenever Mr. Nite would like to see me, I'd be happy to fly east. As I indicated in my cover letter, I'll be graduating next month, and I'd be available to begin work . . . well, really any time thereafter."

" 'Thereafter!' " Cassy sputtered. She choked on her orange juice.

"Yeah," Pitt chimed in. "Where'd that word come from? That doesn't sound like the Beau I've learned to love."

Beau waved them off and shot them a dirty look. "That's correct," he said into the phone. "What I'm looking for is some permutation of the role of personal assistant to Mr. Nite."

"Permutation?" Cassy questioned, suppressing a laugh.

"What I like is the muted but fake English accent," Pitt said. "Maybe Beau should go into acting and forget computers."

"He is a rather good actor," Cassy said, tickling his ear. "This morning he was pretending to be a klutz."

Beau batted away her hand. "Yes, that would be fine," he said into the phone. "I'll make arrangements to be there. Please tell Mr. Nite I look forward to meeting him with great alacrity."

" 'Alacrity'?" Pitt voiced, pretending to gag himself with his index finger.

Beau pressed the end button and flipped his cellular phone closed. He glared at both Cassy and Pitt. "You guys are like really mature. That was possibly the most important call in my life, and you're clowning around."

" 'Like really mature'! That sounds more like the Beau I know," Cassy said.

"Yeah, who was that other guy talking on the phone?" Pitt asked.

"He's the guy who's going to be working for Cipher come June," Beau said. "Mark my word. After that, who knows? While you, my friend, are going to be wasting another four years in medical school."

Pitt laughed out loud. "Waste four years in medical school?" he questioned. "Now that's a curious, albeit twisted perspective."

Cassy slid over next to Beau and started to nibble at his earlobe.

Beau pushed her away. "Jeez, Cass, there are professors in here that I know, people who might be writing me letters of recommendation."

"Oh, don't be so uptight," Cassy said. "We're just teasing you 'cause you're so wired. Actually I'm amazed Cipher called you. It's quite a coup. I'd imagine they'd get lots of job inquiries."

"It's going to be even more of a coup when Randy Nite offers me a job," Beau said. "The experience would be mindboggling. It's a dream job. The man is worth billions."

"It would also be demanding," Cassy said wistfully. "Probably twenty-five hours a day, eight days a week, fourteen months a year. That doesn't leave much time for us, especially if I'll be teaching here."

"It's merely a way to get a jump on a career," Beau said. "I want to do well for us so that we can really enjoy our lives."

Pitt pretended to gag himself again and pleaded with his breakfast companions not to make him sick with mushy romantic stuff.

Once the food came, the threesome ate quickly. They all involuntarily glanced at their respective watches. They didn't have that much time.

"Anybody up for a movie tonight?" Cassy said as she drained her coffee. "I've got an exam today and I deserve a little relaxation."

"Not me, Pumpkin," Beau said. "I got a paper due in a couple of days." He turned and tried to get Marjorie's attention to get the check.

"How about you?" Cassy asked Pitt.

"Sorry," Pitt said. "I'm doing a double shift at the medical center."

"What about Jennifer?" Cassy asked. "I could give her a call."

"Well, that's up to you," Pitt said. "But don't do it on my account. Jennifer and I are on the outs."

"I'm sorry," Cassy said with feeling. "I thought you two guys were a great couple."

"So did I," Pitt said. "Unfortunately she seems to have found someone more to her liking."

For a moment Cassy's and Pitt's eyes held, then they both looked off, feeling a twinge of embarrassment and a mild sense of déjà vu.

Beau got the check and smoothed it out on the table. Despite all three having had various college math courses, it took them five minutes to figure out how much each owed once a reasonable tip had been added.

"You want a ride to the med center?" Beau asked Pitt as they pushed out into the morning sunshine.

"I suppose," Pitt said ambivalently. He was feeling a little depressed. The problem was that he still harbored romantic feelings toward Cassy despite the fact that she had spurned him and Beau was his best friend. He and Beau had known each other since elementary school.

Pitt was a few steps behind his friends. His inclination was to go around to the passenger side of Beau's car to hold the door for Cassy, but he didn't want to make

Beau look bad. Instead he followed Beau and was about to climb into the backseat when Beau put his arm on his shoulder.

"What the hell is that?" Beau asked.

Pitt followed Beau's line of sight. Stuck in the dirt directly in front of the driver's door was a curious, round black object about the size of a silver dollar. It was symmetrically domed, smooth, and in the sunlight it had a dull finish that made it difficult to tell if it were metal or stone.

"I must have stepped on the damn thing when I got out of the car," Beau said. The indentation of a smudged footprint clearly angled off to one side from the object's rounded peak. "I wondered why I slipped."

"Do you think it dropped out from under your car?" Pitt asked.

"It's weird-looking," Beau said. He bent down and, with the side of his hand, brushed away some of the sand from the partially buried curiosity. When he did so he could see eight minute little domes symmetrically arrayed around the object's edge.

"Hey, come on, you guys!" Cassy called from inside the car. "I got to get to my student teaching assignment. I'm already late as it is."

"Just a sec," Beau answered. Then to Pitt he asked: "Any ideas what it is?"

"Not a clue," Pitt admitted. "Let's see if your car starts."

"It's not from my car, you lunkhead," Beau said. With his thumb and index finger of his right hand he tried to pick the object up. It resisted his efforts. "It must be the end of a buried rod."

Using both hands to scrape away the gravel and sand from around the object, Beau surprised himself by quickly upending it. It wasn't part of a rod. The underside was flat. Beau picked it up. At the height of the dome it was about a centimeter thick.

"Shit, it's heavy for its size," Beau said. He handed it to Pitt, who hefted it in the palm of his hand. Pitt whistled and made an expression of amazement. He gave it back to Beau.

"What's it made of?" Pitt asked.

"Feels like lead," Beau said. With his fingernail he tried to scratch it, but it didn't scratch. "But it ain't lead. Hell, I bet it's heavier than lead."

"It reminds me of one of those black rocks you find once in a while at the beach," Pitt said. "You know, those rocks that get rolled around for years by the surf."

Beau hooked his index finger and thumb around the margin of the object and made a motion as if to throw it. "With this flat underside I bet I could skip this thing twenty times."

"Bull!" Pitt said. "With its weight it would sink after one or two skips."

"Five bucks says I could skip it at least ten times," Beau said.

"You're on," Pitt said.

"Ahhh!" Beau cried suddenly. Dropping the object, which again half buried itself in the sand and gravel, Beau grabbed his right hand with his left.

"What happened?" Pitt demanded with alarm.

"The damn thing stung me," Beau said angrily. By squeezing the base of his index finger, he caused a drop of blood to appear at the tip.

"Oh, wow!" Pitt said sarcastically. "A mortal wound!"

"Screw you, Henderson," Beau said, grimacing. "It hurt. It felt like a goddamn bee sting. I even felt it up my arm."

"Ah, instant septicemia," Pitt said with equal sarcasm.

"What the hell's that?" Beau demanded nervously.

"It would take too long to explain, Mr. Hypochondriac," Pitt said. "Besides, I'm just pulling your leg."

Beau bent down and retrieved the black disc. He carefully inspected its edge but found nothing that could have accounted for the sting.

"Come on, Beau!" Cassy called angrily. "I gotta go. What on earth are you two doing?"

"All right, all right," Beau said. He looked at Pitt and shrugged.

Pitt bent down and from the base of the latest indentation the object had made in the sand, lifted a slender shard of glass. "Could this have been stuck to it somehow and cut you?"

"I suppose," Beau said. He thought it unlikely but couldn't think of any other explanation. He'd convinced himself there was no way the object could have been at fault.

"Beauuuuu!" Cassy called through clenched teeth.

Beau swung himself up behind the wheel of his 4×4. As he did so he absently slipped the curious domed disc into his jacket pocket. Pitt climbed into the backseat.

"Now I'm going to be late," Cassy fumed.

"When was your last tetanus shot?" Pitt questioned from the backseat.

A mile from Costa's Diner the Sellers family was in the final stages of its morning routine. The family minivan was already idling thanks to Jonathan, who sat expectantly behind the wheel. His mother, Nancy, was framed by the open front door. She was dressed in a simple suit befitting her professional position as a research virologist for a local pharmaceutical company. She was a petite woman of five foot two with a Medusa's head of tight, blond curls.

"Come on, honey," Nancy called to her husband, Eugene. Eugene was stuck on the kitchen phone, talking with one of the local newspaper reporters whom he knew socially. Eugene motioned he'd be another minute.

Nancy impatiently switched her weight from one foot to the other and eyed her husband of twenty years. He looked like what he was: a physics professor at the university. She'd never been able to coax him out of his baggy corduroy pants and jacket, blue chambray shirt, and knitted tie. She'd gone to the extent of buying him better clothes, but they hung unused in the closet. But she'd not married Eugene for his fashion sense or lack of it. They'd met in graduate school, and she'd fallen hopelessly in love with his wit, humor, and gentle good looks.

Turning around, she eyed her son, in whose face she could definitely see both herself and her husband. He'd seemed defensive that morning when she'd asked him about what he'd been doing the night before at his friend Tim's house. Jonathan's uncharacteristic evasiveness worried her. She knew the pressures teenagers were under.

"Honest, Art," Eugene was saying loud enough for Nancy to hear. "There's no way such a powerful blast of radio waves could have come from any of the labs in the physics department. My advice is to check with some of the radio stations in the area. There are two besides the university station. I suppose it could have been some kind of prank. I just don't know."

Nancy looked back at her husband. She knew it was difficult for him to be rude with anyone, but everybody was going to be late. Holding up a finger she mouthed the words "one minute" to Eugene. Then she walked out to the car.

"Can I drive this morning?" Jonathan asked.

"I don't think this is the morning," Nancy said. "We're already late. Shove over."

"Jeez," Jonathan whined. "You guys never give me any credit for being able to do anything."

"That's not true," Nancy countered. "But I certainly don't think putting you in a situation of having to drive while we are in a hurry is appropriate."

Nancy got in behind the wheel.

"Where's Dad anyway?" Jonathan mumbled.

"He's talking with Art Talbot," Nancy said. She glanced at her watch. The minute was up. She beeped the horn.

Thankfully Eugene appeared at the door, which he turned to and locked. He ran to the car and jumped in the backseat. Nancy quickly backed out into the street and accelerated toward their first stop: Jonathan's school.

"Sorry to keep everybody waiting," Eugene said after they'd driven a short distance in silence. "There was a curious phenomenon last night. Seems that a lot of TVs, radios, and even garage door openers suffered damage in the area around the university. Tell me, Jonathan. Were you and Tim listening to the radio or watching TV around ten-fifteen? As I recall the Appletons live over in that general area."

"Who, me?" Jonathan questioned too quickly. "No, no. We were . . . reading. Yeah, we were reading."

Nancy glanced at her son out of the corner of her eye. She couldn't help but wonder what he really had been doing.

"Whoa!" Jesse Kemper said. He managed to keep a steaming cup of Starbucks coffee from splashing into his lap as his partner, Vince Garbon, bottomed out their cruiser on the lip of the driveway going into Pierson's Electrical Supply. It was located a few blocks away from Costa's Diner.

Jesse was in his middle fifties and was still athletic. Most people thought he was no more than forty. He was also an imposing man with a bushy mustache to offset the thinning hair on the dome of his large head.

Jesse was a detective lieutenant for the city police and was well liked by his colleagues. He'd been only the fifth African-American on the force, but encouraged by his record, the city had commenced a serious recruiting effort toward African-Americans to the point that the department now racially mirrored the community.

Vince pulled the unmarked sedan around the side of the building and stopped outside an open garage door next to a city squad car.

"This I got to see," Jesse said, alighting from the passenger seat.

Coming back from a coffee run, he and Vince had heard on the radio that a repeat, small-time crook by the name of Eddie Howard had been found after having been cornered all night by a watchdog. Eddie was so well known at the police station that he was almost a friend.

Allowing their eyes to adjust from the bright sunlight to the dim interior, Jesse and Vince could hear voices off to the right, behind a bank of massive floor-to-ceiling shelving. When they walked back there they found two uniformed policemen lounging as if on a cigarette break. Plastered to a corner was Eddie Howard. In front of him was a large black-and-white pit bull who stood like a statue. The animal's unblinking eyes were glued to Eddie like two black marbles.

"Kemper, thank God," Eddie said, holding himself rigid while he spoke. "Get this animal away from me!"

Jesse looked at the two uniformed cops.

"We called and the owner's on his way in," one of them said. "Normally they don't get here until nine."

Jesse nodded and turned back to Eddie. "How long have you been in here?"

"All freakin' night," Eddie said. "Pressed up against this wall."

"How'd you get in?" Jesse asked.

"Just walked in," Eddie said. "I was just hanging out in the neighborhood and suddenly the garage door back there opened by itself, like magic. So I came in to make sure everything was okay. You know, to help out."

Jesse gave a short derisive laugh. "I guess Fido here thought you had something else in mind."

"Come on, Kemper," Eddie moaned. "Get this beast away from me."

"In due time," Jesse said with a chuckle. "In due time." Then he turned back to the uniformed officers. "Did you check the garage door?"

"Sure did," the second officer replied.

"Any sign of forced entry?" Jesse asked.

"I think Eddie was telling the truth about that," the officer said.

Jesse shook his head. "More weird stuff happened last night than you can shake a stick at."

"But mostly in this part of the city," Vince added.

Sheila Miller parked her red BMW convertible in her reserved spot near the emergency-room entrance. Flipping the front seat forward, she eyed her stricken VCR. She tried to think of a way of getting it, her briefcase, and a separate stack of folders into her office in one trip. It seemed doubtful until she saw a black Toyota utility vehicle pull up to the unloading bay and discharge a passenger.

"Excuse me, Mr. Henderson," Sheila called out when she recognized Pitt. She made it a point to know everyone by name who worked in her department, whether clerk or surgeon. "Could I see you a moment?"

Although obviously in a hurry, Pitt turned when he heard his name. Instantly he recognized Dr. Miller. Sheepishly he reversed directions, descended the steps from the loading dock, and came over to her car.

"I know I'm a tad late," Pitt said nervously. Dr. Miller had a reputation of being a no-nonsense administrator. Her nickname was "Dragon Lady" among the lower-eschelon staff, particularly the first-year residents. "It won't happen again," Pitt added.

Sheila glanced at her watch, then back at Pitt. "You're slated to start medical school in the fall."

"That's true," Pitt answered with his pulse rising.

"Well, at least you're better-looking than most of the ones in this year's crop," Sheila said, hiding a grin. She could sense Pitt's anxiety.

Confused by the comment, which sounded like a compliment, Pitt merely nodded. In truth he didn't know what to say. He had a sense she was toying with him but couldn't be sure.

"I'll tell you what," Sheila said, nodding toward her back seat. "If you carry that VCR into my office I won't mention this egregious infraction to the dean."

Pitt was now reasonably certain that Dr. Miller was teasing him, but he still felt it better to keep his mouth shut. Without a word he reached in, lifted the VCR, and followed Dr. Miller into the ER.

There was a moderate amount of activity, particularly from a few early-morning fender-benders. Fifteen to twenty patients were waiting in the waiting area, as well as a few more back in the trauma section. The staff present at the front desk greeted Dr. Miller with smiles but cast puzzled looks at Pitt, particularly the person Pitt was scheduled to relieve.

They walked down the main corridor and were about to enter Sheila's office when she caught sight of Kerry Winetrop, one of the hospital's electronic technicians. Keeping all the hospital's monitoring equipment functioning was a full-time job for several people. Sheila called out to the man, and he obligingly came over.

"My VCR had a seizure last night," Sheila said, nodding toward the VCR in Pitt's hands.

"Join the club," Kerry said. "You and a bunch of other people. Apparently there was a surge in the TV cable line around the university area at quarter after ten last night. I've already seen a couple of players that people brought in early this morning."

"A surge, huh," Sheila remarked.

"My TV blew up," Pitt said.

"At least my TV's okay," Sheila said.

"Was it on when the VCR blew?" Kerry asked.

"No," Sheila said.

"Well, that's the reason it didn't pop," Kerry said. "If it had been on you would have lost your picture tube."

"Can the VCR be fixed?" Sheila asked.

"Not without essentially replacing most of the guts," Kerry said. "To tell you the truth it's cheaper to buy another one."

"Too bad," Sheila said. "I'd finally figured out how to set the clock on this one."

Cassy hurried up the steps of Anna C. Scott High School and entered just as the bell announced the beginning of the first period. Reminding herself that getting freaked out was not going to help anything, she rushed up the main stairs and down the hall to her assigned class. She was in the middle of a month-long observation of a junior English class. This was the first time she'd been late.

Pausing at the door to brush hair from her face and smooth the front of her demure cotton dress, she couldn't help but hear the apparent pandemonium going on inside the room. She'd expected to hear Mrs. Edelman's strident voice. Instead there was a mishmash of voices and laughter. Cassy cracked the door and looked within.

Students were haphazardly sprinkled around the room. Some were standing, others were sitting on the radiator covers and on desks. It was a beehive of separate conversations.

Cracking the door further, Cassy could see why there was such chaos. Mrs. Edelman was not there.

Cassy swallowed hard. Her mouth had gone dry. For a second she debated what to do. Her experience with high-school kids was minimal. All her student teaching had been at the elementary-school level. Deciding she had little choice and taking a deep breath, she pushed through the door.

No one paid her any attention. Advancing to Mrs. Edelman's desk in the front of the room she saw a note in Mrs. Edelman's script. It said simply: *Miss Winthrope, I will be delayed for some minutes. Please carry on.*

With her heart accelerating Cassy glanced out at the scene in front of her. She felt incompetent and an imposter. She wasn't a teacher, not yet anyway.

"Excuse me!" Cassy called. There was no response. She called more loudly. Finally she yelled as loudly as she could, which brought forth a stunned silence. She was now graced with close to thirty pairs of staring eyes. The expressions ran the gamut from surprise to irritation at being interrupted to outright disdain.

"Please take your seats," Cassy said. Her voice wavered more than she would have liked.

Reluctantly the students did as they were told.

"Okay," Cassy said, trying to bolster her confidence. "I know what your assignment was, so until Mrs. Edelman arrives, why don't we talk about Faulkner's style in a general sense. Who'd like to volunteer to get us started?"

Cassy's eyes roamed the room. The students who moments earlier were the picture of animation now appeared as if cut from marble. The expressions of those who were still looking at her were blank. One impertinent red-headed boy puckered his lips into a silent kiss as Cassy's eyes briefly locked onto his. Cassy ignored the gesture.

Cassy could feel perspiration at her hairline. Things were not going well. In the back of the second row she could see a blond-headed boy engrossed with a laptop computer.

Stealing a glance at the seating chart in the middle of the desk blotter, Cassy read the boy's name: Jonathan Sellers.

Looking back up, Cassy tried again: "Okay, everyone. I know it's cool to kinda zone out on me. After all I'm just a student teacher and you all know a lot more about what goes on in here than I do, but . . ."

At that moment the door opened. Cassy turned, hoping to see the competent Mrs. Edelman. Instead the situation took a turn for the worse. In walked Mr. Partridge, the principal.

Cassy panicked. Mr. Partridge was a dour man and a strict disciplinarian. Cassy had only met him once when her group of student teachers was going through their orientation. He'd made it very clear that he was not fond of the student-teaching program and only agreed to it under duress.

"Good morning, Mr. Partridge," Cassy managed. "Can I help you in some way?"

"Just carry on!" Mr. Partridge snapped. "I'd been informed of Mrs. Edelman's delay, so I thought I'd stop by to observe for a moment."

"Of course," Cassy said. She turned her attention back to the stony students and cleared her throat. "Jonathan Sellers," she called out. "Perhaps you could start the discussion."

"Sure," Jonathan said agreeably.

Cassy let out an imperceptible sigh of relief.

"William Faulkner was a major American writer," Jonathan said, trying to sound extemporaneous.

Cassy could tell he was reading off his LCD screen, but she didn't care. In fact, she was grateful for his resourcefulness.

"He's known for his vivid characterizations and, like, his convoluted style . . ."

Tim Appleton sitting across from Jonathan tried vainly to suppress a laugh since he knew what Jonathan was doing.

"Okay," Cassy said. "Let's see how that applies to the story you all were asked to read for today." She turned to the blackboard and wrote "vivid characters" and next to it "complex story structure." Then she heard the door to the hall open and close. Glancing over she was relieved to see that gloomy Partridge had already departed.

Facing the class again she was pleased to see several hands up of people willing to get involved in a discussion. Before she called on one of them, Cassy gave Jonathan a tiny but grateful smile. She wasn't sure but she thought she caught a blush before the boy looked back down at his laptop.

CHAPTER 3

11:15 A.M.

Olgavee Hall was one of the largest tiered lecture halls in the business school. Although not a graduate student, Beau had been given special permission to take an advanced marketing course that was extremely popular with the business school students. In fact, it was so popular it needed the seating capacity of Olgavee. The lectures were exciting and stimulating. The course was taught in an interactive style with a different professor each week. The downside was that each class required a lot of preparation. One had to be prepared to be called on at any moment.

But Beau was finding it uncharacteristically hard to concentrate at today's lecture. It wasn't the professor's fault. It was Beau's. To the dismay of his immediate neighbors as well as himself, he couldn't stop fidgeting in his seat. He'd developed uncomfortable aches in his muscles that made it impossible to get comfortable. On top of that he had a dull headache behind his eyes. What made everything worse was that he was sitting in the center of the hall four rows back and directly in the line of sight of the lecturer. Beau always made it a point to get to lecture early to get the best seat.

Beau could tell that the speaker was getting annoyed, but he didn't know what to do.

It had started on his way to Olgavee Hall. The first symptom had been a stinging sensation somewhere up inside his nose causing a wave of violent sneezes. It wasn't long before he was blowing his nose on a regular basis. Initially he'd thought he'd caught a cold. But now he had to admit that it had to be more. The irritation rapidly progressed from his sinuses into his throat, which was now sore, especially when he swallowed. To make matters worse, he began to cough repeatedly, which hurt his throat as much as swallowing.

The person sitting directly in front of Beau turned and gave him a dirty look after Beau let out a particularly explosive cough.

As time dragged on, Beau became particularly bothered by a stiff neck. He tried to rub his muscles, but it didn't help. Even the lapel of his jacket seemed to be exacerbating the discomfort. Thinking that the leadlike object in his pocket might be contributing, Beau took it out and put it on the desk in front of him. It looked odd, sitting on his notes. Its perfectly round shape and exquisite symmetry suggested it was a manufactured piece, yet Beau had no idea if it was. For a moment he thought that perhaps it could have been a futuristic paperweight, but he dismissed the idea as too prosaic. More probable was that it was a tiny sculpture, but he truly wasn't sure. Vaguely he wondered if he should take it over to the geology department to inquire if it could be the result of a natural phenomenon like a geode.

Musing about the object made Beau examine the minute wound on the tip of his index finger. It was now a red dot in the center of a few millimeters of pale, bluish skin. Surrounding that was a two-millimeter halo of redness. To the touch it was mildly sore. It felt like a doctor had poked him with one of those strange little lancets they used to get a small blood sample.

A shaking chill interrupted Beau's thoughts. The chill was followed by a sustained bout of coughing. When he finally got his breath, he acknowledged the futility of attempting to last through the lecture. He wasn't getting anything out of it, and on top of that he was bothering his fellow students and the lecturer.

Beau gathered his papers, slipped his putative mini-sculpture back into his pocket, and stood up. He had to excuse himself multiple times to move laterally along the row. Because of the narrow space his exit caused a signifcant commotion. One student even dropped his looseleaf notebook which opened and sent its contents wafting down into the pit.

When Beau finally got to the aisle, he caught a glimpse of the lecturer shielding his eyes so as to see who was making all the fuss. He was one person Beau wasn't going to ask for a letter of recommendation.

Feeling emotionally as well as physically exhausted at the end of the school day, Cassy made her way down the main stairs of the high school and exited out into the horseshoe drive in front. It was pretty clear to her that from a teaching standpoint she liked elementary school much better than high school. From her perspective high-schoolers generally seemed too self-centered and too interested in constantly challenging their boundaries. She even thought a number of them were downright mean. Give me an innocent, eager third-grader any day, Cassy reflected.

The afternoon sun felt warm on Cassy's face. Shielding her eyes with her hand, she scanned the multitude of vehicles in the drive. She was looking for Beau's 4×4. He insisted on picking her up each afternoon, and was usually waiting for her. Obviously today was different.

Looking for a place to sit, Cassy saw a familiar face waiting nearby. It was Jonathan Sellers from Mrs. Edelman's English class. Cassy walked over and said hello.

"Oh, hi," Jonathan stammered. He nervously glanced around, hoping he wasn't being observed by any classmates. He could feel his face blush. The fact of the matter was, he thought Cassy was the best-looking teacher they'd ever had and had told Tim as much after class.

"Thanks for breaking the ice this morning," Cassy said. "It was a big help. For a moment I was afraid I was at a funeral, my funeral."

"It was just lucky I'd tried to see what it said about Faulkner in my laptop."

"I still think it took a bit of courage on your part to say something," Cassy said. "I appreciated it. It certainly got the ball rolling. I was afraid no one would speak."

"My friends can be jerks at times," Jonathan admitted.

A dark blue minivan pulled up to the curb. Nancy Sellers leaned across the front seat and popped open the passenger-side door.

"Hi, Mom," Jonathan voiced with a little self-conscious wave.

Nancy Sellers's bright, intelligent eyes jumped back and forth between her seventeen-year-old son and this rather sexy college-age woman. She knew his interest in girls had suddenly mushroomed, but this situation seemed a wee bit inappropriate.

"Are you going to introduce me to your friend?" Nancy asked.

"Yeah, sure," Jonathan said, eyeing the crack in the sidewalk. "This is Miss Winthrope."

Cassy leaned forward and stuck out her hand. "Nice to meet you, Mrs. Sellers. You can call me Cassy."

"Cassy it is then," Nancy replied. She shook Cassy's outstretched hand. There was a short but awkward pause before Nancy asked how long Cassy and Jonathan had known each other.

"Mommmm!" Jonathan moaned. He knew instantly what she was implying, and felt mortified. "Miss Winthrope is a student teacher in English class."

"Oh, I see," Nancy remarked with mild relief.

"My mom is a research virologist," Jonathan said to change the subject and help explain how she could say something so stupid.

"Really," Cassy said. "That's certainly an interesting and important field in today's world. Are you at the University Med Center?"

"No, I'm employed at Serotec Pharmaceuticals," Nancy said. "But my husband is at the university. He runs the physics department."

"My goodness," Cassy said. She was impressed. "No wonder you have such a bright son here."

Over the top of the Sellerses' van Cassy caught sight of Beau turning into the horseshoe drive.

"Well, nice meeting you," Cassy said to Nancy. Then turning to Jonathan she said: "Thanks again for today."

"It was nothing," Jonathan insisted.

Cassy half skipped, half ran up to where Beau had pulled to the curb.

Jonathan watched her go, mesmerized by the motion of her buttocks beneath her thin cotton dress.

"Well, am I giving you a ride home or not?" Nancy questioned to break the spell. She was becoming concerned again that there was something going on she didn't know about.

Jonathan climbed into the front of the car after carefully depositing his laptop on the backseat.

"What was she thanking you for?" Nancy asked as they pulled away. She could see Cassy getting into a utility vehicle driven by an attractive male her own age. Nancy's concerns melted again. It was tough raising a teenager: one minute proud, the next concerned. It was an emotional roller coaster for which Nancy felt un-equipped.

Jonathan shrugged. "Like I said, it was nothing."

"Good grief," Nancy said, frustrated. "Getting even a modicum of information from you reminds me of that saying about squeezing water out of a rock."

"Gimme a break," Jonathan said. As they drove past the black 4×4 he stole another glance at Cassy. She was sitting in the vehicle, talking with the driver.

"You look terrible," Cassy said. She was twisted in the seat so she could look directly into Beau's face. He was paler than she'd ever seen him. Perspiration stood on his forehead like tiny cabochon topazes. His eyes were red and rheumy.

"Thanks for the compliment," Beau said.

"Really," Cassy said. "What's the matter?"

"I don't know," Beau said. He covered his mouth while he coughed. "It came on me just before my marketing class, and it's getting worse. I guess I got the flu. You know, muscle aches, sore throat, runny nose, headache, the works."

Cassy stretched out her hand and felt his sweaty brow. "You're hot," she said.

"Funny because I feel cold," Beau said. "I've been having shivers. I even got into bed, but as soon as I was under the covers, I felt hot and kicked them off."

"You should have stayed in bed," Cassy said. "I could have bummed a ride with one of the other student teachers."

"There was no way to get in touch with you," Beau said.

"Men," Cassy voiced as she got out of the car. "You guys never want to admit when you're sick."

"Where are you going?" Beau questioned.

Cassy didn't answer. Instead she walked around the front of the car and opened Beau's door. "Shove over," she said. "I'm driving."

"I can drive," Beau said.

"No arguments," Cassy said. "Move!"

Beau didn't have the energy to protest. Besides, he knew it was probably best even though he wouldn't admit it.

Cassy put the car in gear. At the corner she turned right instead of left.

"Where the hell are you going?" Beau asked. With his head throbbing he wanted to get back to bed.

"You are going to the student infirmary at the University Med Center," Cassy said. "I don't like the way you look."

"I'll be all right," Beau complained, but he didn't protest further. He was feeling worse by the minute.

The entrance to the student infirmary was through the ER, and as Cassy and Beau walked in, Pitt saw them and came out from behind the front desk.

"Good grief!" Pitt said when he took one look at Beau. "Did the Nite organization cancel your interview or did you get run over by the women's track team?"

"I can do without your wisecracks," Beau mumbled. "I think I got the flu."

"You ain't kidding," Pitt said. "Here, come on into one of the ER bays. I don't think they want you down in the student walk-in clinic."

Beau allowed himself to be led into a cubicle. Pitt facilitated the visit by bringing in one of the most compassionate nurses and then by going out to get one of the more senior ER physicians.

Between the nurse and the doctor Beau was quickly examined. Blood was drawn and an IV started.

"This is just for hydration," the doctor said, tapping the IV bottle. "I think you have a bad case of the flu, but your lungs are clear. Still, I think it best for you to stay in the student overnight ward, at least for a few hours to see if we can't bring your fever down and control that cough. We'll also be able to take a look at your blood work in case there's something I'm missing."

"I don't want to stay in the hospital," Beau complained.

"If the doctor thinks you should stay, you're staying," Cassy said. "I don't want to hear any macho bull crap."

Pitt was again able to grease the skids, and within a half hour Beau was comfortably situated in one of the student overnight rooms. It looked like a typical hospital room with vinyl flooring, metal furniture, a TV, and a window that looked south over the hospital lawn. Beau was dressed in hospital-issue pajamas. His clothes were hung in the closet, and his watch, wallet, and the black mini-sculpture were in a metal valuables cabinet affixed to the top of the bureau. Cassy had programmed the combination lock with the last four digits of their home phone number.

Pitt excused himself to get back to the ER desk.

"Comfortable?" Cassy asked. Beau was lying on his back. His eyes were closed. He'd been given a cough suppressant which had already taken effect. He was exhausted.

"As comfortable as can be expected," Beau murmured.

"The doctor said I should come back in a few hours," Cassy said. "All the tests will be available and most likely I'll be able to take you home."

"I'll be here," Beau said. He was enjoying the sensation of a strange languid sleep settling over him like a welcome blanket. He didn't even hear Cassy close the door behind her when she left.

Beau slept more soundly than he'd ever slept. He didn't even dream. After several hours of this comalike trance his body took on a faint phosphorescence. Inside the locked valuables box the black disciform object did the same, particularly one of eight small domed excrescences arrayed around the object's rim. Suddenly the tiny disc detached itself and floated free. Its glow intensified until it became a pinpoint of light like a distant star.

Moving laterally the point of light contacted the side of the valuables box, but it didn't slow. With a muted hissing sound and a few sparks it traveled through the metal, leaving a tiny, perfectly symmetrical hole behind it.

Once free of the confined space, the point of light traveled directly to Beau, causing Beau's luminosity to intensify. It approached Beau's right eye and then hovered a few millimeters away. Slowly the intensity of the point of light decreased until it assumed its normal flat black color.

A few pulses of visible light traveled from the tiny object and impinged on Beau's eyelid. Instantly the eye opened while the other stayed shut. The exposed pupil was maximally dilated with just a bare band of iris visible.

Pulses of electromagnetic radiation were then dispatched into Beau's open eye, mostly in the visible light wavelength. It was one computer downloading to another, and it went on for almost an hour.

"How's our favorite patient?" Cassy asked Pitt when she came through the ER door. Pitt hadn't seen her until she'd spoken. The ER had been busy and he'd had his hands full.

"Fine as far as I know," Pitt said. "I looked in on him a couple of times, as did the nurse. Every time he was sleeping like a baby. I don't think he moved. He must have been exhausted."

"Did his blood work come back?" Cassy asked.

"Yup, and it was pretty normal," Pitt said. "His white count was up slightly but only his mononuclear lymphocytes."

"Hey, remember you're talking to a layperson," Cassy said.

"Sorry," Pitt said. "The bottom line is that he can go home. Then it's the usual. You know: fluids, aspirin, rest, and some TLC."

"What do I have to do to get him released?" Cassy asked.

"Nothing," Pitt said. "I already did all the paperwork. We just have to get him out into the car. Come on, I'll give you a hand."

Pitt got leave from the head nurse to take a break. He found a wheelchair and started down the hall toward the student overnight ward.

"You think a wheelchair is necessary?" Cassy asked with concern.

"We might as well have it just in case," Pitt said. "His legs were pretty wobbly when you brought him in."

They got to the door, and Pitt knocked quietly. When there was no answer he cracked the door and peered inside.

"Just as I thought," Pitt said. He opened the door wide to push in the wheelchair. "Sleeping Beauty still hasn't moved."

Pitt parked the wheelchair and followed Cassy to the bed. Each went to a separate side.

"What did I tell you?" Pitt said. "The picture of tranquility. Why don't you kiss him and see if he turns into a frog."

"Should we wake him?" Cassy asked, ignoring Pitt's attempt at humor.

"It's going to be hard getting him home if we don't," Pitt said.

"He looks so peaceful," Cassy said. "He also looks a hell of a lot better than he did earlier. In fact, his color looks normal."

"I suppose," Pitt said.

Cassy reached out and gently shook Beau's arm while calling his name softly. When he didn't respond, she shook him harder.

Beau's eyes blinked open. He looked back and forth between his two friends. "Hey, how ya doing?" he asked.

"I think the question is how you are doing," Cassy said.

"Me, I'm fine," Beau said. Then his eyes made a rapid sweep around the room. "Where am I?"

"At the med center," Cassy said.

"What am I doing here?" Beau questioned.

"You don't remember?" Cassy asked with concern.

Beau shook his head. He yanked back the covers and threw his feet over the side.

"You don't remember getting sick in class?" Cassy asked. "You don't remember my bringing you here?"

"Oh, yeah," Beau said. "It's coming back. Yeah, I remember. I felt terrible." He looked at Pitt. "Jeez, what did you guys give me? I feel like a new man."

"Seems that you just needed some serious shuteye," Pitt said. "Except for a little hydration, we really didn't treat you."

Beau stood up and stretched. "I might have to come in for hydration more often," he said. "What a difference." He eyed the wheelchair. "Who's that contraption for?"

"You, in case you needed it," Pitt said. "Cassy came to take you home."

"I sure don't need any wheelchair," Beau said. He then coughed and made a face. "Well, my throat's still a little sore, and I still have a cough, but let's get out of here." He stepped over to the closet and grabbed his clothes. He retreated to the bathroom and pushed the door almost closed. "Cassy, could you get my wallet and watch out of that cabinet?" he called through the door.

Cassy stepped over to the bureau and entered the combination.

"If you guys don't need me, I'll head back to the desk," Pitt said.

Cassy turned as she stuck her hand into the valuables box. "You've been a dear," she said as her hand grasped Beau's wallet and watch. She pulled them out and shut the door. Stepping over to Pitt she gave him a hug. "Thanks for your help."

"Hey, any time," Pitt said self-consciously. He looked down at his feet, then out the window. Cassy had a way of making him feel flustered.

Beau came out from the bathroom still tucking in his shirt. "Yeah, thanks, buddy," he said. He gave Pitt a poke in the arm. "Really appreciate it."

"Glad you're feeling better," Pitt said. "See you around." Pitt grabbed the wheelchair and pushed it out the door.

"He's a good guy," Beau said.

Cassy nodded. "He'll make a good doctor. He really cares."

CHAPTER 4

Charlie Arnold had been working for the University Medical Center for thirty-seven years, ever since his seventeenth birthday when he decided to drop out of school. He'd begun with the Building and Grounds Department, mowing lawns, pruning trees, and weeding the flower beds. Unfortunately an allergy to grass drove him out of that line of work. But since he was a valued hospital employee, the administration offered him a housekeeping position instead. Charlie had accepted and enjoyed the work. Particularly on hot days he enjoyed it more than being outside.

Charlie liked working on his own. The supervisor would give him a list of the rooms to clean, and off he'd go. On this particular night he had one more room to go: one of the student overnight rooms. They were always easier than a regular hospital room. In a regular room he never knew what he was going to run into. It depended on the illness of the previous occupant. Sometimes they could be pretty bad.

Whistling under his breath, Charlie cracked open the door, pushed in his mop bucket, and pulled in his cleaning cart. With his hands on his hips he surveyed the room. As he'd expected, it only needed a light disinfectant mopping and dusting. He walked over to the bathroom and glanced in there. It didn't even look as if it had been used.

Charlie always started in the bathroom. After putting on his thick protective gloves, he scrubbed out the shower and the sink and disinfected the toilet. Then he mopped the floor.

Moving out into the room, he peeled off the bed linens and wiped down the mattress. He dusted all other horizontal surfaces, including the windowsill. He was about to start mopping when a glow caught his eye. Turning to face the bureau, he stared at the valuables safe. Although his mind told him it was preposterous, the box seemed to be glowing as if there was an enormously powerful light inside it. Of course that didn't make any sense, since the box was made out of metal, so no matter how bright a light was, even if there was one inside, it wouldn't shine through.

Charlie leaned his mop against the top edge of the bucket, and took a few steps toward the bureau, intending to open the door to the box. But he stopped about three feet away. The glow that surrounded the box had gotten brighter. Charlie even imagined he could feel a warmth on his face!

Charlie's first thought was to get the hell out of the room, but he hesitated. It was a confusing spectacle and mildly frightening, yet curious at the same time.

Then to Charlie's amazement a shower of sparks burst forth from the side of the box accompanied by a hissing sound similar to arc welding. Charlie's hands reflexively shot up to protect his face from the sparks, but they stopped almost the moment they began. From the point of sparking a luminous red spinning disc the size of a silver dollar emerged. It had seared through the metal, leaving a smoking slit.

Completely stunned by this phenomenon, Charlie couldn't move. The spinning disc slowly traveled laterally toward the window, coming within a foot of his arm. At the window it hovered as if it were appreciating the vista of the night sky. Then its color changed from red to white-hot and a corona appeared around it like a narrow halo.

Charlie's curiosity propelled him closer to this mysterious object. He knew no one was going to believe him when he described it. Holding out his hand, palm down, he waved it back and forth over the object to make sure there wasn't a wire or a string. He couldn't understand how it was hanging in the air.

Sensing its warmth, Charlie cupped his hands and slowly brought them closer and closer to the object. It was a peculiar warmth that tingled his skin. When his hands got within the corona, the tingling magnified.

The object ignored Charlie until he inadvertently blocked the object's view of the night sky. The moment he did so, the disc moved laterally, and before Charlie could react, it instantly and effortlessly burnt a hole through the center of his palm! Skin, bone, ligaments, nerves, and blood vessels were all vaporized.

Charlie let out a yelp more in surprise than pain. It had happened so quickly. He staggered back, gaping at his perforated hand in total disbelief and smelling the unmistakable aroma of burnt flesh. There was no bleeding since all the vessels had been heat-coagulated. In the next instant the corona around the luminous object expanded to a foot in diameter.

Before Charlie could react, a whooshing sound commenced and rapidly increased in volume until it was deafening. At the same time Charlie felt a force pulling him toward the window. Frantically he reached out with his good hand and grabbed the bed only to have his feet go out from underneath him. Gritting his teeth, he managed to hang on even though the bed itself moved. The violence of the sound and the movement lasted only seconds before being capped by a noise vaguely reminiscent of the closing of a central vac port.

Charlie let go of the bed and tried to get to his feet, but he couldn't. The muscles of his legs were like rubber. He knew something was horribly wrong and tried to cry out for help, but his voice was weak, and he was salivating so copiously that any speech was nearly impossible. Marshalling what strength he had, he attempted to crawl toward the door. But the effort was in vain. After moving only a few feet he started to retch. Moments later utter darkness descended as Charlie's body was racked by a series of rapidly fatal grand mal seizures.

CHAPTER 5

As far as student apartments went, it was relatively luxurious and spacious, and since it was located on the second floor, it even had a view. Both Cassy's and Beau's parents wanted their children to live in decent surroundings and had been accordingly willing to up their kids' living allowances when they decided to move out of their dorms. Part of the reason for the largesse was that both had stellar academic records.

Cassy and Beau had found the apartment eight months previously and had jointly painted and furnished it. The furniture was mostly garage-sale acquisitions which had been stripped and refinished. The curtains were bedsheets in disguise.

The bedroom faced east which at times was a bother because of the intensity of the morning sun. It wasn't a bedroom that invited late sleeping. But at a little after two in the morning, it was dark save for a swath of light that slanted through the window from a streetlight in the parking lot.

Cassy and Beau were sound asleep: Cassy on her side and Beau on his back. As was normal for her, Cassy had been moving at regular intervals, first on one side, then the other. Beau, on the other hand, had not moved at all. He'd been motionlessly sleeping on his back just as he had that afternoon in the student overnight ward.

At exactly two-ten Beau's closed eyes began to glow, as did the radium dial of an old windup alarm clock Cassy had inherited from her grandmother. After a few minutes of gradually increasing intensity Beau's eyelids popped open. Both eyes were as dilated as his right eye had been that afternoon, and both eyes glowed as if they were light sources themselves.

After reaching a peak of luminosity they began to fade until the pupils were their usual black. Then the irises began to contract until they had assumed a more normal size. After a few blinks, Beau realized he was awake.

Slowly he sat up. Similar to the way he'd awakened in the hospital, he was momentarily disoriented. Sweeping his eyes around the room, he quickly pieced together where he was. Then he lifted his hands and studied them by flexing his fingers. His hands felt different, but he couldn't explain how. In fact, his whole body felt different in some inexplicable way.

Reaching over to Cassy he gently gave her shoulder a shake. She responded by rolling over onto her back. Her heavily lidded eyes regarded him. When she saw he was sitting up, she quickly did the same.

"What's the matter?" she asked huskily. "Are you all right?"

"Fine," Beau said. "Perfect."

"No cough?"

"Not yet. Throat feels fine too."

"Why'd you wake me? Can I get you something?"

"No, thanks," Beau said. "Actually I thought you'd like to see something. Come on!"

Beau got out of bed and came around to Cassy's side. He took her hand and helped her to her feet.

"You want to show me something now?" Cassy asked. She glanced at the clock.

"Right now," Beau said. He guided her into the living room and over to the slider that led to the balcony. When he motioned for her to step outside, she resisted.

"I can't go out," she said. "I'm naked."

"Come on," Beau said. "Nobody's going to see us. It's only going to take a moment, and if we don't go now we'll miss it."

Cassy debated with herself. In the half light she couldn't see Beau's expression, but he sounded sincere. The idea that this was some kind of prank had occurred to her.

"This better be interesting," Cassy warned as she finally stepped over the slider's track.

The night air had its usual chill, and Cassy hugged herself. Even so, everything erectile on the surface of her body popped up. She felt like one big goose pimple.

Beau stepped behind her and enveloped her in his arms to help control Cassy's shivering. They were standing at the railing facing a broad stretch of the sky. It was a cloudless, clear, moonless night.

"Okay, what am I supposed to be seeing?" she asked.

Beau pointed up toward the northern sky. "Look up there toward the Pleiades in the constellation of Taurus."

"What is this, an astronomy lesson?" Cassy questioned. "It's two-ten in the morning. Since when did you know anything about the constellations?"

"Watch!" Beau commanded.

"I'm watching," Cassy said. "What am I supposed to be seeing?"

At that moment there was a rain of meteors with extraordinarily long tails, all streaking from the same pinpoint of sky like a gigantic firework display.

"My God!" Cassy exclaimed. She held her breath until the rain of shooting stars faded. The spectacle was so impressive that she momentarily forgot the chill. "I've never seen anything like it. It was beautiful. Was that what they call a meteor shower?"

"I suppose," Beau said vaguely.

"Will there be more?" Cassy asked, her eyes still glued to the point of origin.

"Nope, that's it," Beau said. He let go of Cassy, then followed her back inside. He closed the slider.

Cassy sprinted back to the bed and dived in. When Beau appeared she had the covers clutched around her neck and was shivering. She ordered him to get under the blanket to warm her up.

"Gladly," he said.

They snuggled for a moment and Cassy's shivering abated. Pulling back from where she had her face tucked into the crook of his neck, she tried to look into Beau's eyes, but they were lost in the gloom. "Thanks for getting me out there to see that meteor shower," she said. "At first I thought you were trying to play a joke on me. But I have one question: How did you know it was going to happen?"

"I can't remember," Beau said. "I guess I heard about it someplace."

"Did you read about it in the paper?" Cassy suggested.

"I don't think so," Beau said. He scratched his head. "I really don't remember."

Cassy shrugged. "Well, it doesn't matter. What matters is that we got to see it. How did you wake up?"

"I don't know," Beau said.

Cassy pushed away and turned on the bedside light. She studied Beau's face. He smiled under her scrutiny.

"Are you sure you feel all right?" she asked.

Beau smiled. "Yeah, I'm sure," he said. "I feel great."

CHAPTER 6

6:45 A.M.

It was one of those cloudless, crystalline mornings with the air so fresh it could almost be tasted. The most distant mountains stood out with shocking clarity. The normally dry ground was covered with a cool layer of dew that sparkled like so many diamonds.

Beau stood for a moment taking in the scene. It was as if he'd seen it for the first time. He couldn't believe the range of colors of the distant hills, and he questioned why he'd not appreciated it before.

He was dressed casually in an Oxford shirt, jeans, and loafers with no socks. He cleared his throat. His cough was all but gone and his throat didn't hurt when he swallowed.

Pushing off from the entrance to his apartment building he walked along the walkway, then up the driveway and into the back parking area. In the sand lining the far periphery he found what he was looking for. Three black mini-sculptures identical to the one he'd found in Costa's parking lot the morning before. He scooped them up, dusted them off, and slipped them into separate pockets.

With his mission accomplished, he turned and retraced his steps.

Inside the apartment the alarm went off next to Cassy's head. The alarm was on her side of the bed because Beau had a bad habit of turning it off so quickly that neither of them truly woke up.

Cassy's hand snaked out from beneath the covers and hit the dream bar. The alarm fell silent for ten luscious minutes. Rolling onto her back, her hand extended toward Beau to give him a shove, the first of many. Beau was not a morning person.

Cassy's exploring hand found empty, cool sheets. The searching arc was extended. Still nothing. Cassy opened her eyes and looked over at Beau, but he was not there!

Surprised by this unexpected turn of events, Cassy sat up and listened for any tell-tale noise from the bathroom. The house was silent. Beau never got up before she did. Suddenly she was worried that his illness had returned.

After slipping on her robe, Cassy padded out into the living room. She was about to call out his name when she saw him over by their fish tank. He was bending down, studying the fish. He was so intent he'd not heard her. While she watched he placed his right index finger against the glass. Somehow his finger concentrated the fluorescent aquarium light so that the tip of his finger glowed.

Mesmerized by this scene, Cassy just stood there continuing to watch. Soon all the fish flocked to the point where Beau's finger touched the glass. When he moved the finger laterally, the fish all dutifully followed.

"How are you doing that?" Cassy asked.

Surprised by Cassy's presence, Beau stood up, letting his hand fall to his side. At the same instant the fish dispersed to the far ends of the tank.

"I didn't hear you come into the room," Beau said with a pleasant smile.

"Obviously," Cassy said. "What were you doing to attract the fish that way?"

"Damned if I know," Beau said. "Maybe they thought I was going to feed them." He came over to Cassy and draped his arms on her shoulders. His smile was radiant. "You look wonderful this morning."

"Oh, yeah, sure," Cassy said jokingly. She tussled her thick hair, then patted it into place. "There, now I'm ready for the Miss America Pageant." She looked up into Beau's eyes. They were a particularly effulgent blue, and the whites were whiter than white.

"You are the one who looks wonderful," Cassy said.

"I feel wonderful," Beau said. He bent down to kiss Cassy on the lips, but she ducked out from beneath his arms.

"Hold on," she said. "This beauty contestant has yet to brush her teeth. I wouldn't want to be disqualified on account of morning breath."

"Not a chance," Beau said with a lascivious smile.

Cassy cocked her head to one side. "You're feeling chipper today," she remarked.

"As I said, I feel great," Beau said.

"That was sure a short course of the flu," Cassy said. "I'd say you made a remarkable recovery."

"I guess I have you to thank for hauling me over to the medical center," Beau said. "That's where things took a turn for the better."

"But the doctor and the nurse didn't do anything," Cassy said. "They admitted so themselves."

Beau shrugged. "Then it's a new strain of a rapid flu. I'm certainly not going to complain about its short course."

"Me neither," Cassy said, starting for the bathroom. "Why don't you make coffee while I take a shower."

"Coffee is already made," Beau said. "I'll bring you a cup."

"Aren't we being efficient," Cassy called on her way through the bedroom.

"Nothing but five-star service in this hotel," Beau said.

Cassy continued to marvel at Beau's quick turnaround. Remembering how he looked when she'd climbed into the car in front of the Anna C. Scott school, she never would have suspected it. She turned on the shower and adjusted the temperature. When it was to her liking, she climbed in. The first order of business was her hair. She washed it every day.

No sooner had she gotten her scalp full of shampoo when she heard knocking on the outside of the shower door. Without opening her eyes, she told Beau to leave her coffee mug on the back of the sink.

Sticking her head under the jet of water, she began to rinse. The next thing she knew was that Beau was in the shower with her.

She opened her eyes with disbelief. Beau was standing right in front of her in the shower fully clothed. He even still had on his loafers.

"What on earth are you doing?" Cassy sputtered. She had to laugh. It was such an unexpected, zany thing for him to do.

Beau didn't say anything. Instead he reached out and hungrily drew Cassy's wet, naked body to him while his lips sought hers. It was a deep, sensual, carnal kiss.

Cassy managed to come up for air, laughing at the absurdity of what they were doing. Beau laughed as well as the water flattened his hair against his forehead.

"You're crazy," Cassy commented. Her hair was still full of soap suds.

"Crazy for you is more accurate," Beau said. He started to fumble with his belt.

Cassy helped by undoing the buttons of his soaked shirt and peeling it from his muscular shoulders. The situation might have been unconventional, especially for the normally neat and compulsive Beau, but for Cassy it was a turn-on. It was so wonderfully spontaneous, and Beau's eagerness added additional spice.

Later, in the midst of their passion, Cassy began to appreciate something else. Not only were they making love in a unique circumstance, but they were making love in an atypical way. Beau was touching her differently. She wasn't able to explain it exactly, but it was marvelous, and she loved it. It had something to do with Beau being more gentle and sensitive than usual even in the midst of his overwhelming ardor.

Reaching his hands over his head, Pitt stretched. He looked at the clock on the ER desk. It was almost seven-thirty and soon his marathon twenty-four-hour shift would be over. He was already fantasizing how good his bed was going to feel when he slid his tired body between the sheets. The idea of the exercise was to give him an idea of what it's like being a resident, when shifts of thirty-six hours are commonplace.

"You should go down to the room where they found that poor guy from house-keeping," Cheryl Watkins said. Cheryl was one of the day staff nurses who'd recently come on duty.

"How come?" Pitt asked. He remembered the patient very well. The patient had been rushed into the ER a little after midnight by someone from housekeeping. The ER doctors had started resuscitation, but had stopped after quickly realizing the patient's body temperature was about the same as room temperature.

Deciding the man was dead had been easy. The hard part was deciding what had killed him other than the apparent seizures he'd had. There'd been a curious blood-less hole through his hand that one of the doctors thought might have been caused by electricity. Yet the history said he'd been found in a room without any access to a high voltage.

Another doctor noticed the patient had particularly dense cataracts. That was strange because cataracts had not been noted on the man's annual employment physical, and his co-workers denied he had any visual handicap. So that suggested the man had suffered sudden cataracts, which the doctors dismissed. They'd never heard of such a thing even when a powerful jolt of electricity was involved.

Confusion about the proximate cause of death lead to wild speculation and even some bets. The only thing that was certain was that no one knew for sure, and the body was sent to the medical examiner's office for the final word.

"I'm not going to tell you why you should see the room," Cheryl said. "Because if I did, you'd say I was pulling your leg. Suffice it to say that it's weird."

"Gimme a hint," Pitt said. He was so tired that the idea of walking all the way over to the hospital proper did not engender a lot of enthusiasm unless it was for something truly unique.

"You have to see for yourself," Cheryl insisted before she headed off to a meeting.

Pitt tapped a pencil against his forehead while he debated. The idea of the cir-cumstance being weird intrigued him. Calling after Cheryl, he asked her where the room was located.

"In the student overnight ward," Cheryl called back over her shoulder. "You can't miss it because there's a ton of people there trying to figure out what hap-pened."

Curiosity overcame Pitt's fatigue. If there were a lot of people involved maybe he should make the effort. He heaved himself to his feet and dragged his tired body down the corridor. At least the student overnight ward was close. While he walked he vaguely thought that if it were truly weird maybe Cassy and Beau would like to hear about it, since they'd just been there the previous afternoon.

As he rounded the final corner that lead to the student infirmary, Pitt could see a small crowd of people milling about. As he came up to the room his curiosity mounted because whatever the situation was, it involved the same room that Beau had occupied.

"What's going on?" Pitt whispered to one of his classmates who also worked in the hospital on a work-study program. Her name was Carol Grossman.

"You tell me," Carol said. "When I got a chance to see I suggested that perhaps Salvador Dali had stopped by, but nobody laughed."

Pitt gave her a quizzical look, but she didn't elaborate. He pushed on, literally. There were so many people he had to worm his way through. Unfortunately in the process he was a bit too aggressive and managed to jostle one of the doctors enough to cause her coffee to slosh out of her cup. When the doctor angrily turned around to glare at Pitt, Pitt caught his breath. Of all the staff, it had to be Dr. Sheila Miller!

"Damn it," Sheila snapped, shaking the hot coffee from the back of her hand. She was in her long white coat. Several fresh coffee stains graced the cuff of her right sleeve.

"I'm terribly sorry," Pitt managed.

Sheila raised her green eyes to Pitt's. She appeared particularly severe with her blond hair pulled tightly back from her face in a compact bun. Her cheeks were flushed with irritation.

"Mr. Henderson!" she snapped. "I hope to God you don't have your sights on a specialty requiring coordination, like eye surgery."

"It was an accident," Pitt pleaded.

"Yeah, that's what people said about World War I," Sheila said. "And think of the consequences! You're the ER clerk. What in God's name are you doing forcing your way in here."

Pitt frantically searched his mind for some reasonable explanation beyond simple curiosity. Simultaneously, his eyes swept the room, hoping to see something that might offer a suggestion. Instead what he saw stunned him.

The first thing that caught his eye was that the shape of the head of the bed was distorted as if it had been heated to the melting point and pulled toward the window. The night table looked the same. In fact as his eyes completed their circuit of the room, he noticed that most of the furniture and fixtures had been twisted out of shape as if they had been made of taffy. The windowpanes, meanwhile, appeared to have melted, with the glass forming stalactite-like formations that hung down from the muntins.

"What on earth happened in here?" Pitt asked.

Sheila spoke through clenched teeth: "Answering that question is why these professionals are standing here talking. Now get back to the ER desk!"

"I'm on my way," Pitt said quickly.

After one more quick glance at the strange transformation of the room, he retreated back through the crowd. He couldn't help but wonder what kind of damage he'd done to his career by pissing off the Dragon Lady.

"I'm sorry for the interruption," Sheila said. She was talking with Detective Lieutenant Jesse Kemper and his partner Vince Garbon.

"No problem," Jesse said. "I wasn't making a lot of sense anyway. I mean, this is a pretty strange situation, but I don't think it's a crime scene. My gut reaction tells me this was not a homicide. Maybe you should get some science experts in here to tell us if a bolt of lightning could have come in through this window."

"But there wasn't a thunderstorm," Sheila complained.

"I know," Jesse said philosophically. He spread his hands like a supplicant. "But you said your engineers ruled out building power. It sure looks like the guy got electrocuted, and if he did, maybe it was lightning."

"I can't buy it," Sheila said. "I'm not a forensic pathologist, but I seem to remember that when lightning strikes an individual, it doesn't make a hole. It grounds, usually coming out the feet, even occasionally blowing the shoes off. There's no evidence of a ground in here. This is more like some powerful laser beam."

"Hey, there you go," Jesse said. "I never thought of that. Don't you have laser beams here in the hospital? Maybe somebody shot one in through the window."

"We've certainly got lasers in the hospital," Sheila admitted. "But nothing that could make the kind of hole we saw in Mr. Arnold's hand. Plus I can't imagine a laser being responsible for these strange distortions that we see with the furniture."

"Well, I'm plumb out of my league here," Jesse said. "If the autopsy suggests we got a corpus delecti and a homicide, we'll get involved. Otherwise I think you have to get the science guys over here."

"We've put in a call to the physics department at the university," Sheila said.

"I think that's the best idea," Jesse said. "Meanwhile, here's my card." He stepped over to Sheila and gave her the business card. He also gave one to Richard Halprin, president of the University Medical Center, and Wayne Maritinez, head of hospital security. "Any of you can call me anytime. I'm interested, really. It's been a strange couple of nights. There's been more weird stuff happening than in all the previous thirty years I've been on the force. Is it a full moon or what?"

At the very end of the show, the music reached a crescendo, and with a final clap of cymbals, the dome of the planetarium went dark. Then the general lights came on. Instantly the auditorium erupted in a smattering of applause, a few whistles, and a babble of excited voices. Most of the seats were occupied by elementary school kids on a field trip. Except for teachers and chaperones, Cassy and Beau were the only adults.

"That was really fun," Cassy said. "I'd forgotten what a planetarium show was like. The last time I'd seen one was in Miss Korth's fourth-grade class."

"I liked it too," Beau said with enthusiasm. "It's fascinating seeing what the galaxy looks like from the point of view of Earth."

Cassy blinked and stared at Beau. All morning long he seemed to have a penchant to pop off with a curious non sequitur.

"Come on," Beau said, oblivious to Cassy's mild perplexity. He stood up. "Let's try to get out of here ahead of these screaming kids."

Hand in hand they exited the auditorium and strolled out onto the expansive lawn that separated the planetarium and the natural history museum. From a pushcart vendor they purchased hot dogs smothered with chili and onions. On a seat in the shade of a large tree they sat down to enjoy their lunch.

"I'd also forgotten how much fun playing hooky can be," Cassy said in between bites of hot dog. "It's lucky that I wasn't scheduled for student teaching today. I mean, skipping class is one thing, but skipping student teaching is something else entirely. I wouldn't have been able to come."

"I'm glad it worked out," Beau said.

"I was surprised when you suggested it," Cassy said. "Isn't this the first time you've ever skipped class?"

"Yup," Beau said.

Cassy laughed. "What is this, a new Beau? First you act like an amorous animal and jump into the shower with your clothes on and now you've willingly missed three classes. But don't get me wrong, I'm not complaining."

"It's all your fault," Beau said. He put down his hot dog and pulled Cassy to him and enveloped her in a playfully sexy embrace. "You're irresistible." He tried to kiss her, but Cassy got her hand up and parried the move.

"Wait a sec," she laughed. "I've got chili all over my face."

"All the more spice," Beau joked.

Cassy wiped her face with her napkin. "What's gotten into you?"

Beau didn't answer. Instead he gave Cassy a long, wonderful kiss. Just like in the shower, the impulsiveness of the gesture was another distinct turn-on for her.

"Wow, you are transmogrifying into a world-class Casanova," Cassy said as she sat back, took a breath, and tried to collect herself. The fact that she could be turned on so easily in public in the middle of the day surprised her.

Beau happily went back to his hot dog. As he chewed he raised his hand to block out the sun while he looked in the sun's direction.

"How far did they say Earth is from the sun?" he asked.

"Jeez, I don't know," Cassy said. Having experienced the stirring of desire, it was hard to change the subject, especially to something as specific as astronomical distances. "Ninety-something million miles."

"Oh, yeah," Beau said. "Ninety-three. That means it would take just a little over eight minutes for the effect of a solar flare to reach here."

"Excuse me?" Cassy asked. There was another one of his non sequiturs. She didn't even know what a solar flare was.

"Look," Beau said excitedly, pointing up into the western sky. "You can see the moon even though it's daylight."

Cassy shielded her eyes and followed the line of Beau's pointing finger. Sure enough, she could just barely make out the gossamer image of the moon. She looked back at Beau. He was enjoying himself immensely in an endearing, almost childlike way. His enthusiasm was infectious, and she couldn't help enjoying herself as well.

"What made you want to come to the planetarium today?" Cassy asked.

Beau shrugged. "Just pure interest," he said. "A chance to learn a little more about this beautiful planet. Let's head over to the museum next. You up for that?"

"Why not?" Cassy exclaimed.

Jonathan carried his lunch outside. On such a day he hated to be in the crowded cafeteria, especially since he'd not seen Candee in there. Skirting the flagpole in the central quad, he headed over to the bleachers alongside the baseball diamond. He knew that was one of Candee's favorite places to get away from the crowd. As he approached he could see that his efforts were to be rewarded. Candee was sitting on the top row.

They waved to each other, and Jonathan started up. There was a slight breeze, and it was snapping the edges of Candee's skirt, revealing tantalizing glimpses of her thighs. Jonathan tried not to make it obvious that he was watching.

"Hi," Candee said.

"Hi," Jonathan answered. He sat down next to her and extracted one of his peanut butter and banana sandwiches.

"Ugh," Candee said. "I can't believe you can eat that stuff."

Jonathan studied his sandwich before taking a bite. "I like it," he said.

"What did Tim say about his radio?" Candee asked.

"He's still pissed," Jonathan said. "But at least he doesn't think it was our fault anymore. The same thing happened to a friend of his brother's."

"Can we still get the car?" Candee asked.

"I'm afraid not," Jonathan said.

"What are we going to do?" Candee asked.

"I don't know," Jonathan said. "I wish to hell my parents weren't so tight-assed about our family car. They treat me like I'm twelve. The only time I can drive the thing is when they are along."

"At least your parents let you get your license," Candee complained. "Mine are making me wait until I'm eighteen."

"That's criminal," Jonathan said. "If they tried that with me, I think I'd run away. But what good is my license without wheels? It's so frustrating my parents won't give me more credit than they do. I mean, I do have a brain. I'm getting good grades, I don't do drugs."

Candee rolled her eyes.

"I don't consider that pot we tried drugs," Jonathan said. "And how many times did we do it: twice!"

"Hey, look," Candee said. She pointed at the receiving dock about seventy-five feet away where trucks made deliveries. It was on the basement level and was approached by a ramp cut into the ground just behind the backstop of the baseball diamond.

"Isn't that Mr. Partridge with the school nurse?" Candee asked.

"It sure is," Jonathan said. "And he doesn't look so good. Look at the way Miss Golden is holding him up. And listen to the old windbag cough."

At that moment an aged Lincoln Town Car pulled around the side of the building and descended the ramp. Behind the wheel Candee and Jonathan recognized Mrs. Partridge, whom the kids in the school called Miss Piggy. Mrs. Partridge seemed to be coughing as much as Mr. Partridge.

"What a pair," Jonathan commented.

While Jonathan and Candee watched, Miss Golden managed to get the sagging Mr. Partridge down a half flight of cement steps and into the car. Mrs. Partridge didn't get out.

"He looks sicker than a dog," Candee said.

"Miss Piggy looks worse," Jonathan said.

The car backed up, turned, and accelerated up the ramp. Halfway up it scraped lightly against the concrete wall. The grating sound made Jonathan wince.

"So much for the paint job," he said.

"What in God's name are you doing back here?" Cheryl Watkins demanded. She was sitting at the ER desk as Pitt Henderson dragged himself through the swinging doors. He looked exhausted with dark circles under his eyes.

"I couldn't sleep," he said. "So I thought I might as well come back and try to salvage what I could of my medical career."

"What on earth are you talking about?" Cheryl asked.

"This morning when I went over to see that room you suggested, I committed a disastrous faux pas."

"Like what?" Cheryl questioned. She could see he was troubled, and she was concerned. Pitt was well liked in the unit.

"I accidentally bumped into the Dragon Lady and spilled her coffee over her and her white coat," Pitt said. "And let me tell you, she was royally pissed. She demanded to know what I was doing there and stupid me couldn't think of a reason."

"Uh oh!" Cheryl commiserated. "Dr. Miller is not fond of getting her white coat dirty, especially early in the morning."

"As we all know!" Pitt said. "She was pretty blunt. Anyway I thought maybe by coming back I could at least impress her with my dedication."

"Can't hurt, although it is above and beyond the call of duty," Cheryl said. "On the other hand, we can always use the help, and I'll make sure our fearless leader hears about it. Meanwhile, why don't you check in a couple of the more routine cases. We had a bad traffic accident an hour ago so we're way behind, and the RNs are all tied up."

Pleased to get a task, especially one that he enjoyed, Pitt grabbed the top clipboard and headed for the patient waiting area. The patient's name was Sandra Evans, aged four.

Pitt called out the name. From the multitude of people impatiently waiting on the hard plastic chairs in the crowded room, a mother and daughter stood up. The woman was in her early thirties and rather bedraggled. The child was darling with tightly curled blond hair, but appeared sick and dirty. She was dressed in soiled pajamas and a tiny robe.

Leading the way, Pitt took them back to an examination bay. He lifted the child up onto the table. Her blue eyes were glassy and her skin pale and moist. She was sick enough not to be overconcerned about the ER environment.

"Are you the doctor?" the mother asked. Pitt appeared much too young.

"The clerk," Pitt announced. Having worked in the ER long enough and having checked in enough prescreened patients Pitt was not self-conscious about his status.

"What's the trouble, sweetheart?" Pitt asked as he wrapped a child's blood pressure cuff around Sandra's arm and inflated it.

"I got a spider," Sandra said.

"She means a bug," the mother interjected. "She can't get that straight. It's the flu or something. It hit her this morning with coughing and sneezing. I tell you, it's always something with kids."

The blood pressure was fine. As Pitt undid the cuff he noted a colorful Band-Aid on Sandra's right palm.

"Looks like you got a booboo too," Pitt said. He got the body temperature instrument and was about to get a reading.

"A rock bit me in the yard," Sandra said.

"Sandra, I told you not to fib," Mrs. Evans said. It was obvious the mother was at the limit of her patience.

"I'm not fibbing," Sandra said indignantly.

Mrs. Evans made an expression as if to say, "What can I do?"

"Have a lot of rocks bitten you?" Pitt teased. He got a reading. The child had a temperature of 103° Fahrenheit. He wrote it and the blood pressure on the chart.

"Just one," Sandra said. "A black one."

"Guess we have to be careful with black rocks," Pitt said. He then instructed the mother to watch the child carefully until the doctor came in.

Pitt headed back to the desk and slipped the chart into the rack where it would be picked up by the next available doctor. He was about to go behind the desk when the swinging doors that led to the outside burst open.

"Help me," cried a man who was carrying a seizing woman. He staggered a few feet into the ER and threatened to collapse himself.

Pitt was the first person to reach the man's side. Without a second's hesitation he relieved the man of his burden by taking the woman into his own arms. It was difficult to hold her because she was still locked in the throes of a seizure.

By then Cheryl Watkins had come around from behind the desk along with several of the ER residents. Even Dr. Sheila Miller had dashed out of her office at the cries for help.

"Into the trauma bay," Dr. Miller commanded.

Without waiting for a gurney, Pitt carried the twitching woman back into the depths of the ER. With the help of Sheila, who'd positioned herself on the other side of the examination table, Pitt put the patient down. As he did so his eyes met

Sheila's for the second time that day. No words were spoken but on this occasion a completely different message was conveyed.

Pitt backed up. Nurses and doctors jumped into the breach. Pitt stood there and watched, wishing he were at a stage in his training where he could participate.

The medical team which Sheila commanded quickly terminated the seizure. But then while they were beginning the evaluation of what caused the seizure, the patient had another, even more violent one.

"Why is she doing this?" the husband moaned. Everyone had forgotten he'd followed the group inside. One of the nurses went over to him and motioned for him to leave. "She's got diabetes, but she's never had a seizure. This shouldn't be happening. I mean, all she got was a cough. She's a young woman. Something is wrong, I know it."

A few minutes after the husband had been led out to the waiting room, Sheila's head snapped up so she could see the cardiac monitor. A sudden change in the sound of the beats had caught her attention.

"Uh oh," she said. "Something's going on here, and I don't like it."

The regular heartbeat had become erratic. Before anybody could react, the monitor's alarm went off. The patient was fibrillating.

"Code red ER!" blared out of the intercom system. More ER doctors flew into the cubicle in response to the cardiac arrest call. Pitt backed up even further so as not to interfere. He found the episode both stimulating and frightening. He wondered if he could ever learn enough to participate capably in such a situation.

The team worked tirelessly but to no avail. Eventually Sheila straightened up and ran her forearm across her sweaty brow.

"OK, that's it," she said reluctantly. "We've lost her." For the previous thirty minutes the monitor had traced a monotonous straight line.

The team hung their heads in dejection.

The old spring-loaded scale squeaked as Dr. Curtis Lapree allowed Charlie Arnold's liver to slosh into its basin. The needle jumped up the scale.

"Well, that's normal," Curtis said.

"Did you expect it to be abnormal?" Jesse Kemper asked. He and Detective Vince Garbon had stopped by to observe the autopsy on the dead University Medical Center housekeeping employee. Both policemen were dressed in disposable contamination suits.

Neither Jesse nor Vince were at all intimidated or sickened by the autopsy. They'd witnessed a hundred or so over the years, especially Jesse, who was eleven years older than Vinnie.

"Nope," Curtis said. "The liver looked normal, felt normal, so I expected it to weigh normal."

"Getting any ideas what killed this poor chap?" Jesse asked.

"Nope," Curtis said. "Looks like it's going to be just another one of those mysteries."

"Don't tell me that," Jesse said petulantly. "I'm counting on you to tell me if this was a homicide or accident."

"Calm down, Lieutenant," Curtis said with a laugh. "I'm just pulling your leg. You should know by now that the dissection part of the autopsy is just the beginning. In this case I expect the microscopic is going to be more important. I mean on gross, I don't know what to make of the hole in the hand. Look at it!"

Curtis held up Charlie Arnold's hand. "The damn hole is a perfect circle."

"Could it be a bullet wound?" Jesse asked.

"You can answer your own question," Curtis said. "With all the bullet wounds you've seen."

"True, it doesn't look like a bullet wound," Jesse said.

"It sure as hell doesn't," Curtis said. "It would have had to be a bullet going the speed of light and hotter than the interior of the sun. Look at how everything got cauterized at the margins. And what happened to the missing tissue and bone? You said there was no blood or tissue at the scene."

"Nothing," Jesse said. "I mean no gore. There was melted glass and melted furniture, but no blood and no tissue."

"What do you mean, melted furniture?" Curtis asked. He wiped his hands on his apron after removing the liver from the scale.

Jesse described the room, to Curtis's utter fascination. "I'll be damned," Curtis said.

"Do you have any ideas?" Jesse asked.

"Sorta," Curtis admitted. "But you're not going to like it. I don't like it either. It's crazy."

"Try me," Jesse said.

"First let me show you something," Curtis said. He went to a side table and brought back a pair of retractors. Putting them inside the deceased's upper and lower lips, he exposed the teeth. The dead man assumed a horrid, grimacing expression.

"Oh, gross," Vinnie said. "You're going to give me nightmares."

"Okay, Doc," Jesse said. "What am I supposed to be looking at other than lousy dental work? Looks like the guy never brushed his teeth."

"Look at the enamel of the front teeth," Curtis said.

"I'm looking," Jesse said. "Looks a little messed up."

"That's it," Curtis said. He withdrew the retractors and returned them to the nearby table.

"Enough of this pussyfootin' around," Jesse said. "What's on your mind?"

"The only thing I can think of that can do that to tooth enamel is acute radiation poisoning," Curtis said.

Jesse's face fell.

"I told you you weren't going to like it," Curtis said.

"Jesse's very close to retirement," Vince said. "It's not nice to tease him like this."

"I'm serious," Curtis said. "It's the only thing that relates all the findings, like the hole in the hand and the changes in the enamel. Even the cataracts that weren't seen on his last yearly physical."

"So what happened to this poor slob?" Jesse asked.

"I know it's going to sound crazy," Curtis warned. "But the only way I can relate all the findings so far is to hypothesize that someone dropped a red-hot pellet of plutonium in his hand that burned through and gave him an enormous dose of radiation in the process. I mean a whopping dose."

"That's absurd," Jesse said.

"I told you you weren't going to like it," Curtis admitted.

"There was no plutonium at the scene," Jesse said. "Did you check if the body was radioactive?"

"I did, actually," Curtis said. "For personal safety concerns."

"And?"

"It's not," Curtis said. "Otherwise I wouldn't be up to my elbows into it."

Jesse shook his head. "This is getting worse instead of better," he said. "Plutonium, shit! That would be some kind of national emergency. Guess I'd better get someone over to that hospital and make sure there's no hot spots. Can I use a phone?"

"Be my guest," Curtis said agreeably.

A sudden burst of coughing got everyone's attention. It was Michael Schonhoff, a mortuary tech, who was over at the sink washing the entrails. The coughing went on for several minutes.

"Jeez, Mike," Curtis said. "You're sounding worse. And pardon my expression, but you look like death warmed over."

"Sorry, Dr. Lapree," Mike said. "I guess I got the flu. I've been trying to ignore it, but now I'm starting to get chills."

"Clock out early," Curtis said. "Get yourself home and in bed, take some aspirin, and drink some tea."

"I want to finish up here," Mike said. "Then I want to label the specimen bottles."

"Forget it," Curtis said. "I'll have someone else finish up."

"Okay," Mike said. Despite his protestations to the contrary, he was happy to be relieved.

CHAPTER 7

8:15 P.M.

"What I keep asking myself is why we never come down here," Beau said. "This is beautiful." He, Cassy, and Pitt were strolling along the pedestrian mall in the city center eating ice cream after a dinner of pasta and white wine.

Five years previously the downtown had looked like a ghost town, with most of the people and restaurants having fled out to suburbia. But like a lot of other American cities, there'd been a reawakening. A few tasteful renovations had started a self-fulfilling prophecy. Now the entire downtown was a feast for the eyes as well as the palate. Crowds milled about, enjoying the spectacle.

"You guys really skipped school today?" Pitt questioned. He was impressed and incredulous.

"Why not," Beau said. "We went to the planetarium, the natural history museum, the art museum, and the zoo. We learned a lot, more than if we'd gone to class."

"That's an interesting rationalization," Pitt said. "I hope you get a bunch of questions about the zoo on your next exams."

"Ah, you're just jealous," Beau said, cuffing the top of Pitt's head.

"Maybe so," Pitt admitted. He stepped out of Beau's reach. "I put in thirty hours in the ER since yesterday morning."

"Thirty hours?" Cassy questioned. "Really?"

"Honest," Pitt said. He then told them the story of the room where Beau had spent the afternoon and about spilling the coffee on Dr. Sheila Miller, the woman in charge of the entire emergency department.

Both Beau and Cassy were entranced, especially about the condition of the room and the death of the housekeeper. Beau asked the most questions, but Pitt had few answers. "They're waiting for the autopsy results," Pitt added. "Everybody's hoping then there will be some answers. Right now no one has any idea of what happened."

"Sounds horrid," Cassy said, making an expression of disgust. "A hole burned through his hand. Gads, I could never be a doctor. No way."

"I got a question for you, Beau," Pitt said after they'd walked a few moments in silence. "How did Cassy manage to talk you into this day of culture?"

"Hey, wait a sec!" Cassy interrupted. "This day wasn't my idea. It was Beau's."

"Get outta here," Pitt said skeptically. "You expect me to believe that . . . Mr. Type A who never misses a day of school."

"Ask him!" Cassy challenged.

Beau just laughed.

Cassy, intent on making her point that she'd not been to blame for the frivolous day and despite the crowded sidewalk, had turned and was walking backward so as to confront Pitt. "Come on, ask him," she urged.

Suddenly Cassy collided with a pedestrian coming in the opposite direction who wasn't paying much attention either. Both were mildly jolted but certainly unhurt.

Cassy immediately apologized as did the individual whom she'd hit. But then she did a double take. It was Mr. Partridge, the dour principal of the Anna C. Scott school.

Ed did a similar double take.

"Wait a second," he said as a smile spread across his face. "I know you. You're Miss Winthrope, the charming student teacher assigned to Mrs. Edelman."

Cassy felt her face flush. Instantly she was aware that she'd possibly blundered into a minor catastrophe. But Mr. Partridge was the picture of gentility. "Such a nice surprise," he was saying. "Here, I'd like you to meet my bride, Clara Partridge."

Cassy dutifully shook hands with Mr. Partridge's wife and suppressed a smile. She was well aware of what the students called the woman.

"And here is a new friend of ours," Mr. Partridge said. He put his arm around his male companion. "I'd like you to meet Michael Schonhoff. He's one of those dedicated civil servants who labors at our medical examiner's office."

Everyone shook hands through their introductions. Beau was particularly interested in Michael Schonhoff, and they fell into their own conversation while Ed Partridge directed his attention to Cassy. "I've certainly been getting some good feedback on your student teaching," he said. "And I was impressed how well you were handling that class yesterday when Mrs. Edelman was delayed."

Cassy didn't know how to respond to these unexpected compliments. She also didn't know how to respond to Mr. Partridge's blatantly lewd inspection. Several times his eyes traveled up and down her body. After the first traverse she thought she could have been overreacting, but after the third time, she knew his behavior was deliberate.

Eventually the two groups said good-bye and went their separate ways.

"Who the hell is Ed Partridge?" Pitt asked as soon as they were out of earshot.

"He's the principal of the high school where I'm student teaching," Cassy said. She shook her head.

"He obviously is impressed with you," Pitt said.

"Did you catch the way he was looking at me?" Cassy asked.

"How could I miss it?" Pitt said. "I was embarrassed for him, especially with his tub of a wife standing right there. What'd you think, Beau?"

"I didn't catch it," Beau said. "I was talking with Michael."

"He's never acted like that before," Cassy said. "In fact he's usually a conservative sourpuss."

"Hey, guys, there's another ice cream place across the street," Beau said enthusiastically. "I'm going to have another. Anybody else?"

Both Cassy and Pitt shook their heads.

"I'll be right back," Beau said. He sprinted across the mall to wait in the ice cream concession line.

"You believe me about this day of playing hooky being Beau's idea?" Cassy questioned.

"If you say so," Pitt said. "But I'm sure you can understand my reaction. It is a little out of character."

"That's an understatement," Cassy said.

They watched while Beau flirted with a couple of attractive co-eds. Even from where they were standing they could hear Beau's characteristic laugh.

"He acts as loose as a goose," Pitt commented.

"That's one way to put it," Cassy said. "We've had a ball today, there's no doubt. But his behavior is starting to make me a little uneasy."

"How so?" Pitt questioned.

Cassy let out a short, mirthless laugh. "He's being too nice. I know that sounds crazy and maybe a little cynical, but he's just not acting normal. He's not acting like Beau normally acts. Skipping classes is just one thing."

"What else?" Pitt asked.

"Well, it's a little personal," Cassy said.

"Hey, I'm a friend," Pitt said encouragingly. At the same time his mouth went dry. He wasn't sure he wanted to hear anything too personal. As much as he tried to deny it, his feelings for Cassy weren't entirely platonic.

"Sexually he's been different," Cassy said haltingly. "This morning he . . ." Cassy stopped in midsentence.

"He what?" Pitt asked.

"I can't believe I'm telling you this," Cassy said. She was abashed. "Let's just say there's something different about him."

"Has it just been today?" Pitt asked

"Last night and today," Cassy said. She considered telling about Beau dragging her out naked onto the balcony in the middle of the night to see the meteor shower but changed her mind.

"All of us have days when we just feel more alive," Pitt said. "You know, when food tastes better and sex . . . seems better." He shrugged. Now he was the embarrassed one.

"Maybe," Cassy said without conviction. "But what I'm wondering is whether his behavior could have something to do with that fleeting flu he had. I've never seen him so sick even though he got over it so quickly. Maybe it scared him. You know, like he thought he was going to die or something. Does that sound reasonable?"

Pitt shook his head. "I didn't think he was that sick."

"Do you have any other ideas?" Cassy asked.

"To be honest I'm a little too tired to think creatively," Pitt said.

"If you . . ." Cassy began, but she stopped. "Look what Beau's doing now!"

Pitt glanced at Beau. He had met up again with Ed Partridge, Mrs. Partridge, and their friend Michael. The foursome were deep in conversation.

"What on earth could he be talking with them for?" Cassy asked.

"Well, whatever it is they all seem to be in agreement," Pitt said. "They're all nodding their heads."

Beau looked at the clock on the dashboard of his 4×4. It was two-thirty in the morning. He was with Michael Schonhoff, and they were parked in the loading dock of the medical examiner's office next to one of the mortuary vans.

"So you think this is the best time?" Beau asked.

"Absolutely," Michael said. "The cleaning crew will be upstairs by now." He opened the passenger door and started to get out.

"You don't need me?" Beau asked.

"I'll be fine," Michael said. "Why don't you wait here. There'll be less explaining to do if I run into security."

"What are the chances of running into security?"

"Small," Michael admitted.

"Then I'm coming," Beau said. He climbed from the car.

"Suit yourself," Michael said agreeably.

Together they advanced to the door. Michael used his keys, and within seconds they were inside.

Without a word, Michael waved for Beau to follow him. Somewhere in the distance a radio could be heard. It was tuned to an all-night talk show.

The route lead through an antechamber, down a small ramp, and into the body holding room. The walls were lined with refrigerator compartments.

Michael knew precisely which compartment to open. The click of the door mechanism was loud in the silence. The body slid out effortlessly on a stainless steel tray.

Charlie Arnold's remains were in a clear plastic body bag. His face was ghostly white.

Intimately familiar with the surroundings, Michael produced a gurney. With Beau's help he got the body onto the gurney and closed the refrigerated compartment.

After a quick check to make sure the anteroom was still vacant, they wheeled the body up the ramp and out the door. It took only a moment to transfer it to the back of the 4×4.

While Beau climbed back into his car, Michael returned the gurney. Soon he was back to the car, and they left.

"That was easy," Beau said.

"I told you it'd be no problem," Michael said.

They drove east out into the desert. Leaving the main road, they took a dirt track until they were in uncontested wilderness.

"This looks okay to me," Beau said.

"I'd say it was perfect," Michael said.

Beau stopped the car. Together they lifted the body out of the car and carried it a hundred feet into the wilderness. They laid it on a ledge of sandstone. Above them stretched the moonless vault of the night sky with its millions of stars.

"Ready?" Beau questioned.

Michael stepped back a few paces. "Ready," he said.

Beau pulled out one of the black discs he'd retrieved that morning and put it on top of the body. Almost immediately it began to glow, and the intensity rapidly increased.

"We'd better get back," Beau said.

They moved about fifty feet away. By now the black disc's glow had reached the point that a corona was beginning to form, and as it did so Charlie Arnold's body also began to glow. The red glow of the disc changed to white and the corona expanded to envelop the body as well.

The whooshing sound started and with it a wind that pulled first leaves, then small stones, and finally larger rocks toward the body. The sound became instantly deafening, like the noise of an enormous jet engine. Beau and Michael hung on to each other to keep from being pulled off their feet.

The sound cut off with such suddenness that it caused a shock wave that jolted both men. The black disc, the body, and a number of stones, leaves, sticks, and other debris were gone. The rock where the body had been was hot, its surface twisted into a spiral.

"That should cause quite a stir," Beau said.

"Indeed," Michael said. "And keep them busy for a time."

CHAPTER 8

8:15 A.M.

"You're not going to tell me where you went last night?" Cassy asked petulantly. She had her hand on the door handle and was about to alight from the car. Beau had pulled into the horseshoe drive in front of the Anna C. Scott school.

"I already told you: just a drive," Beau said. "What's the big deal?"

"You've never gone for a drive in the middle of the night," Cassy said. "Why didn't you wake me and tell me you were going?"

"You were sleeping too soundly," Beau said. "I didn't want to disturb you."

"Didn't you think about me waking up and worrying about you?" Cassy asked.

"I'm sorry," Beau said. He reached over and patted her arm. "I guess I should have awakened you. At the time it seemed better to let you sleep."

"You'll wake me if it ever happens again?" Cassy asked.

"I promise," Beau said. "Jeez, you're making such a big deal out of this."

"It scared me," Cassy said. "I even called the hospital to make sure you weren't there. And the police station too, just to make sure there wasn't an accident."

"All right already," Beau said. "You made your point."

Cassy got out of the van, then leaned back through the window. "But why a drive at two o'clock in the morning? Why not a walk, or if you couldn't sleep, why not watch a little TV? Or better yet, read."

"We're not going over this again," Beau said with conviction but not anger. "Okay?"

"Okay," Cassy said reluctantly. At least she'd gotten an apology and Beau seemed reasonably remorseful.

"See you at three," Beau said.

They waved as Beau pulled away from the curb. When he got to the corner, he didn't look back. If he had he would have seen that Cassy had not moved from the spot where she'd gotten out of the car. She watched him turn the corner, heading away from the university. She shook her head. Beau's strange behavior had not improved.

Beau was whistling softly to himself, blithely unaware of Cassy's concerns as he drove through the downtown. He had a mission and was preoccupied, but not too preoccupied to appreciate how many pedestrians and other drivers were coughing and sneezing, particularly when he stopped for traffic lights. In the very center of town it was as if almost every other person were suffering symptoms of an upper respiratory infection. On top of that many of them were pale and perspiring.

Reaching the outskirts of the city on the side of town opposite the university, Beau turned off Main Street onto Goodwin Place. On his right was the animal shelter, and he pulled through the open chain-link gate. He parked next to the administration building. It was constructed of painted cement block with aluminum jalousie windows.

From behind the building Beau could hear continuous barking. Inside Beau confronted a secretary, told her what he wanted, and was asked to sit in a small waiting area. Beau could have read while he waited, but instead he listened intently to the barking, even the intermittent meow of some cats. He thought it was a strange way to communicate.

"My name is Tad Secolow," a man said, interrupting Beau's thoughts. "I understand you are looking for a dog."

"That's right," Beau said, getting to his feet.

"You've come to the right place," Tad said. "We've got just about any breed you might be looking for. The fact that you are willing to give a home to a full-grown dog gives you a larger selection than if you were intent on a puppy. Do you have an idea of the breed?"

"Nope," Beau said. "But I'll know what I want when I see it."

"Excuse me?" Tad said.

"I said I'll recognize which animal I want when I spot it," Beau repeated.

"Do you want to look at photos first?" Tad asked. "We have pictures of all the dogs that are available."

"I'd prefer to see the animals themselves," Beau said.

"Okay," Tad said agreeably. He escorted Beau past the secretary and through the rear of the building that was filled with animal cages. It had a mild barnyard smell that competed with a cloying odor of deodorant. Tad explained that the dogs housed inside were being treated by the vet who came every other day. Most of these dogs weren't barking. Some looked ill.

The back yard of the shelter had rows of chain-link cages. Down the center were two long runs enclosed with chain-link fences. The floor of the whole complex was concrete. Coils of hose were stacked against the back of the building.

Tad led Beau down the first aisle. The dogs barked wildly at the sight of them. Tad maintained a running commentary on the pluses of each breed they passed. He paused longest at a cage that housed a standard poodle. It was a silver-gray color with dark, pleading eyes. It seemed to understand the urgency of its plight.

Beau shook his head, and they moved on.

While Tad was discussing the good qualities of a black Lab, Beau stopped and gazed in at a large, powerful, fawn-colored dog who returned his stare with mild curiosity.

"How about this one?" Beau asked.

Tad raised his eyebrows when he saw which dog Beau was referring to. "That's a beautiful animal," he said. "But he's big and very strong. Are you interested in a dog that large?"

"What's the breed?" Beau asked.

"Bullmastiff," Tad said. "People are generally afraid of them because of their size, and this guy probably could take your arm off if he were so inclined. But he seems to have a good disposition. The word 'mastiff' actually comes from a Latin word that means 'tame.' "

"How come this dog is here?" Beau asked.

"I'll be honest with you," Tad said. "The previous owners had an unexpected child. They were afraid of the dog's reaction and didn't want to take a chance. The dog loves to hunt small game."

"Open the door," Beau suggested. "Let's see if we get along."

"Let me get a choke collar," Tad said. He went back and disappeared inside the building.

Beau bent down and opened a small feeding door. The dog got up from where he was sitting against the back of the cage and came over to smell Beau's hand. His tail wagged tentatively.

Reaching into his pocket Beau pulled out another of his black discs. Holding it between his thumb and index finger with the index finger on the top of the dome, he pressed it against the dog's shoulder. Almost immediately the dog let out a muffled yelp and took a step back. He tilted his head questioningly.

Beau pocketed the disc just as Tad reappeared with the leash.

"Did he yelp?" Tad asked as he joined Beau.

"I guess I was scratching him too hard," Beau said.

Tad opened the door to the cage. For a moment the dog hesitated, looking back and forth between the two humans.

"Come on, big boy," Tad said. "For the size of you, you shouldn't be so hesitant."

"What's his name?" Beau asked.

"King," Tad said. "Actually it's King Arthur. But that's going a bit far. Can you imagine trying to yell 'King Arthur' out your back door?"

"King's a good name," Beau said.

Tad got the collar on King and led him out of the cage. Beau reached out to pet him, but King hung back.

"Come on, King!" Tad complained. "Here's your big chance. Don't blow it."

"It's okay," Beau said. "I like him. I think he's perfect."

"Does that mean you'll take him?" Tad asked.

"Absolutely," Beau said. He took the leash, then squatted down and gave King a few pats on the head. King's tail slowly rose and then began to wag.

"I don't have much time," Cassy said to Pitt. They were walking down the corridor from the emergency room, heading toward the student overnight ward. "I've only got an hour between classes."

"This will only take a minute," Pitt said. "I just hope we are not too late."

They arrived at the room that Beau had occupied. Unfortunately for the moment they couldn't enter. Two workmen were struggling to carry out the twisted, disassembled bed.

"Look at the headboard," Pitt said.

"Weird," Cassey said. "It does look like it melted."

As soon as they could they stepped inside. Additional workmen were busy removing other warped fixtures including the metal supports for the suspended ceiling. Someone else was reglazing the window.

"Do they have any idea of what happened yet?" Cassy asked.

"Not a clue," Pitt said. "After the autopsy there was a short-lived scare about radiation, but the room and the general area was exhaustively checked and there wasn't any."

"Do you think there is any connection between all this and the way Beau has been acting?" Cassy asked.

"That's why I wanted you to see this," Pitt said. "I can't imagine how, but after you told me he'd been acting differently, I started thinking. After all, he did occupy this room the afternoon before all this happened."

"It is strange," Cassy said. She walked over to look at the twisted arm that previously held the TV. It was as bizarre as the head of the bed. Just as she was about to rejoin Pitt, her eyes happened to meet those of the man replacing the glass.

The workman stared at Cassy for a beat, then eyed her body lasciviously, much the same way Mr. Partridge had leered at her the night before.

Cassy stepped over to Pitt and tugged at his sleeve. He was looking up at the institutional clock on the wall. He'd noticed that the hands had fallen off.

"Let's get out of here," Cassy said. She made a beeline for the door.

Out in the hall Pitt caught up to her. "Hey, slow down," he said.

Cassy slowed. "Did you see the way that man at the window looked at me?" she demanded.

"No, I didn't," Pitt said. "What did he do?"

"He was like Partridge last night," Cassy said. "What is it with these men? It's as if they are reverting to adolescent behavior."

"Aren't construction workers famous for that?" Pitt asked.

"It was more than the proverbial cat-whistle and 'hey baby,'" Cassy said. "This was more like visual rape. Maybe I can't explain it to you. But a woman would know what I'm talking about. It's unpleasant, even frightening."

"You want me to go back in there and confront him?" Pitt asked.

Cassy shot him an "are you crazy" look. "Don't be silly," she said.

They got back to the ER.

"Well, I got to get to school," Cassy said. "Thanks for inviting me over here, although seeing that room has hardly made me feel any better. I don't know what to make of all this."

"I'll tell you what," Pitt said. "Today is the day Beau and I play our three-on-three basketball. It will give me an opportunity to ask him what's up."

"Don't mention that I said anything about sex," Cassy said.

"Of course not," Pitt said. "I'll use the playing hooky to start things off. Then I'll tell him straight out that last night at dinner and when we were walking around, he wasn't the Beau I know. I mean the difference is subtle, but it's real."

"You'll let me know what he says?" Cassy asked.

"Absolutely," Pitt said.

The squad room at police headquarters was always busy, especially around noon. But Jesse Kemper was accustomed to the bustle and could easily ignore it. His desk was in the back, against the glass wall that separated the captain's office from the main room.

Jesse was reading the preliminary autopsy report that Dr. Curtis Lapree had sent over. Jesse didn't like it one bit.

"Doc is still sticking to the idea of radiation poisoning," Jesse called out to Vince, who was at the coffee machine. Vince drank on average fifteen cups a day.

"Did you let him know there was no radiation at the scene?" Vince asked.

"Of course I told him," Jesse said irritably. He tossed the single-page report on the desk and picked up the photo of Charlie Arnold that showed the hole through his hand. Jesse scratched the top of his head where his hair was thinning while he studied the picture. It was one of the strangest things he'd ever seen.

Vince came over to Jesse's desk. His teaspoon clanked against the side of his cup as he stirred.

"This has to be the weirdest damn case," Jesse complained. "I keep seeing in my mind's eye the appearance of that room and ask how."

"Any news from that doctor lady about the science types she was going to have examine the scene?" Vince asked.

"Yeah," Jesse said. "She called and said that no one had any bright ideas. She did say that one of the physicists discovered the metal in the room was magnetized."

"So what does that mean?" Vince asked.

"Not much to me," Jesse admitted. "I called Doc Lapree and told him. His response was that lightning can do that."

"But everybody agrees there wasn't any lightning," Vince said.

"Exactly," Jesse said. "So we're back to square one."

Jesse's phone rang. He ignored it, so Vince picked it up.

Jesse rotated himself around in his swivel chair, tossing the photo of Charlie's hand over his shoulder in the process. It landed back on the desk amid the rest of the clutter. Jesse was exasperated. He still didn't know if he was dealing with a crime or an act of nature. Absently he heard Vince talking on the phone, saying "yeah" over and over. Vince concluded by saying: "Okay, I'll tell him. Thanks for calling, Doc."

Before Jesse could spin back around his eye caught two uniformed officers coming out of the captain's office. What had attracted his attention was that both of them looked terrible, almost as pale as Charlie Arnold in the photo Jesse'd just thrown over his shoulder. The officers were coughing and sneezing like they had the plague.

Jesse was something of a hypochondriac and it irritated him that people were inconsiderate enough to be spreading their germs all over creation. As far as Jesse was concerned they should have stayed the hell home.

A muffled "oww!" emanated from inside the captain's office and diverted Jesse's attention from the two sick officers. Through the window Jesse could see the captain sucking on his finger. In his other hand he was gingerly holding a black disc.

"Jesse, you listening or what?" Vince demanded.

Jesse spun around. "I'm sorry, what were you saying?"

"I said that was Doc Lapree on the phone," Vince said. "There's been a further complication on the Charlie Arnold case. The body disappeared."

"You're joking," Jesse said.

"Nope," Vince said. "Doc said he'd decided to go back and take a bone marrow sample, and when he opened up the refrigerator where Charlie Arnold's body had been placed, it was gone."

"Holy crap," Jesse voiced. He hauled himself to his feet. "We better go down there. This is getting too bizarre."

Pitt changed into his basketball gear and used his bike to travel from the dorm to the courts. He and Beau played frequently in the intramural three-on-three league. The competition was always good. A lot of the players could have played intercollegiate had they had the motivation.

As was his custom, Pitt arrived early in order to practice his shooting. He felt it took him longer than others to warm up. To his surprise Beau was already there.

Beau was dressed to play but was off to the side, behind a chain-link fence, conversing intently with two men and a woman. What was surprising was that the people appeared professional and in their middle to late thirties. All three were dressed in business suits. One of the men was carrying a fancy leather briefcase.

Pitt picked up a ball and began shooting. If Beau noticed him he didn't give any indication. After a few minutes something else about the situation seemed surprising to Pitt. Beau was doing all the talking! The others were simply listening, occasionally responding with nods of agreement.

The other players began to arrive including Tony Ciccone who made up the third person on Pitt and Beau's team. It was only after everyone had arrived including the opposition team and had warmed up that Beau wound up his conversation with the three businesspeople and joined Pitt. Pitt was now doing some stretching exercises.

"Hey, man, good to see you," Beau said. "I was afraid after that marathon you put in at the ER you weren't going to make it today."

Pitt straightened up and lifted a basketball in the process. "The way you were feeling the day before yesterday, you should be surprised you're here," he said.

Beau laughed. "Seems like ages ago. Now I feel terrific. In fact, I've never felt better, and we're going to cream these pansies."

The other three players were continuing to warm up down at the other basket. Tony was tightening the laces of his high-tops.

"I wouldn't be too cocky," Pitt said, squinting against the sun. "See the muscle-bound guy in the purple shorts? Believe it or not, his name is Rocko. He's a ball-breaker and a good shot to boot."

"No problem," Beau said. He snatched the ball away from Pitt and let it sail toward the basket. It went through the goal with a snapping sound having hit nothing but net.

Pitt was impressed. They were standing a good thirty feet away.

"Best of all, we have a cheering section," Beau said. Putting the tip of his thumb and index fingers together and puckering up his mouth, he let loose with a shrill whistle. About a hundred feet away an enormous light-brown dog got up from where he'd been lying in the shade and sauntered over. He collapsed at the edge of the tarmac of the court and lowered his head on his front paws.

Beau squatted down and gave him a series of pats on the top of the head. The tail wagged briefly then went limp.

"Whose dog?" Pitt asked. "If you can call it a dog. It looks more like a small pony."

"He's mine," Beau said. "His name is King."

"You got a dog?" Pitt asked incredulously.

"Yup," Beau said. "I felt like some canine companionship, so I went out to the pound this morning, and there he was, waiting for me."

"A week ago you said you didn't think it was fair to have big dogs in the city," Pitt said.

"I changed my mind," Beau said. "The moment I saw him I knew he was the dog of my dreams."

"Does Cassy know?"

"Not yet," Beau said. He scratched King enthusiastically behind his ears. "Won't she be surprised?"

"That's an understatement," Pitt said, rolling his eyes. "Especially a dog that size. But what's the matter with him? Is he sick? He seems lethargic and his eyes are red."

"Ah, he's just having trouble adjusting," Beau said. "He's just been let out of his cage. I've only had him a few hours."

"He's salivating," Pitt said. "You don't think he has rabies, do you?"

"Not a chance," Beau said. "Of that I'm certain." Beau cupped the dog's large head in his hands. "Come on, King. You should be feeling better by now. We need you to cheer us on."

Beau got to his feet, still gazing at his new companion. "He might be lethargic, but he's a good-looking dog, don't you agree?"

"I suppose," Pitt said. "But listen, Beau. Getting a dog, much less a huge one like this, is an awfully impulsive act, and knowing you the way I do, I'd have to say very unexpected. In fact, from my perspective you've been doing a number of unexpected things lately. I'm concerned, and I think we should have a talk."

"Talk about what?"

"About you," Pitt said. "The way you've been acting, like not going to class. It seems like ever since you had the flu . . ."

Before Pitt could finish Rocko had come up behind Pitt and given him a friendly slap on the shoulder that sent Pitt staggering forward several steps.

"Are you dorks going to play or forfeit?" Rocko jeered. "Pauli, Duff, and I have been ready to take you guys to the cleaners for the last half hour."

"I think we better talk later," Beau whispered to Pitt. "The natives are getting restless."

The game commenced. As Pitt guessed, Rocko dominated the play with his bulldozer tactics. To Pitt's chagrin the burden of covering him had fallen on his shoulders since Rocko had selected to guard Pitt. Every time Rocko got the ball he made it a point to crash right into Pitt before dropping back to put in a jump shot.

Halfway through the game with Rocko et al in the lead, Pitt called a foul after Rocko purposefully elbowed him in the gut in order to get a rebound.

"What?" Rocko demanded angrily. He threw the ball forcibly against the ground so that it bounced some ten feet into the air. "Is the little chicken-shit going to call an offensive foul? No way. Our ball! No way I'm going to honor a call like that."

"It's my call," Pitt persisted. "I say you fouled me. In fact, it's the second time you pulled the same cheap trick."

Rocko stepped over to Pitt and purposefully butted him with his chest. Pitt took a step backward.

"Cheap trick, huh?" Rocko snarled. "All right, tough guy, talk is cheap. Let's see the crybaby take a swing. Come on! I got my arms at my side."

Pitt knew better than to get into a fight with Rocko. Others had tried only to end up with chipped front teeth or black eyes.

"Excuse me," Beau said congenially. He stepped between Pitt and Rocko. "I don't think this issue is worth any hard feelings. I tell you what. We'll give up the ball, but we're going to change who guards whom. I think I'll take a turn guarding you, Rocko, and you can guard me."

Rocko gave a short laugh as he looked Beau up and down. Although they were both about six feet, Rocko outweighed Beau by more than fifteen pounds.

"You don't mind, do you?" Beau asked Pitt.

"Hell no," Pitt said.

With that settled, the game resumed. Rocko's thin-lipped, hard face had settled into a slight smile of anticipation. The next time he got the ball, he charged directly at Beau with his heavy thighs pumping.

With uncanny coordination, Beau managed to step out of the way at the instant Rocko expected contact. The result was almost comical. Expecting the collision, Rocko had his torso way out in front of his center of gravity. When no contact occurred, he sprawled on the pavement.

Everyone, even Pitt, winced, as Rocko skidded across the asphalt. He suffered several large abrasions that were liberally sprinkled with embedded gravel.

Beau was at the downed man's side instantly with an extended hand.

"Sorry, Rocko," Beau said. "Let me help you up."

Rocko glared up at Beau. He ignored the gesture for help and got to his feet under his own power.

"Oww," Beau said with a sympathetic wince. "You got some nasty scrapes there. I think we'd better call the game so you can go over to the infirmary and have them cleaned."

"Hell with you," Rocko said. "Give me the ball. We'll finish the game."

"It's up to you," Beau said. "But it's our ball. You lost it with your little tumble."

Pitt had watched this interchange with growing concern. Beau didn't seem to realize what kind of bully Rocko truly was, and Beau was taunting him. Pitt was afraid the afternoon would end with trouble.

As play resumed Rocko continued to try to use his strong-man tactics, but on each occasion, Beau was able to avoid contact. Rocko fell several more times, which clearly irritated him, and the angrier he got, the more easily Beau was able to deal with him.

Offensively Beau turned into a dynamo. Given the ball he could score at will despite Rocko's efforts to restrain him. On several drives, Beau had gone around Rocko with such a sudden burst of speed, Rocko was left in the dust with a confused expression. By the time Beau put in the final basket to win the game, Rocko's face was suffused with an angry blush.

"Hey, thanks for letting us win," Beau said to Rocko. He stuck out his hand but Rocko ignored it. Rocko and his fellow teammates slunk off to the sideline to towel off.

Beau, Pitt, and Tony walked back to where King was lying in the grass. King seemed even more lethargic than before the game.

"I told you King was going to help," Beau said.

Tony broke out some cold drinks. Pitt was particularly glad to get some fluid, and despite his panting, downed a can in record time. Tony handed him another.

Pitt was about to start on his second drink when he noticed that Beau was casually staring off at a couple of attractive co-eds coming along the track. They were wearing skimpy running gear.

"Great legs," Beau said.

That was when Pitt noticed that Beau was not out of breath like he and Tony were. In fact Beau wasn't even sweating and had yet to take a drink.

Beau caught Pitt staring at him out of the corner of his eye. "Something the matter?" Beau asked.

"You're not sucking air like we are," Pitt said.

"I guess I was loafing out there, letting you guys do all the work."

"Uh oh," Tony said. "Here comes the Sherman tank."

Both Beau and Pitt turned to see Rocko sauntering across the court in their direction.

"Don't taunt him," Pitt whispered forcibly.

"Who, me?" Beau asked innocently.

"We want a rematch," Rocko growled when he reached the group.

"I've had it for today," Pitt said. "I'm through."

"Me too," Tony said.

"I guess that's that," Beau said with a smile. "It wouldn't be quite fair if I played all three of you guys."

Rocko stared at Beau for a beat. "You're mighty arrogant for a little prig."

"I didn't say I'd win," Beau said. "Although I'm sure it would be close, especially the way you guys were playing toward the end of that last game."

"Man, you're looking for it," Rocko snarled.

"I'd rather you didn't raise your voice," Beau said. "My dog's sleeping right next to you, and he's feeling a bit under the weather."

Rocko glanced down at King, then back up at Beau. "I couldn't care a twit about your bag of turd of a dog."

"Wait a sec," Beau said. He got to his feet. "I'm a little confused. Are you calling my new dog a 'bag of turd'?"

"Worse than that," Rocko said. "I think he's a f—"

With hand speed that shocked everyone, Beau reached out and grabbed Rocko by the throat. Rocko reacted quickly as well, clenching his left hand into a tight fist and unleashing a powerful left hook.

Beau saw the blow coming but ignored it. It struck him on the side of his face, just in front of his right ear. The sound was a solid "thunk" that made Pitt wince.

Rocko felt a stab of pain from his knuckles after hitting up against Beau's cheekbone. The punch had been a hefty one and right on target yet Beau's facial expression didn't change. It was as if he'd not felt the blow.

Rocko was shocked by the seeming ineffectiveness of what heretofore had been his best weapon. People never expected a powerful left hook to be the first contact in a fight. It had always worked for Rocko, and more often than not, finished the fight. But with Beau it was different. The only change in Beau's appearance after the punch was that his pupils dilated. Rocko even thought they began to glow.

The other problem Rocko was experiencing was lack of oxygen. His face got redder and his eyes began to bulge. He tried to twist out of Beau's grasp but couldn't. It was as if he were being held by a pair of iron tongs.

"Excuse me," Beau said calmly. "I think you owe my dog an apology."

Rocko grabbed Beau's arm with both hands but still couldn't break Beau's hold around his neck. All Rocko could do was gurgle.

"I can't hear you," Beau said.

Pitt, who moments before had been worried about Beau, was now concerned about Rocko. The man's face was turning blue.

"He can't breathe," Pitt offered.

"You're right," Beau said. He let go of Rocko's neck and grabbed a handful of hair instead. Exerting an upward force, he was able to bring Rocko up onto his tiptoes. Rocko was still clutching Beau's arm with both hands but was unable to free himself.

"I'm waiting for the apology," Beau said. He increased the tension on Rocko's hair.

"I'm sorry about your dog," Rocko managed.

"Don't tell me," Beau said calmly. "Tell the dog."

Pitt was speechless. For a second it almost appeared as if Beau had lifted Rocko off his feet.

"I'm sorry, dog," Rocko squeaked.

"His name is King," Beau said.

"I'm sorry, King," Rocko echoed.

Beau released his hold. Rocko's hands shot to the top of his head. His scalp was burning. With a look that was a combination of anger, pain, and humiliation, Rocko slunk away to join his shocked teammates.

Beau brushed off his hands. "Ugh," he said. "I wonder what kind of goop he uses in his hair."

Pitt and Tony were as shocked as Rocko's teammates and were staring at Beau with their mouths hanging open. Beau noticed their expressions after reaching down for the end of King's leash.

"What is it with you guys?" Beau asked.

"How did you do that?" Pitt asked.

"What are you talking about?" Beau asked.

"How were you able to handle Rocko so easily?" Pitt asked.

Beau tapped the side of his head. "With intelligence," he said. "Poor Rocko uses only brawn. Brawn can be useful but its power pales compared to intelligence. It's why humans dominate this planet. In terms of natural selection, there's nothing that comes close."

All the sudden Beau looked off across the grass toward the library. "Uh oh," he said. "Looks like I'm going to have to leave you guys."

Pitt followed his line of sight. About a hundred yards off and coming in their direction was another group of businessmen types. This time there were six: four men and two women. All were carrying briefcases.

Beau turned back to his teammates. "Great game, guys," he said. He stuck up his hand and high-fived with both. Then he turned to Pitt. "We'll have to have that conversation you suggested another time."

Responding to a tug, King got reluctantly to his feet and followed his master out across the grass to the impromptu conference.

Pitt looked at Tony. Tony shrugged. "I never knew Beau was so strong," he said.

"How the hell can a body disappear?" Jesse asked Dr. Curtis Lapree. "I mean, has it ever happened before?" Jesse and Vince had ridden over to the morgue and were standing on either side of the empty refrigeration compartment where Charlie Arnold's body had been.

"Unfortunately it has happened before," Dr. Lapree admitted. "Not often, thank God, but it has happened. The last time was a little over a year ago. It was the body of a young woman, a suicide case."

"Was the body ever recovered?" Jesse asked.

"No," Dr. Lapree said.

"Was it reported to us?" Jesse asked.

"I don't know, to be truthful," Dr. Lapree said. "It was handled by the commissioner of health, who dealt directly with the commissioner of the police. It was an embarrassment all around and hence was kept as quiet as possible."

"What have you done on this case?" Jesse asked.

"The same thing," Dr. Lapree said. "I've turned it over to the head medical examiner, who's turned it over to the commissioner of health. Before you do anything you'd better check with your bosses. I probably shouldn't have even told you."

"I understand," Jesse said. "And I'll respect your confidence. But have you any suspicions of why someone would steal the body?"

"As a forensic pathologist I know more than most people that the world is full of weird people," Dr. Lapree said. "There are people out there who like dead bodies."

"You think that was the motivation in this instance?" Jesse asked.

"I haven't the slightest idea," Dr. Lapree admitted.

"We're concerned that the disappearance of the body adds weight to the idea that the man's death was a homicide," Jesse said.

"Like the perpetrator didn't want to leave a trail," Vince added.

"I understand," Dr. Lapree said. "But the problem with that line of thinking is that I'd already done the autopsy."

"Yeah, but you were coming back for more tissue," Jesse said.

"True," Dr. Lapree said. "I'd failed to take a sample of bone marrow. But that was just to add more weight to my acute radiation theory."

"If the reason the body was taken was to keep you from getting this final sample, then it sounds as if it were an inside job," Jesse said.

"We are aware of that," Dr. Lapree said. "We're in the process of reviewing everyone who had access to the body."

Jesse sighed. "What a case," he moaned. "The idea of retiring is sounding better and better."

"You'll let us know if you learn anything," Vince said.

"Absolutely," Dr. Lapree said.

Jonathan closed and locked his gym locker. For that semester he'd pulled gym as the last period of the day, and he hated it. He much preferred to have gym sometime in the middle of the day as an oasis between academic subjects.

Leaving the gym wing by the side door he started out across the quad. In the distance he could see a group of kids grouped around the flagpole. As he approached he could hear them cheering. When he got to the base of the flagpole he saw what was going on. A ninth grader, who Jonathan vaguely knew, was in the process of shinnying to the top. His name was Jason Holbrook. Jonathan knew him because he'd played on the freshman basketball team.

"What's happening?" Jonathan asked one of his classmates who was standing off to the side. His name was Jeff.

"Ricky Javetz and crowd have found some new ninth-grader to harass," Jeff said. "The kid's got to touch the eagle on top or he's not going to be allowed in the gang."

Jonathan shielded his eyes from the bright afternoon sun. "That pole's damn high," he said. "Must be fifty, sixty feet or more."

"And it's pretty skinny at the top," Jeff said. "I'm glad I'm not up there."

Jonathan looked around. He was surprised that no teachers had materialized to put a stop to this ridiculous situation. Just then he saw Cassy Winthrope emerge from the north wing. Jonathan elbowed Jeff. "Here comes that sexy student teacher."

Jeff turned to look. Cassy was dressed as usual in a loose-fitting simple cotton dress. As the sun angled through it, the boys could see a silhouette of Cassy's body, including a distinct outline of her high-cut panties.

"Wow," Jeff said. "What a piece of ass."

Mesmerized, the boys watched Cassy melt into the crowd then reappear at the base of the flagpole. She tossed some books she was carrying onto the ground, cupped her hands, and shouted up to Jason to come down.

The crowd hissed at Cassy's interference.

Almost three-quarters of the way to the eagle, Jason hesitated. The pole was beginning to wobble. It seemed higher than he'd expected.

Cassy looked around. The throng of students had closed in. Most of them were seniors and significantly larger than herself. It went through her mind that teachers were assaulted on a daily basis in schools across the United States.

Cassy looked back up the flagpole. From its base the wobbling was apparent.

"Did you hear me," Cassy called again, ignoring the crowd. She had her hands on her hips. "Get down here this instant!"

Cassy felt a hand grab her arm. She jumped. Surprisingly she found herself staring into Mr. Ed Partridge's leering, smiling face. "Miss Winthrope, you're looking delightful today."

Cassy peeled Ed's fingers from her arm. "We've got a student three-quarters of the way up the flagpole," she said.

"I've noticed," Ed said. He chuckled as he tilted his head back and gazed up at the now scared student. "I bet he can make it."

"I hardly think this kind of activity should be condoned," Cassy said in spite of herself.

"Ah, why not?" Ed said. Then cupping his hands he called up to Jason. "Come on, boy, don't fink out now. You're almost there."

Jason looked up. He had another twenty feet or so to go. Hearing the crowd urging him on, he recommenced climbing. The problem was that his hands were perspiring and moist. With each shinny, he slid back half of the gained distance.

"Mr. Partridge," Cassy began. "This isn't . . ."

"Calm down, Miss Winthrope," Ed said. "We have to let our students express themselves. Besides, it's entertaining to see if a prepubescent boy like Jason up there is capable of accomplishing this kind of feat."

Cassy looked up. The wobbling had increased. She shuddered to think of what would happen if the boy fell.

But Jason didn't fall. Benefiting from the crowd's support, he managed to get to the top, touch the eagle, and begin the descent. When he reached the ground, Mr. Partridge was the first to congratulate him.

"Well done, lad," Ed said, giving Jason a pat on the back. "I didn't think you had it in you." Mr. Partridge then looked out over the crowd. "Okay, everybody, time to break it up."

Cassy didn't leave immediately. She watched as Mr. Partridge herded many of the students toward the central wing while maintaining an animated conversation. Cassy was confused. Encouraging such an act seemed irresponsible and certainly out of character for Mr. Partridge.

"I believe these are your books," a voice said.

Cassy turned to see Jonathan Sellers extending her texts to her. She took them and thanked him.

"No problem," he said. He looked off at the fading image of Mr. Partridge. "He's become a different man all of a sudden," Jonathan said, mirroring Cassy's thoughts.

"Just like my parents," another voice said.

Jonathan turned to see Candee. He'd been unaware that she'd been in the crowd from the beginning. Stumbling over his words, he introduced her to Cassy, and as he did so, he noticed her eyes had a red-rimmed, sleepless appearance.

"Are you okay?" Jonathan asked.

Candee nodded. "I'm all right, but I didn't sleep much last night." She stole a self-conscious glance at Cassy, concerned about talking in front of a stranger. At the same time she had a strong urge to unburden herself. As an only child she'd not spoken with anyone, and she was troubled.

"How come you couldn't sleep?" Jonathan asked.

"Because my parents have been acting very strange," Candee said. "It's like I don't know them. They've changed."

"What do you mean 'changed'?" Cassy asked, thinking immediately of Beau.

"They're different," Candee said. "I don't know how to explain it. They're different. Like old Mr. Partridge."

"How long have you noticed this?" Cassy asked. She was amazed; what was happening to people?

"It's been just the last day or so," Candee said.

CHAPTER 9

4:15 P.M.

"Do you want phenytoin?" Dr. Draper yelled at Dr. Sheila Miller. Dr. Draper was one of the senior residents in the emergency medicine program at the University Medical Center.

"No!" Sheila snapped. "I don't want to take any chances on causing an arrhythmia. Give me ten milligrams of Valium IV now that we have the airway secured."

The city ambulance had called earlier to report that they were bringing in a forty-two-year-old diabetic who was in the throes of a major seizure. Considering what had happened with the seizing, diabetic woman the day before, the whole ER team, including Dr. Sheila Miller, had turned out for this new emergency.

Upon arrival the man had been taken directly into one of the bays where his airway had been given top priority. Then stat blood work had been drawn. Concurrently monitors were attached followed by a bolus of IV glucose.

Since the seizing had continued, more medication was necessary. That was when Sheila decided on the Valium.

"Valium given," Ron Severide said. Ron was one of the evening RNs.

Sheila was watching the monitor. Remembering what had happened with the woman the day before, she did not want this patient to arrest.

"What's the patient's name?" Sheila asked. By that time the patient had been in the ER for ten minutes.

"Louis Devereau," Ron said.

"Any other medical history besides the diabetes?" Sheila asked. "Any cardiac history?"

"None that we're aware of," Dr. Draper said.

"Good," Sheila said. She began to calm down. So did the patient. After a few more jerks, the seizing stopped.

"Looking good," Ron said.

No sooner had this positive assessment escaped from Ron's lips than the patient starting convulsing again.

"That's amazing," Dr. Draper said. "He's seizing in the face of both the Valium and the glucose. What's going on here?"

Sheila didn't respond. She was too busy watching the cardiac monitor. There'd been a couple of ectopic beats. She was about to order some lidocaine when the patient arrested.

"Don't do this," Sheila cried as she joined the others in a resuscitation effort.

In a fashion eerily similar to the experience with the woman the day before, Louis Devereau went from fibrillation to flatline no matter what the ER team did. To their great chagrin they had to admit defeat once again, and the patient was pronounced dead.

Feeling anger at the inadequacy of their effort, Sheila snapped her gloves off her hands and threw them forcibly into the appropriate container. Dr. Draper did the same. Together they walked back toward the main desk.

"Get on the phone with the medical examiner," Sheila said. "Make sure you convey to him the necessity of trying to figure out what caused this death. This can't go on. These were both relatively young patients."

"They both were insulin-dependent," Dr. Draper said. "And both had had long-term diabetes."

They reached the expansive ER desk. There was a lot of activity.

"So when has middle-aged diabetes become a fatal illness?" Sheila asked.

"Good point," Dr. Draper said.

Sheila glanced into the waiting room, and her eyebrows lifted. There were so many patients that there was standing room only. Ten minutes previously there'd been the normal number for that time of day. She turned to ask one of the clerks sitting behind the desk if there was some explanation for the sudden crowd and found herself looking at Pitt Henderson.

"Don't you ever go home?" she asked. "Cheryl Watkins told me you were back here hours after a twenty-four-hour shift."

"I'm here to learn," Pitt said. It was a planned retort. He'd seen her approach the desk.

"Well, good grief, don't burn out," Sheila said. "You haven't even started medical school yet."

"I just heard that the diabetic who'd just come in passed away," Pitt said. "That must be very hard for you to deal with."

Sheila looked down at this college senior. He was surprising her. Only the morning before he'd irritated her by sloshing her coffee all over her arm in a room where he had no business being. Now he was being uncharacteristically sensitive for a college-aged male. He was also attractive, with his coal-black hair and dark, liquid eyes. In a fleeting instant, she wondered how she would respond if he were twenty years older.

"I have something here that you will want to see," Pitt said. He handed her a printout from the lab.

Sheila took the sheet and glanced at it. "What is this?" she asked.

"It's the blood work on that diabetic who died yesterday," Pitt said. "I thought you might be particularly interested because all the values are entirely normal. Even the blood sugar."

Sheila scanned the list. Pitt was right.

"It will be interesting to see what today's patient's values are," Pitt said. "From the reading I've done, I can't think of any reason the first patient should have had a seizure."

Sheila was now impressed. None of the other college students who'd come through on the clerking program had shown such a degree of interest. "I'll count on you to get me the blood work on today's patient," she said.

"My pleasure," Pitt said.

"Meanwhile," Sheila said, "do you have any idea why there are so many people in the waiting room?"

"I think so," Pitt said. "It's probably because most of the people delayed coming in until after work. They're all complaining of the flu. Checking through the records from yesterday and today, we've been seeing more and more people with the same symptoms. I think it's something that you should look into."

"But it's flu season," Sheila said. She was even more impressed. Pitt was actually thinking.

"It might be flu season, but this outbreak seems unique," Pitt said. "I checked with the lab, and they have yet to have a positive test for influenza."

"Sometimes they have to grow the influenza virus in tissue culture before they get a positive test. That can take a few days."

"Yeah, I read that," Pitt said. "But in this instance I think it's strange because all these patients have had a lot of respiratory symptoms, so the virus should be there in a high titer. At least that's what it said in the text I was reading."

"I have to say I'm impressed with your initiative," Sheila said.

"Well, the situation worries me," Pitt said. "What if it is a new strain, maybe a new illness? My best friend got it a couple of days ago, and he was really sick, but only for a number of hours. That doesn't sound like regular old flu to me. Besides, after he'd recovered he hasn't been himself. I mean he's been healthy, but he's been acting strange."

"How do you mean strange?" Sheila asked. She began to consider the possibility of viral encephalitis. It was a rare complication of influenza.

"Like a different person," Pitt said. "Well, not totally different, just a little different. The same thing seems to have happened to the principal of the high school."

"You mean like a slight personality change?" Sheila asked.

"Yeah, I suppose you could say that," Pitt said. He was afraid to tell her about Beau's apparent increase in strength and speed and the fact that Beau had occupied the room that had become distorted; Pitt was afraid he'd lose all credibility. He was nervous about talking to Dr. Miller as it was and wouldn't have approached her on his own accord.

"And one other thing," Pitt said, thinking that he'd come this far and might as well let it all out. "I checked the chart of the diabetic woman who died yesterday. She had had flu symptoms before she got her seizure."

Sheila stared into Pitt's dark eyes while she pondered what he'd said. Suddenly she looked up and called out to Dr. Draper, asking him if Louis Devereau had had flu symptoms before he had his seizure.

"Yes, he did," Dr. Draper said. "Why do you ask?"

Sheila ignored Dr. Draper's question. Instead she looked down at Pitt. "About how many patients have we seen with this flu and how many are waiting?"

"Fifty-three," Pitt said. He held up a sheet of paper where he'd kept a tally.

"Jesus H. Christ," Sheila said. For a moment she stared off down the hall with unseeing eyes and chewed the inside of her cheek while she considered the options. Looking back at Pitt she said: "Come with me and bring that sheet of paper!"

Pitt struggled to catch up with Sheila who was moving as if on a power walk. "Where are we going?" Pitt asked as they entered the hospital proper.

"The president's office," Sheila said without elaboration.

Pitt squeezed onto the elevator with Dr. Miller. He tried to read her face but couldn't. He didn't have any idea why he was being taken to the administration. He worried it was for disciplinary purposes.

"I'd like to see Dr. Halprin immediately," Sheila said to the head administrative secretary. Her name was Mrs. Kapland.

"Dr. Halprin is tied up at present," Mrs. Kapland said with a friendly smile. "But I'll let him know you are here. Meanwhile can I get you coffee or perhaps a soft drink?"

"Tell him it's urgent," Sheila said.

They were kept waiting for twenty minutes after which the secretary escorted them into the administrator's office. Both Sheila and Pitt could tell that the man was not feeling well. He was pale and coughing almost continuously.

After Sheila and Pitt had taken chairs, Sheila concisely summarized what Pitt had told her and suggested that the hospital take appropriate action.

"Hold on," Dr. Halprin said between coughs. "Fifty cases of flu during flu season is not a reason to scare the community. Hell, I got the bug myself, and it isn't so bad, although if I had the choice, I suppose I'd be home in bed."

"That's fifty-plus cases at this hospital alone," Sheila said.

"Yes, but we are the major hospital in the community," Halprin said. "We see the most of everything."

"I've had two deaths of previously well-controlled diabetics who've possibly died of this illness," Sheila said.

"Influenza can do that," Dr. Halprin commented. "Unfortunately we all know it can be a nasty illness for the aged and the infirm."

"Mr. Henderson knows of two people who've had the illness and who have demonstrated personality changes as an aftermath. One of those people is his best friend."

"Marked personality change?" Halprin asked.

"Not marked," Pitt admitted. "But definite."

"Give me an example," Dr. Halprin asked while he blew his nose loudly.

Pitt related Beau's sudden carefree attitude and the fact that he'd skipped a whole day of classes to go to museums and the zoo.

Dr. Halprin lowered his tissue and eyed Pitt. He had to smile. "Excuse me, but that hardly sounds earth-shaking."

"You'd have to know Beau to realize how surprising it is," Pitt said.

"Well, we've had some experience with this illness right here in this office," Dr. Halprin said. "Not only do I have it today but both of my secretaries had it yesterday." He bent over and pressed his intercom button. He asked both secretaries to come into his office.

Mrs. Kapland appeared immediately and was followed by a younger woman. Her name was Nancy Casado.

"Dr. Miller is concerned about this flu bug that's going around," Dr. Halprin said. "Perhaps you two could set her mind at ease."

The two women looked at each other, unsure of who should speak. As the more senior employee Mrs. Kapland started.

"It came on sudden, and I felt terrible," she said. "But four or five hours later I was on the mend. Now I feel wonderful. Better than I have in months."

"It was pretty much the same for me," Nancy Casado said. "It started with a cough and sore throat. I'm sure I had a fever although I never took my temperature so I don't know how high it went."

"Do either of you think the other's personality has changed since your recovery?" Dr. Halprin asked.

Both women giggled and covered their mouths with their hands. They looked at each other conspiratorially.

"What's so funny?" Dr. Halprin asked.

"It's just a private joke," Mrs. Kapland said. "But to answer your question, neither of us feel our personalities have changed. Do you think so, Dr. Halprin?"

"Me?" Dr. Halprin questioned. "I don't think I have time to notice such things, but no, I don't think either one of you has changed."

"Do you know others who have been ill?" Sheila asked the women.

"Many," they said in unison.

"Have you noticed a change in anyone's personality?" Sheila asked.

"Not me," Mrs. Kapland said.

"Nor I," Nancy Casado said.

Dr. Halprin spread his hands out, palm up. "I don't think we have a problem here," he said. "But thanks for coming over." He smiled.

"Well, it's your call," Sheila said. She stood up.

Pitt did the same, and he nodded to the president and the secretaries. As his eyes met Nancy Casado's, he noticed that she was looking at him in a curiously provocative way. Her lips were slightly parted and the tip of her tongue played within the shadows. As soon as she could see he was looking at her, she let her eyes roam up and down his body.

Pitt quickly turned and followed Dr. Miller out of the president's office. He felt uncomfortable. All at once he had an appreciation of what Cassy had been trying to tell him that morning after their visit to the room Beau had occupied in the student overnight ward.

Balancing her books, purse, and some take-out chinese food, Cassy managed to get her key in the door and the door open. Entering, she kicked the door closed.

"Beau, are you home yet?" she called as she unburdened herself on the small table next to the door.

A deep, threatening growl made the hairs on the back of Cassy's neck stand straight up. The growl had been very close. In fact it sounded as if it had been right behind her. Slowly she raised her eyes to the decorative mirror above the entrance table. Just to the left of her image was the image of a huge light-brown bull mastiff with its enormous canines bared.

Ever so slowly so as not to upset the already perturbed animal, Cassy rotated to face it. Its eyes were like black marbles. It was a fearsome creature that stood taller than her waist.

Beau, munching an apple, appeared in the kitchen doorway. "Whoa, King! It's okay. This is Cassy."

The dog stopped growling and turned toward Beau and cocked his head to the side.

"It's Cassy," Beau repeated. "She lives here too."

Beau pushed off the doorjamb, gave King a pat and told him "good boy" before giving Cassy a solid kiss on the lips. "Welcome, lover," Beau said breezily. "We've been missing you. Where have you been?"

Beau moved over to the couch and draped himself over the arm.

Cassy hadn't moved a muscle. Nor had the dog except for his brief look at Beau. He wasn't growling any longer, but he'd continued to fix her with his baleful stare.

"What do you mean, where have I been?" Cassy asked. "You were supposed to pick me up. I waited for half an hour."

"Oh yeah," Beau said. "Sorry about that. I had an important meeting and there was no way to get in touch with you. You told me yourself you could get a ride easy enough."

"Yes, when it's planned," Cassy said. "By the time I realized you weren't coming, everyone I knew had left. I had to call a cab."

"Jeez!" Beau said. "I'm sorry. Really I am. There's just a lot going on all the sudden. How about I take you out to dinner tonight to your favorite place, the Bistro?"

"We were just out last night," Cassy said. "Don't you have work to do? I brought home some Chinese food."

"Well, whatever you want, sweetie," Beau said. "I feel badly about leaving you in the lurch this afternoon, so I'd like to make it up to you."

"Just the fact that you're willing to apologize goes a long way," Cassy said. She then looked down at the immobile dog.

"What's the story with this beast?" she asked. "Are you minding it for someone?"

"Nope," Beau said. "He's my dog. His name is King."

"You're joking," Cassy said.

"Hardly," Beau said. He hauled himself from the arm of the couch and stepped over to King. He scratched him roughly behind the ears. King responded with tail wagging and licking Beau's hand with his enormous tongue. "I figured we could use the protection."

"Protection from what?" Cassy asked. She was dumbstruck.

"Just in general," Beau said vaguely. "A dog like this has olfactory and auditory senses far better than ours."

"Don't you think we should have discussed this decision?" Cassy asked. Her fear was turning to anger.

"We can discuss it now," Beau said innocently.

"Good grief!" Cassy voiced angrily. She picked up the Chinese take-out and walked into the kitchen. She took the containers out of the bag and got plates from the cupboard, making sure the door banged against its hinges. From the drawer next to the dishwasher she got flatware and noisily set the table.

Beau appeared at the door. "There's no need to get upset," he said.

"Oh yeah?" Cassy questioned as tears unwillingly welled up. "That's easy for you to say. I'm not the one acting weird, like going out in the middle of the night and coming home with a dog the size of a buffalo."

Beau stepped into the kitchen and tried to put his arms around Cassy. She pushed him away and ran into the bedroom. She was sobbing now.

Beau came in behind her and put his arms around her, and she didn't resist. For a moment he didn't say anything and let her cry. Finally he turned her around and looked into her eyes, and she into his.

"Okay," he said. "I'm sorry about the dog too. I should have talked to you about the idea, but my mind has been so overwhelmed. I've got so many things going on right now. I've heard back from the Nite people. I'll be going out there to meet them."

"When did you hear from them?" Cassy asked, wiping her eyes. She knew how much Beau was counting on getting a job with Cipher Software. Maybe there was an explanation for his odd behavior.

"I heard from them today," Beau said. "It's all so promising."

"When will you go?" Cassy said.

"Tomorrow," Beau said.

"Tomorrow!" Cassy repeated. Things were happening too quickly. It was an emotional overload. "Weren't you going to tell me?"

"Of course I was going to tell you," Beau said.

"And you really want a dog?" Cassy asked. "What will you do with him when you go visit the Nite people?"

"I'll take him," Beau said without hesitation.

"You'll take him on an interview trip?"

"Why not? He's a wonderful animal."

Cassy digested this surprising information. From her perspective it seemed inappropriate to say the least. Having a dog seemed incompatible with their life-style.

"Who's going to walk him when you're in class? And feed him. Having a dog is a lot of responsibility."

"I know, I know," Beau intoned, raising his hands as if to surrender. "I promise to take care of him. I'll take him out, feed him, pick up after him, and punish him if he chews any of your shoes."

Cassy smiled in spite of herself. Beau sounded like the cliché of the small boy pleading with his mother to get a dog while the mother knows full well who will end up assuming the burden of taking care of the pet.

"I got him from the pound," Beau said. "I'm sure you'll like him, but if you don't, we'll take him back. We'll consider the whole thing an experiment. After a week we'll decide."

"Really?" Cassy asked.

"Absolutely," Beau said. "Let me get him so you can meet him properly. He's a great dog."

Cassy nodded, and Beau left the room. Cassy took a deep breath. So much seemed to be happening. Heading for the bathroom to wash her face, Cassy noticed that Beau's computer was running some weird, rapid program. Cassy hesitated and looked at the monitor. Data in the form of text and graphics was appearing and disappearing from the screen at bewildering speed. Then she noticed something else. Sitting in front of Beau's infrared port was the curious black object that Beau had found a few days previously in the parking lot of Costa's Diner. Cassy had forgotten it, and remembering that the men had said it was heavy, she reached for it.

"Here's the monster," Beau called, diverting Cassy's attention. Following Beau's commands, King was happy to bound over to Cassy and lick her hand.

"What a rough tongue," Cassy said.

"He's a great dog," Beau said, beaming.

Cassy patted King's flank. "He is solid," she said. "How much does he weigh?" She was wondering how many cans of dog food he'd need each day.

"I'd guess about one-twenty-five," Beau said.

Cassy scratched King behind the ear, then nodded toward Beau's computer. "What's going on with your PC? It looks like it's running out of control."

"It's just downloading some data off the Internet," Beau said. He stepped over to the machine. "I guess I could turn off the monitor."

"You're going to print all that?" Cassy said. "You'll have to get a lot more paper than we have."

Beau switched off the monitor but made certain the light on the hard drive kept up its rapid blinking.

"So what's it going to be?" Beau said, straightening up. "The Chinese take-out or the Bistro. It's your call."

Beau's eyes snapped open simultaneously with King's. Pushing up on one elbow Beau glanced across Cassy's sleeping form to see the time. It was 2:30 A.M.

Being careful to keep the bedsprings from squeaking, Beau eased his legs from beneath the covers and stood up. He patted King's head before slipping on his clothes. Then he moved over to his computer. A moment earlier the red light on his hard drive had finally stopped blinking.

He picked up the black disc and slipped it into his pocket. Using a notepad next to his computer he scribbled: "Gone for a walk. Be right back. Beau."

After placing the note on his pillow, he and King silently left the apartment.

Beau exited the building and walked around to the parking lot. King stayed at his side without a leash. It was another gorgeous night with the broad stripe of the Milky Way galaxy arching directly overhead. There was no moon, and the stars appeared more dazzling as a consequence.

Toward the rear of the parking lot Beau found an area devoid of cars. Taking the black disc from his pocket, he placed it on the asphalt. Almost the moment it left his hand, it began to glow. By the time Beau and King were fifty feet away it had begun to form its corona and was beginning to turn from red to white-hot.

Cassy had been sleeping restlessly all night with anxiety-filled dreams. She had no idea what had awakened her, but all at once she found herself staring at the ceiling. It was being progressively illuminated by an unusual light.

Cassy sat up. The whole room had a peculiar, mounting glow, and it was apparent that it was streaming in through the window. As she began to slip out of bed to investigate, she noticed Beau was absent just as he'd been the night before. This time, however, she could see that there was a note.

Taking the note with her, Cassy padded across the floor to the window and looked out. She saw the source of the glow immediately. It was a white ball of light which was rapidly increasing its intensity so that the surrounding cars were casting dark shadows.

In the next instant the light disappeared as if it had been suddenly snuffed out. It gave Cassy the impression it had imploded. An instant later she heard a loud whooshing sound that ended equally abruptly.

Having no idea of what she'd just seen, Candy wondered if she should call the police. While debating with herself, she started to turn back into the room when movement out in the parking lot caught her attention. Refocusing her eyes, she saw a man and a dog. Almost immediately she recognized Beau and King.

Certain he must have seen the ball of light, she was about to yell down to him when she saw other figures emerge out of the shadows. To her surprise thirty or forty people mystically appeared.

There were a few streetlights bordering the parking area, so Cassy could just make out some of the faces. At first she didn't recognize anyone. But then she saw two people she thought she knew. She thought she saw Mr. and Mrs. Partridge!

Cassy forced herself to blink several times. Was she really awake or was this a dream? A shudder passed through her. It was terrifying to be confused about her sense of reality. It gave her an immediate appreciation of the horror of psychiatric illness.

Looking again Cassy saw that the people had all congregated in the center of the parking lot. It was as if they were having a clandestine meeting. She thought briefly about putting on her clothes and going out to see what it was all about, but she had to admit to herself that she was frightened. The whole situation was surreal.

Then suddenly she had the sense that King had spotted her at the window. The dog's head had turned in her direction, and his eyes glowed like a cat's eyes when a light is shined in them. A bark from King made all the people look up, including Beau.

Cassy stepped back from the window in shocked surprise. All the people's eyes were glowing like King's. It gave her a shiver, and again she had to wonder if she were dreaming.

She stumbled back to her bed in the darkness and turned on the light. She read the note, hoping there might be some explanation, but it was completely generic. She put the note on the night table and wondered what she should do. Should she call the police? If she did, what would she say? Would they laugh at her? Or if they came would it turn out to be a big embarrassment if there were some reasonable explanation.

All at once she thought of Pitt. Snapping up the phone, she started to dial. But she didn't finish. She remembered it was three o'clock in the morning. What could he do or say? Cassy replaced the receiver and sighed.

Cassy decided she'd just have to wait for Beau to return. She had no idea what was going on, but she was going to find out. She'd confront Beau and demand that he tell her.

Having made a decision, even a passive one, Cassy felt a little less anxious. She leaned back against her pillow and tucked her hands behind her head. She tried not to think about what she'd just seen. Instead she made a conscious effort to relax by concentrating on her breathing.

Cassy heard the front door to the apartment squeak, and she sat bolt upright. She'd been asleep which made her wonder if she been dreaming after all. But a glance at the bedside table revealed Beau's note, and the fact that the light was on told her it had not been a dream.

Beau and King appeared at the doorway with Beau carrying his shoes. He was trying to be quiet.

"You're still awake," Beau said. He sounded disappointed.

"Waiting for you," Cassy said.

"I trust you got my note?" Beau asked. He tossed his shoes into the closet and started peeling off his clothes.

"I did," Cassy said. "I appreciated it." Cassy struggled with herself. She wanted to ask her questions but she felt a reluctance. The whole situation was like a nightmare.

"Good," Beau said. He disappeared into the bathroom.

"What was going on out there?" Cassy called out, marshalling her courage.

"We went for a walk like the note says," Beau called back.

"Who were all those people?" Cassy called.

Beau appeared in the doorway toweling off his face.

"Just a bunch of people out walking like me," Beau said.

"The Partridges?" Cassy questioned sarcastically.

"Yeah, they were there," Beau said. "Nice people. Very enthusiastic."

"What were you talking about?" Cassy asked. "I saw you from the window. It was like a meeting."

"I know you saw us," Beau said. "We weren't hiding or anything. We were just talking, mostly about the environment."

A sardonic half laugh escaped from Cassy. Under the circumstances she couldn't believe Beau would make such a ridiculous statement. "Yeah, sure," she intoned. "Three o'clock in the morning there's a neighborhood meeting on the environment."

Beau came over to the bed and sat on the edge. His expression was one of deep concern.

"Cassy, what is the matter?" he asked. "You're so upset again."

"Of course I'm upset," Cassy yelled.

"Calm down, dear, please," Beau said.

"Oh, come on, Beau. What do you take me for? What's going on with you?"

"Nothing," Beau said. "I feel wonderful, things are going great."

"Don't you realize how strange you've been acting?"

"I don't know what you are talking about," Beau said. "Maybe my value system is shifting, but hell, I'm young, I'm in college, I'm supposed to be learning."

"You haven't been yourself," Cassy persisted.

"Of course I have," Beau said. "I'm Beau Eric Stark. The same guy I was last week and the week before that. I was born in Brookline, Mass., to Tami and Ralph Stark. I have a sister named Jeanine, and I . . ."

"Stop it, Beau!" Cassy cried. "I know your history isn't different, it's your behavior. Can't you tell?"

Beau shrugged his shoulders. "I can't. I'm sorry, but I'm the same person I've always been."

Cassy let out a sigh of exasperation. "Well, you're not, and I'm not the only person who's noticed it. So has your friend Pitt."

"Pitt?" Beau questioned. "Well, now that you mention it, he did say something about me doing some unexpected things."

"Exactly," Cassy said. "That's just what I'm talking about. Listen! I want you to see somebody professional. In fact we'll both go. How's that?" Cassy let out another short sarcastic laugh. "Hell, maybe it's me."

"Okay," Beau said agreeably.

"You'll see someone?" Cassy said. She'd expected an argument.

"If it will make you feel better, I'll see someone," Beau said. "But of course it will have to wait until I get back from meeting with the Nite people, and I don't know exactly when that will be."

"I thought you'd just be going for the day," Cassy said.

"It will be longer than that," Beau said. "But exactly how long I won't know until I get there."

CHAPTER 10

9:50 A.M.

Nancy Sellers worked at home as much as she could. With her computer networked into the mainframe at Serotec Pharmaceuticals and with a superb group of technicians in her lab, she got more work done at home than in her office. The main reason was that the physical separation shielded her from the myriad administrative headaches involved in running a large research lab. The second reason was the tranquility of the silent house fostered her creativity.

Accustomed to absolute silence, the sound of the front door banging closed at ten minutes before ten got Nancy's attention immediately. Pessimistically thinking it could only be bad news, she exited from the program she was working on, and walked out of her home office.

She stopped at the balustrade in the hall and looked down into the front hall. Jonathan came into her line of sight.

"Why aren't you at school?" Nancy called down. Already she'd made a mental assessment of his health. He seemed to be walking okay, and his color was good.

Jonathan stopped at the foot of the stairs and looked up. "We need to talk with you."

"What do you mean, we?" Nancy asked. But no sooner had the question left her lips than she saw a young woman come up behind her son and tilt her head back.

"This is Candee Taylor, Mom," Jonathan said.

Nancy's mouth went dry. What she saw was a pixielike face on top of a well-developed female body. Her first thought was that she was pregnant. Being the mother of a teenager was like a high-wire act: disaster was always lurking around the corner.

"I'll be right down," Nancy said. "I'll meet you in the kitchen."

Nancy made a quick detour into the bathroom, more to get her emotions in check than to attend to her appearance. She'd been worried about Jonathan getting into this kind of a problem for the last year as his interest in girls skyrocketed, and he'd become uncommunicative and secretive.

When Nancy thought she was prepared, she met the kids in the kitchen. They had helped themselves to coffee that she kept on the stove. Nancy poured herself a cup and sat on one of the bar stools along the central island. The kids were sitting in the banquette.

"Okay," Nancy said, prepared for the worst. "Shoot."

Jonathan spoke first since Candee was obviously nervous. He described how Candee's parents were acting out of character. He said that he'd gone over there yesterday afternoon and had witnessed it himself.

"This is what you wanted to talk to me about?" Nancy asked. "About Candee's parents."

"Yes," Jonathan said. "You see, Candee's mom works at Serotec Pharmaceuticals in the accounting department."

"That must be Joy Taylor," Nancy said. She tried to keep the relief she felt out of her voice. "I've talked with her many times."

"That's what we thought," Jonathan said. "We were hoping you might be willing to talk with her because Candee is really worried."

"How is Mrs. Taylor acting that's so strange?" Nancy asked.

"It's both my mother and my father," Candee said.

"I can tell you from my perspective," Jonathan said. "Up until yesterday they didn't want me around. No way. Then yesterday they were so friendly I couldn't believe it. They even invited me to stay overnight."

"Why would they think you'd want to stay overnight?" Nancy asked.

Jonathan and Candee exchanged glances. Both blushed.

"You mean they were suggesting you two sleep together?" she asked.

"Well, they didn't say that exactly," Jonathan said. "But we kinda got that idea."

"I'll be happy to say something," Nancy said, and she meant it. She was appalled.

"It's not only the way they are acting," Candee said. "It's like they are different people. A few days ago they had like zero friends. Now all the sudden they're having people over . . . at all hours of the day and night to talk about the rain forests and pollution and things like that. People I swear they've never even met before who wander around the house. I've got to lock my bedroom door."

Nancy put her coffee cup down. She felt embarrassed about her initial suspicions. She looked at Candee, and instead of a seductress, she saw a frightened child. The image twanged the cords of her maternal instincts.

"I'll be happy to talk with your mother," Nancy repeated. "And you're welcome to stay here if you'd like in our guest room. But I'll be straight with you two. No fooling around, and I think you know what I mean."

———

"What will it be?" Marjorie Stephanopolis asked. Both Cassy and Pitt noticed her radiant smile. "Beautiful day, wouldn't you say."

Cassy and Pitt exchanged glances of amazement. This was the first time Marjorie had ever tried to have a conversation with them. They were in one of the booths at Costa's Diner for lunch.

"I'll have a hamburger, fries, and a Coke," Cassy said.

"Me too," Pitt said.

Marjorie collected the menus. "I'll have your orders out as soon as I can," she said. "I hope you enjoy your lunch."

"At least someone is enjoying the day," Pitt said as he watched Marjorie disappear back into the kitchen. "In the three and a half years I've been coming here, that's the most I've ever heard her say."

"You never eat hamburgers and fries," Cassy said.

"Nor do you," Pitt reminded her.

"It was the first thing that came to my mind," Cassy said. "I'm just so weirded out. And I'm telling you the truth about last night. I wasn't hallucinating."

"But you told me yourself you wondered if you were awake or were dreaming," Pitt reminded her.

"I convinced myself I was awake," Cassy said angrily.

"All right, calm down," Pitt said. He glanced around. Several people in the diner were glaring at them.

Cassy leaned across the table and whispered: "When they all looked up at me, including the dog, their eyes were glowing."

"Aw, Cassy, come on," Pitt said.

"I'm telling you the truth!" she snapped.

Pitt hazarded another look around the room. Even more people were eyeing them now. Clearly Cassy's voice was disturbing people.

"Keep your voice down!" Pitt whispered forcibly.

"Okay," Cassy said. She too could appreciate the stares they were getting.

"When I asked Beau what he was out there talking about at three o'clock in the morning, he told me, 'The environment,' " Cassy said.

"I don't know whether to laugh or cry," Pitt said. "Do you think he was trying to be funny?"

"No, not at all," Cassy said with conviction.

"But the idea of meeting out in the parking lot in the middle of the night to talk about the environment is absurd."

"So is the fact that their eyes were glowing," Cassy said. "But you haven't told me what Beau said when you spoke with him yesterday."

"I didn't get a chance," Pitt said. He then told Cassy everything that happened at the game and after it. Cassy listened with great interest, especially the part about Beau meeting the well-dressed business types on the athletic field.

"Do you have any idea what they were talking about?" Cassy asked.

"Not a clue," Pitt said.

"Could they have been from Cipher Software?" Cassy asked. She kept hoping for a reasonable explanation for everything that had been happening.

"I don't know," Pitt said. "Why would you ask that?" Before Cassy could answer, Pitt noticed Marjorie standing off to the side holding two Cokes. The moment he saw her she came over and placed the drinks on the table.

"Your food will be right out," she said cheerfully.

After Marjorie had again disappeared Pitt said: "I must be getting paranoid. I could have sworn she was standing there listening to us."

"Why would she do that?" Cassy asked.

"Beats me," Pitt said. "Tell me, did Beau go to his classes today?"

"No, he's flown off to Cipher Software," Cassy said. "That's why I asked you about them. He said he'd heard from them yesterday. I assumed they phoned but maybe they came in person. At any rate he's off for an interview."

"When will he be back?"

"He didn't know."

"Well, maybe that's good," Pitt said. "Maybe by the time he gets back he'll be back to normal."

Marjorie reappeared carrying the food. With a flourish she placed their orders before them and even gave their dishes a little spin to orient them perfectly as if Costa's were a fine restaurant.

"Enjoy!" Marjorie said happily before disappearing back into the kitchen.

"It's not just Beau who's been acting differently," Cassy said. "It's Ed Partridge and his wife, and I've heard of others. I think whatever it is, it's spreading. In fact I think it has something to do with the flu that's been going around."

"Amen!" Pitt said. "I have the same feeling. In fact I said as much yesterday to the head of the emergency room."

"And what was the reaction?" Cassy asked.

"Better than I anticipated," Pitt said. "The head of the ER is a rather hard-nosed no-nonsense woman by the name of Dr. Sheila Miller, yet she was willing to listen to me, and even took me over to talk with the president of the hospital."

"What was his response?" Cassy asked.

"He wasn't impressed," Pitt said. "But the man had the flu symptoms while we were talking with him."

"Is something wrong with your food?" Marjorie asked. She'd reappeared at the tableside.

"It's fine," Cassy said with exasperation at the interruption.

"But you haven't touched it," Marjorie said. "If there is a problem I can get you something else."

"We're okay!" Pitt snapped.

"Well, just call if you need me." She hurried off.

"She's going to drive me bananas," Cassy said. "I think I preferred her sullen."

All at once the same idea occurred to Cassy and Pitt.

"Oh my God!" Cassy said. "Do you think she's had the flu?"

"I wonder!" Pitt said with equal concern. "Obviously she's acting very out of character."

"We've got to do something," Cassy said. "Who should we go to? Do you have any ideas?"

"Not really," Pitt said. "Except maybe go back to Dr. Miller. She was at least receptive. I'd like to tell her there are other people with personality changes. I'd only mentioned Beau."

"Would you mind if I came along?" Cassy asked.

"Not at all," Pitt said. "In fact I'd prefer it. But let's do it right away."

"I'm game," Cassy said.

Pitt vainly scanned the room for Marjorie to get the check. When he didn't see her, he sighed with exasperation. It was frustrating that after pestering them for the whole meal, the moment he wanted her, she was nowhere to be seen.

"Marjorie is behind you," Cassy said. She pointed over Pitt's shoulder. "She's at the cash register having an animated chat with Costa."

Pitt twisted in his seat. The moment he did so, Marjorie and Costa both turned their heads in his direction and locked their eyes on his. There was an intensity in their gaze that gave Pitt a chill.

Pitt swung around to face Cassy. "Let's get the hell out of here," he said. "I must be getting paranoid again. I don't know why I'm so sure about this, but Marjorie and Costa were talking about us."

Beau had never been to Santa Fe before, but he'd heard good things about it and had been looking forward to his visit. He wasn't disappointed: he liked the town immediately.

He had arrived on schedule at the modest airport and had been picked up by a stretch Jeep Cherokee! Beau had never seen such a vehicle before, and at first he'd thought it was comical. But after riding in it, he was willing to believe it might be superior to a normal limousine because of its height. Of course he had to admit to himself that he hadn't had much experience with limousines of any sort.

As attractive as Beau found Santa Fe in general, it was only a harbinger of the beauty of the grounds of Cipher Software. After they had passed through a security gate Beau thought the facility had more of a resemblance to a posh resort than to a business establishment. Lush, rolling green lawns stretched between widely dispersed, well proportioned, modern buildings. Dense conifer forests and reflecting pools completed the picture.

Beau was dropped off at the central facility which, like the other buildings, was constructed of granite and gold-tinted glass. Several people who Beau had already met greeted him and told him that Mr. Randy Nite was waiting for him in his office.

As Beau and his escorts rose up in a glass-enclosed elevator through a plant-filled atrium, Beau was asked whether he was hungry or thirsty. Beau told them that he was fine.

Randy Nite's office was huge, occupying most of the west wing of the third and top floor of the building. About fifty feet square, it was bounded on three sides with floor-to-ceiling glass. Randy's desk stood in the center of this expansive space. It was made of a four-inch-thick slab of black and gold marble.

Randy was on the phone when Beau was ushered in, but he stood up immediately and waved Beau over to take a starkly modern black leather chair. He motioned to Beau that he'd be just a few minutes longer. Their job done, the escorts silently withdrew.

Beau had seen photos of Randy innumerable times as well as having seen him on TV. In person he appeared just as young and boyish, with a shock of red hair and a crop of pleasing freckles sprinkled across a wide, healthy-looking face. His gray-green eyes had a hint of merriment. He was about Beau's height but not as muscular although he appeared fit.

"The new software will be shipping next month," Randy was saying, "and the advertising blitz is poised to begin next week. It's a dynamite campaign. Things couldn't look any better. It's going to take the world by storm. Trust me!"

Randy hung up and smiled broadly. He was dressed casually in a blue blazer, acid-washed jeans, and tennis shoes. It was no accident that Beau was dressed in a similar fashion.

"Welcome," Randy said. He extended his hand, and Beau shook it. "I must say that my team has never recommended someone as highly as they have recommended you. Over the last forty-eight hours I've heard nonstop praise. It intrigues me. How has a college senior been able to manage such successful PR?"

"I suppose it's a combination of luck, interest, and old-fashioned hard work," Beau said.

Randy smiled. "Well put," he said. "I've also heard you'd like to start out, not in the mail room, but as my personal assistant."

"Everybody has to start someplace," Beau said.

Randy laughed heartily. "I like that," he said. "Confidence and a sense of humor. Kinda reminds me of myself when I started. Come on! Let me show you around."

"The emergency room looks crowded," Cassy said.

"I've never seen it like this," Pitt said.

They were walking across the parking lot toward the ER dock. Several ambulances were there with their lights blinking. Cars were parked haphazardly, and the hospital security was trying to straighten things out. The dock itself was full of people overflowing from the waiting room.

Climbing the stairs Pitt and Cassy had to literally push their way through to the main desk. Pitt saw Cheryl Watkins and called out to her: "What on earth is going on?"

"We've been inundated with the flu," Cheryl said. She sneezed herself, then coughed. "Unfortunately the staff hasn't been immune."

"Is Dr. Miller here?" Pitt asked.

"She's working along with everyone else," Cheryl said.

"Hang here," Pitt told Casey. "I'll see if I can find her."

"Try to be quick," Cassy said. "I've never liked hospitals."

Pitt got himself a white coat and pinned his hospital ID to the breast pocket. Then he started searching through the bays. He found Dr. Miller with an elderly woman who wanted to be admitted to the hospital. The woman was in a wheelchair ready to go home.

"I'm sorry," Dr. Miller said. She finished writing on the ER sheet and slipped its clipboard into a pocket in the back of the wheel chair. "Your flu symptoms don't warrant an admission. All you need is bed rest, analgesic, and fluids. Your husband will be in here in a moment to take you home."

"But I don't want to go home," the woman complained. "I want to stay in the hospital. My husband frightens me. He's not the same. He's someone else."

At that moment the husband appeared. He'd been brought back to retrieve his wife by one of the orderlies. Although as elderly as his wife, he appeared far more spry and mentally alert.

"No, no, please," the woman moaned when she saw him. She tried to grasp Dr. Miller's sleeve as the husband quickly rolled her out of the bay and toward the exit. "Calm down, dear," the man was saying soothingly. "You don't want to be a bother to these good doctors."

In the process of slipping off her latex examining gloves, Sheila caught sight of Pitt. "Well, you were certainly right about this flu being on the increase. And did you hear the little exchange I just had?"

Pitt nodded. "Sounds suspiciously like there might have been a personality change on the part of the husband."

"My thought as well," Sheila said as she threw away the gloves. "But of course older people can be prone to disorientation."

"I know you are busy," Pitt said, "but could you spare a minute? A friend and I would like to talk with you. We don't know who else to go to."

Sheila agreed immediately despite the chaos in the ER. Pitt's opinions the day before were appearing to be prophetic. She was now convinced this flu was different; for one thing an influenza virus had yet to be isolated.

She took Pitt and Cassy back to her office. As soon as the door closed it was like an island of tranquility in the middle of a storm. Sheila sat down. She was exhausted.

Cassy told the whole story of Beau's transformation after his illness. Although she felt self-conscious about certain parts, she left nothing out. She even related what had happened the previous night, including the strange ball of light, the clandestine meeting, and the fact that everyone's eyes glowed.

When Cassy was finished, Sheila didn't say anything at first. She'd been absently doodling with a pencil. Finally she looked up. "Under normal circumstances with a story like this I'd send you over to psychiatry and let them deal with you. But these are not normal circumstances. I don't know what to think about all this, but we should establish what facts we can. Now, Beau came down with his illness three days ago."

Cassy and Pitt nodded in unison.

"I should see him," Sheila said. "Do you think he'd be willing to come in and be examined?"

"He said he would," Cassy said. "I asked him specifically about seeing someone professional."

"Could you get him in here today?" Sheila asked.

Cassy shook her head. "He's in Santa Fe."

"When will he be back?"

Cassy felt a wave of emotion. "I don't know," she managed. "He wouldn't tell me."

"This is one of my favorite locations in the compound or the Zone as we like to call it," Randy said. He pulled the electric golf cart to a halt and climbed out. Beau got out his side and followed the software mogul up a small grassy knoll. When they reached the top the view was spectacular.

In front of them was a crystalline lake populated with wild ducks. The backdrop was virgin woodland silhouetted against the Rocky Mountains.

"What do you think?" Randy said proudly.

"It's awe-inspiring," Beau said. "It shows what concern for the environment can do, and it provides a ray of hope. It's such an unbelievable tragedy for an intelligent species like human beings to have done the damage they have to this gorgeous planet. Pollution, political strife, racial divisiveness, overpopulation, mismanagement of the gene pool . . ."

Randy had been nodding in agreement until the very last statement. He cast a quick look in Beau's direction, but Beau was dreamily staring off at the distant mountains. Randy wondered what Beau meant by "mismanagement of the gene pool." But before he could ask, Beau continued: "These negative forces have to be controlled, and they can be. I firmly believe there are adequate resources to reverse the harm done to the planet. All it will take is a great visionary man to carry the torch, someone who knows the problems, has the power, and is not afraid to lead."

A smile of acknowledgment spread involuntarily across Randy's face. Beau caught it out of the corner of his eye. The smile alone told Beau that he had Randy exactly where he wanted him.

"These certainly are visionary ideas for a college senior," Randy said. "But do you really think that human nature, such as it is, can be controlled enough to make it happen?"

"I've realized that human nature is a stumbling block," Beau admitted. "But with the financial resources and world community connections that you have amassed with Cipher Software, I think the obstacles can be overcome."

"It's good to have a vision," Randy said. Although he considered Beau overly idealistic, he was nonetheless impressed. But he wasn't impressed enough to start Beau out as his personal assistant. Beau would start in the mail room and work his way up like all his assistants.

"What is that over there on that pile of gravel?" Beau asked.

"Where?" Randy asked.

Beau walked over and bent down. He pretended to pick up one of his black discs that he'd actually pulled out of his pocket. Cradling it in his palm, he returned to Randy, and held it out.

"I don't know what it is," Randy said. "But I've seen some of my assistants with them over the last couple of days. What is it made of?"

"I can't tell," Beau said. "But it's heavy, so maybe it's metal. But take it. Maybe you can tell me."

Randy took the object and tested its weight. "A dense little thing," he remarked. "And what a smooth surface. And look at these symmetrically arranged bumps around the periphery."

"Owwww!" Randy cried. He dropped the disc to grab his finger. A drop of blood rapidly formed.

"The damn thing stung me!"

"That's odd," Beau said. "Let me see."

"There have been other people who have shown personality changes," Cassy told Sheila. "For instance, the principal where I'm student teaching has been acting totally different since his flu episode. I've also heard of others but haven't seen them in person."

"Frankly it is this mental status change that has me the most concerned," Sheila said.

Cassy, Pitt, and Sheila were on their way to Dr. Halprin's office. Armed with new information, Sheila was confident the president of the medical center would have a different response than he'd had the day before. But when they arrived, they were in for a disappointment.

"I'm sorry but Dr. Halprin called this morning to say he was going to take some time off," Mrs. Kapland told them.

"I've never known Dr. Halprin to miss a day at the hospital," Sheila said. "Did he give a reason?"

"He said he and his wife needed to spend some quality time together," Mrs. Kapland said. "But he will be calling in. Would you like to leave a message?"

"We'll be back," Sheila said.

Sheila spun on her heels. Cassy and Pitt hurried after her. They caught up to her at the elevator.

"What now?" Pitt asked.

"It's time someone made a phone call to the people who should be looking into this problem," she said. "Halprin's taking a day off for personal reasons is too weird."

"I hate suicides," Vince said as he turned right on Main. Up ahead was a gaggle of squad cars and emergency vehicles. Crime-scene tape held back a throng of onlookers. It was late afternoon and just getting dark.

"More than homicides?" Jesse asked.

"Yeah," Vince said. "In homicides the victim doesn't have any choice. Suicides are just the opposite. I can't imagine what it's like to kill yourself. It gives me the creeps."

"You're weird," Jesse said. For him it was just the other way around. It was the innocence of the homicide victim that disturbed him. Jesse couldn't conjure up the same sympathy for a suicide. He figured that if someone wanted to do himself in, it was his business. The real problem was making sure the suicide was a suicide and not a homicide in disguise.

Vince parked as close to the scene as he could. On the sidewalk a yellow tarp covered the deceased's remains. The only gore visible was a trail of blood that ran to the curb.

The detectives climbed out of their car and looked up. On a ledge six stories up they saw several crime-scene boys nosing around.

Vince sneezed violently twice in a row.

"Bless you," Jesse said reflexly.

Jesse approached a uniformed officer standing near the crowd barrier.

"Who's in charge here?" Jesse asked.

"Actually, the captain," the officer said.

"Captain Hernandez is here?" Jesse asked with surprise.

"Yup, upstairs," the officer said.

Jesse and Vince exchanged confused glances as they headed toward the entrance. The captain rarely ventured out to scenes.

The building belonged to Serotec Pharmaceuticals. It housed their administrative and research offices. Their manufacturing division was outside the town.

In the elevator Vince started to cough. Jesse moved away as much as the small car would allow. "Jeez," Jesse complained. "What's the matter with you?"

"I don't know," Vince said. "Maybe I'm having an allergic reaction or something."

"Well, cover your mouth when you cough," Jesse said.

They reached the sixth floor. The front of the building was occupied by a research lab. There were several uniformed policemen loitering by an open window. Jesse asked where the captain was and the policemen pointed toward an office off to the side.

"I don't think you guys are going to be needed," Captain Hernandez said when he saw Jesse and Vince enter. "The whole episode is on tape."

Captain Hernandez introduced Jesse and Vince to the half-dozen Serotec personnel in the room as well as the crime-scene investigator who'd found the tape. His name was Tom Stockman.

"Roll that tape once more, Tom," Captain Hernandez said.

It was black-and-white security camera footage taken with a wide-angle lens. The sound had an echolike quality. It showed a short man in a white lab coat facing the camera. He'd backed himself against the window and appeared anxious. In front of him were a number of Serotec people, all in similar white coats. They were seen from the back since they were facing the short man. Jesse guessed they were the same people who were now in the office.

"His name was Sergei Kalinov," Captain Hernandez said. "All of a sudden he started screaming for everyone to leave him alone. That was earlier in the tape. Plainly you can see that no one is touching him or even threatening him."

"He just flipped out," one of the Serotec employees said. "We didn't know what to do."

Sergei then began to sob, saying he knew he was infected and that he couldn't stand it.

One of the Serotec employees was then seen moving forward toward Sergei.

"That's the head tech, Mario Palumbo," Captain Hernandez said. "He's trying to calm Sergei. It's hard to hear his voice because he's speaking so softly."

"I was only telling him that we wanted to help," Mario said defensively.

Suddenly Sergei turned and made a dash for the window. He struggled to get it open. His frantic haste suggested he feared interference. But none of the people present including Mario tried to restrain him.

Once Sergei had the window open, he climbed out on the ledge. With one last glance back at the camera, he leaped off into space.

"Aw, man . . ." Vince voiced and looked away.

Even Jesse felt an unpleasant sinking feeling in his gut having watched this terrified little man kill himself. As the tape continued, Jesse watched as several of the Serotec people, including Mario, walked over to the window and looked down. But they weren't acting as if they were horrified. It was more like they were curious.

Then to Jesse's surprise they closed the window and went back to work.

Tom turned off the tape. Jesse glanced at the Serotec workers. Since they had just watched the harrowing sequence again he would have expected some reaction. There wasn't any. They were all eerily detached from the whole affair.

Tom ejected the tape and was about to slip it into an evidence bag with an attached custody slip when Captain Hernandez took it.

"I'll take care of this," the captain said.

"But that's not . . ."

"I'll take care of it," the captain repeated authoritatively.

"Okay," Tom said agreeably, even though he knew it was not accepted policy.

Jesse watched his captain walk out of the room with the tape in his hand. He looked at Tom.

"He's the captain," Tom said defensively.

Vince coughed explosively directly behind Jesse. Jesse turned and gave him a dirty look. "Jeez," he said. "You're going to get us all sick if you don't cover your mouth."

"Sorry," Vince said. "All of a sudden I feel terrible. Is it cold in here?"

"No it's not cold," Jesse said.

"Shit, I must have a fever," Vince said.

———

"Maybe we should just go out and get some mexican food," Pitt said.

"No, I want to cook," Cassy said. "It always calms me down."

They were walking beneath the bare lightbulbs strung on wires over the European-style outdoor market. The main commodities were fresh produce and fruit brought directly from outlying farms. But there were other stalls as well that sold everything from fish to antiques and objets d'art. It was a colorful, festive environment and popular. At that time in the early evening it was crowded with shoppers.

"Well, what do you want to make?" Pitt asked.

"Pasta," Cassy said. "Pasta primavera."

Pitt held the bag while Cassy made her selections. She was particularly choosy about the tomatoes.

"I don't know what I'm going to do when he does come back," Cassy said. "The way I feel right now, I don't even want to see him. At least not until I'm sure he's back to normal. This whole episode is frightening me more and more."

"I have access to an apartment," Pitt said.

"Really?" Cassy asked.

"It's over near Costa's," Pitt said. "The owner is a second cousin or something like that. He teaches in the chemistry department but is on a semester sabbatical in France. I go in to feed his fish and water his plants. He'd invited me to stay, but it was too much trouble to move at the time."

"You don't think he'd mind if I stayed there?" Cassy asked.

"Nope," Pitt said. "It's a big place. Three bedrooms. I'd stay too if you wanted."

"Do you think I'm overreacting?" Cassy asked.

"Not at all," Pitt said. "After his little demonstration at basketball I'm a bit leery of him myself."

"God! I can't believe we're talking this way about Beau," Cassy said with emotion.

Instinctively Pitt reached out and put his arms around Cassy. Just as instinctively she did the same. They clung to each other, momentarily oblivious to the other shoppers who swirled about them. After several moments Cassy glanced up into Pitt's dark eyes. Both felt a fleeting sense of what might have been. Then, suddenly embarrassed, they released each other and quickly went back to selecting tomatoes.

With their groceries purchased, including a bottle of dry Italian wine, they headed back to the car. The route took them through the flea market section. Pitt suddenly stopped in front of one of the stalls.

"Holy crap!" he exclaimed.

"What?" Cassy demanded. She was ready to flee. As keyed up as she was she expected the worst.

"Look!" Pitt said, pointing toward the stall's display.

Cassy's eyes swept over a bewildering collection of junk that a sign proclaimed to be antiques. There were mostly small items like ashtrays and ceramic animals, but there were a few larger things like plaster garden statues and bedside lamps. There were also several glass boxes of old, cheap costume jewelry.

"What am I supposed to be noticing?" Cassy asked impatiently.

"On the top of the shelf," Pitt said. "In between the beer mug and the pair of bookends."

They moved over to the stall. Cassy now saw what had caught Pitt's eye. "Isn't that interesting," she commented. Lined up in a perfect row were six of the black disc objects like the one Beau had found in the parking lot of Costa's Diner.

Cassy reached out to pick one up, but Pitt grabbed her hand. "Don't touch it!" he said.

"I wasn't going to hurt it," Cassy said. "I just wanted to see how heavy it was."

"I was worried about it hurting you!" Pitt said. "Not vice versa. Beau's stung him somehow. Or at least Beau thought so. What a coincidence seeing these things. I'd forgotten all about Beau's." He bent over and examined one of the discs more closely. He remembered that he and Beau had not been able to decide its composition.

"I saw the one Beau found just last night," Cassy said. "It was sitting in front of his computer when he was downloading a bunch of data from the Internet."

Pitt tried to get the attention of the owner to inquire about the discs, but he was busy with another customer.

While they were eyeing the discs and waiting for the stall keeper to be free, a heavyset man and woman pushed ahead of them.

"Here's some more of those black stones that Gertrude was talking about last night," the woman said.

The man grunted.

"Gertrude said she found four of them in her back yard," the woman said. She then added with a laugh: "She thought they might be valuable until she found out that people had been finding them all over."

The woman picked one of them up. "Wow, it's heavy," she said. She closed her fingers around it. "And it feels cold."

She was about to hand it to her friend when she cried, "Ahhh!" and irritably tossed it back onto the shelf. Unfortunately it skidded off and dropped less than a foot into the bowl of an ashtray. The ashtray shattered into a million pieces.

The sound of the breaking glass brought over the proprietor. Seeing what had happened, he demanded payment for the lost ashtray.

"I ain't paying nothing," the woman said indignantly. "That little black thinga-majig cut my finger." Defiantly she held up her wounded middle finger. The gesture incensed the owner who mistook its motivation as obscene.

While the woman and the owner argued, Pitt and Cassy looked at each other for confirmation about what they'd seen in the gathering gloom. When the woman had held up her finger it had appeared to have a faint blue iridescence!

"What could have caused it?" Cassy whispered.

"You're asking me?" Pitt questioned. "I'm not even sure it happened. It was only for an instant."

"But we both saw it," Cassy said.

It took another twenty minutes for the owner and the woman to come to an agreement. After the woman and her friend had left, Pitt asked the owner about the black discs.

"What do you want to know?" the man said morosely. He'd only gotten half the value of the ashtray.

"Do you know what they are?" Cassy asked.

"I haven't the slightest idea."

"How much do you sell them for?"

"In the beginning I got as much as ten dollars," the man said. "But that was a day or so ago. Now they're coming out of the woodwork, and the market's been flooded. But I'll tell you what. These happen to be exceptional quality. I'll sell you all six for ten dollars."

"Have any of these discs injured anyone else?" Pitt asked.

"Well, one of them stung me too," he said. He shrugged. "But it was nothing: just a pinprick. Yet I couldn't figure out how it happened." He picked up one of the discs. "I mean they're as smooth as a baby's bottom."

Pitt took Cassy's arm and began to lead her away. The man called after them. "Hey, how about eight dollars."

Pitt ignored him. Instead he told Cassy about the little girl in the ER who had been scolded by her mother for saying that a black rock had bitten her.

"Do you think it had been one of those discs?" Cassy asked.

"That's what I'm wondering," Pitt said. "Because she had the flu. That's why she was in the ER."

"Are you suggesting the black disc had something to do with her getting the flu?"

"I know it sounds crazy," Pitt said. "But that was the sequence with Beau. He got stung, then hours later he got sick."

CHAPTER 11

9:15 A.M.

"When did you hear about this Randy Nite news conference?" Cassy asked.

"This morning when I was watching the *Today* show," Pitt said. "The news anchor said NBC was going to be carrying it live."

"And they mentioned Beau's name?"

"That was the astounding thing," Pitt said. "I mean, he only went out there for an interview, and now he's part of a news conference. That's big-time weird."

Cassy and Pitt were in the doctors' lounge in the ER watching a thirteen-inch TV. Sheila Miller had called Pitt early and told him to be there and to bring Cassy. The room was called the doctors' lounge but was used by all the ER personnel for moments of relaxation and for those who brought paper bag lunches.

"What are we here for?" Cassy asked. "I hate to miss class."

"She didn't say," Pitt said, "but my guess is that she's gone over Dr. Halprin's head somehow and wants us to talk with whomever she's contacted."

"Are we going to mention about last evening?" Cassy asked.

Pitt held up his hand to quiet Cassy. The TV anchor was announcing that Randy Nite had entered the room. A moment later Randy's familiar boyish face filled the screen.

Before he began speaking, he turned to the side and coughed. Returning to the microphones he apologized in advance for his voice and said: "I'm just getting over a bout of the flu, so bear with me."

"Uh oh," Pitt said. "He's had it too."

"Now then," Randy said. "Good morning, everyone. For those of you who don't know me, my name is Randy Nite, and I'm a software salesman."

Discreet laughter could be heard from the onscreen audience. While Randy paused the anchor complimented Randy's humorous modesty; he was one of the world's richest men, and there were few people in the industrialized nations who didn't know of Randy Nite.

"I have called a news conference today to announce that I am starting a new venture . . . truly the most exciting, most important undertaking of my life."

An excited murmur erupted from the TV audience. They had expected big news, and it sounded as if they weren't to be disappointed.

"This new venture," Randy continued, "will be called the Institute for a New Beginning, and it will be backed by all the combined resources of Cipher Software. To describe this bold new venture, I would like to introduce a young man of tremendous vision. Ladies and gentlemen, please welcome my new personal assistant, Mr. Beau Stark."

Cassy and Pitt glanced at each other with mouths agape. "I don't believe this," Cassy said.

Beau bounded onto the speaker's platform amid applause. He was dressed in a designer suit with his dark hair slicked back from his forehead. He exuded a politician's confidence.

"Thank you all for coming," Beau boomed with a charming smile. His blue eyes sparkled like sapphires in the midst of his tanned face. "The Institute for a New Beginning is aptly named. We will be seeking the best and the brightest in the fields of science, medicine, engineering, and architecture. Our aim will be to reverse the negative trends that our planet has been experiencing. We can end pollution! We can end social and political strife! We can create a world suitable for a new humankind! We can and we will!"

The reporters present at the news conference erupted in a frenzy of questions. Beau held out his hands to quiet them.

"We will not be entertaining questions today. The purpose of this meeting was merely to make the announcement. One week from today we will hold another news conference in which our agenda will be spelled out in detail. Thank you all for coming."

Despite questions shouted from the news media, Beau stepped from the speakers' platform, embraced Randy Nite, and then the two of them, arm in arm, disappeared from view.

The announcer then tried to fill the gap caused by the precipitous end to the news conference. He began speculating on exactly what the specific goals of the new institute would be and what Randy Nite meant when he said that the venture would be backed by all the combined resources of Cipher Software. He pointed out that those resources were substantial, more than the GNP of many countries.

"My God! Pitt," Cassy said. "What's going on with Beau?"

"My guess is that his interview went okay," Pitt said, trying to be funny.

"This isn't a laughing matter," Cassy said. "I'm getting more and more scared. What are we going to tell Dr. Miller?"

"For the moment I think we've told her enough," Pitt said.

"Come on!" Cassy complained. "We have to tell her about what we saw last night and about the little black discs. We have to . . ."

"Cassy, hold on," Pitt said, taking her by the shoulders. "Think for a second how this is going to sound to her. She's our one chance to get someone important to take notice of what's going on. I don't think we should push it."

"But all she knows right now is that there's this strange flu," Cassy said.

"That's exactly my point," Pitt said. "We've got her attention about the flu and that it seems to cause personality changes. I'm worried if we start talking about far-out stuff like the flu being spread by tiny black discs, or even worse, seeing a fleeting blue light in someone's finger after it had been stung by a black disc, they'll not listen to us. She already threatened to send us to psychiatry."

"But we saw the blue light," Cassy said.

"We think we saw it," Pitt said. "Look, we have to get people involved first. Once they've investigated this flu and know something strange is going on, then we tell them everything."

The door opened and Sheila stuck in her head. "The man I want you two to talk with just arrived," she said. "But he was hungry, and I sent him down to the cafeteria. Let's move into my office so that we'll be prepared for him when he gets back."

Cassy and Pitt got to their feet and followed Sheila.

"All right, you two," Nancy Sellers said to Jonathan and Candee. "I want you to wait here in the van while I go in and talk to Candee's mom. Sound reasonable?"

Both Jonathan and Candee nodded.

"I really appreciate this, Mrs. Sellers," Candee said.

"You don't have to thank me," Nancy said. "Just the fact that your parents were too busy to talk on the phone last night when I called and chose not to call back tells me something is seriously wrong. I mean they didn't even know you stayed over."

Nancy alighted from the van, waved to the kids, and started out toward the front entrance of Serotec Pharmaceuticals. She could still see the stain on the sidewalk where poor Mr. Kalinov had impacted the concrete. She hadn't known the man well since he was a relatively new employee and was in the biochemistry department, but the news had saddened her. She knew he had a family with two teenage daughters.

Entering the building, Nancy wondered what to expect. After the death the day before she was unsure how the whole establishment would be functioning. A memorial service was scheduled for that afternoon. But she immediately sensed that everything was already back to routine.

The accounting department was on the fourth floor, and as she rode up in the crowded elevator, she overheard normal conversation. There was even laughter. At first it made Nancy feel relieved that people had taken the episode in stride. But when the whole car burst into laughter about a comment Nancy hadn't heard well enough to understand, she began to feel uncomfortable. The joviality seemed disrespectful.

Nancy found Joy Taylor with ease. As one of the more senior people she had her own office. When Nancy walked through the open door, Joy was busy at her computer terminal. As Nancy had remembered, she was a mousy person about Nancy's size although much thinner. Nancy guessed that Candee took after her father.

"Excuse me," Nancy called out.

Joy looked up. Her pinched features registered momentary irritation at being disturbed. Then her expression warmed and she smiled.

"Hello," Joy said. "How have you been?"

"Just fine," Nancy said. "I wasn't sure you'd remember me. I'm Nancy Sellers. My son Jonathan and your daughter Candee are classmates."

"Of course I remember you," Joy said.

"Terrible tragedy yesterday," Nancy said while she thought about how to bring up the issues she wanted to discuss.

"Yes and no," Joy said. "Certainly for the family, but I happen to know that Mr. Kalinov had serious kidney disease."

"Oh?" Nancy questioned. The comment confused her.

"Oh yes," Joy said. "He'd been on weekly dialysis for years. There was talk of a transplant. It was bad genes. His brother had the same problem."

"I hadn't heard about his medical problems," Nancy said.

"Is there something I can help you with?" Joy asked.

"Yes, there is," Nancy said, taking a seat. "Well, it's more that I wanted to talk with you. I'm sure it's not serious, but I felt I should at least mention it to you. I'd want you to do the same for me if Jonathan had come to you."

"Candee came to you?" Joy asked. "About what?"

"She's upset," Nancy said. "And frankly, so am I."

Nancy noticed a slight hardening of Joy's features.

"What did Candee say she was upset about?" Joy asked.

"She feels that things have changed at home," Nancy said. "For one thing she said that you and your husband are suddenly doing a lot of entertaining. It's made her feel insecure. Apparently some people have even wandered into her bedroom."

"We have been entertaining," Joy said. "Both my husband and I have recently become very active in environmental causes. It requires work and sacrifice, but we're willing to do both. Perhaps you'd like to come to our meeting tonight."

"Thanks, but some other time," Nancy said.

"Just let me know when," Joy said. "But now I've got to get back to work."

"Just a moment longer," Nancy said. The conversation was going poorly. Joy was not being receptive despite Nancy's diplomatic efforts. It was time for more candor. "My son and your daughter also got the impression that you were encouraging them to sleep together. I'd like you to know that I don't agree with this at all. In fact I'm adamantly against it."

"But they are healthy and their genes are well matched," Joy said.

Nancy struggled to remain calm. She'd never heard such a ridiculous statement. Nancy could not understand Joy's casual attitude about such an issue, especially with the burgeoning problem of teen pregnancy. Just as aggravating was Joy's equanimity in the face of Nancy's obvious agitation.

"Jonathan and Candee do make a cute couple," Nancy forced herself to say. "But they are only seventeen and hardly ready for the responsibilities of adult life."

"If that is how you feel I will be happy to respect it," Joy said. "But my husband and I feel that there are a lot more pressing issues, like the destruction of the rain forest."

Nancy had had enough. It was plain to her that she was not going to have a rational conversation with Joy Taylor. She stood up. "Thank you for your time," she said stiffly. "My only recommendation is that perhaps you might pay a little more attention to your daughter's state of mind. She is upset."

Nancy turned to leave.

"Just a moment," Joy said.

Nancy hesitated.

"You seem to be extremely anxious," Joy said. "I think I can help you." She pulled out the top drawer of her desk and gingerly lifted out a black disc. Placing it in the palm of her hand, she extended it toward Nancy. "Here's a little present for you."

Nancy was already convinced that Joy Taylor was more than a little eccentric, and this unsolicited proffering of a talisman just added to the impression. Nancy leaned over to take a closer look. She had no idea what the strange object was.

"Take it," Joy encouraged.

Out of curiosity Nancy reached for the object. But then she thought better of it and withdrew her hand. "Thank you," she said, "but I think I should just leave."

"Take it," Joy urged. "It will change your life."

"I like my life as it is," Nancy said. Then she turned and walked out of Joy's office. As she descended in the elevator she marveled over the conversation she'd just had. It wasn't anything like she'd expected. And now she had to worry about what she was going to tell Candee. Jonathan, of course, was a different story. She'd tell him to stay the hell away from the Taylor residence.

The door to Dr. Miller's office opened and both Pitt and Cassy got to their feet. A balding yet relatively youthful man walked into the room ahead of Dr. Miller. He was dressed in a nondescript, wrinkled gray suit. Rimless glasses were perched on the end of a broad nose.

"This is Dr. Clyde Horn," Sheila said to Cassy and Pitt. "He's an epidemiological investigative officer from the Centers for Disease Control in Atlanta. He works specifically for the influenza branch."

Clyde was introduced to Pitt and Cassy in turn.

"You two are the youngest-looking residents I think I've ever seen," Clyde commented.

"I'm not a resident," Pitt said. "In fact I'm only starting medical school in the fall."

"And I'm a student teacher," Cassy said.

"Oh, I see," Clyde said, but he was obviously confused.

"Pitt and Cassy are here to put the problem in a personal perspective," Sheila said as she motioned for Clyde to take a seat.

They all sat down.

Sheila then made a presentation of the influenza cases that they had been seeing in the emergency room. She had some charts and graphs which she showed to Clyde. The most impressive was the one that showed the rapid increase in the number of cases over the previous three days. The second most impressive dealt with the number of deaths of people with the same symptoms associated with various chronic disease like diabetes, cancer, kidney problems, rheumatoid arthritis, and liver ailments.

"Have you been able to determine the strain?" Clyde asked. "When you spoke with me on the phone, that had yet to be done."

"It still isn't done," Sheila said. "In fact we still haven't isolated the virus."

"That's curious," Clyde said.

"The only thing we have consistently seen is marked elevation of lymphokines in the blood," Sheila said. She handed Clyde another chart.

"Oh my, these are high titers," Clyde said. "And you said the symptoms are all typical flu."

"Yes," Sheila said. "Just more intense than usual, and generally localizing in the upper respiratory tract. We've seen no pneumonia."

"It certainly has stimulated the immune systems," Clyde said as he continued to study the lymphokine chart.

"The course of the illness is quite short," Sheila said. "In contrast to normal influenza, it reaches a peak in only hours, like five or six. Within twelve hours the patients are apparently well."

"Even better than they were before the illness," Pitt said.

Clyde wrinkled his forehead. "Better?" he questioned.

Sheila nodded. "It is true," she said. "Once recovered the patients exhibit a kind of euphoria with increased energy levels. The disturbing aspect is that many also behave as if they have had a personality change. And that is why Pitt and Cassy are here. They have a mutual friend who they insist is acting like a different person subsequent to his recovery. His case may be particularly important because he might have been the first person to get this particular illness."

"Have there been any neurological workups done?" Clyde asked.

"Indeed," Sheila said. "On a number of patients. But everything was normal including cerebrospinal fluid."

"What about the friend, whatever his name," Clyde said.

"His name is Beau," Cassy said.

"He has not be examined neurologically," Sheila said. "That was planned, but for the moment he's unavailable."

"In what ways is Beau's personality different?" Clyde asked.

"In just about every way," Cassy said. "Prior to his flu he'd never missed a class. After recovery he hasn't gone to any. And he's been waking up at night and going outside to meet strange people. When I asked him what he'd been talking to these people about, he said the environment."

"Is he oriented to time, place, and person?" Clyde asked.

"Most definitely," Pitt said. "His mind seems particularly sharp. He also seems to be significantly stronger."

"Physically?" Clyde asked.

Pitt nodded.

"Personality change after a bout of flu is uncommon," Clyde said while absently scratching the top of his bald pate. "This flu is unique in other ways as well. I've never heard of such a short course. Strange! Do you know if the other hospitals in the area have been seeing the same problem?"

"We don't know," Sheila said. "But finding that out is much easier for the CDC to do."

A loud rap on the door got Sheila out of her chair. Having left specific instructions not to be disturbed, she was concerned a medical emergency had arrived. But instead it was Dr. Halprin. Behind him stood Richard Wainwright, the chief lab tech who had helped draw up the charts Sheila had been presenting. Richard was red-faced and nervously shifting his weight from one foot to the other.

"Hello, Dr. Miller," Dr. Halprin said cheerfully. He had completely recovered from his illness and was now the picture of health. "Richard just informed me that we have an official visitor."

Dr. Halprin pushed into the room and introduced himself as the hospital president to Clyde. Richard self-consciously remained by the door.

"I'm afraid you've been called here under less than forthright pretenses," Dr. Halprin said to Clyde. He smiled graciously. "As Chief Executive Officer any requests for CDC assistance has to come through my office. That's stated in our bylaws. This is, of course, unless it is a reportable illness. But influenza is not."

"I'm terribly sorry," Clyde said. He stood up. "It had been my impression we'd received a legitimate request and all was in order. I don't mean to interfere."

"No problem," Dr. Halprin said. "Just a minor misunderstanding. The fact of the matter is we don't need the services of the CDC. But come to my office, and we can straighten it all out." He put his arm around Clyde's shoulders and urged him toward the door.

Sheila rolled her eyes in frustration. Cassy, already distraught and sensing they were about to lose a significant opportunity, stepped in front of the door, barring egress. "Please, Dr. Horn," she said. "You must listen to us. There is something happening in this city. People are changing with this illness. It's spreading."

"Cassy!" Sheila called out sharply.

"It's true," Cassy persisted. "Don't listen to Dr. Halprin. He's had this flu himself. He's one of them!"

"Cassy, that's enough!" Sheila said. She grabbed Cassy and dragged her aside.

"I'm sorry about this, Clyde," Dr. Halprin said soothingly. "May I call you Clyde?"

"Certainly," Clyde said, nervously looking over his shoulder as if he expected to be attacked.

"As you can see this minor problem has caused significant emotional upset," Dr. Halprin continued as he motioned for Clyde to precede him into the hall. "Unfortunately it has clouded objectivity. But we'll discuss it in my office, and we can make arrangements to get you back to the airport. I've even got something I want you to take back to Atlanta for me. Something I think that will interest the CDC."

Sheila closed the door behind the departing figures and leaned against it. "Cassy, I don't think that was wise."

"I'm sorry," Cassy said. "I couldn't help myself."

"It's because of Beau," Pitt explained to Sheila. "He and Cassy are engaged."

"You don't have to apologize," Sheila said. "I felt equally frustrated. The problem is: now we are back to square one."

The estate was magnificent. Although it had been whittled down to less than five acres over the years, the central house was still standing and in fine condition. It was built in the early nineteen-hundreds in a French château style. The stone was a local granite.

"I like it," Beau said. He spun in the middle of the expansive ballroom with his arms outstretched. King sat near the door as if he feared he was going to be left in the mansion by himself. Randy and a realtor by the name of Helen Bryer were standing off to the side.

"It is four point six acres," Ms. Bryer told Randy. "It is not a lot of land for the size of this house, but it is immediately adjacent to your own holdings at Cipher, so the effective land would be much more."

Beau strolled over to the massive windows and let the sunlight cascade over him. The view was stupendous. With a reflecting pool in the foreground it reminded him of the view from the knoll on the Cipher property.

"I heard your announcement this morning," Ms. Bryer said. "I must tell you, Mr. Nite, I think your Institute for a New Beginning sounds wonderful. Humankind will be grateful."

"New humankind," Randy said.

"Yes, right," Ms. Bryer said. "A new humankind awakened to the needs of the environment. I think something like this has been a long, long time in coming."

"You have no idea how long," Beau called out from where he was standing at the window. Then he strolled over to Randy and Ms. Bryer. "This house is perfect for the institute. We'll take it!"

"Excuse me?" Ms. Bryer said, even though she'd clearly heard Beau. She cleared her throat. She glanced at Randy for confirmation. Randy nodded. Beau smiled and wandered out of the room. King followed.

"Well, this's wonderful!" Ms. Bryer said excitedly when she'd found her voice. "It's a gorgeous property. But don't you want to know how much the seller is asking?"

"Call my lawyers," Randy said. He handed Ms. Bryer a card. "Let them draw up the papers." Randy then left the room looking for Beau.

"Of course, Mr. Nite," Ms. Bryer said. She blinked. Her voice echoed in the now empty ballroom. She smiled to herself. It had been the strangest sale she'd ever made, but what a commission!

The rain sounded like grains of sand as it pummeled the window off to the right of Jesse's desk. Peals of thunder added to the atmosphere. Jesse liked lightning storms. It reminded him of summertime during his childhood back in Detroit.

It was late afternoon and under normal circumstances Jesse would have been ready to head home. Unfortunately Vince Garbon had called in sick that morning, and Jesse had to do work for two. With another hour of paperwork to go, Jesse picked up his empty coffee mug and pushed back from his desk. From years of experience he knew that one more cup wouldn't keep him up that night, and it would help him get through the rest of the day.

On his way to the communal pot, Jesse was struck by how many of his fellow officers were coughing, sneezing, or sniffling. On top of that were all the guys out sick, like Vince. Something was going around, and Jesse considered it a blessing that he'd not been stricken.

On his way back to his desk, Jesse happened to glance through the glass divider into the captain's office. To his surprise the captain was standing at the window facing into the squad room with his hands behind his back and a contented smile glued to his face. When he caught Jesse's eye he waved and flashed a toothy grin.

Jesse waved back. But as he sat down, he wondered what was up with the captain.

First of all, he rarely stayed this late unless there was some special ops, and second of all he was always in a bad mood by the afternoon. Jesse had never seen him smile after twelve.

After getting himself comfortable once again and with his pen in his hand poised above one of the innumerable forms, Jesse hazarded another glance into the captain's office. To his surprise the captain was still in the same spot sporting the same smile. Like a voyeur, Jesse stared at the captain for a beat and tried to divine what on earth the captain was smiling about. It wasn't a humorous smile. It was more a smile of satisfaction.

With a bewildered shake of his head, Jesse refocused his attention to the stack of forms in front of him. He detested paperwork, but it had to be done.

A half hour later, with several of the forms completed, Jesse again got up from his desk. This time it was nature calling. As usual the coffee had gone right through him.

Heading for the men's room at the end of the hall, he glanced into the captain's office and was relieved to see it was empty. Inside the lavatory Jesse didn't dally. He did his thing and got the hell out because there were a half dozen guys in there coughing and sneezing and blowing their noses.

En route back to his desk Jesse passed by the drinking fountain to wet his whistle. That took him by the property booking desk, where he was spotted by Sergeant Alfred Kinsella through the wire mesh of his cage.

"Hey, Jesse!" Alfred called out. "What's up?"

"Not much," Jesse answered. "How's that blood problem of yours?"

"No change," Alfred said. He cleared his throat. "I still have to go in for a transfusion now and then."

Jesse nodded. He had given blood just like most of the guys on the force for Alfred's benefit. Jesse felt sorry for Alfred. He couldn't comprehend what it would be like to have a serious illness the doctors couldn't even diagnose.

"Want to see something bizarre?" Alfred asked. He cleared his throat again and then coughed forcibly several times. He put a hand to his chest.

"You okay?" Jesse asked.

"Yeah, I suppose," Alfred said. "But I've been feeling a little punk over the last hour or so."

"You and everyone else," Jesse said. "What do you have that's bizarre?"

"These little guys," Alfred said.

Jesse moved over to the chest-height counter of the property lockup. He saw that Alfred had a row of black discs in front of him, each about an inch and a half in diameter.

"What are they?" Jesse asked.

"I haven't the foggiest idea," Alfred said. "In fact I was hoping you might be able to tell me."

"Where'd they come from?"

"You know the rash of first-time offenders being brought in the last couple of nights and booked for crazy stuff like lewd behavior or having mass meetings in public spaces without permits."

Jesse nodded. Everybody had been talking about it, and Jesse himself had seen some strange behavior lately.

"Every last one of those people had been carrying one of these black miniature frisbees."

Jesse got his face close to the wire mesh so he could get a better look. The black discs appeared like container tops. There were about twenty of them.

"What are they made of?" Jesse asked.

"Damned if I know, but they are heavy for their size," Alfred said. He sneezed several times and blew his nose.

"Let me see one," Jesse said. He reached through the opening of the wire mesh cage with the intention of picking one of them up. Alfred grabbed his arm.

"Careful!" he warned. "They look perfectly smooth but they can sting. It's kinda spooky because I've not been able to find a sharp edge. Yet I've been stuck several times already. Feels like a bee sting."

Taking Alfred's advice, Jesse took a ballpoint pen from his pocket and used it to push around one of the discs. To his surprise it was not easy. They were indeed heavy. It was particularly hard to get one of them to flip over. Jesse gave up.

"Well, you're on your own," Jesse said. "I don't have any idea what they are."

"Thanks for looking at them," Alfred said in between coughs.

"You sound like you've gotten worse just while I've been standing here," Jesse said. "Maybe you'd better go home."

"I'll stick it out," Alfred said. "I just came on duty at five."

Jesse headed for his desk planning on staying another half hour tops, but he didn't get far. Behind him he heard a fit of coughing and then a crash.

Turning around Jesse saw that Alfred had disappeared from view. Running back to the counter he could hear thumps like someone kicking the cabinets. Pulling himself over the counter Jesse looked down. There on the floor was Alfred with his back arched and his body quivering. He was having a convulsion.

"Hey everybody!" Jesse shouted. "We got a man down in property booking."

Jesse went over the top of the booking desk head first, knocking most of the clutter on its surface to the floor, including the twenty or so black discs. Intent on the convulsing figure of Alfred, Jesse didn't notice that all of the discs landed lightly and right side up.

The first thing Jesse did was get Alfred's keys and plop them on the counter so others could unlock the cage door. Although Jesse had a key, most people didn't. Next he forced a pad of paper between Alfred's tightly clenched jaws. He was about to unbutton the top button of his shirt when he saw something that startled him. A foam was oozing out of Alfred's eyes!

Shocked by this spectacle, Jesse straightened up. He'd never seen anything like it. It was like bubble bath.

Within seconds Jesse was joined by other officers. All were equally amazed at the burgeoning froth.

"What the hell is that foam?" one of the officers asked.

"Who the hell cares," Jesse said, breaking the trance. "Let's get an ambulance. Now!"

There was a loud clap of thunder simultaneous with the gurney as it slammed through the main ER doors of the University Medical Center. It was being pushed by two burly EMTs. A few steps behind was Jesse Kemper. On the gurney Alfred Kinsella was still convulsing. His face was blue, and foam was still bubbling from his eyes like two bottles of disturbed champagne.

Sheila, Pitt, and Cassy emerged from Sheila's office where they'd been most of the day collating all the flu cases, including all the cases seen that day. Sheila had heard the commotion and had responded immediately. She'd been forewarned by the head nurse that a strange case was on its way. The EMTs had called ahead as they'd left the police headquarters.

Intercepting the gurney, Sheila glanced at Alfred. Seeing the foam, she directed the EMTs to take the patient into the bay reserved for contaminated cases. She'd never seen anything like it and wasn't about to take any chances. As the gurney was quickly pushed away, Sheila got the head nurse's attention and told her to page a neurologist stat.

Jesse grabbed Sheila's arm. "Remember me? I'm Detective Lieutenant Jesse Kemper. What's wrong with Officer Kinsella?"

Sheila pulled away. "That's what we would like to find out. Pitt, come on with me; this will be a trial by fire. Cassy, take Lieutenant Kemper into my office. The waiting room is too crowded."

Cassy and Jesse watched Sheila and Pitt run down the hall after the gurney.

"I'm glad I'm not a doctor," Jesse said.

"You and me both," Cassy said. Then she pointed toward Sheila's office. "Come on! I'll show you where you can wait."

The wait was not long. Within a half hour Sheila and Pitt appeared at the door. Their expressions were funereal. It wasn't hard to guess the outcome.

"No luck?" Cassy asked.

Pitt shook his head.

"He never regained consciousness," Sheila said.

"Was it the same flu?" Cassy asked.

"Probably; his lymphokines were very high," Pitt said.

"What the hell are lymphokines?" Jesse asked. "Is that what killed him?"

"Lymphokines are part of the body's defense against invasion," Sheila said. "They are a response, not a cause of disease. But tell me, did Mr. Kinsella have any chronic disease like diabetes?"

"He didn't have diabetes," Jesse said. "But he had a serious problem with his blood. He had to have transfusions every so often."

"I have a question," Cassy said suddenly. "Do you know if Sergeant Kinsella had ever mentioned anything about a black disc about this big." Cassy made a circle about an inch and a half in diameter with her thumbs and forefingers.

"Cassy!" Pitt moaned.

"Quiet!" Cassy said to Pitt. "At this point we don't have much to lose and a lot to gain."

"What's this about a black disc?" Sheila asked.

Pitt rolled his eyes. "Here we go," he said to no one in particular.

"You mean a black disc that's flat on the bottom but has a dome on the top and little nubbin-like bumps around the edge."

"Exactly," Cassy said.

"Yeah, he showed me a bunch of them just before he had his convulsion."

Cassy cast a triumphant look at Pitt whose expression had gone from exasperation to intense interest in the matter of seconds.

"Did he say anything about being stung by one of these discs?" Pitt asked.

"Yeah, a number of times," Jesse said. "He said it was kinda spooky since he couldn't find a sharp edge. And you know something, now that I think about it, I remember the police chief, Captain Hernandez, getting stung by one."

"Somebody better fill me in on these black discs," Sheila said.

"We found one four days ago," Cassy said. "Well, actually it was Beau who found it. He picked it up from the gravel in a parking lot."

"I was there when he found it," Pitt said. "We had no idea what it was. I thought it might have fallen out from beneath Beau's car."

"After just a few minutes Beau said it stung him," Cassy said. "Then a number of hours later Beau came down with his flu."

"We had really forgotten about the disc, to tell the truth," Pitt said. "But then here in the emergency room I was checking in a little girl with the flu who said that a black rock had bitten her."

"But it was an episode just last night that really got us thinking," Cassy said. She went on to describe the incident at the market. She even described the faint blue glow that she and Pitt thought they'd seen.

When Cassy was finished there was a silence.

Sheila finally blew out through pursed lips. "Well, this all sounds crazy, and as I said before, under normal circumstances I'd call in a psychiatry consult for you two. But at this point I'm willing to explore just about anything."

"Tell me," Jesse said. "Does Beau recognize that he's acting differently?"

"He says he doesn't," Cassy said. "But I find it hard to believe. He's doing things he's never done before."

"I agree," Pitt said. "A week ago he was adamantly against large dogs in the city. Suddenly he gets one."

"Yeah, and without discussing it with me," Cassy said. "And we live together. But why do you ask?"

"It would be an important point if the people who are affected are purposefully dissembling," Sheila said. "We'll have to be discreet. But let's get us one of these black discs."

"We can go back to the market," Pitt said.

"I might be able to get one out of property booking," Jesse said.

"Well, try both," Sheila said. She took out a couple of business cards and wrote her home number on the backs. She gave one to Jesse and one to Pitt and Cassy. "Whoever gets one of these discs first, give me a call. But, as I said, let's be discreet about this. It sounds to me that this is the type of thing that could cause a panic if there's any truth to it."

Just before they broke up, Pitt gave both Sheila and Jesse the number of his cousin's apartment. He said that he and Cassy would be staying there. Cassy gave him a questioning look but didn't contradict him.

"Which way do you think the stall was that had the discs?" Pitt asked. They had entered the outdoor market about the same time as the evening before. It was a large area, about the size of two city blocks, and with all the tiny stalls it was like a maze.

"I remember where we got the produce," Cassy said. "Why don't we go there first and follow our trail?"

"Good idea," Pitt said.

They found the stand, where they'd bought tomatoes, with comparative ease.

"What did we do after the tomatoes?" Pitt asked.

"We got the fruit," Cassy said. "It was in that direction." She pointed over Pitt's shoulder.

After they found the fruit stall they both remembered the route into the flea market section. A few minutes later they were standing in front of the booth they sought. Unfortunately it was empty.

"Excuse me," Cassy called to the proprietor of the next stand. "Could you tell me where the man is that runs this empty stall?"

"He's sick," the man said. "I talked with him this morning. He's got the flu like most of us have."

"Thanks," Cassy said. Then to Pitt she whispered: "What do we do now?"

"Hope that Lieutenant Kemper has better luck," Pitt said.

Jesse had driven back to police headquarters directly from the hospital, but he'd hesitated before going in. The news of Kinsella's death had undoubtedly reached the station, and people were going to be upset. It hardly seemed to be the time to be nosing around in Kinsella's cage, especially if the captain was still hanging around. After listening to Cassy and Pitt he'd been reminded of how weird the captain had been acting of late.

So Jesse had driven home. He lived a mile away from headquarters in a small house that was big enough for one person. He'd been living by himself since his wife died of breast cancer eight years previously. They'd had two children but both of them preferred the excitement of Detroit.

Jesse made himself a simple dinner. After a few hours passed he began to entertain the idea of going back to the station, but he knew it would raise a few eyebrows since it was not usual for him to be there unless something out of the ordinary was going on. While he was trying to think up some sort of an explanation, he wondered if Cassy and Pitt had already gotten one of the discs. If they had, there was no need for him to make the effort.

Looking through the scraps of paper in his pocket, he located the kid's telephone number. He placed the call. Pitt answered.

"We bombed," Pitt said. "The guy who had the discs is sick. We asked at other stalls and were told the market had become so flooded, they couldn't sell them. So no one is carrying them anymore."

"Damn," Jesse said.

"You weren't able to get one either?" Pitt asked.

"I haven't tried yet," Jesse admitted. Suddenly an idea occurred to him. "Hey, would there be any chance of you two coming with me to the station? Maybe it sounds funny but if I walk in there by myself, everybody's going to be wondering what I'm doing. If I come in acting like I'm in the process of investigating something, there won't be a problem."

"It's okay by me," Pitt said. "Hang on, let me ask Cassy."

Jesse toyed with the phone cord. Pitt came right back on the line. "She's ready to do anything that might help," Pitt said. "Where should we meet?"

"I'll come and pick you up," Jesse said. "But it will be after midnight. I want the evening gang to have gone home. It will be easier during the graveyard shift. There's a lot less personnel involved." The more Jesse thought about the idea the better it sounded.

It was quarter past one when Jesse pulled into the police headquarters' parking lot and came to a stop in his reserved spot. He killed the engine.

"Okay, guys," Jesse said. "Here's how this is going to play. We're going to walk in the front door. You'll have to go through the metal detector. Then we'll head directly for my desk. If anybody asks you what you're doing, just say you are with me. Okay?"

"Should I be scared about going in there?" Cassy asked. She never thought she'd be concerned about going to police headquarters.

"Nah, not in the slightest," Jesse assured her.

They climbed from the car and entered the station. While Pitt and Cassy were going through the metal detector they overheard the uniformed policeman at the front desk: "Yes, ma'am. We'll be there as soon as we can. We understand that raccoons can be unsettling. Unfortunately we're understaffed with the flu that's going around . . ."

A few minutes later they were sitting around Jesse's desk. The squad room was deserted. "This is better than I thought," Jesse said. "There's hardly anybody here."

"This would be the time to rob the bank," Pitt said.

"That's not funny," Cassy chastised.

"Okay, let's get up and go back to property booking," Jesse said. "Here's my Cross pen. If need be we'll pretend we're booking it in as if it belonged to you."

Pitt took the pen. All three got to their feet.

The property booking cage was locked up tight. Only the light from the hall shone through the wire mesh to illuminate the interior.

"All right, you guys wait here," Jesse said. He used his key to open the door. A quick glance around the floor told him that someone had picked up the discs and the other objects that he'd knocked off the counter when he'd vaulted over to help Alfred. "Damn," he voiced.

"Is there a problem?" Pitt asked.

"Somebody's picked up in here," Jesse said. "The discs must have been placed in envelopes, and there's a whole dad-blasted stack of them in here."

"What are you going to do?"

"Open them up," Jesse said. "There's no shortcut."

Jesse started. It took longer than he expected. He had to twist the clasps, open the envelope, and look inside.

"Can we help?" Pitt offered.

"Yeah, why not," Jesse said. "We'll be here all night."

The kids entered the cage and, following Jesse's lead, began opening envelopes.

"They got to be here someplace," Jesse said irritably.

They worked in silence. After about five minutes Jesse reached out and whispered, "Hold up!"

Slowly Jesse raised himself so he could see over the top of the counter. He'd heard what he thought were footsteps. What he saw made his heart skip a beat. He had to blink to make sure it wasn't an apparition. It wasn't. It was the captain and he was coming in their direction.

Jesse ducked back down. "Jesus," he whispered. "The captain is coming. Move back under the counter and don't move."

As soon as the kids were in position, Jesse stood up. Since there was still time he exited the property booking cage. Walking quickly, he intercepted the captain in the hall.

"The duty officer said you were here, Kemper," the captain said. "What the hell are you doing? It's almost two o'clock in the morning."

Jesse was tempted to turn the question around since it was a lot stranger for the captain to be there than it was for him. But Jesse held his tongue. Instead he said: "Just dealing with a problem involving a couple of kids."

"In the property booking cage?" the captain asked, looking over Jesse's shoulder.

"Yeah, I'm looking for a bit of evidence," Jesse said. But then to change the subject he added: "Terrible tragedy about Kinsella."

"Hardly," the captain said. "He had that chronic illness with his blood. Listen, Kemper, how are you feeling?"

"Me?" Jesse questioned. He was nonplussed by the captain's response concerning Kinsella.

"Of course you," the captain said. "Who else am I talking to."

"I'm fine," Jesse said. "Thank the Lord."

"Well, that's strange," the captain said. "Listen, stop by my office before you leave. I've got something for you."

"Sure thing, Captain," Jesse said.

The captain took another look over Jesse's shoulder before heading back to his office. Jesse watched him leave, perplexed at what was going through his mind.

When the captain had disappeared from view, Jesse hustled back inside the property booking cage. "Let's find one of those discs and get the hell out of here," he said.

Cassy and Pitt emerged from their hiding place in the knee space below the counter. All three went back to opening envelopes.

"Ah ha!" Jesse said as he peered into a particularly heavy one. "Finally!" He reached in to pull it out.

"Don't touch it," Cassy cried out.

"I was going to be careful," Jesse said.

"It happens quickly," Pitt said.

"All right, so I won't touch it," Jesse said. "I'll leave it in the envelope. Let me sign this custody chit and then let's get out of here."

A few minutes later they were back at Jesse's desk in the nearly empty squad room. Jesse glanced into the captain's office. The light was on, but the captain was nowhere to be seen.

"Let's take a look at this thing," Jesse said. He opened the clasp on the envelope and let the disc slide out onto his blotter.

"Looks innocent enough," Jesse commented. As he'd done earlier, he used a pen to push it around. "There's also no opening. How could it possibly sting someone?"

"Both times that I witnessed, the person had wrapped either their fingers or palm around the periphery," Pitt said.

"But if there's no opening it can't happen," Jesse said. "Maybe they're all not the same. Maybe some sting, some don't." He got out his reading glasses, which he detested for vanity reasons, put them on, and then leaned over to get a closer, magnified view. "It looks like polished onyx, only not as shiny." With the tip of his finger he touched the top of the dome.

"I wouldn't do that," Pitt warned.

"It feels cold," Jesse said, ignoring Pitt. "It's also very smooth." Gingerly he moved the very tip of his finger down from the apex of the dome toward the periphery with the intention of feeling the little bumps that lined the edge. The sound of a cabinet banging shut over at the duty officer's desk made him snatch his hand away.

"I guess I'm a little tense," Jesse explained.

"For good reason," Pitt said.

Ready to withdraw his hand at the slightest provocation, Jesse touched one of the little bumps. Nothing happened. Equally carefully he began to run the tip of his finger around the disc's periphery. He got about a quarter of the way around when an extraordinary thing happened. A millimeter-wide slit formed in the seamless surface of the disc's edge.

Jesse yanked his hand away in time to see a chrome-colored needle punch out through the slit a distance of several millimeters. From its tip sprang a single drop of yellowish fluid. In the next instant the needle withdrew and the slit vanished. The whole sequence lasted only a second.

Three pairs of startled eyes rose to regard each other.

"Did you see that?" Jesse asked. "Or am I crazy?"

"I saw it," Cassy said. "And there's proof. There's a wet spot on the blotter."

Nervously Jesse bent his head forward and, with his magnifiers, as he called his glasses, studied the area where the slit had formed. "There's nothing there, not even a seam."

"Wait a sec," Pitt said. "Don't get too close. That fluid must be infectious."

As a hypochondriac Jesse didn't need any more encouragement. He got out of his chair and backed several steps away. "What should we do?"

"We need some scissors and a container, preferably glass," Pitt said. "Plus some chlorine bleach."

"How about a coffee creamer jar?" Jesse suggested. "I don't know about the bleach, but I'll check the janitor's closet. The scissors are in the top drawer."

"A coffee creamer jar is fine," Pitt said. "How about latex gloves?"

"We got those too," Jesse said. "I'll be right back."

Jesse managed to find everything Pitt needed. With the scissors Pitt carefully cut out a circle of the blotter containing the wet dot and deposited it in the jar. The underside of the blotter didn't appear wet, but still he disinfected the area of the desk with the bleach. The gloves and the scissors went into a plastic bag.

"I think we should call Dr. Miller," Pitt said when he was finished.

"Now?" Jesse questioned. "It's after two in the morning."

"She's going to want to know about this right away," Pitt said. "It's my guess she'll want to start immediately trying to grow out whatever is in this sample."

"Okay, you call," Jesse said. "I've got to go in and see the captain. By the time I get back you can tell me if I'm taking you to the med center or home."

Jesse's mind was a jumble of disconnected thoughts as he headed for the captain's office. So much crazy stuff had happened in so short a time, particularly the crack appearing like magic in the black disc, that he felt numb. He was also exhausted since it was way past his bedtime. Nothing seemed real. Even the fact that he was heading in to see the captain after two in the morning.

The captain's office door was ajar. Jesse halted on the threshold. The captain was at his desk busily writing as if it were the middle of the day. Jesse had to admit to himself that the captain looked better than he had in a year despite the hour.

"Excuse me, Captain," Jesse called out. "You wanted to see me?"

"Come in," the captain said, waving Jesse over to the desk. He smiled. "Thanks for coming by. Tell me, how are you feeling now?"

"Pretty tired, sir," Jesse said.

"Not sick?"

"No, thank goodness," Jesse said.

"Get that problem taken care of with the two kids?"

"Still working on it," Jesse said.

"Well, I wanted to reward you for your hard work," the captain said. He opened the center drawer of his desk, reached in and pulled out one of the black discs!

Jesse's eyes widened in shocked surprise.

"I want you to have this symbol of a new beginning," the captain said. He had the disc in the palm of his hand, and he extended it toward Jesse.

Jesse felt a sense of panic. "Thank you, sir, but I can't accept that."

"Of course you can," the captain said. "It doesn't look like much, but it will change your life. Trust me."

"Oh, I believe you, sir," Jesse said. "I just don't deserve it."

"Nonsense," the captain said. "Take it, my man."

"No, thank you," Jesse said. "I'm really tired. I got to get some sleep."

"I'm ordering you to take it," the captain said. A distinct edge had appeared in his voice.

"Yes, sir," Jesse said. He reached forward with a quivering hand. In his mind's eye he saw the glistening chrome needle. At the same time he remembered that to stimulate the mechanism, he'd touched the edge of the disc. He also noticed that the captain was not touching the edge but rather palming the disc in his flattened hand.

"Take it, my friend," the captain urged.

Jesse flattened his own hand palm up and put it next to the captain's. The captain looked him in the eye. Jesse returned the stare and noticed the captain's pupils were widely dilated.

For a few moments it was a Mexican standoff. Finally the captain carefully insinuated his thumb beneath the disc and lifted it with his index finger on top of the dome. He was obviously avoiding the edge. Then he put it in Jesse's palm.

"Thanks, Chief," Jesse said. He avoided looking at the cursed thing and beat a hasty retreat.

"You'll be thanking me," the captain called out after him.

Jesse dashed out to his desk, terrified by the fear of being stung at any moment. But it didn't happen, and he was able to slide the disc out of his hand without incident. It clacked up against its colleague with a sound like two ivory billiard balls colliding.

"What on earth . . ." Pitt remarked.

"Don't ask!" Jesse said. "But I'll tell you one thing. The captain ain't on our side."

Holding the coffee creamer jar up to the light, Sheila looked beneath the label at the scrap of blotter contained inside. "This might be the break we needed," she said. "But tell me again exactly what happened."

Cassy, Pitt, and Jesse all began speaking at once.

"Whoa!" Sheila said. "One at a time."

Cassy and Pitt deferred to Jesse. Jesse retold the episode with Cassy and Pitt adding bits of detail. When Jesse got to describing the part about the slit appearing in the disc, he opened his eyes widely and yanked back his hand in imitation of what he'd done at the time.

Sheila placed the jar on her desk and peered through the oculars of a binocular dissecting microscope. One of the black discs was positioned on the tray.

"This situation gets more and more bizarre," Sheila remarked. "I gotta tell you; the surface appears fault-free. I'd swear it was a solid chunk of whatever it is."

"It may look that way, but it isn't," Cassy said. "It's definitely mechanical. We all saw the slit."

"And the needle," Pitt added.

"Who would make something like this?" Jesse questioned.

"Who could make it?" Cassy asked.

The four people stared at each other. For a few minutes no one spoke. Cassy's rhetorical question was unsettling.

"Well, we won't be able to answer any questions until we find out what's in the fluid that soaked into the blotter," Sheila said. "The problem is I've got to do it myself. Richard, the head tech in the hospital lab, has already blabbed to the CEO about our CDC visitor. I can't trust the people in the lab."

"We need to get other people involved," Cassy said.

"Yeah, like a virologist," Pitt said.

"Considering what happened with the man from the CDC, that's not going to be easy," Sheila said. "It's hard to know who has had this flu and who hasn't."

"Except when it's people we know well," Jesse said. "I knew the captain was acting weird. I just didn't know why."

"But we can't use the fear of not knowing who's been sick as an excuse to sit around and do nothing," Cassy said. "We have to warn people who haven't been infected. I know a couple who could be a great help. She's a virologist and he's a physicist."

"Sounds ideal provided they've not been stung," Sheila said.

"I think I can find out," Cassy said. "Their son is a student in one of the classes I'm student teaching. He has an inkling that something strange is going on because his girlfriend's parents apparently were infected."

"That might be a source of worry," Sheila said. "From what Jesse has told us about the captain, I have a distinct and uncomfortable sense that the infected people feel evangelistic about their condition."

"Amen," Jesse said. "He was not to be denied. He was going to give me that black disc no matter what I said. He wanted me sick, no doubt."

"I'll be wary," Cassy said, "and as you said before, discreet."

"Okay, give it a try," Sheila said. "Meanwhile I'll run some preliminary tests on the fluid."

"What are we going to do with the discs?" Jesse asked.

"The question is more what are they going to do with us," Pitt said. He was looking at the one positioned under the microscope.

CHAPTER 12

9:00 A.M.

It was a glorious morning with a cloudless, crystal-blue sky. The distant saw-toothed purple mountains looked like amethyst crystals bathed in a golden light.

At the gate of the estate an expectant crowd had formed. There were people of all ages and from all walks of life, from mechanics to rocket scientists, from house-wives to presidents of corporations, from high-school students to university professors. Everyone was eager, happy, and glowing with health. The atmosphere was festive.

Beau came out of the house with King at his side, descended the steps, walked fifty feet, then turned around. What he saw pleased him greatly. Overnight a large banner had been made that draped all the way across the front of the building. It said: "The Institute for a New Beginning . . . Welcome!"

Beau's eyes swept around the grounds. He'd accomplished an extraordinary amount in twenty-four hours. He was glad he no longer needed to sleep except for short snatches. Otherwise it wouldn't have been possible.

In the shade of trees or walking through sun-dappled meadows, Beau could see dozens of dogs of various breeds. Most were large dogs, and none had leashes. Beau could see that they were as alert as sentinels, and he was glad.

With a happy spring to his step, he returned to the porch to join Randy.

"This is it," Beau said. "We're ready to begin."

"What a day for the Earth," Randy replied.

"Let in the first group," Beau said. "We'll get them started in the ballroom."

Randy took out his cellular phone, dialed, and told one of his people to open the gate. A few moments later Randy and Beau could hear a cheer rise up into the crisp morning air. From where they were standing they couldn't see the front gate, but they could certainly hear the people shouting as they entered.

Buzzing with excitement, the crowd swarmed to the house and formed a spontaneous semicircle around the front porch.

Beau extended his hand like a Roman general and instantly the crowd went dead silent.

"Welcome!" Beau shouted. "This is the new beginning! You all bear witness that we share the same thoughts and vision. We all know what we must do. Let's do it!"

A cheer and applause erupted from the crowd. Beau turned to Randy, who beamed. He was applauding as well. Beau gestured for Randy to enter the house and then followed him.

"What an electric moment," Randy said as they walked toward the ornate ball-room.

"It's like being one huge organism," Beau said with a nod of understanding.

The two men entered the vast, sun-drenched room and stood off to the side. The crowd followed at their heels, filling the room. Then, responding to an unseen, unspoken cue, they fell to dismantling the room.

Cassy breathed out a silent sigh of relief when she found herself facing Jonathan when the Sellerses' front door had been pulled open. Expecting the worst, she'd anticipated having to face Nancy Sellers right off the bat.

"Miss Winthrope!" Jonathan said with a mixture of surprise and delight.

"You recognized me away from the school," Cassy said. "I'm impressed."

"Of course I recognized you," Jonathan blurted. Consciously he had to resist letting his eyes wander below Cassy's neck. "Come in."

"Are your parents home?" Cassy asked.

"My mom is."

Cassy studied the boy's face. With his flaxen hair hanging down over his forehead and his self-consciously flitting eyes, he looked himself. His manner of dress was reassuring as well. He had on an oversized sweatshirt and a loose-fitting pair of Jams that were just barely hanging on to his buttocks.

"How's Candee?" Cassy asked.

"I haven't seen her since yesterday."

"What about her parents?" Cassy questioned.

Jonathan let out a little sardonic laugh. "They're gonzo. My mom had a talk with Candee's mom, and it was like zero."

"What about your mom?" Cassy asked. She tried to study Jonathan's eyes, but it was like trying to examine a Ping-Pong ball during a game.

"My mom is fine. Why?"

"A lot of people are acting strange lately. You know, like Candee's parents and Mr. Partridge."

"Yeah, I know," Jonathan said. "But not my mom."

"Your dad?"

"He's fine too."

"Good," Cassy said. "Now I'd like to take you up on your invitation to come in. I'm here to talk with your mom."

Jonathan closed the door behind Cassy and then bellowed at the top of his lungs that there was company. The sound echoed around the inside of the house, and Cassy jumped. Despite trying to act calm, she was as taut as a banjo wire.

"Can I get you some water or something?" Jonathan asked.

Before Cassy could respond Nancy Sellers appeared at the balustrade on the second floor. She was dressed casually in acid-washed jeans and loose-fitting blouse.

"Who is it, Jonathan?" Nancy asked. She could see Cassy, but because of the way the sun was coming through the window into the stairwell, Cassy's face was lost in shadow.

Jonathan yelled up who it was and motioned for Cassy to follow him into the kitchen. No sooner had Cassy sat at a banquette than Nancy appeared.

"This is a surprise," Nancy said. "Can I offer you some coffee?"

"Sure," Cassy said. Cassy eyed the woman as she motioned for Jonathan to get a cup while she went to the stove to pick up the coffeepot. As far as Cassy could tell Nancy looked and acted the same as she did when Cassy had first met her.

Cassy was beginning to relax a degree when Nancy reached out to pour the coffee. On her index finger was a fresh Band-Aid, and Cassy felt her own pulse quicken. A wound of any sort on the hands was not what she wanted to see.

"To what do we owe this visit?" Nancy asked as she poured herself a half cup of the coffee.

Cassy stumbled over her words. "What happened to your finger?"

Nancy glanced at her Band-Aid as if it had just appeared. "Just a small cut," she said.

"From some kitchen implement?" Cassy asked.

Nancy studied Cassy's face. "Does it matter?" she asked.

"Well . . ." Cassy stammered. "Yes, it does. It matters a lot."

"Mom, Miss Winthrope is concerned about the people who are changing," Jonathan said, coming to Cassy's aid once again. "You know, like Candee's mom. I've already told her you talked with her and thought that she was out in left field."

"Jonathan!" Nancy snapped. "Your father and I agreed we wouldn't discuss the Taylors outside the home. At least until . . ."

"I don't think it can wait," Cassy interrupted. Nancy's little outburst had encouraged her to trust that Nancy had not been infected. "People are rapidly changing all over the city, not just the Taylors. It might even be happening in other cities. We don't know. It's happening with an illness that resembles the flu, and as far as we can tell it is spread by little black discs that have the capability of stinging people on their hands."

Nancy stared at Cassy. "Are you taking about a black disc with kind of a hump in the middle, about four centimeters in diameter?"

"Exactly," Cassy said. "Have you seen any? Lots of people have them."

"Candee's mother tried to give me one," Nancy said. "Is that why you questioned my Band-Aid?"

Cassy nodded.

"It was a knife," Nancy said. "A recalcitrant bagel and a knife."

"I'm sorry to be so suspicious," Cassy said.

"I suppose it is understandable," Nancy said. "But why did you come here?"

"To enlist your help," Cassy said. "We have a group, a small group, who have been trying to figure out what's happening. But we need help. We have some fluid from one of the discs, and with you being a virologist, you'd know what to do with it. We're afraid to use the hospital lab because we think too many people in the hospital have been infected."

"You suspect a virus?" Nancy questioned.

Cassy shrugged. "I'm not a doctor, but the illness seems like the flu. We also don't know anything about the black discs. That's where we thought your husband might help. We don't know how the things work or even what they are made of."

"I'll have to discuss this with my husband," Nancy said. "How can I get in touch with you?"

Cassy gave the telephone number of Pitt's cousin's apartment where she'd stayed the previous night. She also gave her Dr. Sheila Miller's direct dial number.

"Okay," Nancy said. "I'll be back to you sometime today."

Cassy stood up. "Thank you, and as I've said, we need you. This problem is spreading like a plague."

The street was dark save for the widely dispersed street lights. From the distance two men approached, walking large German shepherds. Both the men and the dogs acted as if they were patrolling the street. Their heads were constantly turning from side to side as if they were searching and listening.

A dark sedan appeared and stopped. The window came down and the pale face a of woman appeared within. The two men stared at the woman but no one spoke. It was as if they were having a conversation without the need for words. After a few minutes the car window soundlessly went back up and the car moved off.

The two men resumed their walk, and as the eyes of one of the men passed by the line of Jonathan's sight, Jonathan thought he saw a glow as if the eyes were reflecting an unseen light source.

Jonathan reflexively pulled back from the window and let the drape fall into place. He didn't know if the man in the street had seen him or not.

After a moment Jonathan carefully parted the center of the drapes with his finger, exposing only the barest crack. Being in a dark room himself, Jonathan was not afraid of light giving him away.

Jonathan brought his eye to the crack. Down in the street he could see that the two men and dogs had continued walking just as they had earlier. Jonathan breathed a sigh of relief. They'd not spotted him.

Letting the curtain fall back into place, Jonathan left the bathroom and went out into the living room to join the others. He and his parents had come to the place where Cassy and her friend Pitt were staying. It was a large three-bedroom flat in a garden apartment complex. Jonathan thought it was cool. There were a number of impressive aquariums and tropical plants.

Jonathan considered telling everyone what he'd just seen, but they were too pre-occupied. At least everybody but his father. His father was standing away from the group with his elbow on the mantel. Jonathan recognized his expression. It was one of those condescending ones he'd assume whenever Jonathan asked him for help with math.

Jonathan had been introduced to the others. He'd seen the black policeman before and had been impressed by him. He'd come to the school the previous autumn for career day. Jonathan had never met Dr. Sheila Miller but was wary of her. Except for her blond hair she reminded him of the witch in the *Snow White* video his parents had made him watch when he was a kid. There wasn't anything feminine about her like there was about Cassy. The long fingernails didn't quite hack it, especially since they were painted a rather dark color.

Cassy's friend Pitt was an okay guy except Jonathan felt a twinge of jealousy because of Cassy. Jonathan didn't know if they were exactly dating, but it seemed like they were living there in the same apartment. Jonathan wished he had a physique like Pitt and maybe even black hair if that was what Cassy liked.

Sheila cleared her throat. "So let's summarize," she said. "What we're dealing with is an infectious agent that rapidly sickened guinea pigs, but the animals produced no detectable microorganisms, specifically no viruses. The illness is not airborne, otherwise we'd all be infected. At least I certainly would be, since I've been essentially living in the ER. It's been literally filled with infected people over the last couple of days who've been continuously coughing and sneezing."

"Have you inoculated any tissue cultures?" Nancy asked.

"No," Sheila said. "I don't think of myself as experienced enough for that type of work."

"So you believe the illness is only spread parenterally," Nancy said.

"Exactly," Sheila said. "By one of these black discs."

Both the discs were sitting in a topless Tupperware container resting on the coffee table. Nancy picked up a fork and began pushing them around so she could examine them. Then she tried to turn one of them over, but being unwilling to touch it with her finger to stabilize it, it seemed impossible. She gave up. "I can't imagine how these things could sting anything. They are so uniform."

"But they most certainly can," Cassy assured her. "We saw it happen."

"A slit opens up at the edge," Jesse said, taking the fork and pointing. "Then a chromelike needle shoots out."

"But I don't see where a slit could be," Nancy said.

Jesse shrugged. "It's got us buffaloed as well."

"The illness is unique," Sheila said, refocusing the discussion. "It basically resembles the flu symptomatically, but its incubation period is only a few hours after injection. Its course is also short and self-limited, again only a few hours except for people with chronic disease like diabetes. Unfortunately, for those people it is rapidly lethal."

"And people with blood disease," Jesse added in memory of Alfred Kinsella.

"True," Sheila agreed.

"And so far no influenza virus has been isolated from any of the victims," Pitt said.

"Also true," Sheila said. "And the most unique and one of the more disturbing aspect of this illness is that after recovery the victim's personality changes. They even profess to feel better generally than they had before the illnesss. And they start talking about environmental problems. Isn't that right, Cassy?"

Cassy nodded: "I discovered my fiancé out in the middle of the night having a conversation with strangers. When I asked him what he'd been talking about, he said the environment. At first I thought he was joking, but he wasn't."

"Joy Taylor told me she and her husband were having environmental meetings every night," Nancy said. "Then with me she brought up the issue about the destruction of the rain forests."

"Just a minute!" Eugene said. "As a scientist all I'm hearing is hearsay and anecdotes. You people are getting way ahead of yourselves."

"That's not true," Cassy said. "We saw the disc open, and we saw the needle. We've even seen people get stung."

"That's not the point," Eugene said. "You don't have any scientific proof that the stinging caused the illness."

"We don't have a lot of proof but the guinea pigs did get sick," Sheila said. "That was for sure."

"You have to establish causality in a controlled circumstance," Eugene said. "That's the scientific method. Otherwise you can't talk about anything except in vague generalities. You need reproducible evidence."

"We got these black discs," Pitt said. "They are not figments of one's imagination."

Eugene pushed off the mantel and bent over to look at the two discs. "Let me understand you: you're trying to say that this solid little thing formed a slit where there is no seam or even microscopic evidence of a door or a flap."

"I know it sounds crazy," Jesse said. "I wouldn't have believed it either if we all hadn't seen it together. It was like it unzipped and then welded itself shut."

"I just thought of something else," Sheila said. "We had a strange episode in the hospital. A man from housekeeping died with an unexplained circular hole in his hand. The room where he'd been found was all strangely twisted out of shape. You remember, Jesse. You were there."

"Of course I remember," Jesse said. "There was some speculation about radiation, but we never found any."

"That was the room which my fiancé was in," Cassy said.

"If that episode is associated with this flu and these black discs, we've got a bigger problem than we think," Sheila said.

Everyone except Eugene, who'd gone back to leaning against the mantel, stared at the two black discs feeling skeptical about what their minds were telling them. Finally Cassy spoke. "I'm sensing that we are all thinking the same thing but are afraid to say it. So I'm going to say it. Maybe these little black discs aren't from around here. Maybe these things are not from this planet."

After an initial impatient sigh from Eugene, Cassy's comments were greeted with total silence. The sounds of respiration and the ticking of a wall clock were the only interior noise. Outside a car horn honked in the distance.

"Come to think about it," Pitt said finally, "the night before Beau found one of these discs, my TV blew up. In fact a lot of us students lost TVs, radios, computers, all sorts of electronic equipment if the equipment happened to be on at the time."

"What time was that?" Sheila asked.

"Ten-fifteen," Pitt said.

"That's when my VCR exploded," Sheila said.

"It's also when my radio blew up," Jonathan said.

"What radio?" Nancy asked. It was the first time she'd heard of it.

"I mean Tim's car radio," Jonathan corrected himself.

"Do you think all those episodes could be related to these black discs?" Pitt asked.

"It's a thought," Nancy said. "Eugene, has that surge of powerful radio waves ever been explained?"

"No, it hasn't," Eugene admitted. "But I wouldn't use that fact to support some half-baked theory."

"I don't know," Nancy said. "I'd say that it makes it at least suspicious."

"Wow," Jonathan commented, "that would mean we're talking about an extraterrestrial virus. Cool!"

"Cool, nothing!" Nancy said. "It would be terrifying."

"Whoa, everybody," Sheila warned. "Let's not let our imaginations run away with themselves. If we start jumping to conclusions and talking about some Andromeda strain it's going to be a lot harder trying to elicit any help."

"This is just what I was trying to warn you about," Eugene said. "You are all beginning to sound like a group of paranormal nuts."

"Whether this illness comes from Earth or outer space, it's here," Jesse said. "I don't think we should be arguing about it. I think we better start finding out what it is and what we can do about it. I don't think we should be wasting a lot of time, because if it is spreading as fast as we think it is, we could be too late."

"You are absolutely right," Sheila said.

"I'll isolate the virus if it's in the sample," Nancy said. "I can use my own lab. No one questions what I do. Once we have the virus we can present our case all the way to Washington and the Surgeon General."

"That's if the Surgeon General isn't already infected by the time we get the information," Cassy said.

"That's a sobering thought," Nancy said.

"Well, we have no choice," Sheila said. "Eugene is right in the sense that if we start calling around now without something more than hearsay and conjecture, no one is going to believe us."

"I'll start the isolation in the morning," Nancy said.

"Is there any chance I could help?" Pitt asked. "I'm a chem major, but I've taken microbiology and worked in the hospital lab."

"Sure," Nancy said. "I've noticed people acting strange at Serotec. I won't know whom to trust."

"I'd like to offer to help figure what these black discs are," Jesse said. "But I wouldn't know where to start."

"I'll take them into my lab," Eugene offered. "Even if it's just to prove to you alarmists that they are not from Andromeda, it will be worth my time."

"Don't touch the edge," Jesse warned.

"No need to worry," Eugene said. "We have the capability of manipulating them from a distance as if they were radioactive."

"It's too bad we just can't talk to one of these infected people directly," Jonathan said. "Heck, we could just ask them what's happening. Maybe they know."

"That would be dangerous," Sheila said. "There's reason to believe they are actively recruiting. They want the rest of us infected. They may even come to view us as an enemy."

"They're recruiting all right," Jesse said. "I think the police chief is actively searching out people on the squad who've yet to get the illness."

"It might be dangerous, but it might also be revealing," Cassy said. She stared off for the moment with unseeing eyes while her mind churned.

"Cassy!" Pitt said. "What are you thinking? I don't like that look on your face."

CHAPTER 13

6:30 A.M.

"These people are with me," Nancy Sellers said. Nancy, Sheila, and Pitt were standing in front of the Serotec Pharmaceutical night security desk. The guard was fingering her ID. Nancy had already shown it at the gate before driving onto the parking area.

"You people have any picture IDs?" the security man asked Sheila and Pitt. Both produced driver's licenses which satisfied the man. The trio trooped to the elevator.

"Security is still on edge after the suicide," Nancy said.

The reason Nancy had them get there so early was to avoid the other workers. And it worked. As yet no one else had arrived, and the entire fourth floor was empty. The fourth floor was reserved entirely for biological research. There was even a small menagerie of experimental animals at one end.

Nancy unlocked her private lab, and they all entered. She locked the door behind them. She did not want any interruptions or questions.

"Okay!" Nancy said. "We are going to wear containment suits and everything will be done under a level three hood. Any questions?"

Neither Sheila nor Pitt had any.

Nancy led them into a side room which had changing cubicles. She gave them appropriate-sized gear and let them change. She changed as well.

Meeting back in the main room Nancy said: "Now, let's have the samples."

Sheila produced the coffee-creamer jar containing the snippet of desk blotter. She also produced multiple blood samples from people who'd acquired the flu. The samples had been drawn at various stages of their illness.

"All right," Nancy said, rubbing her gloved hands together in anticipation. "First I'm going to show you how to inoculate a tissue culture."

"Where the hell did you get this thing?" Carl Maben asked his boss, Eugene Sellers. Carl was a Ph.D. candidate who also worked for the physics department.

With raised eyebrows Eugene glanced over at Jesse Kemper, whom he'd invited to watch the analysis of one of the black discs. Jesse told them that it had been taken from an individual who'd been arrested for lewd behavior.

Both Eugene and Carl expressed interest.

"I don't know the details," Jesse admitted.

Eugene's and Carl's faces fell.

"Well, I do know that the man had been arrested for making love in the park," Jesse said.

"My God! It's amazing the risks people take," Carl said. "It's dangerous just to walk in the park at night, much less make love."

"This wasn't at night," Jesse said. "It was at lunchtime."

"They must have been embarrassed," Eugene said.

"Quite the contrary," Jesse said. "They were irritated at being disturbed. They said that the police should be more concerned about the rising levels of carbon dioxide in the atmosphere and the resultant greenhouse effect."

Both Eugene and Carl laughed.

As soon as Jesse told the story it reminded him of the conversation the previous evening about the infected people's concerns about environmental issues. The possibility that the noontime lovers were infected people had never occurred to him.

Redirecting his attention to the task at hand, Carl said to Eugene: "I don't think this is going to work." At that moment behind a darkly tinted glass screen they were blasting one of the black discs with a high energy laser to knock off some molecules. A gas chromatograph was poised to analyze the resultant gas. Unfortunately the laser wasn't doing the trick.

"All right, turn it off," Eugene said.

The bright beam of coherent light was instantly extinguished when the power was interrupted. The two scientists gazed at the small disc.

"That's one hard surface," Carl said. "What do you think it's composed of?"

"I don't know," Eugene admitted. "But I'm as sure as hell going to find out. Whoever made it better have a patent or I'm going to file one."

"What should we do next?" Carl asked.

"Let's use a diamond drill," Eugene said. "Then we'll vaporize the shavings and let the gas chromatograph do the work."

Slipping an antacid tablet into her mouth, Cassy emerged from the airline terminal building and waited her turn in the taxi line. She'd been anxious from the moment she'd awakened that morning, and the closer she got to Santa Fe the worse it had become. She'd magnified the problem by having coffee on the plane. Now her stomach was in a knot.

"Where to, Miss?" the cab driver asked.

"Do you know anything about this Institute for a New Beginning?" Cassy asked.

"For sure," the driver said. "It's brand new, yet it's the destination of half my fares. Is that where you want to go?"

"Please," Cassy said. She sat back and blankly watched the scenery roll by. Pitt had been adamantly against the idea of Cassy visiting Beau, but once it had taken hold in Cassy's mind, she couldn't let it go. Although she admitted there might be some danger as Sheila predicted, in her heart she could not imagine Beau would ever harm her in any way.

"I have to drop you off here at the gate," the driver said when they had reached the edge of the institute's property. "They don't like car exhaust up near the house. But it isn't far. Only a couple of hundred yards."

Cassy paid the fare and got out. It was a pristine location. There was a white fence as if it were a horse farm. There was also a gate across the driveway, but it was ajar.

Two nicely dressed men about Cassy's age stood off to the side of the gate. They looked tanned and healthy. They were both smiling pleasantly, but as Cassy approached, their smiles didn't change. It was as if their faces were frozen in an expression of gaiety.

Even if the smiles seemed contrived, the two men were cordial. When Cassy said she was hoping to see Beau Stark, they replied that they understood perfectly. They directed her to walk to the house.

Mildly unnerved by this strange interaction, Cassy followed the twisting driveway through the trees. On either side beneath the shade of the trees she caught sight of an occasional large dog. Although every dog she saw turned to watch her, none of them bothered her.

When the shadows of the pines gave way to the sweeping lawns surrounding the mansion, Cassy was impressed despite her anxieties. The only thing that marred the gorgeous scene was the huge banner draped across the entrance.

The moment Cassy started up the front steps a woman appeared who was approximately Cassy's age. She sported a similar smile to the men at the gate. From inside the house Cassy heard sounds of construction.

"I'm here to see Beau Stark," Cassy said.

"Yes, I know," the woman said. "Please follow me."

The woman took Cassy back down the steps and around the enormous house.

"Beautiful home," Cassy commented to make conversation.

"Isn't it," the woman replied. "And to think this is just the beginning. We're all very excited."

The rear of the house was dominated by a large terrace complete with ivy-draped pergolas. Beyond the terrace was a swimming pool. At the edge of the pool was a large umbrella shading a table seating eight. Beau was at the head of the table. About twenty feet away lay King.

As Cassy approached she studied Beau. She had to admit that he looked wonderful. In fact he'd rarely looked so good. His thick hair had more than its usual shine and the skin of his face glowed as if he'd just emerged from a refreshing plunge into the sea. He was carefully dressed in a white billowy shirt. The rest of the people were dressed in suits and ties, including two women.

Several easels were set up to support large pads of paper. The exposed pages were covered with arcane schematics and incomprehensible equations. The table was strewn with papers with similar content. A half dozen laptops were open and humming.

Cassy had never felt more uncertain in her life. Her anxiety had gone up a notch the closer she got to Beau. She had no idea what she was going to say to him. It made it worse that she was interrupting a meeting with important-appearing people. They were all older than Beau and looked professional, like lawyers or doctors.

But before Cassy reached the table, Beau turned toward her, smiled broadly when he recognized her, and leaped to his feet. Without a word to the other people at the table, he ran to Cassy and took her hands. His blue eyes sparkled. For a second Cassy swooned. She felt as if she could have fallen into his huge black pupils.

"I'm so glad you've come," Beau said. "I've been so eager to talk with you."

Beau's words nudged Cassy from her momentary helplessness. "Why didn't you call?" she asked. It was a question she'd not dared ask herself until that moment.

"It's been so hectic," Beau explained. "I've been busy twenty-four hours a day. Believe me."

"I guess I'm lucky to get to see you," Cassy said. She glanced over at the group at the table who were patiently waiting. Same with King who'd raised himself to a sitting position. "You've become quite an important man now."

"There are responsibilities," Beau admitted. He led her a few yards farther away from the group and then pointed up at the house. His other hand still held hers. "What do you think?" he asked proudly.

"I'm a bit overwhelmed," Cassy said. "I'm not sure what to think."

"What you see here is only the beginning. Only the tip of the iceberg. It's so exciting."

"Only the beginning of what?" Cassy asked. "What are you doing here?"

"We are going to make everything right," Beau said. "Remember me telling you over the last six months that I was going to play an important role in the world if I got a job with Randy Nite? Well, it's happening in a way that I never could have anticipated. Beau Stark, the boy from Brookline, is going to help lead the world to a new beginning."

Cassy looked directly into the depths of Beau's eyes. She knew he was in there. If only she could get to him behind this megalomania facade. Lowering her voice and not taking her eyes from his she said: "I know this isn't you talking, Beau. You are not doing this. Something . . . someone is controlling you."

Beau put his head back and laughed heartily. "Oh, Cassy," he remarked. "Always the skeptic! Believe me, no one is controlling me. I'm just Beau Stark. I'm still the same guy you love and who loves you."

"Beau, I do love you," Cassy said with sudden vehemence. "And I think you love me. For the sake of that love come back home with me. Come to the medical center. There is a doctor there who wants to examine you, to find out what's made you change. She thinks it started with that flu you had. Please fight this, whatever it is!"

Despite Cassy's vow to keep her emotions in check, they welled up anyway. Tears came and formed rivulets on her cheeks. She'd not meant to cry but was powerless to prevent it.

"I do love you," she managed.

Beau reached out and wiped the tears from the corners of Cassy's eyes. He regarded her in a truly loving way. He pulled her toward him and enveloped her with his arms, pressing his face against hers.

At first Cassy held back. But as she felt Beau clutching her she relented. She put her own arms around him and, closing her eyes, squeezed him tightly. She didn't want to let him go, ever.

"I do love you," Beau whispered. His lips were brushing her ear. "And I want you to join us. I want you to become one of us because you won't be able to stop us. No one will!"

Cassy stiffened. Hearing Beau's words was like having a knife driven into her heart. Her eyes popped open. With her face still pressed up against his she could see the blurry form of his ear. But what made her blood run cold was a small patch of skin behind his ear that was grayish-blue in color. Reflexively her hand came up and her fingers touched the area. It was rough, almost scaly in texture, and cold. Beau was mutating!

With a rush of revulsion, Cassy tried to extract herself from Beau's grasp, but he held her tightly. He was stronger than she remembered.

"You'll be joining us soon, Cassy," Beau whispered. He acted unaware of her struggles. "Why not let it be now? Please!"

Changing tactics, Cassy abandoned trying to push away from Beau. Instead she quickly ducked beneath his arms and collapsed on the ground. She was up immediately. Her love and concern had turned to terror. She took several steps backward. The only thing that kept her from bolting was the shock of seeing tears had formed in Beau's eyes.

"Please!" Beau pleaded. "Join us, my dearest."

Cassy tore herself away despite Beau's unexpected show of emotion and sprinted beneath the nearest pergola, heading for the end of the house.

The woman who'd met Cassy on the front porch when she had first arrived stepped forward. During Cassy and Beau's conversation she'd stood discreetly to the side. Now her eyes met Beau's, and she motioned toward Cassy's fleeing figure.

Beau understood the meaning of the gesture. She was asking if she should send someone after Cassy. Beau hesitated. He was struggling with himself. Finally he shook his head and turned back to the men and women waiting for him.

Having already found most of the things on the shopping list already, Jonathan rewarded himself by loading up with Coke and then strolling up the aisle with all the potato chips. He selected a few of his favorite types and was nearing the meat department when his cart practically ran into Candee's.

"My God, Candee!" Jonathan blurted. "Where have you been? I've called twenty times."

"Jonathan," Candee said happily. "I'm so glad to see you. I've missed you."

"You have?" Jonathan asked. He couldn't help notice how fantastic Candee looked. She was wearing a miniskirt over a tank top body suit. Every curve of her tight, lithe body was there to see and appreciate.

"Oh yes," Candee said. "I've been thinking about you lots."

"How come you haven't been at school?" Jonathan asked. "I looked for you."

"I've been looking for you as well," Candee said.

Jonathan managed to coax his eyes to travel northward to Candee's elfin face. When he did he noticed her smile. There was something abnormal about it even though he couldn't put his finger on what it was.

"I wanted to tell you that I was wrong about my parents," Candee said. "Totally wrong."

Before Jonathan could respond to this shocking reversal, both of Candee's parents rounded the end of the aisle and came up behind Candee. Her father, Stan, put his hands on Candee's shoulders and beamed.

"Now this is one cute chick, wouldn't you say?" Stan said proudly. "And as an added inducement, there's good, healthy genes in these ovaries."

Candee glanced up into her father's face and gave him an adoring look.

Jonathan averted his eyes. He thought he might puke. These people belonged in a zoo.

"We've missed you at the house," Candee's mother, Joy, said. "Why don't you come over tonight. Us adults will be having a get-together, but it doesn't mean you two youths can't spend some quality time together."

"Yes, well, that sounds great," Jonathan said. He felt a mild degree of panic since Joy had moved to his side, hemming him in against the shelving. Candee and Stan were blocking his way forward.

"Can we count on you?" Joy asked.

Jonathan let his eyes streak past Candee's face. She was still smiling that same smile, and Jonathan realized what it was that was abnormal about it. It was fake. It was the kind of smile people made when they tell themselves to smile. It wasn't a reflection of inner emotion.

"I got a lot of homework tonight," Jonathan said. He started to back up his shopping cart.

Joy gazed into Jonathan's cart. "You certainly are a busy little shopper. Are you having a meeting at your house as well? Perhaps we should all come over there."

"No, no," Jonathan said nervously. "Nobody's coming over. Nothing like that at all. I'm just picking up some TV munchies." Jonathan wondered if these people somehow knew about their little group.

Another glance at their fake smiles gave Jonathan a shiver of fear and propelled him to "make tracks." Abruptly he yanked his cart backward, turned it around, yelled that he had to be going, and rapidly headed toward the check-out lanes. As he walked he could feel the Taylor family's eyes on his back.

"This is the street," Pitt said. He was directing Nancy to his cousin's apartment where they'd all agreed to meet once again. Sheila was in the backseat of the minivan clutching a sheaf of papers.

It was already dark and the streetlamps were lit. As they approached the proper garden apartment complex, Nancy slowed.

"Seems to be a lot of people out tonight," Nancy said.

"You're right," Pitt said. "Looks like noontime in the city center rather than evening in the suburbs."

"I can understand the ones with dogs," Sheila said. "But what are these other people doing? Are they just walking aimlessly?"

"It's weird," Pitt admitted. "No one seems to be talking to anyone, yet they are all smiling."

"So they are," Sheila said.

"What should I do?" Nancy asked. They were almost to their destination.

"Drive around the block," Sheila suggested. "Let's see if they notice us."

Nancy took the suggestion. As they came back to where they'd started, none of the many pedestrians appeared to look in their direction.

"Let's go in," Sheila said.

Nancy parked. They all alighted quickly. Pitt let the women go ahead. By the time he got to the common entry door, the women were already heading up the interior stairway. Pitt looked back out to the street. He'd had the distinct feeling as he'd come up the path that he was being watched, but as he scanned the area, none of the people were looking in his direction.

Cassy opened the door in response to Pitt's knock. Pitt's face brightened. He was relieved to see her. "How'd the trip go?" he asked.

"Not so good," Cassy admitted.

"Did you see Beau?"

"Yes, I saw him," Cassy said. "But I'd rather not talk about it now."

"Okay," Pitt said supportively. He was concerned. He could tell Cassy was truly troubled. He followed her into the living room.

"I'm glad you all are finally here," Eugene said. His blue chambray shirt was open at the neck and his knitted tie was loosened. His dark eyes darted from person to person. He was wired: a far cry from his bored condescension the evening before.

Sitting around the coffee table were Jesse, Nancy, and Sheila. On the table was the Tupperware container with the two black discs along with an assortment of potato chips from Jonathan's shopping foray. Jonathan was at the window intermittently peeking out. Pitt and Cassy took chairs.

"You know there's a shitload of people wandering around outside," Jonathan said.

"Jonathan, watch your language," Nancy scolded.

"We saw them," Sheila said. "They ignored us."

"Can I have everyone's attention," Eugene said. "I've had an interesting day to say the least. Carl and I threw everything we had at this black disc. It is incredibly hard."

"Who's Carl?" Sheila asked.

"My Ph.D. assistant," Eugene said.

"I thought we agreed to keep all this among ourselves," Sheila said. "At least until we know what we're dealing with."

"Carl's fine," Eugene said. "But you're right. Maybe I should have been working by myself. I have to admit I was skeptical about all this, but I'm not now."

"What did you find?" Sheila asked.

"The disc is not made of any natural material," Eugene said. "It's a polymer of sorts. Actually more like a ceramic, but not a true ceramic because there's a metallic component."

"It's even got diamond in it," Jesse said.

Eugene nodded. "Diamond, silicon, and a type of metal that we have yet to identify."

"What are you saying?" Cassy asked.

"We're saying that it's made of a substance that our current capabilities could not possibly duplicate."

"So say it in English," Jonathan voiced. "It's extraterrestrial, that's what it is."

The reality of the confirmation stunned everyone, even though everyone except Eugene had expected as much.

"Well, we've made some progress today as well," Sheila said. She looked at Nancy.

"We've tentatively located a virus," Nancy said.

"An alien virus?" Eugene asked, turning pale.

"Yes and no," Sheila said.

"Come on!" Eugene complained. "Stop teasing us. What are you suggesting?"

"From my initial investigations," Nancy said, "and I have to emphasize initial, there is a virus involved, but it hasn't come in these black discs. At least not now. The virus has been here a long time: a long, long time, because it's in every organism I tested today. My guess is that it is in every earthly organism with a genome large enough to house it."

"So it didn't come in these little spaceships?" Jonathan asked. He sounded disappointed.

"If it's not a virus, what's in the infectious fluid?" Eugene asked.

"It's a protein," Nancy said. "Something like a prion. You know, like what causes Mad Cow disease. But not exactly the same because this protein reacts with the viral DNA. In fact that's how I found the virus so easily. I used the protein as a probe."

"What we think is the protein unmasks the virus," Sheila said.

"So the flulike syndrome is the body reacting with this protein," Eugene said.

"That's my guess," Nancy said. "The protein is antigenic and causes a kind of overcharged immunological insult. That's why the lymphokines are produced in such abundance, and it's the lymphokines that are actually responsible for the symptoms."

"Once unmasked what is this virus doing?" Eugene asked.

"That's a question that's going to take some work," Nancy admitted. "But our impression is that unlike a normal virus which only takes over a single cell, this virus is capable of taking over an entire organism, particularly the brain. So just calling it a virus is misleading. Pitt had a good suggestion. He called it a mega-virus."

Pitt blushed. "It just came to me," he explained.

"This mega-virus has apparently been around way before humans evolved," Sheila said. "Nancy found it in a highly conserved segment of DNA."

"A segment that researchers have ignored," Nancy said. "It's one of those non-coding segments, or so people thought. And it's big. It's hundreds of thousands of base pairs long."

"So this mega-virus has been just waiting," Cassy said.

"That's our thought," Nancy said. "Perhaps some alien viral race or maybe an alien race capable of packaging itself in a viral form for space travel visited the Earth eons ago when life was just evolving. They planted themselves in the DNA like sentinels that waited to see what kind of life might develop. I suppose they could be intermittently awakened with these little spaceships. All they need is the enabling protein."

"And now we've finally evolved into something that they want to inhabit," Eugene said. "Maybe that's what that blast of radio waves was the other night. Maybe these discs can communicate back to wherever they come from."

"Wait a sec," Jonathan said. "You mean that this alien virus is already inside me, like in hibernation?"

"That's what we believe," Sheila said, "provided our initial impressions are correct. The virus's potential to express itself is in our genomes, sort of like an oncogene has the power to express itself as a cancer. We already know that bits and pieces of regular viruses are nestled into our DNA. This just happens to be a humongus piece."

For a few minutes the room was dominated by an awed silence. Pitt took a potato chip. His chewing sounds seemed abnormally loud. He glanced at the others when he became aware they were staring at him. "Sorry," he said.

"I have a feeling that these so called mega-viruses are not content just to take over," Cassy said suddenly. "I'm afraid they have the power to cause organisms to mutate."

All eyes turned to Cassy.

"How do you know that?" Sheila asked.

"Because I went to see my fiancé, Beau Stark, today," Cassy admitted.

"I hardly think that was wise," Sheila said angrily.

"I had to," Cassy said. "I had to try to talk to him and get him to come back and be examined."

"Did you tell him about us?" Sheila demanded.

Cassy shook her head. Thinking about her visit, she fought against tears.

Pitt got out of his chair and sat on the arm of Cassy's. He put his arm around her shoulders.

"What made you think about mutation?" Nancy asked. "Do you mean somatic mutation, like his body changing?"

"Yes," Cassy said. She reached up and took hold of Pitt's hand. "The skin behind his ear has changed. It's not human skin. It's like something I've never felt."

This new revelation brought another period of silence. Now the threat seemed even greater. There was a monster lurking in everyone.

"We have to try to do something about this," Jesse said. "We have to do it now!"

"I agree," Sheila said. "We don't have a lot of data but we have some."

"We've got the protein," Nancy said. "Even if we don't know much about it yet."

"And we have the discs with the preliminary analysis of their composition," Eugene added.

"The only problem is we don't know who is infected and who isn't," Sheila said.

"We'll have to take that chance," Cassy said.

Nancy agreed. "We don't have any choice. Let's put all our data together in a more or less formal report. I want to have something in hand. A good place to do it is in my office at Serotec. We won't be bothered, and we'll have access to word processing, printers, and copiers. What do you all say?"

"I say time's a'wasting," Jesse remarked and got up from the couch.

Eugene put the Tupperware container with the two black discs into a knapsack that also contained printouts of the various tests he'd run. He slung it over his shoulder and followed the others outside.

Everybody squeezed into the Sellerses' minivan. Nancy drove. As they pulled away from the curb, Jonathan looked out the back window. A few of the many pedestrians were watching them but most ignored them.

Within an hour the entire group was hard at work. They divided the task up according to abilities. Cassy and Pitt were busy typing on computer terminals with

Jonathan's technical assistance. Nancy and Eugene were making copies of their test results. Sheila was collating the patients' charts of hundreds of flu cases. Jesse was on the telephone.

"I think you should be the one to speak," Nancy told Sheila. "You're the medical doctor."

"No doubt about it," Eugene said. "You'll be much more convincing. We can back you up by providing details as needed."

"That's a lot of responsibility," Sheila said.

Jesse hung up the phone. "There's a red-eye to Atlanta that leaves in an hour and ten minutes. I booked three seats. I assumed that just Sheila, Nancy, and Eugene were going."

Nancy looked over at Jonathan. "Maybe Eugene or I should stay here," she said.

"Mom!" Jonathan whined. "I'll be fine."

"I think it is important that both you people come," Sheila said. "You're the ones who have done the tests."

"Jonathan can stay with us," Cassy said.

Jonathan's face brightened.

Several cars pulled up to the front of the Serotec building. Pedestrians stopped their wanderings and walked over. They helped open the doors. From the first car emerged Captain Hernandez. His driver got out on the other side. It was Vince Garbon. From the car behind emerged plainclothes officers as well as Candee and her parents.

The pedestrians stood in front of the captain and pointed up to the lights in the fourth-floor windows. They told the captain that all the "unchanged" were up there. The captain nodded, then waved to the others to follow him. En masse they entered the building.

Cassy had finished her typing and was waiting by the printer as it spewed out the pages. Jonathan moved over so he was standing next to her.

"I still don't understand why Atlanta," Jonathan said. "Why not just go to the the health authorities here?"

"Because we don't know whose side the local health people are on," Cassy said. "The problem is here in this city, and we can't risk spilling all we know to somebody who might be one of them."

"But how do you know it's not happening in Atlanta?" Jonathan asked.

"We don't know," Cassy admitted. "At this stage we're just hoping."

"Besides," Pitt said, overhearing, "the CDC is the best bet for handling this kind of problem. It's a national organization. If need be they could quarantine this city or even the whole state. And perhaps most critical of all, they can get the word out. This whole affair has happened so fast here that the media hasn't even picked up on it."

"Either that or the people who control the media are all infected," Cassy said.

Cassy got her pages together and joined them with Pitt's. As she was stapling them together the lights flickered.

"What the hell was that?" Jesse asked. He was tense like everyone else.

For a moment no one moved. Then the lights went out. The only illumination came from computer screens that had backup battery power sources.

"Don't panic," Nancy said. "The building has its own generators."

Jonathan went to the window. He cranked it open and stuck his head out. Below he could see light coming from lower floors. He relayed this disturbing information to the others.

"I don't like this," Jesse said.

The faint but high-pitched whine of the elevator permeated the room. The elevator was coming up.

"Let's get out of here!" Jesse yelled.

Frantically the group threw together all their papers and packed them into a leather briefcase before racing from the room. In the darkened hall they could see from the floor indicator that the elevator was almost there.

With Nancy silently beckoning to show the way, they ran the length of the corridor and burst through the door into the stairwell. They started down but almost immediately heard a door opening three floors below them on the ground level.

Jesse, who was now in the lead, made a snap decision and detoured into the corridor of the third floor. Everyone followed.

They dashed to the stairwell at the opposite end. Jesse held up until Sheila brought up the rear. As Jesse was about to open the door, he caught a glimpse through the door's window of someone coming up the stairs. Quickly he ducked down and motioned frantically for the others to do the same. They all heard the heavy footfalls of several people charging up the stairs, heading to the fourth floor.

The moment Jesse thought he heard the stairwell door above close, he pulled open the door in front of him. He looked up. Satisfied the stairwell was now empty, he motioned for the others to follow him down to the ground level.

They regrouped in front of a door that said it was armed and was restricted for emergency use only.

"Everybody here?" Jesse whispered.

"We're all here," Eugene said.

"We get in that van and we're out of here," Jesse said. "I'll drive. Let me have the keys."

Nancy gladly passed them to him.

"Okay, go!" Jesse said. He burst through the door, setting off the alarm. The others followed closely at his heels. They ran half bent over. Within a few seconds they were inside the car, and Jesse had the engine roaring.

"Hang on," he warned. He gunned the engine. With a screech of tires they rocketed out of the parking lot. Jesse didn't bother to stop at the security gate. The van hit the black-and-white wooden bar and snapped it cleanly off.

Jonathan turned and looked out the rear window. Glancing up at the darkened windows of the fourth floor, he saw several pairs of glowing eyes. They appeared like cats' eyes reflecting the beam of a headlight.

Jesse drove rapidly but purposefully within the speed limit. He'd passed a few squad cars and didn't want to attract their attention.

At a traffic light everyone began to calm down enough to discuss who it could have been that had tried to corner them in the Serotec building. No one had any idea. Nor did anyone know who would have tipped them off. Nancy questioned whether the night security man might be one of "them."

At the next light, Pitt happened to glance over at the car alongside them. When the driver turned to look at Pitt, his face immediately reflected recognition. Pitt saw him reach for his cellular phone.

"This sounds crazy," Pitt said. "But I think the guy next to us recognizes us."

Jesse responded by ignoring the red light. He surged forward between cars, then turned off the main street. They bumped down a back alley.

"Aren't we going the opposite direction from the airport?" Sheila asked.

"Don't worry," Jesse said. "As the expression goes, I know this city like the back of my hand."

They made a few more surprising turns down small, out-of-the-way streets. Then to everyone's surprise they sped up an entrance to the freeway that no one in the car besides Jesse knew existed.

They drove the rest of the way to the airport in silence. It was becoming clear to everyone the extent of the conspiracy and that they could not let down their guard.

Jesse drove up to the departure level of the airport and pulled to a halt at terminal C. Everyone piled out of the van.

"We can take care of ourselves from here," Sheila said, grabbing the briefcase containing the hastily assembled report. "Why don't the rest of you get back home to safety?"

"We're going to see you three off," Jesse said. "I want to make sure there is no more trouble."

"What about the van?" Pitt asked. "Do you want me to stay here with it?"

"No," Jesse said. "I want all of us inside."

The interior of the terminal at that hour was all but deserted. A cleaning crew was polishing the expansive terrazzo floor. The Delta counter was the only one occupied. The monitors said that the Atlanta flight was on time.

"All you people head out to the gate," Jesse said. "I'll get the tickets. Just be sure to have your picture IDs handy."

The group hurried across the terminal and approached airport security. There were a few other passengers who were waiting their turn to put their carry-on baggage into the X-ray detector.

"Where are the black discs?" Cassy whispered to Pitt.

"Eugene has them in his knapsack," Pitt answered.

At that moment Eugene dropped the knapsack on the conveyer, and it disappeared inside the machine. He stepped through the metal detector.

"What if they set off an alarm?" Cassy said.

"I'm more worried that the security personnel might be one of 'them' and recognize the image on X-ray," Pitt said.

Both Pitt and Cassy held their breath as the woman security guard halted the machine. Her eyes were glued to the X-ray image. It seemed like a full minute before the woman restarted the conveyer belt. Cassy sighed in relief. She and Pitt stepped through the metal detector and caught up with the others.

They all avoided locking eyes with any of the other passengers as they walked out the concourse. It was nerve-racking not knowing who was infected and who wasn't. As if reading everybody's mind, Jonathan said: "I think you can tell who they are by either their smiles or their eyes."

"What do you mean?" Nancy asked.

"It's either a fake smile or their eyes glow," Jonathan said. "Of course you can only see the eyes in the dark."

"I think you are right, Jonathan," Cassy said. She'd witnessed both.

They arrived at the gate. The plane was already mostly boarded. They moved to the side to wait for Jesse.

"See that woman over there?" Jonathan said while pointing. "Look at that stupid grin. I bet five bucks she's one of them."

"Jonathan!" Nancy whispered forcibly. "Don't be so obvious."

Vince Garbon pulled the unmarked police car over to the curb, directly behind the Sellerses' minivan.

"Obviously they are here," Captain Hernandez said as he got out of the car. A second car pulled up behind the first. Candee, her parents, and the other plainclothes officers emerged.

Like iron filings being drawn to a magnet, a number of infected airport workers immediately drew around the captain and his group.

"Gate 5, terminal C," one these people said to the captain. "Flight 917 for Atlanta."

"Let's go," Captain Hernandez said. He stepped through the automatic door into the terminal and waved for the others to follow him.

"Now where's Jesse?" Sheila asked. She looked for him back along the concourse toward the main terminal. "I don't want to miss this flight."

"Eugene," Nancy whispered to her husband. "With all that's going on, I'm having second thoughts about leaving Jonathan. Maybe one of us should stay here."

"I'll watch out for him," Jesse said. He'd come up behind the group in time to hear Nancy's comment. "You do your thing in Atlanta. He'll be fine."

"How did you get here?" Sheila asked.

Jesse pointed toward an unmarked, locked door just behind them. "I've been to the airport so many times investigating various crimes that I know the place better than my own basement."

He handed tickets to Nancy, Eugene, and Sheila. Nancy gave her son one last hug. Jonathan remained stiff with his arms at his side.

"You be careful, hear me?" Nancy said, trying vainly to look Jonathan in the eye.

"Mom!" Jonathan complained.

"Let's go," Sheila said. "It's last call."

With Sheila in the lead and Nancy bringing up the rear to give her son a final wave, the three checked in at the gate, showed their picture ID's then disappeared down the jetway. A few minutes later the jetway pulled back from the plane and the plane taxied out into the night.

Jesse turned from the window with a sigh of relief. "They're off, thank God," he said. "But now we . . ."

Jesse didn't get to finish his sentence because he saw Captain Hernandez and Vince Garbon leading a large pack of people. They were walking quickly down the center of the concourse, heading directly toward gate 5.

Cassy saw the cloud descend over Jesse's face and started to ask what was wrong. But Jesse didn't give her a chance. Roughly he herded the group back against the unmarked door.

"What's going on?" Pitt demanded.

Jesse ignored him and quickly punched in the combination on the keypad next to the doorknob. The door opened. "Go!" he commanded.

Cassy was first through the door followed by Jonathan and then Pitt. Jesse pulled the door shut behind himself.

"Come on!" he whispered harshly. He rapidly descended a flight of metal stairs, and ran along a corridor until he came to a door to the outside. On a series of pegs next to the door were yellow rain ponchos with hoods. Quickly he tossed one to each of the others and told them to put them on, including the hoods.

Everyone complied. Cassy asked who he'd seen.

"The chief of police," Jesse said. "And I know for sure he's one of them."

Once again typing the combination onto a keypad, Jesse opened the door to the outside. The group stepped out onto the tarmac. They were directly below the jetway for gate 5.

"See that luggage train over there?" Jesse said as he pointed. It was a tractor-like vehicle hitched to a string of five baggage carts. It was parked about fifty feet away. "We are going to walk over there real casual like. The problem is we'll be visible from the windows above. Once there you all are going to climb into one of the baggage cars. Then, God willing, we'll ride back to terminal A, not C."

"But our car is at terminal C," Pitt said.

"We're leaving the car," Jesse said.

"We are?" Jonathan asked. He was shocked. It was his parents' car.

"Damn right we are," Jesse said. "Let's go!"

They got to the baggage cart without incident. Everyone was tempted to look up into the windows, but no one did.

Jesse started the engine while the others climbed aboard. They were thankful for Jesse's decisive authority. Everyone breathed a sigh of relief as the baggage train twisted around like a snake and then headed for terminal A.

They passed a few airline workers, but no one challenged Jesse's performance. They arrived at terminal A baggage claim without incident. There, they again benefited from Jesse's knowledge of the airport layout and procedure. Within minutes they were outside on the arrival level waiting for the airport bus.

"We'll take the bus back to the city center," Jesse said. "I can get my car from there."

"What about my parents' van?" Jonathan asked.

"I'll take care of it tomorrow," Jesse said.

The sound of a huge jet thundered overhead, making conversation momentarily impossible.

"That must have been them," Jonathan said as soon as he could be heard above the din.

"Now if they can only find receptive people at the CDC," Pitt said.

"They have to," Cassy said. "It could be our only chance."

Beau was occupying the master suite at the château. There were French doors over a balcony that looked down on the terrace and the swimming pool. The doors were ajar and a soft night breeze rustled the papers on the desk. Randy Nite and a few of his more senior people were there, going over the work that had been accomplished that day.

"I'm really pleased," Randy said.

"So am I," Beau said. "Things couldn't be going better." He ran his hand through his hair and his fingers touched the area of altered skin behind his right ear. He scratched it, and it felt good.

The phone rang and one of Randy's assistants answered. After a quick conversation he handed the phone to Beau.

"Captain Hernandez," Beau said happily. "Good of you to call."

Randy tried to hear what the captain was saying, but he couldn't.

"So they are on their way to the CDC in Atlanta," Beau said. "I'm glad you called to let us know, but I assure you there won't be a problem."

Beau disconnected but did not hang up the receiver. Instead he dialed another number with a 404 area code. When the call was answered Beau said: "Dr. Clyde Horn, this is Beau Stark. That group of people I told you about today is on their way to Atlanta as we speak. I imagine they'll be at the CDC tomorrow so handle them as we discussed."

Beau replaced the receiver.

"Do you expect any trouble?" Randy asked.

Beau smiled. "Of course not. Don't be silly."

"Are you sure you should have let that Cassy Winthrope leave today?" Randy asked.

"Goodness, you are a worrywart tonight," Beau said. "But yes, I'm sure. She's been rather special to me, and I decided I didn't want to force her. I want her to embrace the cause voluntarily."

"I don't understand why you care," Randy said.

"I'm not sure why I do either," Beau admitted. "But enough of this talk. Come outside! It's almost time."

Beau and Randy stepped out onto the balcony. After a glance up at the night sky, Beau stuck his head back inside the room and asked one of the assistants to go down and turn off the underwater lights in the pool.

A few minutes later the pool lights went out. The effect was dramatic. The stars were much more intense, especially those in the galactic core of the Milky Way.

"How much longer?" Randy asked.

"Two seconds," Beau said.

No sooner had the words escaped from Beau's lips that the sky lit up with a profusion of shooting stars. Literally thousands of them rained down like a gigantic firework display.

"Beautiful, isn't it?" Beau said.

"Marvelous," Randy said.

"It's the final wave," Beau said. "The final wave!"

CHAPTER 14

8:15 A.M.

"I've never seen anything like this," Jesse said. "You know what I'm saying. I mean, how long does it take three young people to get themselves together to go out for breakfast?"

"It's Cassy's fault," Pitt said. "She was in the bathroom for eight years."

"That's untrue," Cassy said, taking immediate umbrage. "I didn't take as long as Jonathan here. Besides, I had to wash my hair."

"I didn't take long," Jonathan said.

"You most certainly did," Cassy said.

"All right, enough already," Jesse shouted. Then in a more moderate tone he added: "I've just forgotten what it's like having kids around."

They had stayed the night at Pitt's second cousin's apartment, thinking it was the safest place. It had worked out fine with Pitt and Jonathan sharing a bedroom. The only minor problem had been the single bathroom.

"Where should we eat?" Jesse asked.

"We usually eat at Costa's," Cassy said. "But I think the waitress there is an infected person."

"There's going to be infected people no matter where we go," Jesse said. "Let's go to Costa's. I don't want to go anyplace where I might run into any of my fellow officers."

It was a beautiful morning as they emerged into the sunlight. Jesse had them wait by the front door a few minutes while he went out to reconnoiter his car. When he saw no evidence of it having been tampered with, he waved them over. They piled in.

"I got to stop for gas," Jesse informed them as he pulled out into the street.

"There's still a lot of people walking around," Jonathan said. "Just like last night. And they all have that weird shit-eating grin."

"Foul language is no longer cool," Cassy admonished.

"Jeez, you sound like my mother," Jonathan said.

They drove into a gas station. Jesse got out to pump the gas. Pitt got out to keep him company.

"Have you been noticing what I have?" Jesse asked when the tank was almost full. The gas station was very busy at that time in the morning.

"Are you referring to the fact that everybody seems to have the flu?" Pitt commented.

"That's exactly what I'm referring to," Jesse said. Most everyone they saw was either coughing, sneezing, or looking pale.

A few blocks away from the diner, Jesse pulled over to the curb at a newsstand and asked Pitt to get a paper. Pitt got out and waited his turn. Like the gas station, the newsstand was busy. As Pitt got closer to the stacks of papers, he noticed that each was being held down with a black disc!

Pitt asked the proprietor about his paperweights.

"Cute little things, ain't they?" he said.

"Where did you get them?" Pitt asked.

"They were all over my yard this morning," the man said.

Pitt ducked back into the car with the paper and told the others about the black discs.

"Wonderful!" Jesse said sarcastically. He glanced at the headlines: *Mild Flu Spreading*. "As if we didn't know that already," he added.

Cassy took the paper in the back seat and read the article as Jesse drove on to Costa's.

"It says the illness is miserable but short," Cassy said. "At least for healthy people. For people with chronic diseases, it advises them to seek medical attention at the first sign of symptoms."

"A lot of good that's going to do them," Pitt commented.

Once inside Costa's they took a booth toward the front. Pitt and Cassy were on the lookout for Marjorie. They didn't see her. When a boy about Jonathan's age came over to take their order, Cassy asked about the waitress.

"She went to Santa Fe," the boy said. "A lot of our staff went there. That's why I'm working. I'm Stephanos, Costa's son."

After Stephanos disappeared back into the kitchen, Cassy told the others about what she'd seen in Santa Fe. "They're all working at this castlelike house," she added.

"What are they doing?" Jesse asked.

Cassy shrugged. "I asked; it was a natural question. But Beau just gave me platitudes and generalities about a new beginning and making everything right, whatever the hell that meant."

"I thought foul language wasn't cool," Jonathan said.

"You're right," Cassy said. "I'm sorry."

Pitt glanced at his watch for the tenth time since they'd been in the diner. "It shouldn't be too long now before they arrive at the CDC."

"They might be waiting for the place to open," Cassy said. "By now they've been in Atlanta for several hours. With the time difference maybe the CDC doesn't open for another hour or so."

A family of four in the next booth started to cough and sneeze almost simultaneously. The flu symptoms progressed rapidly. Pitt looked over and recognized the pale, feverish appearance, particularly of the father. "I wish I could warn them," he said.

"What would you tell them?" Cassy asked. "That they have an alien monster inside that's now been activated and that by tomorrow they won't be themselves?"

"You're right," Pitt said. "At this stage there's not much that can be said. Prevention is key."

"That's why we've gone to the CDC," Cassy said. "Prevention is what they are about. We just have to keep our fingers crossed that they'll take the threat seriously before it is too late."

Dr. Wilton Marchand leaned back in his high-backed desk chair and folded his hands over his expansive abdomen. He'd never followed any of his own organization's recommendations concerning diet and exercise. He looked more like a successful brewery proprietor of the late nineteenth century than the director of the Centers for Disease Control.

Dr. Marchand had hastily called together some of his department heads for an impromptu meeting. Attending were Dr. Isabel Sanchez, head of the Influenza branch; Dr. Delbert Black, head of Special Pathogens; Dr. Patrick Delbanco, head of virology; and Dr. Hamar Eggans, head of epidemiology. Dr. Marchand would have liked to have included others, but they were either out of town or tied up with other commitments.

"Thank you," Dr. Marchand said to Sheila who'd just finished an impassioned presentation of the entire problem. Dr. Marchand gazed at his branch heads who were looking over each other's shoulders, busily reading the single copy of the report that Sheila had handed them prior to her presentation.

Sheila glanced at Eugene and Nancy who were sitting to her immediate right. The room had gone silent. Nancy nodded to Sheila to convey that she thought Sheila had done an excellent job. Eugene shrugged and raised his eyebrows in response to the silence. He was silently asking the question of how this collection of CDC brass could be taking this information with such apparent composure.

"Excuse me," Eugene said a minute or so later, unable to bear the prolonged silence. "As a physicist, I have to emphasize to you people that these black discs are made of a material that could not have been made on Earth."

Dr. Marchand picked up the Tupperware container on his desk and with lidded eyes gazed in at the two objects.

"And they are definitely manufactured," Eugene continued. "They are not natural. In other words, it would have to be from an advanced culture . . . an alien culture!" It was the first time the trio had used the word "alien." They had implied as much but had avoided being so explicit.

Dr. Marchand smiled to indicate that he understood Eugene's point. He extended the Tupperware container out toward Dr. Black who took it and peered within.

"Quite heavy," Dr. Black commented before handing the container on to Dr. Delbanco.

"And you say that there are many such objects in your city," Dr. Marchand said.

Sheila threw up her hands in exasperation and got to her feet. She couldn't sit a moment longer. "There could be thousands," she said. "But that's not the point. The point that we are making is that we are in the beginning of an epidemic stemming from a provirus in our genomes. In fact, it's in every higher animal's genome that we've tested, suggesting it's been there for maybe a billion years. And the scariest part is that it has to be extraterrestrial in origin."

"Every element, every atom, and every particle of our bodies are 'extraterrestrial,' " Dr. Black said sternly. "Our entire makeup has been forged in the supernova of dying stars."

"That may be," Eugene said. "But we are talking about a life form. Not mere atoms."

"Exactly," Sheila said. "A viruslike organism that has been lying dormant in the genomes of Earth creatures, including human beings."

"Which you purport was transported to Earth in these miniature spaceships in the Tupperware container," Dr. Marchand said wearily.

Sheila rubbed her face to get herself under control. She knew she was exhausted and emotionally drained. Like Nancy and Eugene she'd not slept a wink all night. "I know it sounds implausible," she said, deliberately speaking slowly. "But it is happening. These black discs have the capability of injecting a fluid into living organisms. We were lucky to obtain a drop of the fluid from which we have isolated a protein that we believe functions like a prion."

"A prion only carries one of the spongiform encephalopathies," Dr. Delbanco said with a broad smile. "I doubt your protein is a prion."

"I said, 'Like a prion!'" Sheila added venomously. "I didn't say it was a prion."

"The protein reacts with the particular segment of DNA that was previously considered noncoding," Nancy said. She could see that Sheila was getting angry. "Perhaps it is better to say it's functioning more like a promoter."

"Perhaps we could take a short break," Sheila said. "I know I could use a little coffee."

"Of course," Dr. Marchand said. "How thoughtless of me."

Beau gave King an exuberant scratching behind his ears as he gazed out over the lawns in front of the institute. From the wrought-iron balcony off the library, he and King could see a long stretch of the driveway before it disappeared into the trees. It was clogged with new converts patiently making their way to the château. A few waved up to Beau, and he waved back.

Letting his eyes roam the rest of the grounds, Beau could see his canine friends were reliably on duty. Beau was pleased. He did not want interruptions.

Turning back into the house, Beau descended to the first floor and entered the ballroom. It was jammed with energetically toiling people. Now that the space was almost completely gutted, it looked far different than it had just the day before.

The people working in the room were a remarkably diverse group from all walks of life and of all ages. Yet they were working together like a synchronized swim team. From Beau's perspective it was a sight to behold and the picture of efficiency. No one had to give orders. Like the individual cells of a multicelled organism, each person had in their mind the blueprints of the entire project.

Beau saw Randy Nite laboring happily at a makeshift workbench set up in the center of the room. Randy's team was particularly disparate, with ages ranging from a man in his eighties to a girl less than ten. They were working on banks of sophisticated electronic equipment. Each person wore lighted magnifying headgear reminiscent of a retinal surgeon.

Beau strolled over.

"Hey, Beau!" Randy said cheerfully, catching sight of him. "Great day, huh!"

"Perfect," Beau answered with equal enthusiasm. "Sorry to interrupt, but I'm going to need you this afternoon. Your lawyers are coming by with more papers for you to sign. I'm having the remainder of your assets signed over to the institute."

"No problem," Randy said. He wiped some plaster dust from his brow. "Sometimes I think we should move these electronics away from all this demolition."

"Probably would have been a good idea," Beau admitted. "But the demolition is almost over now."

"The other problem is that these instruments don't have the sophistication we're going to need."

"We'll just use what we can of theirs," Beau said. "We knew there would be problems with their degree of precision. But what we don't have, we'll have to develop ourselves."

"All right," Randy said, although he was less than convinced.

"Come on, Randy," Beau said. "Relax! Everything is going to work out fine."

"Well, at least they're making fantastic progress with the space," Randy said. His eyes roamed the room. "It certainly looks different now. The realtor told me it had been a re-creation of the ballroom of a famous French palace."

"It will serve a far greater purpose once we've finished it," Beau said. He gave Randy a friendly slap on the back. "Don't let me keep you. I'll see you later when the lawyers get here."

Stephanos picked up the soiled dishes from in front of Cassy, Pitt, Jonathan, and Jesse. Jesse asked for another "hit" of coffee. Stephanos went back behind the counter for the coffee pot.

"Did you hear him cough just before he got to our table?" Cassy asked.

Pitt nodded. "He's coming down with it. No doubt about it. But I'm not surprised. Last time we were in here we thought his father was infected."

"Hell with the coffee," Jesse said. "This place is starting to give me the creeps. Let's get."

The group got to their feet. Jesse threw down a tip. "This is my treat," he said. He picked up the check and headed for the cash register by the door.

"What do you think Beau is doing right now?" Pitt asked, as the group followed behind Jesse.

"I don't want to think about it," Cassy said.

"I just can't believe that my best friend is the leader of all this," Pitt said.

"He's not the leader!" Cassy snapped. "He's not Beau any longer. He's being controlled by the virus."

"You're right," Pitt said quickly. He knew he was touching a sore point for Cassy.

"Once the CDC is involved," Cassy said, "do you think they could come up with a cure, like a vaccine?"

"A vaccine is used to prevent an illness," Pitt said. "Not cure it."

Cassy stopped and with eyes that reflected a hint of desperation, looked up into Pitt's face. "You don't think they could come up with a cure?"

"Well, there are antiviral drugs," Pitt said, trying to sound hopeful. "I mean it's possible."

"Oh, Pitt, I hope so," Cassy said, near tears.

Pitt inwardly gulped. There was a nasty part of him that celebrated Beau's departure from the scene because of Pitt's feelings for Cassy. Yet he could see how bad she felt. Reaching out he took her in his arms and hugged her. She hugged him back.

"Hey, guys, take a gander at this," Jesse said, while blindly tapping Pitt on the shoulder. Jesse's eyes were glued to a tiny TV set behind the cash register.

Pitt and Cassy let go of each other. Jonathan crowded in from behind. The TV was tuned to CNN and an instant news break was coming on.

"This is just in to CNN," the announcer said. "There was an unprecedented meteor shower last night seen halfway around the world from the extreme western part of Europe all the way to Hawaii. Astronomers believe it was worldwide but could not be seen in the rest of the world because of sunlight. The cause is unknown since the phenomenon has caught astronomers totally unaware. We will bring more to you about this breaking news as soon as it is available."

"Could that have something to do with you-know-what?" Jonathan asked.

"Maybe more of the black discs?" Jesse suggested. "It must be."

"My God!" Pitt exclaimed. "If it is, then it's now involving the whole world."

"It will be unstoppable," Cassy said. She shook her head.

"Something the matter, folks?" Costa, the owner, asked. It was Jesse's turn at the register. Jesse'd originally lined up behind several other customers.

"Nope," Pitt said quickly. "It was a great breakfast."

Jesse paid the bill, and the group walked outside.

"Did you see his smile?" Jonathan questioned. "Did you see how fake it was? He's one of the infected. I'll bet five bucks."

"You'll have to bet with someone else," Pitt said. "We already knew he was one of them."

After a short break that Sheila and Nancy had used to go into the ladies' room and wash their faces, the trio returned to Dr. Marchand's office. Sheila was still exasperated so Nancy spoke.

"We understand that what we are saying is largely anecdotal and that our report is weak in actual data," Nancy said. "But the fact is that we are three professionals with impeccable credentials who are here because we are concerned. This event is truly happening."

"We certainly are not questioning your motives," Dr. Marchand said. "Just your conclusions. Since we had already dispatched an epidemiological investigative officer to the scene we are understandably dubious. We have his report here." Dr. Marchand raised a single-page memorandum. "It was his feeling that you people were experiencing an outbreak of a mild form of influenza. He described extensive consultation with the CEO of your hospital, Dr. Halprin."

"His visit occurred before we realized what we were dealing with," Sheila said. "Besides, Dr. Halprin had already been a victim of the illness. We tried to make that very clear to your EIS officer."

"Your report is very sketchy," Dr. Eggans said to Sheila, slapping it down onto the edge of Dr. Marchand's desk after he'd read it from cover to cover. "There's too much supposition and very little substance. However . . ."

Sheila had to restrain herself from getting up and angrily walking out. She couldn't believe how these passive intellectual midgets had risen to their current positions within the CDC bureaucracy.

"However," Dr. Eggans repeated, running a hand pensively through his full beard, "it's still compelling enough that I'd like to go and investigate on site."

Sheila turned to Nancy. She wasn't sure she'd heard correctly. Nancy flashed a thumbs up sign.

"Have you circulated this report to any other government agencies?" Dr. Marchand asked. He picked it up from his desk and idly thumbed through it.

"No!" Sheila said emphatically. "We all thought the CDC was the best place to start."

"It hasn't been sent to the State Department or the Surgeon General?"

"No one," Nancy affirmed.

"Did you try to determine the amino acid sequence of the protein?" Dr. Delbanco asked.

"Not yet," Nancy said. "But that will be easy to do."

"Have you determined if the virus is able to be isolated from the patients after they have recovered?" Dr. Delbanco asked.

"What about the nature of the reaction between the protein and DNA?" the willowy Dr. Sanchez asked.

Nancy smiled and held up her hands. She was pleased with the sudden interest. "Slow down," she said. "I can only handle one question at a time."

The queries came fast and furious. Nancy did her best to answer them, and Eugene helped when he could. Sheila initially was as pleased as Nancy, but after ten minutes had passed and the questions were becoming more and more hypothetical, she began to sense that something was wrong.

Sheila took a deep breath. Maybe she was just too tired. Maybe these questions were reasonable from such research-oriented professionals. The problem was that she expected action, not intellectualization. At that point they were busily questioning Nancy how she even came up with the idea of using the protein as a DNA probe.

Sheila let her eyes wander around the room. The walls were decorated with the usual profusion of professional diplomas, licenses, and academic awards. There were pictures of Dr. Marchand with the President and other politicians. Suddenly Sheila's eyes stopped at a door that was open about a foot. Beyond the door she saw the face of Dr. Clyde Horn. She recognized him instantly partially due to his shiny bald pate.

As Sheila's eyes locked onto Dr. Horn's his face twisted into a great smile. Sheila blinked, and when she opened her eyes, Dr. Horn was gone. Sheila closed her eyes again. Was she hallucinating from exhaustion and tension? She wasn't sure, but the image of Dr. Horn's face brought back the memory of him leaving her office with Dr. Halprin. As clearly as if it had been an hour previously, she could hear Dr. Halprin saying: "I've even got something I want you to take back to Atlanta for me. Something I think that will interest the CDC."

Sheila's eyes blinked open. With sudden clairvoyance and absolute certitude she knew what Dr. Halprin had been referring to: a black disc. Sheila glanced at the

CDC people in the room and it dawned on her with equivalent certitude that they were all infected. Instead of being interested in the epidemic in order to contain it, they were grilling Nancy and Eugene to find out how they had learned what they had.

Sheila stood up. She grabbed Nancy's arm and tugged. "Come on, Nancy. Time for us to get some rest."

Nancy pulled her arm free. She was surprised at the interruption. "We're finally making some progress here," she forcibly whispered.

"Eugene, we need a few hours of sleep," Sheila said. "You must understand even if Nancy doesn't."

"Is there something wrong, Dr. Miller?" Dr. Marchand asked.

"Not at all," Sheila said. "I just realized that we're exhausted, and that we shouldn't be taking your time until we've had some rest. We'll make a lot more sense after a little sleep. There's a Sheraton nearby. It will be best for everyone."

Sheila stepped up to Marchand's desk and reached for the report that she and the Sellerses had brought. Dr. Marchand put his hand on it. "If you don't mind, we'd like to peruse this while you're resting."

"That's fine," Sheila said agreeably. She backed away and tugged on Nancy's arm again.

"Sheila, I think . . ." Nancy began but her eyes met Sheila's. She could see Sheila's intensity and resolve. Nancy stood up. It dawned on her Sheila knew something she didn't.

"Why don't we say we'll be back after lunch," Sheila offered. "Say between one and two o'clock."

"I think that will work for us," Dr. Marchand said. He looked at his department heads, and they all nodded.

Eugene crossed his legs. He'd not seen the unspoken communication between his wife and Sheila. "Maybe I'll stay here," he said.

"You are coming with us," Nancy said to Eugene, yanking him to his feet. Then she smiled at her hosts. They smiled back.

Sheila led the way out of Dr. Marchand's office. They passed through the secretarial area and down the pale, institutional green corridor.

At the elevators Eugene started to complain, but Nancy told him to stay quiet.

"At least until we get into the rental car," Sheila whispered.

They boarded the elevator and smiled at the occupants. They all smiled back and commented on how nice the weather was.

By the time they got to the car and climbed in, Eugene was mildly irritated.

"What's wrong with you women?" he said as he put the key in the ignition. "It took us an hour to get them interested and then poof, we have to go rest. This is crazy."

"They are all infected," Sheila said. "Every last one of them."

"Are you sure?" Eugene asked. He was aghast.

"Absolutely," Sheila said. "Not a doubt in my mind."

"I assume we're not going to the Sheraton," Nancy said.

"Hell no!" Sheila said. "Let's get to the airport. We're back to square one."

The reporters had gathered at the gate of the institute. Although they had not been invited, Beau had anticipated their coming, he just didn't know which day. When the young men at the gate had informed Beau they were there, Beau told the gate-keepers to hold them back for fifteen minutes to give Beau a chance to walk out to where the driveway entered the trees. Beau did not want any reporters in the ball-room, at least not yet.

When Beau confronted the group he was mildly surprised by the number. He'd expected ten or fifteen people. Instead there were around fifty. They were equally divided between newspaper, magazine, and TV. There were about ten TV cameras. Everyone had microphones.

"So here you see the new Institute for a New Beginning," Beau said, gesturing toward the château with a sweep of his hand.

"We understand that you are doing a lot of renovation in the building," a jour-nalist said.

"I wouldn't say a lot," Beau said. "But yes, we are making a few changes to suit our needs."

"Can we see the interior?" a journalist asked.

"Not today," Beau said. "It would be too disruptive for the work that is being done."

"So we've come all the way out here for nothing," a journalist commented.

"I hardly think that is the case," Beau said. "You certainly can see that the institute is a reality and not a mere figment of imagination."

"Is it true that all the assets of Cipher Software are now controlled by the Institute for a New Beginning?"

"Most," Beau said vaguely. "Perhaps you should direct that question to Mr. Randy Nite."

"We'd like to," a journalist said. "But he's not been available. I've been trying around the clock to get an appointment to interview him."

"I know he's busy," Beau said. "He has committed himself wholeheartedly to the goals of the institute. But I think I could convince him to talk to you people in the near future."

"What is this 'new beginning,' " a particularly skeptical journalist demanded.

"Exactly that," Beau said. "It is born out of the need to take seriously the ste-wardship of this planet. Human beings have been doing a terrible job up until now as witnessed by pollution, destruction of ecosystems, constant strife, and warfare. The situation necessitates a change, or, if you will, a new beginning, and the institute will be the agent for that change."

The skeptical reporter smiled wryly. "Such practiced rhetoric," he commented. "It certainly sounds highfalutin, maybe even true, at least the part about the mess humans have made of the world. But the idea of an institute accomplishing this out here in an isolated mansion is ludicrous. This whole operation with all these brainwashed people strikes me more as a cult than anything else."

Beau fixed the skeptical reporter with his eyes and his pupils dilated maximally. He walked toward the man, oblivious to the people who were blocking his path. Most stepped aside, a few Beau pushed. He didn't shove them hard but rather eased them out of the way.

Beau reached the reporter who defiantly returned Beau's stare. The whole group of journalists went silent as they watched the confrontation. Beau resisted the temptation to reach out, grab the individual, and demand he show proper respect. Instead Beau decided he would bring this contumacious individual back to the institute and infect him.

But then Beau thought it might be easier to infect them all. He'd just give them each a parting gift of a black disc.

"Excuse me, Beau!" an attractive young woman called who'd just arrived. Her name was Veronica Paterson. She'd run down from the chateau and was out of breath. She was clothed in an alluring one-piece spandex outfit that appeared as if it had been sprayed on her lithe and shapely body. The male reporters in particular were intrigued.

She pulled Beau away from the group so she could tell him in private that there was an important telephone call for him up at the institute.

"Do you think you can handle these reporters?" Beau asked her.

"Most certainly," Veronica said.

"They are not to go inside," Beau said.

"Of course not," Veronica said.

"And they're to leave with gifts," Beau said. "Give them all black discs. Tell them that it is our emblem."

Veronica smiled. "I like that," she said.

"Excuse me, everybody!" Beau called out to the crowd of reporters. "I must leave unexpectedly, but I'm sure I will be seeing each of you again. Miss Paterson will be available for your remaining questions. She will also be handing out small parting gifts for you to take as souvenirs from your day at the institute."

A babble of questions bubbled forth in response to Beau's announcement. Beau merely smiled and moved off. He clapped his hands, and King came bounding to his side. While Beau had been speaking with the reporters he'd had King keep his distance.

A sharp whistle from Beau brought a number of the other dogs from around the grounds. Beau snapped his fingers and pointed toward the group of journalists. The newly summoned dogs quickly moved to positions ringing the reporters and patiently sat on their haunches.

Upon reaching the house, Beau went directly up to the library. He dialed Dr. Marchand's direct number and the line was immediately answered.

"They have left," Dr. Marchand said. "But it was an unexpected ruse. They informed us they were going to the Sheraton, but they did not."

"Do you have their report?" Beau asked.

"Of course," Dr. Marchand said.

"Destroy it," Beau said.

"What do you want us to do about them?" Dr. Marchand asked. "Should we stop them?"

"By all means," Beau said. "You shouldn't ask a question to which you already know the answer."

Marchand laughed. "You are right," he said. "It's just this weird human trait about trying to be diplomatic."

Mid-morning Atlanta traffic wasn't bad compared with rush hour, but it was a lot more than Eugene was accustomed to.

"Everybody seems so aggressive here," Eugene complained.

"You're doing fine, dear," Nancy said, although she hadn't appreciated how close Eugene had come to another car at the previous intersection.

Sheila was busy looking out the back window.

"Anybody following us?" Eugene asked, glancing at Sheila in the rearview mirror.

"I don't think so," Sheila said. "I guess they bought the story about getting some rest. After all, it was reasonable. But what worries me is that now they know that we know! Maybe I should say 'it' knows."

"You make it sound like a single entity," Eugene said.

"All the infected people have a way of working together," Sheila said. "It's spooky. It's like viruses themselves, all working for the collective good. Or like an ant colony where each individual seems to know what everyone else is doing and what they should be doing as a consequence."

"That suggests there is networking among the infected people," Eugene said. "Maybe the alien form is a composite of a number of different organisms. If that were the case, it would be a different dimension of organization than we're accustomed to. Hey, maybe it needs a finite number of infected organisms to reach a critical mass."

"The physicist is getting far too theoretical for me," Sheila said. "And keep your eye on the road! We just came too close to that red car next to us."

"But one thing is for sure," Nancy said. "Whatever the level of organization, we have to remember that we are dealing with a life form. That means that self-preservation will be high on its list."

"And self-preservation depends on recognizing and destroying enemies," Sheila said. "Like us!"

"That's a comforting thought," Nancy said with a shiver.

"Where should we go when we get to the airport?" Eugene asked.

"I'm open to suggestions," Sheila said. "We still have to get to someone or some organization who can do something."

Sheila did a double take when she glanced at the face of the driver in the red car that had been cruising alongside them. It was now pulling ahead.

"My God!" Sheila said.

Nancy's head snapped around. "What's the matter?"

"The driver of the red car," Sheila yelled. "It's the bearded guy: the epidemiologist from the CDC. What's his name?"

"Hamar Eggans," Nancy said. She spun back around and looked. "You're right. It is him. Do you think he's seen us?"

At that moment the red car swerved directly in front of Eugene. He cursed. The bumpers had missed by millimeters.

"There's a black car on our left," Nancy cried. "I think it is Delbanco."

"Oh no! They are on the right too," Sheila shouted. "Dr. Black is in a white car. They have us penned in."

"What should I do?" Eugene yelled in panic. "Is there anybody behind us?"

"There are cars," Sheila said, twisting around in her seat. "But I don't see anyone I recognize."

The moment the words left Sheila's lips, Eugene jammed on the brakes. The tiny four-cylinder rental car shuddered and jackknifed from side to side. Its tires screeched in protest against the pavement, as did the tires of the cars behind.

Eugene did not stop completely, but still the car behind thumped into them. But he had accomplished what he'd wanted to do. The three CDC cars had sped ahead before belatedly putting on their brakes. That gave Eugene the opportunity to turn left across traffic. Nancy screamed as she saw oncoming cars bearing down on her side of the vehicle.

Eugene stomped on the accelerator to avoid a collision and shot into the mouth of a narrow alley. It was filled with trash and several trash barrels. Its width was just adequate for the small car so that all the garbage, cardboard boxes, and barrels were met head on in a flurry of flying debris.

Nancy and Sheila hung on for dear life.

"My God, Eugene!" Nancy shouted as they hit a particularly large barrel that flipped up to bounce off the roof of the car. In the process it shattered the sun roof.

Eugene fought the steering wheel to keep the car going straight despite the rubbish and the containers. Still the car caromed repeatedly off the cement walls with an agonizing scraping sound akin to fingernails on a giant blackboard.

Toward the rear of the alley the way was clear, and Eugene hazarded a glance in the rearview mirror. To his horror he could see the front of the red car just entering the narrow byway.

"Eugene, look out!" Nancy cried, pointing ahead.

Eugene took his gaze away from the rearview mirror in time to see a cyclone fence rushing toward them. Deciding there was little choice, he yelled for the women to hold on and pushed the accelerator to the floor.

The tiny car gained speed. Both Eugene and Nancy were roughly thrown against their seat belts while Sheila bounced off the back of the front seat.

Despite trailing segments of the fence the tiny car sped out into a field churning up plumes of dust. It jackknifed several more times, but on each occasion Eugene was able to steer into the skid to keep the car from rolling over.

The vacant lot was about a hundred yards square and treeless. Ahead Eugene could see a rise stubbled with scraggly vegetation. Beyond the rise was a busy part of the city. Over the crest of the hill the tops of vehicles caught in stop-and-go traffic were visible.

With his mouth dry and forearms aching, Eugene cast another look behind. The red car was attempting to maneuver through the hole in the chain-link fence. The white car was immediately behind it.

Eugene's hastily conceived plan was to rocket over the hill and melt into the traffic. But the terrain had other ideas. The earth was particularly soft, and as the small car's front wheels hit the base of the hill, they dug in. The car spun to the left and lurched to a halt in a cloud of dust. All three of the occupants were severely jolted.

Eugene was the first to recover. He reached out to touch his wife. She responded as if waking from a bad dream. He turned to look at Sheila. She was dazed but okay.

Eugene undid his seat belt and got out on shaky legs and looked toward the chain-link fence. The red car was apparently hung up in the ragged opening: the sound of its tires spinning could be heard across the field.

"Come on!" Eugene called to the women. "We have a chance. Let's get over this hill and melt into the city."

The women emerged on the passenger side of the car. As they did so Eugene nervously glanced back at the red car in time to see the bearded man get out.

"Come on, hurry!" Eugene urged the women. Expecting the bearded man to come running in their direction, Eugene was surprised to see him retrieve something from the car. When he held it aloft, Eugene thought it suspiciously like the Tupperware container they'd brought with them to Atlanta.

Confused by this gesture, Eugene continued to watch while Nancy and Sheila helped each other up the hill. A few seconds later Eugene found himself staring at one of the black discs. To his utter shock it was hovering in midair right in front of his face.

"Come on, Eugene!" Nancy called from near the summit of the rise. "What are you waiting for?"

"It's a black disc," Eugene yelled back.

Eugene noticed that the disc was rotating rapidly. The individual bumps that lined the edge now appeared like a tiny ridge.

The black disc moved closer to Eugene. His skin tingled.

"Eugene!" Nancy called urgently.

Eugene took a step back but did not take his eyes off the disc in front of him, which was now turning red and radiating heat. Slipping off his jacket and rolling it, Eugene swatted at the disc in an attempt to knock it from the air. But it didn't happen. Instead the disc burned a hole through the jacket so quickly, Eugene felt no resistance whatsoever. It had been like a knife through room-temperature butter.

"Eugene!" Nancy shouted. "Come on!"

As a physicist, Eugene was mystified, especially when a corona began to form around the disc and the color began to turn from red to white. The tingling sensation he felt on his skin increased.

The corona rapidly expanded into a glaring ball of light so bright that the image of the disc contained in it was no longer visible.

Nancy could now see what was occupying Eugene's attention. She was about to call out to him again when she saw the bright ball of light suddenly expand to engulf her husband. Eugene's instant scream was immediately choked off and replaced by a whooshing sound. This noise grew deafening, but only for an instant; then it was cut off with such suddenness that Nancy and Sheila felt a concussive force like a silent explosion.

Eugene was gone. The rental car was left as a curiously twisted hulk as if it had been melted and pulled toward the point where Eugene had been standing.

Nancy started to run back down the hill, but Sheila grabbed her.

"No!" Sheila yelled. "We can't." There was now another ball of light forming next to the wreck of the car.

"Eugene!" Nancy cried desperately. Tears had burst forth.

"He's gone," Sheila said. "We have to get out of here."

The second ball of light was now expanding to envelop the car.

Sheila grabbed Nancy's arm and pulled her off the top of the hill toward the busy city. Ahead of them was heavy traffic and, even better, thousands of pedestrians. Behind them they heard the strange whooshing sound again and another concussion.

"What on earth was that?" Nancy asked through tears.

"I believe they thought we were in the car," Sheila said. "And if I had to guess, I'd say we just witnessed the creation of a couple of miniature black holes."

"Why haven't we heard from them?" Jonathan asked. He'd become progressively more worried as the day drew to a close. Now that it was dark, his concerns magnified. "I mean, it's even later in Atlanta."

Jonathan, Jesse, Cassy, and Pitt were in Jesse's car cruising along Jonathan's street. They'd passed his house several times already. Jesse was nervous about making this visit, but he'd relented when Jonathan insisted he needed some more clothes and his laptop. He also wanted to make sure his parents hadn't called and left some kind of message on his computer.

"Your parents and Dr. Miller are probably terribly busy," Cassy said. But her heart wasn't in the explanation. She herself was worried.

"What do you think, Jesse?" Pitt asked as they came to Jonathan's house for the third time. "Do you think it's safe?"

"It looks clear to me," Jesse said. "I don't see anything that looks like a stakeout. All right, let's do it, but we'll make it fast."

They pulled into the driveway and killed the headlights. At Jesse's insistence, they waited for another few minutes to see if there were any changes in the neighboring homes or vehicles parked on the street. All seemed peaceful.

"Okay," Jesse said. "Let's go."

They went in the front door, and Jonathan disappeared upstairs to his room. Jesse turned on the TV in the kitchen and found cold beer in the refrigerator. He offered one to Cassy and Pitt. Pitt accepted. The TV was tuned to CNN.

"This just in," the reporter announced. "A few moments ago the White House canceled the multinational summit on terrorism, saying that the President has come down with the flu. Presidential press secretary Arnold Lerstein said that the meeting probably would have gone on as scheduled without the President except that, by coincidence, most of the other world leaders seemed to be suffering from the same illness. The President's personal physician made the statement that he is convinced the President has the same 'short' flu that has been decimating Washington over the last few days and should resume normal duties in the morning."

Pitt shook his head in dismay. "It's taking over our whole civilization the same way a central nervous system virus takes over a host. It's going for the brain."

"We need a vaccine," Cassy said.

"We needed it yesterday," Jesse said.

The phone startled everyone. Cassy and Pitt looked at Jesse to see if they should answer it. Before Jesse could respond, Jonathan answered it upstairs.

Jesse charged up the stairs with Cassy and Pitt at his heels. He ducked into Jonathan's room.

"Hold on," Jonathan said into the phone, seeing the others. He told everyone that it was Dr. Miller.

"Put her on the speakerphone," Jesse suggested.

Jonathan pushed the button.

"We are all here," Jesse said. "You're on a speakerphone. How did you fare?"

"Miserably," Sheila admitted. "They led us on. It took several hours before I realized that they were all infected. The only thing they were interested in was how we'd found out what was going on."

"Christ!" Jesse mumbled. "Was it hard to get away? Did they try to detain you?"

"Not initially," Sheila said. "We told them we were just going to a motel to get some sleep. They must have followed us because they intercepted us on our way to the airport."

"Was there trouble?" Jesse asked.

"There was," Sheila admitted. "I'm sorry to say we lost Eugene."

The group looked at each other. Everyone had a different interpretation of what "lost" meant. Jesse was the only one who knew for certain.

"Have you looked for him?" Jonathan asked.

"It was like the hospital room," Sheila said. "If you know what I mean."

"What hospital room?" Jonathan asked. He was getting panicky.

Cassy put her arm around Jonathan's shoulder.

"Where are you?" Jesse asked.

"At the Atlanta airport," Sheila said. "Nancy is in kind of a bad way as you might guess, but we're coping. We've decided to come home, but we need someone to call up and prepay some tickets for us. We're afraid to use our credit cards."

"I'll do that right away," Jesse said. "We'll see you as soon as you get back."

Jesse hung up and dialed the airline ticket office. While he was making the arrangements, Jonathan asked Cassy directly if something had happened to his father.

Cassy nodded. "I'm afraid so," she said. "But I don't know what. You'll have to wait until your mother comes back to find out more."

Jesse hung up the phone and looked at Jonathan. He tried to think of something kind to say, but before he was able he heard the sound of skidding tires. From the front window came an intermittant flash of colored lights.

Running to the window Jesse parted the curtains. Outside in the street behind his car was a city police cruiser with its lights flashing. The uniformed occupants were just in the process of getting out, along with Vince Garbon. All had German shepherds on short leashes.

Other police department vehicles appeared, some marked, some not, including a paddy wagon. All pulled to a stop in front of the Sellers house and unloaded.

"What is it?" Pitt asked.

"The police," Jesse said. "They must have been watching the place. I even see my old partner or what's left of him."

"Are they coming here?" Cassy asked.

"I'm afraid so," Jesse said. "Kill all the lights."

The group frantically raced around the house and turned out the few lights they had turned on. They ended up in the darkened kitchen. Flashlight beams from outside stabbed through windows. It was an eerie image.

"They must know we are here," Cassy said.

"What are we going to do?" Pitt asked.

"I don't think there's much we can do," Jesse said.

"This house has a hidden exit," Jonathan said. "It's through the basement. I used it to sneak out at night."

"What are we waiting for?" Jesse said. "Let's go!"

Jonathan led the way, carrying his laptop. They moved slowly and silently, avoiding the flashlight beams that came in through the kitchen bay window. Once they got to the cellar stairs and had closed the door, they felt a bit less vulnerable. But it was difficult going because of the absolute darkness. They were not willing to put on any light because the cellar had several small windows.

They moved in single file. They all hung onto each other to avoid getting lost. Jonathan led them to the back wall of the basement. Once there he opened a massive door that rumbled on its hinges. Cool air flowed out over their ankles.

"In case you are wondering what this is," Jonathan said, "it's a bomb shelter that was built back in the fifties. My parents use it as a wine cellar."

They all entered and Jonathan told whoever was last to close the door. It settled into its jamb with a solid thump.

As soon as the door was closed, Jonathan switched on a light. They were in a cement passageway lined with wood shelving. A few cases of wine were haphazardly scattered about.

"This way," Jonathan said.

They came to another door. Beyond the second door was a step down into a room twelve feet square with bunk beds and an entire wall of cupboards. There was also a well head and a tiny bathroom.

A second chamber had a kitchen. Beyond the kitchen was another solid door. This door lead to another corridor that eventually led outside to a dry river bed behind the Sellerses' house.

"Well, I'll be!" Jesse commented. "Just like the escape route from an old medieval castle. I love it."

CHAPTER 15

9:45 A.M.

"Nancy," Sheila called gently. "We're here."

Nancy's eyes popped open, and she awoke with a start. "What time is it?" she asked, orienting herself to place and person.

Sheila told her.

"I feel awful," Nancy said.

"You and me both," Sheila said.

They had spent the night on the move in the Hartsfield Atlanta International Airport, constantly afraid they would be recognized. Boarding their flight in the wee hours of the morning had been a relief of sorts. Neither had slept for forty hours. Once airborne they had fallen into a deep sleep.

"What am I going to say to my son?" Nancy asked, not really expecting an answer. Every time she thought about the fiery disappearance of her husband, tears came to her eyes.

The women gathered their things and made their way off the plane. They were paranoid of everyone and were sure people were staring at them. When they emerged from the jetway, Nancy saw Jonathan and rushed to him. They hugged silently for several minutes while Sheila greeted Jesse, Pitt, and Cassy.

"Okay, let's move out," Jesse said, tapping the silently grieving mother and child.

They walked in a group toward the terminal. The whole time Jesse's head was a swivel as he constantly evaluated the people around them. He was pleased that no one was paying any attention to them, particularly airport security.

Fifteen minutes later they were in Jesse's personal van heading for town. Sheila and Nancy described in detail their disastrous trip. In a shaky voice Nancy managed to explain Eugene's last moments. The tragedy was greeted with silence.

"We have to decide where to go," Jesse said.

"Our house will be the most comfortable," Nancy said. "It's not elegant but there's a lot of room."

"I don't think that will be wise," Jesse said. He then told Nancy and Sheila what had happened the evening before.

Nancy felt outraged. "I know it's selfish of me to be so upset about a house considering everything that is going on," she said. "But it's my home."

"Where did you all stay last night?" Sheila asked.

"At my cousin's apartment," Pitt said. "The problem is it's only got three bedrooms and one bath."

"Under the circumstances, convenience is a luxury we can't afford," Sheila said.

"This morning on the *Today* show a bunch of health officials told everyone that the flu that was going around was nothing to worry about," Cassy said.

"They were probably from the CDC," Sheila said. "Those bastards."

"What bugs me is that the media hasn't said one word about all the black discs," Pitt said. "Why hasn't the presence of the discs been questioned, especially after so many of them appeared?"

"They're a harmless-appearing curiosity," Jesse said. "People have certainly been talking about them, but it was never considered newsworthy. Unfortunately there's no reason to make a connection between the discs and the flu until it is too late."

"We're going to have to figure out a way to start warning people," Cassy said. "We can't wait any longer."

"Cassy's right," Pitt said. "It's time for us to go public any way we can: TV, radio, newspapers, everything. The public has to know."

"Screw the public," Sheila said. "It's the medical-scientific community we've got to get involved. Pretty soon there won't be anybody left with the skills necessary to figure out a way to stop this thing."

"I think the kids are right," Jesse said. "We tried the CDC and bombed. We got to find some media people who are not infected and just blast this thing around the world. Problem is, I don't know any media people except for a few slimy crime reporters."

"No, Sheila's right . . ." Nancy began.

Jonathan tuned out. He was crushed about his father's fate. As a teenager the concept of death was totally unreal. To a large degree he couldn't accept what he'd been told.

Jonathan's attention drifted from the bickering inside the car to the appearance of the city. There were plenty of people out and about. It seemed from the beginning the streets were always full of people wandering no matter what time of day or night. And everybody was sporting a stupid fake smile.

Jonathan noticed something else as they passed through the downtown. The people were all busily interacting and helping each other. Whether it was a passerby aiding a workman unload his tools or a child helping an older person with a parcel, the people were working together. To Jonathan the city resembled a beehive.

Inside the car the argument reached a crescendo with Sheila raising her voice to drown out Pitt.

"Shut up!" Jonathan cried.

To Jonathan's surprise his outburst worked. Everyone looked at him, even Jesse, who was driving.

"This arguing is stupid," Jonathan said. "We have to work together." He tilted his head to the outside. "They certainly are."

Chastised by a teenager, everyone took his suggestion and looked out at the scene around them. They saw what he meant and were sobered.

"It's scary," Cassy said. "They're like automatons."

Jesse turned onto the street where Pitt's cousin's apartment was located. He started to brake when he saw two cars he was certain were unmarked police cars. From his perspective he was sure that they were staking the place out. It was as if they had signs on their car proclaiming it.

"Here's the apartment complex," Pitt said when he noticed Jesse was about to pass by.

"We're not stopping," Jesse said. He pointed to the right. "See those two stripped-down, late-model Fords. Those are plainclothes officers. I'm sure of it."

Cassy stared at the men.

"Don't look!" Jesse warned. "We don't want to attract their attention."

Jesse kept driving.

"We could go to my apartment," Sheila suggested. "But it's a one-bedroom, and it's high-rise."

"I got a better place," Jesse said. "In fact, it is perfect."

Traveling in a caravan of two of Randy Nite's personal Mercedeses, Beau and a group of close aides drove from the institute to the Donaldson Observatory built on top of Jackson Mountain. The view from the site was spectacular, especially on such a clear day.

The observatory itself was as impressive as the location. It was a huge hemispheric dome set directly on top of the rocky pinnacle of the mountain. It was painted a glistening white that was blinding in the bright sunlight. Its dome shutter was closed to protect the enormous reflective telescope housed within.

As soon as the first car came to a stop, Beau hopped out along with Alexander Dalton. Alexander had been a lawyer in his previous life. Veronica Paterson got out from the driver's side of the car. She was still dressed in her skin-tight spandex outfit. Beau had changed his clothes to a dark print, long-sleeved shirt. He had the collar turned up and the cuffs buttoned at his wrists.

"I hope this equipment is worth this effort," Beau said.

"My understanding is that it is the latest model," Alexander said. He was a tall, thin man with particularly long, spidery fingers. He was currently functioning as one of Beau's closest aides.

The second Mercedes pulled up and a team of technicians got out. They were all carrying their tools.

"Hello, Beau Stark," a voice called.

Everyone turned to see a white-haired man nearly eighty years old standing at an open door at the base of the observatory. His face was creased and creviced like a piece of dried fruit from the intensity of the high-altitude sun.

Beau walked over to the man and shook hands. Then he introduced Veronica and Alexander to Dr. Carlton Hoffman. Beau told his aides that they were meeting the reigning king of American astronomy.

"You're too kind," Carlton said. "Come on in and get started."

Beau waved for his whole team to enter the observatory. They trooped in without a word.

"Do you need anything?" Carlton asked.

"I think we brought the tools we need," Beau said.

The technicians immediately set to work dismantling the giant telescope.

"I'm particularly interested in the prime focus observing capsule," Beau called out to one of the men who had climbed up into the interchangeable end assembly.

Beau turned to Carlton. "Of course you know you're welcome at the institute any time you'd like to come," he said.

"That's kind of you," Carlton said. "I'll be there, especially once you are ready."

"It's not going to be too long," Beau said.

"Stop!" a voice yelled. The sound echoed around inside the domed observatory. The dismantling came to a grinding halt. "What's going on in here? Who are you people?"

All eyes turned to the air lock door. Standing in front of it was a small, mousy man. He coughed violently but continued to fiercely eye the workers who'd taken apart portions of the telescope.

"Fenton, we're over here," Carlton called out to the man. "Everything is okay. There's someone I want you to meet."

The newly arrived individual's name was Fenton Tyler. His position was Assistant Astronomer, and as such, he was the heir apparent of Carlton Hoffman. Fenton cast a quick glance in Carlton's direction, but then quickly looked back at the workers lest they unscrew another single bolt.

"Please, Fenton," Carlton said. "Come over here."

Reluctantly Fenton moved sideways, continuing to keep his beloved telescope in view. As he approached Beau and the others, it was apparent he was sick.

"He has the flu," Carlton whispered to Beau. "I didn't expect him to come over."

Beau nodded knowingly. "I understand," he said.

Fenton reached his boss's side. He was pale and feverish. He sneezed violently. Carlton introduced him to Beau and explained that Beau was borrowing portions of the telescope.

"Borrowing?" Fenton repeated. He was totally confused. "I don't understand."

Carlton put his hand on Fenton's shoulder. "Of course you don't understand," he said. "But you will. I promise you that you will and sooner than you imagine."

"Okay!" Beau called out while clapping his hands loudly. "Back to work, everyone. Let's get it done."

Despite Carlton's comments, Fenton was aghast at the destruction he was witnessing and voiced his confusion. Carlton drew him aside to try to explain it.

"I'm glad Dr. Hoffman was here," Alexander said.

Beau nodded. But he was no longer thinking about the interruption. He was thinking about Cassy.

"Tell me, Alexander," Beau said. "Have you been able to locate that woman I asked you about?"

"Cassy Winthrope," Alexander said. He knew instantly to whom Beau was referring. "She's not been located. Obviously she's not one of us yet."

"Hmm," Beau said pensively. "I never should have let her out of my sight when she made her surprise visit. I don't know what came over me. I supposed it was some vestigial romantic human trait. It's embarrassing. At any rate, find her."

"We'll find her," Alexander said. "No doubt."

The last mile was rough going, but Jesse's van managed to navigate the ruts in the poorly maintained dirt road.

"The cabin is just around the next bend," Jesse said.

"Thank God!" Sheila complained.

Finally the van lurched to a stop. In front of them was a log cabin nestled into a stand of gigantic virgin pines. Sunlight slanted down through the needles in startlingly bright shafts of light.

"Where are we?" Sheila questioned. "Timbuktu?"

"Hardly," Jesse laughed. "It's got electricity, telephone, TV, running water, and a flush toilet."

"You make it sound like a Four Seasons Hotel," Sheila said.

"I think it's beautiful," Cassy said.

"Come on," Jesse said. "Let me show you the inside and the lake that's out back."

They climbed stiffly from the car, especially Sheila and Nancy. All grabbed the meager belongings they had with them. Jonathan carried his laptop.

The air was clean and crisp and smelled of pine needles. The fresh breeze made a slight sighing noise as it passed through the tall evergreen trees. The sound of birds was everywhere.

"How'd you happen to buy this cabin?" Pitt asked as they mounted the front porch. The posts and balustrade were tree trunks. The deck was rough-hewn planks of pine.

"We bought this place mostly for the fishing," Jesse explained. "Annie was the fisherman, not me. After she passed on I couldn't get myself to sell it. Not that I come here that often, especially over the last couple of years."

Jesse wrestled open the front door, and everybody went inside. It smelled mildly musty. The interior was dominated by a huge fieldstone fireplace that went all the way to the peak of the cathedral ceiling. There was a galleylike kitchen to the right, with a hand pump over a soapstone sink. To the left were two bedrooms. The door to the bathroom was to the right of the fireplace.

"I think it is charming," Nancy said.

"Well, it's certainly remote," Sheila said.

"I can't imagine we could have found a better place," Cassy said.

"Let's air it out," Jesse said.

For the next half hour they made the cabin as comfortable as possible. En route from the city they had stopped at a supermarket and loaded up with groceries. The men carried them in from the van and the women put them away.

Jesse insisted on making a fire even though it wasn't cold. "It'll take the dampness out of the place," he explained. "And come evening, you'll be glad it's going. It gets cold here at night, even this time of year."

Finally they all collapsed on the gingham couches and captain's chairs that were grouped around the fireplace. Pitt was using Jonathan's computer.

"We should be safe here," Jonathan said. He'd opened a pack of potato chips and was crunching away.

"For a while," Jesse said. "No one at the station knew about this place to the best of my knowledge. But we ain't here for a vacation. What are we going to do about what's going on out in the world?"

"How fast can this flu spread to everyone?" Cassy asked.

"How fast?" Sheila questioned. "I think we've had ample demonstration."

"With an incubation period of only a few hours," Pitt said, "combined with it being a short illness and the infected people wanting to infect others, it spreads like wildfire." He was typing away on the laptop as he spoke. "I could do some reasonably accurate modeling if I had some idea of how many of the black discs have landed on Earth. But even with a low-ball, rough estimate, things don't look so good."

Pitt turned around the computer screen for the others to see. It was a pie graph with a wedge in red. "This is only after a few days," he said.

"We're talking about millions and millions of people," Jesse said.

"Considering both how well the infected work together and their evangelistic attitude, it's going to be billions before too long," Pitt said.

"What about animals?" Jonathan asked.

Pitt sighed. "I never gave that much thought," he said. "But sure. Any organism that has the virus in its genome."

"Yeah," Cassy said pensively. "Beau must have infected that huge dog of his. I thought it acted weird right from the start."

"So these aliens take over other organisms' bodies," Jonathan said.

"Analogous to the way a normal virus takes over individual cells," Nancy said. "Remember, that's why Pitt called it a mega-virus."

Everybody was glad to hear Nancy's voice. She'd been silent for hours.

"Viruses are parasites," Nancy continued. "They need a host organism. Alone, they are incapable of doing anything."

"Damn right they need hosts," Sheila said. "Especially this alien breed. There's no way a microscopic virus built those spacecraft."

"True!" Cassy said. "This alien virus must have infected some other species somewhere in the universe which had the knowledge, size, and capability of building those discs for them."

"I wouldn't be too sure," Nancy said. "They possibly could have done it themselves. Remember, I suggested that the aliens might be able to package themselves or part of their knowledge into viral form to withstand intergalactic space travel. In that case their normal form could be quite different than viral.

"Eugene, before he disappeared, was hypothesizing that perhaps the alien consciousness could be achieved by a finite number of infected humans working in consonance."

"You all are getting way ahead of me," Jesse commented.

"Anyhow," Jonathan said, "maybe these aliens control millions of life forms around the galaxy."

"And now they view humans as a comfortable home in which to live and grow," Cassy said. "But why now? What's so special now?"

"I'd guess it is just random," Pitt said. "Maybe they've been checking every few million years. They send a single probe to Earth to see what life form has evolved."

"Awakening the sleeping virus," Nancy said.

"The virus takes control of that single host," Sheila said. "And the host observes the lay of the land, so to speak, and reports back home."

"Well, if that's what happened," Jesse said, "the report must have been mighty good because we're knee-deep in those probes now."

Cassy nodded. "It makes sense," she said. "And Beau might have been that first host."

"Possibly," Sheila said. "But if this scenario is correct, then it could have been anyone anyplace."

"Thinking back to everything that has happened," Cassy said more to Pitt than the others, "Beau had to have been the first. And you know something? If it hadn't been for Beau we'd be like everyone else out there, completely unaware of what is going on."

"Or we'd already be one of them," Jesse said.

These sobering thoughts quieted everyone. For a few minutes the only sounds were the crackling of the fire and the chirping of the birds outside the open windows.

"Hey!" Jonathan said, breaking the silence. "What are we going to do about it, just sit here?"

"Hell, no!" Pitt said. "We'll do something. Let's get started fighting back."

"I agree," Cassy said. "It's our responsibility. After all, it's possible that we know more about this calamity right now than anyone else in the world."

"We need an antibody," Sheila said. "An antibody and maybe a vaccine for either the virus or the enabling protein. Or maybe one of the antiviral drugs. Nancy, what do you think?"

"No harm in trying," she said. "But we'll need equipment and luck."

"Of course we'll need equipment," Sheila said. "We can set up a lab right here. We'll need tissue cultures, incubators, microscopes, centrifuges. But it's all available. We just have to get it up here."

"Make a list," Jesse said. "I can probably get most of it."

"I'll have to get into my lab," Nancy said.

"Me too," Sheila said. "We need some of the blood samples from the flu victims. And we have to have the fluid sample from the disc."

"Let's do an abstract of that report we made for the CDC," Cassy said, "and disseminate it."

"Yeah," Pitt said, catching on to Cassy's line of thinking. "We'll put it out on the Internet!"

"Hey, great idea," Jonathan said.

"Let's start by sending it to all the top virology labs," Sheila said.

"Absolutely," Nancy said. "And the research-oriented pharmaceutical houses. All of those sources can't be infected yet. We're bound to get someone to listen to us."

"I can set up a network of 'ghosts,' " Jonathan said. "Or false Internet links. As long as I keep changing them, nobody will ever be able to trace us."

For a beat the group regarded each other. They were a bit giddy and at the same time overwhelmed with the enormity and difficulty of what they were about to undertake. Each had their own assessment of the chances of success, but no matter what the appraisal was, they were all in agreement they had to do something. At that point doing nothing would have been psychologically more difficult.

The sun had just set when Nancy, Sheila, and Jesse trooped out to the van and climbed in. Cassy, Jonathan, and Pitt stood on the porch, waved, and told them to be careful.

After Sheila and Nancy had taken a much-needed nap, it had been decided to make a foraging raid into the city for laboratory equipment. It had also been decided that the kids would remain behind to provide room in the van. At first the kids had objected, particularly Jonathan, but after much discussion they had agreed it was best.

As soon as the van had vanished from sight, Jonathan disappeared back inside. Cassy and Pitt took a brief walk. They skirted the cabin and descended through the pines to the lake. They came to a short dock, and they strolled out to its end. Standing there they silently marveled at the natural beauty of the surroundings. Night

758 / ROBIN COOK

was fast approaching, painting the distant hills with deep purples and dark silver blues.

"Standing here in the middle of this splendid nature makes the whole affair seem like a bad dream," Pitt said. "Like it can't be happening."

"I know what you mean," Cassy said. "At the same time, knowing it is happening and that all humans are at risk, I feel connected in a way I've never felt before. I mean, we're all related. I've never felt like all humans are a big family until now. And to think of what we have done to each other." Cassy visibly shivered at the thought.

Pitt reached out and enveloped her in his arms. It was a gesture to comfort her and keep her warm. As Jesse had promised the temperature had dropped the moment the sun had gone down.

"The threat of losing your identity also makes you look at your life," Cassy said. "It's hard for me to let go of Beau, but I have to. I'm afraid the Beau I knew is no longer around. It's as if he died."

"Maybe we'll develop an antibody," Pitt said. He looked down at Cassy and wanted so much to kiss her, but he didn't dare.

"Oh, yeah, sure," Cassy said scornfully. "And Santa Claus is going to visit us tomorrow."

"Come on, Cassy!" Pitt said, giving her a little shake. "Don't give up."

"Who said anything about giving up," Cassy said. "I'm just trying to deal with reality the best I can. I still love the old Beau, and probably always will. But I've been slowly realizing something else."

"What is that?" Pitt asked innocently.

"I'm realizing that I've always loved you too," Cassy said. "I don't mean to embarrass you, but back when you and I were dating off and on, I didn't think you really cared for me in a serious way, that you purposefully kept things casual. So I didn't question my own feelings. But over the last couple of days I've been getting a different impression of what your feelings might have been, and that maybe I was wrong back then."

A smile erupted from the depths of Pitt's soul and rose up to spread across his face like the rising sun. "I can assure you," he said. "If you thought I didn't care for you, you were absolutely, totally, incontrovertibly wrong."

Pitt and Cassy silently regarded each other in the gathering gloom. They were both experiencing an unexpected exhilaration despite the situation. It was a magical moment until it was shattered by a high-pitched shout.

"Hey, you guys, get your asses up here," Jonathan screamed. "Come and see this!"

Fearing the worst, Pitt and Cassy raced up to the cabin. Just within the few minutes they'd been at the lake, it had gotten considerably darker beneath the lofty pines, and they tripped over the roots. Rushing into the cabin they found Jonathan watching the TV with one leg casually draped over the arm of the sofa. He was eating potato chips mechanically.

"Listen," Jonathan mumbled, pointing to the TV.

". . . everyone agrees that the President is more vibrant and energetic than ever before. To quote a White House staffer, 'He's a changed man.' "

The announcer then had a fit of coughing. She apologized, then continued: "Meanwhile, this curious flu continues to sweep through the nation's capital. High-ranking cabinet officers, as well as most of the key members of both houses of Congress, have all been felled by this swiftly moving illness. Of course the entire country mourns the death of Senator Pierson Cranmore. As a known diabetic he had been an inspiration to others afflicted with chronic illness."

Jonathan clicked the mute button on the remote. "Sounds like they control most of the government," he said.

"I think we already conceded as much," Cassy said. "What about the abstract we did this afternoon? I thought you were going to get it ready to put it out on the Internet."

"I did," Jonathan said. He put his finger on the laptop which was sitting on the coffee table and pushed it around so Cassy could see the screen. The phone line was connected to its side. "All ready," he added.

"Well, then put it out there," Cassy said.

Jonathan hit the proper button, and the first description and warning of what was happening to the world zoomed out over the vast electronic superhighway. Word was now on the Internet.

CHAPTER 16

10:30 A.M.

Beau was sitting in front of a group of TV monitors that he'd had installed in the library. The heavy velvet drapes were drawn across the arched windows to make viewing easier. Veronica stood behind him and massaged his shoulders.

Beau's fingers lightly danced across the control panel and the monitors all came to life. He raised the sound on the top one on the left. It was NBC covering a news conference by the Presidential Press Secretary, Arnold Lerstein.

"There is no need to panic. That is the word from both the President and the Surgeon General, Dr. Alice Lyons. The flu has definitely reached epidemic proportions, but it is a brief illness with no negative side effects. In fact, most people report increased vigor after the illness. Only those people with chronic illness should . . ."

Beau switched the sound to the next monitor. The interviewee was obviously British. He was saying: ". . . over the British Isles. If you or someone you love begins to show symptoms, do not panic. Bed rest, tea, and attention to the fever is recommended."

Beau switched from one monitor to another in rapid succession. The message was similar whether in Russian, Chinese, or Spanish, or any of the other forty-some-odd languages represented.

"That's all reassuring," Beau commented. "The infestation is proceeding as planned."

Veronica nodded and continued her massage.

Beau switched to the monitor for the camcorder at the front gate of the institute. It was a wide-angle shot that included a gang of approximately fifty protesters attempting to heckle the augmented group of young guards. A number of the institute's dogs were in the background.

"My wife is in there," a protester yelled. "I demand to see her. You've no right to keep her."

The smiles on the gatekeepers remained fixed.

"My two sons," another protester screamed. "They're in there. I know it! I want to talk with them. I want to make sure they are okay."

At the same time this group was yelling and screaming, there was a steady stream of calm, smiling people entering through the gate. These were all infected people who'd been summoned for service at the institute, and they were wordlessly recognized by the gatekeepers.

The fact that some people were being allowed entrance without question further inflamed the protesters. They had been ignored since their arrival. Without warning they stormed the gate en masse.

A melee erupted with a lot of yelling and shoving. Even a few fists were thrown. But it was the dogs who quickly determined the outcome. They came charging in from the periphery and attacked. Their vicious snarling and tearing at the legs of the protesters quickly eroded the group's collectively inspired courage. The protesters fell back.

Beau switched off the monitors. He bent his head over onto his chest so Veronica could get at the muscles at the base of his neck. He'd only had one hour of sleep instead of the two he needed.

"You should be pleased," she said. "Everything is going so well."

"I am," Beau responded. Then he changed the subject: "Is Alexander Dalton in the ballroom? Did you see him when you went down there?"

"The answer is yes to both questions," Veronica said. "It's as you wish. He would never contravene your order."

"Then I should go to the ballroom," Beau said. He straightened his neck and stood. A short whistle brought King instantly to his feet. Together they descended the central stairs.

The level of activity in the vast room had increased. Many more workers were involved than the previous day. The support beams of the ceiling were now totally exposed, as were the studs of the walls. The huge chandeliers as well as the massive decorative cornices were all gone. The enormous arched windows were almost completely sealed over. In the center of the room a complicated electronic structure was rising. It was being constructed with all the pirated parts from the observatory, various electronic concerns, and the nearby university physics department.

Observing all the coordinated activity for such great purpose brought a particularly broad smile to Beau's lips. He couldn't help recalling that the room had once been used for something as frivolous as dancing.

Alexander saw Beau standing at the ballroom's entrance and joined him immediately. "Looks good, wouldn't you say?"

"It looks tremendous," Beau said.

"I've got some other good news," Alexander said. "We're effecting immediate closure of most of the highest polluting factories around the Great Lakes. This should be completed within the week."

"What about Eastern Europe?" Beau asked. "They are the ones that have been troubling me the most."

"Same situation," Alexander said. "Particularly Romania. They'll be closed this week."

"Excellent," Beau said.

Randy Nite saw Beau speaking with Alexander and hastened over.

"What do you think?" Randy said, while proudly eyeing the emerging central structure.

"It's coming along well," Beau said. "But I'd appreciate a little more speed."

"I'll need more help then," Randy said.

"Whatever you need," Beau said. "We must be ready for the Arrival."

Randy flashed a smile of appreciation before rushing back to his project.

Beau turned to Alexander. "What about Cassy Winthrope?" he asked. There was a sudden edge to his voice.

"She's not been accounted for as yet," Alexander said.

"How can that be?" Beau asked.

"It is a mystery," Alexander said. "The police and the university officials have been exemplarily cooperative. She'll turn up. Maybe even at the gate on her own accord. I wouldn't worry about it if I were you."

Beau lashed out with his right hand, seizing Alexander's forearm in a powerful grip that immediately cut off circulation to Alexander's hand.

Shocked by this overtly hostile gesture, Alexander looked down at the hand that was holding him. It wasn't a human hand. The fingers were long and wrapped around Alexander like minature boa constrictors.

"This request of mine to find this girl is not an idle whim," Beau said. He regarded Alexander with eyes that were almost all pupil. "I want the girl now."

Alexander raised his eyes to meet Beau's. He knew enough not to struggle.

"We shall make it a top priority," Alexander said.

Jesse had cut pine boughs in the nearby forest, and after parking the van alongside the shed, had covered it with the branches. From the outside the cabin looked completely deserted save for the wisps of smoke rising from the stone chimney.

In marked contrast to the placid exterior, the interior had been transformed into a crowded workstation. Taking up a lion's share of floor space was the makeshift biological laboratory.

Nancy was in charge in that arena with Sheila working closely with her. Everyone suspected that Nancy was redirecting her powerful grief over Eugene's death to the task of finding a way to stop the alien virus. She was a woman possessed.

Pitt was busy with a PC. He was attempting to do more accurate modeling with information that had become available on the TV. The media had finally picked up the story about the black discs, but not in regard to the flu epidemic. The stories were presented more as a way to stimulate the public's interest in going out and finding them.

Jesse recognized that his input was more in logistics, particularly the practical aspects such as food and keeping the fire going. Presently he was busy putting the finishing touches on one of his specialties: chili.

Cassy and Jonathan were sitting at the communal eating table with the laptop. To Jonathan's delight there'd been a distinct role reversal: now he was the teacher. Also to Jonathan's delight, Cassy had on one of her thin cotton dresses. Since it was apparent she had no bra, Jonathan found it excruciatingly difficult to concentrate.

"So what do I do?" Cassy asked.

"What?" Jonathan asked as if waking up from sleep.

"Am I boring you?" Cassy asked.

"No," Jonathan said hastily.

"I'm asking if I change these last three letters in the URL?" Cassy said. She was intent on the LCD screen and oblivious to the effect the physical aspects of her femininity were having on Jonathan. She'd just come in from a swim and her nipples were sticking out like marbles.

"Right . . . uh, yeah," Jonathan said. "Dot G O V. Then . . ."

"Then backslash, 6 0 6, capital R, small g, backslash," Cassy said. "Then I hit Enter."

Cassy looked up at Jonathan and noticed he was blushing.

"Is there something the matter?" Cassy asked.

"Nope," Jonathan said.

"Well, then should I do it?" Cassy asked.

Jonathan nodded, and Cassy hit Enter. Almost simultaneously the printer activated and began spewing out printed pages.

"Voilà," Jonathan said. "We're into our mailbox without anybody being able to trace us."

Cassy smiled and gave Jonathan a friendly poke. "You are one fine teacher."

Jonathan blushed anew and averted his eyes. He busied himself by getting the pages out of the printer. Cassy got up and moved over to Pitt.

"Soup's on in three minutes," Jesse called out. No one responded. "I know, I know," he added. "Everybody's too busy, but you gotta eat. It will be on the table for whoever is interested."

Cassy rested her hands on Pitt's shoulders and looked at his computer screen. He had another pie graph, and now the red was larger than the blue.

"Is this where you think we stand now?" Cassy asked.

Pitt reached up and grasped one of Cassy's hands and gave it a squeeze. "Afraid so," he said. "If the data I got from the TV is reasonable or even if it is low, the projections suggest that sixty-eight percent of the world's population is now infected."

Jonathan tapped Nancy on the back. "Sorry to bother you, Mom," he said. "Here's the latest off the Web."

"Anything from the group up in Winnipeg about the protein amino-acid sequence?" Sheila asked.

"Yeah," Jonathan said. He shuffled the pages and pulled out the one from Winnipeg. He handed it to Sheila who stopped what she was doing to read it.

"I've also connected with a new group in Trondhiem, Norway," Jonathan said. "They're working in a hidden lab beneath the gym in the local university."

"Did you send them our original data?" Nancy asked.

"Yup," Jonathan said. "Just like with the others."

"Hey, they've made some progress," Sheila said. "We now have the entire amino acid sequence of the protein. That means we can start making our own."

"Here's what the Norway people sent," Jonathan said. He started to hand the sheet to Nancy, but Sheila reached over and took it instead. She read it rapidly, then crumpled it. "We've already determined all that," she said. "What a waste of time."

"They've been working in total isolation," Cassy said in their defense, having heard Sheila's remark.

"Anything from the group in France?" Pitt asked.

"A lot," Jonathan said. He separated the French pages from the rest and handed them to Pitt. "Seems that the infestation is still progressing slower there than anyplace else."

"Must be the red wine," Sheila said with a laugh.

"That might be an important point," Nancy said. "If it continues and is not just a random blip on the bell curve and if we can figure out why, it might be useful."

"Here's the bad news," Jonathan said, holding up a sheet of paper. "People with diabetes, hemophilia, cancer, you name it, are dying in record numbers all over the world."

"It's as if the virus is consciously cleaning the gene pool," Sheila said.

Jesse carried the pot of chili to the table and told Pitt to move the PC. As he waited to put the food down he asked Jonathan how many research centers he was in touch with around the world the previous day.

"A hundred and six," Jonathan said.

"And how many today?" Jesse asked.

"Ninety-three," Jonathan said.

"Wow!" Jesse said, putting down the chili. He headed back to the kitchen for dishes and flatware. "That's rapid attrition."

"Well, three of them might still have been okay," Jonathan said. "But they were asking too many questions about who we are and where we are so I cut them off."

"As the saying goes, 'Better to be safe than sorry,' " Pitt said.

"It's still rapid attrition," Jesse said.

"What about the man calling himself Dr. M?" Sheila asked. "Anything from him?"

"A bunch of stuff," Jonathan said.

"Who's Dr. M?" Jesse asked.

"He was the first to respond to our letter on the Internet," Cassy explained. "He responded in the first hour. We think he is in Arizona, but we have no idea where."

"He's given us a lot of important data," Nancy said.

"Enough so he's made me a tad suspicious," Pitt said.

"Come on, everyone," Jesse said. "This chili is going to get cold."

"I'm suspicious of everyone," Sheila said. She walked over to the table and took her usual seat at the end. "But if someone is coming up with useful info, I'll take it."

"As long as contacting him doesn't jeopardize our location," Pitt said.

"Obviously that's a given," Sheila said condescendingly. She took the pages from Dr. M that Jonathan held out for her. Holding them in front of herself, she started reading while shoveling chili into her mouth with her free hand. She acted like a high-school student cramming for exams.

Everyone else sat down at the table in a more civilized manner and spread napkins on their laps.

"Jesse, you've outdone yourself," Cassy said after her first mouthful.

"Compliments are freely accepted," Jesse said.

They ate for a few minutes in silence until Nancy cleared her throat. "I hate to bring this up," she said. "But we're running out of basic lab supplies. We aren't going to be able to continue working much longer unless we make another run into the city. I know it is dangerous, but I'm afraid we have little choice."

"No problem," Jesse said. "Just make out a list. I'll manage it somehow. It's important that you and Sheila keep working. Besides, we need more food."

"I'll go too," Cassy said.

"Not without me you won't," Pitt said.

"And me too," Jonathan said.

"You are staying here," Nancy said to Jonathan.

"Come on, Mom!" Jonathan said. "I can't be coddled. I'm as much a part of this as anybody else."

"If you are going, I'm going too," Nancy said. "Besides, either I or Sheila should go. We're the only ones who know what we need."

"Oh my God!" Sheila said suddenly.

"What's the matter?" Cassy demanded.

"This Doc M guy," Sheila said. "Yesterday he asked us what we had on the sedimentation rate for that section of DNA which we knew contained the virus."

"We sent him our estimate, didn't we?" Nancy asked.

"I sent exactly what you gave me," Jonathan said. "Even the part about our centrifuge not being able to reach such an RPM."

"Well, apparently he has access to one that can," Sheila said.

"Let me see," Nancy said to Sheila. She took the page and read it. "My gosh, we're closer to isolating the virus than we thought."

"Exactly," Sheila said. "Isolating the virus is not an antibody or a vaccine, but it is an important step. Maybe the single largest step."

"What time is it?" Jesse asked.

"Ten-thirty," Pitt said, holding his watch up to his face to see the dial. It was dark beneath the trees on the bluff overlooking the university campus. Jesse, Pitt, Cassy, Nancy, and Jonathan were sitting in the van. They had arrived a half hour earlier, but Jesse had insisted they wait. He didn't want anyone going into the medical center until the eleven o'clock shift change. He was counting on the general confusion at that time to facilitate getting what they needed and getting it out of there.

"We'll start at ten forty-five," Jesse said.

From their vantage point they could see that a number of the university asphalt parking lots had been dug up. Lights were strung across some of the open areas created and infected people were busy planting vegetables.

"They certainly are well organized," Jesse said. "Look at the way they work together without any conversation."

"But where are the cars going to park?" Pitt asked. "That's taking environmentalism to an extreme."

"Maybe they intend not to have cars," Cassy said. "After all, cars are major polluters."

"They do seem to be cleaning up the city," Nancy said. "You have to give them credit for that."

"They're probably cleaning up the whole planet," Cassy said. "In a curious way it's making us look bad. I guess it takes an outsider to appreciate what we've always taken for granted."

"Stop it," Jesse said. "You're starting to sound as if you are on their side."

"It's almost time," Pitt said. "Now here's what I think. Jonathan and I should go into the medical lab in the hospital. I know my way around in there, and Jonathan knows computers. Between the two of us, we'll be able to decide what we need and carry it."

"I think I should stay with Jonathan," Nancy said.

"Mom!" Jonathan moaned. "You have to go to a pharmacy, and you don't need me there. Pitt needs me."

"It's true," Pitt said.

"Cassy and I will go with Nancy," Jesse said. "We'll use the pharmacy in the supermarket, so while she's getting the drugs she needs, we'll load up on groceries."

"All right," Pitt said. "We'll meet back here in thirty minutes."

"Better say forty-five," Jesse said. "We got a little farther to walk."

"Okay," Pitt said. "It's time. Let's go!"

They climbed out of the van. Nancy gave Jonathan a quick hug. Pitt grabbed Cassy's arm.

"Be careful," Pitt said.

"You too," Cassy said.

"Remember, everybody," Jonathan said. "Put a big shit-eating grin on your face and hold it. It's what all of them do."

"Jonathan!" Nancy admonished.

They were about to move off when Cassy grabbed Pitt's arm. When he turned, she gave him a kiss on the lips. Then Cassy ran after Nancy and Jesse while Pitt caught up with Jonathan. They all moved off into the night.

The picture was one of Cassy taken six months previously. It had been shot in an alpinelike meadow with wildflowers forming a natural bed. Cassy was lying down with her thick hair splayed out around her head like a dark halo. She was impishly smiling at the camera.

Beau's wrinkled, rubberlike hand reached out. The long snakelike fingers wrapped around the framed photo and lifted it and drew it closer to his eyes. Their inherent glow served to illuminate the picture so Beau could more clearly make out Cassy's features. He was sitting in the upstairs library with the lights off. Even the bank of monitors was off. The only light was an anemic moonbeam that slanted through the windows.

Beau became aware that someone had entered the room behind him.

"Can I turn on the light?" Alexander asked.

"If you must," Beau said.

Illumination filled the room. Beau's eyes narrowed.

"Is there something wrong, Beau?" Alexander asked before he saw the photo in Beau's hands.

Beau didn't answer.

"If you don't mind me saying," Alexander said, "you shouldn't be obsessing on an individual like this. It is not our way. It is against the collective good."

"I've tried to resist," Beau admitted. "But I can't help it."

Beau slammed the framed photo face down on the table. The glass shattered.

"As my DNA replicates it is supposed to supplant the human DNA, yet the wiring in my brain continues to evoke these human emotions."

"I've felt something of what you speak," Alexander admitted. "But my former mate had a genetic flaw, and she did not pass the awakening stage. I suppose that made it easier."

"This emotionalism is a frightful weakness," Beau admitted. "Our kind has never come up against a species with such interpersonal bonds. There is no precedent to guide me."

Beau's snakelike fingers inserted themselves beneath the broken picture frame. A shard of glass cut him and his finger emitted a green foam.

"You've injured yourself," Alexander said.

"It's nothing," Beau protested. He lifted the broken frame and gazed at the image. "I must know where she is. We have to infect her. Once it's done, then I will be satisfied."

"The word is out," Alexander insisted. "As soon as she is spotted we will be informed."

"She must be in hiding," Beau lamented. "It's driving me mad. I can't concentrate."

"About the Gateway . . ." Alexander began but Beau cut him off.

"I need you to find Cassy Winthrope," Beau said. "Don't talk to me about the Gateway!"

"My god! look at this place!" Jesse said.

They were standing in the parking lot in front of Jefferson's Supermarket. There were a few abandoned cars with their doors ajar as if the occupants had suddenly run for their lives.

Several of the huge plate-glass windows fronting the store were broken and the shattered glass was scattered about the sidewalk. The interior was illuminated only with night lights, but it was adequate to see that the store had been partially looted.

"What happened?" Cassy questioned. It looked like a scene from a third-world country locked in a civil war.

"I can't imagine," Nancy commented.

"Perhaps the few uninfected people panicked," Jesse said. "Maybe law enforcement as we knew it no longer exists."

"What should we do?" Cassy asked.

"What we came here for," Jesse said. "Hell, this makes it easier. I thought I was going to have to break into the place."

The group moved forward tentatively and looked into the store through one of the broken floor-to-ceiling windows. It was eerily quiet.

"It's a mess, but it doesn't look like much of the merchandise has been taken," Nancy said. "It appears that whoever did this was mostly interested in the cash registers."

From where they were standing they could see that the cash drawers on all the registers were open.

"Stupid people!" Jesse commented. "If civil authority breaks down, paper money is going to be worth only what it's printed on."

Jesse took one last look around the empty parking lot. He didn't see a soul. "I wonder why there is no one around here?" he asked. "They all seem to be walking around the rest of the city. But let's not look a gift horse in the mouth. Let's do it."

They stepped through the broken window and headed up the central aisle toward the pharmacy, which was located in the back. The walking was difficult in the half light since the floor was covered with scattered cans, bottles, and boxes of food stuff that had been knocked from the shelves.

The pharmacy section was divided from the rest of the store by a wire mesh grate that rolled out of the ceiling and locked to the floor. Whoever had ransacked the grocery section had also been into the pharmacy. A rough hole was cut in the grate with a pair of chain cutters that were still on the floor.

Jesse held the jagged edges of the hole apart so Nancy could squeeze through. She quickly reconnoitered behind the pharmacy desk.

"What's it look like?" Jesse asked from outside the grate.

"The narcotics are gone," Nancy said, "but that's no problem. The antiviral drugs are here and so are the antibiotics. Give me about ten minutes and I'll have what I need."

Jesse turned to Cassy. "Let's you and I get those provisions," he said.

Cassy and Jesse went back to the front of the store and got bags. Then they started down the appropriate aisles. Cassy selected the items while Jesse played porter.

They were in the middle of the pasta section when Jesse slipped on fluid spilled from a broken bottle. The fluid had made the vinyl floor as slippery as ice.

Cassy managed to grab his arm to help keep him upright. Even after he regained his balance, his feet continued to slide around, forcing him to walk with his legs wide apart. It was like a comedy routine.

Cassy bent over and looked at the bottle. "No wonder," she said. "It's olive oil. So be careful!"

"Careful is my middle name," Jesse said. "How do you think I lasted thirty years as a cop?" He smiled and shook his head. "Funny, I'd been hoping for one big last hurrah before retiring. But I got to tell you, this episode is a lot more than I bargained for."

"It's a lot more than any of us bargained for," Cassy added.

They rounded the corner and entered the aisle with all the cereals. Cassy had to push through an enormous pile of boxes which included some large cardboard containers. All all at once she sucked in her breath as if shocked. Jesse was at her side in an instant.

"What's the matter?" he demanded.

Cassy pointed. In the middle of what had been a crude hut constructed from the boxes was the cherubic face of a young boy. He was no more than five years old. His skin was smudged and his clothing disheveled.

"Good Lord!" Jesse blurted out. "What's he doing in here?"

Cassy instinctively bent down to pick the child up. Jesse grabbed her arm.

"Hold on," Jesse said. "We don't know anything about him."

Cassy made a motion to free her arm, but Jesse held firm.

"He's only a child," Cassy said. "He's terrified."

"But we don't know . . ." Jesse began.

"We can't just leave him here," Cassy said.

Reluctantly Jesse let go of Cassy's arm. Cassy bent over and extracted the child from his house of cereal boxes. The boy instinctively clung to Cassy, burying his face in the crook of her neck.

"What's your name?" Cassy asked the child while gently patting his back. She was surprised by the strength with which he held her.

Cassy and Jesse exchanged glances. They were both thinking the same thing: How was this unexpected event going to impact their already desperate situation?

"Come on, now," Cassy said to the child. "Everything is going to be okay. You're safe, but we need to know your name so we can talk to you."

Slowly the child leaned back.

Cassy smiled warmly at the boy and was about to reassure him again when she noticed the child was smiling as if ecstatic. And even more shocking were his eyes. His pupils were enormous, and they glowed as if illuminated from within.

Feeling an instinctive wave of revulsion Cassy bent over to put the child down. She tried to maintain hold of his arm, but he was unexpectedly strong and twisted from her grip and scurried away toward the front of the store.

"Hey!" Jesse called out. "Come back here!" Jesse started after the boy.

"He's infected," Cassy yelled.

"I know," Jesse said. "That's why I don't want him to get away."

Running down the aisle in the half light was not easy for Jesse. The soles of his shoes still had traces of olive oil, making traction difficult. On top of that were all the cans, bottles, and boxes of scattered merchandise.

The boy seemed to have no problem navigating the obstacles and reached the front of the store well before Jesse. Positioning himself before one of the broken windows, he raised his chubby hand and opened his fingers. A black disc immediately levitated off his palm and disappeared out into the night.

Jesse reached the boy out of breath from all the slipping and sliding he'd been doing. He was also limping slightly from a bruise on his hip. He'd taken a fall near one of the cash registers and had collided with a can of tomato soup.

"Okay, son," Jesse said, trying to catch his breath as he turned the boy around. "What's the story. Why are you in here?"

Sporting the same exaggerated smile the child gazed up into Jesse's face. He didn't say a word.

"Come on, boy," Jesse said. "I'm not asking much."

Cassy came up behind Jesse and looked over his shoulder.

"What did he do?" she asked.

"Nothing as far as I can tell," Jesse said. "He just ran up here and stopped. But I wish he'd wipe that smile off his face. I feel like he's mocking us."

Both Cassy and Jesse saw the headlights at the same moment. A vehicle had turned into the supermarket's parking lot and was coming toward them.

"Oh no!" Jesse said. "Just what we didn't want: company."

It was immediately apparent that the vehicle was coming at a high rate of speed. Both Cassy and Jesse instinctively took several steps backward. A screech of tires against the asphalt heralded the car's sudden halt directly in front of the store. The high beams flooded the interior with blinding light. Both Cassy and Jesse held up their hands to shield their eyes. The child ran toward the light and disappeared in its glare.

"Get Nancy and get out the back of the store!" Jesse forcibly whispered.

"What about you?" Cassy asked.

"I'll keep them company," Jesse said. "If I'm not back at the rendezvous location in fifteen minutes, leave without me. I'll find another vehicle to get back."

"Are you sure?" Cassy questioned. She did not like the idea of leaving without Jesse.

"Of course I'm sure," Jesse snapped. "Now get!"

Cassy's eyes had adjusted enough so that she could just make out indistinct figures climbing down from either side of the vehicle. The headlights' intensity still precluded seeing any details.

Cassy turned and fled back into the depths of the store. Halfway up the aisle, she turned momentarily to see Jesse stepping out through the broken window, heading directly into the blinding light.

Cassy ran as best she could and purposefully collided with the grate separating the pharmacy section from the market. Gripping it with her hands she noisily shook it and called out for Nancy. Nancy's head popped up from behind the pharmacy desk. Nancy immediately saw the light coming from the front of the store.

"What's going on?" she demanded.

Cassy was breathless. "Trouble," she said. "We got to get out of here."

"Okay," Nancy said. "I've got everything anyway." She came from behind the counter and tried to push through the hole in the mesh. The cut ends of the wires had other ideas, and she was snagged.

"Here, take this," Nancy said, handing her sack of drugs to Cassy. Using both hands she tried to extract herself. She found it was not easy.

The light coming from the front of the store was suddenly dramatically augmented. At the same time a whooshing sound commenced and rapidly increased. When it reached earsplitting levels it cut off with such suddenness that its concussive effect knocked some teetering merchandise off shelving.

"Oh no!" Nancy moaned.

"What?" Cassy demanded.

"That was the sound when Eugene was consumed," Nancy said. "Where's Jesse?"

"Come on!" Cassy yelled. "We have to get out of here."

She put down the parcel Nancy had given her and tried to pull back the edges of the wire mesh. Flashlight beams began sweeping around the inside of the store.

"Go!" Nancy cried. "Take the package and run!"

"Not without you," Cassy said, struggling with the stiff wire.

"All right," Nancy said. "You hold this side, and I'll push the other." Working together they were at last able to free Nancy.

Nancy grabbed the bag of drugs and together they began to run along the back of the store. They didn't have a specific destination. They were merely counting on the store having a back entrance. Instead all they found was an interminable frozen food bin.

Reaching the far corner, they turned into the first aisle and headed forward. They thought that by running along the periphery of the building they'd eventually find a door. But they didn't get far. Ahead a shadowy group of people rounded the corner. Most were carrying flashlights.

A simultaneous whimper of fear escaped from both Cassy's and Nancy's lips. What made the group particularly frightening was their eyes. They glowed in the dim light of the store like distant galaxies in a night sky.

Cassy and Nancy simultaneously reversed directions only to be confronted by a second group coming from behind. Huddling together they waited as the two groups closed in on them. When the people were close enough for the women to see their features, it was obvious they were equally divided between male and female, elderly and young. What they had in common was their glowing eyes and their plastic smiles.

For a few moments nothing happened except the infected people completely surrounded the women and pressed in on them. Cassy and Nancy were back to back with their hands clasped over their mouths. Nancy had dropped her bag of drugs.

Terrified at being touched, Cassy screamed when one of the infected people suddenly lunged for her and grabbed her wrist.

"Cassy Winthrope, I presume," the man said with a short laugh. "This is indeed a pleasure. You have been missed."

Pitt drummed his fingers on the steering wheel of Jesse's van. Jonathan fidgeted in the passenger seat. Both were anxious.

"How long as it been now?" Jonathan asked.

"They are twenty-five minutes late," Pitt said.

"What are we going to do?"

"I don't know," Pitt said. "If anybody was going to have trouble I thought it would have been us."

"As long as we kept smiling, nobody seemed to care what the hell we did," Jonathan said.

"Stay here!" Pitt said suddenly. "I got to check on that supermarket. If I'm not back here in fifteen minutes, drive back to the cabin."

"But how will you get back?" Jonathan whined.

"There's plenty of deserted vehicles around," Pitt said. "That won't be the problem."

"But . . ."

772 / ROBIN COOK

"Just do it," Pitt snapped. He climbed out of the van and quickly descended the bluff. He emerged from the trees on a deserted street and set out toward the supermarket. He estimated he had about six blocks before he'd have to turn for the final block.

Ahead an individual came out of a building and turned in Pitt's direction. Pitt could see his eyes glowing. Suppressing an urge to flee Pitt coaxed his face into a broad smile just as he and Jonathan had done in the medical center. Having already smiled so much his facial muscles were sore.

Pitt found it was nerve-racking to walk directly at the changed person. He had to concentrate not only on the smile but also in keeping his eyes directly ahead. He and Jonathan had learned the hard way that any eye contact was viewed suspiciously.

The man passed without incident, and Pitt breathed a sigh of relief. What a way to live, he mused sadly. How long could they survive this cat and mouse game?

Pitt rounded the corner and approached the supermarket. The first thing he saw was a group of cars parked directly in front of the store. What worried him was the fact that their lights were on. As he got closer he could hear their engines were running as well.

Reaching the edge of the parking lot, Pitt saw a tight group of people emerge from the store and begin to climb into the cars. Soon the sound of slamming car doors reached him.

Pitt dashed ahead and ducked into the shadowy doorway of a building at the edge of the entrance to the supermarket's parking lot. Almost immediately the cars began moving and turned in his direction. As they gathered speed they formed into a single line. Pitt pressed himself back into his hiding place as the lights of the leading car swept across the front of him.

Moments later the first of the six cars passed within twenty feet of Pitt. It hesitated momentarily before turning out into the street, giving Pitt a fleeting look at the smiling faces of infected occupants.

Each car in turn passed. As the last car hesitated, Pitt caught his breath. A shiver of abject horror passed down his spine. Seated in the backseat was Cassy!

Unable to restrain himself and without considering the consequences, Pitt took a step forward as if he'd planned on racing to the car and yanking open the door. The low-level ambient light washed over him, and at that moment Cassy glanced in his direction.

For the briefest fraction of a second their eyes met. Pitt urged himself forward, but Cassy shook her head and the moment passed. The car lurched forward and quickly accelerated off into the night.

Pitt staggered back against the darkened door. He was furious with himself for not having done anything. Yet deep down he knew it would have been hopeless. All he could see when he closed his eyes was the image of Cassy's face framed in the car window.

CHAPTER 17

The dazzling desert night sky that had been awash with stars was fast fading to shades of pinkish blue as the promise of another day brightened the eastern sky. Dawn was coming.

Beau had been on the terrace off the master bedroom enjoying the night air since he'd heard the good news. Now he was impatiently waiting for the last few minutes to pass. He knew the meeting was imminent since he'd seen the car come along the driveway and disappear from view in front of the mansion.

Beau heard footfalls through the bedroom and the sound of the latch on the French doors opening. But he didn't turn around. He kept his eyes rooted at the place on the horizon where the sun was about to appear for a new day, a new beginning.

"You have company," Alexander said. Then he withdrew and closed the doors behind him.

Beau watched the first golden rays of sun sparkle forth. He felt a curious stirring in his body that in one sense he understood but in another sense he found mysterious and threatening.

"Hello, Cassy," Beau said, breaking the silence. Slowly he turned around. He was dressed in a dark velvet robe.

Cassy lifted her hands to shield the rays of the sun which silhouetted Beau's face. She couldn't see his features.

"Is that you, Beau?" she asked.

"Of course it is I," Beau said. He moved forward.

Suddenly Cassy could see him clearly and she caught her breath. He'd mutated further. The small patch of skin behind his ear she'd inadvertently seen on her previous visit had spread to the front of his neck up to the line of his jaw. Some fingers of it had even spread up onto his cheeks in a serpiginous margin. His scalp was a patchwork quilt of thinning hair and alien skin. His mouth, although still smiling, was now pinched and thin-lipped, and his teeth had receded and yellowed. His eyes were black holes with no irises, and they blinked continuously, with the lower lid rising up rather than vice versa.

Cassy shrank back in utter horror.

"Don't be afraid," Beau said. He moved up to her and placed his arms around her.

Cassy stiffened. Beau's fingers felt like snakes as they wrapped around portions of her body. And there was an indescribable feral odor.

"Please, Cassy, don't be afraid," Beau said. "It's only me, Beau."

Cassy didn't respond. She had to struggle against an almost irresistible urge to scream.

Beau leaned back, forcing her to again look into his transmogrified face.

"I've missed you so much," Beau said.

With a sudden, unexpected burst of energy, Cassy screamed and pushed herself free. The move caught Beau completely by surprise. "How could you say you missed me?" Cassy cried. "You're not Beau any longer."

"But I am," Beau said soothingly. "I will always be Beau. But I'm also something more. I am a mixture of my former human self and a species almost as ancient as the galaxy itself."

Cassy warily eyed Beau. One part of her told her to flee, another part was paralyzed by the horror of it all.

"You will be part of the new life as well," Beau said. "Everyone will be a part, at least those who are not harboring some terrible genetic flaw. I just had the honor of being the first, but it was a random event. It could have been you or anyone else."

"So, am I talking with Beau now?" Cassy asked. "Or am I talking with the virus's consciousness through the medium of Beau?"

"The answer, as I've already said, is both," Beau said patiently. "But the alien consciousness increases with every person changed. The alien consciousness is a composite of all the infected humans just like a human brain is a composite of its individual cells."

Beau reached out tentatively to avoid frightening Cassy any more than she already was. Compressing his snakelike fingers into a fist of sorts he stroked her cheek.

Cassy had to steel herself against the revulsion she felt to allow this creature to caress her.

"I must make a confession," Beau said. "At first I tried not to think about you. Initially it was easy because of the work that had to be done. But you kept creeping back into my thoughts and made me comprehend the beguiling power of human emotion. It is a weakness unique in the galaxy.

"The human in me loves you, Cassy, and I'm excited about the prospect of being able to give you many worlds. I long for you to want to be one of us."

"They are not coming," Sheila said. "As painful as that reality is, I'm afraid we're going to have to accept it." She stood up and stretched. It had been a sleepless night.

Through the cabin's windows the early morning sun could be seen bathing the tops of the trees on the western shore of the lake. The surface of the lake was covered with a mist that the rising sun would quickly dissipate.

"And if that's reality," Sheila added, "then we have to get our asses out of here before we have uninvited visitors."

Neither Pitt nor Jonathan responded. They were sitting on opposing couches, slouched forward with their chins craddled in their hands and elbows resting on their knees. Their expressions were a mixture of exhaustion, disbelief, and grief.

"Well, we don't have time to take everything," Sheila was saying. "But I think we should take all the data and the tissue cultures that we hope are producing some virions."

"What about my mom?" Jonathan said. "And Cassy and Jesse? What if they come back here looking for us?"

"We've been over this," Sheila said. "Let's not make it more difficult than it already is."

"I don't think we should leave either," Pitt said. Although he'd given up hope about Cassy, he still thought Nancy and Jesse might appear.

"Listen, you two," Sheila said. "Two hours ago you agreed we'd wait until dawn. Now it's dawn. The longer we wait the more chance there is that we will be caught."

"But where will we go?" Pitt asked.

"I'm afraid we'll have to play it by ear," Sheila said. "Come on, let's start getting things ready."

Pitt pushed himself off the couch and stood up. He looked at Sheila, and his expression mirrored his great pain. She softened, stepped over to the couch, and gave him a hug.

Jonathan got up with sudden resolve and went over to his laptop. Flipping it open he began rapidly typing. After sending his message, he stared blankly at the screen. Within minutes an answer came back.

"Hey," he called out to Sheila and Pitt. "I just contacted Dr. M. He's changed his mind. He's willing to meet us. What do you say?"

"I'm naturally skeptical," Sheila admitted. "The idea of putting our lives into the hands of somebody we only know as Doc M sounds absurd. But then again, he's been sending us intriguing data."

"It's not as if we have a lot of choices," Jonathan said.

"Let me see his latest message," Pitt said. He moved over to Jonathan and read over his shoulder. Finishing, he glanced up at Sheila. "I think we should take the chance. I can't imagine he's not legitimate. Hell, Dr. M has been as scared about us as we've been about him."

"It's better than just going out on the road and wandering around," Jonathan said. "Besides, he's obviously connected to the Internet. That means we can leave a message here, so if my mom or the others come back they'll at least be able to contact us."

"All right, you two," Sheila said, relenting. "I suppose it is a compromise. We'll meet this Dr. M, but it means getting the hell out of here, so let's get cracking."

"Cassy, I know it is hard for you," Beau said. "I don't look at myself in the mirror any more. But you have to get beyond that."

Cassy was leaning on the balustrade, looking out over the halcyon view of the institute's grounds. The sun had come up and the morning dew was just about gone. Out in the driveway there was a steady single-file stream of infected people who were arriving from around the globe.

"We are building an amazing environment here," Beau said. "And it is about to spread around the world. It's truly a new beginning."

"I was partial to our old world," Cassy said.

"You can't mean that," Beau said. "Not with all the problems there were. Humans had steered the Earth into a collison course with self-destruction, especially over the last half century. And that shouldn't be, because the Earth is an amazing place. There are innumerable planets in the galaxy but few as warm and wet and as inviting as this one."

Cassy closed her eyes. She was exhausted and needed sleep, yet some of the things Beau was saying did make a modicum of sense. She forced herself to try to think. "When did the virus first come to Earth?" she asked.

"The very first invasion?" Beau asked. "About three billion Earth years ago. It was back when conditions on Earth had reached a point where life was evolving at a fairly rapid clip. An explorer ship released the virions into the primordial seas, and they incorporated into the evolving DNA."

"And this is the first time that a probe ship has returned?" Cassy asked.

"Heavens no," Beau said. "Every hundred million Earth years or so, a probe would return to reawaken the virus and see what form of life had evolved."

"And the virus consciousness didn't remain?" Cassy asked.

"The virus itself remained," Beau said. "But you are right, the consciousness was allowed to lapse. The organisms were always so inconvenient."

"When was the last stopover?" Cassy asked.

"Just about a hundred million Earth years ago," Beau said. "It was a disastrous visit. The Earth had become completely infested with large, reptilian creatures who preyed on each other cannibalistically."

"You mean dinosaurs?" Cassy asked.

"Yes, I believe that is what you have labeled them," Beau said. "But whatever the name, it was a totally unacceptable situation for consciousness. So the infestation was terminated. However, genetic adjustments were made so that the reptilians would die out to allow other species to evolve."

"Like human beings," Cassy suggested.

"Exactly," Beau said. "These are wonderfully versatile bodies and reasonably sized brains. The downside is the emotions."

Cassy let out a short laugh in spite of herself. The concept of an alien culture capable of ranging around the galaxy having trouble with human emotion was preposterous.

"It's true," Beau said. "Primacy of the emotions translates to an exaggerated importance of the individual, which is contrary to the collective good. From my dual perspective it is amazing humans have accomplished as much as they have. In a species in which each individual is striving to maximize his circumstance above and beyond basic needs, war and strife are inevitable. Peace becomes the aberration."

"How many other species in the galaxy has the virus taken over?" Cassy asked.

"Thousands," Beau said. "Whenever we find a suitable envelope."

Cassy continued to stare out into the distance. She didn't want to look at Beau because his appearance was so disturbing that it made it difficult to think, and she wanted to think. She couldn't help but believe that the more she knew the better chance she had of avoiding infection and staying herself. And she was learning a lot. The longer she'd talked with Beau the less she was hearing the human side and the more she was hearing the alien side.

"Where do you come from?" Cassy asked suddenly.

"Where is our home planet?" Beau repeated as if he'd not heard her question. He hesitated, trying to draw upon the collective information available to him. But the answer wasn't forthcoming. "I guess I don't know. I don't even know what our original physical form was. Strange! The question has never come up."

"Does it ever occur to the virus that it is somehow wrong to take over an organism that already has a consciousness?" Cassy asked.

"Not when we are offering something far better," Beau said.

"How can you be so sure?" Cassy asked.

"Simple," Beau said. "I refer back to your history. Look at what you have done to each other and to this planet during your short reign as the dominant creature."

Cassy nodded. Again there was some sense in what she was hearing.

"Come with me, Cassy," Beau said. "There is something I want to show you." Beau went to the door leading to the bedroom and opened it.

Cassy made herself turn around. She steeled herself against Beau's appearance, which she found almost as shocking as when she'd first seen him. He was holding the door for her. He gestured and said, "It's downstairs."

They descended the main stairs. In contrast with the tranquility upstairs, the first floor was filled with busy, smiling people. No one paid any attention to Beau and Cassy. He took her to the ballroom where the level of the activity was almost frantic. It was difficult to comprehend how so many people could work together.

The floor, walls, and ceiling of the enormous room were covered with a maze of wiring. In the middle of the space was a huge structure that appeared to Cassy to be of an otherworldly design and purpose. At its core was a huge steel cylinder that looked vaguely reminiscent of a very large MRI machine. Steel girders angled off in various directions. This superstructure supported what looked to Cassy like equipment for the storage and transmission of high-voltage electricity. A command control center was off to the side, containing a bewildering number of monitors, dials, and switches.

At first Beau didn't speak. He just allowed Cassy to be overwhelmed by the scene.

"It is nearly finished," Beau said finally.

"What is it?" Cassy asked.

"It is what we call a Gateway," Beau said. "It is a formal connection to other worlds that we have infested."

"What do you mean, connection?" Cassy asked. "Is this some communication device?"

"No," Beau said. "Transportation, not communication."

Cassy swallowed. Her throat had gone dry. "You mean other species from other planets that you, I mean, the virus has infected. They will be able to come here. To Earth!"

"And we there," Beau said triumphantly. "The Earth will henceforth be linked to these other worlds. Its isolation is over. It will truly become part of the galaxy."

Cassy felt suddenly weak. The horror of the Earth being invaded by countless alien creatures was now added to the personal fear she had for herself. Combining this with the frantic swirl of nightmarish activity around her and her physical, emotional, and mental exhaustion, Cassy swooned. The room begin to spin and darken, and she fainted.

When she came to, Cassy had no idea how long she'd been unconscious. The first thing she was aware of was a slight nauseousness, but it quickly passed after a shiver. The next thing she sensed was that her right hand was balled into a fist and held firmly.

Cassy's eyes blinked open. She was on the floor in the busy ballroom looking up at a portion of the futuristic, jury-rigged contraption that was allegedly capable of transporting alien creatures to Earth.

"You're going to be okay," Beau said.

Cassy shuddered. It was the cliché that was always told to the patient no matter what the prospective prognosis. Cassy let her eyes fall toward Beau. He was kneeling next to her, clutching her fist closed. That was when Cassy realized there was something in her palm, something heavy and cold.

"No," Cassy cried. She tried to pull her hand free, but Beau would not let it go.

"Please, Beau," Cassy cried.

"Don't be afraid," Beau said soothingly. "You will be content."

"Beau, if you love me don't do this," Cassy said.

"Cassy, calm down," Beau said. "I do love you."

"If you have any control over your actions, let go of my hand," Cassy said. "I want to be myself."

"You will be," Beau said assuringly. "And much more. I do have control. I'm doing what I want. I want the power that has been given me, and I want you."

"Ahhh!" Cassy cried.

Beau immediately let go of her hand. Cassy sat up and with an exclamation of disgust threw the black disc away from herself. It skidded on a small patch of floor before thumping into a bundle of wires.

Cassy grabbed her injured hand with the other and looked at the slowly enlarging drop of blood at the base of her index finger. She'd been stung, and the crushing realization of what that meant caused her to collapse back onto the floor. A single tear rolled out from beneath each eyelid and ran off on either side of her face. She was now one of them.

CHAPTER 18

9:15 A.M.

The gas station looked like a movie set in the nineteen-thirties or the cover of an old *Saturday Evening Post* magazine. There were two old skinny gas pumps that resembled miniature skyscrapers with art deco round tops. In the middle of the tops an image of a red Pegasus still could be discerned despite the peeling paint.

The building behind the pumps was of the same vintage. It defied belief it was still standing. Over the last half century the sand blowing in off the desert had scoured the clapboards of any vestige of paint. The only thing that was reasonably intact was the old asphalt shingle roof. The screen door minus its screens blew back and forth in the hot breeze: a standing tribute to the longevity of its hardware.

Pitt pulled the van over to the side of the road opposite the dilapidated station so that they could look at it.

"What a Godforsaken place," Sheila commented, wiping the sweat out of her eyes. The desert sun was just beginning to give evidence of its noonday power.

They were on an essentially abandoned two-lane road that at one time had been a major route across the Arizona desert. But the interstate twenty miles to the south had changed that. Now cars rarely ventured along this rutted tarmac, as evidenced by the encroaching wisps of sand.

"This is where he said he'd meet us," Jonathan said. "And it is exactly as he described it, screen door and all."

"Well, where is he?" Pitt asked. He ran his eyes around the distant horizon. Except for a few lonely mesas in the distance, there was nothing but flat desert in every direction. The only movement visible was that of clumps of tumbleweed.

"Maybe we should just sit and wait," Jonathan suggested. He was finding it difficult to keep his eyes open from lack of sleep.

"There's no cover out here whatsoever," Pitt said. "It gives me the willies."

"Maybe we should look inside the broken-down station house," Sheila said.

Pitt restarted the van, pulled across the road, and parked between the ancient gas pumps and the dilapidated building. They all eyed the structure with unease. There was something about it that was spooky, particularly with the screen door opening and closing repeatedly. Now that they were close enough they could hear the aged hinges squeaking. The small paned windows, which were surprisingly intact, were too filthy to see through.

"Let's take a look inside," Sheila said.

Hesitantly they climbed out of the van and warily approached the porch. There were two old rocking chairs whose cane seats had long ago rotted out. Next to the door was the rusting hulk of an old-style, ice-cooled Coke dispenser. The sliding lid was open and the interior was filled with all manner of debris.

Pitt propped open the screen door and tried the interior door. It was unlocked. He pushed it open.

"You guys coming or what?" Pitt asked.

"After you," Sheila said.

Pitt stepped inside followed by Jonathan and then Sheila. They stopped just over the threshold and glanced around. With the dirty windows the light was meager. There was a metal desk to the right with a calendar behind it. The year was 1938. The floor was littered with dirt, sand, broken bottles, old newspaper, empty oil cans, and old car parts. Cobwebs hung like Spanish moss from portions of the ceiling joists. To the left was a doorway. The paneled door was partially ajar.

"Looks like nobody's been in here for a long time," Pitt said. "You think this supposed meeting was some kind of setup?"

"I don't think so," Jonathan said. "Maybe he's waiting for us in the desert, watching us to make sure we're okay."

"Where could he be watching us from?" Pitt asked. "It's as flat as a pancake outside." He walked over to the partially opened door and pushed it open all the way. Its hinges protested loudly. The second room was even darker than the first, with only one small window. The walls were lined with shelving, suggesting it had been a storeroom.

"Well, I'm not sure it makes a hell of a lot of difference if we find him or not," Sheila said dejectedly. She nudged some of the trash on the floor with her foot. "I was holding out hope that since he was giving us some interesting information, he had access to a lab or something. Needless to say we're not going to be able to do any work in a place like this. I think we'd better move on."

"Let's wait a little while," Jonathan said. "I'm sure this guy is legit."

"He told us he'd be here when we got here," Sheila reminded Jonathan. "He either lied to us or . . ."

"Or what?" Pitt asked.

"Or they got to him," Sheila said. "By now he could be one of them."

"That's a happy thought," Pitt said.

"We have to deal with reality," Sheila said.

"Wait a second," Pitt said. "Did you hear that?"

"What?" Sheila asked. "The screen door?"

"No, it was something else," Pitt said. "A scraping noise."

Jonathan reached up and felt the top of his head. "Something's fallen on me. Dust or something." He looked up. "Uh oh, there's someone up there."

Everyone looked up. Only now did they appreciate that there was no ceiling. Above the rafters it was darker than below in the room. But now that their eyes had adjusted to the low level of illumination they could just make out a figure in the attic space, standing on the joists.

Pitt reached down and snatched up a tire iron from the debris on the floor.

"Drop it," a raspy voice called down. With surprising speed the figure dropped out of the attic by swinging down on one hand. In his other hand he held an impressive Colt .45. He studied his visitors with a steady eye. He was a man in his early sixties with ruddy skin, curly gray hair, and a wiry frame.

"Drop the club," the man repeated.

Pitt abandoned the tire iron by tossing noisily onto the floor and held up his hands.

"I'm Jumpin Jack Flash," Jonathan said excitedly while repeatedly tapping his chest. "It was my name on the Internet. Are you Dr. M?"

"I might be," the man said.

"My real name is Jonathan. Jonathan Sellers."

"I'm Dr. Sheila Miller."

"And I'm Pitt Henderson."

"Were you checking us out?" Jonathan asked. "Is that why you were hiding up in the rafters?"

"Maybe," the man said. Then he motioned for his three guests to move into the storeroom.

Pitt was hesitant. "We're friends. Really we are. We're normal people."

"Get!" the man said while extending the pistol toward Pitt's face.

Pitt had never seen a .45 before, particularly not from the point of view of looking directly down the dark, threatening barrel.

"I'm going," Pitt said.

"All of you," the man said.

Reluctantly everyone crowded into the dark storeroom.

"Turn around and face me," the man said.

Fearful about what was going to happen, everyone did as he was told. With throats that had gone completely dry they eyed this sinewy man who'd literally dropped in on them. The man returned their stare. There was a moment of silence.

"I know what you are doing," Pitt said. "You're checking our eyes. You're looking to see if our eyes glow!"

The man nodded finally. "You're right," he said. "And I'm pleased to report, they don't shine at all. Good!" He holstered his .45. "My name's McCay. Dr. Harlan McCay. And I guess we'll be working together. I'm glad to see you people, really I am."

With great relief Pitt and Jonathan shadowed the man out into the sunlight where they shook hands enthusiastically. Sheila followed but seemed irritated over the initial reception. She complained that he'd terrified her.

"Sorry," Harlan said. "I didn't mean to scare you, but being careful is a product of the times. But that's all behind us now. Let's get you over to where you'll be working. I'm afraid we don't have a lot of time if we're going to have any effect whatsoever."

"You have a lab or someplace to work?" Sheila questioned. Her mood brightened.

"Yeah," Harlan said. "I got a little lab. But we need to drive a ways. It'll take about twenty minutes." He opened the van's slider and climbed in. Pitt got behind the wheel. Sheila took the front passenger seat, and Jonathan joined Harlan.

Pitt started the van. "Where to?" he asked.

"Straight on," Harlan said. "I'll let you know when to turn."

"Were you in private practice before all this trouble?" Sheila asked as the van pulled out into the road.

"Yes and no," Harlan said. "The first part of my professional life was spent at UCLA in an academic position. I was trained in internal medicine with a subspecialty in immunology. But about five years ago I realized I was burned out, so I came out here and started a general practice in a little town called Paswell. It's just a blip on the map. I worked a lot with Native Americans on the surrounding reservations."

"Immunology!" Sheila commented. She was impressed. "No wonder you were sending us such interesting stuff."

"I could say the same to you," Harlan said. "What's your training?"

"Unfortunately mostly emergency medicine," Sheila admitted. "I did do an internal medicine residency, though."

"Emergency medicine!" Harlan commented. "Then I'm even more impressed with the sophistication of your data. I thought I was communicating with a fellow immunologist."

"I'm afraid I can't take the credit," Sheila said. "Jonathan's mother was with us then, and she was a virologist. She did most of the work."

"Sounds like I shouldn't be asking where she is now," Harlan said.

"We don't know where she is," Jonathan said quickly. "She went to a pharmacy last night to get some drugs and didn't come back."

"I'm sorry," Harlan said.

"She'll contact me on the Internet," Jonathan said, not about to give up hope.

They drove for a few minutes in silence. No one wanted to contradict Jonathan.

"Are we heading for Paswell now?" Sheila asked. The idea of being in a town had a lot of appeal. She wanted a shower and a bed.

"Heavens no," Harlan said. "Everybody's infected there."

"How did you manage to avoid being infected yourself?" Pitt asked.

"Dumb luck at first," Harlan said. "I happened to be with a friend at the moment he got stung by one of those black discs, so I avoided them like the plague. Then when I got an inkling of what was happening and that there wasn't anything I could do, I took to the desert. I've been out here ever since."

"How does being out here in the desert account for the data you were requesting and sending?" Sheila asked.

"I told you," Harlan said. "I got a little lab."

Sheila looked out her side of the van. The featureless desert stretched off toward distant mountains. There weren't any buildings, much less a biological laboratory. She began to worry about how many marbles Harlan McCay was dealing with beneath his shock of gray hair.

"I do have a bit of encouraging news," Harlan said. "Once you were able to give me the amino acid sequence of the enabling protein, and I was able to make some, I've developed a rather crude monoclonal antibody."

Sheila's head spun around. She studied the leathery-faced, blue-eyed, stubbled desert man with disbelief. "Are you sure?" she asked.

"Sure I'm sure," Harlan said. "But don't get bent out of shape, because it's not as specific as I'd like. But it works. The main point is that I've proven the protein is antigenic enough to elicit an antibody response in a mouse. I just have to select out a better B lymphocyte to make my hybridoma cell."

Pitt hazarded a quick glance at Sheila. Despite having had a number of advanced biology courses, Pitt had no idea what Harlan was talking about or even whether he was making sense. Yet Sheila was obviously extraordinarily impressed.

"To make a monoclonal antibody you need sophisticated reagents and materials, like a source of myeloma cells," Sheila said.

"No doubt," Harlan said. "Take a right up here, Pitt, just beyond that cactus."

"But there's no road," Pitt said.

"A mere technicality," Harlan said. "Turn anyway."

Cassy awoke from a short nap, got up from the bed, and went to the large, multi-paned window. She was in a guest room on the second floor of the mansion facing south. To the left she could see a line of pedestrian traffic coming and going on the driveway. Directly ahead, her view of the grounds was limited by a tall, leafy tree. To the right she could see the tip of the terrace that surrounded the pool as well as about a hundred yards of lawn before it butted up against a pine forest.

She looked at her watch. She wondered when she would start feeling ill. She tried to remember the interval that Beau had experienced between being stung and his first symptoms, but she couldn't. All he'd told her was that he'd been in class. She didn't know which class.

Returning to the door, she gave the knob another twist. It was still locked as securely as when she'd been put in the room. Turning around, she leaned against the door and surveyed her surroundings. It was a generous bedroom with a high ceiling, but except for the bed, it was completely empty. And the bed itself consisted of a bare mattress on a box spring.

The short nap had revived Cassy to a point. She felt a mixture of depression and anger. She thought about lying back on the bed but didn't think she could sleep. Instead she returned to the window.

Noticing there was no lock, she tried the sash. To her surprise it opened with ease. Leaning out the window, she looked down. About twenty feet below was a flagstone walkway that connected the back terrace with the front. It was edged with a limestone balustrade. It would be a very hard landing if she tried to jump, but she gave the idea serious thought. Death might be preferable to becoming one of them. The problem was, a twenty-foot fall would probably only maim, not kill.

Cassy raised her eyes and looked more carefully at the tree. One stout branch in particular caught her attention. It grew out of the main trunk, arched directly toward the window, then angled off to the right. Her interest was directed at a short horizontal section that was about six or seven feet away from where she was standing.

The question went through Cassy's mind whether she could leap from the window, catch the branch, and hold on. She didn't know. She'd never done anything like it in her life and was surprised the idea even occurred to her. Yet these were hardly normal circumstances, and she quickly became intrigued. After all it seemed possible, especially with all the working out with weights she'd been doing over the last six months with Beau's encouragement.

Besides, Cassy thought, what if she missed? Her present prospects were dismal. Dashing herself against the balustrade didn't seem much worse and might do more than injure.

Climbing up on the windowsill, Cassy pushed the sash up to its full height to create an opening about five feet square. From that position the ground looked dramatically farther away.

She closed her eyes. Her heart was pounding, and she was breathing rapidly. Her courage vacillated. She recalled going to a circus as a child and seeing the trapeze artists and thinking she could never do anything like that. But then she thought of Eugene and Jesse and what Beau was becoming. She thought of the horror of losing her identity.

With sudden resolve, Cassy opened her eyes and leapt out into the air.

It seemed forever before she made contact. Perhaps drawing on some arboreal instincts she didn't realize she possessed, Cassy had judged the distance perfectly. Her hands made proper contact with the branch, and she grabbed on. Now the question became whether she could hold on as her legs swung beneath her.

There was a few moments of terror before her swinging came to a halt. She'd done it! But it wasn't over. She was still twenty feet off the ground, although now she was suspended over lawn, not flagstone.

Swinging her legs to help her, Cassy moved along the branch until she came to a point where she could get her right foot on a lower branch. From there it was relatively easy to work her way down the tree and eventually jump onto the grass.

The moment her feet touched the ground, Cassy was up and walking. She resisted the temptation to run out across the expansive lawn, knowing full well that it would only draw attention to herself. Instead she forced herself to assume a leisurely pace after climbing over the low balustrade. She followed the walkway to the front of the house.

Mimicking the smiles, the blank staring into the middle distance, and the relaxed walk, Cassy melded into the crowd of infected people heading out the driveway. Her heart was in her throat and she was terrified, but it worked. No one paid her any attention. The hardest part was forcing herself not to look around her, especially not at the dogs.

"How do you know where we are going?" Pitt asked. They had traveled miles on a track that in places was barely discernable from the desert itself.

"We're almost there," Harlan said.

"Oh, please!" Sheila said impatiently. "We're in the middle of the damned desert. Without the paved road this is more Godforsaken than the area around that deserted gas station. Is this some kind of joke?"

"No joke," Harlan said. "Be patient! I'm giving you all a chance to help save the human race."

Sheila glanced over at Pitt, but his attention was glued to the track. Sheila sighed loudly. Just when she'd started feeling good about Harlan, it was becoming apparent he was taking them on a wild-goose chase. There was no lab out there in the desert. The whole situation was absurd.

"Okay," Harlan said. "Stop up 'here next to that flowering cactus."

Pitt did as he was told. He pulled on the brake and cut the engine.

"All right," Harlan said. "Everybody out." He opened the slider and stepped out onto the sand. Jonathan followed at his heels.

"Come on," Harlan encouraged the others.

Sheila and Pitt rolled their eyes for each other's benefit. They were parked in the middle of the desert. Except for a few scattered boulders, a handful of cacti, and some low rolling sand hills, there was nothing around them.

Harlan had walked about twenty feet away before turning back. He was surprised no one was following him. Jonathan had gotten out of the van, but since the others hadn't, he'd hesitated.

"For chrissake!" Harlan complained. "What d'ya need, a special invitation?"

Sheila sighed and alighted from the vehicle. Pitt followed suit. Then all three trudged after Harlan, who was striking out into nowhere land.

Sheila wiped her brow. "I don't know what to make of this," she whispered. "One minute this guy seems like a godsend, the next like a crackpot. And on top of that it's hotter than Hades."

Harlan stopped and waited for the others to catch up to him. He pointed down to the ground and said: "Welcome to the Washburn-Kraft Biological Warfare Reaction Laboratory."

Before anyone could respond to this preposterous statement, Harlan bent down and grasped a camouflaged ring. He pulled up and a circular portion of the desert floor lifted up. Beneath was a round opening lined with stainless steel. Just the tip of a ladder was visible.

Harlan made a sweeping gesture with his hand. "This whole area around here all the way to within a few miles of Paswell is honeycombed with underground facilities. It was supposed to be a big secret, but the Native Americans knew about it."

"It's an operational lab?" Sheila questioned. This indeed was too good to be true.

"It had been mothballed in kind of suspended animation," Harlan said. "It was built back in the height of the cold war but then deemed superfluous when the threat of germ warfare coming to the USA diminished. Except for a few bureaucrats who kept the thing stocked, it was pretty much forgotten about; at least that's my take on the situation. Anyway, after all this trouble started, I got into it and cranked it up to speed. So to answer your question: yes, it is an operational lab."

"And this is the entrance?" Sheila questioned. She leaned out over the rim of the opening and looked down. There were lights below. The ladder went straight down about thirty feet.

"No, this is an emergency exit plus an air vent," Harlan said. "The real entrance is closer to Paswell, but I'm afraid to use that lest I be seen by some of my former patients."

"Can we go inside?" Sheila asked.

"Hey, that's what we're here for," Harlan said. "But before a tour I want to cover the van with a camouflage tarp."

They all climbed down the ladder to a white, high-tech corridor illuminated by banks of fluorescent lights. From a storage locker at the base of the ladder, Harlan got out the tarp he'd mentioned. Pitt returned topside with Harlan to give him a hand.

"Pretty cool," Jonathan said to Sheila while they waited. The corridor seemed to stretch off in either direction to infinity.

"Better than cool," Sheila said. "It's a godsend. And to think it was built to help thwart a germ-warfare attack by the Russians and instead is to be used to do the same thing for aliens is truly ironic."

When Harlan and Pitt returned back down, Harlan led them off in what he said was a northerly direction.

"It will take you a while to orient yourselves," he said. "Until then I recommend you stick together."

"Where are the people that kept this place up?" Sheila asked.

"They came in shifts like the guys that used to man the underground missile silos," Harlan said. "But after they got infected, I guess they either forgot about it or went off someplace. The talk in Paswell was that a lot of people were going to Santa Fe for some reason. Anyway they're not around, and by now I don't expect them."

They came to an air lock. Harlan opened it and had everybody climb into a chamber. Inside the chamber were showers and blue jump suits. Harlan closed the door, then twisted some dials. Air was heard entering the lock.

"This was to make sure none of the biological warfare agents got into the lab except in biohazard containers," Harlan said. "Obviously that's not our worry now."

"Where does the power come from?" Sheila asked.

"Nuclear," Harlan said. "It's kinda like a nuclear submarine. The whole place is independent of what's going on topside."

Everybody had to clear their ears as the pressure built up. When it was equalized with the interior of the lab, Harlan opened the inner door.

Sheila was flabbergasted. She'd never seen such a laboratory in her entire life. It was a series of three large rooms with walk-in incubators and freezers. Adding to her astonishment was the fact that all the equipment was state-of-the-art.

"These freezers are a little scary," Harlan said, tapping one of the stainless steel doors. "They contain just about every known potential biological agent, both bacterial and viral." He then pointed toward another door with large bolts like a walk-in safe. "In there is a library of chemical agents. One of James Bond's villians would have had a ball down here."

"What's through those doors?" Sheila asked, pointing to pressure-sealed hatches with round porthole windows.

"That goes into confinement rooms and a sick bay," Harlan said. "My guess is that they considered such a facility necessary in case any of the people working in here succumbed to whatever they were trying to vanquish."

"Look!" Jonathan said, pointing toward a row of black discs positioned beneath an exhaust hood.

"Don't touch those!" Harlan said anxiously.

"Don't worry," Jonathan said. "We know about them."

Everyone walked over and looked at the collection.

"They can do more than infect people," Sheila said.

"Don't I know," Harlan said. "Come with me. Let me show you something."

Harlan led everyone to a short corridor off of which were several X-ray rooms as well as an MRI scanner. He opened the door to the first X-ray room. Inside the machine had been twisted out of shape as if it had been melted and pulled inward.

"My God!" Sheila said. "This looks just like what happened in a room in the student overnight ward. Do you know how this happened?"

"I think so," Harlan said. "I tried to X-ray one of those black discs, and it didn't like it. This may sound crazy, but I think it created a miniature black hole. My guess is that's how they get here and how they leave."

"Cool," Jonathan said. "How can they do that?"

"I wish I knew," Harlan said. "But I'll tell you how I explained it to myself. Somehow they have the ability to generate enough internal energy to create an instantaneous huge gravitational field so they subatomically implode."

"So where do they go?" Jonathan asked.

"Now you have to go way out on a limb," Harlan said. "And perhaps subscribe to the wormhole theory of the cosmos. In that scenario they'd be in another parallel universe."

"Wow," Jonathan said.

"That's a bit too much for me," Pitt said.

"Me too," Sheila said. "Let's get back to the lab." As they returned she asked: "And there's mice and myeloma cells available down here for monoclonal antibody production?"

"We've got more than mice," Harlan said. "We've got rats, guinea pigs, rabbits, and even a few monkeys. In fact, half my time is taken up feeding the guys."

"What about living quarters?" Sheila asked. As tired and dirty as she was, she couldn't help but think about the pleasure of a shower and a nap.

"This way," Harlan said. He lead them out into the main corridor and through a pair of double doors. The first room they came to was a gigantic living room, complete with a large screen TV and an entire wall filled with books. Next to the living room was a dining area adjacent to a modern kitchen. Beyond the dining room and leading off a central corridor were multiple guest rooms, each with its own bath.

"Hey, this is okay," Jonathan said, seeing that each bedroom had its own computer terminal.

"This is good," Pitt said, eyeing the bed. "This is very good."

Once Cassy had gotten away from the institute, she'd been able to find a car with ease. There were hundreds of them simply abandoned as if many of the infected people weren't interested in them any longer. The people seemed to prefer walking.

As soon as she got to a phone she'd tried calling the cabin. After letting the phone ring twenty times, she'd given up. Obviously no one was there which could only mean one thing: they'd been discovered. Such a realization had been heartbreaking for Cassy, and for over an hour she'd sat in her commandeered car feeling depressed to the point of paralysis. Her wish to at least speak once more with Pitt and the others had been thwarted.

What finally pulled Cassy from the depths of her torpor was a sudden stinging sensation in her nose followed by a series of violent sneezes. Instantly she knew what was happening; the symptoms of the alien flu were starting.

Cassy went back to the telephone, and despite knowing it was in vain, tried calling the cabin again. As she'd expected, there was still no answer. But as the phone rang she thought that there was at least a small possibility that even if the cabin had been discovered, one or more might have gotten away. That was when she thought about what Jonathan had been so patient to teach her: logging onto the Internet.

By the time Cassy got back to the car, the discomfort she felt in her nose had spread down to her throat, and she began to cough. At first it was only a clearing of her throat, but it quickly progressed to a cough.

Cassy drove into the town. There was still some traffic, but it was slight. In contrast there were thousands of people walking about and busily involved with all the necessities of life. A lot of people were gardening. Everyone was smiling, and there was little conversation.

Cassy parked the car and got out onto the sidewalk. Although many businesses were still functioning, others were deserted as if the employees had just stood up at some arbitrary time and walked out the door. Nothing was locked.

One of the empty businesses was a dry-cleaning store. Cassy went inside but didn't find what she was looking for. Instead she found it next door in a copying concern. What she wanted was a computer connected to a modem.

Cassy sat down and activated the screen. When the employees had left they hadn't even turned the equipment off. Remembering Jonathan's Internet name, Jumpin Jack Flash, Cassy began typing.

"This is all you have?" Sheila asked Harlan. She was holding a small vial of clear fluid.

"That's it for now," Harlan said. "But I got a batch of mice with the hybridoma cells implanted in their peritoneal cavities as well as a bunch of cell cultures cooking in the incubator. We can certainly extract more of this monoclonal antibody. But it's only weakly active. I'd much rather try to find a more avid antibody-producing cell."

Sheila, Pitt, and Jonathan had taken showers and rested briefly, but were too wired to sleep. Sheila was especially anxious to get working and had urged Harlan to show her everything he'd done.

Jonathan and Pitt had tagged along. Pitt was having trouble following Harlan's explanations, whereas Jonathan didn't even try. Since he hadn't had much biology, it all sounded like Greek to him. Instead Jonathan ignored the others, sat down at one of the many terminals available, and started typing.

"I'll show you two the process used to select B lymphocytes from emulsified mouse spleen," Harlan said. "Provided you show me the virions you and Jonathan's mother isolated."

"We're not positive the virions are in the tissue culture," Sheila said. "We just suspect they are. We were just about ready to isolate them."

"Well, we can find out simply enough," Harlan said.

"Oh my God!" Jonathan called out suddenly.

Shocked by this outburst, everyone looked across at Jonathan. His eyes were glued to the monitor.

"What's the matter?" Pitt asked nervously.

"It's a message from Cassy!" Jonathan cried.

Pitt practically vaulted over a lab bench to get to Jonathan's side. He stared at the monitor with wide eyes.

"She's typing into the mail drop this instant," Jonathan said. "I mean this is a real-time phenomenon."

"This is fantastic," Pitt managed.

"What a cool girl," Jonathan said. "She's doing just like I taught her."

"What's she saying?" Sheila asked. "Is she saying where she is?"

"Oh no!" Jonathan said. "She says she's been infected."

"Damn!" Pitt agonized, gritting his teeth.

"She says she's already experiencing the first symptoms of the flu," Jonathan continued. "She wants to wish us good luck."

"Contact her!" Pitt shouted. "Now, live, before she signs off."

"Pitt, it's no use," Sheila said. "It will just make it more difficult. She's infected!"

"She might be infected, but obviously she's still Cassy," Pitt said. "Otherwise she wouldn't be wishing us good luck." He forcibly nudged Jonathan aside and started typing furiously.

Jonathan looked up at Sheila. Sheila shook her head. Although she knew it was wrong, she didn't have the heart to stop him.

For Cassy the image on the monitor was intermittently blurry. As she'd typed the tears had come. Closing her eyes for a moment and wiping them with the back of her hand, she tried to get herself under control. She wanted to leave one last message for Pitt. She wanted to tell him that she loved him.

Opening her eyes and returning her hands to the keyboard, Cassy was about to type her last sentence when a live message popped onto her screen. She gazed at it in astonishment. It said: "Cassy, it's me, Pitt. Where are you?"

It was the longest few seconds of Pitt's life. He goggled at the monitor and willed it to respond. Then as if answering a prayer, the black characters began popping out of the luminous background.

"Yes!" Pitt shouted while punching the air with a fist. "I caught her. She knows I'm here."

"What is she saying?" Sheila ventured. She was afraid to ask because she was sure this contact was going to lead to heartache and trouble.

"She's saying she's not too far from here," Pitt said. "I'm going to tell her to meet me."

"Pitt, no!" Sheila shouted. "Even if she's not one of them now, she will be shortly. You can't take the chance. You certainly can't expose this lab."

Pitt looked over at Sheila. His emotional pain was palpable. His breaths were coming in short gasps. "I can't abandon her," he said. "I just can't."

"You must," Sheila said. "You saw what happened to Beau."

Pitt's fingers were poised above the keyboard. He'd never felt such heart-wrenching indecision.

"Wait," Harlan said suddenly. "Ask her how long it has been since she was stung."

"What difference does that make?" Sheila said angrily. She felt irritated that Harlan would interfere at such a moment.

"Just do it," Harlan said. He walked over to stand behind Pitt.

Pitt typed the question. The answer came back instantly: about four hours. Harlan looked at his watch and bit the inside of his cheek while thinking.

"What is going on inside your head?" Sheila demanded, looking Harlan in the eye.

"I have a little confession to make," Harlan said. "I wasn't telling the whole truth about those black discs. One of them did sting me when I was out collecting the last batch."

"Then you are one of them!" Sheila said with horror.

"No, at least I don't think so," Harlan said. "I tied my weak monoclonal antibody to the enabling protein, and I've been giving myself shots ever since. I've had the sniffles but no flu."

"That's fantastic," Pitt said. "Let me tell Cassy."

"Wait!" Sheila commanded. "How long after you were stung did you give yourself the antibody?"

"That's my only concern," Harlan said. "There was a three-hour interval. I was in Paswell at the time it happened. It took me three hours to get back here."

"Cassy has already been four," Sheila said. "What do you think?"

"I think it's worth a try," Harlan said. "We can put her in one of the containment rooms and see what happens. If it doesn't work out, there's no way she can get out of there. They're like dungeons."

Pitt didn't need any more encouragement. Without another word he began telling Cassy they had an antibody to the protein and giving her directions to the deserted gas station.

"Why didn't you tell us you'd been stung?" Sheila questioned. She didn't know whether to be angry or encouraged by this new development.

"To be honest," Harlan said, "I was afraid you wouldn't trust me that I was okay. I was going to tell you sooner or later. Actually the fact that it has seemingly worked makes me feel a bit optimistic."

"Well, I should say so!" Sheila said. "It's the first positive piece of information so far."

Pitt finished his communication with Cassy and came over to Sheila and Harlan.

"I hope you were as discreet as possible with the directions," Harlan said. "We certainly don't want a truckload of infected people to be there at the station waiting for you when you arrive."

"I tried to be," Pitt said. "But at the same time I wanted to make sure Cassy found the place. It is so isolated."

"Actually the risk is probably pretty small," Harlan said. "My feeling is that the infected people aren't using the Net. They don't seem to need it since they appear to know what each other are thinking."

"Aren't you coming with me?" Pitt asked Harlan.

"I don't think I'd better," Harlan said. "There's only a partial dose of my antibody left. I'll have to get busy extracting more so that it's available when your friend gets here. That means you'll have to find your own way. Think you can do it?"

"Sounds like I don't have much choice," Pitt said.

Harlan handed Pitt the vial of what antibody he had along with a syringe. "I hope you know how to give an injection," he said.

Pitt commented that he thought he could do it because he'd been clerking in the hospital for three years.

"You'd better give it IV," Harlan said. "But be prepared for some mouth to mouth if she has an anaphylatic reaction."

Pitt visibly gulped, but he nodded.

"And you might as well take this," Harlan said, unbuckling his holstered Colt .45. "My advice is to use it if you have to. Remember, the infected people feel very strongly about you being infected if they sense you aren't."

"What about me?" Jonathan asked. "I'll go with Pitt. He might have trouble finding his way back here, and four eyes will be better than two."

"I think you'd better stay here," Sheila said. "We can find plenty for you to do." She rolled up her sleeves. "And we are going to be very busy."

Once Cassy had been located, brought to the institute, and subsequently infected, progress on the Gateway speeded up. Although the thousands of workers didn't have to be individually told what to do, ultimately their instructions came from Beau. Consequently it was necessary for Beau to spend a good deal of time in the vicinity of the construction and for his mind to be clear of extraneous thoughts. With Cassy upstairs and soon to be one of the infected, Beau found it easy to fulfill his responsibilities.

Progress had even reached a point where it was possible to energize briefly a portion of the electrical grids. The test was a success although it did indicate that portions of the system needed further shielding. With those instructions communicated, Beau took a break.

He climbed the main stairs in a normal bipedal fashion, although he was conscious of the fact that it would probably be easier for him now to hop up, taking six or eight steps at a time. There had been considerable augmentation of his quadriceps.

Reaching the upper hall he sensed something was wrong. He hadn't felt it downstairs because the level of unspoken communication about the Gateway was so intense. But now that he was alone, it was different. By this time he should have been getting stirrings of Cassy's developing collective consciousness. Since there was none at all he feared she'd died.

Beau quickened his pace. His fear was that perhaps Cassy had been harboring some disastrous gene that had yet to express itself. In that case the virus would have self-destructed.

With a sense of panic that he didn't understand, Beau struggled to open the locked door. Bracing himself to see her lifeless body draped across the mattress, he was even more surprised to find the room empty.

Beau gazed at the open window. He walked over to it and looked down at the ground outside. He saw the walkway and the balustrade. Then his eyes went up the tree, and he looked at the branch. Suddenly he knew. She'd fled.

Letting out a shriek that echoed through the huge mansion, he rushed from the room and charged down the stairs. He was overcome with anger, and anger wasn't healthy for the collective good. The collective consciousness had rarely experienced anger, and it didn't know how to handle it.

Beau entered the ballroom and instantly all work came to a halt. All eyes turned to Beau, feeling the same anger but having no idea why. Beau's nostrils flared as his eyes searched for Alexander. He spotted him at the command control console.

Boldly Beau strode over to his lieutenant and clamped down on his arm with his snakelike fingers. "She is gone! I want her found! Now!"

CHAPTER 19

12:45 A.M.

Pitt kicked a few of the pebbles in the driveway of the old gas station. He bent down and picked up others and threw them absently at the ancient pumps. The stones clanged against the rusting metal.

Shielding his eyes from the sun, which was now significantly more formidable in its heat and intensity then two hours earlier, Pitt scanned the two-lane road to its vanishing point on the horizon. He began to worry. He'd thought she would have been there already.

Just when he was about to retreat back to the shade of the porch, his eye caught the glint of sunlight off a windshield. A vehicle was coming.

Unconsciously Pitt's hand slipped down to envelop the butt of the Colt. There was always the worry that it wasn't Cassy.

As the vehicle got closer, Pitt could make out that it was a late-model recreational vehicle with large tires and a built-in luggage rack on the top. It was coming fast.

For a moment Pitt contemplated hiding inside the building the way Harlan had done, but he dismissed the idea. After all, Jesse's van was sitting right there in plain sight.

The vehicle pulled into the station. Pitt wasn't sure it was Cassy until she opened the door and called out to him. The windows were heavily tinted.

Pitt got to the vehicle in time to help Cassy down. She was coughing and her eyes were red-rimmed.

"Maybe you shouldn't get too close," Cassy said in a deeply nasal voice. "We don't know for sure whether this can spread person to person like an infection."

Ignoring her comment, Pitt enveloped her in an enthusiastic embrace. The only reason he let go of her was concern about her getting the antibody.

"I brought some of the medicine I mentioned on the Internet with me," Pitt said. "Obviously we think it is best to get it into your system as soon as possible and that means intravenous."

"Where should we do it?" Cassy asked.

"In the van," he said.

They walked around the vehicle to its slider.

"How are you feeling?" Pitt asked.

"Terrible," Cassy admitted. "I couldn't get comfortable in that four-by-four; the ride is so stiff. All my muscles ache. I've also got a fever. A half hour ago I was shivering, if you can believe it in this heat."

Pitt opened the van door. He had Cassy lie down on the van's seat. He prepared the syringe, but then, after putting on the tourniquet, he admitted his inexperience at venipuncture.

"I don't want to hear it," Cassy said, looking off in the opposite direction. "Just do it. I mean, you're going to be a doctor."

Pitt had seen medication administered IV thousands of times but never had tried it himself. The idea of puncturing another person's skin was daunting, much less a person he loved. But the consequences of not doing it overwhelmed any timidity he had. Ultimately it went well, and Cassy told him as much.

"You're just being a good sport," Pitt said.

"No, really," Cassy said. "I hardly felt it." No sooner had she complimented him that she had an explosive bout of coughing that left her gasping.

Pitt was momentarily terrified she was having a reaction to the shot as Harlan had warned. Although Pitt had had CPR training, he'd never actually done that, either. Anxiously he held her wrist to feel her pulse. Thankfully it stayed strong and regular.

"Sorry," Cassy managed when she could get her breath.

"Are you okay?" Pitt asked.

Cassy nodded.

"Thank God!" Pitt said. He swallowed to relieve a dry throat. "You stay here on the backseat. We've got about a twenty-minute drive."

"Where are we going?" Cassy asked.

"To a place that's like an answer to a prayer," Pitt said. "It's an underground lab built to deal with a biological or chemical warfare attack. It's perfect for what we have to do. I mean, if we can't do it there, then we can't do it. It's that good. Plus it has a sick bay where we can take care of you."

Pitt started to climb into the front seat when Cassy took hold of his arm. "What if this antibody doesn't work?" she said. "I mean, you warned me it was weak and very preliminary. What will you do with me if I turn into one of them? I don't want to jeopardize what you all are doing."

"Don't worry," Pitt said. "There's a doctor there named Harlan McCay who was stung and is still fine after getting the antibody. But if worst comes to worst, there are what he calls containment rooms. But everything is going to be fine." Pitt gave her shoulder a pat.

"Save the clichés, Pitt," Cassy said. "With everything that has happened, it can't turn out fine."

Pitt shrugged. He knew she was right.

Pitt got behind the wheel, started the van, and pulled out into the road. Cassy remained lying on the backseat. "I hope there's some aspirin where we're going," she said. She was as sick as she'd ever felt in her life.

"I'm sure there is," Pitt said. "If the sick bay is like the rest of the place, it's got everything."

They rode in silence for a few miles. Pitt was concentrating on the driving for fear of missing the turnoff. On his way out he'd built a small cairn of rocks to mark it, but now he was afraid it wouldn't help. The rocks had been small and everything was the same color.

"I can't help but worry that my coming here was a bad idea," Cassy said after another coughing spell.

"Don't talk that way!" Pitt said. "I don't want to hear it."

"It's been more than six hours now," Cassy said. "Maybe even more. I wasn't all that sure of the time when I was stung. So much has been happening."

"What happened to Nancy and Jesse?" Pitt asked. It was a question he'd avoided, but he wanted to change the subject.

"Nancy was stung," Cassy said. "They infected her in my presence. I couldn't figure out why they didn't do it to me until later. Jesse was a different story. I believe the same thing happened to him as to Eugene. But I'm not sure. I didn't see it. I just heard it, and there was a flash of light. Nancy said it was the same as before."

"Harlan thinks those black discs can create miniature black holes," Pitt said.

Cassy shuddered. The idea of disappearing down a black hole seemed like the epitome of destruction. Even one's atoms would be gone from the universe.

"I saw Beau again," Cassy said.

Pitt turned to glance at Cassy before looking back at the road. It was the last thing he expected her to say.

"How was he?" Pitt asked.

"Horrid," Cassy said. "And he's changed visibly. He's mutating progressively. Last time I saw him it was only a patch of skin behind his ear. Now it's most of his body. It's strange because the other infected people didn't seem to be changing. I don't know if they will or if it has something to do with Beau being the first. He's definitely a leader. They all do what he wants."

"Did he have anything to do with your being stung?" Pitt asked.

"I'm afraid so," Cassy said. "He did it himself."

Pitt shook his head imperceptibly. He couldn't believe that his best friend could do such a thing, but then again he was no longer his best friend. He was an alien.

"The most horrid part for me was that there was still some of the old Beau inside," Cassy said. "He even told me that he missed me and that he loved me. Can you believe it?"

"No," Pitt said simply, while fuming that Beau, even as an alien, was still trying to take Cassy away from him.

Beau was standing to the side in the shadows behind the command control unit of the Gateway. His eyes were glowing fiercely. It was hard for him to concentrate on the problems at hand, but he had to. Time was running out.

"Maybe we should try to charge some of the electrical grids again," Randy called over to Beau. Randy was sitting at the controls. A minor glitch had developed, and as of yet, Beau had not suggested a solution.

Yanked from a daydream about Cassy, Beau tried to think. The problem from the beginning had been to create enough energy to turn the powerful, instantaneous gravity of a group of black discs working in concert into antigravity and still have the Gateway stay together. The reaction would only have to last a nanosecond as it sucked matter from a parallel universe into the current one. Suddenly the answer came to Beau; more shielding was needed.

"All right," Randy said, pleased to get some direction. He in turn alerted the thousands of workers who immediately swarmed back up into the superstructure on the gigantic construct.

"Do you think this will work?" Randy called over to Beau.

Beau communicated that he thought it would. He advised to power up all the electrical grids for an instant as soon as the augmented shielding was completed.

"What worries me is that you told me the first visitors are due tonight," Randy said. "It would be a calamity if we weren't ready. The individuals would be lost in the void as mere primary particles."

Beau grunted. He was more interested that Alexander had entered the room. Beau watched him approach. Beau didn't like the vibrations. He could tell they hadn't found her.

"We followed her spoor," Alexander reported. He purposefully stayed out of Beau's reach. "It led us to where she'd taken a vehicle. Now we're looking for the vehicle."

"You will find her!" Beau snarled.

"We will find her," Alexander repeated soothingly. "By now her consciousness should be expanding, and that will help us a great deal."

"Just find her," Beau said.

"You know, I don't have any explanation," Sheila said.

She and Harlan were seated on laboratory stools on wheels that allowed them to zip from bench to bench.

Harlon had his chin cradled in his hand and was chewing the inside of his cheek. It was a habit he'd developed that indicated he was deep in thought.

"Could we have done something stupid?" Sheila asked.

Harlan shook his head. "We've been over our protocol several times. It wasn't technique. It has to be a real finding."

"Let's go over it once again," Sheila said. "Nancy and I had taken a tissue culture of human nasopharyngeal cells and added the enabling protein."

"What was the vehicle for the protein?" Harlan asked.

"Normal tissue culture medium," Sheila said. "The protein is fully soluble in an aqueous solution."

"All right, what next?" Harlan said.

"We simply let the culture incubate," Sheila said. "We could tell that the virus had been activated because of the rapid synthesis of DNA over and above what was needed for cell replication."

"How did you assay that?" Harlan asked.

"We used inactivated adenovirus to carry DNA probes labeled with fluorescein into the cells."

"What next?" Harlan asked.

"That was as far as we got," Sheila said. "We put the cultures aside to incubate further, hoping to get viruses."

"Well, you got them all right," Harlan said.

"Yeah, but look at this image. Under the scanning electron microscope the virus looks like it's been through a miniature meat grinder. This virus is noninfective. Something killed it, but there was nothing in the culture capable of doing that. It doesn't make sense."

"It doesn't make sense, but my gut instinct is that it is trying to tell us something," Harlan said. "We're just too stupid to see it."

"Maybe we should just try it again," Sheila said. "Maybe the culture got too hot riding in the car."

"You'd packed it well," Harlan said. "I don't think that's the answer. But fine, let's do it again. Also, I have some mice that I have been infecting. I suppose we could try to isolate the virus from them."

"Great idea!" Sheila said. "That might be even easier."

"Don't count on it," Harlan said. "The infected mice are amazingly strong and incredibly smart. I have to keep them apart and under lock and key."

"Good Lord," Sheila said. "Are you suggesting the mice are becoming alien too?"

"I'm afraid that's right," Harlan said. "In some form or fashion. My supposition is that if there were enough infected mice all in one location they could collectively act as an intelligent, single individual."

"Maybe we better stick to tissue cultures for the time being," Sheila said. "One way or the other we've got to isolate live, infective virus. It has to be the next step if we're going to do anything about this infestation."

The hiss of the air lock pressurizing sounded.

"That must be Pitt," Jonathan shouted. He ran out to the air lock door and peered through the porthole. "It is Pitt, and Cassy is with him!" he shouted back to the others.

Harlan picked up a vial of newly extracted monoclonal antibody. "I think I'd better put on my physican hat for a little while," he said.

Sheila reached out and motioned for him to give her the vial. "Emergency medicine is my specialty," she said. "We need you as the immunologist."

Harlan handed it over. "Gladly," he said. "I've always been a better researcher than clinician."

The air lock opened. Jonathan helped Cassy step through the hatch. She was pale and feverish. Jonathan's excitement moderated. She was sicker than he'd realized. Still, he couldn't help but ask where his mother was.

Cassy put her hand on his shoulder. "I'm sorry," she said. "We were separated very quickly after we were caught in the supermarket. I don't know where she is."

"Was she stung?" Jonathan asked.

"I'm afraid so," Cassy said.

"Come on!" Sheila said. "We have work to do." She put Cassy's arm over her shoulder. "Let's get you into the infirmary."

With Sheila on one side and Pitt on the other they walked Cassy through the lab to the sick bay. She was introduced to Harlan en route. He held open the door for them.

"I think it best if she occupies one of the containment rooms," Harlan said. He pushed past the group and led the way.

The room looked like a regular hospital room except for its entrance, which had an air lock so the room could be kept at a lower pressure than the rest of the complex. The inner door was also lockable and the glass in the porthole was an inch thick.

Everyone crowded into the room. With help from both Sheila and Pitt, Cassy stretched out on the bed and sighed with relief.

Sheila went right to work. With practiced deftness she started an IV, then gave a sizable dose of the monoclonal antibody. She injected it into the intravenous port on the IV line.

"Did you have any adverse reaction to the first shot?" Sheila asked as she momentarily sped up the IV to carry the last of the antibody into Cassy's system.

Cassy shook her head.

"There was no problem," Pitt said. "Except for a coughing spell which scared me. But I don't think it was related to the medication."

Sheila attached Cassy to a cardiac monitor. The beats were normal and the rhythm regular.

"Have you felt any different since that first shot?" Harlan asked.

"Not that I can tell," Cassy said.

"That's not surprising," Sheila said. "The symptoms are mainly from your own lymphokines, which we know shoot up in the early stages."

"I want to thank you all for letting me come here," Cassy said. "I know you are taking a risk."

"We're glad to have you," Harlan said, giving her knee a squeeze. "Who knows, like me you may be a valuable experimental subject."

"I wish," Cassy said.

"Are you hungry?" Sheila asked.

"Not in the slightest," Cassy said. "But I could certainly use some aspirin."

Sheila looked at Pitt. "I think I'll turn that over to Dr. Henderson," she said with a wry smile. "Meanwhile the rest of us have to get back to work."

Harlan was the first to leave. Sheila paused with one leg into the air lock. Looking back she waved to Jonathan. "Come on. Let's leave the patient to her doctor."

Jonathan reluctantly followed.

"You were right," Cassy said. "This place is unbelievable."

"It's just what the doctor ordered," Pitt said. "Let me get you that aspirin."

It took Pitt a few minutes to find the pharmacy and a few more to locate the aspirin. When he returned to the confinement room, he found that Cassy had been sleeping.

"I don't want to bother you," Pitt said.

"No bother," Cassy said. She took the aspirin, then lay back. She patted the bedside. "Sit down for a minute," she said. "I've got to tell you what I learned from Beau. This nightmare is about to get worse."

The tranquility of the desert was suddenly shattered by the repetitive concussion of the rotor blades and the roar of the Huey military jet engine as the copter swept low across the barren landscape. Inside Vince Garbon held a pair of binoculars to his eyes. He'd told the pilot to follow a strip of black tarmac that cut across the sand from horizon to horizon. In the backseat were two former police officers from Vince's old unit.

"The last word we have is that the vehicle came out this road," Vince shouted to the pilot over the sound of the engine. The pilot nodded.

"I see something coming up," Vince said. "It looks like an old gas station, but there's a vehicle and it fits the description."

The pilot slowed the forward progress. Vince held the binoculars as steady as he could.

"Yup," he said. "I think it's the one. Let's go down and have a look."

The helicopter lowered to the earth, kicking up a horrendous swirl of sand and dust in the process. When the skids were firmly on the ground, the pilot cut the engine. The heavy rotors slowed and came to a stop. Vince climbed out of the cab.

The first thing Vince checked was the vehicle. He opened the door and could immediately sense that Cassy had been in it. He looked in the luggage space. It was empty.

Motioning toward the building, the two former policemen went inside. Vince stayed outside and let his eyes roam around the horizon. It was so hot that he could see heat rising in the air.

The policemen came out quickly and shook their heads. She wasn't in there.

Vince motioned back to the copter. He was close. He could sense it. After all, how far could she get on foot in that heat?

Pitt came into the lab. Everyone was working so intently that they didn't even raise their heads.

"She's finally sleeping," he said.

"Did you lock the outer door?" Harlan asked.

"No," Pitt said. "Do you think I should?"

"Absolutely," Sheila said. "We don't want any surprises."

"I'll be right back," Pitt said. He returned to the air lock and looked in at Cassy. She was still sleeping peacefully. Her coughing had significantly abated. Pitt locked the door.

Returning to the lab, he took a seat. Again no one acknowledged him. Sheila was engrossed, inoculating tissue cultures with the enabling protein. Harlan was extracting more antibody. Jonathan was at a computer terminal wearing earphones and working a joystick.

Pitt asked Jonathan what he was doing. Jonathan took off the earphones. "It's really cool," he said. "Harlan showed me how to connect with all the monitoring equipment topside. There are cameras hidden in fake cacti which can be directed with this joystick. There's also listening devices and motion sensors. Want to try it?"

Pitt declined. Instead he told the others that Cassy had described to him some astounding and disturbing things about the aliens.

"Like what?" Sheila asked while continuing to work.

"The worst thing," Pitt said, "is that they have the infected people building a huge futuristic machine they call a Gateway."

"And what's this Gateway supposed to do?" Sheila asked, while gently swirling a tissue culture flask.

"It's some kind of transporter," Pitt said. "She was told that it will bring all sorts of alien creatures to Earth from distant planets."

"Jesus H. Christ!" Sheila exclaimed. She put down the flask. "We can't face any more adversaries. Maybe we'd better just give up."

"When is this Gateway going to be operational?" Harlan asked.

"I asked the same question," Pitt said. "Cassy didn't know, but she had the impression it was imminent. Beau told her it was almost finished. Cassy said there were thousands of people working on it."

Sheila exhaled noisily in exasperation. "What other charming news did she tell you?"

"Some interesting facts," Pitt said. "For instance, the alien virus first came to earth three billion years ago. That's when it inserted its DNA into the evolving life."

Sheila's eyes narrowed. "Three billion years ago?" she questioned.

Pitt nodded. "That's what Beau told her. He also told her that the aliens have sent the enabling protein every hundred million Earth years or so to 'awaken' the virus to see what kind of life has evolved here and whether it was worth inhabiting. What he meant by Earth years she didn't ask."

"Maybe that relates to their ability to go from one universe to another," Harlan said. "Here in ours we are caught in a space/time freeze. But from the point of view of another universe, what's a billion years here, might only be ten years there. Everything's relative."

Harlan's explanation brought on a moment of silence. Pitt shrugged. "Well, I can't say it makes much sense to me," he said.

"It's like a fifth dimension," Harlan said.

"Whatever," Pitt said. "But getting back to what Cassy was telling me, apparently this alien virus is responsible for the mass extinctions the Earth has witnessed. Every time they came back here, the creatures they infested weren't suitable, so they left."

"And all the creatures they'd infected died?" Sheila asked.

"That's how I understand it," Pitt said. "The virus must have made some lethal change in the DNA causing the disappearance of entire species. That created an opportunity for new creatures to evolve. She told me that Beau had specifically mentioned this with regard to the dinosaurs."

"Well, I'll be," Harlan said. "So much for the asteroid or comet theory."

"How did the creatures die?" Sheila asked. "I mean, what was the specific cause of death?"

"I don't think she knew that," Pitt said. "At least she didn't tell me. But I can ask her later."

"It might be important," Sheila said. She stared off into the middle distance with unseeing eyes. Her mind was churning. "And the virus supposedly came to Earth three billion Earth years ago?"

"That's what she said."

"What are you thinking?" Harlan asked.

"Is there any anaerobic bacteria available in the lab?" Sheila asked.

"Yeah, sure," Harlan said.

"Let's get some and infect it with the enabling protein," Sheila said with mounting excitement.

"Okay," Harlan said agreeably. He stood up. "But what's on your mind? Why do you want bacteria that grows without oxygen?"

"Humor me," Sheila said. "Just get it while I prepare some more enabling protein."

Beau threw open the french doors leading from the sitting room to the terrace surrounding the pool. He stepped out and strode across the terrace. Alexander hurried after him.

"Beau, please!" Alexander said. "Don't go! We need you here."

"They found her car," Beau said. "She's lost in the desert. Only I can find her. By now she should be far on her way to becoming one with us."

Beau descended the few steps from the terrace to the lawn and struck out toward the waiting helicopter. Alexander stayed at his heels.

"Surely this woman cannot be so important," Alexander said. "You can have any woman you want. This is not the time to leave the Gateway. We've not even tested the grids to full power. What if we are not ready?"

Beau spun around. His narrow lips were pulled back in fury. "This woman is driving me mad. I must find her. I'll be back. Until then, carry on without me."

"Why not wait until tomorrow?" Alexander persisted. "By then the Arrival will have occurred. Then you can go look for her. There'll be plenty of time."

"If she's lost in the desert she will be dead by tomorrow," Beau said. "It's decided."

Beau turned back to the copter and quickly closed the distance. For the last few feet he had to duck under the rotating blade. He climbed into the front seat next to the pilot, nodded a greeting to Vince in the backseat, then motioned for the pilot to lift off.

"How long has it been?" Sheila asked.

"About an hour," Harlan said.

"That should be enough time," Sheila said impatiently. "One of the first things we learned was how fast the enabling protein functioned once it was absorbed into a cell. Now let's give the culture a slight dose of soft X-rays."

Harlan looked askance at Sheila. "I'm beginning to get the drift of what's going on in that brain of yours," he said. "You're treating this virus like a provirus, which it is. And now you want to change it from its latent form into its lytic form. But why the anaerobic bacteria? Why no oxygen?"

"Let's see what happens before I explain," Sheila said. "Just keep your fingers crossed. This could be what we are looking for. An alien Achilles' heel."

They gave the infected bacterial culture the dose of X-rays without disturbing its atmosphere of carbon dioxide. As they made mounts for the scanning electron microscope, Sheila found her hands trembling with excitement. She hoped with all her heart that they were on the brink of discovery.

With one of his powerful legs, Beau kicked the door of the deserted gas station. The blow tore it from its hinges and sent it crashing into the far wall of the room. Stepping into the dim interior, Beau's eyes glowed intensely. The helicopter ride had done little to temper his fury.

He stood in the semidarkness for several seconds, then turned around and walked back out into the bright sunshine.

"She was never in there," Beau said.

"I didn't think so," Vince said. He was bending down in the sand on the opposite side of the aged gas pumps. "There are some other fresh tire tracks here." He stood up and looked toward the east. "There must have been a second vehicle. Maybe they picked her up."

"What do you suggest?" Beau asked.

"Apparently she hasn't appeared in any town," Vince said. "Otherwise we would have heard. That means she's out here in the desert. We know there are isolated groups of 'runners' hiding out in the area who've so far avoided infection. Maybe she joined up with one of them."

"But she's infected," Beau said.

"I know," Vince said. "That part is a mystery. Anyway, I think we should head east along this road and see if we can find any tracks going off into the desert. There must be some kind of camp."

"All right," Beau said. "Let's do it. Time is running out."

They climbed back into the helicopter and lifted off. The pilot was ordered to fly high enough to keep from kicking up too much sand and dust yet low enough to see any tracks heading away from the road.

"My gosh, there it is," Harlan said. They had focused in on a virion at sixty thousand times magnification. It was a large filamentous virus that looked like a filoviridae with tiny, cilialike projections.

"It's awesome to think that we are looking at a highly intelligent alien life form," Sheila said. "We've always thought of viruses and bacteria as primitive."

"I don't think it is the alien per se," Pitt said. "Cassy mentioned that the viral form was what enabled the alien to withstand space travel and infest other life forms in the galaxy. Apparently Beau didn't know what the original alien form looked like."

"Maybe that's what the Gateway is for," Jonathan said. "Maybe the virus likes it here so much, the aliens themselves are coming."

"Could be," Pitt said.

"All right," Harlan said to Sheila. "So this little trick with the anaerobic bacteria worked. We've seen the virus. What was your mysterious point?"

"The point is that this virus came to Earth three billion years ago," Sheila said. "At that time the Earth was a very different place. There was very little oxygen in the primitive atmosphere. Since then things have changed. The virus is still fine when it is in the latent form or even when it has been enabled and has transformed the cell. But if it is induced to form virions, it's destroyed by oxygen."

"Interesting idea," Harlan said. He looked down at the culture whose top was now off, exposing its surface to room air. "If that's the case then we'll see damaged, uninfective virus if we make another mount."

"That's exactly what I'm hoping," Sheila said.

Without wasting any time, Sheila and Harlan set to work creating a second sample. Pitt helped as best he could. Jonathan went back to playing with the computer-run security system.

When Harlan focused in on the new mount, it was immediately apparent that Sheila was right. The viruses appeared as if they had been partially eaten.

Sheila and Harlan jumped up from their seats and enthusiastically high-fived and then embraced each other. They were ecstatic.

"What a brilliant idea," Harlan said. "You're to be congratulated. It's a joy to see science in action."

"If we were doing real science," Sheila said, "we'd go back and exhaustively prove this hypothesis. For now, we'll just take it at face value."

"Oh, I agree," Harlan said. "But it makes such sense. It's amazing how toxic oxygen is and how few laypeople know it."

"I don't think I understand," Pitt said. "How does this help us?"

The smiles faded from Sheila's and Harlan's faces. They regarded each other for a beat, then retook their seats. Both were lost in thought.

"I'm not sure how this discovery is going to help us," Sheila said finally. "But it has to. I mean, it must be the alien Achilles' heel."

"It must have been the way that they killed off the dinosaurs," Harlan said. "Once they decided to end the infestation, the viruses all went from being latent to being virions. Then bam! They hit the oxygen and all hell broke loose."

"That doesn't sound very scientific," Sheila said with a smile.

Harlan laughed. "I agree," he said. "But it gives us a hint. We have to induce the virus in the infected people to go from being latent to coming out of the cell."

"How is a latent virus induced?" Pitt asked.

Harlan shrugged. "A lot of ways," he said. "In tissue culture it's usually done with electromagnetic radiation like ultraviolet light or soft X rays like we used with the anaerobic bacterial culture."

"There are some chemicals that can do it," Sheila said.

"That's true," Harlan. "Some of the antimetabolites and other cellular poisons. But that doesn't help us. Neither do X rays. I mean it's not as if we could suddenly X-ray the planet."

"Are there regular viruses that are latent like the alien virus?" Pitt asked.

"Plenty," Sheila said.

"Absolutely," Harlan agreed. "Like the AIDS virus."

"Or the whole herpes viral group," Sheila said. "They can hide out for life or cause intermittent problems."

"You mean like cold sores?" Pitt asked.

"That's right," Sheila said. "That's herpes simplex. It stays latent in certain neurons."

"So when you get a cold sore it means that a latent virus has been induced to form virus particles?" Pitt asked.

"That's right," Sheila said with a touch of exasperation.

"I get cold sores every time I get a cold," Pitt said. "I suppose that's why they're called cold sores."

"Very clever," Sheila said sarcastically. "Pitt, maybe you should leave us alone while we brainstorm. This isn't supposed to be a teaching session."

"Wait a second," Harlan said. "Pitt just gave me an idea."

"I did?" Pitt questioned innocently.

"You know what is the best viral induction agent?" Harlan asked rhetorically. "Another viral infection."

"How is that going to help us?" Sheila asked.

Harlan pointed to the large freezer door across the room. "In there we've got all sorts of viruses. I'm starting to think that we should fight fire with fire!"

"You mean start some kind of epidemic?" Sheila asked.

"That's exactly what I'm thinking," Harlan said. "Something extraordinarily infectious."

"But that freezer is full of viruses designed to be used as biological warfare agents. That will be like going from the frying pan into the fire."

"Hell, that freezer has everything from nuisance viruses to the most deadly," Harlan said. "We just have to pick one that's suitable."

"Well . . ." Sheila mused. "It is true our original tissue culture was probably induced by the adenoviral vehicle we used for the DNA assay."

"Come on!" Harlan said. "Let me show you the inventory."

Sheila stood up. She was very dubious about fighting fire with fire, but she wasn't about to dismiss the idea out of hand.

Next to the freezer was a desk with a bookshelf over it. On the bookshelf were three large, black looseleaf notebooks. Harlan handed one each to Sheila and Pitt. He cracked open the third himself.

"It's like a wine list at a fancy restaurant," Harlan quipped. "Remember, we need something infectious."

"What do you mean, 'infectious'?" Pitt asked.

"Capable of being spread from person to person," Harlan said. "And we need the route to be airborne, not like AIDS or hepatitis. We want a worldwide epidemic."

"God!" Pitt commented, looking at the index of his volume. "I never thought there were so many different viruses. Here's filoviridae. Wow! There's Ebola in there."

"Too virulent," Harlan said. "We want an illness that doesn't kill by itself so that an infected individual can spread it to as many others as possible. The rapidly fatal diseases, believe it or not, tend to be self-limiting."

"Here's arenoviridae," Sheila said.

"Still too virulent," Harlan said.

"How about orthomyxoviridae?" Pitt said. "Influenza is certainly infectious. And there's been some worldwide epidemics."

"That has possibilities," Harlan admitted. "But it has a relatively long incubation period, and it can be fatal. I'd really like to find something rapidly infectious and a bit more benign. Here we go . . . This is what I'm looking for."

Harlan plopped the looseleaf he'd been holding onto the desktop. It was open to page 99. Sheila and Pitt bent over to look at it.

"Picornaviridae," Pitt read, struggling with the pronunciation. "What do they cause?"

"It's this genus that I'm interested in," Harlan said. He pointed to one of the subgroups.

"Rhinovirus," Pitt read.

"Exactly," Harlan said. "The common cold. Wouldn't it be ironic if the common cold were to save mankind?"

"But not everybody gets a cold when it goes around," Pitt said.

"True," Harlan said. "Everyone has different levels of immunity to the hundreds of different strains that exist. But let's see what our microbiologists employed by the Pentagon have come up with."

Harlan flipped through the pages until he came to the rhinovirus section. It comprised thirty-seven pages. The first page had an index of the serotypes plus a short summary section.

Everyone read the summary silently. It suggested that rhinoviruses had limited utility as biological warfare agents. The reason given was that although the upper respiratory infections would affect the performance of a modern army, it would not be to a significant degree, and certainly not as much as an enterovirus causing diarrheal disease.

"Sounds like they were not so high on rhinoviruses," Pitt said.

"True," Harlan said. "But we're not trying to incapacitate an army. We just want the virus to get in there and stir up metabolic trouble to bring the alien virus out in the open."

"Here's something that sounds interesting," Sheila said, pointing to a subsection in the index. It was *artifical rhinoviruses*.

"That's what we need," Harlan said enthusiastically. He flipped through the pages until he came to the section. He read rapidly. Pitt tried to do the same, but the text might as well have been inscribed in Sanskrit. It was all highly technical jargon.

"This is perfect! Absolutely perfect!" Harlan said. He looked at Sheila. "It's tailor-made, both literally and figuratively. They've put together a rhinovirus that has never seen the light of day, meaning no one has any immunity to it. It's a serotype that no one has ever been exposed to so everybody will catch it. It's . . . made to order!"

"Seems to me we're making a rather large leap of faith here," Sheila said. "Don't you think we should somehow test this hypothesis?"

"Absolutely," Harlan said with great excitement. He reached over and put his hand on the latch to the freezer door. "I'll get a sample of the virus for us to grow out. Then we'll test it on those mice that I had infected. Boy, am I glad I did that." Harlan opened the freezer and disappeared inside.

Pitt looked at Sheila. "Do you think it will work?" he asked.

Sheila shrugged. "He seems pretty optimistic," she said.

"If it does work, will it kill the person?" Pitt asked. He was thinking about Cassy and even Beau.

"There's no way to know," Sheila said. "For as much as we know, at this point we're stumbling around in the dark."

"Hold up!" Vince said. He had the binoculars pressed against his eyes. "I think I see some tracks leading off toward the south."

"Where?" Beau asked.

Vince pointed.

Beau nodded. "Take us down to the ground," he told the pilot.

The pilot set the helicopter down on the tarmac. Still, a tremendous amount of sand and dust swirled up into the air.

"I hope all this dirt doesn't cover the tracks," Vince said.

"We're far enough away," the pilot said. He turned off the engine and the rotors came to a halt. Vince and the policeman sitting next to him, named Robert Sherman, immediately got out and jogged up the road to where the tracks were. Beau and the pilot climbed out of the cab as well, but they stayed next to the copter.

Beau was breathing heavily through his mouth with his tongue hanging out like a panting dog. The alien skin was not equipped with sweat glands, and he was beginning to overheat. He looked around for shade, but there was no escape from the merciless sun.

"I want to get back into the chopper," Beau said.

"It'll be too hot in there," the pilot said.

"I want you to start the engine," Beau said.

"But that will make it difficult for the others to return," the pilot said.

"The engine will be started!" Beau growled.

The pilot nodded and did as he was told. The air conditioning came on and quickly lowered the temperature.

Outside the slowly rotating blades kicked up a miniature sandstorm. They could barely see the two men a hundred yards ahead as they bent over to examine the ground.

The radio activated and the pilot slipped on his headset. Beau glanced off at the featureless horizon to the south. Along with his anger he was feeling progressively anxious. He hated these human emotions.

"It's a message from the institute," the pilot told Beau. "There's a problem. They cannot go to full power on the electrical grids. The system trips the circuit breakers."

Beau's long snakelike fingers intertwined to form tight, knotlike fists. His pulse quickened. His head pounded.

"What should I tell them?" the pilot asked.

"Tell them I'll be back soon," Beau said.

After signing off, the pilot removed his headphones. He was experiencing a trace of Beau's mental state via the collective consciousness, and he fidgeted in his seat. He was relieved when he saw the others returning.

Vince and Robert had to cover their faces against the stinging sand as they ducked under the rotating blades to climb into the copter. They didn't try to talk until the door was closed.

"It's the same tracks that were at the old gas station," he said. "They head south. What do you want to do?"

"Follow them!" Beau said.

With great difficulty Harlan, Sheila, Pitt, and Jonathan had managed to get six of the infected mice into a type III biological safety cabinet.

"It's a good thing they weren't rats," Pitt said. "If they had been any larger than mice, I don't think we could have handled them."

Harlan was letting Sheila put disinfectant and bandages on several of the bites he'd gotten. "I knew they were going to be trouble," he said.

"What are we going to do now?" Jonathan asked. He'd become intrigued by the experiment.

"We're going to introduce the virus," Harlan said. "It's in that tissue culture flask that's already inside the hood."

"Where does this cabinet vent?" Sheila asked. "We don't want this virus getting out if it's not going to work."

"The exhaust is irradiated," Harlan said. "No worry there."

Harlan stuck his bandaged hands into the thick rubber gloves that penetrated the front of the cabinet. He grasped the tissue culture flask, pulled out the stopper, and poured the medium out in a flat dish. "There," he said. "That will vaporize rapidly, and then our little furry friends will be breathing in the artificial virus."

"What are the black dots on the back of each mouse?" Jonathan asked.

"Each dot represents how many days ago the mouse was infected," Harlan said. "I was infecting them sequentially so that I could follow the infestation process physiologically. Now I'm glad I did it. There might be a different reaction depending on how much the enabled virus had expressed itself."

For a few minutes all four people stood in front of the cabinet and watched the mice race around the cage.

"Nothing is happening," Jonathan complained.

"Nothing on the level of the entire organism," Harlan said. "But my intuition tells me a lot is happening on a molecular/cellular level."

A few minutes later Jonathan yawned. "Wow," he said. "This is like watching paint dry. I'm going back to the computer."

A few minutes later Pitt broke the silence. "What is interesting is how they are seemingly working together. Look how they are forming a pyramid to explore up the glass."

Sheila grunted. She'd seen the phenomenon but wasn't interested. She wanted to see something physical happen to the mice. Since their level of activity hadn't changed, she was beginning to feel progressively nervous. If this experiment didn't work, they'd be back to square one.

As if reading Sheila's thoughts, Harlan said: "We shouldn't have long to wait. My guess is that it will only take the induction of one cell to initiate a cascade. My only worry is that we didn't test the viability of the virus. Maybe we should do that."

Harlan turned away to do what he'd suggested when Sheila grabbed his arm. "Wait!" she cried. "Look at that mouse with the three dots."

Harlan followed Sheila's pointing finger. Pitt crowded in behind, looking over Harlan's shoulder. The mouse in question had suddenly stopped its incessant rapid wandering around the cage to sit back on its haunches and repeatedly wipe its eyes with its front paws. Then it jerked a few times.

The three observers exchanged glances.

"Are those mouse sneezes?" Sheila asked.

"Damned if I know," Harlan said.

The mouse then swayed and toppled over.

"Is it dead?" Pitt asked.

"No," Sheila said. "It's still plainly breathing, but it doesn't look so good. Look at that foamlike stuff coming out of its eyes."

"And mouth," Harlan said. "And there's another mouse starting to have symptoms. I think it is working!"

"They are all having symptoms," Pitt said. "Look at that one with the most dots. It looks like it is having a seizure."

Hearing the commotion Jonathan returned and managed to squeeze his head between the others. He caught a quick glance at the ailing mice. "Ugh," he said. "The foam has a greenish tinge."

Harlan put his hands back into the gloves and picked up the first mouse. In contrast to its earlier belligerent behavior, it did not resist. It lay calmly in the palm of his hand breathing shallowly. Harlan put the animal down and reached for the one that had had the seizure.

"This one is dead," Harlan said. "Since it had been infected for the longest time, I guess that's telling us something."

"It's probably telling us how the dinosaurs died," Sheila said. "It was certainly rapid."

Harlan put the dead animal down and withdrew his hands. He rubbed them together enthusiastically. "Well, the first part of this experiment has gone very nicely, I'd say. Now that the animal trials are over, I think it's time for the human trials to begin."

"You mean release the virus?" Sheila said. "Like open the door and throw it out."

"No, we're not yet ready for clinical fieldwork," Harlan said with a twinkle in his eye. "I was thinking about the next stage being more close to home. I was thinking about me being the experimental subject."

"Now wait . . ." Sheila protested.

Harlan held up his hand. "There's a long history of famous medical people using themselves as the proverbial guinea pigs," he said. "This is a perfect opportunity to follow suit. I've been infected, and even though it has been a number of days, I've kept the infestation to a minimum by the monoclonal antibody. It's now time for me to rid myself of the virus altogether. So rather than thinking of myself as a sacrificial lamb, I think of myself as a beneficiary of our collective wit."

"How do you propose to do this?" Sheila asked. It was one thing to experiment with mice, quite another with a fellow human being.

"Come on," Harlan said. He grabbed one of the tissue cultures inoculated with the artificial rhinovirus and headed for the sick bay. "We'll do this the same way we did it with the mice. The difference is that you'll lock me into one of the containment rooms."

"Maybe we should use another animal first," Sheila said.

"Nonsense," Harlan said. "It's not as if we have the luxury of a lot of time. Remember that Gateway situation."

Everyone trooped after Harlan, who was obviously intent on using himself as an experimental subject. Sheila tried to talk him out of it all the way to the containment room. Harlan was not to be deterred.

"Just promise me you'll lock the door," Harlan said. "If something really weird were to happen, I don't want to jeopardize all of you."

"What if you need medical attention?" Sheila said. "Like, God forbid, CPR."

"That's a chance I have to take," Harlan said fatalistically. "Now get, so I can catch my cold in peace."

Sheila hesitated for a moment while trying to think of some other way to talk Harlan out of what she thought was a premature folly. Finally she stepped back through the air lock hatch and dogged it closed. She looked through the glass as Harlan gave her a thumbs-up sign.

Admiring Harlan's courage Sheila returned the gesture.

"What's he doing?" Pitt asked from the hallway. The air lock was only big enough for one person.

"He's taking the stopper out of the tissue culture flask," Sheila said.

"I'm going back to the computer," Jonathan said. The tension was making him feel uncomfortable.

Pitt stepped into the neighboring air lock and looked through the porthole at Cassy. She was still sleeping peacefully.

Pitt returned to the air lock occupied by Sheila. "Anything happening?"

"Not yet," Sheila said. "He's just lying down making faces at me. He's acting like he's twelve years old."

Pitt wondered how he'd behave if the situation were reversed, and he was the one in the room. He thought he'd be terrified and unable to joke around like Harlan.

"Wait a second!" Vince said excitedly. "Turn around so I can see where we just passed over."

The pilot banked the copter to the left in a wide circle.

Vince snapped the binoculars to his eyes. The terrain below looked as featureless as it had looked for the previous hour. It had turned out to be extraordinarily difficult to follow the tire tracks from the air, and they'd taken many wrong turns.

"There's something down there," Vince said.

"What is it?" Beau growled. His mood had darkened. What he'd thought was going to be a simple matter of plucking Cassy out of the desert, was turning into a fiasco.

"I can't tell," Vince said. "But it is worth taking a look at. I'd recommend we go down."

"Land!" Beau snarled.

The helicopter settled down in the middle of its own sandstorm. It was worse than earlier, without the tarmac. As the air cleared everyone immediately saw what had attracted Vince's attention. It was a van with a camouflage cover partially blown off by the wind generated by the rotor blades.

"Finally something positive," Beau snapped as he alighted from the helicopter. He strode over to the van. Grasping the tarp he ripped it off. He opened the front passenger-side door.

"She was in here," he said. He looked in the back of the van, then turned to survey the area.

"Beau, there's another communication from the institute," the pilot called out. He'd remained next to the helicopter. "They want you to know that they'd received word that the Arrival is expected in five Earth hours from now. And they want to remind you that the Gateway is not ready. What should I tell them?"

Beau gripped his head with his long fingers and pressed his temples in an attempt to relieve his tension. He breathed out slowly. Ignoring the pilot he yelled to Vince that Cassy was nearby. "I can sense it," Beau added. "But it is strangely weak."

Vince and Robert had wandered away from the van in ever widening circles. Suddenly Vince had stopped and bent down. Straightening up he called for Beau to come over.

Beau joined the two men.

Vince pointed to the ground. "It's a camouflaged hatch," he said. "It's locked from within."

Beau's fingers snaked under the edge. Progressively he applied an upward force until the hatch snapped up into the air. Vince and Beau leaned over and peered down at the lighted corridor below. Then their eyes met.

"She's down there," Beau said.

"I know," Vince said.

"Holy shit!" Jonathan cried. His eyes bulged from their sockets. Then he screamed at the top of his lungs: "Pitt, Sheila, somebody, get over here!"

Pitt slammed down a syringe of antibody he'd been preparing for Cassy and dashed out of the sick bay into the hall en route to the lab where Jonathan was. Pitt had no idea what had happened but there'd been desperation in Jonathan's voice. Pitt heard Sheila running behind him.

They found Jonathan sitting at the computer. His eyes were glued to the monitor, and his face was pale as an ivory cue ball.

"What's the matter?" Pitt demanded as he rushed up to Jonathan.

Jonathan was momentarily tongue-tied. All he could do was motion toward the computer screen. Pitt looked at it and his hand reflexly slapped across his open mouth.

"What is it?" Sheila urged as she arrived at Pitt's side.

"It's a freak!" Jonathan managed.

Sheila sucked in a breath of air when she caught sight of what was on the screen.

"It's Beau!" Pitt said with horror. "Cassy said he'd been mutating, but I had no idea . . ."

"Where is he?" Sheila asked, forcing herself to be practical despite Beau's grotesque appearance.

"It was an alarm that drew my attention," Jonathan said. "Then the computer automatically activated the appropriate minicam."

"I want to know where he is," Sheila repeated frantically.

Jonathan fumbled with the keyboard and managed to bring up a schematic of the facility. A red arrow was blinking at one of the emergency/exhaust vents.

"I think that's the one where we entered," Pitt said.

"I think you're right," Sheila said. "What does the alarm mean, Jonathan?"

"It says 'hatch cover unsealed,'" Jonathan said. "I guess that means they've got the hatch open."

"Good God!" Sheila said. "They'll be coming in."

"What should we do?" Pitt asked.

Sheila ran an anxious hand through her unfettered blond hair; her green eyes darted erratically around the room. She felt like a cornered deer.

"Pitt, go see if you can lock the door to the air lock," she sputtered. "That might delay them for a time."

Pitt dashed from the room.

"Where's Harlan's pistol?" Jonathan asked.

"I don't know," Sheila snapped. "Look for it, Jonathan."

Sheila started for the sick bay.

"Where are you going?" Jonathan called out to Sheila.

"I've got to get Harlan and Cassy out of those containment rooms," Sheila said.

"What do you want me to do, Beau?" Vince asked, breaking what had seemed to be a long silence.

"What do you think this place is?" Beau asked, pointing down the hatch at the gleaming, white, high-tech interior.

"I haven't the slightest idea," Vince said.

Beau glanced back at the helicopter. The pilot was dutifully standing by. Beau returned his gaze down the hatch. His mind was in a turmoil and his emotions frayed.

"I want you and your co-worker to go down in this strange hole and find Cassy," Beau said. He spoke slowly and deliberately as if he were making great effort to restrain himself from flying into a rage. "When you find her, I want you to bring her to me. I must go back to the institute, but I will send the copter back for you."

"As you wish," Vince said warily. He was afraid of saying the wrong thing. The fragility of Beau's emotions was obvious.

Beau reached into his pocket and drew out a black disc. He handed it to Vince. "Use it as you see fit," he said. "But do not harm Cassy!" Then he turned and strode back to the waiting aircraft.

CHAPTER 20

7:10 P.M.

With fumbling hands Sheila unlocked the hatch into Harlan's containment room. By the time she had it open, Harlan was standing next to it. He was surprised and irritated.

"What the hell are you doing?" he questioned. "You've contaminated yourself and the entire facility."

"It can't be helped," Sheila sputtered. "They're here!"

"Who is here?" Harlan asked. His expression rapidly changed to concern.

"Beau and at least one other infected person," Sheila blurted out. "They have the hatch open that we used to come in here. They must have followed Cassy. They'll be here any minute."

"Damn!" Harlan exclaimed. He paused for a second to think, then stepped out through the air lock.

They immediately caught up with Cassy and Pitt as the two emerged from the neighboring containment room. Although Cassy appeared sleepy and confused, her color was better than it had been earlier.

"Where's Jonathan?" Harlan barked.

"Back in the lab," Pitt said. "He was searching for your Colt."

With Harlan leading, the group rushed from the sick bay into the lab proper. They went from room to room. They found Jonathan in the final room, crouching by the door to the corridor. He was holding the pistol in both hands.

"We're getting out of here," Harlan yelled to Jonathan. Harlan ducked into the incubator and emerged seconds later carrying an armload of tissue culture flasks containing the rhinovirus.

A loud sputtering noise was heard from the corridor. Everyone's eyes turned to the open doorway. A shower of sparks shot by as if someone were welding in the hallway. Simultaneously the pressure in the room precipitously dropped, forcing everyone to clear their ears.

"What happened?" Sheila demanded.

"They're cutting through the pressure door," Harlan yelled. "Come on! Hurry!" He motioned for everyone to retreat back toward the infirmary. But before anybody could move a black disc rounded the corner from the corridor and entered the lab. It was glowing bright red and surrounded by a hazy halo.

"It's a disc!" Sheila shouted. "Stay away from it."

"Yes!" Harlan bellowed. "When it's active it's radioactive. It's spewing out alpha particles."

The disc hovered near Jonathan, who ducked away and ran back toward the others. Harlan herded the group through the door into the next lab room. Stepping into the room himself, he slammed the heavy, two-inch-thick fire door.

"Hurry!" he commanded.

The group had gotten halfway across the second lab when the same sputtering noise they'd heard earlier reverberated around the room. There was another shower of sparks. Harlan turned to see the disc passing effortlessly through the door.

Everyone got into the third lab space and raced for the double doors into the infirmary. Harlan took the time to slam the second fire door before running after the others. Behind him he heard the sputtering again. Sparks bounced off the back of his head as he went into the infirmary. The doors swung closed behind him.

"Where to?" Sheila demanded.

"The X-ray room," Harlan barked, pointing with a hand carrying one of the tissue culture flasks. "The one that is still operational."

Jonathan was the first to arrive. He pushed open the shielded door and held it for the others. They all crowded inside.

"This is a dead end!" Sheila shrieked. "Why did you bring us in here?"

"Get over behind the shield," Harlan ordered. Quickly he handed Sheila and Pitt the tissue culture flasks. Then he activated the machine that positioned the X-ray column. He aimed the positioning light directly at the door to the hall before rushing back and crowding behind the screen with the others.

Harlan's hands rapidly flipped switches and spun dials on the X-ray machine's control panel as sparking and sputtering commenced at the door. With the lead shielding it took the disc a few more seconds to burn through the X-ray room door than it had the fire doors. When it emerged inside the room, its red color had slightly paled.

Harlan flipped the switch that sent the high voltage built up in the machine to the X-ray source. There was an electronic buzzing noise and the overhead light dimmed. "These are the hardest X-rays this machine is capable of producing," he explained.

Bombarded with the X-rays, the disc's color instantly changed from pale red to luminous white. The pale halo intensified, expanded, and quickly engulfed the disc. The sound of an enormous furnace igniting was immediately cut off with a thump. At the same instant most of the X-ray machine, the X-ray table, an instrument tray, part of the door, and the light fixture were all pulled out of shape as if they had been sucked toward the point where the disc had been. Even the people had experienced this sudden imploding force and had instinctively braced themselves and grabbed onto whatever they could.

A pall of acrid smoke hung over the room.

Everyone was momentarily dazed.

"Is everyone okay?" Harlan asked.

"My watch exploded," Sheila said.

"So did the wall clock," Harlan said. He pointed up to the institutional clock on the wall. Its glass had been shattered, and its hands were nowhere to be seen.

"That was a miniature black hole," Harlan said.

A loud thump out in the lab shocked everybody back to reality.

"Obviously they've gotten through the air lock," Harlan said. "Come on!" He took the gun away from Jonathan and gave him a tissue culture flask to carry instead. Cassy and Pitt picked up the rest of the flasks. Harlan led everyone from behind the distorted shield toward the door.

"Don't touch anything," he warned. "There still might be some radiation."

It took all three men to get the twisted door open. Harlan leaned out. He could see down to the double doors leading to the lab. There was a small scorched hole in the right one. He looked the other way. It was clear.

"To the left," he barked. "Down through the door at the end and across into the living room. Got it?"

Everyone nodded.

"Go!" Harlan said. He kept his eye on the double doors until the last person had cleared the corridor. He was about to follow them when one of the double doors opened in the opposite direction.

Harlan fired one shot from the huge Peacemaker. The noise was deafening in the hallway. The bullet hit the closed double door and shattered its porthole-like window. The door that had been opened swung shut.

Harlan raced out into the hall and ran its length on legs that had suddenly gone rubbery. He staggered into the living room.

"Harlan?" Sheila questioned. "Have you been shot?" They had all heard the gun go off.

Harlan shook his head. A small amount of foam bubbled out of his mouth and oozed from his eyes. "I think it's the rhinovirus kicking out the alien virus," he managed. He steadied himself against the wall. "It's happening. Unfortunately it's a rather inconvenient time."

Pitt rushed to Harlan's side and draped Harlan's arm over his shoulder. He took the gun from Harlan's limp hand.

"Give me the gun," Sheila commanded. Pitt handed it over.

"How are we going to get out of here?" Sheila asked Harlan.

The sound of breaking glass drifted back from the lab.

"We'll use the main entrance," Harlan said. "My Range Rover should be there. I'd been afraid to go out that way for fear of discovery. Now it doesn't make any difference."

"All right," Sheila said. "How do we get there?"

"We go out in the main hall and turn right," Harlan said. "We pass the storerooms and there'll be another air lock. Then there is a long corridor with electric carts. The exit comes up inside a building that looks like a farmhouse."

Sheila cracked the door to the hall and began slowly to lean her head out to look back toward the lab rooms. She felt the bullet before she heard a distant gun go off. The slug had come so close to her that it had singed some of her hair before burrowing into the partially open door.

She pulled back inside the living room.

"Obviously they know where we are," she said. She wiped her forehead with her hand and examined it. She wouldn't have been surprised to see blood. "Is there another way to get to the exit? We're surely not going to be able to use the hall."

"We have to use the hall," Harlan said.

"Oh screw!" Sheila mumbled. She looked at the gun in her hand, wondering whom she thought she was kidding. She'd never even fired a gun in practice much less gotten into a battle with one.

"We can use the fire system," Harlan said. He pointed toward the security panel on the living-room wall. "If you pull the fire lever, the whole place fills up with fire retardant. The intruders won't be able to breathe very well, if at all."

"Oh that's clever," Sheila said sarcastically. "And, of course, we just walk out holding our breaths."

"No, no," Harlan said. "In the cabinet below the panel are rebreathers that are good for a least a half hour."

Sheila went over to the cabinet and pulled it open. It was filled with gas mask–like apparatuses. She took out five and handed them around. The directions on the long, tubular proboscis were to break the seal, shake, and then don.

"Everybody okay with this?" Sheila asked.

"It's not as if we have a lot of choice," Pitt said.

They all activated their units and then strapped them on. When everyone gave a thumbs-up sign, Sheila yanked down on the fire lever.

An immediate clanging was heard followed by an automated voice that repeated "Fire in the facility" over and over again. A minute later the sprinkler system was activated, sending out billows of fluid that rapidly vaporized. The room filled up with a smoglike haze.

"We have to stick together," Sheila yelled. It was hard to talk in the gas mask, and it was getting hard to see as well. Sheila opened the door to the hall and was pleased to see the hall was as hazy as the living room. She leaned out and looked toward the labs. She couldn't see for more than four or five feet.

Sheila stepped out into the hall. There were no gun shots. "Let's go," she called to the others. "Pitt, you and Harlan go ahead so that we know where we are going. Cassy and Jonathan, you carry the tissue culture flasks."

In a tight group they moved down the hallway. In the haze the corridor seemed interminable. Finally they came to the air lock and climbed in. Sheila pulled the door behind them. Pitt opened the outer door.

Beyond the air lock, the atmosphere progressively cleared, especially when they got on the electric cart. By the time they came to the exit stairs, they could remove their breathing apparatuses.

It was six flights up to the surface. They emerged through a trap door the size of a scatter rug into the living room of a farmhouse. When the trap door was closed, no one would have suspected what it concealed.

"My car should be in the barn," Harlan said. He took his arm off Pitt's shoulder.

"Thanks, Pitt," he said. "I don't think I could have made it without you, but I feel a bit better already." He blew his nose noisily.

"Let's get a move on," Sheila said. "Those people who were after us might have found rebreathers as well."

The group exited the house via the front door and walked back toward the barn. The sun had set and the desert heat was rapidly dissipating. There was a blood-red smear along the edge of the western horizon. The rest of the sky was an inverted bowl of indigo blue. A few stars twinkled overhead.

As Harlan had hoped, his Range Rover was still safely parked in the barn. He put all the tissue culture flasks in the back storage area before getting behind the wheel. He took the Colt from Sheila and slipped it into the door pocket.

"Are you sure you feel up to driving?" Sheila asked. She was amazed at his recovery.

"No problem," Harlan said. "I feel completely different than I did just fifteen minutes ago. The only symptoms I have now are of garden-variety cold. I'd say our human trial was an unmitigated success!"

Sheila got into the front passenger seat. Cassy, Pitt, and Jonathan climbed into the back. Pitt put his arm around Cassy, and she snuggled up against him.

Harlan started the car and backed out of the barn. He made a U-turn and drove to the road.

"This alien infestation certainly has cut down on traffic," he said. "Look at this. Not a car in sight and we're only fifteen minutes out of Paswell."

Harlan turned right and accelerated.

"Where are we going?" Sheila asked.

"I don't think we have a lot of choice," Harlan said. "My sense is that the rhinovirus is going to take care of the infestation. The problem then boils down to the Gateway thing. We got to try to do something about it."

Cassy straightened up. "The Gateway!" she said. "Pitt has told you about it."

"He certainly did," Harlan said. "He said you thought it was almost operational. Did you get any idea when they might use it?"

"I wasn't told specifically," Cassy said. "But my sense is that it will be used as soon as it is finished."

"There you go," Harlan said. "We'll just have to hope we can get there in time and figure out a way to throw a monkey wrench into the works."

"What's this about a rhinovirus?" Cassy asked.

"Some rather good news," Harlan said, glancing at Cassy in the rearview mirror. "Particularly for you and me."

Cassy was then told the whole sequence of events that led to the discovery of a way to rid the human race of the alien viral scourge. Both Harlan and Sheila credited Cassy for the information that she'd given Pitt.

"It was the fact that the alien virus had come here three billion years ago that was so important," Sheila said. "Otherwise we wouldn't have thought about its being sensitive to oxygen."

"Maybe I should be breathing some of that rhinovirus now?" Cassy said.

"No need," Harlan said. "Just riding in the car means all of you are being adequately infected. I imagine it only takes a couple of virions since no one has any immunity to it."

Cassy settled back and snuggled against Pitt. "Only a few hours ago I thought all was lost. It's a shock to be hopeful again."

Pitt squeezed her shoulder. "We've been incredibly lucky."

They arrived at the outskirts of Santa Fe a few minutes after eleven o'clock at night. They had driven straight through, stopping only once at an abandoned service station to fill up the gas tank. They'd also helped themselves to candy and peanuts from a vending machine. There was plenty of change in the cash register.

Cassy had stayed in the car. By then she'd been in the middle of the period of weakness, malaise, and foaming at the mouth and eyes that Harlan had experienced as they'd left the underground laboratory. Harlan had been ecstatic, taking Cassy's temporary misery as further evidence of the efficacy of the "rhino-cure," as he called it.

Skirting the center of Santa Fe, they followed Cassy's directions and drove directly to the Institute for a New Beginning. At this time of night the outer gate was brightly illuminated with flood lights. The daily protesters were gone, but there was a significant number of infected people leaving the grounds.

Harlan pulled over to the side of the road and stopped. He leaned forward and surveyed the scene. "Where's the mansion?" he asked.

En route Cassy had explained to everyone everything she'd been able to remember about the institute's layout particularly the fact that the Gateway was located in the ballroom on the first floor to the right of the front entrance.

"The main building is behind that line of trees," Cassy said. "You can't see it from here."

"Which way did the ballroom windows face?" Harlan asked.

"I believe to the back of the house," Cassy said. "But I'm not positive because they had been boarded up."

"So much for the idea of breaking through the windows," Harlan said.

"Considering what the Gateway is supposed to do," Pitt said, "it must use a lot of energy, and that's got to be electric. Maybe we could unplug it."

"A wonderfully droll suggestion," Harlan quipped. "But to transport aliens through time and space I can't imagine they'll be relying on the same energy as we use to power toasters. Seeing what a single, relatively tiny black disc can do, think of what a whole bunch of them might accomplish if they were working in concert."

"It was just an idea," Pitt said. He felt stupid and decided to keep his thoughts to himself.

"How far is the mansion from the gate?" Sheila asked.

"Quite a ways," Cassy said. "A couple of hundred yards or more. The driveway goes through trees first and then crosses a stretch of wide-open lawn."

"Well, I think that's our first problem," Sheila said. "We have to get to the house if we're going to do anything."

"Good point," Harlan said.

"What about sneaking over the fence somewhere in the back?" Jonathan said. "There are lights here at the gate but I don't see others elsewhere."

"There are big dogs patrolling the grounds," Cassy said. "They're infected just like the people, and they work together. I'm afraid trying to approach the house across the lawn would be dangerous."

Suddenly the night sky above the trees lit up with undulating bands of energy that gave the impression of the northern lights. They formed a sphere and began expanding and contracting, reminiscent of an organism breathing. But each successive expansion was larger so the phenomenon was growing by the second.

"Uh oh," Sheila said. "I have a feeling we're too late. It's starting."

"All right, everybody out of the car!" Harlan commanded.

"What do you mean?" Sheila questioned.

"I want everybody out," Harlan said. "I'm going to do something impulsive. I'm going to drive in there and run this car into the ballroom. I can't let this go on."

"Well, you're not doing it alone," Sheila said.

"Suit yourself," Harlan said. "I don't have time to argue. But the rest of you, out!"

"There's not really anyplace to go," Cassy said. She glanced at Pitt and then Jonathan. Their nods told her she was speaking for them. "I think we're into this thing together."

"Oh for chrissake!" Harlan complained as he put his Range Rover into low range for off roading. "Just what the human race needs: an entire car full of goddamn martyrs." He revved the engine and told everyone to cinch up his seat belt. Harlan yanked his own as tight as he could make it. Then he put on the CD player and selected his favorite: Stravinsky's *Rite of Spring*. He advanced it to a part he especially liked; it was where the kettle drums resound. With the volume at near full blast, he pulled out into the road.

"What are you going to tell the men at the gate?" Sheila yelled.

"I'm going to tell them to eat my dust!" Harlan yelled back.

There was a black-and-white, weighted wooden gate across the driveway. The pedestrian traffic walked around it. Harlan hit it at about forty-five miles per hour and the Rover's bush bars made mincemeat of it. The smiling guards dove out of the way to either side.

Sheila spun around and looked out the back of the car. The guards had recovered and were running after them. Also in pursuit was a pack of wildly barking dogs. Gatekeepers and dogs quickly disappeared as Harlan negotiated an S-curve around some virgin conifers.

The Range Rover rocketed out of the trees. The huge mansion loomed before them in the night. The entire building was glowing, particularly the windows. The undulating bands of light that were rhythmically expanding up into the night sky appeared to be coming from the roof like gigantic flames.

"Aren't you going to slow down a little?" Sheila yelled. The engine was whining like a jet turbine and the kettle drums were pounding. It sounded as if the entire orchestra was inside the car. Sheila reached up and grasped the handle above the passenger-side door to steady herself.

Harlan didn't answer. His expression was one of intense concentration. Up until that moment he'd been steering the vehicle within the confines of the driveway. Now that he had the house in sight, he drove straight toward it across the lawn to avoid the pedestrians. People were streaming from the mansion in single file on the way out of the property.

About a hundred feet from the wide, sweeping steps that led up to the front terrace, Harlan downshifted despite the fact that the engine's RPMs were already close to the red area on the gauge. The car responded by slowing considerably. At the same time significant power was directed to the rear wheels.

"Holy shit!" Jonathan yelled as the distance closed to the front steps. People could be seen diving blindly over the limestone handrails to get away from the three tons of steel hurtling at them.

The Range Rover hit the first step and the front kicked up, launching the entire vehicle into the air. The tires made contact with the earth again at the rear of the front terrace ten feet from the double French door entry. Multipaned side lights surrounded the front door on both sides as well as the top.

Everyone but Harlan squeezed their eyes shut when the collision with the house occurred. There was a muted sound of shattering glass that could be heard above the classical music, but there was surprisingly little effect on the car's forward momentum. Harlan hit the brakes and threw the steering wheel to the right. He was intent on avoiding the grand staircase which was directly ahead.

The car skidded on the black-and-white checkered marble floor, brushed past a large crystal chandelier, and then collided with a marble console table and an interior plastered wall. There was a crunching sound and everyone was thrown against their seat belts. The passenger-side airbag inflated and pressed a startled Sheila back into her seat.

Harlan fought the steering wheel as the car bounced over the crushed table and broken two-by-four studding. The final collision was with a metal and wooden structure draped with electrical cable. The car came to a halt against a steel girder that shattered the windshield, splintering it into a thousand pieces of tempered glass.

Outside the car there was sputtering and sparking as well as a strange mechanical hum that could be felt more than heard over the booming classical music.

"Is everybody okay?" Harlan asked as he disconnected his fingers from the steering wheel. He'd been holding it so tight as to preclude circulation. Both his hands and forearms were stiff. He turned down the volume on the CD player.

Sheila fought with the collapsing airbag. It had abraded her cheek and forearms.

Everyone responded that they had weathered the crash surprisingly well.

Harlan glanced out through the broken front windshield. All he could see were wires and twisted debris. "Do you think this is the ballroom, Cassy?" he asked.

"I do," Cassy said.

"Then mission accomplished," Harlan said. "With all these wires, it certainly appears as if we've collided with some sort of high-tech apparatus. By the looks of all this sparking, we've done something."

Since the Range Rover's engine was still running, Harlan put it in reverse and gave it gas. With a good deal of scraping the car inched backward along its path of destruction. After ten feet the car cleared the superstructure of the Gateway. Everyone could see up to a platform that appeared to be made of Plexiglas. Oval stairs of the same material led up to it. Standing on the platform was a hideous alien creature illuminated by the unabating electrical sparks. Its coal-black eyes regarded those in the car with shocked disbelief.

All at once the creature threw back his head and let out an agonizing cry of grief. Slowly he sank down to the surface of the platform and gripped his head with his hands in utter anguish.

"My God! It's Beau," Cassy said from the backseat.

"I'm afraid it is," Pitt agreed. "Only his mutation has been complete."

"Let me out!" Cassy said. She undid her seat belt.

"No," Pitt said.

"There're too many loose wires," Harlan said. "It's too dangerous, especially with all this sparking going on. The voltage must be astronomical."

"I don't care," Cassy said. She reached across Pitt and opened the door.

"I can't let you," Pitt said.

"Let go of me," Cassy snapped. "I have to get out."

Reluctantly, Pitt let Cassy get out of the car. Gingerly she stepped over the wires and then slowly mounted the steps to the platform. As she got closer she could hear Beau moaning over the mechanical hum and the sputtering wires. She called out to him and he slowly raised his eyes.

"Cassy?" Beau questioned. "Why didn't I sense you?"

"Because I've been freed of the virus," Cassy said. "There's hope! There's hope we can get our old lives back."

Beau shook his head. "Not for me," he said. "I can't go back, and yet I can't go forward. I have failed the trust put in me. These human emotions are a terrible hindrance. They are completely unsuitable. Wanting you I have forsaken the collective good."

A sudden increase in the electrical sparking heralded a vibration. It was slight at first but rapidly gained strength.

"You must flee, Cassy," Beau said. "The electrical grid has been interrupted. There will be no force counteracting the antigravity. There'll be a dispersion."

"Come with me, Beau," Cassy said. "We have a way of ridding you of the virus."

"I am the virus," Beau said.

The vibration had reached a point where Cassy was having trouble maintaining her balance on the translucent steps.

"Go, Cassy!" Beau shouted passionately.

With one final touch of Beau's extended finger, Cassy struggled down to the floor of the ballroom. The room was now shaking as if there were an earthquake.

She managed to get back to the car. Pitt was holding the door open for her. She climbed in.

"Beau said we have to flee," Cassy yelled. "There's going to be a dispersion."

Needing little encouragement, Harlan put the car in reverse and stomped down on the accelerator. There was more bumping and shaking than when the car had come into the building, but soon they were back in the main hall.

Deftly Harlan pulled the car around so that it was facing out through the shattered front entrance. The chandelier above was shaking so badly that bits and pieces of the crystal were flying off in various directions. Sitting in the front seat with no windshield, Sheila had to shield her face.

"Hang on, everybody," Harlan said. With wheels spinning on the slick marble, he rocketed the Range Rover out through the front door, across the terrace, and down the stairs. The jolt from hitting the driveway at the base of the stairs was as bad as the impact had been when they'd slammed into the ballroom wall.

Harlon drove back across the lawn in a beeline toward the cleft in the trees that marked the point where the driveway emerged.

"Must you drive this fast?" Sheila complained.

"Cassy said there was going to be a dispersion," Harlan said. "I figured the greater the distance we're away the better."

"What the hell is a dispersion?" Sheila asked.

"I haven't the foggiest," Harlan admitted. "But it sounds bad."

At that moment there was a tremendous explosion behind them, but without the usual noise or shock wave. Cassy happened to have turned around in time to see the house literally fly apart. There also wasn't any flash of light to indicate the point of conflagration.

At the same time everyone in the Range Rover became aware that they had literally become airborne. Without any traction the engine raced until Harlan took his foot from the accelerator.

The flying lasted only five seconds, and the return to earth was accompanied by a sudden lurch since the wheels had slowed but the forward movement of the car had not.

Bewildered by this strange phenomenon Harlan braked and brought the car to a stop. He was unnerved at having totally lost control of the vehicle even if it had been only for a few seconds.

"We were flying there for a moment," Sheila declared. "How did that happen?"

"I don't know," Harlan said. He looked at the gauges and dials as if they might provide some answers.

"Look what happened to the house," Cassy said. "It's disappeared."

Everyone turned to look. Outside the car the pedestrians were doing the same. There was no smoke and no debris. The house had just vanished.

"So now we know what a dispersion is," Harlan said. "It must be the opposite of a black hole. I guess whatever is dispersed is reduced to all its primary particles, and they are just blown away."

Cassy felt emotion well up inside of her. There was a sudden, intense sense of loss, and a few tears rolled out onto her cheeks.

Out of the corner of his eye, Pitt saw Cassy's tears. He understood immediately and put his arm around her shoulder. "I'll miss him too," he said.

Cassy nodded. "I guess I'll always love him," she said wiping her eyes with a knuckle. But then she quickly added: "But that doesn't mean I don't love you."

With a tenaciousness that took Pitt's breath away, Cassy clasped him in an intense embrace. Tentatively at first and then with equal ardor Pitt hugged her back.

Harlan got out of the car and went around the back. He got out the flasks. "Come on, everybody," he said. "We've got some of our own infecting to do."

"Holy shit," Jonathan cried. "There's my mother."

Everyone looked in the direction Jonathan was pointing.

"You know, I think you are right," Sheila said.

Jonathan alighted from the car with the intention of sprinting across the grass. Harlan grabbed his arm and thrust one of the flasks into his hand.

"Give her a whiff, son," Harlan said. "The sooner the better."